PROTECTOR OF MERCIA

BOOK 5 THE EAGLE OF MERCIA CHRONICLES

MJ PORTER

B

Boldwood

First published in Great Britain in 2023 by Boldwood Books Ltd.

Cover Design by Head Design Ltd

Cover Photography: Shutterstock

A CIP catalogue record for this book is available from the British Library.

Paperback ISBN 978-1-83751-209-6

Large Print ISBN 978-1-83751-208-9

Hardback ISBN 978-1-83751-207-2

Ebook ISBN 978-1-83751-210-2

Kindle ISBN 978-1-83751-211-9

Audio CD ISBN 978-1-83751-202-7

MP3 CD ISBN 978-1-83751-203-4

Digital audio download ISBN 978-1-83751-205-8

Boldwood Books Ltd
23 Bowerdean Street
London SW6 3TN
www.boldwoodbooks.com

This one is for my buddies: the two Js and one C. Thanks for putting up with your mad writer mate.

Designed by Flintlock Covers

CAST OF CHARACTERS

Icel, orphaned youth living in Tamworth, his mother was Ceolburh
Brute, Icel's horse
Cenfrith, Icel's uncle, brother of Ceolburh and one of the Mercian king's warriors, who dies in *Son of Mercia*
Edwin, Icel's childhood friend, although they have been separated
Wine, Cenfrith's horse, now Icel's alongside Brute
Wynflæd, an old herbwoman at the Mercian king's court at Tamworth

The Kings of Mercia
Coelwulf, king of Mercia r.821–825 (deposed)
Beornwulf, king of Mercia r.825–826 (killed)
Lady Cynehild, Beornwulf's wife
Wiglaf, king of Mercia r.827–829 (deposed) r.830–
Queen Cynethryth, Wiglaf's wife
Wigmund, Wiglaf's son, married to Lady Cynehild, sister of Lord Coenwulf
Ecgberht, king of Wessex r.802 onwards, r.829 in Mercia

The Ealdormen/Bishops of Mercia

Ælfstan, one of King Wiglaf's supporters, an ally to Icel
Ælflæd, Lord Coenwulf's sister
Ælfred, ally of Lord Wigmund
Beornoth, one of King Wiglaf's ealdormen
Hunberht, an ally of Lord Wigmund
Muca, one of King Wiglaf's ealdormen
Sigered, a long-standing ealdorman who's survived the troubled years of the 820s
Sigegar, Sigered's grandson
Tidwulf, an ally of King Wiglaf
Wicga, ally of Lord Wigmund

Rulers of other kingdoms

Athelstan, king of the East Angles
Ecgberht, king of Wessex

Ealdorman Ælfstan's Warriors

Cenred, Mercian warrior
Goðeman, Mercian warrior
Kyre, Mercian warrior
Landwine, Mercian warrior
Maneca, Mercian warrior
Ordlaf, Mercian warrior
Oswy, Mercian warrior, once an ally of the queen
Uor, Mercian warrior
Waldhere, Mercian warrior
Wulfgar, Mercian warrior
Wulfheard, Mercian warrior, Ealdorman Ælfstan's oath-sworn man
Bada, Wulfheard's horse

Those living in Kingsholm

Coenwulf and Coelwulf, the sons of Lord Coenwulf and Lady Cynewise
Cuthwahl, Lord Coenwulf's warrior
Deremann, Lord Wigmund's warrior
Eadburg, living in Kingsholm, her mother cares for young Coenwulf and Coelwulf
Eadweard, Lord Wigmund's warrior
Forthgar, Lord Wigmund's warrior
Lady Cynewise, sister of Lord Coenwulf
Mergeat, Lord Wigmund's warrior
Osmod, Lord Coenwulf's warrior
Tatberht, Lord Coenwulf's warrior
Wulfred, Lord Wigmund's warrior

Those living in Hereford

Æthelbald, rogue living in the woodlands
Hywel, rogue living in the woodlands
The Wolf Lady, forest-dweller

Those living in Chester

Æthelgyth, tavern keeper
Godfrith, a young boy
Oswin, tavern stableman

In Northumbria

Wulfnoth, a lord

Those living in Tamworth

Cuthred, training to be a healer with Wynflæd
Eahric, commander of the king's household warriors
Gaya, previously a slave woman with a talent for healing, now freed
Theodore, previously a slave man with a talent for healing, now freed
Wynflæd, a healer

Places mentioned

Eamont, in the north-west, the site of a famous meeting in 927 (if you look at maps of Saxon England, you'll find precious few names on the north-west side of the country)

Hereford, close to the Welsh borders, in Mercia

Kingdom of Wessex, the area south of the River Thames, including Kent at this time, but not Dumnonia (Cornwall and Devon)

Kingsholm, associated with the ruling family of King Coelwulf, close to Gloucester, home to Lord Coenwulf

Lichfield, close to Tamworth and one of the holy sites in Mercia

Londonia, combining the ruins of Roman Londinium and Saxon Lundenwic

Tamworth, the capital of the Mercian kingdom

Winchcombe, the home of a nunnery associated with Mercian royal women

Wroxeter, close to the Welsh borders, in Mercia

THE STORY SO FAR

Icel has retrieved Lord Coenwulf, with the aid of his fellow warriors, from the Viking raiders on the Isle of Sheppey. But in doing so, three men have died, and on returning to Kingsholm, Lady Cynehild, while birthing her second son, has also met her death. But not before finally revealing the truth of Icel's identity as the unacknowledged son of the little lamented King Beornwulf of Mercia, dead for seven years. At the same time, Lady Cynehild has forced Icel to swear an oath to protect her sons and to ensure that they, unlike Icel, will one day claim their birthright as king of Mercia.

THE MERCIAN REGISTER

AD833

In this year, King Wiglaf of Mercia and King Athelstan of the East Angles forged an alliance against the Viking raiders ravaging the kingdom of the East Angles and swore with oaths to always be allies. The Viking raiders captured the Isle of Sheppey but were soon driven from it by men of the Wessex king, King Ecgberht.

1

WINTER AD833, TAMWORTH

'You knew.' The words shoot like seax strikes from my mouth. I've been holding them tight for too long. I should have come to Tamworth from Kingsholm sooner. It should have been the first place I came to when Lady Cynehild first told the truth of my birth – when she told me that my father was King Beornwulf, the king of Mercia who died fighting against the kingdom of the East Angles seven summers ago.

Wynflæd watches me, eyes filled with sorrow I don't want to see. Has she always pitied me? Was our friendship little more than the sympathy of an old woman? Was she training me to become a healer, like her, because she knew I could never claim my birthright?

'I did, boy, I did,' she confirms, her old, thin lips downturned, her eyes hard and flecked with flint.

'You should have told me,' I cry, wishing traitorous tears didn't fall from my eyes. I'm glad young Cuthred isn't here. We're alone in her workshop, and I'm grateful for that. I could have come upon her when she was busy tending to one of the frail within Tamworth. But for once, luck has favoured me. If Cuthred saw me crying, I don't know what I'd do. The rain that's drenched me on my journey here hasn't helped – making it appear as though I'm wreathed in sorrow.

'Why?' I watch Wynflæd as she settles before the hearth, holding out thin, almost translucent hands towards the leaping flames. It's cold, I realise that now. The heat of my fury has driven me onwards, despite the turning season. I sniff, and all I can smell is the scent of wet horses and churned mud. I stink of the cold. 'What good would it have done?' Her words are far from apologetic. I suck in a much-needed breath, seeking some sort of clarity. Why have I come to demand answers from her? What's drawn me to this place? Is it that she's the only person who knows the true identity of my father? Is it that she's my only family, or is it something else? Why am I here?

'I would have known the truth.' My voice is roughened by sorrow. I realise, at that moment, my fear. She must hear it.

'We kept you safe.' Her reply is barely heard above the rain drumming outside. No one is about in Tamworth. The streets are awash with running water and mud. Why then, I consider, does she whisper, even now?

'I wouldn't have been safe?' The words are stark, and I feel my forehead furrow.

'You're the son of a king.' I think she'll leave it there. But she turns away, looking down at her hands before she speaks again. 'The son of a king many blame for the current state of affairs in Mercia. You would have also been blamed.'

'Why would I? I wasn't his son when he was king. I was born before he became king and before he even thought of becoming king.'

'Ah, you've been made to think as the holy men would have it.' Those words spit with more ire than the snapping of the twigs in the heart of the fire. 'A son is a son. In the eyes of some, you would have been throne-worthy, an ætheling. It wouldn't have mattered to many. It still won't.' There's a caution there, one I don't like to hear.

I shake my head, and water pools from my cloak and down my nose. I lick it. I'm thirsty and angry.

'You can use it, you know.' Now I understand all those tales she told me of long-ago kings. I understand her too well, and a shiver of hope and dismissal ripples my spine. She didn't train me because she felt pity for my lost birthright. No, she kept me close so that, when the time came, she could make me Mercia's king.

'I'm no king,' I counter, saying those words enough to assure myself that I speak the truth. I am no king. I'll never be a king. I don't want to rule. I want to be Icel the healer. But I'll be content with Icel the warrior of Mercia. And yet, I'm angry as well. I would have known the truth of my birth. Those decisions should have been mine to make.

'You're an eagle, not a sparrow,' she counters, her words angrier. I eye her as I finally slip the sodden cloak from my shoulders and allow the water to stream onto the floor. There's a hook where other cloaks rest, and I place it on one, ensuring I don't make the others as wet as mine.

'I'm nothing.' I settle before her, sinking gratefully to the stool and the heat of the fire. Running a hand through my black hair, my eyes alight on the scar there, the one that does mark me with Mercia's eagle. But it is Mercia's, not mine.

'You're the son of a king.' She reaches towards me. Her skeletal hands are a too vivid reminder that, should I want to claim Beornwulf as my father, I need to do it quickly before she breathes her last, and there's no one to stand as witness to my claim. But who would accept the words of the old healer woman? Mercia is at peace with itself, almost. Mercia has recovered from the years of uncertainty, the years of too many kings, one after another, falling beneath the blade of the king of the East Angles, Athelstan, the king-killer. Mercia is whole and needs to be, for enemies surround her. Wessex to the south, the kingdom of the East Angles to the east, the Welsh to the west, and the Viking raiders who scurry along rivers, killing and taking people and treasure without thought, leaving bloodshed in their wake.

'I'm the son of my mother, who died birthing me.' I force those words through my tight throat. I've witnessed how my mother died. I watched Lady Cynehild fight her bloody battle on the birthing bed, one she lost, for all her youngest son lives and, I hope, thrives. Her youngest son. Coelwulf. What will his life be like? Who'll protect him from the horrors of who he is and what he did?

'You're the son of Beornwulf, king of Mercia. You have a royal name, for all many have forgotten that.' Once more, the intensity in those words belies the slightness of her frame, the cold etched onto her features as though it were a permanent tattoo emblazoned there with needle and ink. Wynflæd is old, tired and weak. I see it all laid bare before me. What if she doesn't survive the winter? I've always been alone, but I'll be even more alone if she's no longer here.

Edwin isn't my friend. I've shamed the men of Ealdorman Ælfstan's warriors by taking them to the Isle of Sheppey. King Wiglaf's rage is intense. We've all been punished for that act of disobedience, for all we rescued a man who would have died otherwise. Lord Coenwulf, a traitor to Mercia. A man who thought to ally with King Ecgberht of Wessex, or at least, that's what we believe was to happen.

What sort of man is Lord Coenwulf? He wasn't worthy of Lady Cynehild when they married to cement his bargain with King Wiglaf. He was her second husband. In turn, she had been my father's second wife.

Lord Coenwulf will make a poor father to young Coenwulf and Coelwulf, two motherless boys, yet his sister is wed to the king's son, Lord Wigmund. One day Lady Ælflæd will rule Mercia by the side of her husband. I foresee only that she'll be as fearless as the wife of King Offa. She'll not be cowed by a bishop or enemies. She'll be magnificent, for all her husband is a weak, mewling man who'd sooner offer his sword to the enemy than defend his family and kingdom. There is no love lost between myself and Wigmund. We've butted up against one another too many times in the past.

And Lady Ælflæd, I believe, suspects my true identity after her journey to Budworth to pay her respects at my uncle's grave on behalf of Lady Cynehild. Not from witnessing my uncle's grave, but from gazing at my mother's. We can never be friends if that's the case. Not now. I understand so much more since Lady Cynehild informed me of my identity. I wish she hadn't.

'You'll protect Mercia.' Wynflæd's still talking, and I try to listen to her words. 'You'll become her king. No fool, such as young Wigmund, will be able to do what you can. You must.' She almost ends with a shriek. But I'm shaking my head, looking at the fire, focusing on the blue heart of the flame, which should presage warmth but which reminds me only of the frozen world beyond the workshop. Rain might have turned the settlement of Tamworth to dark mud, but winter threatens. When the rain stops, the cold will arrive, and walking anywhere will be dangerous.

Outside, it's white, blue, pale pink and mauve. It's the winter when it's light for a small part of the day and dark for all other times.

'I'm a warrior and a healer able to stitch battle wounds, nothing more,' I counter quickly, swallowing against the spark of hope that Wynflæd's assertion places in the fire of my belly. What could I be if I only had supporters? Could I rule? Could I govern better than King Wiglaf? Perhaps not, but yes, certainly better than his son and the collection of sycophants who've tied themselves to Wigmund, and his mother, Queen Cynethryth, the despised Ealdorman Sigered amongst them. Surely, Sigered should be dead by now. He's old and twisted, but in his heart, not in his body.

Wynflæd's cold hand on mine douses the flames more quickly than an iron blade at my throat. 'Your uncle Cenfrith wanted this for you.'

But I'm shaking my head. My uncle didn't want it for himself. He certainly wouldn't have wanted it for me. He kept me safe. He did his duty. He could have told me himself if he'd wanted me to know. He could have built a collection of ealdormen and warriors around him, but my uncle was a loner. He always thought of Mercia and me, but not in the way Wynflæd thinks. He didn't want me to rule it. I know that for sure.

'My uncle didn't.' I cut her short. 'I don't want it, and anyway,' and this is the pillar of my argument, 'I can't have it. I'm oath-sworn at Lady Cynehild's wishes.'

'Oath-sworn?' Wynflæd's hooded eyes narrow, thin tongue licking at her dry lips. 'Oath-sworn,' she prompts when I offer nothing further.

'To her sons. Coenwulf and Coelwulf. They have a claim to the Mercian kingdom, a stronger one than mine.' Before I'm even aware of what she's doing, Wynflæd is on her feet, her shoulders tight, her stance rigid.

'That bitch.' The words thrum through her body, for all they're hissed with disgust. I feel my forehead furrow at such a reaction. Lady Cynehild and Wynflæd have long since reconciled. I thought them friends, not enemies. Wynflæd rounds on me to bend and grip my hand in her two hands, looking down at the scar from the seax blade when I tried to heal my uncle in the woodlands close to the border with the Welsh kingdoms. It feels as though it were a lifetime ago.

Her cold white fingers trace the edges of the wound. It's long since healed, but it's marked me more than anything else. This makes me Mercian. This makes me an eagle, but it's only skin-deep. It doesn't meet my heart.

'She never wanted you to have anything.' Spittle follows those words, her fingers continuing to trace the scar. I want to pull my hand back and cover the markings with my gloves, as I often do. But her grip's fierce. Her strength surprises me. 'She wasn't your friend, and you're not bound by an oath given to the conniving bitch. Your claim's stronger than her infant sons. You're the son of a king. Her sons are the sons of a son of a king. And what, she's bid you ensure her son is king one day?' Now her words are deathly quiet, the menace making me shiver. I finally snatch back my hand and cover the markings by clenching my fist. 'She would have you fight for her sons when she wouldn't fight for you? She would have you lay down your life to enforce an entitlement that will bring you into conflict with others and a claim that will do you little good but bring more scars to your flesh?' Wynflæd paces as she speaks, no longer whispering. Outside, the sound of the thunderous rain intensifies. I look down, noticing where water encroaches through the doorway. There should be straw there to absorb the water. Something to stop it from getting close to the hearth and compromising the ring of stones in which the wood snaps and crackles, a cheery counterpart to an unpleasant conversation.

'I gave my word,' I murmur. 'She asked, and I gave it.'

'And did you give it before you knew the truth of your birthright, your destiny, or after?' Her eyes blaze into mine.

I shake my head. I won't answer that.

'She was a conniving, lying she-devil until her last breaths.' My sharp intake of shocked breath has Wynflæd laughing. 'You thought her your friend. You thought her last moments a desperate request for you to shield children, æthelings that her disgraced husband will be unable to should King Wiglaf even allow him to live after what he's done? Did you think to feel pity and sorrow for a dying woman? Well, I assure you, she was clearer in those final moments than at any time in the last ten winters. She makes you a protector when she tried to force your uncle to send you from his protection? She demands from you everything that she denied you when you were a boy and needed others to ensure you gained what was rightfully yours.'

Wynflæd's eyes are wild, her fury bringing a glow to her skin that won't have been there since the warmth of the summer. She's enlivened, bold, and very, very scary.

'You won't do it,' she barks, the words a screech louder than an eagle chasing its prey. 'You'll not do it. The boys will become nothing. Their parentage will be forgotten. They'll have no one to speak for them. Had I known her intentions, I would never have allowed you to grow close. I would never have gone to her aid when the birth of her first child approached. I would have let her, and that child, die had I known of this.'

I hang my head low, tears threatening to spill once more. Her harsh words astound me.

'Your uncle would not have wanted this. He esteemed Lady Cynehild but only because she was, for the duration of her first marriage, complicit in keeping your identity a secret. Your father, had he lived, wouldn't have expected this from you. I can assure you of that.' Her words crack with fury.

I came here to tell Wynflæd of my anger, to demand answers, to seek some understanding of the part she willingly played in concealing my identity, but this meeting will be more than that. I know it. Perhaps she fears it too. She asks me for something I can't give. I'm no king. I have no right to rule Mercia, whether I will it or not.

I came here to lay my anger at her feet, but instead, she turns her rage on me.

'I can't deny my oath,' I speak into the silence, my words resounding as though thunder echoes outside, along with the tumultuous downpour. 'I gave my word, admittedly, before I knew the truth of my father's identity,' I say, my voice softer now, not meeting her eyes. I'm not sure it matters. Had I known, I would still have been determined to protect the children. They are like I once was before I became a warrior. They are weak and powerless, and soon, I imagine, they'll lack even the protection of their father. 'I gave my word, and those children are defenceless. I'll protect them.' I speak slowly. I want her to understand. As she kept me safe throughout all these years, I will do the same for those children. To not do so would make me a weak man, no matter my anger at Lady Cynehild for her cruel use of the information she kept from me, or at my uncle for failing to tell me when he evidently knew. At my father for not acknowledging me and then dying before he could.

'Then why did you even come here?' she crows, rage filling the workshop where I spent so much of my childhood. 'Why did you come here if you were only going to disappoint my dreams of many winters?' Her chest heaves as I finally look at her, meet those familiar eyes, and see all that has been consistent until now in my short life.

I stand.

'It was to say goodbye.' And, without looking back, I unhook my dripping cloak and stride from the place.

Wynflæd makes no effort to stop me.

2

'Icel.' My name rings through the damp air from the too-familiar voice, but head down, my cloak failing to shield me from the rain, I push onwards. I tense, fearing that Wulfheard will encourage his stallion, Bada, to race towards me, regardless of the mess of the flooding road. Only when long moments have passed do I appreciate that Wulfheard has made no attempt whatsoever. Perhaps he thinks I'm not whom he thought I was. Maybe he doesn't care.

Tears sting my eyes afresh at this new betrayal, but I don't turn Brute's head and encourage Wine onwards, even when she tries to fight the leading rein and respond to Wulfheard's words. They must know one another of old. Fleeing from Wynflæd and Tamworth has brought me out in the teeming rain. I've taken Wine with me, my uncle's horse. If I never return to Tamworth, I must take responsibility for the animal.

Unbidden, my thoughts tumble to the day of Lady Cynehild's death. My life has changed beyond all recognition since then. I thought of myself as one person, but I'm another, and I'm far from reconciled to it. I consider if this is how my uncle felt when my mother died birthing me. At least he had my father, but then, my father never claimed me, or so it seems. For, had he called me his son, then I'd have long known whom he was and, perhaps, even known him better than that.

My father. A king. The idea is outrageous, and yet, so much makes sense now. Lady Cynehild's interest in me, or lack of interest, would be a better way of describing it. She always hated me, and yet she watched everything I did. She was my father's second wife, once he became king and was expected to birth an heir. Did Lady Cynehild hope I'd falter? Did she wish for me to make mistakes and embarrass the father I didn't know I had but that she did? I struggle to understand her thinking. The conversation I once overheard between her and my uncle during that cold winter rumbles through my mind. She wanted me gone from Tamworth. She wanted my uncle to hide me away, whether because of her failure in regards to an heir for the king, or because when she did have a child, she didn't want another with a prior claim. I wish I could hate her for that.

But it's my father that I hate. He should have claimed me as his son, no matter what. Why didn't he? I was a motherless child, and he cast me aside. Yes, I realise he kept me close and denied his second wife's desire to be rid of me, whatever her reasoning. And he ensured I had what was required, but I needed to know him. I was deprived of truly knowing him. There are so many questions I'd ask him, given half the chance. I'd know why he took the kingdom of Mercia from the rightful king. I would know why he rode to war against the might of the kingdom of the East Angles without so much as a backwards glance. Didn't he even consider the possibility he'd meet his death there? Didn't he think he might make me an orphan if he met his death?

Why? It's the only word that resounds in my head. Why?

'Icel.' The cry is harsh and filled with fury. 'What the bloody hell are you doing?' I look up, rain falling into my eyes to mask the traitor tears that fell when I was feeling sorry for myself, and meet the furious gaze of Wulfheard. Bada drips with rain, pooling onto the broken surface of the stone-built roadway, the gutters so alive with the downpour that they rumble as loud as a river.

'Go away,' I growl at the older man, trying not to see the flash of pain in his eyes, the betrayal in them, and the confusion.

'What do you mean, go away? I'm your commander. You do as I order you to do. Where have you been? Or rather, why do you have Wine and

Brute? It's obvious you've been to Tamworth so where are you going now?'

'Leave me alone.' The words are leaden in my throat, but I must say them all the same. Despite everything I've just thought.

'What's the matter with you?' Wulfheard reaches across the gap between us and grips my arm. I shake him off, feeling the heat of his fingers on my chilled arm.

'I said, go away.' I speak slowly, emphasising the words as I knee Brute forward. Only Wulfheard keeps pace with us; Bada, head down, obeying his master's commands.

'You've been like this ever since Lady Cynehild died,' Wulfheard continues. I wish he'd leave me alone. 'You left Kingsholm without a word to anyone. I see you've been to Tamworth to collect Wine as well. Where do you think you're going.'

'To Kingsholm.'

'Why would you return to Kingsholm? The king's furious with Lord Coenwulf. As soon as he's well enough, it's believed he'll be banished, and the king will confiscate all of his lands. They even say that Lady Ælflæd, will be given the settlement in her own name.' The reminder of Lady Ælflæd, Coenwulf's sister and the wife of the king's son, is an unwelcome one.

'And what of his sons?' I meet Wulfheard's eyes now, seeing the furrow of his eyebrows, and the rain that drips from his nose.

'What of his sons? They're nothing to you.'

'They're Lady Cynehild's sons,' I cry, even though I want to hate her too. She's denied me of so much and now expects me to give it freely. And because I'm a man of my word, I can't refute the final oath she extracted from me.

'The king will care for them. After all, his son is married to their aunt. Their grandfather was once a king, their great-uncle as well.'

I shake my head. I know what will happen to them. I foresee it only too well. It happened to me, and it'll happen to them, no matter the intentions of Lady Ælflæd. She's a strong-willed woman, but she's the wife of the king's son's. One day she'll be queen. Someone, and possibly she's already realised this, will highlight how destructive the boys could be to her son's claim to rule Mercia.

And Lord Coenwulf's a ruin of himself. If I thought him an arrogant, quick-to-rage man when I cared for his father's horse after his father died an old man, he's ten times worse now. He's wrecked.

'The king's son will do all he can to eliminate them. They are but small children. Should they die, no one will think of them. Should someone get their hands on them, one of the other ealdormen, then they'd be a sure way to counter the power of King Wiglaf and his family. Those children are in danger.'

Again, confusion swamps Wulfheard's face. But he doesn't deny my argument, and that hardens my faltering resolve.

'Why should that concern you? What aren't you telling me, Icel? I'm your friend.' The final word's plaintive. I dip my head and focus on my hands, resting on the reins. My gloves are wet through. I can feel the dampness on my skin.

'You're my commander, as you said, when I ride with Ealdorman Ælfstan's warrior band. You're not my friend. You have never been. King Wiglaf and Ealdorman Ælfstan bid you train me to defend myself, and I don't deny that you did a very good job of it, but I'm not one of the warriors. I'm the Lord of Budworth. I should take up that position now.'

'And yet, you head towards Kingsholm and speak of the sons of Lord Coenwulf.' Wulfheard's response is once more rational. I'm aware that he thinks much more clearly than I do.

Silence falls between us, broken only by the sound of heavy rain falling and the rushing water in the blocked drainage channels to the side of the road.

'There is that as well,' I confirm, meeting his eyes, ensuring mine are firm and offer no flicker of my inner turmoil.

'Icel, what's going on?' The booming voice of Oswy cuts the air as he brings his horse into view. I'm aware that the rest of Ealdorman Ælfstan's warriors have halted their journey. All I need now is for Ealdorman Ælfstan to appear.

'Nothing. Leave me alone.' The words aren't easy to say. I've fought beside Oswy, and he's battled to protect me. I healed him and made him whole once more.

'Why's Wine with you?' Once more, confusion covers the other man's face. Wulfheard and Oswy's bewilderment is understandable, but I'm not accountable to them. My oath is to the king.

'She's my horse,' I huff, wishing this was over. The winter days are short enough. I need to resume my journey.

'If you're Lord of Budworth,' Wulfheard demands, and I can tell he's trying to be reasonable, 'why aren't you going there? Why do you head south?'

'I'm going to speak for Lord Coenwulf before the king.'

'The king knows what he plans to do. He's just waiting for Lord Coenwulf to be well enough to leave Mercia before banishing him. Don't tie yourself to Coenwulf. He's no friend of yours.' Wulfheard's words are lucid and sensible, and they echo Wynflæd's when speaking of Lady Cynehild.

'It's the children I must protect,' I retort, aware that my voice screeches with defiance. I sound like a child, not a warrior and lord of Mercia.

'Icel, it's not your role to protect those children. The king will see it done, no matter what happens to Lord Coenwulf. Do you plan on leaving Mercia with him? I don't think you want to do that.'

'The children will remain in Mercia,' I argue. 'I'm sure of it. And they must have protectors.'

'Their aunt will guard them and their other aunt, the young one, I forget her name. They'll be like brother and sister. And anyway, why is this yours to concern yourself with?'

'Lady Cynehild.'

'What of her?' But I can hear the suspicion in Wulfheard's voice. 'What did she say to you as she died? Why were you even there?'

'I...' But I can't find the words. I hate her, miss her, and yet must abide by her wishes simultaneously. Conflict undulates through me, but I know what's right. I need to give voice to my oath to her, and yet I can't. 'I must be there.'

'Ealdorman Ælfstan's there. He'll speak for the children.'

'Ealdorman Ælfstan's position is as untenable as Lord Coenwulf's. Both men will be banished, Coenwulf for his treason, and Ælfstan for going to get him.' Ælfstan is the ealdorman of the Magonsæte, to the north of Kingsholm, an unruly area at the best of times with its borders close to the Welsh kingdoms. The king will want a loyal man as his ally there.

'No, they won't.' Wulfheard dismisses my concerns. 'King Wiglaf needs Ealdorman Ælfstan. The attack on the Isle of Sheppey by the Viking raiders shows how conniving those bastards are. While the king might be furious, he understands we were protecting Mercia with our actions. The same can't be said for Lord Coenwulf. His warriors are all dead, his wife as well. And he's an embarrassment to the king. He must act to protect the union forged between the two families. Better to forget about Lord Coenwulf and focus on his sister, and the children.'

'I think you'll be surprised just what the king thinks.'

'Why, what have you heard? What do you know, Icel? It's not as though you're deep in the king's confidences or even allowed to speak with him other than when you rescue him from the enemy. King Wiglaf wants your blood, not your mind.'

'Perhaps, but all the same.'

'Then very well. Do what must be done. The men and I are sent to Worcester to escort Lady Ælflæd to Kingsholm. Think about what I've said, and I'll see you when we return.' With no more words, Wulfheard turns Bada back towards the road, but Oswy lingers, his gaze keen.

'These women, Icel, they know their worth. Lady Cynehild. The queen. Lady Ælflæd. They make demands on men, and we strive to fulfil those requests, but in the end, we're not their creatures. We know what's right and wrong, as with you and young Edwin. I knew the queen was wrong to belittle your accomplishments. I stepped aside from her control. I don't pretend it wasn't awkward, but it was the right thing to do. I can't deny that she glowers at me whenever I see her, but that is her problem, not mine. Icel, you know the right thing to do more than anyone I've ever known. Tread carefully, my friend.' And with that, Oswy leaves me as well. I linger, against my wishes, watching my fellow warriors ride on, until they disappear beneath the thick clouds, and then, heart hardened, I encourage Brute and Wine onwards to Kingsholm.

I need to reach Kingsholm. I'll add my voice to those few who demand leniency for Lord Coenwulf. I must align myself against the queen and Ealdorman Sigered, even more than now. And I know I must also see what Lady Ælflæd intends to do with regards to her nephews. Will she be swayed by her husband, Lord Wigmund, the king's son? Or will she be honourable, as I hope – though I fear I think too highly of her. With everything that's happened, she too might be desperate to distance herself from her brother's actions.

Oswy's right. These women are ambitious, and they don't care if small children are cast aside in their efforts to maintain a hold on power.

And that's what drives me.

It's not love for Lady Cynehild, for I think, in the end, she didn't love me. Ultimately, she saw me as a means to an end, in much the same way that Wynflæd does. She thought I'd be king. Lady Cynehild hoped the very opposite. Why she told me the truth, with her final words, I don't know. Was it to tie me even more tightly to her children when she knew she was dying? Did she know her husband would be cast aside? So many questions. And no answers, only the silence of the grave.

But those children? Well, they're like I was as a child. Almost orphans, with one parent living who can't protect them, even if he wanted to.

I'll be the shield between Coenwulf and Coelwulf that their father can't be. Even if that brings me into conflict with the king, his wife, his son and Lady Ælflæd. Even if it means I can never wear the warrior helm of Mercia's king which, by my birth, I should be entitled to do.

3

KINGSHOLM

'My lord Coenwulf.' King Wiglaf's words are rich and booming. He speaks as the king of Mercia for all he's in the hall of Coenwulf, heir to his father who ruled as King Coelwulf and, by rights, the man who should be king.

Coenwulf is a ruin of the man he used to be. I thought him bitter and twisted when his father died, and he alleged I killed his father's horse, an accusation for which he later apologised. But now he's truly broken. He might well have wed Lady Cynehild as part of an accord with King Wiglaf. It might have been a union neither had wanted and yet, in the time since her death, I know he loved her. And I know he loves his children, even though he can hardly bear to gaze upon them.

And King Wiglaf? He's grown in stature and command in the years since he became king. He's not the man who ran from the might of King Ecgberht of Wessex. No. He's Mercia's warrior king. He's the man who's now held that position for longer than the two kings who ruled before him.

He's powerful. He's respected. And he knows it.

I eye him warily. I've learned to admire King Wiglaf. As a warrior, he inspires his fellow men. As a king, he's to be esteemed. As a man, he's beset by an over-powerful wife and a useless son. I suppose a man can't have every advantage before him, and Wiglaf certainly doesn't.

And now he must contend with the matter of Lord Coenwulf, a man sworn to him, and yet who was captured by the Viking raiders while agreeing to meet King Ecgberht of Wessex in secrecy.

King Wiglaf has given Lord Coenwulf time to recover from his wounds gained on the Isle of Sheppey and from the death of Lady Cynehild, but it can never be enough. I don't believe that Lord Coenwulf will defend his actions. I almost think he wishes himself dead.

'My lord king.' Lord Coenwulf cannot bow low for fear of falling, and yet he has two of his warriors, one of them my old childhood friend Edwin, to either side so that they can support him all the same. His leg was badly broken by the Viking raiders and allowed to mend at an odd angle. Our rescue of him wasn't gentle. On our journey through Kent, I was forced to re-break his leg and set it correctly again for fear he'd never walk without a limp. It's been slow to heal. Too slow. He might always limp, despite my attempts to prevent it.

The hall at Kingsholm is the fullest I've ever seen it – more of Mercia's noblemen and women crammed into that small space than should be possible. I've found a gap not far from the door to the rear, but I can see well enough. Not that I truly wish to witness this. I would not observe the ruined man cast even lower, but King Wiglaf must punish him. I believe Queen Cynethryth is even more eager to abuse the broken Lord Coenwulf. Now that Lady Cynehild is dead, Queen Cynethryth has only her daughter by marriage, who could possibly claim as much respect as her. Cynehild and the queen were always far from allies. I contemplate whether she exalts in Cynehild's death. Perhaps, I consider, if the child had died as well as the mother, she might. She's a cruel woman, always with both eyes on the future and not just on the here and now. She must see the threat the young boys are to her grandson.

'You may sit,' the king announces, his hand flicking to show servants should bring the lord of Kingsholm a chair upon which to perch. If they don't do so, he'll fall, despite the support of his warriors.

King Wiglaf's dressed in his finest clothes, gold and silver shimmering from his fingers and tunic. His cloak is thick, and a collar of finest white fur lines it. His boots shimmer at the end of thick woollen trews. He wears no warrior helm, but a fine coil of gold slithers through his greying hair, revealing he's king here and no one else. His wife, the queen, sits to his left. She's bedecked in so much finery that I fear she'll tumble if asked to walk far. The weight of the shimmering jewels at her ear and throat must be cold against her skin. Her face is twisted, her silver threaded hair visible beneath the gauze material that covers it. She might look regal, but anger exudes from her. Fingers tapping against the side of the wooden chair she sits within, Queen Cynethyrth can't take her eyes from Lord Coenwulf.

She'd do better to mask her thoughts. I see them too clearly, and so will everyone else.

In the distance, the wail of a child splits the air. I half turn, wincing, before I stop myself. The babe is well, perhaps hungry or dirty, but well. I don't need to leave this place to protect him and his brother. In my self-appointed role, the women caring for the motherless boys are far from welcoming to me. In this, it seems, I lack all of the empathy I once knew when Wynflæd shared her secrets of healing with me.

The sound has heads turning, all apart from mine. The king catches my eye, a perplexed expression on his face. He didn't expect to find me here. He's not alone. I didn't expect to find me here either. No doubt he assumes I'm with Ealdorman Ælfstan's warriors, or perhaps even at Budworth, my estate. But not here, in Kingsholm.

'You've been called to answer to the charges brought against you.' The king quickly returns everyone to the present, talking over the wailing of the babe. 'That of treason.'

The word falls heavily and awkwardly, but the king hasn't finished.

'We must separate the unfortunate outcome of your attempt, your capture by our enemy Viking raiders, from what you intended, which was to speak with the king of Wessex, another enemy of Mercia. For all your wounds would perhaps be seen as punishment enough by some, I can't agree with that. Tell me, Lord Coenwulf, what did you hope to achieve?'

'My lord king.' Coenwulf's voice is frail and little used. 'I was sent word that King Ecgberht of Wessex wished to speak with me regarding the borders between Wessex and Mercia. As you know, there have been difficulties that extend far beyond the reach of the River Thames and include that of the Wansdyke. The land boundary is unruly and has been particularly so since King Ecgberht's incursion inside Mercia. I thought it warranted my attention.'

The words are deceptively bland. They mask the problems on the southern border, where no river exists to act as a natural divide, and instead there is the Wansdyke. As I understand it, thanks to Wulfheard long ago, it's similar to Offa's Dyke, which divides Mercia from the Welsh kingdoms. It's a ditch and a slope, the slope facing northwards, as though to stop any from attacking that way. I don't know who built it. Perhaps the giants who constructed Londinium. If not, then Saxons, like me, under the guidance of a king, long ago, in the far reaches of memory and history.

'And you decided to do so without referring the matter to me?' Again, the words are bland. Both men are trying hard to remove the emotion from the meeting. King Wiglaf feels betrayed. I'm not sure that Lord Coenwulf can feel anything but sorrow for his dead wife and fear for his children.

'I did, my lord king. I knew you were close to Lundenwic. I hoped to contact King Ecgberht, determine his intentions, and seek your advice. It wasn't my objective to act with deception.'

'Hum.' That single word fills the hall. I look up, catching sight of the many eagle-headed shields displayed on the hall's walls above the king's head. Kingsholm has long been the home of Mercia's kings: Coenwulf and then his brother, Coelwulf, both the first of their names. The men who once walked these boards throughout the last thirty winters and warmed themselves before the hearth knew their worth. I still struggle to understand why King Coelwulf relinquished his rights to the kingdom of Mercia. It doesn't help that I know my father, King Beornwulf, was the cause of it.

My father. The thought sends a tremor of fury through my body. If he were here now, I'd kill him. I've no doubts about that. Perhaps Lady Cynehild as well. Both kept their secrets. Of my uncle, I can't decide. Grief for his death makes it impossible for me to hate him, not when, of all those who knew my true identity, he was the one who cared for me the most.

'I've heard a different version of this event.' Of course, I should have expected Ealdorman Sigered to add his voice to the proceedings. The worm is entirely that. I can't be alone in watching the look of smug satisfaction that crosses Queen Cynethryth's face at those words. Ealdorman Sigered is attended upon by his grandson Sigegar, one of Lord Wigmund's allies. Indeed, Lord Wigmund's allies seem to fill the hall: I've seen Ælfred and Hunberht. No doubt there are more of these men and women that I don't recognise who've cast in their lot with Lord Wigmund.

'I'm aware of that, Ealdorman Sigered.' The king isn't to be moved from his interrogation of Lord Coenwulf.

'Then you'll hear me speak,' the old man demands petulantly. He's standing, only just visible above the shoulders of those who sit. He gets smaller each time I see him, shrivelling up like a summer apple during the winter months. No doubt, he'd taste as bitter.

'Indeed, Ealdorman Sigered. Please share what you think you know.' The king speaks with suppressed frustration. I can't believe the ealdorman fails to hear the censure in those words, but he presses on, all the same.

'I've been informed, my lord king, that it was Lord Coenwulf who made overtures of friendship to the Wessex king. Not the other way around. He meant to ally with the Wessex king. His new marriage and the birth of his son had reminded him of all he'd lost.' I perceive a flicker of unease cross King Wiglaf's face. The words of Ealdorman Sigered are eminently feasible. King Wiglaf sees that clearly. If Ealdorman Sigered lies, he's making it as probable as possible.

'And you have witnesses to these accusations?' King Wiglaf speaks quickly before any murmur of unease can begin. My fists clench with outrage, revealing my unsuitability to be in King Wiglaf's position, even if I can claim just as much right to rule as Lord Coenwulf and his sons. Perhaps more right than King Wiglaf, even.

'Alas, only two, my lord king. Lord Coenwulf's men were all murdered by the Viking raiders, as I'm sure you remember.' I feel my forehead crease at those words. All but Edwin, and Edwin is loyal to Lord Coenwulf. He'd never speak out against him. Who then levels the accusation?

'And they'll speak?'

'She will, my lord king, yes. And so will he.' Now my heart stills. My mouth's too dry to swallow. I fear I know who'll be brought forth by Ealdorman Sigered, and I'm not mistaken. Ealdorman Sigered means to lay the most damning evidence against Lord Coenwulf first. I'd hate him, but his planning earns my grudging respect. The damn bastard has survived for decades at the Mercian court. He means to continue to do so.

Lady Ælflæd. She's the wife of the king's son. She's Lord Coenwulf's sister and the aunt to his two small sons, and yet I notice the smirk of triumph on the queen's face and also on that of her son's. Lord Wigmund is a maggot to grind beneath my boots if only I had the opportunity. But I'm devastated that Lady Ælflæd steps forward to denounce her brother. I thought her better than this. I knew his actions would be an embarrassment, but this is too much.

I eye her. She is, as ever, beautiful. My heart thuds loudly in my chest. At this moment, I know I love her, and yet I loathe her as well. More and more, I'm realising the double-edged blade that love and hatred can be.

She shimmers with the wealth of her position, for all her face remains pale. I'm not convinced she's recovered from the birth of her child yet. She need not have travelled to Kingsholm. And yet she did, as soon as she could. It was her that Wulfheard and Oswy escorted to Kingsholm when I last saw them. Well, her and her husband.

'My lord king. I'll speak of my brother's ambitions to drive a wedge between the ancient realm of the kingdom of the Hwicce and that of the rest of the kingdom of Mercia.'

She talks without inflexion as she stands before all assembled. I can't believe what I'm hearing. She sounds nothing like the girl I once knew who berated her brother for his anger towards me. I've been aware of her at Kingsholm, but only in passing. We've managed to avoid one another. She's been secluded with her sickly son. I've been no company for anyone. Wulfheard and Oswy didn't stay, and neither did they approach me. I'm strangely grateful they left me alone.

Perhaps she now seeks a means of gaining revenge against her brother for such a poor marriage that even the progeny brought forth from it fails to thrive. Perhaps. Maybe she's just been turned by her husband's and his mother's wishes.

I can only see Lady Ælflæd's back, shoulders rigid, where she faces the king. Her brother makes a pitiful figure in comparison, his back to me as well, but his shoulders bent on the chair he's been allowed to sit upon. He quivers with the pressure of the trial. If he could, I imagine he'd whimper, as his son does from far away.

I open my mouth and then snap it shut once more. What can I do? I don't know the truth of the allegations. Yet they taste like ash on my too-dry tongue.

'It is specifics I require,' the king tries. I see his eyes flickering between the two. What must he see? What must he surmise from this unexpected discord between the two? Lady Ælflæd is a mother now. Her child is the future king of Mercia, provided Mercia stands united and not divided against its external enemies and its internal ones. Does King Wiglaf wish to bring Kingsholm and the Hwiccan territory more firmly under his command? And if he does, is that through the persuasions of Lady Ælflæd, or would he rather use other means?

'Then, we'll call on Ealdorman Sigered's remaining witness.' Lady Ælflæd is gracious as she inclines her head to her father by marriage, who is also king. I don't miss the look of gratification on Queen Cynethryth's face at her daughter-by-marriage's words.

I don't recognise the man who stumbles to his feet, bowing before he's upright. I thought I had a fairly good grasp of the men and women who made Kingsholm their home, but this man's unknown. It doesn't help that I'm trying to decide who he is just from his back. His hair is long but not unkempt, brown and uninspiring. There's no grey there. He's broad of shoulder and stands upright with a warrior's arrogance.

'My name's Eadbald.' His words are slow and laboured. 'I was once a member of King Coenwulf's loyal household warriors. Now, I'm not.' The words hide much. Where has he been for the last decade since King Coenwulf was removed from the kingship? Has he been inside Kingsholm?

'And you have an eyewitness account of events?' King Wiglaf's poise is assured. Perhaps I shouldn't be surprised that a man who can make decisions in the heat of battle can contend with family discord being played out before him, while the great and good of Mercia watch on.

I eye some of those others, as they sit, avidly watching these events. I know many of them, but there are some new faces. Where, I consider, have they come from? What stone have they crawled from to seek the attention of the king, or his queen, or his son?

'I can, my lord king, for I was the one who was sent to treat with King Ecgberht.' A gasp of outrage floods the hall, no doubt from the men and women of Kingsholm. I look to Lord Coenwulf's back, but he doesn't indicate how he takes the news. I want him to deny the words. I even seek out Edwin amongst the crowd, but he's no longer visible, having left Lord Coenwulf when he was settled on a chair.

I don't believe the lies. But if Lord Coenwulf doesn't speak out for himself, then everyone else will. Lady Ælflæd, and this man that I don't know, denounce him. And with no one decrying the poisonous rumours, which I'm sure they must be, things can only go poorly for Lord Coenwulf.

'My lord Coenwulf, do you have anything to say against such a statement?'

'I don't, my lord king.' I can't believe Lord Coenwulf will allow himself to be treated in such a way. I think of Lady Cynehild. She'd not have allowed her husband to conspire against Mercia. I'm sure of it. But what can I do? I know nothing.

'Then tell me, Eadbald. Where did you seek out King Ecgberht in Wessex?'

'My lord king,' the man queries.

I nod along with King Wiglaf's determination to get to the truth. Queen Cynethryth's face is mutinous for a moment until she remembers to clear it of her anger at her husband's dogged determination. I notice that she stills her son's hand on the chair beside her. His unease is evident.

'I travelled to Winchester, my lord king.' Eadbald doesn't even hesitate. King Wiglaf is far from done.

'And what did you think of Winchester, my good man?' This could almost be two men talking over ale and not discussing the life of another and whether or not treason was intended. 'Is it like Tamworth? Filled with churches?'

'Of course, it is, my lord king. Many churches in Winchester. All of them raised to our heavenly father.' I see Bishop Æthelweald nod as though he expected as much, despite the people of Wessex being enemies of Mercia.

'And they're dedicated to St Peter, as our church in Tamworth, or St Chad, as our church in Lichfield?'

'My, my lord king,' Eadbald stumbles, and now I fix my gaze on Bishop Æthelweald. He's also seated on the dais but further from the king. Does he know the dedications of the churches in Winchester? Does he know to whom the people there pray? Will he mouth those words to Eadbald? I'm convinced Eadbald has never been to Winchester. I can't imagine any man walking into Wessex-held territory when Mercia and Wessex are acknowledged enemies. They hate one another for the violence of Londonia and, before that, in Tamworth and on the borders with the Welsh. 'I didn't frequent the churches, my lord king.' Eadbald tries to equivocate, but I can hear the uncertainty in his voice. Is this, then, how the king will prove that Eadbald is lying?

'Is there not a church dedicated to the blessed Mary?' Queen Cynethryth interjects too quickly. And I sigh heavily. She's determined in her endeavours to oust Lord Coenwulf.

'Of course, my lady. How could I forget?' Eadbald is all bows and sycophantic. I want nothing more than to pummel him to the ground. My fists are so tightly clenched that I can feel my blunt nails digging into my skin. Damn the bastard and the bitch.

'St Mary's. And it is close to the king's residence?' While Wiglaf shows no outward sign of annoyance at his wife's interference, he persists.

'No, my lord king, far from it. And, of course, I didn't go to speak to the king himself, but rather his ealdorman.'

'And the man's name?'

'Was Ealdorman Wilfhardi.'

I sigh. This is no help. Ealdorman Wilfhardi is a name familiar to all in Mercia and Wessex.

'What terms did you carry?'

'A desire to ally against yourself, my lord king.'

'In what way?' The king's becoming ever more persistent.

'Against you, my lord king. To allow King Ecgberht to reclaim Mercia.'

'On what terms, though? What did Lord Coenwulf demand to turn traitor on his king?'

'Um, my lord king, I don't know. It was written on vellum, and I can't read.'

Once more, the king cannot break through Eadbald's façade. I wouldn't be surprised to discover someone has paid him to state all this. I would be even less surprised to discover that someone was Ealdorman Sigered.

Yet, what frustrates me more is that Lord Coenwulf refuses to speak for himself. Why isn't he defending himself before the king? All can see that King Wiglaf wishes him to dismiss the argument.

'Lord Coenwulf, what did you hope to achieve by allying with the Wessex king?'

'It doesn't matter.' The words are so soft, I only just hear them. I see others turning puzzled expressions, one to another, as though unsure whether they heard correctly.

'Repeat yourself so all can hear,' the bishop demands unctuously.

'It doesn't matter.' The mumble is barely louder than the first time.

I don't take my eyes from King Wiglaf's face. A flurry of emotions can be discerned in the tension of his shoulders and the way his fingers drum over his knees. This isn't what King Wiglaf wishes to hear. Far from it.

'Lord Coenwulf, I give you the opportunity to defend yourself for the final time. As it stands, I'll be left with no choice but to banish you from your home and Mercia. You'll be cast out if you've committed treason against the Mercian kingdom and the Mercian people.'

Silence thrums through the hall. I detect the resignation in King Wiglaf's posture. This isn't what he wanted to happen. Indeed, none thought it would be necessary, as Wulfheard argued with me when we last met. The king might have spoken of the need to separate the outcome from the intentions in his case, but all feel sympathy towards Lord Coenwulf. All, it seems, apart from the queen, her son, Ealdorman Sigered and Lord Coenwulf's own sister.

I feel compassion for Lord Coenwulf. He was tricked, and he was stolen away. Lady Cynehild, no matter how I hate her behaviour towards me, was a good, loyal Mercian. Her husband wouldn't have committed treason. She would never have asked us to retrieve him from the Viking raiders on the Isle of Sheppey if that had been his intention. It would have been better for him to die there than to face this. I want the king to be kind to Lord Coenwulf. But the poisonous words of Lady Ælflæd, the political astuteness of the queen and the desire of Ealdorman Sigered to please his ally, the queen, mean that the king has lost that option, especially as Lord Coenwulf won't defend himself, as he should.

Perhaps, if Ealdorman Ælfstan was here, or even others of the ealdormen, the king would have some support. But Ælfstan's been forced to return to his ealdordom of the Magonsæte, due to rumbles from the Welsh, while Tidwulf is in Lundenwic, and Muca is on the borderlands with the kingdom of the East Angles. If I didn't know better, I'd see the queen's hand in that as well. She's isolated Lord Coenwulf.

'Then my decision is this. As is the way of our people, you'll be banished from Mercia for a full seven winters. If, after that time, you still wish to return, you may petition me, provided no further crimes of treason have been uncovered. In your absence, Lady Ælflæd will command Kingsholm and your younger sister, Lady Cynewise.'

'My lord king.' Even now, Lord Coenwulf doesn't attempt to deny the sentence. Once more, the cry of a distressed child rings through the air. The queen leans towards her husband. I see him shake his head at whatever she says, but her words are persistent, as are those of her son. Indeed, Lady Ælflæd rushes forward to offer her support for the queen and her husband, as does another man, one I don't recognise but who seems to be high in the king's favour. Who is he? Why don't I know who he is? Dread grows in my belly, worse than anything I've ever felt.

And then the king breathes deeply and slowly exhales, somehow making sense of those who now bend his ear, demanding something else as punishment for Lord Coenwulf.

'My lord, as an assurance that you'll not enter into negotiations with the enemies of Mercia, and on the advice of Queen Cynethryth, my son and his wife, and Lord Beorhtwulf, your sons will remain behind to act as surety for your good behaviour.' It seems I know the man's name now, but whom he is, I still don't know. Not that I don't miss the similarity of his name to that of my father's. I would look at him further, determine if he might be somehow related to him, but instead, my heart constricts. Not that it's anything compared to the animal roar of outrage from Lord Coenwulf. I thought him dead inside, but that's not the case in the matter of his sons. Not at all.

4

'I'll care for your sons.' Lady Ælflæd's voice lacks all sincerity as I listen – when I shouldn't – to the conversation between her and her brother.

The king's gone, alongside his entourage, swept back to Tamworth with the first flakes of snow to fall this winter. His parting words were that Lord Coenwulf could recover until better weather. But then he'd be expected to be gone, per the terms of the king's sentencing of the traitorous fool.

'You will not. You have your son, and your ambitions are rampant. I want only my sons.' Lord Coenwulf's voice is a howl of agony. His physical wounds are healing. His mind isn't. I know that Theodore and Gaya grew increasingly worried about him while they lingered, to care for his sons and him. They should have returned to Ealdorman Tidwulf, but like me, they played dumb to the messengers sent to seek them out, until it was impossible to ignore those demands and the command of Lady Ælflæd herself.

Lord Coenwulf isn't the man he used to be. I fear for him as well, even more now there's only me here who thinks kindly of him.

'My son, Wigstan, will need supporters when he's old enough to rule. What better than his cousins?'

'No, you conniving bitch.' The malice is impossible to ignore, and I have some sympathy when Lady Ælflæd hisses in response.

'I'm no bitch,' she counters. 'I know the worth of my blood, and I'll use it.'

I'm unsure if it's her brother's erratic behaviour which makes her act as she does, or if she's truly changed.

'You've let the queen into your thoughts, haven't you? Don't deny it. Only from someone as callous as her would such a statement be considered acceptable. You spoke against me, and you lied when you did so. Why, sister, why?' It's clear that Lord Coenwulf has made a decision about his sister. I want to deny his words, but her next comment assures me he's no doubt correct.

'You're no man,' Lady Ælflæd hoots. 'And more, your sons will be my creatures when you're gone. They'll not know you, should you ever be allowed to return. They'll think of me as their mother and my husband as their father. You'll be nothing to them.'

'They'll be coming with me.' Lord Coenwulf's cry is anguished. His hatred has evaporated in the wake of his desperation.

'The king, the queen, my husband and Lord Beorhtwulf, says they won't be, and he has men here to ensure your compliance with that order. There's no one to help you, brother, especially not me. Kingsholm's mine. From here, my son will one day rule.'

'Your son must survive to rule first,' Coenwulf counters. I wince at that harsh retort, but it is the truth. The child, Wigstan, isn't strong. Compared to the shrieks of Coelwulf and his mighty lungs, Wigstan is a wounded lamb, barely able to bleat. Yet Lady Ælflæd has ejected Gaya and Theodore from Kingsholm. She didn't take kindly to their attempts to help. I said my farewells to them, and they smiled and embraced me. Theodore's parting words continue to resonate with me. 'This isn't your fault, young Icel,' he assured me, Gaya nodding along. The wisdom in their eyes tore at me, and yet I couldn't agree with them. I am oath-sworn. I am bound to the children.

'My son will thrive once this blasted cold weather has ended. Unless, brother dearest, that's a threat.'

'No threat, sister. I've heard your exhortations to God. I've heard your promises. Perhaps, if you wanted a son who would be strong and able to lead as his grandfather does, and his other grandfather did, you should have found someone less wormlike to take to your bed.'

The sharp slap of skin on skin assures me that Lady Ælflæd has taken her revenge on her brother for such words. But the slap doesn't bring the conversation to an end. Lord Coenwulf hasn't finished yet.

'Lord Beorhtwulf is no friend of yours,' he adds, the bitterness of the words easy to hear. 'You have more to fear than just the threat from my sons.'

'Lord Beorhtwulf is a man of honour. A friend to my husband.'

'Lord Beorhtwulf has his eyes on the kingship, just as much as your husband does.' I'm startled to hear this. 'And, he has the claim to it as well.'

'He is no ætheling?' Lady Ælflæd retorts. I can imagine the haughty expression on her face.

'Neither was your husband's father. Think on that, sister, dearest.'

I hurry away from the side of the hall, eager to not be caught creeping and listening once more. While few within Kingsholm question my presence, Lady Ælflæd is one of those that does. I'm as eager to avoid her now as I was once eager to be close to her.

Time has made strangers out of both of us. She no longer speaks to me or offers a confidence. She's the wife to the king's heir. The mother of the king's heir, heir. And she knows it. We move around one another. I'm overly alert to her presence. I am overly alert to staying away from her. I don't wish to be forcibly removed from Kingsholm, as Gaya and Theodore were.

Hastily, I scamper through the frozen puddles towards the dubious shelter of the stable. Inside, I can see the heated breath of horses and other men as well. In one of the empty stalls, a collection of warriors, oath-sworn to Lord Wigmund, play games of chance, fight and drink. It upsets the horses, but they won't be told.

I move aside, keen to avoid them, only to collide with Edwin.

'Icel.' His greeting is far from warm, but we're almost friends once more. Almost.

'Edwin, it's a bitter day,' I respond quickly. If I can conclude our conversation and sneak from the stables, then the men of Lord Wigmund won't see me. But it's a futile effort, and with a soft sigh, I hear the movement of wood on wood, and two heads appear above the stable door.

'Ah, Icel, we didn't hear you come in,' one of the men calls. He's angular and bright of cheek, a thick, bushy moustache almost half inside his wide, flat nose. I know why his nose is so flat. He likes to fight, does Eadweard. He relishes the cut and thrust of a good bare-knuckle battle. Why, I don't know. It's not as though he's good at such fights. Perhaps he was when a young man, but those days are long behind him. I think him older than Wulfheard now.

Edwin mouths 'sorry' to me, but it's not his fault. I should have thought more before coming this way. Eadweard and his foul-mouthed collection of friends are usually found here, banished from the hall by Lady Ælflæd, although Lord Wigmund keeps them close.

'Young Icel,' his comrade, Wulfred, echoes, as so often happens with the pair. It's almost as though they're one person, but with two heads – as I've heard is possible. Although their bodies are entirely opposite. Wulfred is short and wiry, lacking all hair, none on his head, none on his face. He doesn't even need to shave.

'You said today would be the day you'd join us,' Eadweard taunts. I've been determined to avoid this collection of warriors. Without my one-time friends at my back – Wulfheard, Oswy and Ealdorman Ælfstan – I've no desire to come up against these six men. All of them are dirty fighters, and it wouldn't bother me so much if they were good at it, but they're poor warriors, resorting to underhand tactics repeatedly to achieve the outcome they want. Wulfred isn't above tripping anyone who almost overpowers Eadweard. Eadweard is happy to thump an enemy of Wulfred's across the back if it appears he won't win the day.

'I must see to my horses,' I counter quickly. It's not a lie.

'But we've no one to fight, young Icel. And we'd like to fight you,' Eadweard whines, his tongue poking at some mark on his face. No doubt, he's cut himself shaving or has a bruise from an earlier fight. 'Edwin can help you, and you can join us then?' Eadweard suggests.

'Perhaps,' is my noncommittal response. I don't want to have anything to do with these men. I beckon to Edwin to join me and walk away, ignoring the catcalls and shouts of derision. I certainly don't respond to the suggestion that I'm too scared to fight Eadweard. I know how this small group conducts itself. And I intend to stay as far away from them as possible.

'Sorry,' Edwin huffs. He still suffers from the wounds he gained on the Isle of Sheppey. His left arm has yet to recover its strength, and his face is no longer smooth and free from scars.

'It's not your fault. I should have gone the other way.' I'm angry at myself, and my tone's short, even to my ears. 'Sorry, Edwin. I was... well, I was listening where I shouldn't have been.'

'Lady Ælflæd?' he questions, and I nod unhappily.

I can no sooner explain what's happened to her since we last met than I can wake the dead. She's a mystery to me, and her brother is right to term her a bitch, for that's what she's become. Or so it seems. I keep trying to excuse her actions, but she snaps at all and sundry. She rules Kingsholm like a vixen, and no one can do right for her. It'll be better when she's gone, only I don't foresee that happening anytime soon. The only person to whom she shows any care is her young son, Wigstan, and he's not appreciative of her gestures. She and her husband might be of one mind with regard to Lord Coenwulf's punishment, but I've never seen a tender look pass between them. I think she hates him as well.

'I hope she becomes a kinder mistress,' Edwin murmurs. I've heard her berate him for his weaknesses since the events that saw him rescue her brother. She has no regard for Edwin, even if her brother would be dead without him. Perhaps that would have made everything easier for her. Maybe that's why she's so evil-tongued towards the wounded warrior.

'I don't see it. I think the queen has her fangs into Lady Ælflæd. She acts with the same regard for man, woman and child as the queen.' I can't forget what I've heard between her and her brother. Does her temper mask her fear, or is she truly so focused on holding Kingsholm that she's angry with her brother for his antics? As to her young sister, Lady Cynewise. I'm well aware that she does her best to stay away from her older sister. Lady Ælflæd wishes to ensure her position by making her young sister a mirror image of her, but Lady Cynewise refuses to conform. Their arguments have also become legendary. All the same, I admire Cynewise. I've heard her inform her sister that she's a twisted shrew. The slap from that encounter was visible on Cynewise's young face for nearly ten days.

Eagerly, I reach up and run my hand along Brute's black neck. He bucks his head at my touch but quickly settles. Beside him, Wine dozes in her stable, head bowed, where she leans against the wooden struts of the building. A welcome grin touches my cheeks to see her in such a way. At least she's comfortable here. She might be the only one of us.

'What will you do?' Edwin has been asking me this for the last few weeks, ever since I made it clear I'd be staying at Kingsholm with Lord Coenwulf.

'I'll know when the time comes,' I murmur. 'What will you do?'

'I'm oath-sworn to Lord Coenwulf. I must escort him.'

'But where will he go? How will he keep you?'

'It doesn't matter. He's my lord, not Lady Ælflæd. There are few enough of his warriors left now. If I don't go with him, he'll be almost unaccompanied.'

I chew my lip as I reach for a brush to begin teasing the knots from Brute's mane. How he manages to become so unruly is beyond me. 'Lady Ælflæd will see him to the River Severn, and if there's no ship for him there, she'll force him into the water,' I argue, although I'd rather not think of her as capable of such.

'There'll be a ship. Its destination will be impossible to determine.'

'You sound so sure of this. Has Lord Coenwulf given you any assurances? Has he even spoken of it?'

'No.' Edwin hangs his head with the admission. 'He won't speak of when he must be parted from his sons.'

His sons. And this is the crux of my problem. I can't leave those children's side. When Lord Coenwulf is gone, no one will care for them. I'll be the person that does.

'And what of Eadburg?' Edwin and Eadburg have an understanding. She was overjoyed to see him returned to Kingsholm, and yet events since then have made it difficult for them.

'She can't come with me.' Edwin sounds mournful.

'I know that. That's what I'm asking. You tell me you love her, yet you'll leave her.'

'I'll have no choice, Icel. You know that. Her place is here, with her mother, the young lord's wet nurse. She won't leave her, just as you won't leave the children.' Edwin's words are reasoned and yet I fear for both of them when they're parted.

I sigh, scattering a cloud of dust released from Brute's coat. Coughing aside the sweet smell, I grimace all the same.

'I still believe you should convince her to go with you,' I try again.

'She won't leave her mother. She's adamant that seven years will pass quickly, and she'll wait for me.'

I shake my head. I know the truth of that, and Edwin's a fool if he believes it. Seven years is an eternity. In seven years, I've come from a boy to a man. Who knows what other changes will overcome me in the next seven years?

'You'll both find love elsewhere then,' I counter aggressively.

'No, we won't.' Edwin's lower lip juts in determination. 'We're in love and will remain true to one another. And anyway, we're talking about you, not me.'

'My place is with Lady Cynehild's sons. She made me swear to that.'

'But that means you must leave Ealdorman Ælfstan's warrior band and remain here with Lady Ælflæd.'

'I've already left it. And I'm not oath-sworn to him, but only to the king.'

'And the king will appreciate you playing nursemaid to the sons of his enemy?' Edwin taunts, eyebrows high.

I managed to evade the king when he was at Kingsholm. I'm hoping thoughts of me are far from his mind. I shake my head. 'No, the king won't appreciate it. But I don't believe the king truly wished to banish Lord Coenwulf. He tried hard to undermine the words of Eadbald and Lady Ælflæd. But Lord Coenwulf wouldn't help himself.' As I speak, I realise I'm gasping, the words flooding from me in a rush. I'm angry at Lord Coenwulf. I knew him when he was a man bowed low with grief, but now he has his sons. He should be prepared to fight for them. He should have told the king that he'd only depart with his children and not leave them behind instead of trying to bend his sister to his will now.

'Maybe,' Edwin admits with a long sigh. 'But the king made his pronouncement. Admittedly, he was coerced by his wife, son, Lady Ælflæd and that Lord Beorhtwulf, whomever he is.'

I'm pleased Edwin doesn't know whom Lord Beorhtwulf is, but it seems that no one else knows whom he is either. I've been unable to find out any more about him. That perplexes me, when I allow myself to think about it.

'Now we must follow those orders or face worse,' he continues. Edwin has evidently reconciled himself to what must happen, but I haven't. I realise that. I want something to occur to ensure Lord Coenwulf can remain with his sons. If that happens, it'll release me from my oath, I hope, for now.

'We must live with the consequences of our actions,' I confirm, wincing at the raucous sound of the warriors in the other half of the stables. If I'm to remain in Kingsholm, I'll need to do something about them, but do I need to ally with them? Perhaps it would be better to show them what sort of warrior I am. Maybe then they might leave me alone. But that's not to be done today. Today, I'll tend to my horses and consider the words of Lady Ælflæd.

I still can't believe how much she's changed. She's become twisted and warped. Is this, I think, what happens to women who marry into the ruling family of Mercia? Certainly, Lady Cynehild, when the wife of King Beornwulf, was far from kind to me. Did her ambition make her bitter? If so, then could I do with separating Lady Ælflæd from the grip of her husband and his mother? If not, she'll never become the girl I once knew, whose horse I once healed, and who spoke to her brother of me and occasioned an apology from him. She'll become as ambitious as the queen, if she hasn't done so already. Her behaviour towards her young sister is already unacceptable.

But Lady Ælflæd and I were children then, untried in the way of kingdoms and politics. Perhaps we've simply grown into the man and woman we were always destined to be – the thought is far from comforting.

5

'Icel.' I turn at the sound of my name, squinting into the fog behind me. It's not a good day to be riding, but I needed to escape the confines of Kingsholm. Everywhere I look is someone whose loyalty I suspect.

'Edwin.' I squint into the whiteness of the cold cloud, not sure if he called me or someone else did. The fog distorts all sound, and I don't even know where he's hailing me from.

'Icel.' The word once more, even though I've not moved. Beneath me, Brute breaths evenly. We've hardly been for a gallop, but instead a careful trot through the shockingly familiar landscape turned strangely haunted, with blackened twigs and branches threatening to pull my cloak free from my head. The air is thick with dampness, and Brute's black and white coat is drenched.

'I'm here,' I call, wincing when my words echo too loudly. I toy with gripping my eagle-headed seax, but here, so close to Kingsholm and with someone calling my name, I must think it's an ally.

Only then, I realise it isn't, as Eadweard and his cronies emerge out of the gloom.

'Ah, there you are,' Eadweard announces, as though he's found treasure. A gleam lights his eyes.

Now I wish I'd allowed Edwin to accompany me, although I denied him, knowing that it still pains him to ride. I'm alone, out here, with Eadweard, Wulfred, Forthgar, Deremann, Mergeat and the other fool whose name I don't know. Whatever's about to happen between us has been in the planning for some time. I've avoided the gang's reach for much of the winter. It was going to end, eventually.

'We thought to join you,' he calls, his voice rich with disdain. 'Fellow warriors should ride together when their winter captivity becomes too much.' He smirks, but his flat nose is bent once more. He's been fighting with anyone who'll try their luck against him. I don't want that person to be me, but if I must, then I must. I'm not sure I'll be able to overpower him, but I'm content to try.

'Then you're welcome. I plan on riding to the river and back again.'

The river isn't far from Kingsholm, but I'm taking a long route, heading towards Gloucester itself, before doubling back on myself. I wanted some solitude, but I'm not to get it.

'Then we should race.' Wulfred chuckles.

I eye him, noticing how water drips from his nose and down onto his chest. It might start to rain soon, and then the fog will be banished.

'It's too dangerous,' I caution. I'll not risk Brute on some stupid game.

'Chicken,' Wulfred whispers.

'If you like,' I counter, not swayed by such a disparaging term, encouraging Brute onwards at our steady pace, overly aware of the men close to my back. I lick my lips, tasting the fog's moisture and the thin line of sweat beading in my black moustache. I shouldn't have called out to these men. I should have remained hidden from them.

'No, no, Wulfred, Icel's correct. It's too dangerous. A gentle trot, nothing more. To the River Severn and back to Kingsholm. It sounds ideal.' Eadweard's delight makes me worry once more. Close to the river, and with the fog as thick as it is, no one will see if we descend into a fight. They won't come looking for me if the six should decide to overpower me. Only Edwin would even notice my disappearance – well, perhaps he and Eadburg, the woman he loves and the daughter of the woman who acts as wet nurse to the children at Kingsholm. They'd miss my unwelcome, loitering presence.

Indeed, it's because of them that I'm here. Eadburg's mother banished me from the children, accusing me of upsetting them with my stink and clank of iron. I didn't argue with her. The children upset me as well, with their constant demands and frailty. Should someone think to end their life, it wouldn't take much. That chafes at me every day. I swore to protect the children. And I must. But I sense betrayal everywhere. I only left because Edwin was there with Eadburg. He might still be weak, but he can stab with his seax. The two are love-struck, and that turns my stomach as well, and I'm aware jealousy is the cause.

I listen to the jangle of harnesses as the other horses follow Brute. Brute, head outstretched, lacks all concern. His gait is smooth, moving at a pace that allows him to ensure the placement of his hooves on the slick ground. I swallow, tasting the saltiness of my sweat. The silence between us grows, and it's far from comfortable.

'They say you fought at Lundenwic,' Eadweard calls from atop his grey stallion. The animal's light-footed despite its bulk. If it came to a race, I don't believe it would stand a chance of winning against Brute. But that's not going to happen. Not today.

'I did, yes, and inside Londinium.' I thought all knew of my battle antics, but perhaps not. I thought all knew of my endeavours for the king, but that must be my conceit. I didn't realise I had any until now. 'Were you there?' I think to ask. They must have been, surely.

'No, we were in Tamworth, protecting the queen and Lord Wigmund.'

Ah, of course, they're the sworn men of Lord Wigmund. Why would they have been close to the threat of actual violence? I consider them once more. Are they fierce warriors, or do they just look the part?

'They also said you healed some bastard Wessex warriors,' Wulfred continues, the edge to his voice impossible to ignore.

'I did, yes, they helped me, and I helped them. Not that it matters. They're all dead now.'

'And against the Viking raiders in the kingdom of the East Angles? You ensured Peterborough remained in the hands of the king?'

I sigh softly, hoping they don't hear me. 'I did, yes. With Ealdorman Ælfstan and his men.' Perhaps it would have been better had Uor not spoken his words to the scop song in praise of my antics.

'And then you went to the Isle of Sheppey to retrieve a traitor, leaving the River Thames open to attack from the enemy?' This comes from Eadweard once more, and now anger infuses his words.

'I did, yes. I retrieved Lord Coenwulf at the request of Lady Cynehild.'

'What a conniving cow she was,' one of the other men calls, Deremann I think, and the others chuckle darkly. The grip on my reins stiffens. I don't like to hear others call the dead woman names even if I think it on a daily basis. 'And that wasn't on the orders of the king?'

'No, it wasn't,' I confirm, gently guiding Brute with my knees. Ahead, I can hear sounds coming from inside Gloucester. I can't see the settlement, but I relax at knowing I'm not alone out here with these six men. I might even make an excuse to go inside the settlement. Perhaps it's a market day despite the fog and gloom?

'And now the king is keen for you to know the full fury of his wrath.'

'The king is, is he?' I counter, turning to observe the leering glower on Eadweard's face but without making it too obvious that I distrust him.

'He is, yes, you little shit.' Before I can react, someone lunges at me. I find myself scrabbling for my reins but knowing I'll fall all the same. The ground veers upwards at me as I land, face down, on the damp grass, coughing aside the force of the impact, even while someone pummels my back.

I wince at the impacts. I should have donned my byrnie, but I didn't. I have my cloak and my weapons belt, but nothing else. No shield. No helm. I thought to use the weather as my protection. And these men mean to batter me. I hear the tread of others dismounting and coming to join the fight. I try and force myself upwards, but Wulfred, for all his slight build, has pinned me to the ground with his legs. Every time I think to catch a deep breath, he thrusts his fists, in tight formation, one-two, one-two, into my back.

I'll be black and blue tomorrow. Should I live until then.

I sense Brute's unease as he veers backwards and then forwards while one of the men tries to take his reins, only I'm still holding them in one hand. I need him to run away. Perhaps even summon help from Kingsholm. With effort, I unclench my left fist and turn my body to allow the leather straps to come free with Brute's actions.

'Go,' I huff, while it feels as though all six men beat me. I see Brute's hooves move out of sight at a quick trot and then consider my enemy.

We're all men of Mercia, but we're not all allies. I replay Eadweard's words to me. This, then, is at the command of Lord Wigmund, or so I assume. I can't genuinely imagine the king setting thugs on me, not when he owes his life to me.

With supreme effort, I suck in a deep breath and then expel it as I force myself to roll free from Wulfred, who still traps me on my back, the damp grass quickly reaching my skin. But, with my hands free, I meet his punches with some of my own, catching sight of the smirking face of Eadweard. I want to rip that expression from his face, lips and all if need be.

When Wulfred deflates before me, thanks to a punishing blow to his nose, I jettison him from my body and surge upwards. Crouching, Eadweard rounds on me, still smirking but with his eyebrows furrowed now. He didn't expect me to put up much of a fight, despite the stories he's heard of me. He kicks out, aiming for my cock and stones, and I just manage to close my legs and turn aside from his attack. With my right fist, I smack his nose. It's hard to miss such a target, and he howls with pain, blood pouring over his thick moustache and down his chest.

But Wulfred's back on his feet, and he leaps at me from behind, his arms circling my neck and pulling me backwards. We land in a crack of bones, and I'm on the bloody ground again. Well, I nearly am – Wulfred's beneath me. I can feel him growing still. Perhaps the damn arse has knocked himself on a stone. Perhaps he's just winded.

Two more of the men come at me. Æthelbald's younger than the others, perhaps the same number of winters to his name as me. He swings with deliberation, economical with his movements, as he reaches down to grab me by the shoulders and haul me upwards. It's my turn to kick out, trying to land a blow on the man whose name I don't know. His nose drips with a stinking cold, and its bright red illuminates him better than any brand. But he skips out of my snaking leg and hooks his own around mine, preventing me from standing.

Eadweard joins them, and it's all I can do to pull my arms around my head and protect it, curling around the hurt of my belly.

Six men against one. Well, five, for I do see when I open my eyes that Wulfred is silent on the ground. If he's dead, this will go very badly. I hope he lives. I don't want to be held accountable for protecting myself from six of my fellow warriors when I was doing little more than taking a ride out on a fog-shrouded day.

My thoughts turn inwards, the pain from the blows becoming less and less, and at some point I lose awareness of where I am, the view around me turning black.

When I wake, everything aches. I'm lying on my back, looking upwards at the still fog-shrouded sky. I don't know how long I've been unaware, but I hear the sound of something close by and reach for my seax blade on my weapons belt, only to feel a thousand different hurts and, worse, to realise my seax isn't there.

A nose comes into view, a questing tongue as well, and I sigh. It's Brute, returned to me. I turn and see that I'm alone. I spare a thought for Wulfred, hoping he still breathes. But it doesn't help me. Everything aches, I can only see a little out of my left eye, and it hurts even to raise my hand to run it over the swelling. My lips are thick and coated with something that I think must be blood.

'Arse,' I exclaim, but even that hurts. 'How long have I been here?' I ask Brute, but get no response. He doesn't lick me any more but watches me from along his long nose, a look of confusion in his familiar eyes. 'Did they hurt you?' I exhale, and when he doesn't move, I take it to mean he escaped as I intended but has since come back to find me. If he thinks I'm going to be able to leap into his saddle and take him back to a warm stable and food, then he's very much mistaken.

I shiver, the cold seeping into my bones and beneath my cloak, drenched from the grasses upon which I lie. It could be worse. I could be on the road, in the gutter, or even lying on a pile of horseshit. I sniff, but my nose is blocked, and instead a wracking cough floods my body. I'm forced to sit upright, despite the pain, or choke on whatever makes me cough.

'Ahhh,' I growl when I can manage words again. Tears drip from my eyes, unbidden, and I lick them from my swollen lips. But the thought of standing is beyond me. I look down at myself, seeing my swollen nose beneath my eyes, and notice the rips on my tunic. My cloak only remains over half of my body. No wonder I'm so damn cold. I try to pull it tighter, but my arms refuse the request, and all I accomplish is to make myself pant, which makes my chest hurt.

'Arse,' I exclaim again, closing my eyes and almost wishing the voice of Wulfheard would appear from the fog. But it won't. He's far from here, close to the king, with Ealdorman Ælfstan. I've made it clear that I want nothing more to do with them. Yet I'd welcome them now. They'd capture Eadweard and his thug friends and see they were punished for what they've done to me. If I return to Kingsholm, or rather, when I do, I'll find nothing but recrimination. No doubt, they'll blame me for what's happened between us. Is my reputation so immense that people will believe I started a fight with six men and expected to triumph?

Not that I have a choice. I've vowed to protect the children of Lady Cynehild, and I will do so. It won't be long until the weather is good enough that Lord Coenwulf must leave his family holdings and begin his seven winters of exile. How he'll cope, I've no idea. He adores his children. He spends more time with them than any other father would do, rarely letting them out of sight. I consider how much he suspects his sister might imperil his children, or whether it was just angry words exchanged between the two. I know that I fear for them. And not just from the queen and Lady Cynehild. There are others. I'm still wary of Lord Beorhtwulf, and even of Lord Wigmund's men. If they can beat me as badly, what could they do to two small children?

Reaching up, wincing at the same time, I reach for the small silver eagle sigil that my uncle bid me return to Lady Cynehild, and which she then gave to me.

It speaks of my heritage as a member of the select few who could rightfully claim the kingdom of Mercia as theirs to rule. Why I wear it, I don't know. I should bury and hide it so no one can suspect my true identity. Yet I think to one day give it to the sons of Lady Cynehild. I think it should be theirs, not mine. But they're mere babes. What if something does befall them? Would that enable me to pursue my claim?

I shake my head. Dismiss the thought. I don't want to be a king. I don't even want to know that I could be king. I close my eyes again, determined to blot out the pain in my body and the hurt in my mind.

Do I wish my uncle had told me? Do I wish that my father had claimed me? If he had, would I have led a life like Lord Wigmund? Pampered and adored by his mother. Kept safe from any hurt or ill that might befall him. Held back from fighting to keep Mercia safe.

I'm denying all that only, unbidden, a stray thought threads into my mind. If I'd been named as an ætheling, throne-worthy, then perhaps I would have been wed to Lady Ælflæd, and not Lord Wigmund. And if that had happened, she'd never have become the conniving, politically astute woman she is now. Perhaps, we might even have been like Edwin and Eadburg.

Once more, a stray tear falls from my closed eye. I don't want to know this. I want to return to when my commitments were much easier. All I needed to do was protect Mercia from her enemies with my sword and seax and nothing else.

How I wish that were all I need to do now.

6

'Bloody hell. What happened to you?' The voice of Cuthwalh on the gate at Kingsholm startles me awake. It's darker than pitch, and I've hardly been aware of Brute's steady hoof falls. If not for him, I'd never have made it here. It took until night had fallen for me to get myself into the saddle. I don't know how long it'll take me to dismount.

'Viking raiders or Wessex scum?' The other man demands, his eyes peering into the darkness as he hastens to close the gate after Brute has walked inside the settlement.

'Just some friendly Mercians,' I wince through my thick lip and aching body.

I feel every single thump and whack that was laid on me.

With the gate shut behind him, Cuthwahl comes closer to me, a brand in his hand making me cringe away from the bright flames.

'Um, so you were involved with those damn fools then, were you?'

'They're here?'

'Aye, came back before noon. They didn't say much. One of them was slumped in his saddle, but he's awake now. You took on all six of them?' I eye the other man. Cuthwalh is about my age, no more and no less. He's newly come to the service of Lord Coenwulf, since so many of his men were killed by the Viking raiders who took him to the Isle of Sheppey.

He's much broader than I am, yet I've watched him with the other warriors. He'll make a good fighter one day. 'They were asked what happened to them, but they were wary about it – passed it off as a little fight with a drunk man in the tavern in Gloucester. I can see why. Do you need help?' He's following me to the stable, and as Brute slows to a stop, aware I can't ride him beneath the low-hanging doorway, Cuthwalh must realise this isn't going to be easy.

I don't want to ask for help, but it's that or sit here all night, getting even colder than I already am.

'Yes, if you could,' I grudgingly admit. 'Even if it's just to keep me on my feet when I slide down Brute's side.'

'Wait a moment.' Hastily, Cuthwalh finds a place to put the brand so that we still have enough light to see by, and then he braces himself close to my leg and Brute. 'When you're ready,' he calls. I take a deep breath, prepare myself for the agony of what's about to happen, and try to force my right leg over the back of Brute's saddle.

It's torture. My chest and leg hurt, and sweat beads down my forehead before I'm even halfway there. Damn, they beat me badly.

'Take your time.' Cuthwalh's tone is patient and filled with understanding. 'Will you demand justice from them?' he continues. My leg still hasn't made it to where it needs to be. I'm considering just falling to the ground, arse first. It's got to hurt less than trying to dismount as usual. Beneath me, Brute's patient, but I'm not.

'Ow,' I huff through tight cheeks, blowing them wide with effort. Finally, my leg comes free and, as I feared, I tumble to the ground, my left leg just about straight, my right leg still far from where it should be. If not for Cuthwalh, I'd be on my arse. But his strong arms keep me upright, and with Brute to the other side, I finally stand, the pain too great to allow me to do more than just breathe for a long moment.

Cuthwalh steps aside slightly when he trusts me to stay upright. I finally hobble towards him, away from Brute. My face is sheeted in perspiration, my legs are trembling, my lips are wobbling with pain, and my chest is so tight it hurts to take even the smallest breaths.

'My thanks,' I eventually manage.

'Here, give me the beast, and I'll take him into the stable. You need to get into the hall, warm up and rest.' I open my mouth to argue with Cuthwalh, but Brute's already moving away, the promise of hay and warmth making him surprisingly placid.

'My thanks,' I wheeze again, my eyes on the hall. Eadweard, Wulfred and the rest of their group of men will be inside. They clearly never intended to tell anyone of what happened between us. Did they hope they'd left me for dead? Did they attack me for the fun of it, or did they, as Eadweard intimated, do so on the orders of the king, or rather, Lord Wigmund? The thought makes me consider Cuthwalh's words. Should I seek justice? I could demand that Lord Coenwulf finds against them, but of course, Lord Coenwulf is unlikely to care, and the men aren't answerable to him, anyway. They owe their oaths to Lord Wigmund, who still makes his home at Kingsholm, ostentatiously, to ensure that Lord Coenwulf doesn't misbehave before he's banished. But all know it's more that, here, Lord Wigmund is far from Tamworth and can imagine he rules as king.

Laboriously, I make my way to the hall, where the door guard, Osmod, allows me entry.

'My thanks,' I whisper. And he grimaces at seeing the state I'm in.

'I'd say the other bastard looks worse, but I'd be lying,' he murmurs, only to quickly stifle a yawn.

'Aye, well. I didn't put up much of a fight in the end.'

'Over there,' and he points to the banked hearth. I'm grateful to see a space for my weary head. My position here is far from regular. I've no dwelling to call my own. I'm not one of Lord Coenwulf's warriors, so I have no place in his bunkhouse either. But I'm not alone in sleeping in the hall, especially not at this time of year, when the hearth is kept burning all day and night long.

Wincing but trying not to shriek with my movements, I limp to the spot and then appreciate I have another problem. It's all but impossible for me to get down on the ground with the agony I'm in. Just like dismounting, this will be excruciating and almost undoable. Gritting my teeth, aware that I don't wish to wake everyone from snoring, I stretch my right leg out before me, my arms reaching for the wooden boards beneath me. And still, they reach. Normally, it would be easy to tumble to the floor, wrap my cloak around me, use another to cushion my head and be asleep in no time. But tonight, I'm sweating and shivering by the time I'm finally prone. Every ache and sting makes itself felt all over again.

I can't even wrap my cloak around me, and it remains bunched beneath my back. I'd fight it, but I can't. Instead, and as uncomfortable as I am, I close my eyes and welcome the warmth. Tomorrow will be soon enough to contend with all my injuries.

Somewhere close by, a child's fretful cry splits the air. I nod in sympathy, reminded again of why I'm enduring this. The child needs me. Of that, I'm sure.

I'm woken by a boot kicking my chest. Pain stabs down towards my legs, and bile rises in my throat. I only just manage to turn aside, to stop the vomit from staining my ripped shirt.

'What are you doing here?'

I meet the angry eyes of Eadweard. From outside, the noise of the settlement waking is easy to hear, the cry of the disturbed chickens, the cockerel with his loud call, the banging of the blacksmith and the humming of the monks. I want to close my eyes and sleep, but I don't trust Eadweard. He's a nasty piece of work, as he showed yesterday.

'I thought we made it clear you weren't welcome here,' Eadweard continues, bending low so no one else can hear the conversation. 'You almost killed Wulfred.' My eyes flicker to my eagle-headed seax, on his weapons belt. He shouldn't be wearing it in Lord Coenwulf's hall. He shouldn't have it at all.

'It was nothing to do with me. He should look where he punches,' I counter, wishing my chest wasn't so tight and I could get up without looking like an aged man. My bruises are making themselves felt. My tongue feels like it's been dipped in dandelion flowers, fuzzy and unwieldy.

'You little turd.' Eadweard launches himself at me, but somehow I manage to scamper away from him, just pulling my legs clear from his unwarranted attack.

'Lads,' a ripe voice calls from the door. I catch the eye of another of the new Kingsholm warriors striding towards us, I think his name is Tatberht, with big meaty fists and a face that looks set to punch and ask questions later. 'This is the lord's hall, not a fighting den,' he shouts. I can feel the eyes of everyone on us, although I can't see that much from my place on the wooden floorboards.

Eadweard stands abruptly, forcing himself upright from where he's almost fallen to the floor. His face is a rictus of fury.

'He almost killed Wulfred yesterday,' Eadweard hollers at the gate warden.

'Well, I'd say there were enough of you to fight off one man,' Tatberht, counters, standing between us, forcing Eadweard to step away from me. I realise how close I am to the hearth as heat suffuses my face. I've been cold all night, and now I'm too bloody hot. 'Now, get out of here, and I don't want to see you until I'm no longer the gate warden for the day.'

With a final backwards glance that assures me this argument is far from finished, Eadweard strides from the hall. As he goes, I hear the scamper of other booted feet and appreciate that he wasn't alone. I consider where Wulfred is.

'Osmod told me about it all, and Cuthwalh,' Tatberht informs me, offering me his hand so I can stand upright. 'We don't want them sort here,' he mutters, but I'm struggling to stand and can't answer straight away.

Only when I'm upright does he step away from me.

'You look like you've been chewed up and spat out by an eagle,' he offers with half a smile. 'I suggest you get yourself cleaned up and sorted out before Lord Coenwulf sees you. And Lady Ælflæd. With her temper, she might lay the blame at you, not at the feet of Eadweard and his lot.'

'My thanks,' I pant, gratefully sinking onto a wooden bench, just far enough away from the fire that I can feel its heat but not sweat from it.

He walks away, and I envy such ease. It'll take me days to get fully back on my feet. Abruptly, I'm aware of someone watching me, and I turn to meet the appraising eyes of Lady Cynewise.

'Lady Cynewise,' I cough, wishing my voice was steadier. She looks like her sister, Lady Ælflæd, only much younger. It's strange to call such a youngster 'lady' but that's what she is. I'm pleased she no longer wears the marks of the slap her sister gave her.

Lady Cynewise nods but, licking her lips, says nothing else until she opens her mouth. 'You need something for the bruising and something to take the swelling from your lips.'

I'd laugh to hear her assessment of me, almost the words of Wynflæd but from a mere slip of a girl. I consider how she knows this and realise it must be because she's needed to make use of the same remedies herself.

'Do you know what those things are?' I ask as she hands me a beaker of water which I drink eagerly.

'I do, yes. I've been studying them. The monks don't realise I'm learning as much as I am. They think only men should know how to heal.' The disgust in her voice has my lips curling wide. 'Theodore and Gaya were teaching me before they were forced to leave on my sister's instructions.' Her tone is filled with remorse. I miss the two healers as well. They were a steadying presence, and somewhere I could go to step away from the scrutiny of those who mean me ill. 'I'll go and find yarrow, woodruff, and wild carrot,' she announces as though I'm testing her. 'And also some garlic and nettles to add to the pottage for you.'

'So, you'll help me? To feel better?'

'I will, Icel, yes. But you smell really bad. Perhaps you could go for a bath first, and I'll prepare a poultice and potion for you.' With those words, the trace of the older woman she'll one day be disappears, and once more, she's just a young girl. She must be about ten winters old, perhaps not quite as old.

'Apologies, my lady.' I try and bow but hiss at the stab of pain elicited along my shoulder blades.

'There's no need to bow to me, Icel. Just do what I say.' And with that, she threads her way through the people in her older brother's hall and ventures outside, once more sounding as though she's the lady of the settlement. I smile and fill another cup of water from the waiting jug before slowly getting to my feet. I'm reminded of when I first met Ælflæd, and she knew how to tend to her horse, or at least how to do some of it. The daughters of the late King Coelwulf, the first of his name, appear well educated and very sure of themselves. I consider why, then, Lord Coenwulf is so very different to them.

The bite of the sharp wind has me shivering and frantically trying to gather together the remnants of my torn tunic as I venture outside. But it's impossible. I need some water to clean myself with, and also some new clothes to wear. My clothes are in the stables with Brute and Wine, so I limp that way, cursing every step that makes me shudder with agony.

Inside, the stablemen are busy with their tasks.

'Hail, Icel,' Pega calls to me while Hatel veers backwards out of one of the stalls and looks me up and down. 'It's true then?' Pega questions me. 'You got into a fight with Eadweard and Wulfred, and the rest of 'em.'

'I think it would be better to say they got into a fight with me.'

Pega's face is rueful. 'A right pair of arseholes, them two,' he mutters. 'Best avoided.'

'I was trying to avoid them. I was far from Kingsholm at the time.'

'A pity they're men of Lord Wigmund,' Pega continues. 'It would be good to have them gone from Kingsholm. They do nothing but cause trouble with their fighting and gambling.'

Pega follows me to where Wine and Brute await me, both heads over the doors of their stables as I labour towards them. From the way Pega and Hatel talk of the other men, I can at least be assured that they're not hiding in the stables today.

'You stink.' Pega echoes young Lady Cynewise, wafting his hand in front of his nose. It must be bad if he's aware of it even over the redolent smell of horses and their shit.

'I'm just getting some clothes, and then I'll do something about the smell.'

'And the bruises and fat lip?'

'Yes, those as well.' He opens the door for me, pushing gently against Wine, who watches me with her intelligent eyes. I consider if the two horses have exchanged stories during the night. Does she know what's happened to me?

'Here.' Pega proffers me my sack of clothes. I take it gratefully, wishing it weighed less. 'I'll tend to your mounts for you, today only. I can't have others seeing me do this for you more than once. Now, away with you, and when I next see you, I hope you'll be only one shade and not every colour of the rainbow.'

I reach out and rub the noses of Wine and Brute and then retrace my steps. I do consider why Pega didn't bid me stay where I was and get my clothes for me, but I don't say anything. He's being too good to me as it is. The stablemen must also avoid Eadweard, Wulfred and the others. Too often they're in the stables, upsetting the horses, and they think nothing of causing problems for the stablemen. Pega's right. They are arseholes.

I go to where the water's stored in huge oak casks, brought here from the river, not far away. Some are for drinking water, and others can be used for anything and added to by leaving the top off the cask's covering and letting the rain fall into it. For now, it's half iced over, and I know that the shock of the cold water will be unpleasant. And will probably hurt like hell.

Pulling my tunic clear, glancing at the array of colours covering my thick chest and the fine down of black hair over it, I plunge my head directly into the cask, seeing stars, my heart pounding with the shock of it all. I stay there longer than I want to, and when I straighten up, I wash my face with my hands, forgetting about my lips. For a moment, pain surges through my body, and I sway slightly and grip the top of the cask to steady myself.

'Good god,' I exhale when I think I can manage rational thought again. 'Good god,' I repeat, pulling a clean tunic over my head after I've run my hands under my armpits, inhaling the familiar smell of horse and hay.

Only then do I retrace my steps back to the hall, smelling better but bitterly cold from the water and the wind. I hardly focus on what's happening around me, content to let the sounds of everyday life wash over me. The gates to the settlement are wide open. People come and go as they wish, leading horses and carts laden with goods to trade. Yesterday's fog has lifted. The days are still long enough to allow men and women to continue their usual tasks. In a few short weeks, it'll be impossible to travel further than to Gloucester without the need to seek shelter elsewhere for the night before returning.

I return to my seat and drink more water, wincing as my chest brushes against the wood of the table before me. There's no sign of young Lady Cynewise. Just as I'm considering gathering my own supplies to help my aches and pains, she appears in the doorway, head downcast, an array of items in her hands. Jars, leaves, scruffy old weeds, or so they appear, and a swathe of white linen. I try to rush to her side, but instead I only manage to knock myself against the wood of the table once more and clatter back to the stool, breathing heavily, eyes downcast.

A crash of clay on the table before me has me lifting my eyes. Lady Cynewise appraises me with the cool eyes of a much older woman. The similarity to Wynflæd astounds me all over again. There must be seven decades between them and at least as many kings. I'd shake my head, but that would hurt.

'At least you smell better,' she assures me, nimble hands gathering together what she needs.

I'm aware of one of the servants hovering close by, a slim hand covering her mouth as she watches Cynewise. I catch her eyes, and they dance with amusement but also respect. Certainly, she doesn't try and stop the youngster. I consider if she's her nursemaid, but surely Cynewise is too old to need a nursemaid. I think to ask Eadburg, when I next see her. And I must check up on the babe and his brother. I've not seen them since the day before yesterday, for all I'm here to ensure they're protected.

'Here.' A murky mixture is presented to me, the sharp smell of birthwort making me want to gag. The scent is too reminiscent of death and decay. 'Put that on your bruises,' she orders me. I want to advise her that perhaps it needs a little more agrimony to drive away the noxious smell, but her face, beneath the façade of someone who knows what they're doing, belies some unease.

'My lady,' I say, and unwillingly scoop the mixture and put it over my shivering chest. The welter of colours there is fiercely illuminated against my pale skin and dark hair covering. She shows no embarrassment at my semi-nakedness; another trait that will make her a good healer. Wynflæd never seems concerned by any body part presented to her, whether intimate or just a grazed elbow.

'Let me help you do your back,' she offers. I shudder away from that and eye the servant woman. Luckily, she's seen my problem.

'My lady, I'll do that for you. You don't want it on your hands.' Soft hands slowly begin to rub the awful-smelling treatment into my back. The servant's hands are cold, my skin is cold, and the lotion is cold and stinks, yet somehow it soothes me.

Lady Cynewise doesn't even watch. Instead, tongue sticking through her thin lips, she begins to work on the next part of her tonic for me. She moves to the hearth, spoons a selection of the pottage into a smaller container and begins to add nettles, far from finely chopped, and garlic, far from finely sliced, into her bowl. I watch her carefully. She seems too small to handle the huge cooking pot, but she manages it well enough.

I eye her cutting knife and quickly realise everything is roughly chopped because it's about as sharp as a branch. Perhaps I might sharpen it for her, or if not, find something more suitable for the task.

'You're done.' The servant quickly steps aside as she speaks. 'You smell like the charnel house,' she winces in sympathy, and I nod. Her eyes stray to Cynewise and once more they sparkle with joy and some trepidation. 'She knows what she's doing, but only the hounds have been subject to her ministrations so far.'

'She does know what she's doing, yes. I have some skill in healing as well,' I offer, although whether I'm reassuring her or me, I'm not sure. Either way, I can already feel the salve taking effect. I find I can breathe more deeply, and my chest isn't as tight as throughout the night.

Not for the first time, I consider how I allowed myself to get into such a state. I should have fought them off harder, even if there were six of them, and I was alone. Even Brute could have become involved, but I sent him away rather than risk him. I regret that now.

'Eat this,' Cynewise commands me. I notice the servant leaving the hall, no doubt to wash her hands clear of the smell.

'It smells good,' I offer, and it does, much better than my skin. But I'm not going to tell her that. She watches me, eyes serious, as I try the first spoonful, which is far too hot. Hastily, I swill more water into my mouth and push the bowl away from me.

'I'll eat it when it's not quite so hot,' I explain, wishing my tongue didn't burn to add to my other miseries.

'Hum,' Cynewise says, eyeing her collection of supplies. 'I think a linen around your chest will help, but I think you smell bad again. I thought you'd washed?'

'I did, yes, all of me. It was cold.'

'Then why do you smell now?'

'Ah, um. Perhaps there's too much birthwort and not enough agrimony in the salve.'

A flicker of uncertainty covers her face, bright eyes shimmering. I fear she might cry. But she doesn't. Instead, she knocks her forehead with her hand, shaking her head.

'Of course. I could think of no reason to add the amount of agrimony they suggested, but it's to counter the smell, isn't it? Agrimony smells of the summer, whereas birthwort smells like death and yarrow more like farts.' She grimaces. 'Sorry. Why didn't you say anything?' Now her eyes are accusing. I appreciate that I've erred in not telling her. 'I've had more than enough of people tolerating what I'm doing as though I'm a babe in the cot and not someone learning how to heal. I know, I know that a girl of my position shouldn't be concerned with healing people, but it's my passion.' Fury covers her face.

'I thought you did a very good job,' I offer, and then hiss sharply. 'Sorry, I didn't mean to sound condescending. I learned about healing from a young age too. But the woman who taught me always let me make mistakes to learn more from them.'

'Well, she was a mean old hag then,' Cynewise announces, elbows on the table, her head in her hands. 'She should have helped you rather than hindered you.'

'I think it did help,' I offer. 'She's a wise woman.'

'She still lives?' This astounds her.

'Yes, at Tamworth. Haven't you heard of Wynflæd? I thought she visited here?'

'Oh her, the really, really old woman? She came with Theodore and Gaya once. The monks disapprove of Theodore and Gaya. They spoke to my brother about banishing them from Kingsholm, but Lady Cynehild was adamant they came. And now, the monks blame them for what happened to Lady Cynehild, and so they've been banished on my sister's orders. I do miss Lady Cynehild.' The words erupt in a gush and with a quiver of her chin.

'I do, too,' I agree.

'What will happen to my brother?' Cynewise demands to know.

'He'll leave here, as the king instructed.'

'But where will he go?' Her voice is plaintive, and no longer assured.

'I don't know, but I'm sure he'll be safe and return soon.'

'It isn't fair.' Small arms cross over her chest, her lower lip jutting out angrily. 'My brother shouldn't have to leave Kingsholm. This is his home, and his children are here. I'm here.' The last ends with a shriek.

I'm not sure what to say to her. I refuse to offer reassurance I don't feel myself. She's right to be worried.

'And my sister, Ælflæd, has become horrible ever since she married the king's son. And her son, well, he's not well at all.' The words erupt in a rush. I can tell she's worried. 'I've told her that Theodore and Gaya should tend to him, but Ælflæd will only let the monks close to Wigstan. What good will prayers do for the poor thing when he struggles to drink his mother's milk?'

I feel my forehead furrow at this. I was aware that Wigstan was failing to thrive. I didn't know it was failure to get enough nourishment that was the problem. Perhaps then, this accounts for Ælflæd's difficult nature. I know I should stop trying to find excuses for her, and yet I do, all the same. 'What do you think ails him?'

'He can't suck as well as he should, or my sister's milk is no good. I've heard the monks talking about it. They seem to believe that prayer will aid him. Theodore and Gaya knew what to do but my sister didn't like what they said, and the monks overruled all they said.'

I lapse into silence, considering her words. I can't say I've ever heard of something like this, but I'm aware that babes can struggle in their first months of life. Some think it's God's will, but I've been taught to heal. Sometimes, I know it's just something lacking in the mother's diet or even the babe. Wynflæd would have suggested lots of meat for the mother. I consider whether Lady Ælflæd would have eaten well while carrying the child. But then, I didn't see her throughout her term. I can't say one way or another.

'Then why were they banished?'

'Lord Wigmund doesn't want to admit there's anything wrong with his firstborn son, and my sister, she's desperate to keep on the right side of him. She's fearful that what my brother did will cause her to be cast aside by the king's son.'

'It seems as though a lot's happening,' I murmur, aware there's much there for someone as young as her to worry about, especially when the death of Lady Cynehild must still pain her, and she and her sister are such opposites.

'The other baby is doing really well.' Lady Cynewise perks up. 'Young Coelwulf eats enough for two babies. Oh, and the poos he does. They stink.' A smile drives the worry from her face.

I hold my tongue, keen to see her happy.

'Come on,' she says. 'I need to put this around you, and then I'll make another pot of salve for you. One that doesn't reek like the charnel house.' Sprightly, she hastens to the task, humming merrily to herself as I try not to wince and groan at the reminder of my bruises.

Much later, she leaves me, bundling up all her supplies, with the aid of the returned servant, and hastens from the hall.

'I'll check on you tomorrow,' she says. 'Now, eat your pottage, and get better soon.'

I chuckle. If she could order me well, then she would. But her words about the two small babies, Coelwulf and Wigstan, concern me. Coelwulf is hale and hearty. Wigstan, the son of the ætheling, isn't; and Lady Ælflæd is remiss not to seek aid from Theodore and Gaya when they have such a wealth of experience. They have far more knowledge than the monks. A tendril of fear coils in my belly.

7

'Bloody hell. Have you shit yourself?' The voice of Eadweard rouses me from where I'm dozing by the hearth. I take a tight breath and meet his taunting gaze. 'I thought only the young and old shit themselves,' he continues. His eyes are bright, his face twisted with desire to belittle me.

'And those who meet their death on the slaughter field,' I counter.

'And you'd know all about that? Wouldn't you?'

Sitting upright, from where my head's been slumped on the board, allows all kinds of agonies to sizzle up my back and down my chest, making my heart thump too loudly.

'Not the shitting myself bit, no, but killing to protect my king? I'd know all about that. Would you? In fact, I did it with that very seax you hold there, and which I'd have back, now.'

I'm in no mind to argue with Eadweard. He beat me with the aid of his friends yesterday. I'll seek my vengeance one day. For now, all I want is my seax returned to me. He has no right to it. If anything, it shows how well he beat me, as opposed to what he's been telling everyone about me overpowering them. If I'd overpowered them, how would I have lost my very distinctive seax, with its eagle emblem made from twisted metal?

The taunting smirk slips from his face as his allies encircle him.

'Why are you here?' he demands to know, his hand reaching for the seax.

'I'm getting warm before the hearth.'

'Why are you here, in Kingsholm?'

'It's none of your concern, Eadweard. But know this, I'm not going anywhere.' I see his fist clench as though he might start a fight with me once more, and I tighten my body to hold myself firm against more punishing blows. 'Return my seax to me, and I'll do nothing further to counter your attack on me, on one of the king's well-known warriors, a man who fought to protect his king's life.' I think Eadweard will argue with me. Certainly, he looks prepared to. I notice, with a wry look, that Wulfred only carries a slight bruise to his cheek, where my head must have hit him as we tumbled backwards. Other than that, and slightly pale skin, he doesn't look as though he's been in a fight.

Only then Lord Wigmund appears in the hall. I've no idea where he's been for half the day. I don't much care.

'Eadweard, a word.' The king's son beckons him closer. Uneasily, Eadweard slips the seax from its place on his weapons belt and places it before me while, trailed by his collection of allies, Ealdorman Sigered's son amongst them, Lord Wigmund strides to the raised dais and seats himself there, ordering food and ale for him and his allies.

I try and make myself as small as possible, as I scoop up my seax, relieved by the familiar weight and feel of the blade in my hand. I'm keen to avoid Wigmund's scrutiny, and some of the others. I have no formal place here. None at all. And with so many months since Lady Cynehild's death, I can't use that as an excuse any more. The rest of the warriors who rescued Lord Coenwulf left months ago. The fact that I linger must be noticed by more than just Eadweard and his cronies.

I would ask Lord Coenwulf for a more permanent position, but he won't be here much longer. No, I just try and keep out of sight as much as possible, spending my time with Edwin and the rest of the warriors of Kingsholm. If it came to it, they could ask me to pay for staying here, eating their food, and sheltering under the hall's roof. I'd have the coin to pay, at least, for while I'm here, in Kingsholm, my estate at Budworth remains under the care of my reeve. He's sent messages to me on a number of occasions, and coins as well. I don't fear for the place, but I don't wish to visit there, not now I know the truth of my identity.

With trepidation, I apply the new, less smelly salve to my chest and what parts of my back I can reach, and then pull my tunic over my head. The linen bandage is more of an encumbrance than an aid, but I don't remove it. If I have to fight Eadweard and his men again, it'll provide another layer of protection from their feet and fists.

I try to hear the words of Lord Wigmund, but it's impossible. The men speak quietly, plotting something that will undoubtedly enhance their prestige, but such politicking is of no concern to me. When some of the Kingsholm warriors - Osmod, Cuthwalh and Tatberht - meander outside, I hasten to join them, merging with them so that I don't catch the eye of either Lord Wigmund or Eadweard.

Once outside, I'm not sure what to do with myself. I find myself close to the building where the small children are cared for, the very same room where Lady Cynehild breathed her last. Aware I won't be any more welcome than usual, I open the door and enter all the same. No one questions me. No one bars my way. There are no wardens, and raucous laughter means my entry is unnoticed. Peering through the wicker screen that divides the door from the smaller rooms, I chuckle to hear young Coenwulf's joyous voice as he giggles while playing with his nurse. I see Eadburg there as well, holding the smaller Coelwulf, although he sits upright, watching his brother with a fierce expression. Coelwulf is desperate to be playing with his older brother.

I seek out the other child, Wigstan, but he's not playing or sitting. Indeed, I suspect he lies in the arms of another of the women, sitting closer to the hearth, murmuring a soft song to the child. I can't think there can be much difference in age between the two small babes. My heart constricts, fearful that perhaps Lady Cynewise's worries are well founded.

I'm not foolish. I'm well aware that not all children are born to flourish and grow to adulthood, but despite Lady Ælflæd's sharp words, and my fears for the person she's become since wedding the king's son, I wouldn't wish such sorrow on her.

Before I'm noticed, I once more slip from the hall, my mind swirling with thoughts, as I make my way to the church and the monks. Never one to think the power of prayer can work unaided, I still offer some words to our Lord God, as Wynflæd might well do, hoping that some good might come of it for Lady Ælflæd's child. Unbidden I consider if our son would have been healthier if we'd had children together. But then I banish the thought. Lady Ælflæd and I are not even friends, and perhaps, we never were.

8

AD834

Lady Cynewise sobs quietly as she stands in the crowded yard outside the hall, watching her much older brother mount up. The weather has changed, the scent of summer is in the air. It'll soon be Eastermonað. Lord Wigmund and his warriors, headed by Eadweard and Wulfred, have demanded it's time for Lord Coenwulf to begin his exile. There's recently been a visit from Lord Beorhtwulf. No doubt he came to add his weight to the decision of Lord Wigmund and Lady Ælflæd to have Lord Coenwulf leave.

No one stands with young Lady Cynewise, not even the servant, who I know is called Gode. All is chaos and angry shouting. I've watched Edwin and Eadburg tearfully part from one another; Edwin, Cuthwalh, Tatberht and Osmod preparing to escort Lord Coenwulf wherever he goes. I decided not to listen to Lord Coenwulf take his leave of his children. That parting will have been bitter and double-edged. When, or rather if, Lord Coenwulf returns to Kingsholm, his children won't know him. They may as well be named orphans now.

Lady Ælflæd has shown herself to be no ally of her brother. She's taken regal command of the children, trying to banish Eadburg and her mother from their side, but there the women refused to be cast aside.

They are, Eadburg said, their carers, placed there by Lady Cynehild, before her death, and have no intention of leaving the children with no one to care for them. While they might hold their places for now, I'm once more suspicious of Ælflæd, especially with her weak son. My prayers did little good for him. The monks prayers are equally ineffective. He needs an experienced healer. One more skilled than me and young Lady Cynewise.

I could weep for what's happening, but I'm as powerless as Lord Coenwulf. The king has been petitioned, and while I think he'd retract his judgement, Lord Wigmund is staunch in demanding the older man leave, and he's supported by others. He has the encouragement of his mother in this, and also Lord Beorhtwulf. The queen doesn't like Lord Coenwulf, and she's not alone in that, for all she brokered the marriage union between him and his wife.

'Take care of yourself,' I murmur to Edwin, mounted on his horse, his face streaked with sorrow.

'And you as well. I suggest you leave this place. With Lord Wigmund in command, you'll only end with more bruises to your name. Return to Ealdorman Ælfstan and his warriors.'

I nod but shake my head sadly. I'm not as angry with them as I once was, our time apart making me appreciate that I miss all of them, even Oswy and his toxic arse. But I have a new oath now, and one I can't easily ignore. 'Don't worry about me, Edwin. Just go carefully. Don't allow Lord Coenwulf to enter into any alliance which the king will use as an excuse to extend his exile or even make it permanent.'

'Then, if you're determined to stay, care for Eadburg for me, her mother and the other children. I fear for them all.'

I reach up and grip Edwin's forearm, feeling his strength there, for all mine is greater. As he's healed, our friendship has also mended. It's felt good to have one friend within Kingsholm throughout the long winter 'I'll do as you ask. And soon, the time will run its course, and we'll be reunited.'

'Perhaps, but if you go to Tamworth, let my mother know this was my choice. It was the honourable action to follow.'

'I will, I assure you.' And with that, Edwin turns his mount, and together with three other men, making the party a total of seven, the horses leave the sanctuary of Kingsholm. I know they plan to find a ship to take them to Frankia or perhaps to one of the Irish kingdoms, but still, I'm fearful. Although, well, at least Lord Coenwulf hasn't sought sanctuary from King Athelstan of the East Angles or King Ecgberht of Wessex. That would have caused enormous problems, and would have ensured he was never allowed to return to Mercia.

I stand and watch the horses' tails until they disappear, and only then realise that only Lady Cynewise and I remain. She still cries, clutching something in her hand.

'My lady.' I walk to her, thinking of taking her hand and offering her some comfort. Furious eyes greet mine, her face red and splotchy with tears. I snatch my hand back. She's not a child to be comforted, for all her next demand is filled with childish sentiments.

'I want my brother back.'

'I know you do, but alas, he must win the king's regard by fulfilling his punishment.' I try to keep my voice even. She's furious. I recognise the emotion too well.

'The king's a horrible man, and his wife is worse,' Lady Cynewise shrieks, startling me. I turn quickly, hoping no one has heard the outburst. Should Lord Wigmund hear, I've no doubt he'd punish the young girl. Should her sister hear, the punishment will be even worse. Should word get back to the queen, I dread to consider what could befall her.

'You don't want anyone to hear you say that,' I murmur. This startles her, and her mouth falls open in shock.

'You didn't berate me for saying it.' Her words are surprised. I consider how many others have tried to stifle her anger and fear and failed to do so, by denying her thoughts.

'No, I didn't,' I confirm, holding her gaze. Now her eyes narrow, and she looks me up and down, perhaps seeing me for the first time since she aided me after I was beaten black and blue by Eadweard and his allies. Her ointment helped me until I could make my own. All the same, it was near enough two weeks before I could mount easily, and all that time, I felt the gaze and the threat from Eadweard. Even now, two months after he beat me, I imagine he plots his next attempt on me. I've ensured I'm never alone, even in the stables when tending to Brute and Wine. I'm aware that will become more difficult now that Edwin, Tatberht and Osmod have left Kingsholm. I can't rely on Haga and Patel getting involved with bloodthirsty warriors.

'Are your bruises all gone?' she queries.

'Yes, thank you. You helped me. You have my thanks.'

Her eyebrows arc. 'Then I knew what I was doing?'

'You did, apart from the problem with the birthwort.'

She grins and uses the cloth she's clutching to wipe the snot from her nose, pleased with my acclaim for her skills. 'My brother gave me this. He said it was my mother's.' Abruptly, she's recalled to what's just happened.

This surprises me. The cloth is as fine as gossamer, as finely spun as a spider's web. I would have expected it to perish in the years since her mother's death, but it seems not.

'I don't remember her. I'm like my nephews. They won't remember their mother either.' Her voice breaks as she speaks. I appreciate that she is another like me. I didn't know my mother. I certainly didn't know my father. Neither, it seems, did she, and certainly not well.

'Perhaps not, but you can tell them stories of her.' I hope this makes her smile. I know I would have appreciated stories of my mother, but mention of my mother was more likely to be met with denial. Not even Wynflæd likes to speak about her.

'I can, can't I?' She looks pleased with the suggestion as we begin walking back to the hall, her tears for now forgotten, as her hand snakes inside mine. Such an action comforts me as well, which I find surprising. I didn't expect to find someone who thought as I did, but Lady Cynewise and I are more alike, for all over a decade separates us in age.

The smell of cooking meat fills the air, reminding me that Lord Wigmund has ordered a feast to celebrate the banishment of Lord Coenwulf. Lord Wigmund's a damn fool, and yet I won't refuse the food. Only then, there's a clatter of horses' hooves, and I turn, expecting to see Lord Coenwulf's return.

But, of course, it's not him. He has determined to face his banishment honourably. Despite his sorrow at leaving his children and his home. Instead, I meet the surprised face of Wulfheard and, behind him, Oswy and Maneca, mounted on their horses.

'What are you doing here?' we ask one another simultaneously.

9

'The king sent us to protect Kingsholm. He knew that Lord Coenwulf was leaving today. Have we missed him?' Wulfheard demands, looking around as though Coenwulf might just appear out of thin air. Behind him are more and more familiar faces. I thrill to see them, even while being careful not to show them how pleased I am that they're here.

'Yes, he left just now. This is his sister, Lady Cynewise.'

'Good day, my lady.' Wulfheard surprises me with his respectful greeting for one so young. 'The king's aware of reports of Viking raiders close to the borders with the Welsh kingdom of Gwent. He's sent my men and me, or rather, Ealdorman Ælfstan's men, under my command, to ensure the king's son is protected, and of course, Lord Coenwulf's children as well.'

'Well met.' The poise of Lady Cynewise doesn't surprise me. She knows whom she is well enough. Her brother might be gone but she's still the daughter of a previous king of Mercia. 'Lord Wigmund is in the hall, celebrating the departure of my brother.' For all the words are laced with tight fury, they remain polite and courtly. I can see Cynewise knows what's expected of a Mercian woman of high birth. I detect the work of Lady Cynehild in her iron resolve, impressive for one so young.

At that moment, a roar of appreciation erupts from the hall.

'Then perhaps, the king's son might think to have men on gate duty.' Wulfheard's lips twist. I see he's about as pleased to be here as an injured man about to have his wounds cleaned with vinegar. 'Maneca, Cenred, dismount, and have the gates closed. Stay on guard until I can sort this mess out,' Wulfheard huffs, his eyes dancing with fury. His gaze sweeps over me, although it lingers for a moment too long, and then he looks to Cynewise.

'My lady, if you could take me to the hall. I'll inform Lord Wigmund of our arrival.'

I don't miss the smirk of triumph on the young woman's lips.

'I'll be having words with you later,' Wulfheard promises me. I watch him go and then look up at Oswy. He evades my gaze. I feel a tremor of unease. I was angry when I last saw Oswy. Angry and fit to fight anyone. He won't know why, and I can't tell him why. The moment elongates for too long, and then he jumps down, throws his reins over his horse's head, and engulfs me in an embrace that stinks of the sharp, biting wind, horse, sweat and the familiarity of Tamworth. I could weep.

'We've missed you in Tamworth,' he announces, stepping back and appraising me to see if I've changed while we've been apart all winter.

'Yes, we have,' Cenred confirms, dismounting as well. I still await some other comment, some slight, but it doesn't come. Indeed, all the men approach me, offering words of greeting, and I feel an unusual smile on my lips. From the hall, I'm aware of the joviality of the situation draining away, the crash of doors being flung open, of furious strides over the courtyard before the hall. Still, through it all, I feel enveloped in warmth from my friends. For a time, I even consider why I left them. With them, I can forget all about Lady Cynehild's dying wish, of the oath she bid me speak before breathing her last.

All until a small boy's giggle and a babe's chuckling permeate my thoughts.

I turn, eyes wide to see young Coenwulf, the older boy, reaching up to touch the noses of the milling horses. Eadburg's there, her cheeks tear-stained, as the look of hope slips from her face. She must have believed Lord Coenwulf, and more importantly, Edwin, had returned to her.

'Eadburg, come meet the warriors of Ealdorman Ælfstan. They've been sent to protect Kingsholm now that Lord Coenwulf's begun his banishment.'

I think she'll shake her head and walk the children away back to her mother, but instead, gripping the babe tightly, she briefly curtsies and comes to my side.

I keep half an eye on young Coenwulf, the older boy, but Oswy's down on one knee beside the diminutive child. I can hear him murmuring about the horses. I never expected to see such a thing.

'That's Oswy,' I inform Eadburg, 'and this is Kyre, Landwine, Waldhere.' I make hasty introductions. Those on their feet stand a little taller, admiring her fine appearance, marred only by the red of her eyes and the splotchy cheeks that shine pink in the bright daylight. She is a fine-looking woman. Edwin is lucky to have found her. I only hope they can survive the coming seven years apart.

I continue my introductions while Maneca and Cenred quickly pull the double gate closed and adopt a position of belligerence on the viewing point just to the side of the gates. I can already hear confused voices from outside Kingsholm. I don't think the gate will remain closed for long. There are too many people working in the fields and about on errands, but as always, Wulfheard has worked quickly to ensure all know there are warriors inside Kingsholm once more and not the useless turds of Eadweard and his cronies.

'They're your friends?' Eadburg asks me, just to be sure.

'Yes, Wulfheard, he's in the hall at the moment, taught me to fight. Oswy helped me as well. And I've stitched up all of them from one wound or another.' A look of confusion touches her face while the babe reaches out as though he too wants to touch one of the horses. She steps closer, but Kyre intervenes.

'Here, the child's heavy. Let me hold him for you. Come on, young man, come and meet Bada. She's Wulfheard's horse and likes littlies.' Hesitantly, Eadburg passes over the precious burden, and abruptly I realise that while I've exiled myself here, to Kingsholm, I've had little to do with the children I'm supposed to be guarding against whatever might harm them.

'Icel, I don't understand why you're here when your friends have only just arrived.' I can hear the confusion in Eadburg's words.

'Don't worry, Eadburg, I don't either, not really. But here's where I must be.' I shrug as I reply. I speak the truth.

But our pleasant exchanges don't last long.

'Get out of here.' The furious voice of Lord Wigmund sends chickens shrieking, and Eadburg instinctively moves to grab hold of both small children. But Oswy holds firm to young Coenwulf while Kyre grips Coelwulf tightly. 'You're not welcome here. And you should leave.'

Behind a furious Wigmund, I see Wulfheard, a frown on his familiar face, his hands resting in a warrior's stance, close to his weapons. In contrast, Eadweard, Wulfred and his allies spill from the hall, grinning with delight at this new development. They're no match for Wulfheard. In fact, if anything, seeing them beside him, I realise what pathetic figures Eadweard and Wulfred make.

'My lord, as I advised you, we're here on the king's instructions.' Wulfheard's words aren't shouted but carry well all the same from where he stands, close to the hall.

'And I'm the king's son, the ætheling, and don't require additional warriors within my own home.'

I'm not alone in wincing at the reminder that, by right, Lord Wigmund is now the master of Kingsholm, although, actually, the king placed it in the hands of his wife, Lady Ælflæd.

'Your gates were open, my lord, and there are reports of Viking raiders and other disturbances along the borders with the Welsh kingdoms. The king, and the queen, both ordered us here. Ealdorman Ælfstan will arrive shortly as well.' If Wulfheard hoped the mention of the queen would sway the matter, he's to be mistaken.

Now Lord Wigmund's face turns purple with rage.

'I don't need someone to stand as my nursemaid. I'm the king's son, a husband and a father. I know how to defend my settlement.'

'But the gates, my lord?' Wulfheard is persistent, and I suddenly appreciate that he has much experience dealing with difficult lordlings. How he doesn't sigh, I don't know.

I notice Lady Cynewise emerging from the hall, and I note her wide eyes as she absorbs what's happening, no doubt keen to avoid the scrutiny of her sister. Even Lady Ælflæd joins the arguing, emerging from the building where the children are cared for. Compared to the chunky child in Oswy's arms, young Wigstan is about half his size and twice as difficult, as he twists in his mother's arms, his cries continuous. A string of wet nurses have tried to tend to him, but he refuses all of them, preferring his mother to all others. Lady Ælflæd, as bitter as she can be, is always tired and lacking in sleep, thanks to her son. He's an awkward and unhappy child. I've heard Eadburg and her mother discussing it at length. Again, I'm aware that Theodore and Gaya would have been able to do more for Ælflæd than her monks and their chanting. Even Wynflæd would have been able to calm the child. There are always remedies but Lady Ælflæd is led by her husband and his mother, the queen. And they both believe they know best.

'What is this?' Lady Ælflæd asks, her words snapping tighter than a war banner in a stiff breeze. She's pale in the bright daylight. While she and her brother have parted on bad terms, this must be difficult for her. Or at least, I hope she has some regret for what's happened. It would perhaps help if her husband showed some regard for her, but he's announced, to all who'll hear, that his wife's no good to him while she tends to their child. They don't share a bed. In fact, they share little but the rule of Kingsholm, and even that's uneven. As such, there'll be no sibling for Wigstan anytime soon.

'My lady, the king has sent my men and me to guard Kingsholm while you and the king's son are in attendance. There are reports of disturbances on the borders with the Welsh kingdoms and some suspected incursions from the Viking raiders. Your gates were wide open.' I'm impressed that Wulfheard has the patience to repeat himself once more.

'Then why are we all arguing about this?' She fixes her husband with a fiery gaze. He subsides, lips tight with fury. 'Find yourselves somewhere for the horses. But you'll have to sleep in the main hall. There are no spare beds to be found anywhere.'

This seems to amuse Lord Wigmund, who turns, his cloak swirling around him, and marches back to his aborted feast, trailed by Eadweard and the others, who don't use all the room in the bunkhouse now that

Edwin and his allies have left to escort Lord Coenwulf, despite Lady Ælflæd's words. For a long moment, no one else moves, but then Wulfheard speaks.

'Men, tend to your horses. If there's no room in the stables, then we'll arrange a temporary paddock for now.'

'I'll take the boys,' Eadburg announces, holding out her hands. She grips the babe tightly, for all I can see he's heavy to carry, even with her hip jutting out to one side to take his weight, while young Coenwulf slips his hand into hers, a joyful look on his bright face. I fear he'll ask after his father, but as they turn, and make their way to where Lady Ælflæd still watches, eyes narrowed, and my fellow warriors start to lead the horses away, I can hear Coenwulf chattering away about the 'big' horses, and how much he likes them. I don't miss the strange look on Lady Ælflæd's face as she eyes young Coelwulf. Does she wish her son was as hale and hearty? I imagine she does, but I also detect another emotion there. Is it hatred or jealousy, or the cold-hearted musings of a woman who knows her son might not survive but that he has two cousins with a claim better than his?

I feel the smile at young Coenwulf's chattering draining from my face, and then Wulfheard's before me, obstructing my view of Lady Ælflæd.

'Right, Icel. It's time me and you talked.' Without waiting for my agreement, he grips my arm tightly and pulls me towards where Cenred and Maneca watch for trouble from outside the gate. He doesn't so much as spare a glance for Lady Ælflæd, and I'm pleased to see Lady Cynewise slowly back away so as to avoid her sister's scrutiny.

Wulfheard forces me up the steep steps that lead to a lookout position to the left-hand side of the gates, I watch Maneca and Cenred slip their way down the stairs.

'Cowards,' I murmur under my breath, but I don't think they hear me. My heart's hammering in my chest. This isn't going to be a nice conversation.

'Ealdorman Ælfstan has forced this godforsaken commission on us because he wants to know what you're doing and when you're returning to Tamworth.' He turns, looking over the landscape surrounding Kingsholm, which is suspiciously flat, the sound of the River Severn close enough that we can hear it. Should it flood, as I know it does, some fields will be inundated, but hopefully not Kingsholm itself.

'I'm not coming back to Tamworth,' I say softly.

'That's what Wynflæd told me. Why?' The fact he's spoken to her of me is a surprise.

'I have to stay here, as I said, guard the children.'

'Why does this fall to you?'

'Lady Cynehild made me swear.'

'And who does she think the children need protecting from?'

This is the question I don't want to answer. Wulfheard doesn't speak, either. When he once more faces me, his eyes flash with respect.

'It's a heavy burden for you. But, if Lady Cynehild suspected the king, the queen, or their pestilent son was a threat to her children, why didn't she do something about it before she died?'

I know my mouth hangs open in shock at his words.

'Really, Icel, you're not the only one with a mind and eyes in your head.' Wulfheard shakes his head at me and waits for a response.

'I... well, I don't know. Of course, she died somewhat unexpectedly. Neither did she, I imagine, think the queen would ensure her husband was sent into exile.'

'Perhaps not, but she was always astute.'

'I was here, and so she laid the oath on me.' I add nothing further. I'd sooner forget why. I'd sooner forget the rest of her admission to me, although the silver eagle hangs heavily around my neck.

'Ealdorman Ælfstan's wary of Lady Ælflæd. He says there are reports that the child she shares with Lord Wigmund is weak and won't survive. As such, until she grows ripe with another babe, the future rule of the Mercians could well be in jeopardy. And, of course, following the last decade of unrest, there are others who think to have a claim to the kingship as well. I'm sure you're aware of Lord Beorhtwulf, as he was in Kingsholm when the king banished Lord Coenwulf. He thinks himself a contender for the kingship of Mercia as well.'

It's good to know Lord Beorhtwulf has come to the attention of Ealdorman Ælfstan and Wulfheard. But I address the issue of the babe, young Wigstan. 'Lord Wigmund is only as young as me. He'll live forever, especially as he seems unable to lift a blade to protect Mercia.'

'Perhaps, Icel, perhaps, but that makes him as weak as the child dependent on his mother's milk to thrive. And Lady Ælflæd will realise this. At the moment, should something happen to her husband, men and women will look to the claim of her brother and not to her. After all, Lord Coenwulf is the son of a king, and he now has sons. Do you know where Lord Coenwulf's gone?'

'No, he took ship this morning. That's all I know. Some said it would take him to Frankia, but I don't know the truth of that.'

Wulfheard is decidedly unhappy about this. 'With Lord Wigmund here and not with his father, Lord Beorhtwulf is gaining in popularity. I've even seen Ealdorman Sigered whispering in corners with him, and all know Sigered was fiercely loyal to the queen.'

'Who is Lord Beorhtwulf? No one in Kingsholm knows.'

'He claims descent from King Beonred, the ill-fated king who ruled for a year only between Æthelbald and Offa last century.' Wulfheard sounds like Wynflæd now, filling me with details of a past I know little about, and in fact, that few will know about, as it's near enough eighty winters ago.

'Then he also claims kinship with King Beornwulf?' The words leave my mouth before I can stop them.

'Aye, he does, but it's so distant, not even the bishops can decipher it,' Wulfheard states, unaware of why I'm asking such questions and why King Beornwulf's name is so readily on my lips.

I chew on my lip, running my hands through my thick beard and moustache. It's kept me warm through the winter, but perhaps it's time to trim it back.

'Then we have many people thinking to claim the kingship of Mercia, and all while King Wiglaf yet lives.'

'We do, yes. Ealdorman Ælfstan cautions us all to be wary. That's why he's stayed at Tamworth, now that affairs in his ealdordom are settled. He doesn't wish to leave while there's so much unease. The king and queen are still unhappy with one another after he was forced to banish Lord Coenwulf when he didn't want to do so. And he's right. All the queen has accomplished is to allow this Lord Beorhtwulf to make an impression on the men and women of the witan. And Lord Beorhtwulf is well oiled and knows how to gain the ear of everyone. I've seen him at work. Few are immune to his charms. And, unlike Lord Wigmund, the king's son, he at least has the look of a warrior about him.'

I breathe deeply, inhaling the cold, fresh scent of the coming spring. I can't help thinking, although I don't want to, that if I made my true origins known, then I too could cause problems for King Wiglaf. If this Beorhtwulf, whomever he is, can claim some tenuous link to a previous king, I can do the same. Only, I really don't want to do so. Wynflæd could speak for me, and all would trust and believe her, I don't deny that, but she would also then be threatened, and not just by the queen, but by any who would think to dispute my claim. I want to ask about her, but I can't bring myself to ask the question, *Does she still live?* I'd sooner think that she does, than know that she doesn't, and surely, when mentioning her earlier, Wulfheard would have told me had she died. Hopefully, one day, I'll be able to reconcile with her, but not yet.

But, as though to prove the point, the pitiful cry of the small child, Wigstan, echoes through the air once more. A reminder that, for the time being, the future of Mercia depends on the life of a child whom everyone fears will die before reaching his first name day.

10

'You're coming with us,' Wulfheard informs me, his legs wide, hands on his hips, brokering no argument. 'We have to ride the borders and ensure all is well.'

'But—' I start.

'I don't really care,' Wulfheard continues, as though I've not spoken, 'why you think you shouldn't. Brute needs a gallop. He's kicking his stall to pieces in the stables. And you need to get away from the crying babes and the presence of Lord Wigmund and those he surrounds himself with.'

Wulfheard only arrived yesterday with the rest of Ealdorman Ælfstan's men, but already I can tell he's restless. The gale of last night won't have helped. With the shrieking of wood, the crash of objects fleeing across the settlement, and the constant draft through the wattle and daub walls, everyone feels twitchy for all the storm has dropped away. The lack of the howling wind means everything seems strangely calm and quiet.

'Fine,' I capitulate, hurrying to Brute's side. Wine watches me with knowing eyes but eagerly pulls at the hay in her stall. She's content. Brute isn't. I'm reminded that Wine is a much older horse. Perhaps it's time to send her to Budworth to be cared for there. Here, I spend too much of my time shovelling shit from the stalls, refusing to allow Pega to do it on my behalf, now that I'm able once more, after my beating. Perhaps, I consider, the next time I receive a message from my reeve at Budworth, I'll arrange for Wine to return with them.

Brute doesn't make it easy. He fights me when I try and saddle him, biting my ear and huffing into it, bashing my back with his long head.

'Do you want to go out?' I eventually exclaim in exasperation, even as Wulfheard calls through the door.

'Hurry up, Icel. Today would be good.'

As though understanding those words, Brute finally allows me to place his saddle, having been forced to loosen off the straps beneath his belly because he's grown fatter during the cold, dark winter months.

I lead him outside and, mounting up, with only a small argument, I join Wulfheard and Oswy as they wait to be allowed to leave the settlement. Sadly, Eadweard and Wulfred are on gate duty, and they take their time so that Wulfheard leaps from Bada's back and opens the gates wide himself. They've not been forced to this duty throughout the long winter, when Edwin, Osmod and Tatberht were usually prevailed upon. But Lord Wigmund, unhappy with Wulfheard's arrival, has assigned them the task. I'd smirk about it, but I don't wish to have anything to do with them.

'If you're this slow when I get back, then you'll be on mucking-out duty for a week,' Wulfheard informs the two men. Neither looks concerned. 'And don't think Lord Wigmund will do anything to intervene. He'll be quieter than a mouse now that I'm here and in overall command,' Wulfheard continues. I'm not convinced that's correct, but there's enough truth in it for both men to look contrite, even while Eadweard arches his eyebrows at me.

'Got your friends to help you, young Icel?' Eadweard taunts. 'I can beat all of them, just like you.'

'I doubt that.' Oswy rides his mount too close to Eadweard, making him step backwards, right into a ripe pile of green horseshit. 'I can pummel your face so your nose lies so close to your face, it'll be no good for breathing through.' The menace in the tone brings a wry smile. It's good to have Oswy beside me, even if it's only for now.

Outside the gates of Kingsholm, Wulfheard turns Bada's head towards the river. There's a bridge within Gloucester, but Wulfheard doesn't go that way, instead heading northwards, which surprises me.

'I thought there were Viking raiders?' I murmur.

'There are reports of Viking raiders,' Oswy informs me, and something in his tone makes me doubt those reports. What is Ealdorman Ælfstan playing at? If there are no Viking raiders, how has he got his warriors assigned to Lord Wigmund?

Beneath me, Brute's restless, and only when we have a clear sight of the river, the fields only just beginning to turn green, apart from those within which the spring crop is slowly becoming ready to harvest, does he eagerly stretch his legs. Quickly, we pass the place where Eadweard almost beat me to death, and I realise I've not been this far outside the settlement since then. I bend low over Brute's shoulder and allow him to set the pace.

Around me, the thunder of hooves assures me that the others do the same.

The thrill of the speed loosens the tension from my shoulder, and by the time Wulfheard calls for us to rein in, I feel more myself than I have since Lady Cynehild's death. How I wish she'd kept the knowledge she knew to herself. I'd never have known, and that would have been acceptable.

'So, men.' Wulfheard beckons us close to him, the horses pawing at the ground, seeking out the few growing strands of grass. 'As you can imagine, our purpose here isn't quite what as it appears. Yes, we must ensure the safety of Lord Wigmund, Lady Ælflæd, and the children, but the ealdorman also commands us to be alert to any indication that all is not as it seems. Now that Mercia has countered the threat of Wessex, if only for the moment, and the aggression of the kingdom of the East Angles, if only for the moment, some grow impatient with the same ruler for the last four years. The ealdorman expects trouble from Lord Wigmund and certainly Lady Ælflæd, and also from Lord Beorhtwulf.'

'What of Viking raiders and Welsh unrest?' Maneca queries, his tone ensuring we all know the idea of playing politics is far from appealing.

'They somehow seem the lesser threat at this time,' Wulfheard admits. I can see it costs him. Mercians should be loyal to Mercians, but of course, my father wasn't loyal to his king. He undermined and then usurped Lord Coenwulf's father. In doing so, he undoubtedly planted the seed that others could do the same.

'I'd sooner run my blade through a Wessex bastard than have to listen to the titters and whispers of those who should know better.' Cenred sounds aggrieved.

I look to Oswy. His clenched hands on his reins show his fury. He's been forced to play this game before. No doubt he thought it was done with. 'Why is nothing ever just accomplished and left as it is?' Oswy questions angrily, assuring me I know his thoughts well.

'Every generation thinks it knows best,' Wulfheard announces, although he's not happy about it. 'We might all be old – well, apart from Icel – and we might all have seen enough to sicken us for one lifetime, but these new ones, who've never been sorely tried, think it little more than a game of kingdoms. As though it were tafl and not people's lives.'

I shudder at Wulfheard's doom-laden tone. I'm not used to seeing my fellow warriors looking so concerned. But then, the enemy they might now face isn't one that comes at them, assesses their weaknesses and strengths, and strikes to undermine them. No, this enemy is something less tangible, hard to grasp and even harder to keep hold of. How else, I realise, was my father's identity kept so secret?

'Then every generation deserves a whack behind the ears from their mother or father, and to be brought to heel. They must understand that good men have died for this stupid fascination with who will rule,' Oswy continues.

'If only they had our wisdom,' Wulfheard muses, and we're all silent.

'So, there are no Viking raiders or unease on the Welsh border?' I ask, just to be sure.

'Oh yes, there are rumours of them, all right,' Wulfheard assures me. 'And those are easy enough to contend with. It's the other whispers we must be alert to. Now, tell us, Icel, who is that woman you spoke to with Lord Coenwulf's children?'

'She's taken,' I hasten to inform them all. 'She and Edwin, they have an arrangement, and although Edwin's gone with Lord Coenwulf, she's sure, as is he, that seven winters will pass quickly, and they'll be reunited.'

'She has a mother, though,' Cenred calls, his approval evident. 'And she's a widow.'

Wulfheard smirks but then faces them all. 'We cause no trouble here. We don't need any women. We can amuse ourselves well enough by riding out and fighting amongst ourselves. I don't want to pull you apart from one another and give Lord Wigmund any opportunity to complain to his father or bloody mother.'

'Where's the queen?' I query instead.

'She's currently in Winchcombe, so not far from here. Worse luck. She and the king are largely separated, but she thinks to have some control over the nunnery there, as Lady Cwenthryth did before her. I wish her luck with that.' I try and bring to mind who Cwenthryth was and then recall she was the daughter of King Coenwulf, the first of his name. I think. She took command of the nunnery where her brother was buried and used his sainted status to add to the troubles in Mercia following her father's demise. She's been dead for some years. Perhaps all the Mercian women are meddlesome, not just the queen and Lady Ælflæd.

'So the king has a disaffected son, wife, and this new lordling, Beorhtwulf, all vying for power, and scattered over Mercia. Isn't that dangerous?'

'Yes, it's very dangerous. That's why we're here. Ealdorman Tidwulf has men with the queen, and in Tamworth, Ealdorman Beornoth keeps his gaze on Ealdorman Sigered as well as Beorhtwulf, whom he's not related to although they share name elements. Sigered is more slippery than a Thames-caught eel. But enough pessimism. Come, we'll ride the boundaries and see what can be seen.'

With that, Wulfheard urges Bada onwards, and the other men hasten to hurry, which makes Brute rush to the front. My horse, catching me unawares, streams onwards, and the landscape, notably flat, passes swiftly before my eyes. In the distance, I can see the Welsh hills, not that they ever come any closer. We'd need to cross the River Severn at one of the bridges to do that.

When Brute eventually slows, I turn him and peer back the way we've come. To the south, hills rise, leading onwards to where I know Wessex must be, while to the west, the hint of cloud suggests the sea isn't far either. Wulfheard's the first to catch me.

'I see he's as well behaved as ever.'

'Nothing changes there,' I confirm.

'Tell me, Icel, I didn't want to ask inside the walls of Kingsholm, but Lady Ælflæd seems greatly changed.'

'She is, yes, I suspect she wishes to be queen more than her brother ever wished to be king. Her son is a poor feeder and lacks strength, or so I've heard. I think she worries he might die, and of course, she does have to live with the odious Lord Wigmund.'

'Perhaps,' Wulfheard muses, but I can see his mind is busy, mulling over all that might be the cause of the current unease running through Mercia. 'Never one to believe a fight can solve everything, I think if, this summer, we have an attack from one of our many enemies, then Mercia will unite, and all will be well again.'

'I doubt you'll get your wish,' I caution him. The Viking raiders, having been attacked on the Isle of Sheppey, haven't been sighted since, at least not close to the River Thames or even to the north, where they might sneak along the River Trent. As for King Ecgberht of Wessex, it's understood that he still struggles to contain the unease from the Viking raider attacks. I can't see that he'll direct his gaze to Mercia anytime soon. Mercia, I fear, will tear itself apart without the aid of any external force.

11

'Wulfheard.' The sharp command of Ealdorman Ælfstan echoes above the clash of training weapons inside Kingsholm, and every man there turns to eye Ælfstan, mounted on his horse.

'My lord. We didn't know to expect you yet,' is the immediate reply from Wulfheard who, cheeks puffing, strides towards his oath-sworn lord, his weapon lowered. 'It's not yet midsummer.'

'Well, I'm here, and now we're commanded to Londonia. Viking raiders along the River Thames. Ealdorman Muca sends word to the king.' Whether Ealdorman Ælfstan approves of this or not is impossible to tell. I note that he rides with two men I don't know. Has he taken on men to replace those lost last year, or are they about some other business?

Such news that the enemy has been sighted should fill me with trepidation, but I'm a warrior, and this is what I do. Anything has to be better than enduring the sour atmosphere at Kingsholm. Young Coenwulf and Coelwulf thrive. Young Wigstan, I believe, is slowly starting to gain on Coelwulf, which cheers me even if his mother remains contrary in her treatment of all, including her young sister. Lady Cynewise has become somewhat of a friend to the men under the command of Wulfheard and also to me. But that's not what makes the atmosphere so difficult. No, that's been caused by the arrival of Queen Cynethryth from Winchcombe with all of her demands. It would have been better for all, including her son, had the queen remained in her manor but she's determined to ensure all know her son is the king's heir, even if neither the queen or his son are with the king.

'When do we leave?' Wulfheard calls to Ælfstan, a very public conversation so that neither of them have to repeat themselves again.

'Tomorrow morning. The queen brought her warriors with her. I carry instructions that she's to remain here, with the king's son, until such time as the Viking raiders are removed from the River Thames.' Now I understand whom the other two warriors are. They must be from the king to the queen, or just the queen's men, encountered on the road by the ealdorman.

Such an accounting is well given, and I nod, conflicted already, despite my urge to be clear of Kingsholm. It's been a long half a year here. I've no true bed to call my own. I'm heartily sick of living from day to day not knowing where I can place my possessions or rest my head each night. It's been easier since the arrival of Wulfheard and the others. But only just.

'And don't think you're not included, Icel,' Ælfstan's calls to me, as though able to hear my thoughts. The command is hardly privately given. 'The king has personally demanded that you're included.' My heart sinks at that, but it's not surprising. I can't help but see the queen's hand at play in this. She was dismayed to find me at Kingsholm when she arrived, just shy of a month ago. I found her watching me. I didn't know she'd sent word to the king.

And yet I gave my oath to Lady Cynehild. Surely, I try and equivocate, I must be fulfilling it by ensuring Mercia remains whole.

'My lord.' I incline my head towards him and note that the tension eases from his shoulders at my easy response. I don't want to leave the children. Even though I hardly see them, at least I'm close if they need me. But equally, I know I must leave Kingsholm. My presence here has outgrown any grudging acceptance it might have initially earned. Eadweard and Wulfred understand to keep their distance, but that's more down to Wulfheard and Oswy than anything I've done. If my fellow warriors leave, and I'm left with Eadweard and Wulfred, I realise I'll be beaten close to death again. Equally, the queen and her son are overly aware of me. Lady Ælflæd, I fear, sees nothing but her son, and her perceived failure, and that of her brother's treason. She wouldn't know whether I was here or not, and that saddens me even now. I've spent so long trying to avoid her, and yet I now realise I needn't have bothered. She doesn't see me. I could have been sat before her for the last half a year, and she still wouldn't have acknowledged my presence.

Later that night, I seek out Eadburg. She and I have become friends in Edwin's absence. It's strange how much easier it is to like him when he's not here. Yes, Edwin and I had been thrust together inside Kingsholm, but all the same, I didn't always find his presence as easy as when we were children. We mended our friendship, but it wasn't quite the same.

'There's still no word from Edwin,' Eadburg frets, as I watch her tending to the children's clothes, needle in hand, ensuring the tears are repaired.

'I don't think there will be, either. Lord Coenwulf knows that his safety depends on no one knowing where he is.' Eadburg and I have had this conversation almost every day since Edwin left.

'Perhaps, but the same can't be true for Edwin, Cuthwalh, and the others who went with him,' she protests.

'If they're all still together, then yes, it must.'

She sighs unhappily at my oft-spoken phrase. She accepts it, and yet, I imagine, late at night, that it taunts her all the same.

'How are the children?'

This question makes her smile. I'm sure, as young as she is, that she must wish to be a mother herself. 'Coenwulf is learning his letters with the monks. Coelwulf's sitting and rolling unaided now. He's a quick boy to learn. And Wigstan is getting there,' she offers with a soft smile. I think all of the women have a soft spot for Wigstan, who's battled through no end of hardships as he appears determined to defy the odds and survive his first year. They don't appreciate his mother, but Wigstan has finally begun to accept the presence of others who care for him, allowing Lady Ælflæd some respite. No matter what people might say about him, he's certainly a fighter. 'And, of course, Lady Cynewise is always with the children, for all she's really one herself.'

I've found occasion to send Lady Cynewise herbs I find on my travels beyond the confines of Kingsholm. I've brought her fennel, yarrow, wild onion, young beech leaves and watercress. I know she still practises on any who'll ask her opinion. She's much better with people than the monks, who think they know all there is to know about healing. Not for the first time, I think she'd have been helpful in Ealdorman Tidwulf's desire to write a leechbook, and she'd certainly have benefited from the presence of Gaya and Theodore. I've still not managed to find her a sharper blade. I really must look for one in Londonia.

'Then you're happy all will be well when we leave?'

Now Eadburg's face twists. 'Provided the queen doesn't interfere. She's only ever birthed one child but believes she knows better than my mother, who birthed six of her own children, and assisted with almost every other woman's child within Kingsholm. She was the woman who tended to the old king's wife, and ensured that Lady Cynewise survived the loss of her mother.' Outrage sparks those words.

I nod. 'Yes, she's somewhat overbearing,' I try and mollify.

'But yes, Icel. Don't worry. Fight the Viking raiders, and all will be well when you return to Kingsholm. Will you be returning here?' Her question's edged with worry.

'I will, yes. Wine's remaining behind. Pega says he'll see to her needs, but I'm sure she'd welcome some attention from young Coenwulf.'

'Of course. She's so gentle with him. I don't think it'll be long until he needs his own pony to ride.'

'You can never start them too young,' I confirm, and then we part. I return to my horses to ensure all is as it should be. I can't say I'm excited to be riding to Londonia and a possible fight with the enemies of Mercia. But I'd sooner face them than the ones within Mercia, who work to undermine all that King Wiglaf has achieved. My opinion of him continues to evolve and change. I admire him for all he's done, and yet wish he was a little more alert to the antics of his wife, son and Ealdorman Sigered. And Lord Beorhtwulf.

King Wiglaf seeks Mercia's enemies at her borders and along her rivers. I'm not sure he's correct to do so.

* * *

I lean over Brute's shoulder, raised in the saddle, trying to make it easier for him as he nears the summit of the huge hill Ealdorman Ælfstan was determined we crested. For all there's another way that misses the hill, the ealdorman wouldn't listen to the complaints of the horses or the men.

'A viewpoint such as this should be examined in detail,' he said obdurately. Now, Brute is the first to near the top of the hill. I know the others are struggling behind me. I did almost consider dismounting and know that others have done so, yet Brute pushed on. He's the most stubborn horse I've ever met.

Finally, as the terrain levels out, I turn and look behind me. Seeing a vast distance to the north and west is possible from here. The hills of the Welsh kingdoms are easy to pick out, as is the patchwork quilt of fields before me. Everything looks tranquil, even the river threading through the land from the sea, all along the River Severn. I'd hoped to search the shoreline for seaweed for Lady Cynewise, but that will have to wait. Perhaps Ealdorman Ælfstan was correct after all. Maybe a permanent watch should be kept here, alert to any possible dangers from Viking raiders using the sea.

'Good God.' Wulfheard is next to arrive, his neck streaming with sweat, where he walks beside Bada, who, head down, looks exhausted. I can see Ealdorman Ælfstan walking beside his mount as well, and determine to hold my tongue when he arrives, although I doubt others will do the same.

The furthest away is Oswy, his horse ploughing ahead of him while, back bent to the slope, he almost crawls on hands and knees.

'It's like the hill on the Isle of Sheppey,' Wulfheard huffs, his face bright pink with the exertion.

'Only five times as long,' I offer resentfully, not wishing to be reminded of the fight and the men we lost there. Sometimes I feel like the others have forgotten all about those who've fallen in the name of Mercia.

But then, one of them will say something, a soft word or two, a cup of ale raised in their memory, and I appreciate that we all carry wounds we keep hidden deep in our hearts.

'Was it worth it?' Wulfheard calls to the ealdorman when he finally arrives. The tone's sharp, and I think the ealdorman will be angry, but instead, he grins, more rictus than joy.

'At least we can say it was indeed worth it,' he calls to Oswy and others still struggling. 'It would have been crap if we'd arrived here and the clouds had descended, and we couldn't see anything.'

He makes a fair point, and as the men collapse to the ground, the horses panting and covered in sweat, I realise we'll be allowed to rest and drink in the view. I swig water from my supplies and look at my fellow warriors.

The years are starting to show on many of them. There's no one here younger than me. I thought the ealdorman would replace those he lost at Sheppey, but he hasn't. Perhaps it would be too much like hard work to whip men into shape so that they fitted with the motley collection of warriors.

The ealdorman is the most changed of all. When I first met him, he was a young man, perhaps with not many more winters to his name than I have now, but time and the fighting we've been forced to endure throughout the last seven summers has left him with physical wounds. His blue eyes are still as bright as ever, but the odd fleck of grey can be seen in his brown beard, and sometimes, when no one's looking, he walks with a slight limp. And, beneath his tunic, I know his chest is criss-crossed with scars from long-since-healed injuries.

Oswy finally emerges only to collapse onto the green tufted grass, his chest heaving beneath his tunic. He started the climb with his byrnie in place, so I hope his horse now carries it, or he'll be retracing his steps. He's a tall man, although I overtop him now. His blond hair masks the streaks of silver that are only visible beneath the bright light of the noon sun. For once, he has no black eye, and his nose is straight. How long that will last is impossible to know. Probably until we encounter one of the Viking raiders or he gets enticed into a fight with someone. Beneath his clothes, his flesh is hard with muscle and the scars of his battles. One of those scars I healed inside Londinium.

'How about it, men, a lookout point, just here?' Ealdorman Ælfstan calls to them.

'As long as we never have to stand a watch,' Maneca huffs. He's on his feet and is recovering more quickly than the others, but it's not that quick.

'The horses need watering,' I call to anyone who'll listen, leading Brute towards where I can hear the rush of tumbling water. Here, a light breeze plays with my dark hair, and I'm grateful I took the time to trim back my beard and moustache. Brute drinks eagerly, for all he seems little concerned by what he's just endured. The other horses follow him without their riders, and I walk amongst them, using a handful of long grasses from the side of the brook to wipe the white foam from their backs, shaking my head at the same time. The men should be here, doing this. Not me.

Eventually, they stagger towards me, even the ealdorman struggling, until they realise it's cooler here, away from the sun's heat, with a collection of branches serving as a shade.

'I think we should move on after we've eaten,' the ealdorman confirms. I look down and smile. All of them have overextended themselves this morning – the damn fools.

Later, as the day begins to close in around us, the horses and men, still languid in their movements, are called to a halt by Wulfheard.

'We sleep here tonight and press on tomorrow to Londonia. It'll take us another three days to get there.' This he directs to Ealdorman Ælfstan. It should have been possible to reach Londonia in three days if we'd taken the other route, and not the four that it now will. There's no response from the ealdorman as we settle for the night. Above my head, the sky's cloudless, stars shimmering brightly as the others grumble and groan, and only when soft snores fill the air do I close my eyes, finding comfort in being with my allies once more and, more importantly, being absent from the oppressive atmosphere inside Kingsholm, where the queen, and her son, plot for when he must become king in the place of his father. I can't see it will happen, but what do I know of politics and kingships?

12

'Where have they been seen?' Ealdorman Ælfstan directs the question to Ealdorman Muca as they greet each other before the hall in Londonia. It seems little has changed since last year when we were here. Although, of course, Frithwine, Æthelmod and Brithelm aren't with us, so there's not likely to be a bloody fight.

'Towards the coast. At least five ships, and sometimes as many as ten.'

The ealdorman looks unhappy at the news.

'They've been disrupting what trading there is at this time of the year when the river levels are so low. The men and women have been vocal in their complaints.'

'So, no fighting, just pillaging?'

'We've found two settlements that have been abandoned, close to the mouth of the river. We found no bodies, so we must assume the inhabitants ran away before they were fired by the enemy.'

'And you have men on watch duty?'

'Yes, we do, and Londinium still possesses a contingent of warriors who use the fort's high walls to watch the river, but the enemy aren't fools. They know to stay out of sight and pick off the ships one by one.'

'Do we have warriors in the ships?'

'Not at this time, no. I don't know many warriors who like to be on a ship, and the traders aren't keen to have a Mercian warrior in there with them. They think one will be no help, although some of them have started to move in convoys, finding safety in numbers.'

I listen with half an ear, eating the fine bread and pottage handed to us after four days of travelling here. Affairs in Londonia sound less fractious than last year, but I can see why Ealdorman Muca wanted reinforcements from the king. The trade that does take place in Londonia is important to Mercia. If the traders stop using the route, even during the summer, then Mercia will suffer, and so will the king's finances.

'And Wessex?'

'Nothing from them. The traders are happy to visit their shore as well as ours. They bring little news, even when I ask specific questions.'

'It's early in the season,' Ælfstan muses. 'Perhaps this is just the beginning, or maybe they've decided on different targets for the remainder of the year. Any news of Lord Coenwulf's whereabouts?' I listen more carefully now. I'd not realised it was something that anyone was genuinely interested in.

'Nothing. It's as though he's disappeared. How was the queen when you saw her?' Ealdorman Muca speaks as though he doesn't truly want the answer.

'Demanding, as to be expected.' Ælfstan lowers his voice. 'There's no sign of another child yet for her son and wife. She grows impatient with Lady Ælflæd, for all she only managed one son with the king. At least it appears as though the child, Wigstan, will survive, after all.'

The two men move aside to discuss matters of taxation and trade, and I stop listening, a pit of unease in my belly.

'What's the matter with you?' Wulfheard queries later when we're preparing to sleep before setting off again in the morning.

'Nothing, really. Just thinking.'

'Well, I'd do less of that if I were you, Icel. I really would. It just seems to get you into trouble.'

* * *

For two months, we ride ever eastward and then back towards Londonia. First one way and then another. The weather gets steadily hotter, the routes familiar beneath the horses' hooves, but we don't see even one Viking raider ship in all that time. The settlements we pass are mostly intact. As Ealdorman Muca said, one or two closer to the mouth of the River Thames have been abandoned and burned. But almost everywhere we visit, the inhabitants are busy in the fields or ensuring their defences are in good condition. Ditches are dug deeper, or at least have the filth of the winter removed from the stinking water lying in the bottom of them, while the ramparts are repaired and the gates made to hang straight where they might have dipped on hinges that creak and complain from the damp winter weather.

'Nothing's happening,' Oswy calls in frustration, far from for the first time. We came here to counter the enemy, but they're non-existent. Whatever ships were plaguing the traders have disappeared as though they were never here. Six times we ride past the location where we first fought the Viking raiders last year, and six times we come to the location where we returned from our foray to the Isle of Sheppey. My skin changes colour beneath the unrelenting heat, but I've no wounds to try and heal other than the odd splinter or knife wound from cutting onions and herbs for the pottage.

The land's hot, the crops ripening, and for once we don't get rained on. We keep our canvases rolled tight on the back of our horses' saddles, and we all grow even more restless than we were in Kingsholm.

'There's nothing,' Wulfheard presses the ealdorman. Ealdorman Ælfstan hasn't remained with us for the entire time. For a month, he kept to Londonia, closeted with Muca, as they discussed court matters.

'No, there isn't,' the ealdorman quickly agrees. 'It's almost as though there never was anything, and we've been summoned here by little more than whispers. Muca fears a substantial attack may be launched against Londonia, but I don't understand how. Surely such an undertaking would require some degree of organisation that I don't see at work here. Not even a scouting vessel. I think the Viking raiders have learned from what happened to them last year. They mean to stay clear of Mercia, and perhaps even Wessex, for they've no way of knowing we retrieved Lord

Coenwulf last year. They might believe it the work of the Wessex king's son.'

'Then we should leave,' Oswy says quickly.

'And go where? Wouldn't you sooner be here than stuck in Tamworth or Kingsholm? I assure you, the queen continues to cause problems if the reports Muca are receiving are correct. Better to stay here, away from the rumour and gossip.'

And so we do. All summer long. For four months, from Eastermonað to Weodmoað, including the most pleasant of all months, Liða, we ride the riverbanks, learning the settlements by name, and recognising people in all of them, who provide us with food and ale, in exchange for our assistance in constructing new defences for them. All of us are shaded by the sun, refusing to wear our byrnies when we ride because they rub against our hot skin. The ealdorman stays with us on some occasions but, on others, remains in Lundenwic or even in Londinium, taking his place on the ancient high stone ramparts, where he says he can see us, no matter how far away we think to be from his scrutiny. He says it to ensure we stay alert, but we don't need such a threat. We've all fought the enemy too many times. We don't fear to do so again.

Time and again, my thoughts turn to Edwin, Lady Ælflæd and the two children. I hope Edwin is well, that young Coenwulf and Coelwulf thrive, and I even hope that Wigstan continues to do well. My feelings towards Lady Ælflæd are ambiguous. She married the king's son. She knew what she was doing. And now, no doubt, she must share his bed once more in the hope of carrying another of his children. I'd pity her if I didn't feel so angry at her for speaking out against her brother. I consider Lady Cynewise as well. I pray that she continues to learn and spend her time with Eadburg and her mother, and that I remember to find her a sharp cutting knife for her herbs before we return to Kingsholm.

Only when the weather takes a decided turn for the worse and the harvest is collected in are we allowed back to Londonia.

'Icel.' The ealdorman beckons me closer, his face revealing nothing of his inner thoughts, as I enter the hall from which Ealdorman Muca controls Londonia for the king. Ealdorman Ælfstan has been absent for much of the last month. I know he planned to travel to Tamworth and seek out the king, and see what was happening amongst those lords not deployed by the king to ensure Mercia was defended.

'What is it, my lord?' I murmur, realising, as he moves away from the rest of the returning men, that this is something he wishes only to tell me.

'I've heard some worrying reports of what's happening at Kingsholm. I know you'd want to know.' Immediately, my stomach fills with unease.

'What sort of reports?'

'The queen, her son, Lady Ælflæd.'

'What of them?'

Now the ealdorman looks away, not wishing to meet my eyes. 'And Lord Coenwulf's children.'

'What of them?' My voice has grown cold.

'I don't know, not for sure, but I thought you should know. I fear. I fear that they mean to take some sort of irrevocable course of action against them now that Wigstan is so much more hale. You know, of course, about Lord Beorhtwulf. I believe they mean to take actions to limit those with a claim to the kingship of Mercia, and they mean to start with the youngest and easiest to contend with. The king will hear nothing against his wife, son and grandson, but Lord Beorhtwulf speaks with all the confidence of a man who knows what's really happening. Of course, he might intend to undermine the queen, I just don't know. It worries me, Icel, it really does.' The ealdorman looks plaintively at me.

'No,' I gasp, all of my previous worries and fears descending upon me. I don't want to suspect Lady Ælflæd of such thoughts towards her nephews, and yet I can't deny that it's not the first time I've feared for them. I'd hoped that Wigstan's better health would prevent the need, but perhaps it's not enough. Once more, I'm reminded of King Offa. He was stringent in disposing of those with any link to the kingship. As such, it's a wonder that Lord Beorhtwulf, and his kinship to King Beonred, has survived to the day. Indeed, it makes me consider that Lord Beorhtwulf might be full of shit with his claims.

'Return to Kingsholm as quickly as you can, if you wish. Wulfheard told me of your bond with them, because of their mother. I'll follow on tomorrow. I must conclude some business here, with Ealdorman Muca.

But I'll come after you. Despite the king's denial, I would see what's happening with my own eyes.'

I nod, already resolved to a long journey north and one that will be too slow, even with Brute as my companion.

'It might all be little and nothing. Whispers from those who mean to smear the name of the king and his wife. But, well...' I can tell he doesn't want to admit this. 'There's enough potential for them to be true that we should ensure nothing ill befalls the children.'

'My thanks for telling me.' I turn aside, but he reaches out and grips my arm.

'Icel, whatever this means to you, do nothing rash. We'll be there in another day, two at most after you arrive. Nothing is happening here. The enemy, wherever they are, aren't about to attack Londonia.'

'I'll do my best,' I inform him, my thoughts already on Kingsholm, the threat of the Viking raiders disappearing, with the fear for the two boys. I don't like to think of what the queen might be capable. Even more, I don't want Lady Ælflæd to be implicated, either. But if it's Lord Wigmund, I wouldn't be surprised. The men he chooses to spend his time with – Ælfred, Hunberht, even Eadweard and Wulfred – lack all honour.

I speak to no one as I slip from the hall again, meeting a surprised-looking Brute in the stables. But he makes no complaint when I quickly saddle him and turn him westwards. While the peak of the summer is passed, there's more than enough daylight to keep up a steady canter, and then, when the darkness finally descends, the moon offers just enough illumination that we can travel at a steady trot. We pause for some rest after over a day's travelling, and then I urge Brute onwards. I don't take the hill route that Ealdorman Ælfstan insisted upon on the way to Londonia. It would only slow us. All the same, we manage to compress three days of travelling into just over two.

We arrive outside Kingsholm when the gates have been opened for the day and elicit no surprise from those who witness us passing beneath them. I note that there are no gate wardens once more. The queen and her son remain too confident of their safety.

'Icel?' Pega calls to me from the stables as I take Brute inside for some much-deserved rest.

I turn and meet his surprised eyes. 'Hello, Pega. How is everyone here at Kingsholm?' I try and keep my voice neutral, hoping he doesn't realise how exhausted Brute and I are. But Pega's face clouds at the question, and he steps close to me, so close that the bristles on his beard touch my ear.

'There's something foul afoot here. I worry for young Lady Cynewise and also for the two little lords. It's not been the same all summer with you and Wulfheard gone.'

'Thank you,' I murmur, surprised by his immediate admission.

'Icel, be wary. The queen's here although she and her son and Lady Ælflæd are preparing to travel to Tamworth on the king's orders. He's summoned them to attend a witan, but they mean to take the children with them, including Lady Cynewise, even though they'd be better left here. Why take such small children on such a journey, especially when two of them have never left Kingsholm before?'

'What? Why?'

Pega shrugs his shoulders, but I already understand too much. Away from Kingsholm and those who care for Lord Coenwulf's children, it'll be much easier for something to befall them. Different scenarios rush through my mind, and none of them are good.

'When do they leave?'

'Today, that's why I'm already saddling the horses.'

'Ealdorman Ælfstan means to follow me here. He should arrive in two days at most. When he does, tell him what you've told me. He'll know what to do.'

'And what will you do?'

'I'll go with them. I'll be their protector,' I announce, not even giving it a moment's thought.

'I suggest you ensure that Lord Wigmund, Lady Ælflæd and the queen don't see you. And Eadweard and the others. Not that it's easy to do. Your horse is unmistakable.' Brute lifts his head at those words, as though he understands them.

'I'll wait outside Kingsholm, and when they leave, I'll keep close, but not too close.' I appreciate he's right to caution me.

'Then go, and quickly.' I turn Brute, wishing I'd thought of this sooner. Quickly, head bowed, I walk Brute to the gate, mindful that I need to evade Eadweard, Wulfred, the queen and her son. Only when I'm once more outside do I take a deep breath. Hastily, I lead Brute to the far side of the road that stretches northwards and into a copse of trees, where we can hide away from those about to travel to see the king.

Eagerly, I wait and watch, the effects of the long days and nights of travel making it hard to stay awake. I allow Brute to doze but don't remove his saddle. The morning moves on apace, and the sun is blindingly hot for once, even though it's moving swiftly towards Haligmonað. I sweat beneath the trees, wishing I could sleep. I stand close to Brute, leaning against a handy tree trunk whose branches start high overhead. I listen to the cries of the men and women of Kingsholm. The shouted commands of those frustrated by one thing or another, and then I startle awake, much, much later, the sky already darkening, and curse myself for a damn fool.

The passage of the convoy north can be clearly seen in the piles of horseshit that splatters the road. I've slept through them leaving, and the fear in my belly hardens to one of sheer terror.

I've lost sight of the children.

'Come on,' I urge Brute, and together, with the blackness of a moonless, cloud-filled sky far overhead, we hurry after the sons of Lady Cynehild.

13

Somehow, I expect to catch them easily. But I don't. The road towards Tamworth is one I've travelled often, with Brute, and Wine.

I push Brute on, aware we've both had time to rest and that my horse never considers his physical limits until it's too late. Eyes wide, I keep alert, noting the drops of horseshit that splatter the road.

Overhead, the halo of shimmering stars moves on apace, and more than once I find myself fixated on one or another of them until the swoop of an owl or bat drags my eyes back to the road. And still, I can hear no sign of the party that's gone on ahead. I consider if they'll stop for the night in Worcester or if they won't make it so far. I didn't see how they intended to travel. Are the children on horses with an experienced rider, or are they in an ox-drawn cart with Eadburg and her mother? I remain alert, looking for signs of either.

All the same, I can't imagine the queen, her son and Lady Ælflæd wanting to camp by the side of the road if they've ridden. Yet I see nothing to give me an idea of where they might stop and so, at the crossroads, where a bridge leads over the River Avon and where I must decide, I glance down, eyeing the horse manure in the moon's glimmer. Which way from here? I wish I hadn't fallen asleep and had stayed alert. Indecision wars inside me, but I press on northwards towards Tamworth. Brute is steady beneath my feet, but I know we've travelled at a warrior's pace and not that of horses carrying children.

Yet the crossroads are too muddled. Anyone could have gone anywhere. There are signs of horses going towards Worcester, but equally, signs of them going towards Tamworth making use of the Fosse Way. Grimacing, I encourage Brute on, more watchful now. Any moment, I expect to encounter the party, sleeping on the side of the road, the smell of smoke alerting me to their presence. But there's nothing. Just a line of horse manure that continues onwards, alongside the occasional hoof print in a pile of mud, washed onto the decaying surface of the uneven road.

I know that Wulfheard would assure me that these roads were built by the giants who constructed Londinium and that they've survived for this long. Still, I can't help thinking, when the road slants to one side, or Brute has to sidestep some of the disturbed stones and gravel, that these roads could do with some repair work if they're to last another five hundred winters, or however long they've been here. Looking upwards, such a span of time seems small and inconsequential, but looking forwards, it seems as though it's been forever. Those men and women who laboured to hack through the hard-packed earth to carry the stones and pebbles to these places are not only long dead, their bodies will have become nought but dust and bones.

Caught up in my reverie, eyes on the heavens above me, I curse when I next glance to the ground. The telltale signs of horse manure have disappeared. Those small pieces that remain have been ground into the stones and surrounding grasses that think to claim the drainage ditches.

I lead Brute on, eyes peering downwards, but there's nothing.

'We've missed them,' I growl deep in my throat, and my horse is unhappy to turn back the way we've just come. I dismount angrily, jarring my knees, and retrace my steps, eyes on the ground. For what feels like half the night, I bend low, looking for what I seek.

'Where have they gone?' I huff more than once, trying to determine how I missed this change beneath me. Why were my thoughts on ancient people when my concern is for those living now?

'Where have they gone?' I repeat, fear suddenly constricting my chest.

I don't want to think anything evil of Lady Ælflæd, but honestly, it's not her that I fear. The queen and her son are ambitious. Too ambitious. And they're not the only ones. Where are they?

'Damn it,' I exclaim, as the grey edges of dawn begin to tint the horizon. Brute follows me. His nose low, reins tied up behind his saddle. More than once, he bumps me, a question on his long, black and white face. But I've no answer for him. Not yet.

'Where have they gone?' I glower, fed up of repeating myself, standing to ease my aching back, pushing my hips forward to lessen the pain there. 'How have I missed them, and where are they going?' Frustrated and angry with myself, I reach for the saddle and help myself to a glug of water before leading Brute towards the welcoming gurgle of a nearby stream.

As he drinks eagerly, I look for signs of horse hooves, but there are none. The riders didn't come this way. Where, then, have they gone? Pega said they were travelling to Tamworth, but unless they've taken some strange route, they've not done so. Perhaps they only travelled some of the distance, turning off to spend the night in a manor somewhere or even visiting Winchcombe. That could, I realise, be my mistake. Or, perhaps, at the crossroads to Worcester, they went that way, keen to speak to the bishop?

'Come on,' I urge Brute, when he's drunk as much as he wants and I've given him some time to tug at the long grasses as well. 'We'll find them at Worcester, I'm sure of it.'

Brute's response is silence, but he does allow me to mount and hastens back towards Worcester, the river at our side offering a low burble of noise until we once more find the crossroads leading to the bridge over the River Avon. Here, with the help of more sunlight, I decide I made my mistake. It's obvious, or so it seems, that most of the traffic went towards the other settlement.

'At this rate,' I muse, 'it'll take them nearly a week to cover a journey we could make in two days at the most. But, of course, the queen is with them. No doubt she expects comfort, not speed.'

Ahead, the settlement of Worcester quickly comes into view, the fields under cultivation, hedges demarcating one crop from another, cows and sheep busy cropping the grasses for it's not yet slaughter month. Some say Worcester is an old settlement, but to me it looks like any other, complete with wooden halls and thatched roofs. But, not wanting to be distracted again, I glance downwards, time and time again, and just before I call for entry into the settlement itself, the smell of the river ripe in the air, I see a trail of horse hooves skirting the settlement. Forehead furrowed, I don't hear the woman speaking to me.

'Move your bloody horse, you great oaf of a man. I can't get my donkey through.' Her words are filled with venom as I peer down and down. She's diminutive, but with hands on hips looks as though she could flay me with her tongue.

Brute eagerly skips out of the way, and she goes to move to the fields and beyond. I consider what the poor donkey carries and where he's going, but call out.

'Is the queen in residence?'

'The queen?' The woman's shocked words assure me that she's not. 'The queen? Why would she come to Worcester? You daft beggar.' And away she goes, encouraging the pliant beast to walk beside her. As I watch, the beast pauses, and a virulent stream of shit hits the ground with a wet thud.

'So that's where all the shit comes from on the road,' I muse.

Ahead, the gates to Worcester are open wide, and I note that some sort of defensive structure encircles parts of the settlement but not all of it. Houses jut up against the ruins of the walls, and the gate really doesn't stop anyone from getting inside. A tumbled-down ruin to the side of it allows entry and exit for those with no goods to convey. I watch a handful of children spider their way over the ruins, chasing a small black and white dog, tail wagging, as it races onwards. They'll have fun catching the little terror.

So, the queen isn't inside Worcester? Where then might she be?

'Are you coming or going?' a grizzled man demands to know. He stands beside me, a wool hat covering sparse hair, his long nose almost touching his lips. His voice is rough, but his eyes are bright with interest.

'I was looking for the queen, but I hear she's not here.'

'The queen? Why would she come to Worcester? No, my lord, last we heard, she was at Winchcombe or Kingsholm with her son, and the king at Tamworth.'

'My thanks,' I call, turning Brute back towards the bridge that leads back to the Fosse Way.

'We've seen no one in these parts other than a group of riders who skirted the settlement yesterday, heading off towards Hereford, I think.'

I stop at those words. Riders? Hereford? 'Is that usual?'

'No, not really. Most people going to Hereford cross the River Severn at Gloucester. It's easier down there. They have to ask some of the river traders to help them up here. The river's wide and there's no bridge.'

'How were they dressed?' I ask the man. I can feel my forehead's furrowed, my eyes narrowed in confusion.

'Like you, my lord. Warriors, I should say.'

'I'm no lord,' I counter, only to shrug my shoulders. I am a lord. I just don't like to think about it.

'Go and see old Leofstan. He'll be upstream a bit. He'll know who they were. He can get information out of a stone, that one.'

I smirk at the rueful tone and dip my head to thank him for his help.

'That way.' He points, showing me where I can bypass the houses and the remnants of the wall on my way to the river. Eyes alert, I look to the settlement as the smoke of cook fires blights the early morning sky. Worcester is much smaller than Gloucester, the village closest to Kingsholm. At Gloucester, much of the old wall remains; inside it, the monks and nuns have built their church and keep very much to themselves. Outside it, the houses of the traders and farmers, complete with workshops and winter enclosures for those animals lucky enough to survive, spread over a wide area, not always close to the old walls.

Here, the buildings that don't belong to the church are pressed up tight to the embankment of the old wall, and there are far fewer of them. That said, the church is visible, its wooden struts and thatched roof peeking over the top of the decaying wall. I ride Brute slowly, mindful of the collection of grazing animals and the runaway dog and children that seem to pay me no heed. This is a place of few defences and even fewer people.

I follow my nose as much as the outskirts of the settlement to where the river is. Once there, I look across it. It's wide. The gate warden's correct to warn me. I can see two ships bobbing in the river and seek out Leofstan. It seems I need not worry that I won't find him.

'My lord.' His voice is firm and filled with command as he steps to the side of me, emerging from a slanting building, inside which I must assume he keeps his stores. There's no cloud of smoke, and neither can I smell it. It's not a dwelling. That's obvious.

'Leofstan?'

'Aye, my lord. Can I assist you in some way?'

'Riders, yesterday? They came this way?'

'They did, yes, off to Hereford, they said. I told 'em to go to Gloucester, but they were having none of it.'

'How many?'

'A dozen of 'em. They weren't happy about the river. Almost as though they didn't know it was here.'

'Did they, excuse the question because it's strange, have a child with them or another lord?'

'A child? Not that I can say. But there was activity on the river overnight. I heard it, but I didn't see it. Others might have crossed later on. It was a clear night. Still, I kept to my bed. But it's impossible not to hear. My home is there.' Leofstan points close to the walls, and I understand. The house, of firm construction, faces westwards, towards the river, but it's just far enough away that I'd not be keen to be roused from my bed to see what was happening. 'I knew it wasn't my boat,' he said. 'I sent it to Gloucester only yesterday.'

'And a lord?'

'Impossible to tell. They might have crossed later, during the night.'

Chewing my lip, I gaze at the view of the river. It's wide here, but nothing compared to the River Thames. Yet I don't know the river.

'Could I swim it with my horse?'

'Why would you want to do that? You're almost in the kingdom of the Welsh, and nothing comes from there but trouble. Mark my words.'

'I think the men are my friends,' I murmur. 'I'm keen to find them.'

'Your friends, are they? Well, I can tell you that one of them was named Wulfred, if that helps you. Had no hair on his head. Surly-faced bastard.'

'Wulfred? Yes, yes, that sounds like him,' I reply, but clearly too quickly. An arched eyebrow, and I think Leofstan is as good at getting the truth out of everyone as the man at the gate informed me.

'Then I can help you. Come with me downstream a little. There's somewhere that the river narrows even more. You'll stand more chance there than you will here. We need a bridge, but no one will part with the coin to build one. Not the bishop. And certainly not the traders, or to be honest, me. I make a living from ferrying people on to the far side of the river, but I give them the opportunity to use the bridge at Gloucester first.'

'Lead on.' I offer an attempt at a smile, but it doesn't touch my lips.

Unlike Leofstan, I know what lies to the west of the river. My uncle and I spent more than enough time close to Hereford. The Welsh kingdoms start some way off yet, but the woodland will be thick, and I'll be alone. And I don't understand what Wulfred and Eadweard are doing. Shouldn't I be turning my head to Tamworth? Only something about that doesn't feel right. I don't believe the queen, Lady Ælflæd and Lord Wigmund are going to Tamworth, not with the children of Lord Coenwulf. It seems they're not crossing the river here either unless they did so during the night. Where, then, are the children? It might be easy enough to hide young Coenwulf and Coelwulf, but not Lady Cynewise.

The strength of the sun gains in intensity, as I walk northwards, Leofstan content to hold his tongue. His gait is firm, for all his legs are more widely spaced than mine. Perhaps, I reason, it's a sign of the time he's spent on board his own ship. I know of mounted warriors who walk similarly, too used to being astride a horse.

'Here you go, my lord.'

I open my mouth to snap back my immediate reply, only to see his eyes shimmering with mirth before I gaze at the river before me. Here, trees grow close to the bank, a tangle of dying summer growth stretching into the river. But – and I smirk to see this – there are two trees, one on each side of the river, and their limbs just about meet and twist together. A bridge for small animals, and I can see where some slight children might think to try their luck.

'Down you go, and then just keep straight,' Leofstan informs me, his eye on the supplies on the back of Brute. 'Have you been to Londonia?' he queries.

'Yes, it's all quiet down there. No sign of the Viking raiders or Wessex warriors.'

'Hum,' he muses. 'This river here. It's been my livelihood since before I could walk, yet I sense its weakness. It's good for trade. It'll be better for those Viking raiders and their ships.'

I startle at that, eyeing him with surprise. 'It won't come to that, surely? The Viking raiders like to stay close to the sea, not the rivers, other than the wide expanse of the Thames.'

'Maybe not. When they tire of such easy targets as the markets and isolated monasteries and nunneries, they'll consider what else they might be able to reach quickly. I've even heard some tell that they lift their ships clear from the rivers when they run out and carry them until they find the next river.'

'No,' I exclaim, astounded by such an idea.

'Yes, my lord. And when you return to King Wiglaf, perhaps you could tell him of such concerns.'

'King Wiglaf?'

'Yes, my lord. I know one of the king's warriors when I see him. You might be alone, but your equipment and horse are of the finest standard. Not for you, a rusty spear or an axe fit for cutting wood, not men.'

'My thanks,' I offer him, suddenly wishing I didn't need to remove my byrnie and tunic to cross the river. But I'll sink if I don't remove my armour. At least, I realise, my body isn't criss-crossed with the many wounds that Oswy or the ealdorman would reveal.

'I'll watch you across. I can't be much help to you if you flounder, but I think your horse will keep you safe.'

And with that, bare-chested and without my boots, for they're tied to the saddle, I clamber down the riverbank, Brute beside me, trying to avoid all the twisting weeds of a full summer's growth, and a thistle, that rears up, almost head height.

Gingerly, I dip a toe in the water, shivering at the coldness of it. I think it's colder than the River Thames. A chuckle reaches my ears. Resolutely,

I ignore it, encouraging Brute into the water, and I follow him, teeth clenched to fight off the breath-stealing cold.

Beneath me, my feet kick up muck and filth from the bottom of the riverbed, and I can feel what I hope are fish shimmering around my legs. Brute eagerly stretches out, and I follow him, staying near his saddle. The water's at least less turbulent here, and I don't feel the tug of the tide around my legs. Perhaps that only happens on the River Thames. I'm sure that if Uor were here he'd tell me all about different rivers, but for now, I focus only on the far shore. In no time at all, before my body can truly warm up in the water, I erupt onto the opposite riverbank, streaming water.

'Well done, my lord. Now, just follow your nose, and it'll take you to Hereford.'

I lift my hand in thanks to Leofstan as he begins his march back towards Worcester. In the distance, the settlement seems both smaller and bigger, the pall of smoke over it informing me that even a small population needs much wood to burn to provide food and keep warm, as well as to work at smelting and whatever trades take place close to the old walls.

Eagerly, I slip my tunic back over my wet back, forcing my byrnie over it as well. And then, feet white with cold, I wince at the unforgiving leather of my boots as I slip them on. Beside me, Brute drips, and I think I should dry him, but it's getting warmer and warmer, almost as though the summer intends to cling on and not allow autumn to turn the leaves a myriad hue of browns and oranges.

'Come on then, lad. Let's see what we can find.' In all honesty, I'm not sure why I'm here. I should be following the Fosse Way to Tamworth, but I'm not. I've never trusted Eadweard and Wulfred or the rest of them. They didn't journey south to help secure Mercia's southern border when it was under threat. No, they stayed at Kingsholm. So why have they finally left it? I'm determined to find out.

Slipping beneath the boughs of the trees that line the river, Brute travels ahead of me, head bowed, forging a path for me to follow. I'm reminded of the time I spent hiding in the woodlands hereabouts when my uncle fled from Tamworth as King Ecgberht of Wessex claimed it for himself. I haven't given much thought to the places I visited since then. For a moment, I fear that I might stumble upon spots we once camped, perhaps even where my uncle met his death.

Angrily, I force myself to continue. What's past is past. I need to determine what Eadweard and Wulfred are up to and what's happening to the children of Lord Coenwulf, and his sister, and perhaps then I might be able to rest and enjoy the peace.

Only, of course, that's not about to happen.

14

The first indication that I'm not alone is the sharp snap of a twig echoing through the treeline. I pause, trying to listen, but Brute hasn't heard it, and he presses on, head bowed, no doubt keen to be free from the trees.

'What was that?' I murmur, but of course, I receive no answer, and eventually I convince myself I've imagined it. Overhead, the interlocking boughs of oak and fir trees block out much of the light, but the strange sepia tones offer just enough visibility to see.

The bank of trees continues, with no sign of it ever thinning, not even the odd stump to assure me that I might be getting close to a place where the locals come to collect their wood for burning. Only then I hear another sharp snap of a breaking twig, this one followed by an exclamation of pain.

'Who's there?' I call, hand reaching for my seax, pleased I tied my weapons belt back in place after my dip in the water.

My words echo back to me, and for all I peer around me, and even Brute's come to a halt, I don't see or hear anything else.

'Whoever you are, know that I'm a warrior of Mercia, and I'm armed. I've killed many men.' My words sound pathetic, even to my ears, but I'll give whomever it is a firm warning. If they attack me now and die on the edge of my blade, they can't say it was entirely unexpected.

'Come on, lad,' I urge Brute on, hopeful that whoever follows me leaves me alone or that we reach a road or designated pathway before I have to shed blood. I distract myself by finding all the mushrooms that Wynflæd might once have asked me to hunt for her. I note the different coloured caps as I go, not bending to pick them but careful not to trample them. Brown, red, thin, curved, I see them all deep in the woodlands. The thought of Wynflæd brings with it sorrow. I left Tamworth on bad terms with her, and I've not yet returned to make my apologies. Perhaps, one day soon, when the mystery of Lord Coenwulf's sons has been resolved, I might visit her with a sack of mushrooms, some horseradish and burdock, alongside other herbs she might need to make my peace with her.

As angry as I was, I'm starting to consider why. What difference does it make to my life whom my father was? He was never really my father. My uncle raised me. Wynflæd and Edwin's mother aided him in that. I should be grateful to them, not angry because they kept such a secret from me.

'Ah, I thought it was.' The words startle me from my thoughts. Looking up, I feel my lips compress on seeing Eadweard, Wulfred and his other warriors in a semicircle, blocking my way ahead.

'Why are you here?' I demand to know. 'What's in Hereford?' I can't see their horses, and I know they've ridden here. So, this isn't all of their force. They've left the horses somewhere else. I strain to hear but can detect no sound of a crying babe or a garrulous small child.

Eadweard chuckles at my questions, revealing his front tooth's been knocked out, no doubt in a fight.

'What does any of this have to do with you, Icel?'

'Do you have Lord Coenwulf's children and his sister?' I persist. I'm convinced they do, but I don't know where.

'Why would we have them?' Wulfred smirks, licking his thin lips with a sliver of tongue. Those with him laugh as well, the sound ripe with derision.

'You left Kingsholm with the queen, and the children?'

'We did, yes, but now we're going to Hereford, on the queen's business.'

'Why are you taking the children to Hereford? What's there?'

'Icel, Icel. Why are you concerned with children that aren't yours? The queen said you would be. I doubted her, as you weren't even in Kingsholm when we left, but she was correct to send us this way. We've been aware of you ever since you crossed the river at Worcester.'

'Wait? What?'

'Icel, you're not quite as clever as you think.' Only now do I hear yet another snap of a broken branch, and I turn, startled to see the huge warrior from Tamworth behind me. Horsa's eyes are as dull as ever, but it doesn't matter because his arms encircle me before I can lash out with my seax as he crushes my arms tighter and tighter to my chest. For the first time in any battle I've ever fought, I wish I wasn't wearing my byrnie. It makes breathing even more difficult.

I kick out with my feet, but I'm like a child lifted by a parent besides the huge warrior. I can't aim a blow on his knees, and I quickly succumb to this unexpected attack, my breath stolen from me in the tight crush.

When I wake again, I'm trussed up like a dead boar, feet together, knees together, my arms above my head, with the rope looped around something in the ground, perhaps even a tree trunk. My mouth tastes of the carding comb. I try to spit aside the woolliness, but there's no moisture to aid me. I think I can hear the nicker of my horse, but in the dark undergrowth, I can see nothing.

'You should be pleased we didn't gag you,' a voice speaks out of the gloom. I'm not alone then. That's something. Not that I can see it'll help me.

'Why are you doing this?'

'Orders,' the voice replies. It's not Eadweard or Wulfred who speaks, but someone else.

'Whose orders?'

'What does it matter? Now, shut up, and go back to sleep.'

'I need to piss and drink.'

'Piss where you are,' the belligerent voice informs me. 'It's only going to be the first of many occasions. Water, I can aid you with. There's a beaker beside your head. If you can reach it, you can drink it.'

'Untie me.'

'No chance. We'll keep you here until we can let you go. No idea how long that will be, or how much of you will still be here by then. Boredom can only be relieved with a few nicks to my enemy.'

The voice, disembodied and coming from further away than I might think, sends a judder of fear through my body. 'Where's Wulfred and Eadweard, and the big man from Tamworth, Horsa?'

'None of your concern,' the disembodied voice again. 'Now shut up before I gag you, and then you'll be in a whole new world of pain.'

Biting my lip, I stop my questions from pouring forth. I should have asked about Brute, but I don't believe any man with half an eye to a good horse would harm him. Brute's more useful to them alive. I might not be.

Sniffing, I scent the damp of the water, and shuffle around, using my feet to drive me backwards so that my arms can bend. Then, I roll over, aiming for where I think a beaker of water waits for me. Licking my lips, I can all but taste it, but it seems impossible to drink the fluid.

Rolling once, twice, trying to ignore the twisting of my left arm, tongue extended, I feel the rim of a wooden beaker. At least it'll be light, I console myself, shuffling closer so that I can just about lift my head and clamp my teeth around it. Unable to sit upright, I have no choice but to force my head back, beaker between my teeth. River water pools into my mouth, but I can't swallow with my mouth open and, instead, it falls into my beard and down my neck, causing an unpleasant coldness. I release the beaker, returning it to its place, where it wobbles precariously. I think it'll fall, but it doesn't.

Swallowing, I get the idea of water, if not the full sensation of sating my thirst. But perhaps I shouldn't be worrying about that. The urge to piss is becoming a pressing concern. I don't wish to soil myself, but there won't be a choice soon. All the same, I try and find a comfortable position, working to ignore the stone or rock that presses against my back, and close my eyes, concentrating on slowing my breathing. When daylight comes, I want to be alert and ready to escape. I won't be kept a captive here. The fact that someone has ordered these men to detain me assures me that I'm correct to suspect the plans for the two sons of Lord Coenwulf. That I'm here, in some part of the woodland that stretches towards Hereford, assures me that Lord Coenwulf's sons and his sister aren't close by. I must escape before the evil machinations of the queen or Lord Wigmund, or even Lady Ælflæd, can take a course they'll have occasion to regret deeply and which will see me fail in my oath to Lady Cynehild.

But damn it, I need to piss first.

Disgusted with myself, I allow the warm liquid to leave my body and only then manage to sleep.

A kick wakes me, and then a face looms so close to me that I have to close my eyes because I can't move my head backwards.

'Wakey, wakey, you stinking turd.' The words are rough, spoken with harsh angles, but all the same, the man's Saxon. He slaps my face with a calloused hand, and I open my eyes once more, eyeing him with disdain. My trews have dried while I've slept, but the stink hasn't left me. And my arms. The agony is intense, painfully tingling, as I try to open and close my hands to get some feeling back into them, but they don't want to move.

'What's all the fuss about you?' the man asks again, and he moves back so I can get a good look at him. He's younger than I first thought, his hair a deep brown, almost black, a fine moustache and beard covering his chin and lower face so that only the thick slits of his lips are visible. They're pink, nearly red, and when he rears back and stands, I appreciate his average height. Probably smaller than me but taller than many others.

'Who are you?' I demand to know.

'None of your damn business.' I expect the reply for all it tells me nothing.

'Where's my horse?'

'He's well.' The response doesn't answer my question, although I hope it's true.

'I need to piss,' I demand, hopeful he might be kinder to me than the man who guarded me last night.

'Ah, well, do it where you are. You're no better than the beasts while you're here.'

'And where is here?'

'Here,' and he lifts his hands to either side of his body and extends them to the side, indicating the woodland. It's light beneath the trees, but not blazing sunlight, more the tones of brown and beige that I noticed yesterday.

'What do you plan on doing to me?'

'No idea, my friend. I'm just being paid to watch you, nothing else, nothing more. And feed you, I suppose.' The scent of smoke belatedly reaches me, and my belly rumbles angrily. 'If you want to eat and drink, you best shut up,' he responds at the noise, but there's humour in his words, not menace. All the same, I stay my tongue, trying to wake up more quickly and reassess my situation now that it's light enough to see.

I remain bound to the tree behind me. I manage to shuffle backwards on my arse, lifting my arms a little so that I can see what's surrounding me, which isn't much. The fire is far enough away from my feet that I can't kick at the flames licking around the wood. The man himself stands to the other side of the fire. He's dressed in a brown tunic and trews and no byrnie, but his weapons belt glitters with enough sharp edges to assure me it's a matter of choice, not for the lack of it.

I consider again whom he is and where he's come from. He must be a Mercian, but perhaps from far north, close to the kingdom of Northumbria. I've never seen him before. Admittedly, there are many Mercians I've never met. Still, I'd have thought, during my time fighting for Mercia, that I've encountered somewhere from everywhere in the vast sprawl of the kingdom over the middle of Britain. But it seems not. Not even when I went to Bardney did I hear a man with such an accent.

'Here. You can have one hand to eat your food and one hand only. If I see you messing around, I'll not give you any more. I'm only to watch you. Not to feed you. I don't think they care if you live or die, although I imagine you do.'

Swiftly, the man comes around my head. I feel him untying the hempen rope that keeps me supine. With relief, my left arm comes free, although it flops like a dying fish on the side of a river. My right arm is quickly retied, causing many sensations to ripple down my arm.

'This is for you.' He thrusts the bowl at me, rich with a fatty pottage, although I don't see any meat in it. I look from him to the bowl, wondering how to hold it when I have only one hand. He sighs softly, the glint of his brown eyes filled with frustration. 'Sit back, and wedge it between your thighs and your belly. That's the best I can do for you.'

With more care than I expect, he holds the bowl while I shuffle around and only then places it on my belly. There's no spoon, so I use my fingers, trying not to think of all the places they've been and how dirty the nails are. Eagerly, I scoop the too-hot mixture, burning my mouth in the process, but not truly caring. I need to eat. I must have the strength to win free when the opportunity presents itself.

He sits by the fire and eats as well. It's hard to hear over the chomping of my jaws, but I'm sure I can hear voices from not far away. And if not voices, then the chatter of hens. Perhaps, for all the trees in front of me seem to go on forever, behind me, if I could only see better, the woodland comes to a halt, and there's a settlement there. I consider whether it'll be a Welsh or a Mercian one. My captor's armed, so perhaps Welsh, although it could equally be that he's expecting trouble from someone thinking to seek me out. Whom that might be, I don't know. No one will know where I am. Pega will think me at Tamworth. The ealdorman will think me at Tamworth. How would anyone know to look for me to the west of the River Severn?

I eat, but even as I do so, a weight of fear settles in my belly beside the food. No one knows where I am. No one will look for me. There's no reason for these men to keep me alive, not if I threaten whatever Eadweard and Wulfred are assisting the queen with.

15

My arm's tied again, but only after I've been given the opportunity to shit as well as piss. The smell's noxious, and the warrior pushes my leavings aside with a branch, his nose wrinkled all the time.

'I didn't realise I'd be a nursemaid to you,' he mumbles, re-securing me. I wince as my right arm's pulled once more, my left having recovered its feeling, but I know it won't be long until it's gone again. My arms are held at an awkward angle above my head, similar to being in the second line of the shield wall. I grit my teeth, but it doesn't help with the pain. I console myself, thinking it'll be better when I can't feel them.

The day drags. The man doesn't speak to me again. No one joins him. He feeds the fire before him, slowly and with only so many twigs, as though there are no more to burn, for all we're surrounded by woodland. He adds more oats to the pot and some chunks of pork, which make my belly rumble again, although I know I won't get any of them. The smell drives me mad. I lick my lips time and time again. He brings me water every so often, holding the beaker before me to my lips so that I can drink more easily than last night. All the same, I never feel truly sated.

I piss again, hating the sharp smell of my body but unable to do anything about it. I do need a nursemaid, after all.

'So, we're just waiting here?'

'Yes.' The quick reply. I want to ask a hundred questions, but I don't. He seems content to leave me alone, provided I'm no trouble. As much as I hate to feel so helpless, with nothing further to give me an idea of what will happen, I decide that ignorance is better. I doze, even as uncomfortable as I am. I count the branches above my head, watching the light seem to bounce from curling leaf to curling leaf. I wish I'd not come alone and that I'd not been fooled by whatever happened outside Worcester. I should have stayed on the Fosse Way and turned Brute's head towards Tamworth. I should have waited for the ealdorman and Wulfheard.

I know why I didn't, and that shames me. I shouldn't have been too embarrassed to face Wynflæd once more. Whether she forgives me for my outburst last year or not, at least I wouldn't have been here, trussed up and helpless, being watched by a man who might sooner kill me should I become too problematic.

The man feeds me once more, releasing my right hand this time so that a thousand shards of metal seem to permeate my flesh. I've long since lost all feeling in my feet. No matter how many times I bang them on the woodland floor, they remain lost to me. My feet and legs are too tightly tied to allow any movement.

'My thanks,' I murmur, delighted to see a piece of succulent pork amongst the oats and onions of the mixture.

A grunt is my only response.

As night falls, I see a flicker of movement by the fireside, more shadows than anything, and the next voice that speaks is that of a different man. I'm sure I heard the other one call him Æthelbald, but I hold that tight. I don't want him to know that I know his name. I can't see him.

'You'll sleep and behave yourself,' he informs me in no uncertain terms. 'Today's gaoler is soft as shite. Hywel's too kind to everyone, but I'm not. I'll beat you to within an inch of your life if necessary. You just need to be alive. They didn't say that you had to be entirely alive.'

The voice is more that of a wounded bear, and I pull my legs up, trying to shield myself from an imaginary blow. I've eaten, and I've drunk well all day. I can't say the same will happen during the night.

And I'm so uncomfortable and in so much pain that sleep's impossible. The movement of animals above my head startles me more than once, the thump of something landing on branches sends a scattering of curling leaves to settle on my face. The occasional spiderweb joins them. I twist and turn, but sleep evades me. Not that Æthelbald, if that's his name, seems to sense my unhappiness. He stays by the fire, feeding it twigs and occasionally a handful of dried leaves so that it flames brightly whenever the loud shriek of an animal sounds too close.

I'd not considered that there might be boars or wolves in the woodland. If one were to attack, I couldn't defend myself. That worry, added to everything else, keeps me awake long into the night until the depth of darkness begins to fade, and only then do I finally manage to sleep. And then, it's not for long. The man from the day before wakes me, as he did the day before. The routine of yesterday repeats itself. My lips are parched, no matter the water given to me. My arms are in a thousand agonies, and now, when I try to move them, it merely sets off a pain in my legs and feet. I've watched men and women die from many wounds and illnesses. I've never seen anyone lose their limbs because they were tied too tightly, but I'm sure it can happen.

Just before darkness falls, I call to the man, my voice broken, my throat dry and my tongue feeling too large for my mouth.

'Hywel, please, my legs, just for a moment or two. They're agony.'

He eyes me with sympathy and comes towards me. He doesn't seem to notice that I know his name.

'If you kick me, I'll stab you,' he menaces.

'I can't even move them,' I mumble. He nods, satisfied with my response, as he undoes the leg bindings. Unable to stop myself, I howl in agony, and his hand clamps over my mouth, his eyes wild with a threat. I nod, gather myself together, and try not to shriek as my foot also comes loose.

Somehow, I manage to move my legs aside. It's not easy. The action is slow and laboured, and I hear a whistle of sympathy from my captor, but he still ties me tightly once more, just as I've managed to regain the feeling in both my legs and feet. I know it'll not be long until I'm as helpless again, but my ears hear the sound of footsteps coming towards us, and my captor hastens to ensure his kindness isn't seen.

The two men speak in low voices, close to the fire. I can't see the man who watches me at night, Æthelbald. He's entirely unknown to me. If I ever escape from here, and I'm not sure I will, I might meet him anywhere and never know we spent this time together.

Hywel leaves without glancing at me, and the night guard hunkers down, feeding more fuel to the flames. Already, I can feel the chill of the coming night. I've survived without my cloak and been almost warm enough. I doubt the same will happen this night. If I could see the heavens from beneath the tree's bough, I imagine they'd be crystalline, not a cloud in sight.

The heat from the fire almost reaches me, but my face is far from warm, and for the rest of my body, it hardly seems to matter. My feet and legs have quickly fallen numb once more, and even though I try to move my fingers occasionally, they're also unresponsive.

I lick my lips. I need more moisture. I can't remember when I last pissed, and that's not a good sign. I've been fed a pottage without even onions to flavour it, and while it was palatable, it only made me more thirsty.

I close my eyes and try to think myself away from this place. Anywhere would be better than here, even fighting on the Isle of Sheppey to rescue Lord Coenwulf. I grimace at the reminder, a slow tear falling down my cheeks at the memory of Frithwine, and before him, Garwulf, losing their lives, fighting for Mercia. I'm weak and feeble. I'm no warrior; here, I've never felt more pathetic, useless, and bloody scared. If they were going to kill me, I just wish they would.

I open my eyes, and my breath blooms before me in the frigid conditions. The icy cold of the ground has numbed my arse and the rest of me as well. I'm nothing but a mouth to breathe with and eyes to see. But I can see more than the previous nights.

I focus on the stars up above. Their persistent glimmer gives me hope, even as I start to shake, each shiver an agony of a hundred tiny wounds. I grit my teeth, my chest rising and falling too quickly as I allow my fears to overwhelm me. Why am I here? More tears form in my eyes, and I can little afford to lose the moisture from my body.

Why am I here? Who'll miss me? Who'll even know of my death when I breathe my last, frozen to the core, strung out, ready for roasting over a pit?

And then I hear it. My eyes start open, and I shuffle backwards, my legs crying, my arse feeling like it belongs to someone else.

It comes again. A crack of a branch? No, it's the snuffling of a creature scenting the air. I glance towards the fire. It doesn't blaze as brightly as before. No, the flames have fallen to a sullen red, the soft shift of the ash dissipating as the final fuel is consumed, a faint shush in an otherwise quiet night. There are no night-time animals. There's no flapping of wings or hoot of owls. I can barely breathe. The man, I realise, is asleep, slumped on his side, his blades flashing in the glimmer of the moon and the stars, and something is coming.

And it's not a man, but a beast.

* * *

I watch the wolf. Its coat is flecked with white at the edges, or so I imagine, the lighter shades the only means of illumination. Its ears are alert, eyes flashing in the darkness. It scents the air. The sound should barely reach me, but it does in the sullen silence of the deepest night. The air is so cold that I can also see where it breathes. I stay still, trying to evade its detection, although it must know I'm there. I stink of my filth and shit. I'm stretched out, ready for it to rip my innards from me. I have no means of defence.

My guard's fast asleep, dreaming of a warm bed and companion, and not of the cold or the hunter that seeks fresh prey. I'm going to die here, and it won't be by blade but by teeth, sharp teeth that yank my flesh from my body. It won't be a clean death but one filled with pain and sorrow. My thoughts flick to the children of Lord Coenwulf, and his sister. I've failed Lady Cynehild. I've failed my uncle. Everything in my life has been a failure, and now it will end, and I can do nothing to stop it.

I can't take my eyes off the animal. It moves so quietly, disturbing neither flame nor guard, its eyes focused on the sleeping man. I hold out half a hope that the wolf will kill the man, and then be sated, and leave me to be found by someone else. The guard in the morning, perhaps. But do I want that?

I fear I'll never fight my way free. So, should I welcome the teeth of the wolf, its sharp jaw and animal urge to sate its hunger? I hear licking and realise the pottage has fallen to one side, and the animal helps itself to the vestiges of the meal. But without meat, I can't see the animal being content with that.

I watch, and I wait. A hundred thoughts tumble through my mind, none as horrifying as the sharp snap of jaws on flesh. I hardly dare look, but I force myself to it.

The animal's no longer grey and flecked with white. Dark fluid coats its snout as it turns, chewing with ferocity. I see the throat of the night guard glinting dully in the moonlight. The man didn't even know, but more importantly, how did the wolf know to take such a clean kill?

I listen to the sharp snap of teeth over bone. My bowels turn to fluid, staining myself once more. But the animal doesn't come towards me. I scurry backwards, desperate now to free my arms or my feet, anything so that I can defend myself. Then the animal stops, head canted to one side, before sitting back and letting loose a sound I don't ever want to hear, and certainly not at such close quarters.

The howl fills the night air: long, loud and clear of all fear. It's a cry of triumph and joy, of satisfaction, and to my horror, as I scream along with it, releasing all of my fear into the crystal-clear night sky, it's joined by others.

'No,' I sob, gasping for breath, my heart hammering, my chest rising and falling too quickly. 'No,' I mutter again and again, the sound ripped from my throat as the wolf savages my night guard. The other animals slink from the undergrowth, heads down, shoulders powerful, all of them grey but edged with white to give away their position on a night such as this.

I count them, one, two, and then there are six of them altogether. The tearing of fabric is loud in my ears, the snap of sharp jaws, the slicing of broken flesh. Vomit fills my mouth. I cough it aside or risk choking. I spit and swallow, but there's only the taste of the foulness of my last meal in my mouth.

I'll die here, somewhere beneath the trees. All that will be found of me will be my gnawed and white bones. I've seen enough bodies to know I'll be unrecognisable. Bad enough to die and have my flesh turn corrupt. But this way, there'll be no flesh left. I'll be dead and eaten. Wulfheard will never know what became of me. Wynflæd will go to her death believing I hated her, and what of those children, with no one to protect them?

I think of Edwin, of my uncle, of Budworth. Who'll claim it as their own? I've written no will. I've made no provision for a death I was arrogant enough to believe would never come. I think of the kingship, of Mercia, of what I might have been had I not become caught up in this foolhardy attempt to rescue children I share no blood with. When Brute is found, he won't be able to answer the questions of those who know I'm missing. No. I'll be lost for all time. And what will become of Brute, and Wine? Horses such as them need good grain and warm stables. What if no one protects them? Before Brute was mine he was known as foul-tempered and unrideable. I wouldn't want that to happen to him once more.

I murmur, soft words beneath my breath, surprised to realise they're the oft-repeated prayers spoken by the holy men in their sumptuous robes that keep the chill of winter from their bodies while they berate the rest of us from their pulpit.

I shudder. My eyes closing and then opening. And then closing at the horror of the scene before me.

One of the wolves knocks the woodpile, and flame springs afresh. They squeal and yip, pulling back from their feast, only to return. So much more is illuminated. I'm only grateful the man was asleep when he died, or his eyes would haunt me.

A raven lands, joining the wolves. They eye one another, but then all return to the feast. Another raven, and even, I notice, some other small creatures, all of them taking their fill, eating of the bounty the first wolf provided.

I'll be next. I know it. They'll eat, and then they'll realise they could eat yet more.

My fear turns to fury. I bend and twist, tugging on the hempen ropes that bind my hands, trying to work them loose, one-handed. The actions never worked during my imprisonment, but that doesn't mean they won't work now. I scrabble with my feet and legs, pulling them close to my belly, for all the movement is torture. I twist and turn. I try and find space between my legs to pull one foot clear of the bindings. Tears blind me, and my breath is faster and faster, the cloud of it almost obscuring the scene before me so that I see shadows and orange flames, bloodied muzzles and little else.

I twist and turn, and it's no good. I can't get free. Whoever tied me ensured that I'd never win free. I curse the man who aided me yesterday, who redid the knots even tighter than the original ones. I thought he did me a kindness but no, he's doomed me to my death.

The ravens fly away, all three of them, the softness of the man's eyes and lips in their bellies, or so I assume. The wolves continue to eat, but not the first one. No, he moves aside, his back legs lithe on a body forged for stealth and speed. He sits beside the fire, closest to me, bending to lick his paws and muzzle, looking little more than a pet dog or a hunting hound, and only then, when he's content that the first man's blood is gone from his fur, does he move towards me. His amber eyes glow as warm as the fire, and I scream. I can't stop myself.

The sound echoes all around the woodlands.

I scream and scream and scream, and the wolf is before me. His meaty breath on my face. His eyes are cold and appraising for all they echo with the warmth of the fire. And I close my eyes as his foul-smelling open mouth comes towards me.

16

The pain doesn't come. That surprises me but doesn't make me open my eyes. Perhaps, I think, my body's just too cold and broken already. I try not to listen to the wet sounds of teeth tearing at my flesh, of my blood spurting free from the confines of the blue ribbons running through my body. I try not to smell the corruption of my flesh, the stink of my bowels being opened and torn asunder.

And then the heat returns to my face, and I open my eyes, peering into the gaze of the wolf, its head canted to one side in confusion, a sliver of something that I fear is my flesh dripping from one side of its open mouth.

I rip my eyes from the gaze and stare down at my legs and feet. I expect to see my innards on display, the grey and red of the ropes of my belly trailing down my legs.

But I see none of those things. My forehead furrows. My legs are free. I bang them against the mulch of the floor, releasing the sharp stink of my piss with the movement. Tears stream down my face as I try to escape this wrathful enemy. The wolf moves towards me. I swallow, aware that my Adam's apple is a perfect inducement to severing my lifeblood there, but the animal, with a swish of its long black tail against my face, merely walks around me.

Ahead, the other animals still feast – well, four of them do. One of them has stepped aside and, in a parody of a man, sits beside the fire, warming itself in the glow from the flames as it licks the blood and flesh from its paws.

A wet tongue on my hand has me wincing, only then my arms collapse above me, freed from the confines of the rope.

'What?' I ask, the sound ragged and guttural. Does the wolf mean to make me run from here? Is he only interested if there's a chase?

Not that I can stand yet. It's agony just to bring my arms back to my side, to look at the whiteness of the flesh, which looks deader than the man the wolves are devouring.

'What?' I ask again. The wolf's returned to my side. He eyes me and then bows his head a little, as I hurry to undo the ties that bind my ankles, the wolf having released my arms and legs.

'How?' I stutter again, fumbling with the knots. I tried this. Not with my hands, admittedly, but how has an animal, who only moments ago mauled my enemy to death while he slept, managed to free me from my ropes? I feel my forehead furrow as the scent of meaty breath combines with my stagnant cloud of air.

Of course, the damn animal can tell me nothing. As much as I wish to scamper away, even if only up high, into the tree on which the ravens now stand guard, squawking one to another as though offering a commentary on what's happening below them, I'm frozen in place, and not just by the cold of the cloudless night. Winter's coming. This is a promise of that, but those thoughts are irrelevant. Why has the animal released me?

'Can I... Can I go?' I ask, my words firmer now, for all I stumble over the sentence. 'My thanks.' I push upwards, using my hands to extend my aching legs. My feet remain clubby appendages, and standing is agony. The wolf does nothing. Neither do the other members of its pack. I wince and stifle another cry of pain as I'm finally upright.

'Thank you.' I offer a bow to the majestic creature, and slowly begin to back away. I'm mindful of the tree trunk at my back and the boughs of the trees that hang low. I remember the sound of hens that I thought I heard. Perhaps there are people there, and they'll aid me. Even if they only tell me where I am, that will be enough.

'Thank you,' I murmur once more, feeling that I'll actually be free from the horrors of my confinement and the terror of the wolf attack. The animal observes me, and then dips its head and turns around languidly, its long legs loping back towards the remainder of the pack. Only then, when all six wolves are once more occupied, do I turn my back on them and race through the tangled limbs and increasingly tighter growth of trees that shields me from wherever the noise of the hens came.

I'm not quiet, far from it, my breath ragged, my limbs still causing me problems, as my feet refuse to work properly, occasionally losing their firm grip or just slipping from beneath me. I try to listen for any sign of being followed, but there's nothing. Not even the yip of the wolves as they call one to another. Neither is there any howling or the swift sound of paws over the soft surface of the woodland floor.

And only then – with my breath tight in my chest, my eyes open so wide that more than once pieces of twig have landed in them, half blinding me – do I erupt into a clearing. The smell of a smoking fire is rife in the air, the cries of hens exploding in a cacophony of riot, as though I'm the wolf and not running from it, and a figure steps into my path.

Long hair, beneath a fur-lined cloak, and a sharp nose are all that's visible.

'Get away from my hens, you monster.'

The voice is distinctly feminine, and I collapse to the ground.

'I'm not a monster. The wolf. The wolf released me.'

'Released you?' The incredulity in her voice is impossible to ignore. For a moment, I fear she won't believe me, and the axe, no doubt for chopping wood, that she holds menacingly takes on huge proportions in my mind. Have I survived the wolf only to be chopped down here?

'Well, sometimes he does that,' she confirms conversationally, arm slowly lowering, the disbelief in her voice gone. I want to ask more about that, but she hasn't finished with her questions yet. 'But why were you in the woodlands?'

'I was held captive,' I pant, my tongue dry in my mouth. 'Two men, they meant to hold me. I don't know if they intended to kill me.'

'So you're the Mercian that the fools were speaking about. I thought they were making it up, although they had silver coins to show for all their talking.' Only now does she fling back the hood on the cloak and eye me. I try not to startle, for half the woman's face is a mass of scar, pink, long since faded to red, one cheek slimmer than the other, the flesh pulled too tight. 'The wolf and its pack and I have something of an agreement,' she murmurs, holding my gaze as though testing me. 'It seems they've included you in that.'

'Are they more reliable than men who can be bought for silver?' I question.

She nods and smiles, her right cheek barely moving, giving her a lopsided expression. 'Come on. I'll feed you and help if I can.' Turning her back on me, she strides out, her legs so long I almost have to run to keep up with her. I look around me. This is a clearing in the heartland of the wood. Far ahead, the shush of trees swaying with the wind can be heard.

'You live here?' I ask.

'I do, yes. Safer here with the beasts than with men. But of course, some know of me. The charcoal burners and the woodsmen. That's who had you, I believe. Poor men, both of them. Eager to earn more, even if they have to hold a man against his will. Mind, the one wasn't beloved by the wolf pack. I imagine that's the one who was attacked. Damn fool, antagonising the beasts by taking their pups and skinning them for a bit of extra meat and fur to sell to men who only give half of what it's worth.'

Ahead, a dwelling appears, cleverly hidden behind a mass of what seems to be hedgerows but isn't. She shows me the way through, a sidestep here, a sidestep there, and then a small wooden gateway to keep the chickens in their pen and, no doubt, away from the hungry appetites of the wolves.

The hall is smaller than some but certainly large enough for a woman if she lives alone. There are also separate buildings, one for the grain, one for the animals, and another one that seems smaller than the others. Perhaps this is where the hens spend their winter months.

'Clean yourself there. I can't allow you inside when you stink of the midden.'

I notice the barrels of water where she points, and shudder at the thought of getting cold and wet, but I do stink, and it's making me feel nauseous. With little enthusiasm, I thrust my head in the barrel and then use a bucket to pour more over me. The woman has gone, and I'm grateful as I shiver and shudder.

* * *

The whiff of woodsmoke hangs in the air as she welcomes me inside through a finely hinged door to the hall. Here I gasp in surprise. The wall furnishings are elaborate, the embroidery showing wolves in all their guises, from vicious warriors to nurturing mothers, and she smiles again.

'They call me the Wolf Lady. It works to keep most of them away from me. I've no control over the wolves, but they aid me on occasion. Here, you look hungry and thirsty.'

She moves around the hearth, finding me water from a jug and then pulling a cauldron free from the fire, from which the most appetising smell I've inhaled in a long time emanates.

'Chicken. It's always chicken unless the wolf catches something else and brings it to me.' Once more she speaks as though she and the wolf do have an agreement. Again, I want to ask more, but I'm hungry and thirsty.

Eagerly, I drink and then eat the food. A low moan escapes my mouth as I savour the succulent chicken and pottage.

'This is fit for a king,' I exclaim, unable to mask my surprise.

'Well, no king is having it. But, tell me, what's your name?'

'I'm Icel, Lord of Budworth, which makes me sound more than I am. I wanted to be a healer, but now I'm a warrior, fighting for the Mercian king.' My relief at being free from my captors and the wolf makes me say too much.

'Do you know you're in the borderlands with the Welsh kingdoms?' she queries.

'I was seeking Hereford with my horse.' At the memory of that, I almost drop my bowl. 'Brute, I don't know where he is.'

'Brute?'

'My horse. The king gifted him to me. He's a beast, as the name implies.'

'Then I imagine he's recognisable?'

'Very.'

'I'll point you in the direction of Hereford in the morning. You'll find him there, no doubt. But why were you going to Hereford and why were you in the woodlands?' And now my arms hang limp, and I remember it all.

'I'm seeking two small boys and a young girl, but I fear I've been misled.'

'Are they your children?'

But I'm already shaking my head. 'No, but I gave my oath to protect them, and I've failed in that already.'

'Æthelbald and Hywel spoke only of a man, not children or even a horse.'

'You knew they held me captive?'

'I thought they were fools who spoke about things that could never be true. I apologise for that.' In the firelight, her savaged face is shadowed.

'How did you know them?'

'I pay them to help me sometimes with the planting out and harvesting. It's much work for one woman, and there are few who think to aid me, even when I can offer eggs and chicken in payment. I almost trusted them.'

'Then you know where they live, well, where the one who yet lives?'

'I do, yes, onwards to Hereford. You'll find them there. Well, you'll find Hywel, I imagine. Æthelbald will be the dead one.'

'What's your name?' I want to ask so much more, but her name will be enough for now.

'They call me the Wolf Lady, and you may do the same. My name is of little importance these days. No one remembers who I used to be, only what I am now. Now, enough talking. Get some rest, and then tomorrow, I'll point you onward. Hopefully, you'll find your horse, and your children, although I think your horse concerns you more.'

Her words unsettle me. I think she's wrong. I hope she's wrong. Or maybe I don't.

17

By the time I've walked to Hereford the following day, the wounds on my wrists and ankles are throbbing. The Wolf Lady escorts me only so far until the denseness of the trees once more gives way to the sky above our heads.

'Just follow the track,' she advises me.

'My thanks,' I offer, but she's already turned, seemingly dismissing me from her thoughts. I consider whom she once was and why she lives the way she does. But more than anything, I'm just grateful she assisted me and didn't sever my head from its neck with her axe. I'm also grateful that she and the wolf have such an agreement, and that, luckily, I seem to have benefited from that as well, even while Æthelbald is more than half-eaten.

Wincing and limping, I amble onwards to where a pall of smoke hangs low in the sky. In no time, I can smell food cooking and the overwhelming stench of many people living in a close community. I see the first building, a stone-built cattle byre, or some such, in a field filled with animals contentedly chewing beneath the pale blue sky. The night wasn't as cold as the previous one, but dew mars the visible grasses. Not that the cows seem to mind. And only then do I remember that only one of the men who held me a prisoner is dead. Will Hywel think to hold me captive once more, or will he hide away, pretend he had nothing to do with it? The sound of running water can also be heard. In the near distance, the river glints at me. I sniff, thinking I could do with dunking my head in it, but really, I must find my horse and my weapons. The eagle-headed seax my uncle gave me is gone. But surprisingly, the silver sigil remains at my neck. I'm grateful for that.

I recall asking my uncle if I could come with him to Hereford. He refused, saying Edwin and I should stay hidden. As such, this is my first sight of the settlement. It seems little different to Worcester or Gloucester, and like those two places, a river provides part of its defence, although not the same river as at Worcester and Gloucester.

This, then, is a border settlement with the Welsh kingdoms across the river. Facing the hills and the Welsh kingdoms, I appreciate how exposed it is. All well and good for the bishop to have his hall and church here but, not far away, I'm sure the Welsh must hunger for a bloody good fight. It makes me feel imperilled just thinking about it. I hasten my steps. The walls and river might only provide the vestige of protection, but it's better than being here alone. Without my weapons.

'Hail,' the call rolls. I meet the eyes of a guard and incline my head.

'Good day,' I offer.

'You been in the wars, my friend?' the man asks. He stands firmly, his stance wide, his feet planted, hand straying to where his weapons hang on his weapons belt. But I wish him luck with finding them, thanks to his overhanging belly. I wonder if he can even see his feet.

'A fight, in the woodlands,' I offer. 'They took my horse. Have you seen a piebald creature? You'll know him. He probably ate your hand.'

'That feisty bugger's yours, is it? Been giving the blacksmith a hard time. Hywel wanted new shoes on the creature, but you can't get near him.'

'And where might that be?'

'Follow the smell of burning ore and, of course, the cries of men trying to tame that damn animal. He's been kicking all night. I hardly got a wink of sleep.'

Despite it all, I grin to hear that. 'Apologies, my friend. But tell me, who brought him here, and did they happen to have any children with them?'

'It was that damn fool Hywel, and no, he came alone, which is unusual as he's usually found with Æthelbald. He told some tale of finding the beast roaming in the woodlands not far from the Wolf Lady.' He shudders as he speaks, and I begin to realise that the woman has quite the reputation. If nothing else, it'll guard her against others thinking to attack her. Wise women aren't to be feared, but sometimes, sometimes, it's good to stir up a little terror. Or so Wynflæd has always told me. 'In you go, and you'll be welcome to him,' he continues.

'And I must tell you that Æthelbald will never step foot here again.'

The man nods, eyes narrowing, and then he indicates that I should enter all the same. I consider if he thinks I killed Æthelbald. Whatever his reasoning, he's keen to have Brute away from Hereford, and I'm as eager to oblige.

'But tell me, what do you know about the Wolf Lady?'

His eyes narrow, and now I think he might refuse me entry, but he sticks out his chest and speaks instead. 'The Wolf Lady is one of ours. She lives how she lives, and we respect that, and so can you. If you go anywhere near her, I assure you, you'll regret it. She knows how to fight. And how to cook,' he adds, and I'm unsure what he means by that. But he clamps his lips tightly shut and I know I'm not going to get anything further from him. I nod, and walk on.

For a moment, on stepping through the gateway, I'm unsure where to go, and then I hear it and, grinning to myself, follow the cries of outrage coming from the northern side of the settlement. People gaze at me with some unease, but no one runs from me, which I take to mean I don't look that bad.

And then I see him. Brute, eyes wild, legs kicking, with a man to either side of him. His shrill cry makes me wince. I realise that many of the people, including the monks from the church just visible from where I walk, have come together to watch the spectacle.

'I say you take him back to where you found him,' a thin woman cries to the blacksmith, and the man, I believe, is Hywel. 'He's more trouble than he's worth, no matter how much you might think to get for selling him.'

'Brute.' I call his name, and the horse immediately stills as I forge a path through the crowd and come to a stop before him, hand extended. The groan of relief from the man I take to be the blacksmith is audible, as is the startled cry from Hywel.

'He's your horse, my lord?' the soot-stained man asks me, but it's more a hopeful statement.

'I lost him in the woodlands,' I counter, not tearing my gaze from Hywel. I'll say nothing for now, but I fully intend to have a conversation with him and soon.

'Then I'm glad you've found him. My stable's all but destroyed, thanks to his hooves.'

'He doesn't like many people,' I reassure, running my hand over Brute's long nose. His eyes watch me, the fury slowly dissipating. 'And did you find my saddlebags as well?' I ask benignly.

'Yes, everything that was on him,' the blacksmith confirms quickly. 'A strange collection of goods for a warrior.'

'Well, sometimes I tend to my fellow warriors' injuries, as well.'

I glance at Hywel again, eyes narrowed. I'm daring him to make a run for it, but he's been kind to me. Perhaps now, if I repay the kindness, he'll assist me.

'Then take him, and be gone. We could all do with some peace and quiet.' With that, the blacksmith turns aside, and I know the crowd's dissipating behind me.

I wait still, and Hywel stays as well.

'Now tell me,' I say softly, my voice filled with menace, 'who paid you, where they went, and what you were to do with me.'

'What's it worth to me?' he demands, chest puffed out.

'Your life,' I reply quickly. 'I'm sure that, round here, thieves are hung for their crimes. I'm not sure what happens to those who detain men and women against their will, but I imagine it'll be even less pleasant.'

His shoulders sag, and I see a younger man than I expected revealed to me.

'I'll buy you a meal from the tavern, and I'll tell you everything.'

'Very well, but I'm not going inside. Brute will also kick the tavern building down if I do so.'

That seems to satisfy him, and together we walk deeper into the settlement.

Small children watch Brute with fearful eyes as he takes my commands and parades beside me. He bristles with pent-up fury but, for now, seems content to behave. While it's warmer than the day before, the thought of sitting outside is far from appealing, but I have little choice.

'Get what you want. I'll have the same. But come back to me, or I'll hunt you down and ensure all know your true nature.'

He shrugs his shoulders and dips his head inside the dark doorway. I consider watching him but instead find a bench to perch on, threading Brute's reins through the wooden legs. He has room to move, but not much.

'We'll be on the way soon,' I reassure him. I'm unsure when he last ate or drank, but for now, he seems content.

I'm holding a wooden beaker of ale in no time, and Hywel's sitting opposite me.

'Tell me everything.' He drinks deeply, wipes his hand on his sleeve and begins to speak.

'It was Æthelbald. He came to me and asked me to help him guard some soft Mercian lord in the woods close to the home of the Wolf Lady. He said I'd get thirty silver coins for my silence. I knew he was getting more, but thirty silver coins is a lot. I agreed. He didn't say much else, just that we were to watch you for a week and then let you go, but he said I could have your horse as well if I wanted him. Mean bastard. It was hardly a good bargain that I struck.'

'And you know Æthelbald is dead.'

'Yes, I went up there to relieve him and found only the remains of him and none of you. I already had the horse, but he seemed lame. That's why I took him to the blacksmith.'

'And these men, did Æthelbald tell you who they were?' I'm relieved to hear they had no intention of killing me. Still, why had I needed to be apprehended for a week? What had Eadweard, Wulfred and the others planned for me? Or rather, what was planned in my absence?

'No. I heard some Mercian voices, but I never saw them.'

'And my weapons?'

'You didn't have any when I found you. I take it the Mercians took them from you.'

I nod, unhappy with the knowledge, even though I suspected it all along. 'So, those Mercians aren't still around?'

'No, we've seen no new warriors of late. The bishop keeps some men for the border skirmishes but no one else.'

I wish I knew where they'd gone, but I can well suspect.

'My thanks for your honesty.' I stand abruptly, bending to retrieve Brute's reins. It's clear to me where I need to go. 'Here.' I place a handful of Londonia struck coins in his hand, the weight pleasing. 'You didn't kill me and almost kept my horse safe. You have my thanks. But now I need to return to Tamworth.'

Hywel's eyes glint at his prize, even as two bowls of pottage are brought outside by a small woman, beady-eyed, a look of displeasure on her face at seeing Hywel.

'He can have it,' I offer her. She gasps at seeing me, so perhaps I look more lordly than I feel, and almost curtsies, in the process slopping the fatty mixture over the side of the bowl. A hound at her feet hastens to lick the spillage. Hywel grabs both bowls eagerly to relieve her of the burden.

'You should eat, my lord,' she says to me. 'The finest pottage this close to the border.'

'I'm sure it is,' I reply, a tight smile on my face. If that's the finest, I muse, I dread to think about the worst. Still, it makes some of my road brothers' attempts seem better in comparison. 'If you hear anything else,' I bend low to Hywel's ear, 'seek me out at Tamworth or Budworth. I'll see you're well recompensed.' Hywel shivers and grins at the menace in my words. 'And don't keep Mercian warriors captive, you damn fool. You never know when you might just need one.'

18

I've never visited Hereford, but leaving and heading slightly northwards, I know a moment of recollection. I've been this way before, with my uncle. We might have kept as close to the trees as possible, but I recognise the ancient road and the view easily enough. That can only mean I'm not actually that far from where my uncle died. Brute, once free from Hereford, is pliable and eager to be on his way. Just for a moment, I consider going back the way I've come, keen to seek out the dead man and hunt for possible tracks that Eadweard, Wulfred and Horsa might have left on their way to wherever it is they're going. But I stop myself. Already I've lost valuable time. I can think of no reason why I might have been persuaded to venture this way other than by people who wanted me to think this was where the children were heading.

Fury stirs in my heart, and with Brute eager to kick the last few days of captivity from him, I bend low over his head and encourage him to ride as fast as his long legs will take him. Any sign of a limp has disappeared. I smirk at that. He thought of playing his own games with the man who took him. My horse is a clever beast. The River Wye quickly disappears from view, heading westwards into the hills, while Brute and I keep our gaze northwards. I'm not going back towards Worcester. I'll cross the River Severn in a different place or avoid it altogether.

I try and clear my thoughts from the memory of my uncle, but it's difficult. Every new corner turned seems to reveal another one of the places we journeyed to together. I think of Edwin as well. Where is he? I never thought to worry about him again, not after we became enemies instead of friends, but the last near-enough year has taught me I should be less hasty. Time heals, and we both need one another. Or we did. He's gone again. I wish I knew where he and Lord Coenwulf were. I should like to seek him out and tell him of my fears. He might think them unfounded, but I don't believe they are. I realise I miss Edwin. That revelation surprises me.

The day stretches on. I have no food, my saddlebags riffled for what I did have, which explains all that's needed about the men who took me. They were hungry. They didn't really want coins, just the means to feed themselves. My belly growls, but it's manageable. Time and time again, Brute and I walk to a stream or a brook, drinking deeply, and then resume our way. As night falls, the moon shimmers above my head, and I reach for my cloak, which was left in my possession in my saddlebags, and wrap it around my body. It's going to be cold, but there's enough moonlight to see by, and so I continue, for now. I know we'll have to stop at some point. And that moment comes when Brute slows to a trot and then hangs his head low, his chest heaving.

'Good lad,' I murmur, dismounting and hastening to remove his saddle so that he can drink from yet another stream. The rush of the water is fierce, and the feel of it on my fingers is chill. I consider whether I should stay awake or not and protect my horse to prevent us both being captured once more, but I dismiss the worry. I walked into that trap. They won't expect me to have escaped. There are still three or four days left of the week the men were to hold me captive. That's to my advantage.

* * *

The closer we get to Tamworth, having turned eastwards when we crossed the River Severn once more at Wroxeter, the faster Brute goes, and yet my fear only intensifies. I need to find Eadweard, Wulfred and their allies, alongside my weapons, but what exactly can I do? If I rush into Tamworth demanding to see the queen, Lord Wigmund and Lady Ælflæd with wild theories about the children and sister of Lord Coenwulf, I imagine even the king will dismiss me.

No, I need to be more subtle than that, but I'm not sure how. And then, as the following day draws to an end, the lights of Tamworth appear before me, having bypassed Lichfield along the way. I could have stayed there for the night and arrived fresh and perhaps even washed. I've changed my clothes from those I wore when forced to piss myself, but I have no others that are clean. I wrinkle my nose. I whiff of horse, sweat and the undergrowth where I was kept tied to the tree. Not even the barrel of cold water that the Wolf Lady allowed me to use could disperse the smell.

But the darkness gives me the cover I need. I won't exactly sneak into Tamworth, but at least few will see me.

I dismount and lead Brute along the walkway that allows entrance inside the settlement's walls. I find a smile on my face as I greet the king's warriors on guard duty. Not that they do much else but acknowledge me with the weary gaze of men who must stand guard duty throughout the long night. It's clear they recognise me, and just before the gates are closed for the night, I slip inside the too-familiar place, exchanging soft words with them, but not more than that. They don't know I shouldn't be here, that I should be tied to a tree. Neither do I ask after those I seek.

Hastily, I take Brute to the stable and leave him there, content with a bag of oats and a bucket of water, while the remainder of the king's horses sleep in their stables. Brute deserves some rest. I run my eyes over the other animals in the gloom, and content I don't recognise Wulfheard's mount, I leave once more. Wherever my fellow warriors are, they're not within Tamworth.

Cuthred hasn't seen me, for which I'm grateful. But now comes the more difficult part. I need to get to Wynflæd, make good on my accusations to her, and find out what she knows about what was planned for the children and sister of Lord Coenwulf.

I hear raucous cries from the king's hall and consider what feast is being celebrated. A firepit assures me that some huge animal has been roasted for the occasion. I lick my lips. Eating would be good, but I have other, more pressing concerns. I realise why the guard men were so unimpressed with their duty. No doubt, they've missed out on free-flowing ale and meat.

I decide against creeping through the buildings to reach Wynflæd's workshop, but I cover my head with my cloak to offer some camouflage as I stride towards it. It's not that I don't want to be seen, but it'll be much easier if I'm not. Outside Wynflæd's door, I pause for a moment, listening to discover if she's alone. I can hear Cuthred talking but little else.

Hesitantly, I bend and knock on the wooden door, and it opens immediately, offering the welcome glow of somewhere I think of as home. Cuthred's eyes boggle wide, and I appreciate that he's grown about a foot since I last saw him. I press a finger to his lips, and he stays his tongue but opens the door wide to allow me entry.

My eyes alight on Wynflæd, and she shows absolutely no surprise at seeing me. If anything, a swift look of relief assures me that I might be welcome.

'At last,' she huffs, as Cuthred quickly closes the door and once more surprises me by lifting a plank of wood across it to further ensure it remains locked. I feel my eyebrows furrow, and Wynflæd cautions me with her finger across her lips, just as I did to Cuthred.

She's aged in my absence, but her wiry strength hasn't left her. There might be more wrinkles around the corners of her eyes and lips, but she's lost none of her quickness of thought.

'Speak in whispers. This place is alive with rumours and gossip. Now, where have you been? I sent for you days ago at Kingsholm. I expected you three days ago, at the latest.'

'I didn't get your message,' I whisper back. 'But I was at Kingsholm before that anyway, my intention to follow them here.' I don't think I need to say more about whom I mean. 'But I was turned around at Worcester and led a merry dance across the River Severn until I was captured outside Hereford. If you believe me, and I scarce do, a wolf set me free.'

Wynflæd's face is a riot of emotion, but my final comment draws a smile from her. 'You met the famous Wolf Lady then?'

'I did, yes. You know of her?' I suppose I shouldn't be surprised.

Wynflæd nods, for a moment amusement in her eyes, that quickly fades as her thoughts must turn to why she sent for me. 'You suspect?'

'I do, yes.'

'Then you're right to. Cuthred has heard rumours. Some of Lord Wigmund's men arrived here three days ago and left very quickly with heavy saddlebags. What were their names?' she questions Cuthred.

He grimaces. 'Wulfred and Eadweard, and some others as well. Horsa was with them. Nasty pieces of work, all of them.'

I nod, unsurprised to discover that they came this way. 'They paid the men near Hereford,' I confirm. Cuthred hands me a beaker of water and then a bowl of pottage, and I eat eagerly.

'And they in turn were paid,' Wynflæd confirms.

'By the queen?' I announce, convinced she is behind all this. Yes, the warriors may nominally owe their allegiance to Wigmund, but I don't think him capable of this. But Wynflæd shakes her head, confusing me.

'By Lord Wigmund.' And again she shakes her head.

I'm forced to say the words I don't want to. I had hoped against hope that she wasn't involved. 'By Lady Ælflæd.'

When she shakes her head once more, I open my mouth to argue, but she hushes me. Cuthred, seeing my rope burns, has brought me a pot of salve, and Wynflæd's strong fingers massage it into my wrists. I won't tell her of my ankles, but I might use it on them when I know what's happening.

'There are very clever people manipulating the royal family, I assure you. I'm unsure of the true power behind it all, but I have my suspicions that Lord Beorhtwulf is involved. He's a wealthy individual, and he's grown in the king's confidence, but what's important is finding those small boys.'

'They came here?' I question, although I'm considering young Lady Cynewise. Wynflæd speaks of the children of Lord Coenwulf, not his sister.

'No, the boys never arrived, and Lady Ælflæd and her sister are most distressed about it all. Lady Ælflæd's son isn't yet strong. I know she hopes to have another child, but in the meantime, her nephews are æthelings, as well as her son. And Lady Cynewise is just as worried, so I've heard.'

'So, Lady Cynewise is here, in Tamworth?'

'Yes, why wouldn't she be?' Wynflæd queries, confused by my question.

'I thought she was taken as well.'

'No, she's with her sister, although she seems unhappy about it. They arrived together. I sent for you because the boys weren't part of the original travelling group, and a messenger was here, on Ealdorman Ælfstan's business, and he said he'd take my request to you.'

I nod again and then eye Cuthred and Wynflæd. 'She has the makings of a healer. While she's here, see if you can bring her into your confidence. As young as she is, I trust her.'

Wynflæd's thin lips part in a smile. 'I will. Thank you, Icel. I thought she was wise.'

'But that doesn't answer the questions of the boys. Has the king sent men to find them? Has Wulfheard set out to find them?' I ask hopefully.

'The king isn't concerned. He believes the children have been forced to stop along the way. They were separate from the majority of the riders, for they were in an ox-cart, not on horseback. He believes they'll arrive imminently. He shows little concern, and no, Wulfheard and the rest of the men haven't been seen all summer. Ealdorman Ælfstan was last here more than three weeks ago. But he was alone. I suspect the boys have been taken northwards to the lands of the Northumbrians, using this journey to Tamworth as a means of covering what's truly happening. It's wild country in Northumbria. They could be lost and never found.' Her words are edged with worry. It seems she's forgotten her rancour towards Lady Cynehild, or has decided the children aren't to be included.

'Then they live?' I scarce say it. All of my fears are in those three words.

'I believe so, yes, but only for now. I wish I knew all the details, but I don't.' Wynflæd sounds confident when she speaks. I take comfort from that.

'I can't just go riding through Northumbria. I hear it's huge. I'll never find them, and stand the chance of encountering the Northumbrian king's warriors.'

'Perhaps, but Cuthred heard a name whispered by those who headed north only three days ago. He was collecting mushrooms for me. He's much better at it than you.' Her ability to berate me even now astonishes me. She winks and then exhales a name, 'Eamont.'

I furrow my forehead at her.

'That's where you'll find them. And it falls to you to do so.'

I nod, considering what I must do. But certainly, it seems I'm to visit Northumbria, whether I want to or not.

19

I leave while it's still dark. Cuthred has spent the grey light of dawn scampering through Tamworth, bringing me bread and cheese while I've borrowed some oats from the grain store. I considered heading towards Budworth, but I don't wish to imperil my people. And there are others, Eadweard and Wulfred amongst them, who might suspect, should I win free, that I'll go there. They wouldn't think to find me at Tamworth. I do need weapons, but again, Wynflæd seems to know better than I do. Cuthred brings me a seax, although not the sharpest, and an old byrnie, rust-stained and no doubt forgotten about by one of the old men who think to never fight again for Mercia. Alongside it is their shield, which is also in a bad way. How Cuthred knew where to find it, I'm unsure. The loss of my seax is a keen one. I know Eadweard will have it. He tried to take it from me once before. No doubt he's taken delight in stealing it again.

For now, I have two days remaining before they told Æthelbald and Hywel to release me. I need to make good on that time to get as far north as possible. It's unfortunate that I'll have to retrace my passage of the previous day, but there's little else I can do. Wynflæd assures me the place I must go to is in the north but on the west, not the east.

'But, are you sure they didn't merely take the children to their father?'

I want to believe it's possible, despite my worries. The news that Lady Ælflæd is concerned for her nephews has me reconsidering my thoughts about her. Perhaps, after all, she does care about them, although I've seen little to assure me of that.

'Yes, I'm confident. I hear Lord Coenwulf's in West Frankia, a guest of King Louis. A messenger brought word from Edwin to his mother.' I startle at that, but it brings me some reassurance even while it increases my worry.

'What will you do when you find them?' Wynflæd questions me.

'I've no idea. But I'll do something.'

She grips my arm before bidding me goodbye. 'Those children are in peril, Icel. Always, and especially without their feeble father to protect them.' I feel my forehead furrow at her words.

'I know.' I murmur.

'Do what you must,' is her parting directive. I'm surprised by the way she reaches up, lips compressed so that I bend to her. She plants a kiss on my beard-fuzzed chin. 'And shave once in a while.' Unexpectedly, a tear slides from her eye, and I swallow against the thickness of my throat. Is this us saying goodbye again? She hasn't even spoken of my outburst last year. Does she mean for me to never return to Tamworth?

'I…' I begin, but she shakes her head.

'Go,' she urges me. 'Go. Lives depend on you.'

So used to obeying her, I'm out of the workshop without considering it, mounted, and on my way northwards before the new dawn even breaks in a welter of cold pinks and reds.

Only at the top of a small rise leading towards Lichfield do I stop and gaze back the way I've travelled. I hope to see Tamworth again. But more, I hope to see Wynflæd once more.

* * *

It starts to rain with the rising of the sun. It's cold and biting, reminding me that it won't be long until the weather becomes miserable, and we all want nothing but to shelter beneath our cloaks. Before that can happen, I need to find the children.

I didn't see the queen, Lady Wigmund or Lady Ælflæd at Tamworth, but I knew they were there, thanks to Wynflæd. Neither did I seek out young Lady Cynewise. I trust Wynflæd to have told me the truth of what's befallen the family. Creeping through the gate, the unmistakable cries of young Wigstan echoing through the wooden buildings, the irony wasn't lost on me that he was safe while his cousins are lost, and the king doesn't even seem to realise.

Huddled inside my cloak, miserable with the ice-cold rain falling into my face, I squint forwards, pitying Brute for having to endure. We pass the ancient settlement of Wall quickly, the place where my uncle, Edwin and I slept on that first night escaping from Tamworth. The similarities to my situation now and then aren't lost on me.

I thought I was done with sneaking around but evidently not.

As the day progresses, the clouds grow greyer and greyer. The downpour drenches me so that I'm so cold I fear it'll be impossible to dismount. I become so used to the susurration of the rain, and little else, that the noise of the trees I guide Brute beneath startles me. I turn, laugh at myself, and slowly dismount, every movement an agony. Of late, I feel I've been used hard. It isn't getting any better.

'Come on, lad.' I take him to the gurgling stream that's pulled me from the road, running with water, the ditches overflowing and sending a summer's worth of dry weeds cascading into every available dip and hollow that marks the ancient roadway.

Brute comes eagerly, and I stand with him, drinking, for all I can't imagine why I need any more water.

'Have you ever been north?' I ask my horse, muzzle dripping with water, his bright eyes glowing in the gloom. His silence is to be expected.

Pulling my gloves free from my hands – luckily, I'd not been wearing them when apprehended, and I found them in my saddlebags – my eyes are drawn to the scar there. I have the scar, but not the blade of my eagle-headed seax. For the first time, I consider why my uncle had it. Was it perhaps a gift from Beornwulf, my father? Was it maybe a promise that he'd acknowledge me one day? Chewing on bread that Cuthred collected for me, I consider. I hope the blade was my uncle's and had nothing to do with my father. I want it to have been Cenfrith's and not Beornwulf's. I also want it back. Not as much as the children, but the desire is there all the same.

Brute settles beneath the trees, undoubtedly grateful to be free from the heavy rain. I watch him, considering my path. It's been a miserable day, and I don't relish spending more time on Watling Street. The road, cut through the landscape, is exposed to the rain. Here, beneath these few trees, the worst of the rain is kept from my shoulders. It almost feels dry.

'Come, we'll stop for the night,' I encourage my horse, leading him away from the water and beneath the low boughs of an elongated fir tree. I have to lift it high, but once underneath, the heavy boughs spread from the tree much higher up, and there's room for us. I only just have to lower my head.

There are traces of others camping here in the past. The soft floor of pine needles is disturbed in some places, a circle of stones showing where others have risked a fire but left no wood for others to burn. Eagerly, I lift some oats from the saddle for Brute, leaving him to eat them while I slump to the ground, happy to be still. Since leaving Londonia, besides when I was tied to the tree, I've done nothing but ride my horse.

Before darkness descends, I inspect the rope-burn marks at my wrists and ankles and smear on more of the salve Cuthred handed me. It's not the same, applying it myself. Wynflæd's fingers might be thin sticks, but they're strong and gentle and know just the right amount of pressure to apply. I lack her skill.

My thoughts turn to the wolf. I'm exposed here, as I was there. I can't imagine I'll be lucky enough to evade another such wolf attack, but perhaps the rain might keep any such denizens away from me while I sleep. Resolved, I settle to sleep.

The following day, the rain has stopped, but in its wake, an icy blast of wind ripples the trees, sending even the great boughs beneath which I slept swaying from side to side.

'Bloody hell,' I murmur to Brute, emerging from the warmth of our night-time sanctuary. Another day of tedium and shivering awaits, and I'm far from happy. Mounting Brute, I gaze onwards. The sky promises nothing but trouble, and indeed, by late afternoon, the wind has brought more rain with it, no doubt from the hills to the west. We've met the road I once took on my journey to Bardney, to inform King Wiglaf of what was happening in the borderlands with the Wessex king as my uncle lay dying. I eye it uneasily. Despite having travelled it only a few days ago in the opposite direction, the memories of that first occasion remain with me, and I find it hard to banish those remembrances.

Shuddering inside my cloak, Brute, somehow sensing my unease, spurs himself onwards, the hope of a warm night driving him, although I can see nowhere that might provide the same. Not yet. Eventually, I pull Brute aside. I've seen no sign of habitation for a long time, and there's no hope of it ahead, but I can sense something out there, and so I direct him from the road. Soon a building emerges from the gloom. I can tell it's been long abandoned, but the roof still holds over at least half of it. And it's better than nothing. With my horse at my side, we enter it and prepare to sleep.

I don't know how much further I need to travel. All Wynflæd could tell me was that it was northwards. I know I'm more north than I've ever been in the past, but whether that's north enough or not, I just don't know.

* * *

It isn't, and a day later, Brute and I have come to the end of the road we followed. Ahead, I can just glimpse what I suspect is the sea and before it – well, quite some distance before it from my vantage point – is a busy settlement. I consider whether I should enter it, but my food supplies are running low, and despite Wynflæd's words, I've yet to see any sign of anything that makes me suspect I'm truly following the path of the lost children.

The rain on that first night washed away all traces of any advance made. The horseshit forced into the drainage ditches, and any stray hoof marks in the mud were lost as well.

'Come on,' I urge Brute. 'A warm meal and some oats wouldn't go amiss.'

I dismount at the gates, supported on either side by ruinous walls, and meet the gaze of one of the guards. He eyes me with feigned nonchalance as I enter.

'Is this Chester?' I call to him and receive a nod in return. I expect something similar to Londinium from the exterior walls but on a less grand scale. Certainly, the current inhabitants occupy the remains of some sort of ordered settlement, but it's more as though they squat amongst the ruins. Few of the buildings are entirely of stone. Instead, many have wood or wattle and daub reinforced wicker fences screening them from others. That said, it's clearly a busy trading day. The smell of meat being roasted, and other less pleasant smells, no doubt from a tannery, pervade the air as I walk along the roadway demarcated by walls running along its sides. It's a ruin, but one more lived in than Londinium. Yet the people here are less settled than those within Lundenwic.

The scent of the river carries on the breeze, but I make my way straight to an alehouse, or so I assume from the men and women converged around its door, sitting on benches.

A small boy runs to me, eyes wide as he looks up and up and up at Brute, who waits patiently, for all the noise of so many people in one place must disturb him after so long on the road with only one another for company.

'Show me the stables, and I'll take him,' I offer, a smile on my face for his unease at seeing a horse such as Brute.

'This way,' and he scampers before me. Not that anyone seems to note us. Well, no one but a woman whose eyes track me from beneath a thick mat of reddish hair. She sits at one of the few stools, and I consider whether she's looking for me or just a curious woman. I know to be wary.

I guide Brute into perhaps the most complete building I've seen so far, redolent with the smell of other horses and hay. He seems content enough, and I pull a silver coin from my money bag and offer it to the boy.

'Watch him, and you'll get another when I return.' His eyes alight with delight. I make my way back to the front of the alehouse, eyes downcast, seeking the woman. She still watches me, although her attempts are well covered by her hair. Only the tension in her shoulders assures me that she's well aware of my return.

'What can I get you?' a man asks me jovially. He has a thin face and a thinner body. His lips curl back over a collection of jagged, uneven teeth.

'Food, ale and water,' I reply, again reaching for coins to offset the cost.

He takes them eagerly, and I find a space to settle on the benches. It's cool, but not cold. The heat in the sun is pleasant after the days of freezing rain and winds, and I don't want to risk being inside should someone try and take Brute away. I've lost him once. I have no intention of making the same mistake again.

I try not to watch the woman as I absorb myself in the conversation between the men and women before me. They're traders, of that I'm sure. Their clothes are better than those who labour in the fields but not so fine as to arouse suspicion in those with half a mind to theft.

I'm not really listening to their words, just pretending to, but then something they say does catch my attention.

'Travelling north at this time of year…' is what permeates my hearing.

'And in this weather. Damn nobility. Got no sense,' a man informs another. 'Mind, I made a pretty coin from them with some of my furs. Top price for them. Told them it was mink, but it was nothing of the sort.' He chuckles, his bearded face alight with the joy of making a good sale. 'You'd think they had no idea of the weather conditions at this time of year. The women were shivering, and the children almost blue with cold.'

I find breathing almost impossible, even as I smile my thanks to the man who brings me what I ordered.

'It's dangerous, to travel so far north. Have you heard of the attacks on the Isle of Sheppey? I know the Wessex scum deserve all they get, but all the same. North of here, they were. Bloody fools.'

With a sense of panic warring inside me, I hastily eat my fill. I want to ask the man more, but equally, I don't want to arouse the suspicion of the woman who still watches me and whose motivations I suspect. Is she merely a thief, out to take what I have from me, or has she been left here to watch out for any sign of the children and their captor being followed?

'Where can I get supplies? Bread and cheese for me and oats for my horse.'

'I can do bread and cheese and some dried meat. The horse, you'll have to visit old Eomer, close to the gate. He keeps such for sale.'

'My thanks. I'll take what I can. I'll go and source the oats first and return here.'

'No need, my lord. I can have them with you in a few moments.'

I remain seated and only stand to return to Brute when I have three loaves of good bread and a round of cheese to add to my sack, alongside a linen that smells of pork. I thought of spending the night here, at the tavern, out of the elements, but know I must continue northwards. The trader has left, and I can't ask him more even if I wanted to, but I believe he saw the children, and perhaps Eadburg and her mother as well. I've given no thought to her, but of course, they will have travelled to Tamworth with the children. Or at least, that must be where they thought they were going.

Palming the coin into the boy's hand as I go to retrieve Brute earlier than expected from his warm stable, I have one more request from him.

'Take me to Eomer.'

'Of course, this way.' He skips ahead, his hand clenched tightly to stop him from losing his precious coins. I imagine he'll eat well tonight, or indeed, for seven days. All the same, his ragged appearance worries me. He has no shoes, and his tunic reveals more of his stomach than it covers. 'Here he is,' the boy grins.

Eomer is a trader of oats and other grains that the farmers must sell to him. His workshop is one of the better ones in Chester, the roof hanging low over the wooden and stone building, and from it, sacks of produce spill, some open, others securely fastened, and five young thugs with mean looking faces move amongst them, checking people who view the produce. Only when they hear the jingle of coin do smiles grace their aspects.

'My thanks. Tell me what's your name and where are your mother and father?'

The boy shrugs his thin shoulders. 'Don't have any. The monks shelter me for the night, and then I work where I can. My name's Godfrith.'

'Then take these, Godfrith.' I offer him another five coins. 'And get yourself some shoes for the winter, a tunic that fits and a cloak as well.' His eyes widen. I'm unsure why I've done this, but the thought of his thin bones shivering all winter worries me. 'Now tell me, where can I find the road that runs north from here?'

'You don't want to go north,' he says too quickly. 'It's wild country there. Even the traders take guards with them.'

'I can look after myself,' I try to reassure. 'And I have my horse. He can gallop very fast.'

'Perhaps, but all the same. I wouldn't. But if you must, leave through the gate here and follow the river. Eventually, you'll meet another road.'

'My thanks.' I smile and turn aside, bartering for oats for Brute, which I should have done before paying my young friend more, and only then manage to leave, passing the same guard from earlier. I glimpse movement from close by and realise the woman still watches me, having moved aside from the alehouse. I consider if she'll follow me and prepare myself for such an occurrence. I can see no evidence that she has a horse, and she'll need one. But perhaps the horse is hidden.

I don't have my usual weapons, but Cuthred and Wynflæd found me some with which to travel. I have the seax with a bone handle, that I've spent time sharpening, although it's still too blunt. I have no sword, but I do have an old and battered shield that might help me, provided my enemy is half-blind and unable to tell one end of a blade from the other. And I have the old byrnie as well. I miss my sword and my seax, but it's been a long time since those were the only ways I knew to kill.

Fighting with Oswy and the others has shown me that, sometimes, a good punch is all that's needed, provided I aim it well.

It's easy enough to pick out the river the young lad directs me to, and Brute shows no concern at having his rest curtailed. With my supplies carefully stowed away, we strike out once more. This time, I'm alert to any sign of others having come this way. The way is liberally supplied with horseshit and the sign of animal hooves and horses' hooves, particularly in the sometimes muddy spots that obscure what was once a much better-maintained trackway.

I listen carefully for any sign of being chased, but it's difficult to hear anything above the noise of Brute's steps. When the settlement has receded behind me, and I'm confident the way onwards isn't as tricky as I first feared, I speed Brute's passage. If someone is following me on foot, they'll struggle to keep pace with my horse, and if they're on horseback, they'll struggle as well. Brute, even at a canter, isn't slow.

Every so often, I risk looking behind me, but I can see no one rushing to follow me. I pass a few people, herding animals back towards their farm-steadings, perhaps from market day. The fields are brown and bare, their crops taken from them. But still, the words of the young lad don't seem to be true. He told me not to come this way. Perhaps he meant to dissuade me from travelling further north than the outlying settlements. Maybe he didn't want me to leave when I was so kind to him.

I'm unsure, but we go onwards until darkness covers the land again, and then I realise that someone is definitely following me.

20

'Hello,' I call into the growing gloom.

The roadway stretches clear before me, but behind it's more shadowed and twisty. Yet I know what a horse hoof sounds like, even one trying not to make too much noise.

'I'm armed,' I call again. I've no intention of being caught unawares. Once was more than enough. Eadweard and Wulfred left me feeling foolish and doubting my skills. But there's no reply. Brute stiffens beneath me but keeps up his steady gait. Not that he can do so forever. We've covered a great distance of late. He'll tire, and so will I. I don't know this landscape. I've no idea where I might be able to seek shelter or even hide away from whoever pursues me. The lack of a response assures me that they mean harm, unfortunately.

And then I have a thought. I hope it's just Eadweard and Wulfred who follow me. I wouldn't like to think it was a Viking raider, perhaps come ashore nearby using the river, as they've done with the River Thames and in the kingdom of the East Angles.

I reach for my seax, the unfamiliar handle settling uncomfortably in my hand. I don't like it, and I'll probably be more of a threat to myself than my pursuer, but it brings some comfort.

Darkness continues to fall, and after nights and nights of the moonlight being good enough to see by, it's eerily dark and quiet. I can see only some distance ahead, and Brute is stepping more carefully, keen not to injure himself. The sounds of the night slowly grow around me, the flap of owl wings, the hoot of the same birds, and the scurrying of animals who hunt at night. I'd welcome the sight of something more familiar, perhaps an eagle far overhead, but there's nothing.

Fear stalks me, as does my hunter, only for a large rock formation to veer upwards from nowhere, just as I'm beginning to worry we might need to travel all night long.

'Here,' I whisper, encouraging Brute off the road. He comes willingly, head bowed low, a sign of his exhaustion. The rock formation is bulky to my right-hand side. It easily hides Brute, who I keep close enough to me that I can mount if needed. I can poke my head clear from its side, but I can see no one. And so, a conundrum, should I wait for them to ride past or hide from them until the morning gives me the light I need to see? My lips twist in thought as I run my hand through my beard. Once more, it's unruly and needs cutting back, but now's hardly the time.

I grip Brute's rein and quietly follow the rock formation until I'm convinced we won't be seen from the road. I can't rightly tell, but from running my hand along it, I think it moves slightly back the further from the road I go, which will hide me. Hopefully.

The sound of the night swells around me, making it impossible to hear what my hunter might be doing. I lean against the rock rather than sit on the ground. Beside me, Brute drowses, also leaning against the rock, and his soft breathing lulls me so that my eyes close as well. I can't stay awake all night, despite my best intentions.

When I open them, at a nudge from Brute, dawn is lightening the horizon, and there's no sign of my pursuer. Forehead furrowed, I look ahead. In the far distance, I can see the orange glow of a fire, perhaps from others forced to stay all night outdoors. But other than that, the area is cast in shadows, dawn yet to steal its way across the unfamiliar landscape. I look to Brute as he nudges me again. He doesn't seem concerned, but neither is he entirely happy about something.

I look behind him then and feel along his muscly frame, but it's not a wound that unsettles him. I strain to hear, but there's no sound either.

Only then do I hear whispers, little more than a soft shush, just out of true hearing. There's someone there, and if they're whispering, there's more than one someone, I must assume.

With Brute behind me, I follow the rock formation further. Above my head, I can sense there's some other mass there. Perhaps these rocks are part of a quarry or have fallen from a hillside. I keep glancing upwards, but until true dawn arrives, I can't see much more. The sound slowly gets louder and louder, and I realise that there's just one voice, and the words they say are repeated over and over again, every so often accompanied by a sob of such desolation that it almost brings a tear to my eye.

'Who's there?' The words are strongly feminine, and I'm sure I recognise the voice.

'Eadburg,' I gasp. She looks up at me from where she sits, huddled on the ground. She has no cloak, and her dress has been ripped, her hair in disarray, but it's whom she sits with that turns my stomach leaden. Her mother. Her flesh white and marbled, the horrifying black bruises of their captivity evident in the rope marks around her neck and wrists, and yet those wounds didn't kill her. No, a bloodied gash is visible, on her chest, and I stumble to my knees and envelop Eadburg in my arms.

She shivers and trembles. I realise that the words I've been hearing have been her soft prayers for her dead mother, the woman who was tasked with being nursemaid to young Coenwulf and Coelwulf. The woman who was wet nurse to the motherless child. My heart stills in fear, even as Eadburg shudders, her words muffled against my shoulder.

What have these people done to the children of Lady Cynehild?

And why have they murdered Eadburg's mother?

Eventually, Eadburg quietens beneath me. I wrap my cloak from my shoulders around her, gently pry her hands from her mother, and move her to one side. The body is cold and rigid, and so is Eadburg.

'How long have you been here?' My words, softly said, break the silence as though thunder rumbling from overhead. She flinches, eyes wild, and I can see the bruises that also scar her body. I shake my head. It's not really important. 'Here, I have food and water.' I place a piece of bread in one hand and my water in the other. 'You need to eat,' I urge her.

She does so, chewing instinctively. I'm sure if I asked her, she wouldn't know what she was eating.

Brute's vigilant beside me. It's clear it wasn't Eadburg who followed me yesterday. Should I be alert to others close by? With the daylight, I glance all around, but there's no one nearby, not even when I step back, shivering in the brisk wind, craning my head as far back as possible to see if there's someone above us.

'They took the children away from us.' Eadburg's words startle me, just as I shocked her earlier.

'When was this?'

'Two days ago, I think. We made it this far, but my mother succumbed to the wounds they inflicted on her.' Her voice catches on saying that.

'I'm so sorry about your mother,' I murmur, and I am, but my thoughts are elsewhere. 'Where did you escape from?' I query.

'Somewhere towards the east. They took the children and then tied us up. We tried to win free. And we nearly made it but then we had to fight. My mother made me run for it, but I went back, and found her, later. I got her this far but I couldn't get her any further, and then, and then...' Eadburg gasps the words, unable to say them. I hold her tight and only when she's recovered do I ask my next question.

'Do you know who it was or where they took the children?'

'No. I didn't know the men. To start with, it was Eadweard and Wulfred, but only for the first day, and then others were responsible. They said we were going to Tamworth, but we never arrived there.'

I crouch before her. 'Would you be able to take me back to where you were held captive?' She's shaking her head before the words leave my mouth.

'No, never. I need to take my mother home to Kingsholm.'

'But we need to find the children.'

She nods miserably, the realisation that she must leave her mother here hardening her features. 'I think... I think they mean to kill them. Why else would they have separated us from them?' Her words are mournful begging me to deny them.

'When did they separate you?'

'Four days ago. We were tied up and couldn't escape for some of that time, no matter how hard we tried.'

I'm unsurprised by her statement that they mean to kill the children. My only real surprise is that, four days ago, they hadn't done so yet. Admittedly, they might have done so by now. I can see what they're thinking. Take the children far away where the blame can never be placed on them and where the bodies will never be found. I clench my fists in a fury, running my fingers over my eagle scar. I'm beyond furious, and not just because Eadburg's mother is dead. These people have no right to meddle in matters of the ruling family of Mercia. The only consolation is that I don't believe Lady Ælflæd is involved, not any more, not if Wynflæd's right when she says she's worried about the children.

'I think they were going north, anyway,' Eadburg murmurs. 'There's no point in going back to where we were captive. There were only two men there. The others had left with the children.'

'Then I'll bury your mother and continue travelling northwards. Will you come with me?' I ask her softly. I'm asking too much of her, but I can't take her back to Chester, not now.

'Yes.' The single word is flecked with rage and resolve. I offer her a sad smile. I can see why Edwin was so enamoured of her. She's not as soft as I thought she was.

'Is there any keepsake you wish to take from her?' I murmur. It's going to be difficult to dig a grave here, but there are more than enough rocks. It'll have to be a cairn for Eadburg's mother. At least, I realise, it'll be easy enough to find, should Eadburg wish to do so. She nods, words beyond her, and moves to her mother. I don't watch what she does. I hear soft kisses and know her goodbyes have been said, although her mourning will be long and hard.

I move the body away from the rocky outcropping just a little, and then, with the hard and unyielding rocky surface beneath her body, I begin to place stones and rocks of all sizes over her. Eadburg doesn't help, and I don't blame her for that. She stands with Brute, her hands on his piebald coat as every rock obscures her mother from view.

Standing, my back crying in pain, I offer her a mournful smile but know I can wait no longer.

'Come, mount Brute. He can take both of us, provided we don't push him too fast.'

Terror fills her eyes, and I wonder if she's ever ridden.

'He'll behave, I promise.' I only hope there's some truth in those words as her warmth settles in front of me, and I direct Brute back to the road we were following yesterday.

I lower my head as the cairn passes out of sight.

I hope this is the only such cairn I need to construct.

Already too many have died while the children of Lady Cynehild remain in the gravest of peril.

I must locate them, even if it makes me a powerful enemy.

I'll find them, I resolve, no matter what trouble it brings to my door. The children are too small and helpless to be part of this game of kingdoms between those who think to rule after King Wiglaf.

21

'Do you know where they were taking them, other than northwards?' I ask Eadburg much later. We've ridden a long way, but not quickly. Brute is firm beneath me, but I'm minded to dismount and give him a break from his heavy burden. He's all I have, and we might need to go a long distance yet.

'I don't think so, no.' Before me, Eadburg has spent time sleeping, finally trusting Brute won't bolt with her on his back. I've been alert, ready to defend us if necessary and, if not, to allow Brute his head so that he can get us away from danger. I look behind us every so often, but I can see no one following us. Still, I can't escape the feeling that someone is there, all the same.

The landscape's growing more and more rugged. To the west, I occasionally catch glimpses of the sea, but my focus is mainly on our surroundings from which our enemy could emerge and catch me unawares. I consider what Wynflæd said to me and what finding Eadburg has revealed to me, and I'm still unsure where to direct Brute other than northwards. I don't know where Eamont is. I didn't ask in Chester, not when I thought the woman paid too much attention to me.

But, at some point, the north will run out, although I imagine not for a long time. Uor and Wulfheard have ensured that I understand the nature of the place I call my home. I might live far from the coast, but nowhere in Britain is truly that far from the sea, not when it's an island.

I wish I knew who had the children. Like Eadburg, I suspected Eadweard and Wulfred, but of course, they were busy misleading me and making me follow them to Hereford, so that they could keep me tied up for seven days. I don't know where they are now. I didn't expect finding the children would be easy, but I didn't believe it would feel this impossible.

The landscape here is ragged. It makes the hills and woodlands of Mercia look tame by comparison. We've seen more sheep than we have people. But there is a roadway, and it stretches onwards.

'Aren't we in the kingdom of Northumbria?' Eadburg eventually asks me, her voice tinged with worry.

'I don't know. There's no marker to show where one kingdom begins and another ends. There are no banners proclaiming that one person or another owns this land.'

The words aren't comforting, but I've been thinking the same for some time. I know Chester is part of Mercia. I'm not sure what the land much further north is. Northumbria is precisely that, the land north of the Humber. While I've never been there, I know that the Humber doesn't run entirely across the kingdom. Like the River Thames, it ends before reaching the western side of the island, but still, the land north of where the Humber lies, regardless of east or west, it still Northumbria. Further north, where the Saxons no longer claim the land as their own, Stratchclyde and the kingdom of Atholl can be found, but that should be far ahead, or so I hope. Bad enough to be a Mercian in Northumbria. To be a Saxon in the kingdom of Atholl or Strathclyde will be much worse.

'If we're Mercians in Northumbria, will the locals not set upon us?' I pause then, mouth open to offer a swift denial, but I genuinely don't know the answer. I've been to the kingdom of the East Angles, to Wessex and, indeed, almost inside some of the Welsh kingdoms. I can't say I was entirely welcomed anywhere that wasn't Mercia.

'We'll see,' is all I can say. I'm not going to offer a reassurance that might not prove to be true. Silence falls once more, and when we stop to relieve ourselves and water Brute, I don't remount, instead walking beside my horse. For all I tell Eadburg to mount, she refuses, and instead we walk onwards.

It all seems hopeless. In this wild, untamed land, how can we find two small children apprehended by who knows whom and, no doubt, taken on fast horses far from where they think we'll look?

'I see smoke.' Eadburg's words rouse me from my wallowing, and I startle. She's correct. There's smoke up ahead, but as we walk, it's clear it's merely a cook fire in one of the dwellings beside the road.

Indeed, now I look, the land here is less wild and more tamed. There are fences built of wattle and daub, and the sounds of animals permeate my hearing. Yet, first, we must counter a collection of men and women who watch us with distrustful eyes. A shiver of fear ripples through my body.

'Good day,' I call to them, wishing my voice didn't catch on those two words.

Eadburg walks so close to Brute that he can hardly move forwards, but he does so, moving her unwillingly on.

'Good day,' a woman calls to me, her words rolling slightly but intelligible enough.

'We seek a party with two small children. Did they pass this way? Both blonde-haired, one not much more than a babe in arms.'

I keep my gaze on the woman. Her hair's streaked with white, but her eyes are bright and alert, and her back isn't bent or twisted by her labour. The dwellings are of firm construction and well maintained, fresh thatch on one of them. This is a prosperous place for all it seems far from Chester.

'What are they to you?' she demands to know, and I feel a spark of hope.

'My children,' Eadburg surprises me by sobbing aloud. Whether she means it or not, it's a good argument. Yet I'm unconvinced that the woman believes her, or those who come closer to us. A huge hound dog comes and sniffs my crotch, and I run my hand over his soft muzzle. He might be welcoming now, but an animal such as that is surely a hunter, like the wolf, and I'm convinced it could sever my throat with a well-placed bite.

'Then, yes, they passed this way. There were many of them. Finely dressed. Why do they want your children?'

'I'm the concubine of a king to the south, and they have a claim to the kingdom.'

At this, the woman spits to the side as though to ward off evil. Her reaction surprises me. 'Men are such fools,' she calls to us. 'They went by two days ago. I don't know where they were heading. I would suggest it must be Strathclyde, or somewhere such as that. The road will take you there. Follow it carefully. There are wild folk in these parts. They won't think to talk to you as we've done.'

'My thanks.' Eadburg lets forth a gentle sob, her anguish clear to hear.

'Good day to you,' I call, the dog backing away at the sound of a guttural cry from one of the men, no doubt its name.

I don't rush to leave the settlement, and I can feel we're being watched for a long time after the smell of smoke has dissipated.

'Do you think they spoke the truth?' I hiss to Eadburg.

'Why wouldn't they? We're not an army of men come to destroy their homes and livelihood.'

'Perhaps,' I counter. The thought of continuing for another two days, taking us further and further from Mercia, is unsettling. I've never been so far from home before. I feel exposed.

'What's Strathclyde?' Eadburg asks me later when we've stopped for the night beneath a spreading oak tree, the only sign of shelter as the sky darkens.

'A kingdom, like the Welsh ones.'

'Not Saxon then?'

'No, not Saxon.'

'Why would they go there? Wouldn't that be a risk?'

'I don't think they are going there. I just think they're going somewhere they believe no one will notice the two small children, or rather, notice when they kill them.'

Her gasp startles me. 'Is that what they mean to do?' she cries, for all she was the one to tell me that.

'I can't think why else they'd have stolen them away,' I counter.

'In my heart, I hoped they were taking them to their father.'

'No, he's in West Frankia. They mean to kill them, I'm sure of it.'

'Why? Because Lady Ælflæd's son is so weak?'

'I don't know. But their claim to the kingship is a good one.' I don't add that mine is as well. I've almost forgotten all about it.

'They wouldn't revert to the old line of the kings, surely?'

'They've done it before, or so Wynflæd would tell you. She knows a great deal about the ruling families.'

Eadburg's face, half-shadowed, looks increasingly unhappy. She hardly eats the bread and cheese I offer her.

'What will you do when you find them?' her voice calls to me long after I think she's fallen asleep. I've determined to stay awake, to provide some protection throughout the long night, although I know I won't be able to survive with none. 'There's only you.' Her words aren't reassuring.

'We'll retrieve them and return them to Mercia.'

'But we're so far from Mercia. There's no one to help us. We only have Brute.'

Her dire assessment of the situation is unnerving but truthful.

'But they don't have Brute. He's the fastest horse I've yet met. He'll get us back to Mercia.' And if not all of us, I think to myself, at least the children and Eadburg.

22

Another day passes with no sign of our quarry, and then, finally, as we're seeking shelter for another night, I hear an unmistakable voice. Young Coenwulf, his childish words lisping through the trees. Eadburg gasps and then thrusts her hands over her mouth to stop more sound gushing forth.

Here, there's a woodland that I thought was all but deserted, but the road surges through them. I don't know if the children are ahead on the road or just deep within the trees as well. The scent of smoke drifts in the air. Wherever they are, they've made camp for the night.

I look to Eadburg and she nods at me, reaching out and taking hold of Brute's reins so that I can slide through the trees and undergrowth, seeking out the children and whoever has them captive.

It's grown dark enough on the road to be unable to see far. Beneath the trees, with little light from the moon, it's even darker. I move quickly but then slow myself. I'll walk into their campsite without realising if I'm not careful. While the smell of smoke is pungent with damp, I can see no light from the fire to guide my steps. I'm grateful for that. Such brightness would blind me more than the darkness.

Around me, animals scurry in the branches, making just enough noise to mask my steps. Hardly daring to breathe, I continue, working my way around and under the reaching boughs of the trees. The childish voice has been shushed, I hope not permanently, and my hand keeps reaching for my blunt seax. Fury thuds in my chest.

While I can't hear young Coenwulf, I can detect the murmur of people talking one to another, the laughter of men sharing some sort of joke, and the more frantic reply of someone shushing them. The sounds guide my steps more than my eyes. And then I crouch low, using a long-since abandoned tree stump to hide behind.

The camp's before me, but far enough away that I won't be seen, provided they don't have guards this far out. Not that I think they will. There are no more than twenty or so people altogether. Their voices are distinctly Mercian. One of the men sits beside the smoking fire. Another figure, with their back to me – perhaps a woman with hair long enough that it moves as the head darts from side to side – sits beside him, a small shape beside them, Coenwulf, I presume. I assume young Coelwulf is in their arms. I can't hear what's being said.

I eye the men. They're the real problem. It's not possible to make out many details. There are enough horses for them all to ride unencumbered, and I also think several pack animals as well. This expedition has been well planned. There's no sign of the original ox-cart. Wherever that was left, it's far from here.

For a moment, I consider if I've got this all wrong. Are they just taking the children to their father but having to employ diversionary tactics to ensure King Wiglaf doesn't hear of it?

Only then I remember that they killed Eadburg's mother. There was no need to do that. She would have happily gone with the children to be reunited with their father.

No, this is something else entirely.

I stay in place long into the night, watching the camp. They all eat, and then most of them turn to sleep, the children with the other figure. I'm still not sure if it's a woman or a man. Not that it matters. I did catch the shimmer of a blade at their waist when they stood to settle the children beneath a canvas to sleep.

Other than the children, everyone in the group carries iron at their waist.

Whatever else, they're expecting trouble. But what can I do? One man against their number?

Only when I can hardly stay awake any longer do I retrace my steps towards where I left Eadburg and Brute. My mind's a riot of fear and resolve. I've found the children, but how can I rescue them? Eadburg's earlier words were stark but true. What can I do alone?

Eadburg, leaning against Brute, where they both sleep beneath a tree, jolts awake when I return, her face pale enough to see even through the blackness.

'Are they there?' she demands to know, her whisper hoarse, as she stifles a yawn.

'Yes, but so are at least sixteen men and possibly a woman protecting them.' She slumps in defeat at that, and I join her on the other side of Brute. He looks at me but then closes his eyes again, no doubt sensing that nothing's about to happen anytime soon. 'Get some more sleep,' I urge her. 'I need some as well. I'm not going to be able to resolve this tonight.' She huffs unhappily but quietens, and I try to calm my breathing and think my way out of this.

What can I do? One man and a woman, with one blunt seax between them. Oh, and a shield, and a rusty byrnie. Against seventeen others. I counted carefully while I watched them. I feared there were twenty but the number is less. Not that it much helps. While I thought the figure with the children might be a woman, the more I've watched, the more I'm convinced that's not the case, which means the children have a warrior, not only guarding them but also taking personal responsibility for their care. I wish I knew whom it was. I'm grateful the children are still alive, but will they remain that way for long? And why all this nurturing for them? Why this huge distance? Why the skulking about taking them so far north? Why not just kill the children and hide their bodies? After all, they killed Eadburg's mother. Why not them as well? Although, of course, they didn't mean to kill Eadburg's mother, did they?

Sleep is long in coming, and when I wake, grit stings my eyes, and Eadburg is pacing the small space.

'It's our duty to get them,' she hisses at me, seemingly unaware that her footsteps are loud while she tries to speak quietly. Anyone close by would hear her movements and come and investigate.

'I know we must get them,' I counter. 'It's not that which worries me, but the how. I am but one man.'

'Well, you have Brute and me.'

'But no other weapons.' I try to explain my reasoning, aware this argument between us has changed. She was concerned to begin with about what I could do. I was convinced I'd be enough, alongside Brute. Yet now she tries to convince me that I am, when I fear the numbers facing us.

'If we sneak in under cover of darkness, then it won't matter.'

'They keep a watch at night,' I inform her.

'So, not all of the warriors, surely?'

I furrow my forehead then, considering how she knows all this. It's not exactly the discussion two lovers would share, but perhaps she asked Edwin about such things. 'And they might move on today.'

'They're not,' she announces staunchly, and my eyes narrow accusingly.

'You went to look? You could have alerted them to our presence.'

'Well, I didn't, and they're busy making pottage, and the children are being amused with games and a small ball. I think they're waiting for someone.'

'Who?' I demand, forgetting my fury at her.

'If I knew that, I'd tell you, but I don't.'

'If they're waiting for someone, then we need to get them before these other people arrive.'

'Exactly,' she counters, hands on her hips. She looks so like her mother at that moment, that I have to blink the shadowed image of the older woman that seems to settle over Eadburg.

'That still doesn't help with how,' I argue.

'No, but I think whoever it is, is travelling from the north, not the south.'

None of this makes sense to me.

'So, if we skirt around them, we might intercept whomever it is,' I muse.

'Why would we do that?' Her response is sharp.

'Ah, well, what if they've never met that person? We could pretend to be them and gain control over the children,' I counter.

'Would you kidnap small children for someone you've never met?' She makes a good point, and my spark of hope evaporates before it can genuinely settle over me. 'And they know me, anyway. They took me and my mother, alongside the children.' Her words are surprisingly bland considering her mother is now dead.

'So we need to retrieve them sooner rather than later,' I conclude.

'Yes, and we should hurry.'

'Why are they arriving today? Did you hear something when you were there?'

'I don't know, but we shouldn't leave them there longer than necessary.' Her words are stubborn, her chin jutting out.

'No, we shouldn't, but I can't just blunder in there. I need to have some idea of what we'll do.' A loud huff of annoyance erupts from her mouth. I'm about to demand to know what she'd do, only a look of worry crosses her face, and she scampers to my side.

I hear it then as well. There's someone walking around not far away. I don't know if they're coming from behind or in front. What if I've been shadowed here? What if the red-haired woman from Chester has finally caught me? What if it's one of the men who has the children captive?

'Damn it,' I exhale, hoping we've not been discovered either by those who have the boys, or by someone who's been tailing me. I don't want to be tied up again, left to feel useless while the children are once more taken from me.

I hold myself still, aware that Brute does the same, although his legs tremble where they extend to the side of him. He wants to stand but can't, not yet.

I grab his long nose, forcing him to look at me. His eyes are furious, but he doesn't buck against me.

A voice calls to another, and I wince, only to hear the reply coming from even further away.

'They've gone,' I mumble, releasing Brute so he can stand. He does so quickly, eager to be on his feet. I'm sure the voices came from ahead, and not behind, but the thought of the red-haired woman reminds me of my fears in Chester and when I first ventured north. What if there is more than one enemy out there?

My gaze settles on Brute. Perhaps he might hold some answers, but I can think of nothing.

I can't ride him through the campsite. They have more than enough horses to chase me, and I don't believe I can burden Brute with two adults and two small children at the same time.

All the same, my eyes appraise him, watching as he nibbles the growth beneath the tree.

Perhaps, I muse.

23

The day's long and tedious. I spend much of it hovering just out of sight of the campsite where the children of Lord Coenwulf are being cared for, even though they're far from Mercia. What I witness doesn't accord with Wynflæd's or my fears, but perhaps one of the warriors has a soft heart.

I watch carefully, with Eadburg out of sight behind me and Brute kept under the tree. I've not tied him to a branch. If he needs to escape, then he can. I won't have him taken from me by those who'd profit from selling him. If he senses danger, I rely on him to do what must be done.

For much of the time, my face is twisted in concentration, assessing my idea from as many different outcomes as possible. Will it work? Won't it? I'm beginning to think there's no chance when the weather offers me a helping hand.

The rain, as it falls, is loud, almost thundering. It's as though every single water barrel has been upended at once, the drumming of a hundred hooves or even the advance of an enemy. I find a smile on my lips, and Eadburg makes her way to my side, assurance on her face. For a woman terrified of Brute only days ago, I'm pleased to see how she's grown in confidence. No doubt, she's determined to secure the children and seek vengeance for her mother's death. I mirror her thoughts.

As darkness covers the land alongside the heavy rain, we move.

The men of the camp have sought shelter beneath canvases. Coenwulf and Coelwulf's voices are muted as they're swallowed beneath the bleached linen. I imagine the smell will be unpleasant.

Rain falls onto my head, the deluge so heavy that the reaching branches overhead can't stop its progress.

'Come on,' I urge Eadburg. I hear angry voices shouting one to another as the guards are forced from their shelter to stand outside, watching northwards and southwards. It'll be difficult to evade them, but I have my blunt seax. If I have to silence them, then I will, using whatever means necessary. Now that the meal for the evening has been consumed, and many of the bored men sleep, I can't think those with the unwelcome duty will be relieved by others happy not to stand in the rain.

All the same, I force us both backwards, watching where I step carefully, although the heavy rain does truly mask all sound. Without the torrent, I don't think my idea would have stood any chance of succeeding, but I'm more hopeful now. It might still fail, but it won't be from lack of trying.

Eadburg moves silently, having hitched her dress through her belt so that she can't trip or snag the weeds and thistles on it. Her face is set with determination. I've no blade to give her, and she wouldn't take it even if I did. She does have a stone to hand should she need to defend herself.

When I'm happy we've moved close enough while still being far enough away, I meet her eyes. She waits, and I continue to circle the camp. We can't see one another, but she has only to recite the familiar prayer always used in church, and she'll continue towards the horses.

The horses.

At the moment, the horses provide our enemy with an advantage over us. They undoubtedly have better blades and are better protected; no matter what we do, they'll also have speed. But without the horses? Then they'll struggle, so we must do all we can to disperse the horses before taking one or two to aid us and, only then, steal the children from beneath their noses.

Happy I'm approaching the horses from a different position to Eadburg, and with the words of the prayer concluded, I fix my eyes on where I want to go. The darkness is becoming all-consuming, the path I want to take slowly disappearing the closer I get. I keep my eyes ahead, trying not to bump into trees or trip over the disturbed ground, and certainly not fall down some burrowing animals' hideaway, but it's hard going. My eyes narrow and then narrow again. I hear one of the guards calling to another, his voice booming above the thundering rain. A reply comes back to him, and both continue with their duties. I know one was sheltering beneath an overhanging branch, but whether he's still there is impossible to tell.

The sound of hooves moving over the ground reaches my ears. The horses have no such protection. The rain coats them, and the animals are unhappy with that. I nod with satisfaction. They're making so much noise, it'll be another means of masking my place amongst them.

The smell of horseshit is ripe in the air. The animals have been penned here for too long, and no one has been caring for them. If they came this way, having lost Eadburg and her mother, whom they must think are both dead following their escape attempts, then they could have been here for five or six days.

Then I'm amongst the animals, my hand trailing along the back of one of the beasts until I reach its head. The animals are tied – loosely, admittedly, but not allowing them as much room as they'd like. They have no saddles, only the leading ropes. This will make it somewhat difficult. The ropes are twisted and threaded, the animals shuffling amongst one another. And that's why my hand follows the animal's body, head, and then the rope tied around a tree stump. I bend and begin to work the tight knot loose with fumbling fingers. Of course, the rope's damp and slick with rain, and it's too dark to actually see, but at least the horses haven't raised any alarm. I'm sure I can hear Eadburg's breaths, but I concentrate on what I'm doing.

We need to free the horses. Have them wander off beneath the heavy clouds and darkness of night, and then, then, we can grab the children, hasten back to Mercia, and return them to Kingsholm. After that, I won't be leaving it again. Not anytime soon.

I feel the knots give beneath my fingers, one horse and then another pulling loose on their ropes. I follow the cords, determined not to wound the animals by having them snag on branches. I loop the rope around my arms, following it back to the animal, and then hastily saw through the hemp with my seax. I could have done that first, but the animals need to leave slowly, not as one. The first animal, realising it's free, eagerly turns aside, forcing a path through the others as it seeks freedom, and, no doubt, respite from the rain.

The second animal is slower, and I wait for it to move on before tracing the rope to another. I'm aware that Eadburg must be with me, but I can't see her. I do hear the soft thud of hooves beneath the thundering rainstorm. I hope it rains all night long. That way, we can accomplish what needs to be done.

Slowly, the herd of horses begins to dissipate. It's so dark that I lose sight of them immediately, but I can just hear them moving further and further from the camp. While the rain's masking our movements, it's also making the horses unwilling to take their chance at freedom. I fear they might find somewhere to shelter beneath the trees and simply stay there.

When I've released six of the animals, I feel a cold hand on mine and meet the blazing eyes of Eadburg.

'They're not going far,' she cautions me in an exhalation.

'Damn it,' I reply, grimacing at the realisation.

'We carry on, all the same. We can release them and then chase them further from the encampment.'

'We need to be careful. One of the guards has been this way once already. He didn't notice anything, but I'm sure he will.'

I don't know how long the tasks take us. It feels like more than half of the night, and I still need to retrieve the children, but I can't hurry any more. The ropes that hold the animals are twisted and refuse to yield to my fingers. The horses are sluggish to rush away, but we can't move to the next part of our plan until this is complete.

'We should move more quickly,' I whisper. She disappears, leaving me with the curious nose of a horse and its warm breath on my cheek. 'Come on then,' and I follow the cord to where it's tied and release it.

Two more of the animals follow, and if my calculations are correct, then that should be more than half of them. That was my part in this, as well as keeping hold of two more animals so that Eadburg could ride with one of the children. I want a spare, just in case the other animal goes lame. We can't afford to be caught with the children and have no means of escape.

I can't tell if I've chosen two horses that will be good to ride in the darkness, but I grip their leading ropes and begin to move aside. The press of horses has long since dissipated. Eadburg has one more horse to remove, as far as I can tell.

Moving backwards, my shoulders tense as I feel the scrutiny of someone. I turn, but it's too dark to see anything. The two horses walk into me, forcing me onwards or risk losing them. The sudden slap of slack rope rings loudly in my ears. Sodden footsteps come my way. My heart pounds too loudly. I know we'll be discovered, and we're not ready yet.

'Who's there?' a voice calls, filled with menace.

'Me, you bloody fool,' a disarticulated voice responds, and the steady stream of someone taking a piss fills my ears.

Once I've heard the steps backtrack, Eadburg hastens to my side, and together we merge back into the treeline, encouraging the milling horses we encounter.

'Can you take them back?' I ask her. This wasn't part of the initial idea, but with the horses reluctant to leave of their own accord, I must make sure they move off.

'What?' she exclaims, snapping the ropes from my hands.

'Lead them back to Brute, and wait for me,' I urge her through lips that hardly move as I try to stay quiet.

'Get the children,' is her parting shot as she merges with the trees. There's no time to argue with me. Even if she's uncomfortable with the animals, there is no other choice to be taken.

Hastily, I reach out and find the other animals. Three of them stand tightly together. I encourage one of them to move onwards, and the other two follow, but the first stops again. I step to it and encourage it once more. However, no sooner are the other two moving than it stops for a second time.

'Come on,' I growl, deciding to lead one of the animals instead. I'm not aware of other horses close by, but three is more than enough for the enemy to chase us once I have the children. The loss of the horses is sure to be discovered soon. I still need to find the children, and that element of this rescue is even more dangerous. Abruptly, I stop and peer backwards. I can't tell which way I've come. I peer into the gloom, but everywhere is murky and damp. I can't even find horse hooves in the forest floor because it's too dark to see them.

'Damn it,' I exclaim softly. I try and retrace my steps, but one of the horses follows me.

'Go away,' I urge the animal. 'Go that way.' But the horse is stubborn and stays where it is. I waver and then determine to strike out the way I think I need to go. I could tie the horse to a tree, but I don't want to. It could be stuck here forever, dying of thirst and starvation, and I can't do that.

On I go, sure I must have missed the campsite, aware that every time I think I've lost the horse, it reappears, its head hanging low, its hoof beats surprisingly soft over the damp forest floor. And then, when I think I've made a huge mistake, I finally see what I need to see. Ahead, the campsite emerges from the dark dankness, and the horse is still with me. Perhaps I can use it after all.

24

The campfire coughs and spits as the rain falls into it. The light it emits is little more than enough to illuminate the ground beside it. But it does show me that no one moves within that small area. Whoever has the unfortunate task of keeping watch doesn't do so from the fire. They must be elsewhere. Not beneath one of the canvases, but perhaps under one of the trees.

I squint into the gloom, wishing I could see more, but aware that now is the time to act. Whatever happens next, it's the opportunity I need to retrieve the children.

I gaze at the horse, head bowed, beside me. It makes no noise. I find its presence comforting.

I intended to scamper between the canvases and trees and retrieve the children on foot. But I have a horse now. I eye the animal. I consider if I recognise it. Is it perhaps an animal from Kingsholm, or have Eadweard and Wulfred's part in this endeavour entirely ended? Does it know me? Does it, more importantly, know the children? It might prove much easier to take the children if they recognise the horse or at least if Coenwulf does. Little Coelwulf will be far too young to identify the animal or even me. And that's a problem. While I've sworn to protect the children, I've done so from a distance, more often than not, unwelcome inside the hall where they spend the majority of their time. Young Coenwulf might simply believe I'm another bad person come to steal him away. He might kick up a fuss. But I can't risk Eadburg here, not with so many warriors carrying iron.

I can protect myself and hopefully the children, but not Eadburg as well.

The beating of my heart slows as I consider my options. I strain to detect the voices of others, but I can barely hear the snoring of those who do sleep. The fire hisses as a sudden deluge tumbles onto it from the branches overhead.

I can't wait any longer.

On stealthy feet, I slide onto the horse's back. The animal's smaller than Brute, perhaps similar to Wine, and easy to mount. With my upper body lying along the damp animal's long neck, my trews even more drenched now, I knee it forward.

'Come on,' I whisper. And it moves out from the shelter of the trees and between the canvases. The animal must be able to see more easily than I can as it avoids all the ropes supporting the canvases, and the seething fire. I direct it towards the canvas I believe the boys are inside from my observations during the day, and then slip from the beast's back again. I'm not waiting to see if anyone hears me. Instead, I duck down to hack through the bindings tying the canvas door closed with my blunt blade. I lack the time to fumble through the toggles of wood. The smell inside the tent is as noxious as I thought it would be, the pig's fat used to proof the tent against the rain mixing with that of bad breath and flatulence and it's impossible to see anything.

I wince as the snoring rumble ceases, only to resume almost immediately.

On my hands and knees, I enter the confines of the canvas. My clothing creaks with the dampness and my trews are too tight around my knees. I look forward, but I can make no sense of the shapes in the gloom. There's no light to see by, none at all.

And then, white eyes greet mine, and I realise I'm being watched.

'Coenwulf,' I whisper, against my better judgement, surprised that he's awake. With hearing like that, he'll one day make a fine warrior to sneak up on his enemies.

'Who are you?' he asks, his words far too loud with his childish shock at being woken in the night.

'I'm a friend of Eadburg's. I've come to take you home.' My words are so soft I'm not sure he hears them. But he must.

'And Coelwulf?' he demands.

'Yes, yes,' I whisper. 'You need to be really quiet. Where's your brother?'

'Here, beside me.'

I can hear Coenwulf moving but can't see what he's doing.

'He's really heavy,' I hear next. My hand has reached for my blunt seax, convinced that we're being too noisy and the warrior who cares for the children will wake. But I can't expect the youngster to carry his brother unaided. Rearing back to waddle into the tent on my feet, my arse almost touching the floor, I make my way to where I think Coenwulf is.

I feel a sodden lump and realise it's his brother. He stinks of piss and shit, and I wrinkle my nose. It's not just the horses that these warriors neglect.

I pat the furs that cover him and, determining which end is which, I scoop him into my arms and turn to leave the tent.

Coelwulf stirs in my arms but doesn't wake.

'Follow me,' I urge his older brother.

Coenwulf hesitates.

'I'll take you to Eadburg,' I promise him hoarsely. I'm convinced that my antics must have been discovered. Yes, the drumming rain has covered our conversation, but I'm sure we're noisier than that.

'What about my toys?'

'We'll leave them, for now.' I try and sound as reassuring as possible, even though I want to do nothing but roar at him to hurry up.

And then I hear a sound I've been fearing.

'Go back to sleep, you little runts,' a heavily accented voice demands as they roll over in their sleeping furs.

Coenwulf stuffs his hand in his mouth but still emits a squeak of fear.

I look down at the sleeping child in my arms, wincing at the movements coming from behind me. I can't let this man discover what I've done. He'll rouse the entire bloody campsite, and even having a horse to speed our escape might be useless to me.

Slowly, I place the sleeping child back on the ground, reaching for my seax. But Coenwulf remains behind me. Should the man realise he's not alone with the children, it'll be easy for him to grab Coenwulf. I can't risk that. I must take both children back to Kingsholm. I can't sacrifice one for the other.

Fear makes my arms leaden and my movements too slow.

'Where are you, you little shit?' the voice asks again. I can sense Coenwulf's shaking. He might not recognise me, but he knows whoever has him captive isn't his friend. Slowly, I turn my head and lift a finger to my lips to urge him to silence. I don't know if he sees me, and I don't appreciate the shriek of my damp clothes as I move. I still can't see where the man lies, but I need to find him.

Slowly, hardly daring to breathe, I turn on my knees, mindful that I might kick Coelwulf. I'm wedged between the two children, and the opening to the tent is so damn close, but I can't risk it. This man must die.

Coenwulf has his wide, frightened eyes fixed on mine. His hand is still in his mouth, trying to stop his whimper of fear from escaping. I can sense the man's hand moving, no doubt feeling for where the children slept. He might expect Coenwulf to move in his sleep, but not Coelwulf, whose soft snores still reverberate through my damp boots.

I beckon Coenwulf to me, but he can't move. Urgently, I reach out to him. I don't want him to see this. It might be dark in here, but he doesn't need to witness my killing his captive. He's but a child. He has no idea of what men will do to one another in the name of war and politics.

His thin body trembles beneath my touch.

'Where are you?' the man grumbles, and I can sense he's stirring to full wakefulness.

Urgently, my knees complaining at the position they're in, I grip Coenwulf, and clasp him to me, the strain in my body from reaching and lifting making me want to stuff my hand in my mouth as well. His body is rigid, which at least helps. I think he's pissed himself with fear as a fresh waft of urine reaches my nose.

'You little shits.' The man must smell it as well. 'I've bloody told you to go outside to piss.'

Carefully, I place Coenwulf beside his brother. I want to tell him to go outside, to take the horse and leave here, but what if there are others outside, disturbed by what's happening inside the shelter?

And then a fresh set of white eyes surges up before me, the warrior's gasp of shock assuring me he didn't know I was there. Hastily, I bring the almost blunt seax up to stab him, but he's quicker than I am. What sort of fool, I manage to think, sleeps with a blade that sharp when there are small children beside him?

The edge of his seax is so sharp, I see it even in the gloom. But it's his mouth that concerns me as I duck below the blade, landing on my arse, legs tangled beneath me. If someone comes at me from the slit entranceway, it'll take me too long to get upright to defend myself. I'll die here in the damp furs of children too young to know where and when to piss.

I want to roar my rage, but he's just one man. If I shout, others will come to his assistance, and I won't be able to win free for myself, let alone the two small children I swore to their mother that I'd protect.

There's nothing for it, as I hear him suck in air to call for help. I leap forward, wary of kicking the children but knowing I have no choice. Spreadeagled, I sprawl on top of the man, sending him back so that his head thuds against the hard ground beneath the furs.

I smell the blood rather than see if I've cut him or he's cut me. I stab down to where his heart must beat, but my hand encounters nothing but the furs. With my other hand scrabbling through the furs, I realise I'm lying on his legs, not his head, and reach upwards frantically, desperate to find his chest.

But it seems I've managed to stun him. He makes no attempt to counter my actions, and finally I work out where he is in relation to my seax and slice the blade into his chest. The hot gush of blood touches my hand, and the scent is ripe enough to drive away the stink of piss that permeates everything.

Breathing heavily, I run my hand over his mouth, eager to assure myself that he's dead. And he is. Thank god.

I suck in a much-needed breath, my hand once more feeling through the furs, seeking the man's seax. But my hand stops on something hard and wooden, and I pull it clear. I can't tell what it is, but I'm sure it's the wooden horse that belongs to Coenwulf. Beside it is another object, clearly metal, but what exactly, I don't know. I scoop them both into my hands. I think of seeking the man's seax but I know I've taken too long. I need to get out of the canvas and back to Eadburg.

Hastily, I return to Coenwulf and Coelwulf. Both children seem well, although Coelwulf's soft snores have stopped.

'Did you kill the bad man?' Coenwulf hiccups in fear.

'I did, yes,' I pant, and then remember the toy. 'Here, did you want this?'

He takes the toy from me but doesn't speak. His eyes remain fearful.

'Take me to Eadburg,' he mutters, thumb in his mouth, or at least, that's what I think he says.

'Come on then. But wait a moment.' I can't just emerge from the tent. I must ensure no one has heard the ruckus from inside. Slowly, endeavouring to hear over the drumming rain and eager to be gone before Coelwulf fully wakes and begins to cry, I poke my head through the ripped canvas.

The fire's entirely gutted. The rain still thuds in a terrible torrent, and I squint into the impenetrable darkness, hoping to see no one and fearing what I'll do if there's someone there.

A movement and I'm gripping my seax tightly, wishing I'd been able to find the dead man's blade, only a whiff of horse breath merges with mine, and I remember the animal.

'Come on,' I urge Coenwulf, as I stand, and add whatever object I've found to my weapons belt to explore later. Perhaps it might tell me whom these men were. Now, I just need to get away from here and join Eadburg and Brute. And then make it home to Kingsholm, where I hope the children will finally be safe.

25

It's easy to seat young Coenwulf on the horse. It's damn near impossible to do anything with Coelwulf. Hands slick with the gore of the dead man, the child slippery and stinking of piss, threatening to wake, I'm once more hobbled.

And the longer it takes to get sorted, the more likely that one of the captors will wake and realise what's happening. That their precious cargo is missing and their comrade is dead.

'Come on,' I eventually huff. 'Hold the horse's neck,' I encourage Coenwulf. He does as I ask one-handed, gripping his toy with the other. I intended to mount up behind him, but it's unachievable with Coelwulf. And I think he's less likely to cry out if I'm holding him. However, he's a dead weight. I never thought such a young child would weigh so much.

'This way,' I encourage the horse, holding Coelwulf one-handed to direct the animal. It would be better if the animal had a name, but I don't know what it is.

The smell of damp smoke fills my nostrils. I risk glancing up, but the night remains black, the canopy of trees above my head doing nothing to stop the incessant rain from falling into my eyes. Disorientated momentarily, it takes me precious time to remember where I've left Brute and told Eadburg to go and join him. But then I reorientate myself. I'm left with no choice but to lead us all directly through the camp, skirting the smoking remains of the fire. I'd like to think it was easier to see, but it isn't. The shadowy trees call to me, but first I have to manoeuvre myself and the horse around the ropes of the tents. Or rather, just me. The horse walks with confidence I admire, the steps gentle with the precious load perched atop it.

Realising the horse is a better guide than I am, I step behind the animal, following the swish of its tail until we're some distance from the camp. Not that I relax. We've still got a long way to go. I might have only killed one man to accomplish this, but that's not an advantage. When they realise their comrade is dead and their horses stolen, they'll come for us. I need to reach Eadburg and Brute before that happens.

The weight of Coelwulf seems to increase with every step I take. Despite the terrible rain, I'm sweating. It's far easier to heft a shield or a sword than to carry this bulky child. At least, I think, he seems to have returned to sleep. I can't have him crying out. He's too young to understand the trouble that would cause us.

On legs growing heavier and heavier, I follow the horse until I realise we're going the wrong way. The horse is returning to where its fellow animals are, and I must reach Eadburg. Hastily, I step in front of the animal.

'This way,' I urge it, and for a moment I fear it will argue with me. Some sound from close by, not a cracking twig, because nothing could snap in this wet, but something else encourages the animal to follow me to where I hope I'll find my allies.

Eventually, I have to stop and look at my surroundings. Have I erred? Did the horse know the way after all? I don't recognise any of the trees I walk beside. They all look the same, from what I can see. Some have pine needles and delicate firs, others are denuded, and others still cling to their golden leaves, which flash white in the darkness.

'Bloody hell,' I explode, only to hear the unmistakable sound of footfall. I turn, expecting to see someone following me from behind, but it's impossible to tell from where the noise comes. My hand lingers on my seax, as I consider how I'll fight with a child in my arms. I must, I caution myself, remember not to use him as a shield. I look at the horse. I wish I could slap it on the rump and send it to Eadburg, but of course, it doesn't know where she is. And neither, it seems, do I.

'Bloody hell,' I repeat more softly. Once more, my heart thuds in my chest. I knew the task was far from complete, but now it feels even further from being accomplished. If the enemy warriors come at me, I'll stand no chance. I might, I appreciate, be able to ensure Coenwulf remains free, provided the horse obeys me, but what of Coelwulf? And he was the child who lived when Lady Cynehild died. It's him I must ensure lives through this.

I hear more steps coming closer. I'm sure of it. The tread is soft but unmistakable. Whomever it is moves carefully, desperate not to make any noise. I look down at the sleeping child in my arms and across to where Coenwulf is half-asleep atop the horse, although remaining upright. The animal, wise eyes on a long face, seems to understand my predicament.

Should I mount up? Should I abandon the children here, and rush with the horse to somewhere else, hopeful that the children won't be found and I can return for them later? That seems like a terrible decision. I can't rely on Coelwulf to keep quiet. If he wakes, he'll cry. I know it. And Coenwulf is too young to protect his brother. He has only a wooden horse.

Impatiently, I turn my head, seeking some way to go, some answer to my problems, but it's unachievable. All is blackness or grey, the trees impossible to see from an arm's length in front of my face.

I thought I'd rescued the children. It seems I've merely brought about their death somewhere else.

'Icel.' The word's harsh while remaining soft, a steadying hand on my arm. 'Come on,' Eadburg urges me. 'You're almost there.' I sag in relief, bending to follow her as she joins Coenwulf and the horse, and quickly directs the animal to where she wants to go. I'm unsure how she's managed to creep up on me, but then, the rain is loud, my heartbeat thuds in my ear, and I have to hear over the noise of three people breathing, not just me.

I can still hear my heart thudding in my ear, and the sweat down my back could cure a fish, but at least I'm not alone any more, with two children and only a blunt seax. And one horse.

Eadburg moves swiftly, her confidence assured, and the soft nicker from Brute assures me I'm nearly at his side, despite the penetrating darkness of night.

'Here, give him to me,' Eadburg demands as soon as possible.

Brute watches with his interested eyes. The two other horses stand, heads hanging low, allowing the water to wash down their necks. I pity them the rain, but I feel just as sorry for myself.

'He stinks,' she mutters. I open my mouth to defend myself, but I'm just grateful to have his weight removed from my arms. Now, should the enemy attack, I'll be able to fight them off without worry that I might forget and use Coelwulf as a shield just because I hold him with my shield arm. 'Come on, little man,' she coos to him. I'd caution her not to wake him, but it's too late. I realise his eyes are wide open but that the presence of Eadburg soothes him.

I can't tell what she's doing in the darkness. I reach out to Coenwulf.

'Are you well?' I demand from him, forcing my voice to be gentle.

'Yes,' he speaks around his thumb, but I understand all the same.

'Do you need to pee or anything? We have to begin our journey home straight away.'

'I did already,' his upset voice mutters.

'It doesn't matter. It happens to everyone.' I hope to console him. Hastily, I run my hands along the bodies of the other horses. Brute will be the fastest, I'm sure of it. And the horse upon which Coenwulf is already mounted will also be fine. I'm concerned about the other two. The one is bent-backed, and the other might be limping slightly, but it's not truly possible to tell in what little light there is.

'I'm ready,' Eadburg announces, her shuffling at an end. 'Will I ride with Coelwulf or Coenwulf?'

'Who can you manage easiest? We can bind Coelwulf to you, but not Coenwulf.'

'Then I'll take the youngest. I'm not the best rider, as it is.'

I agree with her decision but don't say as much. 'You should use the horse Coenwulf's on. Here, young man, come with me. You'll ride Brute with me.'

A shrill shriek erupts from him, but he quickly stuffs his thumb in his mouth.

'Have you heard stories of Brute?' I ask him conversationally. I don't have time for this, but I must soothe him. 'That was when he was younger. Now, he's as staid as your father's mount.' I hope such words will stop him from worrying, but then wince at mentioning his father. That was cruel, and I should have known better than to do so.

'So, he won't go too fast then?'

'Not with me and you, no. He'll do as he's told.' There's iron in my words that I hope my horse hears. We've come all this way. It would be bloody typical if he did something regretful now, but we do have the other horses.

Quickly, I grip Coenwulf, and eyeing Brute firmly, place him on the saddle there. There's no saddle for Eadburg. I'd put Brute's on her horse, but then I'll struggle to ride him, and the saddle is too large for the other animal. I consider what Eadburg's doing. Only then she turns and faces me triumphantly. I should have done this when I gathered Coelwulf to me. She has him held tight to her body, using only a piece of fabric she must have taken from one of the horses. He's held firmly in place there, but she still needs to mount. I also notice that while there's no saddle, there is another piece of cloth over the horse. At least she'll have something to stop her skin from rubbing with the movement of the animal.

'Here, I'll help you,' I urge her, offering my hand for her foot.

'Oh,' and I hear contrition in her voice. She's forgotten about this part of the process. It takes longer than it should to get her on the horse. I'm sure Coelwulf must have been squashed, but he makes no complaint. As soon as she's mounted, the animal pliant beneath her, I hasten to Brute, and carefully settle behind Coenwulf. He tries to shuffle forward to allow me more room, but I hold him tight.

'Stay there. There's more than enough space for the two of us.'

With the leading ropes of the other two horses in my hand, I turn to Eadburg.

'You know the way better than I do,' I grudgingly admit. She's easing herself into position on the horse.

'Then, follow me,' she chuckles softly. I want to relax, as she seems to have done, confident now that she has Coelwulf in her arms that we can manage to escape, but I remain fearful. For someone terrified of horses, she's certainly taken to riding well. Perhaps, after all, Edwin had taught her to ride, but the fear of Brute made her forget. I wish I knew.

I've stolen the children, dispersed the horses, and killed a man. Yet there are still many more of those warriors out there, and we're a bloody long way from home, with no food left, and little to give the children succour until we return to Mercia. We can hope, when they wake, that the enemy will think to find the lost children north from here, but I believe they'll soon realise what's happened. After all, with so many horses and warriors to protect the children, they must be expecting retribution from Mercia.

And even when we return to Mercia, who'll be waiting for the children? And what will they say to explain what's happened to them? I remember the object I took from the canvas. Perhaps that will hold all the answers I need.

With the branches leaving trails of wet to pool down my shoulders and back, I focus on keeping Eadburg in sight. If I lose her, I'll never find my way out of the woodland in the dark.

Our progress is frustratingly slow, but the sound of the rain covers our departure, and finally we win free from the trees. Not that it's daylight beyond the woodland. The sun might have risen, but the clouds remain so low that it could still be night. The rain continues to fall in a torrent, and in moments I'm as wet as I was when I first climbed into the tent to find the children.

I'm aware that young Coenwulf sleeps before me, his head resting on my right arm, his body slumped against mine. He feels so fragile and delicate. How, I think, could anyone mean the two children harm? I find it frightening how easy it would have been to kill them. Perhaps I should be grateful that they allowed the boys to live, despite bringing them so many days north of Mercia.

I'd like to encourage Brute to greater speed, but in the dank day, it's as dangerous as during the night.

'We should go faster,' Eadburg whispers to me, as I draw level. Coelwulf sleeps as well, his cheeks pink against the grey of the day.

'I know, but the roads will be slick and no doubt running with water and mud. And you have no true saddle, only the lead reins of the horse to guide him with.'

The two other horses finally lift their heads. I feel them tugging the lead ropes that I clutch in my hands. I eye them. Both animals look miserable. Whoever rode them here wasn't kind to them. The one, I'm sure, must have been used to carry supplies and not a person. Its coat is rubbed in places, revealing red welts where the skin has been broken. I'd like to tend to the wounds but now isn't the time.

'So, can we go faster or not?' Eadburg asks anxiously.

'A little. No more than a trot. Let me know if you feel your horse start to slow. He's better than the other two and will have more stamina.'

She nods but bites her lip, looking back the way we've come. 'Will they come after us?'

'I imagine so. It's just whether they've found their mounts or not. But, come on, we should hurry as much as we can.'

With my neck itching from being wet, then damp, then dry and then damp again, I grip Coenwulf more tightly, wishing I could trust the horses to follow us without the ropes, but I can't. Encumbered with child, two horses, and no means of reaching my seax for Coenwulf sleeps on my arm, I give Brute a gentle nudge, and he lumbers to a trot.

The sound of his hooves over the uneven stone surface resounds too loudly, but there's nothing for it. We must make more haste.

26

We ride all morning. The clouds never lift, although eventually the rain stops falling. I don't think I've ever been as wet. We stop twice to water the animals, and to allow us all to stretch our legs. There's no food for the children, and I can tell they're hungry. When we ate the last of the bread and cheese, I knew we'd be in trouble. But, then, I hadn't expected to travel so far north. I had no idea of the location that Wynflæd told me to find, only that it was north. In fact, I still don't know if I've reached that location. There are precious few people in this region, and none of them seem keen to share the names of their holdings.

Coenwulf holds his complaints, gripping his wooden horse tightly. Coelwulf, so much younger, doesn't know to stop grouching, and eventually I call a further halt, convinced I've seen a bush ripe with late berries that we can eat.

'Here.' Eagerly, I pull them clear from the barbs of the bush and hand them to Eadburg. She takes them and aids Coelwulf to get them in his mouth. His eyes brighten at the unfamiliar taste, as dark, red juice drips down his chin. Coenwulf takes his fill as well, and as I work my way along the bush, I'm aware of the horses bending to pull at the grasses. I even see Brute helping himself to one of the berries. I can hardly wait to see what colour his shit will be after that.

Not that the berries are that filling, but they're something, and mean we can eat without having to ask any of the few people we see working in fields, or trying to dry out after the deluge. We might be instantly recognisable, should our enemy ask these people if they've seen us, should they think to come south, and I'm doing my best to keep others safe from trouble.

'Will we make it to Chester tonight?' Eadburg asks me. She's released Coelwulf from his sling and now he clings to her skirt, pulling himself up and down with a smile on his face. He's not yet walking, but it won't be long, I'm sure of that. He seems to be robust. I feared for him last night, but perhaps I shouldn't have done. With the chunkiness of childhood, he seems stronger than his older brother who, I note, has begun to lose the chubby cheeks of babyhood.

'No, not a chance. We're still too far from Chester. And, even if we reach there, I don't believe we should risk visiting the place. Our only hope is to get to Kingsholm. There, the people who're loyal to Lord Coenwulf will protect his sons, even in his absence.'

'So you don't mean to seek out the king, then?'

'No. I still don't understand what's at play here. The children will only be safe at Kingsholm and nowhere else.' As I speak, I'm reminded of the item I found in the canvas. I reach into my weapons belt, and pull it forth. It's a brooch, of that I'm sure. Made from gold, and festooned with flashing rubies. It glints even in the dull day, and I show it to Eadburg.

'Did you see them with this?'

She reaches over and grabs the brooch, her eyebrows furrowed in thought. 'No, I didn't. It looks like a family heirloom.'

I nod along with her. She's right, it does, and I don't miss that the rubies are truly eyes on the brooch, the creature, an eagle, I'm sure of it, seeming to look right through me.

I suppress a shudder. This is an expensive item, and it speaks of the family who've taken the children, or so I think. This is something fit for a king, or a family descended from kings. Once more, my thoughts turn to Lord Beorhtwulf. Is this his hand at play, as I suspected? Is this some means of payment for his warriors, or is it something that must be handed over, along with the children, to prove the identity of the warriors who captured the children? I wish I knew. It worries me though. Not having the brooch, but knowing that those involved have something this valuable, means they're wealthy. They can afford to pay a great deal of coin to accomplish their goal, whatever that is.

I eye the children. Were they to be killed, far from Mercia and where their bodies couldn't be found, or did someone want them alive? To what ends, I'm unsure, although, well, they could be thinking far into the future when both children are men and can claim Mercia as their own.

Eadburg nods as she realises that I don't trust the king with the children, and looks unhappy about how much further we still need to travel.

'We need food,' she cautions, her hands sticky with the juices of the berries.

'I know, but we can survive. It's the children I worry about.'

'They'll get poorly bellies if we offer them nothing but berries,' she cautions, as though I'm unaware of that.

'We all will,' I mutter darkly. I swig water from my water bottle and offer the same to Coenwulf. He drinks eagerly. I really look at him in this unguarded moment. His clothes are heavily soiled, and there's a rip running from his neck down his chest. Beneath it, I see a welter of green and yellow bruises, and my fury returns. Whomever these men were, they're lucky to live still. But I don't think they will for long. Once I've returned the children to Kingsholm, I'll seek them out. I must know the truth of what happened here. I need to understand who was at fault. Perhaps Ealdorman Ælfstan will be able to help me with that. He'll know to whom the emblem I have belongs. I place it back in my saddlebags. 'Did you hear the names of the men who took you?'

I realise I've not really asked her what she knew, too determined to find the children.

'Well, yes, but no one I recognised. The men had the usual sorts of names. I heard them mention one name a lot, but he was clearly not there with them. Maybe that was who they were going to meet?'

'What was the name?' I ask, hopeful of finally getting some answers.

'Wulfnoth,' she announces confidently.

'Wulfnoth?' I repeat, trying to determine if I know anyone with such a name, but I don't. It's unusual enough that I would remember someone called that, I'm sure of it. And then Eadburg distracts me from my musings.

'So what now?' she questions.

'We carry on as long as we can and while we can see. Is your horse well? We can put you on one of the others?'

'He's fine. I'll keep him. I'm used to his gait.' Eadburg yawns around the words and I appreciate how little sleep we've had. It's all well and good for the children, they can sleep while we guard them. But Eadburg and I can't sleep on the horses.

I nod. She's right. The other two horses don't share the same rhythm as the one she rides.

'Come on then. We can get further today. I'm sure of it.' But all the same, fear niggles along my spine. We do need to get some sleep. But where? I don't know anyone here. I don't trust anyone, and I'm sure, no matter that we scattered the horses, our enemy will be following us soon enough.

Eadburg nods, but I can tell she's unhappy as she yawns again.

I glance over my shoulder, suddenly feeling like we're being watched. But there's no one there. Not at the moment. I don't know how long that will last.

We could, I consider, hide close to the rocks, but despite the remnants of the stone road we follow, there's enough mud on it for the hoof prints of the horses to be clearly seen. Wherever we go, we'll be easy to track.

We need more people to be about, to confuse the tracks we leave, but with the weather as bad as it is, that's not likely.

'Mount up. Let's be on our way.'

Coenwulf's eager to ride once more, but Coelwulf's unwilling to be bound to Eadburg after his moments of freedom. Face streaked with the purple and reds of the berries, his chunky legs kick out. After long moments, when even Eadburg's stern voice doesn't make him obey, I realise I'll have to have him before me.

'Here, you take Coenwulf, and I'll have Coelwulf.' The thought fills me with trepidation, but we've tarried too long already. Eadburg looks as unhappy as I feel but mounts up, bunching her skirts around her legs and revealing long, pale legs over the blanket that covers her mount's back. I move Coenwulf from Brute to her animal. The horse moves uneasily under the greater weight but settles. I then turn to Coelwulf. 'Come on then.' I heave him into my arms, mindful of holding him too tightly. If Coenwulf's bruised then no doubt Coelwulf is as well. With more luck than skill, I manage to settle myself in the saddle, with Coelwulf wriggling before me. I can't see his face, but Eadburg surprises me by laughing, the unexpected sound a source of delight amongst the stresses and strains of the last few days.

'You should see him,' she giggles. 'His mouth is wide open, his teeth stained red. If he were any older, and you weren't behind him, I'd think he'd battled his enemy and vanquished them.'

'I just hope he sits still,' I grumble, not finding any enjoyment in the feel of him before me. I don't know where to hold him, or how to hold him. I can see why Eadburg bound him to her. His legs are too short, his arms lacking the reach to take hold of the reins, and Brute is much taller than Eadburg's horse. I fear he'll tumble to the ground and be crushed beneath my horse's hooves should we have to hasten on our way.

But Brute, for all his difficult nature, settles with the youngster behind his neck. I loop part of the rein around Coelwulf, binding him to Brute and then to me in such a way. It's far from secure, but I can direct Brute with my knees. The reins are there for when he startles and dashes onwards. I don't believe he'll be doing that. Not at the moment, anyway.

Aware that what daylight there is is beginning to fade, I encourage Brute on. I've no choice but to allow the other horses to follow on if they will. I can't hold Coelwulf as well. I reach over and loop the lead ropes over their necks.

I watch them as Brute moves on. Neither animal seems keen to follow, and I give them up as lost. I should perhaps have sent them running into the wilderness that surrounds us rather than leave them there for our enemy to find. But then, just as I've given up on them, I hear hooves, and turn, expecting trouble, only to find both of them rushing to keep up.

That solves one problem for me.

We ride on. The day grows dark, for all it was hardly light at all. Coelwulf relaxes before me, and I find I can keep a firm hold on him, after all. We ride in silence, other than the beats of the horses' hooves and, eventually, I jolt awake, and return to my musings of who is responsible for stealing the children. I wish I knew whom Wulfnoth was. It wasn't the name that Wynflæd whispered to me. No, that was Eamont.

Overhead, the thick clouds of the last day have finally cleared, and the brightness of the moon and stars ensures we can see well enough to continue riding. Eadburg sleeps, as does Coenwulf. I reach over to touch her shoulder when I fear she might slide from the horse's back. She wakes, sees me and immediately looks guilty.

'Sorry,' she mumbles, yawning around the word.

'It's not a problem. I've been watching you.' The horses have slowed to a walk. We all need some rest, but where still remains a problem. I can't see anywhere that would provide shelter enough for me to protect the children, Eadburg and the horses, should our progress be being tracked. But my eyes are gritty and I can barely sit still any more, my legs thrumming with the pain of being deadened for a long time now.

'We need to stop,' she cautions me.

'I know we do,' I murmur. 'It's more the where that I don't know.'

But, as though summoned, something rears up before me, and I glower at the black maw of the cave. It'll have to do.

'Over there.' I direct her up a steep incline, eyes peering all around me, eager to ensure no wild animals will attack us while we sleep.

The cave itself is partially obscured by huge rocks but if I can see it by moonlight, then anyone else will be able to. It's also well known because when I dismount, holding Coelwulf as securely as I dare, I see the remnants of fires and the detritus of men and women who've used the cave before.

'Get some sleep,' I urge Eadburg and the children. I've hardly finished speaking, and the three of them are curled up on the hard ground. The horses merge together, the two slower animals taking the opportunity to lie down, whereas Eadburg's horse, and Brute, remain standing.

I yawn, reaching for my seax and finding comfort in the blunt blade. I've still not retrieved my treasured stolen eagle-handled seax from Eadweard and Wulfred, who I must assume still have it. The loss of it is upsetting and unsettling. If someone should understand the intent of the eagle handle, I could be in trouble, especially if Eadweard and Wulfred have given it to this Wulfnoth, whomever he is. If I've interpreted the brooch correctly, and his intent behind taking the children, then he knows the significance of my seax's emblem.

I talk to myself, aware I need to stay away. I stand to the side of the cave, and then I walk across it, and then I stand beside Brute, but at some point I must slump to the ground and sleep.

When I wake to the distressed cries of the horses, my hand reaches for my blunt seax, and I'm on my feet immediately. It's still night-time, and the clouds have returned, obscuring the moon and stars. I strain to hear what's upset the horses, and then I see it. Yellow eyes glinting, the wolf slinks towards the cave.

It seems one of the cave's inhabitants has returned.

And he's hungry.

27

'Wake up, Eadburg,' I call to her, not caring if there are others close by who might hear my words as well. 'Eadburg, wake up.' I'm working my way closer to where she lies, blunt seax in hand, but never taking my eyes away from the wolf. The animal, air blowing before it, watches me with disinterest. I wish it were the same animal that I met outside Hereford, the one that seemed to have some connection to the Wolf Lady, but it's not. This creature is younger, more lithe, and its eyes glow orange.

Eadburg rouses quickly, a squeal on her lips as she realises my concern.

'Get the boys off the ground, and hand one of them to me.' I can't risk looking away from the animal to reach for Coenwulf or Coelwulf. I'm daring it to attack me, my thoughts returning to the wolf who aided me in the woodlands close to Hereford. I can't imagine this beast will be as helpful.

A sleepy Coelwulf is placed in my arms while I listen to Eadburg hastening Coenwulf to stand.

'With me, towards the horses.' Blunt seax still menacing, and with Eadburg behind me, we move to where Brute's watching while the other three horses complain against their tethers. I'm just glad I thought to secure them for the night, or they'd be long gone.

I listen to Eadburg calming the animals, and then, what feels a lifetime later, she calls to me.

'We're ready.'

'Then go, and take the two other horses with you. I'll be along shortly.'

The wolf continues to growl, orange eyes wide in the darkness, but it's stayed far enough away that I don't believe it means to attack us. I almost think it wants me to leave without any trouble. Hastily, I fumble for Brute behind me, lifting Coelwulf upwards, hoping he'll be able to grab Brute's mane and stay upright, until I can mount behind him.

I feared our enemy would catch us, but I also appreciated that wolves must inhabit these lands. Now, I need to get away from here without the wolf attacking.

A sudden movement, as I finally turn aside from the animal, and I try to mount up, only I mistime the action, and instead have to reach for Coelwulf or risk him falling. Now I can hear the sharp tapping of the animal's claws over the stones. Sweat beads my face, but I seek calmness, and once more try to mount. This time, my leg swings easily over the saddle, Coelwulf remains upright, and just as the wolf emits a long, bowel-loosening call for its fellow animals, I'm encouraging Brute to move on more quickly than I should.

I don't risk looking behind me. I don't need to. My hearing is alert to the noise of other animals joining the wolf, and sharp yips fill the night air.

How I've escaped again, from the clutches of a wolf, I don't know. I'm grateful as I catch up to Eadburg and the other horses. Her face is pale in the dull light. Coenwulf is again slumped in sleep, but Coelwulf wriggles before me because I've not managed to secure him as I did before.

Once more on the roadway, I take a moment to tangle Coelwulf in the reins and settle myself.

'Are you well?' I call to Eadburg.

'Yes, now. But will they follow us?'

'I doubt it. We've nothing for them to eat.'

'Other than ourselves,' she squeaks, and the sound brings a grin to my tight cheeks.

'Perhaps you. The boys will be little more than a mouthful.' An outraged shriek erupts, but I realise she's smiling as well.

'Bloody hell,' she gasps, a while later, when I feel the tension in my shoulders disperse. 'That was too close.'

'It was, yes, but we've survived that obstacle, and you did get some sleep.'

'Yes,' she confirms. 'Did you?'

'Evidently, yes, for the wolf crept up on me as well.'

'I'm grateful something woke you.' I am as well, although I don't really know what it was. I'm sure the animal could have moved more stealthily if it had wanted to. Maybe, I consider, it didn't fancy eating small children and a muscly warrior.

'We'll ride until daybreak,' I confirm, trying to decide how long that will be. But the clouds are too low and filled with fury. And then, just when I think it can't get any worse, the heavens open, and once more we're covered in rain. It falls so hard, I can hardly see in front of my face. However, the rain has one advantage. It'll cover our tracks from any who think to hunt us, even stirring the muddy hoof prints of the horses.

But it's miserable going. The rain sheets into my face, and Brute's head dips lower and lower. I have a cloak, but it's already swirled over my shoulders, and it doesn't help, not when the rain is coming from the south, instead of the north.

Before me, Coelwulf begins to cry, his sounds soft and filled with misery. It's almost as though he doesn't want to complain, but is left with no choice.

Ahead, Eadburg's head is also down, and every so often I hear her softly singing to Coenwulf. I consider what I could sing to Coelwulf. All the scop songs I know are concerned with war and death. With the Viking raiders, or warrior kings who died many winters ago. I can offer him nothing, but as it seems to be calming Coenwulf, I do think to softly hum the tunes I know. The sound begins deep in my chest, reverberating into the small body held tight to me. It must work, for his cries cease, and I think he sleeps.

Our horses make their way through the settlement with the hound and the woman, but only a mournful cry disturbs the slumbers of those beneath thatch roofs and behind firm walls. I would welcome joining them, but any attempt would be met with force at this time of the day, I'm sure of it.

A hazy grey light begins to turn the world from shadows and blackness to the monochrome of a new day. But the rain doesn't let up, and even I'm hungry now. The berries from yesterday feel like a distant memory.

The smell of woodsmoke slowly permeates my thoughts, and I squint, wishfully hoping that we might be close to somewhere that we can shelter.

I don't believe we've outrun our enemy, not yet, but the weather, and our steady gait southwards, must be giving us some chance of escaping them.

I ride closer to Eadburg. Her eyes shine at me from a face etched in cold, her lips almost blue.

'We'll have to stop,' I call to her. Ahead, the settlement of Chester is finally coming into view. I didn't plan on seeking shelter inside its ancient and tumbled-down walls, for fear the red-haired woman might be there, keen to alert someone to our presence, but there's no choice.

We're too cold and hungry to continue. I risk wounding the children further, and I won't do that. But I do wish I knew more people inside Chester other than young Godfrith and the man at the tavern when I stopped there on my journey north. If I knew the lord here, perhaps I could seek protection from him, but so far from the heart of Mercia, half of the inhabitants perhaps don't even know whom King Wiglaf is, let alone Lord Coenwulf.

'I know,' Eadburg exhales swiftly. I consider what to do, but really, there's little choice. I won't separate us and place us in danger by being apart.

'We ride in together,' I urge her. 'I have some coins, and we have the horses we could sell, if necessary.' I don't want to go to the same tavern as before. Yes, Godfrith would aid us, but what if that red-haired woman is still there? I can't help feeling her interest in me was far from benign. She might know who Wulfnoth is. She might know how to get in touch with him and then we'd be chased back to Mercia. I consider if she did follow me northwards as I attempted to reach Eamont. I'm not sure anyone has been following me, not in the terrible rain, but I suppose it is possible.

'A meal and a fire can't cost the same as a horse?' Eadburg questions me.

'It depends if the people here know who we are and what we're doing, but I hope not,' I agree, and direct Brute towards the gate I exited through on my journey north. The guards watch me approaching from beneath the shelter of an arch where the gate has been opened. At least, I think, it's the time of day when visitors are welcomed inside.

'A grim day,' a rough voice calls to me, but the speaker makes no effort to bar our entrance.

'It's been raining for three bloody days,' the voice of the other guard answers querulously. I don't recognise either of them. I hope they don't recognise me either.

'Where can we find warmth and a dry roof?' I call to them, hopeful of the name of a different tavern.

'You want Æthelgyth at the Broken Ship,' the first man calls, pointing along a road that veers towards the west. 'She has a soft spot for the youngsters, poor woman,' he continues. I consider what he means by that, but I'm already turning Brute the way he directs.

The street's quiet. No one thinks it a good idea to be out in the deluge. With relief, I see a battered sail ahead, hanging limply in the dank conditions, its white linen dyed to yellow and showing some emblem that I can't determine while it's tangled by the storm.

The sound of the horses' hooves occasions a startled face to peer through a doorway, closed, and then opened, but protected by the eaves of the house.

'Oh my goodness,' a stick-thin woman calls, a cloak over her head. 'Oswin, hurry and help these poor people with their horses.' An audible groan greets her words, but I'm dismounting, gripping Coelwulf as I go. I hasten to take Coenwulf from Eadburg, and place him on the mud-churned ground. Only then does Eadburg slide from her horse. By then, poor Oswin, a man, not a boy as I first thought, has grumbled his way outside, entirely covered by a sealskin cloak more likely to be found on the back of a shipman than a stableman in a tavern.

He startles on seeing Brute, a slow smile spreading over his face.

'He's a fine specimen,' Oswin mutters.

'He is, yes, but damn feisty when he's not drenched and miserable.'

'Aye, well, I'll see him well cared for.'

Thinking nothing of it, Oswin gathers the reins of all the horses and leads them to the other side of the street, where I realise a stable stands beneath the shelter of the stone wall.

'Come in, come in. Look at you all. It's not a day to travel.'

Æthelgyth's words are kindly meant, but I don't miss the sharp look she gives me on glimpsing the warrior's belt around my waist.

The heat greeting us is welcome, and quickly we all remove cloaks. Eadburg, after appraising Coenwulf and Coelwulf, and realising that we're alone in the tavern, removes their tunics and trews, leaving them in little more than cloths over their arses, revealing the starkness of the bruises that cover their small bodies. I grumble low in my throat, wishing I could fight the bastards who did that to them here and now.

Coelwulf crawls towards the fire while Coenwulf clutches his wooden horse, eyes wide in a pale face.

Æthelgyth bustles around beside the hearth, watchful, spooning a meaty pottage into four wooden bowls, and handing them to the three of us able to feed ourselves. Coenwulf takes the bowl eagerly, tipping it so he can eat. But Æthelgyth eyes Coelwulf with interest.

'A fine-looking babe,' she acknowledges, face shadowed. I consider what grief she carries with her. 'Come here, little man, and I'll help you.' I watch her as she carefully moves aside morsels too big for his small mouth. He eats eagerly, and I realise I can still see the vestiges of his last berry meal on his chin.

'I won't ask questions,' Æthelgyth murmurs as she feeds him. Eadburg helps Coenwulf, forcing him to use a spoon instead of tipping the food into his belly. 'But we hear strange things in these parts of lost children and Mercian thieves. I take it these are them?'

'Perhaps,' I offer after too long has elapsed. I don't know what to say. I don't know whom she is. At that, the door creaks open, and my hand reaches for my blunt seax, but it's just Oswin. He grumbles beneath his breath, as he swirls the sealskin cloak from his back and hangs it close to the door to drip there.

'Bloody rain,' I hear him mutter as he glances at us. 'Your horses are tired, but I've given them what they need. They require some rest, though. And one of them has a wound on his foreleg. Looks nasty, so I've packed it with some herbs I know.'

'My thanks,' I call to him, hoping Æthelgyth will say nothing further. But, of course, she does.

'You look too young to be the mother of that boy.' Æthelgyth indicates Coenwulf with her chin, her eyes on Eadburg's. 'And neither of you look the sort to beat young babes.'

'She's not my mother.' Coenwulf saves us from having to say anything, and I wish I'd cautioned him before we came inside. 'My mother's dead, and my father's gone away. This is Eadburg. She looks after me, at home. With her mother.' He says 'home' with obvious relish, and Æthelgyth nods along with him, although Eadburg hisses at the reminder of her dead mother.

'So he's not your father?'

'Icel?' Coenwulf gurgles. 'He's a warrior. Have you seen his horse? Brute is a fine animal.' Æthelgyth continues to nod along with him, and I feel a slither of worry worm its way along my spine.

'I did see Brute. And he is a mighty fine beast.' Oswin enters the conversation, having helped himself to a bowl of pottage.

'So, you're returning to your home?' Æthelgyth questions. Coenwulf has taken his wooden horse to Oswin's side, proudly showing it off. Oswin admires the wooden animal. I consider then whom these two are. Are they partners or is Oswin Æthelgyth's servant? It's impossible to tell.

'We are. But the weather's against us.'

'Only the weather?' she queries, her tone deceptively light.

'Perhaps not, I admit.'

'And you bring trouble to my door?'

'Potentially, yes. But it was that or brave the elements for longer, and that imperilled the children.'

'Aye, it did,' she confirms. 'But you'll be safe here for a while. The horses aren't visible from the street, and few come this way. Those at the gate know I only welcome families into my tavern. The men who fight and drink themselves insensible aren't to savour the delights of my cooking, or my ale. Now, you can rest here all day. Oswin told me this morning that the rain would clear by tonight, didn't you, Oswin? That old sea leg of yours?'

'The damn thing aches when it's going to rain, but it doesn't hurt too much today.' Oswin winks as he speaks. 'I'm sure we'll be dry in no time at all.'

'My thanks,' Eadburg finally speaks.

'There's a room through that curtain, and it has beds for all of you. And there's warm water to clean yourselves with. While you rest, I'll prepare some food for you to take with you. I'll wake you when it's time to leave.' With that, she collects Coelwulf in her arms and gives him a hearty cuddle, as she carries his nodding head towards where she indicated.

'She's a good woman,' Oswin speaks into the sudden silence. 'She'll see you right,' he confirms, and then ambles to his feet as well. 'Excuse me, young man, I must get back to the bread.'

I share a glance with Eadburg, but she's too tired to talk.

'Get some rest,' I urge her, and she takes Coenwulf's hand and leads him after Æthelgyth. I take a moment to take a calming breath, and rub my hands over my eyes and shabby-looking beard. I must look a fright, but this journey is far from over, no matter how secure I feel beneath the eaves of Æthelgyth's tavern. All the same, I step towards her as soon as she's back in the main room.

'A red-haired women, at the other tavern, saw me leave here a few days ago. Is she likely to mean me trouble?'

Æthelgyth's eyes narrow at that. 'No, the poor woman sells her body to fill her belly. I doubt she means you ill. And, she's unwelcome here. But, should I see her while you rest, I'll send her on her way, and have Oswin ensure she doesn't mean you harm.'

I feel more relaxed knowing the red-haired woman's story, although I do still fear she might be selling more than her body. But the memory of her reminds me of someone else.

'There's a boy, at the other tavern. He has no mother or father,' I say urgently. 'I gave him coin for a cloak and new shoes, but winter is coming.'

Æthelgyth nods at my words. 'I know him, yes, a sad story. I thought the monks cared for him,' she adds.

'Not enough,' I caution, and her lips twist in thought. 'He's good with horses,' I offer as though this might sway her.

'I'm sure he is.' She smiles, although her eyes remain sad. 'I'll see if Oswin can find him. Now, sleep, before you fall over.' And, with that, she moves away, without a backwards glance, and I follow Eadburg and the children.

If only we could be assured of such a warm welcome at Tamworth, then I could drastically reduce our journey time, but I can't. There's too much at play. I find my hand clutching the brooch one more time, and wish I knew more about the person who had it – the man I killed in a canvas somewhere in the far north who had been in charge of the two children.

28

I don't think I'll sleep, but I do, and a hand on my arm wakes me when I'd still rather be asleep.

'The rain's stopped,' a familiar voice says to me, and I startle awake, opening my eyes on Æthelgyth.

The children wake quickly, as does Eadburg. I'm astounded when Æthelgyth hands Eadburg two small tunics for the boys to wear and two cloaks as well.

'The others are fit for burning,' she mouths, and once more, I recall the words of the gate man that morning. Stepping into the main room of the tavern, a tantalising smell of pottage and pork almost has me salivating. There's still no one else there other than Oswin, and I consider how Æthelgyth makes enough coin to keep the place free from the heavy drinkers. I fumble in my pouch, pleased to feel the weight of coins there. I can pay handsomely for this brief oasis of peace she's given us.

We eat once more, and then I stand, ready to go. From outside, I can hear the sound of heavy rain, but abruptly, it ceases, and Oswin grins.

'I told you, woman,' he calls to Æthelgyth.

She rolls her eyes, even while helping young Coenwulf with his cloak. 'Aye, you did. A pity your damn leg can give you no inkling of when enemies might attack Chester.' The pair have an easy camaraderie, and I find myself pining for Wulfheard, Oswy and the others. With them at my side, I'd have felt far more assured of outrunning whoever must be chasing us. When Ealdorman Ælfstan bid me travel to Kingsholm ahead of the rest of the men, I doubt he anticipated I'd find myself in Chester and halfway to Strathclyde.

'My thanks.' I reach out to grip her hand, a heavy weight of coins in mine. She takes them without even looking and leans towards me.

'Keep them safe, no matter what,' she murmurs. I swallow against the sudden desolation in her words.

'I will. I gave my oath to their mother.'

'Then you're a good man. I'll pray for you,' she offers before bending, kissing both children on the cheek, and purposefully moving back to the hearth. Her back to us, she doesn't watch us leave.

Outside, rain drips from the roofs, and pools in the wooden gutters along the street, but it's stopped falling from the leaden sky. Oswin beckons me over to the stable. I'm greeted by the sight of all four horses, bright-eyed and eager to resume our journey.

'A fine horse, that one,' Oswin confirms. 'Feisty, as you say, but he knows his worth.'

I grin, reaching out to rub my hand along Brute's nose. His nostrils flare at my touch. The stables are warm and dry, not even a trace of water dripping from the tightly woven roof above our head.

Hastily, we mount up, and I see that Oswin has found a saddle for Eadburg which will make it much easier for her. Eadburg takes Coelwulf, wrapped tight to her body, and I have Coenwulf, who can sit well enough himself in the saddle. And then I look to the other horses. A bandage is wrapped around the leg of the one with the bowed back. Her eyes, while keen, also show some fatigue.

'Can you keep her here?' I ask Oswin. 'She's been badly used.'

'I can, yes. She'll do nothing but be pampered, I assure you. As will that boy when I can entice him here. I've found him, be assured. It'll help Æthelgyth to have someone young about the place.' He nods while speaking, and the thought cheers me. Better he's not here to see us leave, but at least we can resume our journey, and I needn't fear Godfrith will succumb to the coming winter weather.

'My thanks.' I reach over to grip his forearm. 'My sincere thanks,' I repeat before releasing my grip and leading Brute from the stable, another handful of good Mercian coins slipping into his hand. I feel refreshed and filled with confidence, as opposed to fear. Let whoever is chasing us come at us. I know I can fight to hold them off now.

Without a backwards glance, we retrace our steps to the gate and emerge into the dull shades of dusk. It's different men on guard duty, but they call farewell to us all the same, without any hint that they might be conniving with those hunting us. Apprehensively, I glance north but see no sign of anyone following us. Perhaps, after all, we might make it home before we're overtaken by the boys' captors.

I regret that thought. We rejoin Watling Street south of Chester, and ride all night, taking advantage of a rapidly clearing sky and a slice of moon to light the way. But we've not gone fast. The horses are rested but still tired from their exertions.

As dawn breaks, the hills to the west greet us, and I'm pleased to be somewhere familiar. Only then, as we pause to relieve ourselves, drink and allow the horses some time to nibble at the grasses, I hear the sound I've been dreading ever since retrieving the boys from the woodlands in the far north.

From behind, the thunder of many hooves sends birds flying high into the sky, denizens of the woodlands, scampering for safety. Squinting back the way we've come, I can't quite see the horses, but there's no other reason for horses to be racing anywhere at this time of the day. They must be hunting us, taking advantage of the clear night, as we've just done.

'Quickly, mount up,' I call to Eadburg. She grips Coelwulf tightly, hands fumbling with the knots to secure him to her. I thrust Coenwulf into the saddle and follow him, ensuring Eadburg's mounted.

I'm unsure where we can seek refuge, but now isn't the time to worry about that. We just need to keep ahead of them and, if possible, slip into the woodlands closer to the Welsh kingdoms. I don't know them well, but I do know a man and two small youths can hide out there for months at a time. My uncle taught me that. It might be harder with two small children and Eadburg, but I've not come so far to lose hope now.

Eadburg, so scared of the horse when I first asked her to mount Brute, bends low and encourages her horse onwards at a speed that Brute struggles to match for a few moments, now that she has a proper saddle. The other horse is quick to follow. The three animals take advantage of the better road construction here to thunder onwards. I can still just about hear the horses coming from behind, but we're certainly maintaining the gap, if nothing else. My biggest fear is that, at some point, the way ahead might be so clear that they can see us. That'll encourage them to ride all the faster, and we can't go any more quickly than we are. Well, Brute could, but I'm not leaving Eadburg behind. Or Coelwulf. Lady Cynehild bid me protect her sons, and Edwin urged me to keep the woman he loves safe. I need to do all of those things.

Once more, I wish I had Wulfheard and Oswy beside me. Ealdorman Ælfstan as well. I'm convinced he could stop those behind from chasing us. He might even be able to bring them before the king to answer for their crimes, provided the queen or her son isn't involved. I consider where he is. He must have arrived at Kingsholm long ago. Is he seeking us, or is he waiting for me to reappear? I wish I knew.

We hurry onwards. The day grows brighter, but the horses eventually slow, only not before I've led them off the side of the road. The ground's churned with the hooves of many horses. Someone must have camped here and not long ago. The mud that's formed has allowed huge impressions of the horses' hooves to remain visible, but where those horses are now, I don't know. In fact, we've seen no one all morning. We've only heard those chasing us. For a moment, I consider what might have happened in my brief absence from the heart of the kingdom. Could the Viking raiders have attacked? Could King Ecgberht have breached the southern borders again? But that's not my concern. The children and Eadburg are.

'This way,' I direct Eadburg, thinking to take advantage of the churned ground to hide our departure from the road. She follows on behind, as does our single spare horse. Immediately, we're shrouded beneath the boughs of huge trees, and in no time at all the way behind us is as dark as night, obscured by the sweeping branches overhead.

I slow Brute so that we don't risk colliding with the lower branches or trunks of the trees. The ground's uneven and spongy, with a fine mat of rich needles embedded with the mud. All sound is muffled as I calm my racing heartbeat.

I strain to hear the hooves from Watling Street, but it's impossible. It's as though we've stepped into another world beneath the trees. There's no one here but the horses, us, and a few small animals that scamper beyond our reach. I don't want to think we've evaded them. I hastily dampen down the spark of hope that surges within me. If the sound of our movements is masked, then the same will apply to those behind – if they were following us, and I'm sure they must have been.

Young Coenwulf, lulled by the slow gait of Brute, slumbers in front of me. I stifle a yawn as well. Turning behind, I realise that I've lost sight of Eadburg. I turn Brute frantically, fearful that we've become parted. That I can't see the other horse either assures me that I've lost them both, although how I don't know.

I hear something scurrying closer, and my hand reaches for the blunt seax. I breathe a sigh of relief when it's the stray horse that emerges from the trees behind me, followed by Eadburg. I see the problem quickly. Eadburg sleeps on the horse's back, head lolling from side to side, Coelwulf silent in her arms. At least he's quiet while he's asleep. His high voice won't give away our location. And Eadburg needs to sleep. She still mourns the loss of her mother and has yet to return to Kingsholm and tell her siblings. I pity her with such sorrow.

'Good horse,' I encourage the one leading the way. Brute touches the other animal's nose, and I consider waking both riders, but there seems little need. They should sleep while they can.

The day advances slowly. I direct Brute in a direction I hope is south when we're deep within the woodlands. I know the treeline won't run to Kingsholm and that, at some point, there'll be rivers and streams to cross, but with the woodlands closing in around me, I allow myself to relax. No one can attack us here. There's hardly room for the horses to pass between the trees, let alone a man with a blade to hand. And if they come in a group, they'll stand no chance.

Eadburg wakes with a yawn and gasps at where we are as she eyes the late afternoon sunlight falling through the dense canopy overhead. I offer her a smirk on meeting her gaze.

'Good sleep?' I call to her. She smiles shyly and bends to check on Coelwulf. He still slumbers. The last few days have taken their toll on everyone. I yawn again. The indeterminate colours of the woodland are fading quickly to darkness. 'We should camp,' I say softly, fearful that if I speak too loudly, I'll disturb the wildlife letting us pass without squawk or shriek to give us away.

'Yes, we should,' she confirms. 'You can get some sleep then. Do you think we're any closer to Kingsholm?' I'm glad Eadburg doesn't ask if we're still being followed because I'm unsure whether we are.

'I don't know. I think our progress will be meandering, as opposed to straight, but at least we're concealed.'

'I just want to get home,' she sighs, dismounting carefully, as I've already done, to lead Brute to a stream.

Coenwulf is on his feet, rubbing his eyes with one hand, his wooden horse clutched in the other, as he looks around in surprise.

'Here you go, little man,' and Eadburg also places Coelwulf on the ground. His brother goes to him and holds out his hands so that the chunky babe can stand upright, although I don't think he can walk yet. I know a moment of sorrow for Lady Cynehild. She should be here to witness this, not me. Indeed, these steps should be taken before his father and mother.

'I do, too,' I confirm. 'The sooner we have armed men to protect the children and you, the better. I hope Ealdorman Ælfstan will be there. He said he'd meet me at Kingsholm when we parted.'

'But we still don't know who these men are who chase us,' she persists. 'We don't know who this Wulfnoth is. I mean' – she retracts some of her statement – 'I know what the men looked like who captured us. I'll never forget their faces, but we don't know why they did what they did and why Eadweard and his allies are involved.' Her voice is filled with anger and sorrow, no doubt her thoughts turning to her mother. I've no answer for her. We don't know whom they are or what they hope to accomplish, which is a problem.

'We'll find out,' I confirm, thinking of the words Wynflæd said to me, naming Eamont, and my suspicions. And of the brooch we have. I'll have to send word to Ealdorman Ælfstan if he's not waiting for me at Kingsholm. He needs to understand what's happening. He might also be able to help me. And if I need to seek out the king, then I will. I believe whatever's going on is concerned with the succession. Not for the first time, I consider my role in that, only to dismiss it. I might know my identity now, but few would believe it. And other than Wynflæd, I don't believe anyone could confirm what Lady Cynehild said to me. The queen, and Lady Ælflæd, would certainly deny it. I'm sure of that. And Lord Wigmund. I shudder to think what his reaction might be. Not that he could wound me, but he has allies aplenty and they could make my life very difficult with their slights and obstruction.

We eat some of the bread and cheese given to us by Æthelgyth, and then I settle to sleep, having handed Eadburg my blunt seax, just in case there's trouble. I think it'll be impossible to get any rest but the thrum of the woodland encloses me. I feel safe and protected.

A shrill shriek has me startling upright. I turn, eyes wide, unsure what's happening as I blink grit from my eyes. I hear the horses moving uneasily where we left them to graze on what they could find near a stream. Only another loud shriek splits the air, and I turn again, eyes wild. That cry is from a young child. Fully upright in a heartbeat, hand reaching for my seax, which I've forgotten I'd given to Eadburg, I hear the gruff voices of men moving quickly away.

'Icel.' Young Coenwulf cries my name in his high voice. I'm standing, looking for anything I can use against the children's captors. How they've managed to creep into the camp without me realising, I don't know, but they have. And now the yells of both children reach me, but they echo, and I don't know from where they come. I rush to Brute, who remains beside the stream, unsure what he can do to help me, but knowing I need him. My foot kicks something and I look down and see Coenwulf's wooden horse. Hastily, I retrieve it, slip the three horses loose from where we tied them up, and bite my lip.

Where's Eadburg? She's not here. My eyes alight on a stretch of red in the mulch of the woodland floor, and my heart thuds in my chest, my mouth filled with bile, as I bend to collect the almost-blunt seax I gave to her. It shimmers with someone's blood, but I don't know whose.

Someone was wounded here. I pray it wasn't the children or her.

'Help me,' I urge Brute. Eyes alert, he sniffs the air, but it's the other horse that none of us has ridden which strides out confidently once more. The animal is clearly used to finding its own way.

'Follow him,' I urge my horse, taking the other animal with me as well. The horse moves with surprising speed. I can't determine whether we travel towards the west or east because I've become turned around, but the horse follows the continuing screaming of the children with unerring ability. I look for Eadburg or for some sign that someone wounded came this way, but the horse moves too quickly to truly see. And the cries of the children urge me to greater speed.

'Damn the bastards,' I mutter to myself. Dawn isn't far off. The sky is edged with an autumn morning's soft purples and pinks. I just wish it would hurry up and get light enough to see better.

The horse continues, tail flashing from side to side, tension evident in how it sometimes stops and then startles forwards again. It's more like a hound on the hunt than a horse, but I don't pause to consider how it knows which way to go.

In half the time it took us to reach where we spent the previous night, I emerge into a clearing close to Watling Street. Ahead, I can see a collection of men on horses, and here the horse I followed emits a shrill neigh, and one of the other animals turns to look at it, despite its rider's commands.

I can see the children enclosed in the arms of two men as they turn to see why the horse makes such a noise, but there's no sign of Eadburg. Have I left her behind in the woodlands? Was she bleeding to death, and I did nothing to help her?

I turn back, uncertain, thinking of Edwin, but my oath is to the children, first and foremost. As much as it pains me to think about it, she might be dead already. The children yet live, and I need to get to them before these men can take them north again.

Ten of them are milling around on horses, seemingly trying to decide which way to go. My arrival occasions no comment other than from the man whose horse moves towards the spare animal. Whatever he does, his horse won't obey him, even when he dismounts and yanks the animal hard with the reins.

If I wasn't so worried about the children, I might laugh at the sight of him falling over as the horse rushes to a gallop and thunders towards me.

'Get here, you bastard,' the man cries. I'd like to think I know him, but I don't. He wears a cloak that covers his clothes, and although I see the flash of blades at his waist, it gives me no idea of his identity or where he's from.

And then another horse rushes towards me, and Brute only just swerves aside. The rider comes with his spear before him, and I feel it graze my shoulder as my eyes open in shock on recognising one of Eadweard's cronies: Mergeat.

Damn it.

Mergeat turns his horse, eyes blazing with fury.

'You damn shit,' the man huffs. 'Days it's taken us to get here, and we don't have days to return before we're supposed to hand the children over. And you killed Wulfgeat, you turd. Wulfnoth won't be happy about that.'

I startle at his words. I didn't realise he'd been in the north. Not that I know him well. But, if he was in the woodland, then perhaps Eadweard was as well. I'd thought him run away, with his coins from Tamworth, but potentially not.

His face is covered in a rough beard, but the spear's finely made. The horse easily takes his directions, turning quickly to come at me again. I have nothing but the blunt seax, and I'll never be able to counter the spear with that. I realise I've lost the shield I did have. I don't know where, and now isn't the time to worry about where I left it, no doubt in the woodlands where I slept last night.

Added to which, the horses are already turning northwards, the two children with the men, I consider if Eadweard, Wulfred and the others of their gang are amongst them. Coenwulf cries my name again, only to be cut off with a wet slap that makes my blood boil. His soft tears turn my heart to iron as I hear the harsh crack of male laughter.

Ignoring Mergeat, who tries to knock me aside, I rush at the other man, who I realise was also at Kingsholm with Eadweard. He's still unseated and out of sorts from the horse rushing southwards. The horse that Eadburg rode follows them quickly. I hear rather than see them, as they make their escape.

Within sight of him, I lean over, seax ready to stab. He sees me at the last moment, and his mouth opens in shock, just in time for my blade to slide into his mouth. He dies with a gasp, and a plume of hot air touches my hand. Quickly aware Mergeat has turned his mount towards me, I jump free of Brute and attempt to take all the blades the dead man has: a seax, a sword and even a war axe are held on his weapons belt. I'd hoped they might be my blades, but they're not. My fingers fumble, the rumble of the other horse getting closer and closer, making my movements too slow.

I grab the man's abandoned shield instead of anything else, and as Mergeat nears me and Brute moves aside, I hold the blade of the bloodied seax before me. Mergeat's spear attempts to knock it aside, but I spin away so that the spear misses me. I manage a glancing blow on Mergeat's thigh.

He howls with rage, turning the horse in such a small space to come back at me, I almost can't believe it. I thought Brute could turn on a Mercian coin, but this animal doesn't even need that much room. The spear threatens me again. Brute's in the way now. I slap his rump to urge him to move, but my horse defies me, rearing on his back legs and kicking out with his front two. Mergeat, expecting my shield, not my horse's hooves, absorbs all of the impact on the left side of his body. But his spear is on the right. His grip falters, his movement already underway. The spear comes perilously close to my ear, and I feel it as a chill wind against my neck.

'Bastard,' I growl, turning because, despite the wounds he's taken, the fight is far from over. I bend quickly, the flash of the dead man's war axe reminding me that I have more than one weapon. Quickly, I pull the dead man's axe into my left hand, half an eye on Mergeat and his mount. The horse is a fine one. I don't recognise it from Kingsholm. Is it perhaps part of the payment for becoming involved in abducting the children?

I don't want to kill the horse, but I will if it gets in the way. Brute rears once more, but the axe is already in flight. It flies through the air, and the man turns into it to avoid Brute's hooves.

The thud impacting Mergeat's forehead is horrifying, but I don't watch. I want the seax the already dead man carries. With it in my hand, I reach for Brute, thinking to calm him, but he's ready for me. Mergeat slowly falls from his horse, leg tangling in the stirrups, landing on his spear with the axe still embedded in his head. The horse, frightened, hears the welcome nicker of the other animals that have fled south and hastens to follow them, Mergeat's head thudding against the stones of the road.

I wince, but the rest of my enemy are already hastening northwards once more.

'Bastards,' I murmur low in my throat. The name of Wulfnoth on Mergeat's lips assures me that he's to blame for this. Well, he and Eadweard, who's in this up to his neck. I need to stop them before I lose Coenwulf and Coelwulf again. I grip the dead man's sword before mounting, and yank the war axe from Mergeat's shattered skull with the loud shriek of iron on bone.

Brute flees northwards, his hooves thundering against the stone of the road. Ahead, I see the men notice they're being chased, urging their horses onwards. One of them lingers as he looks over his shoulder. No doubt, he considers where the two men are who were supposed to stop me, but they're both dead and the horses are gone. I meet his eyes, glower at the man who's also one of Eadweard's allies, and growl low in my throat as he hastens northwards once more.

Crouched low over Brute's long neck, I slip Mergeat's seax into my weapons belt, and the sword as well. The warriors' horses are good, but nothing can truly beat Brute when given his head. He rushes after them, his eyes more able to avoid the pools of lying water than mine and the few holes in the roadway. All the same, I don't believe we're getting closer. The landscape passes in a whirl of green and brown, the colours of autumn and Winterfylleð starting to predominate.

And then, when I think Brute can't go on at such speed much longer, one of the leading horses falters, and then another. Their riders try and urge them onwards, but both animals have limps. The damn fools have ridden them too hard. I watch as the children are exchanged between those with the lame horses and those who can still ride, and then Brute's rearing up before the two stranded men.

Ahead, the others are escaping, but there are only six of them once

I've dealt with these two. I consider the best action to take. Should I avoid them? Take my time to kill them or allow Brute to rush into them? With no real thought, both of those things happen. One of the men, sword extended, thinks to stop our headlong dash, but Brute barrels into him, sending him and his sword clattering against the stone roadway, his head thudding with a wet sound. With a shriek of outrage, the other man tries to spin out of my way, but the sword's ready in my hand, and it ploughs through his neck, not even stopping us. I note that I know neither of these men. Perhaps they belong to Wulfnoth.

Again, I bend low over Brute's neck. I'm breathing as heavily as he is, and a white lather is forming on his neck. I can't keep pushing him like this, but neither can those I follow. Their horses will collapse. I have to hope it's before Brute does.

The road curves ahead, and for a moment I can't see them, and then, when I can, I realise that there are now only four riders. But no sooner have I thought that than a clatter of stones hitting the road brings me to my senses. One of the missiles strikes my leg, another hits Brute's long neck, and he pulls up quickly. I wince at the pain, but only one of the riders threw the stones. Now, another of the men appears before me, perhaps even rearing up from the drainage ditch as I once did in Kent.

'You'll die for this, you interfering bastard,' he cries, his words edged and sharp. He's not Mercian.

He carries a lethal-looking war axe, and he's close enough to menace Brute. I glimpse the two horses, heads down, panting behind a clump of bushes, and lash out with my borrowed sword again. I miss the man as he veers away from my wild strike. Another shower of missiles hits Brute, and me. Brute dances out of the way, sidestepping to avoid the blows. As he does so, he collects the man who tries to attack me. Unaware of what's happening, Brute's back legs knock him sideways, and as he struggles to balance, I pluck the war axe from his hand and use the butt to knock him fully to the ground.

Growling in my chest, I turn back to the man who thinks to attack us from such a distance. A small rise is giving him all the help he needs. Brute eagerly hastens towards him, responding to the squeeze of my knees. Still, missiles aim at us, some of them only clumps of mud and grasses now, but he has eerily good aim. With the sword in one of my hands, and the war axe in the other, Brute thunders towards him, head down, and all I need do is stab down with the long reach of the sword as the man tangles his own legs in haste to get away and Brute knocks him.

I leave him, gurgling bright red blood through his whitening lips, and return to the first man. He's down but not dead, his chest rising and falling. I pause and consider my next actions. I could wake him and demand to know what's happening, or I could kill him.

Looking at the winded horses, I rush to them and remove their saddles and release them from the rope that holds them firm to the tree. I can't do anything else for them, not at the moment, but both animals walk to the road, bend and drink thirstily from the gurgling drainage ditch and a large puddle close by. I eye them, but my fight is on the road ahead. With barely a thought, I bend and take the seax from the unconscious man and use it to slice across his throat.

Now there are only four of them. I'm convinced Eadweard and Wulfred are amongst them. And they do have the children.

In the time it's taken me to kill the men and release the horses, those who went on ahead are out of sight. I push Brute onwards, and as tired as he must be, he eagerly takes my command. The ground flows beneath his hooves as I consider the weapons I now have. It's a pity that none of them is my seax. Not that the war axe is bad or the seaxes I've taken. Or the sword. And at least the seaxes are sharper than the one Wynflæd gave me.

I spare a thought for Eadburg once more, hoping she lives, although I'm fearful that the enemy must have killed her and hidden her body. I don't want to consider that she lives but is cut. I hope she's either escaped or is dead. The other option is too distressing. With all my knowledge of healing, I should have been able to find her and ensure she lived.

Overhead, the sun disappears behind black clouds, and I fear it means another storm. Hunched over Brute, I huddle inside my cloak and try to drive some warmth into my cold limbs. I've not eaten all day, and there's no time now. My mouth's dry as well. I spit aside the taste of blood, unsure if it's mine or one of the men I killed, and then ahead, I hear the cries of warriors and look up. Only for my heart to sink.

29

There might only have been four men racing northwards, but they've been joined now by a group of at least another ten. Where they've come from, I don't know. Maybe they were waiting for them. I'm unsure whether these are the men I first stole the children from. They all seem to have horses, which I wouldn't expect if they were. But then Mergeat implied he'd been in the north. Not for the first time, I consider just how many people are involved in this.

I rein in Brute, when I can still see them, but far enough away that a spear can't be thrown at me or my horse, for some of the men do have spears, as Mergeat did.

The frightened eyes of Coenwulf meet mine. I think he'll cry out to me but he's crushed in front of a large man on a grey horse that paws angrily at the ground. The beast seems ferocious, and there's something about the man that appears familiar, although I can't think why. I consider if this is Wulfnoth. Although, if he is Wulfnoth, then these weren't the men in the north. It was Wulfnoth they were journeying to meet. Wasn't it?

I look for Coelwulf, and see him, almost lifeless, in front of another large man, where he's been tied to him just as Eadburg did, only this man has been much less tender in his ministrations. Their horses seem fresh, and I realise that the four racing horses are to the side of the group, their riders dismounted and coming towards me.

'Arse,' I exclaim. It's easy to see what the plan is here. They've tried to stop me from following, but now they mean to sacrifice the four men in exchange for the children. And I recognise those four men. Eadweard and Wulfred, Forthgar and Deremann from Kingsholm. The rest of the men who beat me up and left me for dead last winter.

I try and smile at Coenwulf, but his face is white and terrified. I note a livid bruise forming on his young cheek. Damn the bastards.

'Give me the children, and you can leave with your lives,' I call to the men. I'm out of all other options. It's time for some bluff.

'You and whose army?' the man who holds Coenwulf demands to know, his voice deep. I already hate him. His familiarity makes my skin crawl, for all I've never met him before. I'd have remembered him. I'm sure of that. He's distinctive. His height makes him perhaps even taller than Horsa.

It's enough that he crushes Coenwulf, but his booming voice, rich with derision, makes me grit my teeth. If I could kill him now, then I would. I don't even want to know his identity or why he's doing this.

'They're coming on behind,' I try to deceive, although I don't know why. It's clear to everyone here that I'm alone.

'You bloody fool,' he rumbles towards me. 'Kill the pestilent cock.' I realise then that Eadweard, Forthgar, Deremann and Wulfred have been advancing on me while I've been looking at the children and wasting my time talking to the man in charge of abducting them. Eadweard looks delighted with the order. Arse. I notice that he has my seax blade at his waist as well. I growl low in my throat. So, he was the one who led me astray and had me tied up. I didn't think I could despise him more than I do, but somehow, I find even more of my fury directed at him.

As I hear heavy hoof beats pounding their way north, I focus on the immediate danger. They all wear byrnies and have a good collection of weapons to hand, but not shields. Brute eyes them with the same unease that I do. He's already saved me more than once today. I can't expect him to keep on putting himself in danger, so I slide from his back.

I have the war axe I took, three seaxes, one blunt and two sharp, and the sword that I hold before me. It's not my favoured weapon, but its reach is long. Brute, despite my intentions, remains at my back.

'Go,' I urge him when the slap to his rump doesn't produce the desired result. 'Go,' I try again, but then there's no more time for Deremann and Forthgar come against me. I can't believe their blatant attack here, in the middle of Watling Street. Anyone could see them and intervene, but they're smug bastards. Deremann smirks at me, revealing that four of his front teeth are missing. Forthgar has a snub nose, more akin to a pig than a man. They also have a collection of scars that mar their faces. Deremann seems to be looking down, his cheek pulled tight. Forthgar has vivid red marks running over his nose, making him appear branded.

But they're quick. Deremann rushes me with a seax in his hand; Frothgar follows behind, a war axe in his. Wulfred stands with his spear pointing at me, a smirk on his face. I can't see Eadweard. I assume he thinks to attack me from behind; only Brute's there. I'd look but there are three men before me, and only one behind. I'd sooner protect myself from the three than the one, even if that one is Eadweard.

I counter Deremann's seax with the sword and Forthgar's war axe with the stolen axe. If the men look surprised that I have their ally's weapons, they don't show it.

Both men hurry to get to me, but my sword keeps Deremann at bay. Forthgar shows less caution, but watching both men simultaneously is difficult. I'm unsurprised when I feel a blow land on my arm. Wulfred thinks of slicing me with his spear while I'm distracted.

'Arsehole,' I roar at him.

I lurch backwards, only to encounter Brute's broad back. He nickers, but not in welcome. As I try and move further back, he attempts to stand where I am. Slowly, I realise we're rotating. I take my three warriors with me while Brute attempts to evade the reach of Eadweard. I can hear his heavy breathing coming from behind.

'You don't want to do this,' I call to them all, knowing it's useless but trying anyway. 'The king will have you killed for this.'

I'm unsurprised when it's Eadweard who responds, his voice rich with derision.

'The king! The king doesn't care, and we'll have our coin and need never step foot in Mercia again once you're bloody dead and have stopped messing everything up. The king has shown himself to be weak. He should have had Lord Coenwulf and his by-blow killed when he had the opportunity.'

Perhaps, I consider, I erred here. It would have been much easier to ride through these men to follow where young Coenwulf and Coelwulf are being taken. Not that I have time to curse myself for a fool.

Wulfred thrusts the spear closer, coming up against my rusty byrnie, which is now even more rusted after days in the wet. My cloak might keep the rain from it, but the damp air is another matter entirely.

The impact is hardly felt, but now Forthgar almost has his war axe free. Quickly, I circle my arm, dropping it low so that the two axes disentangle, and I'm chopping at his neck as he tries to make the same move on me. He's just out of grasp, for I fear to step into his reach in case the spear punctures Brute's side.

'Damn it,' I huff as the seax opens a line down the small area of my arm visible beneath the byrnie. The heat of pain makes me irrational, and without thought, I move forwards, head lowered, and thrust it against Deremann. His nose erupts in a welter of blood and gristle even without my helm. He drops down, the spear that was almost resting on his shoulder following him.

I step into the gap, stamping down with my feet as Deremann moans on the floor. I grip Wulfred's spear. From here, the spear can't hurt Brute. I have my hands on it, just about to wrench it from Wulfred's hands when Forthgar's war axe whistles too close to my neck. I jerk backwards, knocking into Brute, who's about as forgiving as a rock wall at my back.

I'm breathing heavily, the wind taken from me, but far from done.

I jerk the spear, hoping to make Wulfred rear backwards or risk losing his teeth like Deremann. But his grip remains firm. I kick Deremann down on the ground again, wishing I'd done more than break his nose. When he stands up, and he will stand up, he'll be pissed off.

The seax whispers close once more, but I swing my war axe to meet the blade. My sword's on the floor. I dropped it to grab the spear, and now I'm not sure that was a good bargain to make, especially not when

Forthgar surges upwards holding his war axe, and I can't risk bending to grip my sword again.

'Shit,' I mutter to myself. I'm thinking of all the times I fought Oswy and Wulfheard, Garwulf and Frithwine, but I'm not convinced it's fair to compare this to then. I'm entirely outnumbered, with no hope of anyone coming to my assistance. I don't want to think that Eadweard will best me, but it seems increasingly likely, making me even angrier. As does the knowledge that it's not truly Eadweard. He's left Wulfred, Forthgar and Deremann to complete the task. He's already sacrificed Mergeat and the man whose name I don't know as well, and all in the name of coin. He's no better than a bloody Viking raider bastard.

With Brute pressed tightly to me, I don't have room to move. Even evading the advance of the war axe and seax put Brute's life at threat.

The group of us has turned so far now that I'm facing the way I came and can no longer see the horsemen riding north or Coenwulf trying to look at me, head turned, from where he's once more being stolen away.

I growl low in my throat. This isn't going well. And with Eadburg missing, and Wynflæd only knowing the name of Eamont far to the north as my destination, if I die here, on Watling Street, I don't believe anyone will ever know what befell the children, despite my words that others were following on behind. Eadweard will run from here, his saddlebags filled with the coins Cuthred saw him being given in Tamworth, although by whom I'm still not sure, and the children and me will be lost for all time.

Desperation fills my thoughts. I can't die here. I won't allow it. And I won't let Eadweard be the one to end my life.

I meet Deremann's seax with my retrieved seax, the spear forgotten about. Its point still faces downwards, caught between the men advancing on me. I've no idea what Eadweard's doing. Brute turns with me. I wish Brute was Oswy or Wulfheard. Yes, he has his hooves and a nasty bite on him, but we can't shout one to another as I might do with those warriors I've fought with for many winters now.

Sweat beads my face as the two war axes face one another, and while I'm engaged with that blade, I'm aware of the spear coming closer once more. I veer backwards, and it just misses my face because

Wulfred's angle's too tight. Any moment now, he'll realise, and I won't be able to counter his move by just moving my head. And Forthgar leers at me with the war axe, the stink of him filling my nose as I try and break free from where the two axe heads have become entangled. If Wulfred and his spear isn't cause enough to worry, the seax also flashes before me.

'Four men to kill one, you bastards,' I roar, thrusting forwards with the war axe, risking dropping it so it comes free from my foeman's blade. I free my war axe, but not quickly enough, as I feel the burn of a cut on my thigh. Wulfred has realised his mistake and stepped further and further back, thrusting the spear just to the side of Forthgar.

'Four men to kill one Mercian busy-body, yes,' Eadweard bellows in response.

A howl erupts from my mouth, and with it, I hear an answering whinny from Brute. If Eadweard's hurt my damn horse, I'll kill him. But first, I've got to stay alive.

Another burn shudders along my body, this one on my right cheek. I see the blood well from the cut below my eye. I'm just grateful that it didn't take my eye. I raise the war axe to counter Deremann, but he's too quick, and I feel another cut on my chin. Forthgar with the war axe is even closer now. I step back, trying to focus around the pain, expecting to encounter Brute's resistance, but it's not there. Belatedly, I hear the rumble of his hooves over the cobbled road and appreciate that he's finally taken my command to flee. That means Eadweard, who was menacing him, is now behind me.

I swirl my arms, war axe in one hand, seax in the other, but there are four blades against my two, and I'm entirely alone. There's no one to witness this as I stab and slash, but my blood runs more freely for every blow I strike. Not only my arm, cheek and chin but my thigh, calf and even a glancing blow on my back.

I can feel myself weakening. Tears of frustration mingle with my blood and sweat. I lick my lips but taste only the salt of my exertions.

'Why did you take the children?' I cry, determined to have answers before I succumb to this attack.

'They threaten the kingship. And they're weak and useless right now,'

Eadweard cries. 'And what are two young lives? No one will mourn them. And there are others who would rule in their place.'

His words are gratifying to hear, and yet I still don't truly know who's behind all this.

'What's at Eamont?' I try again. If he's shocked that I know the name, he doesn't mention it.

'None of your damn business,' he growls, his attack more frenzied.

More and more, I feel myself weakening. My thoughts turn to the children. Who will find them? Will anyone even care? And I think of my uncle, bleeding his last to defend me. Did he do so for this? I don't believe he did. He wanted me to live to fulfil my destiny, and I want the children to live to fulfil theirs, but it's becoming increasingly unlikely that any of us will be able to do so.

It'll be the small child of Lady Ælflæd who becomes king one day, provided he becomes stronger. Unless, of course, whoever is behind this also means to threaten the weak boy.

Not that any of it should concern me. I'm fighting for my life. Why should matters of the future be a concern for me?

Yet I battle on. I've not given up yet. I won't accept that this is my fate. My seax blade is slick in my hand. The war axe matted with the hair and skin of my enemy. I see Deremann falter, the toothless man with the seax, but the other three remain strong and overwhelming, even the arsehole with the broken nose.

A blow rings resoundingly around my head so that it pulses with the impact. I struggle on. Lashing out wildly. I can hear someone shrieking and roaring and realise it's me. My chest is tight, my heart beating wildly as though I've run from Tamworth to Lichfield and back, and still, I'm being overwhelmed.

'Hurry it up,' Wulfred calls. 'If we don't catch them, you know the bastards will leave us, and take all the coin.'

With his words resounding in my ears, I think to spur myself onwards. They have somewhere to be. Perhaps if I just delay them, they'll tire of this and leave me alone.

Only then, there are two hands around my neck, squeezing, pulling tighter and tighter. I kick and thrash, wild strikes with both blades failing to have any impact because Wulfred, Forthgar and Deremann pull away, their blades glistening with my blood, a reminder of my failure to kill them. And slowly, my struggles lessen, my wild blows falling away, my arms too heavy to lift as I struggle against that bastard, Eadweard. I drop my seax and reach for his hands, but mine are slick with blood and sweat and even with both hands I can't grip his or pull him away.

I'd sob, but I can't even hitch a breath to do so, and slowly the world turns black.

30

I cough and retch, the world around me black, trying to remember where I am, why my body aches and why the bed I lie on has more stones in it than straw.

My throat's raw, the cough sending spasms of pain ricocheting up and down my body to add to all the other hurts and pains.

'Brute,' I try to call, but the sound that comes from my throat is more whisper than shout, and it only makes me cough again.

I'm lying on my face, I think. It feels like pins from the blacksmith's forge stabbing into my face. I can't feel my arms, and I don't know why. I try to move upright, try and see where I am and what I'm doing. And then it all comes back to me.

Young Coenwulf and Coelwulf. Where are they?

And then more comes back to me.

Why am I alive?

With too much haste, I attempt to sit upright, but my arms still won't work. I end up flopping like a fish out of water, my face once more grazing whatever I lie on. My eyes close with the pain, lights flashing behind them. I try to take a deep breath, to will myself upright, but it only makes me cough, and then a thousand other hurts make themselves known. Tears form in my eyes but I can't sob. That would hurt too much.

Instead, I close my eyes and try not to think about everything that aches or pulses, throbs or just makes itself known. I don't think I should feel my tongue, but even it feels huge in my mouth. Huge, and dry, and that sends me into another coughing fit.

Tears continue to fall, and I don't know how. I feel as dry as a husk.

Once more, I will myself to serenity, hoping to find some part of myself that can help me accomplish this. Even without Brute, I must get to my feet. I need to rescue the children. I swore an oath, and the thought of breaking that sends a fresh wave of grief flooding me.

I've failed. I know I have.

But I can't fail. Not now.

I open my eyes, resolved. No matter what. I'm going to get upright. I'll not allow Eadweard and his cronies to triumph. Or this Wulfnoth, whomever he is.

My hands and arms are no longer numb. Now they tingle and hurt all the more. I put some pressure on them, once more feeling the sharp bite of whatever I'm lying on beneath them. It might as well be a thousand blades. That's how pointed the ground is.

With a howl of rage, more akin to a wolf calling for its pack, I make my way onto my bunched knees. A whole host of fresh agony suffuses my body. The hot burn of fresh blood oozing from my many cuts fills my nostrils. I think my eyes are still shut, but they're not. It's night. The moon and stars are obscured by thick cloud with the howl of the wind finally making itself known as a shudder of cold runs through my body.

I focus on my breathing, on trying to tame the agony, but it's no good. Everything hurts. My lips are thick. My stomach aches as though a herd of cows have trampled over me. My knees, well, they feel as though they've been scoured with the very blades beneath my hands.

I reach out, determined to decipher if I'm on the side of the road, or inside a cave or some such. But there's too much air around me, the wind ruffling my sweat-drenched beard and cheeks. Its bite is as sharp as a knife. Reaching out behind me and realising that there's firm ground there, I swivel on my knees to sit on my arse.

I'm panting by the time I've accomplished that. My back aches now, but my knees are no longer as sore, for all I'm sure I must be bleeding from them. My hands snake up towards my neck. I'm remembering Eadweard's hands around me. I'm recalling the sensation of being unable to breathe. Panic makes my chest heave as I relive that moment, but a sharp stab of pain and a warm sensation over my arm and stomach recalls me to the even more frightening reality of now. I've lived through that, but now I need to survive what else they did to me, or my death might have occurred then.

I'm wounded. I'm alone. I've lost my horse and all of my supplies, and I'm shivering. I have no cloak, no means of getting warm and absolutely no chance of seeing where I am. It's just too damn dark. There are nights I wanted it to be so dark, but now, when I need the moon's light to see by, it's abandoned me. And I do feel abandoned.

Once more, panic threatens to envelop me. I'm shivering from cold and fear. And I know, for Wynflæd has told me enough times, that this is a deadly combination.

I force my hands away from my neck, instead examining the cuts I remember taking to my chin and cheek. Both feel as though they've started to scab over. They're filled with filth and muck, but there's no water for me to clean them, so I leave them alone. I have other concerns.

Gingerly, I feel my byrnie and then lower my hands to my belly, forcing myself back to expose it further. Just where my tunic rides free from my taut belly, I can sense the stickiness of a wound. With my hand, I try and determine just how bad it is. It seems to be a good hand long, and it's certainly gaping. I thrust my little finger into it to gauge how wide the wound is, only to feel fresh blood pooling from it.

'Damn it,' I curse. I have only the clothes I'm wearing, and it's bloody frigid, but the wound is a bad one. Running my other hand along the top of my trews, I sense they're sodden with blood and not piss, as I first thought.

Perhaps, I reason, I could do something with my tunic. But no. I'd need to remove it to do that, and I can't. Unless...

My hand scurries to the side. Have they left me with my weapons? I could cut it free. But I find nothing in the close vicinity, and I daren't risk moving any more. I've no idea how much I've bled. I might feel weak from blood loss, but it's impossible to tell with all my other aches and pains. For now, the agony is making me sharp. I appreciate that it might be masking my true state.

With nothing for it, I reach as far forward as I can, prepared to rip my trews to give me something to stem the bleeding. But there's no strength in my hands. I can't rip my trews, and the movement brings a fresh wave of sweat to drip down my nose.

And I've discovered another problem in the process: the cloth of my right trew is stuck in place, no doubt due to bleeding there as well.

My arms shake as I lean backwards. Perhaps I should tear my tunic after all. But no, I've no strength to rip anything.

Defeated, I consider my options. None of them is good, and it's proving impossible to do anything in the dark. Perhaps, I realise, it would be better to just be asleep until dawn breaks. But I can't guarantee I'll live until then.

A shriek of frustration leaves my mouth, making my throat ache as I realise this is futile. I'm alone. There's no one to help me. I don't even know where I am. It doesn't matter how much healing skill I once had because it's impossible to implement any of it. I'm thirsty. I'm in pain. I'm cold. Perhaps it would have been better to die with that bastard's hands around my neck. No one with any honour should kill like that. But Eadweard thought to murder me in such a way. He wounded Brute, he must have done for my fierce horse to leave my side. Eadweard thinks he's killed me. Thoughts of Brute have me worrying all over again. The children. Eadburg. Brute. Wine. Me. If I die here, what will happen to them all?

I grit my teeth. It's impossible to tell how much of the night has passed, but I imagine much of it for it to be so utterly dark. I've no choice but to wait for the morning, if I live to see it. Come the morning, I'll be able to decipher where I am and determine all of my wounds. Come the morning.

Fearful of my belly wound bleeding more, I pull my knees up to my chest and curl into a ball, arms wrapped around my legs. It's uncomfortably tight, but it's the only way I can keep warm and, perhaps, arrest the bleeding. I don't think I'll sleep, what with the blades digging into me, my aches and pains, but at some point I must, because when I wake, driving rain stinging my eyes, it's daylight, and I can see just how precarious my position is.

What I thought were blades sticking into my back are the sharp angles of stones as I lie in what must be a quarry, but a long-abandoned one. There's a sharp edge at my back, down which is a much deeper hole. I'm only grateful the bastards didn't shove me into it as I waken, uncurl my tight, unresponsive body, and try to work out what I should do first.

My body trembles, the rain driving what heat I've been able to generate from it. My clothes are wet, and my hair as well. My hands, which were no doubt bloodied and bruised, look white as dead fish as I examine them. Once more, I grit my teeth, around the thousand different hurts and aches, opening my mouth to try and catch some of the streaming rain to cleanse my mouth and aching throat.

I attempt to stand, swaying alarmingly as I do so. Once upright, I teeter worryingly towards the sharp drop. But there's something close by that I want. A part of the quarry has been worked, but not the area above. It'll allow me to get out of the driving rain if nothing else. Resolved, I stagger forward one step, and then another, knowing that while I'm upright, all of my wounds have the opportunity to bleed once more.

I know my leg bleeds, but I'm not sure about my belly wound.

The distance, which I thought was little more than three horses' lengths, threatens to undo me. It's just too far. I'll never make it. I pause, catch my breath, choke on my crushed throat and then sway. The rain stings my eyes and every hurt on my exposed body. I find a wolf grin on my face. With the force of it, it might clear the muck from my cuts. It hurts like driving sleet, but it spurs me on.

All the same, I need to get out of the rain.

Again, I sway alarmingly from side to side. I look down at my feet, urging them onwards, but they seem wedged in place. Instead, I lean forwards until I almost tumble over, and then my feet finally move, urging me onwards. I make it, the sharp overhang immediately stopping the rain from pelting me. It feels as though I've stepped from outside into a hall with a fiercely blazing hearth. I allow myself to enjoy the sensation, but I'm no fool. I know how dangerous thinking like that can be.

I stand there, catching my breath and looking into the sheeting rain. I can't see Watling Street from here. I can't think they'd have taken the time to move my body far, but all the same, I don't know where I am. I recall Watling Street being bounded mostly by woodland and fields, not a quarry.

Once more, I feel blood seeping from my belly wound and realise it's time to do something about it. Checking my face, I can feel the scabs have moved with the onslaught from the rain, but hopefully, they'll start to seal themselves again now that I'm out of it. Glancing down, I eye my right leg. The cloth's welded tightly to it. I won't be able to remove that, but somehow, and I'm sure it wasn't like that last night, the cloth of my left trew is almost hanging off anyway. I bend and rip it fully off, the biting stab of the cold hitting my skin as my arms protest the movement. Stretching upwards and wincing as I do so, I hold it against my belly wound. Somehow, just doing that makes me feel better. But I'm far from assured of living through this just because I've managed to stem the flow of fresh blood.

Panting, I consider my next objective. I need to move and find people who can help me. But the night made it impossible to see, and the low clouds letting lose their barrage of rain now obscures everything.

I suck my bottom lip, tasting salt and blood once more. I need something to drink. I'm aware I've not pissed for too long. My body, already too dry, will be suffering even more. It's so damn frustrating. The rain is falling in buckets, but I don't have one to hand to capture the water.

Perhaps I should just be pleased to be out of the torrent. I lean back, feeling the marks where the stone's been carved from the wall behind me. Some of it almost feels smooth. I'd run my hand along it, but I don't want to. I'm starting to shake again; this time, it is with the cold. My clothes are drenched. My tunic is stuck to my skin.

I can't go on like this. It might seem madness, but I must get out of my wet clothes.

Growling low in my throat, I force myself to consider removing my byrnie. No matter how I look at it, it's going to hurt. I can allow it to hurt and then recover, or I can ignore the issue, feel warm for a while, and then die in agony because I'm not warm at all, but rather shivering to death.

There's no choice to be made there.

But the wall of the quarry might help me. Leaning against it, I use my numb fingers to release the catch on my weapons belt. It falls to my feet with a loud clang, rubbing against my makeshift bandage as it falls. When my byrnie's removed, I can use the belt to keep the bandage in place.

Leaning back, I allow the quarry to take the weight of my byrnie, lowering my legs in the hope that I'll be able to wriggle out of it like a snake. For a moment, the pain in my knees is too great, and nothing seems to be happening. I almost give up the task but then feel the rusty byrnie start to lift from my shoulders. I continue, and eventually it slips over my head, and I'm beneath it, almost sitting on my arse once more.

I consider staying there, legs before me. But I'm still cold, far too cold. I bend low, moving my body out of the way from where my byrnie will fall, and with relief, hear it thunk to the ground. The next part will hopefully be easier.

Arms juddering, I grip the bottom of my tunic, my eye catching the livid score along my arm, which I think was my first wound, although it might not have been. I've forgotten the order in which I received them. With a grunt of effort, I lift my tunic free from my back, releasing the scent of my wounds and filth, so that I almost gag. The fact it's wet doesn't help either.

A shiver runs over my body, but my eyes catch on the site of the welter of purpling bruises over my chest. I can't imagine my back looking any better.

I work quickly then to secure the strip from my trews in place around my belly wound. I still don't risk looking at it. It's wide but not necessarily deep. While I might stink, I don't smell the shit of the grey coiled ropes inside my belly.

I breathe, once more licking my lips, conscious that when my tunic went over my head, it knocked my facial wounds.

I gaze at my trews, but there's so little of the one leg left that I can't see it will help me to remove them. And, of course, the other side is stuck to my leg anyway, a wound having bled there since yesterday. At least, I consider, I assume it was yesterday. It might be that I was knocked out for longer than that.

What then shall I do now? The options are remarkably few. I can wait here. I can walk out in the rain and see if I can find someone. But I have only my trews and boots to keep me warm, and although I'm glad to be released from my byrnie, I'm still bloody cold.

A whimper leaves my mouth as I tighten the belt around my makeshift bandage.

I'm still buggered. I can't deny that.

Lips trembling, aware I need water, but that even cupping the rain in my hands will result in me being drenched, I hunker down, wincing at the pains as I sit down once more, naked back to the rough stone face, and close my eyes.

I can't do anything in the rain.

I'll sleep awhile.

31

Next time I wake, I know the sun is out, and the rain's stopped, but I find it impossible to open my eyelids. I'm curled tightly in a ball, like a hedgehog keen to evade its hunter but missing the prickles.

If someone attacked me now, I'd have no way of defending myself. I lick my dry lips, dreaming of water, the sound of running water nearby. But it's not enough. My eyes won't open.

* * *

My violent shivering wakes me next, and it's night-time. Or at least I hope it is. My eyes open, gritty and itchy. I'm still curled in a ball. In fact, I think it'd be too hard to uncurl now. My body's adopted this new position. Like dogs who know their time has come, I've chosen the position I mean to die in. I can't escape from this. I'm finished. Hazily, I think of Eadburg, and how I failed her. Of Edwin, and how I failed him. Of Wynflæd, and how I failed her. Of Lady Cynehild, and how I failed her. A broken sob cracks from my sore throat as I consider the two young boys, Coelwulf only just starting to walk. I've failed them more than anyone. Is this all my life was ever meant to be? I'd rage with fury, but I'm just too tired.

* * *

Next time I wake, I'm warm. A soft smile touches my cheeks. It won't be long now. I consider muttering a prayer to God, but it's all I can do even to think the words of the familiar prayer. I don't much agree with his idea of heaven anyway. I think, perhaps, it would be better to go to Valhalla and feast for eternity. But I've no weapon to hand, so that's not going to happen either. I decide to enjoy feeling warm.

Only then I'm aware of voices. They're saying my name. Or so I think. The sound comes from far away.

'Bloody hell. Let me see him.' I smile again, recognising Oswy's voice. I didn't think I'd hear his dulcet tones ever again. It's strange to realise I'm hallucinating him.

Only then I feel hands on my body, a sharp stab of something and I want it to stop.

'What's he saying?' I hear someone else ask. I think it's Wulfheard, but I might be wrong. What's happening to me?

'Gibberish,' Ealdorman Ælfstan confirms. I can hear the concern in his voice. And then Wulfheard speaks again.

'Are you sure you know what you're doing? We should take him to Wynflæd.'

'There's no bloody time for that,' Oswy huffs and, whether I will it or not, my eyes open on the strangest scene I've ever witnessed.

There's a fire in front of me. I can see the welcome reds and yellows dancing on the end of thin sticks and larger pieces of wood, the super-heated blue of its heart assuring me this fire's been burning for some time. It's what Wulfheard, Oswy and Ealdorman Ælfstan are attempting that concerns me more.

'What are you doing?' The words don't sound as though they come out of my mouth. My tongue's so dry it's stuck to the roof of my mouth, and it's an effort to work it loose. Perhaps, I realise, I should greet them with more warmth, but I'm worried about their intentions.

I can tell that Oswy's nervous, his eyes peering down at me and something glinting in his hands.

'Gibberish, but Maneca, hand me the water.'

Gentle hands lift my head above my shoulders, but still, I hiss with pain. Swallowing is torture as I allow the cool fluid inside my mouth. I drink as much as I can, but the beaker is removed too quickly, Maneca snatching it away from me when it's still more than half full.

'What are you doing?' I manage to say this time. Ealdorman Ælfstan, hovering over me, is the one to speak.

'Oswy will stitch your wound.'

'What?' I squeak, meeting the troubled eyes of the man I saved inside Londinium. 'He doesn't know what he's doing.'

'He's watched you perform the task more than enough times,' the ealdorman dismisses. I feel my eyes widen.

'And?'

'And what, Icel? You're lucky we found you. And you're bloody lucky that Oswy is prepared to try this, or you'd be dead by now.'

I eye Oswy, where his lips are pursed in thought, the needle in his hand flashing with all the malice of a bloody seax. 'Is he?'

'What?' Wulfheard demands.

'Is he prepared to try?'

'He has the needle, doesn't he?'

'Yes, he does, but looks like he's about to gut a pig, not stitch me back together.'

Oswy looks at me, with an arched eyebrow. 'For that, little runt, I might just leave you with a message.'

Without further pause, he plunges the needle into my wound, and I shriek, bucking upwards against the pain as Oswy rears backwards, the needle, or so it feels, embedded in my skin.

'Hold his damn legs still,' Wulfheard orders everyone, the words of the ealdorman subsumed beneath his commanding tone. 'Cenred. You're a big bugger. Get over here and hold his leg. Maneca, take his arm. Ealdorman, you can take the other one. Ordlaf, get the other leg. Now, hold him, or Oswy can't stitch him, and then he'll bloody delay us even further.'

'What?' I squawk as rough hands seize my extremities. I try and move, but the men have me held firm. Oswy's going to do his worst, whether I like it or not. 'Not so bloody deep,' I say instead, trying to be reassuring.

I'm aware of others in the campsite and the gentle nicker of horses. It's daylight, but it's bitterly cold. Someone has given me their cloak, the fur collar lining making my nose tickle, but I fear to sneeze while Oswy has his iron embedded in my stomach.

'Like this?' Oswy queries, as I feel the searing pain of my flesh being stabbed with the needle, the pig's gut running through me so that I have to grit my teeth against the painful and disorientating experience.

'How the hell do I know?' I huff, sweat beading my face.

'Yes, like that,' Wulfheard intervenes.

'Small and neat,' I offer again. The pain is immense. I finally understand why the men I treat can never rest easy as I stitch them back together.

The movement of my flesh being tugged is horrific. Instead, I distract myself.

'How did you find me?'

'We came looking,' the ealdorman offers.

'Why?'

'Wynflæd.' It seems then that my fears no one would know where I was were ill-founded. The ealdorman must have gone to Kingsholm, and then to Tamworth.

'So how did you find me?'

'Brute.'

'Did you find him? Is he well?' I attempt to move my head to look, but there are too many people crowding around me to see.

'Of course we found him, or we'd never have found you. He led us straight to you.'

'But he left me?' I feel my forehead wrinkle, only that hurts, so I stop doing it immediately.

'Well, he came back. Poor sod. He was nudging you and you were insensible. Without him, you'd be dead.'

The thought is far from consoling. Still, I wish I could see Brute. My nostrils flare at the familiar stink of heated iron, and I brace myself for what will come next. I've been burnt enough times to know this will hurt.

'I take it you didn't find the boys,' the ealdorman continues first. And now I close my eyes, remembering my failure. While Oswy mutters to himself, and I really fear what he's doing, I think about the last time I saw young Coenwulf wedged into the saddle of the man I think is Wulfnoth.

'I did. I had them.' My voice is broken, the words only just audible even to my ears. I don't want to say them. I don't want to admit to everything I've done wrong. 'But they found us. In the woodlands. There was a woman with me. Eadburg, you met her at Kingsholm. I don't know what happened to her. They killed her mother, but she escaped. She might still be there, not as lucky as me to have Brute to find her, and they took the children away. North again.'

With my eyes closed, I can't see the expressions on the faces of those who help me, or rather, hold me prostrate so that I can't buck and twist against Oswy's less than gentle ministrations. But I hear the heavy silence all the same, and then I feel hands tighten on my arms and legs and I know the worst is to happen.

The pain of the heated blade is like nothing I've ever experienced before. Sweat beads my face as I twist and buck, my roar of outrage so loud I can hear nothing else.

Only when the blade has gone do I open my eyes, sympathy on the faces of those who slowly release me, a look of shock on Oswy's face as he thrusts his seax back into the heat of the fire.

'Do you know who has them?' Wulfheard asks gruffly, when he believes I'm able to answer once more. Perhaps they put the tears that fall from my eyes down to Oswy and my wounds. But I know better.

'Eadweard and Wulfred are involved. But I didn't recognise the man who has the children. A huge man. He rode a huge grey steed. I heard the name Wulfnoth, but I don't know if that was him.'

'It was,' Wulfheard responds angrily. I also hear the others muttering to one another as well, as though they too know who the man is. And still, the pull and twist of the needle is busy at its work. I wonder how big the wound is. I mean, I knew it was large but Oswy has been at the task for a long time now. Only then I feel his hands moving down my leg. He's finished. I breathe more deeply, and feel the tension on my arms and legs ease.

'Why does he want the children?'

'Because the bastard has a black heart and will sell his soul to the highest bidder. But I know where he's going.' At this, I open my eyes and glower at Wulfheard. He wears a smile that presages someone's death, and I shudder at the likeness I see there. I've seen that expression on another man's face, and I feel my forehead wrinkle in consternation.

'Wulfheard—' I open my mouth to ask, but the ealdorman interrupts me.

'We'll go after them as soon as we've got you somewhere safe. And we'll send someone to hunt for this woman.' And my thoughts spiral and I forget what I was going to ask him.

'I'm coming.' I grimace as even saying the words hurts.

'You're not,' the ealdorman replies immediately.

'I bloody am. I don't care if I die.'

'And you will,' Oswy offers, meeting my eyes with his, but he's grinning as he says it.

'Just get on with it, and then we can get going,' I urge him. I'm unsure how many other wounds he needs to tend to, but suddenly, I'm impatient.

'You need to eat and drink,' Ealdorman Ælfstan grudgingly acknowledges. For some time, I've been aware of the smell of something cooking close by. I thought it was Oswy using the herbs to heal me, but perhaps it's a meal. My belly rumbles with the thought of food.

'And sit up,' Oswy glowers, but still he grins.

'And piss,' Wulfheard joins in by repeating my oft-spoken cautions to the men when I tend to them.

'And get some clothes on,' Maneca cackles, and I appreciate that I am, under the fur, entirely, bollock, naked.

32

Sitting is an agony. Standing is sweet torture, but at least I'm reunited with Brute, who comes, with his inquisitive nose, to knock me as I finally release my vivid yellow stream into the nearby undergrowth. I hear the others talking about me, and Oswy hovers close enough to wrinkle his nose at the acrid stench. And, of course, to grab me when Brute's reunion is overenthusiastic and I threaten to tumble into the undergrowth, along with my piss.

'You stink enough without adding to it,' he cautions me, a firm hand on my arm, just about keeping me upright. 'You need to step aside.' He smacks my horse's rump and Brute, teeth bared, snaps at him, causing me to wobble once more as Oswy moves to evade the crotchety animal.

I smirk. Pleased to see my horse.

'Are you wounded?' I ask Brute, and Oswy startles at that.

'I didn't...' Oswy begins.

'I know,' I mollify, using Oswy's firm arm and Brute's own back to allow me to check my mount for injuries. Brute ran. There must have been a reason for that, when he'd stood at my side for so much of the fighting.

Limping, my right leg burning where Oswy's sewn the flaps of skin together, I run my hands along my horse, but as I make my way around his head and to the left side of his body, it doesn't take much investigating to discover why my horse did what he did.

Eadweard appears to have tried to skin my horse. Above his front left leg, a wide cut glimmers red in the daylight, the skin loose, although the wound seems shallow. I wince to see it, and Brute, with his usual mild temper, rears backwards from me, and this time I sway so much that I have to take three rapid steps forward just to stay upright. As Brute's hooves hit the ground, a thud of agony echoes around my body, just to add to the unpleasantness of it all.

'Bloody hell,' Oswy offers, reaching out with his hand as though to touch the wound. Brute repays him with another snap of his teeth. It's a good job that Oswy has the reflexes of a warrior or he'd be missing a hand.

'Come on, boy.' Brute allows me closer, but still backs up away from me. 'I need to see,' I find myself explaining to him, only to cough, painfully, the sound more akin to a stone being pulled over gravel. Brute startles at the noise, and so do I, which makes my stitches and burned flesh twinge. 'Damn it,' I murmur when I can speak again. Oswy's come back to me, and the commotion has also brought Wulfheard and Ælfstan.

'Poor bugger,' Ælfstan murmurs. His words are soft and filled with sympathy for my horse.

'Aye, that'll have made him run,' I confirm. I cursed my horse for leaving me, but I can see exactly why he might have done so. Such a wound would have terrified him. I mean, he runs from a bloody butterfly.

'Will he let Oswy tend him?' Ælfstan queries.

'I doubt it. I'll have to do it.' I'm unsure how. Standing is agony, and my body thrums and shivers beneath the fur cloak that wraps me, but if I want to join the march north, there's little choice.

'Boiled water?' Oswy queries.

'Some linens?' Wulfheard also adds.

'Pig's gut,' the ealdorman concludes, and once more, tears form in my eyes.

I've missed my fellow warriors. Yes, they don't know my identity. But here, with these men, I couldn't give a damn about my birthright. This, I believe, is where I'm meant to be. But only when I've rescued the children, returned them to Kingsholm, and ensured they're never in danger again. And that, I admit, might not be as easy as it should be.

* * *

By the time I've tended to Brute, with the aid of every single member of the war band doing something, I'm exhausted and breathing heavily. My neck still stings, and sometimes my voice is softer than a whisper, and at other occasions it's louder than Oswy in battle. I never know what I'm going to get and, as such, everything disconcerts me.

The day's starting to draw in, and that frustrates me. We need to be going north. I don't know, and neither do the others, just how long's passed since I last saw the children. Wulfheard might be confident he knows where the children are being taken, but what if he's incorrect?

'We need to go,' I urge the ealdorman as we settle before the fire. Well, they do. I'm standing. It's too painful to keep getting up and down. Not that standing is exactly a delight. My leg wound means I limp, and if I don't hold my arm in just the correct position, it throbs. Whatever Oswy's done to my belly wound, and I daren't look, it's not currently hurting too much. In fact, it's the scratches on my hand and face that throb. I've not been able to bathe, but I'm wearing Oswy's spare tunic and Maneca's extra trews, and while they smell faintly of both men, I certainly feel more like myself. After all, my boots are mine.

'We'll eat and then move on. I'm sending Kyre and Landwine ahead. They're going to scout and search for our prey.'

I eye the two men who stand quickly and make their way to the horses. I trust them both, but I must admit, should they find the children first, Coenwulf and Coelwulf will probably be more terrified of them than the men who've captured them.

'How many of them were there?' Kyre questions me, returning to the fire before leaving.

'At least fourteen. I don't think I managed to kill any of Eadweard's cronies who attacked me.'

'Wouldn't know. We don't know where that was.'

'But it was on Watling Street,' I announce, confused. I would have expected there to be some sign of what happened.

'They cleared it up then. That's probably why they moved you as well. They didn't want to leave any obvious signs of their passage.' I shudder at those words. I've killed many warriors in my time, but I'm not sure I've ever done so with the cold-blooded intent these men showed. Certainly, apart from the dead men my uncle killed, and which I forced over the steep incline to ensure the wolves stayed away from my wounded uncle, I've never moved the dead, apart from to bury them.

'We'll keep our eyes peeled,' Landwine murmurs. Both men seem buoyed by the task they've been assigned. As I've come to expect from these warriors. They show no sign of fear even though they might be riding into a great big bloody fight.

'Eat up, young Icel,' Wulfheard urges me. The pottage is delicious, but it's as though I've forgotten how to eat. I'm so tired, and the aches that plague me, even when I swallow, make it hard going. 'You're not going anywhere until you clear that bowl, and even then, you might not be able to mount.'

I've been considering this for some time. But I'm joining them. I don't care how. I'm going.

'I'll walk if I can't ride,' I mutter grumpily.

'You might just be at this rate. Now, eat up, buttercup.'

Growling, and then wishing I hadn't, I hasten to eat, despite how painful it is. I also drink as much water as I can. I still feel dry, and my lips are cracked and sore. I know better than to lick them, but I don't have any salve to rub over them, and so I keep licking them, and that only makes them sorer.

And then there's no more time to procrastinate.

Brute's wound has been tended to as best I could. Given time to rest and recover, I believe he'll be fine, but of course, neither of us has that time. We need to ride on.

Speaking softly and hoping my voice doesn't crack, I run my hand over my horse's back, assessing how I'm going to mount without too much pain. As I recall Waldhere saying to me after the attack on the Isle of Sheppey, once I'm mounted, it might not prove possible to dismount. I might just stay there, hoping the others can return the children without my aid. I don't know if I can hold a seax, and certainly, the thought of wearing a byrnie fills me with shuddering fear. It'll hurt, no matter what. But I must get the children, and my seax, back from Eadweard.

I lead Brute to a handy tree stump and set about mounting, grateful that the others are all busy with other tasks to watch me. Or so I think.

Sweat beads my face, slipping down my back, and still, it's an agony to lift my leg. It doesn't help that I can't grip Brute where I might normally because of his wound.

'Hurry up, Icel. The children will be older than you by the time you get your leg over your horse.' Wulfheard's words are as reassuring as he intends them but it spurs me onwards. Eventually, with some help from Brute, who almost seems to bend at the knees to aid me, I'm finally mounted. I'm absolutely buggered. But I'm on my horse. Now I just need to ride as well.

Ahead, Ealdorman Ælfstan calls his men to order.

'Ride alert to everything. We only found Icel thanks to Brute. These bastards might be hiding the children even better than that.'

'But I doubt it,' we all hear Wulfheard mumble.

'Aye, we all doubt it, but all the same. Let's not allow such assumptions to blind us to the possibility.' There's censure in the ealdorman's words. I consider if I've missed something between the two of them. Have they fallen out in recent days, and I've only just noticed?

But, as Brute steps out, favouring the right side of his body and so making his gait unsteady, the agony that thuds through my body is otherworldly. Whatever's happened between the ealdorman and Wulfheard becomes irrelevant. It's too much effort just to stay seated on my horse.

We ride. Well, I hang on. The others ride, Oswy concerned beside me, his face twisted in consternation and fear. Eventually, I can't help myself. Despite everything, a chuckle blossoms from my mouth.

'What's so damn funny?' Oswy growls.

'Is that what I look like when you lot ignore all my advice?'

'Like what?'

'A mother hen, fussing and biting my tongue.'

Swift fury descends over Oswy's face, the coming night casting his craggy features into a stark contrast of shadows. Only then his face transforms, and he grins. 'Yes. That's it. A mother hen. You always look like you're going to offer us a pillow to take our ease.'

I chuckle again. It's better than bloody crying, which is what I'd like to be doing.

At the sound, I feel Brute relax; suddenly, he's galloping, as usual. It seems, in a moment of levity, both of us have managed to forget our wounds. I only hope it lasts.

33

It doesn't. We ride all night, slower because, while the moon is bright, it's still dark and we need to be careful. We don't see Kyre and Landwine, which means that our prey are still out there. The anger of what they've done goes some way to making me forget my aches and pains, but it's not enough to drive them entirely from my mind.

I stay where I am when the others dismount to water the horses and relieve themselves. Brute doesn't object, and it makes it much, much quicker for all involved.

We continue throughout the next day as well, and I know I sleep in the saddle, Oswy ensuring I don't fall to the ground. We've slept, but only for a small amount of time, making use of the cave where I met the wolf with the children. No wolves trouble us, but the moans and whimpers in my sleep have upset the others. The ealdorman is grim-faced, but it's Wulfheard who's the most sullen, and I'm unsure why. I want to ask, but I don't. I'm loath to draw attention to myself, or I fear they'll leave me.

I order Oswy to find me some moss, wild carrot leaves and dandelions, using the moss on my wound, and adding the dandelions to the pottage we eat when allowed the time to cook it. I'd ask for more, but I know he won't be able to find it. I've already had to stop him adding poisonous mushrooms to the pottage once.

On the second night, we stop in the woodlands where I first found the children, and I discover I can dismount more easily. One of the horses we released finds us during the night, startling Osmod on guard duty, but in the morning, I greet the animal warmly. I hope the others have found their way to some food, perhaps even to the settlement we passed with the hound and the woman. I must have slept through that part of the journey.

Kyre returns to us, his face tight with fury, when we've travelled for half another day.

'We've found them,' he growls, his hand hovering close to his seax.

'Where's Landwine?' Ælfstan demands.

'Watching to make sure we don't lose them. Although, they're hardly hiding,' Kyre complains. His face is twisted, and he keeps licking his lips as though he can taste vengeance. 'They're in a hall, with a fire blazing and men on guard duty around it. They're waiting for someone.'

'Someone with the silver coins to pay the bastards, I imagine.' Wulfheard's furious face has, somehow, become even more twisted with anger.

'Yes, and they're coming today, at some point. We need to get the children before they arrive.'

'How many enemy warriors?'

'I've seen fourteen of them so far, but not the big bloke that Icel spoke about, Wulfnoth. They have horses, but of course, if they escape, they'll miss their rendezvous with whoever's coming to pay them.'

'He won't run,' Wulfheard confirms, as though he knows it for a surety. I'm curious about whom this man is and why Wulfheard knows him so well. Sometimes, I realise, I forget that all these men had lives before I knew them.

'Lead on,' the ealdorman informs Kyre. 'We'll scout the place out and decide what to do then. I don't care if we kill 'em all, as long as the children survive.'

I turn to face the rest of the men I now call friends, even if I know they can kill with their little fingers. I've fought at their side many times, but I've never been the one in stitched-up pieces. Neither, I realise, have I been the one with a huge stake in what was about to happen. The knowledge now is disorientating. Never before have I needed to rely on my fellow warriors as much as I do now. It's a sobering realisation, yet it's not one that worries.

We're the men of Mercia, and if we're fighting to retrieve Mercians from whatever enemy has them, then it doesn't matter if they're children or adults. They're all bloody Mercians.

* * *

Ealdorman Ælfstan sends others to assist Landwine in assessing the hall that the enemy have the children locked up inside. When they return, expressions are grim.

'We can't take the horses.' Kyre is firm on that, as is Oswy. I don't look at them as they say this. I might be able to ride, but running or walking is almost beyond me. Still, I'm not going to be left behind.

'They'll hear us coming if we take the horses,' Oswy echoes again, not looking at me.

'There are two big buggers at the front who actually have their wits about them. The rest, I couldn't say for sure. We've not seen the children, but we've heard them.' Kyre bites down on the rest of that remark, and I consider why. But perhaps it's best if I don't know. For now. I'll kill the bastards, all of them.

'We can circle the property. There's low wicker fences surrounding it. There are pigs in one of the fields, mind. We don't want to make them squeal.' A grin splits Oswy's face as he finds some amusement in that. Ealdorman Ælfstan's face is set in a grimace as he considers.

'Then we split our force. Icel, if you think you can make it, you stay closest to the horses. If we have to run from here, I want you to stand more than half a chance of reaching Brute.' His words are far from reassuring.

'Cenred and Oswy, you stay with Icel. Godeman, Kyre and Osmod, you take the far side. Waldhere, Ordlaf, me and Wulfheard will take the front. The rest of you, it looks like you have to contend with the pigs.'

I would grin at the unhappiness on the faces of Maneca, Uor, Wulfgar and Landwine, but I'm too busy trying to dismount. I'm too slow. When my right foot hits the ground, I think I've done it, only for the delayed pulse of pain to send stars dancing before my eyes and my balance to fail me just as my left leg hits the ground. Somehow, I've also managed to hurt Brute as well, for he veers forwards leaving me with no support.

I hit the ground, jarring my teeth, belly wound, head and everything else as well. Not for the first time, tears fall from my face. I wish none of the men had witnessed that, but I know I've not been so lucky. Strong hands on my arms, and Oswy is beside me, Wulfheard to the other side. I wait for them to tell me to remain behind as they right me and pretend not to see my tears.

'Take this.' Oswy thrusts a seax into my hands as soon as I'm upright. 'You need something to kill the scum with.' I almost choke on his kindness, gripping the well-formed blade hungrily. I've lost too much while trying to track down the children.

'And this.' Wulfheard thrusts a war axe into my other hand. I have my weapons belt, and I've been given my rusted byrnie. My weapons belt is already in place around my waist, but not my byrnie. With fumbling hands, I reach for it, where it's waiting for me, rolled on Brute's back. I wince at the weight, realising how weak I am. It's only been a few days, but my strength has been stolen from me.

Before I can make a further arse of myself trying to shrug into it, the two men are there, taking the weight from me and forcing it over my head. Raising my arms hurts, but it's nothing compared to the feeling of tightening my weapons belt over it, with the added heft of the blades. My belly hurts, but it's only one of so many other aches that they've all merged together.

'You look like a...' Oswy's voice trails off as he eyes me.

'Trussed pig,' Wulfheard offers sourly.

I hold my tongue and limp to where I can empty my bladder. I do, at least, manage to stay upright this time.

Again, I think someone will ask me if I'm sure about this, but no one does, as I limp to where the rest of the men wait. Some of them are clearly impatient. But not all of them.

They eye me, Cenred most carefully.

'Just remember which end to stick 'em with,' is his helpful advice, and then Kyre is leading the way. I follow on last, Cenred and Oswy with me.

Everyone steps carefully, and I try and copy them, but it's difficult with my limp. I try to put weight on my right leg, but it thrums with a nausea-inducing pain, so I continue limping.

I look the part. What I'll be able to accomplish, I'm unsure, but prepared to try. And really, I'm more concerned with ensuring the children recognise me as someone who's come to help them.

I watch the rest of the men scrambling to where they've been told to wait. At some point, the ealdorman alongside, Waldhere, Ordlaf and Wulfheard veer aside, to the settlement's entrance. Ælfstan offers me an appraising glance, but Wulfheard, head down, makes his way without looking at me. I can't help fearing for him. Something about this warrior who has the children means more to Wulfheard than it does to me. I hope he behaves himself. I hope he doesn't take too many chances. I wish one of the others had the stones to tell me what it was.

Overhead, bird call drowns our steps, the harsh cawing of blackbirds high in the trees. Not the best omen, but whether for those we're going to attack or for us, I can't determine.

Through the trees, I catch sight of the hall, and despite the birds, can hear the harsh shriek of young Coelwulf through the wooden walls of the building. My heart thuds loudly in my chest but Cenred and Oswy are no fools.

'Wait for the signal,' Cenred urges me. 'Or die because the others aren't ready yet.'

I nod, but my throat's dry once more.

I run my hand over the borrowed seax and war axe, dreaming of ripping into the flesh of the men who thought to try and kill me. That steadies me. Coelwulf might be distressed, but he won't be for long. Soon I'll have him safely on the way back to Kingsholm, even if when he gets there, he'll have no father to welcome him home. He will, at least, be somewhere safe. Or so I hope.

The day drags. I grow impatient, and thirsty, the raging pain making my head pound in time to my heart. Cenred, beside me, is calmer, his eyes sharp, whereas I'm hazed by pain. I fear my movements will be too slow to attack. Yet the ealdorman has allowed me to remain with the rest of the men. He's a cautious man most of the time. He must trust my abilities, as does Wulfheard. Either that or Oswy's told them that I'm going to die from my wounds regardless and they've decided to allow me to die on the edge of a blade rather than in agony on my deathbed. Either way, I take comfort in knowing the probable outcomes and don't ask Oswy, where he waits with me as well.

I can't see the two men guarding the settlement's approach. It is, as the advance party said, a good place to build a hall. Very secluded for those who don't want to play much part in wider events and who want somewhere defensible as well. There are walls surrounding the settlement, but they're deceptive, woven from hazel, and I can see no ditch, although I might be wrong about there being one. Perhaps, I realise, I should have listened more closely when Kyre was reporting to the ealdorman.

In contrast, the hall's walls are made with thick trunks, the wattle and daub that fills the spaces between fresh and glistening. Whoever lives here is wealthy. But there aren't many outbuildings. My thoughts return to the monastery on the Isle of Sheppey. There were many outbuildings there. Some for the sheep. Others for the monks to sleep within. Perhaps, I consider, those are to the far side of the main building, for I'm sure that someone such as this wouldn't allow the servants, slaves or animals to share the living space with them.

'We go when we get the signal,' Cenred reminds me as I wait impatiently.

'And what is the damn signal?' I ask in a harsh whisper.

'You'll know it when you hear it,' Oswy counters.

'So what, there isn't one?'

'There's always one. You just don't always know what it is. It depends on the circumstances. We can't all bloody hoot like an owl when it's broad daylight.'

I don't know why Cenred mentions an owl, and I feel my forehead furrow.

'Look,' Cenred continues. 'We use an owl sometimes, and of course, none of the daft gits have thought of that until now, so, you know, we'll know it when we hear it and not before.' I nod, lips twisting, as I lick at their cracked surface. I fear they might never feel normal again. Certainly, the women who work in the king's hall in Tamworth won't be looking to kiss me anytime soon. Not that I want to kiss them. Or maybe I do. I don't know and dismiss the thought to focus on what I'm supposed to do.

Only then, a sound thrums through the air. I look to Cenred and Oswy, and they look to me.

'What the hell was that supposed to be?' The call, perhaps meant to be some sort of trill, has the distinct sound of Wulfheard behind it.

'Bloody arseholes,' Cenred complains, checking his weapons belt before striding out from the shelter of the trees, followed by Oswy. Ahead, the fence waits for us, but it takes no time for Cenred to slice through it with his seax. 'Why did they bloody bother?' he grumbles, more to himself than to me.

Cenred doesn't wait for me. Oswy forces his way through, and by the time I happen upon it, my right leg making me wince, both have disappeared. I thrust my arm through it, the pieces of the fencing having knitted back together as though they'd never been forced apart.

'Hurry up,' Oswy hisses. I realise that I'm going to get as much sympathy from Oswy as I've so far received from Wulfheard. Biting my lip, thinking only of the children, I follow the two warriors through.

I glance left and right, considering where the rest of the men are, but I can't see them. Neither, from what I can hear, does it seem that the alarm's been raised. I reach over and touch Cenred's arm.

'Was that the call? None of the others are here.'

'They know what they're doing. Come on. Keep up.'

Cenred moves swiftly, Oswy following him. The fencing that we've come through doesn't allow immediate access to the hall. Instead, Cenred has to force a path through another line of fencing, and then a final one. It's time-consuming, but I still don't understand why they've taken the time to build it when it's about as much use as melted cheese.

It slows us, yes, but only a little. Through the third fence, and I'm finally greeted by the site of the hall and my fellow warriors. The strange bird call must have been the signal, after all. Wulfheard, I see, is already engaged in a fierce fight with someone. Their cries reach me, as does the clash of iron on iron, but it's not the huge man I saw on the horse. That'll annoy Wulfheard.

'Stop dallying, and hurry up,' Cenred urges. Oswy already has weapons ready in his hand. I appreciate then that while there's fighting to the front of the hall, we're faced with the hall itself. The doorway is wide open. I don't know if my fellow warriors have forced it open or if it's just like that. From inside, I can hear the cries of Coelwulf, and they're growing in intensity, and my stomach fills with a leaden weight. If they've done anything to him, I'll kill them all.

With renewed vigour, I hasten to a crab-like run, Cenred and Oswy beside me. Cenred's steps are light compared to mine, and I know he purposefully slows his pace to keep in time with me. Oswy is swifter. He stops at the door, hand blocking our path, as he tries to glimpse the interior. The smell of food cooking stirs my stomach, but that doesn't mean everyone inside doesn't have a blade to hand, ready to kill the enemy.

'Come on.' Oswy moves forward, expecting Cenred and I to stand beside him, and I do, but Oswy's movements are more fluid than mine. I see what I don't want to see as my eyes adjust to the darkness.

A man, who I think is Wulfnoth, holds the two children tightly while wearing a gloating grin. I see the glimmer of iron in his hand and know he means to kill them, given the opportunity.

'Well, well, well, it seems you didn't die, after all.' The words are pointed, aimed at me, and also, I realise, at the shocked expressions of Eadweard and Wulfred who thought to have killed me.

'Give me the children,' I urge him. 'They don't belong to you.' I'm impressed my voice is firm as Cenred and Oswy stiffen beside me. No doubt they're doing a quick assessment of our chances of retrieving the children alive.

The sound of fighting can be heard from outside, but inside, there are more than fourteen men, so our two sides aren't evenly matched. And, of course, the bastard has a blade at the children's throats.

Coenwulf, eyes wide, smiles on seeing me, but the enemy jabs his blade closer. He howls in fear. I'm unsurprised. I'd do the same in his situation. Coelwulf, meanwhile, is held in a tight grip, but he struggles against it. His harsh shrieks would put an eagle to shame or the pigs, knowing they're about to be slaughtered.

Eadweard, Deremann, Wulfred and Forthgar quickly regain their senses, weapons to hand, and move to encircle Cenred, Oswy and me. Apart from Eadweard, they all look like I managed to land a few cuts and blows on their faces before they overpowered me. That makes me smirk. The other men hang back. Perhaps they don't need to act unless these four fail in their attempts to kill us.

'Give the children back, Wulfnoth,' I try once more. 'And you might live to see the sunset.'

'And you and who else are going to see to that? Those men outside? I know them, and I don't believe they're anything to worry about.'

Cenred and Oswy have their eyes on Eadweard and his allies. I take some pleasure in seeing the cuts and abrasions on their faces and exposed arms. I'm glad I gave as good as I got, even if, in the end, they thought they'd won. I'm pleased I didn't just give in to them.

But, as the warrior speaks, there's a crash from outside, and the roar of angry voices. I recognise Ordlaf, and Maneca, Wulfheard and the ealdorman. And every man in that hall looks to the door as though the wall might disappear and reveal to them what's happening. All apart from the man I face. He's heavily scarred. And still, I think I should know him.

'Kill them,' he says, the tone counter to the command. He sounds almost bored.

Eadweard, Wulfred, Forthgar and Deremann advance quickly then. They can't entirely surround us, because the door remains at our backs, and I jab with my seax, frantically trying not to overbalance, as Eadweard skips closer. He laughs at me, spittle flying from his mouth, the smell of ale on his lips, my eagle-headed seax in his hand.

Somehow, my seax hits home, raising a thin line of blood on his left arm. I grimace, trying to find my courage and strength to reclaim the children for a second time even though these men nearly killed me. I try not to look at the boys, no matter their cries. Once I've killed these men, I'll be able to console them. And I will.

Eadweard yelps at my blow and comes at me quickly with my stolen seax. I counter his blows with my blade, curling my left fist, keen to knock his nose aside and have him blinded by the pain. He must sense my intent and jabs out with the seax towards my hand. I smirk, ramming my seax handle into his nose instead. The sound of Eadweard's nose collapsing is audible, and he spits aside blood that runs between his thin lips and into his mouth. Using my elbow, I also knock his forehead, and he stumbles backwards. Unable to stop my forward advance, I follow him, one hand seeking something to steady myself with, but there's only him.

I grab for Eadweard, and follow him down with a heavy thud that reminds me of all my hurts, and sends me into a stabbing frenzy. My body over his, I rear up on my arm and gore him repeatedly, his chest rupturing with each blow despite his byrnie. He tries to counter the attack, but I'm too quick. He's barely raised the stolen seax to counter my blows when his arm crashes to the wooden floor. He's dead, and yet I can't stop spearing him. The feel of his blood on my face spurs me on.

'Bastard,' I shout, my voice raw and strained.

'I think he's bloody dead, Icel.' Oswy's words finally permeate my hearing. I glance up to him, and realise he's fighting two men. One of the others is curled in a ball on the ground, bleeding copiously. I try to stand, but my legs are twisted, and my hands slip in the slickness of Eadweard's blood.

'Here.' Wulfheard is suddenly there, his hand on my arm, pulling me upright. Oswy no longer faces Wulfred and Deremann but only Deremann, Wulfred swaying on his feet, but the light has left his eyes. He's dead before he hits the ground. Cenred has taken on Forthgar.

He bends and takes my eagle-headed seax from Eadweard's lifeless hand, and I welcome the familiar feel of my blade in my hand.

'Kill them,' Wulfnoth rears. I hear Wulfheard's exhalation as more foemen come to meet the attack. These seem to be more seasoned warriors, their blades shimmering in the light from the hearth fire, but we now outnumber them. I'm pushed aside by the rest of my fellow warriors, busy with the task of killing the enemies who believe stealing children is acceptable. And my eyes alight on the man who still holds them.

Somehow, I forge a path through the fighting, being knocked here and there, but staying upright all the same. The man doesn't see me until I'm close to him, Coenwulf almost reaching out to touch me.

'Get back,' Wulfnoth menaces. 'Get back to Wulfheard and his pathetic warriors, or I'll butcher these children.'

I don't glance behind me, as he wants me to do. I know that Wulfheard and the rest of the men are winning the fight. Wulfnoth speaks with bluff and thinks to use the children to stay my hand. It won't bloody work.

Coenwulf watches me fearfully, but Coelwulf still strains against the tight hold of this man, the seax in his right hand, close to Coenwulf's neck. It gives Coelwulf much more room to cause problems.

I consider how best to approach this. I don't want either boy wounded, but Wulfnoth evidently believes I'll play nice and not just attack him. But Wulfnoth's wrong. I'll slice him. I'll risk Coenwulf getting cut because I know I'll be able to heal him if the worst should happen. I take a breath, test my stance to ensure my wounded leg won't fail me, and then, as I lurch at him, Coelwulf, using all of his baby teeth, snaps down on Wulfnoth's exposed hand.

Wulfnoth shrieks, dropping Coelwulf heavily to the floor, who doesn't even seem to notice as he crawls towards me with a gurgle of delight. I jump over him, my seax stabbing down and into the thick seax-holding arm of the man still wincing over the bloody mark on his hand. Coenwulf screams, the sound shocking, but not one of pain, rather one of rage as the blood of his captor gushes over him.

The man's grip on the seax falters, and it's all the opportunity I need. I wrench Coenwulf free, pulling on his arm and knowing I'll leave a mark but not caring. Better a bruise than dead.

With him in my arms, I glower at the other man. His triumph has slid from his face, like wax from a candle, and he's exposed.

'Leave him,' I hear Wulfheard holler. 'Leave him, Icel. He's for me to kill.' Wulfheard speaks with no delight, only conviction. I risk turning, and appreciate that all of the enemy warriors are dead and that Ealdorman Ælfstan cradles Coelwulf in his arms, a strange look on his face, almost as though he's never held a child before.

'Who is he?' I demand from Wulfheard, chest heaving. I want to kill him. I want to use my seax blade with Mercia's eagle emblazoned on it to kill the man who thought to deprive Mercia of her young eaglets.

'A traitor, and always has been,' Wulfheard responds, moving past me and offering nothing further. I hobble backwards, keen to unite the two brothers and not to be a part of whatever vengeance Wulfheard means to exact from the man who stole the children.

'Who is he?' I murmur to Ealdorman Ælfstan, as I reach over and run my hand through Coelwulf's fair hair, as the clash of iron on iron reverberates throughout the hall.

'He's his brother,' Ælfstan admits in a soft voice, and now I understand why he looks at the children as he does. Brothers. But not necessarily allies.

'Why?' I hear Wulfheard demand from his brother as they fight, seaxes twisted together, their fists doing most of the damage. Wulfheard is certainly winning, despite the difference in height between the two.

'Why not, brother?' the other man taunts.

'Who paid you?' Wulfheard demands, but his question is only met with derisive laughter, as the crash of blade on blade intensifies.

'A nastier piece of dung you'd be hard-pressed to find,' Ælfstan continues, as though we talk of small matters, and not two men fighting to the death. 'He has no love for Mercia, or her kings. Some even say he was involved in the murder of King Coenwulf's son near enough twenty years ago.'

I gasp at that. If Coenwulf's son had lived, his brother, Coelwulf, would never have become king. My father would never have usurped him, and the last ten winters need never have happened.

'Aye, Icel. The bastard has a lot to answer for, and Wulfheard is the man to ensure it's done properly. He's waited a long time for this.' While I think to shield Coenwulf's eyes from what's happening before me, he struggles free, and I allow it. After all, he should see this for himself. He might never feel safe again unless he knows his captor has been killed.

And he is being killed. Carefully, precisely, Wulfheard overpowers his brother. With a soft gasp, that could almost be mistaken for a sob, Wulfnoth lies bleeding, one eye missing, his nose broken, and Wulfheard's seax through his neck, cutting off his air with the wet gurgle of a cask of ale being run dry. Wulfnoth's dead, and yet I can't help thinking, we still don't know who paid him, or indeed, any of the men, to capture Mercia's children.

34

It takes more than ten days to return to Kingsholm. Ealdorman Ælfstan leads the way, grim-faced. He's content that Wulfheard killed his brother. But he's dismayed not to know who was the power behind the attempt on the lives of the children, if indeed, that was the intention all along, which appears likely from what Eadweard said to me.

It seems to me, at least, that Lord Wigmund is implicated, but Ælfstan cautions me to silence. He says not enough is known. I disagree with him, but I hold my tongue. For now.

On the journey, Wulfheard is silent. The children are gregarious, and when we seek shelter in Chester for two nights, Æthelgyth cares for them with all the joy she showed previously, and I'm delighted to see young Godfrith with her and Oswin. He shows me his new cloaks and boots with pride, his new tunic and trews as well.

My thoughts turn to Eadburg, time and time again. I fear she's dead. I believe it's my fault, but I only receive an answer when, with the first snowstorms, we ride through the gates of Kingsholm. We find the place hunkering down for the winter months, and Eadburg's there, being tended to by young Lady Cynewise, returned from Tamworth, with some of the king's warriors, on the orders of Lady Ælflæd. I also suspect

Wynflæd's involvement as Cynewise greets me with a smile and a gabble of new knowledge about moss.

Perhaps, after all, my thoughts towards Lady Ælflæd have been blackened by her association with Lord Wigmund, and the precariousness of her position as the sister of a traitor, and wife to the king's son.

Not that Eadburg is well. She's as scarred as I am. While I limp and groan, Eadburg suffers from a deep wound forged through her back. The bastards thought to kill her, and they would have succeeded, if not for the aid of the Wolf Lady, who somehow found her, nursed her, and ensured she was returned to Kingsholm. The woman is powerful in the same way as Wynflæd. I think I'd like to know more about her. When the seasons change, I'll return to Hereford. I'll ask her more about the wolves. I feel I should know about them. And also about her. I would like to know how she came to live as she does. I've used the woods to hide in many times. I can only think she runs from a destiny as momentous as mine might have been.

Eadburg sobs on seeing the children, and they on seeing her, and while all are sombre for the death of Eadburg's mother, as are Eadburg's siblings, even the youngest, not much older than young Coelwulf, there is also much joy. The small children have survived. It's a miracle worthy of one of the priest's sermons.

'Icel.' Ealdorman Ælfstan summons me, two days later, to sit beside him before the hearth. It's piled high with wood, blazing merrily. Outside, the snow has continued to fall. A surprisingly early snowstorm that presages a bleak winter. We're lucky we arrived when we did. If not, it would have been an even more difficult journey here. And it was already hard enough with all our wounds and two small children.

'Ealdorman.' I incline my head, wishing I didn't still feel the crushing weight of Eadweard's fingers at my throat as I do so. It's a constant reminder that not even his death has yet banished.

'Sit with me,' Ælfstan urges me.

We're alone. The other men are in the stables, assisting Pega and Hatel with the increase in the number of horses that must be tended. It's more awkward than it should be, but eventually I'm settled, my right leg before me, my belly stretched slightly backwards to prevent the healing wound from catching and, worse, from itching where it rubs against my trews.

'You did well. I owe you an apology for taking you from the children, dismissing your concerns, and for not hastening back to Kingsholm when you came alone. If they'd died, I'd never have forgiven myself.'

I don't feel I need to add that I wouldn't have forgiven myself either.

'It seems, whether it's men telling you should be the king's commander, or men trying to steal away small children, that you're somehow more closely linked to the ruling house of Mercia than I would have thought possible for someone such as you.'

His fierce eyes blaze into mine. If he's hoping for a confidence, I can't give him one. I must keep my secret. I've seen how much trouble it can cause two small boys. With my reputation as a warrior it would be so much worse.

'I've urged you, in the past, to be careful. To watch what you do, and now I would reiterate that, young Icel. Mercia's enemies are gathering, and as you know only too well, it's not just external enemies, but internal ones as well.' His words are solemn, edged with a warning. 'The king ages. Those who wish to rule after him grow in power and influence. Some, it seems, are more than willing to kill for the chance to rule,' he continues. His voice thrums with intensity. 'Lord Beorhtwulf is a problem. I suspect his ultimate involvement in this, as does Wulfheard. Mind, his brother would sell his soul to the highest bidder, so it is possible it was someone else. I don't suspect Lady Ælflæd.' He says this more softly, eyes alert to those close by. 'I do suspect her husband, and his mother. The queen fears her queenship will be fleeting, and like other Mercian women, especially those associated with Winchcombe, she means to shore up her support and supporters.' I can tell the ealdorman has given the matter a great deal of thought. I nod along with him. I can't deny any of his concerns.

I should have sought out the king, but I've not been able to. Not yet. Perhaps when the snow clears I'll return to Tamworth. Perhaps I'll even inform him of my parentage. No, I could never do that, I realise. I don't want anyone to know. Not now. My future is set. The soft hand of young Coenwulf steals into mine, a cheeky grin on his honey-smeared face,

Coelwulf tottering behind him, with Lady Cynewise holding the youngster's hands to keep him upright, and as much as I want to fear the future, I can't. Not when it might just rest in the hands of these two small boys, and their fierce aunt.

Only time will tell.

HISTORICAL NOTES

This story is mostly fictional, but for fans of the later books which feature Icel, I felt it necessary to build the relationship he shares with both Coenwulf, who we don't really get to know well, and certainly his younger brother, Coelwulf. I also thought it was an excellent way to hold a mirror to his uncle's actions when Ecgberht of Wessex attacked Mercia, and stole Icel away to the borderlands with the Welsh.

As I've said many times before, events in Mercia at this time are not at all well documented. But there is a storm brewing, and I always think it's good to set it up firmly beforehand.

I've always found the title of Northumbria confusing for the area of northern England, but that does indeed seem to be the correct term for all land north of Mercia, once the smaller kingdoms had been merged into the larger ones. It is as simple as my characters say: Northumbria was land north of the River Humber. On occasion, the term Southumbria was also used for all land south of the River Humber. Such huge rivers gave reasonably permanent border features between kingdoms, although, of course, they were on occasion overwhelmed.

The four main roads of Saxon England are well known: Watling Street, Ermine Street, Foss(e) Way and Icknield Way. There are also other well-known roads, such as Dere Street, running through Northumbria to the kingdom of the Scots. There was also a road running north from Chester and through Cumbria towards Carlisle, Akeman Street, and a road running from London towards Winchester, and also one running from London towards Kent are also known. It is believed that the Roman roads were still utilised throughout this period, if not often repaired.

ACKNOWLEDGMENTS

Thanks, as ever, to my editor, Caroline, for a few gentle nudges with this one, and everyone at Boldwood Books for your huge enthusiasm for these tales set in the distant past. A special shout-out to Ross, who has to contend with my 'made-up' words, and inability to get slaughter field, any more and slaughterhouse quite right.

To my fellow authors, thank you for all your support. Elizabeth R. Andersen, Eilis Quinn and Kelly Evans, I'm looking at you there. Also to Donovan Cook, J. C. Duncan and Peter Gibbons, my fellow Boldwood authors, for your encouragement.

And a huge thank you to my other half and (adult) children, for moving 'around me' so that I could get *Protector of Mercia* finished in time. And I'm sorry I have quite so many heavy books.

To my readers, thank you for continuing to enjoy my tales set in Saxon England. I appreciate you and hope you continue to enjoy my stories.

ABOUT THE AUTHOR

MJ Porter is the author of many historical novels set predominantly in Seventh to Eleventh-Century England, and in Viking Age Denmark. Raised in the shadow of a building that was believed to house the bones of long-dead Kings of Mercia, meant that the author's writing destiny was set.

Sign up to MJ Porter's mailing list here for news, competitions and updates on future books.

Visit MJ's website: www.mjporterauthor.com

Follow MJ on social media:

twitter.com/coloursofunison

instagram.com/m_j_porter

bookbub.com/authors/mj-porter

ALSO BY MJ PORTER

The Eagle of Mercia Chronicles

Son of Mercia

Wolf of Mercia

Warrior of Mercia

Eagle of Mercia

Protector of Mercia

The Brunanburh Series

King of Kings

Kings of War

Milton Keynes UK
Ingram Content Group UK Ltd.
UKHW042248080923
428219UK00002BA/7

welcome

Britain's biggest re[illegible] got bigger (again!). [illegible] save at more restaurants than ever before. We've traversed the country to bring you the very best restaurants, recommended by our members. It's heartening to see so many new places joining us; we're truly excited about the establishments that you'll find within these pages and we hope you enjoy dining with them. In this year's guide you'll also see a number of new features, initiatives, and exclusive offers, developed especially for you.

Our members are the backbone of the Gourmet Society. Enjoy the savings.

Contents

How to use your card...

1 Choose + Check > 2 Call + book > 3 Dine + save

It's simple

1. **Choose & Check** - Find a restaurant in this guide, our website or the mobile app and check the offer. Make sure the offer is available on the day you wish to use it.
2. **Call & Book** - Call the restaurant to book your table and let them know that you will be using your Gourmet Society card.
3. **Dine & Save** - Enjoy your meal, show your membership card and get the discount. It's that simple!

Availability

Restaurants welcome Gourmet Society members during the week, and most do during the weekend; each listing has the following symbols for your confirmation.

FRI ✓ SAT ✓	Offer available anytime on Friday/Saturday.
FRI ☀ SAT ☀	Offer not available on Friday/Saturday evenings.
FRI 📱 SAT 📱	Members must call on the day to see if they can use their card that evening, subject to availability and restaurant's discretion.
FRI × SAT ×	Offer not available at anytime on Friday/Saturday.
SUN	Sunday Lunch excluded.
🌲	The Gourmet Society offer is not available throughout December.
✱	The Gourmet Society offer is only available in the evenings.

Don't forget

Always check the individual restaurant's offer and availability prior to booking.
Restaurants may exclude bank holidays and other special days.
Full details are available for every restaurant online at
www.gourmetsociety.co.uk

The Offers explained...

As a Gourmet Society member you'll get up to 50% off meals by showing your card. When you check the restaurant listings you will see a variety of icons. Let's take a look at what they mean...

2-for-1 Offers

2FOR1 MAIN COURSE Purchase one main course and a second will be free.

2FOR1 2 COURSES Purchase one main course with either a starter or dessert, and the second main course and starter/dessert will be free.

2FOR1 3 COURSES Get a free starter, main course and dessert with the purchase of another starter, main course and dessert.

How many people?
One dining card will get you one free meal per party. Restaurants usually allow a maximum of two cards per party, so the purchase of two meals would result in two meals being given for free.

Remember!
The free dish is always the cheapest.

Percentage Offers

25% OFF TOTAL Get **25% off your entire bill**, including your drinks.

50% OFF FOOD Get **50% off your food bill**. Drinks are not included in this offer.

8 **How many people?** Only ONE dining card per party is required for this discount. Some restaurants limit the number of people that the discount applies to and this is indicated by the icon shown.

Don't forget

Always check the individual restaurant's offer details prior to booking.
The Gourmet Society offer is available when dining from the **à la carte menu only**, unless stated otherwise.
It cannot be used in conjunction with set menus or any other offer.

Your Questions Answered...

Helping you get the best deal with every meal...

Why do I need to book in advance?

Quite simply, booking beforehand makes the whole experience more efficient for both members and restaurants. It ensures that the restaurant will apply the discount when they prepare your bill, and it reminds them how valuable our members are to their business. Always remember to call and book, mentioning your Gourmet Society card..

Can I choose any dish from the menu?

Of course! We want to give our members the best possible choice, so the Gourmet Society discount applies to the full a la carte menu, not limited set menus. Enjoy choosing whatever you want every time you dine.

Can I use my dining card every day?

You will find that many of our restaurants are happy to accept Gourmet Society bookings every day of the week, and with almost 7,000 to choose from, you'll be spoilt for choice. Understandably some restaurants do limit use of the cards during their busiest periods, so make sure you check the listings before you book.

Why are there different offers?

We're proud to offer our members a range of discounts as this means the Gourmet Society card is perfect for a variety of different occasions and group sizes. For example, a restaurant offering 25% off the bill is great for a family night out, whereas a 2-for-1 offer is perfect for treating a loved one.

Any more questions?

Give our Member Services team a call on **0845 257 4477.**

Let's work together!

The Gourmet Society is a win-win for everyone; our members get a great deal, and our partner restaurants fill their tables with hungry diners. The restaurants promise you the same high quality of food and service that they would offer to any other guests. All we ask in return is that you, our members, follow the booking instructions and adhere to each restaurant's requirements.

Remember these top tips and help The Society grow...

Treat yourself

You already know that your bill is going to be up to 50% less, so go ahead and indulge a little; choose a decadent dessert, celebrate with a glass of fizz. You'll still be quids in with your Gourmet Society card.

Give a little back

Even though you might have just paid half price, your waiter or waitress has still given 100 percent service. So say "thank you" by tipping based on the full bill before your Gourmet Society discount.

Spread the word!

Things are better, shared. So don't forget to tell your friends and family about the Gourmet Society so they can get involved, too.

Our pledge to you

We'll continue to add new and exciting restaurants for you to try. We'll always try to offer you the biggest discounts and the best availability. If something goes wrong, we'll do our utmost to fix it.

By working together, we'll create a better experience and a bigger, better Society for everyone.

Get the App

- Check out your nearest restaurants
- Read reviews
- Get contact details and directions
- Just flash the app to get the discount!

On the move and fancy eating out for less? There's an app for that, and it's free for all members!

What does it do?

You can search restaurants, find contact details and even get directions, plus it doubles as a Smart Membership card so just show it at the restaurant to get your discount!

How do I get it?

The Gourmet Society dining app is available to download now on all major mobile platforms including Android, iPhone, iPad, Blackberry and Windows. Visit your dedicated app store and search 'Gourmet Society'.

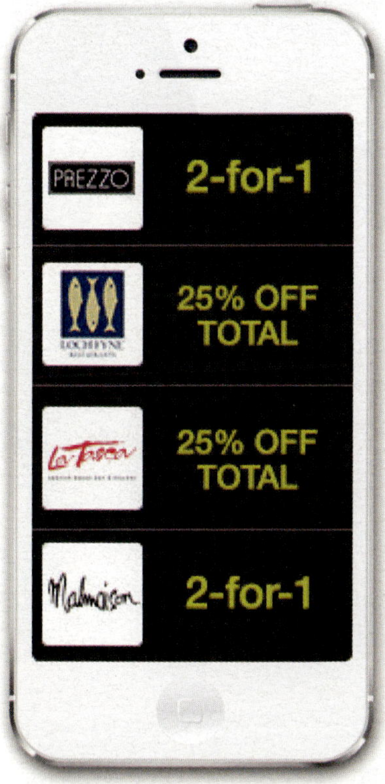

Smart Membership Card

You can access all of the Gourmet Society discounts straight through your mobile phone. Simply download, activate and search for deals, then show the app at the restaurant to get the discount. It's like a super duper digital version of your membership card!

Activating your app

Once you've downloaded your app you must activate it in order to access all the good stuff, including your Smart Membership card (which is personal to you). An Authentication Code is required to do this, you'll find it in the welcome email we sent you when you first joined, and in your welcome letter.

Lost your Authentication Code?

If you can't find your Authentication Code, don't panic - simply log in to the Members' Area to request a new one. Alternatively, give us a call on 0845 257 4477 and we'll provide you with a new one.

www.gourmetsociety.co.uk/apps

Join the Conversation

www.gourmetsociety.co.uk

Your online members' area is a hub for all the benefits of membership

Login today to search restaurants, access exclusive member-only-offers and see what members are saying...

★★★★★

"simply delicious!"

★★★★★

"friendly service"

★★★★★

"fabulous atmosphere"

Advanced Search

Just pop in a location and the restaurant search tool will show you what's available nearby. Results can be filtered by cuisine, offer types and availability.

Restaurant Details

Each one of our restaurants has a dedicated page; here you'll find their address and contact information, along with reviews, the Gourmet Society offer and more.

Member Benefits

Take advantage of exclusive extras; from money off magazine subscriptions, to 2-for-1 entrance on gardens, all available through your members' area.

www.gourmetsociety.co.uk

Forgotten your password?

If you have any problems logging in you can click the link on the login screen or call us on 0845 257 4477 and we'll help you out

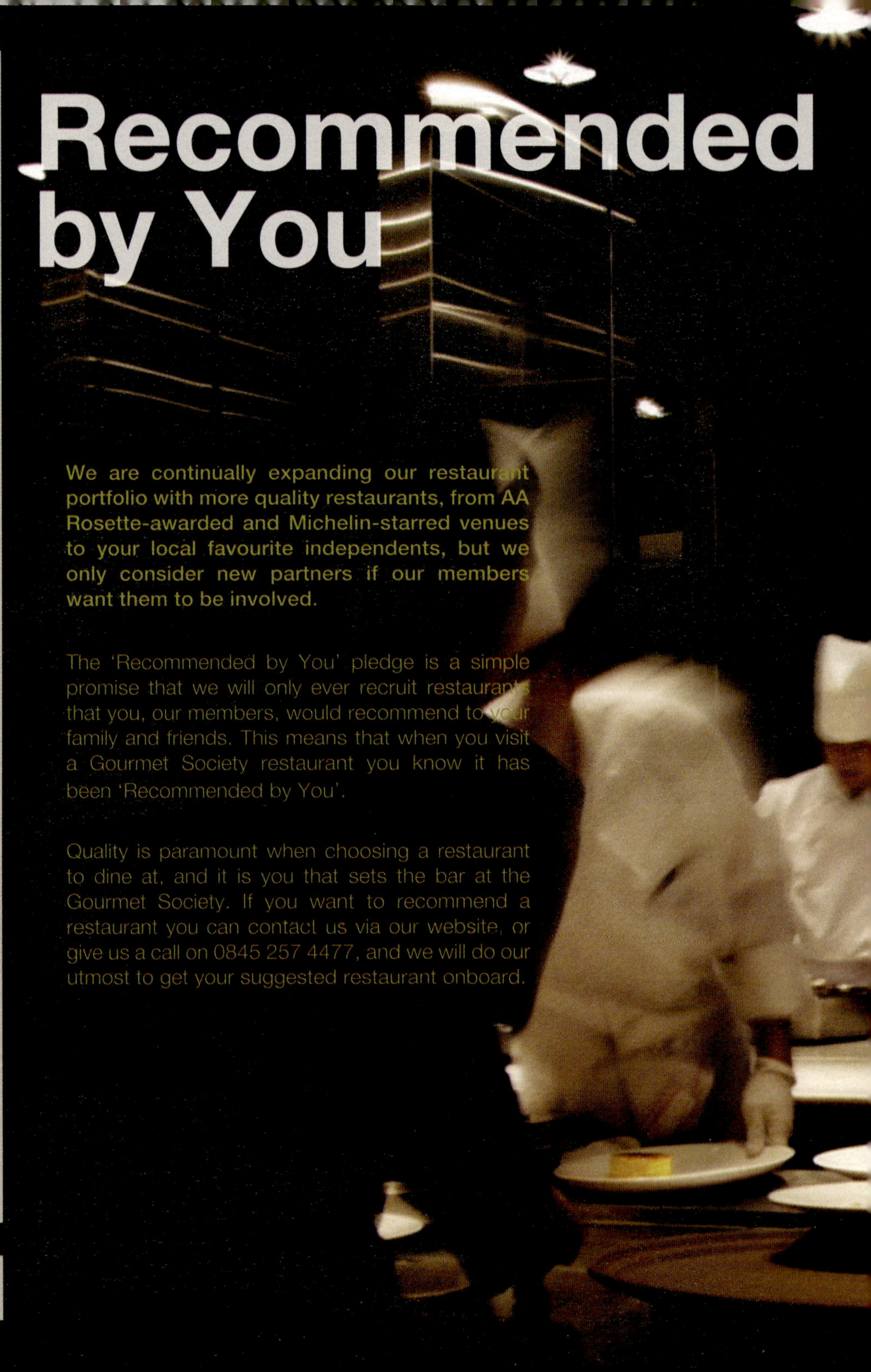

Recommended by You

We are continually expanding our restaurant portfolio with more quality restaurants, from AA Rosette-awarded and Michelin-starred venues to your local favourite independents, but we only consider new partners if our members want them to be involved.

The 'Recommended by You' pledge is a simple promise that we will only ever recruit restaurants that you, our members, would recommend to your family and friends. This means that when you visit a Gourmet Society restaurant you know it has been 'Recommended by You'.

Quality is paramount when choosing a restaurant to dine at, and it is you that sets the bar at the Gourmet Society. If you want to recommend a restaurant you can contact us via our website, or give us a call on 0845 257 4477, and we will do our utmost to get your suggested restaurant onboard.

"... our 'recommended by you' pledge ensures we only recruit restaurants recommended by our members"

Thought the Gourmet Society was all about food?

Think again!

Members now get exclusive discounts on all these tempting treats.

Login at www.gourmetsociety.co.uk for more details and start saving today.

As a Gourmet Society Member you get more than just restaurant savings. Here are some examples of the constantly expanding range of member benefits to help you save money every day.

70% OFF HOTELS

50% OFF THEATRE

50% OFF GARDENS

20% OFF SPAS

2-FOR-1 AIRPORT LOUNGE

£60 OFF WINE

2-FOR-1 AFTERNOON TEA

50% OFF GOLF

25% OFF CINEMA

Check out the latest blockbusting offer!

Members now get 25% off cinema tickets too.

Login at www.gourmetsociety.co.uk for more details and to book your tickets.

Please remember, you must login to our members area and order your cinema tickets <u>in advance</u>; you can't simply arrive at the cinema with your membership card.

Saving refers to average discount off a peak adult ticket. Cinema discounts are only available to full members.

25% OFF
CINEMA
"A FANTASTIC MEMBER BENEFIT"
★★★★★
ODEON
FANATICAL ABOUT FILM
cineworld
CINEMAS
VUE
SHOWCASE
EMPIRE

2-FOR-1 AFTERNOON TEA

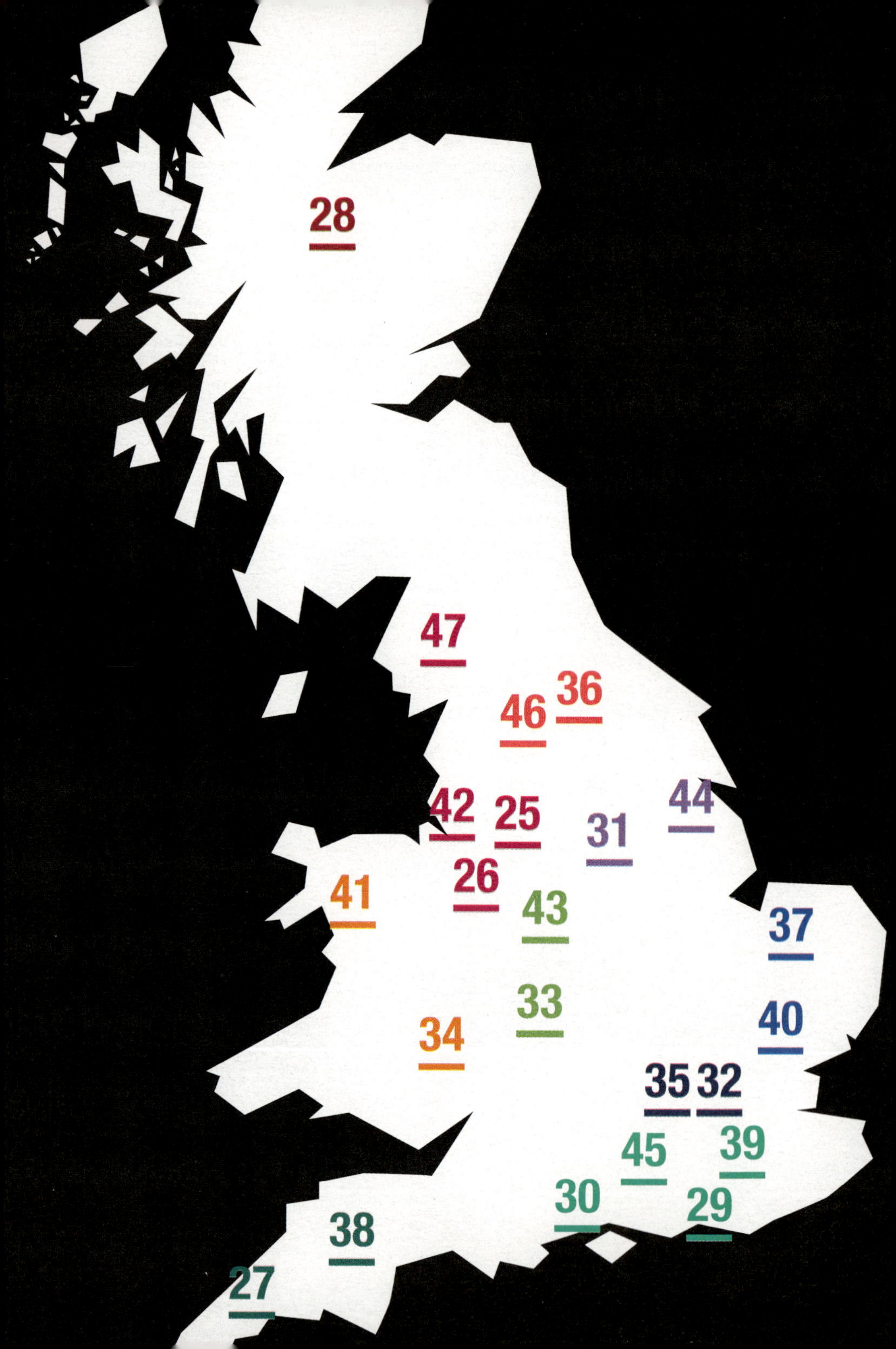
28
47
36
46
44
42
25
31
41
26
43
37
33
40
34
35
32
45
39
30
29
38
27

Editor's Pick

Featured Restaurants

Here at the Gourmet Society we pride ourselves on the quality of participating restaurants throughout the country that our members can dine at.

Take a look at some of our specially chosen restaurants around the country, all boasting awards for menus that are sure to tantalise your taste buds. Feast your eyes on our featured restaurants for 2014...

Room Restaurant

North West, Greater Manchester

25% OFF TOTAL

Room is a thriving 2 AA Rosette restaurant and cocktail bar with a stunning private dining room, situated in the old Manchester Reform Club, where the ambience of this Grade II-listed building is second to none. Whether you are business diners looking to impress, parties of friends, couples looking for a romantic evening or ladies who lunch, Room caters for all dining experiences.

The staff at Room strive to make your time there as enjoyable as possible from the minute you enter until the time you leave. They aim to provide friendly and efficient service coupled with knowledge and pride in the dining experience the team provides. This philosophy doesn't just start and finish in the restaurant but is carried through into the cocktail bar ensuring that all visitors are made to feel welcome.

For booking and address information, see page 322

25% OFF TOTAL | 6 | FRI × | SAT × | SUN |

1851 Restaurant

North West, Cheshire

25% OFF TOTAL

Peckforton Castle's 1851 Restaurant offers a very special dining experience. Featuring modern British cuisine, menus here are brimming with fine dining options.

Holder of 3 AA Rosettes, the 1851 Restaurant treats diners and guests to a gastronomic extravaganza featuring carefully selected, locally grown and reared produce.

The deep plush carpets, tasteful décor and tables adorned with crisp linen and beautiful tableware – all against the magnificent backdrop of Peckforton Castle's impressive architecture – add a welcome touch of magic and glamour to every meal.

For booking and address information, see page 308

25% OFF TOTAL | 4 | FRI ✓ | SAT✓ | SUN | * |

Paul Ainsworth at No 6 ✿

South West, Cornwall

Paul Ainsworth at No.6 serves up Michelin starred cuisine in a splendid Georgian town house in the heart of Padstow. However, this is Michelin starred dining with a twist and a nod to the Cornish way of life: children over four years of age are welcome and there's no dress code.

Paul believes great quality food should be accessible and eaten in an enjoyable environment. So you will be met by relaxed and friendly staff keen to serve you in a warm, cosy and beautifully decorated dining spaces.

No. 6 source brilliant local, seasonal ingredients and then serve them in a simple modern style with a Cornish and British influence.

25% OFF TOTAL

For booking and address information, see page 90

25% OFF TOTAL | 2 | FRI ✓ | SAT

Loch Ness Lodge

Scotland, Highlands

25% OFF TOTAL

An elegant and intimate exclusive retreat in the heart of the Scottish Highlands perched above the western flank of the mysterious and beautiful Loch Ness.

The restaurant's Franco-Scottish double AA rosettes cuisine is sure to grab your attention and stop you searching for the Loch's mythical wildlife.

The Lodge's restaurant utilises the natural environment of the Highlands with its wonderful seasonal range of vegetables and fruit, fabulous local cheeses and of course a fine selection of meats and seafood. The restaurant's chefs use this to their advantage and craft creative, contemporary dishes which taste as good as they look.

For booking and address information, see page 368

25% OFF TOTAL | 4 | FRI ✓ | SAT ✓

Graze

South East, East Sussex

Set in the heart of the Regency Brunswick Hotel, Hove, Graze is a 2 AA Rosette-awarded restaurant that serves a modern British à la carte menu of exceptional quality to go alongside their stunning seven-course tasting menus.

Head Chef Gethin Jones, who trained under celebrity chef Jun Tanaka at Pearl Restaurant in Holborn, shows his experience and art in the neat combinations of fresh, intense flavours. The produce is also notably excellent, with an emphasis on locally sourced, organic and free-range ingredients.

The lavish, Brighton Pavilion-inspired interior gives a modern decadent edge yet manages to achieve a genuine homely feel and guests are made to feel even more welcome by the attentive, friendly and knowledgeable staff.

For booking and address information, see page 153

2FOR1 3 COURSES FRI ☀ SAT ☀ SUN

2-FOR-1

EDITOR'S PICK

The Terrace ✿

South East, Hampshire

25% OFF TOTAL

Situated in Beaulieu in the heart of the New Forest, The Terrace at The Montagu Arms is one of the finest restaurants in Hampshire and the surrounding counties.

The Terrace is a consistently featured in both The Michelin and AA Restaurant Guides and has been awarded a Michelin star and three AA rosettes.

The Terrace's enticing modern menu designed by innovative head chef Matthew Tomkinson and recently voted the Telegraph's Top 50 Summer Restaurants in Britain by Jasper Gerard is undoubtedly the focus of every guests visit to The Montagu Arms.

For booking and address information, see page 131

25% OFF TOTAL | 4 | FRI | SAT

Stones

East Midlands, Derbyshire

Tucked away in the heart of Matlock, Stones restaurant is a cosy and eclectic restaurant with a stylish and welcoming decor of earthy tones of chocolate, toffee and cream, and textures of bare wood and exposed brickwork..

At Stones the philosophy is to provide a fantastic dining experience in a relaxed setting. The dining room offers a perfect place for romantic, family or business meals. Stones boasts a beautiful garden terrace overlooking the River Derwent. A superb modern British menu changes regularly to reflect the very best in seasonal and local produce. Stones has been awarded two AA Rosettes for culinary excellence.

For booking and address information, see page 291

25% OFF TOTAL | 4 | FRI ✓ | SAT ☀ |

25% OFF TOTAL

50% OFF FOOD

The Chancery

Greater London, Central London

A bijou EC4 dining spot that attracts a chic city-centric crowd, The Chancery occupies a small corner site on Cursitor Street that has won rave reviews for its innovative menus, not to mention 2 AA Rosettes.

The restaurant has three dining rooms, two on the ground floor and a smaller more intimate dining room on the lower ground floor suitable for all parties.

Zak Jones, Stephanie Rundle and their team lead the front of house while Head Chef Alice Churchill oversees a creative kitchen and a seasonal menu which will impress the most discerning gourmands.

For booking and address information, see page 179

50% OFF FOOD | 8 | FRI ✓ | SAT ✓ | SUN | * |

Moncreiffe

West Midlands, Warwickshire

The stunning 16th Century Walton Hall has always been a popular destination for food lovers, and with good reason. The majestic grounds and impeccably presented table settings within the Moncreiffe Restaurant set a standard that is hard to rival.

Awarded 2 AA Rosettes, and featuring fresh local ingredients with delicious seasonal menus, this stunning venue is held in high regard.

Moncreiffe Restaurant has elegant surroundings and breathtaking views of the hotels gardens and surrounding countryside.

For booking and address information, see page 269

25% OFF TOTAL

25% OFF TOTAL | 6 | FRI ✓ | SAT × | 🎄 | ✱

The Bell at Skenfrith

Wales, Gwent and Monmouthshire

2-FOR-1

The Bell at Skenfrith, dating from the 17th century, is to be found in the beautiful Monnow Valley. A log fire in the bar, wooden beams and pews, rustic wooden tables and varying styles of chairs in the restaurant create a homely welcoming Welsh environment.

This superb fine-dining restaurant is known for its fresh, varied menu and superbly accomplished cooking, with a focus on sourcing produce locally and serving seasonal classics.

The restaurant at The Bell at Skenfrith has won many awards for its food throughout the years, including 2 prestigious AA Rosettes.

For booking and address information, see page 257

2FOR1 **3 COURSES** FRI ✱ SAT ✱ SUN

Benares

Greater London, Central London

The Michelin-Starred Benares restaurant is one of the top restaurants in the UK. Menus are based on the highest-quality produce and seasonal ingredients from all over India, enhanced with a contemporary twist. Renowned for its subtle spices and authentic flavours, celebrity chef Atul Kochhar's food - all of which is Halal - is faithful to its origins but presented in a style in keeping with the deeply seductive surroundings, marrying tradition with daring modernity.

Proprietor Atul Kochhar is considered one of London's top celebrity chefs, well respected for his masterful use of spicing when creating some of the finest modern British dishes with an innovative Indian twist. Awarded 4 AA Rosettes.

25% OFF TOTAL

For booking and address information, see page 175

25% OFF TOTAL | 6 | FRI | SAT | SUN

EDITOR'S PICK

Clocktower

North East, North Yorkshire

2-FOR-1

Dine at Ruddington Park's double AA Rosette-awarded restaurant underneath the striking centrepiece pink glass chandelier. Relax in the bright and airy conservatory with a 400 year old olive tree in the centre of it. However, most of all enjoy the fabulous food.

The Clocktower serves some of the best food in Harrogate. There is Yorkshire passion in abundance helping to create legendary dishes and menus. The monthly 'food heroes menu' states the number of miles the principal ingredients have journeyed to reach the plate.

Modern Yorkshire British food at its very best ensuring interesting dishes cooked to a consistently high standard.

For booking and address information, see page 346

2FOR1 3 COURSES | FRI | SAT | SUN

Congham Hall

East Anglia, Norfolk

The Restaurant at Congham Hall, which has been awarded 2 AA Rosettes, has large French windows leading directly on to the terrace and beyond to the lawns and parkland. Beautifully light and airy the beige striped Zoffany wallpaper, glass skylight and full-length windows give panoramic views.

The chefs use only the finest seasonal produce, sourced locally where possible, to produce genuinely imaginative dishes that delight and inspire. Indeed the kitchen garden produces over 700 different varieties of herbs, salads and baby vegetables which are picked daily for the chef. A stroll around it during early summer evenings finds the air fragrant with heady aromas.

25% OFF TOTAL

For booking and address information, see page 245

25% OFF TOTAL | 4 | FRI ✓ | SAT ✗

The Arundell Arms

South West, Devon

2-FOR-1

Head Chef Steven Pidgeon, who has the rare honour of being elected one of only 80 Master Chefs of Great Britain, ensures the food on offer is always meticulously prepared and beautifully presented. Using only the finest quality produce, which is sourced from local suppliers, Steven has gained an excellent reputation both locally and nationally for creating outstanding modern British cuisine.

This 2 AA Rosette winning restaurant attracts guests not just with the quality of the food but also the elegant surroundings. Complemented by fine wines and attentive, friendly service The Arundell Arms restaurant is the perfect dining venue for any occasion.

For booking and address information, see page 91

2FOR1 MAIN COURSE | FRI ✓ | SAT ✓

Anise

South East, West Sussex

Recently awarded the 'Best Eating Experience in Sussex at the Sussex Food and Drink Awards, The Anise Fine Dining Restaurant, with 2 AA rosettes, is the jewel in the crown of the Felbridge Hotel & Spa.

Perfect for all those who are passionate about fine food and drink, not only does the restaurant offer the elegance and charm of a top London restaurant, the real reason guests return week after week is the modern focused style and distinctly flavoured cuisine.

The award winning Executive Chef continuously prepares innovative dishes; each beautifully presented and well balanced with a combination of classical techniques and culinary flair.

For booking and address information, see page 156

25% OFF TOTAL | 6 | FRI ✓ | SAT ✓ | *

25% OFF TOTAL

2-FOR-1

The White Hart

East Anglia, Essex

The black and white timbered Tudor fronted White Hart dates from the early 16th Century and is the embodiment of the picture perfect English countryside. The characterful interior is abundant with traditional wooden beams and charming open fireplaces.

Over the last few years the kitchen brigade have ratcheted up the standards cooking with a passion and intelligence that results in flavoursome British and European dishes cooked to a 2 AA rosettes winning standard. With their own beehives and herb field much of the ingredients are not just local, but actually home-grown.

Situated in rural Essex in the attractive village of Great Yeldham on the banks of the River Colne, The White Hart offers great food in a relaxed and historic atmosphere.

For booking and address information, see page 244

2FOR1 MAIN COURSE FRI ✓ SAT SUN

The Royal Sportsman

Wales, Gwynedd

The Royal Sportsman, with Snowdonia as a backdrop, is Porthmadog's premier destination. The unprepossessing former coaching inn has been fully refurbished in recent years to become a first rate hotel.

The 60 cover Peppino's , open to non-residents, is a 2 AA rosettes winning restaurant with a contemporary decoration yet retaining many original lovely features, such as the stone and slate fireplaces and darkwood floor dating back to 1862.

Dan Owen, Head Chef, has earned a reputation for inspirational Modern British cuisine with a heavy Welsh influence. Committed to using fresh Welsh produce the restaurant consistently produces scintillating dishes using local ingredients.

For booking and address information, see page 259

25% OFF TOTAL | 4 | FRI ✓ | SAT ✗

25% OFF TOTAL

London Carriage Works

North West, Merseyside

2-FOR-1

The Good Food Guide sum up LCW perfectly, "Still the city centre's no-brainer for dinner with a sense of occasion, the London Carriage Works has a prime corner spot on the loveliest street in town."

We totally agree and it's no wonder is many people's favourite restaurant in Liverpool. LCW epitomises the very best parts of the culinary revolution that has taken Liverpool by storm over the last 15 years.

Paul Askew is in a league of his own when it comes to sourcing and cooking food; this is demonstrated when tasting the Modern European dishes from his menu.

For booking and address information, see page 331

2FOR1 3 COURSES | FRI ✓ | SAT ✗

The Old Vicarage

West Midlands, Staffordshire

Pascal Arnoux is a not a man who seeks publicity and as such his restaurant, Pascal At The Old Vicarage, is, amazingly, not featured in any of the major guides.

However, he is a man who knows how to run a restaurant delivering consistently high standards. It's a travesty that Pascal's restaurant hasn't received more accolades.

Pascal at The Old Vicarage is the perfect blend of French and English cuisine and service. It's genuinely one of the best restaurants within a hundred miles radius.

For booking and address information, see page 266

25% OFF TOTAL

25% OFF TOTAL | 4 | FRI ✓ | SAT ☀ | SUN

EDITOR'S PICK

Winteringham Fields

East Midlands, Lincolnshire

25% OFF TOTAL

Three AA rosettes, Alice in Wonderland themed menu and the North Lincolnshire flatlands could only mean one thing: Colin McGurran's Winteringham Fields.

Winteringham Fields is truly a one-off, but still maintains the highest levels and standards of cuisine and service. Fortunately for McGurran, he is able to utilise the abundant local produce to create amazing dishes that are prepared with ingredients that have travelled less than 5 miles!

If Winteringham Fields was in South East England it would be one of the most famous restaurants in the country. This stylish restaurant-with-rooms is worth making the journey for.

For booking and address information, see page 298

25% OFF TOTAL | 10 | FRI | SAT | SUN

Oakley Hall

South East, Hampshire

Oakley Hall in North Hampshire is a grand old house, built in 1795, with literary connections to Jane Austen. The Winchester Restaurant has been awarded 2 AA rosettes for it high culinary and service standards.

The restaurant is designed in a modern contemporary way with banquette seating, wall mirrors and unclothed tables creating a perfect stage for Head Chef Justin Mundy's inspiring cuisine.

The menu draws on local suppliers, such as Laverstoke Park Farm, to ensure food miles are kept to a minimum; however, this does not stop Justin from utilising global influences in his creations.

For booking and address information, see page 132

50% OFF FOOD

50% OFF FOOD | 4 | FRI × | SAT × | SUN |

The Devonshire Fell

North East, North Yorkshire

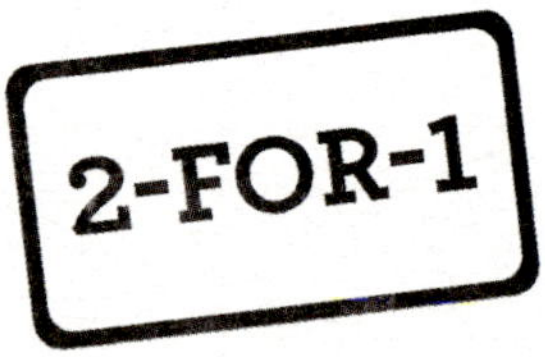

Set in a grand old Edwardian manor in the Yorkshire Dales, The Devonshire Fell is a charming hotel that plays host to a double AA Rosette-winning restaurant.

The Restaurant is light and airy with The Duchess of Devonshire's trademark bright colours and striking artwork, as well as stunning views into the gardens, up the fell, and across the Dales. Smart bright decor with colourful suede seating the design is akin to a city centre brasserie but the setting is unbeatable.

By using local suppliers who care about animal husbandry and the quality of their stock you really will be able to "taste the difference".

For booking and address information, see page 346

2FOR1 3 COURSES | FRI ✱ | SAT ✱

Linthwaite House

North West, Cumbria

The Lake District is awash with country house hotels. However, the are few, if any, better than Linthwaite House. An unstuffy boutique hotel with stunning views over Lake Windermere, this is a true gem of a find.

The real piece de resistance is the triple AA rosette winning restaurant. Even when the fiercest storm is howling across the lake you will find the restaurant a picture of the utmost tranquility serving sublime cuisine and wine in a friendly and inviting way.

This is fine dining at its best. If you're visiting The Lakes it's worth planning your trip around your meal at Linthwaite.

For booking and address information, see page 314

25% OFF TOTAL

25% OFF TOTAL | 6 | FRI ✓ | SAT ✓

Mercure
Di Maggio's
Malmaison
WALKABOUT
handmade burger Cº
La Tasca
CAFÉ ROUGE
LOCH FYNE
BEEFEATER GRILL
VINTAGE INNS
Bella Italia
STRADA
PREZZO
Table Table
Chino Latino
Modern Pan-Asian Cuisine and Latin Bar
Hotel du Vin & Bistro
FISH WORKS
17 77
HALL & WOODHOUSE
Hand PICKED HOTELS

National Chains

25% OFF TOTAL

La Tasca

spanish tapas bar & kitchen

La Tasca has been reinvigorated with a new emphasis on fresh, Iberian-sourced ingredients resulting in a culinary 'Spanish Revolution'.

Quintessentially Spanish, their fresh and exciting menu offers something for everyone. With dishes from the sea, the field and the garden, La Tasca's tapas dishes are sincerely Spanish, while their paellas always deliver on flavour.

Antonio Bennetto, Executive Chef, has travelled throughout Spain to find the best local producers and has sourced some truly authentic produce to use in each of his new dishes.

If you haven't been to La Tasca for a while now's the perfect time to go and experience Antonio's fantastic menu, crafted with some of the finest produce from across Spain.

25% OFF TOTAL | 8 | FRI ✓ | SAT ✗

"THE VERY BEST FRESH QUALITY INGREDIENTS
+ REGIONAL SPANISH PRODUCE + LOVING PREPARATION
= GREAT SPANISH FOOD"

CAFÉ ROUGE

25% OFF TOTAL

A high street favourite with more than 125 restaurants in the UK, Café Rouge has been serving up modern and classic French dishes for over 20 years.

A relaxed, friendly bistro, the extensive, seasonally changing menu includes classics such as Steak Frites, Beouf Bourguignon and Duck Confit, alongside hearty Salads, tasty Croques and Baguettes, reflecting the fresh flavours of the season.

There is a French dominated wine list offering some little gems of wines and well-known favourites, to sip as you enjoy relaxing at one of the many pavement terraces, watching the world go by.

Inside the restaurants you will find cosy booths where you can bring your friends or family to celebrate something special. Whatever your reason, you'll find a friendly, continental welcome at Café Rouge.

25% OFF TOTAL | 6 | FRI ✓ | SAT ✓ | * |

"CAFÉ ROUGE OFFERS A RELAXING ENVIRONMENT, UNIQUE SELECTION OF WINES AND TOP QUALITY CUISINE, WITH A SOPHISTICATED PARISIAN CHARM"

2-FOR-1

PREZZO

Our partnership with Prezzo enters into yet another year allowing our members to enjoy great quality Italian food, created using the finest Italian seasonal products all set in stylish and contemporary surroundings.

From the signature Executive V.I.Pizza which include Posh Pepperoni with its Salami milano, calabrese sausage, salsiccia picanti pepperoni, prosciutto, roquito chilli peppers, fresh rocket, mozzarella and tomato to a traditional lasagne or lobster and crab tortelli, the menu is packed full of tempting options. In many of the restaurants you can witness the chefs in their open kitchens hand stretching the dough to create one of their freshly baked pizzas, cooked to perfection in traditional stone ovens.

There are now three ways to enjoy Prezzo Pizza. The CLASSIC, hand stretched and stone baked to order. LIGHT, a smaller flatbread pizza served with mixed salad and low calorie dressing or V.I.Pizza, the Ultimate Prezzo pizza - bigger and crispier.

2FOR1 MAIN COURSE | FRI × | SAT ×

"SIGNATURE PASTAS, STONE-BAKED PIZZAS AND CLASSIC ITALIAN DISHES PROMISE A PERFECT DINING CHOICE FOR THE WHOLE FAMILY"

LOCH FYNE®
SEAFOOD & GRILL

25% OFF TOTAL

Loch Fyne Seafood & Grill are all about great food and great flavours. The superb seafood dishes are simply prepared with a focus on high-quality, fresh ingredients and choices to suit all tastes and appetites.

The business originated at Loch Fyne on the West Coast of Scotland where its founders started out by selling fresh oysters from a small roadside shack. Times moved on and this original oyster bar became increasingly successful, spawning a group of over 30 restaurants across the UK - all taking their core produce of shellfish and smoked fish direct from the shores and smokehouse of Loch Fyne.

There's something for everyone on the menu – not just for the seafood lovers. The à la carte menu includes a courgette & ricotta tortellini with wild mushrooms, butternut squash and toasted pine nuts, while meat lovers will be delighted to see a 28 day aged sirloin steak, Barbary duck breast or a char-grilled Aberdeen Angus burger. Plenty of the restaurants are open all day. So whatever time you pop in, you'll be assured of a friendly welcome.

25% OFF TOTAL | 4 | FRI | SAT

"ALL THE PRODUCE SERVED AT LOCH FYNE IS SUSTAINABLY SOURCED AND THEY HAVE BEEN A PIONEER IN SUPPORTING UK-BASED, SMALL FISHING BOATS"

STRADA

In more than 60 stylish sites across the UK, many with outdoor seating for *al fresco* dining, Strada offers fresh, bold dishes inspired by the modern flavours of Italian city life.

Strada restaurants serve a wide range of seasonal share plates, pastas, seafood and grills, and are especially known for their incredible Italian style pizzas. Made to order using hand-stretched dough, and topped with the finest of Italian ingredients like Buffalo Mozzarella and their top secret tomato sauce blend, Strada's pizzas and 'Schiacciatella' flatbreads are stone-baked in a fiery oven at over 500 degrees to golden bubbly perfection.

25% OFF TOTAL

There is also a fantastic selection of Italian wines to enjoy, from luscious berry reds to crisp citrusy whites, as well as Italian beer.

To finish, try one of their hand-crafted, gourmet coffees (made with Musetti beans roasted in Italy) and addictive desserts like their *Chocolate Fondente*, and the popular *Limoncello Trifle*.

25% OFF TOTAL | 6 | FRI ✓ | SAT ×

"FRESH ITALIAN FLAVOURS,
GOOD TIMES!"

handmade burger Cº

handmade burger Co. are passionate about great, fresh, food and use only the finest ingredients for you to enjoy.

Famous for burgers handmade from traditionally reared, 100% prime Scotch beef, the chefs make over 40 varieties of hand pressed burgers everyday. The sourdough burger buns come from a fourth generation family bakery and are made from a recipe developed in partnership. The menu also boasts a wide selection of fabulous vegetarian options and a great range for children all made from the finest fresh ingredients.

2-FOR-1

As each burger is made by hand, you can tailor your burger with a range of toppings to have it just how you like it! Like everything else they serve, the relishes used are handmade to guarantee great flavours every time, they add red peppers to their handmade coleslaw to give it that special touch.

Every restaurant receives deliveries of farm fresh potatoes to ensure the chips are as fresh as possible. Each potato is peeled, cut and double fried to give you fresh chips that will rival any homemade ones!

2FOR1 MAIN COURSE | FRI ✓ | SAT × | SUN

"BEAUTIFULLY HANDMADE, CHARGRILLED BURGERS, MADE FROM TRADITIONALLY REARED, GRASS FED, 100% FULLY TRACEABLE PRIME SCOTCH BEEF"

25% OFF TOTAL

VINTAGE INNS

Discover real ales, real fires and pub food as hearty and warming as the welcome at a Vintage Inn country dining pub near you.

Imagine it... a cosy corner of a perfect country pub, gazing at the sunset, sitting round an old wooden table and chatting with the family and friends you treasure, savouring your last mouthful of a superb pie, enjoying another contented sip from your glass of wine, and feeling utterly relaxed... After all, why leave now? There's no rush... You're in a Vintage Inn.

Vintage Inns are the perfect country retreat, deliciously traditional, with a contemporary twist. Ideal for an intimate evening meal in stylish, authentic surroundings, an idyllic place to catch up with old friends, or a memorable lunch in a picturesque country setting.

Whichever one you choose to visit, you'll discover British inn keeping at its very finest.

25% OFF TOTAL | FRI ✓ | SAT ✓ | SUN | ▲

"PICTURESQUE SURROUNDINGS PROVIDE THE PERFECT BACKDROP FOR SAVOURING THE HEARTY, SEASONAL PUB-FOOD ON THE MENU"

Hotel du Vin & Bistro

2-FOR-1

Think quintessential British style, elegant and unpretentious. Combine this with great spirit, wit, and an unquestionable devotion to wine, and you have captured the essence of Hotel du Vin.

With nationally acclaimed bistros, Hotel du Vin promises an exceptional dining experience time and time again. Many of the Hotel du Vin bistros have been awarded at least one AA Rosette, while others such as Winchester and Edinburgh boast a well-deserved two. Absolute validation that Hotel du Vin's philosophy, to serve good food produced using the finest and freshest local produce, cooked simply and sensibly priced, has been achieved.

Each bistro has an extensive and varied wine list, including an impressive array of by-the-glass options and a selection of good value bottles. A master Sommelier is also on hand to help you match your wine with a course from the menu.

No matter where you find yourself, if you are in need of stylish hospitality... The answer is simple. Think du Vin.

2FOR1 MAIN COURSE

Check the listings for full offer details.

"IF YOU ARE IN NEED OF STYLISH HOSPITALITY... THE ANSWER IS SIMPLE. THINK HOTEL DU VIN"

2-FOR-1

BEEFEATER GRILL

Experience the special flavour of the chargrill, freshly prepared using the finest cuts of prime beef, succulent chicken and seasonal produce.

Seared on the outside, succulent throughout, seasoned for extra flavour and chargrilled to perfection. Beefeater Grill pride themselves as being the experts in steak. In every restaurant you'll find a Steakmaster who will advise you on the best cuts for your taste. Just choose your cut and tell them how you'd like it.

But it's more than just great steak, there's delicious chicken and fish dishes, pasta, salads and vegetarian options too. Of course you can also spoil yourself rotten with an indulgent selection of desserts to choose from.

There's also a wide selection of quality White, Red, Rose, Sparkling wine and Champagnes to complement your choice.

2FOR1 MAIN COURSE | 6 | FRI ✓ | SAT ×

"EXPERIENCE THE TASTE OF CHARGRILL, FROM SIZZLING STEAKS TO SUCCULENT FISH, PREPARED JUST THE WAY YOU LIKE IT"

25% OFF TOTAL

Bella Italia

Pizza ♥ Pasta ♥ Grill

For decades Bella Italia has been bringing the authentic taste of Italy to the UK, and there's no better place to enjoy the simple pleasure of eating out with family and friends.

The menu has something for everyone, with Italian classics, healthier options and a great selection for the kids. Pizza lovers can choose from a traditional thin and crispy, delicious Calzone or enjoy all the taste without the guilt with a lighter Pizza Vita.

And of course there's pasta; generous bowls of steaming hot and tasty dishes, created with ingredients from Agnesi - Italy's oldest pasta maker. There's also a range of grills and perennial favourites from the classic Milanese, succulent steaks and warming stews to healthy salads.

25% OFF TOTAL | 6 | FRI × | SAT × | SUN |

"BELLA ITALIA HAS BEEN A FAMILY FAVOURITE FOR NEARLY 20 YEARS, SERVING DELICIOUS ITALIAN FOOD, JUST LIKE MAMA MAKES IT"

2-FOR-1

Malmaison

Malmaison dares to be different at every level, and this philosophy is echoed in its food and drink. Guests regularly find some of the region's most delectable food secrets served on their plates; such is the commitment of individual chefs to consistently source local specialities to add to the already outstanding Mal menu.

The compelling combination of expert cuisine and some of the world's finest wines is carried off to perfection, ensuring high praise from both guests and critics. Eight of the group sport AA Rosettes, with the London and Edinburgh brasseries both having received two each.

All the Mal bars have lashings of attitude, and have been designed with an eye to the hip, chic and trendy. They are uber-cool venues in which to sip delicious cocktails or to try a glass or two of excellent vino from their extensive wine list.

2FOR1 MAIN COURSE **Check listings for full offer details.**

"MALMAISON DARES TO BE DIFFERENT AT EVERY LEVEL, AND THIS PHILOSOPHY IS ECHOED IN ITS FOOD AND DRINK."

Table Table

2-FOR-1

Table Table is a pub restaurant serving great value, quality classics with a modern twist. The menu has been lovingly developed and prepared using seasonal ingredients.

Table Table pride themselves on delivering great pub food in a place you'll love. The main menu includes sharing platters, tasty starters and nibbles along with all your pub classics and some tempting desserts. There's also a yummy children's menu with heaps of choice and healthy options too.

It almost goes without saying that you're spoilt for choice when it comes to drinks, whether it's a local beer, soft drink or wine that's been chosen to match your meal, there's something for everyone.

There's a relaxed and friendly atmosphere, with consistently excellent service, making Table Table the perfect place for family gatherings and meeting friends alike, whatever the occasion. Get together with a few friends and chill out at the bar, share an intimate dinner for two, or enjoy a meal with the whole family in contemporary dining rooms.

2FOR1 MAIN COURSE | FRI ✓ | SAT✓

"QUALITY PUB CLASSICS WITH MODERN TWISTS MEET WITH A FRIENDLY AND RELAXED ATMOSPHERE THAT IS PERFECT FOR ANY OCCASION"

Hand PICKED HOTELS

The award-winning Hand Picked Hotels collection, are luxurious country houses renowned for exquisite food, fine wines and excellent service in stylish, architecturally stunning surroundings.

Hand Picked Hotels focus on the quality of service and cuisines; all hotels have achieved AA Rosette status, with the Norton House Hotel and Spa in Edinburgh having won three, and five of them have achieved Red Star status, being recognised as amongst the AA's top 200 hotels in the UK and Ireland.

Great dining and fine wine define the Hand Picked Hotels experience and, where possible, produce is sourced from local farmers who often produce smaller yields to a very high standard to ensure the very best in quality and flavour.

These great venues invite their talented chefs to re-invent the British dining experience, and their guests to simply indulge.

Check the listings for full offer details.

"GREAT DINING AND FINE WINES DEFINE THE HAND PICKED HOTELS EXPERIENCE... FANATICAL ABOUT GREAT FOOD AND WINE"

25% OFF TOTAL

WALKABOUT

Walkabout is a nationwide chain of Australian bars serving food inspired by Australia and the Australian spirit.

There's loads to choose from; a great selection of small boards and larger sharers for those just looking for a snack. A wide range of burgers including Australian delicacies – Kangaroo and Wild Boar and the more traditional style plated meals with a twist – try the Chicken Parmagiano an Italian dish adopted by Australians as their own.

Whatever the dish Walkabout makes it their own; freshness and fun are the key components of the menu. The Walkabout Salad is a real treat combining avocado, pomegranate seeds, asparagus spears and cooked beetroot; you can even top your salad with grilled chicken or halloumi to make it even better.

There is an extensive wine and cocktail list which feature Australian inspired cocktails and a range of accessible wines from down under – perfect to accompany any meal.

25% OFF TOTAL | 10 | FRI ✓ | SAT ✓

Please note: not all dishes are not available in every Walkabout and menus are subject to regular change. Please visit www.walkaboutbars.co.uk to check out the menu prior to your visit.

"WHATEVER THE DISH WALKABOUT MAKES IT THEIR OWN; FRESHNESS AND FUN ARE THE KEY COMPONENTS OF THE MENU"

25% OFF TOTAL

1777

HALL & WOODHOUSE

Hall & Woodhouse is a renowned independent family brewer, with a variety of public houses that deliver a traditionally English eating and drinking experience.

Each house is different; many steeped in history and nostalgia, creating a unique atmosphere and environment to share with friends, colleagues, or just your own solitude. It's their food, hospitality and heritage that really set them apart from their rivals, as well as being one of the few remaining regional family brewers.

Hall and Woodhouse work with regional food partners, typically from family businesses like their own, who provide quality ingredients that their teams of talented chefs use to create fresh, unpretentious and seasonal dishes. Taking real pride in the food that they serve; these public houses do simple things extremely well, delivering a variety of traditional dishes that are crafted to perfection.

25% OFF TOTAL | FRI × | SAT ×

Please see the listings for individual participating pubs.

"HALL & WOODHOUSE BRING THE FINEST ASPECTS OF THE TRADITIONAL BRITISH PUB TOGETHER UNDER ONE ROOF"

25% OFF TOTAL

Di Maggio's

'Our family serving your family'

Independent family oriented pizzerias.

Located in the Strathclyde region, Di Maggio's offers the finest in Italian cuisine at their neighbourhood pizzerias, and the essence of the Italian family is absolutely paramount to the workings of every single one of them.

Although each restaurant has its own character according to its locale, they all provide the same exacting standards of quality, freshly cooked food and first-rate service.

Di Maggio's have a great reputation that has been built over generations and thus it should come as no surprise that they have been hailed as Scotland's best Italian.

Try a different home-made pizza at each of the seven Di Maggio's that offer Gourmet Society members a great discount.

25% OFF TOTAL | 6 | FRI | SAT

DI MAGGIO'S HAVE A GREAT REPUTATION THAT HAS BEEN BUILT OVER GENERATIONS AND ARE NOW HAILED AS SCOTLANDS BEST ITALIAN"

FISH WORKS

FishWorks is an award-winning restaurant group whose ethos is all about eating and enjoying the freshest, highest-quality seasonal seafood.

Daily deliveries from day-boat vessels landing in Brixham fish market and the South coast area means that they only serve the freshest produce available, and by working closely with suppliers can ensure their seafood is honestly and sustainably harvested.

Each of the restaurants have their own fishmonger with a wet fish counter where you can select any fish or crustacean and have it cooked to your liking, right there and then.

25% OFF TOTAL

FishWorks have restaurants in Marylebone, Richmond, and Piccadilly, each allowing Gourmet Society members a chance to dine on outstanding dishes while receiving a great discount.

Blackboards display daily landings, and diners can choose from a classic menu that boasts delights such as piled-high fruits de mer, scrumptious River Exe mussels, or simply the best cod and chips you will ever taste.

25% OFF TOTAL | 6 | FRI | SAT | SUN

"EACH RESTAURANT HAS THEIR OWN FISH COUNTER WHERE YOU CAN SELECT ANY FISH OR CRUSTACEAN AND HAVE IT COOKED TO YOUR LIKING"

Mercure Hotels can be found in some of the leading cities in the UK and are becoming well-recognised for providing welcoming stays for all.

Each one of the 26 venues has its very own in-house restaurant serving delectable, well-rounded food to both hotel guests and non-residents alike. Imaginative talent resides in every hotel kitchen with chefs aiming to provide unbeatably delicious food, guaranteeing a return visit from every diner.

When heading for the sea, the Mercure Brighton Seafront Hotel eagerly awaits your arrival with its breathtakingly British Victorian façade and well-established Brasserie Restaurant. If you find yourself escaping from the city lights and heading for the country, be sure to stop off at the Mercure Newbury Elcot Park where the Orangery Restaurant works to produce delicious flavours and vibrant cuisine.

Check the listings for full offer details.

"IMAGINATIVE TALENT RESIDES IN EVERY HOTEL KITCHEN WITH CHEFS AIMING TO PROVIDE UNBEATABLY DELICIOUS FOOD EVERY TIME"

25% OFF TOTAL

Chino Latino

Modern Pan-Asian Cuisine and Latin Bar

Chino Latino is a modern Pan-Asian cuisine restaurant with a Latin cocktail bar, boasting understated elegance and urban styling with gunmetal, cream and crimson interiors.

These multi award-winning restaurants offer something new – a sophisticated twist on the traditional Pan-Asian style of informal eating and drinking, combining the distinctive yet delicate flavours of China, South-East Asia and modern Japan.

The constantly evolving menu ranges from sushi, dim sum, tempura, meat and seafood. Signature dishes include their critically acclaimed Black Cod with spicy miso, and the succulent Sirloin steak, which is marinated in a soy mirin with garlic and brought the table sizzling on hot stones.

The food is carefully complemented by a cocktail menu created by talented mixologists using only the finest and freshest ingredients.

25% OFF TOTAL **Check the listings for full offer details.**

"THESE MULTI AWARD-WINNING RESTAURANTS OFFER A SOPHISTICATED TWIST ON THE TRADITIONAL PAN-ASIAN STYLE OF INFORMAL EATING AND DRINKING"

South West

Cornwall

BALTI CURRIES
☎ 01326 317 905
47 Arwenack Street, Falmouth, TR11 3JH
The oldest curry house in Cornwall and conveniently located right in the heart of Falmouth just near the Sea Front. Balti Curries has added the colour and flavour of spice to Cornish life.

2FOR1 MAIN COURSE | FRI ✓ | SAT ✓ — Indian

BARCLAY HOUSE
☎ 01503 262 929
St Martins Road, Looe, PL13 1LP
Magnificent river views are the perfect counterpart to the delightful Cornish coastal cuisine. Highlights are Looe Day-Boat fish matched with Camel Valley wines from nearby Bodmin. Awarded 2 AA Rosettes.

2FOR1 3 COURSES | FRI ✱ | SAT ✱ | SUN — Fine Dining

THE BAY RESTAURANT
☎ 01736 366 890
Britons Hill, Penzance, TR18 3AE
Enjoy magnificent views across Mount's Bay as you indulge in divine European cuisine. The knowledgeable waiting staff will help you choose from the many regional and modern dishes. 2 AA Rosettes.

25% OFF TOTAL | 👤 2 | FRI ▮ | SAT ▮ — European

BEAUCLIFFES RESTAURANT
☎ 01637 873 274
Porth Veor Manor, Porth Way, Porth, TR7 3LW
A fine attribute of Porth Veor Manor, Beaucliffes Restaurant offers stunning views of Porth beach and outstanding coastal views. Enjoy fine dining and exceptionally well-prepared Cornish cuisine.

2FOR1 3 COURSES | FRI ✓ | SAT ✓ — International

BRITANNIA HOTEL
☎ 01872 560 546
Fore Street, Truro, TR4 8LN
Seafood lovers are in their element at this renowned hotel. Substantial and wholesome portions promise to satisfy rumbling tummies. The cuisine is sourced from the nearby sea to ensure tastiness.

2FOR1 MAIN COURSE | FRI × | SAT × — Seafood

THE CALLYWITH
01208 264698
Launceston Road, Bodmin, PL31 2AR
Quality pub classics with modern twists meets with a friendly and relaxed atmosphere to make this Table Table venue the perfect place for any occasion. *Excludes daytime & evening deals and festive menus.

2FOR1 MAIN COURSE | FRI ✓ | SAT ✓ — Modern British

THE CARCLAZE
01726 624 010
Treverbyn Road, Carclaze, St Austell, PL25 4EJ
Quality pub classics with modern twists meets with a friendly and relaxed atmosphere to make this Table Table venue the perfect place for any occasion. *Excludes daytime & evening deals and festive menus.

2FOR1 MAIN COURSE | FRI ✓ | SAT ✓ — Modern British

CARNON INN
01872 863370
Old Carnon Hill, Carnon Downs, Truro, TR3 6JT
Quality pub classics with modern twists meets with a friendly and relaxed atmosphere to make this Table Table venue the perfect place for any occasion. *Excludes daytime & evening deals and festive menus.

2FOR1 MAIN COURSE | FRI ✓ | SAT ✓ — Modern British

GOLDEN LION INN & LAKESIDE RESTAURANT
☎ 01209 860 332
Stithians Lake, Redruth, TR16 6NW
Boasting 4 'Cornwall Tourism Awards', this inn is nestled in the quaint hills of Redruth. Dine al fresco overlooking the exquisite gardens or in the traditional bar complete with a roaring log fire.

2FOR1 MAIN COURSE | FRI ✱ | SAT ✱ — English and Continental

INDIAN DINING CLUB
☎ 01637 839 125
Station Approach, Newquay, TR7 2NG
Priding themselves on quality, the staff at this Indian eatery take kindly to anyone who appreciates good food. Welcoming families, couples and businesses alike.

2FOR1 3 COURSES | FRI × | SAT × — Indian

THE JOURNEYMAN
☎ 01841 540 604
Mellingey Mill, Mellingey, St Issey, PL27 7QU
Choose from over 50 dishes that have been specially selected from the world's finest cuisines. Long summer nights and cosy winter evenings can enjoyably be spent here, whatever your party size.

25% OFF TOTAL | 👤 8 | FRI ▮ | SAT ▮ | SUN | ✱ — Multi-Cuisine

LISKEARD TAVERN
01579 341 752
Liskeard Retail Park, Haviland Road, Liskeard, PL14 3FG
Quality pub classics with modern twists meets with a friendly and relaxed atmosphere to make this Table Table venue the perfect place for any occasion. *Excludes daytime & evening deals and festive menus.

2FOR1 MAIN COURSE | FRI ✓ | SAT ✓ — Modern British

MANGO'S BAR & CLUB
01326 316 909
5-7 Church St, Falmouth, TR11 3DP
The Mango Tango Bar and Cafe in Falmouth is an unusual but very friendly and relaxed place to enjoy good food.

25% OFF TOTAL | 👤 10 | FRI ✓ | SAT ✓ — American

MAY TREE
01326 555 000
Clodgey Lane, Helston, TR13 0QD
Quality pub classics with modern twists meets with a friendly and relaxed atmosphere to make this Table Table venue the perfect place for any occasion. *Excludes daytime & evening deals and festive menus.

2FOR1 MAIN COURSE | FRI ✓ | SAT ✓ — Modern British

THE OLD PLOUGH INN
☎ 01872 273 001
Church Road, Truro, TR4 9DY
Enjoy a great home-cooked menu with traditional pub food at reasonable prices. This wonderful local venue also boasts a fine range of real ales, lagers, ciders, wines and spirits.

2FOR1 MAIN COURSE | FRI × | SAT ✓ | SUN | ✱ | ▲ — British

PAUL AINSWORTH AT NO 6
☎ 01841 532 093
6 Middle Street, Padstow, PL28 8AP
Michelin starred dining where customer experience and value for money are the key features. Delicious British cuisine served by diligent staff in a beautifully converted Georgian town house.

25% OFF TOTAL | 👤 2 | FRI ✓ | SAT ▮ — British

PREZZO
01326 314 564
The Old Post Office, The Moor, Falmouth, TR11 3QA
With a character all of its own, Prezzo oozes contemporary style and enduring charm. Signature pastas, stone-baked pizzas and classic Italian dishes promise a perfect dining choice for the whole family.

2FOR1 MAIN COURSE | FRI × | SAT × | ▲ — Italian

THE RESTAURANT AT THE HEADLAND
☎ 01637 872 211
Fistral Beach, Newquay, TR7 1EW
This venue oozes intimacy, ideal for romantic dinners for two. Cosy up with a loved one whilst admiring the spectacular views of the setting sun and tuck into Newquay Bay lobster.

2FOR1 MAIN COURSE | FRI ▮ | SAT ▮ | ✱ — British

ROSEWARNE MANOR RESTAURANT
☎ 01209 610 414
Gwinear Road, Hayle, TR27 5JQ
Priding themselves on using only fresh and local ingredients, this venue offers an array of fish and meats. Enjoy a plump and juicy venison steak whilst taking in the stunning Cornish countryside scenery.

25% OFF TOTAL | 👤 6 | FRI ✓ | SAT ▮ — British

SAMPHIRE RESTAURANT
☎ 01326 210 759
36 Arwenack Street, Falmouth, TR11 3JF
Exerting no culinary boundaries, the chefs at the Samphire kitchen pride themselves on their locally sourced, delicious dishes.

25% OFF TOTAL | 👤 4 | FRI × | SAT × — British

ST AUBYN ARMS
☎ 01209 831 425
The Square Praze, Camborne, TR14 0JR
This historic coaching inn oozes character and hosts a sizable beer garden alongside a children's games room. Head Chef Niel Carter prepares fresh dishes, supporting the local farmers and fishermen.

2FOR1 3 COURSES | FRI × | SAT ✱ | ▲ — British

ST MICHAEL'S MOUNT INN
☎ 01209 716 640

9 Fore Street, Camborne, TR14 0QR

Serving delicious home-made dishes in a comfortable, relaxing atmosphere, St Michael's Mount is the perfect place to enjoy lunch whether you are visiting during the week or for a family meal on a Sunday.

25% OFF TOTAL | 8 | FRI | SAT | * — British

TABB'S RESTAURANT
☎ 01872 262 110

85 Kenwyn Street, Truro, TR1 3BZ

For a truly home-made dining experience, chef-patron Nigel Tabb ensures that everything from the bread accompanying the starters to the chocolates served with coffee are made in the heart of the kitchen.

2FOR1 MAIN COURSE | FRI | SAT | SUN — British

TAVISTOCK ARMS HOTEL
☎ 01822 832 217

Fore Street, Gunnislake, PL18 9BN

Take refuge in a picturesque Cornish village and allow this charming restaurant to provide an intriguingly tasty menu and a ranging drinks selection. A warm welcome and pleasurable visit guaranteed.

2FOR1 MAIN COURSE | FRI ✓ | SAT ✓ — International

TREFFRY TAVERN
01637 839 560

Quintrell Downs, Newquay, TR8 4LE

Quality pub classics with modern twists meets with a friendly and relaxed atmosphere to make this Table Table venue the perfect place for any occasion. *Excludes daytime & evening deals and festive menus.

2FOR1 MAIN COURSE | FRI ✓ | SAT ✓ — Modern British

TREVALSA COURT HOTEL
☎ 01726 842 468

School Hill, St Austell, PL26 6TH

Take in views of the sea in the romantic restaurant whilst relishing fish caught earlier that same day. Unwind on the roof terrace, reassured in the knowledge that all produce is reared and grown locally.

2FOR1 3 COURSES | FRI ✓ | SAT ✓ — International

TREVITHICK INN
08715 279 308

Treswithian Road, Camborne, TR14 7NF

Quality pub classics with modern twists meets with a friendly and relaxed atmosphere to make this Table Table venue the perfect place for any occasion. *Excludes daytime & evening deals and festive menus.

2FOR1 MAIN COURSE | FRI ✓ | SAT ✓ — Modern British

WALKABOUT
☎ 01637 853 000

The Crescent, Newquay, TR7 1DS

Walkabout is famous for its characteristically Australian atmosphere and well-rounded menu. From live sport with a juicy burger to some Aussie kangaroo skewers, you'll find it hard to tear yourself away.

25% OFF TOTAL | 10 | FRI ✓ | SAT ✓ | ▲ — International

THE WATERLOO RESTAURANT
☎ 01840 250 202

The Wellington Hotel, Boscastle, PL35 0AQ

By offering a mix of modern and traditional British cuisine in a more formal yet relaxed environment, this hotel-restaurant hopes guests will thoroughly enjoy a fine dining experience.

2FOR1 3 COURSES | FRI ✓ | SAT ✓ — International

YAK AND YETI TRURO
☎ 01872 272 363

10 Kenwyn Street, Truro, TR1 3DJ

Bringing Nepal a little closer to the western world, Yak and Yeti in Truro draws upon the subtle yet recognisable flavours that are uniquely owned by this patch of Asia.

2FOR1 3 COURSES | FRI × | SAT × — Nepalese

Devon

ARGEE BHAJEE
☎ 01392 495 577

13 Buddle Lane, St Thomas, Exeter, EX4 1JU

With a loyal following of curry fans, Argee Bhajee has a winning formula: fantastic Indian food, great service and reasonable prices. Excellent cuisine and outstanding flavours.

2FOR1 MAIN COURSE | FRI × | SAT ✓ | ▲ — Indian

ARUNDELL ARMS HOTEL AND RESTAURANT
☎ 01566 784 666

1 Fore Street, Lifton, PL16 0AA

Meticulously prepared fine dining is the hallmark of this stand-out restaurant. The cuisine is imaginative and superbly conceived. 2 AA Rosettes. *Offer available in the main restaurant only.

2FOR1 MAIN COURSE | FRI ✓ | SAT ✓ | ▲ — Modern British

THE BABA INDIAN RESTAURANT
☎ 01752 250 677

17 Bretonside, Plymouth, PL4 0BB

There is something very homely about this Indian restaurant; you can count on being well treated and well fed, with their plethora of classic curry dishes cooked swiftly, freshly and to superb effect.

25% OFF TOTAL | 4 | FRI ✓ | SAT ✓ | * | ▲ — Indian

BALTI KING
☎ 01803 868 095

5 Ticklemore Street, Totnes, TQ9 5EJ

A terrific Indian restaurant perfect for a quiet evening out. Alternatively, take your delicious dishes home with you and take delight in familiar comforts as you enjoy your feast.

2FOR1 MAIN COURSE | FRI | SAT — Indian

BARN OWL
☎ 01803 872 130

Aller Road, Newton Abbot, TQ12 5AN

Here at the Barn Owl they understand that sometimes simplicity is most effective. Enjoy traditionally English dishes in a pub-restaurant that is enveloped in historical wealth.

25% OFF TOTAL | FRI × | SAT × | SUN | ▲ — British

THE BARN OWL
01392 449 011

Guardian Road, Exeter Business Park, Exeter, EX1 3PE

This Vintage Inn oozes rural charm and rustic character. The picturesque surroundings provide the perfect backdrop for savouring the hearty, seasonal pub-food on the menu.

25% OFF TOTAL | FRI ✓ | SAT ✓ | SUN | ▲ — Modern British

BARUM GATE
01271 377 830

Whiddon Valley, Barnstaple, EX32 8RY

Quality pub classics with modern twists meets with a friendly and relaxed atmosphere to make this Table Table venue the perfect place for any occasion. *Excludes daytime & evening deals and festive menus.

2FOR1 MAIN COURSE | FRI ✓ | SAT ✓ — Modern British

BELGRAVE
01803 202 282

Seafront, Belgrave Road, Torquay, TQ2 5HE

Beefeater Grill are one of the UK's best-loved restaurants welcoming guests for almost 40 years in over 130 locations nationwide. *Excludes Breakfast, Light Bites, Bar menu, set menus and all other offers.

2FOR1 MAIN COURSE | 6 | FRI ✓ | SAT × | ▲ — Modern British

BELLA ITALIA
01392 211 778

92 Queen Street, Exeter, EX4 3RP

Accessible Italian cuisine on the British high street - indulge in authentic sharing platters, hand stretched pizzas and hearty pasta dishes, served with a healthy dose of gregarious Italian hospitality.

25% OFF TOTAL | 6 | FRI × | SAT × | SUN | ▲ — Italian

BELLA ITALIA
01752 662 143

30-33, Derrys Cross, Plymouth, PL1 2SW

Accessible Italian cuisine on the British high street - indulge in authentic sharing platters, hand stretched pizzas and hearty pasta dishes, served with a healthy dose of gregarious Italian hospitality.

25% OFF TOTAL | 6 | FRI × | SAT × | SUN | ▲ — Italian

BIANCO'S RISTORANTE
☎ 01803 293 430

38 Torwood Street, Torquay, TQ1 1EB

Enjoyment of fine Italian cuisine and wines is of utmost importance here. The proprietor Mauro gives a warm welcome to all; those celebrating a special occasion are in excellent hands.

2FOR1 MAIN COURSE | FRI | SAT * | * — Italian

BISTRO 67
☎ 01803 862 604

67 Fore Street, Totnes, TQ9 5NJ

Hearty meals and epic desserts. An inviting atmosphere can be enjoyed as soon as the warm welcome greets you at the door. Bistro-style dishes are tenderly prepared by a highly experienced chef.

2FOR1 MAIN COURSE | FRI | SAT | * — British

BISTRO ONE
☎01752 313 315

68 Ebrington Street, Plymouth, PL4 9AQ

This hidden gem in one of Plymouth's memorable districts is sure to guarantee a good time, delivering dishes that surprise and delight, all locally sourced to ensure the best of flavours.

25% OFF TOTAL | 6 | FRI ✓ | SAT ✓ — Bistro

BLACK HORSE INN
☎01392 366 649

Old Honiton Road, Sowton, Exeter, EX5 2AN

A pub-restaurant that has re-opened following a comprehensive, fantastic refurbishment, The Black Horse offers an extensive range of beers, fresh and fabulous food and fine wines in a relaxed atmosphere.

25% OFF TOTAL | 4 | FRI × | SAT × | SUN — British

BLACKBERRIES
☎01398 331 842

19 Fore Street, Bampton, Tiverton, EX16 9ND

Part of the distinct attractiveness of the local area, this family-run establishment not only looks exceptional, but also offers fantastic food and personal service that will guarantee maximum enjoyment.

2FOR1 2 COURSES | FRI ✓ | SAT ✓ | ✱ — British

THE BRASSERIE @ ELEPHANT RESTAURANT
☎01803 200 044

3-4 Beacon Terrace, Torquay, TQ1 2BH

A sublime seafront restaurant amongst the burgeoning culinary scene of the English Riviera. Diners in the Brasserie can enjoy the delicious menu, in an informal and attractive setting.

25% OFF TOTAL | 4 | FRI ✓ | SAT ✱ — Contemporary

BRASSERIE RESTAURANT
☎01752 336 428

The Elfordleigh Hotel, Colebrook, Plympton, PL7 5EB

Leave the world behind as you indulge in a well-deserved break. Try your hand at golf, go for a swim or treat yourself to a facial in the Hotel spa. The restaurant holds theme nights for guests to enjoy.

25% OFF TOTAL | 10 | FRI ▯ | SAT ▯ | ✱ — British

THE BRAUNTON INN
01271 816 547

Braunton Road, Barnstaple, EX31 4AX

This Vintage Inn oozes rural charm and rustic character. The picturesque surroundings provide the perfect backdrop for savouring the hearty, seasonal pub-food on the menu.

25% OFF TOTAL | FRI ✓ | SAT ✓ | SUN | ▲ — Modern British

THE BRILL PLAICE
☎01803 770 007

1 New Road, Dartmouth, TQ6 0NR

The Brill Plaice is a small bistro style restaurant in Stoke Fleming, just 3 miles from Dartmouth. Specialising in locally caught fish, seafood, local meats and produce from within the local area.

2FOR1 3 COURSES | FRI ▯ | SAT × | SUN | ✱ — British

CAFÉ ASIA
☎01803 868 803

46 The High Street, Totnes, TQ9 5SQ

Café Asia proudly captures new Asian tastes that provide the well-travelled diner with culinary delights from the Far East. Those new to Asian cuisine will be blown away by exotic treats.

2FOR1 MAIN COURSE | FRI ✱ | SAT ✱ — Pan-Asian

CAFÉ ROUGE
01392 251 042

24 Bedford Street, Princesshay, EX1 1GJ

French sophistication on the British high street - enjoy seasonally changing French dishes and a continental wine selection, served in a relaxed environment with an undeniable flair of Parisian chic.

25% OFF TOTAL | 6 | FRI ✓ | SAT ✓ | ✱ | ▲ — French

CAFÉ ROUGE
01752 665 522

11 Whimple Street, St Andrews Close, Plymouth, PL1 2DH

French sophistication on the British high street - enjoy seasonally changing French dishes and a continental wine selection, served in a relaxed environment with an undeniable flair of Parisian chic.

25% OFF TOTAL | 6 | FRI ✓ | SAT ✓ | ✱ | ▲ — French

THE CHINA HOUSE
01752 661 592

Sutton Wharf, Plymouth, PL4 0DW

This Vintage Inn oozes rural charm and rustic character. The picturesque surroundings provide the perfect backdrop for savouring the hearty, seasonal pub-food on the menu.

25% OFF TOTAL | FRI ✓ | SAT ✓ | SUN | ▲ — Modern British

CINNAMONS
☎01297 631 175

10 South Street, Axminster, EX13 5AD

Warm and down-to-earth Indian restaurant in Axminster which successfully brings together dishes from different parts of the subcontinent. They've an especial line in creamy, rich Makhani and Xakuti dishes.

2FOR1 MAIN COURSE | FRI ✓ | SAT ✓ | ✱ | ▲ — Authentic Indian

COUNTESS WEAR
01392 428 000

398 Topsham Road, Exeter, EX2 6HE

Beefeater Grill are one of the UK's best-loved restaurants welcoming guests for almost 40 years in over 130 locations nationwide. *Excludes Breakfast, Light Bites, Bar menu, set menus and all other offers.

2FOR1 MAIN COURSE | 6 | FRI ✓ | SAT × | ▲ — Modern British

DADA INDIAN
☎01803 551 166

4a Parkside Road, Paignton, TQ4 6AE

Smart and serious but very convivial Indian restaurant in Paignton that looks to distinguish itself in the quality of its ingredients and preparation. Enjoy a delicious meal in, or partake of the takeaway.

2FOR1 MAIN COURSE | FRI ✓ | SAT ✓ — Indian

THE DOLPHIN HOUSE BRAZZERIE
☎01752 254 879

Dolphin House, Plymouth, PL4 0DW

Ethically sourced fresh food with integrity, from the day boat fish to the local farm assured meat. Specialising in modern British cuisine with international flavours.

25% OFF TOTAL | 6 | FRI ▯ | SAT ▯ — British

THE DRUM INN
01803 690 264

Cockington Village, Torquay, TQ2 6XA

This Vintage Inn oozes rural charm and rustic character. The picturesque surroundings provide the perfect backdrop for savouring the hearty, seasonal pub-food on the menu.

25% OFF TOTAL | FRI ✓ | SAT ✓ | SUN | ▲ — Modern British

THE DUKE OF CORNWALL HOTEL
☎01752 275 850

Millbay Road, Plymouth, PL1 3LG

Elegant, extravagant, and famous for its grand design; the food, influenced by West Country produce, emphasises quality and freshness. All to be enjoyed in the warm and inviting atmosphere. One AA Rosette.

25% OFF TOTAL | 10 | FRI ▯ | SAT ▯ | ✱ | ▲ — European

THE EASTERN EYE
☎01752 262 948

57 Notte Street, Plymouth, PL1 2AG

Featuring in multiple food guides, this venue has a fantastic reputation for obvious reasons. Cuisine is cooked to an exceptional standard and is served by the most knowledgeable and inviting of staff.

2FOR1 3 COURSES | FRI ✱ | SAT ✱ | ✱ — Indian

ELLIOT'S RESTAURANT
☎01752 639 900

Armada Way, Plymouth, PL1 2HJ

With stunning views over Plymouth Sound, Elliott's restaurant provides a relaxing, welcoming atmosphere. This venue provides a modern yet warm reception, serving a delicious menu and of course, fresh fish.

25% OFF TOTAL | 6 | FRI ✓ | SAT ✓ — International

EPICENTRE
☎01803 553 790

59 Torquay Road, Paignton, TQ3 3DT

Friendly, charismatic place to eat. A vegetarian café as well as a great book shop, with the excellent feel of a neighbourhood, community venue. Serves a range of café-style snacks and sweet treats.

50% OFF FOOD | 10 | FRI ✱ | SAT ✱ — Vegetarian

FISH ON THE HARBOUR
☎01598 753 600

1 Riverside Road, Lynmouth, EX35 6EX

Bright and airy space in this beautiful seaside location for classic, fresh, delicious fish and chips as well as neat, sophisticated seafood dishes.

25% OFF TOTAL | 2 | FRI ✓ | SAT ✓ — British

FRENCH'S COSMOPOLITAN BISTRO
☎01769 580 023

Combe House, Fore Street, Chulmleigh, EX18 7BR

Wholesome, full-bodied French-style bistro food in this warm, friendly and accommodating Devon restaurant.

25% OFF TOTAL | 6 | FRI ✓ | SAT ✓ — European

THE GALLEY RESTAURANT
☎01392 876 078

41 Fore Street, Topsham, Exeter, EX3 0HU

This venue, run by celebrity Master Chef Paul Da Costa Greaves, brings a contemporary twist and unique style to their seafood dishes. *Advance booking mentioning Gourmet Society is essential.

25% OFF TOTAL | 4 | FRI ✓ | SAT ▯ | SUN — Seafood

THE GEORGE INN
☎01803 712 342

Main Street, Blackawton, Totnes, TQ9 7BG

Tucked away in a lovely little Devon village, you'll enjoy a warm welcome at The George. For locals and visitors alike, this is your first port of call for a superbly ranging menu of fulsome, tasty food.

2FOR1 MAIN COURSE | FRI ▯ | SAT ✱ | SUN | ▲ — Fresh Fish/Pub Classics

THE GLOBE HOTEL
☎01805 624 424

Fore Street, Torrington, EX38 8H

The Globe Hotel is situated in a white-wash building and is a notable feature of the area. The restaurant has been beautifully adorned with tapestries and Greek vases that altogether create warm vibes.

2FOR1 MAIN COURSE | FRI ✓ | SAT ▯ | ▲ — British

THE GRANDSTAND
01626 883 300

Newton Abbot Racecourse, Newton Abbot, TQ12 3AF

Beefeater Grill are one of the UK's best-loved restaurants welcoming guests for almost 40 years in over 130 locations nationwide. *Excludes Breakfast, Light Bites, Bar menu, set menus and all other offers.

2FOR1 MAIN COURSE | 6 | FRI ✓ | SAT × | ▲ — Modern British

HAWKINS MEETING HOUSE
☎01752 222 919

5 Buckwell Street, Plymouth, PL1 2DA

Taking pride in bold, vibrant flavours, Hawkins does traditional British fare perfectly whilst providing a positive and diverse atmosphere for all cultures.

2FOR1 3 COURSES | FRI ✓ | SAT ✓ | SUN — British

HAZELWOOD HOUSE
☎01548 821 232

Loddiswell, South Hams, Kingsbridge, TQ7 4EB

Worth the trip, this country house hotel-restaurant is set in 67 acres of Outstanding Natural Beauty. Pay attention to the daily changing menus which are composed of locally sourced produce.

2FOR1 3 COURSES | FRI ▯ | SAT ▯ — British

HENNESSY RESTAURANT
☎01803 290 900

41 Torwood Street, Torquay, TQ1 1DZ

Ascend the elegant staircase to the expansive restaurant with a fresh and fruity cocktail in hand. Indulge in the innovative and chic menu which guarantees local sourcing and freshness.

25% OFF TOTAL | 6 | FRI ▯ | SAT ▯ | SUN | ✱ | ▲ — British

ILFRACOMBE TANDOORI RESTAURANT
☎01271 866 453

13-14 High Street, Ilfracombe, EX34 9DF

A unique and modern dining venue where chefs demonstrate the ability to craft and serve an exquisite array of Bangladeshi and Indian cuisine. Experience fine Eastern food in a sophisticated atmosphere.

2FOR1 2 COURSES | FRI ✓ | SAT ✓ | ✱ — Indian

THE JACK RABBIT
01752 783 585

7-9 Howeson Lane, Derriford, Plymouth, PL6 8BD

This Vintage Inn oozes rural charm and rustic character. The picturesque surroundings provide the perfect backdrop for savouring the hearty, seasonal pub-food on the menu.

25% OFF TOTAL | FRI ✓ | SAT ✓ | SUN | ▲ — Modern British

JD'S GRILL
☎01752 601 605

17-19 Derrys Cross, Plymouth, PL1 2SW

JD's Grill serves delicious gourmet burgers and American influenced food in a cool, fresh and modern environment. With over 30 burgers to choose from you will surely find your perfect match.

2FOR1 MAIN COURSE | FRI ✱ | SAT × | ▲ — American

LA ROSETTA
☎01395 568 136

High Street, Newton Poppleford, EX10 0DW

A fine Italian restaurant housing a kitchen driven by passion for food and a team of staff committed to its diners. Dishes are impressively prepared and cooked in a traditionally authentic Italian way.

25% OFF TOTAL | 10 | FRI × | SAT × | SUN — Italian

LA TASCA
☎01392 434 488

26 Bedford Street, Exeter, EX1 1GJ

Quintessentially Spanish, La Tasca's fresh and exciting menu offers something for everyone. Their tapas dishes are sincerely authentic, while their paellas always deliver on flavour.

25% OFF TOTAL | 8 | FRI ✓ | SAT × | ▲ — Spanish

LAKEVIEW MANOR
☎01404 891 287

Near Dunkeswell, Honiton, EX14 4SH

Open to residents and non-residents alike serving mouthwatering, locally sourced dishes-Lakeview Manor is a hidden gem in an oasis of stunning countryside calm.

25% OFF TOTAL | 8 | FRI ✓ | SAT ✓ — European

LAVANI
☎01803 203 040

35 Ilsham Road, Wellswood Village, Torquay, TQ1 2JG

Experience the power of culinary India at Lavani. They create fiercely authentic home cooked offbeat dishes with an accent on regional cuisine and Anglo-Indian cuisine of the British Raj.

2FOR1 MAIN COURSE | FRI × | SAT × | ✱ | ▲ — Indian

LIGHTER INN
☎01392 875 439

The Quay, Exeter, EX3 0HZ

Hall & Woodhouse owned, this beautiful venue is situated on the water and boasts exquisite views of the Rive Exe estuary. Serving locally sourced English cuisine, this restaurant welcomes all.

25% OFF TOTAL | FRI × | SAT × | SUN | ▲ — British

LIVE & LET LIVE INN
☎01803 762 663

Landscove, Newton Abbot, TQ13 7LZ

Welcoming smiles, undoubtedly good food and an affable atmosphere makes this pub an ideal location in which to catch-up with friends or refuel after a long day.

2FOR1 MAIN COURSE | FRI ▯ | SAT ▯ — British

LOCKYERS QUAY
01752 664 353

1 Lockyers Quay, Coxside, Plymouth, PL4 0DX

Quality pub classics with modern twists meets with a friendly and relaxed atmosphere to make this Table Table venue the perfect place for any occasion. *Excludes daytime & evening deals and festive menus.

2FOR1 MAIN COURSE | FRI ✓ | SAT ✓ — Modern British

LYDFORD COUNTRY HOUSE
☎01822 820 347

Lydford, Okehampton, EX20 4AU

The prestigious menu created by Hugo Gouveia is exploding with fresh and seasonal recipes, ensuring diners are repeatedly thrilled. Whether staying for the night or simply dining, this venue is a must.

25% OFF TOTAL | 4 | FRI ✓ | SAT ✓ — International

MACARI'S ITALIAN
☎01803 295 627

17 Victoria Parade, Habourside, Torquay, TQ1 2BB

Taste the real Italy at Macari's Italian Restaurant, Pizzeria & Bar. By day, a cafe bar with a varied lunchtime menu, and by night, a fine dining Italian restaurant with full waiter service.

2FOR1 MAIN COURSE | FRI ✓ | SAT ✓ | ✱ | ▲ — Italian

MARSH MILLS
01752 600 660

300 Plymouth Road, Crabtree, Plymouth, PL3 6RW

Beefeater Grill are one of the UK's best-loved restaurants welcoming guests for almost 40 years in over 130 locations nationwide. *Excludes Breakfast, Light Bites, Bar menu, set menus and all other offers.

2FOR1 MAIN COURSE | 6 | FRI ✓ | SAT × | ▲ — Modern British

MILL STREET STEAKHOUSE
☎01548 857 788

9-11 Mill Street, Kingsbridge, TQ7 1ED

Dine on succulent steaks cooked to your liking, served with a number of exquisite side dishes. Choose an excellent wine from their select list to perfectly complement your meal.

2FOR1 3 COURSES | FRI ✓ | SAT ✓ — International

MIRCH MASALA
☎01803 311 296

44 Babbacombe Road, Torquay, TQ1 3SN

Mirch Masala is confident that it can satisfy any curry lover with its expansive selection of Indian delights. Renowned for its traditional recipes, this venue is a popular local destination.

2FOR1 3 COURSES | FRI × | SAT × — Indian

THE NESS
☎ 01626 873 480

Ness Drive, Shaldon, Teignmouth, TQ14 0HP

The temptingly fresh aromas of morning coffee initiate the start of the day at this elegant Georgian pub. After having your daily kick-start, indulge in a casual lunch as you take in the unmissable views.

25% OFF TOTAL | ♟ 6 | FRI × | SAT × | SUN — European

OLD INN
☎ 01364 621 207

Widecombe in the Moor, Newton Abbot, TQ13 7TA

Hall & Woodhouse, a family-owned brewer, focus upon locally sourced produce at an affordable price. Attracting a variety of diners, this venue is situated at the heart of the Dartmoor National Park.

25% OFF TOTAL | FRI × | SAT × | SUN | ▲ — British

POOPDECK RESTAURANT
☎ 01803 858 681

14 The Quay, Brixham, TQ5 8AW

A little quayside restaurant whose speciality, naturally, is seafood, offering sublimely fresh fish, superbly cooked to bring out the subtle texture and flavours of each variety.

25% OFF TOTAL | ♟ 4 | FRI ✓ | SAT ✱ — Seafood

SAFFRON
☎ 01626 363 963

104 Queen Street, Newton Abbot, TQ12 2EU

With its great food and friendly, inviting atmosphere, this restaurant is extremely popular and enjoys an admirably varied clientèle. Successfully caters for meat lovers and vegetarians alike.

2FOR1 MAIN COURSE | FRI 📱 | SAT 📱 — Indian

SAILS RESTAURANT
☎ 01803 839 281

22 South Embankment, Dartmouth, TQ6 9BB

A tranquil haven offering the most delectable of dishes. Local fish is used to create divine meals, whilst an enticing wine list provides a suitable beverage. *Must order a minimum of two courses.

2FOR1 3 COURSES | FRI × | SAT × | SUN — International

THE THATCHED COTTAGE RESTAURANT
☎ 01626 365 650

9 Crossley Moor Road, Newton Abbott, TQ12 3LE

A family-run establishment where dining in a relaxed, warm and comfortable environment is a real pleasure. All food is freshly prepared and cooked with carefully sourced, often organic, ingredients.

25% OFF TOTAL | ♟ 4 | FRI 📱 | SAT × | SUN | ▲ — Fine Dining

THE SAINT GEORGE AND DRAGON
01392 876 121

Clyst St George, Exeter, EX3 0QJ

This Vintage Inn oozes rural charm and rustic character. The picturesque surroundings provide the perfect backdrop for savouring the hearty, seasonal pub-food on the menu.

25% OFF TOTAL | FRI ✓ | SAT ✓ | SUN | ▲ — Modern British

THE SEA TROUT INN
☎ 01803 762 274

Staverton, Totnes, TQ9 6PA

Top-notch modern British cuisine in this homely Devon inn, beautifully set in an area that supplies the vast majority of its fresh produce. *Advance booking mentioning Gourmet Society is essential.

2FOR1 MAIN COURSE | FRI × | SAT × | SUN | ✱ | ▲ — Modern British

THE SEVEN STARS
☎ 01548 852 331

13 Mill Street, Kingsbridge, TQ7 1ED

Firm and versatile modern British cuisine; interesting chef's specials as well as some tasty traditional favourites. Flaky, creamy fish pie or a zingy fajita, you'll be well oriented with the Seven Stars.

2FOR1 3 COURSES | FRI 📱 | SAT 📱 | ▲ — Contemporary

STRADA
01392 432 727

Princesshay Square, Bedford Street, Exeter, EX1 1AH

Offering fresh, bold dishes inspired by flavours of Italian city life - Strada serves a selection of indulgent tastes, to those seeking a blissful escape to laidback Italian life. *Excludes Pizzettas.

25% OFF TOTAL | ♟ 6 | FRI ✓ | SAT × | ▲ — Italian

TYME RESTAURANT
☎ 01271 862 841

Trimstone, Woolacombe, EX34 8NR

French windows lead to the lovely gardens in this pretty restaurant within the 17th-century Trimstone Manor hotel. Brasserie-style menu features fresh, clear flavours.

50% OFF FOOD | ♟ 2 | FRI ✓ | SAT ✓ — British

VICEROY DUNKESWELL
☎ 01404 891 341

4 Culme Way, Honiton, EX14 4JP

Innovative and indulgent, this contemporary restaurant boasts an authentic and fresh Indian menu. The modern and sensual interior make this venue an ideal location for the sophisticated diner.

50% OFF FOOD | ♟ 4 | FRI × | SAT × — Indian

WALKABOUT
☎ 01392 410 965

99-101 Fore Street, Exeter, EX4 3HY

Walkabout is famous for its characteristically Australian atmosphere and well-rounded menu. From live sport with a juicy burger to some Aussie kangaroo skewers, you'll find it hard to tear yourself away.

25% OFF TOTAL | 10 | FRI ✓ | SAT ✓ | ▲ — International

WALKABOUT
☎ 01752 825 650

5 Union Street, Plymouth, PL1 2SU

Walkabout is famous for its characteristically Australian atmosphere and well-rounded menu. From live sport with a juicy burger to some Aussie kangaroo skewers, you'll find it hard to tear yourself away.

25% OFF TOTAL | 10 | FRI ✓ | SAT ✓ | ▲ — International

WHITE ROCK
01803 698 930

White Rock, Long Road South, Paignton, TQ4 7AZ

Beefeater Grill are one of the UK's best-loved restaurants welcoming guests for almost 40 years in over 130 locations nationwide. *Excludes Breakfast, Light Bites, Bar menu, set menus and all other offers.

2FOR1 MAIN COURSE | 6 | FRI ✓ | SAT × | ▲ — Modern British

ZENA'S RESTAURANT
☎ 01271 378 844

1 Market Street, Barnstaple, EX31 1BX

Mellow and warm-toned atmosphere, well-drilled service and eclectic, elegant Mediterranean cuisine. Try the excellent pan-roasted gnocchi with roasted vegetables and a beurre blanc sauce.

50% OFF FOOD | 2 | FRI ✱ | SAT ✱ — Mediterranean

Dorset

THE ANGEL INN
☎ 01202 873 778

Ringwood Road, Longham, Wimborne, BH22 9AP

A classically English pub serving fine cask ales and freshly cooked food at affordable prices. The owners focus on the maintenance of the traditional village pub by providing a warm homely atmosphere.

25% OFF TOTAL | 6 | FRI × | SAT × | SUN | ▲ — British

ARUBA RESTAURANT & BAR
☎ 01202 554 211

Pier Approach, Bournemouth, BH2 5AA

Marvellously louche beach bar and restaurant. Serves breakfasts, snacks, lunches and dinners from a series of menus ranging from classic bistro-style fare to some fine oriental dishes. Open and welcoming.

25% OFF TOTAL | 6 | FRI ✱ | SAT × — International

AVON CAUSEWAY HOTEL
☎ 01202 482 714

Hurn, Christchurch, BH23 6AS

This beautiful, traditional, four-star hotel is home to a restaurant serving a wholesome, broad array of classic pub grub. *Offer not available on Christmas Menus.

25% OFF TOTAL | 4 | FRI × | SAT × | SUN — British

BAILEY BRIDGE
01202 485 215

Barrack Road, Christchurch, BH23 2BN

Quality pub classics with modern twists meets with a friendly and relaxed atmosphere to make this Table Table venue the perfect place for any occasion. *Excludes daytime & evening deals and festive menus.

2FOR1 MAIN COURSE | FRI ✓ | SAT ✓ — Modern British

THE BAKER'S ARMS
01202 622 900

Dorchester Road, Lytchett Minster, Poole, BH16 6JF

This Vintage Inn oozes rural charm and rustic character. The picturesque surroundings provide the perfect backdrop for savouring the hearty, seasonal pub-food on the menu.

25% OFF TOTAL | FRI ✓ | SAT ✓ | SUN | ▲ — Modern British

THE BALTI HOUSE
☎ 01202 422 634

865 Christchurch Road, Bournemouth, BH7 6AT

Creative and thoughtful full-flavoured balti dishes in this traditional, unpretentious and friendly Indian restaurant situated in the heart of Boscombe.

2FOR1 MAIN COURSE | FRI ✱ | SAT ✱ | ✱ | ▲ — Indian

BEIRUT LOUNGE
☎ 01202 311 388

232 Old Christchurch Road, Bournemouth, BH1 1PE

The perfect location for a relaxing night with friends, with excellent Lebanese food and wide selection of boutique wines, Beirut Lounge is perfect for those seeking something a little out of the ordinary.

25% OFF TOTAL | 2 | FRI ✓ | SAT ✓ — Middle Eastern

BELLA ITALIA
01202 296 993

84 Old Christchurch Road, Bournemouth, BH1 1LR

Accessible Italian cuisine on the British high street - indulge in authentic sharing platters, hand stretched pizzas and hearty pasta dishes, served with a healthy dose of gregarious Italian hospitality.

25% OFF TOTAL | 6 | FRI × | SAT × | SUN | ▲ — Italian

BELLA ITALIA
01305 778 424

104 St Mary Street, Weymouth, DT4 8NY

Accessible Italian cuisine on the British high street - indulge in authentic sharing platters, hand stretched pizzas and hearty pasta dishes, served with a healthy dose of gregarious Italian hospitality.

25% OFF TOTAL | 6 | FRI × | SAT × | SUN | ▲ — Italian

BLUE MANGO BOURNEMOUTH
☎ 01202 280 206

37 Exeter Road, Bournemouth, BH2 5AF

The Blue Mango is a restaurant with a takeaway menu as well. It offers food from various regions of Thailand and provides diners with freshly prepared authentic Thai cuisine.

25% OFF TOTAL | 6 | FRI ✓ | SAT ✓ | ✱ | ▲ — Thai

CAFÉ ROUGE
01202 757 472

67-71a Seamoor Rd, Westbourne, Bournemouth, BH4 9AE

French sophistication on the British high street - enjoy seasonally changing French dishes and a continental wine selection, served in a relaxed environment with an undeniable flair of Parisian chic.

25% OFF TOTAL | 6 | FRI ✓ | SAT ✓ | ✱ | ▲ — French

THE CANOPY RESTAURANT @ PENN CENTRAL
☎ 01202 710 888

Penn Hill Avenue, Poole, BH14 9NA

The attentive staff at The Canopy Restaurant at Penn Central welcome you to the contemporary steakhouse filled with atmosphere, great lighting and beautiful decor.

2FOR1 3 COURSES | FRI ✓ | SAT ✓ | SUN | ▲ — British

CHACHY
☎ 01202 293 355

148 Old Christchurch Road, Bournemouth, BH1 1NL

Sophisticated Indian restaurant where the chefs do not shy away from imaginative flavours and well-balanced recipes. The menu accommodates a whole host of Indian spices and creative influences.

2FOR1 3 COURSES | FRI ▯ | SAT ✓ | SUN — Indian

CHILLIES
☎ 01305 766 602

10 Queen Street, Weymouth, DT4 7HZ

Warmly recommended by local diners, Chillies in Weymouth serves up delectable Indian dishes, not only fixed on the old favourites but with some more expansive and intriguing alternatives.

25% OFF TOTAL | 4 | FRI ✓ | SAT ✓ — Indian

CIAO
☎ 01202 555 657

144 Old Christchurch Road, Bournemouth, BH1 1NL

This restaurant offers a variety of Italian and Mediterranean cuisine in a modern and stylish setting. With fresh, seasonal ingredients imported from Italy they offer a great menu and daily specials.

2FOR1 MAIN COURSE | FRI ✱ | SAT ▯ — Italian

THE CLIFF PANORAMIC RESTAURANT
☎ 01305 826 060

Southwell Park, Portland, DT5 2NA

The Cliff Panoramic Restaurant stands proudly on the historic Portland cliff-tops, boasting fantastic views over the Jurassic coast. A passionate team, committed to providing local sourced innovative food.

25% OFF TOTAL | 6 | FRI × | SAT ▯ | ✱ | ▲ — British

CLIFFHANGER CAFÉ
☎ 01425 278 058
Waterford Road, Highcliffe, Christchurch, BH23 5JA
Delicious food and outstanding views are guaranteed to take your breath away. Enjoy breakfast, lunch or an evening meal with the intimate company of another or a large celebratory party.

2FOR1 MAIN COURSE | FRI ✓ | SAT ✓ | ✱ — British

CORIANDER RESTAURANT
☎ 01202 552 202
22 Richmond Hill, Bournemouth, BH2 6EJ
With a vibrant and fun atmosphere, Coriander offers a light siesta menu and traditional Mexican meals. Its unique décor with cacti, sombreros and traditional woven blankets offer an authentic experience.

2FOR1 MAIN COURSE | FRI ✱ | SAT ✱ | SUN | ▲ — Mexican

CORKERS RESTAURANT
☎ 01202 681 393
1 High Street, Poole, BH15 1AB
Revel in the superb harbour and quayside views at Corkers Restaurant while feasting on delicious dishes that reflect the seasons. *Offer excludes Shellfish and Dover Sole.

25% OFF TOTAL | 👤 2 | FRI ✱ | SAT ✱ — European

THE CROWN
01425 672 279
Ringwood Road, Bransgore, Christchurch, BH23 8AA
This Vintage Inn oozes rural charm and rustic character. The picturesque surroundings provide the perfect backdrop for savouring the hearty, seasonal pub-food on the menu.

25% OFF TOTAL | FRI ✓ | SAT ✓ | SUN | ▲ — Modern British

CROWN HOTEL
☎ 01258 456 626
8 West Street, Blandford Forum, DT11 7AJ
Gastronomic menu in a classic, elegant English coaching house: try a silken Stargazy Pie or the tender roast monkfish, washed down with one of their deep, golden cask ales.

25% OFF TOTAL | 👤 6 | FRI × | SAT × | SUN | ▲ — European

THE CURLEW
01202 594 811
287 Christchurch Rd, West Parley, Bournemouth, BH22 8SQ
This Vintage Inn oozes rural charm and rustic character. The picturesque surroundings provide the perfect backdrop for savouring the hearty, seasonal pub-food on the menu.

25% OFF TOTAL | FRI ✓ | SAT ✓ | SUN | ▲ — Modern British

CYGNETS RESTAURANT
☎ 01305 208 979
Weymouth College, Cranford Ave, Weymouth, DT4 7LQ
Support the talented chefs of the future at this terrific on-site restaurant. Wonderful dishes are prepared by chefs-in-training, guaranteeing guests a first-class dining experience.

2FOR1 MAIN COURSE | FRI ✓ | SAT ✓ | ✱ — Classic British/French

DEAUVILLE RESTAURANT
☎ 01202 552 262
5-7 Priory Road, Bournemouth, BH2 5DH
Acclaimed restaurant renowned for its varied and imaginative menus. Sophisticated Art Deco surroundings are coupled with great views across the town. The food, in turn, is stylish and very tempting.

25% OFF TOTAL | 👤 10 | FRI ✓ | SAT ✓ | ▲ — Contemporary

DEAN PARK INN
☎ 01202 552 941
41 Wimborne Road, Bournemouth, BH2 6NB
A friendly, local pub with a good selection of Wadworth ales to complement the home cooked food. *Offer available from 1st December 2013. Excludes Christmas menu's.

25% OFF TOTAL | 👤 4 | FRI × | SAT × | SUN — British

THE DROVERS INN
☎ 01258 840 084
Gussage All Saints, Wimborne, BH21 5ET
The Drovers Inn is a traditional 17th Century country pub in the heart of Dorset, serving good food, locally sourced and a great seasonal menu, real ale and opens with a warm welcome.

25% OFF TOTAL | 👤 6 | FRI 📱 | SAT 📱 | SUN — British

THE EYE OF THE TIGER
☎ 01202 780 900
207 Old Christchurch Road, Bournemouth, BH1 1JZ
Established venue that offers a range of gourmet Indian and Bangladeshi dishes, its speciality being the 'Tiger Special'. Large capacity, and renowned for once cooking the biggest curry in the world.

2FOR1 MAIN COURSE | FRI ✱ | SAT ✱ — Indian

FRAMPTON ARMS
☎ 01305 852 253
Queens Dr, Hurst Rd, Moreton, Dorchester, DT2 8BB
Hardy Country is the perfect home for this traditional family-run inn which sits across from the old railway station in Moreton village. It serves creative, well-conceived menus in a welcoming atmosphere.

25% OFF TOTAL | 👤 4 | FRI 📱 | SAT 📱 | SUN — British

GLOBE INN
01425 271 360
266 Lymington Road, Highcliffe, Christchurch, BH23 5ET
Quality pub classics with modern twists meets with a friendly and relaxed atmosphere to make this Table Table venue the perfect place for any occasion. *Excludes daytime & evening deals and festive menus.

2FOR1 MAIN COURSE | FRI ✓ | SAT ✓ — Modern British

GOAT & TRICYCLE
☎ 01202 314 220
27-29 West Hill Road, Bournemouth, BH2 5PF
Often described as Bournemouth's hidden gem, The Goat & Tricycle serves a regularly updated menu, with everything from bangers and mash to goat curry. *Excludes Christmas Menus.

25% OFF TOTAL | 👤 4 | FRI × | SAT × | SUN — British

GRASSHOPPER
☎ 01202 741 463
141 Bournemouth Road, Poole, BH14 9HT
Perfect for lunch and dinner, the Grasshopper is just a short drive from Bournemouth and Poole. Hall & Woodhouse owned, this pub serves locally sourced food and English cuisine. Welcoming to all.

25% OFF TOTAL | 👤 6 | FRI × | SAT × | SUN | ▲ — British

THE GREYHOUND INN
☎ 01929 480 205
The Square, Corfe Castle, Wareham, BH20 5EZ
Shipped straight from the bay, the vast range of seafood on offer here is guaranteed to be fresh, locally sourced, and deliciously flavoursome. Exquisite afternoon Dorset cream teas can also be enjoyed.

25% OFF TOTAL | 👤 4 | FRI ✓ | SAT ✓ | ✱ — British

GURKHA 2
☎ 01202 922 173
683 Christchurch Road, Bournemouth, BH7 6AA
One of Bournemouth's best Nepalese and Indian restaurants, Gurkha 2 offers enjoyable, memorable dining experiences with delicious cuisines, an exciting environment & amazing hospitality.

2FOR1 MAIN COURSE | FRI ✓ | SAT × — Indian

HALF MOON
☎ 01747 852 456
Salisbury Road, Shaftesbury, SP7 8BS
Part of the Hall & Woodhouse family brewer, only the finest of traditional English cuisine is served. Sourced locally, the freshest of food is offered to a variety of clientèle in a historical pub.

25% OFF TOTAL | FRI × | SAT × | SUN | ▲ — British

HALFWAY INN
☎ 01929 480 402
Norden Nr Corfe Castle, Wareham, SP7 8BS
Located in the heart of the Isle of Purbeck, this historical venue is part of the Hall & Woodhouse family brewer. Locally sourced food is served in a welcoming, family environment.

25% OFF TOTAL | FRI × | SAT × | SUN | ▲ — British

HALLMARK HOTEL BRASSERIE
☎ 01202 751 000
7 Durley Chine Road, Bournemouth, BH2 5JS
The restaurant at Bournemouth's Hallmark Hotel is stylish but relaxed in feel. The accomplished kitchen prepares consistently excellent food from an extended brasserie menu that appeals to every guest.

50% OFF FOOD | 👤 6 | FRI 📱 | SAT 📱 | ▲ — European

HOLES BAY
01202 669 944
Holes Bay Road, Poole, BH15 2BD
Quality pub classics with modern twists meets with a friendly and relaxed atmosphere to make this Table Table venue the perfect place for any occasion. *Excludes daytime & evening deals and festive menus.

2FOR1 MAIN COURSE | FRI ✓ | SAT ✓ — Modern British

HOTEL DU VIN ☎01202 785 570
Thames Street, the Quay, Poole, BH15 1JN
The finest, freshest local produce, simple European recipes, a stunning choice of wines; these are the elements of the trademark Hotel du Vin bistro. A fine eatery awarded 1 AA Rosette.

2FOR1 MAIN COURSE | FRI × | SAT × | SUN | ▲ — European

INDIAN OCEAN ☎01202 311 222
4 West Cliffe Road, Bournemouth, BH2 5EY
A premier destination for authentic Indian cuisine prepared by expert chefs, providing diners with a variety of tastes and aromas from across India. Both classics and specialities will delight your palate.

2FOR1 2 COURSES | FRI ▯ | SAT ✱ — Indian

KAYLA BRASSERIE ☎01202 554 300
42 Holdenhurst Road, Bournemouth, BH8 8AD
Well known for its elegant and contemporary vibes, Kayla Brasserie serves delectable Italian dishes to a fine cohort of guests. Expect first-class dining without breaking the bank.

2FOR1 MAIN COURSE | 4 | FRI ✓ | SAT × | ▲ — Italian

THE KITCHEN CLUB ☎01202 436 430
Riverside Avenue, Bournemouth, BH7 7ES
Inspired by the Italian cuisine with a little added from the Continent and a few tasteful creations, the style is both rustic and contemporary and seek to make guests feel cozy and trendy.

25% OFF TOTAL | 4 | FRI ✱ | SAT × | ▲ — British

LA GONDOLA RESTAURANT ☎01202 558 079
9-10 Lansdowne House, Christchurch Rd, BH1 3JP
Bearing his extensive experience and masterful expertise, owner Luca arrived at La Gondola to provide diners with the most phenomenal Italian dining experience and cuisine.

25% OFF TOTAL | 4 | FRI ✓ | SAT ✱ | SUN | ✱ | ▲ — Italian

LA PICCOLA ITALIA 01202 551 510
23 Holdenhurst Rd, Bournemouth, BH1 3QJ
A long-established Bournemouth restaurant, decked out with iconic columns and rich claret tones, boasting an excellent reputation in the town for its atmosphere and delicious food.

25% OFF TOTAL | 6 | FRI ✓ | SAT × | SUN | ▲ — Italian

LA STALLA ☎01202 535 642
270a Wallisdown Road, Bournemouth, BH10 4HZ
La Stalla provides an amiable atmosphere that offers exquisite cuisine in a home away from home. Whilst a warm ambience will completely relax you, the food will have you jumping for joy.

2FOR1 MAIN COURSE | FRI ✓ | SAT ✓ | SUN | ▲ — Italian

LA TASCA ☎0845 126 2960
23-27 Bourne Avenue, Bournemouth, BH2 6DT
Quintessentially Spanish, La Tasca's fresh and exciting menu offers something for everyone. Their tapas dishes are sincerely authentic, while their paellas always deliver on flavour.

25% OFF TOTAL | 8 | FRI ✓ | SAT × | ▲ — Spanish

LA TRATTORIA ☎01929 423 784
10-12 High Street, Swanage, BH19 2NT
An array of Italian treats bursting with flavour are on offer at this intimately small evening restaurant. Local crab and lobster make tremendous dishes for the avid seafood fan.

2FOR1 MAIN COURSE | FRI ▯ | SAT ✱ — Italian

THE LAMBS' GREEN INN 01202 881 974
Lambs Green Lane, Corfe Mullen, Wimborne, BH21 3DN
This Vintage Inn oozes rural charm and rustic character. The picturesque surroundings provide the perfect backdrop for savouring the hearty, seasonal pub-food on the menu.

25% OFF TOTAL | FRI ✓ | SAT ✓ | SUN | ▲ — Modern British

LE CAFÉ BAR AT THE TRUOVILLE HOTEL ☎01202 552 262
5-7 Priory Road, Bournemouth, BH2 5DH
Enjoy a glass of wine in hand as you watch the world go by, or sit back and relax with a light bite or luxurious coffee. The perfect location for pre-show meals and after-show drinks.

25% OFF TOTAL | 8 | FRI ✓ | SAT ✓ | ▲ — Contemporary

LOCH FYNE ☎01202 609 000
47 Haven Rd, Canford Cliffs BH13 7LH
From the roadside oyster bar that once was, Loch Fyne restaurants now successfully inject energy and passion into great food and wonderful flavours, whilst ensuring their seafood is sustainably sourced.

25% OFF TOTAL | 4 | FRI ✱ | SAT ✱ | ▲ — Seafood

LULWORTH COVE INN ☎01929 400 333
Main Road, Wareham, BH20 5RQ
A family-owned brewer, Hall & Woodhouse focus on locally sourced ingredients at an affordable price. Attracting a variety of guests, this friendly venue is located in a picturesque, historical village.

25% OFF TOTAL | FRI × | SAT × | SUN | ▲ — British

LYNTON COURT 01202 293 992
47 Christchurch Road, Boscombe, Bournemouth, BH1 3PA
Quality pub classics with modern twists meets with a friendly and relaxed atmosphere to make this Table Table venue the perfect place for any occasion. *Excludes daytime & evening deals and festive menus.

2FOR1 MAIN COURSE | FRI ✓ | SAT ✓ — Modern British

MINT ☎01202 733 438
4 Station Road, Poole, BH14 8UB
Mint is an exciting new Indian contemporary restaurant that brings the old and new together. The kitchen has produced a menu of Indian treats that demonstrate revamped traditional favourite flavours.

2FOR1 MAIN COURSE | FRI × | SAT × — Indian

MONMOUTH ASH ☎01202 822 227
Manor Road, Verwood, BH31 6DT
Perfect for a few drinks with dinner, the Monmouth Ash overlooks the New Forest National Park. Hall & Woodhouse owned, this venue serves local ingredients and traditional English food. All welcome.

25% OFF TOTAL | FRI × | SAT × | SUN | ▲ — British

MONTY'S LOUNGE ☎01202 241 415
926-928 Christchurch Road, Bournemouth, BH7 6DL
Monty's Lounge in Bournemouth - where good food comes naturally. Lovely local restaurant and lounge bar, serving up locally sourced food and drinks in a warm, friendly lounge.

25% OFF TOTAL | 8 | FRI × | SAT × | SUN | ✱ — British

THE NEW INN PORTLAND ☎01305 821 232
35 Easton Street, Portland, DT5 1BS
The New Inn is a newly refurbished, family run Freehouse with a cosy snug with a real wood burning stove and is listed in The Good Pub Guide. Serving fresh locally sourced produce, in bistro style dishes.

25% OFF TOTAL | 4 | FRI × | SAT × | SUN | ▲ — Bistro

NEW QUEEN INN ☎01425 672 432
Ringwood Road, Christchurch, BH23 7BG
Beautifully located on the riverside, this rural pub overlooks the New Forest National Park. Hall & Woodhouse owned, this venue serves local food served in traditional English dishes. All are welcome.

25% OFF TOTAL | FRI × | SAT × | SUN | ▲ — British

OCEAN BAY RESTAURANT ☎01929 422 222
2 Ulwell Road, Swanage, BH19 1LH
Situated in the picturesque town of Swanage, this fabulously modern restaurant offers wonderful views to be enjoyed while you savour the fantastic food - whether you arrive by land or by sea.

25% OFF TOTAL | 4 | FRI ▯ | SAT ▯ | ✱ — British

OLD GRANARY ☎01929 552 010
The Quay, Wareham, BH20 4LP
A talented team of chefs now operate under the roof of this old grain store. An indulgent menu offers traditional dishes and adventurous Mediterranean cuisine.

25% OFF TOTAL | 6 | FRI × | SAT × | SUN | ▲ — European

OLIVE BRANCH ☎01202 884 686
East Borough, Wimborne, BH21 1PF
Once believed to be the home of an infamous 19th century smuggler, this traditional pub serves wholesome, flavourful food and offers a range of fabulous wines to suit all tastes and pockets.

25% OFF TOTAL | 6 | FRI × | SAT × | SUN | ▲ — European

PREZZO

2FOR1 MAIN COURSE | FRI ✗ | SAT ✗ | ▲

2-FOR-1 MAIN COURSE

6 restaurants in Dorset

56 St Thomas Street, Weymouth, DT4 8EQ	☎ 01305 787 600
Purbeck House, 5 West Borough, Wimborne, BH21 1LT	☎ 01202 881 119
Judge Jeffreys, 6 High West St, Dorchester DT1 1UJ	☎ 01305 259 678
43 East Street, Blandford Forum, DT11 7DX	☎ 01258 489 625
3 Bridge Street, Christchurch, BH23 1DY	☎ 01202 496 100
58 Westover Road, Bournemouth, BH1 2BZ	☎ 01202 556 399

PACIFIC 23 ☎01202 485 105
75 Mudeford, Mudeford, Christchurch, BH23 3NJ

An attractive menu offering traditional pub food and tasty Thai cuisine. This popular bar offers both set and à la carte menus which present dishes such as spicy king prawns or delicious duck.

25% OFF TOTAL | 6 | FRI ✓ | SAT ✓ — International

PEPPINO'S ITALIAN FUSION RESTAURANT ☎01202 292 727
27-37 Charminster Road, Bournemouth, BH8 8UE

The motto at Peppino's is Eat, Drink, Dance. They serve traditional Italian cuisine as well as creatively designed Fusion dishes from the talented and experienced team of chefs!

2FOR1 MAIN COURSE | FRI ✗ | SAT ✗ | ✱ | ▲ — Italian

PIZZA STEAK HOUSE ☎01297 444 788
2 Drakes Way, Broad Street, DT7 3QP

An outstanding choice of heavenly pizzas and local steaks of the finest quality, as well as other delectable Mediterranean dishes. The emphasis is on quality food at a sensible price.

25% OFF TOTAL | 4 | FRI ✓ | SAT ✓ — Italian

THE PRINT ROOM ☎01202 789 669
Richmond Hill, Bournemouth, BH2 6HH

This Rosette-winning venue boasts historicism in the forms of architecture and art-décor. Lavishly decorated with Swarovski crystal chandeliers and gleaming tiles, The Print Room is delightfully debonair.

2FOR1 3 COURSES | FRI ✓ | SAT ✗ | ▲ — Brasserie

RAJPOOT RESTAURANT ☎01305 257 492
43 High West Street, Dorchester, DT1 1UT

Exclusive and exciting Indian restaurant in Dorchester, looking to move a degree beyond the classic British Indian dining scene. Its cool, calm atmosphere hosts some scintillating, imaginative dishes.

25% OFF TOTAL | 4 | FRI ✱ | SAT ✱ | ✱ | ▲ — Indian

SAKIB SPICE 01202 582 880
183 Tuckton Road, Tuckton, BH6 3LA

Customers can delight in a fantastic quality of Indian fare at a pocket-friendly price. Feast upon exciting new blends of spices that tempt and tease the palate.

2FOR1 3 COURSES | FRI ✗ | SAT ✗ — Indian

SENSE ☎01305 777 222
46 St Mary Street, Weymouth, DT4 8PU

Offers fantastic European dishes in a warm and friendly atmosphere. The carefully selected wines, the deliciously satisfying food and the accommodating staff make every experience here a special occasion.

25% OFF TOTAL | 4 | FRI ✱ | SAT ✱ | SUN | ▲ — European

SHIP INN WEYMOUTH ☎01305 773 879
Custom House Quay, Weymouth, DT4 8BE

Hall & Woodhouse are dedicated to locally sourced ingredients at pocket-friendly prices in a welcoming environment. This favourable venue is beautifully located on Custom House Quay.

25% OFF TOTAL | FRI ✗ | SAT ✗ | SUN | ▲ — British

SIAM THAI RESTAURANT ☎01202 731 010
129 Parkstone Road, Poole, BH15 2PB

A calm and intimate atmosphere, with fresh and delicious Thai food in the heart of Poole. With an extensive menu, the dishes are beautifully presented and perfect for a authentic Thai dining experience.

25% OFF TOTAL | 8 | FRI ✓ | SAT ✓ — Thai

SMUGGLERS HAUNT 01202 874 210
Ringwood Road, Tricketts Cross, Ferndown, BH22 9BB

Beefeater Grill are one of the UK's best-loved restaurants welcoming guests for almost 40 years in over 130 locations nationwide. *Excludes Breakfast, Light Bites, Bar menu, set menus and all other offers.

2FOR1 MAIN COURSE | 6 | FRI ✓ | SAT ✗ | ▲ — Modern British

SMUGGLERS INN
☎01305 833 125

Osmington Mills, Weymouth, DT3 6HF

Nestled between cliffs, this Hall & Woodhouse owned pub is both famous and historic. Serving locally sourced food from its regional food partners, the Smugglers Inn offers traditional English food to all.

25% OFF TOTAL | FRI × | SAT × | SUN | ▲ — British

SOMERFORD
01202 485 376

Somerford Road, Christchurch, BH23 3QG

Beefeater Grill are one of the UK's best-loved restaurants welcoming guests for almost 40 years in over 130 locations nationwide. *Excludes Breakfast, Light Bites, Bar menu, set menus and all other offers.

2FOR1 MAIN COURSE | 6 | FRI ✓ | SAT × | ▲ — Modern British

THE SPICE CENTRE
☎01305 267 450

37-38 High West Street, Dorchester, DT1 1UP

Great Indian cuisine is served at The Spice Centre, where dishes of all spice levels are on offer. Friendly staff are happy to cater to your every need.

25% OFF TOTAL | 10 | FRI ✱ | SAT ✱ — Indian

THE SPRINGHEAD
☎01305 832 117

Sutton Road, Sutton Poyntz, Weymouth, DT3 6LW

Beautifully and intimately tucked away beneath the chalk downs, this village pub provides the warmest of welcomes. The freshest of food can be enjoyed all year round, from light bites to hearty meals.

25% OFF TOTAL | 4 | FRI ✓ | SAT ✓ | SUN — European

ST PETER'S FINGER
☎01202 622 275

Dorchester Road, Lytchett Minster, Poole, BH16 6JE

Unique by name, this inn delivers scrumptious food, award-winning beers, and unbeatable hospitality to every one of its guests. All ingredients are regionally sourced, even their delicious ice cream.

25% OFF TOTAL | 6 | FRI × | SAT × | SUN | ▲ — British

STANDARD BENGAL RESTAURANT
☎01202 490 084

105 Bargates, Christchurch, BH23 1QH

Combining the values of style, quality, creativity and refinement, the chefs prepare beautifully balanced food. Treat yourself to the ultimate dining experience with your favourite curry dish.

25% OFF TOTAL | 6 | FRI | SAT | ✱ — Indian

THE THREE LEGGED CROSS
01202 826 052

Ringwood Road, Three Legged Cross, Wimborne, BH21 6RE

This Vintage Inn oozes rural charm and rustic character. The picturesque surroundings provide the perfect backdrop for savouring the hearty, seasonal pub-food on the menu.

25% OFF TOTAL | FRI ✓ | SAT ✓ | SUN | ▲ — Modern British

TIIEN
☎01202 299 412

105 St Michael's Road, Bournemouth, BH2 5DU

Beautiful canopied sofas, soft cushions and authentic pots and vases create an enviable recreation of the treasures of the East. The most sublime Thai flavours can be found in every dish on the menu.

2FOR1 2 COURSES | FRI × | SAT × — Thai

VIA VENETO
☎01202 707 321

Harbourside Hotel, 38 Salterns Way, Poole, BH14 8JR

The panoramic sea views that accompany the outstanding contemporary Italian cuisine will leave you wanting to come back here over and over again. Perfect for that special occasion.

2FOR1 MAIN COURSE | FRI | SAT ✱ | SUN — Italian

WALKABOUT
☎01202 295 072

156-164 Old Christchurch Road, Bournemouth, BH1 1NL

Walkabout is famous for its characteristically Australian atmosphere and well-rounded menu. From live sport with a juicy burger to some Aussie kangaroo skewers, you'll find it hard to tear yourself away.

25% OFF TOTAL | 10 | FRI ✓ | SAT ✓ | ▲ — International

WESTBEACH
☎01202 587 785

Pier Approach, Bournemouth, BH2 5AA

Exceptional fish and seafood restaurant in a spectacular south coast setting. Metres from the sandy shore by Bournemouth Pier, it's consistently innovative in its use of the daily catch. 2 AA Rosettes.

2FOR1 3 COURSES | FRI | SAT × | ▲ — Seafood

WEYMOUTH
01305 831 241

Gateway Business Park, Mercury Road, Weymouth, DT3 5HJ

Beefeater Grill are one of the UK's best-loved restaurants welcoming guests for almost 40 years in over 130 locations nationwide. *Excludes Breakfast, Light Bites, Bar menu, set menus and all other offers.

2FOR1 MAIN COURSE | 6 | FRI ✓ | SAT × | ▲ — Modern British

WORLDS END ALMER
☎01929 459 671

Almer, Blandford Forum, DT11 9EW

Family owned brewer Hall and Woodhouse devote themselves to locally sourced food at affordable prices in an affable atmosphere. This stunning Dorset pub is considered a local landmark.

25% OFF TOTAL | FRI × | SAT × | SUN | ▲ — British

YACHTSMAN
☎01202 674 568

Lake Road, Poole, BH15 4LW

Merely minutes from the sea on the Dorset coast, this Hall & Woodhouse venue is both contemporary and friendly. Serving locally sourced food, this pub welcomes everyone who enjoys traditional food.

25% OFF TOTAL | FRI × | SAT × | SUN | ▲ — British

Gloucestershire

BABURCHI CUISINE
☎01452 300 615

42 Bristol Road, Gloucester, GL1 5SD

Specialising in balti dishes, the cuisine here is authentic and celebratory of the Indian continent. Long-established, this venue has a reputable name for all the right reasons.

25% OFF TOTAL | 4 | FRI ✓ | SAT ✓ — Indian

THE BECKFORD INN
☎01386 881 532

Cheltenham Road, Tewkesbury, GL20 7AN

The Beckford Inn sits on the northern edge of the beautiful Cotswolds. It is a stunning 18th Century coaching inn set in the open countryside.

25% OFF TOTAL | 6 | FRI × | SAT × | SUN — British

BELLA ITALIA
01242 584 341

70-72 High Street, Cheltenham, GL50 1EG

Accessible Italian cuisine on the British high street - indulge in authentic sharing platters, hand stretched pizzas and hearty pasta dishes, served with a healthy dose of gregarious Italian hospitality.

25% OFF TOTAL | 6 | FRI × | SAT × | SUN | ▲ — Italian

BELLA ITALIA
01242 577 417

23 The Promenade, Cheltenham, GL50 1LE

Accessible Italian cuisine on the British high street - indulge in authentic sharing platters, hand stretched pizzas and hearty pasta dishes, served with a healthy dose of gregarious Italian hospitality.

25% OFF TOTAL | 6 | FRI × | SAT × | SUN | ▲ — Italian

THE BROWN JUG
☎01242 521 736

242 Bath Road, Cheltenham, GL53 7NB

Renowned for its real ales and award-winning British cuisine, The Brown Jug has a loyal following of regulars who appreciate an authentic traditional pub.

25% OFF TOTAL | 10 | FRI ✓ | SAT ✓ | SUN — British

THE BUMBLE BEE
01452 727041

Waterwells Business Park, Quedgeley, GL2 4AB

This Vintage Inn oozes rural charm and rustic character. The picturesque surroundings provide the perfect backdrop for savouring the hearty, seasonal pub-food on the menu.

25% OFF TOTAL | FRI ✓ | SAT ✓ | SUN | ▲ — Modern British

C & W'S AFRICAN EXP
☎01452 387 911

8-10 St Catherine Street, Gloucester, GL1 2BX

Showcasing the vibrant highlights of African cuisine, C & W's focuses on specific culinary traditions, drawing on choice ingredients and styles of preparation. End the evening with a special African brew.

50% OFF FOOD | FRI ✓ | SAT ✓ — African

CAFÉ ROUGE
01242 529 989
31-41 The Promenade, Cheltenham, GL50 1NW
French sophistication on the British high street - enjoy seasonally changing French dishes and a continental wine selection, served in a relaxed environment with an undeniable flair of Parisian chic.

25% OFF TOTAL | 6 | FRI ✓ | SAT ✓ | ✱ | ▲ — French

CHARINGWORTH MANOR HOTEL
☎ 01386 593 555
Charingworth, Chipping Campden, GL55 6NS
Quintessential Cotswold manor house with historical architecture and a fine ambience. The restaurant is held in high regard; crisp and clean flavours feature highly on its seasonal menus. 1 AA Rosette.

25% OFF TOTAL | 6 | FRI ✓ | SAT × | ✱ — Classic British/ French

CHELTENHAM BALTI
☎ 01242 227 772
2 Great Norwood Street, Cheltenham, GL50 2AN
A balti house that, appealingly, doesn't make a song and dance about itself and gets on with serving a good curry. It's on that basis that the restaurant has won itself such a good reputation in the town.

2FOR1 3 COURSES | FRI ✱ | SAT ✱ — Indian

CONNOISSEUR TANDOORI
☎ 01452 304 003
22 London Road, Gloucester, GL1 3NR
Unassuming tandoori restaurant that serves up a superb selection of Indian dishes in pleasant, homely surroundings. It's a simple, effective place for a good, spicy meal out.

2FOR1 3 COURSES | FRI ✱ | SAT ✱ — Indian

CROSS HANDS
01242 233 847
Tewkesbury Road, Uckington, Cheltenham, GL51 9SL
Beefeater Grill are one of the UK's best-loved restaurants welcoming guests for almost 40 years in over 130 locations nationwide. *Excludes Breakfast, Light Bites, Bar menu, set menus and all other offers.

2FOR1 MAIN COURSE | 6 | FRI ✓ | SAT × | ▲ — Modern British

DEARMANS @ MERCURE
☎ 0844 815 9077
Bondend Lane, Gloucester, GL4 8ED
Enveloped by elegance, this period Hotel maintains all of the characteristically Regent features. With the Cotswolds nearby, the Hotel and the Dearmans Restaurant capture the area's exquisite beauty.

2FOR1 3 COURSES | FRI ✓ | SAT ✓ — International

THE FOUNTAIN INN
☎ 01452 522 562
53 Westgate Street, Gloucester, GL1 2NW
The Fountain is pretty little 17th century pub located in a quiet courtyard, serving good food, with a range of cask ales and friendly service.

2FOR1 MAIN COURSE | FRI ✓ | SAT ✓ | ✱ — Multi-Cuisine

THE GRAPEVINE HOTEL
☎ 01451 830 344
High Street, Bourton-on-the-Water, GL54 2AN
Beautiful hotel in idyllic surroundings with elegant dining rooms that provide a perfect backdrop for the excellent cuisine. Menus are seasonal and feature outstanding, understated cooking. 2 AA Rosettes.

25% OFF TOTAL | 10 | FRI ✓ | SAT ✓ — British

THE GREYHOUND
☎ 01285 653 573
Ashton Road, Siddington, Cirencester, GL7 6HR
Home-cooked food, exciting specials, including market fish dishes, a wide range of real ales and choice of fine wines makes The Greyhound an excellent venue for warmth and hospitality. Family friendly.

25% OFF TOTAL | 4 | FRI × | SAT × | SUN — Modern Pub

GRILLE RESTAURANT
☎ 01242 771 444
49 Winchcombe Street, Cheltenham, GL52 2NE
A lively restaurant serving traditional dishes from this delicious cuisine. Let the warmth of the open fire envelop you and relax into the great food, drink, service and décor.

25% OFF TOTAL | 10 | FRI ✓ | SAT ✓ — Turkish

HOTEL DU VIN
☎ 01242 588 450
Parabola Road, Cheltenham, GL50 3AQ
The finest fresh local produce, simple European recipes, a stunning choice of wines; these are the trademark of a fine Hotel du Vin bistro. This venue boasts a cigar shack for the aficionado. 1 AA Rosette.

2FOR1 MAIN COURSE | FRI × | SAT × | SUN | ▲ — European

JEWEL IN THE CROWN
☎ 01452 310 366
88 Westgate Street, Gloucester, GL1 2NZ
Jewel in the Crown is a popular haunt for locals and has a reputation, not only for flavoursome food but friendly staff.Well worth a visit for a tasty curry in a relaxed environment.

25% OFF TOTAL | 4 | FRI × | SAT × — Indian

LA TASCA
☎ 01242 220 775
70 Regents Street, Cheltenham, GL50 1HW
Quintessentially Spanish, La Tasca's fresh and exciting menu offers something for everyone. Their tapas dishes are sincerely authentic, while their paellas always deliver on flavour.

25% OFF TOTAL | 8 | FRI ✓ | SAT × | ▲ — Spanish

LINDEN TREE
☎ 01452 527 869
73 Bristol Road, Gloucester, GL1 5SN
This traditional country style pub, set in a Georgian Grade II listed building, offers a warm and friendly atmosphere, good food, comfortable accommodation and a wide range of ales. *Excludes Christmas Menus.

25% OFF TOTAL | 4 | FRI × | SAT × | SUN — British

LONGFORD INN
01452 523 519
Tewkesbury Road, Longford, GL2 9BE
Beefeater Grill are one of the UK's best-loved restaurants welcoming guests for almost 40 years in over 130 locations nationwide. *Excludes Breakfast, Light Bites, Bar menu, set menus and all other offers.

2FOR1 MAIN COURSE | 6 | FRI ✓ | SAT × | ▲ — Modern British

THE MALT HOUSE
☎ 01453 511 177
22 Marybrook Street, Berkeley, GL13 9BA
Boasting a comfortable interior, tasteful furnishings and intimate, relaxing surroundings, this family hotel and restaurant offers delicious food and a great place to stay in the heart of the Cotswolds.

2FOR1 MAIN COURSE | FRI ✓ | SAT ✓ | ▲ — English and Continental

MARINADES RESTAURANT
☎ 01242 578 811
56 High St, Cheltenham, GL50 1EE
Tempting, exotic aromas seep into the restaurant from the kitchen at this fantastic colourful restaurant. Vibrant dishes bursting with extraordinary flavours serve the place with a popular reputation.

2FOR1 3 COURSES | FRI × | SAT × — Caribbean

MARK @ STREET
☎ 01453 839 251
Bath Road, Stroud, GL6 0BX
Nearby sourcing is at the heart of the ethos here, as Chef Mark Payne uses the finest local cheeses, meats and beers for his vivacious menu. *Check the website for further details.

2FOR1 MAIN COURSE | FRI ▯ | SAT ▯ | ▲ — British

MASALA BITES
☎ 01242 530 531
22-24 Albion Street, Cheltenham, GL52 2LP
Rather than focusing upon heat intensity, the chefs at this eatery strive to wow guests with flavoursome dishes that tempt and tantalise the palate. Expect an informal, friendly ambience.

2FOR1 3 COURSES | FRI ▯ | SAT ▯ — Indian

MY GREAT GRANDFATHERS
☎ 01684 292 687
84 Church Street, Tewkesbury, GL20 5RX
A modern restaurant set against the historical backdrop of the medieval town of Tewkesbury. Here you'll find British food with a delightful exotic twist. The Thai-style lobster fish cakes are heavenly.

25% OFF TOTAL | 4 | FRI ▯ | SAT ✱ | ✱ — Contemporary

THE NAPIER RESTAURANT
☎ 01242 307 800
The Promenade, Cheltenham, GL50 1NN
The Mercure Queen's Hotel is an elegant luxury hotel; the AA rosette awarded Napier Restaurant & Conservatory offers traditional & contemporary cuisine.

25% OFF TOTAL | FRI ✓ | SAT × | ▲ — Contemporary

THE NEW INN AT COLN
☎ 0844 815 3434
Coln St Aldwyns, Cirencester, GL7 5AN
Adding to the charm and character of its location, the New Inn at Coln is well suited to its pretty village location. Distinguished food and first-class service has awarded it 2 AA Rosettes.

25% OFF TOTAL | 4 | FRI ✱ | SAT × | SUN | ▲ — European

THE OAKWOOD
01452 730 266
Tewkesbury Road, Twigworth, Gloucester, GL2 9PG
Quality pub classics with modern twists meets with a friendly and relaxed atmosphere to make this Table Table venue the perfect place for any occasion. *Excludes daytime & evening deals and festive menus.

2FOR1 MAIN COURSE | FRI ✓ | SAT ✓ — Modern British

THE PARROT BAR AND GRILL
☎ 01242 526 965
4 North Place, Cheltenham, GL50 4DW
Bar and grill that prides itself on a philosophy of provenance, entailing authenticity, assurance and rigorous attention to obtain the finest local ingredients at source. Tasty range of well-cooked dishes.

25% OFF TOTAL | 6 | FRI ▯ | SAT ▯ | SUN | ▲ — Steakhouse/Seafood

PREZZO
01242 227 703
1 The Brewery, Henrietta St, Cheltenham, GL50 4FA
With a character all of its own, Prezzo oozes contemporary style and enduring charm. Signature pastas, stone-baked pizzas and classic Italian dishes promise a perfect dining choice for the whole family.

2FOR1 MAIN COURSE | FRI × | SAT × | ▲ — Italian

PREZZO
01242 524 437
99-101 The Promenade, Cheltenham, GL50 1NW
With a character all of its own, Prezzo oozes contemporary style and enduring charm. Signature pastas, stone-baked pizzas and classic Italian dishes promise a perfect dining choice for the whole family.

2FOR1 MAIN COURSE | FRI × | SAT × | ▲ — Italian

PREZZO
01452 414 022
46 Southgate Street, Gloucester, GL1 2DR
With a character all of its own, Prezzo oozes contemporary style and enduring charm. Signature pastas, stone-baked pizzas and classic Italian dishes promise a perfect dining choice for the whole family.

2FOR1 MAIN COURSE | FRI × | SAT × | ▲ — Italian

THE RESTAURANT AT COTSWOLD HOUSE
☎ 01386 840 330
The Square, Chipping Campden, GL55 6AN
Strikingly beautiful, this hotel offers guests a tranquil retreat from every day stress. Celebrating British cuisine, chunks of crusty bread are served alongside creamy churned cheeses - all made locally.

2FOR1 MAIN COURSE | FRI ✓ | SAT × | SUN | ▲ — International

THE RESTAURANT AT NOEL ARMS HOTEL
☎ 01386 840 330
Lower High St, Chipping Campden, GL55 6AN
Savour an authentic Indian dish expertly prepared by Head Chef Indunil Upatissa who boasts the Best Pub Curry Chef Award. Treat a sweet tooth with a scrumptious home-made cake and a velvety coffee.

2FOR1 MAIN COURSE | FRI ✓ | SAT × | SUN | ▲ — International

SEBZ
☎ 01452 310 599
93 Northgate Street, Gloucester, GL1 2AA
Tasty tapas treats on offer at this fantastic Portugese and Mediterranean restaurant in Gloucester. Fresh fish, tender meat and well-sourced vegetables combine with tasty sauces, herbs and spices.

2FOR1 MAIN COURSE | FRI ✓ | SAT × — Mediterranean

THE SEVERN BORE INN
☎ 01452 750 318
Main Road, Minsterworth, Gloucester, GL2 8JX
The Severn Bore Inn is situated on the banks of the River Severn and offers traditional home cooked food, locally sourced where possible, a wide range of real cask ales, beer garden and children's playarea

2FOR1 3 COURSES | FRI ✓ | SAT ✓ | SUN — British

SHAHI BALTI
☎ 0871 432 0500
72 Westgate Street, Gloucester, GL1 2NZ
Indian restaurant in the heart of Gloucester that's garnered itself a good reputation for doing the simple things well. Great range of dishes on the menu, plentiful portions, and a relaxed buzz about it.

2FOR1 3 COURSES | FRI ✱ | SAT ✱ — Indian

SOPHIE'S RESTAURANT
☎ 01453 885 188
The Priory, 20 High Street, Stroud, GL6 9BN
A popular family-run French restaurant serving simple, traditional cuisine that is high-quality, well-cooked, and affordable. Accompanied by a 100% French wine list. *Offer excludes special event nights.

2FOR1 2 COURSES | FRI ✓ | SAT ✓ — French

SPICE LODGE
☎ 01242 226 300
Montpellier Drive, Cheltenham, GL50 1TY
Premier pan-Asian cuisine provides an exciting taste of the Orient. In a majestic setting chefs craft delicious, traditional food to delight and satisfy diners, providing a unique and luxurious experience.

2FOR1 MAIN COURSE | FRI ✱ | SAT ✱ — Thai/Indian

STRADA
01242 253 410
6-7 Montpellier Street, Cheltenham, GL50 1SX
Offering fresh, bold dishes inspired by flavours of Italian city life - Strada serves a selection of indulgent tastes, to those seeking a blissful escape to laidback Italian life. *Excludes Pizzettas.

25% OFF TOTAL | 6 | FRI ✓ | SAT × | ▲ — Italian

THE SWAN AT WOTTON UNDER EDGE
☎ 01453 843 004
16 Market St, Wotton-under-Edge, GL12 7AE
Whether staying the night at this 17th Century coaching inn or simply treating yourself to dinner, be sure to sample a delectable dish off of the chef's speciality board, promising to be locally sourced.

2FOR1 MAIN COURSE | FRI ▯ | SAT ▯ | SUN | ▲ — British

TASTE OF INDIA
☎ 01452 300 772
38 Worcester Street, Gloucester, GL1 3AG
Visit Taste of India and join them in an exciting culinary journey which is a result of centuries of patronage to the art of cooking and a large repertoire of delicious recipes.

2FOR1 2 COURSES | FRI × | SAT × | ✱ — Indian

TEWKESBURY PARK HOTEL
☎ 01684 295 405
Lincoln Green Lane, Tewkesbury, GL20 7DN
Experience a variety of English dishes, created with skill and passion from locally sourced produce, all within the restaurant of this fine Hotel.

25% OFF TOTAL | FRI ✓ | SAT ✓ — Modern British

THE TWELVE BELLS
01452 862 521
Witcombe, Gloucester, GL3 4SS
Beefeater Grill are one of the UK's best-loved restaurants welcoming guests for almost 40 years in over 130 locations nationwide. *Excludes Breakfast, Light Bites, Bar menu, set menus and all other offers.

2FOR1 MAIN COURSE | 6 | FRI ✓ | SAT × | ▲ — Modern British

WESLEY HOUSE RESTAURANT
☎ 01242 602 366
High Street, Winchcombe, Cheltenham, GL54 5LJ
An extremely popular restaurant; a treat whether for a light lunch or a romantic meal for two. Enjoy the open fire in the winter and the marvellous views from the Atrium in the summer. 2 AA Rosettes.

2FOR1 MAIN COURSE | FRI ✱ | SAT ✱ | ▲ — European

THE WHEATSHEAF
☎ 01242 521 736
283 Old Bath Road, Cheltenham, GL53 9AJ
An intimate, stylish bar and restaurant that draws on classic British flavours and excellent wines. Quintessentially English, the Wheatsheaf Inn is a great place to spend an evening.

25% OFF TOTAL | 10 | FRI ✓ | SAT ✓ | SUN — British

WILD GARLIC RESTAURANT & ROOMS
☎ 01453 832 615
3 Cossack Square, Nailsworth, GL6 0DB
Within only three months of opening in November 2007, the AA took the unprecedented step of awarding Wild Garlic Restaurant 2 AA Rosettes for food. An absolute must.

25% OFF TOTAL | 4 | FRI ✓ | SAT ✓ — British

WYCK HILL HOUSE
☎ 01451 831 936
Wyck Hill House Hotel, Stow-on-the-Wold, GL54 1HY
Boasting an AA 2 Rosette Award, this venue hosts accomplished Head Chef Mark who offers locally sourced, contemporary cuisine. Intimate and scenic, Wyck Hill is the perfect setting for any occasion.

2FOR1 MAIN COURSE | FRI ✓ | SAT × | SUN | ▲ — International

To understand what the restaurant icons mean, please see the inside back cover.

THE YEW TREE
☎01531 820 719

The Yew Tree, Cliffords Mesne, GL18 1JS

A characterful old building plays host to this classic pub-restaurant whose menu takes the hearty classics and adds a contemporary inflection to each. Try out this glorious Gloucestershire outpost.

25% OFF TOTAL | 4 | FRI ✓ | SAT ✱ | SUN — British

TAILORS EATING HOUSE
☎01242 255 453

4 Cambray Place, Cheltenham, GL50 1JS

If you love good homecooked food, you'll love Tailors. Situated in a paved shopping area and covered in rich green ivy, this local favourite offers a wide range of real ales and wine. *Excludes Christmas Menus.

25% OFF TOTAL | 4 | FRI × | SAT × | SUN — British

Guernsey/Jersey

BELLA ITALIA
01534 725 478

10-12 York Street, St Helier, Jersey, JE2 3RQ

Accessible Italian cuisine on the British high street - indulge in authentic sharing platters, hand stretched pizzas and hearty pasta dishes, served with a healthy dose of gregarious Italian hospitality.

25% OFF TOTAL | 6 | FRI × | SAT × | SUN | ▲ — Italian

THE BRASSERIE AND THE GRILL
☎01534 743 101

L'Horizon, La Route de la Baie, St Brelade, JE3 8EF

Overlooking the beautiful bay in St. Brelade, this Hand Picked Hotels venue boasts a dashing restaurant specialising in fresh, local seafood, and a genial brasserie for informal eating. 2 AA Rosettes.

25% OFF TOTAL | 4 | FRI ✱ | SAT ✱ — British

THE GARDEN @ ST. MARGARET'S LODGE
☎01481 235 757

Forest Road, St Martin, Guernsey, GY4 6UE

A wonderful retreat at the end of the day, this hotel-based restaurant offers a brilliant range of options. Making use of fresh local seafood and produce, its dishes keep the flavours clear and clean.

2FOR1 3 COURSES | FRI ▯ | SAT ▯ — French

Somerset

ACORN RESTAURANT @ MERCURE
☎0844 815 9063

Bristol North The Grange, Northwoods, Bristol, BS36 1RP

Set back within acres of fresh green land, the Mercure Bristol North The Grange Hotel is an old country manor house with 4-stars held to its name. The Acorn Restaurant offers spectacular views of outside.

2FOR1 3 COURSES | FRI ✓ | SAT ✓ — International

AHMED'S CURRY CAFÉ
☎01179 466 466

1e Chandos Road, Bristol, BS6 6PG

Authentic food, expertly prepared to bring forward the exotic flavours and textures of fine Indian cooking. Renowned for their special haandi dishes.

2FOR1 MAIN COURSE | FRI ✓ | SAT ✓ | ✱ — Indian

AHMED'S MASALA CAFÉ
☎01179 304 194

2 Jacob Wells Road, Hotwells, Bristol, BS8 1EA

A cosy curry café; relaxed and unpretentious. Great food, perfect for a pop-in 'nosh. *Offer not available for takeaway.

2FOR1 MAIN COURSE | FRI ▯ | SAT ▯ | ✱ — Indian

AIRFIELD TAVERN
01935 476 311

Alvington Lane, Brympton, Yeovil, BA22 8UX

Quality pub classics with modern twists meets with a friendly and relaxed atmosphere to make this Table Table venue the perfect place for any occasion. *Excludes daytime & evening deals and festive menus.

2FOR1 MAIN COURSE | FRI ✓ | SAT ✓ — Modern British

AKASH
☎01935 472 352

101 Middle Street, Yeovil, BA20 1NA

Imaginative, philosophical Indian and Bangladeshi restaurant serving a panoply of excellent food. Old favourites like the dhansak are done beautifully; the raan mussallam stands out among the specialities.

2FOR1 MAIN COURSE | FRI × | SAT × | ▲ — Indian/Bangladeshi

ASSILAH BISTRO
☎01179 095 419

194 Wells Road, Totterdown, Bristol, BS4 2AX

With 30 years experience to hand, this family-run restaurant specialises in home-made Moroccan cuisine. Boasting a menu of traditional dishes at moderate prices, diners can simply sit back and enjoy.

25% OFF TOTAL | 2 | SUN — Moroccan

BADMINTON ARMS
☎01454 772 132

Badminton Road, Coalpit Heath, BS36 2QJ

A friendly and welcoming pub situated on the edge of Bristol City. The Badminton Arms serves great food along with a selection of wines and real ales. *Excludes Christmas Menus.

25% OFF TOTAL | 4 | FRI × | SAT × | SUN — British

BAR @ MERCURE
☎01179 689 900

Holland House Hotel, Redcliffe Hill, Bristol, BS1 6SQ

Enjoy simple, light bites to eat alongside a sip of wine or two the bar at this excellent contemporary hotel in the centre of Bristol.

50% OFF FOOD | 4 | FRI ✓ | SAT ✓ — International

BAR @ RADISSON
☎01179 349 500

The Radisson Blu Bristol, Broad Quay, Bristol, BS1 4BY

With spectacular views of the Bristol waterfront, this hotel bar does a range of custom cocktails, wines and spirits and serves delicious light dishes through the day, from antipasti to home-made burgers.

50% OFF FOOD | 6 | FRI ✱ | SAT ✓ — Brasserie

BARLOW'S BISTRO @ OLD VICARAGE HOTEL
☎01278 458 891

45-51 St Mary Street, Bridgwater, TA6 3EQ

At Barlow's Bistro,the chef describes his food as Modern British. He aims to serve fresh locally sourced food cooked to order and generous portion sizes. One of Bridgwater's best kept secrets revealed.

2FOR1 MAIN COURSE | FRI ▯ | SAT ▯ | SUN | ✱ | ▲ — British

THE BAY BAR AND KITCHEN
☎01179 531 446

4-6 North Street, Bedminster, Bristol, BS3 1HT

Try this warm, contemporary restaurant in Bristol for thoroughgoing British and modern European food, from Angus to lamb shank, brie tart to Greek salad.

25% OFF TOTAL | 8 | FRI ✱ | SAT ✱ — European

BELLA ITALIA
01179 293 278

8-10 Baldwin Street, Bristol, BS1 1SA

Accessible Italian cuisine on the British high street - indulge in authentic sharing platters, hand stretched pizzas and hearty pasta dishes, served with a healthy dose of gregarious Italian hospitality.

25% OFF TOTAL | 6 | FRI × | SAT × | SUN | ▲ — Italian

BELLA ITALIA
01179 277 230

Unit SU79, Cabot Circus, Bristol, BS1 3BX

Accessible Italian cuisine on the British high street - indulge in authentic sharing platters, hand stretched pizzas and hearty pasta dishes, served with a healthy dose of gregarious Italian hospitality.

25% OFF TOTAL | 6 | FRI × | SAT × | SUN | ▲ — Italian

BELLA ITALIA
01179 590 982

Venue Leisure Complex, Merlins Road, Bristol, BS10 7SR

Accessible Italian cuisine on the British high street - indulge in authentic sharing platters, hand stretched pizzas and hearty pasta dishes, served with a healthy dose of gregarious Italian hospitality.

25% OFF TOTAL | 6 | FRI × | SAT × | SUN | ▲ — Italian

THE BLACK STEER BAR & GRILL
☎01173 295 685

219 Henleaze Road, Bristol, BS9 4NQ

Quality is certainly not compromised at this affordable eatery. Carnivorous diners can sink their teeth into thick steaks and wholesome side dishes. Certain to appease larger-than-life appetites.

50% OFF FOOD | 6 | FRI ✓ | SAT ✓ | SUN — Steakhouse

BOMBAY BOULEVARD ☎ 01179 273 544
4 Denmark Street, Bristol, BS1 5DQ
Bombay Boulevard's charm is in simple, no-nonsense Indian takeaway food, with good service, plenty of choice and eclectic, rich flavours.

50% OFF FOOD | 2 | FRI ✱ | SAT ✱ — Indian

BORDEAUX QUAY BRASSERIE & RESTAURANT ☎ 01179 431 200
V-Shed, Canons Way, Bristol, BS1 5UH
Superb independent restaurant specialising in traditional, provincial European dishes. A popular local spot by the water's edge, it has also received accolades for sustainability and 2 AA Rosettes.

2FOR1 MAIN COURSE | FRI ✓ | SAT × | SUN | ▲ — European

BRASSERIE BRUNEL @ THE ROYAL HOTEL ☎ 01225 463 134
Manvers Street, Bath, BA1 1JP
Brassiere Brunel is casual dining in a French brasserie setting with a menu to match. Wherever possible the food is sourced locally and the majority of dishes are freshly produced by a first class team.

25% OFF TOTAL | 8 | FRI ▯ | SAT ✓ — European

THE BRASSMILL 01179 867 280
Avon Mill Lane, Keynsham, Bristol, BS31 2UG
This Vintage Inn oozes rural charm and rustic character. The picturesque surroundings provide the perfect backdrop for savouring the hearty, seasonal pub-food on the menu.

25% OFF TOTAL | FRI ✓ | SAT ✓ | SUN | ▲ — Modern British

BRIDGEWATER STEAKHOUSE ☎ 01278 455 454
17 Penel Orlieu, Bridgwater, TA6 3PF
The Bridgewater Steakhouse has fantastic reviews. The food is lovingly prepared and freshly cooked. The steaks are top quality and melt in the mouth, there is also a good variety of none steak dishes.

25% OFF TOTAL | 10 | FRI ✓ | SAT ✓ — British

BRISTOL FASHION 01179 298 953
The Haymarket, Bristol, BS1 3LR
Beefeater Grill are one of the UK's best-loved restaurants welcoming guests for almost 40 years in over 130 locations nationwide. *Excludes Breakfast, Light Bites, Bar menu, set menus and all other offers.

2FOR1 MAIN COURSE | 6 | FRI ✓ | SAT × | ▲ — Modern British

BRUNEL'S HAT RESTAURANT @ HILTON ☎ 01454 201 144
Hilton Bristol Hotel, Woodlands Lane, Bristol, BS32 4JF
Simple, smart restaurant in the Bristol Hilton. Serves both a buffet and an à la carte menu featuring traditional West Country specialities among its range of well-cooked international dishes.

50% OFF FOOD | 4 | FRI ✱ | SAT ✱ — British

BSB BAR ☎ 01179 114 950
41 Corn Street, Bristol, BS1 1HT
Vibrant modern bar that's branched out to this Corn Street location. Expect a broad crowd who enjoy the menu made up of locally sourced food, cooked with accomplishment, tasty and unfussy.

2FOR1 MAIN COURSE | FRI ✓ | SAT ✓ | ▲ — European

BSB BAR ☎ 01179 114 950
Canons Road, Bristol, BS1 5UH
Vibrant modern bar that's set in the old tobacco shed down at the historic harbour. Expect a broad crowd who enjoy the menu made up of locally sourced food, cooked with accomplishment, tasty and unfussy.

2FOR1 MAIN COURSE | FRI ✓ | SAT ✓ | ▲ — European

CAFÉ PIANO ☎ 01749 677 772
9 Heritage Courtyard, Tenbury Wells, BA5 2RR
Smooth, low-key and contemporary café tucked away in a quiet courtyard. Makes excellent use of its calm setting with a hugely appealing bistro-style menu. Some delicious rustic flavours are their staple.

50% OFF FOOD | 2 | FRI ✓ | SAT × | ▲ — Modern European

CARRIAGES RESTAURANT ☎ 01454 415 050
Alveston, Thornbury, Bristol, BS35 2LA
AA Rosette winning restaurant offering both formal and informal dining experiences. Immerse yourself in the relaxed conservatory as you enjoy drinks and canapés and browse the scintillating menu

25% OFF TOTAL | 2 | FRI ✓ | SAT ✓ | SUN | ▲ — European

THE CASINO RESTAURANT ☎ 01179 069 970
Gala Casino, Explore Lane, Bristol, BS1 5TY
Drink and dine in style at this fabulous casino restaurant, where juicy steaks, giant king prawns and tender char-grilled lamb cutlets line the menu. Round your evening off in the casino.

50% OFF FOOD | 4 | FRI × | SAT × — International

CASSIA ☎ 01179 690 907
79 Gloucester Road, Bristol, BS34 5JQ
Imaginatively created recipes are used in this terrific Indian restaurant. Unique flavours characterise each dish.

25% OFF TOTAL | 4 | FRI ✓ | SAT ✓ — Indian

CENTRAL BAR ☎ 01225 333 939
10 Upper Borough Walls, Bath, BA1 1RG
Breathing beauty, Bath is a wonderful city that must be enjoyed, and Central Bar will help you make the most of it. Here you'll find a careful blend of relaxed energy and lively vibes.

2FOR1 3 COURSES | FRI ✓ | SAT × — European

CAFÉ ROUGE

25% OFF TOTAL | 6 | FRI ✓ | SAT ✓ | ✱ | ▲

25% OFF TOTAL

4 restaurants in Somerset

15 Milsom Street, Bath, BA1 1DE ☎ 01225 462 368
Cabot Circus, Bristol, BS1 3BD ☎ 0117 954 4808
Unit R4, The Mall, The Avenue, Bristol, BS34 5UR ☎ 0117 950 8730
85 Park Street, Bristol, BS1 5PJ ☎ 0117 929 2571

CITY CAFÉ
☎01179 102 700

Temple Rose Street, Bristol, BS1 6BF

Set in a stylish, art-deco hotel, this superb restaurant is headed up by Matt Lord, ex of Michelin-starred restaurant Arkle. 2 AA Rosettes. *Offer Friday-Sunday only.

25% OFF TOTAL | 8 | FRI ✓ | SAT ✓ | ✱ — International

CLIFTON WINE BAR
☎01179 732 069

3-5 Richmond Terrace, Queens Road, Clifton, BS8 1AB

The Clifton Wine Bar has a contemporary feel and a welcoming atmoshphere, the hidden vine garden is the perfect place to relax and unwind. *Excludes Christmas Menus.

25% OFF TOTAL | 4 | FRI × | SAT × | SUN — British

COMBE HOUSE RESTAURANT
☎01278 741 382

Holford, Bridgwater, TA5 1RZ

Delightful country getaway set against the woody backdrop of Somerset countryside. A restaurant that features modern, European cuisine and makes especially good use of the region's produce. 1 AA Rosette.

50% OFF FOOD | 4 | FRI ▯ | SAT ✱ — British

CURRY HOUSE
☎01179 779 090

393 Bath Road, Brislington, Bristol, BS4 3EQ

This award-winning restaurant offers a varied menu, from Indian classics to specials such as quail and kangaroo. The modern and comfortable décor help build a relaxing atmosphere with a fine wine list.

25% OFF TOTAL | 4 | FRI ✱ | SAT ✱ | ✱ | ▲ — Indian

DELMONICO
☎01179 445 673

217A Gloucester Road, Bristol, BS7 8NN

Offering regularly changing menus that are based on locally sourced produce. Guests love the extensive array of food on offer, from classic Anglo-French cuisine to Asian and Italian influenced dishes.

25% OFF TOTAL | 6 | FRI ✓ | SAT ✱ | SUN | ✱ | ▲ — International

THE DINING ROOMS
☎01179 238 788

44 St Pauls Rd, Bristol, BS8 1LR

With dishes prepared by their well-known 'mystery chef' The Dining Rooms promise to astound you with their selection of freshly prepared contemporary British dishes.

50% OFF FOOD | 4 | FRI ✓ | SAT ✓ — European

THE DOVECOTE
01275 392 245

Long Ashton, Bristol, BS41 9LX

This Vintage Inn oozes rural charm and rustic character. The picturesque surroundings provide the perfect backdrop for savouring the hearty, seasonal pub-food on the menu.

25% OFF TOTAL | FRI ✓ | SAT ✓ | SUN | ▲ — Modern British

THE DOWER HOUSE
☎01225 823 333

16 Royal Crescent, Bath, BA2 8AW

Head Chef David Campbell blends together various elements to enhance, yet not overpower, the main ingredients. Presented to perfection, the food is sourced locally and put together with passion.

25% OFF TOTAL | 4 | FRI × | SAT × | ▲ — Modern British

ELLIPSE
☎01179 291 030

4 Welsh Back, Bristol, BS1 4SP

Waterside dining on the popular Welsh Back, renowned for a stylish atmosphere with an ever-changing menu that reflects the seasons. Only the finest, freshly cooked food is served. 1 AA Rosette.

25% OFF TOTAL | 6 | FRI ▯ | SAT ▯ | SUN | ▲ — European

EMERSONS GREEN
01179 564 755

200-202 Westerleigh Road, Bristol, BS16 7AN

Beefeater Grill are one of the UK's best-loved restaurants welcoming guests for almost 40 years in over 130 locations nationwide. *Excludes Breakfast, Light Bites, Bar menu, set menus and all other offers.

2FOR1 MAIN COURSE | 6 | FRI ✓ | SAT × | ▲ — Modern British

ENTELIA
☎01179 466 793

50 Whiteladies Road, Bristol, BS8 2NH

Cuisine with a twist; regional Greek dishes are endorsed, and the menu is constantly tweaked to mirror traditional methods. *Booking is essential. Always mention your GS card.

2FOR1 3 COURSES | FRI × | SAT × — Greek

THE FARMERS ARMS
☎01823 480 980

Slough Hill, Taunton, TA3 5RS

The Farmers Arms has a light and airy restaurant which overlooks the garden, where you can enjoy a full 3 course meal or something lighter.

2FOR1 3 COURSES | FRI × | SAT × | SUN | ✱ | ▲ — British

FILINI @ RADISSON
☎01179 349 500

The Radisson Blu, Broad Quay, Bristol, BS1 4BY

The concept here is based on the simplicity and authenticity of beautiful food. Dishes here are inspired by contemporary Italian cuisine, an aromatic fusion of authentic flavours and modern practices.

50% OFF FOOD | 6 | FRI ✓ | SAT ✓ — Italian

THE FOOD HUT
☎07516 035 717

Cleeve Nursery & Garden Centre, Bristol, BS49 4PW

Known for its exciting and adventurous menus, the Food Hut Café experiments with many different genres and styles, offering light lunches, snacks, and drinks from fresh weekly menus.

25% OFF TOTAL | 4 | FRI ✓ | SAT ✓ | ▲ — European

THE FOX DEN
01179 791 861

New Road, Stoke Gifford, Bristol, BS34 8RQ

This Vintage Inn oozes rural charm and rustic character. The picturesque surroundings provide the perfect backdrop for savouring the hearty, seasonal pub-food on the menu.

25% OFF TOTAL | FRI ✓ | SAT ✓ | SUN | ▲ — Modern British

FROME FLYER
01373 468 980

Commerce Park, Jenson Avenue, Frome, BA11 2LD

Quality pub classics with modern twists meets with a friendly and relaxed atmosphere to make this Table Table venue the perfect place for any occasion. *Excludes daytime & evening deals and festive menus.

2FOR1 MAIN COURSE | FRI ✓ | SAT ✓ — Modern British

THE FULL MOON AT RUDGE
☎01373 830 936

Lower Rudge, Frome, BA11 2QF

Classic pub-restaurant fare is to be found in this pretty coaching inn near Frome. Its food is sourced locally, in a good spirit of community it is cooked freshly and with skill, and is supremely hearty.

2FOR1 MAIN COURSE | FRI ▯ | SAT ▯ | ▲ — British

GANESHA AUTHENTIC INDIAN CUISINE
☎01179 533 990

54-56 Bedminster Parade, Bedminster, BS3 4HS

This Bristol-based Indian restaurant prides itself on the imaginativeness of its menu, moving away from curry house staples with piquant, authentically Indian recipes.

2FOR1 MAIN COURSE | FRI ▯ | SAT ✱ | ✱ — Indian

THE GANGES
☎01179 245 234

368 Gloucester Road, Bristol, BS7 8TP

The Ganges provides a rich mix of classic dishes from the Indian Sub-Continent, reflecting its history and culture. Curry connoisseurs will find their favourite dishes as well as new ones to tantalise.

2FOR1 MAIN COURSE | FRI × | SAT × | SUN | ▲ — Indian

GARAM MASSALA
☎01179 237 585

37 Cotham Hill, Cotham, Bristol, BS6 6JY

A quality Indian restaurant with a full and wide-ranging menu that leaves you with a fantastic choice. The service is first-class, while the ambience is welcoming and low-key.

2FOR1 3 COURSES | FRI ✱ | SAT ✱ | ▲ — Indian/Punjabi

GEORGE HOTEL
☎01373 462 584

5 Market Place, Frome, BA11 1AF

A relaxed and friendly Frome hotel which offers delicious home-cooked food, fine wine and some great beers. Welcoming and hospitable, you're sure to enjoy a languid drink and a sumptuous dinner.

25% OFF TOTAL | 4 | FRI × | SAT × | SUN — British

GEORGE INN
☎01373 834 224

High Street, Norton St Philip, Bath, BA2 7LH

A relaxed inn that places its emphasis on good food and drink, and on a hospitable welcome for all, whether it be for a drink, a coffee, a bite for lunch, a languid dinner or a more prolonged stay.

25% OFF TOTAL | 4 | FRI × | SAT × | SUN — British

GIUSEPPES ☎01179 264 869
59 Baldwin Street, Bristol, BS1 1QZ
With a menu that combines clear, fresh-to-the-palate flavours and fulsome, rich meats and sauces, this welcoming, cosy restaurant is a hidden gem in the centre of Bristol.

2FOR1 MAIN COURSE | FRI ✓ | SAT ✱ | ▲ — Italian

THE GLOBE 01225 872 891
Newton St Loe, Bath, BA2 9BB
This Vintage Inn oozes rural charm and rustic character. The picturesque surroundings provide the perfect backdrop for savouring the hearty, seasonal pub-food on the menu.

25% OFF TOTAL | FRI ✓ | SAT ✓ | SUN | ▲ — Modern British

GOODFELLOWS ☎01749 673 866
5 Sadler Street, Wells, BA5 2RR
2 AA Rosette brasserie-style venue whose delicate pàtisserie vie for attention with superb dishes, refined in both flavour and presentation; a menu deep-seated in classic French country cooking.

25% OFF TOTAL | ♟ 4 | FRI ✓ | SAT × | SUN — Seafood

HALL & WOODHOUSE BATH ☎01225 469 259
1 Old King Street, Bath, BA1 2JW
A family-owned brewer, Hall & Woodhouse are devoted to good quality food at affordable prices for the whole family. Locally sourced, the food is guaranteed to be of exceedingly good value.

25% OFF TOTAL | FRI × | SAT × | SUN | ▲ — British

HALO 01179 442 504
141 Gloucester road, Bristol, BS7 8BA
Halo restaurant serves breakfast through to fine dining in the evening and open to the early hours for a sociable drinks. Typical fare are burgers, steaks, sandwiches and salads in a relaxed setting.

50% OFF FOOD | ♟ 10 | FRI ✓ | SAT ✓ | ▲ — Continental

HOBBS BOAT 01934 812 782
Bridgwater Road, Lympsham, Weston Super Mare, BS24 0BP
Quality pub classics with modern twists meets with a friendly and relaxed atmosphere to make this Table Table venue the perfect place for any occasion. *Excludes daytime & evening deals and festive menus.

2FOR1 MAIN COURSE | FRI ✓ | SAT ✓ — Modern British

HOLLYWOODS RESTAURANT ☎01934 424 600
44 Boulevard, Weston-super-Mare, BS23 1NF
Hollywoods American Themed Family Restaurant offers a true taste of the USA, right in the heart of Weston-super-Mare. The huge menu features all your American favourites.

25% OFF TOTAL | ♟ 4 | FRI ▯ | SAT ▯ | ✱ — American

HOMEWOOD PARK HOTEL ☎01225 723 731
Abbey Lane, Hinton Charterhouse, Bath, BA2 7TB
Taste English cuisine at this graceful country house hotel. The technique and imagination which goes into each dish is self-evident in both taste and presentation. 2 AA Rosettes. *Booking is essential.

25% OFF TOTAL | ♟ 4 | FRI ▯ | SAT × | SUN | ▲ — British

HOPHOUSE ☎01179 237 390
16 Kings Road, Clifton, Bristol, BS8 4AB
A vibrant pub situated in a lovely, lively area of Bristol. Take advantage of an excellent array of quality food and fine beers, with enough choice to cater for every guest.

25% OFF TOTAL | ♟ 4 | FRI × | SAT × | SUN — British

HOTEL DU VIN ☎01179 255 577
Sugar House, Narrow Lewins, Mead, Bristol, BS1 2NU
The finest, freshest local produce, simple European recipes, a stunning choice of wines; these are the elements of the trademark Hotel du Vin bistro. A magnificently restored Bristol venue. 1 AA Rosette.

2FOR1 MAIN COURSE | FRI × | SAT × | SUN | ▲ — European

INDIAN OCEAN ☎01179 237 861
44 Cotham Hill, Cotham, Bristol, BS6 6LA
The taste and aroma from the many different coasts of the Indian Ocean are recreated in this wonderful restaurant. One of the oldest and most well-reputed establishments in Bristol.

2FOR1 3 COURSES | FRI ▯ | SAT ▯ — Indian

INNER FIRE ☎01179 657 999
367 Fishponds Road, Bristol, BS5 6RD
No-nonsense, bright and brassy Indian restaurant in Bristol, whose fish paneer shashlik is among the great finds of its ranging menu, as is the fresh-flavoured dil cush, not to mention the edgy maricha.

2FOR1 MAIN COURSE | FRI ✱ | SAT ✱ | SUN — Indian

JAMUNA INDIAN CUISINE ☎01225 464 631
9-10 High Street, Bath, BA1 5AQ
A classic combination of knowledge, tradition and unique experience. Guests are offered sophisticated fine dining with effortlessly charming staff, discreet service and tantalising food.

2FOR1 MAIN COURSE | FRI ✓ | SAT ✱ — Indian

JUNCTION RESTAURANT @ HOLIDAY INN ☎0871 942 9014
Holiday Inn Bristol, Filton Road, Bristol, BS16 1QX
Modern takes on classic dishes can be expected in this open-plan hotel-restaurant. The sizzling cumberland sausages, for example, feature highly on the favourites list.

25% OFF TOTAL | ♟ 6 | FRI ✓ | SAT ✓ — International

KASHMIR ☎01179 520 004
15 High Street, Easton, Bristol, BS5 6DL
A popular eatery serving classic and regional dishes from the foothills of the Himalayas. Curries are divided into spice levels for both the initiated and newcomers, and all can expect a real Indian feast.

25% OFF TOTAL | ♟ 2 | FRI ✱ | SAT ✱ — Indian

THE KNOWLE INN ☎01278 683 330
115 Bath Road, Bridgwater, TA7 8PN
The Knowle Inn is a delightful country pub situated just a few minutes from Junction 23 of the M5 motorway in Somerset. They offer a warm friendly atmosphere coupled with an extensive menu.

25% OFF TOTAL | ♟ 8 | FRI ✱ | SAT ✱ | SUN

KRISHNA'S INN 01179 276 864
4 Byron Place, Clifton, Bristol, BS8 IJT
While Krishna's Inn caters for those diners seeking a classic curry favourite, the kitchen also offers more exotic, adventurous options, such as the malabar served with vellapam (rice pancakes).

2FOR1 2 COURSES | FRI ✱ | SAT ✱ | ▲ — Indian

LA BISALTA ☎01373 464 238
6 Vicarage St, Frome, BA11 1PX
Enter the quaint canvassed doorway, enjoy a pre-dinner drink in the rustic bar and select an authentic dish created by chef Luigi. Named after the Italian mountain range, this venue encourages relaxation.

2FOR1 MAIN COURSE | FRI ▯ | SAT × | SUN | ✱ — Italian

LA TASCA ☎01225 466 477
The Empire, Bath, BA2 4DF
Quintessentially Spanish, La Tasca's fresh and exciting menu offers something for everyone. Their tapas dishes are sincerely authentic, while their paellas always deliver on flavour.

25% OFF TOTAL | ♟ 8 | FRI ✓ | SAT × | ▲ — Spanish

LA TERRE ☎01458 834 959
22 High Street, Glastonbury, BA6 9DU
Drawing on elements of Spanish tapas dishes, La Terre operates morning, noon and night to bring hearty breakfasts, wholesome lunches and decadent dinners to the diners of Glastonbury.

2FOR1 MAIN COURSE | FRI ▯ | SAT ▯ | * — Mediterranean

LIME RESTAURANT AT HOMEWOOD PARK ☎01225 723 731
Abbey Lane, Hinton Charterhouse, Bath, BA2 7TB
Awarded 3 AA Rosettes in recognition of the technique, flair and imagination of the dishes. Head Chef Daniel Moon designs the menus, taking great pride in everything he creates and serves for guests.

25% OFF TOTAL | 👤4 | FRI × | SAT × | SUN — English and Continental

LOCH FYNE ☎01225 750 120
24 Milsom Street, Bath, BA1 1DG
From the roadside oyster bar that once was, Loch Fyne restaurants now successfully inject energy and passion into great food and wonderful flavours, whilst ensuring their seafood is sustainably sourced.

25% OFF TOTAL | 👤4 | FRI ✱ | SAT ✱ | ▲ — Seafood

LOCH FYNE ☎01179 307 160
The Granary, 51 Queen Charlotte St, Bristol, BS1 4HQ
From the roadside oyster bar that once was, Loch Fyne restaurants now successfully inject energy and passion into great food and wonderful flavours, whilst ensuring their seafood is sustainably sourced.

25% OFF TOTAL | 👤4 | FRI ✱ | SAT ✱ | ▲ — Seafood

LOUNGE BAR @ HILTON ☎01454 201 144
Hilton Bristol, Woodlands Lane, Bradley Stoke, BS32 4JF
Bright, smart lounge bar in the Bristol Hilton whose signature burger and the fresh-flavoured chicken caesar salad make for some tasty light meals to enjoy with a drink.

50% OFF FOOD | 👤4 | FRI ✱ | SAT ✱ — British

LOUNGE COCKTAIL BAR ☎01225 424 321
43 St James's Parade, Bath, BA1 1UQ
A secret gem of a bar where classic cocktails, tasty pizzas and creamy risottos feature strongly on the menu. Highly experienced staff are always eager to ensure every experience is memorable.

50% OFF FOOD | 👤2 | FRI × | SAT × — International

MALIHA ☎01823 322 722
52 Station Road, Taunton, TA1 1NS
Maliha is an Indian restaurant and takeaway, where each and every meal is prepared to order using only the freshest, finest and most delicious ingredients.

2FOR1 2 COURSES | FRI ✓ | SAT × | * — Indian

MARCO PIERRE WHITE BRISTOL ☎01934 839 019
Cadbury House, Bristol, BS49 5AD
This popular venue boasts a dark and sultry ambiance that radiates charm and charisma. Ethically sourced and reared, diners can feast upon 28-day aged steaks and fish specials at pocket-friendly prices.

25% OFF TOTAL | 👤10 | FRI ▯ | SAT ▯ | ▲ — Steakhouse

THE MILL AT RODE ☎01373 831 100
Rode, Frome, BA11 6AG
Whilst maintaining the external character and charm of its industrial past, this charismatic restaurant renders a more modern feel inside. Renowned for its great food and relaxed atmosphere.

25% OFF TOTAL | 👤4 | FRI ✱ | SAT ✱ | SUN | ▲ — British

MILLERS AT THE ANCHOR ☎01643 862 753
Porlock Weir, Porlock, Minehead, TA24 8PB
Chef Andrew Clark brings a wealth of high-level experience as well as his enthusiasm; the fine dining on offer here is all about quality of produce, prepared simply and superbly.

2FOR1 MAIN COURSE | FRI ✱ | SAT ✱ — British

MOUCHUCK INDIAN RESTAURANT ☎01225 333 449
136 Wells Road, Bath, BA2 3AH
Mouchuck Takeaway in Bath is an authentic Indian Takeaway serving the finest in Indian takeaway cuisine.

2FOR1 MAIN COURSE | FRI × | SAT × | ▲ — Indian

MOUNT SOMERSET HOTEL & SPA ☎01823 442 500
Lower Henlade, Taunton, TA3 5NB
A lovely fine-dining restaurant situated in a superbly tranquil location overlooking the Somerset countryside, with a menu that combines tradition with some imaginative new dishes. 2 AA Rosettes.

25% OFF TOTAL | 👤4 | FRI ✓ | SAT ✓ | * — European

MULBERRYS RESTAURANT AND GRILL ☎01935 434 188
9 Union Street, Yeovil, BA20 1PQ
Sample the outstanding quality of local meats available in this exceptional bistro. Specialising in grills and steaks, the kitchen proudly balances tasty and delicious food with healthy ingredients.

25% OFF TOTAL | 👤2 | FRI ▯ | SAT ▯ | SUN | ▲ — European

MUMTAZ RESTAURANT ☎01454 411 764
7 St Mary Street, Bristol, BS35 2AB
If classic and flavoursome is what you're looking for then this popular Indian restaurant is for you. Exceptional service, good quality food and a warm atmosphere underpins its popularity.

2FOR1 MAIN COURSE | FRI ✱ | SAT ✱ | ▲ — Indian

MUMTAZ RESTAURANT ☎01179 503 084
61 High Street, West-on-Trym, Bristol, BS9 3ED
Skilled chefs cook traditional recipes to perfection, producing classic dishes that are bursting with aromatic flavours and a smack of authenticity. A critically acclaimed fine Indian dining experience.

2FOR1 MAIN COURSE | FRI ✱ | SAT ✱ | ▲ — Indian

NAMASTE NEPAL ☎01179 300 779
Unite House, Frogmore Street, Bristol, BS1 5NA
A wonderful family-run establishment offering fine Nepalese and Indian cuisine. Take note of the original Nepalese sculptures and paintings that altogether create a unique dining environment.

25% OFF TOTAL | 👤2 | FRI ✓ | SAT ✓ | ▲ — Indian/Nepalese

NATRAJ TANDOORI ☎01823 288 876
148 East Reach, Taunton, TA1 3HT
A successful Indian restaurant, serving a wide variety of Indian and tandoori staple dishes. The special clay oven dishes are very popular, with the marinated lamb proving to be a firm favourite.

2FOR1 MAIN COURSE | FRI ✓ | SAT ✓ | ▲ — Indian

NO4 CLIFTON VILLAGE ☎01179 706 869
4 Rodney Place, Bristol, BS8 4HY
No.4 is an award-winning restaurant in Bristol located in a beautiful Georgian mansion house set in the heart of Clifton village. A daily changing menu with locally sourced produce, a true delight!

2FOR1 MAIN COURSE | FRI ✓ | SAT ✓ | SUN | * | ▲ — European

NOA JAPANESE RESTAURANT ☎01179 732 881
12-13 Waterloo Street, Clifton, BS8 4BT
Smooth and sultry, Noa is known for its low-fi modern style. Serves a fine range of dishes with the ramen particularly popular, not to forget the miso soup, sashimi, or slightly richer chicken katsu curry.

25% OFF TOTAL | 👤4 | FRI × | SAT × | ▲ — Japanese

OH CALCUTTA ☎01179 240 458
216 Cheltenham Road, Bristol, BS6 5QU
Fresh ingredients and loving preparation makes the food here extremely tasty. A local favourite, the high-quality food and exceptional service make this an extremely popular Indian restaurant.

25% OFF TOTAL | 👤8 | FRI ▯ | SAT ✱ | SUN | * | ▲ — Indian

OLD INDIA ☎01179 221 136
34 Saint Nicolas Street, Bristol, BS1 1TG
Belies the name by serving avant-garde Indian cuisine. In practice, this emerges in the highly distinctive menu, featuring less the curry staples and more dishes like the anari chops or the dal-ki-ta.

2FOR1 MAIN COURSE | FRI ✱ | SAT ✱ — Indian

OPA ☎01225 317 900
14 North Parade, Bath, BA2 4AJ
Every last week of the month, the menu has a new Greek island recipe to ensure guests experience an authentic taste of Greece. Opa source only the finest of wines and ingredients from the native homeland.

2FOR1 3 COURSES | FRI × | SAT × | SUN — Greek

PALM COURT
☎ 01179 255 100

Bristol Marriott Royal Hotel, Bristol, BS1 5TB

AA Rosette-awarded restaurant offering elegant dining in exquisite surroundings. The menu features locally-inspired dishes with a focus on fresh, seasonal produce, while the mood is formal and elegant.

25% OFF TOTAL | 4 | FRI ✓ | SAT ✓ | International

PANASIA
☎ 01225 481 001

2 George Street, Bath, BA1 2EH

Take a whistle-stop tour of the Far East without having to leave the country. Panasia stays true to traditional and authentic recipes, spices and ingredients to provide truly memorable cuisine.

2FOR1 3 COURSES | FRI ✗ | SAT ✗ | Thai

THE PAVILION
01934 622 625

Hutton Moor Road, Weston-super-Mare, BS22 8LY

Beefeater Grill are one of the UK's best-loved restaurants welcoming guests for almost 40 years in over 130 locations nationwide. *Excludes Breakfast, Light Bites, Bar menu, set menus and all other offers.

2FOR1 MAIN COURSE | 6 | FRI ✓ | SAT ✗ | Modern British

PENNY FARTHING
☎ 01179 733 539

115 Whiteladies Road, Clifton, Bristol, BS8 2PB

With an excellent range of classic pub grub and quality ales, the Penny Farthing is the perfect place to meet for a quick lunchtime drink or a relaxing catch up after work. *Excludes Christmas Menus.

25% OFF TOTAL | 4 | FRI ✗ | SAT ✗ | SUN | British

PHOENIX RESTAURANT @ MERCURE
☎ 01179 689 900

Holland House Hotel, Redcliffe Hill, Bristol, BS1 6SQ

Bustling hotel-based restaurant with plenty of light, comfortable surroundings and some excellent cuisine. Wide-ranging menu with a number of international styles; emphasis on simple, clear flavours.

50% OFF FOOD | 4 | FRI | SAT | International

PINK GARLIC
☎ 01823 279 558

53 Hamilton Road, Taunton, TA1 2EL

Pink Garlic uses the best selection of fresh spices to create mouthwatering flavours to suit all taste buds. Each dish is prepared using the perfect combination of spices to create this delectable menu.

2FOR1 2 COURSES | FRI ✓ | SAT ✓ | Indian

PLANET PIZZA
☎ 01179 444 717

187 Gloucester Road, Bishopston, Bristol, BS7 8BG

Planet Pizza is a vibrant restaurant serving out-of-this-world pizzas and heavenly salads, all in a contemporary and friendly setting.

25% OFF TOTAL | 6 | FRI ✱ | SAT ✱ | Pizza

THE PRIORY
01275 376 307

Station Road, Portbury, Bristol, BS20 7TN

This Vintage Inn oozes rural charm and rustic character. The picturesque surroundings provide the perfect backdrop for savouring the hearty, seasonal pub-food on the menu.

25% OFF TOTAL | FRI ✓ | SAT ✓ | SUN | Modern British

RACKS BAR AND KITCHEN
☎ 01179 741 626

St Paul's Road, Clifton, Bristol, BS8 1LX

In a building bursting with character, this is the perfect place to eat, drink and be merry. Diners can sample the tasty English and continental dishes whilst enjoying the fine selection of beverages.

2FOR1 MAIN COURSE | FRI ✓ | SAT ✓ | English and Continental

RAJ RESTAURANT
01179 291 132

35 King Street, Bristol, BS1 4DZ

A passion for food and excellent service is clear from the moment you step inside Raj Restaurant. the Indian cuisine on offer is spectacular, while the staff are more than inviting and helpful.

25% OFF TOTAL | 10 | FRI ✓ | SAT ✓ | ✱ | Indian

PREZZO

2FOR1 MAIN COURSE | FRI ✗ | SAT ✗

2-FOR-1 MAIN COURSE

6 restaurants in Somerset

30 Cornhill, Bridgwater, TA6 3BY	☎ 01278 433 600
25 Fore Street, Taunton, TA1 1JW	☎ 01823 339 233
Old Sarum House, 49 Princes Street, Yeovil, BA20 1EG	☎ 01935 426 381
6-7 Brunel Square, Bath, BA1 1SX	☎ 01225 310 222
Anchor Square, Bristol, BS1 5DB	☎ 0117 909 1926
37c Clarks Village, Street, BA16 0BB	☎ 01458 440 053

To understand what the restaurant icons mean, please see the inside back cover.

RAJPOOT
☎ 01225 466 833
4 Argyle Street, Bath, BA2 4BA
Established in 1980, Rajpoot has been providing a high-class South Asian dining experience to food lovers ever since.

25% OFF TOTAL | 4 | FRI × | SAT × | SUN — Indian

RAJPOOT RESTAURANT
☎ 01179 733 515
52 Upper Belgrave Road, Clifton, Bristol, BS8 2XP
Rewind back to the colonial past whilst dining at this delightful Indian restaurant, marvellously located in a beautiful Georgian house. Rajpoot celebrates both its admirable setting and exquisite food.

25% OFF TOTAL | 4 | FRI ✓ | SAT × | ✱ | ▲ — Indian/Nepalese

THE REAL ITALIAN PIZZA CO
☎ 01225 330 121
16 York Street, Bath, BA1 1NG
Choose from a bursting menu of delicious pizzas created with a range of traditional and modern toppings, as well as a great selection of starters and Italian options at this great local restaurant.

2FOR1 3 COURSES | FRI 📱 | SAT × | SUN | ▲ — Italian

RED LION
☎ 01373 830 350
Bath Road, Woolverton, Bath, BA2 7QS
A traditional pub delivering flavoursome, home-cooked food and delicious local beers all day long. Enjoy food and drink in the wonderful garden area in summer, or by roaring log fires in the winter.

25% OFF TOTAL | 4 | FRI × | SAT × | SUN — British

RENATOS NUMERO UNO
☎ 01179 744 484
203 Whiteladies Road, Bristol, BS8 2XT
A restaurant that consistently offers exquisite Italian food and charmingly attentive service. Everything from the pasta sauces to the pizza doughs are freshly made on the premises.

25% OFF TOTAL | 4 | FRI 📱 | SAT 📱 — Italian

RESTAURANT AT THE GRANGE
☎ 01373 836 522
Combe Farm, Frome, BA11 3JU
With a vast open kitchen, diners can watch and learn as their favourite dishes are prepared before their very eyes. Guests should sample the log fire oven-baked pizzas, prepared with undoubted passion.

25% OFF TOTAL | 4 | FRI 📱 | SAT 📱 | SUN | ▲ — British

RING O' BELLS
☎ 01458 210 232
High St, Ashcott, TA7 9PZ
A real family-affair of a pub, this charming 18th-century treasure is everything it should be for its location. Traditionally cosy, here you'll find light snacks, main meals and a fine array of drinks.

25% OFF TOTAL | 4 | FRI ✱ | SAT ✱ | SUN | ▲ — Modern Pub

THE RIVER GRILLE
☎ 01179 230 333
The Bristol Hotel, Prince Street, Bristol, BS1 4QF
A light, airy quayside restaurant within a luxurious hotel, delivering wholesome hand crafted dishes using the finest ingredients such as fresh fish, juicy steak, and divine West Country cheeses.

25% OFF TOTAL | 4 | FRI ✓ | SAT ✓ | ✱ — British

THE RIVERSIDE RESTAURANT
☎ 01749 672 100
Glastonbury Road, Wells, BA5 1QT
Riverside Indian Restaurant is a valued place in Wells. Serving superbly made Indian dishes to a small dining room of patrons, the restaurant is proud of its kitchen talent and friendly front of house.

2FOR1 MAIN COURSE | FRI × | SAT × — Indian

THE ROCKFISH GRILL & SEAFOOD MARKET
☎ 01179 737 384
128 Whiteladies Road, Clifton, Bristol, BS8 2RS
The Rockfish Grill and Market specialise in fresh seafood and quality meat cooked over a charcoal burning fire, served in beautiful dining room.

25% OFF TOTAL | 4 | FRI 📱 | SAT × | SUN — British

ROMA TRATTORIA
☎ 01179 619 311
91 Regent Street, Kingswood, Bristol, BS15 8LJ
A strikingly classy interior and a vibrant bar scene make this a wonderful place to enjoy excellent food. Dishes are imaginatively infused with a Latin zest making each and every choice a great one.

25% OFF TOTAL | 6 | FRI ✓ | SAT ✓ | ✱ | ▲ — Spanish

THE RUMMER HOTEL
☎ 01179 290 111
All Saints Lane, Bristol, BS1 1JH
Whatever you fancy to eat, head here for a choice of hot and cold dishes for breakfast through to supper. Emphasis is placed on the hearty seasonal British fare with a little continental panache thrown in.

25% OFF TOTAL | 6 | FRI ✓ | SAT ✓ | SUN | ▲ — Modern British

RUPSHA
☎ 01179 739 937
3a Regent Street, Bristol, BS8 4HW
Lovers of south Asian cuisine are in for a treat at this venue, located in the stunning setting of Clifton. Soak up the warm and friendly atmosphere and feast upon the finest of ingredients.

2FOR1 MAIN COURSE | FRI × | SAT × — Indian

SAMPAN RESTAURANT @ HOLIDAY INN
☎ 0871 942 9014
Holiday Inn Bristol, Filton Road, Bristol, BS16 1QX
Open to both hotel guests and non-residents, Sampan Oriental Restaurant serves Chinese, Malaysian and Thai cuisine, offering guests a real taste and flavour of Asia.

25% OFF TOTAL | 6 | FRI ✓ | SAT ✓ — Oriental

SHEZAN
☎ 01761 479 888
28 Meadgate, Bath, BA2 0NW
Shezan is a contemporary restaurant offering dining experience to satisfy all aspects of fine cuisine: food, wine selection, service, ambience, and atmosphere

50% OFF FOOD | 10 | FRI 📱 | SAT 📱 — Indian

SIGNATURE VICEROY
☎ 01935 426 210
98 Middle Street, Yeovil, BA20 1NE
Yeovil's Signature Viceroy warms the heart with its healthy portions of dazzlingly flavoured Indian dishes. It's accommodating and friendly, with a low-key thrum about it, and promises a good, tasty meal.

2FOR1 MAIN COURSE | FRI ✓ | SAT ✓ | ✱ | ▲ — Authentic Indian

SOLO RESTAURANT BATH
☎ 01225 444 439
2 Milsom Place, Bath, BA1 1BZ
Located in the prestigious Milsom Place, Solo Pizza Restaurant sits facing a beautiful courtyard where you can enjoy a morning coffee or enjoy an alfresco lunch, pizza or tapas dishes.

25% OFF TOTAL | 8 | FRI ✓ | SAT × | ▲ — Italian

THE SORREL RESTAURANT
☎ 01761 241 631
Ston Easton Park, Ston Easton, Nr Bath, BA3 4DF
Splendid Georgian restaurant looking out across the cascading River Norr; the perfect tone for a place known for its absolutely superb cuisine. Great base ingredients cooked with precision. 2 AA Rosettes.

25% OFF TOTAL | FRI 📱 | SAT 📱 | SUN | ▲ — Fine Dining

SPICE CLUB
☎ 01278 433 334
10 Eastover, Bridgwater, TA6 5AB
Spice Club specialises in contemporary modern Indian cuisine. They use the best selection of fresh ground spices to create mouth watering flavours to suit all taste buds.

2FOR1 3 COURSES | FRI ✓ | SAT ✓ — Indian

SPICE OF INDIA
☎ 01179 299 222
13 Small Street, Bristol, BS1 1DE
Incredible value for money can be found at this brilliant Indian restaurant. Unusual yet tasty dishes such as curried salmon with home-made chutney have guaranteed this restaurant an admirable reputation.

2FOR1 MAIN COURSE | FRI ✱ | SAT ✱ — Indian

STRADA
01179 237 224
34 Princess Victoria Street, Bristol, BS8 4BZ
Offering fresh, bold dishes inspired by flavours of Italian city life - Strada serves a selection of indulgent tastes, to those seeking a blissful escape to laidback Italian life. *Excludes Pizzettas.

25% OFF TOTAL | 6 | FRI ✓ | SAT × | ▲ — Italian

www.gourmetsociety.co.uk

STRADA
01225 337 753

Beau Nash House, Bath, BA1 1EU

Offering fresh, bold dishes inspired by flavours of Italian city life - Strada serves a selection of indulgent tastes, to those seeking a blissful escape to laidback Italian life. *Excludes Pizzettas.

25% OFF TOTAL | 6 | FRI ✓ | SAT ✗ | Italian

TAJ MAHAL
☎ 01643 704 857

9a The Avenue, Minehead, TA24 5AY

Long and lush Indian restaurant with comfortable booths and elegant design. A much-loved spot to enjoy a low-key, convivial Indian meal in company. Distinctive menu with an emphasis on authentic dishes.

2FOR1 MAIN COURSE | FRI ✗ | SAT ✗ | SUN | Indian

TAJ MAHAL
☎ 01823 253 590

3 Staplegrove Road, Taunton, TA1 1DE

Vivacious and vibrant, the interior here is warm and inviting. The cuisine is contemporary and based upon culinary values that are unique to the Taj Mahal. Expect service with a smile.

50% OFF FOOD | 2 | FRI | SAT | Indian

THAI EDGE BRISTOL
☎ 01179 276 088

Broad Quay, South Block, Bristol, BS1 4DA

Every dish combines a unique array of herbs, roots and spices such as galangal and krachai to create a subtle blend of flavours. The authentic Thai cuisine will have you coming back for more.

25% OFF TOTAL | 4 | FRI ✱ | SAT ✱ | ✱ | Thai

TIKKA FLAME
☎ 01173 169 393

South Building, Anchor Square, Canons Rd, BS1 5UH

Winning the 'Healthy Eating Award' for 4 years running, the kitchen ensures its produce is fresh and ingredients well-sourced. Chefs from Pakistan work hard to recreate a true taste of the subcontinent.

2FOR1 3 COURSES | FRI ✗ | SAT ✗ | Indian

UDDINS
☎ 01823 351 555

23 East Reach, Taunton, TA1 3EP

Committed to making every dining occasion special, Uddins provides tasty Indian cuisine in a vibrant, inviting atmosphere. Staff are eager to please, while the food is sure to bring you back for more.

50% OFF FOOD | 8 | FRI ✓ | SAT ✓ | Indian

UDDINS
☎ 01934 707 072

15-18 Alexandra Parade, Western-Super-Mare, BS23 1QT

Devoted to making every guest feel special, the staff at Uddins are dedicated to exceptional customer service. The vibrant and aromatic menu will ensure diners go back for more.

50% OFF FOOD | FRI ✓ | SAT ✓ | Indian

VICEROY INDIAN RESTAURANT
☎ 01935 421 758

100 Middle Street, Yeovil, BA20 1NE

Yeovil's Viceroy Indian Restaurant has a welcoming ambience, with something of a buzz about the place. They've an especial line in creamy, rich Makhani and Xakuti dishes.

2FOR1 MAIN COURSE | FRI ✗ | SAT ✗ | ✱ | Indian

WALKABOUT
☎ 01179 300 181

40 Corn Street, Bristol, BS1 1HQ

Walkabout is famous for its characteristically Australian atmosphere and well-rounded menu. From live sport with a juicy burger to some Aussie kangaroo skewers, you'll find it hard to tear yourself away.

25% OFF TOTAL | 10 | FRI ✓ | SAT ✓ | International

THE WHITE HORSE
☎ 01179 566 902

Bristol Road, Bristol, BS16 1RY

If patron satisfaction is top of the list, then the White Horse delivers accordingly. Feast on wholesome favourites and an ice cold pint whilst chatting to friends, or enjoy a slice of quiet time.

2FOR1 3 COURSES | FRI ✓ | SAT ✓ | English/Gastro pub

Gourmet Society discount applies to the à la carte menu only, unless stated otherwise.

WHITE LODGE 01823 321 112
81 Bridgewater Road, Taunton, TA1 2DU
Beefeater Grill are one of the UK's best-loved restaurants welcoming guests for almost 40 years in over 130 locations nationwide. *Excludes Breakfast, Light Bites, Bar menu, set menus and all other offers.

2FOR1 MAIN COURSE | 👤 6 | FRI ✓ | SAT × | ▲ — Modern British

THE WILLY WICKET 01179 567 308
Badminton Road, Downend, Bristol, BS36 1DP
This Vintage Inn oozes rural charm and rustic character. The picturesque surroundings provide the perfect backdrop for savouring the hearty, seasonal pub-food on the menu.

25% OFF TOTAL | FRI ✓ | SAT ✓ | SUN | ▲ — Modern British

WINE & SAUSAGE 01823 422 333
Corner House Hotel, Park Street, Taunton, TA1 4DQ
Following the success of the first Wine and Sausage, this Taunton restaurant follows suit with its unfussy but magnificent food, underpinned by a thorough investment in quality regional produce.

2FOR1 MAIN COURSE | FRI ▯ | SAT ▯ | SUN — British

WORLD'S END TAUNTON 01823 462 928
Bradford-on-Tone, Taunton, TA4 1ET
Hall and Woodhouse, a family owned brewer, devote themselves to locally sourced food at affordable prices in an affable atmosphere. Converted from a Victorian house, this pub is exquisite.

25% OFF TOTAL | 👤 6 | FRI × | SAT × | SUN | ▲ — British

YUM YUM THAI RESTAURANT 01179 290 987
50 Park Street, Bristol, BS1 5JN
Charming restaurant that serves delicious, authentic Thai flavours. The menu is filled with familiar dishes and a range of lesser known delicacies, not to mention the wide selection of organic wines.

2FOR1 MAIN COURSE | FRI × | SAT × | * | ▲ — Thai

Wiltshire

ALEXANDRA HOUSE 01793 819 000
Whittingham Drive, Wroughton, Swindon, SN4 0QJ
Perfectly positioned hotel for a short break away, Alexandra House is a popular venue situated within 20 acres of beautifully landscaped grounds. Dine in the Orangery Restaurant for a real treat.

25% OFF TOTAL | 👤 6 | FRI ✓ | SAT ✓ | ▲ — British

THE BARGE INN 01380 828 230
Seend Cleeve, Melksham, SN12 6QB
Set in beautiful surroundings on the Kennet and Avon Canal, the Barge offers excellent food everyday along with great Wadworth beers and an extensive wine list. *Excludes Christmas Menus.

25% OFF TOTAL | 👤 4 | FRI × | SAT × | SUN — British

THE BECKFORD ARMS 01747 870 385
Fonthill Gifford, Tisbury, SP3 6PX
A traditional yet stylish country pub. Whole suckling pig spit-roasting on the bar's open fire, their own hams and piccalilli, game pies with home-made pastry and aged Wiltshire steaks are all available.

25% OFF TOTAL | 👤 6 | FRI × | SAT × — British

BOATHOUSE GASTROPUB 01722 414 782
Mill Stream Approach, Castle St, Salisbury, SP1 3TA
The Boathouse Cafe Bar & Gastro Pub with it's fabulous riverside setting is the perfect place to wine, dine and relax in style and comfort.

2FOR1 3 COURSES | FRI ✓ | SAT ✓ | SUN | * | ▲ — Mediterranean

BUCA DI BEPPO 01793 878 785
De Vere Village Swindon, Swindon, SN5 7DW
Drawing on the culture of Italian dining, the dishes at Buca Di Beppo are intended for sharing. Perfect for an evening out with family or friends, the food is delicious and the staff courteous.

2FOR1 MAIN COURSE | FRI × | SAT × | SUN | ▲ — Italian

CAFÉ ROUGE 01722 330 417
19-21 High Street, Salisbury, SP1 2
French sophistication on the British high street - enjoy seasonally changing French dishes and a continental wine selection, served in a relaxed environment with an undeniable flair of Parisian chic.

25% OFF TOTAL | 👤 6 | FRI ✓ | SAT ✓ | * — French

CONNIE'S 01793 521 515
53 Devizes Road, Swindon, SN1 4BG
Infusing Szechuan, Cantonese and south-east Asian cuisine, Connie's is both a distinctive and memorable experience. Promising satisfaction, the dishes are wholesome and bursting with flavour.

50% OFF FOOD | 👤 4 | FRI × | SAT × | ▲ — Oriental

CROWN INN 01380 722 692
19 New Park Street, Devizes, SN10 1EA
The Crown is a friendly local situated in the pretty market square of Westbury where good food and ale are served with a smile. *Offer available from 1st December 2013. Excludes Christmas menu's.

25% OFF TOTAL | 👤 4 | FRI × | SAT × | SUN — British

THE CROWN INN 01722 780 335
Alvediston, Salisbury, SP5 5JY
Appealingly selective menu shows this restaurant's keen investment in its dishes. The steak and kidney pudding is rich and sumptuous; the chef's fish pie warming and tender with a personal touch.

2FOR1 MAIN COURSE | FRI ✓ | SAT ✓ | ▲ — Traditional English

FAT FOWL 01225 863 111
Silver Street, Bradford-on-Avon, BA15 1JX
Inviting restaurant with a ranging menu; specialises in vibrant tapas and fulsome mains. Also stages great live music.

25% OFF TOTAL | 👤 4 | FRI ▯ | SAT ▯ | SUN | ▲ — European

GLASSHOUSE RESTAURANT & BAR 01793 842 800
Marsh Farm Hotel, Wootton Bassett, Swindon, SN4 8ER
A historically-recognised grade II listed farmhouse forms the centrepiece of the hotel and grounds where this great restaurant is situated. Fresh produce is used to craft an excellent international menu.

50% OFF FOOD | 👤 4 | FRI × | SAT ✓ | SUN | ▲ — International

HAMPTON INN 01722 339 836
Pearce Way, Off London Road, Salisbury, SP1 3YU
Quality pub classics with modern twists meets with a friendly and relaxed atmosphere to make this Table Table venue the perfect place for any occasion. *Excludes daytime & evening deals and festive menus.

2FOR1 MAIN COURSE | FRI ✓ | SAT ✓ — Modern British

THE HARROW INN 01793 791 792
High Street, Swindon, SN4 0AE
The Harrow Inn is a fine dining restaurant with parts dating back to 1747 and is known for fine wines and cask ales. The Inn sources premium quality produce locally to produce fresh and exciting food.

2FOR1 3 COURSES | FRI ✓ | SAT × — British

HORSE AND GROOM INN 01666 823 904
The Street, Malmsbury, SN16 9DL
Original flagstone floors, open log fires and award-winning menus make this venue an impeccable dining experience. Friendly and attentive staff are habitually hospitable.

2FOR1 MAIN COURSE | FRI ✓ | SAT × | SUN | ▲ — International

HOX BRASSERIE 01722 341 600
155 Fisherton Street, Salisbury, SP2 7RP
A restaurant with a focus on South Indian food. The spices used in their dishes are traditional and authentic, and can truly be described as real, quality Indian food in a modern, contemporary environment.

2FOR1 MAIN COURSE | FRI * | SAT * | SUN — Indian

THE LANSDOWNE ARMS 01249 812 422
Derry Hill, Calne, SN11 9NS
Built in 1843, this pub has outstanding views of the Avon Valley. Take a break from countryside walking and indulge in traditional British fare. *Offer not available on Christmas Menus.

25% OFF TOTAL | 👤 4 | FRI × | SAT × | SUN — British

LYDIARD
01793 881 490

Lydiard Fields, Great Western Way, Swindon, SN5 8UY

Beefeater Grill are one of the UK's best-loved restaurants welcoming guests for almost 40 years in over 130 locations nationwide. *Excludes Breakfast, Light Bites, Bar menu, set menus and all other offers.

2FOR1 MAIN COURSE | 👤 6 | FRI ✓ | SAT × | ▲ — Modern British

MONSOON CONTEMPORARY INDIAN CUISINE
☎ 01793 422 455

13 Faringdon Road, Swindon, SN1 5AR

A stylish and contemporary Indian restaurant in Swindon, Monsoon's just the place to enjoy a superior kind of curry, in both the quality of the food and the elegant ambience of the dining room.

2FOR1 3 COURSES | FRI ✱ | SAT ✱ — Indian

NEEL AKASH
☎ 01722 743 553

14 North Street, Salisbury, SP2 0HE

Affable surroundings and talkative, friendly staff will guarantee an agreeable eating experience. Curry lovers receive an impeccable standard of food.

2FOR1 MAIN COURSE | FRI ✓ | SAT ✓ — Indian

THE NIGHTINGALE BAR @ MERCURE
☎ 01793 833 700

South Marston Hotel, Old Vicarage Lane, Swindon, SN3 4SH

A contemporary bar and lounge where relaxation is entirely encouraged. Enjoy an afternoon or early evening drink, or take a light lunch from the snack menu before heading out for the day.

50% OFF FOOD | 👤 4 | FRI ✓ | SAT ✓ | ▲ — British

THE NIGHTINGALE RESTAURANT @ MERCURE
☎ 01793 833 700

South Marston Hotel, Old Vicarage Lane, Swindon, SN3 4SH

Contemporary setting and relaxed atmosphere in which to enjoy a menu comprised of many great options, from simple and light meals to more sophisticated modern British cuisine.

50% OFF FOOD | 👤 4 | FRI ✓ | SAT ✓ | ✱ | ▲ — British

OLD BELL
☎ 01985 216 611

42 Market Place, Warminster, BA12 9AN

The Old Bell is a traditional coaching inn dating back to 1483. Situated in the town of Warminster, it's a comfortable inn enjoying an excellent reputation for good food. *Excludes Christmas Menus.

25% OFF TOTAL | 👤 4 | FRI × | SAT × | SUN — British

PHEASANT
☎ 01249 444 083

Bath Road, Chippenham, SN14 0AE

With roaring log fires and cosy corners in the winter yet cool and relaxing in the summer, The Pheasant is the perfect place to relax and unwind after a hard day. *Excludes Christmas Menus.

25% OFF TOTAL | 👤 4 | FRI × | SAT × | SUN — British

PREZZO
01722 341 333

52 High Street, Salisbury, SP1 2PF

With a character all of its own, Prezzo oozes contemporary style and enduring charm. Signature pastas, stone-baked pizzas and classic Italian dishes promise a perfect dining choice for the whole family.

2FOR1 MAIN COURSE | FRI × | SAT × | ▲ — Italian

PREZZO
☎ 01672 511 181

90 High Street, Marlborough, SN8 1HD

With a character all of its own, oozes contemporary style and enduring charm. Signature pastas, stone-baked pizzas and classic Italian dishes promise a perfect dining choice for the whole family.

2FOR1 MAIN COURSE | FRI × | SAT × | ▲ — Italian

PURPLE MANGO
☎ 01793 526 161

1 Victoria Road, Swindon, SN1 3AJ

A fusion of traditional and modern India finds its way into the cuisine and the décor at Purple Mango. The Head Chef heads a kitchen full of talent, where passion goes into creating every dish.

2FOR1 MAIN COURSE | FRI ✓ | SAT ✓ | ✱ | ▲ — Indian

RAFU'S
☎ 01793 780 300

22 High Street, Shrivenham, Swindon, SN6 8AA

Delicately prepared and spiced food served within an intimate setting. Helpful staff guide diners through an accommodating menu that covers all tastes and preferences, including vegetarian options.

2FOR1 MAIN COURSE | FRI ✓ | SAT ✓ — Indian

RAFU'S
☎ 01793 765 320

29-30 High Street, Highworth, Swindon, SN6 7AQ

Delicately spiced and prepared food served within an intimate setting. Helpful staff guide diners through an accommodating menu that covers all tastes and preferences, including vegetarian options.

2FOR1 MAIN COURSE | FRI × | SAT × | SUN — Indian

THE RED LION AXFORD
☎ 01672 520 271

Axford, Marlborough, SN8 2HA

Cosy up by the inglenook fires under the exposed beams of this 16th Century inn. This Michelin Guide featured venue serves local game which can be enjoyed al fresco by the River Kennett.

25% OFF TOTAL | 👤 6 | FRI ✓ | SAT ✓ | SUN — British

SOLSTICE BAR & GRILL @ HOLIDAY INN
☎ 0845 241 3535

Midsummer Place, Solstice Park, Salisbury, SP4 7SQ

Cosy and intimate favourite among the town's restaurants, pairing classic comfort food and innovative new specialities with an extensive wine list. Deservedly awarded one AA rosette.

25% OFF TOTAL | 👤 10 | FRI ✓ | SAT ✓ — English and Continental

SQUIRES RESTAURANT @ MERCURE
☎ 01722 327 476

White Hart Hotel, 1 St John Street, Salisbury, SP1 2SD

Restaurant in the elegant dining rooms of a fine Georgian building in Salisbury. Similarly classic in the food, whether it be their refined breakfasts, carvery lunches or a full seasonal à la carte menu.

50% OFF FOOD | 👤 4 | FRI ✓ | SAT ✓ | ▲ — International

STRADA
01722 321 213

32 Market Place, Salisbury, SP1 1TL

Offering fresh, bold dishes inspired by flavours of Italian city life - Strada serves a selection of indulgent tastes, to those seeking a blissful escape to laidback Italian life. *Excludes Pizzettas.

25% OFF TOTAL | 👤 6 | FRI ✓ | SAT × | ▲ — Italian

THE SWAN
☎ 01225 868 686

1 Church Street, Bradford-on-Avon, BA15 1LN

A wonderful family-friendly pub situated in a beautiful listed building. Children can enjoy smaller portions of the freshly cooked dishes which are all made with the finest local ingredients.

25% OFF TOTAL | 👤 6 | FRI ▯ | SAT ▯ | ✱ — British

THE SWAN AT STOFORD
☎ 01722 790 236

Warminster Road, Salisbury, SP2 0PR

Situated close to the beautiful Cathedral city of Salisbury, the Swan at Stoford provides delicious food and excellent accommodation. The menu presents a host of delicious culinary creations.

50% OFF FOOD | 👤 4 | FRI ✓ | SAT ✓ | ✱ — British

TRADERS RESTAURANT @ HOLIDAY INN
☎ 0871 942 9072

Marlborough Road, Swindon, SN3 6AQ

Situated in the wonderful Holiday Inn Swindon, Traders Restaurant proudly accommodates both hotel guests as well as walk-in diners. A fine blend of European and classic dishes occupy the menu.

50% OFF FOOD | 👤 4 | FRI ✓ | SAT ✓ — British

THE VINE TREE
☎ 01666 837 654

Foxley Road, Norton, Near Malmesbury, SN16 0JP

The Vine Tree is an award-winning Free House and was awarded 'The Wine Pub of the Year for Great Britain 2008' by The Good Pub Guide but retains a traditional pub atmosphere.

25% OFF TOTAL | 👤 4 | FRI ✓ | SAT × | SUN | ▲ — British

WHEATSHEAF INN
☎ 01722 782 203

Woodford, Salisbury, SP4 6NQ

Family owned brewer Hall & Woodhouse believe in pub favourites that are locally sourced at an affordable price. Nestled in the heart of the Woodford Valley, this venue is delectable and unspoiled.

25% OFF TOTAL | FRI × | SAT × | SUN | ▲ — British

ZEN
☎ 01793 486 223

109-111 Cricklade Road, Gorse Hill, Swindon, SN2 1AB

Smart, up-to-date Chinese restaurant that serves up reams of well-seasoned, quality dishes. Lively and welcoming with a very attentive staff team, it is a great place to enjoy a good Chinese meal.

2FOR1 3 COURSES | FRI ✓ | SAT ▯ — Chinese

South East

All restaurants listed within the M25 are listed within the Greater London region. Members looking for restaurants in the Home Counties should also check the Greater London section, as some area of these counties are within the M25.

Bedfordshire

BALTISTAN
☎ 01582 413 025

317 Hitchin Road, Luton, LU2 7SL

Versatile curry place that does a fine selection of dishes across the board. Try the nargis kebab - like a scotch egg only with more pizzazz - or a popular speciality like the king prawn suka.

2FOR1 3 COURSES | FRI ✓ | SAT ✓ — Indian

BAR ESPRESSO
☎ 01582 459 823

39-41 New Bedford Road, Luton, LU1 1SE

A cracking little café and sports bar that offers smooth vibes by day and an informal, relaxed atmosphere by night. The perfect place to enjoy a casual breakfast, lunch or dinner.

50% OFF FOOD | ♟10 | FRI ✓ | SAT ✓ — Mediterranean

THE BELL BEDFORD
☎ 01234 768 310

2 Bedford Road, Marston Moretain, MK43 0ND

Classic and homely local pub serving real ales that provide an accompaniment to the hale and hearty English fare served up by the kitchens; great meals of beef, you'll eat like wolves.

2FOR1 MAIN COURSE | FRI ✓ | SAT ✓ | SUN — British

BENGAL BRASSERIE
☎ 01234 340 888

9 The Broadway, Bedford, MK40 2TJ

Bengal Brasserie offers a new concept in culinary fare to Bedfordshire. They believe they have created an Indian restaurant for tomorrow which is traditional yet modern, authentic yet innovative.

2FOR1 MAIN COURSE | FRI ✗ | SAT ✗ | ✱ | ▲ — Indian

BOUNTY'S CARIBBEAN
☎ 01582 526 986

194 Dunstable Road, Luton, LU4 8JJ

Restaurant known for its homely, tasty, full-flavoured Caribbean dishes. You'll find all the classics here, from rice and peas to jerk chicken and excellent goat curry.

50% OFF FOOD | ♟8 | FRI ▯ | SAT ▯ — Caribbean

THE BRACHE
01582 420 208

Osborne Road, Luton, LU1 3HJ

Beefeater Grill are one of the UK's best-loved restaurants welcoming guests for almost 40 years in over 130 locations nationwide. *Excludes Breakfast, Light Bites, Bar menu, set menus and all other offers.

2FOR1 MAIN COURSE | ♟6 | FRI ✓ | SAT ✗ | ▲ — Modern British

BRAMINGHAM
☎ 01582 788 230

1 Quantock Rise, Luton, LU3 4AB

A Great British Carvery pub and restaurant with a relaxed 'home from home' feel, making for a perfect meeting place when you want to relax and enjoy freshly cooked food. *Booking is essential.

2FOR1 MAIN COURSE | FRI ✓ | SAT ✓ | SUN — Carvery

CAFÉ GOA
☎ 01582 883 934

2 Bedford Road, Barton-le-Clay, MK45 4JU

The success of this restaurant's style of cooking depends on the very best ingredients being crafted with expertise and care to enhance their natural flavours. Indulge in a truly authentic curry.

25% OFF TOTAL | ♟6 | FRI ✗ | SAT ✗ | SUN | ✱ — Indian

CALZONE & CO
☎ 01234 341 414

28 Castle Lane, Bedford, MK40 3US

Calzone & Co is simple restaurant that focuses on serving fantastic calzone and pizza to using the very best ingredients, made to true Italian style, where families and romantic diners are invited alike.

25% OFF TOTAL | ♟8 | FRI ✗ | SAT ✗ | SUN — Italian

CHOUDHURY
☎ 01234 356 162

32 The Broadway, Bedford, MK40 2TH

Curry-hungry diners are well-catered for at Choudhury Restaurant, where an eclectic menu provides a wide variety of dishes ranging from the fiery hot to the cautiously creamy.

2FOR1 3 COURSES | FRI ✗ | SAT ✗ | SUN | ✱ — Indian

COCONUT GARDEN
☎ 01582 472 688

212 High Street North, Dunstable, LU6 1AU

Indulge in the fragrant and exotic flavours of South-east Asian food. Delight in a traditional menu of favourites that also includes specialised vegetarian dishes recognised by The Vegetarian Society.

2FOR1 MAIN COURSE | FRI ✱ | SAT ✱ | ▲ — Thai

DONATELLOS
☎ 01582 475 797

204a High Street North, Dunstable, LU6 1AU

Trattoria-style Italian restaurant, tables dotted about the converted cottage's dining rooms. Varied and traditional menu with an especially good line in pizzas and pastas, staple of any good Italian.

25% OFF TOTAL | ♟4 | FRI ✓ | SAT ✓ — Italian

DROVER'S ARMS
☎ 01525 715 697

Flitwick Road, Steppingley, Bedford, MK45 5BA

Popular inn of long standing, with a reputation for producing flavoursome, rich Indian cuisine. Enjoys an appealing atmosphere, with some excellent Indian cuisine and well-drilled service.

2FOR1 3 COURSES | FRI ✱ | SAT ✱ — Indian

DUNSTABLE TANDOORI
☎ 01582 471 912

21 Vernon Place, Dunstable, LU5 4HA

Fabulous Tandoori restaurant that offers superbly tasty dishes, where customers are guaranteed to be well received and thoroughly looked after. The dhansak curries come highly recommended.

2FOR1 3 COURSES | FRI ✱ | SAT ✱ — Indian

FAJITAS MEXICAN RESTAURANT
☎ 01525 404 303

4 The Kings Arms Yard, Ampthill, MK45 2PJ

Fine Mexican cuisine and drinks are served in the rather surprising yet wonderfully preserved home of a former workhouse. The interior is replete with original features that create intimate dining spaces.

25% OFF TOTAL | ♟4 | FRI ✱ | SAT ✱ | ✱ | ▲ — Mexican

FIGARO RESTAURANT
☎ 01234 211 411

67 Commercial Road, Bedford, MK40 1QS

A warm and welcoming ambience comes as standard at this traditional family-run restaurant. Offers a menu and specials selection to tempt everyone's taste buds, with choice wines to complement each dish.

2FOR1 MAIN COURSE | FRI ✓ | SAT ✱ | ▲ — Italian

FROG & RHUBARB
01582 452 722

Church Road, Slip End, Luton, LU1 4BJ

A cosy country pub combining a traditional bar with quality dining, a selection of beers and wines from around the globe and a great choice of hearty, well-prepared dishes from around the continent.

2FOR1 MAIN COURSE | FRI ✗ | SAT ✱ | SUN | ▲ — English and Continental

THE FRONTIER LOUNGE
☎ 01582 414 028

39 Alma Street, Luton, LU1 2PL

With a menu hand-crafted to include numerous secret recipes, so every bite carries rich flavours, aromas and spices, Frontier Lounge is a definitive gateway to the rich heritage of Indian cuisine.

2FOR1 2 COURSES | FRI ✗ | SAT ✗ | SUN | ✱ | ▲ — Indian

HALFWAY HOUSE
01582 609 938

350 Luton Road, Dunstable, LU5 4LL

Quality pub classics with modern twists meets with a friendly and relaxed atmosphere to make this Table Table venue the perfect place for any occasion. *Excludes daytime & evening deals and festive menus.

2FOR1 MAIN COURSE | FRI ✓ | SAT ✓ — Modern British

HARPURS
☎ 01234 347 877

46 Tavistock Street, Bedford, MK40 2RD

Let your taste buds run wild with freshly prepared foods, and enjoy a specially selected wine list in an atmosphere perfect for relaxation. Varied menus to cater for all tastes and budgets.

2FOR1 MAIN COURSE | FRI ✗ | SAT ✗ | SUN — British

THE HEATH INN
☎ 01525 237 390

76 Woburn Road, Leighton Buzzard, LU7 0AR

Wide-ranging menu on offer at the Heath Inn, where warm and comforting classics meet the more formal, refined of dishes. The inn is also a great place to rest on your travels.

50% OFF FOOD | ♟4 | FRI ✗ | SAT ✗ — British

HORSE & JOCKEY
01582 841 488

125 Watling Street, Kensworth, Dunstable, LU6 3QP

Quality pub classics with modern twists meets with a friendly and relaxed atmosphere to make this Table Table venue the perfect place for any occasion. *Excludes daytime & evening deals and festive menus.

2FOR1 MAIN COURSE | FRI ✓ | SAT ✓ — Modern British

INDIAN SUMMER
01234 351 251

69 Tavistock Street, Bedford, MK40 2RR

Guests can sink their teeth into juicy lamb chops and fabulously fresh seafood at this newly refurbished eatery. Enjoy chef specials prepared using only the most invigorating ingredients.

2FOR1 MAIN COURSE | FRI ✓ | SAT ✓ — Indian

ISHA BAR & RESTAURANT
01296 688 258

10 Aylesbury Road, Leighton Buzzard, LU7 0PB

Over an ice-cold kingfisher beer, peruse the well-executed menu before making a selection. Chef specials and tandoori mixed grills appear as firm favourites with regular diners.

2FOR1 MAIN COURSE | FRI × | SAT × — Indian

IVEL RESTAURANT & BAR
01767 692 220

Girtford Bridge, Sandy, SG19 1NA

There is something for everyone at the Ivel Restaurant, where an extensive menu entices both locals and newcomers. Satisfaction guaranteed, this venue boasts popularity.

25% OFF TOTAL | 6 | FRI ✓ | SAT ✓ — International

JAYRAJ
01582 734 455

636 Hitchin Road, Stopsley, Luton, LU2 7UG

Jayraj is offers is a fine Indian restaurant and takeaway. The menu features authentic and imaginative traditional Indian foods, cooked to a high standards using the best quality and freshest ingredients.

2FOR1 MAIN COURSE | FRI ✓ | SAT ✓ | ✱ — Indian

KING WILLIAM HOTEL
01582 728 086

Mangrove Green, Cockernhoe, Luton, LU2 8QE

The King William has the air of a traditional country pub, with all its homely colours and smells. The food has all the British pub classics, and if you're up for it, an enormous 20oz rump steak.

50% OFF FOOD | 6 | FRI ✓ | SAT ✓ — British

LA CAMPANA
01582 872 460

The Bell, Dunstable Road, Dunstable, LU6 2QG

An excellent restaurant situated in idyllic countryside. The Sicilian-trained chef cooks up divinely tasty rustic Italian dishes full of intense rich flavours.

2FOR1 MAIN COURSE | FRI ✱ | SAT × | SUN — Italian

LEBANON GRILL
01582 412 411

14 Wellington Street, Luton, LU1 2QH

This venue entices both family and friends with lavish Moroccan décor coupled with a heated garden and authentic shisha pipes. The fusion dishes are a must, as they only use the best quality produce.

25% OFF TOTAL | FRI | SAT — Lebanese

THE MELODIA RESTAURANT
01582 455 325

30 Guildford Street, Luton, LU1 2NR

Well-regarded Italian restaurant in Luton. Cool, low-key tones set the scene, with offbeat black and white photos on the walls. The menu features a great selection of pizza and pasta, plus specials.

50% OFF FOOD | 8 | FRI ✓ | SAT ✱ — Italian

MEM-SAAB BEDFORD
01234 344 440

4 Kimbolton Road, Bedford, MK40 2NR

This award-winning chain is popular for its contemporary design, including an oriental garden area featuring tranquil water fountains. The expertly prepared cuisine is both authentic and exquisite.

2FOR1 3 COURSES | FRI ✓ | SAT × | SUN | ✱ — Indian

MILLIE BACI CAFÉ BAR & PIZZERIA
01234 345 491

32-34 St Loyes Street, Bedford, MK40 1EP

Mille Bacci is a superb Italian café and restaurant, popular for its family-run operations and delectable food offerings. Freshly cooked pastas and crispy home-made desserts to round your evening off.

25% OFF TOTAL | 6 | FRI ✓ | SAT ✓ | SUN — Italian

MIRAJ
01582 576 200

249 Birdsfoot Lane, Luton, LU3 2HX

Miraj restaurant and takeaway was established in 2001 offers a range of authentic & imaginative traditional Indian foods, cooked to a high standard only using the best quality & freshest ingredients.

2FOR1 MAIN COURSE | FRI ✓ | SAT ✓ | ✱ — Indian

MOJA
01525 377 715

1 Mill Road, Leighton Buzzard, LU7 1AU

While the bright, stock colours create a contemporary feel to the restaurant, the menu is made up of traditional Indian dishes, serving staple curries and family favourites.

50% OFF FOOD | FRI × | SAT × — Indian

MORETEYNE MANOR
01234 767 003

Woburn Rd, Marston Moretaine, Bedford, MK43 0NQ

Set in a 16th Century Tudor manor house, dine in one of the most picturesque locations in England at Moreteyne Manor, where classic comfort meets modern, sophisticated service.

50% OFF FOOD | 4 | FRI ✓ | SAT × — European

THE PARK PUB AND KITCHEN
01234 273 929

98 Kimbolton Road, Bedford, MK40 2PF

There's an emphasis on local suppliers here, with the freshest ingredients and seasonal produce used to create the menu on offer. The wine list is carefully sourced and includes boutique wineries.

25% OFF TOTAL | 6 | FRI × | SAT × — British

THE PLOUGH
01582 720 923

Woodside Road, Woodside, Luton, LU1 4LU

The Plough is a good, friendly pub, offering a broad menu and a good range of very tasty, hearty pub classics. It's a family-friendly place, with a great garden and some quality ales on tap

2FOR1 MAIN COURSE | FRI ✓ | SAT ✓ | SUN — British

PRIORY MARINA
01234 352 883

Priory Country Park, Barkers Lane, Bedford, MK41 9RQ

Beefeater Grill are one of the UK's best-loved restaurants welcoming guests for almost 40 years in over 130 locations nationwide. *Excludes Breakfast, Light Bites, Bar menu, set menus and all other offers.

2FOR1 MAIN COURSE | 6 | FRI ✓ | SAT × — Modern British

RAJ LUTON
01582 734 455

37 Adelaide Street, Luton, LU1 5BD

The Raj Indian Restaurant was established in 2008 & offers a range of authentic & imaginative fusion dishes. The food is cooked to the highest standards only using the best quality & freshest ingredients.

2FOR1 MAIN COURSE | FRI ✓ | SAT ✓ | ✱ — Indian

RBG BAR AND GRILL @ PARK INN
01234 799 988

The Park Inn, 2 St Marys Street, Bedford, MK42 0AR

Wonderfully located place to stay in the town centre of Bedford. For casual dining head to the RBG Bar & Grill, where classic burgers, crispy fish & chips and great grills can all be found and devoured.

25% OFF TOTAL | 6 | FRI ✓ | SAT ✓ — European

RIOBELLO
01234 364 430

6 St Mary's Street, Bedford, MK42 0PS

Simply authentic Italian cuisine served in a beautiful location, combined with impeccable service and fine choice wines. Sample a true taste of Italy at the Riobello.

2FOR1 MAIN COURSE | FRI | SAT ✱ | SUN — Italian

THE RIVER ROOM
01234 346 565

Bedford Swan Hotel, The Embankment, Bedford, MK40 1RW

This 18th-century hotel is truly fabulous. Occupying a formidable location with spectacular views, this is a superb place to dine, drink, celebrate and stay. 1 AA Rosette.

2FOR1 MAIN COURSE | FRI ✓ | SAT | SUN — Modern British

ROGON RESTAURANT
01582 348 111

Marsh Road, Luton, LU3 2RW

Many subsections of curry types feature on the menu at Rogon; whether you fancy a fruity or a hot and fiery dish, the kitchen can cater for you. Chef specialities make popular choices.

2FOR1 MAIN COURSE | FRI ✓ | SAT ✓ — Indian

SAFFRON
01234 326 394

64 Tavistock Street, Bedford, MK40 2RG

Providing regular local diners and visitors from afar with exceptional Indian cuisine, Saffron offers an extensive range of classic dishes made from free range and organic produce where possible.

50% OFF FOOD | FRI × | SAT × — Indian

SPICE FUSION
☎ 01582 662 551

4-6 Albion Street, Dunstable, LU6 1SA

Playing up to its name, this restaurant is proud of its unique fusion of flavoursome spices that give each and every dish its authentic taste. A vast range of popular and more unusual Indian dishes.

25% OFF TOTAL | 10 | FRI 📱 | SAT × — Indian

STAR AND GARTER
☎ 01525 860 250

14-16 High Street, Silsoe, MK45 4DR

In a gorgeous location, packed with history, this pub-restaurant serves seasoned and savoury home-cooked specialities, to be washed down with a fine pint of something starry-eyed.

25% OFF TOTAL | 6 | FRI 📱 | SAT 📱 | SUN | ▲ — British

TOFF'S INDIAN LOUNGE
☎ 01582 729 526

41 Wellington Street, Luton, LU1 2QH

Step into the world of Toff's, where the fusion of both Bangladesh and India are incorporated into its Bengali cuisine. Here you will be amazed by the diversity and quality of the many different dishes.

25% OFF TOTAL | 10 | FRI ✓ | SAT ✓ | ✱ — Indian

TONG SAM
☎ 01582 666 880

84 High Street North, Dunstable, LU6 1LH

A fantastic family-run establishment where the authenticity of the food proves to be more than satisfying. Experience delicious and flavoursome dishes from a variety of Asian countries.

25% OFF TOTAL | 10 | FRI ✱ | SAT ✱ — Oriental

THE TRAVELLER'S REST
01525 221 841

Tring Road, Edlesborough, Dunstable, LU6 2EE

This Vintage Inn oozes rural charm and rustic character. The picturesque surroundings provide the perfect backdrop for savouring the hearty, seasonal pub-food on the menu.

25% OFF TOTAL | FRI ✓ | SAT ✓ | SUN | ▲ — Modern British

THE WARDEN
01582 591 277

129 Barton Road, Luton, LU3 2BL

Beefeater Grill are one of the UK's best-loved restaurants welcoming guests for almost 40 years in over 130 locations nationwide. *Excludes Breakfast, Light Bites, Bar menu, set menus and all other offers.

2FOR1 MAIN COURSE | 6 | FRI ✓ | SAT × | ▲ — Modern British

WINEGLASS RESTAURANT
☎ 01234 270 044

Cardington Road, Bedford, MK44 3SA

A sleek and stylish restaurant in this characterful hotel plays host to some modern classic dishes, cooked freshly to order. Kick back and enjoy the ranging menu.

25% OFF TOTAL | 4 | FRI ✓ | SAT ✓ — European

Berkshire

ASIAN FUSION
☎ 01628 822 140

Bath Road, Littlewick Green, Maidenhead, SL6 3QR

Asian Fusion has broken away from a traditional all-Indian menu and combined some of the finest dishes from Bangladesh, China and Thailand. They offer an extensive menu, first class service and atmosphere.

25% OFF TOTAL | 6 | FRI × | SAT × | SUN — Asian

AVANTI BISTRO BAR CAFÉ
☎ 01753 866 338

98 Peascod Street, Windsor, SL4 1DH

The divine tastes of Italy are brought to the historical town of Windsor. From Italian classics to old favourites, this venue caters for every palate. The brûlée cheesecake is a popular tasty treat.

2FOR1 MAIN COURSE | FRI ✓ | SAT ✓ | ✱ | ▲ — Italian

BAR ONE ASCOT
☎ 01344 875 123

1 High Street, Ascot, SL5 7JF

A wide menu accommodating popular tastes and Mediterranean recipes, from salmon and calamari to pizzas and pastas. Proud of its range of dishes, Bar One is popular for quiet nights to lively beginnings.

50% OFF FOOD | 10 | FRI ✓ | SAT ✓ — Italian

BARANDA
☎ 0118 977 6100

48-50 Peach Street, Wokingham, RG40 1XG

Oozing sophistication and authenticity, Baranda prepares Indian and Bangladeshi fare in a spacious and ambient setting. The carefully selected menu is composed of an array of classic regional dishes.

2FOR1 MAIN COURSE | FRI × | SAT × — Indian

BEAUMONT ESTATE
☎ 01753 640 000

Burfield Road, Windsor, SL4 2JP

Be inspired by the enchanting and awe-inspiring Beaumont Estate, where class and charm come naturally. Rest in luxury, dine in elegance, and create memories that will last a lifetime.

25% OFF TOTAL | 6 | FRI ✓ | SAT ✓ | ▲ — British

BEIJING RESTAURANT
☎ 01344 778 802

103 Old Wokingham Road, Crowthorne, RG45 6LH

An enjoyable evening is guaranteed at this marvellous Chinese restaurant. Szechuan and Peking dishes make up a comprehensive à la carte menu, which offers over 170 dishes.

2FOR1 MAIN COURSE | FRI ✱ | SAT ✱ | ▲ — Chinese

THE BELL AT BOXFORD
☎ 01488 608 721

Bell at Boxford, Newbury, RG20 8DD

Long-established and award-winning, this venue prides itself on providing a 'home away from home' ambiance complete with home-cooked food and complementary Wi-Fi. Contemporary, International dishes served.

2FOR1 3 COURSES | FRI ✓ | SAT ✓ | SUN | ▲ — International

BINA TANDOORI
☎ 01189 462 116

21 Prospect Street, Caversham, Reading, RG4 8JB

An effective combination of good food and great service, this modern restaurant has many fans and offers a mix of both traditional Indian specialities and Anglicised dishes.

2FOR1 MAIN COURSE | FRI ✱ | SAT ✱ | 🌲 — Indian

BOUCHRA INDIAN RESTAURANT
☎ 01628 782 455

Westborough Road, Maidenhead, West Berkshire, SL6 4A

Blending the classic with the contemporary, Bouchra serves delectable Indian cuisine in a charming and thoroughly inviting atmosphere. Make use of the garden during those warm, balmy evenings.

2FOR1 3 COURSES | FRI 📱 | SAT 📱 — Indian

BRIDGES
☎ 01189 484 550

2 Bridge Street, Caversham, RG4 8AA

If you're not hungry when you arrive at Bridges, you will be when you see their menu. Each dish is cooked to perfection and served with a smile by one of their friendly staff who will gladly attend to your every need.

25% OFF TOTAL | FRI 📱 | SAT 📱 — British

BROAD STREET TAVERN
☎ 01189 773 706

29 Broad Street, Wokingham, RG40 1AU

Situated in the heart of Wokingham town centre; good food, a selection of quality real ales and a warm welcome awaits you at the Broad Street Tavern. *Excludes Xmas menus.

25% OFF TOTAL | 👤 4 | FRI × | SAT × | SUN — British

BURGHFIELD SPICES
☎ 01189 834 040

The Hatch Gate Inn, Burghfield Village, RG30 3TH

Attracting sophisticated clientele, Burghfield Spices host charming, attentive staff who will ensure a fantastic dining experience. The Indian cuisine is guaranteed to be scrumptious.

2FOR1 MAIN COURSE | FRI × | SAT × — Indian

CAFÉ MADRAS
☎ 0118 975 8181

73 Whitley Street Reading, Reading, RG2 0EG

Known for its variety of spices and exceptional flavours, South Indian cuisine is becoming more popular in the western world. Café Madras draws on the tastes and traditional dishes known in South India.

2FOR1 2 COURSES | FRI 📱 | SAT 📱 — Indian

CANTLEY HOUSE HOTEL
☎ 01189 789 912

Milton Road, Wokingham, RG40 5QG

This enchanting Victorian mansion in Berkshire offers exquisite scenery and the Milton's restaurant is privately located for serene bliss. Hearty meals by roaring fires are this venue's niche.

2FOR1 MAIN COURSE | FRI ✓ | SAT × | SUN | 🌲 — International

CAPRICE RESTAURANT @ HOLIDAY INN
01189 440 444

Holiday Inn Reading, Wharfedale Rd, Reading, RG41 5TS

Prestigious and long-established, the Executive Head Chef Graham Weston prepares contemporary dishes which are internationally influenced. This 2 AA Rosette-winning venue promises a fine-dining experience.

25% OFF TOTAL | 👤 6 | FRI ✓ | SAT ✓ — Modern British

CERISE @ THE FORBURY
☎ 01189 527 770

26 The Forbury, Reading, RG1 3EJ

Cerise is a stylish brasserie; low-key, offbeat and contemporary. The menu is seasonal and accomplished, with a focus on modern British cuisine, with influences from around the world. 1 A Rosette.

2FOR1 MAIN COURSE | FRI × | SAT × — Fine Dining

THE CLOVES
☎ 01753 830 003

85b, Clewer Hill Road, Windsor, SL4 4DE

Cloves is a wonderfully popular restaurant in Windsor where effective recipes and impressive ingredients contribute to the tasty Indian food. Perfect for special occasions and mid-week treats.

50% OFF FOOD | 👤 6 | FRI ✓ | SAT ✓ | ✱ | 🌲 — Indian

THE CROOKED HOUSE OF WINDSOR
☎ 01753 857 534

51 High Street, Windsor, SL4 1LR

The Crooked House of Windsor is a quintessential English tea room. This historic building with its quaint and quirky interior is the ideal venue for a breakfast, lunch, afternoon tea or bespoke dinner to remember.

25% OFF TOTAL | 👤 2 | FRI × | SAT × | SUN | 🌲 — British

CROWN AND GARTER
☎ 01488 668 325

Inkpen Common, Inkpen, Hungerford, RG17 9QR

The experienced Head Chef creates exquisite classic dishes using the best local produce. They aim to provide a gastronomic experience with a traditional country inn décor and atmosphere.

2FOR1 MAIN COURSE | FRI 📱 | SAT 📱 | SUN — British

THE CROWN INN
☎ 01753 647 714

Crown Lane, Farnham Royal, Slough, SL2 3SQ

Friendly country pub serving an extensive range of dining options, from hearty pies to tapas sharing platters. Great food, service and atmosphere; the jewel in Farnham's crown.

50% OFF FOOD | 👤 6 | FRI 📱 | SAT 📱 | SUN — British

THE CUNNING MAN
01189 598 067

Burghfield Road, Burghfield Bridge, Reading, RG30 3BR

This Vintage Inn oozes rural charm and rustic character. The picturesque surroundings provide the perfect backdrop for savouring the hearty, seasonal pub-food on the menu.

25% OFF TOTAL | FRI ✓ | SAT ✓ | SUN | 🌲 — Modern British

DOWNSHIRE ARMS
01344 423 585

Downshire Way, Bracknell, RG12 4AA

Beefeater Grill are one of the UK's best-loved restaurants welcoming guests for almost 40 years in over 130 locations nationwide. *Excludes Breakfast, Light Bites, Bar menu, set menus and all other offers.

2FOR1 MAIN COURSE | 👤 6 | FRI ✓ | SAT × | 🌲 — Modern British

EDEN BAR & RESTAURANT
☎ 01753 896 400

Wexham Park Lane, George Green, Slough, SL3 6AP

AA Rosette-winning hotel-based restaurant with a stylish, contemporary feel. Freshly flavoured starters and robust, earthy mains characterise the menu.

25% OFF TOTAL | 👤 6 | FRI 📱 | SAT 📱 — Fine Dining

CAFÉ ROUGE

25% OFF TOTAL | 👤 6 | FRI ✓ | SAT ✓ | ✱ | 🌲

25% OFF TOTAL

Parkway Shopping, 74-75 Marsh Lane, Newbury RG14 1AY — ☎ 0163 535 670

Unit R16, The Oracle Centre, Reading RG1 2AG — ☎ 0118 957 5223

31-32 Royal Station Parade, Thames St, Windsor, SL4 1PJ — ☎ 01753 831 100

30 Market Place, Wokingham, RG40 1AP — ☎ 0118 979 9128

FOX & HOUNDS
☎01189 302 295

Hangar Road, Sunnyside, Theale, Reading, RG7 4BE

A traditional country pub serving a wide range of real ales along with an extensive menu and homemade specials. It's located directly opposite the picturesque Hosehill Lake - a protected bird reserve. *Excludes Xmas menus.

25% OFF TOTAL | 4 | FRI ✗ | SAT ✗ | SUN — British

FRANCESCO'S MAIDENHEAD
01628 777 815

73-75 King St, Maidenhead, SL6 1DU

In a restaurant where even the pizza dough is made at least twice a day, it's no surprise that the food is amazing. Enjoy delicious dishes in a style in keeping with the Italian way of life.

2FOR1 MAIN COURSE | FRI ✓ | SAT ✓ | ▲ — Italian

FRANCESCO'S WINDSOR
☎01753 863 773

53 Peascod Street, Windsor, SL4 1DE

In a restaurant where even the pizza dough is made at least twice a day, it's no surprise that the food is amazing. Enjoy delicious dishes in a style in keeping with the Italian way of life.

2FOR1 MAIN COURSE | FRI ✓ | SAT ✓ | ▲ — Italian

FUSIONZ INDIAN RESTAURANT
☎01753 593 333

260 Trewlaney Avenue, Slough, SL3 7UD

A traditional Indian and Bangladeshi restaurant in the heart of Langley, Fusionz serves an excellent selection of mouth-wateringly authentic dishes in sumptuous surroundings.

2FOR1 3 COURSES | FRI ✓ | SAT ✓ — Indian

THE GARDEN ROOM AT STOKE PLACE
☎01753 534 790

Stoke Place, Stoke Poges, Slough, SL2 4HT

Holder of three prestigious AA Rosettes, this superb restaurant boasts a menu of contemporary dishes that showcase quality, seasonal ingredients and classical cooking techniques

50% OFF FOOD | 6 | FRI ✓ | SAT ✱ | SUN — Modern European

GAYLORD TANDOORI
☎01189 345 511

26 London Road, Reading, RG10 9ER

The team welcome you to the Gaylord Tandoori, temping you with an unrivalled range of authentic and imaginative traditional Indian foods. So enjoy your meal and have a memorable experience.

50% OFF FOOD | 10 | FRI ✗ | SAT ✗ — Indian

GODARI RESTAURANT
☎01753 536 606

54 Park Street, Slough, SL1 1PS

For your fill of fine Indian food, head to Godari, where flavoursome dishes appear strongly on a well put together menu. Sample traditional South Indian curries, crisp sundries and fresh naan breads.

2FOR1 3 COURSES | FRI ✗ | SAT ✗ — Indian

THE GOLDEN RETRIEVER
01344 868 535

Nine Mile Ride, Bracknell, RG40 3DR

This Vintage Inn oozes rural charm and rustic character. The picturesque surroundings provide the perfect backdrop for savouring the hearty, seasonal pub-food on the menu.

25% OFF TOTAL | FRI ✓ | SAT ✓ | SUN | ▲ — Modern British

THE GURU
01635 269 999

The Harrow, Newbury Road, Headley, Thatcham, RG19 8LG

Using the finest spices and the freshest ingredients, The Guru offers superbly tasty Indian cuisine for dining in and taking away. The staff are always eager to advise you on the menu.

2FOR1 MAIN COURSE | FRI 📱 | SAT ✗ — Indian

HANDMADE BURGER CO.
01189 588 106

Unit 10 The Riverside, Reading, RG1 2AG

With over 40 varieties on offer, the combination of fresh sourdough buns, 100% Scotch beef burgers and unusual toppings you're truly spoilt for choice. *Menu exclusions apply.

2FOR1 MAIN COURSE | FRI ✓ | SAT ✗ | SUN — International

THE HARE RESTAURANT AND BAR
☎0148 871 386

Ermin Street, Lambourn Woodlands, Hungerford, RG17 7SD

In an area of outstanding beauty, delivering fine dining with a tempting choice of traditional and contemporary cuisine. Carefully selected ingredients are used to create stunning dishes. 2 AA Rosettes.

25% OFF TOTAL | 6 | FRI ✱ | SAT ✱ | SUN | ✱ | ▲ — European

HUNGRY RICE
01753 830 099

1 Church Lane, Windsor, SL4 1PA

An accomplished Indian restaurant with a menu that features a fine selection of dishes, some especially good marinades, and a firm emphasis on freshness of produce and flavour.

2FOR1 MAIN COURSE | FRI ✗ | SAT ✗ | SUN — Indian

INDIAN PARADISE
☎07925 449 688

28 Farnham Drive, Reading, RG4 6NY

Tapas with a twist; this venue offers flavoursome Indian cuisine on tapas-sized plates created by a team of devoted chefs. The succulent spiced lamb comes highly recommended.

50% OFF FOOD | 6 | FRI 📱 | SAT 📱 — Indian

ISLAND BAR AND RESTAURANT
☎01189 479 530

Pipers Island, Reading, RG4 8AH

Situated on Pipers Island, the spectacular Island Bar and Restaurant enjoys uninterrupted views of the River Thames. Robust mains courses, tapas and meze dishes available along with al fresco dining.

25% OFF TOTAL | 2 | FRI ✗ | SAT ✗ | SUN — International

JP'S BISTRO
☎0163 538 000

6-8 Oxford Street, Newbury, RG14 1JB

Ideal restaurant for a relaxed dining experience, with a menu that makes use of seasonal ingredients. For a casual atmosphere, the bar is the place to unwind with a drink and a choice of light snacks.

50% OFF FOOD | 2 | FRI ✗ | SAT ✗ — International

KHUKURI
☎01189 511 881

82 London Street, Reading, RG1 4SJ

Experience faithful versions of Nepalese and Thai classics that are fresh, healthy and delectable. A family-run restaurant that has offered authentic dishes of the highest quality since 1990.

25% OFF TOTAL | 10 | FRI ✓ | SAT ✓ | ✱ — Nepalese

LA PRIMAVERA
☎01488 682 588

16 Charnham Street, Hungerford, RG17 0AE

Savour sumptuous Italian cuisine in continental surroundings. Admire the eye-catching wall prints and enjoy regional wine from the heart of Italy. La Primavera welcomes the entire family.

2FOR1 MAIN COURSE | FRI 📱 | SAT 📱 | ▲ — French

LA TASCA
☎0163 534 279

32 Market Place, Newbury, RG14 5AG

Quintessentially Spanish, La Tasca's fresh and exciting menu offers something for everyone. Their tapas dishes are sincerely authentic, while their paellas always deliver on flavour.

25% OFF TOTAL | 8 | FRI ✓ | SAT ✗ | ▲ — Spanish

LA TASCA
☎01753 852 288

Windsor Royal Station, Windsor, SL4 1PJ

Quintessentially Spanish, La Tasca's fresh and exciting menu offers something for everyone. Their tapas dishes are sincerely authentic, while their paellas always deliver on flavour.

25% OFF TOTAL | 8 | FRI ✓ | SAT ✗ | ▲ — Spanish

LANKA'S FINEST
☎01189 261 199

83 Wokingham Road, Reading, RG6 1LH

The menu at Lanka's Finest is filled with exotic choices of authentic, freshly prepared recipes. Using the finest blend of herbs and spices, the chefs create mouth watering dishes of Sri Lankan cuisine.

25% OFF TOTAL | 4 | FRI 📱 | SAT 📱 | SUN — Sri Lankan

LOCH FYNE
☎01189 185 850

The Maltings, Bear Wharf, Fobney St, Reading, RG1 6BT

From the roadside oyster bar that once was, Loch Fyne restaurants now successfully inject energy and passion into great food and wonderful flavours, whilst ensuring their seafood is sustainably sourced.

25% OFF TOTAL | 4 | FRI ✱ | SAT ✱ | ▲ — Seafood

LOCH FYNE
☎01189 123 260

Plough, London Road, Wokingham, RG40 1RD

From the roadside oyster bar that once was, Loch Fyne restaurants now successfully inject energy and passion into great food and wonderful flavours, whilst ensuring their seafood is sustainably sourced.

25% OFF TOTAL | 4 | FRI ✱ | SAT ✱ | ▲ — Seafood

LOCH FYNE
☎ 01344 894 760

The Crispin, Windsor Rd, Winkfield, Windsor, SL4 2DE

From the roadside oyster bar that once was, Loch Fyne restaurants now successfully inject energy and passion into great food and wonderful flavours, whilst ensuring their seafood is sustainably sourced.

25% OFF TOTAL | ♟ 4 | FRI ✱ | SAT ✱ | ▲ — Seafood

THE LONG WALK BRASSERIE
☎ 01753 863 916

46 Kings Road, Windsor, SL4 2AG

Adhering strictly to its philosophy which insists on fresh, seasonal dishes in an inviting atmosphere, this restaurant is always pleasing. A fine, exclusive wine will add the finishing touch to your meal.

2FOR1 MAIN COURSE | FRI 📱 | SAT 📱 — British

MALMAISON
☎ 01189 562 300

18-20 Station Road, Reading, RG1 1JX

Relax in inimitable Malmaison style and savour deliciously contemporary brasserie dishes, whilst enjoying the marvellous surroundings of this newly refurbished, richly historical building. 1 AA Rosette.

2FOR1 MAIN COURSE | FRI × | SAT × | SUN | ▲ — European

MANGAL RESTAURANT
☎ 01189 504 039

60 St Mary's Butts, Reading, RG1 2LG

Whether you are in hope of recreating holiday memories or simply fancy flavours from across the sea, the kitchen make offerings of barbecued meats to tasty moussaka and lamb shank.

2FOR1 MAIN COURSE | FRI ✓ | SAT × | ▲ — Mediterranean

MASALA 22
☎ 01189 672 710

22 Hildens Drive, Reading, RG31 5HU

As the name suggests, this Indian eatery prepares a cracking masala. For guests whose palates require something with a bit of a kick, the menu is bursting with a sumptuous variety.

2FOR1 3 COURSES | FRI ✓ | SAT ✓ — Indian

MEGHNA TANDOORI
☎ 01753 521 674

7 Upton Lea Parade, Slough, SL2 5JU

Long-established, the Head Chef infuses every dish with aromatic and effluvious flavours. Guests must sample the Tandoori Murgh Masala, traditionally a wedding feast dish but perfect for any occasion.

2FOR1 3 COURSES | FRI ✓ | SAT ✓ | ✱ — Indian

MEMORIES OF INDIA
☎ 01753 644 166

The Broadway, Farnham Common, SL2 3PQ

Smart modern Indian restaurant with an open and spacious feel, warm tones and low lighting. Broad-based menu features all the old favourites, but also some much more interesting eclectic options.

2FOR1 2 COURSES | FRI ✓ | SAT ✓ — Indian

MILTONS RESTAURANT
☎ 01189 791 666

Cantley House Hotel, Milton Road, Wokingham, RG40 5QG

Housed in a stunning converted 17th Century barn, with its own secluded courtyard garden, Milton's specialises in modern British cuisine with a locally sourced and seasonally changing menu.

50% OFF FOOD | ♟ 8 | FRI ✱ | SAT × | ▲ — European

THE OAKLEY COURT
☎ 01753 609 988

Windsor Road, Water Oakley, Windsor, SL4 5UR

The Oakley Court is a well-cherished member of the Principal Hayley hotel group, offering beautifully serene surroundings and excellent facilities. Enjoy exquisite 2 AA Rosette-awarded British cuisine.

25% OFF TOTAL | ♟ 6 | FRI ✓ | SAT ✓ | ▲ — British

OCEAN VILLAGE
☎ 01628 638 129

117 Bridge Road, Maidenhead, SL6 8NA

Both local curry lovers and guests from further afield have professed admiration for the fantastic Indian cuisine on offer at this popular restaurant. Wash down your meal with an authentic Indian beer.

25% OFF TOTAL | ♟ 4 | FRI ✓ | SAT ✓ — Indian

THE OLIVE TREE
☎ 01635 273 074

Best Western, Cox's Lane, Migham, Reading, RG7 5UP

Allow the tranquil ambience to envelop you as you dine in a beautifully charismatic restaurant overlooking an enclosed courtyard. Dishes demonstrate their own modern interpretation of European cuisine.

25% OFF TOTAL | ♟ 4 | FRI ✓ | SAT ✓ — British

OMNIA BAR @ HILTON
☎ 01189 772 550

Hilton St Annes, London Road, Wokingham, RG40 0GQ

Enjoy a pre-dinner drink or unwind over cocktails at the Omnia Bar and Lounge. Ideal for a mid-morning coffee or an afternoon snack, choose from sandwiches to salads from the contemporary menu.

50% OFF FOOD | ♟ 6 | FRI ✓ | SAT ✓ — British

OMNIA RESTAURANT @ HILTON
☎ 01189 772 550

Hilton St Annes, London Road, Wokingham, RG40 1ST

Grand old country house also featuring an elegant restaurant, smart after the fashion of a club dining room. Serves an excellent selection of British dishes, cooked superbly, like the tender trio of lamb.

50% OFF FOOD | ♟ 6 | FRI 📱 | SAT 📱 — International

THE ORANGERY @ MERCURE
☎ 0844 815 9060

Newbury Elcot Park Hotel, Elcot, Newbury, RG20 8NJ

An exceptional 4-star country retreat, the Mercure Newbury Elcot Park hotel is situated in a splendid Georgian Manor house. The Orangery Restaurant is a grove in itself, full of colour and vibrancy.

2FOR1 3 COURSES | FRI ✓ | SAT ✓ — International

ORANGERY LOUNGE @ RAMADA
☎ 0845 815 9060

Ramada Newbury Elcot Park, Elcot, Newbury, RG20 8NJ

Relaxing, cosy neo-Georgian lounge area where you can enjoy a cafetière of good coffee or a crisp glass of wine together with some simple, tasty light bites.

50% OFF FOOD | ♟ 10 | FRI ✓ | SAT ✱ — Modern European

ORANGERY RESTAURANT @ RAMADA
☎ 0844 815 9060

Ramada Newbury Elcot Park, Elcot, Newbury, RG20 8NJ

Bright bay windows look out over the Berkshire countryside from a well-spaced, warm dining room. Brasserie-style dishes across the menu, the likes of pan-fried sea bass or calves liver with bacon and mash.

50% OFF FOOD | ♟ 10 | FRI ✓ | SAT ✱ — British

PREZZO

2FOR1 MAIN COURSE | FRI × | SAT × | ▲

2-FOR-1 MAIN COURSE

4 restaurants in Berkshire

58 Cheap Street, Newbury, RG14 5DH	☎ 0163 531 957
10-12 King Street, Reading, RG1 2HF	☎ 0118 959 6092
9-10 Bridge Street, Maidenhead, SL6 8LR	☎ 01628 780 227
31 Broad Street, Wokingham, RG40 1AU	☎ 0118 978 5139

To understand what the restaurant icons mean, please see the inside back cover.

PAPA GEE
☎ 0118 9556 906

138 Caversham Road, Reading, RG1 8AY

Either sourced locally or direct from Italy, this bistro promises authentic dishes. Grab a light lunch or indulge in an intimate dinner with a loved one at this idyllic Caversham road retreat.

2FOR1 3 COURSES | FRI ✓ | SAT ✓ | SUN | ✱ — Italian

PEACOCK FARM
☎ 01344 423 481

Peacock Lane, Bracknell, RG12 8SS

A traditional, rustic open-plan interior where original beams and wood burners create a warm and welcoming environment. Wonderful home-made food features highly on the restaurant's list of attributes.

25% OFF TOTAL | 6 | FRI × | SAT × | SUN | ▲ — British

PIANO BAR @ HILTON
☎ 01635 529 000

Hilton Newbury, Pinchington Lane, Newbury, RG2 0GQ

Sip a cocktail and listen to gentle piano music at the Hilton Newbury Centre hotel. Guests and visitors alike can enjoy contemporary snacks under the chandeliers at this wood-panelled Newbury bar.

2FOR1 3 COURSES | FRI ✓ | SAT ✓ — British

RACKSTRAWS FARM
01252 878 181

221 Yorktown Road, College Town, Sandhurst, GU47 0RT

Beefeater Grill are one of the UK's best-loved restaurants welcoming guests for almost 40 years in over 130 locations nationwide. *Excludes Breakfast, Light Bites, Bar menu, set menus and all other offers.

2FOR1 MAIN COURSE | 6 | FRI ✓ | SAT × | ▲ — Modern British

THE RESTAURANT
☎ 0843 357 5518

Thames Riviera Hotel, The Bridge, Maidenhead, SL6 8DW

Overlooking the River Thames, this chic and modish venue is perfect for an evening of unwinding whilst boat-watching. Banquet upon modern British dishes and make use of the complimentary Wi-Fi.

2FOR1 MAIN COURSE | FRI ✓ | SAT × | SUN | ▲ — International

THE ROSE AND CROWN ASCOT
☎ 01344 882 051

Woodside Road, Winfield, Ascot, Windsor, SL4 2DP

A delightful traditional inn that prides itself in offering friendly service, fine ales, wines and fresh food, supplied exclusively by the 'Royal Farms Windsor.'

25% OFF TOTAL | 4 | FRI 📱 | SAT 📱 | SUN | ▲ — British

THE ROYAL ADELAIDE BAR
☎ 01753 863 916

46 Kings Road, Windsor, SL4 2AG

The Head Chef here has created a tempting, mouth-watering menu that offers sumptuous dishes for a delightful evening meal. Classic Sunday brunch is a must for those dining at the weekend.

50% OFF FOOD | 6 | FRI ✓ | SAT ✓ — International

ROYAL FORESTERS
01344 884 747

London Road, Ascot, SL5 8DR

Beefeater Grill are one of the UK's best-loved restaurants welcoming guests for almost 40 years in over 130 locations nationwide. *Excludes Breakfast, Light Bites, Bar menu, set menus and all other offers.

2FOR1 MAIN COURSE | 6 | FRI ✓ | SAT × | ▲ — Modern British

SASSO
☎ 01635 297 446

10-12 George Street, Kingsclere, RG20 5NQ

A lovely local Italian restaurant offering a carefully fashioned menu. Succulent meat, fresh fish and creamy pasta dishes are to be enjoyed by every guest. *Offer excludes 'Specials of the Day'.

2FOR1 MAIN COURSE | FRI ✱ | SAT ✱ | SUN | ▲ — Italian

SILSILA TANDOORI
☎ 01189 417 551

100 Royal Avenue, Calcot, Reading, RG31 4UT

Lovely, well-established Indian restaurant with a real emphasis on the freshness of its ingredients and the depth of its flavours. Friendly, convivial and homely atmosphere for an enjoyable curry.

2FOR1 MAIN COURSE | FRI 📱 | SAT 📱 | ✱ — Indian

SOUTHCOTE READING BEEFEATER GRILL
01189 572 685

Southcote Lane, Reading, RG30 3AB

Beefeater Grill are one of the UK's best-loved restaurants welcoming guests for almost 40 years in over 130 locations nationwide. *Excludes Breakfast, Light Bites, Bar menu, set menus and all other offers.

2FOR1 MAIN COURSE | 6 | FRI ✓ | SAT × | ▲ — Modern British

THE SPACE @ HILTON
☎ 01635 247 010

Hilton Newbury, Oxford Road, Newbury, RG20 8XY

In-house restaurant at the Hilton Newbury North, just on the edge of the market town. Ideal for meetings, with plenty of space and large tables; also does a good selection of light, bistro-style dishes.

50% OFF FOOD | 10 | FRI ✓ | SAT ✓ — International

SPICE ROUTE
☎ 01753 860 720

18a Thames Street, Windsor, SL4 1PL

Explore the taste sensations of India at Spice Route. Tantalizing aromas seeping from the kitchen will leave you pondering over the extensive menu a while longer before you make your choice.

25% OFF TOTAL | 10 | FRI ✓ | SAT ✓ — Indian

SPICES RESTAURANT
☎ 01753 581 008

Silver Cottage, The Green, Datchet, SL3 9BJ

Spices Indian restaurant specialises in creating superb dishes, home-made sauces and crisp, fresh sundries. Each dish reflects the aromas and tastes of authentic Indian street-food stalls.

2FOR1 MAIN COURSE | FRI 📱 | SAT 📱 — Indian

THE SPRING INN
☎ 01189 303 440

Bath Road, Reading, RG7 5HP

Renowned for its friendly staff, this country pub promises to source local produce to ensure a regional taste. Indulge in a crispy pizza or a hearty portion of fish and chips.

2FOR1 MAIN COURSE | FRI ✓ | SAT ✓ | SUN | ▲ — British

STANDARD TANDOORI
01189 590 093

141-145 Caversham Rd, Reading, RG1 8AU

An attractive blend of Nepalese and Indian dishes occupy an extensive menu. The chefs make full use of the finest ingredients, and proudly grind their own herbs and spices to create unique flavours.

25% OFF TOTAL | 6 | FRI × | SAT × | ▲ — Indian/Nepalese

THE STAR INN
01635 296 241

Newbury Road, Kingsclere, Newbury, RG20 4SY

This Vintage Inn oozes rural charm and rustic character. The picturesque surroundings provide the perfect backdrop for savouring the hearty, seasonal pub-food on the menu.

25% OFF TOTAL | FRI ✓ | SAT ✓ | SUN | ▲ — Modern British

STRADA
01635 569 193

21-25 Market Place, Newbury, RG14 5AA

Offering fresh, bold dishes inspired by flavours of Italian city life – Strada serves a selection of indulgent tastes, to those seeking a blissful escape to laidback Italian life. *Excludes Pizzettas.

25% OFF TOTAL | 6 | FRI ✓ | SAT × | ▲ — Italian

STRADA
01189 394 861

The Oracle Shopping Centre, Reading, RG1 2AG

Offering fresh, bold dishes inspired by flavours of Italian city life – Strada serves a selection of indulgent tastes, to those seeking a blissful escape to laidback Italian life. *Excludes Pizzettas.

25% OFF TOTAL | 6 | FRI ✓ | SAT × | ▲ — Italian

STUBBS RESTAURANT @ HILTON
☎ 01635 529 000

Hilton Newbury, Pinchington Lane, Newbury, RG14 7HL

Elegant wood-panelling and casual low-slung chairs, a dining room with a touch of the 1920s about it. Columns, Art Deco details and low, warm tones are the setting for a broad-based menu of English dishes.

2FOR1 3 COURSES | FRI 📱 | SAT 📱 — International

THE SWAN INN
☎ 0163 540 313

Newtown, Newbury, RG20 9BH

When done right, there are few things to match a good pub meal; the Swan Inn does it perfectly. Succulent meats and beautifully fresh vegetables, a ranging menu and array of ales, it's a place to savour.

25% OFF TOTAL | 6 | FRI × | SAT × | SUN | ▲ — European

THE TEMPLE MONKEY
☎ 01753 528 797

39 Upton Park, Slough, SL1 2DA

In-house bar and restaurant of the Upton Park Hotel. The Temple Monkey has a relaxed atmosphere and serves an array of traditional pub dishes alongside a great Indian menu.

2FOR1 3 COURSES | FRI × | SAT × | ✱ | ▲ — Indian

TOWER BRASSERIE
☎ 0844 855 9131

Harte & Garter Hotel, High Street, Windsor, SL4 1PH

Grand in design, grand in gesture at this luxuriously decadent hotel brasserie. Polite, welcoming staff are always eager to assist you in your choices, where the menu leaves you spoilt for choice.

50% OFF FOOD | 4 | FRI ✱ | SAT × | SUN — British

THE UNION INN
☎ 01753 861 955

Free House and Country, 17 Crimp Hill, Windsor, SL4 2QY

Straddling the borders of Berkshire and Surrey, The Union Inn hosts outstanding views of the countryside. A perfect setting to enjoy fresh seafood, succulent steaks and imaginative dishes.

25% OFF TOTAL | 6 | FRI | SAT | SUN — British

UNIQUE SPICE
☎ 01628 660 741

109 High Street, Burnham, SL1 7JZ

Unique Spice is dedicated to producing Indian and Bangladeshi dishes that are brimming with flavour, texture and high quality produce. After dinner, put on your dancing shoes and dance the night away.

2FOR1 MAIN COURSE | FRI × | SAT × — Indian/Nepalese

VEERAJ
☎ 01753 831 234

4 Datchet Road, Windsor, SL4 2RQ

Situated in the heart of Old-Windsor, Veeraj serves modern Indian cuisine with a contemporary British twist. The head chef Abdul Asik has a wealth of experience which is reflected in the innovative menu.

25% OFF TOTAL | FRI ✓ | SAT ✓ — Indian

VIVA L'ITALIA SLOUGH
☎ 01753 206 344

19-21 London Road, Slough, SL3 7RL

This hidden gem, Viva L'Italia is no longer a secret. The locals of Slough flock to this delightful Italian eatery. Friendly knowledgeable staff serving up high quality Italian cuisine at affordable prices.

25% OFF TOTAL | 10 | FRI ✓ | SAT ✓ — Italian

WALKABOUT
☎ 01189 530 000

Wiston Terrace, Reading, RG1 1DG

Walkabout is famous for its characteristically Australian atmosphere and well-rounded menu. From live sport with a juicy burger to some Aussie kangaroo skewers, you'll find it hard to tear yourself away.

25% OFF TOTAL | 10 | FRI ✓ | SAT ✓ | ▲ — International

YE OLDE GEORGE INN
☎ 01753 682 010

146 High Street, Colnbrook, SL3 0LX

The Ye Old George is much loved by regulars and occasional visitors alike; their high standards and excellent reputation mean that all guests are sure to come back time and time again.

50% OFF FOOD | 4 | FRI × | SAT × | SUN — British

ZAMAN OF DATCHET
☎ 01753 596 057

147 Horton Road, Slough, SL3 9HU

Perfect for fans of Indian cuisine, Zaman of Datchet recently been awarded as one of the best restaurants in the South East Region of England and is well worth a visit.

2FOR1 MAIN COURSE | FRI × | SAT × — Indian

Buckinghamshire

ATRIUM BAR @ HOLIDAY INN
☎ 0871 942 9057

500 Saxon Gate, West Central, Milton Keynes, MK9 2HQ

Located in the hotel's central atrium, guests will enjoy the light airiness of the lounge and the tranquil ambience this creates. Hot and cold snacks, sandwiches and drinks are available.

25% OFF TOTAL | 6 | FRI ✓ | SAT ✓ — British

THE BARGE
01908 233 841

15 Newport Road, Woolstone, Milton Keynes, MK15 0AE

This Vintage Inn oozes rural charm and rustic character. The picturesque surroundings provide the perfect backdrop for savouring the hearty, seasonal pub-food on the menu.

25% OFF TOTAL | FRI ✓ | SAT ✓ | SUN | ▲ — Modern British

THE BARN
01908 663 388

Secklow Gate West, Milton Keynes, MK9 3BZ

Beefeater Grill are one of the UK's best-loved restaurants welcoming guests for almost 40 years in over 130 locations nationwide. *Excludes Breakfast, Light Bites, Bar menu, set menus and all other offers.

2FOR1 MAIN COURSE | 6 | FRI ✓ | SAT × | ▲ — Modern British

BEKASH RESTAURANT
☎ 01908 562 249

50 High Street, Stony Stratford, Milton Keynes, MK11 1AQ

Combining the exotic tastes of India and Bangladesh, this elegant venue oozes charm and sophistication. Priding themselves on maintaining the heritage of Asian cooking, the chefs are wholly dedicated.

2FOR1 MAIN COURSE | FRI ✓ | SAT ✓ | ✱ | ▲ — Indian

BELLA ITALIA
01908 395 369

12 Savoy Crescent, Milton Keynes, MK9 3PU

Accessible Italian cuisine on the British high street – indulge in authentic sharing platters, hand stretched pizzas and hearty pasta dishes, served with a healthy dose of gregarious Italian hospitality.

25% OFF TOTAL | 6 | FRI × | SAT × | SUN | ▲ — Italian

BISTRO LIVE
☎ 0845 331 1500

488 Midsummer Boulevard, Milton Keynes, MK9 2EA

Bright and buzzy place to enjoy live music, a fun evening out and a selection of remarkably tasty bistro-style food. *Essential to mention GS when booking. £10 entertainment fee is also required.

25% OFF TOTAL | FRI ✓ | SAT ✓ — International

BLACK HORSE IVER HEATH
☎ 01753 652 631

95 Slough Road, Iver Heath, SL0 0DH

Hall & Woodhouse, a family-owned company, concern themselves with locally sourced food at an affordable price in a friendly environment. The Black Horse is contemporary and held dear by locals.

25% OFF TOTAL | FRI × | SAT × | SUN | ▲ — British

BLUE ORCHID
☎ 01908 282 877

The Square, Aspley Guise, MK17 8DF

Inside the listed 19th-century building you'll find Thai furnishings and exotic foliage that enhance the character and atmosphere of this delightful restaurant. *See the website for further info.

25% OFF TOTAL | 4 | FRI ✱ | SAT ✱ | ✱ — Thai

BOWATERS
☎ 0844 879 9128

The Compleat Angler Marlow Bridge, Marlow, SL7 1RG

In the beautiful Macdonald Compleat Angler Hotel sits this stunning AA Rosette-rated restaurant, proudly offering delectable British food in an idyllic location by the River Thames.

25% OFF TOTAL | 6 | FRI ✓ | SAT × | SUN — International

THE BRASSERIE
☎ 01908 637 373

Bletchley Campus, Milton Keynes, MK3 6DR

Support the talented chef of the future at this terrific training college restaurant. Wonderful dishes are prepared by chefs-in-training, guaranteeing guests a first-class dining experience.

25% OFF TOTAL | 6 | FRI | SAT × | SUN | ▲ — British

THE BUGLE HORN
01296 747 594

Oxford Road, Hartwell, Aylesbury, HP17 8QP

This Vintage Inn oozes rural charm and rustic character. The picturesque surroundings provide the perfect backdrop for savouring the hearty, seasonal pub-food on the menu.

25% OFF TOTAL | FRI ✓ | SAT ✓ | SUN | ▲ — Modern British

THE BULL INN
☎ 01234 711 470

9 Market Place, Olney, MK46 4EA

A stand-out pub. Menu comprises the likes of roast venison saddle with juniper and redcurrant sauce, or an apricot, almond and aubergine tagine with saffron couscous. Superb food and a friendly charm.

2FOR1 MAIN COURSE | FRI × | SAT × | SUN | ▲ — British

CAFÉ BALTI
☎ 01908 311 188

52 Church Street, Wolverton, MK12 5JW

Bright, modern Indian restaurant with a sprightly atmosphere and eclectic range of tasty dishes. Worthy of note are the excellent garlic chicken and the rich sagwala, with lots of spinach.

2FOR1 MAIN COURSE | FRI × | SAT × | SUN — Indian

Gourmet Society discount applies to the à la carte menu only, unless stated otherwise.

CAFÉ ROUGE
01753 880 601

25-27 Station Road, Gerrards Cross, SL9 8ES

French sophistication on the British high street – enjoy seasonally changing French dishes and a continental wine selection, served in a relaxed environment with an undeniable flair of Parisian chic.

25% OFF TOTAL | 6 | FRI ✓ | SAT ✓ | ✱ | ▲ — French

CAFÉ ROUGE
01908 605 282

Queens Court, Milton Keynes, MK9 3ES

French sophistication on the British high street – enjoy seasonally changing French dishes and a continental wine selection, served in a relaxed environment with an undeniable flair of Parisian chic.

25% OFF TOTAL | FRI ✓ | SAT ✓ | ✱ | ▲ — French

CAFÉ ROUGE
01908 241 709

Building 500, Avebury Boulevard, Milton Keynes, MK9 2FB

French sophistication on the British high street – enjoy seasonally changing French dishes and a continental wine selection, served in a relaxed environment with an undeniable flair of Parisian chic.

25% OFF TOTAL | 6 | FRI ✓ | SAT ✓ | ✱ | ▲ — French

CALCUTTA BRASSERIE
☎ 01908 566 577

7 St Pauls Court, Stony Stratford, MK11 1LJ

By its use of a myriad of delectable tastes and flavours, this Indian brasserie reveals a culture that boasts a spectacular array of rich ingredients, spices and cooking styles.

2FOR1 MAIN COURSE | FRI 📱 | SAT ✱ | ▲ — Indian

CAMERON'S BRASSERIE
☎ 01908 568 000

5 Odells Yard, Milton Keynes, MK11 1AQ

Masterchef's very own Dan Cameron works his magic in the kitchen of Cameron's Brasserie. Boasting both seasonal and diverse menus from Tuesday to Saturday, guests are certain to be satisfied.

25% OFF TOTAL | 10 | FRI × | SAT × | SUN | ▲ — European

THE CHARTER
01296 336 855

2 Rimmington Way, Aylesbury, HP19 8AW

Quality pub classics with modern twists meets with a friendly and relaxed atmosphere to make this Table Table venue the perfect place for any occasion. *Excludes daytime & evening deals and festive menus.

2FOR1 MAIN COURSE | FRI ✓ | SAT ✓ — Modern British

THE CORIANDER AMERSHAM
☎ 01494 726 370

Metro Court, Station Approach, Amersham, HP6 5AZ

Catering for both the curry lover and the novice, the chefs at this Indian and Bangladeshi eatery are devoted to pleasing diners no matter their palate. The tandoori sea bass comes highly appraised.

2FOR1 MAIN COURSE | FRI × | SAT × | ▲ — Indian

THE CORIANDER BOURNE END
☎ 01628 522 734

58-60 The Parade, Bourne End, SL8 5SS

Catering for both the curry lover and the novice, the chefs at this Indian and Bangladeshi eatery are devoted to pleasing diners no matter their palate. The tandoori sea bass comes highly appraised.

2FOR1 MAIN COURSE | FRI × | SAT × | ▲ — Indian

THE CROSS KEYS
☎ 01908 679 404

34 Newport Road, Milton Keynes, MK15 0AA

The Cross Keys offers a regularly-changing menu, with specialties ranging from classic pub-style favourites to more inspired dishes. Although food is the focus, their roots as a country ale house have not been forgotten.

2FOR1 MAIN COURSE | FRI ✓ | SAT ✓ | ▲ — British

ENIGMA TAVERN
☎ 01908 645 523

Albert Street, Milton Keynes, MK2 2EN

Priding themselves on a warm and friendly welcoming coupled with a guaranteed smile, Enigma Tavern offer an authentic tavern experience specialising in both local and traditional British dishes.

2FOR1 MAIN COURSE | FRI ✓ | SAT ✓ | ▲ — British

THE FIRECREST
01296 628 041

London Road, Wendover, Aylesbury, HP22 6QG

This Vintage Inn oozes rural charm and rustic character. The picturesque surroundings provide the perfect backdrop for savouring the hearty, seasonal pub-food on the menu.

25% OFF TOTAL | FRI ✓ | SAT ✓ | SUN | ▲ — Modern British

THE FIVE ARROWS HOTEL
☎ 01296 651 727

High Street, Waddesdon, HP18 0JE

This versatile restaurant caters for a range of occasions but maintains its thoughtful, imaginative style and technical accomplishment throughout. You'll enjoy a relaxed ambience and great range of dishes.

2FOR1 MAIN COURSE | FRI 📱 | SAT ✱ | SUN | ▲ — European

THE FIVE BELLS
01296 613 131

40 Main Street, Weston Turville, Aylesbury, HP22 5RW

This Vintage Inn oozes rural charm and rustic character. The picturesque surroundings provide the perfect backdrop for savouring the hearty, seasonal pub-food on the menu.

25% OFF TOTAL | FRI ✓ | SAT ✓ | SUN | ▲ — Modern British

THE FLYING FOX
01525 290 444

Sheep Lane, Woburn, Milton Keynes, MK17 9HD

This Vintage Inn oozes rural charm and rustic character. The picturesque surroundings provide the perfect backdrop for savouring the hearty, seasonal pub-food on the menu.

25% OFF TOTAL | FRI ✓ | SAT ✓ | SUN | ▲ — Modern British

THE FOUNDRY ARMS
☎ 01908 377 621

32 Victoria Road, Fenny Stratford, MK2 2NQ

A true community pub in Fenny Stratford, The Foundry Arms combines great pub grub with excellent beers and live entertainment. Delicious food, entertainment and the warmest of welcomes await you here.

2FOR1 3 COURSES | FRI ✓ | SAT ✓ — British

FOUR PILLARS TANDOORI
☎ 01234 714 083

60 High Street, Olney, MK46 4BE

Flavoured with the finest herbs and spices, dishes on offer here are carefully prepared with fresh produce, and are influenced and adapted from all over the vast Indian subcontinent.

2FOR1 MAIN COURSE | FRI ✱ | SAT ✱ | ✱ — Indian

FRANCESCO'S MARLOW
01628 473 532

13 Spittal Street, Marlow, SL7 3HJ

In a restaurant where even the pizza dough is made at least twice a day, it's no surprise that the food is amazing. Enjoy delicious dishes in a style in keeping with the Italian way of life.

2FOR1 MAIN COURSE | FRI ✓ | SAT ✓ | ▲ — Italian

FUSIONS RESTAURANT
☎ 01494 430 378

145 West Wycombe Road, High Wycombe, HP12 3AB

Imaginative, lively combinations of flavours in this AA Rosette-recognised restaurant. Fine dining with a thoroughgoing attention to fresh, seasonal and high-quality produce.

25% OFF TOTAL | 10 | FRI ✓ | SAT ✓ | SUN — Fine Dining

GEORGE & DRAGON
01628 814 312

The Causeway, Marlow, SL7 2AA

Quality pub classics with modern twists meets with a friendly and relaxed atmosphere to make this Table Table venue the perfect place for any occasion. *Excludes daytime & evening deals and festive menus.

2FOR1 MAIN COURSE | FRI ✓ | SAT ✓ — Modern British

GRAYS RESTAURANT
☎ 01628 600 150

Grove Road, Burnham, SL1 8DP

Located within an original Georgian mansion, elegant surroundings are combined with contemporary cuisine. Enjoy the ambience and the mouth-watering food of a deservedly AA Rosette-awarded restaurant.

25% OFF TOTAL | 4 | FRI ✓ | SAT ✓ | ✱ | ▲ — British

HORWOOD HOUSE
☎ 01296 722 100

Little Horwood, Milton Keynes, MK17 0PH

Nestled in the countryside of Buckinghamshire, yet only 11 miles from the cosmopolitan city of Milton Keynes, Horwood House offers the best of both worlds. A seasonal menu that accommodates local produce.

25% OFF TOTAL | 6 | FRI ✓ | SAT ✓ | ▲ — British

INDIAN COTTAGE
☎ 01908 217 778

122 High Street, Newport Pagnell, MK16 8EH

If the expansive menu dazzles diners, the knowledgeable and attentive staff will advise on an enjoyable dish. From fiery contenders to creamy curries, Indian Cottage is passionate about authentic cuisine.

2FOR1 MAIN COURSE | FRI 📱 | SAT 📱 | ✱ — Indian

INDIAN NIGHTS
☎01753 651 351

75 Slough Road, Tiverton, SL0 0DW

Lamb bhujon keeps the regulars at this venue returning time after time. Prepared using secret ingredients, guests are always thrilled by this popular, authentic restaurant.

50% OFF FOOD | FRI ✓ | SAT ✓ — Indian

INDIGO
☎01753 883 100

Indigo House, Gerrards Cross, SL9 7AL

Authentic cuisine in a contemporary setting is the ethos behind Indigo. For Indian food with a twist, diners should try grilled chicken smothered in zesty chutney or a generous helping of sea bass.

2FOR1 MAIN COURSE | FRI × | SAT × | ✱ — Indian

JUNCTION RESTAURANT @ HOLIDAY INN
☎0871 942 9057

Holiday Inn, 500 Saxon Gate, Milton Keynes, MK9 2HQ

Sip on your favourite evening drink before heading to Junction Restaurant, where delicious steaks and creamy curries appear as strong contenders on the menu. Great quality food for any occasion.

25% OFF TOTAL | 6 | FRI ✓ | SAT ✓ — British

KARDAMOM LOUNGE
☎01908 567 538

34 High Street, Stony Stratford, MK11 1AF

A fantastic place to enjoy truly authentic Bangladeshi and Indian cuisine served in a welcoming environment. The menu is a diverse mix of authentic and regional dishes with a major focus on quality.

2FOR1 MAIN COURSE | FRI ✓ | SAT ✓ | ✱ — Indian

KASHMIR GARDENS
☎01296 415 644

120 High Street, Aylesbury, HP20 1RB

Well-drilled, attentive service, a low-key, subtly designed interior, and some excellent Indian cuisine including a good selection of alternative options, going a bit beyond the usual curry house fare.

2FOR1 3 COURSES | FRI ✱ | SAT ✱ — Indian

KEN'S BEIJING
☎01494 433 059

131 Station Road, Amersham, HP7 0AH

Ken's Beijing has been serving the people of Amersham with fresh, tasty Chinese and East Asian cuisine for many years, making this family-run restaurant a firm local favourite.

25% OFF TOTAL | 10 | FRI × | SAT × — Chinese

THE KING AND QUEEN
☎01296 623 272

17 South Street, Wendover, HP22 6EF

A local pub serving an extensive menu of good, hearty food. With an outdoor seating area, guests can enjoy real ales in the open air when the sun shines.

25% OFF TOTAL | 4 | FRI ✓ | SAT ✓ | ✱ | ▲ — Seafood

THE KING'S ARMS BISTRO
☎01494 723 989

30 High Street, Old Amersham, HP7 0DJ

Nestled in the heart of Amersham, The King's Arms Bistro beautifully resides in an 18th Century Tudor-style building. Choice cuts of meat from the surrounding counties make fantastic dishes.

2FOR1 MAIN COURSE | FRI ✓ | SAT ✓ — British

LA TASCA
☎01908 331 920

Xscape, Avebury Boulevard, Milton Keynes, MK9 3XS

Quintessentially Spanish, La Tasca's fresh and exciting menu offers something for everyone. Their tapas dishes are sincerely authentic, while their paellas always deliver on flavour.

25% OFF TOTAL | 8 | FRI ✓ | SAT × | ▲ — Spanish

MELA RESTAURANT
☎01296 630 110

103 London Road, Aston Clinton, HP22 5LD

Unique Indian restaurant offering delightful authentic cuisine. The staff value good service and are dedicated to ensuring all guests feel entirely at home. The Bengal fish curry is not to be missed.

2FOR1 MAIN COURSE | FRI ✱ | SAT ✱ | SUN | ✱ | ▲ — Indian

MOM'S DINER
☎01494 257 011

3-4 Queens Square, High Wycombe, HP11 2BP

A lively all-American diner offering the best grub in town. Head on down with a large appetite and the food will soon satisfy any hungry bellies. Offers scrumptious bagels, pizzas, burgers and shakes.

50% OFF FOOD | 4 | FRI | SAT — American

MUMBAI 2 SHANGHAI
☎01908 645 000

16 Buckingham Road, Milton Keynes, MK3 5HL

Mumbai 2 Shanghai draws on the influence of its name, gathering flavours and spices from the different places en route. Focuses on the lighter, healthier elements of Asian cuisine.

2FOR1 MAIN COURSE | FRI ✓ | SAT × — Indo-Chinese

NEW HORIZONS BAR AND LOUNGE @HILTON ☎01908 694 433
Hilton Milton Keynes, Timbold Dr, Milton Keynes, MK7 6HL

Colourful and contemporary with a low-key feel, this bar is ideal for relaxing with a light bite to eat and a quiet drink. A fully-stocked bar complete with tasty snacks and sandwiches awaits any guests.

50% OFF FOOD | 4 | FRI ✱ | SAT ✱ | ▲ — Bistro

NEW HORIZONS RESTAURANT @HILTON ☎01908 694 433
Hilton Milton Keynes, Timbold Dr, Milton Keynes, MK7 6HL

The New Horizon restaurant is a warm and sophisticated place to eat, with its menu largely characterised by classic British dishes together with an array of more eclectic global flavours.

2FOR1 3 COURSES | 2 | FRI ✱ | SAT ✱ | ▲ — International

PASSAGE TO INDIA ☎01908 567 610
10-11 Cotteridge Close, Stony Stratford, MK11 1BY

With a chef who has won a prestigious local award for his cooking, this restaurant consistently offers wonderfully tasty Indian cuisine. Customers will enjoy restaurant-quality takeaway food.

25% OFF TOTAL | 10 | FRI ✓ | SAT ▯ | ✱ — Indian

PEPPERS FINEST INDIAN CUISINE ☎01628 605 511
69 High Street, Burnham, SL1 7JX

Peppers provide a steadfast line in quality Indian cuisine, fine wine and beers. All food is prepared using only the freshest herbs and finest spices, with an emphasis on slow-cooked, succulent dishes.

25% OFF TOTAL | 4 | FRI ▯ | SAT ▯ | ✱ — Indian

THE POMEROY INN 01494 766 845
131 White Lion Road, Amersham, HP7 9JY

This Vintage Inn oozes rural charm and rustic character. The picturesque surroundings provide the perfect backdrop for savouring the hearty, seasonal pub-food on the menu.

25% OFF TOTAL | FRI ✓ | SAT ✓ | SUN | ▲ — Modern British

THE POTTERS ARMS ☎01494 726 222
Fagnall Lane, Winchmore Hill, HP7 0PH

The Potter's Arms is a village pub set in glorious rural Buckinghamshire. Characterful and personable, the pub boasts a delicious traditional British menu for families and friends alike.

2FOR1 3 COURSES | FRI × | SAT × | SUN | ▲ — British

RAJDHANI ☎01908 392 299
706 Midsummer Boulevard, Milton Keynes, MK9 3NT

Enjoy luxury banquet menus, deluxe buffets and chef specialities at this wonderful Indian restaurant. Ideally located in the cosmopolitan hub of Milton Keynes, this is a great place to dine.

2FOR1 MAIN COURSE | FRI ✓ | SAT ✓ | SUN | ✱ — Indian

SAFFRON SPICE ☎01908 240 600
2 Pimlico Court, Milton Keynes, MK10 9RH

This perfect blend of Indian flavours gives guests a sample of some of the best Asian dishes in town, lovingly prepared and exquisitely presented. Enjoy sumptuous food in beautifully decorated surroundings

25% OFF TOTAL | 4 | FRI ▯ | SAT ▯ | ✱ — Indian

SAM'S 01908 866 800
31 Singleton Drive, Milton Keynes, MK8 0PX

Specialises in all forms of comfort food. Tucked away in the residential area of Grange Park, offering simple, unfussy and satisfying food.

25% OFF TOTAL | 10 | FRI × | SAT × — British

SILK ROAD RESTAURANT ☎01908 200 522
151 Grafton Gate East, Milton Keynes, MK9 1AE

Smart and sophisticated restaurant in Milton Keynes that offers a fusion menu of Indian, Chinese and Thai dishes. Altogether, a place to enjoy some excellent food of eclectic origin.

2FOR1 MAIN COURSE | FRI ✓ | SAT ✓ | ▲ — Multi-Cuisine

THE SPICE COTTAGE ☎01296 625 202
57 Tring Road, Aylesbury, HP22 6NU

Veggies can feast upon vegetable biryani, whilst the carnivorous devour succulent lamb rogan josh. For the audacious diner, there is an expansive menu consisting of unparalleled curries.

25% OFF TOTAL | 10 | FRI ▯ | SAT ▯ — Indian

SPICE GRILL ☎01908 377 704
182 Queensway, Bletchley, MK2 2SW

Laid-back Indian restaurant with discreet service that's nonetheless right on hand and very well drilled. More than just the Indian classics, with dishes hailing from East Africa and the Middle East.

2FOR1 MAIN COURSE | FRI × | SAT × | SUN — Indian

STRADA 01908 238 900
500 The Hub, Milton Keynes, MK9 2BE

Offering fresh, bold dishes inspired by flavours of Italian city life – Strada serves a selection of indulgent tastes, to those seeking a blissful escape to laidback Italian life. *Excludes Pizzettas.

25% OFF TOTAL | 6 | FRI ✓ | SAT × | ▲ — Italian

THE SWAN AT IVER ☎01753 655 776
2 High Street, Iver, SL0 9NG

Fine dining in the à la carte restaurant offers the very best of English and Italian dishes. This welcoming pub also serves delightful food.

2FOR1 2 COURSES | FRI ▯ | SAT ▯ | ▲ — Italian

THE THAI LOUNGE ☎01753 648 764
7 Ashley House, Farnham Common, SL2 3PQ

Wonderful Thai restaurant that prides itself on the quality of food and service provided to each diner. Expect contemporary design with a genuine warm and welcoming atmosphere.

2FOR1 MAIN COURSE | 10 | FRI ✓ | SAT ✓ — Thai

THAI THAI RESTAURANT ☎01628 523 331
Heart in Hand, Cores End Road, Bourne End, SL8 5HH

Vividly contemporary but thoroughly authentic Thai cuisine; Thai Thai's kitchen shows great skill at drawing out the eclectic, vibrant flavours and colours in these beautifully presented dishes.

50% OFF FOOD | 10 | FRI ✱ | SAT ✱ — Thai

THE TREE AT CADMORE END ☎01494 881 183
Marlow Road, Stokenchurch, High Wycombe, HP14 3PF

This gastro-pub takes pride in its exquisite quality of food and the charming ambience it exudes. Placing emphasis on comfort, the interior décor is captivating and ensures a winning experience.

2FOR1 MAIN COURSE | FRI ✱ | SAT ✱ — International

THE TWO BREWERS ☎01234 711 393
34 High Street, Olney, MK46 4BB

Homely and welcoming village pub that serves a great array of tasty, wholesome traditional fare - all with a focus on fresh and locally sourced produce.

2FOR1 MAIN COURSE | FRI ✓ | SAT ✓ | SUN | ▲ — British

THE VILLAGE HALL ☎01753 887 596
Gold Hill West, Chalfont St Peter, SL9 9HH
Award-winning family pub set on the corner of the idyllic Gold Hill Common, famous for its grill menu, ales and wines, live music and sport, while also offering excellent private functions.

2FOR1 3 COURSES | FRI ✓ | SAT ✱ | SUN — British

THE WHITE HART 01494 671 211
Aylesbury End, Beaconsfield, HP9 1LW
Enjoy a spot by the roaring log-fire, or make the best of the British summertime by eating alfresco in the pretty beer garden.

25% OFF TOTAL | FRI ✓ | SAT ✓ | SUN | ▲ — Modern British

THE WOBURN BRASSERIE ☎01525 290 260
13 Bedford Street, Woburn, Milton Keynes, MK17 9QB
Receive a warm welcome whether it be for a leisurely lunch, an evening meal, or simply a relaxing drink. Become accustomed with the diverse choice of local, fresh produce used to craft each delicious dish.

25% OFF TOTAL | 2 | FRI ▮ | SAT ▮ | SUN | ▲ — British

THE WOBURN FORT ☎01908 282 002
33 High Street, Woburn Sands, MK17 8RB
Unafraid to try out new and exciting ventures when it comes to food, guests enjoy the innovative ways in which the chefs often use fruit to enhance the flavours of their dishes. A fabulous place to dine.

2FOR1 MAIN COURSE | FRI ✱ | SAT ✱ | SUN | ✱ | ▲ — Indian

ZINGA ☎01908 522 524
20 Redgrove Drive, Oxley Park, Milton Keynes, MK4 4JB
Zinga is a terrific Indian restaurant in Milton Keynes, popular for its amiable staff and exquisite curry dishes. Soft, tender chicken tandoori to a juicy, melt-in-the-mouth lamb rogan josh.

2FOR1 MAIN COURSE | FRI ✓ | SAT ▮ — Indian

Hampshire/Isle of Wight

ANTICO ☎02380 333 260
13-14 Terminus Terrace, Southampton, SO14 3DT
Located closely to the popular Oxford Street, Antico is beautifully decorated and offers a delicious menu. While steak is the speciality, the large menu accommodates every appetite.

25% OFF TOTAL | 6 | FRI × | SAT × | ▲ — Steakhouse

APPLEGARTH FARM ☎01428 712 777
Headley Road, Grayshott, GU26 6JL
The British menu is given a thrilling Mediterranean twist at this stunning eatery. Kick start the weekend with a crisp glass of wine from the sophisticated wine list.

2FOR1 MAIN COURSE | FRI ✓ | SAT ✓ — British

AVIATOR BRASSERIE ☎01252 555 895
55 Farnborough Road, Farnborough, GU14 6EL
Exuding intimacy, the two private dining rooms are perfect for the sophisticated clientele. Exquisite decor and French wine make an ideal setting in which customers can feast on the 5 course tasting menu.

25% OFF TOTAL | 6 | FRI ▮ | SAT ▮ | ▲ — European

BADI MIRCHI ☎02380 612 174
190 Leigh Road, Eastleigh, SO50 9DX
The chefs at Badi Mirchi bring their experience to the kitchen pot, using their many years in first-class Indian restaurants to create sensational dishes. The flavours represent India's culinary diversity.

2FOR1 MAIN COURSE | FRI × | SAT × — Indian

THE BALMORAL 02380 732 262
Romsey Road, Nursling, Southampton, SO16 0XJ
Beefeater Grill are one of the UK's best-loved restaurants welcoming guests for almost 40 years in over 130 locations nationwide. *Excludes Breakfast, Light Bites, Bar menu, set menus and all other offers.

2FOR1 MAIN COURSE | 6 | FRI ✓ | SAT × | ▲ — Modern British

BANKS BAR BISTRO ☎01489 896 352
The Old Granary, Bank St, Bishops Waltham, O32 1AE
Michelin-star trained chefs bring to the kitchen their extensive experience to create exquisite dishes for lunch and evening meals. The menu focuses on modern British dishes with a continental twist.

25% OFF TOTAL | 10 | FRI ▮ | SAT ▮ | SUN | ▲ — British

BARTONS MILL ☎01256 331 153
Bartons Lane, Old Basing, Basingstoke, RG24 8AE
A country pub haven set within a conservation area near to the historical Basing house ruins. Enjoy delicious home-made food and Wadworth ales by the calming waters of the River Loddon.

25% OFF TOTAL | 4 | FRI × | SAT × | SUN — British

BASMATI INDIAN RESTAURANT ☎01489 575 556
10a Centre Way, Locks Heath, SO31 6DX
The combination of fine, fresh ingredients with traditional herbs and spices is the secret to these flavoursome recipes. This award-winning establishment offers a wide variety of dishes for you to enjoy.

2FOR1 MAIN COURSE | FRI ▮ | SAT ▮ | ✱ — Indian

THE BELL INN ☎02380 812 214
Brook, New Forest, Nr Lyndhurst, SO43 7HE
A firm favourite with the locals, this AA Rosette awarded restaurant menus are prepared with seasonal choices from the New Forest and the country estate to which it belongs.

25% OFF TOTAL | 6 | FRI × | SAT × | ▲ — English/Gastro pub

BELLA ITALIA 02380 227 664
107 Above Bar, Southampton, SO14 7FH
Accessible Italian cuisine on the British high street – indulge in authentic sharing platters, hand stretched pizzas and hearty pasta dishes, served with a healthy dose of gregarious Italian hospitality.

25% OFF TOTAL | 6 | FRI × | SAT × | SUN | ▲ — Italian

BELLA ITALIA 02380 339 215
19 Hanover Buildings, Southampton, SO14 1JX
Accessible Italian cuisine on the British high street – indulge in authentic sharing platters, hand stretched pizzas and hearty pasta dishes, served with a healthy dose of gregarious Italian hospitality.

25% OFF TOTAL | 6 | FRI × | SAT × | SUN | ▲ — Italian

BENGAL BRASSERIE ☎02380 230 988
7 Bedford Place, Southampton, SO15 2DB
A great local restaurant serving terrific Indian cuisine. Friendly staff are happy to cater to your every need.

2FOR1 MAIN COURSE | FRI ▮ | SAT ▮ | ✱ — Indian

BENGAL SAGE ☎01962 862 173
72-74 St George's Street, Winchester, SO23 8AH
Restaurateur Miff Kayum, once semi-finalist on Gordon Ramsay's F-Word Restaurant of the Year, is proud to bring his cooking to Winchester. Subtle textures and complex flavours characterise the curries.

2FOR1 MAIN COURSE | FRI × | SAT × | ✱ | ▲ — Indian

BERESFORD'S ☎01590 623 116
Balmer Lawn Hotel, Lyndhurst Rd, Brockenhurst, SO42 7ZB
An AA Rosette-winning restaurant for fine dining, Beresford's menu is updated daily using fresh local produce wherever possible. The wine list offers a great range of fine wines catering for all tastes.

25% OFF TOTAL | 6 | FRI × | SAT × | SUN — British

BLISS @THE BLUE BELL ☎01730 893 104
Farnham Road, Liss, GU33 6JU
Bliss @ The Blue Bell has a warm and welcoming atmosphere with an extensive a la carte menu to satisfy your hunger. Whatever the occasion, the team at Bliss look forward to welcoming you soon.

50% OFF FOOD | 4 | FRI × | SAT × | SUN | ✱ — British

BRITANNIA THAI ☎01590 642 226
1 High Street, Milford on Sea, Lymington, SO41 0QF
A most exquisite dining experience for any guest as expert chefs immaculately execute and present a wide selection of authentic dishes in a stylish venue, offering fantastic value for money.

2FOR1 MAIN COURSE | 4 | FRI ✓ | SAT × | ✱ — Thai

THE BUGLE HOTEL
☎01329 841 888
High Street, Fareham, PO14 4AF
Head to The Bugle Hotel to experience the delightful food they have on offer. From a leisurely breakfast, to a special celebration, The Bugle offers a delicious selection of food for all occasions.

2FOR1 3 COURSES | FRI | SAT | British

BUON GUSTO
☎02380 331 543
1 Commercial Road, Southampton, SO15 1GF
This classic, authentic Italian restaurant serves hearty, wholesome and traditional dishes in a superb location, whether as part of your night at the theatre, or simply for an intimate meal.

25% OFF TOTAL | 4 | FRI ✓ | SAT ✱ | SUN | ✱ | Italian

THE BUSH INN
☎01962 732 764
Ovington, Alresford, SO24 0RE
Ensconced in beautiful Hampshire countryside, this pub restaurant is an inviting place for that languid drink or dinner. The menu is fresh and accomplished, serving thoroughly tasty gastro-pub fare.

25% OFF TOTAL | 4 | FRI × | SAT × | SUN | British

CAFÉ ROUGE
01256 334 556
20a Winchester Street, Basingstoke, RG21 7DZ
French sophistication on the British high street – enjoy seasonally changing French dishes and a continental wine selection, served in a relaxed environment with an undeniable flair of Parisian chic.

25% OFF TOTAL | 6 | FRI ✓ | SAT ✓ | ✱ | French

CAFÉ ROUGE
02392 754 849
Gunwharf Quays, Portsmouth, PO1 3FA
French sophistication on the British high street – enjoy seasonally changing French dishes and a continental wine selection, served in a relaxed environment with an undeniable flair of Parisian chic.

25% OFF TOTAL | 6 | FRI ✓ | SAT ✓ | ✱ | French

CAFÉ ROUGE
02380 331 152
Food Terrace, Westquay, Southampton SO15 1QF
French sophistication on the British high street – enjoy seasonally changing French dishes and a continental wine selection, served in a relaxed environment with an undeniable flair of Parisian chic.

25% OFF TOTAL | 6 | FRI ✓ | SAT ✓ | ✱ | French

CANTINA
☎02380 220 500
2a-3a Bedford Place, Southampton, SO15 2BY
Whether it's a light bite with friends or a hearty Mexican banquet, this venue promises to spoil diners for choice with its diverse menu. Reasonably priced, the cuisine is fresh and bursting with flavour.

25% OFF TOTAL | 6 | FRI × | SAT × | Mexican

THE CHILLIES
☎01264 339 211
10-12 Winchester Street, Andover, SP10 2EA
Infusing traditional Indian curry dishes with contemporary sophistication. The Himalayan chicken curry is a popular choice with diners who love their Indian food hot and fiery.

25% OFF TOTAL | 4 | FRI ✓ | SAT ✓ | Indian

CHOWDHURY'S CURRY LOUNGE
☎02380 338 833
206 Shirley Road, Southampton, SO15 3FH
A large number of loyal diners as well as new guests are accommodated at this impressive Indian restaurant. The adventurous curry fan will love the wide range of unusual, less well-known dishes.

2FOR1 MAIN COURSE | FRI | SAT | ✱ | Indian

THE CLEVELAND BAY
☎02380 269 814
1 Pilgrims close, Valley Park, Chandlers Ford, SO53 4ST
Warm yourself by the open fire during winter months or sit out in the large garden in the summertime. Whatever the weather, a superb choice of fresh, wholesome, homemade food is always available. *Excludes Xmas menus.

25% OFF TOTAL | 4 | FRI × | SAT × | SUN | British

THE CONSERVATORY BRASSERIE
☎01256 817 555
Audley Wood Hotel, Alton Road, Basingstoke, RG25 2JY
Breathtakingly situated in seven acres of extensive woodland, this traditional country estate blends the customary with the contemporary. Fresh, local ingredients are served a midst flickering candles.

25% OFF TOTAL | 6 | FRI ✓ | SAT ✱ | European

THE CONSERVATORY RESTAURANT @ HILTON
☎01256 460 460
Hilton Basingstoke, Old Common Rd, Basingstoke, RG21 3PR
The Conservatory Restaurant is a fine attribute of the Hilton Basingstoke. With views out onto the hotel grounds, the restaurant is light and airy and provides a perfect backdrop to a relaxed evening.

50% OFF FOOD | 10 | FRI ✓ | SAT ✓ | European

THE COWHERDS
02380 558 405
The Common, Southampton, SO15 7NN
This Vintage Inn oozes rural charm and rustic character. The picturesque surroundings provide the perfect backdrop for savouring the hearty, seasonal pub-food on the menu.

25% OFF TOTAL | FRI ✓ | SAT ✓ | SUN | Modern British

CROOKHORN INDIAN TAKEAWAY
☎02392 240 066
1 Purbrook Way, Waterlooville, PO7 5QH
Crookhorn Indian has a gentle touch when it comes to curries, with a holistic menu that has a bit of fire and spice where it's needed but does the subtler, more flavourful dishes with skill. Popular local.

2FOR1 MAIN COURSE | FRI × | SAT × | SUN | Indian

CURRYLICIOUS TAKEAWAY
01252 544 222
1 Salisbury Road, Farnborough, GU14 7AN
Back to basics at this curry house in Farnborough. Menu full of rich and flavourful dishes, among which the shahi lamb korma and the sizzling lahsuni chicken tikka (with a garlic-laden marinade) stand out.

2FOR1 MAIN COURSE | FRI ✓ | SAT ✓ | Indian

DE HAVILLAND ARMS
☎01252 628 102
The Key, Elvetham Health, Fleet, GU51 1HA
Hall & Woodhouse owned, the De Havilland Arms is ideally situated in the heart of Elvetham Heath and offers a friendly environment perfect for all. Local ingredients make up the traditional English dishes.

25% OFF TOTAL | FRI × | SAT × | SUN | British

DHAKA INDIAN CUISINE
☎02380 336 662
11 Onslow Road, Southampton, SO14 0JD
Sometimes there is nothing better than a simple curry, created and served by passionate staff in a welcoming environment.

2FOR1 MAIN COURSE | FRI ✓ | SAT ✓ | ✱ | Bangladeshi/Indian

DILJAS
☎02380 584 674
104 Portswood Road, Southampton, SO17 2FW
Often described as a hidden gem, Diljas Indian Restaurant treats guests to authentic Punjabi cuisine served with warmth and care.

2FOR1 MAIN COURSE | FRI ✓ | SAT ✓ | ✱ | Indian

THE DUKE OF YORK
☎01252 321 150
248 Weybourne Road, Aldershot, GU11 3NF
Much loved by the residents of Aldershot, this pub-restaurant boasts an exciting menu composed of a variety of international cuisines. The Thai green curry is a must-try.

2FOR1 MAIN COURSE | FRI × | SAT × | British

EMPRESS OF BLANDINGS
☎02380 812 321
Romsey Road, Copythorne, Southampton, SO40 2PF
Hall & Woodhouse, a family owned brewer, focus on locally sourced cuisine at pocket-friendly prices in a welcoming environment. This friendly New Forest pub is named after PG Wodehouse's legendary pig.

25% OFF TOTAL | FRI × | SAT × | SUN | British

EVEREST SPICE
☎02392 654 940
180 Kingston Road, Portsmouth, PO2 7LP
A wonderful restaurant in the heart of the beautiful Portsmouth, where quality of produce and ingredients are the key focus. Enjoy Indian and Nepalese cuisine in a comfortable and relaxing environment.

2FOR1 3 COURSES | FRI ✓ | SAT ✓ | Nepalese

FARRINGFORD GARDEN RESTAURANT
☎01983 752 700
Farringford, Bedbury Lane, Freshwater Bay, PO40 9PE
A warm, contemporary venue serving elegant and supremely accomplished modern British cuisine. Beautifully cooked and thoughtfully presented, it is a very distinctive and deeply satisfying place to dine.

2FOR1 MAIN COURSE | FRI ✓ | SAT ✓ | SUN | Modern British

THE FISHER'S POND — 02380 692 209
Main Road, Fishers Pond, Eastleigh, SO50 7HG

This Vintage Inn oozes rural charm and rustic character. The picturesque surroundings provide the perfect backdrop for savouring the hearty, seasonal pub-food on the menu.

25% OFF TOTAL | FRI ✓ | SAT ✓ | SUN | ▲ — Modern British

THE FOX & GOOSE — ☎ 01256 702 062
The Street, Greywell, Hook, RG29 1BY

Family run pub set in the heart of the tranquil village of Greywell. This superb example of a 16th Century inn offer traditional English fare with the emphasis very much on home-made dishes.

50% OFF FOOD | 6 | FRI ✱ | SAT × | SUN — British

THE GATEWAY — 02380 650 541
Leigh Road, Eastleigh, Southampton, SO50 9YX

Quality pub classics with modern twists meets with a friendly and relaxed atmosphere to make this Table Table venue the perfect place for any occasion. *Excludes daytime & evening deals and festive menus.

2FOR1 MAIN COURSE | FRI ✓ | SAT ✓ — Modern British

THE GEORGE — ☎ 01730 233 343
28 The Square, Petersfield, GU32 3HH

Imaginative chefs prepare an innovative menu of hearty pies and meaty burgers with contemporary twists. *Advance booking mentioning Gourmet Society is essential.

2FOR1 MAIN COURSE | FRI × | SAT ▯ | ✱ | ▲ — British

THE GEORGE & FALCON — ☎ 01730 829 623
Warnford Road, Warnford, Southampton, SO32 3LB

Rural inn with a cosy snug area, two separate dining rooms and a continental-style decking area overlooking the River Meon. Serves a range of freshly cooked, high-quality food from a seasonal menu.

25% OFF TOTAL | 10 | FRI ✓ | SAT ✓ | ✱ | ▲ — Modern British

GOURMET PIZZA — 01962 842 553
21 The Square, Winchester, SO23 9EX

Nestled among local boutiques, this family-friendly venue offers a hearty and creative menu filled with heavenly pizzas and other classic options, served in a rustic dining room to an unpretentious crowd.

2FOR1 MAIN COURSE | FRI ✓ | SAT ✱ — Pizza

THE GRAPEVINE BISTRO — ☎ 01256 701 122
121 High Street, Odiham, RG29 1LA

Long-established by Andrew and Katie, the menu at this idyllically situated bistro is subject to seasonal change, ensuring freshness and plenty of room for innovation. The fresh fish is highly appraised.

50% OFF FOOD | 4 | FRI × | SAT × — British

THE GREAT MOGHUL — ☎ 02380 612 018
1 High Street, Eastleigh, SO50 5LB

Eastleigh's longest established Tandoori Restaurant - The Great Mogul has been serving delicious Indian cuisine since 1990. A local favourite that's not to be missed.

2FOR1 2 COURSES | 10 | FRI × | SAT × | ✱ | ▲ — Indian

GREAT OAK — 01730 230 480
Buckmore Farm, Winchester Road, Petersfield, GU32 3BS

Quality pub classics with modern twists meets with a friendly and relaxed atmosphere to make this Table Table venue the perfect place for any occasion. *Excludes daytime & evening deals and festive menus.

2FOR1 MAIN COURSE | FRI ✓ | SAT ✓ — Modern British

THE GREYFRIAR — ☎ 0142 083 841
Winchester Road, Chawton, GU34 1SB

A superb public house directly opposite the original home of Jane Austen. Classic wood beams and warmth in this beautiful Hampshire village; it serves some exceptionally tasty home-made food.

2FOR1 2 COURSES | FRI × | SAT × | SUN | ✱ — European

GURKHA CHAUTARI — ☎ 01428 729 355
18 Station Road, Liphook, GU30 7DR

Take shelter on the trails of Nepal and sample the culinary delights on offer. An authentic atmosphere serving the finest, most delicious Nepalese cuisine.

2FOR1 MAIN COURSE | FRI ☎ | SAT ✱ — Nepalese

GUSTO RESTAURANT — ☎ 01730 892 411
41 Station Road, Liss, GU33 7DP

Co-owners Daniele and Jonathan understand the importance of family eateries and endeavour to make Gusto a rounded venue. Daniele hand-stretches the dough to make authentic pizzas and specialty dishes.

2FOR1 MAIN COURSE | FRI ✓ | SAT ✓ | ▲ — Italian

HARBOUR LIGHTS — 02392 321 122
1 Southampton Road, Cosham, Portsmouth, PO6 4SA

Beefeater Grill are one of the UK's best-loved restaurants welcoming guests for almost 40 years in over 130 locations nationwide. *Excludes Breakfast, Light Bites, Bar menu, set menus and all other offers.

2FOR1 MAIN COURSE | 6 | FRI ✓ | SAT × | ▲ — Modern British

HEATH HOTEL — 02380 842 275
Beaulieu Road, Dibden Purlieu, Southampton, SO45 5PW

Quality pub classics with modern twists meets with a friendly and relaxed atmosphere to make this Table Table venue the perfect place for any occasion. *Excludes daytime & evening deals and festive menus.

2FOR1 MAIN COURSE | FRI ✓ | SAT ✓ — Modern British

THE HIGH CORNER INN — ☎ 01425 473 973
Linwood, Ringwood, BH24 3QY

This beautiful country inn is ensconced in the New Forest and serves as a calming, welcoming retreat. A great place to take a room and explore the local area, it also serves fabulous, classic British fare.

25% OFF TOTAL | 4 | FRI × | SAT × | SUN — British

HOBBITS RESTAURANT BAR — ☎ 02380 848 524
6b High Street, Hythe, Southampton, SO45 6AH

A totally unique venue that delivers simple, fresh food every single day of the week. A great atmosphere is coupled with friendly staff who endeavour to ensure every guest is relaxed and content.

25% OFF TOTAL | 4 | FRI ✱ | SAT ✱ | ▲ — European

HOTEL DU VIN — ☎ 01962 841 414
Southgate Street, Winchester, SO23 9EF

The finest, fresh local produce, simple European recipes, and stunning choice of wines; the trademark Hotel du Vin bistro. The original Hotel Du Vin wrought in Georgian splendour. Winner of 2 AA rosettes.

2FOR1 MAIN COURSE | FRI × | SAT × | SUN | ▲ — European

HOUSE MARTIN — ☎ 01425 618 521
Christchurch Road, New Milton, BH25 6QF

Hall & Woodhouse owned, this contemporary pub-restaurant is only moments away from the sea front at Barton-on-Sea. Welcoming to all, this venue serves local food and traditional English dishes.

25% OFF TOTAL | FRI × | SAT × | SUN | ▲ — British

HUMBLE PLUMB — ☎ 02380 437 577
Commercial Street, Bitterne, Southampton, SO18 6LY

With open fires during the winter months and superb floral displays in the summer months you are guaranteed the warmest of welcomes in the friendliest of surroundings - no matter what the weather. *Excludes Xmas menus.

25% OFF TOTAL | 4 | FRI × | SAT × | SUN — British

THE HUT — 02380 266 626
Bournemouth Road, Chandlers Ford, Eastleigh, SO5 3DJ

Beefeater Grill are one of the UK's best-loved restaurants welcoming guests for almost 40 years in over 130 locations nationwide. *Excludes Breakfast, Light Bites, Bar menu, set menus and all other offers.

2FOR1 MAIN COURSE | 6 | FRI ✓ | SAT × | ▲ — Modern British

ISTANBUL RESTAURANT — ☎ 02392 753 490
40 Osborne Road, Portsmouth, PO5 3LT

The Istanbul Restaurant is a jewel of restaurant in Southsea's town centre. This fully licensed restaurant offers a relaxing and quaint dining experience, serving fine quality Turkish and Kurdish cuisine.

25% OFF TOTAL | 8 | FRI ✓ | SAT ✓ — Mediterranean

JASPER'S RESTAURANT — ☎ 02392 463 226
54 Station Road, Hayling Island, PO11 0EL

Flair and imagination ignite the many dishes on offer in this fabulous restaurant. With a bar, À la carte and Sunday lunch menus, it is no surprise that this venue has a strong, loyal following.

25% OFF TOTAL | 4 | FRI ✓ | SAT ✱ | SUN | ✱ — British

JEKYLL & HYDE
☎01256 882 442
Hartley Wespall, Liphook, RG27 0AX
A family owned brewer, Hall & Woodhouse devote themselves to locally sourced food at affordable prices in an affable atmosphere. Situated next to the beautiful Duke of Wellington's estate.

25% OFF TOTAL | FRI × | SAT × | SUN | ▲ — British

JKS WINEBAR
☎02381 220 485
3 High Street, Eastleigh, SO50 5LB
JKS Wine Bar is Eastleigh's newest wine bar and prides itself on offering an impressive selection of high quality food and drinks at affordable prices and is inviting, comfortable and friendly.

50% OFF FOOD | 👤10 | FRI ✓ | SAT ✓ | SUN — British

JOLLY SAILOR
☎02380 405 557
Lands End Road, Southampton, SO31 8DN
Overlooking the Hamble Estuary and situated on the water, the Jolly Sailor is an exceptional pub-restaurant. Hall & Woodhouse owned, the cuisine is traditionally British and locally sourced.

25% OFF TOTAL | FRI × | SAT × | SUN | ▲ — British

THE JOSHUA TREE
☎02380 211 889
70 Millbank Street, Southampton, SO14 5QN
A tranquil live music venue that delivers simple, home-cooked classics, including vegetarian options. A great place to unwind throughout the whole day, with a vast selection of beverages available.

50% OFF FOOD | 👤6 | FRI 📱 | SAT 📱 — British

JSW
☎01730 262 030
20 Dragon Street, Petersfield, GU31 4JJ
A Michelin-starred, 3 AA Rosette restaurant offering exceptional seasonal British dishes that are crafted with passion, using the finest produce, to reach the highest culinary standards. Short for Jake Saul Watkins, its proprietor, this venue is a highly stylish and provides the perfect backdrop for modern eating and drinking.

*Please note that in this instance the 2-for-1 offer is on a notional main course, meaning that a £25 discount on the bill will be applied when 2 people dine using 1 Gourmet Society card. This offer is available from either the tasting menus or the à la carte menu.

2FOR1 MAIN COURSE | FRI ✱ | SAT ✱ | SUN | ▲ — British

JUNCTION RESTAURANT @ HOLIDAY INN
☎08719 429 029
Holiday Inn Lynchford Road, Farnborough, GU14 6AZ
This Farnborough hotel is located close to the town centre and provides a fantastic place to rest and eat. The restaurant offers a balanced menu serving contemporary British dishes and New World Wines.

50% OFF FOOD | 👤4 | FRI 📱 | SAT 📱 | ✱ | ▲ — British

KISMET
01252 861 151
66b Reading Road, Yately, GU46 7UH
A great little tandoori restaurant that shows good attention to detail and serves an excellent range of simple, effective tandoori dishes, as well as a select range of house specials.

2FOR1 MAIN COURSE | FRI × | SAT × | SUN — Indian

LA MARGHERITA
☎02380 333 390
1 Town Quay, Southampton, SO14 2AQ
Combining terrific Italian cuisine with superb entertainment, this wonderfully popular restaurant offers great service and wonderful hospitality. A perfect venue to dine, drink and dance the night away.

2FOR1 MAIN COURSE | FRI ✓ | SAT 📱 | ▲ — Italian

LA ORIENT
☎01329 234 682
138 West Street, Fareham, PO16 0EL
Offers a menu bursting with the finest Eastern dishes. Staff are incredibly helpful and are committed to ensuring every guest has a happy dining experience that exceeds satisfaction.

2FOR1 MAIN COURSE | FRI ✱ | SAT ✱ | ✱ — Chinese

LA TASCA
☎02392 864 444
Gun Wharf Quays, Portsmouth, PO1 3TA
Quintessentially Spanish, La Tasca's fresh and exciting menu offers something for everyone. Their tapas dishes are sincerely authentic, while their paellas always deliver on flavour.

25% OFF TOTAL | 👤8 | FRI ✓ | SAT × | ▲ — Spanish

LA TASCA
☎01256 477 949
Festival Square, Basingstoke, RG21 7BB
Quintessentially Spanish, La Tasca's fresh and exciting menu offers something for everyone. Their tapas dishes are sincerely authentic, while their paellas always deliver on flavour.

25% OFF TOTAL | 👤8 | FRI ✓ | SAT × | ▲ — Spanish

LA TAVERNETTA
☎02380 635 185
1-3 Civic Centre Road, Southampton, SO14 7FJ
Contemporary Italian cuisine served in a calm, relaxing environment. From vibrant, bursting to the brim pizzas to creamy tagliatelle dishes, La Tavernetta offers something for all diners.

2FOR1 MAIN COURSE | FRI ✓ | SAT ✓ | ▲ — Italian

LANES OF LYMINGTON
☎01590 672 777
Ashley Lane, Lymington, SO41 3RH
Discover this charming haven of a restaurant, located inside an architecturally stunning 19th-century building. A simply elegant interior offers guests a calm and serene environment to enjoy.

25% OFF TOTAL | 👤6 | FRI ✓ | SAT × — British

THE LECONFIELD
☎01983 852 196
85 Leeson Road, Ventnor, PO38 1PU
Breathtaking panoramic views of the sea can be enjoyed from the comfort of the restaurant at Leconfield Hotel. Serenely peaceful in atmosphere, the dining room is a fantastic place to spend an evening.

25% OFF TOTAL | 👤4 | FRI ✓ | SAT ✓ — Fine Dining

LEMONGRASS THAI RESTAURANT
☎01425 478 254
17 Market Place, Ringwood, BH24 1AN
Welcome to Lemongrass Thai Restaurant and Lounge Bar in Hampshire, on the edge of the stunning New Forest. Exceptional service and Thai culinary delights created by highly skilled Thai chefs.

25% OFF TOTAL | 👤4 | FRI 📱 | SAT 📱 — Thai

LOCH FYNE
☎01962 872 930
18 Jewry Street, Winchester, SO23 8RZ
From the roadside oyster bar that once was, Loch Fyne restaurants now successfully inject energy and passion into great food and wonderful flavours, whilst ensuring their seafood is sustainably sourced.

25% OFF TOTAL | 👤4 | FRI ✱ | SAT ✱ | ▲ — Seafood

LOCH FYNE
☎02392 778 060
Gunwharf Quays, Portsmouth, PO1 3BF
From the roadside oyster bar that once was, Loch Fyne restaurants now successfully inject energy and passion into great food and wonderful flavours, whilst ensuring their seafood is sustainably sourced.

25% OFF TOTAL | 👤4 | FRI ✱ | SAT ✱ | ▲ — Seafood

THE LONGBRIDGE MILL
01256 883 483
Hook, Sherfield on Lodden, Hook, RG27 0DL
This Vintage Inn oozes rural charm and rustic character. The picturesque surroundings provide the perfect backdrop for savouring the hearty, seasonal pub-food on the menu.

25% OFF TOTAL | FRI ✓ | SAT ✓ | SUN | ▲ — Modern British

THE LOUNGE @ HILTON
☎01256 460 460
Hilton Basingstoke, Old Common Rd, Basingstoke, RG21 3PR
This newly developed Sport Media Bar hosts a modern, contemporary décor comprising of stylish furniture and a great atmosphere and is perfect to enjoy a drink with business colleagues or friends.

50% OFF FOOD | 👤10 | FRI ✓ | SAT ✓ — European

LUPA ITALIAN RESTAURANT
☎02380 331 849
123-124 High Street, Southampton, SO14 2AA
With a lively and contemporary continental ambience, Lupa serves classical, richly flavoured Italian dishes, including a broad and inviting array of pizzas.

25% OFF TOTAL | 👤6 | FRI × | SAT × | ▲ — Italian

MANZIL TANDOORI
☎02380 227 423
54 Onslow Road, Southampton, SO14 0JN
A treasured curry house that is extremely popular with the local community. Reasonably priced Indian cuisine is available until late, making it the perfect place to dine either before or after a night out.

2FOR1 MAIN COURSE | FRI ✱ | SAT ✱ | ✱ | ▲ — Indian

MARCO PIERRE WHITE
☎ 01252 873 275

Handford Lane, Yateley, GU46 6BT

Prestigious and sophisticated, Marco Pierre White's chain of restaurants ooze culinary excellence. Combining French and British classics, the menu is locally sourced and appeases all palates and pockets.

25% OFF TOTAL | 6 | FRI 📱 | SAT 📱 | SUN — Classic British/ French

MARWELL HOTEL
☎ 08433 575 502

Thompsons Lane, Winchester, SO21 1JY

Feast your eyes upon the elegantly presented dishes, guaranteed to taste as good as they look. Ravenous appetites appeased, guests can take an unhurried stroll through the surrounding woodlands.

2FOR1 MAIN COURSE | FRI ✓ | SAT × | SUN | ▲ — International

MAYFLOWER
☎ 01256 328 989

1 May Place, Basingstoke, RG21 7NX

This accommodating restaurant, perfectly sited in Basingstoke, provides a broad-based menu of dishes from the different regions and culinary traditions in China; fragrant, seasoned and delicious Chinese.

2FOR1 MAIN COURSE | FRI ✱ | SAT ✱ | SUN | ✱ | ▲ — Chinese

THE MEAD END
☎ 02392 264 593

22 Mead End Road, Waterlooville, PO7 6PZ

Local pub-restaurant serving a traditional menu of hearty dishes, perfectly complemented by a selection of real ales and a well-stocked line of beers, wines and spirits.

25% OFF TOTAL | 6 | FRI ✓ | SAT ✓ | SUN | ✱ — British

MELA INDIAN RESTAURANT
☎ 02392 427 772

40 Drift Road, Waterlooville, Portsmouth, PO7 6UP

Taking you on a culinary journey through the culture and tradition of the Indian subcontinent, the chefs at Mela are proud to produce truly authentic cuisine made from age-old recipes.

2FOR1 3 COURSES | FRI 📱 | SAT 📱 | ✱ — Indian

MONSOON THALI HOUSE
☎ 02392 826 343

54 Albert Road, Southsea, PO5 2SJ

Boasting a full house nearly every time, Monsoon Thali regards quality as the key to their ethos. With a fantastic choice of scrumptious and mouth-watering dishes, the menu is sure to entice.

2FOR1 3 COURSES | FRI ✓ | SAT ✓ — Indian

MORN HILL BRASSERIE
☎ 01962 670 700

Holiday Inn, Telegraph Way, Winchester, SO21 1HZ

Al fresco dining on the terrace of this award-winning venue makes Morn Hill Brasserie a very popular hot spot. Ideal for families and business lunches alike, guests are urged to try the hand-made desserts.

25% OFF TOTAL | 6 | FRI ✓ | SAT × | SUN — British

MOWCHAK TANDOORI
☎ 02392 375 007

270 Havant Road, Portsmouth, PO6 1PA

Add a touch of spice to your life with the award-winning Mowchak Tandoori restaurant which provides exquisite, stylish Indian food, modern surroundings and warm, friendly staff.

2FOR1 MAIN COURSE | FRI ✱ | SAT ✱ — Indian

MOZZARELLA JOES
02392 295 004

Clarence Esplanade, Southsea, Portsmouth, PO5 3AE

Insists upon great food and superb service in a fresh and contemporary atmosphere. Offering fabulous stone-baked pizzas and enormous gourmet burgers cooked in a lively open-plan kitchen.

25% OFF TOTAL | 10 | FRI ✓ | SAT ✓ — Italian

MR SO CHINESE RESTAURANT
☎ 01962 861 234

3 Jewry Street, Winchester, SO23 8RZ

Providing dishes from different provinces of China, this authentic restaurant maintains its popular reputation for offering meals to suit every taste. The crackling pork is superbly tasty.

25% OFF TOTAL | 4 | FRI × | SAT × | ✱ — Chinese

NAMASTE KERALA
☎ 02380 224 422

4 Civic Centre Road, Southampton, SO14 7FL

Namaste Kerala is a modest very friendly upstairs restaurant, serving vibrantly flavoured South Indian cooking using authentic South Indian recipes passed down through generations

25% OFF TOTAL | 6 | FRI × | SAT × | ▲ — Indian

NASHAA
☎ 02380 651 861

51 Leigh Road, Eastleigh, SO50 9DF

A fabulous subcontinental cuisine restaurant with a full open-view kitchen where you can see the skilled chefs at work, preparing mouth-watering traditional and modern Indian dishes.

25% OFF TOTAL | 10 | FRI ✓ | SAT ✱ | ✱ — Indian

NEW RIMJHIM PORTSOLENT
☎ 02392 370 720

22-23 Broadwalk, Portsmouth, PO6 4TP

New Rimjhim pride themselves in serving the West a true taste of India. Experience a different class of dining for yourself - the team await to deliver you a service that cannot be matched.

25% OFF TOTAL | 6 | FRI ✱ | SAT ✱ — Indian

THE NEW TAJ MAHAL RESTAURANT
☎ 02392 661 021

54 Kingston Road, North End, PO2 7PA

A welcome commingling of the opulent old with the bang up to date at the New Taj Mahal. Enjoy the breadth of their menu and the depth of their flavours with rich spice, silky sauce and piquant marinades.

2FOR1 MAIN COURSE | FRI ✓ | SAT ✓ | ✱ — Indian

NIMBU
☎ 02380 233 433

1 Oxford Street, Southampton, SO14 3DJ

At Nimbu, they endeavour to source the best possible ingredients, from local suppliers. One of their signature dishes uses Buffalo meat supplied by Broughton Water Buffalo in Stockbridge.

2FOR1 MAIN COURSE | FRI ✓ | SAT ✓ | ▲ — Indian

NINETY DEGREES
☎ 02380 234 664

24 Carlton Place, Southampton, SO15 2DY

Guests can enjoy an all-encompassing list of cocktails in one of Bedford's premier bars. Effortlessly chic and vaunting a contemporary ambience, this bar guarantees an exceptional night out.

50% OFF FOOD | 8 | FRI ✓ | SAT ✓ — British

OAST AND SQUIRE
01329 844 377

Peak Lane, The Avenue, Fareham, PO14 3AA

Beefeater Grill are one of the UK's best-loved restaurants welcoming guests for almost 40 years in over 130 locations nationwide. *Excludes Breakfast, Light Bites, Bar menu, set menus and all other offers.

2FOR1 MAIN COURSE | 6 | FRI ✓ | SAT × | ▲ — Modern British

ODDBALLS WINE BAR AND RESTAURANT
☎ 02392 755 291

12 Clarendon Road, Southsea, Portsmouth, PO5 2EE

An impressive, eclectic menu drawing on global influences, providing a refreshing variety of imaginative and creative dishes. Successfully caters for parties large or small, lively or intimate.

2FOR1 MAIN COURSE | FRI ✓ | SAT ✓ | ▲ — International

OLIVETREE
02380 343 333

29 Oxford Street, Southampton, SO14 3DJ

Locals are well acquainted with the delights of this fine Mediterranean restaurant, while newcomers rapidly become familiar with its excellence. *Excludes fixed priced menu's.

25% OFF TOTAL | 10 | FRI 📱 | SAT 📱 — French

OSBORNE VIEW
☎ 01329 664 623

Hill Head Road, Fareham, PO14 3JP

Located on the beach at Osborne view, this Hall & Woodhouse owned pub is perfect for seaside drinks. Serving only the best of the locally sourced food, diners can enjoy traditional English dishes.

25% OFF TOTAL | FRI × | SAT × | SUN | ▲ — British

PAVILLION RESTAURANT @ HILTON
☎ 02380 702 700

Hilton Southampton, Chilworth, Southampton, SO16 3RB

Indulge in a Sunday carvery at this plush venue, set in luscious landscaped gardens. For any other day of the week, the à la carte menu is delectable and can be enjoyed on a picturesque raised terrace.

50% OFF FOOD | 2 | FRI ✓ | SAT ✓ | ✱ — Bistro

POP
☎ 02380 233 323

3-4 Vernon Walk, Southampton, SO15 2EJ

Popular cocktail lounge, bijou discotheque, gourmet pizza parlour; altogether Pop is a down-to-earth, tongue-in-cheek kind of a place that serves some flavourful, stone-baked pizzas and other tasty dishes.

2FOR1 3 COURSES | FRI ✱ | SAT ✱ | ▲ — International

PREZZO

2FOR1 MAIN COURSE | FRI × | SAT × | ▲

2-FOR-1 MAIN COURSE

11 restaurants in Hampshire

16 Jewry Street, Winchester, SO23 8BB	☎ 01962 864 256
1-2 Market Square, Alton, GU34 1HD	☎ 0142 085 580
The Old Pump House, 20 High Street, Lyndhurst, SO43 7BD	☎ 02380 282 680
43 The Boardwalk, Port Solent, Portsmouth, PO6 4TP	☎ 02392 387 951
21 Palmerston Street, Romsey, SO51 8GF	☎ 01794 517 353
27 Market Place, Ringwood, BH24 1AN	☎ 01425 471 200
25 Oxford Street, Southampton, SO14 3DJ	☎ 02380 226 181
55 High Street, Lymington, SO41 9AH	☎ 01590 677 910
Unit L1A, Swan Leisure Centre, Eastleigh, SO50 5FX	☎ 02380 610 772
10 Westgate, Aldershot, GU11 1WG	☎ 01252 338 771
Whiteley Shopping Centre, Whiteley, PO15 7PD	☎ 01489 886 702

THE POPLAR FARM
01264 710 424

Old Salisbury Road, Abbotts Ann, Andover, SP11 7NJ

This Vintage Inn oozes rural charm and rustic character. The picturesque surroundings provide the perfect backdrop for savouring the hearty, seasonal pub-food on the menu.

25% OFF TOTAL | FRI ✓ | SAT ✓ | SUN | ▲ — Modern British

PORTSMOUTH ARMS
☎ 01256 334 036

Hatch Warren Lane, Basingstoke, RG22 4RA

Hall & Woodhouse, a family owned brewer, devote themselves to locally sourced food at pocket-friendly prices in a welcoming environment. Boasting a thatched roof, this pub is a picturesque haven.

25% OFF TOTAL | FRI × | SAT × | SUN | ▲ — British

PUNJAB SPICE
☎ 02380 222 218

56-58 Bevois Valley Road, Southampton, SO14 0JR

Punjab Spice is well known in the area for its fantastic Indian cuisine, that characterises the Punjab region and draws on the distinctive flavours associated with it.

25% OFF TOTAL | 10 | FRI | SAT — Indian

QUEEN'S COLLEGE ARMS
☎ 01256 850 071

Aldermaston Road, Tadley, RG26 5QR

Owned by Queen's College, Oxford, this historical venue is part of the Hall & Woodhouse family brewer. Welcoming families and colleagues alike, this restaurant serves traditional food sourced locally.

25% OFF TOTAL | FRI × | SAT × | SUN | ▲ — British

THE QUEENS HEAD
☎ 01252 613 531

Pilcot Lane, Hook, RG27 8SY

An incredible array of delicious sounding and even better tasting dishes are on offer at the Queens Head. Traditional pub furniture highlights the establishment's focus on providing wholesome experiences.

25% OFF TOTAL | 2 | FRI × | SAT × | SUN | ▲ — Bistro

RAJDHANI
☎ 02380 231 002

21 Bevois Valley Road, Southampton, SO14 0JP

Excellent food until 3am, seven days a week. Renowned for distinctive flavourings and tender meat, the menu is prepared and cooked to perfection, served by friendly staff in a contemporary atmosphere.

2FOR1 MAIN COURSE | FRI | SAT | * — Indian

RED LION
02392 593 202

2 Havant Road, Horndean, Portsmouth, PO8 0DT

Quality pub classics with modern twists meets with a friendly and relaxed atmosphere to make this Table Table venue the perfect place for any occasion. *Excludes daytime & evening deals and festive menus.

2FOR1 MAIN COURSE | FRI ✓ | SAT ✓ — Modern British

THE REGENCY ISLAND ROOM
☎ 01983 613 146

Priory Bay Hotel, Seaview, PO34 5BU

Wild sea bass, roasted venison and pan-seared pigeon breast are just some of the delights to feature on the prestigious menu. Admire 70 acres of charming landscape with a glass of carefully selected wine.

25% OFF TOTAL | 4 | FRI ✓ | SAT ✓ — Modern British

RHINEFIELD HOUSE HOTEL
☎ 0845 072 7516

Armada, Rhinefield Rd, Brockenhurst, SO42 7QB

The blend of fine dining and a special atmosphere at this Hand Picked Hotels restaurant has 2 AA rosettes testifying to its exceptional quality. Settle in for sophisticated, nuanced British recipes.

25% OFF TOTAL | 4 | FRI * | SAT * | SUN — Fine Dining

RIMJHIM COLDEN COMMON
☎ 01962 713 389

Main Road, Winchester, SO21 1RR

Describing themselves as 'food artists', the chefs carefully select the finest of natural ingredients to create effluvious and redolent curries. Vaunting elegant surroundings, Rimjhim promises excellence.

2FOR1 MAIN COURSE | FRI | SAT — Indian

RIMJHIM WINCHESTER
☎ 01962 868 352

1 City Road, Winchester, SO23 8SD

Elegantly decorated, the interior exudes a soothing and relaxing ambiance in which to savour a contemporary Indian dish. Cooking techniques closely mirror those found in an Asian domestic kitchen.

2FOR1 MAIN COURSE | FRI | SAT — Indian

ROOM FOR FOOD
☎ 02380 233 523

81 Bedford Place, Southampton, SO15 2DF

Situated in the heart of Bedford Place, flourishing with bars and restaurants at night and favoured by shoppers during the day; Room for Food can cater to your every requirement.

25% OFF TOTAL | 2 | FRI | SAT × | SUN | — International

THE RUSTY CUTTER
02392 472 619

65 Bedhampton Hill Road, Bedhampton, Havant, PO9 3JN

Beefeater Grill are one of the UK's best-loved restaurants welcoming guests for almost 40 years in over 130 locations nationwide. *Excludes Breakfast, Light Bites, Bar menu, set menus and all other offers.

2FOR1 MAIN COURSE | 6 | FRI ✓ | SAT × | — Modern British

SARA'S THAI CUISINE
☎ 02380 676 063

273 Portswood Road, Southampton, SO17 2LD

This intimate restaurant comes well recommended for its reasonable prices and glorious Thai food. Their vegetarian, stir-fried and Thai grill dishes are all scrumptiously good.

25% OFF TOTAL | 2 | FRI | SAT — Thai

SCURES BRASSERIE
☎ 01256 764 161

Basingstoke Country Hotel, Scures Hill, Liphook, RG27 9JS

Laid-back, charming restaurant in this excellent retreat of a hotel, perfectly geared for a calm, quiet bite to eat. Their ranging menu emphasises clear flavours and quality ingredients.

2FOR1 3 COURSES | FRI ✱ | SAT ✱ | — British

SEVEN FISH
☎ 01425 480 472

Southampton Road, Ringwood, BH24 1HY

Bright, fresh and full of flavour aptly describes not only the excellent seafood at this neighbourhood restaurant, but the atmosphere of the place itself. An easy place to warm to, with a broad menu.

2FOR1 MAIN COURSE | FRI | SAT — Seafood

SEVEN STARS
☎ 01730 264 122

56 Winchester Road, Petersfield, GU32 3PG

Hall & Woodhouse owned, this friendly pub restaurant near Petersfield is ideal for winding down. Perfect for the more traditional experience, this venue serves classic English dishes.

25% OFF TOTAL | FRI × | SAT × | SUN | — British

THE SHOE INN
☎ 01794 322 397

The Shoe Inn, Plaitford, SO51 6EE

Kerry and Kevin run this traditional pub where hospitality is central to their ethos. Enjoy a dazzling array of real ales and fresh, crisp wines to accompany home-cooked food.

25% OFF TOTAL | 2 | FRI × | SAT × | SUN | — British

THE SIMONDS ROOM
☎ 01256 817 555

Audleys Wood, Cliddesden, RG25 2JT

Situated in the historic Audleys Wood Hotel, this venue hosts Chef Adam Fargin who's signature dishes include Hampshire Rabbit. Picturesque and intimate, this is ideal for special occasions and business.

25% OFF TOTAL | 4 | FRI ✓ | SAT × | SUN | ✱ | — British

SPRUCE GOOSE
01256 811 477

Worthing Road, Basingstoke, RG22 6PG

Beefeater Grill are one of the UK's best-loved restaurants welcoming guests for almost 40 years in over 130 locations nationwide. *Excludes Breakfast, Light Bites, Bar menu, set menus and all other offers.

2FOR1 MAIN COURSE | 6 | FRI ✓ | SAT × | — Modern British

SQUIRES AT THE RED LION HOTEL
☎ 01256 328 525

Red Lion Hotel, Basingstoke, RG21 7LX

Indulge in an exquisite evening dinner for two at this picturesque venue set in the heart of Basingstoke. For peckish guests, a light bite can be enjoyed with a velvety, aromatic coffee.

2FOR1 MAIN COURSE | FRI ✓ | SAT ✓ | ✱ | — European

STACJA PL
☎ 02380 633 339

15 Onslow Road, Southampton, SO14 0JD

This Polish-inspired eatery prides itself on great food and service at an affordable price. Boasting a varied menu from both Poland and Eastern Europe, the cuisine is authentic and exceptionally prepared.

2FOR1 MAIN COURSE | FRI ✓ | SAT ✓ — Polish

STRADA
02392 817 278

R2-R3 City Quay, Portsmouth, PO1 3TZ

Offering fresh, bold dishes inspired by flavours of Italian city life – Strada serves a selection of indulgent tastes, to those seeking a blissful escape to laidback Italian life. *Excludes Pizzettas.

25% OFF TOTAL | 6 | FRI ✓ | SAT × | — Italian

TALISMAN
☎ 01489 572 614

Bridge Road, Park Gate, Southampton, SO31 7GD

Held dear by its guests, the Talisman in Southampton is part of the Hall & Woodhouse family. Serving only the freshest of local ingredients, the venue prides itself in traditional English dishes.

25% OFF TOTAL | FRI × | SAT × | SUN | — British

THE TAP
☎ 02392 655 739

17 London Road, Portsmouth, PO2 0BQ

Great good-value-for-money venue with a welcoming atmosphere making it perfect for a quick drink, bite to eat or full evening meal. Catch up with friends over an extensive menu of home-cooked dishes.

2FOR1 MAIN COURSE | FRI ✓ | SAT ✓ | SUN — British

TARIQ MANZIL'S INDIAN
☎ 02380 231 002

21 Bevois Valley Road, Southampton, SO14 0JP

Personable, approachable Indian restaurant in Southampton whose eclectic menu has all the classic dishes in good-sized portions, with the hot, sweet and sour pathia dishes especially worth a try.

2FOR1 3 COURSES | FRI ✱ | SAT ✱ — Indian

THE TERRACE AT THE MONTAGU ARMS
☎ 01590 612 324

Montagu Arms Hotel, Palace Lane, Beaulieu, SO42 7ZL

Awarded a Michelin Star in only its first year under the direction of Roux Scholar Matthew Tomkinson, this superb restaurant is unmissable for the discerning. *Check website for further details.

25% OFF TOTAL | 4 | FRI ✱ | SAT ✱ | — Fine Dining

THATCHED COTTAGE
☎ 01590 623 090

16 Brookley Road, Brockenhurst, SO42 7RR

Infusing historic charm with modern essentials, a sumptuous menu is brought to this 1627 built venue. Enjoy a brisk walk in the New Forest before refuelling with a hearty main course.

50% OFF FOOD | 2 | FRI ✱ | SAT ✱ — British

THE TITCHFIELD MILL
01329 840 931

Mill Lane, Titchfield, Fareham, PO15 5RF

This Vintage Inn oozes rural charm and rustic character. The picturesque surroundings provide the perfect backdrop for savouring the hearty, seasonal pub-food on the menu.

25% OFF TOTAL | FRI ✓ | SAT ✓ | SUN | — Modern British

TK SNAX
02392 170 208

Unit 2 Gosport Bus Station, Gosport, PO12 1EP

When heading out on an adventure or on a long journey, hunger must be kept at bay. TK Snax provides everything you need for the bus or ferry, from soft filled rolls to delicious Caribbean street food.

2FOR1 MAIN COURSE | FRI ✱ | SAT ✱ | SUN — Mexican

TRADERS RESTAURANT @ HOLIDAY INN
☎ 08719 429 065

Holiday Inn, Pembroke Road, Portsmouth, PO1 2TA

The restaurant in this Portsmouth hotel offers a range of tantalising dishes from the à la carte menu plus a complementary wine selection.

25% OFF TOTAL | 6 | FRI ✓ | SAT ✓ — International

TRADERS RESTAURANT @ HOLIDAY INN
☎ 08719 429 028

Holiday Inn, Cartwright Drive, Fareham, PO15 5RJ

Guests of the hotel's Traders Restaurant and Bar will love the wide choice of wholesome dishes on offer. The kitchen ensures it rotates its menu every eight weeks to keep it fresh and vibrant.

25% OFF TOTAL | 6 | FRI ✓ | SAT ✓ — European

TRADEWINDS RESTAURANT @ HILTON ☎ 02392 219 111
Hilton Portsmouth, Eastern Road, Portsmouth, PO6 1UN
Bright and breezy in-house restaurant of the Hilton Portsmouth hotel. Has a spacious feel about it, and serves a good selection of classic British fare, both buffet breakfast and for evening meals.

50% OFF FOOD | 4 | FRI ✓ | SAT ✓ | SUN — International

THE TROOPER INN ☎ 01730 827 293
Alton Road, Froxfield, Peterfield, GU32 1BD
This beautiful pub is high up in Hampshire; steal a march and enjoy its location while you take your choice of classic pub fare or something more eclectic. Exceptionally welcoming and accomplished inn.

25% OFF TOTAL | 6 | FRI 📱 | SAT ✱ | SUN — British

THE VESTRY BAR AND RESTAURANT ☎ 02380 231 101
61 Commercial Road, Southampton, SO15 1GG
Buzzing with a cosmopolitan crowd, this venue hosts live entertainment and offers exclusive hire. Devour a well-deserved Sunday lunch or a speciality dish whilst absorbing the ambiance.

25% OFF TOTAL | 8 | FRI ✱ | SAT ✱ | ▲ — British

THE WATERMARK ☎ 02392 377 422
36-38 The Boardwalk, Portsmouth, PO6 4TP
Boasting an award for 'Britain's Best Burger', the cuisine at this venue is locally sourced. Portchester sausages, cheese and real ales all feature on the menu which hosts favourites such as fish pie.

25% OFF TOTAL | FRI 📱 | SAT 📱 | ▲ — British

WATERS EDGE ☎ 02380 457 220
Mercury Yacht Harbour, Satchell Lane, Hamble, SO30 4HQ
A restaurant set on the famous river Hamble where the dazzling variety of wildlife meets with the bustle of the yachting fraternity. Here dining can be enjoyed any time of the day. *A la carte menu only.

25% OFF TOTAL | 2 | FRI ✓ | SAT ✓ — European

THE WELLINGTON ARMS ☎ 01256 882 214
Stratfield Turgis, Hook, RG27 0AS
In the exceptionally elegant, charming Wellington Arms Hotel, you can enjoy quality, refined food that won't leave you thinking of the proverbial boot, but rather the fabled beef.

25% OFF TOTAL | 6 | FRI × | SAT × | SUN | ▲ — European

THE WINCHESTER RESTAURANT ☎ 01256 783 350
Oakley Hall Hotel, Rectory Road, Basingstoke, RG23 7EL
Oakley Hall Hotel truly is a hidden treasure amongst the rolling countryside of North Hampshire. Using only the best local ingredients, Head Chef Justin Mundy creates contemporary dishes that are sure to delight. 2 AA Rosettes.

50% OFF FOOD | 4 | FRI × | SAT × | SUN | ▲ — British

WHITE HORSE INN ☎ 01489 877 490
South Hill, Droxford, SO32 3PB
Down-to-earth village pub that serves a tasty array of Indian food along with some pub classics. Enjoy the easy feel and the accommodating atmosphere.

2FOR1 MAIN COURSE | FRI ✓ | SAT ✓ — Indian

THE WHITE LION 01252 890 840
104-108 Reading Road, Yateley, GU46 7RX
This Vintage Inn oozes rural charm and rustic character. The picturesque surroundings provide the perfect backdrop for savouring the hearty, seasonal pub-food on the menu.

25% OFF TOTAL | FRI ✓ | SAT ✓ | SUN | ▲ — Modern British

WHITELEY'S FAMILY RESTAURANT ☎ 01428 751 635
Standford Lane, Bordon, GU35 8RA
Oozing innovation and imagination, Peter Whiteley's menu is bursting with culinary delights inspired by his experience in the Far East. *Cannot be used in conjunction with any other offer.

2FOR1 3 COURSES | FRI ✓ | SAT ✓ | SUN — British

WIGHT MOUSE INN ☎ 01983 730 431
Newport Road, Chale, PO38 2HA
Family owned brewer Hall & Woodhouse devote themselves to locally sourced ingredients at pocket-friendly prices in a welcoming environment. This pub is held dear by diners for its beautiful views.

25% OFF TOTAL | FRI × | SAT × | SUN | ▲ — British

THE WINCHESTER ☎ 01489 780 888
Macdonald Botley Park Hotel, Southampton, SO32 2UA
Savour delightful dishes and fine wines at the elegant, AA Rosette award-winning Winchester Restaurant based right in the heart of the Hampshire countryside.

25% OFF TOTAL | 8 | FRI 📱 | SAT 📱 | ✱ — European

YENZ ☎ 01590 622 005
Lyndhurst Road, Brockenhurst, SO42 7RL
A conveniently located gem serving great Cantonese cuisine. The tastefully decorated restaurant as well as the function room means that this restaurant is suitable for all party sizes.

25% OFF TOTAL | 10 | FRI 📱 | SAT 📱 | ✱ — Chinese

THE CASTLE INN ☎ 01983 522 528
91 High Street, Newport, PO30 1BQ
Newport's oldest pub provides a relaxed atmosphere with an excellent menu of freshly prepared dishes including fish, poultry, game and vegetarian options.

2FOR1 MAIN COURSE | FRI × | SAT × | SUN — British

DAN'S KITCHEN ☎ 01983 872 303
Lower Green Road, St Helens, PO33 1TS
Whether its food for carnivores or vegetarians, Dan's Kitchen cooks up delicious dishes for all, using only the freshest of local ingredients. Guests can expect imaginative and innovative cuisine.

25% OFF TOTAL | 4 | FRI × | SAT × | SUN — British

LUGLEY'S OF COWES ☎ 01983 299 618
Osborne Court, The Parade, Cowes, PO31 7QS
Beautiful modern British cuisine served in gorgeous surroundings, Lugley's of Cowes is a gem, not to be missed. Welcoming staff, delicious food and beautiful ambience is sure to make Lugley's a favourite.

2FOR1 3 COURSES | FRI × | SAT × | SUN | ▲ — British

LUGLEY'S OF NEWPORT ☎ 01983 822 994
33 Lugley Street, Newport, PO30 5ET
Beautiful modern British cuisine served in gorgeous surroundings, Lugley's of Newport is a gem, not to be missed. Welcoming staff, delicious food and beautiful ambience is sure to make Lugley's a favourite.

2FOR1 3 COURSES | FRI × | SAT × | SUN | ▲ — British

MEDINA QUAY 01983 825 082
Seaclose, Fairlee Rd, Newport, Isle of Wight, PO30 2DN
Quality pub classics with modern twists meets with a friendly and relaxed atmosphere to make this Table Table venue the perfect place for any occasion. * Excludes daytime & evening deals and festive menus.

2FOR1 MAIN COURSE | FRI ✓ | SAT ✓ — Modern British

Hertfordshire

THE ABBOTTS SPICE ☎ 01920 870032
73 High Street, Ware, SG12 8AS
The Abbotts Spice restaurant is eager to welcome you to an ultimate experience of Indian fine dining using the finest herbs, spices, and cuts of meat, and the most traditional of cooking techniques.

25% OFF TOTAL | 10 | FRI ✓ | SAT ✓ | ✱ — Indian

THE ALBANY RESTAURANT & BAR ☎ 01727 730 888
7 George Street, St Albans, AL3 4ER
French-inspired, this venue oozes Parisian charm. Indulge in seared scallops with cauliflower puree or a rich sea bass ratatouille. Perfect for business meetings and evenings out with a touch of panache.

50% OFF FOOD | 4 | FRI 📱 | SAT 📱 | SUN | ▲ — Modern European

THE BAR @ IBIS ☎ 01438 779 955
Ibis Hotel, Stevenage, SG1 1EJ
A well-loved attribute of the Ibis Stevenage Centre, The Bar serves a great selection of drinks and a wide range of snacks available 24 hours a day.

50% OFF FOOD | 6 | FRI 📱 | SAT 📱 — British

THE BEAN TREE RESTAURANT
☎01582 460 901

20a Leyton Road, Harpenden, AL5 2HU

Treat yourself to al fresco dining within the terrace garden of this 18th Century eatery. Offering prestigious French cuisine, diners can also enjoy live music on a Wednesday and a monthly jazz night.

2FOR1 MAIN COURSE | FRI × | SAT × | SUN | ✱ | ♠ — Fine Dining

BELLA ITALIA
01707 251 990

The Galleria, Unit 63, Comet Way, Hatfield, AL10 0XY

Accessible Italian cuisine on the British high street – indulge in authentic sharing platters, hand stretched pizzas and hearty pasta dishes, served with a healthy dose of gregarious Italian hospitality.

25% OFF TOTAL | ♟6 | FRI × | SAT × | SUN | ♠ — Italian

BOMBAY BISTRO
☎01462 491226

8 Bell Row, Baldock, SG7 6AP

The Bombay Bistro is a new Indian restaurant in Baldock, which offers traditional Indian cuisine, in a sophisticated setting, which turns the perception of most Indian restaurants on its head!

2FOR1 2 COURSES | FRI × | SAT × | ✱ — Indian

BORDERS RESTAURANT
☎01582 449 988

London Road, Markyate, AL3 8HH

A superb hotel surrounded by quiet countryside. Borders offers an informal ambience that is perfect for an enjoyable meal en route to nearby visitor attractions or simply to while away an evening.

25% OFF TOTAL | ♟6 | FRI ✓ | SAT ✓ — International

THE CHEQUERS IN STEVENAGE
01438 817 814

Bragbury End, Stevenage, SG2 8TH

This Vintage Inn oozes rural charm and rustic character. The picturesque surroundings provide the perfect backdrop for savouring the hearty, seasonal pub-food on the menu.

25% OFF TOTAL | FRI ✓ | SAT ✓ | SUN | ♠ — Modern British

CHESHUNT TANDOORI
☎01992 628701

187 Windmill Lane, Cheshunt, EN8 9AW

Cheshunt Tandoori offer traditional Indian food in a contemporary setting. It has recently been refurbished and has some new additions to the menu and continue to serve older classics.

50% OFF FOOD | FRI ✓ | SAT ✓ — Indian

THE COLNEY FOX
01727 823 698

1 Barnet Road, London Colney, St Albans, AL2 1BL

This Vintage Inn oozes rural charm and rustic character. The picturesque surroundings provide the perfect backdrop for savouring the hearty, seasonal pub-food on the menu.

25% OFF TOTAL | FRI ✓ | SAT ✓ | SUN | ♠ — Modern British

THE COMET BRASSERIE & BAR
☎01707 252 400

The Ramada Hatfield Hotel, Hatfield, AL10 9RH

This hotel-based brasserie in Hatfield serves a large array of dishes that have been inspired by the flavours of all seven continents. Experienced staff have been trained to cater to your needs.

2FOR1 3 COURSES | FRI ✓ | SAT ✓ — British

COREYS MILL
01438 351 318

Coreys Mill Lane, Stevenage, SG1 4AA

Beefeater Grill are one of the UK's best-loved restaurants welcoming guests for almost 40 years in over 130 locations nationwide. *Excludes Breakfast, Light Bites, Bar menu, set menus and all other offers.

2FOR1 MAIN COURSE | ♟6 | FRI ✓ | SAT × | ♠ — Modern British

THE CROOKED CHIMNEY
01707 397 021

Cromer Hyde Lane, Lemsford, Welwyn Garden City, AL8 7XE

This Vintage Inn oozes rural charm and rustic character. The picturesque surroundings provide the perfect backdrop for savouring the hearty, seasonal pub-food on the menu.

25% OFF TOTAL | FRI ✓ | SAT ✓ | SUN | ♠ — Modern British

THE CROWN
01992 462 244

Old Nazing Road, Broxbourne, EN10 6QT

This Vintage Inn oozes rural charm and rustic character. The picturesque surroundings provide the perfect backdrop for savouring the hearty, seasonal pub-food on the menu.

25% OFF TOTAL | FRI ✓ | SAT ✓ | SUN | ♠ — Modern British

CROWS NEST
01442 824 819

Tring Hill, Tring, HP23 4LD

Beefeater Grill are one of the UK's best-loved restaurants welcoming guests for almost 40 years in over 130 locations nationwide. *Excludes Breakfast, Light Bites, Bar menu, set menus and all other offers.

2FOR1 MAIN COURSE | ♟6 | FRI ✓ | SAT × | ♠ — Modern British

DARCY'S RESTAURANT
☎01727 730 777

2 Hatfield Road, St Albans, AL1 3RP

Independent restaurant in picturesque St Albans. Drawing imaginatively on culinary influences from Asia, Australia and Europe, Darcy's puts together stylish and contemporary dishes in a warm ambience.

2FOR1 MAIN COURSE | FRI ▯ | SAT ✱ | SUN | ♠ — European

DE JA VU
☎01992 636 325

19 High Street, Cheshunt, EN8 0BX

De Ja Vu brings the best of exotic Indian cuisine to the beating heart of Hertfordshire. Flawless service and a laid-back vibe have made it a firm favourite with the locals.

2FOR1 MAIN COURSE | FRI × | SAT × — Indian

DESTINATIONS
☎01438 722 727

St Georges Way, Stevenage, SG1 1HS

Dine at Destinations and you won't be disappointed. An ideal venue for private dining events, the restaurant offers a differently themed menu every night of the week. Sumptuous exotic dishes guaranteed.

2FOR1 MAIN COURSE | FRI ✓ | SAT ✓ | ✱ — International

ELEMENTS BAR @ NOVOTEL
☎01438 346 100

Knebworth Park, Stevenage, SG1 2AX

This cosmopolitan bar and restaurant offers its guests a tempting array of naughty nibbles and contemporary lunch-time delights. Relax with friends and enjoy a drink from the extensive bar menu.

50% OFF FOOD | ♟4 | FRI ✓ | SAT ✓ — International

ELEMENTS RESTAURANT @ NOVOTEL
☎01438 346 100

Knebworth Park, Stevenage, SG1 2AX

Tuck into a sumptuous abundance of international dishes at pocket-friendly prices. Whether it's a weekend treat with friends or a romantic dinner, Elements provide a sensational night out.

50% OFF FOOD | ♟4 | FRI ✓ | SAT ✓ — International

THE FISH AND EELS
01992 466 073

Dobbs Weir Road, Hoddesdon, EN11 0AY

This Vintage Inn oozes rural charm and rustic character. The picturesque surroundings provide the perfect backdrop for savouring the hearty, seasonal pub-food on the menu.

25% OFF TOTAL | FRI ✓ | SAT ✓ | SUN | ▲ — Modern British

FREDDIE'S
☎01727 811 889

52 Adelaide Street, St Albans, AL3 5BG

Bright, smart and contemporary European-style restaurant that serves an eclectic array of beautifully realised and presented dishes in a cosy, welcoming atmosphere. *Offer not available on event nights.

2FOR1 3 COURSES | FRI × | SAT × | SUN | ▲ — European

THE GRILL @ THE BOBSLEIGH
☎01442 833 276

The Bobsleigh Hotel, Bovingdon, HP3 0DS

Set in the supreme rural location of Bovingdon, by the Chiltern Hills, The Bobsleigh Hotel is recognised for providing some of the finest food and drink near Hemel

25% OFF TOTAL | 6 | FRI × | SAT × | SUN | ✱ | ▲ — Modern British

HARPENDEN HOUSE HOTEL
☎01582 449 955

18 Southdown Road, Harpenden, AL5 1PE

A new outpost of the exceptional team from the Vineyard at Stockcross, this exceptional hotel-based restaurant is unfussy in manner and deliciously precise in execution.

25% OFF TOTAL | 4 | FRI ✓ | SAT ✓ — British

IL GIARDINO
☎01279 657 316

9 Northgate End, Bishops Stortford, CM23 2ET

Established chef Pedro prepares only the most authentic of dishes using age-old recipes. Guests savour rich pasta sauces and those with a sweet-tooth can indulge in a naughty treat of velvety ice creams.

2FOR1 3 COURSES | FRI | SAT | ▲ — Italian

JADE GARDEN
☎01727 856 077

16 Spencer Street, St Albans, AL3 5EG

A popular restaurant within the city allowing guests to indulge in predominately Cantonese-style cooking enhanced by the tasteful décor. A wonderful selection of dishes offers something new every time.

2FOR1 3 COURSES | FRI ✱ | SAT ✱ | ✱ — Oriental

JUBRAJ TANDOORI RESTAURANT
☎01442 825 368

53a High Street, Tring, HP23 5AG

Exceeding in quality cuisine, customers dine on prime tandoori meats and unusual curries while the more refined palate can feast upon a classic dish. Whatever the occasion, Jubraj is a fine evening out.

2FOR1 MAIN COURSE | FRI × | SAT × — Indian

KATMANDU RESTAURANT
☎01992 633 558

160 High Street, Waltham Cross, EN87DF

Diners can enjoy the fresh and saporous tastes of traditional Nepalese cuisine from a varied menu. Savour prime cuts of meat and wholesome rice dishes.

25% OFF TOTAL | 4 | FRI ✓ | SAT ✓ — Indian

KIPPINGS BISTRO AND WINE BAR
☎01582 833 122

54 High Street, St Albans, AL4 8AR

Kippings Bistro and Wine Bar was born out of a passion for good food and wine served in a relaxed but engaging atmosphere to like-minded customers.

25% OFF TOTAL | 6 | FRI ✱ | SAT ✱ | ▲ — British

LE MOULIN
☎01582 831 988

3 Mill Walk, Wheathampstead, St Albans, AL4 8DT

Bijou little restaurant with attached patisserie offering beautifully cooked French and modern European cuisine, from delicate tapas dishes to a full-bodied cassoulet.

2FOR1 2 COURSES | FRI ✓ | SAT ✓ | SUN | ✱ — European

THE LEMON TREE
☎01279 757 788

14-16 Water Lane, Bishops Stortford, CM23 2LB

Dine in the most pleasurable surroundings at The Lemon Tree. Situated within a well-preserved 16th Century building, the modern British-themed menu offers exquisite dishes for lunch and dinner.

25% OFF TOTAL | 10 | FRI ✓ | SAT ✱ | SUN | ▲ — British

LOCH FYNE
☎01727 799 050

5-5b Verulam Road, St Albans, AL3 4DA

From the roadside oyster bar that once was, Loch Fyne restaurants now successfully inject energy and passion into great food and wonderful flavours, whilst ensuring their seafood is sustainably sourced.

25% OFF TOTAL | 4 | FRI ✱ | SAT ✱ | ▲ — Seafood

LOCH FYNE
☎01992 585 440

130 Fore Street, Hertford, SG14 1AJ

From the roadside oyster bar that once was, Loch Fyne restaurants now successfully inject energy and passion into great food and wonderful flavours, whilst ensuring their seafood is sustainably sourced.

25% OFF TOTAL | 4 | FRI ✱ | SAT ✱ | ▲ — Seafood

LYTTON'S @ MERCURE
☎01462 683 747

Letchworth Hall Hotel, Letchworth Lane, SG6 3NP

Set within 8 acres of magnificent surroundings, Lytton's Restaurant at Mercure Letchworth Hall Hotel offers the perfect destination to wine and dine in luxury. An ever-evolving experience not to be missed.

2FOR1 3 COURSES | FRI ✓ | SAT ✓ | ▲ — European

MARINA SPICE LOUNGE
☎01442 270 603

20 Dickinson Quay, Apsley Lock, HP3 9WQ

Specialising in Indian and Bangladeshi cuisine, Marina Spice Lounge offers freshly cooked, expertly spiced sub-continental dining in the beautiful settings of Hemel Hempstead's Dickinson Quay.

25% OFF TOTAL | 10 | FRI × | SAT × — Indian

MEDUSA BAR RESTAURANT
☎01438 360 500

1 Queensway, Stevenage, SG1 1DA

Sleek, modern ambience in this restaurant whose emphasis is on an array of Mediterranean flavours along with classic grill fare. *Only 1 card can be used per table.

2FOR1 3 COURSES | FRI ✓ | SAT × | SUN | ✱ — Mediterranean

MINT LEAF RESTAURANT
☎01992 639 988

284 High Street, Waltham Cross, EN8 7EA

An excellent Indian restaurant boasting a huge variety of different dishes, from classic curries to more contemporary options. Helpful staff offer advice on choosing the perfect dish.

2FOR1 3 COURSES | FRI ✓ | SAT ✓ — Indian

MUMBAI BRASSERIE
☎01707 878 744

20 Station Road, Pottersbar, EN6 4HT

When only a curry will do, Mumbai Brasserie delivers. Divine creamy korma to rich madras and rogan josh make the mark, with alternative choices originating from the chef's own specialities.

2FOR1 MAIN COURSE | FRI × | SAT × | ✱ | ▲ — Indian

MUMTAJ
☎01727 843 691

115 London Road, St Albans, AL1 1LR

Mumtaj have been offering award winning, Indian cuisine since 1983, with a warm and friendly atmosphere. If you are looking for a quality Indian restaurant in St Albans, look no further than Mumtaj.

25% OFF TOTAL | FRI × | SAT × | ▲ — Indian

NIRVANA FINE INDIAN DINING
☎01438 365 445

The Roebuck Inn, London Road, Stevenage, SG2 8DS

Hotel-restaurant named after the great Dick Turpin, probably the most famous highwayman of the time. Turpins' professional team of chefs have carefully created a choice menu of traditional favourites.

50% OFF FOOD | 2 | FRI × | SAT × | SUN — Indian

OUTSIDE IN
☎01707 288 500

Beales Hotel, Comet Way, Hatfield, AL10 9NG

Beautifully prepared food that has earned the restaurant 2 AA Rosettes. The dishes available have been specifically designed so that accompaniments enhance the intense flavours of the main ingredient.

25% OFF TOTAL | 4 | FRI ✓ | SAT ✓ | ▲ — Locally Sourced

THE PAVILION
☎01582 841 843

38 High Street, Markyate, AL3 8PB

Bright and vital Indian restaurant in Markyate with a strong sense of unity and commitment in purpose. The restaurant puts together warm and richly spiced recipes in a thoroughly accommodating ambience.

2FOR1 MAIN COURSE | FRI ✱ | SAT ✱ | ✱ | ▲ — Indian

PREZZO

2FOR1 MAIN COURSE | FRI × | SAT × | ▲

2-FOR-1 MAIN COURSE

9 restaurants in Hertfordshire

15 Leyton Road, Harpenden, AL5 2HX	☎ 01582 469 007
Stevenage Leisure Park, Stevenage, SG1 2UA	☎ 01438 355 591
15 Bancroft, Hitchin, SG5 1JQ	☎ 01462 453 366
128 High Street, Old Town, Stevenage, SG1 3DB	☎ 01438 361 576
3 The Colonnade, St Albans, AL3 4DD	☎ 01727 859 050
1 North Street, Bishops Stortford, CM23 2LD	☎ 01279 656 784
17-21 Fore Street, Hertford, SG14 1DH	☎ 01992 504 674
69 The High Street, Tring, HP23 4AB	☎ 01442 822 610
15 Howardsgate, Welwyn Garden City, AL8 6AL	☎ 01707 325 321

THE PLOUGH AND HARROW ☎ 01582 715 844
88 Southdown, Harpenden, AL5 1PR

Atmospheric and lively local pub with live music, quiz, and a genial, appealing relationship with its regulars. Enjoy a hearty and classic pub meal as part of a great night.

2FOR1 MAIN COURSE | FRI ✱ | SAT ✱ | ▲ — British

PONSBOURNE PARK ☎ 01707 876 191
Newgate Street Village, Hertford, SG13 8RF

Ponsbourne Park's restaurant is smart and elegant in style, complementing the fine surroundings. The menu plays on this English location with some excellent takes on local meat and game. 2 AA Rosettes.

25% OFF TOTAL | 👤 4 | FRI ✓ | SAT ✓ | SUN | ▲ — British

RESTAURANT 65 ☎ 01442 239 010
65 High Street, Hemel Hempstead, HP1 3AF

A restaurant specialising in contemporary British cuisine. Wears its values on its sleeve: freshness, seasonal produce, and a belief in 'balance, moderation and variety'. An inviting place to eat.

25% OFF TOTAL | 👤 4 | FRI 📱 | SAT × — British

SEATTLE STEAKHOUSE ☎ 01442 264 846
10 St Johns Road, Hemel Hempstead, HP1 1JR

Interesting and exciting range of steaks on offer, serving everything from cuts of juicy Aberdeen Angus to kangaroo for the more adventurous. The restaurant's strong following preserves its reputation.

2FOR1 MAIN COURSE | FRI × | SAT ✱ — Steakhouse

SITAR 2 ☎ 01462 451 896
3a Sun Street, Hitchin, SG5 1AE

An exciting take on contemporary Indian cuisine, The Sitar really pushes the boundaries of classic Asian flavouring to deliver a truly unique dining experience.

2FOR1 MAIN COURSE | FRI × | SAT × | ✱ — Indian

THE STANBOROUGH 01707 391 345
Stanborough Road, Welwyn Garden City, AL8 6XE

Beefeater Grill are one of the UK's best-loved restaurants welcoming guests for almost 40 years in over 130 locations nationwide. *Excludes Breakfast, Light Bites, Bar menu, set menus and all other offers.

2FOR1 MAIN COURSE | 👤 6 | FRI ✓ | SAT × | ▲ — Modern British

STRADA 01462 457 746
25b-26 Sun Street, Hitchin, SG5 1AH

Offering fresh, bold dishes inspired by flavours of Italian city life – Strada serves a selection of indulgent tastes, to those seeking a blissful escape to laidback Italian life. *Excludes Pizzettas.

25% OFF TOTAL | 👤 6 | FRI ✓ | SAT × | ▲ — Italian

STRADA 01582 462 793
Victoria Works, Harpenden, AL5 2BS

Offering fresh, bold dishes inspired by flavours of Italian city life – Strada serves a selection of indulgent tastes, to those seeking a blissful escape to laidback Italian life. *Excludes Pizzettas.

25% OFF TOTAL | 👤 6 | FRI ✓ | SAT × | ▲ — Italian

TEMPLE FUSION AT WARE ☎ 01920 484 675
1-4 Tudor Square, Ware, SG12 9XF

The Temple Bar & Restaurant has been designed to give customers a comfortable and unique dining experience. Their 'Indian Fusion' style cuisine contains dishes from the Indian sub-continent including Bangladesh, India and Nepal.

50% OFF FOOD | 👤 4 | FRI × | SAT × | ▲ — Indian

THE THREE HORSESHOES ☎ 01462 742 280
74 High Street, Hinxworth, Baldock, SG7 5HQ

From classic, fluffy breaded mushrooms to the superbly savoury twang of their ham, eggs and chips, this pub-restaurant is a warm and lovely place to eat, in a charismatic old thatched building.

2FOR1 MAIN COURSE | FRI ✓ | SAT ✓ — Traditional English

THE THREE HORSESHOES 01727 851 608
612 Hatfield Road, Smallford, St Albans, AL4 0HP

This Vintage Inn oozes rural charm and rustic character. The picturesque surroundings provide the perfect backdrop for savouring the hearty, seasonal pub-food on the menu.

25% OFF TOTAL | FRI ✓ | SAT ✓ | SUN | ▲ — Modern British

THE THREE TUNS ☎ 01763 852 768
30 High Street, Royston, SG8 0JP

Situated in an early 19th Century building, the establishment proudly plays up to its historic location offering warm, welcoming and hearty food and service. A varied menu accommodates traditional dishes.

2FOR1 MAIN COURSE | FRI ✓ | SAT ✓ | SUN | ▲ — Traditional English

THE WAGGONERS ☎ 01707 324 241
Brickwall Close, Welwyn Garden City, AL6 9AA

Run by the long-established Aude and Laurent Brydniak, this 17th Century coaching inn is steeped in historicism. The French staff are attentive and ensure that guests have the ultimate dining experience.

2FOR1 MAIN COURSE | FRI 📱 | SAT 📱 | ▲ — French

www.gourmetsociety.co.uk

Always mention your Gourmet Society card when booking a table.

THE WHITE HORSE
☎01992 586 791
White Horse Hotel, Hertingfordbury, SG14 2LB
The White Horse Hertingfordbury offers traditional cuisine with a modern British theme, which varies to reflect the changing season. Great food served in welcoming and tranquil surroundings.
50% OFF FOOD | 6 | FRI ✓ | SAT ✓ | ▲ — European

Kent

ALEXANDRA RISTORANTE ITALIANO
☎01843 590 595
70 Harbour Parade, Ramsgate, CT11 8LP
A Ramsgate restaurant offering diners a wide choice of authentic Italian pizza, pasta, meat, fish and vegetarian specialities, all exceptionally prepared and creatively produced.
2FOR1 3 COURSES | FRI ✓ | SAT ✱ — Italian

THE AMBRETTE
☎01843 231 504
44 King Street, Margate, CT9 1QE
Stunning fine-dining Indian restaurant with a clipped, eclectic menu of artful and delicious dishes by chef Dev Biswal. With exceptionally seasoned, crafted cuisine, The Ambrette is a special experience.
25% OFF TOTAL | 10 | FRI ✓ | SAT ✱ | ✱ — Indian

THE ARTS BAR @ RAMADA
☎0845 815 9045
Ramada Maidstone, Hollingbourne, Maidstone, ME17 1RE
With modern art lining the walls, this hotel restaurant combines a laid-back setting among plenty of greenery and a selection of simple, light bites to eat, alongside a fine wine or tasty cocktail.
50% OFF FOOD | 6 | FRI ✗ | SAT ✗ — British

THE ARTS BRASSERIE @ RAMADA
☎0844 815 9045
Ramada Maidstone, Hollingbourne, Maidstone, ME17 1RE
In-house brasserie of the Ramada Maidstone, overlooking green fields and serving a range of dishes from fresh fish to succulent cuts of meat. A smart, comfortable place to eat.
50% OFF FOOD | 6 | FRI 📱 | SAT ✗ — British

ATRIUM RESTAURANT
☎01634 847 776
86 High Street, Rochester, ME1 1JY
A modern venue run by a former army veteran who once cooked for the Queen, serving a unique fusion of British and Mediterranean cuisine. Service is great while the breadth of the wine list is unparalleled.
25% OFF TOTAL | 6 | FRI ✓ | SAT ✱ — Contemporary

BAITHAK
☎01843 580 290
6-8 Westcliffe Arcade, Ramsgate, CT11 8LH
Perfectly located restaurant for those who wish to enjoy the harbour and waterfront. This Indian restaurant never fails to impress, serving fresh and tasty classic curries and the more unusual dishes.
50% OFF FOOD | 4 | FRI ✗ | SAT ✗ — Indian

THE BANGLA GARDEN RESTAURANT
01322 386 833
39 High Street, Swanscombe, DA10 0AG
Friendly Indian restaurant in Swanscombe that serves a range of dishes across their eclectic menu.
2FOR1 MAIN COURSE | FRI ✗ | SAT ✗ | SUN — Indian

BANGLA LOUNGE
☎07944 329 500
1-3 Prospect Road, Hythe, CT21 5NS
The head chef's enthusiasm to cook delicious food using timeless classic flavours and techniques means the menu is filled with creative and innovative recipes that will pamper your taste buds.
2FOR1 MAIN COURSE | FRI 📱 | SAT 📱 — Indian

THE BARN RESTAURANT
☎01634 361 363
507 Lower Rainham Road, Rainham, ME8 7TN
This family-run restaurant takes delight in exceeding customer expectations. Inspired traditionally English meals are balanced by modern presentation, bringing old dishes into the 21st-century.
25% OFF TOTAL | 4 | FRI ✓ | SAT ✱ | SUN | ▲ — British

BEECHES
☎01622 813 038
501 Seven Mile Lane, Mereworth, ME18 5QY
Classic European cuisine is the order of the day, while a vast selection of shellfish and seafood dishes cater for diners who enjoy the daily catch. Veal, venison and Aberdeen angus also appear.
2FOR1 MAIN COURSE | FRI ✗ | SAT ✗ — Steakhouse/ Seafood

BELL'S FISH BAR
☎01892 838 472
56-60 Maidstone Road, Tonbridge, TN12 6AF
Savour chunky pieces of haddock with a generous stack of piping hot chips in true British style. Appease grumbling stomachs and warm your cockles with a hearty helping of one of the nation's favourites.
2FOR1 MAIN COURSE | FRI ✗ | SAT ✗ | SUN — British

BEST WESTERN DONNINGTON MANOR
☎01732 462 681
London Road, Dunton Green, Sevenoaks, TN13 2TD
A wood-beamed, classically styled restaurant in a plush Best Western hotel, offering freshly cooked, locally sourced dishes every evening, in a thoroughly relaxing, traditional English atmosphere.
25% OFF TOTAL | FRI ✗ | SAT ✗ | ✱ | ▲ — European

BRANDSHATCH PLACE HOTEL & SPA
☎0845 072 7395
The Dining Room, Brands Hatch Rd, Fawkham, DA3 8NQ
Traditional favourites meet new creations at this Hand Picked Hotels group establishment. Find exceptionally satisfying dishes that make use of quality local produce. Awarded 2 AA Rosettes.
25% OFF TOTAL | 6 | FRI ✓ | SAT ✱ | ✱ — British

THE BRASSERIE @ MERCURE
☎0844 815 9045
Mercure Hotel, Hollingbourne, Maidstone, ME17 1RE
The Mercure Maidstone Hotel revels in its location and aims to mimic its natural surrounds, being situated in the 'Garden of England'. The Brasserie offers freedom and relaxation to every patron.
2FOR1 3 COURSES | FRI ✓ | SAT ✓ — International

CAFÉ ROUGE

25% OFF TOTAL

25% OFF TOTAL | 6 | FRI ✓ | SAT ✓ | ✱ | ▲

Bluewater Centre, Greenhithe, DA9 9SJ — ☎ 01322 624 427
Unit 3-5, Longmarket, Canterbury, CT1 2JS — ☎ 01227 784 984
42-44 Earl Street, Maidstone, ME14 1PS — ☎ 0162 276 9928
Bligh's Meadow, Pembroke Road, Sevenoaks, TN13 1AS — ☎ 01732 450 395
43 High Street, Tenterden, TN30 6BJ — ☎ 01580 763 029

THE BRASSERIE ON THE BAY
☎ 01304 611 118

The Lodge at Prince's Golf Club, Sandwich, CT13 9QB

An intimate venue nestled on the Bay of Sandwich, The Lodge offers an all new option to diners in this modern, contemporary Brasserie on the Bay. Menus are created to coincide with local produce.

2FOR1 MAIN COURSE | FRI ✓ | SAT ✱ | ▲ — British

BRICKFIELD TAVERN
01303 273 620

Cherry Garden Lane, Folkestone, Kent, CT19 4AP

Quality pub classics with modern twists meets with a friendly and relaxed atmosphere to make this Table Table venue the perfect place for any occasion. *Excludes daytime & evening deals and festive menus.

2FOR1 MAIN COURSE | FRI ✓ | SAT ✓ — Modern British

BYBROOK TAVERN @HOLIDAY INN
☎ 08719 429 001

Holiday Inn Hotel, Canterbury Road, Ashford, TN24 8QQ

Lofty, wood beamed ceilings create an open, inviting ambience at the Bybrook Tavern, where guests can expect to find a lounge and bar menu available until 10pm.

25% OFF TOTAL | 6 | FRI ✓ | SAT ✓ — International

CHILSTON PARK HOTEL
☎ 08450 727 426

Culpeper Restaurant, Sandway, Lenham, ME17 2BE

Whether you arrive with a firm favourite dish in mind, or you fancy being a little more adventurous, the chef aims to please all at this Hand Picked Hotels group venue. Awarded 2 AA Rosettes.

25% OFF TOTAL | 10 | FRI ✱ | SAT ✱ | SUN | ▲ — British

CHOM CHOM CANTERBURY
☎ 01227 450 200

10-11 Burgate Lane, Canterbury, CT1 2HH

You now no longer need to be a jet-setting globetrotter in order to taste the best cuisine the world has to offer. Eating at Chom Chom is simple, just pick your fresh ingredients and enjoy!

2FOR1 3 COURSES | FRI ✓ | SAT ✗ | SUN | ▲ — International

COCHIN MARINE
☎ 01892 616 742

49 Grosvenor Road, Tunbridge Wells, TN1 2AY

Appetising south Indian cuisine available at Cochin Marine. Superb aromas only hint at the tastiness of each and every dish that is on offer, whilst the vibrancy of the curries will make your mouth water.

50% OFF FOOD | 2 | FRI ✗ | SAT ✗ — Seafood

CONFUCIUS RESTAURANT
☎ 01634 817 867

342 High Street, Chatham, ME4 4NR

Well-loved and always popular with the locals, Confucius Restaurant takes great delight in serving terrific Chinese cuisine to both regular and first-time diners. Dishes loaded with flavour and produce.

2FOR1 3 COURSES | FRI ✗ | SAT ✗ — Chinese

CONICAL GRILL
☎ 01622 734 334

Tudor Park Hotel, Ashford Road, Bearsted, ME14 4NQ

Maintaining simplicity at the core, the rustic menu at the Tudor Park is careful not to overcomplicate its dishes, and service is friendly and efficient. Only the very best seasonal produce is used.

25% OFF TOTAL | 10 | FRI ✓ | SAT ✱ — British

THE COURT BAR @ HILTON
☎ 01622 734 322

Hilton Maidstone, Bearsted Road, Maidstone, ME14 5AA

Relaxing and airy place to eat and enjoy a quiet drink in company at the Hilton Maidstone. Opt for a simple snack, one of the hotel's bespoke burgers, or something more substantial from their evening menu.

50% OFF FOOD | 4 | FRI ✓ | SAT ✓ | ▲ — British

THE COURTYARD
☎ 01795 530 013

Brogdale Farm, Brogdale Road, Faversham, ME13 8XZ

You'll find yourself the beneficiary of a full-throated breakfast or a delightful, fulsome lunch at this charming little eatery in Kent. *In winter, only open daytimes (Weather based).

2FOR1 MAIN COURSE | FRI ✓ | SAT ✓ — British

THE CROWN AND HORSESHOES
☎ 01622 861 958

Sutton Road, Maidstone, ME17 3LZ

The Crown and Horseshoes is a charming country pub, perfect for that country lunch or evening meal. Traditional in appearance, this is a great place when only the English countryside spirit will do.

2FOR1 MAIN COURSE | FRI ✓ | SAT ✓ | ▲ — British

DAME TARTINE
☎ 01892 553 330

Five Ways, Lime Hill Road, Tunbridge Wells, TN1 1LJ

Bridging the gap between sandwich bar and restaurant, Dame Tartine serves distinctive, flavoursome fresh snacks and bites alongside the eatery's namesake; the French tartine.

50% OFF FOOD | 8 | FRI ✓ | SAT ✗ — French

DE HONOURABLES
☎ 01634 577 786

10 High Street, Gillingham, ME7 1BB

Buzzy Afro-Caribbean cuisine on offer in this fun-filled, quirky Gillingham restaurant. Perfect for those wanting to sample something new, to satisfy adventurous palates.

50% OFF FOOD | 4 | FRI 📱 | SAT 📱 — African

THE DOG INN AT WINGHAM
☎ 01227 720 339

Canterbury Road, Wingham, CT3 1BB

A picturesque inn with an enviable reputation for their excellence and variety, as dishes benefit from the freshest local produce available. Highly regarded for the depth and range of their wine cellar.

25% OFF TOTAL | 10 | FRI ✓ | SAT ✱ — Fine Dining

DRAGON INN
☎ 01634 829 828

236 High Street, Rochester, ME1 1HY

A taste of the Orient is brought to one of Britain's most historic places. No matter the palate, guests are certain to be satisfied by the pocket-friendly menu. Dine in a friendly atmosphere.

2FOR1 3 COURSES | FRI ✗ | SAT ✗ — Pan-Asian

THE DUCK INN
☎ 01227 830 354

Pett Bottom, Canterbury, CT4 5PB

Supremely picturesque, a favourite haunt of James Bond author Ian Fleming and mentioned in You Only Live Twice, The Duck Inn takes its name from the low doorway, and serves thoroughly tasty English fare.

2FOR1 3 COURSES | FRI ✓ | SAT ✓ | SUN — British

EUREKA PARK BEEFEATER GRILL
01233 739 282

Eureka Leisure Park, Ashford, TN25 4BN

Beefeater Grill are one of the UK's best-loved restaurants welcoming guests for almost 40 years in over 130 locations nationwide. *Excludes Breakfast, Light Bites, Bar menu, set menus and all other offers.

2FOR1 MAIN COURSE | 6 | FRI ✓ | SAT ✗ | ▲ — Modern British

EVEREST KITCHEN
☎ 01622 765 999

Maidstone West Railway Station, Maidstone, ME16 8RJ

Not just a fantastic dining experience, this venue also offers an authentic exposure of Nepalese culture. Fabulously fresh ingredients and vivacious spices create tasty dishes.

2FOR1 MAIN COURSE | FRI 📱 | SAT 📱 — Indian/Nepalese

FISHERMANS WHARF
☎ 01304 613 636

The Quay, Sandwich, CT13 9RU

With its idyllic waterfront location, flower-filled courtyard and unique atmosphere, this is a perfect venue to sample their succulent contemporary menu. *Advance booking is essential.

2FOR1 MAIN COURSE | FRI ✓ | SAT ✓ — Contemporary

THE FOX AND HOUNDS
☎ 01732 750 328

Toys Hill, Westerham, TN16 1QG

In an area of outstanding beauty, a superb menu offers fresh local produce and wonderful fish dishes prepared by an excellent chef. A good selection of wine, lager, and ales accompanies the food here.

2FOR1 MAIN COURSE | FRI ✓ | SAT ✓ | SUN | ✱ | ▲ — European

FRENCH CONNECTION
01233 500 755

Hall Avenue, Orbital Retail Park, Ashford, TN24 0GA

Quality pub classics with modern twists meets with a friendly and relaxed atmosphere to make this Table Table venue the perfect place for any occasion. *Excludes daytime & evening deals and festive menus.

2FOR1 MAIN COURSE | FRI ✓ | SAT ✓ — Modern British

FUSION RESTAURANT
☎ 01227 273 034

55 Canterbury Road, Whitstable, CT5 4HH

Fusion Lounge is known for its friendly and homely atmosphere, but above all for its unique and tasty Indian cuisine. All of the items are made with fresh ingredients by experienced chefs.

50% OFF FOOD | 4 | FRI ✗ | SAT ✗ | SUN | ▲ — Indian

To understand what the restaurant icons mean, please see the inside back cover.

THE GEORGE HOTEL
☎ 01580 713 348
Stone Street, Cranbrook, TN17 3HE
Drawing on his native Portuguese culinary style and blending it with a modern English flavour, Head Chef Paulo Fernandes has created an impressive menu at The George Hotel.

2FOR1 MAIN COURSE | FRI ✓ | SAT × | SUN — British

THE GREEN MAN
01474 702 234
Main Road, Longfield Hill, Longfield, DA3 7AS
This Vintage Inn oozes rural charm and rustic character. The picturesque surroundings provide the perfect backdrop for savouring the hearty, seasonal pub-food on the menu.

25% OFF TOTAL | FRI ✓ | SAT ✓ | SUN | ▲ — Modern British

GROUND ZERO RESTAURANT & BAR
☎ 01474 356 610
20 High Street, Gravesend, DA11 0BA
Guests are transported to the Big Apple at this American diner, complete with traditional booths ideal for private occasions. As expected, the menu hosts treats such as milkshakes and juicy burgers.

50% OFF FOOD | FRI ✓ | SAT ✓ — International

THE GURKHA VILLAGE
☎ 01634 666 054
Victoria Cross, 614 Lords Wood Lane, Chatham, ME5 8QX
Unbeatable air of a good local Nepalese restaurant. Fresh flowers, crisp white linen, warm, luxurious fabrics, a cosy atmosphere about the place, and some curries full of flavour and in plentiful portions.

2FOR1 3 COURSES | FRI ✱ | SAT ✱ — Nepalese

HALLETT'S LOUNGE AND RESTAURANT
☎ 01303 256 001
35 The Old High Street, Hallett's, Folkestone, CT20 1RL
Nestled in the Bohemian Quarter on the Old High Street lies one of the best experiences Folkestone has to offer. South African inspired, the menu is innovative and accompanied by an extensive wine list.

2FOR1 3 COURSES | FRI ✱ | SAT × — Modern British

HERNE BAY
01227 289 352
Blacksole Farm, Margate Road, Herne Bay, CT6 6LA
Quality pub classics with modern twists meets with a friendly and relaxed atmosphere to make this Table Table venue the perfect place for any occasion. *Excludes daytime & evening deals and festive menus.

2FOR1 MAIN COURSE | FRI ✓ | SAT ✓ — Modern British

HILDEN MANOR
01732 362 784
London Road, Tonbridge, TN10 3AN
Beefeater Grill are one of the UK's best-loved restaurants welcoming guests for almost 40 years in over 130 locations nationwide. *Excludes Breakfast, Light Bites, Bar menu, set menus and all other offers.

2FOR1 MAIN COURSE | 👤 6 | FRI ✓ | SAT × | ▲ — Modern British

HOP PICKERS PUB
☎ 01233 713 333
Holiday Inn Ashford North, Ashford, TN26 1AR
Set in the hotel grounds, this restaurant offers a unique stone grill menu and traditional pub grub for both guests and visitors to enjoy. A delicious Carvery is available every Sunday.

25% OFF TOTAL | 👤 6 | FRI ✓ | SAT ✓ — International

HOTEL DU VIN
☎ 01892 526 455
Crescent Road, Tunbridge Wells, TN1 2LY
The finest, freshest local produce, simple European recipes, a stunning choice of wines; these are the elements of the trademark Hotel du Vin bistro. A fine grade II listed mansion house. 1 AA Rosette.

2FOR1 MAIN COURSE | FRI × | SAT × | SUN | ▲ — European

JASIN'S RESTAURANT
☎ 01304 366 820
Deal Pier, Beach Street, CT14 6HZ
Get ready to face the day with a hearty breakfast at this delectable 'end of the pier' eatery. Perfect for children and vegetarians, the menu is brimming with an array of favourites such as home-made pies.

25% OFF TOTAL | 👤 2 | FRI ✓ | SAT × | SUN — International

JUNCTION RESTAURANT @ HOLIDAY INN
☎ 08719 429 001
Holiday Inn, Canterbury Road, Ashford, TN24 8QQ
Unwind at the end of the day by rounding it off with a superb, fulfilling meal at the Junction Restaurant. Tempting dishes line the menu, and can be enjoyed with a glass of your favourite wine.

25% OFF TOTAL | 👤 6 | FRI ✓ | SAT ✓ — International

KALARED BAR AND RESTAURANT
☎ 01622 686 683
83 Bank Street, Maidstone, ME14 1SD
Quench your thirst and feed your appetite in this stylish bar and restaurant. Luxurious settings provide guests with the perfect backdrop to their dining experience. Oriental set feasts are available.

2FOR1 MAIN COURSE | FRI 📱 | SAT 📱 | ✱ | ▲ — Chinese

KARMA INDIAN CUISINE
☎ 01634 400 450
74 High Street, Chatham, ME4 4DS
Cracking Indian restaurant in Chatham that combines traditional classics with smart, contemporary flavours. Fine line in vegetable dishes, with the squash and pumpkin-based curries very well regarded.

2FOR1 3 COURSES | FRI ✓ | SAT ✓ — Indian

KASHMIR TANDOORI
☎ 01227 462 050
20 Palace Street, Canterbury, CT1 2DZ
It is no wonder Kashmir Tandoori are held dear by the locals, with a varied menu of Indian classics and unusual recipes. This venue continues to thrill and delight both its regulars and new clientèle.

2FOR1 MAIN COURSE | FRI 📱 | SAT 📱 — Indian

KING CHARLES HOTEL
☎ 01634 830 303
Brompton Road, Gillingham, ME7 5QT
A beautiful hotel houses this wonderful restaurant that serves English and International dishes. Both guests and non-residents can enjoy the extensive à la carte menu created by highly imaginative chefs.

2FOR1 MAIN COURSE | FRI 📱 | SAT ✱ | SUN — British

KOHINOOR SPICE
☎ 01474 833 247
60 Istead Rise, Gravesend, DA13 9JF
A friendly curry place in Gravesend that distinguishes itself from the crowd by the freshness of flavour in its cuisine and their down-to-earth welcome.

50% OFF FOOD | 👤 4 | FRI ✱ | SAT ✱ — Indian

LA CASA VECCHIA
☎ 01892 544 700
70-72 The Pantiles, Tunbridge Wells, TN25TW
Vaunting an expansive, international wine list, this venue is perfect for a sophisticated evening of dining. Mediterranean inspired, the food is authentic yet reasonably priced.

50% OFF FOOD | 👤 6 | FRI × | SAT × | ▲ — Mediterranean

LA TASCA
☎ 01322 423 902
Water Circus, Dartford, DA9 9SE
Quintessentially Spanish, La Tasca's fresh and exciting menu offers something for everyone. Their tapas dishes are sincerely authentic, while their paellas always deliver on flavour.

25% OFF TOTAL | 👤 8 | FRI ✓ | SAT × | ▲ — Spanish

LIGHT OF INDIA
☎ 01304 241 066
Burlington House Complex, Dover, CT16 1JR
Gratify a rapacious stomach at this Indian eatery where the cuisine is mouth-watering and promises to have diners returning time after time to appease curry cravings.

2FOR1 MAIN COURSE | FRI × | SAT × — Indian

THE LIGHTHOUSE INN
☎ 01303 254 080
111 Old Dover Road, Folkestone, CT18 7HT
A family run business with comfortable rooms, friendly staff and an expert kitchen serving locally produced food. The bar features a wide selection of beers and award-winning local wines.

25% OFF TOTAL | 👤 6 | FRI 📱 | SAT 📱 — British

THE LION
01322 860 621
High Street, Farningham, DA4 0DP
This Vintage Inn oozes rural charm and rustic character. The picturesque surroundings provide the perfect backdrop for savouring the hearty, seasonal pub-food on the menu.

25% OFF TOTAL | FRI ✓ | SAT ✓ | SUN | ▲ — Modern British

LOCH FYNE
☎ 01732 467 140
63-65 High Street, Sevenoaks, TN13 1JY
From the roadside oyster bar that once was, Loch Fyne restaurants now successfully inject energy and passion into great food and wonderful flavours, whilst ensuring their seafood is sustainably sourced.

25% OFF TOTAL | 👤 4 | FRI ✱ | SAT ✱ | ▲ — Seafood

LOCH FYNE
☎01322 623930

West Village Bluewater, Bluewater, DA9 9SE

From the roadside oyster bar that once was, Loch Fyne restaurants now successfully inject energy and passion into great food and wonderful flavours, whilst ensuring their seafood is sustainably sourced.

25% OFF TOTAL | 4 | FRI ✱ | SAT ✱ | ▲ — Seafood

LODOS MEZE GRILL
☎01843 869 222

117 High Street, Broadstairs, CT10 1NQ

Traditional Turkish cuisine is served in this intimate restaurant. Lodos is fast becoming a favourite with locals and visitors alike due to the fantastic reviews it has received from customers.

25% OFF TOTAL | 6 | FRI × | SAT × | SUN | ✱ | ▲ — Turkish

LONG REACH
01227 272 459

Thanet Way, Whitstable, CT5 3DB

Beefeater Grill are one of the UK's best-loved restaurants welcoming guests for almost 40 years in over 130 locations nationwide. *Excludes Breakfast, Light Bites, Bar menu, set menus and all other offers.

2FOR1 MAIN COURSE | 6 | FRI ✓ | SAT × | ▲ — Modern British

THE MALLOWS RESTAURANT @ MERCURE
☎0844 815 9074

Tonbridge Road, Pembury, Tunbridge Wells, TN2 4QL

The Mallows Restaurant offers comfortable and relaxed dining, perfectly blending an intimate degree of formality with a splash of the informal. Make sure you save room for the desserts; they are delicious.

2FOR1 3 COURSES | FRI ✓ | SAT ✓ — International

MALTA INN
01622 717 251

Allington Lock, Sandling, Nr Maidsone, ME14 3AS

Beefeater Grill are one of the UK's best-loved restaurants welcoming guests for almost 40 years in over 130 locations nationwide. *Excludes Breakfast, Light Bites, Bar menu, set menus and all other offers.

2FOR1 MAIN COURSE | 6 | FRI ✓ | SAT × | ▲ — Modern British

MAMMA MIA
☎01634 827 027

4 High Street, Rochester, ME1 1PT

Sometimes it's difficult to differentiate between the large numbers of Italian restaurants; rest assured, this is not the case with Mamma Mia. Exceptionally showcases the very best flavours of Italy.

2FOR1 MAIN COURSE | FRI ✱ | SAT ✱ | ✱ | ▲ — Italian

MANOR FARM
01634 373 230

High Street, Rainham, Gillingham, ME8 7JE

Beefeater Grill are one of the UK's best-loved restaurants welcoming guests for almost 40 years in over 130 locations nationwide. *Excludes Breakfast, Light Bites, Bar menu, set menus and all other offers.

2FOR1 MAIN COURSE | 6 | FRI ✓ | SAT × | ▲ — Modern British

MARINE COURT
01304 218 260

Marine Parade, Dover, CT16 1LW

Quality pub classics with modern twists meets with a friendly and relaxed atmosphere to make this Table Table venue the perfect place for any occasion. *Excludes daytime & evening deals and festive menus.

2FOR1 MAIN COURSE | FRI ✓ | SAT ✓ — Modern British

THE MARQUIS AT ALKHAM
☎01304 873 410

Alkham Valley Road, Alkham, CT15 7DF

Awarded 2 AA Rosettes, great flavour is everything at The Marquis. Seasonally inspired menus make use of locally sourced ingredients, whilst every dish is elegant in appearance and delicious in taste.

25% OFF TOTAL | 10 | FRI ✓ | SAT ✱ — English and Continental

MAZA INDIAN
☎01892 520 600

72 London Road, Tunbridge Wells, TN4 0PR

Located on London Road in Tunbridge Wells, Maza Indian specialises in providing fine Indian dining in a warm environment. For a delicious Indian meal in Tunbridge Wells, Maza Indian is not to be missed!

25% OFF TOTAL | 4 | FRI ✓ | SAT ✓ — Indian

MEXXA MEXXA
☎01622 662 020

40 Earl Street, Maidstone, ME14 1PS

A wide range of favourite and the less well-known dishes are on offer in this efficient and friendly Mexican restaurant. The paella and patata con carne come highly recommended.

25% OFF TOTAL | 10 | FRI ▯ | SAT ✱ | ▲ — Mexican

MOAT
☎01732 882 263

London Road, Sevenoaks, TN15 7RR

Idyllically set just outside of Wrotham, this friendly village pub-restaurant is part of the Hall & Woodhouse family group. Traditional English dishes are locally sourced in a welcoming environment.

25% OFF TOTAL | FRI × | SAT × | SUN | ▲ — British

MULLINS BRASSERIE
☎01843 295 603

6 Market Place, Margate, CT9 1EN

A charming, accommodating place to eat in this pretty part of Margate, where you can sit back and enjoy some flavourful, tasty brasserie-style food, and watch the world go by.

25% OFF TOTAL | 6 | FRI × | SAT × | SUN — Modern European

NORTHGATE CAFÉ & RESTAURANT
☎01227 636 839

110-111 Northgate, Canterbury, CT1 1BH

Dine al fresco with a hearty, home-made dish that appeases even the most ravenous of diners. Casual and relaxed, guests are sure to have a pleasing experience at NorthGate.

25% OFF TOTAL | FRI ✓ | SAT ✓ — International

NOWREIN RESTAURANT
☎01634 400 450

74 High Street, Chatham, ME4 4DS

The award winning chef and the friendly staff at Nowrein deliver a truly outstanding atmosphere with exceptional Indian cuisine catered specifically to your needs.

2FOR1 3 COURSES | FRI ✓ | SAT ✓ — Indian

THE NURSERY
☎01634 386 111

Dunn Street Road, Gillingham, ME7 3ND

Recently under new management, this venue delivers a wonderful menu of tasty options, from a fresh mixed seafood grill to mouth-watering Cajun chicken. Enjoy great food and value for money.

25% OFF TOTAL | FRI ✓ | SAT ✓ — British

THE OAK
☎01233 712 612

5 High Street, Ashford, TN27 0HU

Situated on the High Street in the historical village of Charing, The Oak exudes Kentish charm and traditional English character. Head here when you're in need of some soothing, comforting food.

25% OFF TOTAL | 8 | FRI ▯ | SAT ▯ — British

THE OAKS BAR AND GRILL
☎01732 451 109

High Street, Sevenoaks, TN13 1HY

The No 5 Bistro in a fine hotel is a popular choice locally and for visitors; well known for its excellent food, wine and service, delivered in a highly stylish and airy dining room.

25% OFF TOTAL | 4 | FRI ✓ | SAT ✓ — European

THE OLD BREWERY TAVERN
☎01227 826 682

Stour Street, Canterbury, CT1 2NR

Soak up the sunshine on the decking or cosy up by the inviting fireplace at this 'gastro-cool' pub. Dishes are substantial, wholesome and undoubtedly fresh. Kick start the weekend with a perfect pint.

25% OFF TOTAL | 6 | FRI ✱ | SAT × | SUN | ▲ — British

THE OLD GATE INN
01227 829 951

162-164 New Dover Road, Canterbury, CT1 3EL

This Vintage Inn oozes rural charm and rustic character. The picturesque surroundings provide the perfect backdrop for savouring the hearty, seasonal pub-food on the menu.

25% OFF TOTAL | FRI ✓ | SAT ✓ | SUN | ▲ — Modern British

OLIVER'S BAR & RESTAURANT
☎01634 847 629

Oliver's Bar & Restaurant, Rochester, ME1 1EY

The philosophy at Oliver's Bar & Restaurant is to only offer the best to their patrons; from their extensive range of wines, beers and spirits, to their locally sourced and inspired restaurant menu.

25% OFF TOTAL | 10 | FRI ✱ | SAT ✱ | ▲ — British

ORCHARD RESTAURANT @ HOLIDAY INN
☎01233 713 333

Holiday Inn Ashford North, Ashford, TN26 1AR

A quality restaurant where guests can enjoy meals throughout the day. Choose from an extensive selection of well-prepared dishes for breakfast, lunch and dinner, including some great healthy options.

25% OFF TOTAL | 6 | FRI ✓ | SAT ✓ — International

PALIO
☎ 01892 515 558
84-86 Grosvenor Road, Tunbridge Wells, TN1 2AS

The Italian cuisine on offer at this inviting, contemporary restaurant is broad and accomplished, with all the classics present and correct together with a number of delicious specialities.

2FOR1 MAIN COURSE | FRI ✱ | SAT ✱ — Italian

THE PARK GATE INN
01622 880 985
Ashford Road, Hollingbourne, Maidstone, ME17 1PG

This Vintage Inn oozes rural charm and rustic character. The picturesque surroundings provide the perfect backdrop for savouring the hearty, seasonal pub-food on the menu.

25% OFF TOTAL | FRI ✓ | SAT ✓ | SUN | ▲ — Modern British

PATOGH
☎ 01843 852 631
2 Effingham Street, Ramsgate, CT11 9AT

Patogh is Persian for a place to relax and unwind and that is exactly what you will find at this stylish Ramsgate favourite. Delicious Persian food makes this a must-visit restaurant.

50% OFF FOOD | 👤 6 | FRI ✓ | SAT ✓ — Persian

PITCHER & PIANO
☎ 01892 510 555
3-5 Church Road, Tunbridge Wells, TN1 1HT

Graze leisurely on your lunch-break or satisfy a grumbling stomach with a home-made prime beef burger. For a naughty yet scrumptious treat, be sure to sample a white chocolate and honeycomb cheesecake.

50% OFF FOOD | 👤 4 | FRI ▯ | SAT ▯ — British

THE PLOUGH
01304 213 339
Folkestone Road, Dover, CT15 7AB

Beefeater Grill are one of the UK's best-loved restaurants welcoming guests for almost 40 years in over 130 locations nationwide. *Excludes Breakfast, Light Bites, Bar menu, set menus and all other offers.

2FOR1 MAIN COURSE | 👤 6 | FRI ✓ | SAT × | ▲ — Modern British

PRINCE OF INDIA
☎ 01795 535 359
70 Preston Street, Faversham, ME13 8PA

Prince of India first opened in 2006 and immediately gained a reputation for quality food and service. They have an extensive Bangladeshi and Indian menus with unique dishes and traditional favourites.

2FOR1 MAIN COURSE | FRI × | SAT × — Indian

RAJ PAVILION
☎ 01892 533 153
20 Grove Hill Road, Tunbridge Wells, TN1 1RZ

At this award-winning establishment, with an unrivalled range of authentic and imaginative Indian foods, the food is cooked to the highest standards only using the best quality and freshest ingredients.

2FOR1 3 COURSES | FRI × | SAT × | ✱ | ▲ — Indian

THE RESTAURANT AT HAMLETS HOTEL
☎ 01732 846 858
Hamlets Hotel, 802 London Road, Maidstone, ME20 6HJ

A welcoming eatery which offers superb food set within the plush greenery of the garden of England. Hamlets Hotel is an 18th Century building with a modern twist giving it a cosy, intimate feel.

50% OFF FOOD | 👤 10 | FRI ▯ | SAT ▯ | ▲ — British

RIGGINGS
☎ 01227 361 880
6 East Street, Herne Bay, CT6 5HN

A family-run continental restaurant specialising in fresh local fish straight from the water, complemented with thirty-two different varieties of wine from all over the globe. *À la carte menu only.

25% OFF TOTAL | 👤 10 | FRI ✓ | SAT ✱ | SUN | ✱ | ▲ — Seafood

RINGLESTONE INN
☎ 01622 859 900
Ringlestone Road, Maidstone, ME17 1NX

Still endorsing its original features, this 14th-century hospice for monks is now a fabulous eatery which prides itself on 'Kentish fare with flare'. Locally sourced, the dishes celebrate British heritage.

2FOR1 MAIN COURSE | FRI ✓ | SAT ✓ — British

RIVA WATERSIDE RESTAURANT & BAR
☎ 01474 364 694
Town Pier, West Street, Gravesend, DA11 0BJ

Broad array of Mediterranean cuisine cooked freshly with good produce and plenty of verve. Occupies a superb location, with a smartly designed contemporary style about it.

25% OFF TOTAL | 👤 8 | FRI ✓ | SAT ✱ — Modern European

THE RIVERSIDE TAVERN
☎ 01634 719 949
8 Canal Road, Rochester, ME2 4DR

The Riverside Tavern is a friendly Bar and Grill situated by Strood train station. Enjoy the extensive menu which offers fantastic value, great tasting dishes by the banks of the river.

25% OFF TOTAL | 👤 6 | FRI ✓ | SAT ✓ — British

THE ROSE AND CROWN
01732 462 343
London Road, Dunton Green, Sevenoaks, TN13 2TH

This Vintage Inn oozes rural charm and rustic character. The picturesque surroundings provide the perfect backdrop for savouring the hearty, seasonal pub-food on the menu.

25% OFF TOTAL | FRI ✓ | SAT ✓ | SUN | ▲ — Modern British

ROYAL OAK
01732 884 214
London Road, Wrotham Heath, Nr Sevenoaks, TN15 7RX

Beefeater Grill are one of the UK's best-loved restaurants welcoming guests for almost 40 years in over 130 locations nationwide. *Excludes Breakfast, Light Bites, Bar menu, set menus and all other offers.

2FOR1 MAIN COURSE | 👤 6 | FRI ✓ | SAT × | ▲ — Modern British

PREZZO

2FOR1 MAIN COURSE | FRI × | SAT × | ▲

2-FOR-1 MAIN COURSE

7 restaurants in Kent

52 High Street, Tenterden, TN30 6AU	☎ 01580 764 769
16 Albion Street, Broadstairs, CT10 1LU	☎ 01843 871 188
45 Earl Street, Maidstone, ME14 1PD	☎ 01622 677 499
29 High Street, Canterbury, CT1 2AZ	☎ 01227 379 571
1-3 High Street, Whitstable, CT5 1AP	☎ 01227 276 508
84 Mount Pleasant Road, Tunbridge Wells, TN1 1RT	☎ 01892 547 558
8 London Road, Sevenoaks, TN13 1AJ	☎ 01732 463 127

SAMPHIRE AT HAM
☎ 01304 617 362

Hay Hill, Ham, Sandwich, CT14 0ED

Delightful cuisine is proudly presented as being 'Kentish with a twist' at this charmingly charismatic restaurant. Every hint of creativity and thought can be tasted in all dishes.

25% OFF TOTAL | 10 | FRI ✓ | SAT ✱ — British

THE SANDGATE HOTEL
☎ 01303 220 444

8-9 Wellington Terrace, Folkestone, CT20 3DY

Sophisticated and accommodating hotel-restaurant focusing on the quality of its produce to concoct superbly savoury, supremely cooked dishes. Draws on classic recipes and adds contemporary nuance.

25% OFF TOTAL | 6 | FRI ✓ | SAT ✓ — European

SEASONS RESTAURANT @ HILTON
☎ 01623 734 322

Hilton Maidstone, Bearsted Road, Weavering, ME14 5AA

Taste the difference at this fantastic eatery. Oozing charm and elegance much like the hotel it resides in, Seasons Restaurant is an ideal place to relish a superb meal whatever the occasion.

2FOR1 3 COURSES | FRI ✓ | SAT ✱ — British

THE SHAPLA TANDOORI
01227 770 811

36 Harbour Street, Whitstable, CT5 1AJ

Tandoori specialist not far from the seafront. Serves authentic Indian cuisine and some distinctive dishes that you won't find just anywhere and that really stand out.

2FOR1 MAIN COURSE | FRI × | SAT × | SUN — Indian

SIR THOMAS WYATT
01622 752 515

London Road, Maidstone, ME16 0HG

Beefeater Grill are one of the UK's best-loved restaurants welcoming guests for almost 40 years in over 130 locations nationwide. *Excludes Breakfast, Light Bites, Bar menu, set menus and all other offers.

2FOR1 MAIN COURSE | 6 | FRI ✓ | SAT × | (bell) — Modern British

SMUGGLERS RETREAT
01843 820 700

Tothill Street, Minster, Ramsgate, CT12 4AG

Quality pub classics with modern twists meets with a friendly and relaxed atmosphere to make this Table Table venue the perfect place for any occasion. *Excludes daytime & evening deals and festive menus.

2FOR1 MAIN COURSE | FRI ✓ | SAT ✓ — Modern British

SOPRANO TAPAS & WINE BAR
☎ 01892 535 842

56 The High Street, Tunbridge Wells, TN1 1XF

Vegetarian diners are catered for just as thoroughly as the carnivorous at this Spanish-inspired tapas venue. Whether it's a nibble or a hearty dinner, the vast array of plates spoil guests for choice.

25% OFF TOTAL | 4 | FRI × | SAT × | SUN — Tapas

SOPRANO TAPAS & WINE BAR
☎ 01732 741 333

8 Dorset Street, Sevenoaks, TN13 1LL

Terrific tapas and wine bar that arrived in Sevenoaks after Soprano's success in Tunbridge Wells. Divine cakes, exciting pasta combinations and tasty tapas dishes make this a must visit.

25% OFF TOTAL | 4 | FRI × | SAT × | SUN — Spanish

THE SPICE COURT
☎ 01634 850 150

56-58 Balmoral Road, Gillingham, ME7 4PG

Fresh and colourful Indian restaurant with a distinctive air about it. Serves a marvellous selection of classic dishes as well as some fine tandoori plates. Full, friendly and flavourful.

2FOR1 MAIN COURSE | FRI (phone) | SAT (phone) — Indian

SPICES RESTAURANT
01227 282 814

83 Canterbury Road, Whitstable, CT5 4HQ

Friendly Indian restaurant in Whitstable that knows its audience and does an excellent job of catering to all tastes. Plenty of flavour in the dishes and good-sized portions, together with engaged service.

2FOR1 MAIN COURSE | FRI × | SAT × | SUN — Indian

STRADA
01227 472 089

10-11 Sun Street, Canterbury, CT1 2HX

Offering fresh, bold dishes inspired by flavours of Italian city life – Strada serves a selection of indulgent tastes, to those seeking a blissful escape to laidback Italian life. *Excludes Pizzettas.

25% OFF TOTAL | 6 | FRI ✓ | SAT × | (bell) — Italian

STRADA
01732 461 706

3c Dorset Street, Sevenoaks, TN13 1LL

Offering fresh, bold dishes inspired by flavours of Italian city life – Strada serves a selection of indulgent tastes, to those seeking a blissful escape to laidback Italian life. *Excludes Pizzettas.

25% OFF TOTAL | 6 | FRI ✓ | SAT × | (bell) — Italian

STRADA
01892 520 007

74-76 Mount Pleasant Road, Tunbridge Wells, TN1 1RJ

Offering fresh, bold dishes inspired by flavours of Italian city life – Strada serves a selection of indulgent tastes, to those seeking a blissful escape to laidback Italian life. *Excludes Pizzettas.

25% OFF TOTAL | 6 | FRI ✓ | SAT × | (bell) — Italian

SURIN
☎ 01843 592 001

30 Harbour Street, Ramsgate, CT11 9QD

Chef-proprietor Miss Damarong counts the Thai Royal family amongst her patrons; regularly praised in the press, join her for excellent Thai, Cambodian and Laotian cuisine.

2FOR1 MAIN COURSE | FRI ✱ | SAT ✱ | SUN — Thai

TABLA BAR & INDIAN RESTAURANT
☎ 01303 268 263

Best Western, West Parade, Hythe, CT21 6DT

A contemporary lounge, bar and Indian restaurant offering guests a wonderful place to drink and dine. Spectacular views of the English Channel can be taken in as you savour a taste of India.

2FOR1 MAIN COURSE | FRI ✓ | SAT ✓ | ✱ — Indian

TACOS LOCOS
☎ 01622 759 555

29 Lower Stone Street, Maidstone, ME15 6LH

The ultimate Mexican party venue. Experience huge variety with a menu boasting over 70 succulent dishes and tapas, as well as an extensive cocktail menu, not forgetting their famous Margaritas.

25% OFF TOTAL | 8 | FRI ✱ | SAT ✱ | SUN | ✱ | (bell) — Mexican

TANDOORI NITE
☎ 01843 848 244

64 Station Road, Birchington, CT7 9RA

Adventurous guests can expect to be thrilled and enchanted by the unusual variety featuring on the menu. For the more refined palate, traditional curries are also prepared to an exceptional standard.

2FOR1 MAIN COURSE | FRI × | SAT × — Indian

TRIPLE J'S
☎ 01634 577 786

10 High Street, Gillingham, ME7 1BB

Down-home African Caribbean cuisine on the High Street in Gillingham, from the warm tang of a good goat curry to rice & peas with little or no nonsense about it. You'll not feel a jerk at Triple J's.

25% OFF TOTAL | 6 | FRI ✓ | SAT ✱ | SUN | (bell) — Caribbean

TURNING TABLES RESTAURANT
☎ 01622 763 777

62-63 High Street, Maidstone, ME14 1SR

Turning Tables is a Fresh Produce Restaurant, where the restaurant also houses a farm shop offering fresh produce in the heart of Maidstone.

25% OFF TOTAL | 6 | FRI (phone) | SAT (phone) | SUN — British

WHEATSHEAF AT BOUGH BEECH
☎ 01732 700 254

Hever Road, Edenbridge, TN8 7NU

Ivy-bedecked traditional inn in a notable building dating all the way back to the 16th-century. Now a traditional and charming pub with a spacious feel, serving a varied and tasty menu.

50% OFF FOOD | 4 | FRI ✱ | SAT ✱ — British

THE WHITE HORSE INN
☎ 01227 751 343

The Street, Boughton-under-Blean, Faversham, ME13 9AL

Revelling in its classic Englishness, The White Horse Inn is beautifully traditional and effortlessly inviting. Roaring log fires make for a welcoming indoors, while the gardens are quaint and comforting.

2FOR1 MAIN COURSE | FRI ✓ | SAT × | SUN | (bell) — British

THE WHITE RABBIT
01622 692 212

Sandling Road, Maidstone, ME14 2RF

This Vintage Inn oozes rural charm and rustic character. The picturesque surroundings provide the perfect backdrop for savouring the hearty, seasonal pub-food on the menu.

25% OFF TOTAL | FRI ✓ | SAT ✓ | SUN | (bell) — Modern British

THE WIFE OF BATH
☎ 01233 812 232

4 Upper Bridge Street, Ashford, TN25 5AF

With a character not quite so frank as Chaucer's famous figure, this restaurant is full of smooth charisma and admirable gentility. 2 AA Rosettes. *Offer not available on lunchtime set menus.

25% OFF TOTAL | 4 | FRI ✱ | SAT ✱ | SUN | ✱ — European

THE WINE KITCHEN
☎ 01580 762 075

75 High Street, Tenterden, TN30 6BB

Serving up delicious modern British cuisine, in the heart of Tenterden, The Wine Kitchen is a popular choice with locals and travellers alike. The Wine Kitchen cannot come more highly recommended.

25% OFF TOTAL | 2 | FRI × | SAT × | SUN — British

THE WOODLANDS
01474 533 556

Wrotham Road, Gravesend, DA11 7LF

Beefeater Grill are one of the UK's best-loved restaurants welcoming guests for almost 40 years in over 130 locations nationwide. *Excludes Breakfast, Light Bites, Bar menu, set menus and all other offers.

2FOR1 MAIN COURSE | 6 | FRI ✓ | SAT × | ▲ — Modern British

THE WOOLPACK
01233 713 000

Maidstone Road, Hothfield, Nr Ashford TN26 1AP

Beefeater Grill are one of the UK's best-loved restaurants welcoming guests for almost 40 years in over 130 locations nationwide. *Excludes Breakfast, Light Bites, Bar menu, set menus and all other offers.

2FOR1 MAIN COURSE | 6 | FRI ✓ | SAT × | ▲ — Modern British

YANTZE RESTAURANT
☎ 01227 771 786

144 Tankerton Road, Whitstable, CT5 2AN

Explore the oriental methods of Cantonese, Peking and Szechuan cooking. The expert chefs have carefully composed the à la carte menu which guarantees to immerse diners in authentic Chinese culture.

50% OFF FOOD | 4 | FRI × | SAT × | ▲ — Chinese

ZARA CUISINE
☎ 01474 707 777

73 Station Road, Longfield, DA3 7QA

Devoted to impeccable hospitality, the staff will ensure guests have an exceptional dining experience. Chefs are dedicated to preparing heavenly dishes in a debonair setting.

50% OFF FOOD | FRI ▮ | SAT ▮ — Indian

ZEE RESTAURANT
☎ 01732 363 680

7 Railway Approach, Tonbridge, TN9 2RQ

Look for the podina chops (with a bouquet of mint, cooked over charcoal), the limboo chicken (with lime and fresh coriander to take the edge off), or content yourself with their range of Indian classics.

2FOR1 MAIN COURSE | FRI × | SAT × | SUN — Indian

ZEST
☎ 01580 766 696

4 Manor Row, High Street, Tenterden, TN30 6HP

Making good use of the produce from 'The Garden of England', Zest places a slight twist on tasty English classics. Be sure to try the scrumptious home-made desserts and the classic French wines.

25% OFF TOTAL | 8 | FRI ✱ | SAT ✱ — British

Oxfordshire

THE ANGEL AT BURFORD
☎ 01993 822 714

14 Witney Street, Burford, OX18 4SN

Offering an exceptional array of simple, well-designed dishes, the AA Rosette awarded, The Angel at Burford is perfect for a hearty, high-quality meal in a classic and relaxed setting.

2FOR1 MAIN COURSE | FRI ✱ | SAT ✱ | SUN | ▲ — British

ANICA RESTAURANT
☎ 01869 324 094

3-4 Deans Court, Bicester, OX26 6RD

Refreshingly original Indian restaurant offering an eclectic menu of authentic dishes, including a distinctive range of curries alongside a fine selection of freshly made sundries.

2FOR1 3 COURSES | FRI ▮ | SAT ▮ — Indian

ANNORA INTERNATIONAL
☎ 01865 775 974

The Tree Hotel, 63 Church Way, OX4 4EY

The restaurant is proud to present a menu bursting full of exciting and interesting flavours. Try exceedingly tasty, quirky English dishes as well as divine, authentic Indian and Thai cuisine.

2FOR1 MAIN COURSE | FRI ✱ | SAT ✱ | SUN | ▲ — International

THE APPLECART
01235 835 168

Milton Interchange, Milton, Abingdon, OX14 4DP

Quality pub classics with modern twists meets with a friendly and relaxed atmosphere to make this Table Table venue the perfect place for any occasion. *Excludes daytime & evening deals and festive menus.

2FOR1 MAIN COURSE | FRI ✓ | SAT ✓ — Modern British

ARZOO OXFORD
☎ 01865 554 905

107-108 Walton Street, Oxford, OX2 6AJ

A family run restaurant, located in the heard of Oxford, let Arzoo awaken your senses to the delights of authentic, contemporary Indian cuisine.

25% OFF TOTAL | 4 | FRI ▮ | SAT ▮ — Indian

AVANTI
☎ 01491 835 500

85 High Street, Wallingford, OX10 0BW

Fresh Italian cuisine created with pride, offering a vast menu with an emphasis on fish and seafood. This venue caters for all, not least with the temptation of its indulgent home-made desserts.

2FOR1 MAIN COURSE | FRI ▮ | SAT ✱ — Italian

THE BEEHIVE
☎ 01993 840 813

Black Bourton Road, Carterton, OX18 3HA

The Beehive is a traditional pub with a lively twist. Good food is served daily along with a great selection of wines and Wadworth real ales. *Excludes Xmas menus.

25% OFF TOTAL | 4 | FRI × | SAT × | SUN — British

BELLA ITALIA
01865 791 032

6 George Street, Oxford, OX1 2AF

Accessible Italian cuisine on the British high street – indulge in authentic sharing platters, hand stretched pizzas and hearty pasta dishes, served with a healthy dose of gregarious Italian hospitality.

25% OFF TOTAL | 6 | FRI × | SAT × | SUN | ▲ — Italian

BOMBAY RESTAURANT
01865 511 188

82 Walton Street, Oxford, OX2 6EA

A great choice of dishes are offer in this successful Indian restaurant, where the 'BYO' policy proves extremely popular. Try the chicken shashlik to be guaranteed a fabulous dining experience.

25% OFF TOTAL | 10 | FRI ✱ | SAT ✱ — Indian

BRANCA
☎ 01865 556 111

111 Walton Street, Oxford, OX2 6AJ

Impressive service provides exquisite tasting food in this informal Italian restaurant. Regular diners enjoy the complementary focaccia bread, before feasting on one of the many favourite dishes on offer.

2FOR1 MAIN COURSE | FRI ✱ | SAT ✱ | ▲ — Italian

BROOKES RESTAURANT
☎ 01865 483 803

Gipsy Lane, Headington, Oxford, OX3 0BP

One of the finest commercial restaurants in the city and at the same time a teaching resource for up-and-coming students in the hospitality trade. A superb seasonal menu keeps everyone on their toes.

2FOR1 3 COURSES | FRI ✱ | SAT × | SUN | ▲ — Locally Sourced

BROTHERTONS BRASSERIE
☎ 01993 811 114

1 High Street, Woodstock, OX20 1TE

Deeply burnished timber and glowing gaslight create a heart-warming environment in which guests can enjoy delicious dishes. The wild boar casserole and the char grilled swordfish are both great choices.

25% OFF TOTAL | 2 | FRI ▮ | SAT ▮ | ▲ — Contemporary

CAFÉ ROUGE
01491 411 733

37 Hart Street, Henley-on-Thames, RG9 2AR

French sophistication on the British high street – enjoy seasonally changing French dishes and a continental wine selection, served in a relaxed environment with an undeniable flair of Parisian chic.

25% OFF TOTAL | 6 | FRI ✓ | SAT ✓ | ✱ | ▲ — French

CAFÉ ROUGE
01865 310 194

11 Little Clarendon Street, Oxford, OX1 2HP

French sophistication on the British high street – enjoy seasonally changing French dishes and a continental wine selection, served in a relaxed environment with an undeniable flair of Parisian chic.

25% OFF TOTAL | 6 | FRI ✓ | SAT ✓ | ✱ | ▲ — French

CAFÉ ROUGE
01993 775 014

Marriott's Close, Woodford Way, Oxford, OX28 6GW

French sophistication on the British high street – enjoy seasonally changing French dishes and a continental wine selection, served in a relaxed environment with an undeniable flair of Parisian chic.

25% OFF TOTAL | 6 | FRI ✓ | SAT ✓ | ✱ | ▲ — French

THE CHEQUERS INN
01608 644 717

Goddard's Lane, Chipping Norton, OX7 5NP

A pub with a long history that now features a fine restaurant in its old courtyard. Serves traditional pub food and supports local suppliers. Quality is high, with seasonal menus and a fine specials board.

2FOR1 MAIN COURSE | FRI ✓ | SAT ✓ | ▲ — Modern British

CHERRY TREE
☎ 01235 831 222

33 High Street, Steventon, OX13 6RZ

This oak-beamed, low, cosy inn is a past master in the arts of a quiet drink, a homely and hearty meal, and a friendly, accommodating welcome. Settle back and enjoy a classic pub dinner.

25% OFF TOTAL | 4 | FRI × | SAT × | SUN — British

CHOPSTICKS RESTAURANT
☎ 01235 813 333

126 Broadway, Didcot, OX11 8AB

Great little characterful Chinese restaurant in Didcot. Serves an array of colour-filled, spicy dishes; a selection of menus are also on offer, ideal for business lunches or a relaxed evening meal

2FOR1 MAIN COURSE | FRI ✱ | SAT ✱ | ▲ — Chinese

COCKADOO BAR & RESTAURANT
☎ 01865 341 030

Nuneham Courtenay, Oxford, OX44 9NX

A fine dining restaurant boasting contemporary yet authentic décor and a great selection of Asian fusion dishes. Experience an array of delicately enchanting flavours created by truly experienced chefs.

25% OFF TOTAL | 6 | FRI ✓ | SAT ✓ — Oriental

CORI
☎ 01295 263 664

53 High Street, Banbury, OX16 5JJ

A warm and welcoming family-run Italian restaurant, whose traditional and authentic food includes freshly made pizzas. A culinary treat in the centre of Banbury, where all occasions are catered for.

2FOR1 MAIN COURSE | FRI ✱ | SAT ✱ | SUN ✱ | ✱ — Italian

THE COTTAGE IMPERIAL
☎ 01235 538 338

17a Bridge Street, Abingdon, OX14 3HN

Simple and thoroughly tasty Chinese takeaway food. Has a good reputation for the overall quality of its dishes. and for their swiftness in delivering. A smart, effective little eatery.

2FOR1 MAIN COURSE | FRI ✓ | SAT × | ✱ — Chinese

DOOR 74
☎ 01865 203 374

74 Cowley Road, Oxford, OX4 1JB

Dedicated to serving the finest contemporary British cuisine all day long, using seasonal and locally sourced ingredients. Beautiful presentation of each dish sets Door 74 apart.

25% OFF TOTAL | 4 | FRI ✱ | SAT ✱ | ▲ — British

THE DUCK ON THE POND
☎ 01295 721 166

Main Street, South Newington, OX15 4JE

This wonderfully located pub and restaurant has been lovingly maintained. The original features enhance the interior cosiness, and offer a perfect backdrop to a fabulous dining experience.

25% OFF TOTAL | 4 | FRI × | SAT × | SUN | ▲ — English and Continental

THE DUKE'S CUT
☎ 01865 204 060

1 Park End Street, Oxford, OX1 1HH

Be sure to stop at The Duke's Cut whilst in the prestigious city of Oxford for a refuel after a busy day of sightseeing. Choose from sandwiches that are fit to burst or juicy bangers and creamy mash.

2FOR1 MAIN COURSE | FRI ▯ | SAT × | SUN | ▲ — British

EDEN BAR AND GRILL
☎ 01844 213 661

Spread Eagle Hotel, 16-17 Cornmarket, Thame, OX9 2BW

Haute cuisine inflected in a contemporary British style at this charismatic inn in Thame. Accomplished, sophisticated flavours, along with a down-home 'comfort cooking' section of the menu.

25% OFF TOTAL | 4 | FRI ✓ | SAT ✓ | ▲ — British

ELAICHI
☎ 01235 772 010

9 Millbrook Square, Grove, Wantage, OX12 7JZ

Holding a great reputation, this establishment delivers affordable Bangladeshi cuisine that showcases an array of flavours and spices to satisfy every individual taste. A high standard of food and service.

2FOR1 MAIN COURSE | FRI ✓ | SAT ▯ | ▲ — Bangladeshi/Indian

EVEREST NEPALESE
☎ 01865 251 555

147-151, Howard Street, Oxford, OX4 3AZ

Using only the freshest ingredients, the recipes here are created for a cleaner, crisper, more balanced taste - all resulting in the most delightful food you will discover between oxford and Kathmandu.

25% OFF TOTAL | FRI × | SAT × | ▲ — Indian

FALKLAND ARMS
☎ 01608 683 653

Gret Tew, Chipping Norton, OX7 4DB

A traditional local pub that thrives on those well-established values of hospitality and sociability. It also serves some delicious pub food. Grab a moment's serenity, a bite to eat and a leisurely drink.

25% OFF TOTAL | 4 | FRI × | SAT × | SUN — British

FALLOWFIELDS COUNTRY HOUSE
☎ 01865 820 416

Faringdon Road, Kingston Bagpuize, OX13 5BH

The aim of the team at Fallowfields is to be recognised as one of the best fine dining restaurants in Oxfordshire. Seasonal fruit, vegetables and herbs are grown in the hotel's kitchen gardens and orchards.

2FOR1 MAIN COURSE | FRI ✓ | SAT ✱ | SUN — Modern British

THE FLOWING WELL
☎ 01865 735 846

Sunningwell, Abingdon, OX13 6RB

Stunningly situated, this venue is held dear by the locals of Sunningwell. Prepared in the open kitchen, the stone-baked pizzas and burgers are divine. A warm welcome ensures this venue appeals to all.

2FOR1 3 COURSES | FRI ✓ | SAT ✱ | SUN — Modern Pub

THE GRIFFIN INN
☎ 01295 660 311

9 Culworth Road, Chipping Warden, OX17 1LB

Allow yourself to be engrossed by the tremendous atmosphere that awaits you in this commendable bistro pub. The attractiveness of its location is transferred to the interior décor and the outstanding menu.

2FOR1 MAIN COURSE | FRI ✓ | SAT ✓ — European

GURKHA VILLAGE NEPALESE RESTAURANT
☎ 01865 378 180

174 Oxford Road, Kidlington, Oxford, OX5 1EA

In the heart of the cosmopolitan city of Oxford sits the Gurkha Village Restaurant. Decadent Nepalese cuisine is memorable, flavourful and wholly deserving of its popularity.

2FOR1 MAIN COURSE | FRI × | SAT × | ▲ — Nepalese

THE HIGH TABLE
☎ 01865 248 695

71-73 High Street, Oxford, OX1 4BE

One of Oxford's best-kept secrets. A brasserie and bar that is all about fresh ingredients, simple, quality cooking, and switched-on service. British and French-influenced cuisine awarded 1 AA Rosette.

25% OFF TOTAL | 4 | FRI ✱ | SAT ✱ | SUN — British

HI-LO JAMAICAN EATING HOUSE
☎ 01865 725 984

68-70 Cowley Road, Oxford, OX4 1JB

A popular venue that appeals to all ages, delivering traditional Jamaican home cooking that includes jerk pork and Caribbean sea fish. Live music offers an authentic and entertaining night.

25% OFF TOTAL | 2 | FRI ✱ | SAT ✱ | ✱ — Caribbean

HIMALAYAN TANDOORI
☎ 01491 410 939

16 Reading Road, Henley-on-Thames, RG9 1AG

Enjoy fine traditional Indian and Nepalese cuisine superbly crafted and delivered by exemplary staff in a great atmosphere. A varied choice of vegetarian dishes ensures all tastes are catered for.

2FOR1 MAIN COURSE | FRI ✓ | SAT ✓ — Nepalese

To understand what the restaurant icons mean, please see the inside back cover.

THE HORNTON BAR @ MERCURE
☎01295 253 261
Whately Hall Hotel, 17-19 Horse Fair, Banbury, OX16 0AN
The Hornton Bar serves simple, tasty light bites and lunches to go with the array of excellent wines in this magnificent 17th-century hotel on Horse Fair in Banbury.

25% OFF TOTAL | ♟ 4 | FRI ✓ | SAT ✓ | ▲ — International

HOTEL DU VIN
☎01491 848 400
New Street, Henley-on-Thames, RG9 2BP
The finest, freshest local produce, simple European recipes, a stunning choice of wines; these are the elements of the trademark Hotel du Vin bistro. Housed in a converted riverside brewery. 2 AA Rosettes.

2FOR1 MAIN COURSE | FRI ✱ | SAT ✱ | SUN | ▲ — European

INDIAN DREAM
☎01235 817 711
32-34 Wantage Road, Didcot, OX11 0BT
Prepared and served following the traditions of India, the food here is simple, authentic, and provides a real taste of India's excellent culinary culture. An ideal venue for any occasion, even a takeaway.

2FOR1 2 COURSES | FRI ✱ | SAT ✱ — Indian

JEE SAHEB RESTAURANT
☎01865 513 773
15 North Parade Avenue, Oxford, OX2 6LX
Classic Asian cuisine from across the subcontinent. An array of traditional and creative dishes from Bangladesh, India and Pakistan that have been beautifully crafted from fresh, quality produce.

2FOR1 MAIN COURSE | FRI ✱ | SAT ✱ — Indian

JUNCTION RESTAURANT @ HOLIDAY INN
☎08719 429 086
Holiday Inn, Woodstock Road, Oxford, OX2 8JD
The Holiday Inn Oxford hosts a modern contemporary restaurant, where a British-themed menu offers delectable favourites and comforting treats. Imaginative international flavours also influence the food.

50% OFF FOOD | ♟ 4 | FRI × | SAT × | SUN — Modern British

KADAI & NAAN
☎01865 244 555
209 Cowley Road, Oxford, OX4 1XF
Authentic dishes achieved through the use of the finest ingredients and cooking techniques allow you to savour both the contemporary and familiar tastes of India.

25% OFF TOTAL | FRI × | SAT × | ✱ | ▲ — Indian

KARMA RESTAURANT
☎01865 777 402
152 Oxford Road, Oxford, OX4 2EA
Speciality dishes such as the murgh mirchi or the Goa maachli curry give this Indian eatery a very reputable name indeed. Chefs guarantee happy and satisfied diners at the Karma Restaurant.

2FOR1 2 COURSES | FRI × | SAT × — Indian

LA TASCA
☎01865 246 464
5 Oxford Castle, Oxford, OX1 1AY
Quintessentially Spanish, La Tasca's fresh and exciting menu offers something for everyone. Their tapas dishes are sincerely authentic, while their paellas always deliver on flavour.

25% OFF TOTAL | ♟ 8 | FRI ✓ | SAT × | ▲ — Spanish

LAMB INN HOTEL
☎01993 823 155
Sheep Street, Burford, OX18 4LR
This stunning restaurant, recognised by 2 AA Rosettes, allows visitors to dine on contemporary English cuisine and enjoy quality real ales. *Offer available in the restaurant only. Booking is essential.

25% OFF TOTAL | ♟ 4 | FRI ✓ | SAT ✱ | SUN — Modern British

LAMBERT ARMS
☎01844 351 496
London Road, Oxon, OX49 5SB
Steeped in historicism, this original coaching inn is located in an area of breathtaking scenery. Relax by the open fires and indulge in a British seasonal dish prepared from the à la carte menu.

2FOR1 MAIN COURSE | FRI ✓ | SAT × | SUN | ▲ — International

LE KESH
☎01865 202 077
180 Cowley Road, Oxford, OX4 1UE
Be transported to Beirut and Marrakesh in this fabulous Arabic-inspired eatery. Serving only the most vibrant of dishes, diners can expect generous meat kebabs and fresh vegetable tagines.

2FOR1 MAIN COURSE | FRI × | SAT × — Mediterranean

LOCH FYNE
☎01491 845 780
20 Market Street, Henley-on-Thames, RG9 2AH
From the roadside oyster bar that once was, Loch Fyne restaurants now successfully inject energy and passion into great food and wonderful flavours, whilst ensuring their seafood is sustainably sourced.

25% OFF TOTAL | ♟ 4 | FRI ✱ | SAT ✱ | ▲ — Seafood

LOCH FYNE
☎01865 292 510
55 Walton Street, Oxford, OX2 6AE
From the roadside oyster bar that once was, Loch Fyne restaurants now successfully inject energy and passion into great food and wonderful flavours, whilst ensuring their seafood is sustainably sourced.

25% OFF TOTAL | ♟ 4 | FRI ✱ | SAT ✱ | ▲ — Seafood

THE LONGWALL
01865 779 230
Oxford Business Park, Garsington Road, Oxford, OX4 2JT
Beefeater Grill are one of the UK's best-loved restaurants welcoming guests for almost 40 years in over 130 locations nationwide. *Excludes Breakfast, Light Bites, Bar menu, set menus and all other offers.

2FOR1 MAIN COURSE | ♟ 6 | FRI ✓ | SAT × | ▲ — Modern British

MALIKAS
☎01865 723 029
218 Cowley Road, Oxford, OX4 1UQ
Well-regarded Indian restaurant in Oxford that provides a fine line in traditional dishes and creative flavours. Talented chefs and attentive waiting staff are a further two firm attributes of Malikas.

25% OFF TOTAL | ♟ 6 | FRI ✓ | SAT ✓ | ▲ — Indian

MALMAISON
☎01865 268 400
3 Oxford Castle, New Road, Oxford, OX1 1AY
Guests will want to lock themselves up and throw away the key in this magnificent 'Mal', impeccably transformed from a prison. The brasserie features mouth-watering food and fantastic wine. 1 AA Rosette.

2FOR1 MAIN COURSE | FRI × | SAT × | SUN | ▲ — European

MAXWELL'S
☎01865 242 192
36 Queen Street, Oxford, OX1 1ER
A well-established late night bar and grill. The winning formula of top-quality service and a famous burger menu satisfies every guest, whilst the stylishly chic interior provides a relaxing ambience.

2FOR1 MAIN COURSE | FRI ✓ | SAT ✓ | ▲ — American

THE MAYTIME INN
☎01993 822 068
Asthall Burford, Oxford, OX18 4HW
Nestled in the heart of the beautiful, peaceful and historic village of Asthall, this great establishment uses only the finest local produce so you can be ensured of a quality meal.

25% OFF TOTAL | ♟ 4 | FRI 📱 | SAT × | SUN — British

MEMORIES OF BENGAL
☎01491 652 399
12 Wallingford Road, Cholsey, Wallingford, OX10 9LQ
Be tempted by an unrivalled range of authentic and imaginative fusion dishes, delicately crafted to reveal the true tastes and aromas of a culture with an exemplary culinary history.

25% OFF TOTAL | ♟ 4 | FRI ✱ | SAT ✱ | ✱ — Indian

THE MIRABAI RESTAURANT
☎01865 762 255
70 London Road, Headington, Oxford, OX3 7PD
A wide selection of both Bangladeshi and Indian dishes are on offer in this popular tandoori restaurant. Its many regular diners testifies to its excellence.

25% OFF TOTAL | ♟ 2 | FRI ✱ | SAT ✱ — Indian/Bangladeshi

THE MITRE
01865 244 563
High Street, Oxford, OX1 4AG
Beefeater Grill are one of the UK's best-loved restaurants welcoming guests for almost 40 years in over 130 locations nationwide. *Excludes Breakfast, Light Bites, Bar menu, set menus and all other offers.

2FOR1 MAIN COURSE | ♟ 6 | FRI ✓ | SAT × | ▲ — Modern British

THE MOON & SIXPENCE
☎01295 730 544
Main Street, Hanwell, Banbury, OX17 1HW
A highly popular place to eat, run by Chef Hylton Bradley, is situated on the outskirts of Banbury, in the beautiful village of Hanwell. *Advance booking mentioning Gourmet Society is essential.

50% OFF FOOD | ♟ 4 | FRI ✓ | SAT × | SUN | ▲ — British

MOTI MAHAL INDIAN RESTAURANT
☎01844 339 245
Oxford Road, Tiddington, Thame, OX4 3HU
An excellent Indian restaurant set in the old Fox pub, Tiddington, offering diners the chance to experience the true scope of Indian cuisine, with a menu bursting with spice and flavour.

2FOR1 MAIN COURSE | FRI ✓ | SAT ✓ — Indian

NEW MOGUL TANDOORI
☎01295 251 920
58 Parson Street, Banbury, OX16 5NB
A wonderful Banbury restaurant that serves classic Indian dishes and tasty tandoori cuisine. Whether you fancy a creamy masala or a tandoori-grilled chicken with thick naan bread, you'll find it here.

50% OFF FOOD | 8 | FRI | SAT — Indian

NO.1 FOLLY BRIDGE
☎01865 201 293
1 Folly Bridge, Oxford, OX1 4LB
Café and brasserie restaurant serving a wide range of food and drink to be enjoyed on the beautiful pontoon or in the stylish dining area. A relaxed, rustic and welcoming experience by the river.

2FOR1 MAIN COURSE | FRI ✓ | SAT ✓ | ▲ — Mediterranean

THE NUT TREE INN
☎01865 331 253
Main Street, Murcott, Kidlington, Oxford, OX5 2RE
This double AA Rosette, Michelin starred venue is part of the local community, and an extraordinary fine dining spot. Its quality brooks no debate; the food - featuring rare breed pigs speaks for itself.

2FOR1 MAIN COURSE | FRI * | SAT × | SUN — British

THE OCK MILL
01235 554 148
Marcham Road, Abingdon, Oxford, OX14 1AD
Beefeater Grill are one of the UK's best-loved restaurants welcoming guests for almost 40 years in over 130 locations nationwide. *Excludes Breakfast, Light Bites, Bar menu, set menus and all other offers.

2FOR1 MAIN COURSE | 6 | FRI ✓ | SAT × | ▲ — Modern British

THE OLD RED LION
☎01844 281 274
40 High Street, Tetsworth, Thame, OX9 7AS
Radiating a magic and welcoming character, the lively atmosphere is just one of the pub's appealing factors. The patio area is perfect for summer barbecues and spit roasts.

2FOR1 3 COURSES | FRI | SAT — British

THE OLD SWAN
☎01993 774 441
Old Swan & Minster Mill, School Hill, Witney, OX29 0RN
The Old Swan is the latest of the de Savary Family's boutique inns, situated next to the River Windrush in the Cotswolds, serving delicious gastro pub food, using local produce as well as a la carte menu.

25% OFF TOTAL | 6 | FRI ✓ | SAT | ▲ — British

THE OXFORD BLUE
☎01865 460 215
32 Marston Street, Oxford, OX4 1JU
The vision of Oxford Blue is to be a pub that serves great food, beers and wines in a friendly atmosphere. They certainly do not fail to deliver. An eclectic menu that highlights quality local produce.

2FOR1 MAIN COURSE | FRI × | SAT × | SUN | * | ▲ — British

OXFORD GRILL
☎01865 201 120
21 Cowley Road, Oxford, OX4 1HP
Guaranteeing authentic and affable surroundings, this Mediterranean-inspired brasserie specialises in Turkish cuisine prepared from fresh, prime ingredients.

25% OFF TOTAL | 4 | FRI ✓ | SAT ✓ — Mediterranean

THE OXFORD RETREAT
☎01865 250 309
1-2 Hythe Bridge Street, Oxford, OX1 2EW
The Oxford Retreat is a beautiful traditional pub with warm eclectic furnishings, set on the river in Oxford, serving delicious, fresh, and locally sourced produce every day.

2FOR1 MAIN COURSE | FRI × | SAT × | SUN — British

PORTABELLO
☎01865 559 653
7 South Parade, Summertown, Oxford, OX2 7JL
Cooked with imagination and flair, the food is fresh and flavourful, whilst the service is markedly efficient. Unwind in a calm atmosphere with the pick of some delicious dishes and watch the world go by.

25% OFF TOTAL | 4 | FRI × | SAT × | SUN | * | ▲ — Modern British

PREZZO
01865 791 748
2 Oxford Castle, Oxford, OX1 1AY
With a character all of its own, Prezzo oozes contemporary style and enduring charm. Signature pastas, stone-baked pizzas and classic Italian dishes promise a perfect dining choice for the whole family.

2FOR1 MAIN COURSE | FRI × | SAT × | ▲ — Italian

PREZZO
01844 218 542
12a Buttermarket, Thame, OX9 3DX
With a character all of its own, Prezzo oozes contemporary style and enduring charm. Signature pastas, stone-baked pizzas and classic Italian dishes promise a perfect dining choice for the whole family.

2FOR1 MAIN COURSE | FRI × | SAT × | ▲ — Italian

PREZZO
☎01235 511 271
8 Market Place, Didcot, OX11 7LE
With a character all of its own, Prezzo oozes contemporary style and enduring charm. Signature pastas, stone-baked pizzas and classic Italian dishes promise a perfect dining choice for the whole family.

2FOR1 MAIN COURSE | FRI × | SAT × | ▲ — Italian

QUISINE
☎01295 276 203
24 Cornhill, Banbury, OX16 5NG
Guests can expect fine-dining at this British eatery. Devour baked chestnut portobello mushrooms or blackened chicken.

50% OFF FOOD | 4 | FRI × | SAT × — British

THE RED LION
☎01865 890 625
115 High Street, Chalgrove, OX44 7SS
Lovely village pub, all ivy-coated outer walls, beautiful gardens and a cosy, traditional space inside. Down-to-earth, simple but always fresh and thoughtful style in the exceptional pub food.

2FOR1 MAIN COURSE | FRI * | SAT * | ▲ — British

THE RED LION
☎01869 340 225
South Side, Steeple Aston, OX25 4RY
Unspoilt pub that provides a peaceful and relaxing space to eat and drink. Sumptuously furnished, the light and airy restaurant is naturally warm, and serves a range of neatly accomplished dishes.

25% OFF TOTAL | 10 | FRI ✓ | SAT ✓ — English/Gastro pub

RIVER ROOM RESTAURANT
☎01865 334 444
Henley Road, Sandford-on-Thames, OX4 4GX
Restaurant in the stately and stylish Oxford Thames Four Pillars Hotel. Overlooks the river and picturesque grounds, and features a varied menu of both classic and contemporary dishes.

25% OFF TOTAL | 10 | FRI ✓ | SAT ✓ | ▲ — Contemporary

RIVERVIEW RESTAURANT
☎01865 858 567
Shillingford Bridge Hotel, Wallingford, OX10 8LZ
The Riverview Restaurant with its superb views across the grounds, offers an extensive a la carte menu together with an excellent and imaginative wine list.

25% OFF TOTAL | 8 | FRI ✓ | SAT ✓ | ▲ — British

SAFFRON RESTAURANT
☎01865 512 211
204-206 Banbury Road, Oxford, OX2 7BY
At the Saffron Restaurant, you will experience the finest food, which perfectly combines the ancient traditions and authentic flavours of India and Bangladesh, fused exotically with a unique ethnic edge.

2FOR1 MAIN COURSE | FRI × | SAT ✓ | SUN | * | ▲ — Indian

SAN CARLO
☎01295 703 073
36-37 Parsons Street, Banbury, OX16 5NA
Traditional Italian home-made food that will have you coming back time and time again. Scrumptious stone-baked pizzas and tasty salads as well as pastas from all regions of Italy.

2FOR1 MAIN COURSE | FRI * | SAT * | SUN | * | ▲ — Italian

SAN SICARIO
☎01491 834 078
28 High Street, Wallingford, OX10 0BU
A highly popular Italian restaurant where traditional culinary methods are used to ensure authentic tastes and flavours are locked into every dish. The fabulous menu represents all regions of Italy.

2FOR1 MAIN COURSE | FRI ✓ | SAT * — Italian

SHANGHAI 30'S
☎01865 242 230

82 St Aldates, Oxford, OX1 1RA

Provides a menu that focuses on both classic and contemporary dishes. Cuisine from Shanghai and the surrounding areas is met by better-known food from Szechuan and Canton.

2FOR1 3 COURSES | FRI ✱ | SAT ✱ | ▲ — Chinese

SPICE LOUNGE
☎01865 510 072

193 Banbury Road, Summertown, Oxford, OX2 7AR

Chefs produce stunningly delicious dishes with an emphasis on organic and creative food. Traditional recipes are used providing customers with a diverse, unusual menu while focusing on healthy eating.

2FOR1 MAIN COURSE | FRI ✱ | SAT ✱ | SUN — Indian

SPIRES RESTAURANT
☎01865 553 461

Linton Lodge, 11-13 Linton Road, Oxford, OX2 6UJ

Contemporary and accomplished dining in this hotel-based restaurant in Oxford. Modern and open styling with a wide-ranging menu to match.

25% OFF TOTAL | 10 | FRI ✓ | SAT ✓ | SUN | ▲ — British

STRADA
01491 571 497

49-51 Bell Street, Henley-on-Thames, RG9 2BG

Offering fresh, bold dishes inspired by flavours of Italian city life – Strada serves a selection of indulgent tastes, to those seeking a blissful escape to laidback Italian life. *Excludes Pizzettas.

25% OFF TOTAL | 6 | FRI ✓ | SAT × | ▲ — Italian

STRADA
01865 514 468

1-2 Little Clarendon St, Oxford, OX1 2HP

Offering fresh, bold dishes inspired by flavours of Italian city life – Strada serves a selection of indulgent tastes, to those seeking a blissful escape to laidback Italian life. *Excludes Pizzettas.

25% OFF TOTAL | 6 | FRI ✓ | SAT × | ▲ — Italian

THE SWAN INN
☎01993 823 339

Swinbrook, Burford, OX18 4DY

A perfect 'bubble' - with 2 AA Rosettes - to forget the world, catch up with friends, escape for a drink, dine on locally sourced, excellent food and enjoy the beautiful Cotswold countryside.

50% OFF FOOD | FRI × | SAT × | ✱ | ▲ — Modern British

SWIFT RESTAURANT @ MECURE
☎01295 253 261

Whately Hall Hotel, 17-19 Horse Fair, Banbury, OX16 0AN

Spare and elegant in its design with oak panelling, cosy intimate tables and a cluster of paintings on one wall. The menu features a range of subtle, refined dishes together with some excellent wines.

50% OFF FOOD | 4 | FRI ✓ | SAT ✓ | ▲ — International

TASTE OF INDIA
☎01865 874 800

34 The Green, Oxford, OX33 1RP

A convivial and informal Indian restaurant and takeaway. Enjoy their curry and spices in the comfortable dining area or public bar.

2FOR1 MAIN COURSE | FRI ✱ | SAT ✱ | ▲ — Indian

THE TURNPIKE
01865 847 666

2 Woodstock Road, Yarnton, Kidlington, OX5 1PJ

This Vintage Inn oozes rural charm and rustic character. The picturesque surroundings provide the perfect backdrop for savouring the hearty, seasonal pub-food on the menu.

25% OFF TOTAL | FRI ✓ | SAT ✓ | SUN | ▲ — Modern British

VERDE PIZZERIA
☎01865 246 222

212-214 Cowley Road, Oxford, OX3 1UQ

Doing exactly what its name promises, this cracking pizzeria offers a terrific array of choices, from salads to exciting pizzas. Amiable staff and an inviting atmosphere are added bonuses.

25% OFF TOTAL | FRI ▯ | SAT ▯ — Italian

VICTORIA ARMS
☎01865 241 382

Mill Lane, Old Marston, Oxford, OX3 0PZ

A picturesque pub priding themselves on a perfect pint and a perfect view. Dine on classic, hearty pub food and settle back and enjoy a Cask Marque-credited Wadworth ale to wash it all down.

25% OFF TOTAL | 4 | FRI × | SAT × | SUN — British

THE WHITE HART HOTEL
☎01865 340 074

26 High Street, Dorchester-on-Thames, OX10 7HN

An AA Rosette-awarded restaurant in a gorgeous old coaching inn. Plush and cosy inside, its menus are all about simplicity and subtlety, with light sauces and little variations making all the difference.

2FOR1 MAIN COURSE | FRI ▯ | SAT ✱ — European

Surrey

39PRIME
☎01737 237 977

39 Church Street, Reigate, RH2 0AD

39 Prime invites you to enjoy the finest steaks and a mouth-watering choice of the best and most tender cuts of beef from around the world.

2FOR1 3 COURSES | FRI ✓ | SAT ✱ | SUN | ✱ | ▲ — Steakhouse

ANCHOR
☎01932 342 507

Pryford Lock, Woking, GU23 6QW

Suitably named for its location on the River Wey, The Anchor is a fine place to enjoy an afternoon or early evening. Delivers a traditionally English dining and drinking experience.

25% OFF TOTAL | FRI × | SAT × | SUN | ▲ — British

THE ANCIENT RAJ
☎0127 621 503

9 The Parade, Frimley, GU16 7HY

Carefully selected spices are traditionally blended to add the most wonderful flavours to every dish. Generous portions are served by courteous staff in a relaxed environment.

2FOR1 MAIN COURSE | FRI ✱ | SAT ✱ — Indian

ANGEL DINING ROOMS
☎01483 533 537

91 High Street, Guildford, GU1 3DS

Set within the historic Angel Posting House on a charming cobbled street, The Angel Dining Rooms showcases gourmet British dishes. With a weekly changing menu and fine produce, The Angel is a delight.

2FOR1 3 COURSES | 8 | FRI ▯ | SAT ▯ | ▲ — British

ASIANA RESTAURANT
☎01483 488 122

114 Hermitage Road, St Johns, Woking, GU21 8TT

Experience true Indian spice and fragrance, with every dish being of sublime quality. Whether an intimate meal or a family gathering, this venue offers a unique Indian fine dining experience.

2FOR1 MAIN COURSE | FRI ✱ | SAT ✱ | ✱ | ▲ — Indian

BELLA ITALIA
01276 686 724

The Atrium, Camberley, GU15 3PT

Accessible Italian cuisine on the British high street – indulge in authentic sharing platters, hand stretched pizzas and hearty pasta dishes, served with a healthy dose of gregarious Italian hospitality.

25% OFF TOTAL | 6 | FRI × | SAT × | SUN | ▲ — Italian

THE BENCH BAR AND RESTAURANT
01483 683 888

Surrey Sports Park, Guildford, GU2 7AD

The Bench Bar and Restaurant at the Surrey Sports Park is a great place to wind down after a game. Panoramic views of the outdoor pitches and the rolling Surrey hills provide a unique aspect to the place.

2FOR1 MAIN COURSE | FRI ✓ | SAT ✓ — British

BEST WESTERN GATWICK MOAT HOUSE
☎08712 261 931

Gatwick, Horley, RH6 0AB

Harriett's Restaurant is a refreshing alternative to typical airport eateries. Named for the first woman to fly across the Channel, the mouth watering menu and daily specials are worth flying in for.

25% OFF TOTAL | 6 | FRI ✓ | SAT ✓ — International

BINAKA RESTAURANT
01483 740 686

18 High Street, Woking, GU21 6BW

Indian restaurant whose charm is the attention to detail it brings to bear. Excellent selection of dishes to go with a friendly atmosphere and switched-on service. Fresh-flavoured dishes across the board.

2FOR1 MAIN COURSE | FRI × | SAT × | SUN — Indian

BLACK HORSE HOOKWOOD
☎ 01293 773 611

Reigate Road, Gatwick, RH6 0HU

Idyllically set on the edge of the rolling countryside of Surrey, this famous Hall & Woodhouse pub provides a menu full of traditional English dishes sourced locally. An ideal eatery for everyone.

25% OFF TOTAL | FRI × | SAT × | SUN | ▲ — British

THE BLACK SWAN OCKHAM
☎ 01932 862 364

Old Lane, Ockham, KT11 1NG

The Black Swan Ockham nestled in the idyllic Surrey countryside is the local culinary hotspot, offering an inventive British menu using some of the best in fresh local & seasonal produce.

25% OFF TOTAL | ♟ 6 | FRI × | SAT × | SUN | ✱ — British

BLACKHORSE REIGATE
☎ 01737 245 694

93 West Street, Reigate, RH2 9JZ

Pretty Reigate pub that does a fine range of traditional fare and slightly more unusual offerings. Favourites include crayfish with honey and mustard, or the traditional liver and bacon with onion gravy.

2FOR1 MAIN COURSE | FRI × | SAT × | SUN — Modern Pub

THE BLACKSMITHS HEAD
☎ 01342 833 697

Newchapel Road, Lingfield, RH7 6LE

Lawrence and Catherine welcome you to their recently refurbished restaurant, The Blacksmiths Head. They offer quality home cooked food where everything is prepared fresh to order.

50% OFF FOOD | ♟ 4 | FRI ✓ | SAT ✓ | SUN | ✱ — British

BRIDGE BARN
01483 763 642

Bridge Barn Lane, Horsell, Woking, GU21 6NL

Beefeater Grill are one of the UK's best-loved restaurants welcoming guests for almost 40 years in over 130 locations nationwide. *Excludes Breakfast, Light Bites, Bar menu, set menus and all other offers.

2FOR1 MAIN COURSE | ♟ 6 | FRI ✓ | SAT × | ▲ — Modern British

CAFE RIALTO
☎ 01306 742 885

55 South Street, Dorking, RH4 2JX

Flagship Café Rialto. Friendly and unpretentious, its Italian menu is excellent. The classic scaloppa alla Milanese, for instance, is beautifully tender; the atmosphere of the place helps make the evening.

2FOR1 MAIN COURSE | FRI ✱ | SAT ✱ | ▲ — Italian

CEYLON TAVERN
☎ 01306 886 000

53-55 South Street, Dorking, RH4 2JX

Originally known as Ceylon in its ancestral days, Sri Lanka is renowned for its beauty, splendour and its fantastic food culture. Ceylon Tavern draws on the exciting flavours known on the island.

2FOR1 3 COURSES | FRI × | SAT × — Sri Lankan

CINNAMON LOUNGE
☎ 01883 722 700

5-6 Hoskins Walk, Oxted, RH8 9HR

This wonderful venue has attempted, with great success, to recreate the ambiance, atmosphere and the flavours that make a visit to India so memorable. Visit Cinnamon and catch a real glimpse of India's rich cultures.

2FOR1 MAIN COURSE | FRI ✓ | SAT ✓ — Indian

CJ'S RESTAURANT @ MINERS ARMS
☎ 01252 509 088

2 Mytchett Road, Mytchett, GU16 6EZ

CJ's has an extensive Mediterranean menu with great selection of starters, delicious pastas, salads and meat dishes to ensure that there is something for everyone.

25% OFF TOTAL | FRI ✱ | SAT ✱ | SUN — Mediterranean

CLOISTERS RESTAURANT
☎ 08450 727 485

Nutfield Priory Hotel, Nutfield, Redhill, RH1 4EL

Whether you fancy a four-course gourmet meal or are craving a simple snack, the kitchen can cater for you, with a range of dining options on offer at this Hand Picked Hotels restaurant. 2 AA Rosettes.

25% OFF TOTAL | ♟ 10 | FRI ✱ | SAT ✱ | ✱ — Fine Dining

COACH HOUSE RESTAURANT @ MERCURE
☎ 01306 881 138

Mercure White Horse Hotel, High St, Dorking, RH4 1BE

Housed in an 18th Century coaching inn, the Coach House Restaurant resides in the White Horse Hotel in Dorking. Low ceiling beams and log fires create a traditional air to match the food.

25% OFF TOTAL | ♟ 8 | FRI ✓ | SAT ✓ — British

THE CRICKETERS
01276 473 196

1 London Road, Bagshot, GU19 5HR

Beefeater Grill are one of the UK's best-loved restaurants welcoming guests for almost 40 years in over 130 locations nationwide. *Excludes Breakfast, Light Bites, Bar menu, set menus and all other offers.

2FOR1 MAIN COURSE | ♟ 6 | FRI ✓ | SAT × | ▲ — Modern British

THE CYDER HOUSE INN
☎ 01483 810 360

Peper Harow Lane, Godalming, GU8 6AN

Nestled in an area of Outstanding Natural Beauty, this venue boasts snug seating and a cosy ambiance. The cuisine is honestly simple, and diners should try the game casserole or the roasted sea bass.

50% OFF FOOD | ♟ 2 | FRI ✓ | SAT ✓ | SUN — British

THE DONKEY
☎ 01252 702 124

Charles Hill, Tilford, Farnham, GU10 2AU

The owner and Head Chef Lee Francis prepares dishes of outstanding quality and the joint owner Helen Francis and her professional team will always give you a warm welcome and fantastic service.

25% OFF TOTAL | ♟ 6 | FRI ✓ | SAT × | SUN | ▲ — British

DORKING BRASSERIE
☎ 01306 742 448

Highland Cottage, Junction Road, Dorking, RH4 3HB

This renowned Indian restaurant has a reputation for one of the best curries in Surrey. Their traditional menu and diverse daily specials promise a delicious, exciting, healthy experience for every diner.

2FOR1 MAIN COURSE | FRI ✱ | SAT ✱ | ▲ — Indian

EVEREST SPICE
☎ 01737 789 599

39 Holland Close, Redhill, RH1 1HT

Everest Spice has been influenced by a long history of various groups and cultures interacting with the Asian subcontinent, leading to the diversity of flavours and regional cuisines of Nepal and India.

25% OFF TOTAL | ♟ 4 | FRI × | SAT × | ✱ | ▲ — Nepalese

FLAVOUR OF GOA
☎ 01276 671 555

3 Frimley Road, Camberley, GU15 3EN

Passionate and contemporary Indian restaurant serving a proper range of dishes at good value for money.

25% OFF TOTAL | ♟ 4 | FRI ✱ | SAT ✱ | ▲ — Indian

Always mention your Gourmet Society card when booking a table.

FRASCATI RESTAURANT
☎01372 373 950

London Road, Mickleham, Dorking, RH5 6EH

Reputable for its sizable portions, this restaurant serves delicious and wholesome cuisine. Italian inspired, this restaurant cooks up classical dishes from the heart of a lovingly preserved cottage.

25% OFF TOTAL | 10 | FRI ✓ | SAT ✓ | SUN — Italian

THE GALLERY RESTAURANT
☎01306 734 661

Denbies Wine Estate, London Road, Dorking, RH5 6AA

Situated on the top floor of England's largest vineyard, Denbies Wine Estate, The Gallery Restaurant is one of the most unique venues in Surrey with 360° panoramic views of the vineyard.

2FOR1 MAIN COURSE | FRI ✓ | SAT ✓ | ♣ — International

GURKHA DURBAR
☎01428 605 855

30 Headley Road, Grayshott, GU26 6LD

Dine on cuisine that exhibits delicate, simple flavours and a touch of spice. Cooking combines fine Chinese and Indian cuisine with an approach that relies on skilfully blending ingredients.

2FOR1 MAIN COURSE | FRI | SAT ✱ — Nepalese

THE HARE AND HOUNDS
☎01883 742 296

Bletchingley Road, Godstone, RH9 8LN

A pretty Surrey pub with a good atmosphere that accompanies a good range of wine and beers with a selection of simple and satisfying, freshly made pub food. Check out the specialities.

25% OFF TOTAL | 8 | FRI ✓ | SAT × | SUN — Traditional English

THE HORNS
☎01252 850 560

Bowling Alley, Farnham, GU10 5RJ

Escape every day life at this cosy retreat, idyllically set in a picturesque village. Traditional palates will enjoy genuine pub favourites, whilst the more adventurous can devour a speciality dish.

2FOR1 MAIN COURSE | FRI × | SAT × | SUN — British

HOTEL DANIELE ITALIAN RESTAURANT
☎01252 728 603

Lower Hale, Farnham, GU9 9RP

Exposed wooden beams, stunning décor and a chic bar create the perfect atmosphere at this country venue. Exploding with choice, the menu can be enjoyed al fresco.

25% OFF TOTAL | 4 | FRI ✱ | SAT ✱ | ✱ | ♣ — Italian

THE HUB @ HOLIDAY INN
☎0872 942 9030

Holiday Inn Gatwick, Povey Cross Rd, Horley, RH6 0BA

Serving a great variety of light snacks, meals and drinks in a comfortable and friendly environment, this smart hotel-bar is a great place for winding down after a long day or busy week.

25% OFF TOTAL | 6 | FRI ✓ | SAT ✓ — International

THE HUNTER'S LODGE
01483 474 602

Bagshot Road, Knaphill, Woking, GU21 2RP

This Vintage Inn oozes rural charm and rustic character. The picturesque surroundings provide the perfect backdrop for savouring the hearty, seasonal pub-food on the menu.

25% OFF TOTAL | FRI ✓ | SAT ✓ | SUN | ♣ — Modern British

JAIPUR RESTAURANT
☎01483 772 626

49 Chertsey Road, Woking, GU21 5AJ

The subtle tastes and flavours of this restaurant's cuisine differs from many others. Drawing influences from all five regions of India, a menu of culinary delights has been crafted to satisfy all palates.

2FOR1 MAIN COURSE | FRI ✱ | SAT ✱ | ♣ — Indian

JJ'S AMERICAN DINER
☎01932 355 151

18 Station Approach, West Byfleet, KT14 6NF

JJ's American Diner is Surrey's home of tasty American food, homemade and cooked to perfection. They serve an exciting all American menu and they are open for breakfast, lunch and dinner.

25% OFF TOTAL | 2 | FRI × | SAT × | SUN — American

KHARI
☎0127 626 868

The Atrium, Camberley, GU15 3GP

The Khari is a excellently reviewed Indian restaurant and takeaway in Camberley, where dishes are based on authentic flavours of the Khari Baolo spice street market in Delhi.

25% OFF TOTAL | 8 | FRI | SAT | ♣ — Indian

LA BARBE RESTAURANT
☎01737 241 966

71 Bell Street, Reigate, RH2 7AN

Well deserving of its loyal, appreciative following, this truly French restaurant offers delectable, classical and provincial cuisine. Wonderful French and New World wines are also on offer.

25% OFF TOTAL | 6 | FRI ✱ | SAT ✱ | ♣ — French

LA LANTERNA
☎01737 245 113

73 Bell Street, Reigate, RH2 7AN

Whether you require a perfect venue for an intimate evening out, or a relaxed setting for an important business lunch, La Lanterna can cater for you. Outstanding Italian dishes that are irresistibly tasty.

2FOR1 MAIN COURSE | FRI ✱ | SAT ✱ | SUN | ♣ — Italian

LA LUNA
☎01483 414 155

10 Wharf Street, Godalming, GU7 1NN

Classic flavours of Italy are a priority in this charming Italian restaurant. Fish dishes are especially superb, with the scallops in dry Martini being particularly popular. Awarded 2 AA Rosettes.

25% OFF TOTAL | 6 | FRI ✱ | SAT ✱ | ♣ — Italian

THE LAKESIDE RESTAURANT
☎01483 689 655

University of Surrey, Guildford, GU2 7XH

The Lakeside Restaurant at the University of Surrey offers a modern à la carte dining experience. Everything is made in-house, from the bread to begin to the biscuit with your coffee.

25% OFF TOTAL | 4 | FRI ✓ | SAT × | SUN — European

L'AROMA RESTAURANT
☎01483 770 742

16 High Street, Woking, GU21 6BW

Completely Neapolitan, the menu is composed of authentic recipes and superb-quality cuisine. Culinary talent and unique flavours makes L'Aroma a popular choice with the locals.

2FOR1 MAIN COURSE | FRI × | SAT × | SUN — Italian

THE LION BREWERY
☎01252 650 486

104 Guildford Road, Ash, Aldershot, GU12 6BT

Traditional English public house located in the rural Surrey countryside. Feast on classic pub fare while enjoying a selection of fine wines and ales in a congenial and pleasant atmosphere.

50% OFF FOOD | 2 | FRI ✓ | SAT ✱ — English/Gastro pub

LOCH FYNE
☎01784 414 890

5-6 High Street, Egham, TW20 9EA

From the roadside oyster bar that once was, Loch Fyne restaurants now successfully inject energy and passion into great food and wonderful flavours, whilst ensuring their seafood is sustainably sourced.

25% OFF TOTAL | 4 | FRI ✱ | SAT ✱ — Seafood

LOCH FYNE
☎01483 230 550

Centenary Hall, Chapel Street, Guildford, GU1 3UH

From the roadside oyster bar that once was, Loch Fyne restaurants now successfully inject energy and passion into great food and wonderful flavours, whilst ensuring their seafood is sustainably sourced.

25% OFF TOTAL | 4 | FRI ✱ | SAT ✱ — Seafood

LOCH FYNE
☎01252 748 030

3 Downing Street, Farnham, GU9 7NX

From the roadside oyster bar that once was, Loch Fyne restaurants now successfully inject energy and passion into great food and wonderful flavours, whilst ensuring their seafood is sustainably sourced.

25% OFF TOTAL | 4 | FRI ✱ | SAT ✱ — Seafood

THE LOCK BAR AND KITCHEN
☎01784 436 171

Runnymede Hotel, Windsor Road, Egham, TW20 0AG

This unpretentious bar is stunningly located on the banks of the River Thames. Cuisine inspired by British domestic kitchens, diners are guaranteed hearty and substantial dishes that reflect the seasons.

25% OFF TOTAL | 4 | FRI ✓ | SAT × | SUN — English and Continental

M.BRASSERIE
☎01483 303 030

36-40 London Road, Guildford, GU1 2AE

A truly memorable gastronomic experience awaits you in this treasured venue. Traditional and contemporary cuisine makes the most of the fresh, local produce that the area has to offer.

2FOR1 3 COURSES | FRI × | SAT × — Brasserie

MANOR INN
01483 427 134

Guildford Road, Godalming, GU7 3BX

Beefeater Grill are one of the UK's best-loved restaurants welcoming guests for almost 40 years in over 130 locations nationwide. *Excludes Breakfast, Light Bites, Bar menu, set menus and all other offers.

2FOR1 MAIN COURSE | 6 | FRI ✓ | SAT × — Modern British

MELA REDHILL
☎01737 766 154

1 Linkfield Street, Redhill, RH1 1HQ

Sister of the Shaftesbury Mela, doing a similarly fine line in subtle, accomplished Indian cuisine. Features high windows and warm tones, as well as a fantastic outdoor patio area for the balmy days.

2FOR1 3 COURSES | FRI × | SAT × — Indian

THE MERRY HARRIERS
☎01428 682 883

The Merry Harriers, Hambledon, GU8 4DR

Absolute classic of a village pub: big open fire, array of real ales, low key, relaxing ambience and great home cooking. Pub staples are the order of the day, drawing on fresh local produce.

25% OFF TOTAL | 6 | FRI ✱ | SAT ✓ | SUN — Traditional English

MERSTHAM TANDOORI
☎01737 644 670

14-16 Portland Drive, Merstham, RH1 3HY

Contemporary Indian cooking with the added zest of spice, the menu changes regularly ensuring there is always something new for customers to enjoy.

25% OFF TOTAL | 8 | FRI | SAT — Indian

MILL HOUSE
01737 767 277

Brighton Road, Salfords, Redhill, RH1 5BT

Beefeater Grill are one of the UK's best-loved restaurants welcoming guests for almost 40 years in over 130 locations nationwide. *Excludes Breakfast, Light Bites, Bar menu, set menus and all other offers.

2FOR1 MAIN COURSE | 6 | FRI ✓ | SAT × — Modern British

NAMASTE NEPALESE & INDIAN
☎01483 773 311

21 High Street, Woking, GU21 6BW

Exciting Nepalese and Indian dishes award this restaurant an enviable reputation. Locally renowned for providing one of the very best curries in the area.

25% OFF TOTAL | 4 | FRI | SAT ✓ — Indian

PREZZO

2FOR1 MAIN COURSE | FRI × | SAT ×

2-FOR-1 MAIN COURSE

8 restaurants in Surrey

260-262 High Street, Guildford, GU1 3JL	☎ 01483 569 199
7 The Borough, Farnham, GU9 7NA	☎ 01252 737 849
11 The Atrium, Park Street, Camberley, GU15 3GP	☎ 0127 623 945
8 Queen Street, Godalming, GU7 1BD	☎ 01483 428 746
33 London Road, Redhill, RH1 1NJ	☎ 01737 779 927
21-25 Church Street, Leatherhead, KT22 8DN	☎ 01372 379 625
59 High Street, Reigate, RH2 9AE	☎ 01737 242 525
2 Egham Hill, Egham, TW20 0AY	☎ 01784 472 628

To understand what the restaurant icons mean, please see the inside back cover.

NEW DIWAN-E-KHAS
0127 623 500

413 London Road, Camberley, GU15 3HZ

Offers fine Indian cuisine, suitable for both meat lovers and vegetarians. Exciting, creative meals sit alongside the traditional favourites to be found on their excellent, eclectic menus.

2FOR1 MAIN COURSE | FRI | SAT — Indian/Bangladeshi

OLIVO RISTORANTE ITALIANO
01483 303 535

53 Quarry Street, Guildford, GU1 3UA

A delightful haven of understated sophistication. Guests enjoy authentic cuisine cooked by talented Italian chefs who insist on using the freshest ingredients. Passion for food can be tasted in every dish.

2FOR1 2 COURSES | FRI ✱ | SAT ✱ — Italian

PALETTE RESTAURANT
01483 737 829

The Lightbox, Woking, GU214AA

As the name suggests, this venue promises to tantalise the taste buds. With quality at the forefront of their ethos, chefs are dedicated to preparing an expansive menu bursting with international dishes.

2FOR1 3 COURSES | FRI × | SAT × — Multi-Cuisine

THE PARKWAY
01483 304 932

Parkway, Guildford, Surrey, GU1 1UP

Quality pub classics with modern twists meets with a friendly and relaxed atmosphere to make this Table Table venue the perfect place for any occasion. *Excludes daytime & evening deals and festive menus.

2FOR1 MAIN COURSE | FRI ✓ | SAT ✓ — Modern British

THE PLOUGH
01306 611 348

Church Road, Leigh, Reigate, RH2 8NJ

Highly regarded that has the balance of food and drink just right. Place that shows great taste in its range of ales and beers on tap; caters to all sorts with a range of well-prepared, home-cooked food.

2FOR1 MAIN COURSE | FRI ✓ | SAT ✓ | SUN — English/Gastro pub

PRIDE OF THE VALLEY
01428 605 799

Tilford Road, Churt, Farnham, GU10 2LH

A luxurious and stylish environment where chefs use fresh produce to craft a menu filled with high-quality food, and diners can choose select wines direct from the wall. Reasonable prices guaranteed.

25% OFF TOTAL | 6 | FRI ✓ | SAT ✓ | SUN — British

THE PURPLE KITCHEN
02089 411 444

119b Walton Road, East Molesey, KT8 0DT

The Purple Kitchen is a lovely cafe on Walton road that ticks all the right boxes. Serving great British food with a smile, you will be welcomed with open arms and given top notch table service.

50% OFF FOOD | 4 | FRI ✓ | SAT × — International

RANIA RESTAURANT
01483 267 800

184 High Street, Cranleigh, GU6 8RL

Ensuring that the menu does not overpower the diner, the chefs at Rania have worked hard to create a well-balanced selection of dishes that provide a variety of tastes and spices.

2FOR1 MAIN COURSE | FRI × | SAT × — Indian

RED CHILLI
01306 644 816

Horsham Road, Mid-Holmwood, Dorking, RH5 4EH

Immaculately presented, the food served here is simple and delicious, offering diners a taste of Indian culture. Authentic cooking, fresh ingredients and wonderful spices mould each dish to perfection.

2FOR1 MAIN COURSE | FRI ✱ | SAT ✱ | SUN | ✱ — Indian

THE RED LION
01483 423 428

1 Mill Lane, Godalming, GU7 1HF

Carnivorous diners can sink their teeth into a juicy treat from the world burger menu, whilst veggies can savour a hand-stretched margherita stone-baked pizza. Ideal for a refreshing drink with friends.

50% OFF FOOD | 4 | FRI ✓ | SAT ✓ — British

RED LION INN
01483 892 202

The Green, Shamley Green, Guildford, GU5 0UB

With a view of the village and beautiful cricket green, enjoy hearty, traditional dishes throughout the year, combined with a variety of lagers and choice wines. *Check website for further details.

2FOR1 MAIN COURSE | FRI | SAT × | SUN — British

RED ROSE
01784 434 303

87 High Street, Egham, TW20 9HF

Expertly crafted Bangladeshi and Indian cuisine, with a myriad of dishes on offer that represent the variety of tastes and cultures found across the Indian subcontinent.

25% OFF TOTAL | 10 | FRI | SAT | ✱ — Indian

THE ROSE VALLEY
01483 572 572

50 Chertsey Street, Guildford, GU1 4HD

A well-respected restaurant serving only the finest Indian-Bangladeshi cuisine. Occupying an enviable position as a restaurant of the highest quality, the helpful staff further its excellence.

2FOR1 2 COURSES | FRI × | SAT × — Indian

ROYAL OAK INN
01883 722 207

Caterfield Lane, Staffhurst Wood, Oxted, RH8 0RR

Capturing the very essence of classic English and European dishes, the menu at this award-winning restaurant provides a superb selection of locally sourced meat, game, fresh fish and lobster.

2FOR1 MAIN COURSE | FRI | SAT ✱ | SUN — European

SHAHIN RESTAURANT
01483 570 137

29 Woodbridge Hill, Guildford, GU2 9AA

Ideally located Indian restaurant, where diners will be happily met by some deliciously tasty cuisine. Excellent curry selection means that every guest will be suitably catered for.

2FOR1 2 COURSES | FRI | SAT — Indian

SON OF SOMBRERO
01483 453 434

52a Chertsey Street, Guildford, GU1 4HD

A highly popular restaurant where tantalising food is plentiful, with a quality of service to match. A great venue with lively, authentic surroundings.

2FOR1 MAIN COURSE | FRI | SAT — Mexican

THE SPOTTED COW
01252 726 541

Bourne Grove, Lower Bourne, Farnham, GU10 3QT

Be enchanted as you discover the magical location of this idyllic country pub. The surrounding grounds are perfect for families with children and dogs. Inside, you will be met by great food and fine wines.

2FOR1 2 COURSES | FRI ✱ | SAT ✱ | SUN — European

THE STAR
01428 684 656

Petworth Road, Witley, GU8 5LU

A traditional local pub offering visitors a good range of real ales and lagers, a classic menu and a wide variety of wines. Hearty pub grub is served all day long.

25% OFF TOTAL | 4 | FRI ✓ | SAT ✓ | SUN — British

THE STEPHAN LANGTON INN
01306 730 775

Friday Street, Abinger Common, Dorking, RH5 6JR

Situated in the beautiful woodland around Abinger Common, this is a perfect spot for an escape into peace and quiet. Besides some great beers on tap, the inn serves excellent fresh-cooked food.

25% OFF TOTAL | 6 | FRI ✓ | SAT × | SUN — Modern British

THE STOKE PUB & PIZZERIA
01483 504 296

103 Stoke Road, Guildford, GU1 4JN

An exciting, refreshing, vibrant place to eat out, The Stoke Pub & Pizzeria offers diners a fantastic experience and wonderful fresh food.

2FOR1 MAIN COURSE | FRI ✓ | SAT × | SUN — International

STRADA
01737 240 089

12 Church Street, Reigate, RH2 0AN

Offering fresh, bold dishes inspired by flavours of Italian city life – Strada serves a selection of indulgent tastes, to those seeking a blissful escape to laidback Italian life. *Excludes Pizzettas.

25% OFF TOTAL | 6 | FRI ✓ | SAT × — Italian

SURREY PENANG
01306 711 522

Horsham Road, Capel, Dorking, RH5 4PG

Distinctive Malaysian restaurant, a brassy and colourful venue. Bold and eclectic menu with the rendang padang and ayam bumbu bali a couple of the stand-out options.

2FOR1 MAIN COURSE | FRI × | SAT × — Malaysian

THACKERAYS RESTAURANT @ MERCURE ☎01252 715 237
Mecure Farnham Bush, The Borough, Farnham, GU8 6DU
The Thackeray Restaurant is a wonderful attribute of the Mercure Farnham Bush Hotel. Overlooking the magnificent gardens, the restaurant offers a classic setting where one can enjoy good British cuisine.

50% OFF FOOD | 6 | FRI ✓ | SAT ✓ | SUN | ✱ | ▲ — British

THALI THALI ☎01483 755 210
33 Chertsey Road, Woking, GU21 5AJ
Standing out for its subtle flavours and quality of produce, Thali Thali is an Indian restaurant where regional vegetarian dishes are its speciality. Try the hyderabadi bagahre baingan for a real treat.

2FOR1 3 COURSES | FRI ✓ | SAT ✓ | ▲ — Indian

TUDOR LOUNGE ☎01483 300 999
144 High Street, Guildford, GU1 3HJ
Spoil yourself at brunch with a towering stack of eggy bread, pork sausages and crispy bacon drizzled with maple syrup. For dinner, interactive furniture and thrilling illuminations transform the venue.

50% OFF FOOD | 4 | FRI × | SAT × — International

WATERMARK RESTAURANT ☎01252 795 161
Frensham Pond Hotel, Bacon Lane, Farnham, GU10 2QD
The Watermark Restaurant's menu is wide-ranging, accomplished, and strongly individual- the kind that makes it hard for you to rule things out. The restaurant space is charming, refined and welcoming.

2FOR1 MAIN COURSE | FRI ✓ | SAT ✷ | SUN | ✱ | ▲ — British

THE WHITE HART 01883 742 521
71 High Street, Godstone, RH9 8DU
Beefeater Grill are one of the UK's best-loved restaurants welcoming guests for almost 40 years in over 130 locations nationwide. *Excludes Breakfast, Light Bites, Bar menu, set menus and all other offers.

2FOR1 MAIN COURSE | 6 | FRI ✓ | SAT × | ▲ — Modern British

WOTTON HOUSE ☎01306 730 000
Guildford Road, Dorking, RH5 6HS
Standing proud in all its glory, Wotton House is unashamedly breathtaking. The spectacular grounds make this an idyllic place to relax and unwind during a short break, while making the most of the area.

25% OFF TOTAL | 6 | FRI ✓ | SAT ✓ | ▲ — British

YE OLDE SIX BELLS 01293 825 028
Church Road, Horley, RH6 8AD
This Vintage Inn oozes rural charm and rustic character. The picturesque surroundings provide the perfect backdrop for savouring the hearty, seasonal pub-food on the menu.

25% OFF TOTAL | FRI ✓ | SAT ✓ | SUN | ▲ — Modern British

East Sussex

A TASTE OF SAHARA ☎01273 911 843
103 Western Road, Brighton, BN1 2AA
Collection of flavours from North African and Middle Eastern cuisine, including excellent tagines and some fine shish kebabs. Comfortable, robust furniture sets the scene for the truly superb food.

25% OFF TOTAL | 4 | FRI × | SAT × | ▲ — Lebanese

ABERDEEN STEAK HOUSE 01273 326 892
27 Preston Street, Brighton, BN1 2HP
If you like a steak, then this is a great choice. High-quality cuts, great sides, all at reasonable prices. Attentive and friendly staff ensure diners have a memorable experience.

25% OFF TOTAL | 10 | FRI ✷ | SAT ✷ — British

ADA RESTAURANT BEXHILL ☎01424 212 189
60 Devonshire Road, Bexhill-on-Sea, TN40 1AX
Food is an integral part of the Turkish culture and Ada Restaurant has recreated the passion and integrity that is maintained in Turkish cooking. Spicy koftas feature alongside Middle Eastern casseroles.

25% OFF TOTAL | FRI ▯ | SAT ▯ — Turkish

ADA RESTAURANT HASTINGS ☎01424 422 423
42 Robertson Street, Hastings, TN34 1HL
Food is an integral part of the Turkish culture and Ada Restaurant has recreated the passion and integrity that is maintained in Turkish cooking. Spicy koftas feature alongside Middle Eastern casseroles.

25% OFF TOTAL | FRI ▯ | SAT ▯ — Turkish

AL DUOMO ☎01273 326 741
7 Pavilion Buildings, Brighton, BN1 1EE
Sure to suit all tastes and pockets, this Italian restaurant boasts a menu of huge variety from fresh pizzas to tempting desserts, all representing good value for money. Perfect for all occasions.

2FOR1 MAIN COURSE | FRI ✓ | SAT ✷ | ▲ — Italian

ALROUCHE RESTAURANT ☎01273 734 810
44 Preston Street, Brighton, BN1 2HP
A cosy and friendly family-run restaurant that showcases the qualities of Lebanese cuisine. Choose from an array of well-prepared dishes that offer diners a host of divine flavours.

25% OFF TOTAL | 8 | FRI ✷ | SAT ✷ — Lebanese

THE AMBRETTE AT RYE ☎01797 222 043
White Vine House, Rye, TN31 7JF
Award-winning chef Dev Biswal prides himself on exotic recipes infused with innovation. This fine dining venue uses the most refined of ingredients to create beautifully presented cuisine.

25% OFF TOTAL | FRI ✓ | SAT ✷ — Fine Dining

ANATOLIA BRIGHTON ☎01273 693 467
51 St James Street, Brighton, BN2 1QG
The open fire, flexibility of dishes and attentive staff enhance the tantalizing array of truly authentic Turkish dishes on offer. An undiscovered gem in the heart of Brighton.

50% OFF FOOD | 6 | FRI × | SAT × | ✱ | ▲ — Turkish

ANFORA RESTAURANT ☎01273 721 182
64 Western Road, Hove, BN3 2JQ
Highly enjoyable experiences are guaranteed at Anfora, where charm and simplicity come together. Expect attentive staff and delectable Mediterranean cuisine, with a ranging menu to suit your every need.

25% OFF TOTAL | 10 | FRI × | SAT × | SUN | ▲ — Mediterranean

ARISTOCRATS SIZZLING RESTAURANT ☎01273 748 388
54 Preston Street, Brighton, BN1 2HE
A lively establishment, perfect for dining with family and friends. The menu offers a delightful assortment of mouth-watering dishes, and is accompanied by a fine selection of wines and beers.

25% OFF TOTAL | 10 | FRI ✓ | SAT ✓ | SUN | ✱ — Filipino

AROMA SPICE ☎01273 677 608
4 Lewes Road, Brighton, BN2 3HP
Secret spice blends and a warm family welcome are the key ingredients to this delightful Indian restaurant, situated moments away from the centre of Brighton.

2FOR1 3 COURSES | FRI × | SAT × | ✱ | ▲ — Indian

ASHOKA ☎01273 202 112
95-97 Church Road, Hove, BN3 2BA
Perfect for intimate evenings for two or a more animated group outing, with Ashoka both the food and the service are second to none.

2FOR1 3 COURSES | FRI × | SAT × | ▲ — Indian

BALI BRASSERIE ☎01273 323 810
Kingsway Court, First Avenue, Hove, BN3 2LR
Great example of often-overlooked Indonesian and Malaysian cuisine. At this seafront restaurant you'll find an eclectic selection, from rendang to mee goreng. Contemporary styling with a hint of kitsch.

25% OFF TOTAL | 4 | FRI × | SAT × | ▲ — Indonesian

THE BEACHY HEAD 01323 728 060
Beachy Head Road, Beachy Head, Eastbourne, BN20 7YA
This Vintage Inn oozes rural charm and rustic character. The picturesque surroundings provide the perfect backdrop for savouring the hearty, seasonal pub-food on the menu.

25% OFF TOTAL | FRI ✓ | SAT ✓ | SUN | ▲ — Modern British

Gourmet Society discount applies to the à la carte menu only, unless stated otherwise.

THE BELL AT IDEN
☎01797 280 242
Church Lane, Iden, Rye, TN31 7PU
From tender, flaky home-made steak and Hobgoblin pie to home-baked ham, egg and chips, The Bell is rooted in classic British home cooking. Wholesome and delicious menu in a charming location.

2FOR1 MAIN COURSE | FRI ✱ | SAT ✱ | SUN — British

BELLA ITALIA
01273 777 607
24 Market Street, Brighton, BN1 1HH
Accessible Italian cuisine on the British high street – indulge in authentic sharing platters, hand stretched pizzas and hearty pasta dishes, served with a healthy dose of gregarious Italian hospitality.

25% OFF TOTAL | 6 | FRI × | SAT × | SUN | ▲ — Italian

BENGAL BRASSERIE
☎01424 736 007
66 London Road, Bexhill-on-Sea, TN39 3LE
A variety of Indian dishes are on offer at Bengal Brasserie. Curry lovers will be impressed by the wide-ranging menu.

2FOR1 MAIN COURSE | FRI ✓ | SAT ☎ — Indian

BENGAL CURRY HOUSE
☎01424 465 076
7 Marine Court, St Leonards-on-Sea, TN38 0DX
Restaurant that runs the gamut of essential Indian dishes, from delicious butter chicken to the friskier methi curry. An authentic Indian restaurant not far from the seafront in St Leonards.

2FOR1 3 COURSES | FRI ✱ | SAT ✱ — Indian

THE BLACK PEARL
☎01424 719 919
9 George Street, Hastings, TN34 3EG
Like a home from home, The Black Pearl successfully offers an intimately cosy atmosphere while maintaining high standards of dining. For a post-dinner beverage, head to the ground floor wine bar.

2FOR1 MAIN COURSE | FRI ✓ | SAT × | SUN — Contemporary

BLENIO BISTRO
☎01273 220 220
87 Dyke Road, Brighton, BN1 3JE
Catch the scent of fresh rosemary and thyme and savour delectable, rustic dishes based on the best natural ingredients. A welcoming, stylish bistro serving flavoursome food from breakfast till dinner.

2FOR1 MAIN COURSE | FRI ✱ | SAT ✱ — European

BOMBAY INDIAN CUISINE
☎01273 721 199
85-87 Preston Street, Brighton, BN1 2HG
The Bombay has been one of the most popular restaurants in Brighton and Hove for nearly 20 years. The Indian menu focuses on dishes unique to the Bombay, such as Butter Paneer or Chilli Paneer.

25% OFF TOTAL | 10 | FRI ✓ | SAT ✓ — Indian

THE BRASSERIE @ MECURE
☎0844 815 9061
Mercure Brighton Hotel, Kings Rd, Brighton, BN1 2PP
With a breathtaking Victorian façade, the Mercure Brighton is characteristically British when it comes to its status as a seaside hotel. The Brasserie is a great place to seize hold of your appetite.

2FOR1 3 COURSES | FRI ✓ | SAT ✓ — International

BRASSERIE FISH AND GRILL
☎01273 698 989
3a Waterfront, Brighton Marina, Brighton, BN2 5WA
Fine fish dishes are on offer in this wonderful seafood restaurant. Enjoy the relaxing ambience as you take in the views of the nautical world of Brighton marina.

25% OFF TOTAL | 6 | FRI ✓ | SAT ✱ — Seafood

CAFÉ ROUGE
01273 774 422
24 Prince Albert St, Brighton, BN1 1HF
French sophistication on the British high street – enjoy seasonally changing French dishes and a continental wine selection, served in a relaxed environment with an undeniable flair of Parisian chic.

25% OFF TOTAL | 6 | FRI ✓ | SAT ✓ | ✱ | ▲ — French

CAFÉ ROUGE
01273 622 423
The Waterfront, Brighton Marina, Brighton, BN2 5WA
French sophistication on the British high street – enjoy seasonally changing French dishes and a continental wine selection, served in a relaxed environment with an undeniable flair of Parisian chic.

25% OFF TOTAL | 6 | FRI ✓ | SAT ✓ | ✱ | ▲ — French

CINNAMON SPICE ST LEONARDS ON SEA
☎01424 433 059
18 Kings Road, St Leonards-on-Sea, TN37 6DU
A friendly restaurant with a high standard of cooking and presentation, the dishes are packed with flavours and spices in this Indian eatery where nothing is too much trouble.

25% OFF TOTAL | FRI ✓ | SAT ✓ — Indian

COAST BRIGHTON
☎01272 723 256
28 East Street, Brighton, BN1 1HL
Located in the heart of the lane, Coast is an independent restaurant that works with local farmers and fishmongers to bring delectable meals and satisfy your palate.

2FOR1 3 COURSES | FRI × | SAT × | SUN | ▲ — British

COMO BRASSERIE
☎01273 945 045
41 Market Street, Brighton, BN1 1HH
Honouring simple and age-old cuisine, the menu infuses French, Belgian and Italian food. Revel in an organic pizza from the tavern whilst pondering over which of the 40 European beers to savour.

50% OFF FOOD | 4 | FRI ✓ | SAT ☎ — European

THE CROW AND GATE
01892 603 461
Ukfield Road, Crowborough, TN6 3TA
This Vintage Inn oozes rural charm and rustic character. The picturesque surroundings provide the perfect backdrop for savouring the hearty, seasonal pub-food on the menu.

25% OFF TOTAL | FRI ✓ | SAT ✓ | SUN | ▲ — Modern British

CURRY LEAF
☎01323 727 890
8 Susan's Road, Eastbourne, BN21 3HA
Curry Leaf is a break from the stereotypical Indian restaurant and instead offers an intimate, beautiful and elegant space, full of inviting warmth, whilst feeling open and spacious.

50% OFF FOOD | 6 | FRI ✓ | SAT ✓ — Indian

THE DEVIL'S DYKE
01273 857 256
Dyke Road, Poynings, Brighton, BN1 8YJ
This Vintage Inn oozes rural charm and rustic character. The picturesque surroundings provide the perfect backdrop for savouring the hearty, seasonal pub-food on the menu.

25% OFF TOTAL | FRI ✓ | SAT ✓ | SUN | ▲ — Modern British

THE DINING ROOM RESTAURANT
☎08450 727 412
Buxted Park Hotel, Buxted, Uckfield, TN22 4AY
Enjoy your favourite classic British dish with a modern twist, or indulge in one of the chef's many creations at this Hand Picked Hotels group restaurant that will delight and excite you. 2 AA Rosettes.

25% OFF TOTAL | 6 | FRI ✱ | SAT ✱ — British

DODO
☎01273 933 137
84a Dyke Road, Brighton, BN1 3JD
Think British, think fish and chips. Dodo makes no mistakes when it comes to producing and serving this national treasure, with fresh fish and home-made chips making the mark.

25% OFF TOTAL | 10 | FRI ✓ | SAT ✓ — British

ESTIA
☎01273 777 399
3 Hampton Place, Brighton, BN1 3DA
Modern, stylish restaurant that serves mellow, fragrant Greek Cypriot cuisine in a warm, welcoming ambience.

25% OFF TOTAL | 10 | FRI ☎ | SAT ☎ | SUN | ✱ | ▲ — Greek

FLACKLEY ASH HOTEL
☎01797 230 651
Peasmarsh, Rye, TN31 6YH
This Michelin-recommended restaurant focuses on traditional English recipes and Mediterranean twists. Customers can enjoy full, natural, flavoursome dishes in a serene, stately location.

25% OFF TOTAL | 10 | FRI ✓ | SAT × | SUN | ✱ — European

FOXY'S ROAST & GRILL
01273 776 661
90 Goldstone Villas, Hove, BR3 3RU
Take a good luck at the menu here at Foxy's, where roasts, grills and steaks appear prominently. With ample portions and impressive prices, this is the place to come for post-work food and fun.

2FOR1 MAIN COURSE | FRI ✓ | SAT ✓ | SUN — British

THE GARDEN RESTAURANT
☎ 01323 412 345

The Grand Hotel, Eastbourne, BN21 4EQ

Guests can enjoy the best of both worlds in this opulent venue which boasts an informal ambiance. Gorge on a British classic with a contemporary twist. The innovative chefs are inspired by local produce.

2FOR1 MAIN COURSE | FRI × | SAT × | ✱ | ▲ — European

GB1 RESTAURANT
☎ 01273 224 300

97-99 King's Road, Brighton, BN1 2FW

Set in the Grand Hotel, which iconically covers the waterfront, this restaurant has just the right degree of grandeur together with a classic British menu with suitable twists through the seasons.

2FOR1 MAIN COURSE | FRI ✓ | SAT ✓ — British

THE GOLDEN GALLEON
01323 892 247

Exceat Bridge, Cuckmere Haven, Seaford, BN25 4AB

This Vintage Inn oozes rural charm and rustic character. The picturesque surroundings provide the perfect backdrop for savouring the hearty, seasonal pub-food on the menu.

25% OFF TOTAL | FRI ✓ | SAT ✓ | SUN | ▲ — Modern British

GRAZE RESTAURANT
☎ 01273 823 707

42 Western Road, Hove, BN3 2FD

A lavish interior gives a modern edge as the Head Chef combines fresh and intense flavours to create seasonally based menus using locally sourced, organic and free-range produce. Awarded 2 AA Rosettes.

2FOR1 MAIN COURSE | FRI ✓ | SAT ✱ — Modern British

THE GREENHOUSE
☎ 01323 738 228

10 Station Street, Eastbourne, BN21 4RG

Delivers great food and drink and excellent service, in stylish and pleasing surroundings. The customer's requirements are first on the agenda here, with all visitors being exceptionally looked after.

2FOR1 MAIN COURSE | FRI ✱ | SAT ✱ | SUN | ▲ — European

GURKHA CHEF NEPALESE CUISINE
☎ 01424 444 440

20 Grand Parade, St Leonards-on-Sea, TN37 6DN

Indulge in unique Nepalese cuisine filled with delicious, authentic flavours that combine an array of traditional herbs and spices. A large selection of regional dishes offer a real taste of Nepal.

25% OFF TOTAL | 4 | FRI ✱ | SAT ✱ | ✱ — Nepalese

HANGLETON MANOR
☎ 01273 413 266

Hangleton Valley Drive, Hove, BN3 8AN

In the oldest secular building surviving in Brighton and Hove this restaurant delivers real food by talented chefs. A classic yet inspiring menu with dishes including the renowned Tanglefoot ale pie.

25% OFF TOTAL | 6 | FRI × | SAT × | SUN | ▲ — British

HARRIS RESTAURANT
☎ 01424 437 221

58 High Street, Hastings, TN34 3EN

Look no further for a well-established venue offering the finest selection of authentic Spanish tapas. Well-priced food, all freshly prepared to the highest culinary standards.

2FOR1 MAIN COURSE | FRI ✱ | SAT ✱ | SUN | ✱ — Spanish

HASTINGS INDIAN CUISINE
☎ 01424 439 493

177a Queens Road, Hastings, TN34 1RN

Excellent choices offered by Hastings Indian Cuisine include contemporary meals, tandoori specialities and traditional Indian dishes, prepared by their award-winning chefs

2FOR1 MAIN COURSE | FRI ✓ | SAT ✓ — Indian

HOTEL DU VIN
☎ 01273 718 588

Ship Street, Brighton, BN1 1AD

The finest, fresh local produce, simple European recipes, a stunning choice of wines; these are the elements of the trademark Hotel du Vin bistro. Situated in the heart of the famous 'Lanes'. 1 AA Rosette.

2FOR1 MAIN COURSE | FRI × | SAT × | SUN | ▲ — European

IL BISTRO
☎ 01273 324 584

6-7a Market Street, Brighton, BN1 1HH

A genuine Mediterranean experience where the Head Chef utilises his experiences in the kitchen. Set in a beautiful 18th century cottage, this restaurant boasts a delicious menu and excellent service.

2FOR1 2 COURSES | FRI ✱ | SAT ✱ — Mediterranean

IN VINO VERITAS
☎ 01273 622 522

103 North Road, Brighton, BN1 1YW

This restaurant is all about good food and wine without the expensive price tag. Diners can enjoy tapas-sized continental food and a glass of wine from the vast Old and New world selection.

25% OFF TOTAL | 6 | FRI ✱ | SAT ✱ | ▲ — European

INDIAN OCEAN
☎ 01424 844 977

17-21 Cooden Sea Road, Bexhill-on-Sea, TN39 4SJ

Passionate about sharing their love of food with ravenous diners, the chefs at this venue strive to impress each guest with an array of striking and fragrant dishes.

2FOR1 MAIN COURSE | FRI × | SAT × — Indian

INDIAN PARADISE
☎ 01323 735 408

166 Seaside, Eastbourne, BN22 7QW

Go on an adventure to India at Indian Paradise. Guests are recommended to start with crunchy poppadoms and then select a curry from the delectable menu: fiery and hot or smooth and creamy.

2FOR1 MAIN COURSE | FRI ▯ | SAT ▯ | SUN — Indian

INDIAN SUMMER
☎ 01273 711 001

69 East Street, Brighton, BN1 1HG

Popular, authentic Indian restaurant with all the staple favourites along with some stand-out specialities; try the classic East Indian chingri malai, or one of the richly spiced vegan options. A hot spot.

25% OFF TOTAL | 8 | FRI ✱ | SAT ✱ — Indian

JALI
☎ 01424 457 300

The Chatsworth Hotel, Hastings, TN34 1JG

An AA Rosette-rated restaurant serving only the finest dishes made from authentic ingredients, inspired by India's culinary traditions. A memorable experience setting the new standard for Indian cuisine.

2FOR1 MAIN COURSE | FRI ✱ | SAT ✱ — Indian

K2 INDIAN @ HOLIDAY INN
☎ 01323 483 844

Holiday Inn, Nightingale Hill, Polegate, BN26 6RF

K2's a big, easygoing Indian restaurant that does a fine selection of classic and speciality dishes. It's known for food with lots of flavour, a dash of spice where needed, and well-sized portions.

2FOR1 MAIN COURSE | FRI ▯ | SAT × | SUN — Indian

KAVI RESTAURANT
☎ 01424 220 176

27 Sea Road, Bexhill-on-Sea, TN40 1EE

A neat little restaurant with a welcoming café-style frontage, an accommodating, low-key vibe, and a good range of contemporary cuisine, making it a popular spot for both locals and visitors.

25% OFF TOTAL | 6 | FRI ✱ | SAT ✱ — European

LA CAVE À FROMAGE
☎ 01273 725 500

34-35 Western Road, Hove, BN3 1AF

Friendly and relaxing tasting café offering some of the best cheese platters in Sussex, along with wines from small vineyards across France. Excellent cheese and friendly yet unobtrusive service.

25% OFF TOTAL | 6 | FRI ▯ | SAT × | ▲ — British

THE LAMB INN
01424 848 649

Pevensey Marsh, Hooe, Battle, TN33 9HH

This Vintage Inn oozes rural charm and rustic character. The picturesque surroundings provide the perfect backdrop for savouring the hearty, seasonal pub-food on the menu.

25% OFF TOTAL | FRI ✓ | SAT ✓ | SUN | ▲ — Modern British

THE LECTERN
☎ 01273 685 258

5 Pelham Terrace, Brighton, BN2 4AF

Possibly the best student boozer in town, The Lectern is fun, friendly, legendary food, a full range of beers and spirits and live sports showing on big screens.

2FOR1 MAIN COURSE | FRI ✓ | SAT ✓ — British

MEMORIES OF INDIA
☎ 01273 600 088

The Board Walk, Brighton Marina, Brighton, BN2 5WA

An exciting culinary journey through India and the sub-continent - Memories of India aim to share their vast experience and modern culinary expertise with their customers. A restaurant not to be missed.

25% OFF TOTAL | 6 | FRI × | SAT × — Indian

THE MERRIE HARRIERS
☎01323 833 108
Cowbeech, Herstmonceux, BN27 4JQ
Both setting and food offer a quintessentially English experience at this delightful village inn. New British classics appear on the extensive menu, whilst lighter bites to eat can be enjoyed at the bar.

25% OFF TOTAL | 2 | FRI | SAT | SUN — British

MICHELANGELO RESTAURANT
☎01323 724 345
89 South Street, Eastbourne, BN21 4LR
Come and enjoy fresh homemade pasta dishes and traditional Italian cooking combined with friendly, attentive service in one of the Eastbourne's finest Mediterranean restaurant, Michelangelo Restaurant.

25% OFF TOTAL | 4 | FRI ✓ | SAT × — Italian

MIRABELLE RESTAURANT
☎01323 412 345
The Grand Hotel, Eastbourne, BN21 4EQ
Prestigious and award-winning, this AA Rosette venue oozes opulence and sophistication. The seasonal European menu thrills the taste buds and is complemented by an expansive, carefully selected wine list.

2FOR1 MAIN COURSE | FRI × | SAT × | ✱ | ▲ — European

MO MAMBO
☎01323 732 832
71 Seaside Road, Eastbourne, BN21 3PL
Cosy, colourful place to eat in Eastbourne. A lively Italian restaurant with a bright and friendly atmosphere. Great selection of pasta dishes and some excellent meat and fish options to boot.

2FOR1 3 COURSES | FRI | SAT | ▲ — Italian

MOONSTONE SRI LANKAN RESTAURANT
☎01273 202 151
208 Church Road, Hove, BN3 2DJ
Traditionally mild, the expert chefs prepare Sri-Lankan curries to the required spice intensity. Attentive staff serve authentic Lion Beer in this habitually hospitable eatery.

2FOR1 MAIN COURSE | FRI ✱ | SAT ✱ — Sri Lankan

THE MUDDY DUCK
☎01797 253 540
3 Main Street, Northiam, TN31 7DJ
When only good-quality food and friendly service will do, head to The Muddy Duck in Northiam. Whitewash walls and wooden beer tables makes it an ideal place to set up camp during those lazy summer months.

25% OFF TOTAL | 10 | FRI | SAT — English/Gastro pub

NEIGHBOURHOOD RESTAURANT
☎01273 673 891
101 St James's Street, Brighton, BN2 1TP
A NEIGHBOURHOOD restaurant, with a vintage industrial feel that is comparable to bars of Brooklyn and East London hang-outs. Serving delicious brunch and an evening menu with Americana classics.

2FOR1 MAIN COURSE | FRI ✓ | SAT × — British

NEW STEINE BISTRO
☎01273 681 546
10-11 New Steine, Brighton, BN2 1PB
Award-winning hotel restaurant offering the most delicious continental fare from breakfast to dinner. Guests will love the extensive breakfast buffet which will ensure you get the most out of your day.

2FOR1 MAIN COURSE | FRI ✱ | SAT ✱ | ✱ — French

NOORIS
☎01273 329 405
70-71 Ship Street, Brighton, BN1 1AE
With flavoursome signature dishes and a variety of Indian beers, Noori's welcome you with aromatic spices, warm surroundings and the freshest original cuisine.

50% OFF FOOD | 10 | FRI × | SAT × | ▲ — Indian

THE OLD SHIP INN
☎01273 814 223
Uckfield Road, Ringmer, BN8 5RP
Classic country inn with a welcoming atmosphere that's a pleasure to enjoy. Changing regularly, their menu can see you pass from the juicy twang of steak Diane to the zip of fruit pavlova.

2FOR1 MAIN COURSE | FRI ✓ | SAT × | SUN — British

THE OLD VINE
☎01892 782 271
Cousley Wood Road, Wadhurst, TN5 6ER
Owners Matthew and Gillian have successfully created a hub for the community focusing on traditional homemade food sourced with the best of British and Irish ingredients at affordable prices.

25% OFF TOTAL | 10 | FRI | SAT | ▲ — British

PELHAM HOUSE RESTAURANT
☎01273 488 600
St Andrews Lane, Lewes, BN7 1UW
The Pelham House Hotel is stunning in many ways, and its restaurant certainly contributes to its appeal. Beautiful views of the hotel gardens can be thoroughly enjoyed as you dine.

25% OFF TOTAL | 6 | FRI | SAT ✱ — Fine Dining

PICCOLO RESTAURANT
☎01273 380 380
56 Ship Street, Brighton, BN1 1AF
Simple and authentic, this Italian restaurant delivers delicately flavoured food combined with competitive prices, attentive service, and a friendly atmosphere.

25% OFF TOTAL | 10 | FRI ✱ | SAT ✱ — Italian

PIER NINE AT ZANZIBAR
☎01424 460 109
Zanzibar Hotel, St Leonards-on-Sea, TN37 6BY
Corn-fed chicken and Sussex beef carpaccio are both highly appraised in this white-wash beach house setting. At pocket friendly prices, this venue exudes quality within every dish.

2FOR1 MAIN COURSE | FRI | SAT × | SUN | ▲ — British

PREZZO
01273 472 179
173 High Street, Lewes, BN7 1YE
With a character all of its own, Prezzo oozes contemporary style and enduring charm. Signature pastas, stone-baked pizzas and classic Italian dishes promise a perfect dining choice for the whole family.

2FOR1 MAIN COURSE | FRI × | SAT × | ▲ — Italian

PREZZO
01323 722 667
Terminus Building, Upperton Rd, Eastbourne BN21 1BA
With a character all of its own, Prezzo oozes contemporary style and enduring charm. Signature pastas, stone-baked pizzas and classic Italian dishes promise a perfect dining choice for the whole family.

2FOR1 MAIN COURSE | FRI × | SAT × | ▲ — Italian

PREZZO
01323 442 010
The Old School House, High Street, Hailsham, BN27 1AR
With a character all of its own, Prezzo oozes contemporary style and enduring charm. Signature pastas, stone-baked pizzas and classic Italian dishes promise a perfect dining choice for the whole family.

2FOR1 MAIN COURSE | FRI × | SAT × | ▲ — Italian

PREZZO
01273 680 582
The Waterfront, Brighton BN2 5WA
With a character all of its own, Prezzo oozes contemporary style and enduring charm. Signature pastas, stone-baked pizzas and classic Italian dishes promise a perfect dining choice for the whole family.

2FOR1 MAIN COURSE | FRI × | SAT × | ▲ — Italian

THE PRINCE ARTHUR
☎01273 205 797
38 Dean Street, Brighton, BN1 3EG
Located in central Brighton, The Prince Arthur is a sophisticated venue that doesn't shy away from the excellency of traditional British dishes. Inviting surrounds makes it a warm welcoming place to all.

50% OFF FOOD | 6 | FRI ✓ | SAT ✓ | SUN | ▲ — British

THE PROMENADE RESTAURANT
☎01273 206 700
Thistle Brighton, King's Road, Brighton, BN1 2GS
On the lovely Promenade, offering unrivalled views of the famous Brighton Pier and the sea, guests here can dine on great dishes from home-cooked British favourites to delicious European cuisine.

50% OFF FOOD | 8 | FRI ✓ | SAT ✓ | ✱ | ▲ — European

PUB DU VIN
☎01273 718 588
7 Ship Street, Brighton, BN1 1AD
A combination of classic British tradition with modern style gives this converted venue undeniable charm. Features a wide selection of locally sourced ales and a hearty and satisfying menu.

2FOR1 MAIN COURSE | FRI × | SAT × | SUN | ▲ — European

THE RAJPOOT
☎01892 654 631
3 London Road, Crowborough, TN6 2TT
The chefs at this Indian venue offer a delectable variety of creamy curries and succulent sundries, whilst the staff guarantee a friendly and attentive service.

2FOR1 MAIN COURSE | FRI × | SAT × — Indian

THE REGENCY RESTAURANT
☎01273 325 014
131 Kings Road, Brighton, BN1 2HH
Supremely charismatic and highly regarded seafront restaurant where the fish is of fabulous quality, simply cooked and deliciously so. The price, too, is right: something as fresh as the sea air.

25% OFF TOTAL | 8 | FRI ✓ | SAT ✱ | SUN — Seafood

RIDGWAYS
☎01323 726 805
42-44 Meads Street, Meads, Eastbourne, BN20 7RG
Sample the delights of this traditional, high-quality restaurant that specialises in beautifully crafted English cuisine. They offer a diverse, good-value menu with a continental element.

2FOR1 MAIN COURSE | FRI ✓ | SAT ✱ | SUN | ✱ — British

RINGLES CROSS HOTEL
☎01825 765 428
London Road, Uckfield, TN22 1HG
Favourites such as thick, juicy sausages and creamy mash or internationally-inspired spicy chili con carne are just some of the culinary temptations aligning the menu a this charming eatery.

50% OFF FOOD | 4 | FRI | SAT — British

RIVER SPICE
☎01273 739 183
17 Preston Street, Brighton, BN1 2HN
A stunning contemporary interior awaits you at this marvellous Indian restaurant. The kitchen hosts a talented team of chefs who place all of their energy and passion into creating the most divine dishes.

2FOR1 MAIN COURSE | FRI ✓ | SAT ✓ | ✱ — Indian

RIVERSIDE BRASSERIE
☎01273 472 247
Riverside, Cliffe Bridge, Lewes, BN7 2AD
This most delightful of venues offers a riverside view that guarantees to leave you feeling calm, relaxed and refreshed. Peruse the menu or enjoy a steaming hot cappuccino with a heavenly pastry.

25% OFF TOTAL | 4 | FRI ✱ | SAT ✱ | SUN — Brasserie

SEAFRONT TANDOORI
☎01323 720 084
63 Seaside Road, Eastbourne, BN21 3PL
Ideally situated on the Eastbourne coast, Seafront Tandoori vaunts a loyal following of guests. Diners can expect habitually welcoming staff who can help you select a dish from their expansive menu.

2FOR1 3 COURSES | FRI ✓ | SAT ✓ — Indian

SHANAZ INDIAN CUISINE
☎01273 488 038
83 High Street, Lewes, BN7 1XN
Cosy, slightly kitsch Indian restaurant in Lewes. Foliage decks the ceiling, crisp linen the tables. The menu runs the gamut of curry house classics and stretches out with some really interesting specials.

2FOR1 3 COURSES | FRI ✱ | SAT ✱ — Indian

THE SMUGGLER'S REST
01273 586 593
South Coast Rd, Telscombe Cliffs, Peacehaven, BN10 7BE
This Vintage Inn oozes rural charm and rustic character. The picturesque surroundings provide the perfect backdrop for savouring the hearty, seasonal pub-food on the menu.

25% OFF TOTAL | FRI ✓ | SAT ✓ | SUN — Modern British

SQUARE BAR & RESTAURANT
☎01273 772 777
79-80 Western Road, Hove, BN3 2JQ
Treat yourself to a flaky pastry and a velvety coffee for brunch, or a few cheeky cocktails after work. The afternoon tea is particularly popular, boasting finger-sandwiches and home-made cakes.

50% OFF FOOD | 4 | FRI × | SAT × — Italian

THE STAR INN
☎01323 762 648
Normans Bay, Pevensey, B24 6QG
Both adults and children are well catered for at this delightful family-friendly pub. With stunning views of the East Sussex countryside, the garden at The Star Inn provides the perfect spot for al fresco dining.

2FOR1 MAIN COURSE | FRI ✓ | SAT ✱ | SUN — English and Continental

THE STAR INN
☎01435 812 495
Waldron, Nr Heathfield, TN21 0RA
At the recently refurbished, Star Inn Restaurant, chef Nick Botting heads a team that produces fabulous gastro pub food with a big emphasis on flavour through the use of quality ingredients.

2FOR1 3 COURSES | FRI ✓ | SAT × | SUN — British

STRADA
01273 202 070
160-161 North Street, Brighton, BN1 1EZ
Offering fresh, bold dishes inspired by flavours of Italian city life – Strada serves a selection of indulgent tastes, to those seeking a blissful escape to laidback Italian life. *Excludes Pizzettas.

25% OFF TOTAL | 6 | FRI ✓ | SAT × — Italian

THAI KITCHEN @ THE IRON DUKE
☎01273 734 806
3 Waterloo Street, Hove, BN3 1AQ
Based at the Iron Duke pub, The Thai Kitchen is a wonderful place to head for a tasty and authentic Thai meal. The staff aim to delight all guests with a genuine Thai culinary experience.

2FOR1 3 COURSES | FRI | SAT | SUN — Thai

THE TOWNHOUSE RESTAURANT
☎01273 693 216
81-82 St James Street, Brighton, BN2 1PL
A homely, unprepossessing bar and restaurant with simple wooden furniture complementing the open brick fireplaces. Features a high-class menu of classic dishes done with flair. *A la carte menu only.

25% OFF TOTAL | 8 | FRI × | SAT × | SUN — Classic British/French

TREACLE MINE
01323 489 520
Hailsham Road, Polegate, East Sussex, BN26 6QL
Quality pub classics with modern twists meets with a friendly and relaxed atmosphere to make this Table Table venue the perfect place for any occasion. *Excludes daytime & evening deals and festive menus.

2FOR1 MAIN COURSE | FRI ✓ | SAT ✓ — Modern British

V-BAR
☎01323 492 574
Pelham Yard, High Street, Seaford, BN25 1PQ
Great little bar tucked away in Seaford where you can count on a simple, unfussy drink and bite to eat; a welcoming and friendly local spot.

2FOR1 MAIN COURSE | FRI ✓ | SAT ✱ | SUN — British

VBITES
☎01273 933 757
Hove Lagoon, Kingsway, Hove, BN3 4LX
Bright, enthusiastic and committed vegan restaurant in Hove Lagoon owned by Heather Mills; with a great range of dishes whose vibrant flavours will both surprise and delight you.

25% OFF TOTAL | 4 | FRI ✓ | SAT ✓ — Vegan

THE VICEROY
☎01273 513 308
4a Bridge Street, Newhaven, BN9 9PJ
This regionally inspired menu successfully offers an authentic taste of India. Appeasing both carnivorous diners and veggies, this venue promises that nobody will go home hungry.

2FOR1 2 COURSES | FRI ✓ | SAT ✓ — Bangladeshi/Indian

WARUNG TUJUH
☎01273 720 784
7 Pool Valley, Brighton, BN1 1NJ
This Indonesian restaurant gains rave reviews for its intriguing, thoroughly tasty dishes and for its excellent service. Their signature, slow-cooked beef in coconut milk hits home. *1 card per party.

2FOR1 MAIN COURSE | FRI ✱ | SAT ✱ — Indonesian

WATERSIDE SEAFOOD RESTAURANT
☎01323 646 566
11-12 Royal Parade, Eastbourne, BN22 7AR
Set fair on Eastbourne's Royal Parade, the Waterside is a boutique hotel and restaurant that's bright and welcoming in feel. The flavours are clear and the restaurant holds a well-deserved AA Rosette.

25% OFF TOTAL | 6 | FRI × | SAT × | SUN | ✱ — Seafood

WHEATSHEAF RESTAURANT
☎01424 842 004
2 Barnhorn Road, Bexhill-on-Sea, TN39 4LR
Beautifully situated in the heart of Little Common village, this pub-restaurant is steeped in British tradition. Sip a beer whilst devouring a substantial and wholesome dish at a pocket-friendly price.

2FOR1 MAIN COURSE | FRI ✓ | SAT ✓ | SUN — British

THE WHITE HART
01424 813 187
Winchelsea Road, Guestling, Hastings, TN35 4LW
Beefeater Grill are one of the UK's best-loved restaurants welcoming guests for almost 40 years in over 130 locations nationwide. *Excludes Breakfast, Light Bites, Bar menu, set menus and all other offers.

2FOR1 MAIN COURSE | 6 | FRI ✓ | SAT × — Modern British

To understand what the restaurant icons mean, please see the inside back cover.

YE OLDE PUMPHOUSE
01424 422 016
64 George Street, Hastings, TN34 3EE
From a daytime moment of calm to a buzzy night out, Ye Olde Pump House puts together an array of classic English dishes with an especial line in hearty, wholesome Sunday roasts.

2FOR1 MAIN COURSE | FRI | SAT ✱ | SUN — British

YPRES CASTLE INN
01797 223 248
Gun Garden, Rye, TN31 7HH
Seafood lovers can savour the fresh tastes of scallops, plaice and John Dory direct from the Rye Bay. Indulge in fresh produce whilst dining al fresco, overlooking the Romney Marsh and flowing rivers.

2FOR1 MAIN COURSE | FRI | SAT — British

ZAFFERELLI
01273 206 662
31-32 New Road, Brighton, BN1 1UG
Don't think twice: this warmly atmospheric Italian restaurant in the heart of Brighton stands out for its fresh, flavoursome dishes with a lot of unpretentious, genial and authentic character.

25% OFF TOTAL | 4 | FRI ✱ | SAT ✱ | ▲ — Italian

West Sussex

THE ACORN
01444 237 720
Charles Avenue, Burgess Hill, RH15 9TQ
Beefeater Grill are one of the UK's best-loved restaurants welcoming guests for almost 40 years in over 130 locations nationwide. *Excludes Breakfast, Light Bites, Bar menu, set menus and all other offers.

2FOR1 MAIN COURSE | 6 | FRI ✓ | SAT × | ▲ — Modern British

AL'S DINER
01903 367 313
23 Marine Parade, Worthing, BN11 3PS
Come on down to this classic American diner, serving all-American dishes that are too good to resist. From juicy hamburgers to maple syrup pancakes, here you'll find something to suit any appetite.

50% OFF FOOD | 10 | FRI ✓ | SAT × — American

AMELIE AND FRIENDS
01243 771 444
31 North Street, Chicester, PO19 1LY
Whether you visit for an indulgent dinner, pre-theatre treat, tasty lunch, or even just coffee and cake, you can expect a warm and efficient service and some very fine food indeed from Amelie and Friends.

2FOR1 3 COURSES | FRI ✓ | SAT ✓ — British

THE ANCHOR INN
01243 641 373
Selsey, Sidlesham, Chichester, PO20 7QU
Pretty roadside pub in Selsey, near Chichester, that does a good range of classic pub food through the week, as well as a plentiful, delicious carvery on select days.

2FOR1 MAIN COURSE | FRI ✓ | SAT ✓ — Fresh Fish/Pub Classics

ANISE RESTAURANT
01342 337 700
London Road, Felbridge, RH19 2BH
Highly distinctive flavours and a focused, modern style make this a popular place to dine out. Elegant, charming and individual, the mood and the cuisine are both exceptional. 2 AA Rosettes.

25% OFF TOTAL | 6 | FRI ✓ | SAT ✓ | ✱ — European

BADGERS
01798 342 651
Coultershaw Bridge, Petworth, GU28 0JF
One of the best pubs in the area. A truly charming venue known for high quality, hearty food matched by diligent service, providing assistance to help choose that perfect wine or beer.

25% OFF TOTAL | 4 | FRI ✓ | SAT — European

BASMATI INDIAN RESTAURANT
01798 343 414
Swan House Cellars, Petworth, GU28 0AH
This cool cellar serves some of the hottest curries in town. The menu features a blend of old and new, with traditional Indian cuisine sitting comfortably next to some British inventions.

2FOR1 MAIN COURSE | FRI ✓ | SAT | ✱ — Indian British

BASMATI INDIAN RESTAURANT
01243 543 400
83 Nyton Road, Chichester, PO20 3UG
Taste India, Pakistan and Bangladesh as chef Nasar Miah expertly prepares delectable dishes from the sub-continent. Mirroring Asian domestic methods, the food is authentic and undoubtedly mouth-watering.

2FOR1 MAIN COURSE | FRI × | SAT × | ✱ | ▲ — Indian

BAYTREE RESTAURANT
0134 233 700
London Road, Felbridge, RH19 2BH
Stylish and intimate restaurant in the Felbridge Hotel. Serves an accomplished menu of classic dishes with imaginative accompaniments. Try the superb confit leg of duck with its cassoulet side.

25% OFF TOTAL | 6 | FRI ✓ | SAT ✓ — European

THE BEACH HOUSE
01243 514 800
77 Rookwood Road, West Wittering, PO20 8LT
A New England style café and restaurant located in a coastal Area of Outstanding Natural Beauty. Outstanding British cuisine can be enjoyed outdoors on the heated veranda during those bright days.

2FOR1 MAIN COURSE | FRI ✓ | SAT ✱ | SUN — British

THE BEACH HOUSE
01273 440 902
16-18 East Street, Shoreham-by-Sea, BN43 5ZE
Beach House is Shoreham-by-Sea's newest restaurant, bar and café. Located in the heart of the historic old town, they serve freshly-prepared locally-sourced food in a relaxed and friendly atmosphere.

25% OFF TOTAL | 2 | FRI × | SAT × | ✱ — British

BELLA ITALIA
01293 521 974
Crawley Leisure Park, Crawley, RH10 8LR
Accessible Italian cuisine on the British high street – indulge in authentic sharing platters, hand stretched pizzas and hearty pasta dishes, served with a healthy dose of gregarious Italian hospitality.

25% OFF TOTAL | 6 | FRI × | SAT × | SUN | ▲ — Italian

BENTLEYS AT THE ANGEL HOTEL
01730 812 421
North Street, Midhurst, GU29 9DN
A distinctive experience at this hotel-based restaurant specialising in exceptional Argentinian steaks. Dining room features a stunning brick fireplace and golden wood panelling; a calm and lovely space.

25% OFF TOTAL | 6 | FRI ✓ | SAT ✓ | SUN — Steakhouse

BEST WESTERN THE BIRCH HOTEL
01444 451 565
Lewes Road, Haywards Heath, RH17 7SF
In the heart of West Sussex, in the beautiful Hayward Heath, The Birch Hotel is a wonderful place to stay if you wish to explore the local area. The restaurant offers divine food in an amiable environment.

50% OFF FOOD | 4 | FRI | SAT | SUN — British

THE BLACK HORSE INN
01403 891 272
Nuthurst Street, Horsham, RH13 6LH
The Black Horse Inn is a traditional English pub situated in the delightful Sussex village of Nuthurst, surrounded by countryside, walks and cycle paths. Wide selection of beers and wines on offer.

50% OFF FOOD | 8 | FRI × | SAT × | SUN — Modern European

BLACK RABBIT
01903 882 828
Mill Road, Offham, Arundel, BN18 9PB
Owned by Hall & Woodhouse, this historical pub is situated beautifully on the River Arun. Traditional English cuisines are made from only the freshest, most locally sourced food. Welcoming to all.

25% OFF TOTAL | FRI × | SAT × | SUN | ▲ — British

BLACK SWAN
01293 612 261
Pease Pottage, Crawley, RH11 9AJ
Hall & Woodhouse owned, this historic Sussex pub-restaurant is beautifully located at the gateway of the South Downs. Traditionally English, expect to find pub favourites which have been locally sourced.

25% OFF TOTAL | FRI × | SAT × | SUN | ▲ — British

THE BOATHOUSE BRASSERIE
01798 831 059
Houghton Bridge, Arundel, BN18 9LR
Appease a ravenous appetite with a succulent joints of meat whilst admiring the views of the Arun Valley on the open patio. Be sure to finish the meal in style with a naughty-but-nice home-made dessert.

25% OFF TOTAL | 6 | FRI | SAT | SUN | ▲ — British

THE BOSHAM INN 01243 575 027
Main Road, Bosham, Chichester, PO18 8PW
This Vintage Inn oozes rural charm and rustic character. The picturesque surroundings provide the perfect backdrop for savouring the hearty, seasonal pub-food on the menu.

25% OFF TOTAL | FRI ✓ | SAT ✓ | SUN | ▲ — Modern British

CAFÉ ROUGE 01243 781 751
30 Southgate, Chichester, PO19 1DP
French sophistication on the British high street – enjoy seasonally changing French dishes and a continental wine selection, served in a relaxed environment with an undeniable flair of Parisian chic.

25% OFF TOTAL | 6 | FRI ✓ | SAT ✓ | ✳ | ▲ — French

CAFÉ ROUGE 01444 440 888
33 The Broadway, Haywards Heath, RH16 3AS
French sophistication on the British high street – enjoy seasonally changing French dishes and a continental wine selection, served in a relaxed environment with an undeniable flair of Parisian chic.

25% OFF TOTAL | 6 | FRI ✓ | SAT ✓ | ✳ | ▲ — French

CARMELA RISTORANTE ☎ 01403 275 375
3 Denne Road, Horsham, RH12 1JE
Modern, charming Sicilian ristorante in a lovely Tudor building. Serves a great selection of staple pizzas and pastas, plus traditional specialities. Also a great place to work over coffee during the day.

2FOR1 MAIN COURSE | FRI ✱ | SAT × | ▲ — Italian

THE CEDAR RESTAURANT @ HILTON ☎ 01243 558 300
Hilton Avisford Park, Yapton Lane, Arundel, BN18 0LS
Elegant but relaxed venue featuring burnished wood-panelled walls adorned with the names of past head boys. Distinct emphasis on classic and contemporary English cooking, with market-fresh ingredients.

50% OFF FOOD | 6 | FRI ✱ | SAT ✱ | SUN | ▲ — European

CHAMBERS BISTRO ☎ 01273 446 677
Old Town Hall, High Street, Shoreham-by-Sea, BN43 5DD
Seasonal and refreshing contemporary bistro-style food at this little restaurant in the old Town Hall of picturesque Shoreham-by-Sea. Simple dishes, cooked beautifully to bring out the best in the produce.

2FOR1 MAIN COURSE | FRI ✱ | SAT ✱ | SUN — Bistro

CHINA BRASSERIE HORSHAM ☎ 01403 218 218
33-35 North Street, Horsham, RH12 1RJ
China Brasserie is a contemporary Chinese restaurant, well known for superb menus, featuring a selection of healthy, quality local produce used in every dish.

25% OFF TOTAL | 8 | FRI ✓ | SAT × | SUN | ▲ — Chinese

THE CROSSBUSH 01903 882 655
Crossbush Lane, Arundel, BN18 9PQ
Beefeater Grill are one of the UK's best-loved restaurants welcoming guests for almost 40 years in over 130 locations nationwide. *Excludes Breakfast, Light Bites, Bar menu, set menus and all other offers.

2FOR1 MAIN COURSE | 6 | FRI ✓ | SAT × | ▲ — Modern British

THE CROWN INN ☎ 01403 710 902
Worthing Road, Dial Post, Horsham, RH13 8NH
Fabulous food-led pub with an imaginative, accomplished chef-patron. The pub has a great sense of heritage and personability about it; enjoy, for example, the musky and creamy Sussex Smokie, a crown jewel.

25% OFF TOTAL | 6 | FRI ▯ | SAT ▯ | SUN — British

THE CURRY INN ☎ 01444 415 141
58 Commercial Square, Haywards Heath, RH16 1EA
Smart, bright and popular Indian restaurant in Haywards Heath; mouth-wateringly piquant and rich curry dishes with a freshness in their flavours.

2FOR1 MAIN COURSE | FRI ✓ | SAT ▯ | ✳ — Indian

DA PEPPINO ☎ 01293 516 677
7 High Street, Crawley, RH10 1BH
Da Peppino's longevity of over 25 years illustrates the quality and passion that exudes from the kitchen. Including authentic pizzas, risotto and plates of hearty meat, the menu is bursting with variety.

50% OFF FOOD | FRI ✱ | SAT ✱ — Italian

DRAGON ☎ 01903 773 354
125 Sea Lane, Rustington, Littlehampton, BN16 2SG
Set sail on your voyage in this delightful South Coast restaurant. Cantonese, Peking and Szechuan dishes can be accompanied by one of the many fine wines from the extensive drinks menu.

25% OFF TOTAL | 10 | FRI ✓ | SAT ✓ | ✳ — Cantonese

THE FRIAR'S OAK 01273 847 801
London Road, Hassocks, BN6 9NA
This Vintage Inn oozes rural charm and rustic character. The picturesque surroundings provide the perfect backdrop for savouring the hearty, seasonal pub-food on the menu.

25% OFF TOTAL | FRI ✓ | SAT ✓ | SUN | ▲ — Modern British

GARDENERS ARMS ☎ 01444 892 328
Selsfield Road, Ardingly, RH17 6TJ
Found in a rural location, this venue serves traditional pub food, satisfying diners with real hearty meals. A listed building with some original features, also offering a beer garden and patio area.

25% OFF TOTAL | 6 | FRI × | SAT × | SUN | ▲ — British

THE GEORGE & DRAGON ☎ 01798 831 559
Houghton, Arundel, BN18 9LW
Exceedingly beautiful, one of Sussex's oldest pubs welcomes guests to admire the rolling hills of the Sussex Downs. The menu guarantees quality and promises dishes to be locally sourced and seasonal.

2FOR1 MAIN COURSE | FRI ✓ | SAT × | SUN | ▲ — British

GIUSEPPES ☎ 01903 212 780
8 Warwick Lane, Worthing, BN11 3DP
Giuseppes is an intimate and friendly Italian restaurant in Worthing, serving authentic and rustic food.

2FOR1 3 COURSES | FRI ✱ | SAT ✱ | ▲ — Italian

GOFFS MANOR ☎ 01293 540 982
Old Horsham Road, Southgate, Crawley, RH11 8PE
Traditional English dishes have given this 16th Century pub-restaurant a reputation to be proud of. Perfect for any occasion, this Hall & Woodhouse venue caters for all clientèle.

25% OFF TOTAL | FRI × | SAT × | SUN | ▲ — British

THE GREETS INN 01403 265 047
47 Friday Street, Warnham, Horsham, RH12 3QY
Historic inn with an enviable reputation for serving fabulous Sussex fare. Quintessentially English village pub with a magnificent menu crammed with locally sourced produce.

25% OFF TOTAL | 8 | FRI ▯ | SAT ✱ | SUN — Traditional English

THE GRILL AT ARORA CRAWLEY ☎ 01293 530 000
Southgate Avenue, Crawley, RH10 6LW
The Grill is a great local restaurant celebrating the fantastic produce that Sussex and the surrounding counties are famed for, contemporary design and good service.

25% OFF TOTAL | 4 | FRI ✓ | SAT ✓ — British

THE GROVE INN ☎ 01798 343 659
Grove Lane, Petworth, GU28 0HY
An inn sat in beautiful countryside, featuring a menu based on local, fresh produce with creative cooking and a calm, accommodating ambience.

2FOR1 MAIN COURSE | FRI ✓ | SAT ✱ | ▲ — English/Gastro pub

HALLIDAYS RESTAURANT ☎ 01243 575 331
Watery Lane, Funtington, Chichester, PO18 9LF
A small intimate restaurant in a quiet West Sussex village, with a chef whose natural talent combined with hard-won expertise provides teasing combinations of flavours. Awarded 2 AA Rosettes.

25% OFF TOTAL | 6 | FRI ✓ | SAT × | SUN | ✳ — Fine Dining

HAMILTON ARMS NAVA THAI ☎ 01730 812 555
School Lane, Stedham, GU29 0NZ
A unique place for a traditional country pub combined with a Thai restaurant. Indulge in an extensive range of succulent and authentic dishes served by Thai staff in traditional Thai dress.

2FOR1 MAIN COURSE | FRI ✓ | SAT ✱ — Thai

Gourmet Society discount applies to the à la carte menu only, unless stated otherwise.

THE HILLSIDE INN
01293 883 346

Balcombe Road, Crawley, RH10 7SX

This Vintage Inn oozes rural charm and rustic character. The picturesque surroundings provide the perfect backdrop for savouring the hearty, seasonal pub-food on the menu.

25% OFF TOTAL | FRI ✓ | SAT ✓ | SUN — Modern British

THE HORNBROOK
01403 252 638

Brighton Road, Horsham, RH13 6QA

Good old-fashioned English pub that is nevertheless bang up to date in its quality of service and welcome. Serves hearty British pub fare, which you can enjoy in the company of a great real ale.

25% OFF TOTAL | 6 | FRI × | SAT × | SUN — British

THE HUNGRY GUEST CAFE
01798 344 564

Lombard Street, Petworth, GU28 0AG

The Hungry Guest Café offers an exciting and fresh menu for you to enjoy in a modern and beautifully designed environment. Named by The Times in 2012 as one of the 30 Best Places for Brunch in Britain.

25% OFF TOTAL | 4 | FRI ✓ | SAT ✓ — British

THE JOLLY TANNERS
01444 400 335

Handcross Road, Staplefield, RH17 6EF

Endorsing traditional British culture, this renowned pub serves a dazzling array of real ales and genuinely mouth-watering dishes sourced locally.

25% OFF TOTAL | 4 | FRI ✓ | SAT ✓ — Traditional English

LA BRASSERIE @ SOFITEL GATWICK
01293 567 070

Sofitel London Gatwich, Gatwick Airport, RH6 0PH

La Brasserie is an award-winning, French fine dining restaurant within the Sofitel London Gatwick Luxury Hotel. It is set around the central atrium just off Gatwick's North Terminal exit

25% OFF TOTAL | 4 | FRI ✓ | SAT ✓ — French

LYTTON'S BRASSERIE @ HOLIDAY INN
01293 884 806

Crabbet Park, Crawley, Turners Hill Road, RH10 4SS

Be sure to try the house speciality, Oak Smoked Welsh Lamb Shank braised until tender and succulent, served on creamy mash with honey glazed root vegetables.

2FOR1 MAIN COURSE | FRI ✓ | SAT ✓ | ✱ — Brasserie

MAE PING THAI RESTAURANT
01342 327 244

16 Railway Approach, East Grinstead, RH19 1BP

Attractive English countryside town with a fine Thai restaurant frequented by local patrons and their honoured guests to enjoy freshly-cooked dishes in a traditional atmosphere.

2FOR1 MAIN COURSE | FRI × | SAT × | SUN — Thai

NIZAM INDIAN RESTAURANT
01444 457 527

139 South Road, Haywards Heath, RH16 4LY

A wonderful menu accommodating outstandingly tasty dishes can be found at this excellent Indian restaurant. A light and contemporary environment makes this an idyllic place to relax and enjoy great food.

2FOR1 MAIN COURSE | FRI × | SAT × — Indian

OLD FORGE RESTAURANT
01903 743 402

6 Church Street, Storrington, RH20 4LA

Owners Cathy and Clive Roberts have expanded their Old Forge restaurant by adding a delicatessen and wine cellar.

2FOR1 MAIN COURSE | FRI ✓ | SAT [icon] | SUN — British

THE OLD STABLES
01243 543 082

Fontwell Park, Fontwell Avenue, Fontwell, BN18 0SY

This Vintage Inn oozes rural charm and rustic character. The picturesque surroundings provide the perfect backdrop for savouring the hearty, seasonal pub-food on the menu.

25% OFF TOTAL | FRI ✓ | SAT ✓ | SUN — Modern British

OM RESTAURANT
01903 233 300

67 Rowlands Road, Worthing, BN11 3JN

OM are incredibly proud to offer authentic Nepalese cuisine to the people of Worthing and visitors from afar. With friendly staff and delicious food, this charming restaurant sets out to impress.

2FOR1 MAIN COURSE | FRI ✓ | SAT ✓ | SUN — Nepalese

THE OYSTERCATCHER
01903 726 354

Yapton Road, Climping, Littlehampton, BN17 5RU

This Vintage Inn oozes rural charm and rustic character. The picturesque surroundings provide the perfect backdrop for savouring the hearty, seasonal pub-food on the menu.

25% OFF TOTAL | FRI ✓ | SAT ✓ | SUN — Modern British

REINA
01403 265 894

7-9 Park Place, Horsham, RH12 1DF

A shrine for House music lovers, Reina in Horsham is your number one stop for great music, your favourite cocktails and some really tasty food.

50% OFF FOOD | 6 | FRI ✱ | SAT ✱ — Italian

THE ROUNDSTONE
01903 785423

Roundstone Lane, East Preston, Littlehampton, BN16 1EB

Quality pub classics with modern twists meets with a friendly and relaxed atmosphere to make this Table Table venue the perfect place for any occasion. *Excludes daytime & evening deals and festive menus.

2FOR1 MAIN COURSE | FRI ✓ | SAT ✓ — Modern British

PREZZO

2FOR1 MAIN COURSE | FRI × | SAT ×

2-FOR-1 MAIN COURSE

7 restaurants in West Sussex

61 South Street, Chichester, PO19 1EE	01243 536 951
13 High Street, East Grinstead, RH19 3AF	01342 300 211
60 The Broadway, Haywards Heath, RH16 3AR	01444 451 001
46 Carfax, Horsham, RH12 1EQ	01403 230 245
Ground Floor, West Street, Midhurst, GU29 9NQ	01730 817 040
60 High Street, Crawley, RH10 1BT	01293 512 459
61 High Street, Arundel, BN18 9AJ	01903 884 793

THE SERGISON ARMS
01444 413 768
Butlers Green Road, Haywards Heath, RH16 4AH
This Vintage Inn oozes rural charm and rustic character. The picturesque surroundings provide the perfect backdrop for savouring the hearty, seasonal pub-food on the menu.

25% OFF TOTAL | FRI ✓ | SAT ✓ | SUN | ▲ — Modern British

SEVEN FISH
☎ 01730 716 280
North Street, Midhurst, GU29 9DN
Bright, fresh and full of flavour aptly describes not only the excellent seafood at this neighbourhood restaurant, but the atmosphere of the place itself. An easy place to warm to, with a broad menu.

2FOR1 MAIN COURSE | FRI ✸ | SAT × — Seafood

SHAFIQUES RESTAURANT
☎ 01903 504 035
42 Goring Road, Worthing, BN12 4AD
A family run Indian restaurant that has become some what of an institution in Worthing. Try Shafiques for attentive service, delicious food and lovely ambiance.

2FOR1 3 COURSES | FRI × | SAT × — Indian

SHANGHAI COTTAGE
☎ 01798 343 949
Market Square, Petworth, GU28 0AH
A wonderful restaurant offering tasty Chinese cuisine. Enjoy an evening out with great food and good company, or opt for the takeaway option and feast in the comfort of your own home.

25% OFF TOTAL | 👤10 | FRI ✓ | SAT ✓ | ✱ — Chinese

SHIMLA INDIAN RESTAURANT
☎ 01293 518 866
Apple Tree Pub, West Green, Crawley, RH11 7DL
Shimla Indian Restaurant at The Apple Tree pub offers homemade Indian cuisine in a relaxed atmosphere also with a takeaway and delivery service.

25% OFF TOTAL | 👤6 | FRI ✓ | SAT ✓ | ✱ | ▲ — Indian

SILK ROAD RESTAURANT
☎ 01903 722 055
8-10 Arcade Road, Littlehampton, BN17 5AP
Guests who dine here will fall in love with the Mediterranean delights and attention to detail. Enjoy magnificently tasty cuisine served on your own unique antique plate. Weekly live entertainment.

25% OFF TOTAL | 👤4 | FRI ✓ | SAT ✸ | ▲ — Turkish

SO INDIA
☎ 01798 874 748
Stane Street, Codmore Hill, Pulborough, RH20 1BG
With a taste of authentic cuisine of the Grand Moghuls, So India offers dishes such as Ostrich Tikka, Crab Malibar and Swordfish Bhuna. Straying from the usual fare and sure to tickle your taste buds.

2FOR1 3 COURSES | FRI × | SAT × | ▲ — Indian

THE SPORTSMAN
☎ 01444 233 460
Cuckfield Road, Hassocks, BN6 9LQ
Situated in a grade II listed pub, this 19th Century pub plays home to extremely talented chefs. From a spiced potted crab starter to a creamy panna cotta dessert, dishes are sure to be remembered.

2FOR1 MAIN COURSE | FRI 📱 | SAT 📱 | SUN | ▲ — British

THE SPOTTED COW
☎ 01243 786 718
Selsey Road, Chichester, PO20 1PD
The Spotted Cow is full of charm and history. The menu consists of traditional favourites and contemporary dishes made with fresh locally sourced produce. A true gem!

2FOR1 3 COURSES | FRI ✓ | SAT ✸ | SUN | ▲ — British

THE STATION
01403 250 141
57 North Street, Horsham, RH12 1RB
Beefeater Grill are one of the UK's best-loved restaurants welcoming guests for almost 40 years in over 130 locations nationwide. *Excludes Breakfast, Light Bites, Bar menu, set menus and all other offers.

2FOR1 MAIN COURSE | 👤6 | FRI ✓ | SAT × | ▲ — Modern British

STRADA
01403 248 887
5 East Street, Horsham, RH12 1HH
Offering fresh, bold dishes inspired by flavours of Italian city life – Strada serves a selection of indulgent tastes, to those seeking a blissful escape to laidback Italian life. *Excludes Pizzettas.

25% OFF TOTAL | 👤6 | FRI ✓ | SAT × | ▲ — Italian

THE SWALLOW'S RETURN
01903 506 346
1 Titnore Lane, Worthing, BN12 6PB
This Vintage Inn oozes rural charm and rustic character. The picturesque surroundings provide the perfect backdrop for savouring the hearty, seasonal pub-food on the menu.

25% OFF TOTAL | FRI ✓ | SAT ✓ | SUN | ▲ — Modern British

TAKANZO
☎ 01798 874 141
19 Swan Corner, Pulborough, RH20 1RJ
A vibrant blend of oriental cuisines can be enjoyed in this relaxing and comfortable restaurant and bar. Chinese, Malaysian, Thai and Japanese dishes feature highly on the eclectic menu.

25% OFF TOTAL | 👤10 | FRI ✓ | SAT ✓ | ✱ — Pan-Asian

TASTE OF BENGAL
01903 238 400
203 Heene Road, Worthing, BN11 4NN
Friendly, long-established Indian takeaway in Worthing with a bubbly persona and a great menu. There's lots to choose from, good quality ingredients, and an experienced eye for spice and flavour.

25% OFF TOTAL | 👤6 | FRI × | SAT × | SUN — Indian

TOUCH OF SPICE
☎ 01903 212 666
8 Downlands Parade, Worthing, BN14 9JH
Drawing its name from the ethos held in the kitchen, Touch of Spice provides delicately infused Indian dishes to a regular influx of diners. Exotic spices are combined in an imaginative way.

2FOR1 2 COURSES | FRI ✓ | SAT ✓ — Indian

VARDAR RESTAURANT
☎ 01903 721 226
3 Selborne Place, Littlehapton, BN175NH
Dine on mouth-watering steaks and crispy vegetables bakes at this venue, where British cuisine is given a charismatic twist. The expansive menu plays host to memorable flavours and aromas.

2FOR1 2 COURSES | FRI 📱 | SAT 📱 | SUN | ✱ | ▲ — British

WABI
☎ 01403 788 140
38 East Street, Horsham, RH12 1HL
Named after the Wabi-Sabi aesthetic movement, diners can expect to find chic and elegant surroundings accompanied by an award-winning menu. Watch, open-mouthed, as food is prepared before your very eyes.

25% OFF TOTAL | 👤6 | FRI 📱 | SAT × | SUN | ▲ — Japanese

WELLIES RESTAURANT
☎ 01243 819 007
Oldwick Farm, Chichester, PO18 9AA
Martin and Charlotte welcome you to Wellies Restaurant & Tea Rooms. Their cosy restaurant and sunny terrace are the perfect place for you to enjoy your meal from their extensive menu.

50% OFF FOOD | 👤4 | FRI ✓ | SAT ✓ | ▲ — British

WOODIES WINE BAR AND BRASSERIE
☎ 01243 779 895
10-13 St Pancras, Chichester, PO19 7SJ
From an ever-varying menu and in deeply lit, relaxing and ambient surroundings, enjoy the imaginative and stylish combinations of contemporary flavours at this chic Chichester brasserie.

25% OFF TOTAL | 👤6 | FRI ✓ | SAT ✸ | SUN | ✱ | ▲ — English and Continental

WORLDS END PATCHING
☎ 01903 871 346
Arundel Road, Patching, Worthing, BN13 3UQ
Family owned brewer Hall & Woodhouse devote themselves to locally sourced food at affordable prices in an affable atmosphere. This beautiful Sussex longhouse caters for all.

25% OFF TOTAL | FRI × | SAT × | SUN | ▲ — British

YE OLDE HOUSE AT HOME
☎ 01903 232 661
77 Broadwater Street East, Worthing, BN14 9AD
As the name suggests, this pub provides a homely atmosphere in traditional surroundings. Enjoy the exquisite exposed beams by the glowing log fire whilst tucking into genuine old favourites.

2FOR1 MAIN COURSE | FRI × | SAT × | SUN | ▲ — British

Greater London

All restaurants inside the M25 are listed in the Greater london region, and are arranged into geographic zones. Do be sure to browse East Anglia and the South East regions too, for restaurants near the boundary.

All central London restaurants have a grid reference that refers to the map included in this section, and are ordered from the centre of the map outwards. Page numbers are also included on the map to aid your search for a particular area. Also, every London restaurant has their nearest tube/train station listed to help you navigate to your chosen restaurant.

A
B
C
D
E
F
1
2
3
4
St.Johns Wood
p. 183
p. 183
REGENT'S PARK
Mornington Crescent
p. 183
Somers Town
Maida Vale
MAIDA VALE
St John's Wood
EUSTON STATION
Euston Square
p. 189
p. 183
p. 177
Warren Street
p. 177
MARYLEBONE STATION
Regents Park
Great Portland Street
Warwick Ave
Baker Street
Fitzrovia
Goodge Street
Lisson Grove
Edgware Road
MARYLEBONE
Royal Oak
PADDINGTON
Tottenham Court Rd
PADDINGTON STATION
p. 176
p. 182
Oxford Circus
p. 170
p. 188
Paddington
Bond Street
Marble Arch
SOHO
Bayswater
Lancaster Gate
Bayswater
MAYFAIR
Piccadilly Circus
HYDE PARK
p. 188
GARDENS
p. 175
Green Park
p. 174
St James's
Hyde Park Corner
GREEN PARK
ST.JAMES' PARK
Knightsbridge
KENSINGTON
Knightsbridge
St.James Park
p. 187
p. 181
p. 181
WESTMINSTER
p. 181
VICTORIA STATION
Gloucester Road
South Kensington
South Kensington
Sloane Square
Belgravia
Pimlico
Pimlico
p. 186
CHELSEA
p. 187
p. 186
Brompton
CHELSEA BRIDGE

A
B
C
D
E
F
5
6
7
8
p. 183
KINGS CROSS
p. 183
Angel
Pentonville
p. 184
Hoxton
p. 189
Hoxton
FINSBURY
Old Street
SHOREDITCH
p. 178
Russell Square
BLOOMSBURY
Clerkenwell
p. 178
p. 184
Shoreditch High St
p. 189
Spitalfields
Farringdon
Barbican
Chancery Lane
Holborn
Holborn
LIVERPOOL STREET
Moorgate
p. 185
Liverpool Street
THE CITY
Aldgate East
St Giles
p. 172
p. 179
St.Pauls
Aldgate
Bank
p. 190
Covent Garden
COVENT GARDEN
Strand
Temple
Mansion House
Cannon Street
Monument
Whitechapel
Tower Hill
BLACKFRIARS BRIDGE
MILLENNIUM BRIDGE
SOUTHWARK BRIDGE
LONDON BRIDGE
WATERLOO BRIDGE
CHARING CROSS STATION
Embankment
p. 174
p. 180
London Bridge
p. 192
Waterloo
Southwark
p. 186
WATERLOO STATION
Borough
Westminster
WESTMINSTER BRIDGE
LAMBETH
Lambeth North
p. 181
Elephant & Castle
p. 186
p. 180
LAMBETH BRIDGE
Newington
Walworth
p. 186
VAUXHALL BRIDGE
Vauxhall
Kennington

CENTRAL LONDON RESTAURANT INDEX

RESTAURANT NAME	GRID REF
The Aviary	C4
B-Soho	C4
Bellaria Restaurant & Wine Bar	C4
Bistro 1 @ Beak Street Soho	C4
Café Rouge	C4
Café Rouge	C4
Cape Town Fish Market	C4
Carnaby	C4
Costa Dorada	C4
Degò Restaurant	C4
The Delhi Brasserie	C4
Denise's Restaurant	C4
Elena's L'etoile	C4
Elysee Restaurant	C4
Gay Hussar	C4
Haozhan	C4
Heliot Steak House	C4
Jerusalem	C4
Josephine's Restaurant	C4
The Landseer British Kitchen	C4
Little Sicily	C4
Match	C4
Mediterranean Cafe	C4
Mela Shaftesbury	C4
Ora	C4
Ozer Restaurant	C4
Pierre Loti	C4
The Red Fort	C4
Reynolds Restaurant	C4
Salsa!	C4
Silk	C4
SIX Soho	C4
Soho Theatre Bar	C4
Souk Bazaar	C4
Strada	C4
Sweetspot	C4
Trattoria da Aldo	C4
Yumchaa Soho	C4
Zebrano	C4
Zebrano	C4
Bacco Restaurant & Wine Bar	C5
Bella Italia	C5
Bella Italia	C5
Bhatti Indian Cuisine	C5
Bistro 1 @ Covent Garden	C5
Boulevard Brasserie	C5
Brasserie @ Holborn House	C5
Café des Amis	C5
Café Mode	C5
Café Mode	C5
Café Rouge	C5
Café Rouge	C5
Covent Garden Cocktail Club	C5
Daawat at Johnstons	C5
Gandhi's Restaurant	C5
Giotto	C5
Grand Connaught Rooms	C5
Il Castelletto	C5
Kingsley Two Brasserie	C5
La Piazzetta	C5
La Tasca	C5
The Level Restaurant	C5
Los Locos	C5
Maxwell's Bar and Grill	C5
Navajo Joe	C5
Piazza Restaurant	C5
Prezzo	C5
Prezzo	C5
Salvador and Amanda	C5
Sofra	C5
Souk Medina	C5
Strada	C5

RESTAURANT NAME	GRID REF
Strada	C5
Strand Carvery	C5
Takari Covent Garden	C5
Tandoori Nights	C5
Tandoori Raj	C5
Tea Room at The Arts	C5
Walkabout	C5
Bella Italia	D5
Bella Italia	D5
Boyd's Brasserie	D5
Café Rouge	D5
Chilli Chutney	D5
Gibson's at The Yacht London	D5
Prezzo	D5
Smollensky's on The Strand	D5
Zen China	D5
Albannach	D4
Bella Italia	D4
Belowzero Restaurant & Lounge	D4
Bistro 1 @ Frith Street Soho	D4
Blue Lagoon Thai @ Haymarket	D4
Café Rouge	D4
Chowki	D4
Fishworks	D4
Franco's Ristorante Pizzeria	D4
Henry's Café Bar	D4
House Lounge @Thistle	D4
La Locanda	D4
Library Lounge @ Hilton	D4
L'Ulivo	D4
Mint Leaf Restaurant	D4
Nightingales Restaurant & Bar	D4
Planet Hollywood	D4
Prezzo	D4
Prezzo	D4
The Restaurant	D4
So Restaurant	D4
The Sports Cafe	D4

RESTAURANT NAME	GRID REF
Squares Restaurant	D4
Strada	D4
Terrace Restaurant	D4
Tiger Green Brasserie	D4
Wheelers of St. James's	D4
Woodlands Restaurant	D4
Avista	D3
Benares	D3
The Chesterfield Mayfair	D3
Citrus	D3
Greig's Grill & Restaurant	D3
Madisons Restaurant	D3
Prezzo	D3
Sofra Mayfair	D3
108 Marylebone Lane	C3
140 Park Lane Restaurant & Bar	C3
Brasserie at the Cumberland Hotel	C3
Café Rouge	C3
Carmina Café	C3
Colony Bar and Grill	C3
The Crescent at Montcalm Hotel	C3
Fire and Spice	C3
Fishworks	C3
Gaylord Restaurant	C3
The Grill at the Montcalm	C3
La Tasca	C3
The Marmor Grill @ Thistle	C3
Original Tagines	C3
Prezzo	C3
Prezzo	C3
Rasa W1	C3
The Running Horse	C3
Seymour Restaurant	C3
Sherlock's Grill	C3
Strada	C3
Woodlands	C3
Zayna	C3
Base Brasserie	B3

RESTAURANT NAME	GRID REF
La Tasca	E4
Spicy World Balti House	E4
Café Rouge	E3
da Scalzo	E3
Lowndes Bar & Kitchen	E3
MU Restaurant and Cocktail Bar	E3
Sobranie Russian Restaurant	E3
Spicy World	E3
Awana Malaysian Restaurant	E2
Beiteddine	E2
Bella Italia	E2
Bistro Fifteen	E2
Brompton Quarter Brasserie	E2
Café Rouge	E2
Caffe Concerto Kensington	E2
Chicago Rib Shack	E2
The Delhi Brasserie	E2
The Dorsia	E2
Frankie's Criterion	E2
Haandi	E2
The Hour Glass	E2
Kumo	E2
Laya'Lina	E2
Mamounia Lounge	E2
Monza Restaurant	E2
Off the Hook @ The Paxtons Head	E2
Shezan	E2
Cheminee Persian Restaurant	C2
Dolce	C2
Fantasia Palace	C2
Fiamma Restaurant @Hilton	C2
London St Brasserie	C2
Maximini Chinese Restaurant	C2
Pak Awie	C2
Ryath Indian Tandoori	C2
See Japanese Fusion Restaurant	C2
Dar Marrakesh	B2

RESTAURANT NAME	GRID REF
Mumtaz London	B2
Café Rouge	A2
Mezza Express	A3
Namaaste Kitchen	A3
Strada	A3
Yumchaa Parkway	A3
Andy's Taverna	A4
Elixir Bar	A4
Hellenic Restaurant	A4
Karavas	A4
The Maharani	A4
Rodon Live	A4
Central Station	A5
Mediterraneo	A5
Rasa Maricham	A5
Taste Of Asia	A5
Anam Bar	A6
Axis Bar & Kitchen	A6
Bombay Lounge	A6
Di Monforte	A6
Dolcetto Restaurant	A6
Gufaa	A6
Miz en Bouche	A6
Parveen Tandoori	A6
Pasha	A6
Spices	A6
Strada	A6
Bacchus Pub and Kitchen	A7
Ribeira	A7
Bogayo	B7
Chico Bandito	B7
Floripa London	B7
Lena	B7
Mai'da London	B7
New Regency	B7
Thai Thai East	B7
Yard	B7

RESTAURANT NAME	GRID REF
1901 at The Andaz Hotel	C7
Bonds Restaurant & Bar	C7
Caffe Concerto St. Paul's	C7
Catch at The Andaz Hotel	C7
Clause	C7
The Cuban Bar	C7
Eastway at The Andaz Hotel	C7
Goldfish	C7
Gow's Restaurant & Oyster Bar	C7
Harry's Abchurch Yard	C7
Harry's Ironmonger Lane	C7
La Tasca	C7
Luc's Brasserie	C7
Off The Wall Restaurant	C7
Ortega	C7
Osteria Del Mercato	C7
Rucola Italian Restaurant	C7
Saffron Red	C7
Swithins Restaurant	C7
Yager	C7
The Borough Bar and Dining	D7
Café Rouge	D7
Champor-Champor	D7
Londinium	D7
Northbank Restaurant & Bar	D7
Quarter Bar and Lounge	D7
Roast	D7
The Shad Indian	D7
Silka	D7
Southwark Rooms	D7
Antico Restaurant and Lounge Bar	E7
Gregg's Bar and Grill	E7
Chino Latino	F5
The Coriander	F5
Caffe Concerto Kings Road	F3
The Cadogan Arms	F2
Jakobs Cafe & Deli	F2
JuJu	F2

RESTAURANT NAME	GRID REF
Kings Road Steakhouse & Grill	F2
La Pizzeria	F2
Marco Pierre White	F2
Osteria dell'Arancio	F2
Three5 World Tapas	F2
Bella's Restaurant	F1
Coquine	F1
Couscous Darna Restaurant	F1
Dall'Artista	F1
Peridot	F1
Strada	F1
As Greek As It Gets	E1
The Atrium Restaurant	E1
Aubrey	E1
Café Rouge	E1
Caffe Concerto Knightsbridge	E1
Consortia @ Holiday Inn	E1
Five 25 Lounge @ Harrington Hall	E1
Five 25 Restaurant @ Harrington Hall	E1
The Jam Cupboard	E1
Light Of India	E1
Memories of India	E1
Pasha Lounge & Restaurant	E1
The Patisserie	E1
Prezzo	E1
Strada	E1
The Brasserie	D1
Curry Place	D1
Antony's	C1
Ariana Restaurant	C1
Bel Canto	C1
Bella Italia	C1
Bella Italia	C1
Café Rouge	C1
cherryjam	C1
The Dining Room @ Hilton	C1
Elements Restaurant @ Novotel	C1
The Golden Horseshoe	C1

RESTAURANT NAME	GRID REF
Golden Shalimar	C1
La Suite West	C1
Lagenda @ Holiday Villa Hotel	C1
Massis Lebanese Grill & Bar	C1
Med Mezze Restaurant	C1
Mr Fish Bayswater	C1
Olio's Brasserie	C1
Taormina Restaurant	C1
The Union Bar & Grill	C1
Whites Restaurant	C1
Akash Tandoori	B1
Café Rouge	B1
Le Cochonnet	B1
Agra Tandoori	A8
The Waterhouse	A8
Aladin	B8
Azka Mediterranean Meze	B8
Bengal Village	B8
Brick Lane Brasserie	B8
The Brickhouse	B8
Cinnamon Brick Lane	B8
City Spice	B8
Curry and Tandoori	B8
The Drunken Monkey	B8
The Famous Curry Bazaar	B8
The Globe	B8
Juno	B8
The Light Bar and Restaurant	B8
Muhib Indian Restaurant	B8
Nazrul Restaurant	B8
Preem and Prithi	B8
Preem Restaurant	B8
Reema Balti House	B8
Rocket Bishopsgate	B8
Sahara Hoxton	B8
Sahara Shoreditch	B8
Shampan	B8
Sheba Restaurant	B8

RESTAURANT NAME	GRID REF
Addendum Restaurant	C8
Barcelona Tapas Bar	C8
Bengal Cuisine	C8
Brick Lane Clipper	C8
Bundu Khan	C8
Bury Court	C8
Cafe Bangla	C8
Café Spice Namasté	C8
Chillies	C8
City Café Restaurant	C8
Clifton Restaurant	C8
The Empress	C8
The Famous Moonlight	C8
Gilt London	C8
Hemingways Wine Bar and Restaurant	C8
Jamies	C8
Kasturi	C8
La Fenice Rossa	C8
Liberty Lounge	C8
The Lloyds Club London	C8
Mango Brick Lane	C8
Marco Pierre White Steak & Alehouse	C8
Masala Brick Lane	C8
Monsoon	C8
Mumbai Square	C8
Papadoms	C8
Pause	C8
Red Chilli	C8
Saffron	C8
Sajna Grill Restaurant	C8
Sheraz Bangla Lounge	C8
Strada	C8
Taste of India	C8
Bengal Clipper	D8
Café Rouge	D8
Indian Fusion	D8
Tentazioni Restaurant	D8

Central

THE AVIARY
☎020 7538 8503
16 Little Portland Street, W1W 8BW
Nearest Station: Oxford Circus Map: C4
The Aviary Restaurant prides itself on serving excellent cuisine. Pop in for lunch, an excellent coffee, or book a table in the evening for a meal.

50% OFF FOOD | 4 | FRI ✓ | SAT × | SUN | ▲ — European

B-SOHO
☎020 7287 1661
Poland Street, W1F 8QQ
Nearest Station: Oxford Circus Map: C4
Combining the most authentic Italian pizzas, the coolest drinks and the hottest vibes, dynamic new cocktail bar and pizzeria, B-Soho, are breathing new life into the capital's dining scene.

50% OFF FOOD | 6 | FRI × | SAT × | SUN — Italian

BELLARIA RESTAURANT & WINE BAR
☎020 7580 8075
71 Great Titchfield Street, W1W 6RB
Nearest Station: Goodge Street Map: C4
Fine-looking street restaurant that's a perfect haunt to sit outside and watch the world by, or just as well to enjoy an outstanding Italian meal in their cosy, catacomb-like dining rooms.

50% OFF FOOD | 10 | FRI ✓ | SAT ✓ | ✱ — Italian

BISTRO 1 @ BEAK STREET SOHO
☎020 7287 1840
75 Beak Street, W1F 9SS
Nearest Station: Oxford Circus Map: C4
With European café vibes, this Bistro 1 venue in Soho is ideally located between Oxford Circus and Piccadilly. Serving exquisite, decently-priced Mediterranean cuisine to a buzzing audience.

25% OFF TOTAL | 2 | FRI × | SAT × | ▲ — Mediterranean

CAFÉ ROUGE
020 7434 2635
43 Charing Cross Road, WCH2 0AP
Nearest Station: Leicester Square Map: C4
French sophistication on the British high street – enjoy seasonally changing French dishes and a continental wine selection, served in a relaxed environment with an undeniable flair of Parisian chic.

25% OFF TOTAL | 6 | FRI ✓ | SAT ✓ | ▲ — French

CAFÉ ROUGE
020 7631 3075
264 Tottenham Court Road, W1T 7RH
Nearest Station: Tottenham Court Road Map: C4
French sophistication on the British high street – enjoy seasonally changing French dishes and a continental wine selection, served in a relaxed environment with an undeniable flair of Parisian chic.

25% OFF TOTAL | 6 | FRI ✓ | SAT ✓ | ✱ | ▲ — French

CAPE TOWN FISH MARKET
☎020 7437 1143
5-6 Argyll Street, W1F 7TE
Nearest Station: Oxford Circus Map: C4
Eclectic kind of a place that combines the eponymous fish market, a great seafood restaurant, and a sushi bar, all part of a very South African concern. *Offer excludes Lobster.

2FOR1 MAIN COURSE | FRI ✓ | SAT ✱ — Seafood

CARNABY
☎020 7297 5568
19 Great Marlborough Street, W1F 7HL
Nearest Station: Oxford Circus Map: C4
Uncluttered and pared-down contemporary styling that is reflected in the restaurant's thoroughly unfussy menu of smooth, appealingly flavourful dishes. *Minimum of two courses must be purchased.

2FOR1 3 COURSES | FRI ☎ | SAT ☎ — European

COSTA DORADA
☎020 7631 5117
47-55 Handway Street, W1T 1UX
Nearest Station: Tottenham Court Road Map: C4
Enjoy freshly prepared authentic Spanish cuisine and breathtaking live entertainment at Costa Dorado.

2FOR1 3 COURSES | FRI ✱ | SAT ☎ — Spanish

DEGÒ RESTAURANT
☎020 7636 2207
4 Great Portland Street, W1W 8QJ
Nearest Station: Oxford Circus Map: C4
Derived from the Italian word for 'tavern' and 'tasting', this cosmopolitan, AA Rosette-winning venue plays host to a prestigious Italian menu. *Offer available in the restaurant only.

25% OFF TOTAL | 6 | FRI ✓ | SAT ✓ — Italian

THE DELHI BRASSERIE
☎020 7437 8261
44 Frith Street, W1D 4SB
Nearest Station: Tottenham Court Road Map: C4
Serving diners with a broad range of North Indian cuisine in the heart of the most fashionable part of London's trendy Soho. Well established with food of exceptionally high quality.

2FOR1 MAIN COURSE | FRI ✱ | SAT ✱ — Indian

DENISE'S RESTAURANT
☎020 7436 1562
79 Southampton Row, WC1B 4ET
Nearest Station: Russell Square Map: C4
Whether you are hungry for a scrumptious lunch, or require an evening meal in a reliable restaurant, Denise's never fails to please. Healthy fresh dishes are prepared to perfection.

25% OFF TOTAL | 10 | FRI ✓ | SAT ✓ — European

ELENA'S L'ETOILE
☎020 7636 7189
30 Charlotte Street, W1T 2NG
Nearest Station: Goodge Street Map: C4
Well-balanced, charismatic bistro that serves superbly realised, thoroughgoing French cuisine; a relaxed and appealing touch of nostalgia in its styling and its dishes.

25% OFF TOTAL | 6 | FRI ✓ | SAT ✓ | SUN | ✱ | ▲ — French

ELYSEE RESTAURANT
☎020 7636 4804
13 Percy Street, W1T 1DT
Nearest Station: Goodge Street Map: C4
Effortlessly elegant restaurant with quite a history. First opened in 1936 and known as a spot for artists, writers and Greek royalty, its bay-windowed charm is mirrored in a fine, ranging Greek menu.

25% OFF TOTAL | 4 | FRI ✱ | SAT ✱ — Greek

GAY HUSSAR
☎020 7439 4788
2 Greek Street, W1D 4NB
Nearest Station: Tottenham Court Road Map: C4
For over 50 years this venue has served exquisite Hungarian cuisine, from national specialities to the finest Hungarian wines. The unique décor is on par with the food, and the service is impeccable.

25% OFF TOTAL | 6 | FRI ✓ | SAT ✓ | SUN | ▲ — Hungarian

HAOZHAN
☎020 7434 3838
8 Gerrard Street, W1D 5PJ
Nearest Station: Leicester Square Map: C4
Exquisite Chinese fusion food brimming with great warmth and charm. Truly exemplary food served with great care and attention, providing diners with a modern oriental dining experience.

25% OFF TOTAL | 4 | FRI ✱ | SAT ✱ | ▲ — Chinese

HELIOT STEAK HOUSE
☎020 7769 8844
The Hippodrome, Leicester Square, WC2H 7JH
Nearest Station: Leicester Square Map: C4
Executive Chef Barry Vera at Heliot Steakhouse has taken inspiration from the building's heritage and offers an alluring menu with something for everyone, including interesting twists on British classics.

25% OFF TOTAL | 8 | FRI ✓ | SAT ✓ — British

JERUSALEM
☎020 7255 1120
33-34 Rathbone Place, W1T 1JN
Nearest Station: Goodge Street Map: C4
A delightful haven of quietly cultured sophistication. This stylishly simple eatery offers a mouth-watering menu of wholesome, hearty and reasonably priced food.

2FOR1 3 COURSES | FRI ✓ | SAT ✓ | ✱ | ▲ — European

JOSEPHINE'S RESTAURANT
☎020 7580 6551
4 Charlotte Street, W1T 2LP
Nearest Station: Goodge Street Map: C4
Highly experienced chefs serve delicious Filipino cuisine in an inviting and friendly atmosphere. Guests can taste the talent that can be found in the kitchen as they enjoy tasty authentic meals.

25% OFF TOTAL | 4 | FRI ☎ | SAT ✓ | ▲ — Filipino

THE LANDSEER BRITISH KITCHEN
☎ 020 7347 1222

The Bloomsbury, 16-22 Great Russell Street, WC1B 3NN
Nearest Station: Tottenham Court Road Map: C4

An architecturally stunning neo-Georgian building houses this charming hotel. Explore the myriad of local treasures before taking a well-earned break in the exceptional restaurant and bar.

25% OFF TOTAL | 👤10 | FRI ✓ | SAT ✓ — British

LITTLE SICILY
☎ 020 7287 8989

36-40 Rupert Street, W1D 6DW
Nearest Station: Piccadilly Circus Map: C4

A stunning restaurant spread over two floors, where every dish is beautiful in appearance and delicious to taste. Vibrant colours will fill your plate, while welcoming staff will warm your heart.

50% OFF FOOD | 👤8 | FRI ✓ | SAT ✓ — Italian

MATCH
☎ 020 7629 7551

37-38 Margaret Street, W1G 0JF
Nearest Station: Oxford Circus Map: C4

Basing their menu on the four seasons, Match ensures that the food on offer reflects the produce and flavours that are associated with the time of year. Home-made soups, sauces and burgers.

50% OFF FOOD | 👤10 | FRI ✓ | SAT ✓ | 🌲 — British

MEDITERRANEAN CAFE
☎ 020 7437 0560

18 Berwick Street, W1F 0PX
Nearest Station: Piccadilly Circus Map: C4

A Soho favourite, the Mediterranean Café and its menu take you on a grand tour of the tastes and style of the Med. Dishes have been selected from Italy, Greece and Turkey for all their unique flavours.

2FOR1 2 COURSES | FRI ✱ | SAT ✱ | SUN | 🌲 — Mediterranean

MELA SHAFTESBURY
☎ 020 7836 8635

152-156 Shaftesbury Avenue, WC2H 8HL
Nearest Station: Covent Garden Map: C4

Highly regarded Shaftesbury Avenue restaurant. Features a choice menu of high-class curries (not least the kozi vertha with coconut and fennel, or the Hyderabadi crab curry), and a calm, lovely atmosphere.

2FOR1 3 COURSES | FRI × | SAT × — Indian

ORA
☎ 020 7637 0125

6 Little Portland Street, W1W 7JE
Nearest Station: Oxford Circus Map: C4

Ora is the latest addition to the growing contemporary Thai offering in London, delivering innovative yet classic cuisine in a stylish setting. The perfect retreat after a long day in the capital.

25% OFF TOTAL | 👤10 | FRI ✓ | SAT ✓ — Thai

OZER RESTAURANT
☎ 020 7323 0505

5 Langham Place, W1B 3DG
Nearest Station: Oxford Circus Map: C4

Ozer is a sumptuous, atmospheric restaurant that draws on the vast culinary influences of the Ottoman Empire. Chefs combine interesting ingredients, serving unique dishes with a modern touch. 1 AA Rosette.

2FOR1 MAIN COURSE | FRI ✓ | SAT ✓ | 🌲 — Middle Eastern

PIERRE LOTI
☎ 020 3417 6164

31 Rathbone Place, W1T 1JH
Nearest Station: Tottenham Court Road Map: C4

Sparkling Turkish restaurant just up from Oxford Street. Classic and unprepossessing by turns, edgy and asymmetric in places, the ambience is perfect for the range of subtle and excellent Turkish dishes.

2FOR1 3 COURSES | FRI ✓ | SAT ✓ — Turkish

THE RED FORT
☎ 020 7437 2525

77 Dean Street, W1D 3SH
Nearest Station: Tottenham Court Road Map: C4

Open-grills and tandoor ovens cook exciting, fresh cuisine to Mughal Court standards. Complete with fresh bread made daily, the food at this venue is exploding with culinary excellence. 1 AA Rosette.

2FOR1 3 COURSES | FRI ✱ | SAT × | 🌲 — Indian

REYNOLDS RESTAURANT
☎ 020 7580 2290

53 Charlotte Street, London, W1T 4PA
Nearest Station: Goodge Street Map: C4

At Reynolds, they do things a little differently.They believe in grazing. Their foodie items are wholesome and packed with flavour. All ingredients are locally sourced and served with a smile. Let's graze!

25% OFF TOTAL | 👤6 | FRI ✓ | SAT × | SUN | ✱ — International

SALSA!
☎ 020 7379 3277

96 Charing Cross Road, WC2H 0JG
Nearest Station: Tottenham Court Road Map: C4

Sizzling lamb steaks marinated in garlic and paprika, king prawns with hot Spanish guindilla peppers and superbly tasty fajitas can all be found at this colourfully cultural venue.

50% OFF FOOD | 👤10 | FRI ✱ | SAT ✱ | ✱ | 🌲 — Tex-Mex

SILK
☎ 020 7297 5538

19-21 Great Marlborough Street, W1F 7HL
Nearest Station: Oxford Circus Map: C4

A Michelin-recommended, Hilton hotel-based restaurant whose imaginative Asian-fusion cuisine jostles for your attention with the magnificent vaulted glass ceiling of its former courthouse setting.

2FOR1 2 COURSES | FRI ✓ | SAT ✓ | SUN | ✱ — Pan-Asian

SIX SOHO
☎ 020 7734 3888

6 Greek Street, W1D 4DE
Nearest Station: Tottenham Court Road Map: C4

Already revered as one of the finest Italian restaurant in trendy Central London's Soho district, SIX Soho offers an array of freshly prepared Italian dishes to savour and enjoy.

25% OFF TOTAL | 👤4 | FRI 📱 | SAT ✓ | SUN — Italian

SOHO THEATRE BAR
☎ 020 7434 9393

21 Dean Street, W1D 3NE
Nearest Station: Tottenham Court Road Map: C4

A theatre bar perfect for daytime meetings and drinks before or after a show. The drinks menu offers an extensive list of cocktails, bottled and draught beers, wines, fair-trade coffees and teas.

2FOR1 3 COURSES | FRI 📱 | SAT 📱 — Modern European

SOUK BAZAAR
☎ 020 7240 1796

27 Litchfield Street, WC2H 9NJ
Nearest Station: Leicester Square Map: C4

Bringing the exquisite tastes of North Africa to London, Souk Bazaar offer a selection of tapas alongside a vast array of tagines in an ideal location. *Must show membership card upon arrival.

50% OFF FOOD | 👤8 | FRI 📱 | SAT 📱 | 🌲 — Moroccan

STRADA
020 7580 4644

9-10 Market Place, W1W 8AQ
Nearest Station: Oxford Circus Map: C4

Offering fresh, bold dishes inspired by flavours of Italian city life - Strada serves a selection of indulgent tastes, to those seeking a blissful escape to laidback Italian life. *Excludes Pizzettas.

25% OFF TOTAL | 👤6 | FRI ✓ | SAT × | 🌲 — Italian

SWEETSPOT
☎ 020 7580 4684

60 Great Titchfield Street, W1W 7QF
Nearest Station: Oxford Circus Map: C4

Diners with a sweet tooth will adore the vast array of crepes and waffles. Start the day right with a banana, pecan and whipped cream pancake, which is enough to make anyone smile.

50% OFF FOOD | 👤10 | FRI ✓ | SAT ✓ — Belgian

TRATTORIA DA ALDO
☎ 020 7437 3985

51 Greek Street, W1D 4EH
Nearest Station: Tottenham Court Road Map: C4

The combination of a relaxing atmosphere and tasty food make this a great Italian restaurant to visit in London.The philosophy on cooking is simple, quality and seasonality of produce with minimum fuss.

25% OFF TOTAL | 👤4 | FRI 📱 | SAT 📱 — Italian

YUMCHAA SOHO
☎ 020 7209 9641

45 Berwick St, W1F 8SF
Nearest Station: Tottenham Court Road Map: C4

Yumchaa Soho, much like its sister branches, serves tea like no other, where a wide variety of loose leaf teas appear in quaint milk jugs. Sample the cakes to really polish your afternoon off.

2FOR1 3 COURSES | FRI ✓ | SAT ✓ — British

ZEBRANO
☎ 020 7287 5267

18 Greek Street, W1D 4DS
Nearest Station: Tottenham Court Road Map: C4

The place where a fun-filled time is always on the table. The Zebrano chefs have it covered, whether you want a casual dinner or a celebration with friends. The cocktails are sure to satisfy all.

50% OFF FOOD | 👤4 | FRI ✱ | SAT ✱ | ✱ | 🌲 — Modern European

ZEBRANO
☎020 7287 5267
14-16 Ganton Street, W1F 7BT
Nearest Station: Oxford Circus Map: C4
The place where a fun-filled time is always on the table. The Zebrano chefs have it covered, whether you want a casual dinner or a celebration with friends. The cocktails are sure to satisfy all.

50% OFF FOOD | 4 | FRI ✱ | SAT✱ | ✱ | Modern European

BACCO RESTAURANT & WINE BAR
☎020 7242 7900
25-26 Red Lion Street, WC1R 4PS
Nearest Station: Holborn Map: C5
The perfect place for pre-theatre dinners. Quality Italian food to be enjoyed with a glass from the carefully selected regional Italian wine list. *Must order starter and main course for 50% discount.

50% OFF FOOD | 4 | FRI ✓ | SAT✓ | SUN | ✱ | Italian

BELLA ITALIA
020 7836 8396
30 Henrietta Street, WC2E 8NA
Nearest Station: Covent Garden Map: C5
Accessible Italian cuisine on the British high street – indulge in authentic sharing platters, hand stretched pizzas and hearty pasta dishes, served with a healthy dose of gregarious Italian hospitality.

25% OFF TOTAL | 6 | FRI × | SAT× | SUN | Italian

BELLA ITALIA
020 7836 0484
70 St Martins Lane, WC2N 4JS
Nearest Station: Leicester Square Map: C5
Accessible Italian cuisine on the British high street – indulge in authentic sharing platters, hand stretched pizzas and hearty pasta dishes, served with a healthy dose of gregarious Italian hospitality.

25% OFF TOTAL | 6 | FRI × | SAT× | SUN | Italian

BHATTI INDIAN CUISINE
☎020 7831 0817
37 Great Queen Street, WC2B 5AA
Nearest Station: Holborn Map: C5
Snack on an Indian appetizer or simply savour a delicious main meal. Whether you like your food nice and spicy or meek and mild, the many dishes on offer provide something for everyone.

2FOR1 3 COURSES | FRI ✱ | SAT✱ | ✱ | Indian/Punjabi

BISTRO 1 @ COVENT GARDEN
☎020 7379 7585
33 Southampton Street, WC2E 7HE
Nearest Station: Covent Garden Map: C5
Situated in Covent Garden, this is one of three Bistro 1 venues. Serving exquisite Mediterranean cuisine to a vibrant audience, this place caters for hungry bellies that demand great food at good prices.

25% OFF TOTAL | 2 | FRI × | SAT× | Mediterranean

BOULEVARD BRASSERIE
☎020 7240 2992
40 Wellington Street, WC2E 7BD
Nearest Station: Covent Garden Map: C5
Classically simple French brasserie dishes are served in this popular eatery. Hearty beef bourguignon and succulent steaks are delightful choices, whilst the wine list offers an accompaniment for any dish.

25% OFF TOTAL | 4 | FRI | SAT✱ | French

BRASSERIE @ HOLBORN HOUSE
☎020 7242 4350
266-267 High Holborn, WC1V 7EE
Nearest Station: Chancery Lane Map: C5
Find a sophisticated clientele dining al fresco on the bijou terrace at this venue. Boasting a menu composed of both classic and contemporary Mediterranean cuisine, this eatery is effortlessly chic.

50% OFF FOOD | FRI × | SAT× | Modern European

CAFÉ DES AMIS
☎020 7379 3444
11-14 Hanover Place, WC2E 9JP
Nearest Station: Covent Garden Map: C5
A Covent Garden classic. Modern European cuisine is subjected to a divine French twist, which ensures every dish locks in delicious flavours. Enjoy a tasty cheese platter in the champagne bar.

50% OFF FOOD | 8 | FRI ✓ | SAT✓ | French

CAFÉ MODE
☎020 7831 2255
170A Drury Lane, WC2B 5PD
Nearest Station: Holborn Map: C5
Café Mode offers a fusion of tasty, fresh Italian food and delicious grills all served in a friendly setting with exceptional service.

2FOR1 MAIN COURSE | FRI ✓ | SAT✓ | Italian

CAFÉ MODE
☎020 7240 8085
57-59 Endell Street, WC2H 9AJ
Nearest Station: Covent Garden Map: C5
Perfectly situated for the theatres, this welcoming little red restaurant is bright and cheerful inside and serves a mean array of flavour-filled, herby Italian dishes and juicy grill-time specialities.

2FOR1 MAIN COURSE | FRI ✓ | SAT✓ | Mediterranean

CAFÉ ROUGE
020 7430 1416
77 Kingsway, WC2B 6SR
Nearest Station: Holborn Map: C5
French sophistication on the British high street – enjoy seasonally changing French dishes and a continental wine selection, served in a relaxed environment with an undeniable flair of Parisian chic.

25% OFF TOTAL | 6 | FRI ✓ | SAT✓ | ✱ | French

CAFÉ ROUGE
020 7836 0998
34 Wellington Street, WC2E 7BD
Nearest Station: Covent Garden Map: C5
French sophistication on the British high street – enjoy seasonally changing French dishes and a continental wine selection, served in a relaxed environment with an undeniable flair of Parisian chic.

25% OFF TOTAL | 6 | FRI ✓ | SAT✓ | ✱ | French

COVENT GARDEN COCKTAIL CLUB
☎020 7836 9533
6-7 Great Newport Street, WC2H 7JB
Nearest Station: Covent Garden Map: C5
A fabulous bar and kitchen that serves food and drink with a splash of verve and bundles of panache. Fantastic mini-bites to eat alongside the more substantial, while the cocktails take precedent.

2FOR1 3 COURSES | FRI × | SAT× | SUN | British

DAAWAT AT JOHNSTONS
☎020 7379 4737
372 Strand, WC2R 0JJ
Nearest Station: Covent Garden Map: C5
Whether you prefer something light, blended with fragrant spices and swirled with cream, or you seek the richness and heady aroma of a full bodied dish, Daawat have created a menu to tempt and indulge.

25% OFF TOTAL | 10 | FRI | SAT | British

GANDHI'S RESTAURANT
☎020 7831 6208
35 Grays Inn Road, WC1X 8PG
Nearest Station: Chancery Lane Map: C5
This restaurant has a unique friendly ambience that closely mirrors the warm hospitable nature of Indian culture. Every dish is infused with the finest ingredients, herbs and spices.

25% OFF TOTAL | 10 | FRI ✓ | SAT✓ | Indian

GIOTTO
☎020 7323 0891
52-54 New Oxford Street, WC1A 1ES
Nearest Station: Tottenham Court Road Map: C5
Keeping a firm hold on the culinary traditions of Italy, Giotto brings an authentic taste to the heart of London. What better place to step into after a day's shopping or an afternoon at the theatre.

25% OFF TOTAL | FRI | SAT | Italian

GRAND CONNAUGHT ROOMS
☎020 7405 7811
Great Queen Street, WC2B 5DA
Nearest Station: Holborn Map: C5
The Grand Connaught Rooms have to be seen to be believed. Breathtaking in appearance and stunning in all of its glory, this is a prime venue for important conferences and high-profile events.

25% OFF TOTAL | 6 | FRI ✓ | SAT✓ | British

IL CASTELLETTO
☎020 7405 2232
17 Bury Place, WC1A 2JB
Nearest Station: Holborn Map: C5
A rustic décor matches this restaurant's traditional culinary values. Fantastically located for both tourists and residents of the city, Il Castelletto has an attractive cohort of diners.

25% OFF TOTAL | 4 | FRI | SAT | Italian

KINGSLEY TWO BRASSERIE
☎0871 376 9006
Kingsley Hotel by Thistle, Bloomsbury Way, WC1A 2SD
Nearest Station: Holborn Map: C5
Light, elegant lines and high ceilings set the tone. Broad and inviting menu backs this up with a selection of brasserie dishes prepared and presented with verve and accomplishment.

2FOR1 MAIN COURSE | FRI ✓ | SAT✓ | SUN | ✱ | Brasserie

LA PIAZZETTA
☎020 7240 1168
13 Neal's Yard, WC2H 9DP
Nearest Station: Covent Garden Map: C5
This is is a bright and relaxed little place where the food is simple and Italianate, with some beautiful light options together with more wholesome dishes. A lovely setting for a bite to eat with friends.
50% OFF FOOD | FRI ✓ | SAT × — Italian

LA TASCA
☎0845 126 2950
23-24 Maiden Lane, WC2E 7NA
Nearest Station: Covent Garden Map: C5
Quintessentially Spanish, La Tasca's fresh and exciting menu offers something for everyone. Their tapas dishes are sincerely authentic, while their paellas always deliver on flavour.
25% OFF TOTAL | 8 | FRI ✓ | SAT × — Spanish

THE LEVEL RESTAURANT
☎020 7242 2828
Double Tree by Hilton, 92 Southampton Row, WC1B 4BH
Nearest Station: Holborn Map: C5
Be tempted by an innovative and exciting international menu as you relax in the eclectic ambiance of this vibrant and stylish restaurant. The perfect venue for socialising with friends or colleagues.
50% OFF FOOD | 6 | FRI ✓ | SAT ✓ | SUN — International

LOS LOCOS
☎020 7379 0220
24 Russell Street, WC2B 5HF
Nearest Station: Covent Garden Map: C5
A brilliantly lively place for tasty, thoroughbred Tex-Mex food; the spicy signature dishes and hearty, home-made accompaniments are an especial pleasure.
2FOR1 3 COURSES | FRI | SAT | SUN | * — Mexican

MAXWELL'S BAR AND GRILL
☎020 7836 0303
8 James Street, WC2E 8BH
Nearest Station: Covent Garden Map: C5
The vibrant atmosphere at Maxwell's is a great setting for the hearty, classic American food it serves. Come here for its major helpings of a wide range of freshly cooked, fulsome grill dishes.
25% OFF TOTAL | 4 | FRI * | SAT * — American

NAVAJO JOE
☎020 7240 4008
34 King Street, WC2E 8JD
Nearest Station: Covent Garden Map: C5
On the cusp of Covent Garden's famous piazza, experience a blend of Pacific Rim and South West American flavour. Renowned for its extensive range of tequilas, rum, and other world favourites.
25% OFF TOTAL | 4 | FRI * | SAT * — Southwestern American

PIAZZA RESTAURANT
☎020 7379 6867
35 Cranbourn Street, WC2H 7AD
Nearest Station: Leicester Square Map: C5
Long-established, this family-run restaurant has a reputable name based on its welcoming and attentive staff. Home-made pizzas and rustic pasta dishes line the carefully selected menu.
50% OFF FOOD | 6 | FRI ✓ | SAT × — Italian

PREZZO
020 7436 6641
34 New Oxford Street, WC1A 1AP
Nearest Station: Holborn Map: C5
With a character all of its own, Prezzo oozes contemporary style and enduring charm. Signature pastas, stone-baked pizzas and classic Italian dishes promise a perfect dining choice for the whole family.
2FOR1 MAIN COURSE | FRI × | SAT × — Italian

PREZZO
☎020 7240 0352
116 St Martins Lane, WC2N 4BF
Nearest Station: Leicester Square Map: C5
With a character all of its own, Prezzo oozes contemporary style and enduring charm. Signature pastas, stone-baked pizzas and classic Italian dishes promise a perfect dining choice for the whole family.
2FOR1 MAIN COURSE | FRI × | SAT × — Italian

SALVADOR AND AMANDA
☎020 7240 1551
8 Great Newport Street, WC2H 7JA
Nearest Station: Leicester Square Map: C5
Spanish passion is aplenty in this extraordinarily outstanding restaurant. A menu that boasts an eclectic variety of Spanish dishes such as prawns seared in garlic and mouth-watering paella.
50% OFF FOOD | 4 | FRI * | SAT * | SUN | * — Spanish

SOFRA
☎020 7240 3773
36 Tavistock Steet, WC2E 7PB
Nearest Station: Covent Garden Map: C5
Sofra promises high-quality recipes with an accent on healthy options, choice and uncompromising tastes. Order a feast of mezzes or savour a succulent tagine, and experience Turkish dining redefined.
2FOR1 MAIN COURSE | FRI ✓ | SAT ✓ — Middle Eastern

SOUK MEDINA
☎020 7240 1796
1A Short Gardens, WC2H 9AT
Nearest Station: Covent Garden Map: C5
North African restaurant full of character and charm, one that has won itself a fine reputation for its atmosphere and cooking. *Must show membership card upon arrival.
50% OFF FOOD | 8 | FRI | SAT — Moroccan

STRADA
020 3077 1127
13-15 Tavistock Street, WC2E 7PS
Nearest Station: Covent Garden Map: C5
Offering fresh, bold dishes inspired by flavours of Italian city life - Strada serves a selection of indulgent tastes, to those seeking a blissful escape to laidback Italian life. *Excludes Pizzettas.
25% OFF TOTAL | 6 | FRI ✓ | SAT × — Italian

STRADA
020 7405 6293
6 Great Queen Street, WC2B 5DH
Nearest Station: Holborn Map: C5
Offering fresh, bold dishes inspired by flavours of Italian city life - Strada serves a selection of indulgent tastes, to those seeking a blissful escape to laidback Italian life. *Excludes Pizzettas.
25% OFF TOTAL | 6 | FRI ✓ | SAT × — Italian

STRAND CARVERY
☎020 7497 4158
372 Strand, WC2R 0JJ
Nearest Station: Covent Garden Map: C5
In the heart of London's theatre land, this carvery restaurant serves big and bold, succulent roast dinners; the Shakespearean injunction for 'great meals of beef and iron and steel' chimes beautifully.
25% OFF TOTAL | 10 | FRI ✓ | SAT ✓ | * — British

TAKARI COVENT GARDEN
☎020 7836 1628
22 Drury Lane, WC2B 5RH
Nearest Station: Covent Garden Map: C5
Using traditional Indian cooking methods, this eatery boasts affable surroundings and a team of staff devoted to providing impeccable service. The attention to culinary detail is unmistakable.
50% OFF TOTAL | 10 | FRI ✓ | SAT ✓ — Indian

TANDOORI NIGHTS
☎020 7831 2558
35 Great Queen Street, WC2B 5AA
Nearest Station: Holborn Map: C5
This venue offer diners a splendid range of curries and Tandoori specialities prepared by master chefs . A rendezvous for all who enjoy the exotic, spicy and healthy dishes of the Indian subcontinent.
25% OFF TOTAL | 10 | FRI ✓ | SAT ✓ — Indian

TANDOORI RAJ
☎020 7405 8072
65 Red Lion Street, WC1R 4NA
Nearest Station: Holborn Map: C5
Warm and well-thought-out Indian restaurant in Holborn, where dishes are classic, exceptionally well flavoured and concocted with care; the place is atmospheric, well-located and very accommodating.
2FOR1 MAIN COURSE | FRI ✓ | SAT ✓ | * — Indian

TEA ROOM AT THE ARTS
☎020 7836 9533
6-7 Great Newport Street, WC2H 7JB
Nearest Station: Covent Garden Map: C5
Classic English tea, divine cakes and delicious sandwiches make this an ideal place to spend the afternoon with friends and loved ones. Lounge on the soft cushioned sofas for an hour of bliss.
50% OFF FOOD | FRI ✓ | SAT ✓ — British

WALKABOUT
☎020 7395 3690
Temple Station, WC2R 2PH
Nearest Station: Temple Map: C5
Walkabout is famous for its characteristically Australian atmosphere and well-rounded menu. From live sport with a juicy burger to some Aussie kangaroo skewers, you'll find it hard to tear yourself away.
25% OFF TOTAL | 10 | FRI ✓ | SAT ✓ — International

BELLA ITALIA
020 7494 0288

61-63 Shaftsbury Avenue, W1D 6LG

Nearest Station: Charing Cross Map: D5

Accessible Italian cuisine on the British high street – indulge in authentic sharing platters, hand stretched pizzas and hearty pasta dishes, served with a healthy dose of gregarious Italian hospitality.

25% OFF TOTAL | 6 | FRI × | SAT × | SUN | ▲ — Italian

BELLA ITALIA
020 7839 3705

65 The Strand, WC2N 5LR

Nearest Station: Charing Cross Map: D5

Accessible Italian cuisine on the British high street – indulge in authentic sharing platters, hand stretched pizzas and hearty pasta dishes, served with a healthy dose of gregarious Italian hospitality.

25% OFF TOTAL | 6 | FRI × | SAT × | SUN | ▲ — Italian

BOYD'S BRASSERIE
☎ 020 7808 3344

The Northumberland, WC2N 5BY

Nearest Station: Charing Cross Map: D5

Ideally located in the business centre of London, this excellent brasserie offers something for everyone. Boyd's continues to deliver a quality breakfast, lunch and dinner.

2FOR1 3 COURSES | FRI ✓ | SAT ✓ | ▲ — British

CAFÉ ROUGE
020 7925 2142

9-11 Villiers Street, WC2N 6NA

Nearest Station: Charing Cross Map: D5

French sophistication on the British high street – enjoy seasonally changing French dishes and a continental wine selection, served in a relaxed environment with an undeniable flair of Parisian chic.

25% OFF TOTAL | 6 | FRI ✓ | SAT ✓ | ✱ | ▲ — French

CHILLI CHUTNEY
☎ 020 8633 1779

47 York Road, SE1 7NJ

Nearest Station: Waterloo Map: D5

Encapsulating a century-long tradition of Mughlai cooking, Chilli Chutney boasts a fine menu of mouth-watering dishes based on the extensive use of barbecuing techniques provided by tandoor.

2FOR1 3 COURSES | FRI ✓ | SAT ✓ — Indian

GIBSON'S AT THE YACHT LONDON
020 7836 1566

Temple Pier, WC2R 2PN

Nearest Station: Temple Map: D5

With some of the most glorious views in London spanning the River Thames, the Yacht offers a modern World class European menu and exceptional service. *Book online up to 10 days in advance.

50% OFF FOOD | 2 | FRI × | SAT × | ▲ — European

PREZZO
020 7930 4288

31-32 Northumberland Avenue, WC2N 5BW

Nearest Station: Charing Cross Map: D5

With a character all of its own, Prezzo oozes contemporary style and enduring charm. Signature pastas, stone-baked pizzas and classic Italian dishes promise a perfect dining choice for the whole family.

2FOR1 MAIN COURSE | FRI × | SAT × | ▲ — Italian

SMOLLENSKY'S ON THE STRAND
☎ 020 7497 2101

105 The Strand, WC2R 0AA

Nearest Station: Temple Map: D5

One of the great names in grill restaurants and has been at the forefront of the London bar and restaurant scene for over 20 years. Simply fantastic food, superb service and great value for money.

50% OFF FOOD | 4 | FRI ✱ | SAT ✱ | ▲ — International

ZEN CHINA
☎ 020 7261 1196

Riverside Building, Queens Walk, SE1 7PB

Nearest Station: Waterloo Map: D5

Zen China is a conveniently located restaurant on Southbank. Try the authentic Beijing roasted duck for a real Chinese feast. *A la carte menu only. Must book at least 2 hours in advance.

50% OFF FOOD | 6 | FRI ▯ | SAT ▯ — Chinese

ALBANNACH
☎ 020 7930 0066

66 Trafalgar Square, WC2N 5DS

Nearest Station: Charing Cross Map: D4

Seasonal and British, the menu is accompanied by a prestigious selection of Scotch whiskies. Perfect for all events, the venue hosts private rooms, a vaulted cocktail bar and an intimate restaurant.

50% OFF FOOD | 6 | FRI ✓ | SAT ✱ | ▲ — British

BELLA ITALIA
020 7495 1110

66-66 Duke Street, W1K 6JD

Nearest Station: Leicester Square Map: D4

Accessible Italian cuisine on the British high street – indulge in authentic sharing platters, hand stretched pizzas and hearty pasta dishes, served with a healthy dose of gregarious Italian hospitality.

25% OFF TOTAL | 6 | FRI × | SAT × | SUN | ▲ — Italian

BELOWZERO RESTAURANT & LOUNGE
☎ 020 7478 8910

31-33 Heddon Street, W1B 4BN

Nearest Station: Piccadilly Circus Map: D4

A venue that embodies its title. Boasting a unique bar made out of ice, here you are guaranteed a great time, so good you'll be wishing you could freeze the moment. Snacks and meals are available.

25% OFF TOTAL | 8 | FRI × | SAT × | ✱ | ▲ — European

BISTRO 1 @ FRITH STREET SOHO
☎ 020 7734 6204

27 Frith Street, W1D 5LE

Nearest Station: Leicester Square Map: D4

For a lunch date or evening out in this trendy part of the city, Bistro 1 serves exceptionally tasty Mediterranean cuisine to a vibrant crowd. Happily feeds hungry bellies at good prices.

25% OFF TOTAL | 2 | FRI × | SAT × | ▲ — Mediterranean

BLUE LAGOON THAI @ HAYMARKET
☎ 020 7930 7800

23 Haymarket, SW1Y 4DG

Nearest Station: Piccadilly Circus Map: D4

Blue Lagoon offers exquisite Thai cuisine at superb prices, drawing on the exotic flavours of the increasingly popular south east Asian country of Thailand. Divine coconut and cream sauces.

50% OFF FOOD | 10 | FRI ✓ | SAT ✓ — Thai

CAFÉ ROUGE
020 7930 9135

17-18 Irving Street, WC2H 7AT

Nearest Station: Leicester Square Map: D4

French sophistication on the British high street – enjoy seasonally changing French dishes and a continental wine selection, served in a relaxed environment with an undeniable flair of Parisian chic.

25% OFF TOTAL | 6 | FRI ✓ | SAT ✓ | ✱ | ▲ — French

CHOWKI
☎ 020 7439 1330

2-3 Denman Street, W1D 7HA

Nearest Station: Piccadilly Circus Map: D4

No slap-up curry house, featuring a menu that changes regularly and features all sorts of eclectic dishes from across the subcontinent. The restaurant has carved itself a niche and has a cult following.

2FOR1 MAIN COURSE | FRI ✱ | SAT ✱ — Indian

FISHWORKS
☎ 020 7734 5813

7-9 Swallow Street, W1B 4DE

Nearest Station: Piccadilly Circus Map: D4

A sleek seafood restaurant with its own fish counter where you can buy fresh from a full cohort; vivid, classic dishes populate the menu and the restaurant is serenely ensconced just away from Piccadilly.

25% OFF TOTAL | 6 | FRI ✱ | SAT ✱ | SUN | ▲ — Seafood

FRANCO'S RISTORANTE PIZZERIA
☎ 020 7734 9415

30 Rupert Street, W1D 6DL

Nearest Station: Piccadilly Circus Map: D4

With chianti bottles lining the ceiling and jars of olives running along the walls, Franco's is a superb place to fulfil those cravings for a real Italian dining experience. Delicious, authentic cuisine.

2FOR1 3 COURSES | FRI ✓ | SAT ✓ — Italian

HENRY'S CAFÉ BAR
☎ 020 7491 2544

80 Piccadilly, W1J 8HX

Nearest Station: Green Park Map: D4

An oasis for every type of person with a delicious, well-prepared menu; ideal for lunch, dinner or a light snack. Henry's also boasts an extensive wine and champagne list and array of cocktails to die for.

25% OFF TOTAL | 10 | FRI ✓ | SAT ✓ | ▲ — European

HOUSE LOUNGE @ THISTLE
☎ 0871 376 9031

Thistle Piccadilly, Coventry Street, W1D 6BZ

Nearest Station: Piccadilly Circus Map: D4

With its authentic Victorian exterior, Thistle Piccadilly is a hotel oozing beauty and class. The restaurant here is the perfect place to feed your appetite before exploring the city delights.

50% OFF FOOD | 6 | FRI ✓ | SAT ✓ — International

LA LOCANDA
☎020 7734 6689

35 Heddon Street, W1B 4BR
Nearest Station: Piccadilly Circus Map: D4

One of the area's best kept secrets. Veal escalope with mozzarella and Parma ham, baked mushrooms with spinach and parmesan and tagliatelle are just some of the restaurant's specialities.

25% OFF TOTAL | 4 | FRI | SAT — Italian

LIBRARY LOUNGE @ HILTON
☎020 7221 2217

Hilton Hyde Park, 129 Bayswater Road, W2 4RJ
Nearest Station: Queensway Map: D4

Charming place to drink before or after an evening dinner, or alternatively to grab a light snack throughout the day. Traditional, warm and inviting, this is a fantastic attribute of the Hilton Hyde Park.

50% OFF FOOD | 10 | FRI ✓ | SAT × — International

L'ULIVO
☎020 7930 3279

14-15 Irving Street, WC2H 7AU
Nearest Station: Leicester Square Map: D4

A fantastically located Italian eatery, perfect for rounding off a day sightseeing or for a pre-theatre meal. Serves deliciously hearty cuisine that has been given the ultimate authentic edge.

2FOR1 3 COURSES | FRI × | SAT × — Italian

MINT LEAF RESTAURANT
☎020 7930 9020

Suffolk Place, SW1Y 4HX
Nearest Station: Piccadilly Circus Map: D4

An outstanding menu tenderly prepared by the kitchen's talented Head Chef at this traditional Indian restaurant. The stylish, sophisticated interior is only one of the highlights. 1 AA Rosette.

25% OFF TOTAL | 8 | FRI × | SAT × | ▲ — Indian

NIGHTINGALES RESTAURANT & BAR
☎0871 423 4876

3 Berkeley Street, W1J 8NE
Nearest Station: Green Park Map: D4

A centrally located hotel in the heart of the capital city, with great public transport links extremely nearby. Nightingales Restaurant is a great attribute, serving juicy steaks in an elegant interior.

25% OFF TOTAL | 6 | FRI ✓ | SAT ✓ — European

PLANET HOLLYWOOD
☎020 7287 1000

57-60 Haymarket, SW1Y 4QX
Nearest Station: Piccadilly Circus Map: D4

Experience the glamour of Hollywood with a large cocktail bar and extravagantly themed rooms filled with mega-star memorabilia. Freshly prepared, quality American food delivering a taste of the States.

25% OFF TOTAL | 8 | FRI ✓ | SAT × | ▲ — American

PREZZO
020 7839 1129

Kinghouse, 8 Haymarket, SW1Y 4BP
Nearest Station: Piccadilly Circus Map: D4

With a character all of its own, Prezzo oozes contemporary style and enduring charm. Signature pastas, stone-baked pizzas and classic Italian dishes promise a perfect dining choice for the whole family.

2FOR1 MAIN COURSE | FRI × | SAT × | ▲ — Italian

PREZZO
☎020 7287 8429

36-38 Glasshouse Street, W1B 5DL
Nearest Station: Piccadilly Circus Map: D4

With a character all of its own, oozes contemporary style and enduring charm. Signature pastas, stone-baked pizzas and classic Italian dishes promise a perfect dining choice for the whole family.

2FOR1 MAIN COURSE | FRI × | SAT × | ▲ — Italian

THE RESTAURANT
☎020 7499 3464

The Athenaeum Hotel, 116 Piccadilly, W1J 7BJ
Nearest Station: Piccadilly Circus Map: D4

This debonair venue hosts a menu consisting of innovative twists on the classic notions of British cuisine. Braised venison and pan-fried sole tempt the palettes of guests in the beautiful surroundings.

50% OFF FOOD | 6 | FRI × | SAT × | ▲ — Modern British

SO RESTAURANT
☎020 7292 0767

3-4 Warwick Street, W1B 5LS
Nearest Station: Piccadilly Circus Map: D4

Sophisticated Japanese cuisine infused with unique European flavours. Select dishes are prepared on a customised grill and cooked over volcanic rocks imported from Mt. Fuji. Awarded 2 AA Rosettes.

25% OFF TOTAL | 4 | FRI × | SAT × | SUN | ✱ | ▲ — Japanese

THE SPORTS CAFE
020 3137 2636

80 Haymarket, SW1Y 4TE
Nearest Station: Piccadilly Circus Map: D4

From succulent steaks to the signature chicken wings, Sports Café offers something for everyone. Come and relax in front of the 65 screens to watch the latest sport whilst enjoying your favourite American meal.

50% OFF FOOD | FRI ✓ | SAT × | SUN | ▲ — American

SQUARES RESTAURANT
☎0871 376 9037

Thistle London Royal, Whitcomb Street, WC2H 7HG
Nearest Station: Piccadilly Circus Map: D4

Upmarket restaurant located within the Royal Trafalgar Hotel. Modern takes on classic British and European dishes guarantee Squares Restaurant an admirable reputation for quality cuisine.

50% OFF FOOD | FRI × | SAT × — English and Continental

STRADA
020 7930 8535

Panton House, 39 Panton Street, SW1Y 4EA
Nearest Station: Piccadilly Circus Map: D4

Offering fresh, bold dishes inspired by flavours of Italian city life - Strada serves a selection of indulgent tastes, to those seeking a blissful escape to laidback Italian life. *Excludes Pizzettas.

25% OFF TOTAL | 6 | FRI ✓ | SAT × | ▲ — Italian

TERRACE RESTAURANT
☎020 7851 3085

Le Meridien, 21 Piccadilly, W1J 0BH
Nearest Station: Green Park Map: D4

A wonderful place to take a break from the hustle and bustle of the city without removing yourself from it. The soothing, relaxed ambience provides a great contrast to the activity of London Piccadilly.

50% OFF FOOD | FRI ✱ | SAT ✱ | ▲ — International

TIGER GREEN BRASSERIE
☎020 7965 1841

Hilton London Green Park, W1J 7BN
Nearest Station: Green Park Map: D4

This chic Georgian townhouse exudes an authentic cosmopolitan feel. Dine on Hilton classics such as Caesar salad and an array of specialty grills to sink your teeth into. Be sure to leave room for dessert.

50% OFF FOOD | FRI ✓ | SAT ✓ — International

WHEELERS OF ST. JAMES'S
☎020 7408 1440

72-73 St James Street, SW1A 1PH
Nearest Station: Green Park Map: D4

A revival of the world's oldest and finest fish restaurant in a distinguished location. With its traditional exterior and its glamorous interior, this is an extremely popular destination. 2 AA Rosettes.

25% OFF TOTAL | 10 | FRI | SAT ✱ | ▲ — Seafood

WOODLANDS RESTAURANT
☎020 7839 7258

37 Panton Street, SW1Y 4EA
Nearest Station: Piccadilly Circus Map: D4

South Indian vegetarian cuisine at its very best. The award-winning kitchen accommodates chefs with at least 15 years of experience from other Woodlands restaurants.

25% OFF TOTAL | 8 | FRI | SAT — South Indian Vegetarian

AVISTA
☎020 7596 3399

39 Grosvenor Square, W1K 2HP
Nearest Station: Bond Street Map: D3

A fine Italian restaurant in Mayfair whose menu combines a variety of both rustic and contemporary dishes. Understated and stylish in mood, the food is of rare quality, the wine list superb. 2 AA Rosettes.

25% OFF TOTAL | 10 | FRI ✓ | SAT ✓ | SUN — Italian/ Mediterranean

BENARES
☎020 7629 8886

12A Berkeley Square, W1J 6BS
Nearest Station: Green Park Map: D3

Atul Kochhar's Michelin-starred and 4 AA Rosettes restaurant serving phenomenal Indian cuisine with subtle spices and authentic flavours. Admire the menu which is based on ingredients from all over India.

25% OFF TOTAL | 4 | FRI ✱ | SAT ✱ | ▲ — Indian British

THE CHESTERFIELD MAYFAIR
☎020 7514 5706

35 Charles Street, W1J 5EB
Nearest Station: Green Park Map: D3

An integral part of the Chesterfield Hotel, the luxurious Butlers Restaurant offers a carefully selected array of dishes that provide satisfaction for all palates and appetites. Awarded 2 AA Rosettes.

25% OFF TOTAL | 4 | FRI ✓ | SAT ✓ — British

To understand what the restaurant icons mean, please see the inside back cover.

CITRUS
020 7499 6321

The Park Lane Hotel, 112 Piccadilly, W1J 7BX
Nearest Station: Green Park Map: D3

Distinctively offbeat Piccadilly restaurant in the Park Lane Hotel. Serves high-quality Italian cuisine, ranging from beef carpaccio with pecorino to pork belly brasato with fragula.

50% OFF FOOD | 8 | FRI ✱ | SAT ✱ — Italian

GREIG'S GRILL & RESTAURANT
020 7629 5613

26-28 Bruton Place, W1J 6NG
Nearest Station: Bond Street Map: D3

Established in the 1950s by Alistair Greig, serving some of the best steaks in London. Half a century later the steaks are still cooked on a coal grill; the restaurant also offers great British classics.

50% OFF FOOD | 6 | FRI ✓ | SAT ✓ | ▲ — British

MADISONS RESTAURANT
020 7499 7000

The Washington Mayfair Hotel, 5 Curzon Street, W1J 5HE
Nearest Station: Green Park Map: D3

Madisons Restaurant is one of the most calm, airy and comfortable restaurants in Mayfair. The eclectic international menu focuses on seasonal produce which is served by a friendly professional team.

50% OFF FOOD | 6 | FRI (phone) | SAT (phone) | ▲ — International

PREZZO
020 7499 4690

17 Hertford Street, W1J 7RS
Nearest Station: Hyde Park Corner Map: D3

With a character all of its own, Prezzo oozes contemporary style and enduring charm. Signature pastas, stone-baked pizzas and classic Italian dishes promise a perfect dining choice for the whole family.

2FOR1 MAIN COURSE | FRI × | SAT × | ▲ — Italian

SOFRA MAYFAIR
020 7493 3320

18 Shepherd Street, W1J 7JG
Nearest Station: Green Park Map: D3

Sofra promises high-quality recipes with an accent on healthy options, choice and uncompromising tastes. Order a feast of mezzes or savour a succulent tagine and experience Turkish dining, redefined.

2FOR1 MAIN COURSE | FRI ✓ | SAT ✓ | ▲ — Turkish

108 MARYLEBONE LANE
020 7969 3900

108 Marylebone Lane, W1U 2QE
Nearest Station: Bond Street Map: C3

A fine addition to Marylebone's culinary scene. Their food philosophy is simple, using only the best ingredients to create simple, classic dishes, sourcing from local supplier when possible.

50% OFF FOOD | 4 | FRI × | SAT × | ▲ — Modern British

140 PARK LANE RESTAURANT & BAR
020 7647 5664

140 Park Lane, W1K 7AA
Nearest Station: Marble Arch Map: C3

Something of the feel of a relaxed French restaurant; a menu populated by classic dishes, largely British but with distinct international influences. Worthy of note is the excellent seafood. 2 AA Rosettes.

50% OFF FOOD | 8 | FRI ✓ | SAT ✓ | ▲ — British

BRASSERIE AT THE CUMBERLAND HOTEL
020 7616 5930

Great Cumberland Place, W1H 7DL
Nearest Station: Marble Arch Map: C3

Defined by its relaxed, informal setting, The Brasserie serves a menu of European classics with a distinctly British twist. Awarded 1 AA Rosette.

25% OFF TOTAL | 10 | FRI ✓ | SAT ✱ | SUN | ▲ — British

CAFÉ ROUGE
020 7487 4847

46-48 James St, W1U 1HA
Nearest Station: Bond Street Map: C3

French sophistication on the British high street – enjoy seasonally changing French dishes and a continental wine selection, served in a relaxed environment with an undeniable flair of Parisian chic.

25% OFF TOTAL | 6 | FRI ✓ | SAT ✓ | ✱ — French

CARMINA CAFÉ
020 7224 3771

88 Wigmore Street, W1U 3RB
Nearest Station: Bond Street Map: C3

Lovely neighbourhood street café with a well-spaced, well-paced atmosphere geared towards settling in and watching the world bustle by. Great selection of sandwiches, light dishes, pizzas and the like.

50% OFF FOOD | 6 | FRI ✓ | SAT ✓ — Brasserie

COLONY BAR AND GRILL
020 7935 3353

8 Paddington Street, W1U 5QH
Nearest Station: Baker Street Map: C3

Created by acclaimed, twice Michelin-starred chef Atul Kochhar and celebrated restaurateur Carlo Spetale, this fine restaurant does a spectrum of Asian flavours combined with French gastronomic techniques.

25% OFF TOTAL | 10 | FRI ✓ | SAT ✓ | SUN — Indian British

THE CRESCENT AT MONTCALM HOTEL
020 7958 3220

34-40 Great Cumberland Place, W1H 7TW
Nearest Station: Marble Arch Map: C3

Spoilt for choice, diners can expect to be dazzled by the array of International cuisine on offer at this venue. From Middle Eastern meze platters to simmering curries, there is something for everyone.

25% OFF TOTAL | 4 | FRI ✓ | SAT ✓ | SUN | ▲ — International

FIRE AND SPICE
020 7487 0678

4 Bryanston Street, W1H 7BY
Nearest Station: Marble Arch Map: C3

Nestled away near Marble Arch, this restaurant serves full-bodied grill food with delicious, piquant marinades in a cool, cosy setting.

2FOR1 MAIN COURSE | FRI ✓ | SAT ✓ — International

FISHWORKS
020 7935 9796

89 Marylebone High Street, W1U 4QW
Nearest Station: Baker Street Map: C3

A sleek seafood restaurant with its own fish counter where you can buy fresh from a full cohort; vivid, classic dishes populate the menu and the restaurant is serenely ensconced just off Oxford Street.

25% OFF TOTAL | 6 | FRI ✱ | SAT ✱ | SUN | ▲ — Seafood

GAYLORD RESTAURANT
020 7580 3615

79-81 Mortimer Street, W1W 7SJ
Nearest Station: Oxford Circus Map: C3

With a particular specialisation in tandoori recipes, this North Indian restaurant covers the gamut of classic dishes, adding distinctive flavours into the mix.

2FOR1 MAIN COURSE | FRI (phone) | SAT (phone) | ▲ — Indian

THE GRILL AT THE MONTCALM
020 7958 3216

34-40 Great Cumberland Place, W1H 7TW
Nearest Station: Marble Arch Map: C3

No matter the occasion, this venue superbly caters to every need. Preparing the most exclusive of British cuisine, all of the dishes are presented with a contemporary twist and a sophisticated wine list.

25% OFF TOTAL | 10 | FRI ✓ | SAT ✓ — Modern British

LA TASCA
020 7486 3314

30-34 James Street, W1U 1ER
Nearest Station: Bond Street Map: C3

Quintessentially Spanish, La Tasca's fresh and exciting menu offers something for everyone. Their tapas dishes are sincerely authentic, while their paellas always deliver on flavour.

25% OFF TOTAL | 8 | FRI ✓ | SAT × | ▲ — Spanish

THE MARMOR GRILL @ THISTLE
0871 376 9027

Thistle Marble Arch, Bryanston Street, W1H 7EH
Nearest Station: Marble Arch Map: C3

This 4-star hotel plays host to a fabulous 1930s themed eatery. The more adventurous can feast on potted duck with grape chutney, whilst ravenous stomachs can be filled with a hearty steak and kidney pie.

50% OFF FOOD | 4 | FRI (phone) | SAT (phone) — British

ORIGINAL TAGINES
020 7935 1545

7a Dorset Street, W1U 6QN
Nearest Station: Baker Street Map: C3

A restaurant boasting all the qualities of a good, friendly local. Sample the culinary delights of Morocco in a contemporary venue that delivers a truly authentic, well-executed menu.

25% OFF TOTAL | 4 | FRI ✓ | SAT ✓ — Moroccan

PREZZO
020 7723 7172

7-9 Great Cumberland Street, W1H 7LU
Nearest Station: Marble Arch Map: C3

With a character all of its own, Prezzo oozes contemporary style and enduring charm. Signature pastas, stone-baked pizzas and classic Italian dishes promise a perfect dining choice for the whole family.

2FOR1 MAIN COURSE | FRI × | SAT × | ▲ — Italian

PREZZO
020 7493 4990

15 North Audley Street, W1K 6WZ
Nearest Station: Bond Street Map: C3

With a character all of its own, Prezzo oozes contemporary style and enduring charm. Signature pastas, stone-baked pizzas and classic Italian dishes promise a perfect dining choice for the whole family.

2FOR1 MAIN COURSE | FRI × | SAT × | ♟ — Italian

RASA W1
☎020 7629 1346

6 Dering Street, W1S 1AD
Nearest Station: Bond Street Map: C3

Inspired by the authentic home cooking of beautiful, spice-rich Kerala, this restaurant's passion is food prepared always with devotion, love, and the finest ingredients. Experience the essence of India.

2FOR1 MAIN COURSE | FRI ✱ | SAT ✱ | SUN | ♟ — Indian

THE RUNNING HORSE
☎020 7493 1275

50 Davies Street, W1K 5JE
Nearest Station: Bond Street Map: C3

Trusty and timeless, The Running Horse menu offers dishes like Cumberland sausage ring with mash and grain mustard or grilled spring lamb chop with baby carrots.

25% OFF TOTAL | ♟ 6 | FRI × | SAT ✓ | SUN | ♟ — British

SEYMOUR RESTAURANT
☎020 7935 2010

15 Seymour Street, W1H 7JW
Nearest Station: Marble Arch Map: C3

Elegant dining room in the heart of London. A welcome retreat, dining room complete with open fireplaces, antique art and crisply dressed tables. Menu ranges from fisherman's pie to sausage pappardelle.

2FOR1 3 COURSES | FRI ✓ | SAT ✓ | ✱ — International

SHERLOCK'S GRILL
☎020 7958 5103

108 Baker Street, W1U 6LJ
Nearest Station: Baker Street Map: C3

Cool, relaxed styling that befits the restaurant's namesake and its Baker Street location. Dining of the highest order, featuring subtle starters and refined mains on a ranging menu. 1 AA Rosette.

50% OFF FOOD | ♟ 4 | FRI ✓ | SAT ✓ | ♟ — Modern European

STRADA
020 7935 1004

31 Marylebone High Street, W1U 4PP
Nearest Station: Baker Street Map: C3

Offering fresh, bold dishes inspired by flavours of Italian city life - Strada serves a selection of indulgent tastes, to those seeking a blissful escape to laidback Italian life. *Excludes Pizzettas.

25% OFF TOTAL | ♟ 6 | FRI ✓ | SAT × | ♟ — Italian

WOODLANDS
☎020 7486 3862

77 Marylebone Lane, W1U 2PS
Nearest Station: Bond Street Map: C3

South Indian vegetarian cuisine at its very best. The award-winning kitchen accommodates chefs with at least 15 years of experience from other Woodlands restaurants.

25% OFF TOTAL | ♟ 10 | FRI ✓ | SAT ✓ — South Indian Vegetarian

ZAYNA
☎020 7723 2229

25 New Quebec Street, W1H 7SF
Nearest Station: Marble Arch Map: C3

A highly regarded restaurant serving North Indian and Pakistani food as its speciality, demonstrating great attention to detail with vibrant and rich dishes. *Min 2 courses must be ordered.

2FOR1 2 COURSES | FRI ✱ | SAT ✱ | ♟ — Indian

BASE BRASSERIE
☎020 7486 7000

195 Baker Street, NW1 6UY
Nearest Station: Baker Street Map: B3

Base Brasserie has been established for 7 years and serves delicious Mediterranean cuisine. Food is sourced from local markets, and the specials board changes daily to offer the freshest dishes.

25% OFF TOTAL | ♟ 6 | FRI ✱ | SAT ✱ — Mediterranean

CINNAMON SPICE
☎020 7935 0212

12-14 Glentworth Street, NW1 5PG
Nearest Station: Baker Street Map: B3

A delicate blend of contrasting flavours makes the most exquisite tasting dishes in this wonderful Indian restaurant. Curry fans will fall head over heels for the lamb moslini or the cinnamon chicken.

2FOR1 3 COURSES | FRI ✱ | SAT ✓ | ♟ — Indian

L'ULIVO
☎020 7935 0194

194 Baker Street, NW1 5RT
Nearest Station: Baker Street Map: B3

Clients can choose from an abundance of classical Italian dishes and watch as they are prepared in the great open kitchen. Contemporary and ideally situated, L'Ulivo caters for all. Live entertainment.

2FOR1 3 COURSES | FRI × | SAT × — Italian

QUEEN'S HEAD & ARTICHOKE
☎020 7916 6206

30-32 Albany Street, NW1 4EA
Nearest Station: Great Portland Street Map: B3

One of London's best gastro pubs, serving delightful modern English food as well as a delicious tapas menu. Excellent service and an extensive beverages selection.

2FOR1 MAIN COURSE | FRI ✱ | SAT ✓ | SUN | ♟ — Modern European

STRADA
020 7935 7071

100 Baker Street, W1U 6TW
Nearest Station: Baker Street Map: B3

Offering fresh, bold dishes inspired by flavours of Italian city life - Strada serves a selection of indulgent tastes, to those seeking a blissful escape to laidback Italian life. *Excludes Pizzettas.

25% OFF TOTAL | ♟ 6 | FRI ✓ | SAT × | ♟ — Italian

ANWAR RESTAURANT
☎020 7387 6664

64 Grafton Way, W1T 5DP
Nearest Station: Warren Street Map: B4

Anwar's is a pleasurable dining experience for all. The menu is well suited to a variety of palettes with a particular focus on vegetarian and vegan cuisine. Delicious authentic Indian served with a smile.

2FOR1 MAIN COURSE | FRI ✓ | SAT ✓ | SUN | ✱ | ♟ — Indian

ARCHIPELAGO
☎020 7383 3346

110 Whifield Street, W1T 5ED
Nearest Station: Warren Street Map: B4

A sensual dining experience as an indulgence of tantalising global dishes awaits you, featuring hallmark exotic dishes such as crocodile and kangaroo. World cuisine awarded 2 AA Rosettes.

50% OFF FOOD | ♟ 2 | FRI ✱ | SAT ✱ | SUN | ♟ — European

BRASSERIE 43 @ THISTLE
☎0871 376 9017

Thistle Euston, Cardington Street, NW1 2LP
Nearest Station: Euston Map: B4

Brasserie 43 restaurant offers a choice of British and European dishes in comfortable and contemporary surroundings. The hotel restaurant also keeps an extensive cellar of classic and New World wines.

25% OFF TOTAL | FRI ✓ | SAT ✓ — International

CAFÉ ROUGE
020 7388 9100

Euston Station, NW1 2RT
Nearest Station: Euston Square Map: B4

French sophistication on the British high street – enjoy seasonally changing French dishes and a continental wine selection, served in a relaxed environment with an undeniable flair of Parisian chic.

25% OFF TOTAL | ♟ 6 | FRI ✓ | SAT ✓ | ✱ | ♟ — French

HANDMADE SUSHI
☎020 7383 0602

339 Euston Road, NW1 3AD
Nearest Station: Warren Street Map: B4

Providing an authentic Japanese eating experience, Handmade Sushi is perfect for those seeking something a little different. *Offer applicable to the Sushi Bar menu only. Not available on take-away.

50% OFF FOOD | FRI ✓ | SAT ✓ — Japanese

JUNCTION RESTAURANT @ HOLIDAY INN
☎020 7874 9011

Carburton Street, W1W 5EE
Nearest Station: Great Portland Street Map: B4

The Junction is a stylish establishment built with both the individual traveller and families in mind. With a menu comprised of many old favourites and great service, this London eatery is set to impress.

50% OFF FOOD | ♟ 6 | FRI ✓ | SAT ✓ | SUN | ✱ | ♟ — European

LAL QILA INDIAN RESTAURANT
☎020 7388 3877

117 Tottenham Court Road, W1T 5AL
Nearest Station: Warren Street Map: B4

Long-established, Lal Qila oozes sophistication as it transports guests on a magical journey through the regions of India with its expertly prepared array of dishes. The cuisine is vibrant and fresh.

50% OFF FOOD | ♟ 8 | FRI ✓ | SAT ✓ — Indian

Gourmet Society discount applies to the à la carte menu only, unless stated otherwise.

MASSALA HUT
☎020 7387 6699
161-163 Drummond Street, NW1 2PB
Nearest Station: Euston Square Map: B4
Famed by locals for its authentic curries, Massala Hut delivers a menu of traditional classics and chef's specials, all freshly prepared and cooked as truly intended.
50% OFF FOOD | 10 | FRI ✓ | SAT ✓ | ✱ — Indian

MUSHU
☎020 7388 3629
53 Warren Street, W1T 5NL
Nearest Station: Warren Street Map: B4
Relaxed bar-restaurant serving a diverse menu of oriental tapas; great-tasting, simple, honest food, ranging from fresh sushi and tempura to handmade dumplings and slow-cooked Chinese meatballs.
25% OFF TOTAL | 4 | FRI ✓ | SAT ✓ | ✱ — Japanese

NUMBER TWELVE RESTAURANT & BAR
☎020 7693 5423
12 Upper Woburn Place, WC1H 0HX
Nearest Station: Euston Map: B4
Smart Bloomsbury restaurant with more than half an eye on the area's cultural history. Subtle and understated in style, the menu features refined, well-spaced flavours, from minestrone to roasted figs.
2FOR1 3 COURSES | 4 | FRI ✓ | SAT ✓ — European

PREZZO
020 7387 5587
161 Euston Road, NW1 2BD
Nearest Station: Euston Map: B4
With a character all of its own, Prezzo oozes contemporary style and enduring charm. Signature pastas, stone-baked pizzas and classic Italian dishes promise a perfect dining choice for the whole family.
2FOR1 MAIN COURSE | FRI × | SAT × | ▲ — Italian

RAGAM
☎020 7636 9098
57 Cleveland Street, W1T 4JN
Nearest Station: Goodge Street Map: B4
Renowned reputation for producing delectable South Indian cuisine whilst demonstrating variety on their cheerful menu. A light, healthy, and delicious dining experience.
2FOR1 MAIN COURSE | FRI ✱ | SAT ✱ | ▲ — Indian

THE UNION BAR & GRILL
☎020 7387 0361
11 Triton Street, NW1 5YA
Nearest Station: Great Portland Street Map: B4
Situated in Regents Place, The Union Bar and Grill is known for its mix of modern Mediterranean food, providing a relaxed eating environment for business and leisure alike.
2FOR1 3 COURSES | FRI × | SAT × | ✱ — British

THE BAR @ MERCURE
☎020 7833 3691
Mercure Bloomsbury, 130-134 Southampton Row, WC1B 5AF
Nearest Station: Russell Square Map: B5
Sharp lines and strong colours make this a cool, contemporary and sophisticated hotel-bar. Situated in the Mercure Hotel, Bloomsbury, here you'll find a great array of pre or post-dinner drinks.
50% OFF FOOD | 4 | FRI ✓ | SAT ✓ — British

THE BLOOMSBURY ROOM
☎020 7833 1881
61-66 Russell Square, WC1B 5JS
Nearest Station: Russell Square Map: B5
A lively brasserie that is always filled with a fun crowd. Colourful and relaxed in style, this dining room is the perfect place to celebrate your luck at the roulette table.
50% OFF FOOD | 4 | FRI ✓ | SAT ✓ | ▲ — International

THE BRASSERIE @ MERCURE
☎020 7833 3691
Mercure Bloomsbury, 130-134 Southampton Row, WC1B 5AF
Nearest Station: Russell Square Map: B5
Stylish hotel-restaurant serving a well-executed menu of tasty brasserie classics and international cuisine. Offsetting the modern dining room, a picturesque terrace makes for tranquil al fresco dining.
25% OFF TOTAL | 10 | FRI ✓ | SAT ✓ — International

CHUTNEY RAJ
☎020 7831 1149
137 Grays Inn Road, WC1X 8TU
Nearest Station: Chancery Lane Map: B5
Bangladeshi fish dishes appear strongly on the menu at this terrific central London restaurant. With specific ingredients being flown in fresh from the East, vivid tastiness is guaranteed in every dish.
2FOR1 MAIN COURSE | FRI ✓ | SAT ✓ | ▲ — Indian

HASON RAJA RESTAURANT
☎020 7242 3377
84 Southampton Row, WC1B 4BB
Nearest Station: Russell Square Map: B5
Located in Holborn, close to the British Museum and Holborn Underground Station, Hason Raja specialize in authentic Indian Fine Dining using the freshest, highest,quality, locally sourced ingredients.
25% OFF TOTAL | 10 | FRI ✓ | SAT ✓ | ✱ — Indian

HOTEL RUSSELL
☎020 7837 6470
Russell Square, WC1B 5BE
Nearest Station: Russell Square Map: B5
Peace and tranquility can often be hard to find in a city; Hotel Russell offers the perfect solution. With its majestic appearance and fashionable location, this is a fantastic inner-city retreat.
25% OFF TOTAL | 6 | FRI ✓ | SAT ✓ | ▲ — British

JUNCTION RESTAURANT @ HOLIDAY INN
☎0871 942 9222
Coram Street, WC1N 1HT
Nearest Station: Russell Square Map: B5
At this sleek Bloomsbury hotel you will find a restaurant serving delicious favourites from around the world; sizzling fajitas and traditional British fare including the hearty steak and ale pie.
50% OFF FOOD | 6 | FRI ✓ | SAT ✓ | ✱ — International

NORFOLK ARMS
☎020 7388 3937
28 Leigh Street, WC1H 9EP
Nearest Station: Kings Cross St Pancras Map: B5
Combining traditional English food with a Spanish serving style. Tapas dishes can be ordered at the bar, allowing you to experience all the comforts of England in an enjoyable European way.
2FOR1 MAIN COURSE | FRI ✱ | SAT ✓ | ▲ — Modern European

SALAAM NAMASTE
☎020 7405 3697
68 Millman Street, WC1N 3EF
Nearest Station: Russell Square Map: B5
With a a sterling reputation for its excellent food and unpretentious atmosphere, Salaam Namaste is proud of its ability to produce high quality food all year round.
2FOR1 3 COURSES | FRI ✱ | SAT ✱ — Indian

STRADA
020 7278 2777
15-17 The Brunswick Centre, Marchmont Street, WC1N 1AF
Nearest Station: Russell Square Map: B5
Offering fresh, bold dishes inspired by flavours of Italian city life - Strada serves a selection of indulgent tastes, to those seeking a blissful escape to laidback Italian life. *Excludes Pizzettas.
25% OFF TOTAL | 6 | FRI ✓ | SAT × | ▲ — Italian

CAFÉ TIFFIN
☎020 7490 2883
69 Compton Street, EC1V 0BN
Nearest Station: Barbican Map: B6
At this charming Indian eatery, the creamy chicken korma and the village-style begon are must-tries for any avid curry lover. With an extensive menu under their belt, this venue comes highly recommended.
2FOR1 3 COURSES | FRI ✓ | SAT ✓ — Authentic Indian

CAFÉ VN ☎020 7278 4123

144 Clerkenwell Road, EC1R 5DP
Nearest Station: Farringdon Map: B6
An authentic Vietnamese café, bar and restaurant specialising in traditional pho, bun and salads. Enjoy a tasty dish from the divine menu or sample gourmet coffee direct from Vietnam.

2FOR1 2 COURSES | FRI ✓ | SAT ✓ | SUN | ✱ | ▲ — **Vietnamese**

CINNAMON TREE ☎020 7837 6000

14 Exmouth Market, EC1R 4QE
Nearest Station: Farringdon Map: B6
Fresh-faced modern Indian restaurant. Spacious, warm and subtle in style, it has gained a good local reputation for simple, fresh flavours and plenty of spice where it's called for.

50% OFF FOOD | ♟10 | FRI ✓ | SAT ✓ — **Indian**

CLERKENWELL HOUSE ☎020 7404 1113

23-27 Hatton Wall, EC1N 8JJ
Nearest Station: Farringdon Map: B6
This fresh and funky venue's décor reflects the vibrancy of the local area thanks to the support of local artists. Their freshly prepared mezze dishes offer variety and flavour for the delighted diner.

2FOR1 MAIN COURSE | FRI ▯ | SAT ✱ | SUN | ▲ — **Italian/ Mediterranean**

THE COACH AND HORSES ☎020 7278 8990

26-28 Ray Street, EC1R 3DJ
Nearest Station: Farringdon Map: B6
Time Out award-winning gastro-pub in historic, lively Clerkenwell. Attractive Victorian interior, decked out with original Eduardo Paolozzi prints. Balanced, modern British menu with seasonal emphasis.

2FOR1 MAIN COURSE | FRI ▯ | SAT ✓ | ✱ | ▲ — **British**

GULSHAN TANDOORI ☎020 7833 2436

15-17 Exmouth Market, EC1R 4QD
Nearest Station: Farringdon Map: B6
Combining the flavours of India with Bangladesh, this long-established venue boasts traditional cuisine in a friendly setting. A friendly and welcoming environment in which to dine.

2FOR1 MAIN COURSE | FRI ✓ | SAT ✓ | ✱ — **Indian**

MALMAISON ☎020 7012 3700

18-21 Charterhouse Square, EC1M 6AH
Nearest Station: Barbican Map: B6
Divinely tasty, beautifully presented cuisine prepared with incredible local ingredients, served with professionalism and passion. A beautifully chic brasserie with a lively atmosphere. 2 AA Rosettes.

2FOR1 MAIN COURSE | FRI × | SAT × | SUN | ▲ — **European**

NEO BARBICAN ☎020 7726 8925

14-17 Carthusian Street, EC1M 6AD
Nearest Station: Barbican Map: B6
Coiling downstairs off the main road you'll find the sultry, stylish Neo Barbican. The bar does a fine line in Italian food, with some fresh and tasty paninis, pizzas and platters, plus great bruschetta.

2FOR1 3 COURSES | FRI ✓ | SAT ✓ — **International**

RANGO'S HOT STONE KITCHEN ☎020 3417 2031

59 Mount Pleasant, WC1X 0AY
Nearest Station: Chancery Lane Map: B6
Rango's have turned a primeval method of cooking into a unique dining concept in which your meal is served to you on a bed of lava rock held within the recess of a bamboo board for your dining pleasure.

25% OFF TOTAL | ♟4 | FRI ✓ | SAT ✓ | SUN | ▲ — **British**

SADE RESTAURANT 020 7833 1111

21 Exmouth Market, EC1R 4QD
Nearest Station: Farringdon Map: B6
A restaurant specialising in healthy food made from natural ingredients, served in superbly pleasant surroundings. The Mediterranean menu is warm and wide-ranging, perfect for a relaxing meal in company.

2FOR1 MAIN COURSE | FRI × | SAT ✓ | ▲ — **Mediterranean**

THE SAMUEL PEPYS ☎020 7489 1871

Stew Lane, EC1V 0BY
Nearest Station: Farringdon Map: B6
On the fabulously monikered Stew Lane, tucked away across from South Bank, you can enjoy rich and classic English flavours - like a beauty of a herby Cumberland - along with broader cosmopolitan flavours.

2FOR1 MAIN COURSE | FRI ▯ | SAT ✓ | SUN | ▲ — **European**

THE SHAKESPEARE 020 7253 6116

2 Goswell Road, EC1M 7AA
Nearest Station: Barbican Map: B6
Sophisticated diners gravitate towards The Shakespeare to sip on cocktails and Scottish malt whiskies from an overwhelming drinks list. The menu successfully infuses the tastes of Britain and Italy.

2FOR1 MAIN COURSE | FRI ✱ | SAT × | SUN — **English and Continental**

STRADA 020 7278 0800

8-10 Exmouth Market, EC1R 4QA
Nearest Station: Farringdon Map: B6
Offering fresh, bold dishes inspired by flavours of Italian city life - Strada serves a selection of indulgent tastes, to those seeking a blissful escape to laidback Italian life. *Excludes Pizzettas.

25% OFF TOTAL | ♟6 | FRI ✓ | SAT × | ▲ — **Italian**

VECCHIO PARIOLI ☎020 7253 3240

129 Aldersgate Street, EC1A 4JQ
Nearest Station: Barbican Map: B6
Classic feel to this on-the-corner Italian joint right by the Barbican. Cool and calm atmosphere, flexible with their menu, and a trattoria vibe between the whitewashed walls and the colourful plates.

2FOR1 MAIN COURSE | FRI ✓ | SAT ✓ | SUN — **Italian**

THE WELL ☎020 7251 9363

108 St John Street, EC1V 4JY
Nearest Station: Farringdon Map: B6
A neighbourhood gem boasting the very best in British food served up with good, honest hospitality.

50% OFF FOOD | ♟8 | FRI ✱ | SAT ✱ | SUN | ▲ — **British**

ZEN GARDEN ☎020 7242 6128

88 Leather Lane, EC1N 7TT
Nearest Station: Farringdon Map: B6
Zen Garden's eclectic menu contains some real treats of unique and distinctive flavours; it has a good array of dishes that are skilfully and attentively produced and packed with full, rich tastes.

25% OFF TOTAL | ♟4 | FRI ✓ | SAT ✱ | SUN | ✱ — **Chinese**

CAFÉ ROUGE 020 7489 7812

5 Condor House, St Paul's Churchyard, EC4M 8AY
Nearest Station: St. Paul's Map: C6
French sophistication on the British high street – enjoy seasonally changing French dishes and a continental wine selection, served in a relaxed environment with an undeniable flair of Parisian chic.

25% OFF TOTAL | ♟6 | FRI ✓ | SAT ✓ | ✱ | ▲ — **French**

CHAMBERS BAR AND RESTAURANT ☎020 3004 4141

Apex Temple Court, 1-2 Serjeants Inn, EC4Y 1LL
Nearest Station: Blackfriars Map: C6
Feast like a king at this European-inspired eatery where full-length banqueting seats create a fine dining experience. Be sure to indulge in a bottle of the finest wine from the astounding beverage list.

50% OFF FOOD | ♟6 | FRI ▯ | SAT ▯ | ▲ — **Modern European**

THE CHANCERY ☎020 7831 4000

9 Cursitor Street, EC4A 1LL
Nearest Station: Chancery Lane Map: C6
An elegant little restaurant serving exceptional, sophisticated flavours by its talented and experienced chef-patrons. Fine dining in a cosy, personable environment off Chancery Lane. 2 AA Rosettes.

50% OFF FOOD | ♟8 | FRI ✓ | SAT ✓ | SUN | ✱ | ▲ — **Modern European**

CHARTERHOUSE BAR ☎020 7608 0858

38 Charterhouse Street, EC1M 6JH
Nearest Station: Barbican Map: C6
A stylish place to party as well as eat. From lunchtime into the evening, guests can enjoy great quality food and a fabulous choice of beverages. Allow the fun-filled atmosphere ease away the day.

2FOR1 MAIN COURSE | FRI ▯ | SAT ✓ | SUN | ▲ — **English/Gastro pub**

CHINESE CRICKET CLUB ☎020 7438 8052

Crowne Plaza London, EC4V 6DB
Nearest Station: Blackfriars Map: C6
Against a relaxed and calming backdrop decorated with a warm simplicity, the AA awarded Rosette, Chinese Cricket Club offers a mouth-watering range of Sichuan fare with a modern twist.

25% OFF TOTAL | ♟10 | FRI ✓ | SAT ✓ | ✱ | ▲ — **Chinese**

THE CITY LOUNGE
☎020 7438 8052

Crowne Plaza London, EC4V 6DB
Nearest Station: Blackfriars Map: C6

Serving a wide variety of cuisine from the famous One Pounder burger to the traditional Club Sandwich, the City Lounge offers a hand-crafted taste of British comfort food.

25% OFF TOTAL | FRI ✓ | SAT ✓ | ✱ | ▲ — British

DICIANNOVE
☎020 7438 8052

Crowne Plaza London, EC4V 6DB
Nearest Station: City Thameslink Map: C6

Set against a backdrop of an elegant, homely interior, Diciannove restaurant is a dynamic showcase for instinctively Italian food.

25% OFF TOTAL | ♟10 | FRI ✓ | SAT ✓ | ✱ | ▲ — Italian

THE DISTILLERS
☎020 7600 2705

66 West Smithfield, EC1A 9DY
Nearest Station: Barbican Map: C6

Launched by the team behind The Distillers In Hammersmith and The Bedford in Balham, The Distillers Smithfield offers a fresh take on the modern British pub on the edge of London's financial district.

25% OFF TOTAL | ♟4 | FRI × | SAT ✓ | ▲ — British

GRAPPOLO
☎020 7842 0510

1 Plough Place, EC4A 1HY
Nearest Station: Chancery Lane Map: C6

Energetic and flamboyant, the chefs at this Italian venue are nothing short of authentic. Choose tender meat that falls off the bone, or succulent seafood. The cuisine is fresh and sourced locally.

50% OFF FOOD | ♟8 | FRI ✓ | SAT ✓ — Italian

KURZ & LANG
020 7993 2923

1 St John Street, EC1M 4AA
Nearest Station: Farringdon Map: C6

Kurz & Lang is 'The Bratwurst Company', and brings a welcome aspect of authentic German cuisine to Smithfield. The principle is quite simple: if it's wurst you like, try out this refreshing restaurant.

25% OFF TOTAL | ♟2 | FRI × | SAT ✓ — German

PATCH
☎020 7489 7777

58-60 Carter Lane, EC4V 5EA
Nearest Station: Blackfriars Map: C6

Aiming to steer clear of the usual city-centre bars, Patch brings something alive and exciting to the capital. Combining style with quirkiness, Patch offers fantastic cocktails and delicious tapas dishes.

50% OFF FOOD | ♟10 | FRI 📱 | SAT 📱 | SUN — Multi-Cuisine

THE PUNCH TAVERN
☎020 7353 6658

99 Fleet Street, EC4Y 1DE
Nearest Station: City Thameslink Map: C6

Situated in an architecturally beautiful building steeped in history, the kitchen ensures fresh produce is used in all of its home-made cooking. A popular venue for parties and corporate functions.

2FOR1 MAIN COURSE | FRI ✓ | SAT ✓ | ▲ — British

SEEMA TANDOORI
☎020 7236 3663

41 Farringdon Street, EC4A 4AN
Nearest Station: Chancery Lane Map: C6

Being spoilt for choice by the expansive menu, allow the attentive and amiable staff to advise accordingly. A restaurant designed to help you relax and settle down for the evening.

50% OFF FOOD | ♟6 | FRI ✓ | SAT ✓ | ▲ — Indian

STRADA
020 7248 7178

4 St Paul's Churchyard, EC4M 8AY
Nearest Station: St. Paul's Map: C6

Offering fresh, bold dishes inspired by flavours of Italian city life - Strada serves a selection of indulgent tastes, to those seeking a blissful escape to laidback Italian life. *Excludes Pizzettas.

25% OFF TOTAL | ♟6 | FRI ✓ | SAT × | ▲ — Italian

VOLUPTE
☎020 7831 1622

7-9 Norwich Street, EC4A 1EJ
Nearest Station: Chancery Lane Map: C6

Prepare to enter a complete world of pleasure and exquisite delight. Volupte offers everything from old movie clips to accompany your cocktail, to all day afternoon tea to complete your day out.

25% OFF TOTAL | ♟4 | FRI 📱 | SAT 📱 | SUN — European

THE WHITE SWAN
☎020 7248 1782

20 Farringdon Street, EC4A 4AB
Nearest Station: Chancery Lane Map: C6

The White Swan serves up delicious, freshly prepared dishes in a smooth, serene atmosphere. The décor strongly reflects the charmingly contemporary feel that the staff aim to preserve.

2FOR1 3 COURSES | FRI 📱 | SAT 📱 | SUN — British

THE WHITE SWAN
☎020 7242 9696

108 Fetter Lane, EC4A 1ES
Nearest Station: Chancery Lane Map: C6

The White Swan serves the very best in modern British cuisine. Menus are complemented by an extensive wine list comprising of 150 wines as we all as an impressive selection of real ales.

50% OFF FOOD | ♟8 | FRI ✓ | SAT ✓ | ✱ | ▲ — British

ANOKHA
020 7236 3999

4 Burgon Street, EC4V 5DR
Nearest Station: City Thameslink Map: D6

Sultry modern Indian restaurant with a two-tone balance of dark and light. They specialise in dishes from across India and the subcontinent. Among the best are the jhinga malabar and the hot Goan xacuti.

50% OFF FOOD | ♟10 | FRI ✓ | SAT ✓ | SUN — Indian

BALTIC
☎020 7928 1111

74 Blackfriars Road, SE1 8HA
Nearest Station: Southwark Map: D6

Baltic's cuisine is full of the strong flavours and robustness of great country cooking from the east of Europe, with a menu changing monthly reflecting the seasonal influences. Awarded 1 AA Rosette.

50% OFF FOOD | ♟4 | FRI 📱 | SAT 📱 | ▲ — European

ELEMENTS RESTAURANT @ NOVOTEL
020 7633 2617

46 Blackfriars Road, SE1 8NZ
Nearest Station: Southwark Map: D6

Elements Restaurant and Bar is perfect for a meal, coffee or drinks through the day in a cosy atmosphere with the latest Microsoft Surface table in the lobby and the iPad table in the restaurant.

25% OFF TOTAL | ♟4 | FRI ✓ | SAT ✓ — International

GOURMET PIZZA - GABRIEL'S WHARF
020 7928 3188

Gabriel's Wharf, SE1 9PP
Nearest Station: Southwark Map: D6

Popular with pizza lovers and people watchers alike, this buzzy city restaurant offers lavish pizzas heaped with colour in spacious and comfortable surroundings. A special menu offers alternative treats.

2FOR1 MAIN COURSE | FRI ✓ | SAT × — Pizza

INDIGO
☎020 7593 0009

56 Stamford Street, SE1 9LX
Nearest Station: Southwark Map: D6

A contemporary environment for you to relax and enjoy superb Indian and Bangladeshi cuisine. Choose a great meal from a selection of classic curries and other dishes, as well as starters and naan breads.

2FOR1 MAIN COURSE | FRI ✓ | SAT ✓ — Bangladeshi/Indian

JACK'S LOUNGE
020 7928 0678

96 Isabella Street, SE1 8DA
Nearest Station: Southwark Map: D6

Treat friends to a delectable array of sharing platters and fantastic finger goods at Jack's Lounge - a transformed railway arch that oozes character. Relax in an antique chair in this family-run venue.

2FOR1 MAIN COURSE | FRI ✱ | SAT ✓ | SUN | ▲ — British

THE WHARF
☎020 7401 7314

Riverside Walk, Gabriel's Wharf, SE1 9PP
Nearest Station: Southwark Map: D6

Breathe in panoramic riverbank views as you peruse the modern and innovative Euro-Asian menu. Situated in a converted old boathouse, The Wharf is proud of its exceptionally bold menu and fine service.

2FOR1 3 COURSES | FRI 📱 | SAT 📱 — Seafood

IVORY ARCH
☎020 7703 0182

80-82 Walworth Road, SE1 6SW
Nearest Station: Elephant &Castle Map: E6

A vibrant Indian restaurant that hosts a fine selection of great, tasty dishes. Perfect for a midweek feast or weekend treat, Ivory Arch offers diners the chance to experience high-quality cuisine.

50% OFF FOOD | FRI ✓ | SAT ✓ — Indian

LA DOLCE VITA
020 7928 7138
4-5 London Road, SE1 6JZ
Nearest Station: Elephant &Castle Map: E6
Genuine Italian fare is prepared by expert chefs at this venue alongside a selection of carefully chosen wines. With a vast menu at an affordable price, La Dolce Vita is perfect for any occasion.
50% OFF FOOD | FRI ✓ | SAT ✓ | SUN | ✱ — Italian

MY BIG FAT GREEK
020 7252 5250
16 Elephant and Castle, SE1 6TH
Nearest Station: Elephant &Castle Map: E6
As the name suggests, this eatery prepares only the most authentic and substantial of Greek dishes. Greek chefs serve juicy, succulent grills in a friendly and hospitable setting.
50% OFF FOOD | 2 | FRI × | SAT × — Greek

SPHINX ALSULTAN
020 7582 6333
82 Kennington Road, SE11 6NL
Nearest Station: Lambeth North Map: E6
Lavishly colourful restaurant serving Egyptian cuisine. Restaurant replete with colourful fabrics, plush cushions and curious trinkets. An evening here is a warm affair, with some fine cuisine to boot.
2FOR1 3 COURSES | FRI ✱ | SAT ✱ — International

LOCALE COUNTY HALL
020 7401 6734
3b Belvedere Road, SE1 7GP
Nearest Station: Waterloo Map: E5
Cool and collected Italian restaurant with all the classic dishes and flavours; hearty and flavourful pasta and risotto, and a line in beautifully seasoned meat and fish with smart accompaniments.
25% OFF TOTAL | 6 | FRI ✓ | SAT ✓ — Italian

2 AMICI RISTORANTE
020 7976 5660
48a Rochester Row, SW1P 1JU
Nearest Station: Victoria Map: E4
2 Amici offers a unique, friendly ambience and provides the finest Italian cuisine. The tasty dishes are supported by an exclusive range of Italy's most excellent wines.
25% OFF TOTAL | 10 | FRI | SAT | SUN — Italian

2 BRIDGE PLACE
020 7802 8555
2 Bridge Place, SW1V 1QA
Nearest Station: Victoria Map: E4
European influences reign supreme at the hotel restaurant. 2 Bridge Place has an à la carte menu that combines locally sourced ingredients and a seasonal selection of succulent meat, poultry, and seafood dishes.
2FOR1 3 COURSES | FRI ✓ | SAT ✓ | SUN | ✱ — European

LA TASCA
020 7828 5515
6 Cathedral Walk, SW1E 5JE
Nearest Station: Victoria Map: E4
Quintessentially Spanish, La Tasca's fresh and exciting menu offers something for everyone. Their tapas dishes are sincerely authentic, while their paellas always deliver on flavour.
25% OFF TOTAL | 8 | FRI ✓ | SAT × — Spanish

SPICY WORLD BALTI HOUSE
020 7630 9951
76 Wilton Road, SW1V 1DE
Nearest Station: Victoria Map: E4
A culmination of popular dishes, rich with succulent flavours and spices, have been created through years of experimentation to bring out the incomparable taste of India in every mouthful.
2FOR1 MAIN COURSE | FRI | SAT | ✱ — Indian

CAFÉ ROUGE
020 7931 9300
Victoria Place Ctr., Buckingham Palace Rd, SW1W 9SJ
Nearest Station: Victoria Map: E3
French sophistication on the British high street – enjoy seasonally changing French dishes and a continental wine selection, served in a relaxed environment with an undeniable flair of Parisian chic.
25% OFF TOTAL | 6 | FRI ✓ | SAT ✓ | ✱ — French

DA SCALZO
020 7730 5498
2a Elizabeth Street, SW1W 9RB
Nearest Station: Victoria Map: E3
Combining contemporary art with exceptional cuisine is the ethos of this restaurant, run by two brothers with an infectious passion for art and food. The listed building venue adds to the charm.
25% OFF TOTAL | 4 | FRI ✓ | SAT ✓ — Italian

LOWNDES BAR & KITCHEN
020 7858 7223
21 Lowndes Street, SW1X 9ES
Nearest Station: Knightsbridge Map: E3
Creamy risottos, pan-fried prawns or prime beef burgers all align the menu at this stylish eatery. Whatever the time, Head Chef Martin has crafted a menu to appease ravenous stomachs in a relaxed setting.
25% OFF TOTAL | 2 | FRI ✓ | SAT ✓ — Modern British

MU RESTAURANT AND COCKTAIL BAR
020 7201 6330
17 Sloane Street, SW1X 9NU
Nearest Station: Knightsbridge Map: E3
A restaurant with an appealing warmth, MU delivers an eclectic menu of fantastic Asian-influenced tapas and other vibrant dishes in one of London's most celebrated locations. *Excludes set menu.
2FOR1 MAIN COURSE | FRI ✓ | SAT ✱ | SUN — Pan-Asian

SOBRANIE RUSSIAN RESTAURANT
020 7233 7000
123-151 Buckingham Palace Road, SW1W 9SH
Nearest Station: Victoria Map: E3
Lavish reds and deep mahogany browns set the warm tone and atmosphere at Sobranie. Allow yourself to be spoiled by the glowing Russian fare, such as the aubergine caviar and chicken kiev.
50% OFF FOOD | 6 | FRI | SAT — European

SPICY WORLD
020 7630 9668
1 Gillingham Street, SW1V 1HN
Nearest Station: Victoria Map: E3
Aiming to provide something to suit all palates, Spicy World serves up delicious curries ranging from a mild, creamy korma, to a spicy madras. Amiable staff will enhance your overall experience.
50% OFF FOOD | 4 | FRI ✓ | SAT ✓ — Indian

AWANA MALAYSIAN RESTAURANT
020 7584 8880
85 Sloane Avenue, SW3 3DX
Nearest Station: South Kensington Map: E2
Awaken to the world of Malaysian cuisine, some of Asia's most exciting food. Adapting rich culinary history this venue creates flavoursome dishes using innovative modern interpretations. 1 AA Rosette.
25% OFF TOTAL | 8 | FRI | SAT — Malaysian

BEITEDDINE
020 7235 3969
8 Harriet Street, SW1X 9JW
Nearest Station: Knightsbridge Map: E2
Taking its inspiration from the grand palace of its namesake, Beiteddine aims to treat each and every guest like Royalty. Outstanding cuisine that draws on the culture and traditions of Lebanon.
50% OFF FOOD | FRI ✓ | SAT ✓ — Lebanese

BELLA ITALIA
020 7584 4028
60 Old Brompton Road, SW7 3DY
Nearest Station: South Kensington Map: E2
Accessible Italian cuisine on the British high street – indulge in authentic sharing platters, hand stretched pizzas and hearty pasta dishes, served with a healthy dose of gregarious Italian hospitality.
25% OFF TOTAL | 6 | FRI × | SAT × | SUN — Italian

BISTRO FIFTEEN
020 7589 8288
15 Cromwell Place, SW7 2LA
Nearest Station: South Kensington Map: E2
Contemporary cuisine meets an Italian twist at this popular bistro. From early morning breakfast buffets to delicious à la carte menu's, this venue caters for an assortment of tastes. Perfect for hire.
25% OFF TOTAL | 4 | FRI ✓ | SAT ✓ — International

BROMPTON QUARTER BRASSERIE
020 7225 2107
223-225 Brompton Road, SW3 2EJ
Nearest Station: Knightsbridge Map: E2
From crumbly pastries and oriental lunches to succulent oysters and creamy risottos, this venue has it all. Boasting a cosmopolitan atmosphere and chic interior, a sophisticated clientèle is guaranteed.
25% OFF TOTAL | 10 | FRI ✓ | SAT × | SUN — Locally Sourced

CAFÉ ROUGE
020 7584 2345
27-31 Basil Street, SW3 1BB
Nearest Station: Knightsbridge Map: E2
French sophistication on the British high street – enjoy seasonally changing French dishes and a continental wine selection, served in a relaxed environment with an undeniable flair of Parisian chic.
25% OFF TOTAL | 6 | FRI ✓ | SAT ✓ | ✱ — French

To understand what the restaurant icons mean, please see the inside back cover.

CAFFE CONCERTO KENSINGTON
☎0844 335 8403
152 Brompton Road, SW3 1HX
Nearest Station: Knightsbridge Map: E2
Luxurious, contemporary dining with a focus on favourites from the Italian table. Carbonara to chicken Milanese along with some outstanding vegetarian, seafood, and salad options.

25% OFF TOTAL | 👤4 | FRI ✱ | SAT ✓ — Italian

CHICAGO RIB SHACK
☎020 7591 4664
145 Knightsbridge, SW1X 7PA
Nearest Station: Knightsbridge Map: E2
A slice of America in London. Two floors of restaurant and bar that offer a unique experience with a lively soundtrack, authentic American drinks, and some of London's best barbecue and smoked meats.

2FOR1 3 COURSES | FRI ✱ | SAT ✱ | ▲ — American

THE DELHI BRASSERIE
☎020 7370 7617
134 Cromwell Road, SW7 9HA
Nearest Station: South Kensington Map: E2
A fabulous Indian restaurant in the heart of Kensington. Guests will love the exotic spiciness of the dishes available. For a more unusual dining experience, try the quails marinated in yoghurt.

2FOR1 MAIN COURSE | FRI ▯ | SAT ▯ | SUN — Indian

THE DORSIA
☎020 7590 4630
3 Cromwell Road, SW3 2HR
Nearest Station: South Kensington Map: E2
Opulently decorated and boasting exquisite views over the Natural History Museum, guests feast upon modern European cuisine prepared by Head Chef Alexander Baillieu. Be sure to visit the Onyx Bar.

50% OFF FOOD | 👤4 | FRI × | SAT × — European

FRANKIE'S CRITERION
☎020 7590 9999
3 Yeoman's Row, SW3 2AL
Nearest Station: Knightsbridge Map: E2
Flagship restaurant of the Marco Pierre White-Frankie Dettori axis, the vibrant American styling of Frankie's Criterion is home to a range of tasty and rich Italian fare.

25% OFF TOTAL | 👤10 | FRI ▯ | SAT ▯ | ▲ — Italian

HAANDI
☎020 7823 7373
7 Cheval Place, SW7 1EW
Nearest Station: South Kensington Map: E2
A restaurant specialising in North Indian cuisine, producing fine food cooked to order in an open-plan kitchen, that allows you to view expert chefs at work. An exemplary venue where quality is paramount.

25% OFF TOTAL | 👤6 | FRI ✱ | SAT ✱ | ▲ — Indian

THE HOUR GLASS
☎020 7581 2840
279-283 Brompton Road, SW3 2DY
Nearest Station: South Kensington Map: E2
Down-to-earth, delicious dishes at this traditional-style pub in SW3. Open fires will warm you against the cold, whilst the outside seating is a sun-trap in summer. Enjoy locally sourced classics.

2FOR1 MAIN COURSE | FRI ✱ | SAT ✱ | SUN | ▲ — British

KUMO
☎020 7225 0944
11 Beauchamp Place, SW3 1NQ
Nearest Station: Knightsbridge Map: E2
Adhering to the glitz and glamour of its location, this stylish Japanese-inspired sushi bar is an ideal place to drink, dine and dance. Evocative and attractive surroundings to enjoy a classic cocktail.

25% OFF TOTAL | 👤10 | FRI ▯ | SAT ▯ — Japanese

LAYA'LINA
☎020 7581 4296
2-3 Beauchamp Place, SW3 1NG
Nearest Station: Knightsbridge Map: E2
Reflecting the glamour and sophistication of its location, this attractive restaurant and bar is stylish yet intimate enough to relax in. Relish delightful cocktails and mouth-watering Lebanese canapés.

50% OFF FOOD | 👤10 | FRI ▯ | SAT ✱ | ▲ — Lebanese

MAMOUNIA LOUNGE
☎020 7581 7777
136 Brompton Road, SW3 1HY
Nearest Station: Knightsbridge Map: E2
Stylish bar and restaurant that offers a fusion of Middle Eastern cuisine alongside a varied drinks list and shisha in a range of flavours. Be swept away by traditional Arabic charm and magnificent food.

50% OFF FOOD | 👤4 | FRI ▯ | SAT ▯ — Moroccan/ Lebanese

MONZA RESTAURANT
☎020 7591 0210
6 Yeoman's Row, SW3 2AH
Nearest Station: South Kensington Map: E2
Tucked away in Knightsbridge, Monza is known for its rich milanese dishes, along with the full range of flavourful and hearty Italian recipes. The restaurant has a homely feel for a cosy dining experience.

2FOR1 MAIN COURSE | FRI ✱ | SAT ✱ | SUN — Italian

OFF THE HOOK @ THE PAXTONS HEAD
☎020 7589 6627
153 Knightsbridge, SW1X 7PA
Nearest Station: Knightsbridge Map: E2
A traditional English pub and restaurant presenting an instant interest to all who are keen to sample a slice of English gastronomic heritage. The food is fresh, uncomplicated, and reasonably priced.

2FOR1 2 COURSES | FRI ✓ | SAT ✓ — European

SHEZAN
☎020 7584 9316
16-22 Cheval Place, SW7 1ES
Nearest Station: Knightsbridge Map: E2
In the heart of London's prestigious Knightsbridge sits a wonderful restaurant serving fabulous Indian cuisine. This well-established venue hosts live classical music in a relaxed atmosphere.

50% OFF FOOD | 👤10 | FRI ▯ | SAT ▯ | ▲ — Indian/Punjabi

CHEMINEE PERSIAN RESTAURANT
☎020 7402 1313
17 Bouverie Place, W2 1RD
Nearest Station: Paddington Map: C2
Enjoy the delights of an authentic Persian meal.The food at Cheminee is made using the freshest ingredients, prepared for you while you wait.Immerse yourself in the friendly Middle Eastern atmosphere.

2FOR1 2 COURSES | FRI ▯ | SAT ▯ | ✱ — Middle Eastern

DOLCE
☎020 7262 9623
30 Connaught Street, W2 2AF
Nearest Station: Marble Arch Map: C2
From classic pasta dishes to sumptuous steaks, there will be something at Dolce to tempt your tastebuds.The menu coupled with the cool and modern ambience that is rapidly gaining Dolce a great reputation.

25% OFF TOTAL | FRI ✓ | SAT ✓ | SUN | ✱ — Italian

FANTASIA PALACE
☎020 8127 5422
28 Praed Street, London, W2 1NH
Nearest Station: Edgware Road (Bakerloo) Map: C2
Fantasia Palace serves delicious Greek food, along with traditional entertainment-with their popular music experience and belly dancers. Often referred to as a 'jewel' of a Greek restaurant.

25% OFF TOTAL | FRI ▯ | SAT ▯ — Greek

FIAMMA RESTAURANT @ HILTON
☎020 7402 4141
Hilton London Metropole, 225 Edgware Road, W2 1JU
Nearest Station: Edgware Road (Bakerloo) Map: C2
A light, open and spacious restaurant that provides the perfect atmosphere for any occasion. Rich reds and cool greys create a relaxing ambience, while the menu offers a wide variety of divine dishes.

50% OFF FOOD | 👤6 | FRI ✓ | SAT ✓ — International

LONDON ST BRASSERIE
☎020 7706 4444
Hotel Indigo, 16 London Street, W2 1HL
Nearest Station: Paddington Map: C2
Trendy restaurant with a friendly atmosphere offering diners great value for money. Situated close to Paddington Station, London Street Brasserie is a popular destination with tourists and locals alike.

25% OFF TOTAL | 👤4 | FRI ✓ | SAT ✓ — English and Continental

MAXIMINI CHINESE RESTAURANT
☎020 7402 6263
31-33 Sussex Place, W2 2TH
Nearest Station: Lancaster Gate Map: C2
Blending chic with old-fashioned colonial style, Malaysian dishes are prepared to culinary impeccability by master chef Albert Koh. The menu, which is Chinese-infused, is sure to appease hungry diners.

25% OFF TOTAL | 👤10 | FRI ✓ | SAT ✓ — Chinese

PAK AWIE
☎020 7402 8055
36 Southwick Street, W2 1JQ
Nearest Station: Edgware Road (Bakerloo) Map: C2
Beautifully presented, deliciously tasty Malaysian cuisine is featured at Pak Awie. The kitchen works exceptionally hard to produce signature flavours and memorable appearances in every dish.

2FOR1 MAIN COURSE | FRI × | SAT × | ✱ — Malaysian

RYATH INDIAN TANDOORI
☎020 7723 8954
32 Norfolk Place, W2 1QH
Nearest Station: Paddington Map: C2
Clean plates are always the outcome of every diner's experience at this popular Indian restaurant. Generous portions of freshly made Indian halal dishes are presented with impeccable service.
50% OFF FOOD | 4 | FRI ✓ | SAT ✓ — Indian

SEE JAPANESE FUSION RESTAURANT
☎020 7724 7358
4D Praed Street, W2 1JX
Nearest Station: Edgware Road (Bakerloo) Map: C2
A featured restaurant on UKTV Food's Market Kitchen, See Restaurant really does have to be seen to be believed. Sit in a soothing ambience while chowing down on yummy Japanese cuisine.
25% OFF TOTAL | 4 | FRI ✓ | SAT ✓ | SUN | * — Japanese

DAR MARRAKESH
☎020 7262 0560
422 Edgware Road, W2 1EG
Nearest Station: Edgware Road (Bakerloo) Map: B2
Unwind in the bar and enjoy an array of freshly prepared food, from authentic Moroccan cuisine to classic home-made burgers. A unique atmosphere that suits every occasion.
25% OFF TOTAL | FRI | SAT — Moroccan

MUMTAZ LONDON
☎020 7723 0549
4-10 Park Road, NW1 4SH
Nearest Station: Baker Street Map: B2
Conveniently located restaurant serving a superbly delicious array of authentic North Indian cuisine. Named after the Queen Mumtaz Mahal, the restaurant prides itself on its warm Moghal style ambience.
25% OFF TOTAL | 10 | FRI | SAT — Indian

CAFÉ ROUGE
020 7722 8366
120 St John's Wood High Street, NW8 7SG
Nearest Station: St John's Wood Map: A2
French sophistication on the British high street – enjoy seasonally changing French dishes and a continental wine selection, served in a relaxed environment with an undeniable flair of Parisian chic.
25% OFF TOTAL | 6 | FRI ✓ | SAT ✓ | * — French

MEZZA EXPRESS
☎020 7267 7111
47 Parkway, NW1 7PN
Nearest Station: Camden Town Map: A3
Dine-in and takeaway options are both highly popular at this fantastic Lebanese restaurant. The hot and cold mezze selection is phenomenal, whilst the vast main menu offers delicious chargrilled dishes.
25% OFF TOTAL | 6 | FRI | SAT — Lebanese

NAMAASTE KITCHEN
☎020 7485 5977
64 Parkway, NW1 7AH
Nearest Station: Camden Road Map: A3
A stylish setting - a balance of bare brick walls and sultry modern styling - to enjoy a pleasing curry, whether you plump for the creamier kind of dish or a more fiery set of flavours.
2FOR1 3 COURSES | FRI ✱ | SAT ✱ — Indian

STRADA
020 7428 9653
40-42 Parkway, Camden, NW1 7AH
Nearest Station: Camden Town Map: A3
Offering fresh, bold dishes inspired by flavours of Italian city life - Strada serves a selection of indulgent tastes, to those seeking a blissful escape to laidback Italian life. *Excludes Pizzettas.
25% OFF TOTAL | 6 | FRI ✓ | SAT × | ▲ — Italian

YUMCHAA PARKWAY
☎020 7209 9641
35-37 Parkway, NW1 7PN
Nearest Station: Camden Town Map: A3
Yumchaa Parkway, much like its sister branches, serves tea like no other. With a wide variety of loose leaf teas appearing in quaint milk jugs, sample the cakes to really polish your afternoon off.
2FOR1 3 COURSES | FRI ✓ | SAT ✓ — British

ANDY'S TAVERNA
☎020 7485 9718
81-81a Bayham Street, NW1 0AG
Nearest Station: Camden Town Map: A4
Feel at home in this fantastic taverna that offers good food and wine to go with great company. The friendly relaxed atmosphere has maintained its fantastic reputation and regular clientà¨le.
50% OFF FOOD | 2 | FRI ✱ | SAT ✱ — Greek

ELIXIR BAR
☎020 7383 0925
162 Eversholt Street, NW1 1BL
Nearest Station: Mornington Crescent Map: A4
A versatile entertainment venue that serves excellent, fresh food; home-baked bread and tasty, eclectic Mediterranean and Middle Eastern dishes.
2FOR1 3 COURSES | FRI ✓ | SAT ✱ — Mediterranean

HELLENIC RESTAURANT
☎020 7388 8595
9a Delancey Street, NW1 7NL
Nearest Station: Camden Town Map: A4
Hellenic Restaurant invites you to enjoy a selection of home-made Greek dishes, which are cooked using the highest quality local ingredients and authentic recipes.
2FOR1 3 COURSES | FRI ✓ | SAT ✓ — Mediterranean

KARAVAS
☎020 7388 4121
87-88 Plender Street, NW1 0JN
Nearest Station: Camden Town Map: A4
The centrality of its location is not this restaurant's only outstanding attribute. The fresh and tasty Greek cuisine on offer also guarantees guests a great evening out.
25% OFF TOTAL | 10 | FRI ✱ | SAT ✱ — Greek

THE MAHARANI
☎020 7387 6551
109a Camden High Street, NW1 7JN
Nearest Station: Mornington Crescent Map: A4
Indulge in a menu that successfully fuses traditional and contemporary dishes, all made from the freshest ingredients and finest spices. Taste the care and attention that goes into every single meal.
2FOR1 MAIN COURSE | FRI ✓ | SAT ✓ — Indian

RODON LIVE
☎020 7267 8088
7 Pratt Street, NW1 0AE
Nearest Station: Camden Town Map: A4
Treat your friends and family to an exceptionally special dining experience at this wonderful Greek restaurant. A fun and lively venue that offers traditional cuisine as well as fantastic entertainment.
2FOR1 2 COURSES | FRI ✓ | SAT ✓ | ▲ — Greek

CENTRAL STATION
☎020 7278 3294
37 Wharfdale Road, N1 9SD
Nearest Station: Kings Cross St Pancras Map: A5
Renowned as one of the most exciting venues in the area, this recently renovated eatery is making a name for itself in the food industry. Cracking food and wine can be enjoyed on the terrace.
2FOR1 3 COURSES | FRI ✓ | SAT ✓ | SUN — European

MEDITERRANEO
☎020 7837 5108
112 Kings Cross Road, WC1X 9DS
Nearest Station: Kings Cross St Pancras Map: A5
Focusing on the clear, straightforward flavourfulness of traditional Italian cooking, this trattoria places emphasis on quality cooking, a personal touch in its service, and a homely Italian setting.
50% OFF FOOD | 10 | FRI ✓ | SAT ✓ — Italian

RASA MARICHAM
☎020 7833 9787
Holiday Inn, 1 Kings Cross Road, WC1X 9HX
Nearest Station: Kings Cross St Pancras Map: A5
Inspired by the authentic home cooking of beautiful, spice-rich Kerala, this restaurant's passion is food prepared always with devotion, love, and the finest ingredients. Experience the essence of India.
2FOR1 MAIN COURSE | FRI ✓ | SAT ✓ | SUN | ▲ — Indian

TASTE OF ASIA
☎020 7713 0055
126 Kings Cross Road, WC1X 9DS
Nearest Station: Kings Cross St Pancras Map: A5
Something of a local favourite, with that unquantifiable edge of quality in its dishes. Crisp, comfortable atmosphere, with high ceilings, light colour scheme, excellent service and generous portions.
50% OFF FOOD | 10 | FRI ✓ | SAT ✓ | ▲ — Indian

ANAM BAR
☎020 7278 1001
3a Chapel Market, N1 9EZ
Nearest Station: Angel Map: A6
A funky cocktail bar mixing a blend of soulful uplifting dance music with an exquisite selection of premium spirit-based cocktails, plus freshly cooked dishes. The life and soul of the party.
50% OFF FOOD | 2 | FRI ✱ | SAT ✱ | SUN | ▲ — English and Continental

Gourmet Society discount applies to the à la carte menu only, unless stated otherwise.

AXIS BAR & KITCHEN
020 7354 7739
53 Upper Street, N1 0UY
Nearest Station: Angel Map: A6
Undoubtedly chic, this cosmopolitan bar is ideally nestled between boutiques and shops. Contemporary delights such as sautéed baby artichoke hearts are served along side an assortment of light bites.
50% OFF FOOD | 10 | FRI | SAT
Fusion

BOMBAY LOUNGE
020 7278 5080
3 Penton Street, N1 9PT
Nearest Station: Angel Map: A6
A taste of India can be found in this attractive restaurant. The kitchen overflows with enthusiasm from the chefs, who work hard to bring diners an enjoyable meal and an unforgettable experience.
50% OFF FOOD | 4 | FRI ✓ | SAT ✓ | ✱
Indian

DI MONFORTE
020 7226 1475
70-72 Liverpool Road, N1 0QH
Nearest Station: Angel Map: A6
A perfect dining venue, encompassing the true authenticity of an Italian restaurant whilst also offering a blend of sophistication and ambience for intimate dining. Fine ingredients imported from Italy.
2FOR1 MAIN COURSE | FRI | SAT
Italian

DOLCETTO RESTAURANT
020 7278 2825
18 Chapel Market, N1 9EZ
Nearest Station: Angel Map: A6
Typically rustic, the Head Chef brings a genuine taste of Italy to Islington. Blending the classic with the contemporary, the menu is bursting with favourites and specialties. Try home-made desserts.
2FOR1 3 COURSES | FRI × | SAT × | ▲
Italian

GUFAA
020 7354 5465
39 Upper Street, N1 0PN
Nearest Station: Angel Map: A6
A colourful restaurant where great tasting food is certainly on the cards, ranging through all the traditional favourites and edging into the more unfamiliar territory of some regional delicacies.
2FOR1 3 COURSES | FRI ✱ | SAT ✱ | ▲
Indian

MIZ EN BOUCHE
020 7998 0640
316 St John Street, EC1V 4NT
Nearest Station: Angel Map: A6
Bringing a fun element to French cuisine, Miz en Bouche have created an eclectic menu that focuses on authentic French food whilst adding a contemporary twist.
50% OFF FOOD | FRI ✱ | SAT ✱
European

PARVEEN TANDOORI
020 7354 5993
6 Theberton Street, N1 0QX
Nearest Station: Angel Map: A6
The oldest Indian restaurant in Islington enjoys an excellent reputation amongst locals for their mouth-watering cuisine, prepared on site since 1977.
25% OFF TOTAL | 10 | FRI | SAT | ✱
Indian

PASHA
020 7226 1454
301 Upper Street, N1 2TU
Nearest Station: Angel Map: A6
Deliciously tasty Turkish delights to be discovered in a fashionable location. Traditional influences are married with modern tastes, bringing Turkish cuisine with a difference.
2FOR1 3 COURSES | FRI ✱ | SAT ✱
Turkish

SPICES
020 7837 7151
10 Chapel Market, N1 9EZ
Nearest Station: Angel Map: A6
Step into the ruby red shop-front and indulge in a freshly cooked curry. Guaranteeing to please you with flavour in every dish, chefs promise that diners will be consistently delighted with their choices.
2FOR1 3 COURSES | FRI ✓ | SAT ✓
Indian

STRADA
020 7226 9742
105-106 Upper Street, N1 1QN
Nearest Station: Angel Map: A6
Offering fresh, bold dishes inspired by flavours of Italian city life - Strada serves a selection of indulgent tastes, to those seeking a blissful escape to laidback Italian life. *Excludes Pizzettas.
25% OFF TOTAL | 6 | FRI ✓ | SAT × | ▲
Italian

BACCHUS PUB AND KITCHEN
020 7613 0477
177 Hoxton Street, N1 6PJ
Nearest Station: Hoxton Map: A7
Escape the hustle and bustle of daily life and revive yourself with good, honest, and simple cooking. The perfect place to relax and unwind with cool interior, great music, good beers, and hearty food.
25% OFF TOTAL | 6 | FRI ✓ | SAT ✓ | SUN | ▲
Modern British

RIBEIRA
020 3119 0037
46a De Beauvoir Crescent, N1 5RY
Nearest Station: Haggerston Map: A7
Ribeira is a hidden sanctuary, nestled in London's East End. Open for breakfast lunch and dinner - serving unique and modern dishes alongside South American tapas and sharing platters.
25% OFF TOTAL | 6 | FRI ✱ | SAT × | SUN
South American

BOGAYO
020 7012 1226
320 Old Street, EC1V 9DR
Nearest Station: Old Street Map: B7
Restaurant rooted in the warm, mellow flavours of Morocco. Food comes in generous portions whether you plump for their excellent tagines or a big plate of couscous. Real rustic charm in a very urban spot.
50% OFF FOOD | 10 | FRI | SAT
Moroccan

CHICO BANDITO
020 7613 1230
74 Luke Street, EC2A 4PY
Nearest Station: Shoreditch High Street Map: B7
Bursting burritos and flavoursome fajitas can be found in this fun-filled Mexican joint. Top off your experience by ordering one of the delicious cocktails and you'll have yourself the perfect evening out.
50% OFF FOOD | 6 | FRI ✓ | SAT ✓ | ▲
Mexican

FLORIPA LONDON
020 7613 4228
91-93 Great Eastern Street, EC2A 3HZ
Nearest Station: Old Street Map: B7
Fusing together Brazil and London, this eatery is a music venue, an international bar and an Ipanema-inspired bordello. Guests can indulge in a Brazilian Sunday Roast whilst savouring a cocktail.
50% OFF FOOD | 6 | FRI ✓ | SAT ✓ | ✱
Portuguese

LENA
020 7739 5714
66 Great Eastern Street, EC2A 3JT
Nearest Station: Old Street Map: B7
Specialising in the earthy, full flavours of southern Italian cuisine, Lena is run with a keen investment in traditional hospitality, in a light, vibrant Shoreditch space.
2FOR1 MAIN COURSE | FRI | SAT | ▲
Italian

MAI'DA LONDON
020 7739 2645
148-150 Bethnal Green Road, E2 6DG
Nearest Station: Shoreditch High Street Map: B7
Mai'da London is a fantastic restaurant that serves a fine line in Indian and Indo-Chinese cuisine. Popular with good reason, the food is superbly fresh and excels in taste and flavour.
2FOR1 3 COURSES | FRI ✓ | SAT ✓
Indian

NEW REGENCY
020 7336 8636
93 Old Street, EC1V 9AY
Nearest Station: Old Street Map: B7
A great little classic Indian restaurant set among the shops, cafés and restaurants of Old Street, where the flavours are rich and the spices well judged, resulting in a superbly satisfying meal.
25% OFF TOTAL | 2 | FRI ✓ | SAT ✓ | ✱
Indian

THAI THAI EAST
020 7490 5230
110 Old Street, EC1V 9BD
Nearest Station: Old Street Map: B7
Stay healthy whilst being blown away by the excellent culinary skill that goes into each dish. Here, you will be guaranteed a highly enjoyable dining experience in an elegantly decorated restaurant.
25% OFF TOTAL | 10 | FRI ✓ | SAT ✓
Thai

YARD
020 7336 7758
140 Tabernacle Street, EC2A 4SD
Nearest Station: Old Street Map: B7
A trendy pizza joint located in a converted fire station. An extremely popular restaurant renowned for its yard-length pizzas and the shredded duck or Parma ham toppings.
2FOR1 MAIN COURSE | FRI ✓ | SAT ✱
Pizza

1901 AT THE ANDAZ HOTEL
☎020 7618 7000

40 Liverpool Street, EC2M 7QN
Nearest Station: Liverpool Street Map: C7
Introducing an entirely fresh and dynamic approach to fine dining, with sumptuous dishes created using the most diverse home-grown produce, cooked simply and delivered with style. Awarded 3 AA rosettes.

2FOR1 MAIN COURSE | FRI ✓ | SAT ✓ | SUN | ▲ — British

BONDS RESTAURANT & BAR
☎020 7657 8088

5 Threadneedle Street, EC2R 8AY
Nearest Station: Bank Map: C7
At the very heart of Threadneedles, Bonds provides a fresh approach to modern European cuisine. This modern restaurant and the superb cuisine makes it a long time favourite with locals and visitors alike.

25% OFF TOTAL | 10 | FRI ✓ | SAT × | SUN — European

CAFFE CONCERTO ST. PAUL'S
☎0844 335 8403

1 New Change, EC2V 6DL
Nearest Station: St. Paul's Map: C7
Luxurious, contemporary dining with a focus on favourites from the Italian table. Carbonara to chicken Milanese along with some outstanding vegetarian, seafood, and salad options.

25% OFF TOTAL | 4 | FRI ✓ | SAT ✓ — Italian

CATCH AT THE ANDAZ HOTEL
☎020 7618 7200

40 Liverpool Street, EC2M 7QN
Nearest Station: Liverpool Street Map: C7
A shrine to the sea, the stunning stained glass windows and wood panelled walls create an exceptional atmosphere in which sensational seafood dishes can be thoroughly enjoyed. Awarded 1 AA Rosette.

2FOR1 MAIN COURSE | FRI ✓ | SAT ✱ | SUN | ▲ — Seafood

CLAUSE
☎020 7283 5181

1 Lovat Lane, EC3R 8DT
Nearest Station: Monument Map: C7
Having spent the day dealing with deadlines and copious work-related demands, it seems fair that the evening is spent playing just as hard. Clause serves delicious cocktails and tasty, no nonsense food.

2FOR1 3 COURSES | FRI ☎ | SAT ☎ | SUN — Multi-Cuisine

THE CUBAN BAR
☎020 7256 2202

1 Ropemaker Street, EC2Y 9AW
Nearest Station: Moorgate Map: C7
Stylish bar with lots of vitality where you can enjoy bright, zingy Cuban tapas and grill-style mains with fruity, spicy marinades. Worth topping off with a sparkling Habanero cocktail.

2FOR1 MAIN COURSE | FRI ✱ | SAT ✱ | SUN — Cuban

EASTWAY AT THE ANDAZ HOTEL
☎020 7618 7400

40 Liverpool Street, EC2M 7QN
Nearest Station: Liverpool Street Map: C7
Eclectic, full-bodied food at this New York-style brasserie. Distinctive grill dishes and signature cocktails top things off in a stylish and lively atmosphere.

2FOR1 MAIN COURSE | FRI ✓ | SAT ✓ | ▲ — Brasserie

GOLDFISH
☎020 7726 0308

46 Gresham Street, EC2V 7AY
Nearest Station: Bank Map: C7
Simple stained-glass effects and a spare, open layout give Goldfish City a distinctive mood. The food is roundly excellent, with their bento boxes and ramen soups, particularly hitting the spot.

2FOR1 3 COURSES | FRI ✓ | SAT × | SUN — Chinese

GOW'S RESTAURANT & OYSTER BAR
☎020 7920 9645

81 Old Broad Street, EC2M 1PR
Nearest Station: Liverpool Street Map: C7
Classic, long-established restaurant whose speciality is fresh, flavourful seafood of exceptional quality. Ideal for oyster lovers and those who like to watch the world go by.

2FOR1 MAIN COURSE | FRI ✓ | SAT ✱ | SUN | ✱ | ▲ — Seafood

HARRY'S ABCHURCH YARD
☎020 7623 2355

5 Abchurch Yard, EC4N 7BA
Nearest Station: Monument Map: C7
Whether you visit for a glass of wine with friends or a meal with the family, home-made flavoursome food and a friendly welcome awaits you in this charming, rustic restaurant and bar.

50% OFF FOOD | 10 | FRI ✓ | SAT × | SUN | ✱ | ▲ — British

HARRY'S IRONMONGER LANE
☎020 7600 0300

17-20 Ironmonger Lane, EC2V 8EP
Nearest Station: Bank Map: C7
Sophisticated restaurant, sleek service and contemporary cocktail lounge, fine food, eclectic wines and cool cocktails. Perfect for a refined lunch or funky late night dancing.

50% OFF FOOD | FRI ✓ | SAT × | SUN | ▲ — British

LA TASCA
☎020 7256 2381

16 Eldon Street, EC2M 7LA
Nearest Station: Liverpool Street Map: C7
Quintessentially Spanish, La Tasca's fresh and exciting menu offers something for everyone. Their tapas dishes are sincerely authentic, while their paellas always deliver on flavour.

25% OFF TOTAL | 8 | FRI ✓ | SAT × | ▲ — Spanish

LUC'S BRASSERIE
☎020 7621 0666

17-22 Leadenhall Market, EC3V 1LR
Nearest Station: Monument Map: C7
The handsome dining room of this Parisian-style brasserie goes with its classical, appetising French dishes for an uncluttered, refined meal in the centre of London.

50% OFF FOOD | 6 | FRI ✱ | SAT ✱ | SUN | ✱ | ▲ — French

OFF THE WALL RESTAURANT
☎020 7562 3030

Apex London Wall Hotel, 7-9 Copthall Avenue, EC2R 7NJ
Nearest Station: Moorgate Map: C7
Considerate of special dietary requirements, the menu is European and oozes finesse. Private dining is available in an effortlessly chic room for those precious celebrations deserving of a touch of class.

50% OFF FOOD | 6 | FRI ☎ | SAT ☎ | ▲ — Modern European

ORTEGA
☎020 7623 1818

26-27 Leadenhall Market, EC3V 1LR
Nearest Station: Monument Map: C7
A vibrant tapas bar that captures the magical liveliness of a bustling Spanish city. Accompany your array of dishes or sizzling grill with freshly made Sangria or a premium Spanish beer.

50% OFF FOOD | 4 | FRI ☎ | SAT ✱ | SUN | ▲ — Spanish

OSTERIA DEL MERCATO
☎020 7929 6742

13-15 Leadenhall Place, EC3V 1LR
Nearest Station: Monument Map: C7
A perfect location in the heart of the City of London for those seeking an escape from the 'hustle and bustle' of city life; Osteria del Mercato is an ideal location for relaxing Italian meal.

25% OFF TOTAL | 6 | FRI × | SAT × | SUN — Italian

RUCOLA ITALIAN RESTAURANT
☎020 7600 7776

6 Foster Lane, EC2V 6HH
Nearest Station: St. Paul's Map: C7
Rucola, Italian for rocket leaf, is a well-established eatery that puts a contemporary spin on classic dishes. Relax with a crisp glass of carefully selected wine in the shadow of St. Paul's cathedral.

2FOR1 3 COURSES | FRI ✓ | SAT × | SUN | ✱ — Italian

SAFFRON RED
☎020 7283 4376

78-79 Leadenhall Street, EC3A 3DH
Nearest Station: Aldgate Map: C7
A member of the well-reputed Saffron Restaurant Group, Saffron Red in London is a popular addition to the whole host and variety of Asian and Indian restaurants in the capital.

50% OFF FOOD | 10 | FRI ✓ | SAT ✓ | SUN | ✱ | ▲ — Indian

SWITHINS RESTAURANT
☎020 7623 6853

21 St Swithins Lane, EC4N 8AD
Nearest Station: Bank Map: C7
One of London's finest seafood restaurants specialising in fish and crustacea. Situated in an elegant dining room, diners can enjoy divine food with complementing fine wines and vintage champagnes.

50% OFF FOOD | 4 | FRI ✓ | SAT ✓ | ✱ — Seafood

YAGER
☎020 7236 5318

2-3 Old Change Peters Hill, EC4M 8EN
Nearest Station: Mansion House Map: C7
Unique hidden gem that is truly one of a kind. Professional, comfortable, embracing and friendly, Yager Bar is where good food and drink meets excellent service in a great environment.

25% OFF TOTAL | 6 | FRI ✱ | SAT × | ▲ — Contemporary

THE BOROUGH BAR AND DINING ☎020 7407 6962
10-18 London Bridge Street, SE1 9SG
Nearest Station: London Bridge Map: D7
A comfortable bar and restaurant with its own unique character. Enjoy a snack at the bar or a meal in the raised dining area, taking advantage of the English and continental cuisine and the nightly music.

2FOR1 MAIN COURSE | FRI ✓ | SAT ✱ | SUN | ✱ — English and Continental

CAFÉ ROUGE 020 7378 0097
Hays Galleria, Tooley Street, SE1 2HD
Nearest Station: London Bridge Map: D7
French sophistication on the British high street – enjoy seasonally changing French dishes and a continental wine selection, served in a relaxed environment with an undeniable flair of Parisian chic.

25% OFF TOTAL | 6 | FRI ✓ | SAT ✓ | ✱ | ▲ — French

CHAMPOR-CHAMPOR ☎020 7403 4600
62-64 Weston Street, SE1 3QJ
Nearest Station: London Bridge Map: D7
Be seated at a uniquely decorated table, where select dishes are created and served in their own unique way. Tribal artefacts and statues rub shoulders with stylish modern art pieces. 1 AA Rosette.

2FOR1 2 COURSES | FRI | SAT | SUN | ✱ | ▲ — Asian

LONDINIUM ☎020 7855 2225
8-18 London Bridge Street, SE1 9SG
Nearest Station: London Bridge Map: D7
Roman history mixed with contemporary design, delivering patrons an astonishing selection of delectable dishes, complemented by relaxing music and a welcoming ambience. A recipe for an enjoyable evening.

2FOR1 MAIN COURSE | FRI ✓ | SAT ✓ | ✱ — British

NORTHBANK RESTAURANT & BAR ☎020 7329 9299
1 Pauls Walk, EC4V 3QH
Nearest Station: Mansion House Map: D7
Tucked under the Millennium Bridge with outstanding Thameside views, Northbank is a friendly, stylish modern British restaurant and bar, passionate about sourcing fresh ingredients for their dishes.

50% OFF FOOD | 4 | FRI ✓ | SAT ✓ — International

QUARTER BAR AND LOUNGE ☎020 7855 2200
London Bridge Hotel, 8-18 London Bridge Street, SE1 9SG
Nearest Station: London Bridge Map: D7
Find a chic, sophisticated atmosphere at The Quarter Bar and Lounge, where you can enjoy large platters to light bites, cakes and pastries and sandwiches and salads.

50% OFF FOOD | 6 | FRI ✓ | SAT ✓ — International

ROAST ☎0845 0347 300
The Floral Hall, Borough Market, Stoney Street, SE1 1TL
Nearest Station: London Bridge Map: D7
Here there is something to see from every seat, be it the liveliness of the open kitchen to the beauty of St Paul's Cathedral. Serves gutsy food and delicious drinks. Awarded 1 AA Rosette.

2FOR1 MAIN COURSE | FRI × | SAT × | SUN | ▲ — British

THE SHAD INDIAN ☎020 7407 9555
96 Tooley Street, SE1 2TH
Nearest Station: London Bridge Map: D7
Unique cooking methods and authentic Indian recipes create outstanding dishes on offer at this central London restaurant. The house specialities are worth a try, from a lamb shank to a chicken pasanda.

2FOR1 2 COURSES | FRI ✓ | SAT ✓ — Indian

SILKA ☎020 7378 6161
6-8 Southwark Street, SE1 1TL
Nearest Station: London Bridge Map: D7
Enter this relaxing haven of a restaurant, where the calm and soothing atmosphere provides a perfect antidote to the hustle and bustle of the city. Eclectic Indian dishes make for a divine menu.

2FOR1 3 COURSES | FRI ✓ | SAT ✓ | SUN | ✱ — Indian

SOUTHWARK ROOMS ☎020 7357 9301
60 Southwark Street, SE1 1UN
Nearest Station: London Bridge Map: D7
Lively bar and restaurant in Southwark, where patrons often spill out onto the patio and take in the vibrancy of the capital city. Enjoy the modern European menu that is lined with tasty tempting treats.

2FOR1 3 COURSES | FRI × | SAT × | SUN | ▲ — International

ANTICO RESTAURANT AND LOUNGE BAR ☎020 7407 4682
214 Bermondsey Street, SE1 3TQ
Nearest Station: Borough Map: E7
Antico delivers rustic Italian cuisine, giving traditional dishes a modern flair such as the ever-popular ragu pappardelle and slow-roasted pork tortelloni. Also serves up cleverly crafted cocktails.

25% OFF TOTAL | 6 | FRI × | SAT × | ▲ — Italian

GREGG'S BAR AND GRILL ☎020 7378 24 56
Bermondsey Square, Tower Bridge Road, SE1 3UN
Nearest Station: London Bridge Map: E7
Gregg Wallace, co-presenter of MasterChef, prides himself on the contemporary European menu composed of honest food. Guests should sample the spinach and goats cheese lasagne or the hearty lamp chops.

50% OFF FOOD | 4 | FRI ✓ | SAT ✓ — British

CHINO LATINO ☎020 7769 2500
18 Albert Embankment, SE1 7TJ
Nearest Station: Vauxhall Map: F5
Another great Chino Latino venue offering contemporary Pan-Asian cuisine and divine cocktails. The constantly evolving menu delivers an option for every appetite. Awarded 2 AA Rosettes.

25% OFF TOTAL | 4 | FRI × | SAT × | ▲ — Asian

THE CORIANDER ☎020 7582 9569
332 Kennington Lane, SE11 5HY
Nearest Station: Vauxhall Map: F5
Stylish and sophisticated Indian restaurant with a focus on superb service and a specialisation in the richness and piquancy of North Indian and Bangladeshi cuisine.

2FOR1 MAIN COURSE | FRI ✱ | SAT ✱ | ▲ — Indian/Bangladeshi

CAFFE CONCERTO KINGS ROAD ☎0844 335 8403
52 King's Road, SW3 4UD
Nearest Station: Sloane Square Map: F3
Luxurious, contemporary dining with a focus on favourites from the Italian table. Carbonara to chicken Milanese along with some outstanding vegetarian, seafood, and salad options.

25% OFF TOTAL | 4 | FRI ✱ | SAT ✓ — Italian

THE CADOGAN ARMS ☎020 7352 6500
298 King's Road, SW3 5UG
Nearest Station: South Kensington Map: F2
Homely restaurant in the heart of Chelsea; expect a menu of British seasonal produce sourced from select UK farms, excellent cocktails and real ales.

50% OFF FOOD | 8 | FRI ✱ | SAT ✱ | SUN | ▲ — British

JAKOBS CAFE & DELI ☎020 7998 3797
84 Fulham Road, SW3 6HR
Nearest Station: South Kensington Map: F2
A friendly establishment showcasing quality Middle Eastern food and classical food dishes. Everything is freshly prepared and cooked beautifully, delivering delicious tastes at a most reasonable price.

25% OFF TOTAL | 4 | FRI ✓ | SAT ✓ | ✱ — Middle Eastern

JUJU ☎020 7351 5998
316-318 King's Road, SW3 5UH
Nearest Station: South Kensington Map: F2
A stunningly sleek, acclaimed addition to London's bar scene, JuJu is renowned for its mixology, but can also be relied upon for some outstandingly tasty, Far East-influenced sharing platters.

50% OFF FOOD | 10 | FRI | SAT × | ✱ | ▲ — Pan-Asian

KINGS ROAD STEAKHOUSE & GRILL ☎020 7351 9997
386 King's Road, SW3 5UZ
Nearest Station: South Kensington Map: F2
Succulent juicy steaks will have your mouth watering and your taste buds tingling at this traditional steakhouse. Timeless English dishes are also available in this popular vibrant restaurant.

25% OFF TOTAL | 10 | FRI ✱ | SAT ✱ | ▲ — Steakhouse

LA PIZZERIA ☎020 7823 3878
125 Sydney Street, SW3 6NR
Nearest Station: Sloane Square Map: F2
Take delight in authentic Italian tastes as this restaurant cooks pizza to perfection in their traditional wood-fired oven. When the sun prevails the garden area makes for fine al fresco dining.

25% OFF TOTAL | 8 | FRI ✓ | SAT ✓ — Italian

MARCO PIERRE WHITE
☎020 7352 3435

4 Sydney Street, SW3 6PP
Nearest Station: South Kensington Map: F2
The Sydney Street Grill is a traditional restaurant on the border of Chelsea and South Kensington, serving a mouth-watering range of classic steak cuts, as well as a variety of hot dishes from the grill.

25% OFF TOTAL | 6 | FRI | SAT — British

OSTERIA DELL'ARANCIO
☎020 7349 8111

383 King's Road, W10 0LP
Nearest Station: South Kensington Map: F2
Experience Italian culinary traditions at Osteria dell'Arancio. Designed to allow guests to sample multiple courses, the menu is authentic and all ingredients are sourced from Marche and Tuscany.

2FOR1 MAIN COURSE | FRI × | SAT * — Italian

THREE5 WORLD TAPAS
☎020 7225 7535

35 Ixworth Place, SW3 3QX
Nearest Station: South Kensington Map: F2
Experience something unique at Three5, where an array of international dishes are served in tapas-sized portions. Perfect for sampling a little piece of everything.

25% OFF TOTAL | 10 | FRI ✓ | SAT ✓ — European

BELLA'S RESTAURANT
☎020 7351 7370

323 Fulham Road, SW10 9QL
Nearest Station: Gloucester Road Map: F1
Bella's is a lovely authentic Sicilian bistro and restaurant. Available for breakfast, lunch and dinner, there is a delightful selection of Italian dishes to tempt your palate.

50% OFF FOOD | 6 | FRI × | SAT × | SUN | * — Italian

COQUINE
☎020 7341 7678

160 Old Brompton Road, SW5 0BA
Nearest Station: Gloucester Road Map: F1
Whether guests are seeking a small Mediterranean bite upstairs or a party downstairs, this chic venue caters for all. With a cocktail list created by Thierry Brocher, Coquine is fabulously popular.

2FOR1 2 COURSES | FRI ✓ | SAT ✓ | SUN | * — Mediterranean

COUSCOUS DARNA RESTAURANT
☎020 7584 2919

91 Old Brompton Road, SW7 3LD
Nearest Station: South Kensington Map: F1
The distinctive aromas, colours and textures of Morocco are brought out to their full extent in this restaurant that sets its stall on an authentic experience. *Booking is essential. Always mention GS.

25% OFF TOTAL | 8 | FRI * | SAT * | * — Moroccan

DALL'ARTISTA
☎020 7373 1659

243 Old Brompton Road, SW5 9HP
Nearest Station: Earl's Court Map: F1
Guests at this wonderful local restaurant are always delighted with the genuine Italian experience it offers. An honest and authentic taste of Italy can be enjoyed by all the family.

25% OFF TOTAL | 4 | FRI ✓ | SAT — Italian

PERIDOT
☎020 7244 5555

The Bentley Hotel, SW7 4JX
Nearest Station: Gloucester Road Map: F1
Delightfully charming and oozing with class, Peridot is typically characteristic of the hotel it resides in. Guests will marvel over the delicate pastries and delectable sandwiches during afternoon tea.

2FOR1 3 COURSES | FRI | SAT — Fine Dining

STRADA
020 7835 1180

237 Earls Court Road, SW5 9AH
Nearest Station: Earl's Court Map: F1
Offering fresh, bold dishes inspired by flavours of Italian city life - Strada serves a selection of indulgent tastes, to those seeking a blissful escape to laidback Italian life. *Excludes Pizzettas.

25% OFF TOTAL | 6 | FRI ✓ | SAT × — Italian

AS GREEK AS IT GETS
☎020 7244 7777

233 Earl's Court Road, SW5 9AH
Nearest Station: Earl's Court Map: E1
A truly authentic Greek experience. Perfect for lunch or dinner boasting a delectable menu filled with Greek flavours and specialities, most definitely to be enjoyed with classic wine or some feisty ouzo.

25% OFF TOTAL | 6 | FRI ✓ | SAT — Greek

THE ATRIUM RESTAURANT
☎020 7341 6205

147 Cromwell Road, SW5 0TH
Nearest Station: Earl's Court Map: E1
Modern takes on American classic dishes are on offer in the recently transformed restaurant of this beautiful Kensington hotel. Enjoy the drama of the live-theatre kitchen while sipping a yummy cocktail.

2FOR1 MAIN COURSE | FRI ✓ | SAT ✓ | SUN — North American

AUBREY
☎020 7589 6300

109-113 Queens Gate, SW7 5LR
Nearest Station: South Kensington Map: E1
Memorable surroundings to enjoy food at breakfast, lunch, dinner, choosing from the restaurant's eclectic menu, which blends fresh British fare with flavours from around the world.

50% OFF FOOD | 2 | FRI * | SAT * — European

CAFÉ ROUGE
020 7938 4200

2 Lancer Square, W8 4EH
Nearest Station: High Street Kensington Map: E1
French sophistication on the British high street – enjoy seasonally changing French dishes and a continental wine selection, served in a relaxed environment with an undeniable flair of Parisian chic.

25% OFF TOTAL | 6 | FRI ✓ | SAT ✓ | * — French

CAFFE CONCERTO KNIGHTSBRIDGE
☎0844 335 8403

88-90 Kensington High Street, W8 4SG
Nearest Station: High Street Kensington Map: E1
Luxurious, contemporary dining with a focus on favourites from the Italian table. Carbonara to chicken Milanese along with some outstanding vegetarian, seafood, and salad options.

25% OFF TOTAL | 4 | FRI * | SAT ✓ — Italian

CONSORTIA @ HOLIDAY INN
☎0871 942 9100

97 Cromwell Road, SW7 4DN
Nearest Station: Gloucester Road Map: E1
Smartly decked-out, unfussy and welcoming restaurant in the Holiday Inn Kensington Forum. Serves a strong array of contemporary European dishes in its well-lit, open surroundings.

25% OFF TOTAL | 6 | FRI ✓ | SAT ✓ | * — International

FIVE 25 LOUNGE @ HARRINGTON HALL
☎020 7396 9696

5-25 Harrington Gardens, SW7 4JW
Nearest Station: Gloucester Road Map: E1
A combination of warmth and elegance, with comfortable traditional furnishings. Enjoy a leisurely drink or simply relax by the beautiful marble fireplace; a calm and warming spot to unwind.

50% OFF FOOD | FRI ✓ | SAT ✓ — British

FIVE 25 RESTAURANT @ HARRINGTON HALL
☎020 7396 9696

5-25 Harrington Gardens, SW7 4JW
Nearest Station: Gloucester Road Map: E1
After browsing all of the shops that the local area has to offer, what better place to unwind than the restaurant at Harrington Hall Hotel. Feast to fill your appetite or simply sip your favourite drink.

50% OFF FOOD | 4 | FRI ✓ | SAT ✓ — British

THE JAM CUPBOARD
☎020 7584 8100

61 Gloucester Road, SW7 4PE
Nearest Station: Gloucester Road Map: E1
In the heart of one of the most exclusive area's in London, Rydges is an amiable place to rest and dine after a long day exploring the area. The Jam Cupboard offers early breakfasts to evening dinners.

50% OFF FOOD | FRI ✓ | SAT ✓ — Modern European

LIGHT OF INDIA
☎020 7584 7654

67-69 Gloucester Road, SW7 4PG
Nearest Station: Gloucester Road Map: E1
Located in the prestigious area of Kensington, this long-established eatery vaunts elegant décor and an affable ambiance. Chef Kumar is renowned for fusing original flavours with a contemporary style.

25% OFF TOTAL | 10 | FRI ✓ | SAT ✓ — Indian

MEMORIES OF INDIA
☎020 7589 6450

18 Gloucester Road, SW7 4RB
Nearest Station: Gloucester Road Map: E1
Memories of India serves a range of classic, flavourful curries in unfussy, smart surroundings.

25% OFF TOTAL | 10 | FRI ✓ | SAT ✓ — Indian

To understand what the restaurant icons mean, please see the inside back cover.

PASHA LOUNGE & RESTAURANT ☎020 7589 7969
1 Gloucester Road, SW7 4PP
Nearest Station: Gloucester Road Map: E1
Cosy and exotic North African restaurant with plush cushions and authentic design. Boasts broad-based and tasty food, packed with the mild-spiced flavours that characterise North African cuisine.
50% OFF FOOD | FRI ✱ | SAT ✱ — African

THE PATISSERIE ☎020 7835 1990
77a Gloucester Road, SW7 4SS
Nearest Station: Gloucester Road Map: E1
Gloucester Road favourite, popular with students, tourists, business folk and weekend munchers alike. Visit any time of day, take the weight off your feet and enjoy some tasty food.
50% OFF FOOD | ♟ 4 | FRI ▯ | SAT ▯ — International

PREZZO 020 7930 4288
35a Kensington High Street, W8 5BA
Nearest Station: High Street Kensington Map: E1
With a character all of its own, Prezzo oozes contemporary style and enduring charm. Signature pastas, stone-baked pizzas and classic Italian dishes promise a perfect dining choice for the whole family.
2FOR1 MAIN COURSE | FRI × | SAT × | ▲ — Italian

STRADA 020 7938 4648
29 High Street Kensington, W8 4NP
Nearest Station: High Street Kensington Map: E1
Offering fresh, bold dishes inspired by flavours of Italian city life - Strada serves a selection of indulgent tastes, to those seeking a blissful escape to laidback Italian life. *Excludes Pizzettas.
25% OFF TOTAL | ♟ 6 | FRI ✓ | SAT × | ▲ — Italian

THE BRASSERIE ☎020 7262 4461
Thistle Kensington Gardens, W2 3HL
Nearest Station: Queensway Map: D1
From afternoon tea with a friend, or an intimate dinner with a loved one - this venue pleases an array of guests with its expansive menu and its fantastic view of Kensington Gardens.
2FOR1 MAIN COURSE | FRI ✱ | SAT ✱ — International

CURRY PLACE ☎020 7243 8992
36 Queensway, W2 3RX
Nearest Station: Queensway Map: D1
The luxurious décor and delightful aromas offer a warm welcome to this Indian-inspired venue. They infuse passion and experience into every dish to create a gourmet experience that won't be forgotten.
2FOR1 MAIN COURSE | FRI ✱ | SAT ✱ — Indian

ANTONY'S ☎020 7243 8743
54 Porchester Road, W2 6ET
Nearest Station: Royal Oak Map: C1
Mellow and cosy little restaurant with a superb reputation among diners for its food and welcome. Authentic Polish dishes are the staple, with a wholesome and homely approach to their cooking and service.
2FOR1 MAIN COURSE | FRI ✓ | SAT ✓ — European

ARIANA RESTAURANT ☎020 7266 9200
108 Bourne Terrace, W2 5TH
Nearest Station: Royal Oak Map: C1
An excellent Iranian/Afghan restaurant with authentic décor and a warm, friendly atmosphere. Fine Persian cuisine at great prices, complemented by traditional live music.
2FOR1 3 COURSES | FRI ✱ | SAT ✱ — Middle Eastern

BEL CANTO ☎020 7262 1678
Corus Hotel Hyde Park, 1 Lancaster Gate, W2 3LG
Nearest Station: Lancaster Gate Map: C1
A theatrical dining experience, where your waiters are opera singers and their performance and service perform a rondo, conjuring up an unforgettable night of music and food. *Entertainment fee excluded.
50% OFF FOOD | ♟ 4 | FRI ✓ | SAT ✓ | SUN | ✱ | ▲ — French

BELLA ITALIA 020 7229 2439
108-110 Queensway, W2 3RR
Nearest Station: Bayswater Map: C1
Accessible Italian cuisine on the British high street – indulge in authentic sharing platters, hand stretched pizzas and hearty pasta dishes, served with a healthy dose of gregarious Italian hospitality.
25% OFF TOTAL | ♟ 6 | FRI × | SAT × | SUN | ▲ — Italian

BELLA ITALIA 020 7792 2880
55-57 Queensway, W2 4QH
Nearest Station: Bayswater Map: C1
Accessible Italian cuisine on the British high street – indulge in authentic sharing platters, hand stretched pizzas and hearty pasta dishes, served with a healthy dose of gregarious Italian hospitality.
25% OFF TOTAL | ♟ 6 | FRI × | SAT × | SUN | ▲ — Italian

CAFÉ ROUGE 020 7221 1509
Whiteleys Centre, Queensway, W2 4SB
Nearest Station: Bayswater Map: C1
French sophistication on the British high street – enjoy seasonally changing French dishes and a continental wine selection, served in a relaxed environment with an undeniable flair of Parisian chic.
25% OFF TOTAL | ♟ 6 | FRI ✓ | SAT ✓ | ✱ | ▲ — French

CHERRYJAM ☎020 7727 9950
58 Porchester Road, W2 6ET
Nearest Station: Royal Oak Map: C1
With zingy tapas and tongue-tingling Thai bites, cherryjam is all about the vim and verve of the venue.
50% OFF FOOD | ♟ 4 | FRI ✓ | SAT ✓ | ✱ — International

THE DINING ROOM @ HILTON ☎020 7221 2217
Hilton Hyde Park, 129 Bayswater Road, W2 4RJ
Nearest Station: Queensway Map: C1
Light and high-ceilinged restaurant of the tall, striking Hilton Hyde Park. Smartly arrayed tables and splashes of colour set a convivial tone; the menu is simple, classic and very popular.
50% OFF FOOD | ♟ 10 | FRI ✓ | SAT ✓ — International

ELEMENTS RESTAURANT @ NOVOTEL 020 7266 6000
Novotel Paddington, 3 Kingdom Street, W2 6BD
Nearest Station: Paddington Map: C1
Old favourites receive a contemporary twist at this exciting venue. From light bites to hearty, wholesome meals, diners can enjoy the dishes alongside an extensive array of beverages.
50% OFF FOOD | ♟ 8 | FRI ✓ | SAT ✓ — International

THE GOLDEN HORSESHOE ☎020 7221 8788
Gala Casino, 79-81 Queensway, W2 4QH
Nearest Station: Bayswater Map: C1
A great place to spend your winnings, this casino restaurant and grill serves up seriously tasty meals. Succulent steaks and char-grilled burgers make up a fantastic part of the menu.
50% OFF FOOD | ♟ 4 | FRI ▯ | SAT ▯ — International

GOLDEN SHALIMAR 020 7262 3763
6 Spring Street, W2 3RA
Nearest Station: Paddington Map: C1
The aim at Golden Shalimar is to make your visit an enjoyable and memorable experience that leaves a lasting impression. The unrivalled customer service and imaginative fusion will see you return!
25% OFF TOTAL | ♟ 4 | FRI ✓ | SAT ✓ — Indian

LA SUITE WEST ☎020 7666 8484
41-51 Inverness Terrace, W2 3JN
Nearest Station: Bayswater Map: C1
Situated in a boutique, minimalist hotel close to Hyde Park, Suite West offers a menu that is as fresh and sophisticated as the building's design itself. International flavours touch down on every dish.
25% OFF TOTAL | FRI ▯ | SAT ▯ — Modern European

LAGENDA @ HOLIDAY VILLA HOTEL ☎020 7258 0269
Holiday Villa Hotel, 37 Leinster Gardens, W2 3AN
Nearest Station: Bayswater Map: C1
Enjoy an authentic Malaysian menu that includes chef specialities such as the delicious nasi lemak, bursting with traditional flavour and leaving you spoilt for choice. Expect a warm Malaysian welcome.
50% OFF FOOD | ♟ 4 | FRI ▯ | SAT ▯ — Chinese

MASSIS LEBANESE GRILL & BAR ☎020 7286 8000
9 Sheldon Square, W2 6HY
Nearest Station: Paddington Map: C1
This cosy, welcoming Lebanese restaurant is ensconced just off Oxford Street and offers all the mix of mellowness and zest that characterises Lebanese cuisine.
2FOR1 MAIN COURSE | FRI ✱ | SAT ✓ — Lebanese

MED MEZZE RESTAURANT
☎020 7221 5055

22 Queensway, W2 3RX

Nearest Station: Queensway Map: C1

Embracing the colours and textures of Morocco and Lebanon, Med Mezze's interior matches the cuisine in authenticity. Distinctive flavours from the Med and the Middle East characterise the food.

50% OFF FOOD | 4 | FRI ✓ | SAT × | SUN — Moroccan

MR FISH BAYSWATER
☎020 7229 4161

9 Porchester Road, W2 5DP

Nearest Station: Royal Oak Map: C1

Traditional methods are used to prepare the tastiest, freshest of fish and chips. Long-established, Mr Fish uses a unique recipe batter and only perfect potatoes to make exceedingly good food.

2FOR1 MAIN COURSE | FRI ✓ | SAT ✓ — British

OLIO'S BRASSERIE
☎0844 736 8601

1-7 Lancaster Gate, W2 3LG

Nearest Station: Lancaster Gate Map: C1

Combining British and Malaysian cuisine, the authentic chef at this venue cooks up a storm in the kitchen. Enjoy either classic or oriental dishes in this chic, ideally located restaurant.

25% OFF TOTAL | 4 | FRI ✓ | SAT ✓ | ✱ — Malaysian

TAORMINA RESTAURANT
☎020 7262 2090

19 Craven Terrace, W2 3QH

Nearest Station: Lancaster Gate Map: C1

A family-run restaurant where chefs create a stunning range of mouth-watering, traditional Italian dishes. Warm, friendly and stylish décor creates an air of authenticity for all diners.

50% OFF FOOD | 2 | FRI ✱ | SAT ✱ | SUN — Italian

THE UNION BAR & GRILL
☎020 7289 3063

4 Sheldon Square, W2 6EZ

Nearest Station: Paddington Map: C1

Situated alongside the canal at Paddington Waterside, The Union Bar and Grill provides the ideal location for a relaxed meal or drink, amidst the hustle and bustle of city life. *Not available on Thursdays

2FOR1 3 COURSES | FRI × | SAT ✓ | ✱ — British

WHITES RESTAURANT
☎0871 376 9022

Hyde Park Hotel, 90-92 Lancaster Gate, W2 3NR

Nearest Station: Lancaster Gate Map: C1

Priding themselves on their prime location, this venue is perfect for refuelling after sightseeing or light lunches with colleagues. British and European inspired, the menu oozes unmistakable finesse.

50% OFF FOOD | 8 | FRI ✓ | SAT ✓ | ▲ — British

AKASH TANDOORI
☎020 7706 1788

500a Edgeware Road, W2 1EJ

Nearest Station: Edgware Road (Bakerloo) Map: B1

Real home-made Indian food, prepared and presented in the true Indian way, including a great selection of appetising starters, delicious curries and fresh poppadoms, all delivering great value for money.

2FOR1 MAIN COURSE | FRI ✓ | SAT ✓ | ✱ | ▲ — Indian

CAFÉ ROUGE
020 7286 2266

30 Clifton Road, W9 1ST

Nearest Station: Warwick Avenue Map: B1

French sophistication on the British high street – enjoy seasonally changing French dishes and a continental wine selection, served in a relaxed environment with an undeniable flair of Parisian chic.

25% OFF TOTAL | 6 | FRI ✓ | SAT ✓ | ✱ | ▲ — French

LE COCHONNET
☎020 7289 0393

1 Lauderdale Parade, W9 1LU

Nearest Station: Maida Vale Map: B1

A welcoming, vital and colourful little restaurant specialising particularly in fresh-cooked, tasty and eclectic pizzas, alongside an array of hearty breakfasts, deli dishes, and English and Italian mains.

25% OFF TOTAL | 6 | FRI ✱ | SAT ✱ — Italian

AGRA TANDOORI
020 7613 2613

277 Hackney Road, E2 8NA

Nearest Station: Hoxton Map: A8

Simple, savvy and well-established neighbourhood tandoori restaurant on the Hackney Road, which is ideal to drop in for an easy, substantial and filling curry.

50% OFF FOOD | 2 | FRI ✱ | SAT ✱ — Indian

THE WATERHOUSE
☎020 7033 0123

10 Orsman Road, N1 5QJ

Nearest Station: Haggerston Map: A8

Environmentally conscious diners can feast innocently in this eco-friendly training restaurant. Exceptionally prepared food composes the seasonal menu in this sustainable venue.

50% OFF FOOD | 4 | FRI ✱ | SAT ✱ | ✱ | ▲ — Locally Sourced

ALADIN
☎020 7247 8210

132 Brick Lane, E1 5DD

Nearest Station: Bethnal Green (NR) Map: B8

Traditionally a meeting place for the settling community of Brick Lane, where residents could enjoy home-spun Bangladeshi cuisine; that fine Indian cooking is still available here today.

25% OFF TOTAL | 10 | FRI ✱ | SAT ✱ — Indian

AZKA MEDITERRANEAN MEZE
☎020 3556 3497

267 Bethnal Green Road, E2 7JR

Nearest Station: Shoreditch High Street Map: B8

From an intimate meal with a loved one to a catch up with friends, Aska provides a relaxed haven from the bustling streets. Cooked on an open charcoal grill, diners can enjoy a variety of spicy kebabs.

25% OFF TOTAL | 4 | FRI × | SAT × | SUN — Mediterranean

BENGAL VILLAGE
☎020 7366 4868

75 Brick Lane, E1 6QL

Nearest Station: Shoreditch High Street Map: B8

Authentic venue with a great reputation for both quality of food and service, with an emphasis on healthy eating that is achieved through careful ingredient selection and expert cooking methods.

25% OFF TOTAL | 2 | FRI ✓ | SAT ✓ — Bangladeshi/Indian

BRICK LANE BRASSERIE
☎020 7377 8072

67 Brick Lane, E1 6QL

Nearest Station: Shoreditch High Street Map: B8

Fine member of the restaurant fraternity on this famous London street. Well regarded for its richly flavourful, tenderly cooked Indian dishes. All the usual suspects are present along with a warm ambience.

50% OFF FOOD | 2 | FRI ✱ | SAT ✱ — Indian

THE BRICKHOUSE
☎020 7247 0005

152c Brick Lane, E1 6RU

Nearest Station: Shoreditch High Street Map: B8

Vibrant and sassy venue on Brick Lane where the verve of their live entertainments in no way overshadows the superb quality of the food on offer, produced by acclaimed and talented chef Matt Reuter.

50% OFF FOOD | 10 | FRI 📱 | SAT ✱ | SUN | ✱ | ▲ — Modern European

CINNAMON BRICK LANE
☎020 7377 5526

134 Brick Lane, E1 6RL

Nearest Station: Aldgate East Map: B8

The contemporary cuisine is characterised by its delicate blend of herbs and spices, fused to create rich and unique dishes. The staff take great care to provide an enjoyable and modern experience.

25% OFF TOTAL | 4 | FRI ✓ | SAT ✓ — Indian

CITY SPICE
☎020 7247 1012

138 Brick Lane, E1 6RU

Nearest Station: Shoreditch High Street Map: B8

This Bangladeshi-inspired restaurant combines traditional dishes and décor to create an authentic experience. The relaxed atmosphere and friendly service provide a memorable night out.

25% OFF TOTAL | 10 | FRI ✓ | SAT ✓ — Indian

CURRY AND TANDOORI
☎020 7247 3713

118 Brick Lane, E1 6RU

Nearest Station: Shoreditch High Street Map: B8

With most of their dishes oven-cooked and oil kept to a minimum, this Balti house offers fresh and original curries. The kind, knowledgeable staff are always on hand to guide you and even offer lessons.

25% OFF TOTAL | 10 | FRI 📱 | SAT 📱 | ▲ — Indian

THE DRUNKEN MONKEY
☎020 7392 9606

222 Shoreditch High Street, E1 6PJ

Nearest Station: Shoreditch High Street Map: B8

An early pioneer of the drinking and dim sum trend in London, serving potent cocktails and a tantalising selection of delicious Chinese food. This innovative bar is firmly the king of the swingers.

2FOR1 2 COURSES | FRI ✓ | SAT ✱ | ▲ — Chinese

THE FAMOUS CURRY BAZAAR
020 7375 1986
77 Brick Lane, E1 6QL
Nearest Station: Shoreditch High Street Map: B8
Large selection of Indian dishes providing succulent flavours at reasonable prices. Using only traditional ingredients, dishes are prepared by experienced chefs and an exceptional menu caters for all.
2FOR1 MAIN COURSE | FRI ✓ | SAT ✓ — Indian/Bangladeshi

THE GLOBE
020 7613 9816
100 Shoreditch High Street, E1 6JQ
Nearest Station: Shoreditch High Street Map: B8
Breathtaking views of the city are more than enough to ensure you a wonderful dining experience at this top-floor restaurant. Delicious breakfasts, lunches and evening meals are equally superb.
25% OFF TOTAL | 4 | FRI ✓ | SAT ✓ | SUN | ✱ — European

JUNO
020 7729 2660
134-135 Shoreditch High Street, E1 6JE
Nearest Station: Shoreditch High Street Map: B8
An internationally inspired menu combining elements of modern European and North African cuisine. Enjoy a cocktail or cold beer as you lounge in the intimate basement or try your luck on arcade classics.
50% OFF FOOD | 2 | FRI ✱ | SAT ✱ — International

THE LIGHT BAR AND RESTAURANT
020 7247 8989
233 Shoreditch High Street, E1 6PJ
Nearest Station: Shoreditch High Street Map: B8
Head Chef Mark Caplin and his capable team have created a tempting menu of classic dishes which sit comfortably alongside the wide array of wines, beers and cocktails.
50% OFF FOOD | 10 | FRI ✓ | SAT ✓ | SUN — International

MUHIB INDIAN RESTAURANT
020 7247 7122
73 Brick Lane, E1 6QL
Nearest Station: Shoreditch High Street Map: B8
A fine member of the Brick Lane culinary community, Muhib serves staple Indian classics alongside the more unusual dishes, all served by amiable and welcoming staff in a buzzy atmosphere.
50% OFF FOOD | 4 | FRI × | SAT × — Indian

NAZRUL RESTAURANT
020 7247 2505
130 Brick Lane, E1 6RU
Nearest Station: Shoreditch High Street Map: B8
Nazrul have created a number of unique dishes to reflect the unusual and vibrant cuisine of the Indian sub-continent. Plush and intimate surroundings make this a dining experience not to be missed.
25% OFF TOTAL | FRI ✓ | SAT ✓ — Indian

PREEM AND PRITHI
020 7377 5252
124 Brick Lane, E1 6RL
Nearest Station: Aldgate East Map: B8
The secret is in the cooking, providing diners with enhanced flavours and unquestionable quality of taste. All vegetables are organic, and attentive staff are happy to advise the indecisive guest.
25% OFF TOTAL | 10 | FRI 📱 | SAT 📱 — Indian

PREEM RESTAURANT
020 7247 0397
120 Brick Lane, E1 6RL
Nearest Station: Aldgate East Map: B8
The secret is in the cooking, providing diners with enhanced flavours and unquestionable quality of taste. All vegetables are organic, and attentive staff are happy to advise the curious guest.
25% OFF TOTAL | 10 | FRI 📱 | SAT 📱 — Indian

REEMA BALTI HOUSE
020 7655 4544
48 Hanbury Street, E1 5JL
Nearest Station: Aldgate East Map: B8
One of the longest serving and most popular Indian Restaurants in London's famous Brick Lane. Relax in comfortable surroundings whilst the kitchen serves up culinary wonders.
25% OFF TOTAL | 10 | FRI ✓ | SAT ✓ | ✱ — Indian

ROCKET BISHOPSGATE
020 7377 8863
201 Bishopsgate, EC2M 3AB
Nearest Station: Shoreditch High Street Map: B8
Fresh, bright venue conveniently located close to Liverpool Street Station. Fantastic dishes make the mark, from the caramelised chicken and mango to start to the crayfish and salmon cakes for mains.
25% OFF TOTAL | 6 | FRI × | SAT ✓ | SUN — Modern Italian

SAHARA HOXTON
020 7033 4044
48 Great Eastern Street, EC2A 3EP
Nearest Station: Shoreditch High Street Map: B8
Moroccan restaurant and cafe offering an array of authentic meals, light bites and shisha throughout the day. With its relaxing ambience and welcoming staff, Sahara is ideal for any occasion.
25% OFF TOTAL | FRI ✓ | SAT ✓ | ✱ — Moroccan

SAHARA SHOREDITCH
020 7426 0838
61 Hanbury Street, Brick Lane, E1 5JP
Nearest Station: Shoreditch High Street Map: B8
For the best in Moroccan Lebanese cuisine, Sahara creates an inspiring menu with fresh ingredients and traditional Middle Eastern flavours- try ordering number of the speciality dishes and sharing.
25% OFF TOTAL | FRI ✓ | SAT ✓ — Moroccan/ Lebanese

SHAMPAN
020 7375 0475
79 Brick Lane, E1 6QL
Nearest Station: Shoreditch High Street Map: B8
Captures the very essence of Bangladeshi culture and tradition through its delicious dishes, cooked to perfection. Perfectly located to bring out the special character and flavour of the subcontinent.
25% OFF TOTAL | 10 | FRI ✓ | SAT ✓ — Indian

SHEBA RESTAURANT
020 7247 7824
136 Brick Lane, E1 6RU
Nearest Station: Shoreditch High Street Map: B8
Passionate about attending to customer's needs, desires and appetites, the staff at Sheba are welcoming, attentive and efficient. Both regular and new guests enjoy the fine Indian cuisine on offer.
25% OFF TOTAL | 10 | FRI ✓ | SAT ✓ — Indian/Bangladeshi

ADDENDUM RESTAURANT
020 7977 9500
Apex London Hotel, 1 Seething Lane, EC3N 4AX
Nearest Station: Tower Hill Map: C8
A restaurant with understated, modern décor and a menu that seduces an ever-increasing crowd of gastronomic disciples due to the chef's passion and extensive experience. Proudly awarded 1 AA Rosette.
50% OFF FOOD | 6 | FRI 📱 | SAT 📱 | SUN | ✱ | ▲ — European

BARCELONA TAPAS BAR
020 7377 5111
15 St Botolph Street, EC3A 7DT
Nearest Station: Aldgate Map: C8
An expanding family business offering delicious Spanish food in an authentic atmosphere. Barcelona boasts a bright, colourful interior and hosts a vibrant display of original flamenco costumes.
25% OFF TOTAL | 4 | FRI ✓ | SAT ✱ | SUN | ▲ — Spanish

BENGAL CUISINE
020 7377 8405
12 Brick Lane, E1 6RF
Nearest Station: Aldgate East Map: C8
The colourful history and culture of the Bengal region is fully reflected in its diverse cuisine. Enjoy the delights of Bengali food lovingly and authentically cooked by award-winning chef Mrs Kazi.
50% OFF FOOD | 10 | FRI ✓ | SAT ✓ | ✱ — Indian

BRICK LANE CLIPPER
020 7377 0022
104 Brick Lane, E1 6RL
Nearest Station: Aldgate East Map: C8
Complete your experience of the city by heading to the curry capital of London. This fabulous Brick Lane restaurant offers contemporary Indian cuisine in elegant surroundings.
2FOR1 MAIN COURSE | FRI ✱ | SAT ✱ | SUN | ✱ | ▲ — Indian

BUNDU KHAN
020 7375 2595
43 Commercial Street, E1 6BD
Nearest Station: Aldgate East Map: C8
A great environment to eat, relax, and host a special event in. The superb menu offers an outstanding array of dishes and specialities which are completely unique to the restaurant.
25% OFF TOTAL | 4 | FRI ✓ | SAT ✱ — Indian

BURY COURT
020 7929 6660
38 St Mary Axe, EC3A 8EX
Nearest Station: Aldgate Map: C8
Diners can enjoy the spacious surroundings at the latest addition to the Balls Brothers estate, whilst watching in anticipation as their food is prepared in the open kitchen.
50% OFF FOOD | 6 | FRI ✓ | SAT × | SUN | ✱ — British

CAFE BANGLA ☎020 7247 8981
128 Brick Lane, E1 6RL
Nearest Station: Shoreditch High Street Map: C8
With a warm and friendly atmosphere in the dining room, combined with the amazing food served from the kitchen, a night at Cafe Bangla is a memorable experience for all.
25% OFF TOTAL | FRI ✓ | SAT ✓ — Indian

CAFÉ SPICE NAMASTÉ ☎020 7488 9242
16 Prescot Street, E1 8AZ
Nearest Station: Aldgate East Map: C8
Chef Cyrus Todiwala's (OBE) elaborate menu demonstrates the kitchen's passion for redefined Indian cuisine. Expect unusual meats and unique spice fusions at this award winning AA Rosette restaurant.
2FOR1 MAIN COURSE | FRI ✓ | SAT ✓ | ▲ — Indian

CHILLIES ☎020 7247 7539
76 Brick Lane, E1 6RL
Nearest Station: Aldgate East Map: C8
Freshly prepared dishes can be tailored to every palate, whether you enjoy your curry exceptionally spicy or gentle and mild. Speciality, seafood and vegetarian dishes are available.
25% OFF TOTAL | 👤8 | FRI 📱 | SAT 📱 — Indian

CITY CAFÉ RESTAURANT ☎020 7709 1040
7 Pepys Street, EC3N 4AF
Nearest Station: Tower Hill Map: C8
Exceptional values are endorsed at this prestigious Tower of London venue. From business breakfasts at 6am to the à la carte evening menu, this award-winning restaurant oozes luxury.
25% OFF TOTAL | FRI ✓ | SAT ✓ | ▲ — European

CLIFTON RESTAURANT ☎020 7377 5533
1 Whitechapel Rd, E1 6TY
Nearest Station: Aldgate East Map: C8
The Bangladeshi, Pakistani and Indian-inspired menu promotes the unique cuisine of South Asia. Natural and organic spices are used in the creation of healthy dishes. Watch chefs in the open-plan kitchen.
25% OFF TOTAL | 👤10 | FRI ✓ | SAT ✓ — Indian

THE EMPRESS ☎020 7265 0745
141 Leman Street, E1 8EY
Nearest Station: Aldgate East Map: C8
Previous winners at the British Curry Awards, this family-run restaurant prides itself in delivering exceptional food. Astonishingly diverse flavours offered to diners alongside a great wine list.
2FOR1 MAIN COURSE | FRI ✱ | SAT 📱 | ▲ — Indian

THE FAMOUS MOONLIGHT ☎020 7247 6606
8 Brick Lane, E1 6RF
Nearest Station: Aldgate East Map: C8
The Famous Moonlight stands out from the crowd. With professional staff and plentiful portions, The Famous Moonlight is perfect for a quick bite or an extended dinner with family and friends.
25% OFF TOTAL | FRI ✓ | SAT ✓ — Indian

GILT LONDON ☎020 7264 1910
14 New London Street, EC3M 2RY
Nearest Station: Tower Hill Map: C8
In the heart of the city, Gilt Bar and Restaurant is the perfect place to lunch or dine in the evening. A select menu accommodates all palates and appetites, from creamy pasta to fish and chips.
25% OFF TOTAL | 👤6 | FRI ✱ | SAT ✗ | SUN | ▲ — European

HEMINGWAYS WINE BAR AND RESTAURANT ☎020 7220 7170
19 Bevis Marks, EC3A 7JB
Nearest Station: Aldgate Map: C8
A privately owned independent wine bar, restaurant and function room where high quality food is made from fine seasonal ingredients. Simply great food and wine, offering excellent value.
25% OFF TOTAL | 👤6 | FRI ✓ | SAT ✱ | SUN — European

JAMIES ☎020 7256 7279
155 Bishops Gate, EC2A 2AA
Nearest Station: Old Street Map: C8
With a reputation for delivering quality and value to all of their customers, this venue offers a unique environment for casual dining. Unfussy food and an eclectic mix of wine, champagne, and cocktails.
25% OFF TOTAL | 👤6 | FRI 📱 | SAT ✱ | SUN | ▲ — British

KASTURI ☎020 7480 7402
57 Aldgate High Street, EC3N 1AL
Nearest Station: Aldgate Map: C8
Focusing on the special qualities of Pakhtoon cuisine, Kasturi aims to preserve the glorious heritage of Indian subcontinental cuisine by retaining its authentic nature.
25% OFF TOTAL | 👤10 | FRI ✓ | SAT ✓ | SUN | ▲ — Indian

LA FENICE ROSSA ☎020 7621 0545
19 Bevis Marks, EC3A 7JA
Nearest Station: Aldgate Map: C8
La Fenice Rossa is a classic authentic Italian Restaurant, newly opened in the City of London. Offering their customers only the best and highest quality products and ingredients direct from Italy.
25% OFF TOTAL | 👤4 | FRI ✓ | SAT ✓ | SUN — Italian

LIBERTY LOUNGE ☎020 7377 5118
1a Bell Lane, E1 7LA
Nearest Station: Aldgate East Map: C8
Relaxed and friendly lounge in a stylish, modern and cosy basement setting. Perfect for an after-work drinking retreat with an array of beverages served alongside delicious Moroccan tapas.
50% OFF FOOD | 👤6 | FRI ✓ | SAT ✓ — Indian

THE LLOYDS CLUB LONDON ☎020 7863 6680
42 Crutched Friars, EC3N 2AP
Nearest Station: Fenchurch Street Map: C8
Seasonal menus feature contemporary and traditional cuisine to the highest standard, using only the finest ingredients available. The talented team of chefs at Lloyds Club will stimulate your senses.
25% OFF TOTAL | FRI ✓ | SAT ✗ | SUN — British

MANGO BRICK LANE ☎020 7247 9686
90 Brick Lane, E1 6RL
Nearest Station: Aldgate East Map: C8
With cheerful service, Indian classical music and a colourful dining room this is a suitable place for informal lunches. The decor is vibrant with vermilion feature walls and glossy wooden floors.
50% OFF FOOD | 👤10 | FRI ✓ | SAT ✓ — Indian

MARCO PIERRE WHITE STEAK & ALEHOUSE ☎020 7247 5050
East India House, Middlesex Street, E1 7JF
Nearest Station: Liverpool Street Map: C8
The name needs no introduction; this open, airy steakhouse combines the full cohort of cuts, perfectly cooked and stylishly accompanied, with an array of melting, savoury English classics. 2 AA Rosettes.
25% OFF TOTAL | 👤10 | FRI 📱 | SAT 📱 — British

MASALA BRICK LANE ☎020 7539 9448
88 Brick Lane, E1 6RL
Nearest Station: Aldgate East Map: C8
A cool and contemporary interior with a neutral décor allows diners to relax and unwind as they enjoy the authentic Indian cuisine on offer. The roop chanda is delicious and highly recommended.
25% OFF TOTAL | 👤4 | FRI 📱 | SAT 📱 — Indian

MONSOON ☎020 7375 1345
78 Brick Lane, E1 6RL
Nearest Station: Aldgate East Map: C8
Channelling their energy into the traditional culinary art of Bangladeshi cooking, the chefs at The Monsoon produce divine dishes, making use of wonderful fragrant spices and fresh ingredients.
25% OFF TOTAL | 👤10 | FRI ✓ | SAT ✓ — Bangladeshi

MUMBAI SQUARE ☎020 7247 6461
7 Middlesex Street, E1 7AA
Nearest Station: Aldgate Map: C8
Passionate about providing an impeccable dining experience, the boundaries of culinary excellence are constantly pushed. Stunning dining rooms, flawless service and a bursting menu make this venue a must.
2FOR1 2 COURSES | FRI ✓ | SAT ✓ — Indian

PAPADOMS ☎020 7377 9123
94 Brick Lane, E1 6RL
Nearest Station: Aldgate East Map: C8
Boasting an award-winning curry chef, it's not surprising that this restaurant is known for its exceedingly tasty food. Fine ingredients and exotic spices come together to create irresistible flavour.
50% OFF FOOD | 👤8 | FRI ✓ | SAT ✓ — Indian/Bangladeshi

PAUSE ☎020 7621 0850
80-84 Leadenhall Street, EC3A 3DH
Nearest Station: Aldgate Map: C8
Sometimes it's difficult to grab that well-deserved and much needed break from the trials of everyday life: Pause encourages all to take a breather and relax. Contemporary décor promotes relaxing vibes.
50% OFF FOOD | 10 | FRI | SAT | SUN — Multi-Cuisine

RED CHILLI ☎020 7481 3300
137 Leman Street, E1 8EY
Nearest Station: Aldgate East Map: C8
Traditional Indian cuisine transported to London with vivacious staff and clientèle, as well as a modern, sleek interior. The menu boasts Indian favourites, popular monthly menus and various specialities.
2FOR1 MAIN COURSE | FRI | SAT ✓ — Indian

SAFFRON ☎020 7247 2633
53 Brick Lane, E1 6PU
Nearest Station: Aldgate East Map: C8
Open until late, Saffron guarantees to be buzzing with a varied clientèle. Indian and Bangladeshi curries galore, the classic dishes such as lamb passanda with nuts has set the bar high on Brick Lane.
50% OFF FOOD | 4 | FRI ✓ | SAT ✓ — Indian

SAJNA GRILL RESTAURANT ☎020 7392 2100
30 Osbourne Street, E1 6TD
Nearest Station: Aldgate East Map: C8
Rooted in the regions of Bengal and Northern India, the dishes here are bursting with eastern promise. A sophisticated blend of spices creates elegantly prepared dishes, guaranteed to satisfy diners.
50% OFF FOOD | 4 | FRI ✓ | SAT ✓ | * — Indian/Bangladeshi

SHERAZ BANGLA LOUNGE ☎020 7247 5755
13 Brick Lane, E1 6PU
Nearest Station: Aldgate East Map: C8
One of the very first Indian restaurants in the area. Proud to be a founding part of the East End's rich heritage, the kitchen focuses its energy on customer preferences and informed choices.
25% OFF TOTAL | 10 | FRI | SAT | * | ▲ — Bangladeshi/Indian

TASTE OF INDIA ☎020 7481 4010
76 Aldgate High Street, EC3N 1BD
Nearest Station: Aldgate Map: C8
Step aside from busy Aldgate High Street for a well-conceived classic Indian meal in this bright, accommodating restaurant. It's tandoori specialities are well worth checking out.
25% OFF TOTAL | 4 | FRI ✓ | SAT ✓ — Indian

BENGAL CLIPPER ☎020 7357 9001
1-12 Cardamon Building, Shad Thames, SE1 2YR
Nearest Station: London Bridge Map: D8
Traditional, flavoursome dishes are created by chefs who draw their inspiration from across the subcontinent. The Sunday buffet is a great way to sample many dishes, such as the creamy murgh sagrana.
2FOR1 MAIN COURSE | FRI ✓ | SAT ✓ | ▲ — Indian

CAFÉ ROUGE 020 7702 0195
St Katharines Docks, Quayside Road, E1W 1AN
Nearest Station: Tower Hill Map: D8
French sophistication on the British high street – enjoy seasonally changing French dishes and a continental wine selection, served in a relaxed environment with an undeniable flair of Parisian chic.
25% OFF TOTAL | 6 | FRI ✓ | SAT ✓ | * — French

INDIAN FUSION ☎020 7403 9242
214 Tower Bridge Road, SE1 2UP
Nearest Station: London Bridge Map: D8
The tastes of Asia are combined in this chic venue, as Indian and Bangladeshi dishes are fused to culinary impeccability. Striving for healthier cuisine, dishes contain no artificial colours.
2FOR1 3 COURSES | FRI ✓ | SAT ✓ | ▲ — Indian

STRADA 020 7702 0123
2 Tower Bridge House, E1W 1AA
Nearest Station: Tower Hill Map: D8
Offering fresh, bold dishes inspired by flavours of Italian city life - Strada serves a selection of indulgent tastes, to those seeking a blissful escape to laidback Italian life. *Excludes Pizzettas.
25% OFF TOTAL | 6 | FRI ✓ | SAT × | ▲ — Italian

TENTAZIONI RESTAURANT ☎020 7237 1100
2 Mill Street, SE1 2BD
Nearest Station: Bermondsey Map: D8
This warm, familial Italian restaurant boasts a signature menu with an array of strong, colourful dishes that bring out all the deep and rich flavours that characterise authentic Italian cuisine.
2FOR1 3 COURSES | FRI ✓ | SAT ✓ | SUN — Italian

North East

36 ☎020 8361 1411
36 Queen Parade, Friern Barnet, N11 3DA
Nearest Station: Arnos Grove
A contemporary venue delivering fine Italian cuisine from a menu showcasing an eclectic mix of flavours and textures with a variety of authentic dishes. Complement your meal with a pick of choice wines.
2FOR1 MAIN COURSE | FRI × | SAT × | SUN — Italian

44 RESTAURANT ☎01708 441 231
44 High Street, Hornchurch, RM12 4UN
Nearest Station: Emerson Park
Roux Scholar Frederick Forster heads this fine restaurant in Hornchurch. Smart and spare in design, it is a truly high-class affair both in style and in cuisine. A sprightly, exceptional place to dine.
2FOR1 3 COURSES | FRI ✱ | SAT ✱ — International

AFRICAN TORCH RESTAURANT ☎020 8808 8166
135-137 High Cross Road, Seven Sisters, N17 9NU
Nearest Station: Tottenham Hale
A torch-bearer for West-African cooking. The menu features many traditional dishes and the akonfem platter with yam and salad exemplifies the rich flavours that characterise this cuisine.
50% OFF FOOD | 6 | FRI ✓ | SAT ✓ | ▲ — African

ALEXANDRA TANDOORI 020 8365 2666
126 Alexandra Park Road, Haringey, N10 2AH
Nearest Station: Alexandra Palace
Alexandra Tandoori's Tron-like exterior opens up into a welcoming local Indian restaurant whose stock-in-trade is substantial, full-flavoured and full-bodied curries at a good price.
2FOR1 MAIN COURSE | FRI × | SAT × | SUN — Indian

AMURG ☎020 8556 9602
579 High Road, Leytonstone, E11 4PB
Nearest Station: Leytonstone High Road
A Romanian restaurant serving fabulously tasty national cuisine in a charismatic environment. Star-like lights line the ceiling, whilst Friday's live music provides a great start to the weekend.
2FOR1 2 COURSES | FRI | SAT | SUN — Romanian

ANATOLIA ☎020 8558 0401
277 High Road, Leyton, E10 5QN
Nearest Station: Leyton
Great Turkish restaurant moments from the tube, with a large variety of cuisine prepared by Turkish chefs. The cakes are not to be missed.

25% OFF TOTAL | 👤 2 | FRI ✓ | SAT ✓ — Turkish

ANGORA TURKISH RESTAURANT ☎020 7790 3312
337 Commercial Road, Tower Hamlets, E1 2PS
Nearest Station: Shadwell
Turkish cuisine at its very best, Angora Restaurant has much in the way of tasty, authentic food at decent prices. Distinctive Middle Eastern flavours characterise the aromatic dishes.

25% OFF TOTAL | 👤 6 | FRI × | SAT ✓ | SUN — Turkish

AROMA INDIAN RESTAURANT ☎01708 732 345
55 High Street, Romford, RM1 1JL
Nearest Station: Romford
A local favourite having garnered a reputation for a combination of excellent curry and cheerful staff. A familiar and exquisite menu, every dish rich in aromatic Indian flavours and spice.

2FOR1 MAIN COURSE | FRI ✓ | SAT ✓ — Indian

THE BANC ☎020 8888 8898
261-263 West Green Road, Haringey, N15 3BH
Nearest Station: Seven Sisters
Memorable dining experiences to be had at The Banc, where the staff work exceptionally hard to ensure all diners are well catered for and wholly satisfied. Strokes of Mediterranean influences.

25% OFF TOTAL | 👤 6 | FRI × | SAT × — Mediterranean

BEJOY TANDOORI RESTAURANT ☎020 8888 1268
78 Bounds Green Road, Bounds Green, N11 2EU
Nearest Station: Bounds Green
Simple and effective tandoori restaurant in Bounds Green that serves a good selection of classic dishes together with some more eclectic offerings. Great service is a given, flavours and portions generous.

2FOR1 MAIN COURSE | FRI × | SAT × | SUN — Indian

BENGAL LANCER ☎020 8594 9598
84 Longbridge Road, Barking, IG11 8SF
Nearest Station: Barking
Bengal Lancer is a Tandoori Restaurant featuring classic dishes such as dopiaza, biriyani and house specialities.

2FOR1 MAIN COURSE | FRI ✱ | SAT ✱ | ✱ | ▲ — Indian

BENGAL SPICE & MASALA ☎01708 452 439
17 Station Parade, Hornchurch, RM12 5AD
Nearest Station: Elm Park
Enjoy authentic Indian cuisine cooked using the freshest ingredients by the highly experienced chef. This restaurant offers customers fantastic service and dishes of excellent quality.

25% OFF TOTAL | 👤 10 | FRI 📱 | SAT 📱 | ✱ — Indian

BHANGRA BEAT ☎020 8989 8909
49 Chigwell Road, South Woodford, E18 1NG
Nearest Station: South Woodford
Enjoy superb Indian cuisine as the sounds of Bollywood style music fill the air around you. Meat lovers will fall head over heels for the special balti, which incorporates succulent lamb, chicken and duck.

25% OFF TOTAL | 👤 10 | FRI 📱 | SAT 📱 | ✱ — Indian

BHANGRA BEAT ☎020 8590 2503
108 High Road, Chadwell Heath, RM6 6NX
Nearest Station: Chadwell Heath
A cosy, family-run establishment serving tasty Indian subcontinental cuisine. With an award-winning chef in the kitchen, it is unsurprising that this restaurant increases in popularity by the day.

2FOR1 MAIN COURSE | FRI ✱ | SAT ✱ | ✱ | ▲ — Indian

BIRASHWAMYS ☎020 8500 1570
4 Broadway Market, Ilford, IG6 2JT
Nearest Station: Fairlop
Birashwamys is a hidden gem in Ilford. With unassuming decor, friendly efficient staff and flavoursome curries on offer, this local Indian is about to be discovered and gain more loyal followers.

50% OFF FOOD | 👤 8 | FRI 📱 | SAT 📱 | ✱ — Indian

BOLLYWOOD BRASSERIE ☎020 7473 5004
2 Western Gateway, Excel West, E16 1DR
Nearest Station: Custom House for ExCeL
Guests enjoy the luxuriously decorated waterfront dining room whilst unwinding in the hands of the efficient service. Completely cosmopolitan, diners should expect Indian cuisine with a contemporary twist.

50% OFF FOOD | 👤 4 | FRI ✱ | SAT ✱ — Indian

BOMBAY PALACE ☎01708 371 866
45 Station Road, Harold Wood, RM3 0BS
Nearest Station: Harold Wood
Feed your senses at this wonderful Indian restaurant, where the focus remains on traditional cooking methods and the ancient Indian philosophy behind the culinary experience.

2FOR1 MAIN COURSE | FRI 📱 | SAT × — Indian

BOUGA ☎020 8348 5609
1 Park Road, Crouch End, Haringey, N8 8TE
Nearest Station: Crouch Hill
Beautiful mosaic floors, silk drapes and ornate handicrafts provide an enchanting atmospheric haven. The menu draws upon the richness of Moroccan culture and cuisine, providing exquisite food for all.

25% OFF TOTAL | 👤 4 | FRI ✱ | SAT ✱ — Moroccan

BRODIE'S BAR AND RESTAURANT ☎020 7719 0202
43-44 Fisherman's Walk, Canary Wharf, E14 5HD
Nearest Station: Canary Wharf
Bursting with vibrant energy, Brodie's is proud of its character that attracts both small and large parties for all occasions. Main dishes, gourmet sandwiches and delicious desserts are all on offer.

2FOR1 MAIN COURSE | FRI ✱ | SAT ✱ | SUN | ▲ — International

CAFE LA DIVINA ☎020 8616 4149
134 Upper Street, Islington, N1 1QP
Nearest Station: Essex Road
Cracking little restaurant with open-brick walls, photos, posters and paraphernalia. Well regarded for its Italian cuisine, with the pizza toscana and boccouncini alla romana two of the leading lights.

50% OFF FOOD | 👤 4 | FRI ✓ | SAT ✱ — Italian

CAFE RODI ☎020 8527 4541
16 Blackhorse Lane, Walthamstow, E17 6HJ
Nearest Station: Blackhorse Road
This relaxed retro restaurant Cafe Rodi, has all the British classics. Whether you fancy a big English breakfast or a quality panini with a side of crispy chips, Cafe Rodi delivers tasty food.

25% OFF TOTAL | FRI ✓ | SAT ✓ | SUN — British

CANECAO BRAZILLIAN PUB ☎020 7485 4738
17 York Way, Camden Town, N7 9QG
Nearest Station: Caledonian Road
One capital meets another at this Brazilian pub in London. Portugese and South American style tapas dishes and a fine host of beers and beverages can be found at this fun place in Camden.

50% OFF FOOD | 👤 8 | FRI ✓ | SAT ✓ — Brazilian

CAFÉ ROUGE

25% OFF TOTAL | 👤 6 | FRI ✓ | SAT ✓ | ✱ | ▲

3 restaurants in North East London

29-35 Mackenzie Walk, Canary Wharf, E14 4PH
Canary Wharf ☎ 020 7537 9696

179-181 High Road, Loughton, IG10 4LF
Loughton ☎ 020 8502 2011

45-46 Cannon Hill, Southgate, Barnet, N14 6LH
New Southgate ☎ 020 8886 3336

To understand what the restaurant icons mean, please see the inside back cover.

CARIBBEAN SCENE FAMILY
020 8522 8660
Gerry Raffles Square, Stratford, E15 1BG
Nearest Station: Stratford
Celebrates all that is wonderful about Caribbean culture. Stimulate all of your senses with exquisite food, delectable cocktails, aromatic rums and lively music, all in the most vibrant of settings.

2FOR1 MAIN COURSE | FRI | SAT ✱ | Caribbean

CARIBBEAN SCENE ROYALE
020 7511 2023
17 Western Gateway, Royal Victoria Docks, E16 1AQ
Nearest Station: Royal Victoria
Allow the allusive Caribbean theme of the restaurant transport you straight to the islands. From the natural herbs and spices used in the food, to the music and décor, you'll enjoy being in paradise.

2FOR1 MAIN COURSE | FRI | SAT | SUN | ✱ | Caribbean

CHANDNI CHOWK INDIAN RESTAURANT
020 3222 2000
754/756 Green Lane, Dagenham, RM8 1YT
Nearest Station: Chadwell Heath
Taking its name from the old Delhi trading square, Chandni Chowk restaurant recreates traditional Indian cuisine and sweets. Sample the tastes of a world far away without leaving the country.

25% OFF TOTAL | 4 | FRI | SAT | Indian

CHASE SIDE INDIAN RESTAURANT
020 8367 9919
135-137 Chase Side, Enfield, EN2 0PN
Nearest Station: Gordon Hill
The authentically trained chefs offer a classical and surprising take on the traditional Indian and Bangladeshi style of cooking, with an extensive menu catering for all tastes.

2FOR1 3 COURSES | FRI × | SAT × | ✱ | Indian

CHEZ TONTON
020 8440 2696
182 East Barnet Road, New Barnet, EN4 8RD
Nearest Station: New Barnet
Classic and charming French restaurant in New Barnet with a real air of the bleu blanc rouge. Superbly cooked French fare combines with a choice wine list for a convivial evening or a romantic dinner.

2FOR1 MAIN COURSE | FRI ✱ | SAT ✱ | SUN | French

CINNAMON SPICE
01708 478 510
10 Tadworth Parade, Elm Park, Hornchurch, RM12 5AS
Nearest Station: Elm Park
Cheerful staff enhance the amiable ambience of this restaurant. Local diners regularly flock to this eatery for its chilled atmosphere and satisfying food. The cinnamon garlic chicken is outstanding.

2FOR1 MAIN COURSE | FRI ✓ | SAT ✓ | Indian

CIRRIK RESTAURANT
020 8985 2879
1-3 Amhurst Road, Hackney, E8 1LL
Nearest Station: Hackney Central
This authentic Turkish restaurant greets you with a mouth-watering aroma of herbs and spices from the grill. Their wide selection of delicious dishes offer something for everyone. Families most welcome.

25% OFF TOTAL | 2 | FRI | SAT | ✱ | Mediterranean

CLIFTON DOCKLANDS
020 7001 2999
32 Westferry Rd, Canary Wharf, E14 8LW
Nearest Station: South Quay
The innovative South Asian cuisine is complemented by the refined and sophisticated décor. The friendly and knowledgeable staff ensure that every guest has a relaxing and delicious experience.

25% OFF TOTAL | 10 | FRI ✓ | SAT ✓ | Indian

COMEDOR GRILL AND BAR
020 7354 2843
176 Upper Street, Islington, N1 1RG
Nearest Station: Highbury & Islington
Coming from the Spanish word for 'dining room', Comedor Grill and Bar will make you feel at ease. Vibrant colours and flavours characterise the South American cuisine on offer.

50% OFF FOOD | 6 | FRI × | SAT × | South American

THE CORIANDER
020 8504 2671
40 Victoria Road, Buckhurst Hill, IG9 5ES
Nearest Station: Buckhurst Hill
The gleaming reputation of The Coriander is entirely well deserved. Serving fine Northern Indian and Bangladeshi cuisine, this suitably located restaurant shines out from the crowd.

2FOR1 2 COURSES | FRI × | SAT × | SUN | ✱ | Indian

CORNELIUS RESTAURANT
020 8885 2829
Heron House, Hale Wharf, Ferry Lane, N17 9NF
Nearest Station: Tottenham Hale
Light, open continental restaurant specialising in Romanian cuisine, with some equally excellent Italian and other European flavours to boot. Try the excellent polenta cake and the great pork fillet.

50% OFF FOOD | 2 | FRI | SAT | European

DAR MARRAKECH
020 8221 0113
403 High Street, Stratford, E15 4QZ
Nearest Station: Stratford
Beautifully adorned with characteristically Moroccan décor, the food at Dar Marrakech is equally characteristic of Moroccan and North African culture and cuisine. Delectable dishes make it worth a visit.

25% OFF TOTAL | FRI ✓ | SAT ✓ | Moroccan/ Lebanese

DOCKMASTERS HOUSE
020 7345 0345
1 Hertsmere Road, Docklands, Tower Hamlets, E14 8JD
Nearest Station: Westferry
Classic Indian dishes with an expressive contemporary twist in this charming restaurant and bar. Guests will fall in love with the stunning dining rooms. *Only 1 card per party may be used.

2FOR1 MAIN COURSE | 2 | FRI | SAT | SUN | Indian

THE DRUNKEN MONKEY
020 7882 8797
Sir Christopher France House, Westfield Way, E1 4QA
Nearest Station: Mile End
The Drunken Monkey has a chic modern interior bathed in sunlight during the day. Alongside St. Regent's Canal, this Drunken Monkey blends accents of modern Riviera and Chinese funk.

2FOR1 2 COURSES | FRI ✓ | SAT ✓ | Chinese

EL MERCADO BAR AND CANTINA
020 7923 0555
26-30 Stoke Newington Church St, Hackney, N16 0LU
Nearest Station: Stoke Newington
Exciting and vibrant blend of Mexican street food with cuisine that has been influenced by modern tastes. Desirable, spicy dishes are made authentically and with the verve that Mexican cuisine demands.

25% OFF TOTAL | 4 | FRI × | SAT × | SUN | ✱ | Mexican

THE EMPRESS
020 8533 5123
130 Lauriston Road, Hackney, E9 7LH
Nearest Station: London Fields
Stylish eatery where brunches, roasts and light snacks are whipped up and plated, oozing flavour and quality. Interesting dishes made from alternative meats, such as the beef cheek with turnip.

25% OFF TOTAL | 4 | FRI ✱ | SAT × | SUN | Modern British

EUREKA TASTE
020 8888 8857
77 Westbury Avenue, Haringey, N22 6SA
Nearest Station: Turnpike Lane
Guests feast upon authentic Polish cuisine in this chic London bistro. The entirely home-made menu consists of only the most time-tested recipes such as hearty soups and stews. Expect service with a smile.

2FOR1 3 COURSES | FRI | SAT | European

EXCELINE AFRICAN CUISINE
020 8525 9222
175 Mare Street, Hackney, E8 3RH
Nearest Station: London Fields
From a goat stew to tilapia fish, Exceline proudly presents the very best of east African cuisine. Exotic food available in a city that thrives upon its vibrant cultural blend.

2FOR1 MAIN COURSE | FRI × | SAT × | SUN | African

EYE 2 RESTAURANT
020 8508 7799
159a High Road, Loughton, IG10 4LF
Nearest Station: Loughton
Passionate chefs use their expertise to create an authentic home-style Indian menu, served courteously in a relaxed atmosphere. Expect a variety of unusual, delicately spiced dishes.

50% OFF FOOD | 6 | FRI ✓ | SAT ✓ | Indian

FISH FISH
020 8348 3121
179 Archway Road, Haringey, N6 5BN
Nearest Station: Highgate
A homely-looking restaurant serving an array of classic fish dishes, cooked and served simply and freshly. With a laid-back and quirky ambience, Fish Fish is an enjoyable place to eat.

25% OFF TOTAL | 4 | FRI ✓ | SAT ✓ | Seafood

FLAMIN STEAK GRILL
020 8521 3456
328 Hoe Street, Walthamstow, E17 9PX
Nearest Station: Walthamstow Central
Whether you're looking for a family gathering, or a private night's dining for two, Walthamstow's newest steakhouse, Flamin' Steak Grill is the perfect venue for you. A traditional steakhouse experience.

2FOR1 MAIN COURSE | FRI × | SAT × | SUN — American

FLAVOUR-E-AZAM
☎020 8523 9799
65 Old Church Road, Chingford Mount, E4 6ST
Nearest Station: Highams Park
From the Himalayas to the Bay of Bengal, Flavour-E-Asam draws on the characteristically rich flavours and spices found in Indian dishes. Vibrant colours and exquisite aromas.

50% OFF FOOD | 👤10 | FRI ✓ | SAT ✓ | ✱ — Indian

FOREST TANDOORI
☎020 8520 8080
102 Wood Street, Waltham Forest, E17 3HX
Nearest Station: Wood Street
A hidden gem of an Indian restaurant. The food, service and interior are top notch, with the quality of the takeaway being equally excellent.

2FOR1 MAIN COURSE | FRI ✱ | SAT ✱ | ▲ — Indian

FORTUNE INN
☎020 8594 3311
14 London Road, Barking, IG11 8AG
Nearest Station: Barking
Spanning the gamut of different flavours from regions of China, the Fortune Inn is lucid in the way it goes about preparing its dishes. Calm and collected, flavourful and piquant, altogether balanced food.

25% OFF TOTAL | 👤10 | FRI 🍾 | SAT 🍾 | ✱ — Chinese

GEORGE'S FISH AND SOUVLAKI BAR
☎020 8989 3970
164 George Lane, South Woodford, E18 1AY
Nearest Station: South Woodford
Taking pride in local sourcing is imperative at this Greek-Cypriot venue, where traditional fish and chips receive a Mediterranean twist. Seafood lovers can savour the chunky calamari and plush prawns.

2FOR1 3 COURSES | FRI ✱ | SAT ✱ | ▲ — Traditional fish & chips/Greek

GLOBE CAFE BISTRO
☎020 7354 1400
231 Blackstock Road, Highbury, N5 2LL
Nearest Station: Arsenal
Whether visiting for breakfast, lunch or dinner, this restaurant is a place where you can truly explore and ignite your senses by trying many of the mouth watering dishes.

25% OFF TOTAL | 👤4 | FRI 🍾 | SAT 🍾 | SUN — Turkish

GURKHA'S NAMASTE
☎020 8591 5237
31 Longbridge Road, Barking, IG11 8TN
Nearest Station: Barking
Nepalese food is unique and at this restaurant they are passionate about retaining its authenticity. Some of the spices are imported directly from Nepal to create the unique flavours found in the dishes.

2FOR1 3 COURSES | FRI ✓ | SAT ✓ — Nepalese

HENRY'S CAFÉ BAR
☎020 7515 8361
16 Hertsmere Road, Canary Wharf, E14 4AX
Nearest Station: West India Quay
Enjoy cocktails or a chic coffee at this member of the Henry's group. Diners can banquet on a chunky burger or deli sandwich whilst sipping your favourite drink. Located near to the Westfield Centre.

2FOR1 3 COURSES | FRI × | SAT × | SUN | ▲ — British

I PAPARAZZI ROMFORD
☎01708 751 901
33 Main Road, Romford, RM1 3DL
Nearest Station: Romford
Residing in a fabulous Victorian location, I Paparazzi has a kitchen brimming full of culinary talent. Serving moreish Italian dishes alongside seasonal English cuisine.

2FOR1 3 COURSES | FRI ✓ | SAT ✓ | ▲ — Italian

IBLEO
☎020 8529 9329
1 Station Approach, Station Road, Chingford, E4 6AL
Nearest Station: Chingford
Influenced by Sicilian cuisine, Ibleo hosts a unique blend of Mediterranean flavours. Renowned chefs Antonio and Giovanni's lastest venture, Ibleo is devoted to quality and service. *Booking is essential.

2FOR1 3 COURSES | FRI 🍾 | SAT 🍾 — Italian

IL BACIO
☎020 7249 3933
61 Stoke Newington Church St, Stoke New'ton, N16 0AR
Nearest Station: Stoke Newington
Experience the taste of the entire Italian peninsula all under one roof. The skilful hands of the chefs prepare delectable dishes that emanate Italian culture, with a menu filled with all the classics.

25% OFF TOTAL | 👤6 | FRI ✱ | SAT ✱ | ✱ — Italian

INDIA GARDEN
☎020 7609 7052
6 Brecknock Road, Kentish Town, N7 0DD
Nearest Station: Kentish Town
Sophistication without the price-tag, this venue guarantees a touch of class with every dish. The chef specials attract a faithful crowd, whilst the menu vaunts Indian favourites.

50% OFF FOOD | FRI × | SAT × — Indian

INDIANA
☎020 7987 2576
129 Salmon Lane, Tower Hamlets, E14 7PG
Nearest Station: Limehouse
A real local institution with chic interior and neon lighting. An interesting menu offers traditional cuisine but also delivers unique creations inspired by the many different flavours of the subcontinent.

50% OFF FOOD | 👤6 | FRI ✱ | SAT ✱ | ✱ — Bangladeshi/Indian

INN ON THE PARK
01992 718 481
2 Solar Way, Enfield, EN3 7NJ
Nearest Station: Brimsdown
Quality pub classics with modern twists meets with a friendly and relaxed atmosphere to make this Table Table venue the perfect place for any occasion. *Excludes daytime & evening deals and festive menus.

2FOR1 MAIN COURSE | FRI ✓ | SAT ✓ — Modern British

IZNIK
☎020 7704 8099
19 Highbury Park, Islington, N5 1QJ
Nearest Station: Drayton Park
An authentic restaurant with rich, deep colours, arabesque jali screens, and warm lanterns, coupled with an outstanding atmosphere and a top-notch menu that delivers for all kind of tastes.

50% OFF FOOD | 👤8 | FRI ✓ | SAT ✓ — Turkish

JUBORAJ
☎020 8363 6294
12 Cambridge Parade, Enfield, EN1 4JU
Nearest Station: Enfield Town
Great quality Indian food to be enjoyed in the warmth and comfort of the restaurant. Enjoy house specials, such as the jalfrezi dishes or the special rezala. Tasty flavours guaranteed.

2FOR1 2 COURSES | FRI ✓ | SAT ✓ — Indian

JUNCTION ROOM
☎020 7241 5755
578 Kingsland Road, Dalston, E8 4AH
Nearest Station: Dalston Junction
A cosy, homely venue with wooden beams, warm tones and kitschy lampshades, the Junction Room is a great spot to meet up with friends for a drink or some simple, yet highly-satisfying food.

25% OFF TOTAL | 👤8 | FRI ✓ | SAT ✓ — International

KAFTAN RESTAURANT
☎020 8911 6543
253 High Road, Ilford, IG1 1NE
Nearest Station: Ilford
Enjoy a mixture of exquisite Turkish and Mediterranean dishes created by chefs who boast a wealth of international kitchen experience. The charcoal grill ensures perfectly cooked, sizzling meats.

25% OFF TOTAL | 👤10 | FRI 🍾 | SAT 🍾 | ✱ | ▲ — Turkish

KAJAL
☎020 8365 7771
4 Green Lane, Palmers Green, N13 6UT
Nearest Station: Palmers Green
Find excellence in Indian cuisine here, and treat yourself to one of many fine curry and tandoori dishes, perfectly complemented by a list of fresh, tasty sundries and an extensive drinks selection.

2FOR1 3 COURSES | FRI 🍾 | SAT 🍾 — Indian

KOKEB ETHIOPIAN CUISINE
☎020 7609 9832
45 Roman Way, Islington, N7 8XF
Nearest Station: Caledonian Road
Ethiopian cuisine is often overlooked, but Kokeb Restaurant strives to put it firmly on the table. Complex flavours feature in every dish, while the crucial element berbere is made full use of.

2FOR1 MAIN COURSE | FRI 🍾 | SAT 🍾 — Ethiopian

KUKU'S NEST
020 8590 6064
69-71 Goodmayes Road, Ilford, IG3 9UB
Nearest Station: Goodmayes
Soak up the atmosphere at this two-storey restaurant and bar, where the live music and delicious European food have earned it a well-deserved reputation. Fabulously designed and a cordial atmosphere.
50% OFF FOOD | 10 | FRI | SAT
European

KUSADASI TAVERNA
01708 524 437
90a Rainham Road, Rainham, RM13 7RJ
Nearest Station: Rainham
The Kusadasi Taverna has been serving mouth-watering Turkish dishes for 20 years and the winners of Archant London's Best Modern European Restaurant Award for Food and Drink in our area in 2008 and 2009.
2FOR1 3 COURSES | FRI × | SAT ×
Turkish

LA FAVORITA
020 7272 5040
174 Tollington Park, Finsbury Park, N4 3AJ
Nearest Station: Crouch Hill
La Favorita is a new Italian Restaurant offering affordable, high quality Italian cuisine. They pride themselves on serving delicious food, providing first class hospitality and informed hospitality.
50% OFF FOOD | 10 | FRI | SAT × | SUN
Italian

LA PAELLA TAPAS BAR
020 8882 7868
9 The Broadway, Southgate, N14 6PH
Nearest Station: Southgate
Authentically decorated, this Spanish inspired venue serves food prepared by Head Chef Angel Torres in traditional hand-made ceramic dishes. Perfect for a romantic dinner, the house paella feeds two.
25% OFF TOTAL | 4 | FRI ✓ | SAT × | ✱
Spanish

LA TASCA
020 7531 9990
Hertsmere Road, Canary Wharf, E14 4AE
Nearest Station: West India Quay
Quintessentially Spanish, La Tasca's fresh and exciting menu offers something for everyone. Their tapas dishes are sincerely authentic, while their paellas always deliver on flavour.
25% OFF TOTAL | 8 | FRI ✓ | SAT ×
Spanish

LAHORE ONE RESTAURANT
020 7791 0112
218 Commercial Road, Tower Hamlets, E1 2JT
Nearest Station: Shadwell
A restaurant that has proudly pioneered a new approach towards traditional Indian cooking. The various flavours of Indian, British, Arabic and Chinese go towards making each dish tasty and delicious.
25% OFF TOTAL | 4 | FRI ✱ | SAT ✱
Indian

LEYTONSTONE SPICE
020 8558 4275
639 Leytonstone High Road, Leytonstone, E11 4RD
Nearest Station: Leytonstone High Road
Unsuspectingly tucked away on Leytonstone High Road, the Leytonstone Spice offers diners delicious Indian cuisine. Fast becoming a favourite for many, Leytonstone Spice comes highly recommended.
50% OFF FOOD | 10 | FRI ✓ | SAT ✓
Indian

THE LIBERTY BELL
01708 760 570
Mercury Gardens, Romford, RM1 3EN
Nearest Station: Romford
Quality pub classics with modern twists meets with a friendly and relaxed atmosphere to make this Table Table venue the perfect place for any occasion. *Excludes daytime & evening deals and festive menus.
2FOR1 MAIN COURSE | FRI ✓ | SAT ✓
Modern British

L'INFINITO
020 8530 5057
27 High Street, Wanstead, E11 2AA
Nearest Station: Snaresbrook
Brand new Italian restaurant with the age-old Italian passion for taste, art and pleasure. It is the portrait of true Italian dining that brings the best food and hospitality to one unique environment.
2FOR1 3 COURSES | FRI | SAT
Italian

LOCH FYNE
020 8532 5140
280-282 High Road, Loughton, IG10 1RB
Nearest Station: Loughton
From the roadside oyster bar that once was, Loch Fyne restaurants now successfully inject energy and passion into great food and wonderful flavours, whilst ensuring their seafood is sustainably sourced.
25% OFF TOTAL | 4 | FRI ✱ | SAT ✱
Seafood

MAHAL
020 7226 5551
108 Essex Road, Islington, N1 8LX
Nearest Station: Essex Road
Mahal is a wonderful new Indian restaurant which will welcome you into a relaxed and comfortable surroundings tempted by an unrivalled range of authentic and imaginative dishes.
25% OFF TOTAL | FRI ✓ | SAT ✓ | ✱
Indian

MASALA KING
020 8514 2446
8 Chapel Road, Ilford, IG1 2AG
Nearest Station: Ilford
Sample a fusion of authentic and Sri Lankan cuisine from the exceptional range on offer, experiencing the divine tastes of different cultures, prepared well to produce a high standard of satisfying cuisine.
2FOR1 2 COURSES | FRI ✓ | SAT
Indian

MAZA DESI EATERY
020 7539 3433
97 New Road, Whitechapel, E1 1HJ
Nearest Station: Whitechapel
Maza Desi Eatery combines an authentic mix of herbs and spices to create an array of sizzling grills and mouth-watering curries which show off the best of Pakistani cuisine.
25% OFF TOTAL | FRI ✓ | SAT ✓
Indian

MEMSAHEB ON THAMES
020 7538 3008
65-67 Amsterdam Road, Docklands, E14 3UU
Nearest Station: Canary Wharf
Memsaheb on Thames is a traditional Indian curry house restaurant located on the banks of the River Thames, serving fantastic food in relaxed style.
25% OFF TOTAL | FRI | SAT
Indian

METOLINO
020 7923 9200
162 Stoke Newington Road, Hackney, N16 7UY
Nearest Station: Rectory Road
Metolino offers a refreshing take on Italian and Mediterranean cuisine. Quickly obtaining a great name for itself, this stylish and contemporary eatery is popular from breakfasts to evening dinners.
50% OFF FOOD | 4 | FRI ✓ | SAT ✓ | ✱
Italian

MOSAICA @ THE FACTORY
020 8889 2400
The Chocolate Factory, Haringey, N22 6XJ
Nearest Station: Alexandra Palace
The impeccably composed menu combines the best of modern European cuisine, from creamy seafood risotto to succulent rib-eye steak. This alluringly decorated venue is both cosmopolitan and sophisticated.
2FOR1 MAIN COURSE | FRI ✓ | SAT ×
Modern European

MUNA'S RESTAURANT
020 8340 8411
599 Green Lanes, Haringey, N8 0RE
Nearest Station: Harringay Green Lanes
Extremely hearty and flavoursome food will tantalise even the most sophisticated of palates. Whether you enjoy your food mild or exceedingly spicy, the kitchen can cater for all tastes and preferences.
25% OFF TOTAL | 8 | FRI ✱ | SAT ✱ | ✱
Sudanese/Eritrean

MUYA RESTAURANT
07852 151871
13 Brecknock Road, Camden, N7 0BL
Nearest Station: Kentish Town
You may not have thought about trying Ethiopian food before, but now's the time! Go and enjoy this unique opportunity to savour the unrivalled sounds, tastes, and aromas of Ethiopian culture and cuisine.
2FOR1 3 COURSES | FRI | SAT
Ethiopian

THE OLD SHIP
020 8986 1641
2 Sylvester Path, Hackney, E8 1EN
Nearest Station: Hackney Central
Genial and accommodating urban inn in Hackney where you can enjoy a ranging, seasonal menu that celebrates classic British cuisine while looking to keep it up to date with modern touches.
2FOR1 MAIN COURSE | FRI ✓ | SAT ✓ | SUN | ✱
British

THE OLIVE BRANCH
020 8886 3688

222 Green Lanes, Palmers Green, N13 5UD
Nearest Station: Palmers Green

Zingy tzatziki, rich halloumi and grilled pitta breads are staple classics at this Turkish restaurant, where you'll be tempted to order a whole host of starters before even beginning on the mains.

50% OFF FOOD | FRI ✗ | SAT ✗ — **British**

THE OLIVE TREE
☎ 020 8502 3332

258 High Road, Loughton, IG10 1RB
Nearest Station: Loughton

Broad menu of Greek cuisine with some other Mediterranean influences. Smart, sensitive service; a dining space that feels both easygoing and sophisticated. Effortlessly warm, with some beautiful food.

25% OFF TOTAL | 4 | FRI ✱ | SAT ✱ | 🌲 — **Mediterranean**

OMI RESTAURANT
☎ 020 7923 1273

84 Stoke Newington High Street, Hackney, N16 7PA
Nearest Station: Rectory Road

Perfect for those seeking something a little out of the ordinary, Omi Restaurant presents an authentic Moroccan dining experience in North London.

25% OFF TOTAL | 4 | FRI ✗ | SAT ✗ — **Moroccan**

OSIDGE ARMS
☎ 020 8361 4611

Hampden Square, Southgate, N14 5JP
Nearest Station: Southgate

The Osidge Arms is a brilliant restaurant with an appealing local vibe to it. Head here for a traditionally warm, inviting experience be it on a cold winter's night or hot summer's day.

50% OFF FOOD | 10 | FRI ✓ | SAT ✓ | 🌲 — **Mediterranean**

PANDOOS
☎ 020 8518 6677

112 Cranbrook Road, Ilford, IG1 4LZ
Nearest Station: Ilford

Pandoo's aim is to provide quality food, an enjoyable atmosphere and customer satisfaction. The fusion menu features a selection of freshly prepared food and mouth-watering dishes from around the world.

25% OFF TOTAL | 4 | FRI ✗ | SAT ✗ | SUN — **Mediterranean**

PANNA'S RESTAURANT
☎ 020 8924 2255

The City Pavilion, Romford, RM5 2BH
Nearest Station: Fairlop

Indo-Chinese inspired, this venue is ideally located in the City Pavilion entertainment complex. Start your evening's events in style by feasting upon oriental delights and exotic dishes.

2FOR1 2 COURSES | FRI 📱 | SAT ✗ | SUN | ✱ | 🌲 — **Indian**

PASA
☎ 020 7607 6511

10 Brecknock Road, Kentish Town, N7 0DD
Nearest Station: Kentish Town

North African inspired, the cuisine is created for sharing with family and friends. Food comes to the table in a continuous flow in the opulent surroundings. The staff are habitually hospitable.

25% OFF TOTAL | 4 | FRI ✗ | SAT ✗ — **Nepalese**

PASTA RUSTICA
☎ 020 7359 9773

67-69 Newington Green Road, Islington, N1 4QU
Nearest Station: Canonbury

Guaranteeing to appease grumbling stomachs, the menu consists of rustic herbs and quality meats. Diners are transported to Italy in the inviting atmosphere.

2FOR1 3 COURSES | FRI ✗ | SAT ✗ | 🌲 — **Italian**

PIN-PETCH THAI
☎ 020 7354 8546

39 Newington Green Road, Islington, N1 4QT
Nearest Station: Canonbury

Pin-Petch use only fresh ingredients locally sourced wherever possible. Experienced fans of Asian cuisine are sure to find their favourites dishes, as well as a few new ones!

2FOR1 2 COURSES | FRI ✓ | SAT ✓ — **Thai**

PIZZA BELLA
☎ 020 8342 8541

4-6 Park Road, Hornsey, N8 8TD
Nearest Station: Crouch Hill

Priding itself on providing local diners with truly authentic Italian cuisine, Pizza Bella are a family friendly restaurant that always provide a warm welcome and top-quality service to every guest.

25% OFF TOTAL | 4 | FRI 📱 | SAT 📱 — **Italian**

PRADERA TAPAS BAR
☎ 020 8340 9400

14 High Street, Crouch End, N8 7PB
Nearest Station: Hornsey

With flavours as vibrant as the Spanish sun, this restaurant introduces an authentic setting with a host of dishes to choose from. All food is finely produced and pan-fried to deliver an original taste.

25% OFF TOTAL | 2 | FRI ✗ | SAT ✗ | ✱ — **Spanish**

THE PRINCE ARTHUR
☎ 020 7249 9996

5 Forest Road, Hackney, E8 3BH
Nearest Station: London Fields

This classic Victorian pub from 1861 has been carefully restored retaining all of the original features. The Prince Arthurs hosts a delightful menu, alongside an excellent selection of real ales, wines and spirits.

50% OFF FOOD | 8 | FRI ✓ | SAT ✱ | SUN | 🌲 — **British**

PREZZO

2FOR1 MAIN COURSE | FRI ✗ | SAT ✗ | 🌲

2-FOR-1 MAIN COURSE

8 restaurants in North East London

Elmhurst, 98 High Road, South Woodford, E18 2QH	South Woodford	☎ 020 8559 0192
8 Johnson Road, Woodford Green, IG8 OXA	South Woodford	☎ 020 8505 2400
189 High Street, Hornchurch, RM11 3XT	Upminster Bridge	☎ 01708 455 501
53 Corbets Tey Road, Upminster, RM14 2AJ	Upminster	☎ 01708 642 096
127-129 Cockfoster Road, Cockfosters, EN4 0DA	Cockfosters	☎ 020 8441 6917
The Coach House, 26 The Town, Enfield, EN2 6LU	Enfield Town	☎ 020 8366 8817
1a The Green, Chingford, E4 7ES	Chingford	☎ 020 8559 3593
63 Queens Road, Buckhurst Hill, IG9 5BU	Buckhurst Hill	☎ 020 8505 6593

QUEENS BRITISH STEAK HOUSE & GRILL ☎020 8530 8861
63 New Wanstead, Wanstead, E11 2SA
Nearest Station: Wanstead
Guests can expect a cracking time with some genuinely good food at this British steak house. Dry aged for at least 35 days, the steaks are reared locally and guarantee a succulent, juicy texture.

2FOR1 MAIN COURSE | FRI | SAT ✗ | SUN | British

RABIENG ☎020 7226 2014
143 Upper Street, N1 1QY
Nearest Station: Essex Road
Fine Thai cuisine served in a stylish and funky setting, with a wide range of modern and traditional dishes to choose from. Try the highly recommended Thai red curry with coconut rice.

2FOR1 2 COURSES | FRI | SAT | Thai

RADHUNI ☎01708 739 292
206 Main Road, Romford, RM2 5HA
Nearest Station: Gidea Park
Contemporary Indian cuisine that will completely stimulate your palate. Kind, welcoming staff are happy to ensure you have a pleasing dining experience.

2FOR1 MAIN COURSE | FRI ✱ | SAT ✱ | Indian

RAIZES BRAZILIAN ☎020 7739 2009
460 Hackney Road, Bethnal Green, E2 9EG
Nearest Station: Cambridge Heath
An original and delicious gastronomic experience. Raizes use carefully selected high quality meat, with many cuts to choose from. All cooked on a grill or griddle and served at your table from skewers.

25% OFF TOTAL | 8 | FRI ✓ | SAT ✓ | South American

RASA MUDRA ☎020 8539 1700
715 High Road, Leytonstone, E11 4RD
Nearest Station: Leytonstone High Road
Inspired by the authentic home cooking of beautiful, spice-rich Kerala, this restaurant's passion is food prepared always with devotion, love, and the finest ingredients. Experience the essence of India.

2FOR1 MAIN COURSE | FRI ✓ | SAT ✓ | Indian

RED HOUSE 020 8550 6451
Redbridge Lane East, Ilford, IG4 5BG
Nearest Station: Redbridge
Beefeater Grill are one of the UK's best-loved restaurants welcoming guests for almost 40 years in over 130 locations nationwide. *Excludes Breakfast, Light Bites, Bar menu, set menus and all other offers.

2FOR1 MAIN COURSE | 6 | FRI ✓ | SAT ✗ | Modern British

RED MANTRA ☎020 8989 7711
103-105 George Lane, South Woodford, E18 1AN
Nearest Station: South Woodford
The menus have been developed by the highly experienced chefs with unique takes on classical dishes influenced by Punjabi, Gujarati and South-East Asian Cuisine.

50% OFF FOOD | 6 | FRI ✗ | SAT ✗ | SUN | ✱ | Asian

RESTAURANT @ SOUTHGATE COLLEGE ☎020 8982 5068
High Street, Henfield, N14 6BS
Nearest Station: Southgate
The fresh talent of the trainee chefs at this eatery keep the guests consistently thrilled with an ever-changing, innovative menu. *Cannot be used in conjunction with any other offer.

2FOR1 3 COURSES | FRI ✓ | SAT ✓ | International

RIVER VIEW ☎020 7480 6026
New Crane Wharf, New Crane Place, Wapping, E1W 3TU
Nearest Station: Wapping
Enjoy great river views whilst dining at this well-established venue that delivers quality authentic Chinese cuisine. Offers a vast menu specialising in seafood and other fine dishes.

25% OFF TOTAL | 10 | FRI ✓ | SAT ✓ | Chinese

RIYADZ ☎01708 449 777
96 Ardleigh Green Road, Hornchurch, RM11 2LG
Nearest Station: Gidea Park
Bringing a unique experience with flavours inspired by culinary delights found in the heart of Asia, all dishes are made from over 30 spices and herbs, freshly cooked by an award-winning chef.

2FOR1 MAIN COURSE | FRI ✓ | SAT | ✱ | Indian

ROUGE ☎020 8548 7400
Redbridge College, Barley Lane, Little Heath, RM6 4XT
Nearest Station: Chadwell Heath
Support the talented chefs of the future at this college-based restaurant. Wonderful dishes are prepared by chefs-in-training, guaranteeing guests a first-class dining experience.

2FOR1 MAIN COURSE | FRI | SAT ✱ | SUN | International

ROYAL INDIA ☎020 7249 7025
47 Stoke Newington Church St, Stoke New'ton, N16 0NX
Nearest Station: Stoke Newington
Enjoy the luxurious furnishings that create a warm and inviting ambience at this phenomenal Indian restaurant. The takeaway option means delicious food can be enjoyed in the comfort of your own home.

25% OFF TOTAL | 6 | FRI | SAT | ✱ | Indian

ROYAL SPICE ☎020 7536 9902
815 Commercial Road, Tower Hamlets, E14 7HG
Nearest Station: Westferry
Combining the tastes of Bangladesh and India, chefs infuse each dish with aromatic and piquant flavours. Renowned for quality cuisine and impeccable service, weekend bookings are essential.

50% OFF FOOD | 4 | FRI ✓ | SAT ✓ | Indian

RUM & SUGAR ☎020 7538 2702
No. 1 Warehouse, West India Quay, E14 4AL
Nearest Station: West India Quay
Lovingly created using locally sourced, seasonal produce, Rum and Sugar's menu features British dishes with a contemporary twist. *Not available on Thursdays after 5pm.

2FOR1 MAIN COURSE | FRI ✓ | SAT ✓ | British

RUMAN ☎020 7359 5388
130 Black Stock Road, Finsbury Park, N4 2DX
Nearest Station: Finsbury Park
An excellent choice for authentic Indian cuisine in North London, Ruman gives all its attention to offering its diners the perfect, traditional Indian meal. *Not available on Match Days.

25% OFF TOTAL | 6 | FRI ✓ | SAT ✓ | ✱ | Indian

SAFFRON CROUCH END ☎020 8348 9412
33 Broadway Parade, Crouch End, N8 9DB
Nearest Station: Hornsey
Located in the heart of Crouch End, Saffron provides authentic Bangladeshi and Indian cuisine in sumptuous surroundings.Staff are friendly, attentive and happy to share their knowledgeable recommendations.

50% OFF FOOD | 6 | FRI ✓ | SAT ✓ | ✱ | Indian

SALAAM NAMASTE ☎01992 815 555
13 Forest Drive, Theydon Bois, CM16 7EX
Nearest Station: Theydon Bois
Exceeding guest expectations time and time again, Salaam Namaste offers great tasting food and a smooth table service. Impressive in appearance and taste, each dish is made to the highest standard.

25% OFF TOTAL | 10 | FRI ✓ | SAT ✓ | Indian

SERENE FISH AND CHIPS ☎020 8551 5655
27 Woodford Avenue, Ilford, IG2 6UF
Nearest Station: Gants Hill
Established in 1974, Serene take great pride not only in the high quality of produce, but also in the level of service they provide in creating mouthwatering fish & chips and other irresistible dishes.

25% OFF TOTAL | 10 | FRI | SAT | Seafood

SHAPLA INDIAN ☎020 8597 9933
612 Longbridge Road, Barking, RM8 2AJ
Nearest Station: Upney
Fully licensed restaurant in Dagenham serving a range of the traditional dishes with no frills, lots of flavour and in generous portions. Also does a takeaway service that is becoming increasingly popular.

50% OFF FOOD | 6 | FRI ✱ | SAT ✱ | Indian

SHAWARMA GRILL ☎020 8221 1881
72 High Road, Stratford, E15 2BP
Nearest Station: Leyton
Shawarma Grill is one of the best halal restaurants in London. Their namesake signature dish, Shawarma consists of succulent meat, Lebanese favourites such as hummus and an array of toppings.

2FOR1 MAIN COURSE | FRI ✓ | SAT ✓ | Middle Eastern

SHIMLA PUNJABI RESTAURANT & BAR
☎020 8360 1799

752 Green Lanes, Enfield, N21 3RE
Nearest Station: Winchmore Hill
Honest food from the Punjab region of India comes to London in the form of Shimla Punjabi. Sensational and scrumptious cuisine entices diners into returning time and time again for a beloved curry fix.

2FOR1 3 COURSES | FRI × | SAT × | ▲ — Indian

SILK RESTAURANT
☎020 8422 4477

2 Berther Road, Havering, RM11 3HS
Nearest Station: Emerson Park
Tuck into deep-fried scallops in batter served with a chilli and tamarind sauce at this Thai-inspired eatery, where diners can savour an abundance of dishes. Be sure not to miss the cracking entertainment.

25% OFF TOTAL | 10 | FRI ✱ | SAT ✱ — Asian

SMOLLENSKY'S
☎020 7719 0101

1 Reuters Plaza, Canary Wharf, E14 5AJ
Nearest Station: Canary Wharf
Cosmopolitan dining in a stylish environment offering diners stunning, modern food. With over 20 years experience, this restaurant continues to offer exceptional dishes perfect for any occasion.

25% OFF TOTAL | 4 | FRI ✓ | SAT ✓ | SUN | ▲ — American

SRI RATHIGA
☎020 8478 7272

312 High Road, Ilford, IG1 1QW
Nearest Station: Ilford
Affable staff provide an efficient service and warm friendly smiles in this wonderfully well-maintained restaurant. Ancient traditional recipes are used to create authentic South Indian cuisine.

2FOR1 MAIN COURSE | FRI | SAT | SUN | ✱ — Indian

STAR OF INDIA
☎020 8989 4028

875 High Rd, Leytonstone, E11 1HR
Nearest Station: Leytonstone
One of the best Indian restaurants in London boasting two award-winning chefs. Excellent staff provide a friendly atmosphere, serving diners with a huge array of full-flavoured dishes and beverages.

2FOR1 MAIN COURSE | FRI | SAT | ✱ — Indian

STRADA
020 7538 9435

12 Hertsmere Road, E14 4AE
Nearest Station: West India Quay
Offering fresh, bold dishes inspired by flavours of Italian city life – Strada serves a selection of indulgent tastes, to those seeking a blissful escape to laidback Italian life. *Excludes Pizzettas.

25% OFF TOTAL | 6 | FRI ✓ | SAT × | ▲ — Italian

SUNSET GRILL & MEZE BAR
☎020 8804 9055

500-504 Hertford Road, Enfield, EN3 5SS
Nearest Station: Turkey Street
Delectable cuisine that offers a real taste of Turkey. The succulent tapas dishes will transport you to a place that is warm, relaxing and entirely loveable.

50% OFF FOOD | FRI × | SAT × — Turkish

SWEET HANDZ RESTAURANT
☎020 7700 6427

148 Holloway Road, Holloway, N7 8DD
Nearest Station: Holloway Road
A wonderful restaurant situated in the heart of London. An extensive menu of traditional and modern Ghanaian cuisine is to be enjoyed with imported African beers, tropical cocktails and fine wine.

25% OFF TOTAL | 10 | FRI | SAT — African

TA DILINA
☎020 8368 6864

10 Hampden Square, East Barnet, N14 5JR
Nearest Station: Southgate
Authentic Greek food, with a comfortable and relaxing atmosphere - Ta Dalina brings friendly Greek hospitality and sumptuous food to North London.

2FOR1 2 COURSES | FRI | SAT — Greek

TABLE 7
☎020 8524 8438

1 Church View, The Green, Chingford, E4 7EL
Nearest Station: Chingford
Expect to find a beautiful picture on your plate. Specialising in modern British and European cuisine, a personal finishing touch goes a long way in the kitchen. *25% off for parties of 4 or more.

2FOR1 3 COURSES | FRI | SAT | SUN | ✱ | ▲ — European

TAJ MAHAL
☎01708 752 218

6 Station Parade, Victoria Road, Romford, RM1 2JA
Nearest Station: Romford
Classic Indian restaurant and takeaway near to Romford station, that serves a good selection of tasty, satisfying curries without undue bells and whistles, in good-sized portions and with sharp service.

50% OFF FOOD | FRI ✓ | SAT ✓ — Indian

THE TALE OF INDIA
☎020 7537 2546

53 India Dock Road, Isle of Dogs, E14 8HN
Nearest Station: Westferry
Classic Indian and Bangladeshi cuisine on the Isle of Dogs; all the array of spices marking out subcontinental cuisine, in a vibrant, buzzy and welcoming setting.

2FOR1 MAIN COURSE | FRI ✱ | SAT ✱ | ✱ | ▲ — Indian

TAMARIND INDIAN CUISINE
☎020 8599 1763

246-248 High Road, Romford, RM6 6AP
Nearest Station: Chadwell Heath
Classic Indian restaurant serving a fine line in traditional flavours and spices. Amiable staff serve with happy smiles and a good knowledge of the menu to help you make your choice.

2FOR1 3 COURSES | FRI × | SAT × — Indian

TANDOORI NIGHTS
☎020 8441 2131

27 Station Parade, Cockfosters, EN4 0DW
Nearest Station: Cockfosters
This venue offer diners a splendid range of curries and Tandoori specialities prepared by master chefs . A rendezvous for all who enjoy the exotic, spicy and healthy dishes of the Indian subcontinent.

25% OFF TOTAL | 8 | FRI | SAT — Indian

TARANTINO RESTAURANT
☎01708 504 030

51 High Street, Hornchurch, RM11 1TP
Nearest Station: Emerson Park
A well-rounded dining experience is what guests are guaranteed to receive. Adorned with native pictures, the walls are traditional and vibrant. Steaks, pizzas, and fish specials leave diners spoilt.

25% OFF TOTAL | 4 | FRI ✱ | SAT ✱ | ▲ — Italian

TASTE OF KERALA
☎020 8590 3770

1177 High Road, Chadwell Heath, Romford, RM6 4AL
Nearest Station: Chadwell Heath
Kerala has really taken on board its own meaning. Standing for 'where taste meets tradition', Kerala has a healthy combination of contemporary tastes and flavours with classic traditions.

50% OFF FOOD | 6 | FRI ✓ | SAT ✓ — Indian

TASTE OF NAWAB
☎020 8883 6429

97 Colney Hatch Lane, Muswell Hill, N10 1LR
Nearest Station: Bounds Green
Award-winning restaurant with an excellent reputation. Prepare yourself for a gastronomical journey through India and indulge your senses with an extensive menu offering spice-infused authentic dishes.

25% OFF TOTAL | 10 | FRI ✱ | SAT ✱ | SUN | ✱ | ▲ — Indian

TEMPLE FUSION AT WOODFORD
☎020 8504 4380

Old Parcel Office, Woodford, IG8 7QF
Nearest Station: Woodford
The Temple Bar & Restaurant serves 'Indian Fusion' style cuisine, which samples dishes from the Indian sub-continent including Bangladesh, India and Nepal.

50% OFF FOOD | 4 | FRI × | SAT × | ▲ — Indian

THE THATCHED HOUSE
01708 641 408

St. Marys Lane, Upminster, RM14 3LT
Nearest Station: Upminster
This Vintage Inn oozes rural charm and rustic character. The picturesque surroundings provide the perfect backdrop for savouring the hearty, seasonal pub-food on the menu.

25% OFF TOTAL | FRI ✓ | SAT ✓ | SUN | ▲ — Modern British

THEYDON BOIS BALTI HOUSE
☎01992 814 104

Station Approach, Coppice Row, Theydon Bois, CM16 7EU
Nearest Station: Epping
The oldest Tandoori restaurant in the area offering innovative takes on authentic Indian, Persian and Kashmiri dishes. Attentiveness is a key attribute of all the staff at this local friendly restaurant.

2FOR1 MAIN COURSE | FRI ✱ | SAT ✱ | ✱ — Indian

To understand what the restaurant icons mean, please see the inside back cover.

THE THREE JOLLY WHEELERS 020 8502 9296
735 Chigwell Road, Woodford Green, IG8 8AS
Nearest Station: Chigwell
This Vintage Inn oozes rural charm and rustic character. The picturesque surroundings provide the perfect backdrop for savouring the hearty, seasonal pub-food on the menu.

25% OFF TOTAL | FRI ✓ | SAT ✓ | SUN | ▲ — Modern British

TIERRA PERU ☎020 7354 5586
164 Essex Road, Islington, N1 8LY
Nearest Station: Essex Road
Tierra Peru is a new restaurant in the heart of Islington, serving authentic Peruvian cuisine in a modern and relaxed atmosphere.

2FOR1 2 COURSES | FRI ✱ | SAT ✱ — South American

TOPGOLF CHIGWELL ☎020 8500 2644
TopGolf Game Centre, Abridge Road, Chigwell, IG7 6BX
Nearest Station: Debden
What better way to top off your game of golf than with a fantastic meal. Head to the Bayview Café Bar where you can find a variety of food available all day long.

50% OFF FOOD | 👤 4 | FRI ✱ | SAT × | SUN — British

TRADERS RESTAURANT @ HOLIDAY INN ☎020 7791 9010
261-267 Commercial Road, Tower Hamlets, E1 2BT
Nearest Station: Shadwell
The superb in-house restaurant at Holiday Inn London - Commercial Road,Traders Restaurant & Bar offers internationally-inspired food and drink, created with both the individual traveller and families in mind.

50% OFF FOOD | 👤 4 | FRI ▮ | SAT ▮ — British

THE TRIANGLE ☎020 8292 0516
1 Ferme Park Road, Crouch End, N4 4DS
Nearest Station: Crouch Hill
Through an esoterically patterned front door into a lush space of lanterns and varia, this is a quirky, appealing place. The lively kitchen serves eclectic cuisine, from Mediterranean to Moroccan to Thai.

50% OFF FOOD | 👤 2 | FRI ✱ | SAT ✱ — International

TWENTY TWELVE RESTAURANT ☎020 3301 4040
Holiday Inn Stratford City, Stratford, E20 1GL
Nearest Station: Stratford
Twenty Twelve Restaurant is located in The Holiday Inn. The menu features dishes of European cuisine and visitors can enjoy alfresco dining on The Stadium terrace with panoramic views over the Olympic Park

50% OFF FOOD | 👤 6 | FRI ✓ | SAT ✓ — European

VERTIGO LOUNGE 01708 479 609
17-19 Station Lane, Hornchurch, RM12 6JL
Nearest Station: Emerson Park
A contemporary al fresco roof terrace makes this venue a hot spot for dining with friends. With sophistication at the forefront, Vertigo is ideal for evening drinks and social functions.

2FOR1 3 COURSES | FRI ✱ | SAT ✱ — Modern European

THE VILLAGE GREEK ☎020 8449 1341
24 Lytton Road, Barnet, EN5 5BY
Nearest Station: New Barnet
Concerned solely with the quality of the cuisine, the décor at this authentic Greek eatery is contemporary yet simple. Mediterranean inspired, guests feast on tender kebabs and creamy home-made dips.

25% OFF TOTAL | 👤 4 | FRI × | SAT × | ✱ — Greek

VILLAGE TANDOORI ☎020 8531 3835
Burnside Avenue, Chingford, E4 8YJ
Nearest Station: Highams Park
Well-established Indian takeaway in Chingford with a heady selection of dishes and a strong emphasis on quality ingredients and cutting down on grease.

2FOR1 MAIN COURSE | FRI × | SAT × | SUN — Indian

THE WESTBRIDGE ☎020 3327 4969
335-337 High Street, Stratford, E15 2TF
Nearest Station: Stratford
A favourite with guests and locals alike, the menu boasts a good selection of British classics using only the finest local ingredients as well as an impressive selection of wines and ales.

25% OFF TOTAL | 👤 2 | FRI ✓ | SAT ✓ | ▲ — European

WILLOW FARM 01708 634 825
New Road, Wennington, Rainham, RM13 9ED
Nearest Station: Rainham
Quality pub classics with modern twists meets with a friendly and relaxed atmosphere to make this Table Table venue the perfect place for any occasion. *Excludes daytime & evening deals and festive menus.

2FOR1 MAIN COURSE | FRI ✓ | SAT ✓ — Modern British

WINDMILL TAPAS RESTAURANT ☎020 8521 8544
18 High Street, Walthamstow, E17 7LD
Nearest Station: St James Street
Bringing a taste of Portugal and Madeira to London, Jose and Regina serve a tempting terrine of tasty tapas dishes. Dubbed a well-kept-secret by locals, this venue guarantees a good night out.

25% OFF TOTAL | 👤 2 | FRI × | SAT × | SUN | ▲ — Tapas

WOLKITE KITFO ☎020 7700 3055
82 Hornsey Road, Islington, N7 7NN
Nearest Station: Arsenal
Delicious food and a hearty serving of warm, welcoming Ethiopian hospitality makes Wolkite Kitfo a must for all adventurous diners.

2FOR1 MAIN COURSE | FRI ✓ | SAT × | SUN — Ethiopian

YE OLDE CHERRY TREE 020 8886 1808
The Green, Southgate, N14 6EN
Nearest Station: Southgate
This Vintage Inn oozes rural charm and rustic character. The picturesque surroundings provide the perfect backdrop for savouring the hearty, seasonal pub-food on the menu.

25% OFF TOTAL | FRI ✓ | SAT ✓ | SUN | ▲ — Modern British

ZAMAN RESTAURANT ☎020 8366 3474
101 St Marks Road, Enfield, EN1 1BJ
Nearest Station: Bush Hill Park
When the only thing that will satisfy your hunger is a delicious Indian feast, head to Zaman Restaurant. Here you will find sensational flavours and fine spices, every dish proving to be wholly moreish.

2FOR1 MAIN COURSE | FRI ▮ | SAT ▮ | ✱ — Indian

ZARANA INDIAN RESTAURANT ☎01708 456 000
55 High Street, Hornchurch, RM11 1TP
Nearest Station: Emerson Park
Superbly blending age-old Indian recipes with a contemporary spin, Zarana provides a concise menu to tempt an array of curry lovers.

2FOR1 MAIN COURSE | FRI ✓ | SAT ✓ — Indian

ZAYNZAH ☎020 8444 9808
148 Colney Hatch Lane, Muswell Hill, N10 1ER
Nearest Station: Alexandra Palace
A modern, refreshing Indian restaurant that offers all of the classic favourites in a contemporary open atmosphere. Guests might like to choose the supremely tasty channa gosht.

25% OFF TOTAL | 👤 4 | FRI ▮ | SAT ▮ — Indian

ZIAS ☎020 7263 9955
680 Holloway Road, Archway, N19 3NP
Nearest Station: Upper Holloway
High-quality, fresh-faced Indian restaurant that serves some excellent food to go with the cosy and colourful atmosphere. Standards are high, from simple yellow lentil dhal to the aromatic jafarani duck.

50% OFF FOOD | 👤 10 | FRI ▮ | SAT ▮ | SUN | ▲ — Indian

ZIGNI HOUSE ☎020 7226 7418
330 Essex Road, Islington, N1 3PB
Nearest Station: Canonbury
Cultural trinkets and fitting décor enhance the culinary adventure that Zigni House offers. Be prepared for an East African whirlwind, with mild to fiery flavours being well-accommodated on the menu.

25% OFF TOTAL | 👤 4 | FRI ▮ | SAT ▮ — African

ZOE RESTAURANT ☎020 7354 0087
149a Upper street, Islington, N1 1RA
Nearest Station: Essex Road
Make time to visit Zoe without any regrets; the food here has been inspired by the colours and flavours of France and the Mediterranean, while the interior décor has the warmth of a far-away land.

25% OFF TOTAL | 👤 6 | FRI ▮ | SAT ▮ | ▲ — French

North West

A DIL SE
☎020 8515 0825
56-60 Northolt Road, South Harrow, HA2 0DW
Nearest Station: South Harrow
From business meetings to intimate meals for two, this Indo-Chinese-inspired venue dazzles guests with a strikingly vivacious interior. Chefs prepare the cuisine to the highest of culinary expectations.

25% OFF TOTAL | 10 | FRI ✱ | SAT ✱ — Indian/Chinese

THE ADAM & EVE
☎020 8959 1553
The Ridgeway, Mill Hill, NW7 1RL
Nearest Station: Mill Hill East
The Adam and Eve is very proud of its monthly changing menus (both a la carte and set menus) that feature fresh, seasonal and wherever possible, locally sourced ingredients.

25% OFF TOTAL | 4 | FRI × | SAT × | SUN | ▲ — British

AKKADIA
☎020 7938 1547
221 Kensington High Street, Kensington, W8 6SG
Nearest Station: Kensington
Akkadia Lebanese restaurant in London's Kensington High Street has been a local favourite. The Lebanese menu here is authentic and loaded with favourites, from beautiful lamb dishes to many mezze dishes.

25% OFF TOTAL | FRI × | SAT × | SUN | ▲ — Lebanese

ALIBABA
☎01923 229 793
13 King Street, Watford, WD18 0BW
Nearest Station: Watford High Street
Long-established, the chefs use authentic Indian recipes that stand the test of time. With quality at the forefront of their ethos, you can ensure dishes of an impeccable standard on every visit.

2FOR1 MAIN COURSE | FRI ✓ | SAT ✓ — Indian

ANAR PERSIAN KITCHEN
☎020 8960 6555
349 Portobello Road, Notting Hill, W10 5SA
Nearest Station: Ladbroke Grove
Anar's flawless backdrop is the perfect atmosphere to surround you in rich and modern Persian culture and to indulge in traditional and mouth watering Persian cuisine.

50% OFF FOOD | 4 | FRI 📱 | SAT 📱 — Middle Eastern

ANARKALI INDIAN CUISINE
☎020 8748 1760
303-305 King Street, Hammersmith, W6 9NH
Nearest Station: Ravenscourt Park
Reasonably priced Indian restaurant serving a menu of quintessential Indian food.

2FOR1 MAIN COURSE | FRI ✓ | SAT ✓ — Indian

ANJANAAS INDIAN CUISINE
☎020 7624 1713
57-59 Willesden Lane, Kilburn, NW6 7RL
Nearest Station: Brondesbury Park
The philosophy at Anjanaas is to convey passion for Indian cuisine by questing for the perfect ingredients and using expert techniques to craft dishes that satisfy each and every one of their patrons.

25% OFF TOTAL | 6 | FRI ✓ | SAT ✓ — Indian

THE ARENA CLUB
☎020 8202 0128
17 Central Circus, Barnet, NW4 3AS
Nearest Station: Hendon Central
Sports lovers are in their element at this modish bar complete with Sky Sports and ESPN licences, showcasing football, rugby and much more. Grab a bite to eat and a cold pint whilst watching the game.

2FOR1 2 COURSES | FRI 📱 | SAT 📱 | ✱ | ▲ — Indian

AREN'S BAR AND RESTAURANT
☎020 8868 3092
Joel Street, Pinner, HA5 2PR
Nearest Station: Northwood Hills
With beautifully decorated bar lounges, a state of the art dance room and a 40 seater dining area serving only the best European dishes, Arens Bar & Restaurant is perfect for any special occasion.

25% OFF TOTAL | 6 | FRI × | SAT × | SUN | ▲ — British

AROMA SPICE
☎020 7267 0444
98 Fleet Road, Hampstead, NW3 2QX
Nearest Station: Hampstead Heath
Renowned for its welcoming staff, this long-established eatery endorses family recipes that have been passed down through the generations. Fill your appetite with an authentic, hearty curry.

25% OFF TOTAL | 6 | FRI 📱 | SAT 📱 | ▲ — Indian

THE ART OF PIZZA
☎020 8450 3644
73 Cricklewood Lane, NW2 1HR
Nearest Station: Cricklewood
The Art of Pizza offers diners a fresh approach to the pizzeria. A great venue for family and friends, the restaurant offers delicious Italian fare for everyone.

50% OFF FOOD | 4 | FRI 📱 | SAT 📱 — Italian

ATELIER
☎01923 235 881
Elton Way, Watford, WD25 8HA
Nearest Station: Watford
Enjoy some of the best French cuisine this side of the Channel here at Atelier Restaurant. Proud in-house eatery at the Hilton Watford Hotel, you'll find French onion soups and creamy crème brulees.

25% OFF TOTAL | 6 | FRI ✓ | SAT ✓ — French

AURA AT HA5
☎020 8868 6101
99 Field End Road, Pinner, HA5 1QG
Nearest Station: Eastcote
A fine Indian restaurant where crispy, fresh poppadoms, tasty sundries and home-made dips are guaranteed to start your evening out on the right foot. Tasty curries and succulent tandoori options.

25% OFF TOTAL | 8 | FRI ✓ | SAT ✓ | ✱ | ▲ — Indian

BALTI NAZ
☎020 8560 5900
185 South Ealing Road, Ealing, W5 4RH
Nearest Station: South Ealing
Massive array of Indian dishes at this friendly restaurant. Balti dishes are their speciality, among which the spicy lamb rezzala is particularly worth a try.

2FOR1 MAIN COURSE | FRI ✓ | SAT ✓ — Indian

BAR UNO
☎020 7428 0546
4 Inverness Street, Camden, W5 1ED
Nearest Station: Camden Town
With 35 years experience, the chef at Bar UNO rustles up Mexican cuisine to an impeccable standard. Whatever the dish, it is assured to be authentic and mouth-watering.

25% OFF TOTAL | 8 | FRI ✓ | SAT ✓ — Tex-Mex

BARBARELLA
☎020 7385 9434
428 Fulham Road, Fulham, W6 1DU
Nearest Station: Fulham Broadway
Combining elegant Italian cuisine with late night entertainment, this bar and restaurant has proven an iconic night-life venue in the surrounding area. Devour great food before dancing the night away.

2FOR1 MAIN COURSE | FRI ✱ | SAT 📱 | SUN — Italian

BARISTA
☎020 8371 6644
24 Ballards Lane, Finchley, N3 2BJ
Nearest Station: Finchley Central
Barista, conveniently located a short walk from Finchley Central tube station, serves freshly made food, prepared with the greatest care and attention in the hope that they will exceed expectations.

50% OFF FOOD | FRI × | SAT × | SUN | ✱ | ▲ — International

BASIL & MINT BAR AND RESTAURANT
☎020 7381 8150
238-240 Munster Road, Fulham, SW6 6BA
Nearest Station: Parsons Green
Basil and Mint may seem an unusual combination, yet at this Fulham restaurant the choice of rarely combined herbs is a reflection of a successfully executed fusion.

2FOR1 2 COURSES | FRI ✓ | SAT ✓ | ✱ — Indian

BAY OF BENGAL
☎020 8451 4666
21 Walm Lane, Willesden, NW2 5SH
Nearest Station: Willesden Green
Indulge in authentic Indian cuisine at this fabulous eatery where dishes guarantee to be aromatic and piquant. The friendly and affable staff ensure a fantastic dining experience.

2FOR1 3 COURSES | FRI ✓ | SAT ✓ — Indian

Gourmet Society discount applies to the à la carte menu only, unless stated otherwise.

BEIRUT NIGHTS ☎020 8961 2101
19 Abbey Road, Brent Park, NW10 7RB
Nearest Station: Park Royal
With relaxed surroundings nestled in between Mediterranean and Middle Eastern ambience, you will be transported to another world of culinary delight by enjoying an assortment of Lebanese delicacies.
25% OFF TOTAL | FRI × | SAT × | ✱ — Middle Eastern

BELLA ITALIA 020 8579 7089
36 New Broadway, Ealing, W5 2XA
Nearest Station: Ealing Broadway
Accessible Italian cuisine on the British high street – indulge in authentic sharing platters, hand stretched pizzas and hearty pasta dishes, served with a healthy dose of gregarious Italian hospitality.
25% OFF TOTAL | 👤6 | FRI × | SAT × | SUN | ▲ — Italian

BELLISSIMO RESTAURANT & PIZZERIA ☎01923 232 223
The Parade, Watford High Street, Watford, WD17 1AW
Nearest Station: Watford
Italian restaurant with high, bright murals, open-face brickwork, low, cosy light and sharp service. The menu in turn is broad and appealing, primarily Italian; the quality is good and the place a delight.
50% OFF FOOD | 👤4 | FRI ✷ | SAT ✷ — Italian

BENGAL SPICE ☎020 7794 3744
245 West End Lane, Camden, NW6 1XN
Nearest Station: West Hampstead
Curry house with a choice menu, attentive and knowledgeable waiters, and smart, skilful cooking values. There are also a good selection of alternatives for those who are willing to go off the beaten track.
2FOR1 3 COURSES | FRI ✷ | SAT ✷ — Indian

BINA TANDOORI ☎01923 823 412
110 High Street, Northwood, HA6 1BJ
Nearest Station: Northwood
A family-run business for the past 30 years, Bina has the experience and skill to ensure an enjoyable visit, whatever your preference.
50% OFF FOOD | FRI 📱 | SAT 📱 — Indian

BLACK PEPPER RESTAURANT ☎020 8421 4349
461 Uxbridge Road, Hatch End, HA5 4JS
Nearest Station: Hatch End
Ideally located in the heart of Hatch End, this prestigious Italian restaurant and bar boasts a dazzling selection of champagnes with which to accompany a sophisticated dish.
2FOR1 3 COURSES | FRI ✷ | SAT ✷ | ▲ — Italian

BLOODY FRENCH CANTINE ☎020 7727 7770
149 Westbourne Grove, W11 2RS
Nearest Station: Notting Hill Gate
French chic meets bohemian bistro in this bustling venue, popular among locals for its stylish and elegant interior as well as the taste of Europe in a quirky and authentic menu that is fit for foodies.
2FOR1 3 COURSES | FRI ✓ | SAT × | ✱ — European

BLUE LAGOON THAI RESTAURANT ☎020 7603 1231
284 Kensington High Street, Kensington, W14 8NZ
Nearest Station: Kensington
With an array of seafood, meat and vegetarian dishes, Blue Lagoon is enough to excite and entice any diner. Ingredients are fresh from Thailand, and the Thai chef guarantees the most oriental of flavours.
50% OFF FOOD | 👤6 | FRI ✓ | SAT ✓ — Thai

BODEANS BBQ ☎020 7610 0440
4 Fulham Broadway Chambers, Fulham, SW6 1EP
Nearest Station: Fulham Broadway
Bodeans is the brainchild of Andre Blais who set out in 2002 to bring the taste and the style of classic Kansas City barbecue to London. A fresh twist on Americana that makes for a great place to relax.
2FOR1 MAIN COURSE | FRI × | SAT × | SUN | ▲ — American

BOMBAY BISTRO ☎020 8992 5131
47 High Street, Acton Trussell, W3 6ND
Nearest Station: Acton Central
Imaginative approach to Indian cuisine at this great little bistro that has won a fine reputation in the area. Broad-based menu that's not unmanageable, and cooking marked by exceptional production values.
2FOR1 MAIN COURSE | FRI 📱 | SAT 📱 | ▲ — Indian

BOMBAY FLAME ☎020 7625 5522
74 Kingsgate Road, West Hampstead, NW6 4TE
Nearest Station: Brondesbury
Offering everything for the meek and mild palate to the chilli fiend, Bombay Flame knows how to cater for all. Boasting highly experienced chefs who serve up tasty regional specialities.
50% OFF FOOD | 👤10 | FRI ✓ | SAT ✓ | ✱ — Indian

BOMBAY NIGHTS ☎020 7431 4802
90 Fortune Green Road, West Hampstead, NW6 1DS
Nearest Station: West Hampstead
Award-winning chef Jude Pinto creates mouth-watering Indian dishes that can be adjusted to each individual palate. Expect nice smiles and warm welcomes as you enter the night.
2FOR1 MAIN COURSE | FRI 📱 | SAT 📱 | ✱ | ▲ — Indian

THE BRASSERIE @ MERCURE ☎0844 815 9056
Mercure London Watford Hotel, Watford, WD25 8JH
Nearest Station: Watford
Combining comfort with its close proximity to the centre of the Big Smoke, the Mercure London Watford Hotel is an ideal place to stay. The Brasserie serves delectable appetising cuisine.
2FOR1 3 COURSES | FRI ✓ | SAT ✓ — Brasserie

BROADWAY BRASSERIE ☎020 8748 3899
58 Fulham Palace Road, Hammersmith, W6 9PH
Nearest Station: Hammersmith
Experience perfectly cooked and presented Indian cuisine in the heart of Hammersmith. The menu boasts a wide range of traditional Indian dishes, plus many other Indian specialities.
25% OFF TOTAL | 👤10 | FRI ✓ | SAT ✓ — Indian

BUMBU RESTAURANT ☎020 8965 3938
39 Station Road, Willesden, NW10 4UP
Nearest Station: Willesden Junction
Highly popular with locals and diners from surrounding areas. Each dish is thoughtfully prepared, using only the finest ingredients to create the most delicious of tastes.
25% OFF TOTAL | FRI ✓ | SAT ✓ | SUN — Caribbean

CAFÉ BUKUSHI ☎01923 859 911
245 Watling Street, Radlett, WD7 7AL
Nearest Station: Radlett
A unique fusion of a New York deli and a contemporary sushi bar. Scrumptious sandwiches and salads, burgers and ribs can be enjoyed if the fresh fish sushi and bukushi sauces aren't for you.
25% OFF TOTAL | 👤4 | FRI ✓ | SAT ✷ — Japanese

CAFE DE THAI RESTAURANT ☎020 7243 3001
20 All Saints Road, Westbourne Park, W11 1HE
Nearest Station: Westbourne Park
Exquisite and unique Thai restaurant showcasing an array of intense and flavourful dishes, with fresh ingredients being their essential secret. A venue that ensures diners a memorable experience.
50% OFF FOOD | 👤10 | FRI ✓ | SAT ✓ | ▲ — Thai

CAFÉ MEZZA ☎01923 211 500
144 High Street, Watford, WD17 2EN
Nearest Station: Watford
A traditional café offering delicious Lebanese food in an amiable environment. Dine on a Friday and Saturday evening and be entertained by authentic belly dancing and Lebanese music.
2FOR1 MAIN COURSE | FRI 📱 | SAT 📱 | ✱ | ▲ — Lebanese

CAFE RIALTO ☎020 7736 9429
825 Fulham Road, Fulham, SW6 5HG
Nearest Station: Parsons Green
Welcoming little café whose strengths are in its hospitality and quality of dishes across an eclectic Italian menu. On Saturdays and Sundays they also do a great brunch menu out of the English top drawer.
2FOR1 MAIN COURSE | FRI ✷ | SAT ✷ | ▲ — Italian

CAFFE CONCERTO WESTFIELD ☎ 0844 335 8403
Westfield Shopping Centre, Hammersmith, W12 7GE
Nearest Station: Wood Lane
Luxurious, contemporary dining with a focus on favourites from the Italian table. Carbonara to chicken Milanese along with some outstanding vegetarian, seafood, and salad options.
25% OFF TOTAL | 4 | FRI ✓ | SAT ✓ — Italian

CAFFE PICCOLO ☎ 020 8747 9989
26 Chiswick High Road, Chiswick, W4 1TE
Nearest Station: Stamford Brook
A characterful Italian restaurant that oozes a personality all of its own. Generous portions of delicious food are served by terrific waiting staff who will brighten even the dullest of days.
2FOR1 MAIN COURSE | FRI ✓ | SAT ✓ — Italian

CARLTON LOUNGE ☎ 020 8205 3112
232-234 Kingsbury Road, Kingsbury, NW9 0BH
Nearest Station: Kingsbury
The Carlton Lounge bestows upon its diners the finest selections of scrumptious North Indian cuisines, freshly and expertly prepared by their chefs. Fine Indian cuisine, service and atmosphere.
25% OFF TOTAL | FRI × | SAT × — Indian

CARTHAGE TAPAS AND MEZE BAR ☎ 020 8567 3427
99 Uxbridge Road, Hanwell, W7 3ST
Nearest Station: Hanwell
Promising to transport you to the Mediterranean, this venue offers meze classics and tapas to share. Soak up the holiday atmosphere without the price-tag.
50% OFF FOOD | 8 | FRI 📱 | SAT 📱 — Mediterranean

CASA BATAVIA ☎ 020 7221 7348
135 Kensington Church Street, Kensington, W8 7LP
Nearest Station: Notting Hill Gate
Devour succulent baby squid and wild fennel, or tender rabbit salad prepared by Michelin recognised Nicola Batavia. Beautifully decorated, this venue oozes cool sophistication and overlooks Kensington.
25% OFF TOTAL | 6 | FRI ✓ | SAT ✓ — Italian

CASARECCIA ☎ 020 7328 0800
267 Kilburn High Road, Kilburn, NW6 7JR
Nearest Station: Brondesbury
A pleasant and friendly atmosphere in which you'll find infectiously happy staff. Well accomplished recipes make use of the freshest natural ingredients. A perfect place to create special memories.
25% OFF TOTAL | 8 | FRI ✓ | SAT ✓ — Italian

CEDAR TREE LEBANESE RESTAURANT ☎ 01895 631 401
80 Victoria Road, Ruislip, HA4 0AL
Nearest Station: Ruislip
The staff at Cedar Tree understand the importance of every dining experience; that's why they are proud to serve sensational Lebanese food in a warm inviting atmosphere, where service is second to none.
2FOR1 MAIN COURSE | FRI × | SAT × | 🌲 — Lebanese

CELEBRITY RESTAURANT ☎ 020 8204 0444
714-716 Kenton Road, Kenton, HA3 9QX
Nearest Station: Kingsbury
Subtle tones and stylish design make this a really calm, comfortable place to enjoy dinner. The menu is broad and eclectic, while the dishes are done with care and professionalism, and are full of taste.
25% OFF TOTAL | 2 | FRI ✱ | SAT × | SUN | ✱ | 🌲 — Indian

CHAUDHRY'S TKC RESTAURANT ☎ 020 8571 5738
161-163 The Broadway, Southall, UB1 1LR
Nearest Station: Southall
The menu here is filled with Punjabi dishes of outstanding quality which have been popular in Southall for more than four decades.
25% OFF TOTAL | FRI ✓ | SAT ✓ — Indian

CHEHEL SOTOUN ☎ 020 7221 3598
108 Holland Park Avenue, Notting Hill, W11 4UA
Nearest Station: Holland Park
Bringing the delicious and unusual flavours of Persia to Notting Hill,Chehel Sotoun offers the best in this exotic cuisine. If you fancy something a little different, be sure to give Chehel Sotoun a whirl.
25% OFF TOTAL | 2 | FRI ✓ | SAT ✓ — Middle Eastern

CAFÉ ROUGE

25% OFF TOTAL

25% OFF TOTAL | 6 | FRI ✓ | SAT ✓ | ✱ | 🌲

9 restaurants in North West London

Address	Station	Phone
227-229 Chiswick High Road, Chiswick, W4 2DW	Turnham Green	020 8742 7447
17 The Green, Ealing, W5 5DA	Ealing Broadway	020 8579 2788
Leisure Way, Finchley, N12 0QZ	West Finchley	020 8446 4777
98-100 Shepherds Bush Rd, Hammersmith, W6 7PD	Goldhawk Road	020 7602 7732
38-40 High Street, Hampstead, NW3 1QE	Hampstead	020 7435 4240
6-7 South Grove, Highgate, N6 6BP	Highgate	020 8342 9797
85 Strand on the Green, Kew, W4 3PU	Kew Bridge	020 8995 6575
13-13a High Street, Pinner, Harrow, HA5 5PJ	Pinner	020 8429 4424
10 High Street, Ruislip, Hillingdon, HA4 7AW	Ruislip	01895 678 572

CHUTNEY'S RESTAURANT
01923 254 900
6 Chalk Hill, Watford, WD19 4BL
Nearest Station: Watford High Street
Devoted to providing an authentic Indian experience, Chutney's serves delicious food in a charming environment. When hungry bellies are grumbling for food, this venue will not fail to impress.
2FOR1 MAIN COURSE | FRI | SAT | ✱ — Indian

CIRRIK FULHAM
020 7381 1154
297 Northend Road, Fulham, W14 9NS
Nearest Station: West Brompton
Specialising in kebabs, this Turkish menu hosts authentic masterpieces such as tender lamb kebabs and adana kebabs. The ocakbasi grill adds a Mediterranean feel to the cuisine.
2FOR1 MAIN COURSE | FRI ✓ | SAT ✓ — Turkish

THE CLARENDON
020 7229 1500
123a Clarendon Road, Notting Hill, W11 4JG
Nearest Station: Latimer Road
All-in-one pub, cocktail lounge bar and restaurant providing a welcome oasis of calm. Offers an exciting menu that changes seasonally with different exquisite dishes on offer to satisfy all guests.
2FOR1 3 COURSES | FRI ✱ | SAT ✱ | SUN — European

CLAYE CHEF
020 8861 5772
391 High Road, Harrow Weald, HA3 6EL
Nearest Station: Headstone Lane
Curry lovers unite at this amiable Indian restaurant. A vast menu presents a wide range of dishes that caters for all tastes, appetites and palates.
50% OFF FOOD | 10 | FRI ✓ | SAT ✓ — Indian/Bangladeshi

CLUB TREE'S
020 8907 4448
406 Kenton Lane, Harrow, HA3 8RQ
Nearest Station: Canons Park
Experience an invigorating and innovative menu that is bursting with piquant flavours. This venue boasts dishes that taste just as authentic as those prepared in a domestic Indian kitchen.
25% OFF TOTAL | 10 | FRI ✱ | SAT ✱ — Indian

COCO BAMBOO
020 7267 6613
48 Chalk Farm Road, Chalk Farm, NW1 8AJ
Nearest Station: Chalk Farm
A family-run bar and restaurant serving the finest Brazilian and Caribbean cuisine and a superb selection of exotic cocktails. An authentic South American experience.
2FOR1 3 COURSES | FRI ✓ | SAT ✓ | ✱ — Brazilian

THE CORIANDER LEAF
020 8560 6660
158 South Ealing Road, South Ealing, W5 4QL
Nearest Station: South Ealing
At The Coriander Leaf, the aim is to stay true to the revered authentic taste and cooking preparations of the Indian sub-continent, whilst bringing a fresh level of innovation to the traditional menu.
25% OFF TOTAL | FRI | SAT — Indian

THE COY CARP
01895 821 471
Copperhill Lane, Harefield, Uxbridge, UB9 6HZ
Nearest Station: Rickmansworth
This Vintage Inn oozes rural charm and rustic character. The picturesque surroundings provide the perfect backdrop for savouring the hearty, seasonal pub-food on the menu.
25% OFF TOTAL | FRI ✓ | SAT ✓ | SUN — Modern British

THE CUBAN CAMDEN
020 7424 0692
Stables Market, Chalk Farm Road, Camden, NW1 8AH
Nearest Station: Chalk Farm
An authentic and unique experience for diners, who can enjoy the Cuban cuisine while admiring the Che Guevara-inspired dining and bar areas. Draws a relaxed, informal crowd for a truly chilled evening.
2FOR1 MAIN COURSE | FRI ✓ | SAT ✓ — Cuban

DALCHA
020 7731 6066
636 Fulham Road, Fulham, SW6 5RT
Nearest Station: Parsons Green
The cooking is distinctive yet familiar at this noteworthy neighbourhood restaurant. Each and every dish from the menu has been given a mouth-watering and flavoursome spin
25% OFF TOTAL | 8 | FRI × | SAT × — Indian

DAR'S
020 7482 1029
2 Elm Terrace, Constantine Road, NW3 2LL
Nearest Station: Hampstead Heath
Dar's is a family run Pakistani & Indian Restaurant offering tasty and traditional food. Authentic and delicious; the team at Dar's bring you the real taste of Punjab.
2FOR1 3 COURSES | FRI ✓ | SAT ✓ | ✱ — Indian

D'DEN
020 8830 5000
47 Cricklewood Broadway, Cricklewood, NW2 3JX
Nearest Station: Kilburn
A charismatic little restaurant serving distinctive, spicy, fizzing Nigerian-based dishes in an especially vibrant, inviting atmosphere.
2FOR1 MAIN COURSE | FRI ✓ | SAT ✓ | ✱ — African

DELHI SPICEE
01895 624 700
136 High Street, Ruilsip, HA4 8LL
Nearest Station: Ruislip
Experience a fusion of western presentation, Indian cuisine and contemporary ambience, at Delhi Spicee, where traditional favourites and contemporary options are presented with more than a hint of style.
25% OFF TOTAL | 8 | FRI × | SAT × | SUN | ✱ — Indian

DES PARDES
020 8905 0940
248 Kingsbury Road, Kingsbury, NW9 0BG
Nearest Station: Kingsbury
Des pardes is an authentic Indian Pakistani takeaway restaurant, using the most traditional herbs, spices and cooking techniques, the staff at Des Pardes create an extensive menu that will suit everyone.
25% OFF TOTAL | 10 | FRI ✓ | SAT — Indian

THE DISTILLERS
020 8748 2834
64 Fulham Palace Road, Hammersmith, W6 9PH
Nearest Station: Hammersmith
The Distillers is a bar meets pub venue with chandeliers and atmospheric lighting, this carefully chosen decor sets the scene for guests to enjoy meals that are freshly prepared with local produce.
25% OFF TOTAL | 4 | FRI × | SAT ✓ — British

DONBOIS THAI RESTAURANT
020 7736 8833
311 New Kings Road, Fulham, SW6 4RF
Nearest Station: Parsons Green
Lovers of tasty Thai cuisine will be extremely pleased with the flavourful dishes on offer here. Dishes overflow with deliciousness and are served in generous portions.
25% OFF TOTAL | 4 | FRI | SAT | ✱ — Thai

DOOEY'S RESTAURANT
020 8861 3030
41-43 Station Road, Harrow, HA1 2UA
Nearest Station: Harrow & Wealdstone
Drawing on the traditional flavours and recipes of Northern India, Dooey's serves delicious Indian cuisine while also offering a plentiful seafood menu. Also offers a bar area for after dinner drinks.
50% OFF FOOD | 6 | FRI ✓ | SAT × | ✱ — Indian

THE DURELL ARMS
020 7736 3014
704 Fulham Road, Fulham, SW6 5SB
Nearest Station: Parsons Green
Quality menu with daily specials, produced using the freshest ingredients, including their renowned Sunday roast where diners get a true taste of home-cooking. Historical setting with contemporary touch.
50% OFF FOOD | 8 | FRI ✓ | SAT ✓ — British

THE EALING PARK TAVERN
020 8758 1879
222 South Ealing Road, Ealing, W5 4RL
Nearest Station: South Ealing
An open kitchen, slouchy sofas and blazing fireplaces are just a handful of the fantastic features of the Ealing Park Tavern. Pan fried salmon to pancetta wrapped pork, the menu is plentiful.
2FOR1 MAIN COURSE | 4 | FRI ✱ | SAT ✱ | SUN — English and Continental

EL METRO
020 7384 1264
10 Effie Road, Fulham, SW6 1TB
Nearest Station: Fulham Broadway
With a keen sense of place and an ambition to be its own little 'Castle in Spain', El Metro serves vital, zesty Spanish classics along with juicy gourmet burgers and other dishes for breadth.
2FOR1 MAIN COURSE | FRI ✱ | SAT ✱ — Spanish

EL PASO MEXICANA 020 8741 9913
24 Fulham Palace Road, Hammersmith, W6 9PH
Nearest Station: Hammersmith
Experience varied flavours, colourful decoration, and a variety of spices and ingredients, all at this authentic Mexican restaurant that delivers an exemplary list of expertly prepared dishes.
50% OFF FOOD | 2 | FRI ✓ | SAT ✓ | ✱ — Mexican

EL TORO STEAKHOUSE 020 7602 5161
87 Hammersmith Road, West Kensington, W14 0QH
Nearest Station: Kensington (Olympia)
An authentic Argentinian restaurant, the team at El Toro are devoted to providing an unique dining experience with excellent quality of food coupled with warm and friendly atmosphere.
25% OFF TOTAL | 10 | FRI ✓ | SAT ✓ | ▲ — South American

THE ELEPHANT 020 8422 5323
20 Station Parade, South Harrow, HA2 8HB
Nearest Station: Northolt Park
Real Indian food in a real Indian atmosphere, this excellent restaurant bears Indian artefacts and paraphernalia in its warm dining room, and serves authentic regional specialities of real quality.
50% OFF FOOD | FRI ✓ | SAT ✓ — Indian

EMPEROR'S KITCHEN 020 8205 3272
163 Edgware Road, Colindale, NW9 6LP
Nearest Station: Colindale
Vegetarians and families are catered for at this exotic eatery where dishes can be custom made to suit. Expert chefs ooze flair and panache in the kitchen, where authenticity is unmistakable.
50% OFF FOOD | 6 | FRI ✷ | SAT ✷ | ✱ — Indian

FAIT MAISON 020 7937 2777
3 Stratford Road, W8 6RQ
Nearest Station: High Street Kensington
Be it for a brief lunch date or an afternoon coffee catch up, Fait Maison is a unique eatery that serves tasty salads, pastries and desserts: perfect for any time and all occasions.
25% OFF TOTAL | 2 | FRI | SAT — Mediterranean

FAIT MAISON 020 8222 8755
245 Goldhawk Road, Hammersmith, W12 8EU
Nearest Station: Goldhawk Road
Be it for a brief lunch date or an afternoon coffee catch up, Fait Maison is a unique eatery that serves tasty salads, pastries and desserts: perfect for any time and all occasions.
25% OFF TOTAL | 2 | FRI | SAT — Mediterranean

THE FEST 020 7736 5293
678-680 Fulham Road, Fulham, SW6 5SA
Nearest Station: Parsons Green
An authentic Oktoberfest experience outside of Munich. Enjoy a sample of the world's biggest party all year round, with imports from beer to pork knuckles. Caters for all events.
2FOR1 MAIN COURSE | FRI ✓ | SAT ✷ | ✱ | ▲ — German

FEZ RESTAURANT 020 8563 7176
32 Fulham Palace Road, Hammersmith, W6 9PH
Nearest Station: Hammersmith
Well-regarded Moroccan and Lebanese restaurant serving superb quality traditional cuisine and boasting an especial line in outstanding couscous. A charismatic, charming place to eat.
25% OFF TOTAL | 6 | FRI ✓ | SAT ✓ | ▲ — Moroccan

THE FIDDLERS RESTAURANT 020 8863 6066
221-227 High Road, Harrow Weald, HA3 5EE
Nearest Station: Harrow & Wealdstone
From your fundamentally Italian Rognoncini Trifolati to the crumbling, sweet lamb of a Greek Kleftiko, you'll enjoy something very authentic, very warm, rich and colourful in this charismatic restaurant.
50% OFF FOOD | 10 | FRI | SAT — Mediterranean

FIESTA HAVANA 020 7381 5005
490 Fulham Road, Fulham, SW6 5NH
Nearest Station: Fulham Broadway
A lavishly decked out bar and restaurant with barrels, bunting, murals and Cuban paraphernalia. It's a place with a great atmosphere that also does a fine range of Latin American dishes.
50% OFF FOOD | FRI ✗ | SAT ✗ — Cuban

FINE BURGER CO. 020 7433 0700
O2 Centre, 255 Finchley Road, Swiss Cottage, NW3 6LU
Nearest Station: Finchley Road
This classic, burgeoning burger kitchen sets its stall on fresh, high quality ingredients. Try the quirky milkshakes and crisp, flavourful onion rings.
25% OFF TOTAL | 6 | FRI ✓ | SAT ✓ — American

FIRST FLOOR RESTAURANT 020 7243 0072
186 Portobello Road, Notting Hill, W11 1LA
Nearest Station: Ladbroke Grove
Marvellously elegant, charismatic restaurant on the Portobello Road; well-conceived and proportioned dishes can be found on the à la carte menu of this popular local spot.
25% OFF TOTAL | 4 | FRI ✷ | SAT ✷ | SUN | ▲ — Modern European

FLAMINGO 020 8740 7865
31 Goldhawk Road, Shepherd's Bush, W12 8QQ
Nearest Station: Shepherd's Bush
A kitchen dedicated to the exotic flavours of North Africa can be found at this charming Shepherd's Bush restaurant. Of note is the doro ingudai.
25% OFF TOTAL | 10 | FRI ✓ | SAT ✓ — African

FLEET TANDOORI 020 7485 6402
104 Fleet Road, Hampstead, NW3 2QX
Nearest Station: Hampstead Heath
Step into the ruby red shop front and find yourself in the heart of India at this authentic eatery. Recommended by the chef, the lamb shahi monipuri slow cooked in tomato, garlic and mint is mouthwatering.
25% OFF TOTAL | 10 | FRI ✗ | SAT ✗ | ✱ — Indian

THE FOUNTAIN 020 8898 2382
Corner Sixth Cross & Staines Road, Twickenham, TW2 5PE
Nearest Station: Fulwell
Beefeater Grill are one of the UK's best-loved restaurants welcoming guests for almost 40 years in over 130 locations nationwide. *Excludes Breakfast, Light Bites, Bar menu, set menus and all other offers.
2FOR1 MAIN COURSE | 6 | FRI ✓ | SAT ✗ | ▲ — Modern British

FOUR FACES CONTEMPORARY THAI KITCHEN 020 8960 1022
536-538 Harrow Road, Westminster, W9 3QF
Nearest Station: Westbourne Park
The innovative menu is bursting with imaginative Thai dishes to excite and please guests. Awaken the senses and try something new, as all of the dishes are fabulously fresh and healthy.
25% OFF TOTAL | 2 | FRI ✷ | SAT ✓ | ▲ — Thai

FRANKIE'S SPORTS BAR & GRILL 020 7957 8298
Stamford Bridge, Fulham Road, Fulham, SW6 1HS
Nearest Station: Fulham Broadway
Sleek and hip sports bar from the Marco Pierre White-Frankie Dettori stable, home to a range of rich, tasty Italian fare.
25% OFF TOTAL | 10 | FRI | SAT ✷ | ▲ — Italian

THE GATE 020 7727 9007
87 Notting Hill Gate, Notting Hill, W11 3JZ
Nearest Station: Notting Hill Gate
A place for the chic, gorgeous, cosmopolitan party crowd, offering a night of fine dining, chilled lounge atmosphere and all-night dancing. Enjoy delicious Asian cuisine and a formidable cocktail bar.
25% OFF TOTAL | 10 | FRI ✓ | SAT ✓ | SUN | ✱ | ▲ — Pan-Asian

GENIES RESTAURANT 020 7229 3130
6 Portland Road, Holland Park, W11 4LA
Nearest Station: Holland Park
This long-established bar, recently combined with Genie's, is an intimate hot spot in which to unwind. Enjoy the scenic views of the conservatory and gallery whilst tucking into Far Eastern cuisine.
50% OFF FOOD | 4 | FRI ✓ | SAT ✓ — Thai

GOSTOSA PIZZERIA 020 8963 1400
159 High Street, Harlesden, NW10 4TR
Nearest Station: Willesden Junction
Brazil is not known for its pizzas but Gostosa Pizzeria is here to change that, with a menu filled with a cornucopia of delicious pizzas alongside a dizzying array of other flavourful dishes.
25% OFF TOTAL | 10 | FRI ✓ | SAT ✗ — Brazilian

To understand what the restaurant icons mean, please see the inside back cover.

GRAND JUNCTION ARMS
☎020 8965 5670

Acton Lane, Park Royal, NW10 7AD
Nearest Station: Harlesden

The Grand Junction Arms is a traditional and picturesque canal side pub boasting one of the biggest and best beer gardens in all of London.

2FOR1 MAIN COURSE | FRI × | SAT ✱ | ✱ | ▲ — British

THE GRAPES
020 8573 7479

362 Uxbridge Road, Hayes, UB4 0HF
Nearest Station: Southall

Beefeater Grill are one of the UK's best-loved restaurants welcoming guests for almost 40 years in over 130 locations nationwide. *Excludes Breakfast, Light Bites, Bar menu, set menus and all other offers.

2FOR1 MAIN COURSE | 6 | FRI ✓ | SAT × | ▲ — Modern British

THE GREEDY BUDDHA
☎020 7751 3311

144 Wandsworth Bridge Road, Fulham, SW6 2UH
Nearest Station: Parsons Green

A sleek, smart, contemporary corner restaurant, and rare purveyor of real Nepalese food. All dishes are authentic and freshly prepared. They also have live music nights here.

2FOR1 MAIN COURSE | FRI ✱ | SAT ✱ | SUN | ✱ — Indian/Nepalese

GURKHA'S PRIDE
☎01895 622 801

148 High Street, Ruislip, HA4 8LJ
Nearest Station: Ruislip

Nepalese-inspired, the menu is prepared to perfection by the award-winning chefs. With exceptional service guaranteed, guests can relax in the tranquil settings that reflect the peaceful nature of Nepal.

2FOR1 MAIN COURSE | FRI ✓ | SAT ✓ — Indian

HAANDI HOUSE
☎020 8452 1369

89 Cricklewood Broadway, Cricklewood, NW2 3JG
Nearest Station: Cricklewood

Named after a traditional cooking pot, this venue specialises in strikingly fragrant cuisine. Bringing an authentic taste of Pakistan to the table, Khurram Mirza provides hearty, substantial portions.

2FOR1 2 COURSES | FRI ✓ | SAT ☎ — Indian/Pakistani

HATCHETS
☎020 8428 9973

513 Uxbridge Road, Hatch End, Pinner, HA5 4JS
Nearest Station: Hatch End

Mrs Beeton, a former resident of Hatch End, would have approved of this family-friendly neighbourhood restaurant where the emphasis is on good, home-cooked food and welcoming service.

2FOR1 MAIN COURSE | FRI ✓ | SAT ✱ — European

HENDON HALL HOTEL
☎020 8203 3341

The Fringe, Ashley Lane, Barnet, NW4 1HF
Nearest Station: Hendon Central

Passionately crafted British cuisine served with charm in this magnificent country house of the Hand Picked Hotels group, offering contemporary dining with classic and inventive dishes. 2 AA Rosettes.

25% OFF TOTAL | 10 | FRI ✱ | SAT ✱ | SUN — European

THE HILL BAR AND BRASSERIE
☎020 7267 0033

94 Haverstock Hill, Camden, NW3 2BD
Nearest Station: Chalk Farm

Influenced by North American cuisine, this venue hosts an innovative menu composed of traditional and honest dishes. The Raw Bar oysters come highly appraised by Vancouver-born chef Michael Parker.

25% OFF TOTAL | FRI × | SAT × | SUN — British

THE HORSE AND CHAINS
☎020 8421 9907

79 High Street, Bushey, WD23 1BL
Nearest Station: Bushey

Dating back to the 17th century this old inn has been lovingly redesigned, the pub offers a 'restaurant' experience within the cosy confines of a real pub and a market menu which changes weekly.

2FOR1 3 COURSES | FRI ✱ | SAT ✱ | SUN | ▲ — British

HOT RED CHILLIES
☎020 8868 0900

219 Field End Road, Pinner, HA5 1QZ
Nearest Station: Eastcote

A top-notch Punjabi restaurant with a bright and spacious dining room. The menu is diverse and accomplished, complete with well-balanced flavours and plenty of heat where it's needed.

25% OFF TOTAL | 8 | FRI ✓ | SAT ✓ — Indian

THE HUB @ RAMADA
☎020 8753 0800

Ramada Encore London West, 4 Portal Way, Ealing, W3 6RT
Nearest Station: North Acton

A simply arranged, comfortable and relaxing bar and lounge in the Ramada Encore London West hotel, The Hub serves a range of light bites together with its selection of drinks.

50% OFF FOOD | 4 | FRI ✓ | SAT ✓ | ✱ — Modern Pub

HUM TUM
☎020 8579 2666

175 Uxbridge Road, Hanwell, W7 3TH
Nearest Station: Hanwell

Hum Tum is a little jem of a restaurant, serving authentic Asian fusion cuisine to many delighted diners in Hanwell.

50% OFF FOOD | 4 | FRI × | SAT × | ✱ | ▲ — Indian

HUNGRY YETI
☎020 8840 7888

79 New Broadway, Ealing, W5 5AL
Nearest Station: Ealing Broadway

Combining the tastiest of spices with age-old recipes, the Hungry Yeti works hard to strike a balance between appealing to the contemporary palate and drawing on the fine attributes of Oriental cuisine.

50% OFF FOOD | 2 | FRI × | SAT × — Oriental

INDIAN CINNAMON
☎020 8994 0544

42 Devonshire Road, Chiswick, W4 2HD
Nearest Station: Turnham Green

Priding themselves on good quality cuisine, this venue is treasured by its neighbourhood. Whether diners are seeking a striking curry or a naughty sweet treat, this restaurant will satisfy.

2FOR1 3 COURSES | FRI ☎ | SAT ☎ | ✱ — Indian

INDIAN COTTAGE FULHAM
☎020 7384 2165

67 Fulham High Street, Fulham, SW63JJ
Nearest Station: Putney Bridge

Classic, down-to-earth Indian restaurant that combines a cosy, low-key atmosphere with colourful, rich dishes across the menu. The dansaks are excellent, while the chicken dhaka steals the show.

50% OFF FOOD | 4 | FRI ✱ | SAT ✱ — Indian

THE INDIAN PRINCE
☎020 7384 3382

164 Wandsworth Bridge Road, SW6 2UQ
Nearest Station: Parsons Green

Drawing on the warmth of traditional Indian hospitality, diners will enjoy the mouth-watering selection of dishes that occupy a well thought-out menu. Informal enough to relax and completely unwind.

50% OFF FOOD | FRI ✓ | SAT ✓ | ✱ — Indian

INDIAN SIZZLER
☎01923 630 111

97 Longspring, Watford, WD24 6PU
Nearest Station: Watford Junction

A stylishly designed restaurant with crisp white linen, sharp modern lighting, and most importantly, excellent traditional Indian cuisine. The menu is wide-ranging and includes select signature dishes.

50% OFF FOOD | 8 | FRI ☎ | SAT ☎ — Indian

INDIAN STAR
☎020 7386 9693

102a Lillie Road, Fulham, SW6 7SR
Nearest Station: West Brompton

Placing an emphasis on spices and unique, memorable flavours, The Indian Star restaurant is truly one of a kind. Head Chef Mr Bari is well known in the industry for his deliciously tasty Indian dishes.

50% OFF FOOD | 2 | FRI ✓ | SAT ✓ | ▲ — Indian

INDIAN SUMMER DENHAM
☎01895 232 332

96 Oxford Road, Uxbridge New Denham, UB9 4DW
Nearest Station: Uxbridge

At Indian Summer, the staff are passionate about their food and relish in their customers enjoying the experience of eating their exquisite dishes. Come and try their sumptuous range of food!

2FOR1 MAIN COURSE | FRI × | SAT × — Indian

INSPIRAL LOUNGE
020 7428 5875

250 Camden High Street, Camden, NW1 8QS
Nearest Station: Camden Town

A wonderfully innovative dining and entertainment concept. A unique restaurant, bar and music venue that reinforces the importance of personal and planetary health.

2FOR1 MAIN COURSE | FRI ✓ | SAT ✓ — Contemporary

JAIME'S SPANISH TAPAS
020 8563 0869
28 Fulham Palace Road, Hammersmith, W6 9PH
Nearest Station: Hammersmith
While away the time eating delicious tapas from an extensive array of traditional and modern choices, and drinking choice wines, all at reasonable prices.
50% OFF FOOD | FRI ✓ | SAT ✓ | ✱ — Spanish

JAKARTA
☎020 8205 3335
7 Shaveshill Parade, Colindale, NW9 6RS
Nearest Station: Colindale
Jakarta is a restaurant full of character with a menu replete with the tangs and tastes of Indonesian cuisine. Artefacts and art-work make this place a welcoming, singular pleasure to dine.
2FOR1 MAIN COURSE | FRI × | SAT × | SUN — Asian

JONGLEURS HAMMERSMITH
☎0870 011 1960
Rutland Grove, Hammersmith, W6 9DJ
Nearest Station: Hammersmith
Great entertainment and food is delivered at all of these premier comedy clubs. An excellent selection of sharing platters, gourmet burgers and freshly made pizzas to enjoy while you watch the show.
50% OFF FOOD | 8 | FRI ✱ | SAT ✓ | SUN | ▲ — International

JOYA TANDOORI
☎01923 249 374
37 Market Street, Watford, WD18 0PN
Nearest Station: Watford
Diners seeking an affordable meal without compromising on quality need look no further. Creating authentic dishes in contemporary Indian surroundings, this family-run venue is held dear by locals.
2FOR1 3 COURSES | FRI ✓ | SAT ✓ — Indian

KABUL CITY
☎020 8952 6036
34 Station Road, Edgware, HA8 7AB
Nearest Station: Edgware
Kabul City offers true Afghan dining in a comfortable setting, appropriate for all occasions. It features both the traditional and the more contemporary Afghan dishes at affordable prices.
25% OFF TOTAL | 10 | FRI | SAT — Afghani

KARAAM LEBANESE RESTAURANT
☎020 8566 4433
71 New Broadway, Ealing, W5 5AL
Nearest Station: Ealing Broadway
Deriving its influences from the ethos of Lebanese culture, the kitchen at Karaam takes generosity as its care value in achieving great food, service, and quality of presentation.
50% OFF FOOD | 2 | FRI | SAT | ✱ — Lebanese

KATHMANDU RESTAURANT
☎020 8840 1634
86 Northfield Avenue, West Ealing, W13 9RR
Nearest Station: Northfields
For lovers of South Asian cuisine, the Nepalese food offered at Kathmandu Restaurant is truly enjoyable.
2FOR1 3 COURSES | FRI × | SAT × | ✱ | ▲ — Nepalese

KATTARA LEBANESE
☎020 8846 9010
130 King Street, Hammersmith, W6 0QU
Nearest Station: Ravenscourt Park
From the Heart of Lebanon to the Heart of London, Kattara is pleased to provide its customers with real taste of Lebanon. Every meal is a celebration of taste, texture and family values.
25% OFF TOTAL | 4 | FRI | SAT | ▲ — Middle Eastern

KENSINGTON TANDOORI
☎020 7937 6182
1 Abingdon Road, Kensington, W8 6AH
Nearest Station: High Street Kensington
It will be tempting to fill up on the deliciously tasty starters, which are freshly prepared and cooked to perfection. However, the speciality North Indian dishes are worth saving room for.
50% OFF FOOD | 4 | FRI ✓ | SAT ✓ — Indian

KENTISH CANTEEN
☎020 7485 7331
300 Kentish Town Road, Kentish Town, NW5 2TG
Nearest Station: Kentish Town
Embracing modern dining, in the up and coming Kentish Town area, Kentish Canteen brings stylish and quality food to the area.
2FOR1 3 COURSES | FRI × | SAT × — Contemporary

KHAO SAN
☎020 7221 9984
108 Chepstow Road, Notting Hill, W2 5QS
Nearest Station: Westbourne Park
Experienced kitchen staff produce a fine menu of traditional Thai dishes, each brimming with various sweet, sour and spicy flavours that define the cuisine of South-East Asia.
50% OFF FOOD | 6 | FRI ✓ | SAT × | SUN | ✱ — Thai

KISHMISH
☎020 7385 6953
448-450 Fulham Road, Fulham, SW6 1DL
Nearest Station: Fulham Broadway
Passionately dedicated to providing classic and contemporary Indian cuisine, this restaurant serves beautiful dishes that capture the essence of real authentic subcontinental flavour.
25% OFF TOTAL | 10 | FRI | SAT | ✱ — Indian

KLEFTIKO
☎020 7603 0807
186 Holland Park Avenue, Holland Park, W11 4UJ
Nearest Station: Shepherd's Bush
A classic Greek eatery boasting a fine assortment of dishes including succulent meats with fragrant juices, served within comfortable surroundings, all delicious and modestly priced.
25% OFF TOTAL | 10 | FRI ✓ | SAT ✓ — Greek

KOI SUSHI & NOODLE BAR
☎020 7433 1321
Unit 5-6, Palace Court, Hampstead, NW3 6DN
Nearest Station: Finchley Road & Frognal
Striving to bring the healthy Japanese eating style to the British Mainstream, Koi Sushi offers a casual dining experience, whilst emphasising the health benefits of their freshly made food.
50% OFF FOOD | 10 | FRI | SAT | SUN — Japanese

KONA KAI
☎020 7385 9991
515 Fulham Road, SW6 1HD
Nearest Station: Fulham Broadway
Polynesian-inspired, the interior boasts Tiki features and exotic music to lift your mood. Have a miniature holiday without the expense as you indulge in fresh cocktails and authentic Oceania cuisine.
25% OFF TOTAL | 4 | FRI × | SAT × | ✱ — Mediterranean

KONKAN
☎0189 542 0973
107 Station Road, West Drayton, UB7 7LT
Nearest Station: West Drayton
Drawing on the delicious tastes found in the Konkan area, the owners of this fantastic restaurant invite you to enjoy an exotic celebration of fabulously tasty Indian and Goan cuisine.
2FOR1 MAIN COURSE | FRI ✓ | SAT ✓ — Indian

KOOBLA BAR & RESTAURANT
☎020 3011 1000
26-42 Bond Street, Ealing, W5 5AA
Nearest Station: Ealing Broadway
The 19th century Silk Routes introduced Western Europe to the exotic wares and spice-rich cuisine of China and Asia; today the Koobla Restaurant embraces those influences in its décor and menu.
50% OFF FOOD | 6 | FRI × | SAT × | ✱ — Asian

KUZNIA SMAKU
☎020 8847 1740
175 South Ealing Road, Ealing, W5 4QP
Nearest Station: South Ealing
Serving wholesome soups and traditional goulash, this Polish venue has an extensive wine list. Whether it's friends or dinner parties, Kuznia Smaku sees that no one goes home hungry.
25% OFF TOTAL | FRI ✓ | SAT ✓ — Polish

LA PICCOLA PIZZERIA
☎020 8563 7360
243 King Street, Hammersmith, W6 9LP
Nearest Station: Ravenscourt Park
Wonderfully homely atmosphere that enhances the terrifically tasty dishes on offer. A main menu bursting with deliciously tempting pizzas, pastas and meat dishes accompanies a daily specials board.
2FOR1 MAIN COURSE | FRI ✓ | SAT ✓ | SUN — Italian

LA PROVENCE
☎020 7433 3055
116 Heath Street, Hampstead, NW3 1DR
Nearest Station: Hampstead
Enjoy fabulous French cuisine at La Provence. For those who enjoy delicious, fresh food, cooked to perfection using authentic ingredients and served beautifully, this is the place.
25% OFF TOTAL | 4 | FRI | SAT | ▲ — European

LAGUNA RESTAURANT ☎020 8579 9992
1-4 Culmington Parade, Ealing, W13 9BD
Nearest Station: West Ealing
Holding a desire to exceed guest expectations, the staff at this Indian restaurant go out of their way to ensure every diner has an unforgettable experience. A popular choice for many occasions.
25% OFF TOTAL | 8 | FRI ✓ | SAT ✓ | SUN — Indian

THE LAMB BREWERY ☎020 8994 1880
9 Barley Mow Passage, Chiswick, W4 4PH
Nearest Station: Chiswick Park
Good honest food, freshly prepared using seasonal ingredients is the perfect complement to The Lamb's home brewed beers. Their quality menu is varied enough to satisfy even the most discerning grazer.
25% OFF TOTAL | 4 | FRI ☎ | SAT ☎ — British

THE LAZY FOX 020 7386 3783
18 Farm Lane, Fulham, SW6 1PP
Nearest Station: Fulham Broadway
The Lazy Fox is the latest addition to Fulham's eating and drinking scene. Relax with a glass of wine in front of an open fire, tuck into a freshly cooked meal from the seasonal British menu.
25% OFF TOTAL | 10 | FRI ✓ | SAT ✓ | ▲ — British

LIBERTY KEBABISH RESTAURANT ☎020 7267 2000
56 Chetwynd Road, Kentish Town, NW5 1DJ
Nearest Station: Tufnell Park
Exotic Punjabi dishes are on offer for you to enjoy at this wonderful restaurant and takeaway. Kebabish draws on the culinary influences and age-old traditions of North West India and Eastern Pakistan.
50% OFF FOOD | 6 | FRI ☎ | SAT ☎ — Pakistani

LITTLE BENGAL RESTAURANT ☎020 7371 7839
45 Fulham High Street, Hammersmith, SW6 3JJ
Nearest Station: Putney Bridge
A fun, friendly Bengali restaurant whose menu isn't all clod-hopping curries but features instead some delicately and diversely flavoured, skilfully and imaginatively prepared local specialities.
25% OFF TOTAL | 10 | FRI ✓ | SAT ✓ | ✱ | ▲ — Indian/Nepalese

LOCALE ☎020 7381 6137
222 Munster Road, Fulham, SW6 6AY
Nearest Station: Parsons Green
Cool and collected Italian restaurant with all the classic dishes and flavours; hearty and flavourful pasta and risotto, and a line in beautifully seasoned meat and fish with smart accompaniments.
25% OFF TOTAL | 6 | FRI ✓ | SAT ✓ — Italian

LONG ISLAND HOTEL ☎01923 779 466
2 Victoria Close, Rickmansworth, WD3 4EQ
Nearest Station: Rickmansworth
Appease a grumbling stomach with a generous helping of award-winning fish and chips. Carnivorous diners can feast upon mouth-watering steaks before the late night DJ set on Friday and Saturday.
2FOR1 MAIN COURSE | FRI ✓ | SAT ✓ | ✱ — British

THE LONSDALE ☎020 7727 4080
48 Lonsdale Road, Notting Hill, W11 2DE
Nearest Station: Ladbroke Grove
Whether you are looking for a gastronomical feast or a glamorous evening cocktail, The Lonsdale is a culmination of the very best dining experiences. *You are advised to book 24 hours in advance.
50% OFF FOOD | 6 | FRI ☎ | SAT × — International

L'ORIENT INDIAN CUISINE ☎020 8991 1966
9 Hanger Green, Ealing, W5 3EL
Nearest Station: Park Royal
Fine Indian cuisine on offer at L'Orient. Special spices and authentic recipes create divine dishes. Crispy fresh starters will provide the perfect opening to your evening meal.
2FOR1 MAIN COURSE | FRI ✓ | SAT ☎ — Indian

LUMBINI ☎01895 230 059
12 Oxford Road, New Denham, Uxbridge, UB9 4DQ
Nearest Station: Uxbridge
Beautiful little Nepalese restaurant whose ambience, openness and superb menu - a range of classic Indian dishes alongside some more distinctive regional recipes - are the reasons behind its popularity.
2FOR1 2 COURSES | FRI ✱ | SAT ✱ | SUN — Nepalese

LUNA NUOVA ☎020 7371 9774
773 Fulham Road, Hammersmith, SW6 5HA
Nearest Station: Parsons Green
Bang in the heart of Fulham, Luna Nuova is no twilight of the idols; rather, it's a superbly fun, buzzy place with a friendly feel that serves fresh and imaginative Italian cuisine with a touch of pizzazz.
50% OFF FOOD | 4 | FRI ☎ | SAT ☎ | ✱ | ▲ — Italian

MACHAAN CHISWICK ☎020 8994 6022
12 Chiswick High Road, Chiswick, W4 1TH
Nearest Station: Stamford Brook
The richness and diversity of Indian cuisine demands perfect understanding of spices and their melange for each delicacy, as demonstrated by Head Chef Pradeep Asawa at Machaan Chiswick.
25% OFF TOTAL | 2 | FRI × | SAT × | ▲ — Indian

MAHI'S RESTAURANT ☎020 8830 3914
371-373 High Road, Willesden, NW10 2JR
Nearest Station: Dollis Hill
Mahi's delicious, mouth watering food consists of a range of authentic Indian dishes, made with fresh ingredients from fragrant spices to succulent meats. One of London's finest Indian dining experiences.
25% OFF TOTAL | FRI ✓ | SAT ✓ — Indian

MALAY CHINESE ☎020 8236 2388
42 Shenley Road, Borehamwood, WD6 1DR
Nearest Station: Elstree & Borehamwood
With Malaysian and Chinese dishes to tickle your taste-buds, the staff are knowledgeable and always happy to help. Within a homely atmosphere, Malay Chinese also offers karaoke for an unforgettable night.
25% OFF TOTAL | 4 | FRI ☎ | SAT ☎ — Asian

THE MALT SHOVEL 01895 812 797
69 Iver Lane, Uxbridge, UB8 2JE
Nearest Station: Uxbridge
This Vintage Inn oozes rural charm and rustic character. The picturesque surroundings provide the perfect backdrop for savouring the hearty, seasonal pub-food on the menu.
25% OFF TOTAL | FRI ✓ | SAT ✓ | SUN | ▲ — Modern British

MANZARA ☎020 7727 3062
24 Penbridge Road, Notting Hill, W11 3HL
Nearest Station: Notting Hill Gate
With a diverse menu that expands beyond its Turkish staple dishes, this characterful café has a bright, lively setting and an emphasis on organic produce; it offers full, flavoursome Mediterranean tastes.
25% OFF TOTAL | 10 | FRI ✓ | SAT ✓ | ✱ | ▲ — Turkish

MARAMIA CAFÉ ☎020 3181 0030
48 Golborne Road, Kensington and Chelsea, W10 5PR
Nearest Station: Westbourne Park
The first of its kind in the UK, this Palestinian venue prepares authentic and charming Arabic inspired cuisine to tantalise the more curious of palates. Whatever the occasion, this restaurant is a must.
25% OFF TOTAL | 4 | FRI ☎ | SAT ☎ — Palestinian

MARCO BY MARCO PIERRE WHITE ☎020 7915 2929
Stamford Bridge, Fulham Road, Fulham, SW6 1HS
Nearest Station: Fulham Broadway
Culinary delights from both sides of the Channel are fused to create divine French cuisine with some modern British flair. Another Marco Pierre White success. Awarded 2 AA Rosettes.
25% OFF TOTAL | 6 | FRI ✓ | SAT ✓ | SUN | ✱ | ▲ — Classic British/French

MARCO'S ITALIAN RESTAURANT & BAR ☎020 7352 7252
Harbour Yard, Chelsea Harbour, Lots Road, SW10 0XD
Nearest Station: Imperial Wharf
Admirably located in the heart of the stunning Chelsea Harbour, Marco's maintains simplicity by blending the base flavours associated with Italy's culinary culture. Home-made pasta defines the standard.
25% OFF TOTAL | FRI ✓ | SAT ✓ | SUN — Italian

MAREMOTO RESTAURANT ☎020 7731 8685
562 King's Road, Chelsea, SW6 2DZ
Nearest Station: Fulham Broadway
Described by connoisseurs as a sparkle of Los Angeles on the King's Road, the food here is classically Italian, with modern twists, to create a mouth-watering menu of fresh and healthy dishes.
25% OFF TOTAL | 6 | FRI ☎ | SAT ☎ | SUN | ✱ | ▲ — Italian

ME LOVE SUSHI
☎020 7483 0888
100 Avenue Road, Swiss Cottage, NW3 3HF
Nearest Station: Swiss Cottage
With three London restaurants and more on the way, Me Love Sushi is the ultimate experience for sushi lovers. The Swiss Cottage branch maintains the reputable standards and affordable prices.

25% OFF TOTAL | 4 | FRI × | SAT × | * — Japanese

ME LOVE SUSHI
☎020 8958 0055
307 Hale Lane, Edgware, HA8 7AX
Nearest Station: Edgware
With three London restaurants and more on the way, Me Love Sushi is the ultimate experience for sushi lovers. The Edgware branch maintains the reputable standards and affordable prices.

25% OFF TOTAL | 4 | FRI × | SAT × | * — Japanese

MEGHNA HAMPSTEAD INDIAN CUISINE
☎020 7433 3355
113 Boundary Rd, St John's Wood, London, NW8 0RG
Nearest Station: Hampstead
Well-established Indian restaurant serving a huge variety of fine, authentic North Indian dishes, including a number of meat, seafood, and vegetarian delicacies.

2FOR1 3 COURSES | FRI ✓ | SAT ✓ — Indian

MERIBEL BRASSERIE
☎020 7267 7360
47-49 Camden Road, Camden, NW1 9LS
Nearest Station: Camden Road
Named after a French town in the alps, this venue prepares delectable cuisine that is fresh and seasonal. The brasserie is open at all hours, so guests can enjoy a continental coffee whatever the time.

2FOR1 3 COURSES | FRI × | SAT × | ▲ — French

MEZZOROMA 2
☎020 3583 8595
36 High Road, Willesden Green, W10 2QD
Nearest Station: Willesden Green
Whether you are looking for a relaxed and sophisticated coffee, or an atmospheric family dinner, Mezzoroma strive to provide the very best environment for your dining experience.

2FOR1 3 COURSES | FRI ✓ | SAT ✓ | * — Turkish

MIMINO GEORGIAN RESTAURANT
☎020 7937 1551
197C Kensington High Street, Kensington, W8 6BA
Nearest Station: High Street Kensington
Zauri Goreli's passion for Georgian food translates into a distinctive experience of this little-known cuisine and culture. His knowledge and enthusiasm are infectious; the dishes are hearty and delicious.

2FOR1 3 COURSES | FRI × | SAT × | SUN | * — Georgian

MISSION
☎020 7736 3322
116 Wandsworth Bridge Road, Hammersmith, SW6 2TF
Nearest Station: Parsons Green
Globally inspired cuisine delivered in a modern environment, offering a huge breadth of tastes and textures. Quality food, well-prepared and cooked to perfection, with a great outside terraced area.

50% OFF FOOD | 8 | FRI ✓ | SAT ✓ | * — Oriental

MONTY'S USHA
☎020 8567 1441
146 Boston Road, Ealing, W7 2HJ
Nearest Station: Hanwell
Nepalese and Indian cuisines are blended to create a menu with a twist. Family-run, the dishes are both affordable and reputable.

50% OFF FOOD | 10 | FRI ✓ | SAT ✓ | * — Indian/Nepalese

MOOR MILL
01727 875 557
Smug Oak Lane, Bricket Wood, Radlett, AL2 3PN
Nearest Station: Radlett
Beefeater Grill are one of the UK's best-loved restaurants welcoming guests for almost 40 years in over 130 locations nationwide. *Excludes Breakfast, Light Bites, Bar menu, set menus and all other offers.

2FOR1 MAIN COURSE | 6 | FRI ✓ | SAT × | ▲ — Modern British

MOROCCAN SAHARA RESTAURANT
☎020 7792 0770
39 Hereford Road, Notting Hill, W2 4AB
Nearest Station: Bayswater
Extravagant décor with vibrant colours give this restaurant an authentic feel. Diners are transported to the Sahara desert as they indulge in home-made Moroccan tangines prepared by expert chefs.

50% OFF FOOD | 2 | FRI ✓ | SAT ✓ — Moroccan

NAKED NOSH
☎020 7736 7007
606 Fulham Road, Fulham, SW6 5RP
Nearest Station: Parsons Green
The Naked Nosh philosophy is simple: good, fresh, locally sourced produce and deliciously authentic recipes delivered to your door. Special fixed price menus are perfect if you are catering for friends.

2FOR1 MAIN COURSE | FRI ✓ | SAT ✓ — English and Continental

NAPA RESTAURANT
☎020 8996 5200
Moran Hotel, 626 Chiswick High Rd, Chiswick, W4 5RN
Nearest Station: Gunnersbury
Quality seasonal produce is the driving force behind the modern British menu at this fantastic Chiswick restaurant. Breakfast and dinner is served on a daily basis.

50% OFF FOOD | 6 | FRI ✓ | SAT ✓ — British

NAYAAB INDIAN RESTAURANT
☎020 7731 6993
309 New King's Road, Fulham, SW6 4RF
Nearest Station: Parsons Green
A menu that fully achieves the kitchen's goal to maintain traditional Indian favourites whilst leaving room for the culinary adventurous, who desire to explore new styles of cuisine.

25% OFF TOTAL | 4 | FRI * | SAT * | * — Indian

NEPALESE TANDOORI RESTAURANT
☎020 8740 7551
121 Uxbridge Road, Shepherds Bush, W12 8NL
Nearest Station: Shepherd's Bush Market
An outstanding restaurant that is committed to preserving the Nepalese culture and tradition. The kitchen passionately recreates daal, bhaat and tarkari dishes for diners to devour.

25% OFF TOTAL | 4 | FRI * | SAT * | * | ▲ — Nepalese

NOTTING HILL TANDOORI
☎020 7727 9999
23 All Saints Road, Notting Hill, W11 1HE
Nearest Station: Ladbroke Grove
Preparing all food with care and attention, not to mention the freshest ingredients, this local Indian restaurant serves quality curries, rice dishes and sundries to the diners of Notting Hill and beyond.

25% OFF TOTAL | FRI ▯ | SAT ▯ — Indian

THE ORCHARD
01895 633 481
Ickenham Road, Ruislip, HA4 7DR
Nearest Station: West Ruislip
Beefeater Grill are one of the UK's best-loved restaurants welcoming guests for almost 40 years in over 130 locations nationwide. *Excludes Breakfast, Light Bites, Bar menu, set menus and all other offers.

2FOR1 MAIN COURSE | 6 | FRI ✓ | SAT × | ▲ — Modern British

ORKIDEH RESTAURANT
☎020 8731 9921
746 Finchley Road, Golders Green, NW11 7TH
Nearest Station: Golders Green
Orkideh welcomes you to the finest Iranian cuisineA warm welcome and extensive menu greets all diners. You are certainly guaranteed excellent food and a warm welcome at Orkideh.

25% OFF TOTAL | 6 | FRI ▯ | SAT ▯ | SUN — Middle Eastern

O'SULLIVAN'S @ HOLIDAY INN
☎08719 429 071
Barnet Bypass, Elstree, WD6 5PU
Nearest Station: Elstree & Borehamwood
O'Sullivan's restaurant boasts a spacious eatery that offers a contemporary menu in modern surroundings. Choose from a range of culinary treats, suiting tastes from across the world and closer to home.

25% OFF TOTAL | 6 | FRI ✓ | SAT ✓ — International

PALKI INDIAN CUISINE
☎020 8968 8764
44 Golborne Road, Kensington, W10 5PR
Nearest Station: Westbourne Park
Palki is a warmly welcoming restaurant which values and cherishes its customers. Unbeatable authentic Indian dishes are made with the finest produce and minimal artifical ingredients.

2FOR1 MAIN COURSE | FRI ▯ | SAT × — Indian

PEARL WATER RESTAURANT
☎020 8993 7977
51-53 Steyne Road, Acton, Ealing, W3 9NU
Nearest Station: Acton Central
Tasty, accomplished Chinese food in a restaurant characterised by a tranquil, settling ambience.

25% OFF TOTAL | 10 | FRI * | SAT ✓ — Chinese/Malaysian

PEPPERS
☎ 020 8995 3535

10 Fauconberg Road, Chiswick, W4 3JY
Nearest Station: Gunnersbury

Celebrate the specialised "Dumpukht" style of cooking, originating from the Moghul Emperors. Focusing on clarity, the expert chefs at this venue focus only on cuisine that is fragrant and tantalising.

25% OFF TOTAL | 4 | FRI ✓ | SAT ✓ — Indian

PINNER TANDOORI
☎ 020 8866 5474

141-143 Marsh Road, Pinner, HA5 5PB
Nearest Station: Pinner

Dining at the Pinner Tandoori Restaurant is a rare treat for all those who appreciate authentic and healthy Indian/Bangladeshi cuisine. Truly a hidden gem in the heart of Pinner.

2FOR1 MAIN COURSE | FRI ✗ | SAT ✗ | SUN | ✱ — Indian

PIZZA FORMAGGIO
☎ 020 8446 6998

2a Lodge Lane, North Finchley, N12 8JR
Nearest Station: Woodside Park

Pizza Formaggio is an Italian restaurant and takeaway located in Finchley, North London, serving fresh stone baked pizza.

50% OFF FOOD | 10 | FRI ✓ | SAT ✓ — Italian

PIZZA METRO PIZZA
☎ 020 7727 8877

147 - 149 Notting Hill Gate, Notting Hill, W11 3LF
Nearest Station: Notting Hill Gate

The second Pizza Metro in London where Italian chefs use their passion for food to create tasty dishes. Freshly prepared ingredients contribute to the tastiness of every meal.

50% OFF FOOD | 2 | FRI ✗ | SAT ✗ — Italian

POEM BAR & GRILL
☎ 020 7372 3897

94 Boundary Road, St John's Wood, NW8 0RH
Nearest Station: Kilburn

A glossy modern Steak House restaurant close to London's famed Abbey Road Studios and crossing, Poem Bar and Grill is a popular meeting place for the St John's Wood gourmet set.

25% OFF TOTAL | 10 | FRI ✓ | SAT ✓ — European

POMODORINO
☎ 020 7221 7348

135 Kensington Church Street, Kensington, W8 7LP
Nearest Station: Notting Hill Gate

Pomodorino is ran the Italian way,passionate and homely with a little flair and always taking great pride in what comes out of the kitchen. You'll be hard pressed to find a more genuine Italian restaurant.

25% OFF TOTAL | 4 | FRI ✗ | SAT ✗ | SUN — Italian

THE PRINCE OF BENGAL
☎ 01923 253 538

51 Langley Way, Watford, WD17 3EA
Nearest Station: Watford

Unfussy, deliciously tasty Indian dishes are to be found at this versatile Bengali restaurant in Watford. *Essential to book in advance. Buffet and Banquet are excluded.

2FOR1 MAIN COURSE | FRI ✓ | SAT ✓ — Indian

PRINCE OF PERSIA
☎ 020 8861 5555

7-9 Sheepcote Road, Harrow, HA1 2JN
Nearest Station: Harrow-on-the-Hill

Decorated accordingly, the Prince of Persia is authentic and ambient. Feast on stews, grills and an abundance of home-cooked dishes steeped in tradition.

25% OFF TOTAL | 4 | FRI ✓ | SAT ✓ — Persian

THE QUEEN ADELAIDE
☎ 020 8746 2573

412 Uxbridge Road, Hammersmith, W12 0NR
Nearest Station: Shepherd's Bush

An exquisite chandelier and opulent wood panelling add a touch of class to this contemporary pub. Fresh and innovative, the menu entices diners with dishes such as smoked haddock and hearty cottage pie.

25% OFF TOTAL | 2 | FRI ✗ | SAT ✗ | ▲ — Modern Pub

RABBANI
☎ 01923 250 800

167-169 The Parade, Watford, WD17 1NJ
Nearest Station: Watford Junction

Family-run, this eatery uses hand-picked herbs and aromatic spices from the heart of India. Substantial portions and authentic flavours from the Bangladeshi Head Chef will ensure diners are satisfied.

25% OFF TOTAL | 10 | FRI 📱 | SAT 📱 — Indian

THE RAJ BALTI HOUSE
☎ 020 8960 7090

43 Chamberlyane Road, Brent, NW10 3NB
Nearest Station: Kensal Rise

Raj Balti has worked hard to receive an impeccable name for itself. Sourcing only the freshest of ingredients, the dishes exude excellence and flavour. The exquisite Goan fish is not to be missed.

2FOR1 MAIN COURSE | FRI ✓ | SAT ✓ — Indian

THE PRINCE ALBERT CAMDEN
☎ 020 7485 0270

163 Royal College Street, Camden, NW1 0SG
Nearest Station: Camden Road

The Prince Albert is a pub and restaurant of quality and character serving local brews and fine British cuisine, locally sourced and lovingly prepared.

25% OFF TOTAL | 4 | FRI ✗ | SAT ✗ | SUN | ▲ — British

PREZZO

2FOR1 MAIN COURSE | FRI ✗ | SAT ✗ | ▲

2-FOR-1 MAIN COURSE

9 restaurants in North West London

Address	Station	Phone
36 High Street, Pinner, HA5 5PW	Pinner	☎ 020 8966 9916
29 Green Lane, Northwood, HA6 2PY	Northwood	☎ 01923 829 941
St George's Centre, St Ann's Rd, Harrow, HA1 1HS	Harrow-on-the-Hill	☎ 020 8427 9588
67-69 The Broadway, Stanmore, HA7 4DJ	Stanmore	☎ 020 8416 0213
London Designer Outlet Ctr, Wembley, HA9 0FD	Wembley Park	☎ 020 8795 3377
97-101 The Broadway, Mill Hill, NW7 3TG	Mill Hill Broadway	☎ 020 8959 0336
9 & 11 Belmont Road, Uxbridge, UB8 1QS	Uxbridge	☎ 01895 257 939
238-240 High Street, Barnet, EN5 5TD	High Barnet	☎ 020 8441 7156
82 Watling Street, Radlett, WD7 7AB	Radlett	☎ 01923 853 566

RAM'S RESTAURANT ☎020 8907 2022
203 Kenton Road, Kenton, HA3 OHD
Nearest Station: Kenton
Hand-picked chefs bring the finest Punjabi, South Indian and Surti cuisine to their diners. Guests can arrive expecting welcoming, friendly staff who go out of their way to provide an incomparable service.
25% OFF TOTAL | 4 | FRI ✓ | SAT ✱ — Indian

RAW LASAN ☎020 8954 3335
154 Stanmore Hill, Stanmore, HA7 3DA
Nearest Station: Stanmore
Lasan, meaning 'garlic' in Gujarati, is widely used in Indian cuisine. One of the many flavours that characterise the food at Raw Lasan, the kitchen offers a unique fusion of Indian and Indo-Chinese.
50% OFF FOOD | 4 | FRI × | SAT × | ▲ — Indian

RAW MANGO ☎020 8424 8300
190-194 Station Road, Harrow, HA1 2RH
Nearest Station: Harrow-on-the-Hill
Raw Mango, the latest addition to the Raw venture, brings quick and convenient food to Central Harrow and boasts an impressive salad bar, fat-free frozen yoghurts and outstanding healthy snack options.
50% OFF FOOD | 4 | FRI × | SAT × | ▲ — Indian

RAW SPICE ☎020 8202 6793
117-125 West Hendon Broadway, Edgware, NW9 7BP
Nearest Station: Hendon
Raw Restaurants are all about great tastes, contemporary recipes and invigorating flavours. Raw Spice brings the divine fusion of Indo-Chinese cuisine to the table, using only the finest ingredients.
50% OFF FOOD | 4 | FRI × | SAT × | ▲ — Indian

RBG @ PARK INN WATFORD ☎01923 429 988
30-40 St Albans Road, Watford, WD17 1RN
Nearest Station: Watford Junction
Eclectic, extensive menu that takes in a number of different international flavours. Lively and relaxed, the gourmet burgers are a particular treat; the blackened salmon salad also deserves mention.
25% OFF TOTAL | 4 | FRI ✓ | SAT ✓ | ▲ — International

REEF ☎020 8994 1988
1 Station Parade, Burlington Lane, Chiswick, W4 3HD
Nearest Station: Chiswick
Infusing the traditionally British fish and chips dish with a hint of contemporary glamour, Reef offers a tempting array of seafood alongside classic favourites in a stylishly decorated, relaxed interior.
25% OFF TOTAL | 4 | FRI ✓ | SAT ✓ — British

RENI'S CAFÉ ☎020 8449 6211
182 High St, Barnet, EN5 5SZ
Nearest Station: High Barnet
Attentive and efficient staff give Reni's Café a reputable name for fantastic dining experiences. The cuisine is created using fresh and authentic spices, served up in quaint surroundings.
2FOR1 MAIN COURSE | FRI ✓ | SAT × | SUN | ▲ — International

RISTORANTE BELVEDERE ☎020 8998 9786
11-12 Abbey Parade, Ealing, W5 1EE
Nearest Station: Hanger Lane
A fine family-run Italian restaurant situated in a most distinctive part of the city. The Neapolitan menu includes fabulous home-made pastas, traditional salads and amazing meat and fish dishes.
25% OFF TOTAL | 4 | FRI ✱ | SAT ✱ | SUN | ▲ — Italian

ROBERTO'S ☎01923 774 440
153 Uxbridge Road, Rickmansworth, WD3 7DW
Nearest Station: Rickmansworth
Inspired by his own mother's traditional northern Italian home cooking and trained at the savoy, Roberto, a Michelin-starred chef, brings the classic flavours of Italy together with flair.
50% OFF FOOD | 4 | FRI × | SAT × | SUN | ▲ — Italian

ROMANOS RISTORANTE ITALIANO ☎020 7937 8752
32 Kensington Church Street, W8 4HA
Nearest Station: High Street Kensington
Priding themselves in a selection of wines imported directly from Italy, this eatery offers fresh and authentic Italian cuisine. Perfect for a treat after visiting the vivacious array of nearby shops.
50% OFF FOOD | FRI ✓ | SAT ✓ — Italian

ROWANS CAFE BAR ☎020 8742 1649
8 Stile Hall Parade, Hounslow, W4 3AG
Nearest Station: Kew Bridge
A diverse venue that can cater at any time of day. Whether you fancy a midday coffee or a few drinks in the evening, this restaurant and bar serves sumptuous food and thirst-quenching beverages.
2FOR1 3 COURSES | FRI ✓ | SAT ✱ — International

THE ROYALS ☎020 8908 5306
769 Harrow Road, Sudbury, HA0 2LW
Nearest Station: Sudbury & Harrow Road
Royals is a family run business which adopts a philosophy of wholesomeness, well-being and creates a strong traditional ambience, accompanied by a chef with 32 years of experience.
50% OFF FOOD | 10 | FRI ✓ | SAT ✓ — Indian

RUBY & SEQUOIA ☎020 7243 6363
6-8 All Saints Road, Westbourne Park, W11 1HH
Nearest Station: Westbourne Park
A bright and lively restaurant in a glamorous venue, offering a mixture of tables and booths alongside a divine menu making this restaurant great for a meal, drinks or any occasion.
50% OFF FOOD | 10 | FRI ✱ | SAT ✱ | ▲ — Modern European

RUMI LOUNGE ☎020 7349 0810
531 King's Road, Fulham, SW10 0TZ
Nearest Station: Fulham Broadway
A cool urban hangout where a mellow atmosphere and deliciously chilled cocktails will completely relax you. The Lebanese and Middle Eastern menu offers an abundance of mezze-style dishes for you to enjoy.
50% OFF FOOD | 10 | FRI ✓ | SAT ✓ | SUN ✱ | ▲ — Lebanese

SABROSO TAPAS BAR ☎020 7221 3598
108 Holland Park Avenue, Kensington, W11 4UA
Nearest Station: Holland Park
From Barcelona to the Big Smoke, this authentic Spanish bar serves tapas to enjoy with friends. Hungrier appetites are satisfied with the main courses, and fish lovers can tuck into succulent sea bass.
50% OFF FOOD | 4 | FRI ✓ | SAT ✓ — Tapas

SEASONING RESTAURANT ☎020 7386 0303
84-86 Lillie Road, Fulham, SW6 1TL
Nearest Station: West Brompton
Asian-fusion dishes express the kitchen's culinary prowess and a passion for cultural transfusion. The menu also plays home to exotic Mughlai recipes and traditional northern Indian dishes.
25% OFF TOTAL | 4 | FRI ✓ | SAT ✓ — Indian

SEASONS DINING ROOM ☎020 8748 2002
323 King Street, Hammersmith, W6 7PU
Nearest Station: Goldhawk Road
Enticing dishes make the most of seasonal British and European produce and the very best natural flavours. Try the tasty cheeses and even a fine British wine to round off your main meal.
50% OFF FOOD | 10 | FRI ✓ | SAT ✓ — British

SEAWISE ☎020 7428 5835
726 Stables Market, Camden, NW1 8AH
Nearest Station: Chalk Farm
Seawise does exactly what it says on the tin; bringing the freshest produce from the sea, the kitchen are wise about the fish they serve. Cockles and whelks to traditional British fish and chips.
25% OFF TOTAL | FRI ✓ | SAT ✓ | ▲ — Seafood

To understand what the restaurant icons mean, please see the inside back cover.

SECRETS OF INDIA
☎01923 841 561

36 High Street, Northwood, HA6 1BN
Nearest Station: Northwood Hills

At Secrets of India you will find classical Indian dishes with a contemporary twist. Exquisite cuisine combines with a relaxed and friendly atmosphere to provide the perfect casual dining experience.

25% OFF TOTAL | 4 | FRI ✓ | SAT × | ✱ — Indian

SEVENTEEN RESTAURANT
☎020 7985 0006

17 Notting Hill Gate, Notting Hill, W11 3JQ
Nearest Station: Notting Hill Gate

Indulge on an eclectic mix of popular authentic Chinese cuisines including Cantonese and Shanghai options, including an emphasis on Szechuan dishes for true spice-lovers.

50% OFF FOOD | 4 | FRI | SAT — Pan-Asian

SHAHRZAD PERSIAN RESTAURANT
☎020 8446 3535

281 Ballards Lane, North Finchley, N12 8NR
Nearest Station: West Finchley

Shahrzad Restaurant draws diners to enjoy some of the finest Persian cuisine in North London. Using the finest and authentic produce, Shahrzad Restaurant serves delicious, flavoursome dishes.

2FOR1 MAIN COURSE | FRI × | SAT × — Middle Eastern

SHAKA ZULU
☎020 3376 9911

Stables Market, Camden, NW1 8AH
Nearest Station: Chalk Farm

One of London's most stylish hangouts, combining a lounge bar, restaurant and club in one unique venue. Experience culinary delights ranging from gourmet sharing platters to Cape-inspired seafood.

50% OFF FOOD | 10 | FRI ✱ | SAT ✱ | ▲ — Steakhouse/ Seafood

SHILPA INDIAN RESTAURANT
☎020 8741 3127

206 King Street, Hammersmith, W6 0RA
Nearest Station: Ravenscourt Park

A delightful menu accommodating the very best Indian dishes. Specialists in South Indian and Kerala recipes in particular, the food here is honest, tasty and exceedingly satisfying.

25% OFF TOTAL | 10 | FRI | SAT — Indian

SHIMLA MIRCH
☎020 7602 8899

158a Shepherds Bush Road, Hammersmith, W6 7PB
Nearest Station: Hammersmith

Classic Indian restaurant where you'll find a fine selection of curries and other delicacies. The restaurant is distinguished by full flavours and plenty of spice.

50% OFF FOOD | 2 | FRI ✱ | SAT ✱ — Indian

SHISH
☎020 8371 4375

26 Ballands Road, Finchley, N3 2BJ
Nearest Station: Finchley Central

Curry lovers are in their element at this exotic eatery, where dishes range from the seductively creamy to the flaming hot. Undoubtedly fresh and aromatic, the cuisine is sure to hit the spot.

50% OFF FOOD | FRI ✓ | SAT ✓ — Indian

SIAIM RESTAURANT
☎020 8346 3022

59 Ballards Lane, Finchley, N3 1XP
Nearest Station: West Finchley

A stylish venue that serves a diverse selection of dishes influenced from all around the globe, Siaim is an excellent choice for those seeking something a little out-of-the-ordinary.

2FOR1 MAIN COURSE | FRI ✱ | SAT × | ✱ — Mediterranean

THE SITAR
☎020 8348 7755

25 Aylmer Parade, East Finchley, N2 0PE
Nearest Station: East Finchley

The modern interior keeps things fresh, and the polite and attentive service coupled with the delicious menu means that The Sitar is fast becoming somewhat of a hotspot in East Finchley.

2FOR1 MAIN COURSE | FRI ✓ | SAT ✓ | ✱ — Indian

SOCIETY BAR & RESTAURANT
☎020 7856 1980

380 Kensington High Street, Kensington, W14 8NL
Nearest Station: Kensington

The à la carte menu is innovative and bursting with variety. Sample the gurnard fillet with celeraic and grain mustard for an exquisite taste sensation. Quintessentially British and perfect for all.

25% OFF TOTAL | 4 | FRI | SAT | ▲ — British

THE SOUTHERN BELLE
☎020 7381 8682

175-177 Fulham Palace Road, Hammersmith, W6 8QT
Nearest Station: Hammersmith

Classic down-home diner fare near Roehampton University at this vibrant and buzz-filled restaurant. Dig into succulent chicken wings, a quirky pizza or a cracking rack of ribs.

50% OFF FOOD | 4 | FRI ✓ | SAT ✓ — American

SPICE 6
☎020 8208 2026

22 Station Parade, Willesden Green, NW2 4NH
Nearest Station: Willesden Green

Become immersed in rich Indian heritage and enjoy a sophisticated fine dining experience where passion and spice are infused together. Continues a legacy of delicious food and great attention to detail.

25% OFF TOTAL | 10 | FRI ✓ | SAT ✓ | ✱ — Indian

SPICE GARDEN
☎020 8863 9888

33 Station Road, North Harrow, HA2 7SU
Nearest Station: North Harrow

Spice Garden offers the an authentic taste of India. Their very skilled chefs prepare delicious, fresh and healthy dishes. *Offer not applicable with BYO promotion.

50% OFF FOOD | 10 | FRI ✓ | SAT ✓ — Indian

SPICE LOUNGE WATFORD
☎01923 236 500

36 Market Street, Watford, WD18 0PY
Nearest Station: Watford High Street

The Spice Lounge Indian Restaurant & takeaway has a menu offering a wide range of authentic & imaginative traditional Indian dishes, using the best quality & freshest ingredients.

2FOR1 MAIN COURSE | FRI ✓ | SAT ✓ | ✱ — Indian

SPICE MAGIC
☎020 8840 7503

122 Northfield Avenue, Ealing, W13 9RT
Nearest Station: Northfields

Bringing a new dimension to Indian cuisine in Ealing, this venue delivers a fresh and stylish menu with decor to match, appealing to families, party types and discerning diners alike.

25% OFF TOTAL | FRI × | SAT × | ✱ — Indian

SPICE OF INDIA
☎020 7736 0077

7 The Boulevard, Fulham, SW6 2UB
Nearest Station: Imperial Wharf

Dine al fresco or in the warmth of the charming interior at this splendid Indian restaurant in Imperial Wharf. Feast on fresh sundries, crispy naans and creamy masalas.

2FOR1 3 COURSES | FRI ✓ | SAT ✓ — Indian

THE SPICE ROOM
☎020 8868 8835

12 Kaduna Close, Pinner, HA5 2PZ
Nearest Station: Northwood Hills

In a contemporary setting, a unique and innovative spin has been placed on typically traditional North Indian dishes at The Spice Room. An ideal location for any event and any party size.

25% OFF TOTAL | 6 | FRI ✱ | SAT ✱ | ✱ | ▲ — Indian

SPICE TREE
☎020 7431 1841

32 Mill Lane, London, NW6 1NR
Nearest Station: Kilburn

Praises have long been sung for Spice Tree's traditional Indian dishes, cooked to order using fresh, high quality ingredients. A firm local favourite - why not join them for an authentic Indian experience?

2FOR1 MAIN COURSE | FRI ✓ | SAT ✓ | ✱ | ▲ — Indian

SPIRITUAL CAIPIRINHA BAR
☎020 7485 6791

4 Ferdinand Street, Camden, NW1 8ER
Nearest Station: Chalk Farm

Enjoy a selection of Brazilian delicacies such as exquisite grilled meats and fish, with a drinks list you would expect from a Latin American venue. The world famous Caipirinha cocktail is a must.

50% OFF FOOD | 8 | FRI ✱ | SAT ✱ | ▲ — Brazilian

STEAKHOUSE
☎01923 247 750

195 St Albans Road, Watford, WD24 5BH
Nearest Station: Watford Junction

Sample something unique at this steakhouse, where the cuisine is served up on a sizzling volcanic slab. From kangaroo to camel, the choice is astoundingly varied. Vegetarians can savour meat-free fajitas.

50% OFF FOOD | 10 | FRI ✓ | SAT ✓ | ▲ — Steakhouse

STRADA 020 8995 0004
156 Chiswick High Road, W4 1PR
Nearest Station: Turnham Green
Offering fresh, bold dishes inspired by flavours of Italian city life – Strada serves a selection of indulgent tastes, to those seeking a blissful escape to laidback Italian life. *Excludes Pizzettas.
25% OFF TOTAL | 6 | FRI ✓ | SAT × | Italian

STRADA 020 8347 8686
4 Southgrove, Highgate, N6 6BS
Nearest Station: Highgate
Offering fresh, bold dishes inspired by flavours of Italian city life – Strada serves a selection of indulgent tastes, to those seeking a blissful escape to laidback Italian life. *Excludes Pizzettas.
25% OFF TOTAL | 6 | FRI ✓ | SAT × | Italian

STRADA 020 7731 6404
175 New King's Road, Parsons Green, SW6 4SW
Nearest Station: Parsons Green
Offering fresh, bold dishes inspired by flavours of Italian city life – Strada serves a selection of indulgent tastes, to those seeking a blissful escape to laidback Italian life. *Excludes Pizzettas.
25% OFF TOTAL | 6 | FRI ✓ | SAT × | Italian

SUNDARBAN TANDOORI 020 8902 4706
5 Sudbury Heights Avenue, Greenford, UB6 0LZ
Nearest Station: Sudbury Town
Smart Bangladeshi restaurant that is as welcoming on arrival as it's been made to look from the outside. The food is rich and tasty, authentically Bangladeshi with all the various flavours of the region.
25% OFF TOTAL | FRI × | SAT × | SUN | Indian

TARA TARI WORLD BUFFET 020 7483 4282
117 Finchley Road, Swiss Cottage, NW3 6HY
Nearest Station: Swiss Cottage
Sample all the culinary delights the world has to offer here at Tara Tari, in a relaxed and fun setting. Perfect for families.
50% OFF FOOD | 2 | FRI × | SAT × | International

TATRA RESTAURANT 020 8749 8193
24 Goldhawk Road, Shepherd's Bush, W12 8DH
Nearest Station: Goldhawk Road
Modern and stylish interior to match the outstandingly well-prepared Polish and East European cuisine. With a vast selection of vodkas including home-made flavoured varieties, this venue is truly unique.
25% OFF TOTAL | 4 | FRI ✓ | SAT | * | Modern Polish

THE THREE COMPASSES 01923 857 655
Pegmire Lane, Watford, WD25 8DR
Nearest Station: Radlett
Whilst still serving traditional British favourites, The Three Compasses now brings a taste of India to its menu for the first time with its unrivalled, authentic Northern Indian cuisine.
2FOR1 MAIN COURSE | FRI ✓ | SAT ✓ | British

TIGER CUBS 01895 239 503
74 Oxford Road, Uxbridge, UB9 4DN
Nearest Station: Uxbridge
Modern Indian brasserie set in a traditional-looking, neo-Tudor building. Has a cosy atmosphere to go with trendy styling and excellent service. Appealing and eclectic menu that goes beyond the familiars.
50% OFF FOOD | 6 | FRI | SAT * | Indian

TOKYO JOE'S 020 8440 0180
192-194 High Street, Barnet, EN5 5SZ
Nearest Station: High Barnet
This Japanese restaurant is a new addition to Barnet's bustling restaurant scene, aiming to bring guests a large variety of vibrant, flavoursome dishes and sumptuous regional specialities.
25% OFF TOTAL | 4 | FRI | SAT | Japanese

TOMMY FLYNNS BAR AND STEAK HOUSE 020 8991 0760
253 Ealing Road, Brent, HA0 1ET
Nearest Station: Alperton
Grill and charcoal dishes make this a steakhouse well worth the trip out. There is also a pub-grub menu which offers sandwiches, paninis, sausages & mash and many more wholesome treats.
25% OFF TOTAL | 2 | FRI ✓ | SAT ✓ | * | Steakhouse

TOPGOLF WATFORD 01923 222 045
Bushey Mill Lane, Watford, WD24 7AB
Nearest Station: Watford
What better way to top off your game of golf than with a fantastic meal or a round of celebratory drinks. Head to the Bayview café-bar where you can find a variety of food available all day long.
2FOR1 MAIN COURSE | FRI ✓ | SAT ✓ | American

TRATTORIA SORRENTINA 020 8427 9411
6 Manor Parade, Sheepcote Road, Harrow, HA1 2JN
Nearest Station: Harrow-on-the-Hill
The most authentic Italian restaurant in Harrow, this establishment truly delivers the best of Mediterranean cooking; from steak to pasta, as well as some outstanding fish dishes.
2FOR1 MAIN COURSE | FRI × | SAT × | SUN | Italian

TRAVELLERS REST 020 8907 1671
Kenton Road, Harrow, HA3 8AT
Nearest Station: Northwick Park
Beefeater Grill are one of the UK's best-loved restaurants welcoming guests for almost 40 years in over 130 locations nationwide. *Excludes Breakfast, Light Bites, Bar menu, set menus and all other offers.
2FOR1 MAIN COURSE | 6 | FRI ✓ | SAT × | Modern British

TURMERIC BAR & RESTAURANT 020 8868 6838
434 Rayners Lane, Harrow, HA5 5DX
Nearest Station: Rayners Lane
Bright and brassy Indian restaurant in Harrow. Unfussy dishes are the order of the day, with a good selection ranging from lamb saagwala to a great black lentil dal makhni.
50% OFF FOOD | 6 | FRI ✓ | SAT ✓ | * | Indian

THE UNION BAR & GRILL 020 8995 9056
566 Chiswick High Road, Chiswick Park, W4 5YA
Nearest Station: Chiswick Park
Situated in Chiswick Park, The Union Bar and Grill is known for its mix of modern Mediterranean food, providing a relaxed eating environment for business and leisure alike.
2FOR1 3 COURSES | FRI ✓ | SAT × | SUN | * | British

URBAN KARAHI 020 8579 4474
47 Greenford Avenue, Hanwell, W7 1LP
Nearest Station: Hanwell
An emphasis on refined yet creative Indian cuisine leads to a menu which incorporates both traditional classic favourites and original new dishes that apply Eastern flavours with a Western twist.
50% OFF FOOD | 4 | FRI × | SAT × | * | Indian

VICINO 020 7736 1145
189 New King's Road, Fulham, SW6 4SW
Nearest Station: Parsons Green
Lucid, bright and pretty neighbourhood restaurant with a friendly buzz and a line in fluid, fresh, mellow and authentically Italian flavours through all its dishes.
25% OFF TOTAL | 8 | FRI | SAT | Italian

W5 GRILL BAR @ HILTON 020 8896 8400
DoubleTree by Hilton, 2-8 Hanger Lane, Ealing, W5 3HN
Nearest Station: Ealing Broadway
Memorable meals start in the W5 Grill & Bar, decorated with original paintings and vibrant colours, followed by coffee in the cosy Bar at the DoubleTree by Hilton London Ealing.
25% OFF TOTAL | 6 | FRI ✓ | SAT ✓ | British

WALKABOUT 020 8743 2006
56 Shepherds Bush Garden, Shepherd's Bush, W12 8QE
Nearest Station: Shepherd's Bush
Walkabout is famous for its characteristically Australian atmosphere and well-rounded menu. From live sport with a juicy burger to some Aussie kangaroo skewers, you'll find it hard to tear yourself away.
25% OFF TOTAL | 10 | FRI ✓ | SAT ✓ | International

WALKABOUT 01923 240 688
76 The Parade, Watford, WD17 1AW
Nearest Station: Watford High Street
Walkabout is famous for its characteristically Australian atmosphere and well-rounded menu. From live sport with a juicy burger to some Aussie kangaroo skewers, you'll find it hard to tear yourself away.
25% OFF TOTAL | 10 | FRI ✓ | SAT ✓ | International

WALKABOUT ☎020 7433 6570
o2 Centre, West Hampstead, NW3 6LU
Nearest Station: Finchley Road
Walkabout is famous for its characteristically Australian atmosphere and well-rounded menu. From live sport with a juicy burger to some Aussie kangaroo skewers, you'll find it hard to tear yourself away.
25% OFF TOTAL | 10 | FRI ✓ | SAT ✓ | ▲ — International

WESTELEVEN ☎020 7603 3355
Hilton Kensington, Kensington, W11 4UL
Nearest Station: Holland Park
Nestled in one of Britain's most plush hotels, this venue boasts simple and honest cuisine. Gorge on a satisfying Shepherd's Bush pie and then treat yourself with a naughty-but-nice sticky toffee pudding.
50% OFF FOOD | 10 | FRI ✓ | SAT ✓ | * — British

WHIP AND COLLAR ☎01923 774 946
367 Uxbridge Road, Rickmansworth, WD3 8DT
Nearest Station: Rickmansworth
Thoroughly encapsulating classic British charm, The Whip and Collar is admirably located on the river and serves up some truly scrumptious dishes, from home-made pizzas to pub classics.
2FOR1 3 COURSES | FRI | SAT | SUN — British

WILLIAMS OF EALING ☎020 8567 4219
12 Bond Street, Broadway, W5 5AA
Nearest Station: Ealing Broadway
Dishes are carefully created by the experienced team of chef who work hard to create meals that will tantalise your taste buds at Ealing's one and only restaurant dedicated to fresh and delicious seafood.
25% OFF TOTAL | 6 | FRI ✓ | SAT ✓ — Seafood

WINE AND BREAD CAFÉ RESTAURANT ☎020 3490 2721
41 Church Road, Hendon, NW4 4EB
Nearest Station: Hendon Central
Specialising in Portuguese and vibrant Mediterranean cuisine, this popular family-run restaurant has many different parts to it: a quirky bar, a friendly café and a cosy lounge.
50% OFF FOOD | 4 | FRI ✓ | SAT ✓ — Mediterranean

WINE AND BREAD LOUNGE BAR ☎020 3490 2721
41 Church Road, Hendon, NW4 4EB
Nearest Station: Hendon Central
This intimate lounge bar is a fantastic attribute of Wine and Bread. Cosy up in a well-lit corner as you sip a fine wine or rich whisky, and feast on sumptuous Portuguese stews or piri-piri chicken dishes.
50% OFF FOOD | 4 | FRI ✓ | SAT ✓ — Mediterranean

WOK AROUND THE WORLD ☎020 8753 0800
4 Portal Way, Acton, W3 6RT
Nearest Station: North Acton
An informal venue serving a fusion of quality Asian and European cuisine. The theatre of the open kitchen makes this an exciting experience as you watch your meal being prepared before your eyes.
50% OFF FOOD | 4 | FRI ✓ | SAT ✓ | * — Oriental

WOODLANDS RESTAURANT ☎020 7794 3080
102 Heath Street, Hamstead, NW3 1DR
Nearest Station: Hampstead
South Indian vegetarian cuisine at its very best. The award-winning kitchen accommodates chefs with at least 15 years of experience from other Woodlands restaurants.
25% OFF TOTAL | 4 | FRI | SAT — South Indian Vegetarian

XIAN RESTAURANT ☎020 8445 8125
862 High Road, Finchley, N12 9RH
Nearest Station: Woodside Park
A local favourite crafting simple yet delicious Chinese cuisine, offering diners an eclectic, flavoursome menu to choose from. Good value and attentive service add to the appeal of this restaurant.
25% OFF TOTAL | FRI ✓ | SAT ✓ — Chinese

YAMAL ALSHAM ☎020 3010 1100
5 The Boulevard, Imperial Wharf, SW6 2UB
Nearest Station: Imperial Wharf
Restaurant offering an inspired Lebanese & Syrian culinary experience, which combines the sophistication and subtleties of European cuisines with the exotic ingredients of the Middle and Far East.
25% OFF TOTAL | 10 | FRI ✓ | SAT ✓ — Lebanese

YE OLDE GREENE MANNE 01923 826 433
Batchworth Heath, Rickmansworth, WD3 1QB
Nearest Station: Northwood
This Vintage Inn oozes rural charm and rustic character. The picturesque surroundings provide the perfect backdrop for savouring the hearty, seasonal pub-food on the menu.
25% OFF TOTAL | FRI ✓ | SAT ✓ | SUN | ▲ — Modern British

YUMCHAA CAMDEN LOCK ☎020 7209 9641
91-92 Camden Lock Place, Camden, NW1 8AF
Nearest Station: Camden Town
Yumchaa Camden, much like its sister branches, serves tea like no other. With a wide variety of loose leaf teas appearing in quaint milk jugs, sample the cakes to really polish your afternoon off.
2FOR1 3 COURSES | FRI ✓ | SAT ✓ — British

ZAYKA INDIAN CUISINE ☎020 8579 7278
8 South Ealing Road, Ealing, W5 4QA
Nearest Station: South Ealing
Bright and welcoming Nepalese and Indian restaurant that serves delicious, fresh-flavoured and finely spiced dishes. They also focus on healthy choices for ingredients, without sacrificing flavour.
2FOR1 MAIN COURSE | FRI ✓ | SAT ✓ | ▲ — Indian

ZENNY'S ☎020 8994 1988
1 Station Parade, Chiswick, W4 3HB
Nearest Station: Chiswick
An innovative and modern restaurant situated in the west London borough of Chiswick with a warm and welcoming atmosphere, excellent service and great-tasting foods from the Med.
50% OFF FOOD | FRI ✓ | SAT ✓ — Mediterranean

ZENSAI ☎020 7424 9527
16 Inverness Street, Camden, NW1 7HJ
Nearest Station: Camden Town
Superb Malaysian restaurant in Camden Town, where superbly delicious cocktails meet terrific cuisine. Perfect for a mid-week treat, the food here is renowned across the city for being exceptionally tasty.
2FOR1 MAIN COURSE | FRI × | SAT × | SUN | ▲ — Malaysian

South East

ADWOA'S KITCHEN ☎020 8771 9444
35 White Horse Lane, Croydon, SE25 6RD
Nearest Station: Thornton Heath
Be enticed by the vibrant interiors and authentically warm welcome, to sample the deliciously authentic African culinary treats that Adwoa's Kitchen has to offer you.
2FOR1 3 COURSES | FRI ✓ | SAT ✓ — African

ALBERT'S TABLE ☎020 8680 2010
49C Southend, Croydon, CR0 1BF
Nearest Station: South Croydon
Expert chef Joby Wells prepares the renowned roast Hereford beef with hand-cut chips at this popular eatery. Guests can expect a sophisticated crowd savouring naughty treats such as treacle tart.
2FOR1 MAIN COURSE | FRI ✱ | SAT ✱ | SUN | ▲ — British

ANGEL BBQ KEBAB ☎020 8778 6823
179 Penge High Street, Penge, SE20 7PF
Nearest Station: Kent House
If you are seeking a delicious Mediterranean eatery in Beckenham, Angel BBQ Kebab is an excellent find.If you are seeking an effortless meal out, with simply delicious food, look no further than Angel BBQ.
25% OFF TOTAL | 10 | FRI | SAT | * — Mediterranean

THE APERFIELD 01959 542 565
311 Main Road, Biggin Hill, TN16 2HN
Nearest Station: Whyteleafe South
This Vintage Inn oozes rural charm and rustic character. The picturesque surroundings provide the perfect backdrop for savouring the hearty, seasonal pub-food on the menu.
25% OFF TOTAL | FRI ✓ | SAT ✓ | SUN | ▲ — Modern British

AQUA BRASSERIE
☎020 8667 0070

33 South End, Croydon, CR0 1BE
Nearest Station: South Croydon
First-class dining with a selection of Modern European dishes that combine fresh, simple ingredients with a genuine love for creating exquisite cuisine, perfectly cooked and beautifully presented.

25% OFF TOTAL | 10 | FRI ✓ | SAT × | ▲ — European

AQUA MEDITERRANEAN BAR AND GRILL
☎020 8460 2346

4-6 Market Parade, Bromley, BR1 1QN
Nearest Station: Sundridge Park
The kitchen's centrepiece is a bespoke charcoal grill, giving each dish a unique flavour by cooking over the smoked embers to bring you the insatiable taste of Mediterranean cuisine.

25% OFF TOTAL | 10 | FRI ✓ | SAT ✓ | ▲ — Mediterranean

BARCELONA TAPAS BAR
☎020 8693 5111

481 Lordship Lane, Dulwich, SE22 8JY
Nearest Station: Forest Hill
An expanding family business offering delicious Spanish food in an authentic atmosphere. Watch the world go by as you relax on the outdoor terrace area, and experience real Spanish flavour.

25% OFF TOTAL | 4 | FRI ✓ | SAT ✓ | ▲ — Spanish

THE BEACON
01322 629 022

Halcrow Avenue, Dartford, DA1 5FX
Nearest Station: Dartford
Beefeater Grill are one of the UK's best-loved restaurants welcoming guests for almost 40 years in over 130 locations nationwide. *Excludes Breakfast, Light Bites, Bar menu, set menus and all other offers.

2FOR1 MAIN COURSE | 6 | FRI ✓ | SAT × | ▲ — Modern British

BELLA ITALIA
020 8688 5787

18 George Street, Croydon, CR0 1PA
Nearest Station: East Croydon
Accessible Italian cuisine on the British high street – indulge in authentic sharing platters, hand stretched pizzas and hearty pasta dishes, served with a healthy dose of gregarious Italian hospitality.

25% OFF TOTAL | 6 | FRI × | SAT × | SUN | ▲ — Italian

BENGAL BRASSERIE
☎020 8244 2442

79 Springbank Road, Hither Green, SE13 6SS
Nearest Station: Hither Green
Extremely talented chefs work hard in the kitchen to create a variety of tasty dishes originating from all parts of India. A well-established restaurant, popular with both locals and guests from afar.

25% OFF TOTAL | 10 | FRI ✓ | SAT ✓ | ✱ — Indian

THE BENGALI KITCHEN
☎020 8650 6434

406 Upper Elmer's End Road, Beckenham, BR3 3HG
Nearest Station: Eden Park
The Bengali Restaurant and takeaway is located on Upper Elmer's End Road in Beckenham offering delicious Indian cuisine with a warm welcome and great service.

25% OFF TOTAL | FRI ✓ | SAT ✓ | ✱ — Indian

BHARAT BHAVAN
☎020 8688 6239

10 Lower Addiscombe Road, Croydon, CR0 6AA
Nearest Station: East Croydon
The Bharat Bhavan is a traditional Indian restaurant that serves authentic South Indian dishes. It also has a wide selection of wines, spirits and beers.

25% OFF TOTAL | 4 | FRI ✓ | SAT ✓ — Indian

BIANCO 43 RISTORANTE
☎020 8858 2668

43 Greenwich Church Street, Greenwich, SE10 9BL
Nearest Station: Cutty Sark for Maritime Greenwich
A perfect location for those seeking out true authentic Italian food amongst today's many high-street chains, Bianco 43 is an ideal choice for anyone who enjoys good Italian food.

25% OFF TOTAL | 6 | FRI × | SAT × — Italian

BIANCO 43 RISTORANTE
☎020 8305 1558

79 Lassell Street, Greenwich, SE10 9PJ
Nearest Station: Maze Hill
A perfect location for those seeking out true authentic Italian food amongst today's many high-street chains, Bianco 43 is an ideal choice for anyone who enjoys good Italian food.

50% OFF FOOD | 8 | FRI ✓ | SAT ✓ | ✱ — Italian

BLEND BAR & GRILL
☎020 8298 0284

272-274 Broadway, Bexleyheath, DA6 8BE
Nearest Station: Bexleyheath
From China to South America, this venue infuses the flavours of a variety of countries to create a new taste experience that doesn't cost the Earth. Diners can enjoy a warm and relaxed atmosphere.

2FOR1 MAIN COURSE | FRI × | SAT × — British

BLUE WAVES RESTAURANT
020 8686 7468

60 Southend, Croydon, CR0 1DP
Nearest Station: South Croydon
Experienced chef Mangal Kumar has gained a reputable name through preparing honest and healthy dishes. From fresh seafood to tender meats, this venue serves food to soothe the mind and soul.

25% OFF TOTAL | FRI 📱 | SAT 📱 — Indian

BRAZAS
☎020 8678 0697

45 Tulse Hill, Herne Hill, SW2 2TJ
Nearest Station: Herne Hill
Meat lovers can feast upon scrumptious burgers and char-grilled piri-piri chicken: favourites on the restaurants seasonal menu. Inspired by both Portuguese and British cuisine, this venue suits all.

2FOR1 3 COURSES | FRI ✓ | SAT × | SUN | ✱ — European

25% OFF TOTAL

CAFÉ ROUGE

25% OFF TOTAL | 6 | FRI ✓ | SAT ✓ | ✱ | ▲

7 restaurants in South East London

16-18 Montpelier Vale, Blackheath, SE3 0TA
Blackheath ☎ 020 8297 2727

12-13 Market Square, Bromley, BR1 1NA
Bromley South ☎ 020 8460 0470

9 The High Street, Chislehurst, BR7 5AJ
Chislehurst ☎ 020 8295 5000

84 Park Hall Road, Dulwich, SE21 8BW
West Dulwich ☎ 020 8766 0070

96-98 Dulwich Village, Dulwich, SE21 7AQ
North Dulwich ☎ 020 8693 9316

Hotel Ibis, 30 Stockwell Street, SE10 9JN
Cutty Sark/Greenwich ☎ 020 8293 6660

Peninsular Square, Greenwich, SE10 0EN
North Greenwich ☎ 020 8305 0203

BUBBAS RESTAURANT
☎020 8674 44114

7A Station Rise, Tulse Hill, SE27 9BW
Nearest Station: Tulse Hill

From apple and chili jam to curried goat - this Caribbean eatery promises to thrill even the most bold of diners. Combining the most unsuspecting of flavours, this exotic menu is bursting with finesse.

50% OFF FOOD | 6 | FRI ✓ | SAT ✓ — Caribbean

THE BULL
01322 610 021

London Road, Swanley, BR8 7QD
Nearest Station: Swanley

Beefeater Grill are one of the UK's best-loved restaurants welcoming guests for almost 40 years in over 130 locations nationwide. *Excludes Breakfast, Light Bites, Bar menu, set menus and all other offers.

2FOR1 MAIN COURSE | 6 | FRI ✓ | SAT ✗ | ▲ — Modern British

CAFFEE ELIZEE RESTAURANT
☎020 3609 1982

226 High Street, Bromley, BR1 1PQ
Nearest Station: Bromley North

Wholesome and affordable food is proudly served at Caffee Elizee. The menu draws on the speciality dishes found in countries across the world, from a Hungarian goulash soup to a British bangers and mash.

25% OFF TOTAL | 4 | FRI ✓ | SAT ✓ | ✱ — International

CAPRICE RESTAURANT
☎020 8127 4808

108a High Street, Croydon, CR0 1ND
Nearest Station: East Croydon

Mediterranean and Balkan cuisine make this an unusual yet exciting venue, where succulent meats and spice-infused dips meet a variety of tasty breads. An informal setting allow guests to feel comfortable.

25% OFF TOTAL | 8 | FRI ✓ | SAT ✱ | ▲ — Mediterranean

CHAI CORNER
☎020 8633 1779

2 North End, Croydon, CR9 1SB
Nearest Station: East Croydon

Set against a harmonious backdrop of lush tea gardens from afar, Chai Corner provides a relaxed environment with excellent value, heart-warming halal food and refreshing beverages.

2FOR1 3 COURSES | FRI ✓ | SAT ✓ — Indian

THE CHILLI ROOM
☎020 8686 4422

24 South End, Croydon, CR0 1DN
Nearest Station: South Croydon

Fine Indian chefs create inspirational dishes from all over India. Food is freshly prepared, and caters for all tastes by bringing new and exotic cuisines to to the table. An authentic Indian experience.

2FOR1 2 COURSES | FRI ✱ | SAT ✱ | ✱ — Indian

CHOM CHOM BECKENHAM
☎020 8650 5072

8-12 Bromley Road, Beckenham, BR3 5JE
Nearest Station: Beckenham Junction

You now no longer need to be a jet-setting globetrotter in order to taste the best cuisine the world has to offer. Eating at Chom Chom is simple, just pick your fresh ingredients and enjoy!

2FOR1 3 COURSES | FRI ✓ | SAT ✗ | SUN | ▲ — International

CINNAMON CULTURE
☎020 8289 0322

46 Plaistow Lane, Bromley, BR1 3PA
Nearest Station: Sundridge Park

With a fine-dining attitude to catering and presentation, Cinnamon Culture offer the most exquisite takes on Asian dishes, from tender meats to juicy, flavoursome vegetable dishes.

2FOR1 3 COURSES | FRI ✗ | SAT ✗ — Indian

CON AMORE
☎020 8466 8820

250 High Street, Bromley, BR1 1PG
Nearest Station: Bromley North

If you enjoy the taste of true Italian cuisine then Con Amore is the place for you. Discover authentic Sicilian flavours that will tantalise your taste buds and melt your heart.

25% OFF TOTAL | 6 | FRI ✗ | SAT ✗ | SUN — Italian

COOMBE LODGE
020 8686 2030

104 Coombe Road, Croydon, CR0 5RB
Nearest Station: South Croydon

Beefeater Grill are one of the UK's best-loved restaurants welcoming guests for almost 40 years in over 130 locations nationwide. *Excludes Breakfast, Light Bites, Bar menu, set menus and all other offers.

2FOR1 MAIN COURSE | 6 | FRI ✓ | SAT ✗ | ▲ — Modern British

THE CORIANDER BLACKHEATH
☎020 8858 7878

1-3 Station Crescent, Blackheath, SE3 7EQ
Nearest Station: Westcombe Park

Blending Northern Indian and Bangladeshi flavours, this restaurant produces some distinctive dishes to tantalise the palate. The Coriander always uses fresh, locally sourced produce.

2FOR1 MAIN COURSE | FRI ✗ | SAT ✗ | SUN | ▲ — Indian

CRYSTAL PALACE TANDOORI
☎020 8761 1515

24 Weston Hill, Crystal Palace, SE19 1RX
Nearest Station: Crystal Palace

Renowned in South London as one of the finest Indian and Bangladeshi restaurants. A wide range of traditional dishes use only the freshest ingredients and free range meat and eggs.

2FOR1 MAIN COURSE | FRI ✱ | SAT ✱ | ▲ — Indian

CUMMIN' UP CARIBBEAN
☎020 8690 9167

389 Lewisham High Street, Lewisham, SE13 6NZ
Nearest Station: Lewisham

Offering traditional Caribbean cuisine, this vibrant restaurant brings the warm culture and rich flavours of the islands to London. Jamaica's national dish, ackee, saltfish and rice, is a firm winner.

50% OFF FOOD | 10 | FRI ✓ | SAT ✓ — Caribbean

DA PEPPINO
☎020 3417 0468

125-129 Bellegrove Road, Welling, DA16 3QS
Nearest Station: Welling

Charming Italian restaurant in Welling with an excellent range of dishes. Enjoy the carpaccio di manzo, tart and tasty linguine vodka & gamberetti, or the excellent, fleshy monkfish tail in white wine.

50% OFF FOOD | 2 | FRI ✱ | SAT ✱ — Italian

DESPERADOS RESTAURANT
☎020 8853 4880

33-35 Greenwich Church St, Greenwich, SE10 9JB
Nearest Station: Cutty Sark for Maritime Greenwich

Tex-Mex inspired, this restaurant oozes flair and panache. Guests banquet upon exploding burritos, sizzling fajitas and tapas ideal for sharing. Awaken the senses with bold colours and vibrant aromas.

2FOR1 MAIN COURSE | FRI ✗ | SAT ✗ — Mexican

EASTERN CURRY
020 8317 7576

130 Upper Wickham Lane, Welling, DA16 3DP
Nearest Station: Welling

Light, bright restaurant and simple, spicy Indian cuisine are the two main ingredients of this neat little curry house in Welling. Runs through a range of traditional classics and specials.

2FOR1 MAIN COURSE | FRI ✗ | SAT ✗ | SUN — Indian

EL SOMBRERO
☎020 8686 8030

281 High Street, Croydon, CR0 1QH
Nearest Station: South Croydon

Rich tacos and edgy fried mussels in a chilli salsa stand out among others at this popular, buzzy Mexican place in Croydon. Check out their chilli con carne, cooked in Sol beer with surprising success.

50% OFF FOOD | 8 | FRI ✱ | SAT ✱ — Mexican

ELEMENTS RESTAURANT & BAR
☎020 8312 6800

173-185 Greenwich High Road, Greenwich, SE10 8JA
Nearest Station: Greenwich

Calm and relaxed hotel-based restaurant that serves hearty, warming international food from an eclectic à la carte menu.

2FOR1 3 COURSES | FRI ✓ | SAT ✓ — International

EVEREST INN RESTAURANT BLACKHEATH
☎020 8852 7872

431 Montpelier Vale, Blackheath, SE3 0TJ
Nearest Station: Blackheath

The fresh flavours of Nepal and India are combined in this award-winning venue. Chef Shanker Pandey blends the traditional with the contemporary in an ambient and inviting atmosphere.

2FOR1 MAIN COURSE | FRI ✗ | SAT ✗ | ▲ — Indian

FERRARIS RESTAURANT
☎020 8464 8877

39 East Street, Bromley, BR1 1QQ
Nearest Station: Bromley North

Earthy, authentic Italian food in this spruce restaurant in Bromley. A range of dishes from classic staples to more contemporary flavours; menus follow the seasons with a focus on freshness.

25% OFF TOTAL | 6 | FRI | SAT ✱ | SUN — Italian

FLAVOURS OF MOROCCO ☎01322 551 005
73 High Street, Bexley, DA5 1AA
Nearest Station: Bexley
Flavours of Morocco is a chic boutique café inspired by the owners countless trips to their favourite country. Offers tasty dishes oozing in unique tastes and extraordinary flavours.
25% OFF TOTAL | 4 | FRI × | SAT × | SUN — Moroccan

FRIENDS OF MINE ☎020 8658 6650
72-74 High Street, Beckenham, BR3 1ED
Nearest Station: Beckenham Hill
Stylish Restaurant and Bar that blends the nuances of London and New York's ultra-chic bar scene. The menu here is bursting with classic and traditional modern European dishes.
50% OFF FOOD | 4 | FRI | SAT × — European

FUSHIA RESTAURANT ☎020 8680 8833
3 Brighton Road, Croydon, CR2 6EA
Nearest Station: South Croydon
A restaurant with an emphasis on refined yet creative Indian cuisine and a menu incorporating both classic favourites and new dishes, applying Eastern flavours with a Western twist.
50% OFF FOOD | FRI ✓ | SAT ✓ — Indian

GANDHI TANDOORI ☎020 8855 5179
8 Plumstead High Street, Plumstead, SE18 1SN
Nearest Station: Plumstead
The Gandhi Tandoori takeaway offers Indian cuisine using fresh ingredients and without the grease that can be found in Indian food. The staff are friendly and happy to help.
50% OFF FOOD | FRI ✓ | SAT ✓ — Indian

GINGER ☎020 8462 7611
36 Station Approach, Hayes, BR2 7EJ
Nearest Station: Hayes
At Ginger, they are proud to offer a fine selection of authentic Indian cuisine dishes. Generally believed to be one of the best Indian restaurant in the Bromley area, Ginger is popular and welcoming.
2FOR1 MAIN COURSE | FRI × | SAT × | SUN | ✱ — Indian

GREENZ ☎020 8678 0569
5 Station Rise, Tulse Hill, SE27 9BW
Nearest Station: Tulse Hill
This vegetarian and vegan restaurant serves delicious fare, inspired by travels around the world and a Caribbean heritage, ranging from rice 'n' peas to vegan paella, lasagne, salad and burgers.
2FOR1 2 COURSES | FRI × | SAT ✓ — Vegetarian

GURKHA SQUARE ☎020 8467 6878
13 Belmont Parade, Chislehurst, BR7 6AN
Nearest Station: Elmstead Woods
Experience an authentic Nepalese taste as the ingredients are sourced directly from Asia. A diverse menu is prepared by talented chefs, inspired by the highest regions to the Kathmandu valleys of Nepal.
2FOR1 MAIN COURSE | FRI ✓ | SAT ✓ | ✱ — Indian

THE GURKHA'S FLAVOUR ☎020 8314 0614
297a Stanstead Road, Forest Hill, SE23 1JB
Nearest Station: Catford
Infusing the exotic tastes of Nepal with India, the long-established Mr. Aryal boasts Michelin-star experience and a work ethos dedicated to healthy cuisine. Diners must sample the unique masu bhutuwa.
50% OFF FOOD | FRI ✓ | SAT ✓ — Indian/Nepalese

GURKHA'S INN ☎020 8293 5464
17 Colomb Street, Greenwich, SE10 9HA
Nearest Station: Maze Hill
Gurkha's Inn draw on the regional flavours of Nepal to showcase the country's diverse cuisine and the team invite you to join them for a truly Nepalese experience, delicious food and friendly service.
2FOR1 3 COURSES | FRI × | SAT × | SUN | ✱ — Indian

THE HARROW 01883 627 565
309 Farleigh Road, Warlingham, CR6 9EL
Nearest Station: Upper Warlingham
This Vintage Inn oozes rural charm and rustic character. The picturesque surroundings provide the perfect backdrop for savouring the hearty, seasonal pub-food on the menu.
25% OFF TOTAL | FRI ✓ | SAT ✓ | SUN — Modern British

HENRY'S CAFÉ BAR ☎020 8313 0980
2 Ringers Road, Bromley, BR1 1HT
Nearest Station: Bromley South
Enjoy cocktails or a chic coffee at this award-winning Café Bar. Diners can banquet on a chunky, fleshy burger or a bursting deli sandwich whilst idly browsing on the free Wi-Fi service.
25% OFF TOTAL | 10 | FRI ✓ | SAT ✓ — European

THE HERNE TAVERN ☎020 8299 9521
2 Forest Hill Road, Southwark, SE22 0RR
Nearest Station: Honor Oak Park
Allow your children to enter the magical landscaped garden as you relax over a glass of wine and feast on a divine lunch or evening meal. Traditionally English dishes make up an admirable menu.
25% OFF TOTAL | 4 | FRI ✓ | SAT ✱ | SUN — British

THE HIDEOUT ☎01322 224 691
70 Spital Street, Dartford, DA1 2DT
Nearest Station: Dartford
More-than-generous portions of sumptuous, salty, spicy Tex-Mex dishes come as no surprise in this rewarding little gem of a restaurant. It's worth settling in for a cocktail or two, besides the great food.
2FOR1 3 COURSES | FRI ✓ | SAT ✓ | ✱ — Mexican

HIGH CHAPPARRAL MEXICAN RESTAURANT ☎020 8293 9143
35 Greenwich Church Street, Greenwich, SE10 9JB
Nearest Station: Cutty Sark for Maritime Greenwich
Recognised as one of the great restaurants in the area, High Chapparral Mexican Restaurant serves delightfully vibrant Mexican and Spanish cuisine alongside superb cocktail creations.
2FOR1 MAIN COURSE | FRI × | SAT × — Mexican

HIMALAYA INDIAN RESTAURANT ☎020 8690 2863
393 Lewisham High Street, Lewisham, SE13 6NZ
Nearest Station: Lewisham
Boasting a long-established reputation, this venue provides diners with an affordable yet authentic dining option. Experienced chefs create fine cuisine that is locally recommended.
25% OFF TOTAL | 6 | FRI ✱ | SAT ✱ — Indian

HOMESDALE TANDOORI ☎020 8290 0671
28 Homesdale Road, Bromley, BR2 9LD
Nearest Station: South Bermondsey
Convivial staff and expert chefs give this venue a very reputable name. Expect to be spoilt for choice by the striking menu. The mouth-watering tandoori meat dishes are popular with the regulars.
25% OFF TOTAL | 10 | FRI ✓ | SAT ✓ | ✱ — Indian

ISLAND FUSION ☎020 8761 5544
57b Westow Hill, Crystal Palace, SE19 1TS
Nearest Station: Crystal Palace
Masterfully blending a mix of cultures, this innovative marriage of West Indian traditional and European modern is fresh, stimulating and sensual. Deliciously unique dining.
25% OFF TOTAL | 2 | FRI ✱ | SAT ✱ — Caribbean

JAFFLONG ☎01322 293 858
58 Spital Street, Dartford, DA1 2DT
Nearest Station: Crayford
Vibrantly decked-out Indian restaurant in Dartford. Serves some great leftfield Indian dishes alongside the usual suspects. Thaali selection platters and the tart rezalla curry tip the balance.
2FOR1 3 COURSES | FRI × | SAT × — Indian

JOANNA'S ☎020 8670 4052
56 Westow Hill, Crystal Palace, SE19 1RX
Nearest Station: Crystal Palace
A well-loved restaurant where diners can enjoy stunning city views as they dine. Guests will love the irresistible treats that can be found on the breakfast, brunch and à la carte menus.
2FOR1 MAIN COURSE | FRI ✓ | SAT ✱ | SUN — European

JUDAH AND ZULA'S CARIB INN ☎020 8305 2500
135-137 Trafalgar Road, Greenwich, SE10 9TX
Nearest Station: Maze Hill
Classic Caribbean cuisine on offer at this colourfully vibrant restaurant in Greenwich. Bright dishes match the staff smiles that will warmly welcome you to a taste of Jamaica.
50% OFF FOOD | FRI | SAT — Caribbean

To understand what the restaurant icons mean, please see the inside back cover.

KAMANA
☎020 8851 6728
350 Baring Road, Grove Park, SE12 0DU
Nearest Station: Grove Park
Combining the exotic tastes of India and Nepal, this eatery is perfect for a romantic treat or a weekend takeaway. Using age-old family recipes, the place is sure to be every curry lover's paradise.

2FOR1 MAIN COURSE | FRI × | SAT × — Indian

KATHMANDU MASALA
☎020 8658 6812
263 Croydon Road, Beckenham, BR3 3PS
Nearest Station: Elmers End
Using local suppliers, this venue infuses the sensational tastes of India and Nepal to create culinary excellence. Focusing on a variety of regional recipes, the dishes here are made with passion.

25% OFF TOTAL | 6 | FRI | SAT — Indian

KEMER RESTAURANT
☎020 8658 1679
133 Croydon Road, Beckenham, BR3 3RB
Nearest Station: Beckenham Road
Kemer serves traditional Turkish meals which are prepared and cooked by a native chef using the freshest ingredients. A popular dish is the restaurant's charcoal grilled lamb served with fresh salad.

25% OFF TOTAL | 4 | FRI ✓ | SAT × | ▲ — Turkish

KERALA ZONE
☎020 8293 9158
119 Trafalgar Road, Greenwich, SE10 9TX
Nearest Station: Maze Hill
Wholeheartedly abiding by the ancient mantra 'treat your guest like God', the staff are renowned for their excellence in Indian hospitality, while Ayurvedic traditions are maintained in the kitchen.

25% OFF TOTAL | 10 | FRI | SAT | ✱ — Indian

KHANA PEENA
☎020 8688 9123
177-179 Brighton Road, Croydon, CR2 6EG
Nearest Station: South Croydon
The tastiness of the traditional Indian food has awarded this restaurant its popular reputation. Excellent hospitality guaranteed.

2FOR1 MAIN COURSE | FRI ✓ | SAT ✓ — Indian

KHYBER
☎020 8681 6565
284 High Street, Croydon, CR0 1NG
Nearest Station: South Croydon
With a formidable reputation for high quality food, this restaurant proudly serves Indian cuisine at reasonable prices. The kitchen freshly grinds its own spices to ensure distinct flavour in every dish.

2FOR1 MAIN COURSE | FRI ✓ | SAT ✓ | ✱ | ▲ — Indian

KING WILLIAM RESTAURANT
☎020 8269 2131
Old Royal Naval College, Greenwich, SE10 9LW
Nearest Station: Cutty Sark for Maritime Greenwich
Situated within the Old Royal Navy College, this restaurant is steeped in history. Offering a fine British lunch menu, guests enjoy divine food that is matched by the surroundings.

25% OFF TOTAL | 8 | FRI ✓ | SAT ✱ — British

THE KING'S ARMS
☎01959 572 080
Leaves Green Road, Biggin Hill, BR2 6DU
Nearest Station: Hayes
The King's Arms is a modest pub in Biggin Hill, serving wholesome British cuisine to the people of the local area. Perfect for a bite to eat and a thirst-quencher as you are passing through.

50% OFF FOOD | 4 | FRI | SAT | SUN — British

KYRGYZ KAZAKH HOUSE
☎020 7277 2228
158 Camberwell Road, Southwark, SE5 0EE
Nearest Station: Oval
Authentic Mediterranean cuisine is rustled up in a vivacious and vibrant setting. Nestled in a boutique hotel, the cuisine is innovative and fresh.

25% OFF TOTAL | 4 | FRI × | SAT × — Turkish

THE LARDER AND RUBA BAR @ HILTON
☎020 3002 4300
Hilton London Tower Bridge, Southwark, SE16 5HW
Nearest Station: Canada Water
Satisfy a ravenous appetite with the contemporary European menu on offer at this ideally located eatery. Cosmopolitan and chic, this venue vaunts impressive city views for a contemporary feel.

25% OFF TOTAL | 10 | FRI ✓ | SAT ✓ | ▲ — European

LE BON CAFÉ
☎020 8760 5191
61 South End, Croydon, CR0 1BF
Nearest Station: South Croydon
The most acclaimed Moroccan Restaurant in Croydon; Le Bon are committed to serving traditional Mediterranean and Moroccan cuisine at its best.

2FOR1 2 COURSES | FRI ✓ | SAT ✓ — Moroccan

LE CHARDON
☎020 8299 1921
65 Lordship Lane, Dulwich, SE22 8EP
Nearest Station: East Dulwich
Formerly a grocer's shop with many of the Victorian features still intact, but also decked out for a warmly authentic French feel. Classic French cuisine, from bistro favourites to intriguing specialities.

50% OFF FOOD | 4 | FRI | SAT — French

LOCALE
☎020 8852 0700
1 Lawn Terrace, Blackheath, SE3 9LJ
Nearest Station: Blackheath
One bella ristorante, this classic Italian neighbourhood joint is full of colour, verve and vitality, as well as offering a warm and chilled out space to bask in the fabulously fresh, homely Italian food.

25% OFF TOTAL | 6 | FRI ✱ | SAT ✱ | SUN — Italian

LOCALE
☎020 7732 7575
58-60 East Dulwich Road, Dulwich, SE22 9AX
Nearest Station: East Dulwich
With an open kitchen and a passion for fine food, Locale is a quintessential Italian neighbourhood restaurant. Scrumptiously tasty pasta, fish and meat dishes can be accompanied by fresh fruit cocktails.

25% OFF TOTAL | 6 | FRI | SAT ✱ | SUN — Italian

LUIGI'S RESTAURANT
☎020 8670 1843
129 Gipsy Hill, Dulwich, SE19 1QS
Nearest Station: Gipsy Hill
Open and unpresupposing Italian ristorante in West Dulwich. Serves excellent dishes across a broad menu. Highlights include the stinco d'agnello and fine gnocchi. A place that tends to garner regulars.

25% OFF TOTAL | 6 | FRI ✱ | SAT ✱ | ▲ — Italian

MADHUWAN
☎020 8466 7431
20-22 Bromley Hill, Bromley, BR1 4JX
Nearest Station: Beckenham Hill
Exceedingly debonair, this chic Nepalese-inspired eatery oozes a cosmopolitan feel. Devour a beautifully presented oriental dish whilst admiring the interior design of Vincent Tsang and Miho Sakamoto.

2FOR1 2 COURSES | FRI ✓ | SAT ✓ — Indian

MAE PING THAI RESTAURANT
☎020 8650 7887
16 High Street, Beckenham, BR3 1AY
Nearest Station: Beckenham Junction
Striving to maintain traditional cooking methods and recipes, Mae Ping Beckenham caters for a vast clientele of families and friends, allowing them to relax and savour sumptuous dishes.

2FOR1 MAIN COURSE | FRI × | SAT × | SUN | ▲ — Thai

MAE PING THAI RESTAURANT
☎020 8760 0278
16-18 South End, Croydon, CR0 1DN
Nearest Station: South Croydon
Established over 15 years ago, this restaurant has a firm following of old and new customers in the local area who enjoy the culinary excellence of the traditional Thai food on offer here.

2FOR1 MAIN COURSE | FRI × | SAT × | SUN | ▲ — Thai

MONKEYS INDIAN CUISINE
☎020 8670 0101
4 Crown Point Parade, West Norwood, SE19 3NG
Nearest Station: West Norwood
Offers both in-house dining and takeaway options, Monkeys Indian Cuisine provides a vast menu that does not exhaust every option: the staff are more than happy to cater to your palate's desires.

50% OFF FOOD | 8 | FRI ✓ | SAT ✓ — Indian

MY BIG FAT GREEK AT DULWICH
☎020 8693 0505
11-15, Melbourne Grove, Dulwich, SE22 8RG
Nearest Station: East Dulwich
It's hard to recreate your holiday experiences, but My Big Fat Greek certainly helps you give it a good go. A charcoal grill and traditional menu guarantees a close fit to a Mediterranean experience.

50% OFF FOOD | FRI × | SAT × — Greek

NA PURA PORTUGUESE CUISINE
☎ 020 7732 7344
30 Nunhead Green, Nunhead, SE15 3QF
Nearest Station: Nunhead
Na Pura is a brilliant restaurant that offers tasty and delicious Portugese cuisine alongside a wide range of pizzas and pasta dishes. Spicy piri-piri chicken dishes feature as particular highlights.
25% OFF TOTAL | 10 | FRI ✓ | SAT ✓ — Portuguese

NENE RESTAURANT
☎ 020 8658 1014
159 High Street, Beckenham, BR3 1AE
Nearest Station: Beckenham Junction
The Turkish for 'nana', Nene endorses family recipes and wholesome food. Specialising in Mediterranean cuisine, there is a vast selection of both modern and traditional recipes to tickle the taste buds.
25% OFF TOTAL | 4 | FRI ✱ | SAT × | ▲ — Mediterranean

NEO INDIA
☎ 020 8670 2552
78 Westow Hill, Crystal Palace, SE19 1SB
Nearest Station: West Norwood
Blending the culinary cultures of Mauritius and India, Neo India is a unique restaurant that thrives on its blend of two exciting and vibrant cuisines. The extensive seafood menu is highly admirable.
50% OFF FOOD | 4 | FRI ▯ | SAT ▯ — Indian

NEW DEWANIAM
☎ 020 7703 9318
225a Camberwell New Road, Camberwell, SE5 0TH
Nearest Station: Oval
The taste of India brings to you splendid curries and excellent Indian starter treats, from a crispy onion bhaji to a sizzling kebab. Take friends and choose a selection of dishes to sample.
2FOR1 MAIN COURSE | FRI ✓ | SAT ✓ | ✱ — Authentic Indian

THE NEW INDIA RESTAURANT
☎ 020 8460 9793
24 East Street, Bromley, BR1 1QU
Nearest Station: Bromley North
At the oldest Indian in Bromley, the chefs are devoted to preparing authentic and healthy food. Banishing additives and colourings from the menu, The New India promises to make a friend of every diner.
2FOR1 MAIN COURSE | FRI ▯ | SAT ▯ — Indian

NORTH POLE BAR & RESTAURANT
☎ 020 8853 3020
131 Greenwich High Road, Greenwich, SE10 8JA
Nearest Station: Greenwich
Drink, dine and dance all under one roof at the fantastic North Pole. The restaurant offers divine European cuisine and great world wines, while the bar serves easy dining options and classic cocktails.
50% OFF FOOD | FRI ✓ | SAT ✱ — Modern European

ORIENTAL FUSION RESTAURANT
☎ 020 8699 0887
25 Dartmouth Road, Lewisham, SE23 3HN
Nearest Station: Forest Hill
Dine on authentic and flavourful dishes originating from a comprehensive range of Asian and Pan-Pacific countries. Chefs here pride themselves on catering for the gourmet as well as the casual diner.
25% OFF TOTAL | 10 | FRI ✓ | SAT ✓ | ✱ — Chinese

PANAS GURKHA RESTAURANT
☎ 020 8852 9891
318 Lee High Road, Lewisham, SE13 5PJ
Nearest Station: Lewisham
Savour a menu of traditional recipes crafted by native chefs to produce delicious dishes that are low in fat. Be greeted by the world famous Gurkha warmth and hospitality.
2FOR1 3 COURSES | FRI ✓ | SAT ✓ | ✱ — Nepalese

PASTA HOUSE RISTORANTE
☎ 01883 330 137
20 Godstone Road, Caterham, CR3 6RA
Nearest Station: Caterham
Wonderfully authentic, family-run pasta house with a pleasant clientà¨le and warm atmosphere. Choose from a variety of modern and traditional dishes all bursting with rich Italian flavour.
2FOR1 MAIN COURSE | FRI ✓ | SAT ✓ | ▲ — Italian

PLANET SPICE
☎ 020 8651 3300
88 Selsoon Park Road, Addington, CR2 8ST
Nearest Station: Sanderstead
Expert chefs, with invaluable previous experience in Madras, delicately prepare dishes cooked in a contemporary style with the added zest of spice. Some of the most authentic cuisine possible.
2FOR1 2 COURSES | FRI ▯ | SAT ▯ — Indian

PREZZO
2FOR1 MAIN COURSE | FRI × | SAT × | ▲

4 restaurants in South East London

35 Bugsby Way, Greenwich, SE10 0QJ
⊖ Westcombe Park ☎ 020 8858 2760

95-97 High Street, Chislehurst, BR7 5AG
⊖ Elmstead Woods ☎ 020 8295 4565

145-151 High Street, Beckenham, BR3 1AG
⊖ Beckenham Junction ☎ 020 8658 0747

183-185 High Street, Eltham, SE9 1TS
⊖ Eltham ☎ 020 8294 2010

THE RECREATION GROUND
☎ 020 7277 2601
65 Camberwell Church Street, Camberwell, SE5 8TR
Nearest Station: Denmark Hill
For dinner and dancing, head to The Recreation Ground, where fun and play are a guarantee. Fresh food, delicious drinks and great music make this an ideal place any time of the week.
50% OFF FOOD | 8 | FRI ✓ | SAT ✓ — Modern European

REYNA
☎ 020 8692 1263
379 New Cross Road, New Cross, SE14 6AT
Nearest Station: New Cross
Enjoy the pleasures of the open kitchen at this cracking Turkish and Mediterranean café-restaurant. Caters for breakfast, late evening dinners, and everything in-between.
25% OFF TOTAL | 4 | FRI × | SAT × | SUN | ▲ — Turkish

RISHTA
☎ 020 8302 8934
3 Marechal Niel Parade, Sidcup, DA14 6QF
Nearest Station: Sidcup
Rishta is an Indian and Bangladeshi restaurant, ideally located in the centre of Sidcup and offers a takeaway and delivery service to customers as well as a sit down restaurant environment.
2FOR1 3 COURSES | FRI ▯ | SAT ▯ — Indian

ROYAL GARDEN RESTAURANT
☎ 020 8654 6491
Shirley Hills Road, Croydon, CR0 5HQ
Nearest Station: South Croydon
A terrific restaurant offering a tranquil retreat in a stunningly unique location. Enjoy an exquisite Chinese feast of all of your favourites dishes in a place that is hard to leave.
25% OFF TOTAL | 4 | FRI ✱ | SAT ✱ | SUN — Chinese

ROYAL GURKHA
☎ 020 8461 4819
419 Bromley Road, Bromley, BR1 4PL
Nearest Station: Beckenham Hill
At Royal Gurkha, you have the choice of wholesome Nepalese fare, the earthy delights of Tandoori (clay oven), as well as the robust cuisine of the frontiers and of course, local favourites. Enjoy!
50% OFF FOOD | 8 | FRI × | SAT × | ✱ | ▲ — Indian

THE ROYAL OAK
01689 852 519
High Street, Green Street Green, Orpington, BR6 6BJ
Nearest Station: Chelsfield
This Vintage Inn oozes rural charm and rustic character. The picturesque surroundings provide the perfect backdrop for savouring the hearty, seasonal pub-food on the menu.
25% OFF TOTAL | FRI ✓ | SAT ✓ | SUN | ▲ — Modern British

SAFA RESTAURANT ☎020 7701 6004
22 Camberwell Church Street, Southwark, SE5 8QU
Nearest Station: Denmark Hill
Superb Indian restaurant serving a fine array of curry staples, crispy sundries and excellent tandoori dishes. Dine in the restaurant for some evening luxury.

2FOR1 MAIN COURSE | 4 | FRI × | SAT ✓ — Indian

SAGGOR TANDOORI ☎020 8303 2904
145 Blendon Road, Bexleyheath, DA5 1BT
Nearest Station: Albany Park
Popular, experienced restaurant specialising in tandoori dishes. Freshly cooked and full-flavoured, served in comfortable, cool surroundings. Try the substantial mutton tikka musalla with its creamy sauce.

50% OFF FOOD | 4 | FRI ✱ | SAT ✱ — Indian

SEASONS RESTAURANT @ HILTON ☎01322 284 444
Hilton Dartford Bridge, Masthead Cl, Dartford, DA2 6QF
Nearest Station: Dartford
Indulge in the à la carte menu, boasting an overwhelming array of International dishes. Health conscious diners can gorge on the low-fat buffet whilst admiring the views of Dartford Bridge.

50% OFF FOOD | 6 | FRI × | SAT × — British

SELSDON PARK HOTEL & GOLF CLUB ☎020 8657 8811
Addington Road, Sanderstead, CR2 8YA
Nearest Station: Sanderstead
At Secrets of India you will find classical Indian dishes with a contemporary twist. Exquisite cuisine combines with a relaxed and friendly atmosphere to provide the perfect casual dining experience.

25% OFF TOTAL | 6 | FRI ✓ | SAT ✓ | ▲ — British

SELSDON SPICE ☎020 8651 6602
4 Selsdon Parade, Croydon, CR2 8LH
Nearest Station: South Croydon
This small friendly Indian restaurant in Selsdon Croydon is well known locally for the first rate food and service.

25% OFF TOTAL | 2 | FRI × | SAT × — Indian

SPICELAND ☎020 8649 8895
212 London Road, Croydon, CR0 2TE
Nearest Station: West Croydon
Whether you enjoy your curry meek and mild or hot and spicy, Spiceland can accommodate every palate. Enjoy South Indian cuisine in the relaxed restaurant or in the warmth of your own home.

25% OFF TOTAL | 10 | FRI ▯ | SAT ✓ — Indian British

STRADA 020 8318 6644
5 Lee Road, Blackheath, SE3 9RQ
Nearest Station: Blackheath
Offering fresh, bold dishes inspired by flavours of Italian city life – Strada serves a selection of indulgent tastes, to those seeking a blissful escape to laidback Italian life. *Excludes Pizzettas.

25% OFF TOTAL | 6 | FRI ✓ | SAT × | ▲ — Italian

SULTAN RESTAURANT ☎020 8466 8486
32 East Street, Bromley, BR1 1QU
Nearest Station: Bromley North
Guests need not travel to Turkey to experience an authentic taste. Specialising in genuine cuisine, this venue uses original Turkish cooking methods. Ottoman themed, the décor is tasteful and elegant.

25% OFF TOTAL | 6 | FRI ✓ | SAT × | ▲ — Indian

SURUCHI RESTAURANT ☎020 8698 7174
466 Bromley Road, Bromley, BR1 4PP
Nearest Station: Beckenham Hill
Simply decorated, colourfully lit modern Indian restaurant with a spacious feel about it. Smart, professional service, and a selection of excellent dishes including some fantastic less familiar options.

50% OFF FOOD | FRI ✱ | SAT ✱ — Indian

SWADESH ☎020 8613 1500
120 Lordship Lane, East Dulwich, SE22 8HD
Nearest Station: East Dulwich
With a modern kitchen and elegant surroundings, Swadesh produce sumptuous Indian cuisine. Simply fine food created by a dedicated chef, with each dish being full of flavour and delicate spice.

2FOR1 2 COURSES | 10 | FRI ✱ | SAT ✱ — Indian

TAMASHA HOTEL AND RESTAURANT ☎020 8460 3240
131 Widmore Road, Bromley, BR1 3AX
Nearest Station: Bromley North
Expect unusual dishes whose flavours range from delicate to robust, all prepared by expert chefs. There's a special warmth waiting for you at Tamasha - in the ambiance, in the service and in the welcome.

2FOR1 MAIN COURSE | FRI ✱ | SAT ✱ | SUN | ▲ — Indian

TANDOORI KNIGHTS ☎020 8777 0844
576 Wickham Rd, Croydon, CR0 8DN
Nearest Station: West Wickham
Diners faithful to curry dishes flock to this restaurant's doors to indulge in deliciously tasty Indian cuisine. Traditional favourites and rarer North Indian delicacies appear on the menu.

2FOR1 2 COURSES | FRI ▯ | SAT ▯ | ✱ — Indian

TASTE OF BANGLA ☎020 8671 5589
196 Norwood Road, Lambeth, SE27 9AU
Nearest Station: Tulse Hill
Passionate about sharing the sensational tastes of Bangla cuisine with their guests, the team of chefs at this venue succesfully master the perfect combinations of heat and spice. Chicken rezala is a must.

50% OFF FOOD | 6 | FRI ✱ | SAT ✱ | ▲ — Indian

TERRACE BAR @ HILTON ☎020 7231 1001
265 Rotherhithe Street, Southwark, SE16 5HW
Nearest Station: Canada Water
Epic views of the Thames and the City act as the ideal backdrop for enjoying a cold beer, glass of wine or bite to eat at this relaxed lounge area, especially on the al fresco terrace.

50% OFF FOOD | 4 | FRI × | SAT × — International

TRATTORIA RAFFAELE ☎020 8778 6262
94 Syndenham Road, Sydenham, SE26 5JX
Nearest Station: Lower Sydenham
Fresh, hand-made pizza bases and breads ensure every guest has the tastiest meal. A family-run Italian restaurant where authentic, top-quality dishes are anything but hard to come by.

25% OFF TOTAL | 4 | FRI ✱ | SAT ✓ — Italian

TRY TAPAS ☎020 8291 2822
37-39 Honor Oak Park, Honor Oak, SE23 1DZ
Nearest Station: Honor Oak Park
Priding themselves on being a friendly neighbourhood tapas bar, Try Tapas offers an informal approach to dining with their customers being allowed great choice and flexibility.

25% OFF TOTAL | 6 | FRI ✱ | SAT ✓ — Tapas

THE TUDOR KITCHEN ☎020 8302 1529
20 Sidcup High Street, Sidcup, DA14 6EH
Nearest Station: Sidcup
Eggs benedict, hot Arboath smokies and Welsh rarebit are just some of the breakfast delights at this Tudor-inspired eatery. For a hearty dinner, the chef recommends coq au vin and beef bourguignon.

2FOR1 3 COURSES | FRI ▯ | SAT ▯ | ▲ — British

THE UNION TAVERN ☎020 7091 0447
146 Camberwell New Road, Camberwell, SE5 0RR
Nearest Station: Oval
Delicious stone-baked pizzas, tasty salads and wonderful pasta dishes are all available in the midst of Victorian surroundings. Why not sample the lively salsa classes held in the ball room.

2FOR1 MAIN COURSE | FRI ✱ | SAT ✓ — Italian

VAEL-N-DINE ☎020 8681 7943
62a South End Road, South Croydon, CR0 1DP
Nearest Station: South Croydon
Nordic for 'enjoy and dine', Vael-n-Dine is a South Indian venue which explores regional dishes that complement each other. Culturally inclined to fantastic food, the chefs deliver exceptional quality.

2FOR1 3 COURSES | FRI ▯ | SAT ▯ | ▲ — South Indian/Sri Lankan

VILLA ROMANA ☎020 7252 3465
58-60 Bush Road, Surrey Quays, SE8 5AP
Nearest Station: Surrey Quays
Fresh as you like and packed with all the vibrancy of real, down-home Italian cooking, you'll enjoy the breadth of rich options available to you in Villa Romana's cosy, friendly dining room.

2FOR1 MAIN COURSE | FRI ✓ | SAT ✓ | ✱ — Italian

VILLAGE CUISINE
☎01689 851 077

145 High Street, Farnborough, BR6 7AZ
Nearest Station: Orpington
Having opened its doors in 1992, Village Cuisine has been offering superb Indian dishes to a loyal following for many years. Successful in many ways, the food served is characterised by Indian spices.

2FOR1 MAIN COURSE | FRI | SAT — Bangladeshi

VIVA GOA
☎020 8761 1515

24 Westow Hill, Crystal Palace, SE19 1RX
Nearest Station: Crystal Palace
Bright and vivacious restaurant that serves the sumptuous amalgam of flavours characterising Goan cuisine; with warm and attentive service and stylish presentation, it's a place to savour.

2FOR1 3 COURSES | FRI | SAT | * — Indian

YAK AND YETI BROMLEY
☎020 8290 6386

16 Bromley Hill, Bromley, BR1 4JX
Nearest Station: Ravensbourne
With an attention to detail and special flavours, Yak and Yeti pride themselves on good quality wonderfully fresh food served on a daily basis to their customers. Be sure to try this local favourite.

25% OFF TOTAL | 10 | FRI | SAT | * — Nepalese

YAK AND YETI CRYSTAL PALACE
☎020 8771 6898

107 Church Road, Crystal Palace, SE19 2PR
Nearest Station: Crystal Palace
The Yak and Yeti offers diners in south London the opportunity to taste and enjoy authentic Nepalese, Indian and Tibetan cooking, any night of the week.

25% OFF TOTAL | 2 | FRI × | SAT × — Indian

ZEERA
☎020 8462 1433

12 Addington Road, West Wickham, BR4 9BS
Nearest Station: Hayes
Aromatic and fragrant, the dishes here are bursting with exotic flavours and vivacious colours. From fiery to creamy, there are curries to suit every palate.

25% OFF TOTAL | 10 | FRI ✓ | SAT ✓ | * — Indian

South West

143 THE CANOPY RESTAURANT
☎01372 745 330

143 High Street, Epsom, KT19 8EH
Nearest Station: Epsom Downs
143 The Canopy Restaurant specialises in providing customers with English and contemporary cuisine with healthier choices, it is welcoming and traditional decorated with contemporary artworks.

2FOR1 MAIN COURSE | FRI ✱ | SAT ✱ | SUN | * — Contemporary

A TASTE OF MCCLEMENTS
☎020 8940 6617

8 Station Approach, Kew, TW9 3QB
Nearest Station: Kew Gardens
Excellent food prepared to the highest of standards, complete with a popular tasting menu of 18 dishes, all beautifully presented and coupled with by-the-glass matching wine suggestions.

25% OFF TOTAL | 8 | FRI ✱ | SAT ✱ | SUN — European

AL FORNO RESTAURANT
☎020 8439 7555

1-2-3a Townsend Parade, Kingston, KT1 1LY
Nearest Station: Kingston
Wholesome Italian cooking in a comfortable and relaxing atmosphere. Whether it's a spot of lunch, a family gathering or a romantic dinner, all diners are treated to a truly perfect experience.

2FOR1 MAIN COURSE | FRI ✱ | SAT ✱ — Italian

AL ROLLO RICHMOND
020 8940 8951

20 Hill Street, Richmond, TW9 1TN
Nearest Station: Richmond
Pizza Al Rollo will have pizza lovers in a twist. Famous for its delicious by-the-yard thin-crust authentic pizzas and bonhomie, its a popular venue that also serves other fine Italian classics.

2FOR1 MAIN COURSE | FRI ✓ | SAT × — Italian

ALLEPPEY RESTAURANT
☎020 8394 1012

332 Kingston Road, Ewell, KT19 0DT
Nearest Station: Stoneleigh
Alleppey Restaurant offer you the distinct taste of South Indian cuisine. Rich in spice and flavour, Alleppey Restaurant creates carefully balanced dishes to showcase the region's fine cuisine.

2FOR1 MAIN COURSE | FRI ✓ | SAT × — Indian

AMADORA
020 8940 1806

9 Paved Court, Richmond, TW9 1LZ
Nearest Station: Richmond
Simple elegance characterises this fine little Richmond restaurant, neatly tucked away in Paved Court. Ranging Italian menu yields some excellent choices, marked by simple accomplishment in the cooking.

2FOR1 3 COURSES | FRI ✓ | SAT ✓ — Italian

AMAIYA
01372 466 617

51 High Street, Esher, KT10 9RQ
Nearest Station: Esher
Pan-Asian street food is on the rise in Britain and Amaiya has the ability to bring the very best treats from across the continent. The kitchen fuses ingredients and flavours to create a unique experience.

50% OFF FOOD | 4 | FRI | SAT — Pan-Asian

AMBIENCE RESTAURANT
☎020 8946 4300

12 Leopold Road, Wimbledon, SW19 7BD
Nearest Station: Wimbledon Park
As the name suggests, Ambience provide an authentic, relaxed Mediterranean atmosphere. Complete with a Shisha Lounge and a chic cocktail bar, this venue also combines traditional and contemporary dishes.

25% OFF TOTAL | 10 | FRI ✱ | SAT ✱ | * — Mediterranean

AMIRAH'S KITCHEN
☎020 8874 8008

356 Old York Road, Wandsworth, SW18 1SS
Nearest Station: Wandsworth Town
A unique Indian dining experience in London, Amirah's Kitchen's mix of authentic Indian street food along with tried and tested favourites is sure to satisfy.

25% OFF TOTAL | 4 | FRI | SAT | * — Indian

ASHNA RESTAURANT
☎020 8577 0771

368 Staines Road, Hounslow, TW4 5BD
Nearest Station: Hounslow West
Passionate about serving authentic Indian food, this family-run restaurant is dedicated to producing sensational vegetarian dishes in a welcoming atmosphere. The delicious Indian sweets are a must.

2FOR1 MAIN COURSE | FRI | SAT × — Indian

ATITHI INDIAN CUISINE
☎020 8744 3868

27 York Street, Twickenham, TW1 3JX
Nearest Station: Twickenham
Meaning 'guest' in old Sanskrit, Atithi is dedicated to customer service. Award-winning chef Krisnipal Negi, experienced in both London and India, prepares the most original and delectable of dishes.

25% OFF TOTAL | 8 | FRI × | SAT × | SUN — Indian

B@JUANS
☎020 8780 3989

240 Upper Richmond Road, Wandsworth, SW15 6TG
Nearest Station: Putney
B@Juans is a vibrant take on European cuisine. Enjoy an array of intense culinary experiences selected from Europe's finest cuisines: classic dishes cooked with precision and packed with powerful flavour.

2FOR1 3 COURSES | FRI × | SAT × | * — European

BANYAN ON THE THAMES
☎020 7801 3600

Hotel Rafayel, 34 Lombard Road, Battersea, SW11 3RF
Nearest Station: Clapham Junction
A fantastically stylish restaurant in the Hotel Rafayel that overlooks the Thames and the London Heliport. High, panoramic windows set the scene for dining from a sophisticated, diverse international menu.

50% OFF FOOD | 10 | FRI ✓ | SAT ✓ — Fine Dining

BATTERSEA SPICE
☎020 7978 6663

63 Battersea Bridge Road, Battersea, SW11 3AU
Nearest Station: Battersea Park
Providing the local neighbourhood and surrounding areas with high quality Indian and Bangladeshi cuisine. A well-regarded restaurant that serves fine food that captures exciting and authentic flavours.

25% OFF TOTAL | 4 | FRI | SAT — Indian

BELLA ITALIA 020 8681 2144
Valley Leisure Park, Hesterman Way, Croydon, CR0 4YA
Nearest Station: Waddon
Accessible Italian cuisine on the British high street – indulge in authentic sharing platters, hand stretched pizzas and hearty pasta dishes, served with a healthy dose of gregarious Italian hospitality.
25% OFF TOTAL | 👤6 | FRI × | SAT × | SUN | ▲ — Italian

THE BELLE VUE ☎020 7498 9473
1 Clapham Common Southside, Clapham, SW4 7AA
Nearest Station: Clapham Common
Great little low-key pub in Clapham Common where sizeable portions of thoroughgoing, filling fare will leave you sated after one of those lazy, cosy lunches or an evening retreat to the sanctum.
50% OFF FOOD | 👤4 | FRI ✓ | SAT ✓ | ✱ | ▲ — British

BENGAL NAZ ☎020 8647 0088
3 Manor Road, Wallington, SM6 0BW
Nearest Station: Wallington
A winning balance of creative dishes, high-quality ingredients and beautifully designed interiors, Bengal Naz proves for an unforgettable dining experience.
25% OFF TOTAL | FRI ✓ | SAT ✓ — Indian

THE BES BBQ RESTAURANT ☎020 8665 1115
1064 London Road, Thornton Heath, CR7 7ND
Nearest Station: Norbury
Serving a collection of eastern Mediterranean food, this restaurant is a welcoming local place with dishes filled with flavour.
25% OFF TOTAL | 👤10 | FRI ✓ | SAT ✓ | ✱ — Mediterranean

THE BINGHAM ☎020 8940 0902
61-63 Petersham Road, Richmond, TW10 6UT
Nearest Station: Richmond
Shay Cooper and his team at the 3AA Rosette award winning establishment at The Bingham, expertly create Modern British Cuisine using the finest locally sourced sustainable ingredients.
2FOR1 MAIN COURSE | FRI 📱 | SAT × | ▲ — Contemporary

BLADES ☎020 8789 0869
94 Lower Richmond Road, Wandsworth, SW15 1LL
Nearest Station: East Putney
An open grill is the centrepiece of this convivial restaurant. Chefs prepare your food to taste as you nibble on delicious antipasti with a refreshing glass of wine.
25% OFF TOTAL | 👤8 | FRI ✓ | SAT ✓ — Italian

BLAH BLAH BLAH ☎020 8892 0888
157 Heath Road, Twickenham, TW1 4BH
Nearest Station: Strawberry Hill
Blah Blah Blah Vegetarian restaurant offers casual dining Monday to Sunday, a weekend brunch and an all-day mezze bar menu.
2FOR1 3 COURSES | FRI 📱 | SAT 📱 | ▲ — Vegetarian

BOMBAY DINE ☎020 7228 9628
133 Lavender Hill, Battersea, SW11 5QJ
Nearest Station: Clapham Junction
A perfect place in Lavender Hill for a relaxing evening, Bombay Dine is a popular, well-decorated restaurant that serves traditional, comforting curries alongside more innovative dishes.
50% OFF FOOD | 👤8 | FRI ✓ | SAT ✓ | ▲ — Indian

BOMBAY INN ☎020 8674 4736
220 Brixton Hill, Lambeth, SW2 1HE
Nearest Station: Brixton
The menu consists of Tandoori and Bengali dishes, a sample of the classic Indian food found in the Indian sub-continent, including the Tandoori king prawn korai and special mint sauce.
2FOR1 2 COURSES | FRI 📱 | SAT × — Indian

BOMBAY WOK ☎020 8577 9087
50-52 Bell Road, Hounslow, TW3 3PB
Nearest Station: Hounslow
Adapting Chinese cooking techniques to Indian flavours and tastes, Bombay Wok draws on the vibrant culinary culture of Bombay (now Mumbai) and uses the classic Chinese wok to produce fantastic dishes.
2FOR1 MAIN COURSE | FRI ✱ | SAT ✱ — Indian

THE BOSCO BAR & LOUNGE 020 8339 5720
St Marks Hill, Surbiton, KT6 4LQ
Nearest Station: Surbiton
Keeping it simple, but with the same verve that characterises the place as a whole, Bosco delivers delicious food, both well-prepared and presented, in a stylish yet comfortable setting.
50% OFF FOOD | 👤4 | FRI × | SAT × — European

BOSCOREALE ☎01737 351 157
12 Waterhouse Lane, Kingswood, Tadworth, KT20 6EQ
Nearest Station: Tadworth
Beautiful Italian restaurant in the leafy suburbs, with a menu going a little beyond standard Italian fare. Dishes like the fichi ripiene gratinati and pollo montebianco stand out from the crowd.
50% OFF FOOD | 👤4 | FRI ✓ | SAT ✱ | ▲ — International

BRAVO! BRAVO! ☎020 8283 2038
Park Inn Heathrow, Bath Rd, West Drayton, UB7 0DU
Nearest Station: Heathrow Terminals 1, 2, 3
Expect all-round entertainment and to be tempted by the buffet or the gourmet à la carte menu, dining in stylish and chic surroundings. As the music volume increases, liven up and dance the night away.
25% OFF TOTAL | 👤10 | FRI ✓ | SAT ✓ | ✱ — European

BROADWAY BAR CAFE ☎020 8399 7698
43-51 Tolworth Broadway, Tolworth, KT6 7DW
Nearest Station: Surbiton
Contemporary and stylish café bar that shows live sporting events and serves straight up, straight down tasty and hearty pub food, along with good and spicy fresh curries.
2FOR1 2 COURSES | FRI ✓ | SAT ✓ — British

BROADWAY TANDOORI ☎020 8542 7697
250-252 The Broadway, Wimbledon, SW19 1SB
Nearest Station: South Wimbledon
Large and small party sizes alike can enjoy the vast array of exquisite Indian dishes on offer in this wonderful restaurant. Daily happy hours and a delivery service are further highlights of this venue.
2FOR1 MAIN COURSE | FRI ✓ | SAT ✓ — Indian

BROUGE @ THE OLD GOAT ☎020 8977 2698
241 Hampton Road, Twickenham, TW2 5NG
Nearest Station: Fulwell
Brouge @ The Old Goat offers high quality Belgian-influenced British cuisine, prepared daily using fresh ingredients. They specialise in cooking with Belgian beer and complementing your drink to your meal.
50% OFF FOOD | 👤10 | FRI ✱ | SAT ✱ | SUN — European

CAFÉ ROUGE

25% OFF TOTAL | 👤6 | FRI ✓ | SAT ✓ | ✱ | ▲

4 restaurants in South West London

96-98 High Street, Epsom, KT19 8BR
Epsom Downs ☎ 01372 749 131

Portsmouth Road, Esher, KT10 9AD
Stoneleigh ☎ 01372 465 550

85 Queens Road, Weybridge, KT13 9UG
Walton-on-Thames ☎ 01932 851 777

26 High Street, Wimbledon Village, SW19 5BY
South Wimbledon ☎ 020 8944 5131

BUGATTI PIZZERIA
☎020 8870 9000

145-147 Wandsworth High Street, Wandsworth, SW18 4JB

Nearest Station: Wandsworth Town

This Italian pizzeria takes great pride in using only the freshest, quality ingredients to create flavoursome dishes that reflect the varied tastes of the Italian pizza.

2FOR1 2 COURSES | FRI ✓ | SAT ✓ — Italian

CAFE MASALA
☎020 8948 0055

113 Kew Road, Richmond, TW9 2PN

Nearest Station: Richmond

A rich variety of Indian dishes are on offer at this wonderful restaurant. Accommodating staff are eager to ensure every guest has a memorable dining experience.

25% OFF TOTAL | 4 | FRI | SAT — Indian

CAFÉ RICCO
01784 463 300

133 High Street, Staines, TW18 4PD

Nearest Station: Staines

Friendly and accommodating café serving simple yet great-tasting food, made fresh and how you like it. Whether you are in a hurry or have time to spare, this is an ideal spot to get your fill.

2FOR1 3 COURSES | FRI | SAT | SUN | * — Mediterranean

CAFÉ ZIA
☎020 3202 0077

811-813 Wandsworth Road, Battersea, SW8 3JH

Nearest Station: Wandsworth Road

Distinctive dishes are offered with impeccable service. A blend of traditional ingredients are combined with contemporary recipes to create fresh and imaginative dishes.

25% OFF TOTAL | 10 | FRI ✓ | SAT ✓ | * — Indian

CAFFE PICCOLO
☎01372 465 596

10 High Street, Esher, KT10 9RT

Nearest Station: Stoneleigh

With a warm and welcoming ambience and terrific Italian cuisine, this restaurant offers the perfect venue to enjoy an evening of great food with your favourite company. Children are well catered for.

2FOR1 MAIN COURSE | FRI ✓ | SAT ✱ | ▲ — Italian

CAMINATA
☎020 8772 0701

96 Bedford Hill, Wandsworth, SW12 9HR

Nearest Station: Balham

Breezy pizzeria in Balham. Ideal to drop in for a low-key coffee, to shoot the breeze and watch the world by; also for their fine selection of pizzas. A well-loved independent restaurant.

50% OFF FOOD | 6 | FRI ✱ | SAT ✱ — Italian

CARNEVALE'S RESTAURANT
☎020 8944 9351

558-560 Garratt Lane, Earlsfield, SW17 0NU

Nearest Station: Earlsfield

Lively, robust Italian restaurant, the food is marked by fresh, clear flavours; their wine list is selected by Gabriele Rappo, one of the world's top sommeliers. *Offer does to apply to the specials' menu.

50% OFF FOOD | 8 | FRI ✓ | SAT ✓ — Italian

CHEZ LALEE
☎020 8549 5314

6 Griffin Centre, Kingston-upon-Thames, KT1 1JT

Nearest Station: Kingston

Located in Kingston, Chez Lalee serves a wide selection of Mexican dishes including fajitas, burritos and enchilladas. Deliciously prepared and presented food, with choices to suit every palate.

2FOR1 MAIN COURSE | FRI × | SAT × — Mexican

CHEZ MANNY
☎020 7223 4040

145-149 Battersea High Street, Battersea, SW11 3JS

Nearest Station: Clapham Junction

Much-loved neighbourhood restaurant run by brothers Manny and Guillaume. Serves a brilliant array of French dishes with a fine balance, as they aptly put it, between the "gastronomique" and the "rustique".

25% OFF TOTAL | 6 | FRI ✓ | SAT ✓ — French

CHINA BOULEVARD ON THE RIVER
☎020 8874 9878

1 Smuggler's Way, Wandsworth, SW18 1DE

Nearest Station: Wandsworth Town

Sensational panoramic views of the river Thames can be enjoyed as you dine in this superbly spacious restaurant. Here you will be delighted at the wide range of both traditional and exotic dishes.

2FOR1 MAIN COURSE | FRI ✓ | SAT ✓ | * | ▲ — Chinese

CHINA ROYAL
☎020 8541 1988

110 Canbury Park Rd, Kingston-upon-Thames, KT2 6JZ

Nearest Station: Kingston

A charming restaurant serving scrumptiously tasty Chinese cuisine. Guests will enjoy the small cosiness of the interior and the warmly welcoming ambience.

2FOR1 MAIN COURSE | FRI ✓ | SAT ✓ | * — Chinese

THE CHUTNEY
☎020 8870 4588

11 Alma Road, Wandsworth, SW18 1AA

Nearest Station: Wandsworth Town

At The Chutney, the emphasis has and will always be to provide authentic Indian cuisine without the use of artificial colourings or ingredients. The menu consists of carefully chosen regional dishes.

50% OFF FOOD | FRI | SAT | * — Indian

CHUTNEY TANDOORI
☎020 7622 1122

9 Wilcox Road, Vauxhall, SW8 2XA

Nearest Station: Vauxhall

Be prepared to relax and experience authentic cuisine from the many regions of India, delivered with hospitable service in stylish surroundings.

2FOR1 MAIN COURSE | FRI ✓ | SAT ✓ — Indian

CHUTNEYS RESTAURANT
☎020 8540 9788

31A Hartfield Road, Merton, SW19 3SG

Nearest Station: Wimbledon

Highly spacious and contemporary in design, Chutneys offers excellent quality cuisine and guaranteed good times. Highly experienced chefs thrive upon serving exquisite, mouth-watering dishes every time.

2FOR1 3 COURSES | FRI | SAT — Indian

CINI KEBAB
☎020 7350 0424

33 Lavender Hill, Clapham, SW11 5QW

Nearest Station: Clapham Common

Smart, beautifully lit, balanced Turkish restaurant that serves some superb food in a low-key, appealing atmosphere. Wide-ranging menu that offers an excellent introduction to all sorts of Turkish dishes.

2FOR1 3 COURSES | FRI ✓ | SAT ✓ — Turkish

CIRRIK RICHMOND
☎020 8940 0033

94 Kew Road, Richmond, TW9 2PQ

Nearest Station: Richmond

Turkish cuisine at its finest with authentic recipes and dishes inspired by the great Ottoman Empire, combining fresh aromatic spices and herbs, cooked on an open charcoal grill.

50% OFF FOOD | 10 | FRI ✓ | SAT ✓ — Mediterranean

CITIZEN SMITH
☎020 8780 2235

160 Putney High St, Putney, SW15 1RS

Nearest Station: East Putney

Offering a menu based around its pizza oven, the quirky and tasty cuisine brings a unique feel to Citizen Smith. The fun and friendly service complemented by the delicious food guarantee a great meal.

50% OFF FOOD | 4 | FRI ✓ | SAT ✱ | * | ▲ — Pizza

CLAPHAM TANDOORI
☎020 7498 8489

10 Clapham Common, Clapham, SW4 7AA

Nearest Station: Clapham Common

Classic tandoori dishes in a stripped-down but accommodating restaurant right on the edge of Clapham Common. Long-established restaurant with a sound reputation for good quality preparation and service.

2FOR1 3 COURSES | FRI | SAT — Indian

THE COACH AND HORSES
☎020 7622 3815

173-175 Clapham Park Road, Clapham, SW4 7EX

Nearest Station: Clapham Common

The Coach and Horses offers fantastic service and dishes of excellent quality in a relaxing atmosphere, perfect for romantic evenings, family gatherings or just friendly catch-ups.

2FOR1 3 COURSES | FRI ✓ | SAT ✓ | SUN | * — British

COBHAM SPICE OVEN
☎01932 863 666

40 Portsmouth Road, Cobham, KT11 1HZ

Nearest Station: Cobham

Let the efficient staff attend to your every need as you unwind from the stresses of every day life in this relaxed eatery. Using age-old recipes, the dishes ooze Indian authenticity.

25% OFF TOTAL | 10 | FRI ✓ | SAT ✓ — Indian/Bangladeshi

To understand what the restaurant icons mean, please see the inside back cover.

COCHIN BRASSERIE ☎020 8785 6004
193 Lower Richmond Rd, Wandsworth, SW15 1HJ
Nearest Station: East Putney
Named after a vibrant city in Southwest India, the cuisine is characterised by a blend of spices and coconut. The traditional methods and soft taste of the meat and fish offer a delicious combination.
2FOR1 3 COURSES | FRI | SAT | ✱ — Indian

CURRY CENTRE ☎01737 362 648
169 High Street, Banstead, SM7 2NT
Nearest Station: Banstead
Situated in a picturesque village on the outskirts of London, this restaurant offers authentic Bangladeshi dishes prepared with passion, experience and fine ingredients.
2FOR1 MAIN COURSE | FRI | SAT | SUN — Bangladeshi

CURRY KITCHEN ☎020 8751 6655
487c Staines Road, Bedfont, TW14 8BN
Nearest Station: Feltham
Vibrant and pleasant place to eat with a generous selection of traditional Indian dishes, curries and other delicacies. A colourful place that provides a fine setting for an evening in company.
2FOR1 3 COURSES | FRI ✓ | SAT ✱ — Indian

CURRY LEAF ☎020 7585 0703
135a Saint Johns Hill, Clapham Junction, SW11 1TD
Nearest Station: Clapham Junction
Neat little curry house set back off the main drag. Has a good selection of flavourful, tasty dishes in bright but cosy surroundings. *Available on the à la carte only menu.
50% OFF FOOD | 6 | FRI ✓ | SAT ✓ — Indian

CURRY MAHAL ☎020 8788 7880
294 Upper Richmond Road, Wandsworth, SW15 6TH
Nearest Station: Putney
Reputable through longevity and culinary excellence, perfectly executed Tandoori classics are brought to the table. Head Chef Himmat Singh recommends the sea bass infused with coconut and mustard.
2FOR1 MAIN COURSE | FRI × | SAT × | SUN | ✱ — Indian

DA VINCI RESTAURANT ☎020 8744 9910
39 Heath Road, Twickenham, TW1 4AW
Nearest Station: Twickenham
Reputable for their attentive service and distinguished food, Da Vinci Italian uses a wood-burning oven to give pizzas a fresh and crispy base. Steaks and seafood aplenty, all taste buds are tickled.
2FOR1 MAIN COURSE | FRI ✱ | SAT ✱ — Italian

DAAL HANDI ☎020 8481 0008
206 Cambridge Road, Kingston-upon-Thames, KT1 3LU
Nearest Station: Norbiton
An authentic Indian restaurant situated in the heart of Kingston-upon-Thames, Daal Handi serve a range of traditional and delicious Indian dishes.
2FOR1 3 COURSES | FRI × | SAT × | ✱ — Indian

DALCHINI ☎020 8947 5966
147 Arthur Road, Merton, SW19 8AB
Nearest Station: Wimbledon Park
A pioneering restaurant offering Hakka cuisine. An exciting marriage of oriental techniques and Indian ingredients characterises the cuisine. *Check availability on the day during Wimbledon fortnight.
25% OFF TOTAL | 10 | FRI | SAT — Indo-Chinese

DEEA ☎020 8974 5388
145-147 Richmond Road, Kingston-upon-Thames, KT2 5BZ
Nearest Station: Kingston
Whilst striving to improve ancient recipes that have been handed down through generations, the kitchen ensures it maintains all of the traditional flavours that make each dish sumptuous and delicious.
2FOR1 MAIN COURSE | FRI ✱ | SAT ✱ | SUN | ✱ | ▲ — Bangladeshi

DELHI CHEFS 020 8337 5322
20 Cheam Common Road, Sutton, KT4 8RW
Nearest Station: Worcester Park
A stunning contemporary Indian Restaurant priding themselves on innovative cuisine from all across India, truly impeccable service and gorgeous interiors.
2FOR1 2 COURSES | FRI | SAT — Indian

DELHI HEIGHTS BAR & GRILL ☎020 8543 3123
222 High Street, Colliers Wood, SW19 2BH
Nearest Station: Colliers Wood
Endorsing traditional values and putting them into the cuisine makes Delhi Heights an exceptional venue. Tantalising dishes satisfy the palate, whilst the service is effortlessly charming.
2FOR1 2 COURSES | FRI × | SAT × — Indian/Punjabi

DELHI ORCHID ☎020 8948 8790
5 Petersham Road, Richmond, TW10 6UH
Nearest Station: Richmond
Delhi Orchid in Richmond is a wonderful restaurant serving signature North Indian dishes. Located within close proximity of the Thames, every diner will be pleased with the chefs and their offerings.
25% OFF TOTAL | 10 | FRI ✓ | SAT ✓ | ✱ — Indian

DONNA MARGHERITA ☎020 7228 2660
183 Lavander Hill, Clapham Jct, Wandsworth, SW11 5TE
Nearest Station: Clapham Junction
Donna Margherita brings Neapolitan cuisine to London with its Southern Italian influence. Its menu offers a wide choice of exciting and unusual dishes with a fantastic atmosphere and friendly service.
2FOR1 MAIN COURSE | FRI ✓ | SAT ✓ — Italian

DON'T TELL FRED ☎020 8878 8266
40 Sheen Lane East, Richmond, SW14 8LW
Nearest Station: Mortlake
Thrives on a contemporary, stylish tone, with high-backed white chairs, ceiling-high murals and a sparkling chandelier. Brasserie-style European dishes; fine cooking and a good eye for produce.
2FOR1 3 COURSES | FRI ✱ | SAT ✱ | SUN — Bistro

EAST INDIA ☎020 8683 2234
842 London Road, Croydon, CR7 7PA
Nearest Station: Thornton Heath
The kitchen is constantly overflowing with the delectable aromas of authentic Indian spices, and the bold, vibrant colours are enough to entice any diner. Creamy, tomato bases tantalise the taste buds.
2FOR1 MAIN COURSE | FRI ✓ | SAT ✓ — Indian

EASTERN EMPIRE ☎020 8673 8880
57 Bedford Hill, Balham, SW12 9EZ
Nearest Station: Balham
Light, airy Indian restaurant with a low-key atmosphere. A popular place in this corner of London for its fresh-flavoured, subtle and, where necessary, spicy curries. Excellent service, never obsequious.
50% OFF FOOD | 10 | FRI ✓ | SAT ✓ — Indian

EL PEYOTE ☎020 8549 4988
37 Richmond Road, Kingston, KT2 5BW
Nearest Station: Kingston
Introducing a unique cuisine to the restaurant industry, El Peyote draws on the spicy zing of Mexican dishes and expertly blends them with the smooth, rich tastes of the Mediterranean.
2FOR1 3 COURSES | FRI × | SAT × | SUN | ▲ — Mexican

EMPRESS OF INDIA ☎020 8641 4949
77 Stonecot Hill, Sutton, SM3 9HJ
Nearest Station: St. Helier
Echoing the days of the Raj to bring fabulous cuisine enjoyed by the privileged few, here you will find the very best of India, carefully prepared with the finest ingredients to captivate your palate.
2FOR1 2 COURSES | FRI | SAT — Indian

EVEREST ☎020 8296 6669
Ross Parade, Wallington, SM6 8QG
Nearest Station: Wallington
Locally renowned for crafting exceptional food at very good prices, using recipes and spices from all over the rich and diverse Indian subcontinent. Truly a jewel in the crown.
25% OFF TOTAL | 10 | FRI ✱ | SAT ✱ | ✱ — Indian

EVEREST SPICE ☎01372 727 444
3 Derby Square, Epsom, KT19 8AG
Nearest Station: Epsom Downs
With a simple goal to excite and delight diners, Everest Spice Restaurant serves a fine blend of Indian and Nepalese cuisine. Creamy bases and spicy sauces characterise the food on offer.
25% OFF TOTAL | 6 | FRI × | SAT × | SUN | ✱ — Indian/Nepalese

THE EWE ☎020 8398 3182
Hampton Court Way, Thames Ditton, KT7 0JW
Nearest Station: Esher
Renowned for obvious reasons, The Ewe has a loyal following of diners who return on a regular basis to feast upon traditional dishes with a dash of contemporary glamour.
2FOR1 MAIN COURSE | FRI ✓ | SAT × | SUN | ▲ — European

FIRST EDITION RESTAURANT @ THISTLE ☎08713 769 021
Thistle London Heathrow, Bath Rd, West Drayton, UB7 0EQ
Nearest Station: Heathrow Terminal 5
With superb views of Heathrow's runway, guests can enjoy contemporary dishes and capacious wine list whilst watching the world fly by.
50% OFF FOOD | 4 | FRI ✓ | SAT ✓ — International

FISHWORKS RICHMOND ☎020 8948 5965
13-19 The Market, The Square, Richmond, TW9 1EA
Nearest Station: Richmond
A sleek seafood restaurant with its own fish counter where you can buy fresh from a full cohort; vivid, classic dishes populate the menu and the restaurant is serenely ensconced just off the High Street.
25% OFF TOTAL | 6 | FRI ✱ | SAT ✱ | SUN | ▲ — Seafood

THE FOX 01883 340 737
Coulsdon Common, Caterham, CR3 5QS
Nearest Station: Whyteleafe South
This Vintage Inn oozes rural charm and rustic character. The picturesque surroundings provide the perfect backdrop for savouring the hearty, seasonal pub-food on the menu.
25% OFF TOTAL | FRI ✓ | SAT ✓ | SUN | ▲ — Modern British

THE GARDENERS PUB ☎020 8875 1524
268 Merton Road, Southfields, SW18 5JL
Nearest Station: Southfields
Make the most of the weather by dining al fresco in the courtyard garden. Guaranteed to satisfy even the most discerning of diners, the menu is extensive and exceedingly tasty.
2FOR1 MAIN COURSE | FRI × | SAT ✓ | SUN — British

THE GAYLORD BATTERSEA ☎020 7228 3981
44 Battersea Rise, Clapham, SW11 1EE
Nearest Station: Clapham Junction
The Gaylord's menu is amongst the best in the area. Their fresh and traditional food, is paired well with warm and friendly service to provide an exceptional Indian dining experience in busy Clapham.
50% OFF FOOD | 4 | FRI 📱 | SAT 📱 | ✱ — Indian

GLO WALTON-ON-THAMES ☎01932 222 004
The Heart Centre, Walton-on-Thames, KT12 1GH
Nearest Station: Shepperton
Contemporary, casual eating. A place for guests to relax in style with good food and great company. Indulge your palate with some fine pan-Asian cuisine and enjoy this fresh dining experience.
2FOR1 3 COURSES | FRI 📱 | SAT ✱ | ▲ — Pan-Asian

GOLDEN CURRY ☎020 8979 4358
19 Hampton Court Parade, East Molesey, KT8 9HB
Nearest Station: Hampton Court
Utilising recipes past down from generations, the dishes created here are traditionally cooked and truly authentic. Menu includes specials, with a popular Sunday buffet and a comprehensive drinks list.
2FOR1 MAIN COURSE | FRI ✱ | SAT ✱ | ✱ — Indian

GOURMET CREATION ☎020 8780 3279
140 Upper Richmond Road, Wandsworth, SW15 2SW
Nearest Station: East Putney
Recognised for its crispy poppadoms and juicy relishes, this venue promises to satisfy even the most stubborn of palates. The creamy lamb with crunchy cashews comes highly rated.
25% OFF TOTAL | 4 | FRI ✓ | SAT ✓ — Indian

GOZ MEZE BAR & RESTAURANT ☎020 8763 8787
204 Brighton Road, Coulsdon, CR5 2NF
Nearest Station: Coulsdon South
With friendly staff, expert chefs, a warm atmosphere and tasty food, Goz Restaurant promises to be an exciting and dynamic addition to the area and provide an authentic and warm eating experience.
50% OFF FOOD | 6 | FRI × | SAT × — Turkish

THE GRANGE ☎020 8773 8195
Beddington Park, London Road, Wallington, SM6 7BT
Nearest Station: Hackbridge
A menu that accommodates everything from Continental to Indo-Chinese cuisine. Globally inspired dishes make use of the freshest ingredients.
2FOR1 MAIN COURSE | FRI ✓ | SAT ✓ | SUN | ▲ — Pan-Asian

THE GRILL DINER ☎020 3556 7614
Lampton Road, Hounslow, TW3 4EZ
Nearest Station: Hounslow
Based in West London, The Grill has established itself as a place for people to come and socialize over great food. The relaxed atmosphere and friendly staff makes The Grill ideal for a casual dinner.
2FOR1 3 COURSES | FRI × | SAT × | SUN | ✱ — International

THE GURKHA'S INN ☎020 8892 4535
25 York Street, Twickenham, TW1 3LP
Nearest Station: Twickenham
Experience exquisite Nepalese cuisine within an elegantly decorated venue that oozes luxury. Devoted to preparing healthier dishes, chefs cook with ghee-butter over oil and grind all of their own spices.
25% OFF TOTAL | 6 | FRI 📱 | SAT 📱 — Nepalese

HAMPTON RESTAURANT 08445 678 955
20-30 Beaufort Road, Kingston-upon-Thames, KT1 2TQ
Nearest Station: Kingston
Offering diners a carefully selected international menu, this venue prides itself on choice and piquant flavours. Every palate is sure to be gratified at this fine dining restaurant.
2FOR1 3 COURSES | FRI ✓ | SAT ✓ | SUN | ✱ — Bistro

HAND AND FLOWER ☎020 8332 2022
24 Upper Ham Road, Richmond, CR4 4JA
Nearest Station: Teddington
A stunning pub and kitchen that boasts spectacular garden areas and cosmopolitan interior dining spaces. Serves everything from meze to seafood chowder, Jamaican jerk chicken to rump steak.
2FOR1 3 COURSES | FRI × | SAT × | SUN — British

HAWELI OF CLAPHAM ☎020 8673 4900
3 Cavendish Parade, Clapham, SW4 9DW
Nearest Station: Clapham South
Haweli pride themselves on Indian dishes that ooze sophistication and taste. Combining fresh ingredients with authentic spices, this eatery is perfect for midweek treats or special occasions.
2FOR1 MAIN COURSE | FRI 📱 | SAT 📱 | ✱ — Indian

HAZAR MEZE ☎020 8669 9119
9-10 The Parade, Carshalton, SM5 3RL
Nearest Station: Carshalton Beeches
Come along to Hazar Meze and experience the finest that the charcoal grill has to offer. Delicious kebabs with lovingly made sauces feature highly on a well-balanced menu.
2FOR1 3 COURSES | FRI × | SAT × | SUN — Med/Meze

HENRY J BEAN'S BAR & GRILL ☎020 8543 5083
153-161 The Broadway, Wimbledon, SW19 1NE
Nearest Station: South Wimbledon
A unique brand that can best be described as a typical bar and grill. Simply classic American food complemented by a vast array of beverages, all served with flair in a vibrant and lively atmosphere.
25% OFF TOTAL | 10 | FRI ✱ | SAT ✱ | ▲ — American

THE HG WELLS ☎020 8337 4784
101 Cheam Common Rd, Worcester Park, KT4 8TA
Nearest Station: Worcester Park
Wooden floorboards and charming lighting create a warm, inviting feel to this pub and restaurant. In honour of its legendary namesake, this establishment has gained enviable popularity for its excellence.
2FOR1 3 COURSES | FRI 📱 | SAT 📱 | SUN — British

THE HOGARTH ☎020 8943 9192
58 Broad Street, Teddington, TW11 8QY
Nearest Station: Teddington
A small stylish pub in Teddington, The Hogarth is a central meeting point in town perfect for getting together with friends over lunch or a pint. Traditional British food and stone baked pizzas are served.
2FOR1 3 COURSES | FRI × | SAT × | ▲ — British

Gourmet Society discount applies to the à la carte menu only, unless stated otherwise.

HOP AND SPICE ☎020 8675 3121
53 Bedford Hill, Balham, SW12 9EZ
Nearest Station: Balham
Outstanding restaurant serving up something more than your typical curry. With a cuisine based around Sri Lankan origins, explore a deliciously light and healthy tapas menu with a unique edge.

2FOR1 3 COURSES | FRI × | SAT × — Pan-Asian

HOUSE OF ROXY ☎020 8785 9203
141 Upper Richmond Road, Wandsworth, SW15 2TX
Nearest Station: Putney
The House of Roxy is Putney's newest eatery, it is a Tapas Kitchen and cocktail bar. Featuring world class entertainers and a fantastic range of classic and bespoke cocktails.

50% OFF FOOD | 4 | FRI × | SAT × | SUN | ✱ | ▲ — British

IL CARRETTO ☎020 8660 5056
121 Brighton Road, Coulsdon, CR5 2NG
Nearest Station: Coulsdon South
Adored by its locals for obvious reasons, this restaurant is well-rounded and caters to a variety of palates. Serving saporous pasta dishes to crunchy salads and everything in-between.

50% OFF FOOD | FRI | SAT — Italian

INDIAN FLAVOURS ☎020 7622 4003
5 Clapham High Street, Lambeth, SW4 7TS
Nearest Station: Clapham North
There is no need to travel to India for authentic, professionally prepared cuisine. Indian Flavours provides diners with a genuine taste of the country's finest delicacies and a memorable experience.

50% OFF FOOD | FRI ✓ | SAT ✓ — Indian

INDIAN PALACE TANDOORI RESTAURANT ☎020 8751 5822
414 Staines Road, Bedfont, TW14 8BT
Nearest Station: Heathrow Terminal 4
Crisp poppadoms, succulent sundries and creamy curries burst out of the menu at the Indian Palace Tandoori Restaurant. Chefs promise fabulous flavours from quality ingredients.

2FOR1 MAIN COURSE | FRI ✓ | SAT ✓ — Indian

INDIAN ROOM ☎020 8675 8611
59 Bedford Hill, Balham, SW12 1AD
Nearest Station: Balham
Award-winning Indian restaurant serving delicious, flavoursome food. Feel guilt-free as you savour the scrumptious dishes which are created using a lower fat, lower oil style of cooking.

25% OFF TOTAL | 10 | FRI ✱ | SAT ✱ | ✱ — Indian

INDIAN SPICE ☎01932 222 317
13 Church Street, Walton-on-Thames, KT12 2QP
Nearest Station: Walton-on-Thames
A bright and friendly Indian restaurant in Walton that serves a good selection of dishes, ranging from the expected standard curries, to the more imaginative specialities that make it well worth a visit.

25% OFF TOTAL | 10 | FRI ✓ | SAT ✓ | ▲ — Indian

INLUST ☎020 7018 2621
487c Staines Road, Feltham, TW14 8BN
Nearest Station: Heathrow Terminal 4
In Lust is a restaurant that uses the magic of traditional Indian food with a combination of distinctive Chinese & specialist seafood dishes to craft a diversified dining experience for its food lovers.

25% OFF TOTAL | 10 | FRI | SAT — Indian

THE ITALIAN TASTE ☎020 8241 2105
44 Victoria Road, Surbiton, KT6 4JL
Nearest Station: Surbiton
Authentic Italian food served in a relaxed and pleasant atmosphere. Established for 11 years, the chefs here prepare beautiful fresh dishes including a fantastic fish selection.

25% OFF TOTAL | 4 | FRI ✱ | SAT ✱ | ✱ | ▲ — Italian

IVORY LOUNGE SUTTON ☎020 8642 4930
33-35 High Street, Sutton, SM1 1DJ
Nearest Station: Sutton
Offering something for everyone, the Ivory Lounge serves old favourites from sausage and mash to vegetarian delights such as a five-bean chilli. This venue will certainly tickle everyone's taste buds.

2FOR1 MAIN COURSE | FRI ✓ | SAT ✓ — British

JACKSON'S 020 7819 9700
62 Clapham High Street, Clapham, SW4 7UL
Nearest Station: Clapham North
A little café with a big heart, this delightfully pleasant venue offers scrumptious Caribbean food for the soul. Try the jerk chicken and you won't be disappointed.

2FOR1 MAIN COURSE | FRI ✱ | SAT ✱ | SUN — Caribbean

JAIPUR ☎020 8399 9165
90 The Broadway, Surbiton, KT6 7HT
Nearest Station: Tolworth
A classic Indian restaurant serving tasty and authentic Indian food, from traditional favourites to more unknown yet delicious regional specialities. Tantalising cuisine cooked to perfection.

2FOR1 3 COURSES | FRI | SAT | ✱ — Indian

JOY ☎020 8390 3988
37 Brighton Road, Surbiton, KT6 5LR
Nearest Station: Surbiton
A gastronomic taste of India's fabulous culinary regions. Using the finest ingredients and authentic recipes, Joy has become the byword for high quality Indian food set in a contemporary environment.

2FOR1 2 COURSES | FRI | SAT — Indian

JUNCTION RESTAURANT @ HOLIDAY INN ☎020 8234 1100
Holiday Inn London Sutton, Gibson Rd, Sutton, SM12RF
Nearest Station: Sutton
The Junction is a contemporary and stylish restaurant serving modern British cuisine in the evenings.

25% OFF TOTAL | 10 | FRI ✓ | SAT ✓ | ✱ | ▲ — British

K&S REIGN ☎07860 461 935
540 Streatham High Road, Lambeth, SW16 3QF
Nearest Station: Streatham Hill
Quirky and creative surroundings provide a fantastic interior to dine in here. Mouth-watering food from the grill has made this eatery one of the most up and coming places to dine in South London.

25% OFF TOTAL | 6 | FRI | SAT | ✱ — Fusion

KARACHI CUISINE ☎020 8689 6868
1033 London Road, Thornton Heath, CR7 6JF
Nearest Station: Thornton Heath
Karachi Cuisine boasts knowledgeable staff who pride themselves on customer service and offer a guaranteed smile. The kebabs come most recommended, as do the creamy bhunas.

2FOR1 3 COURSES | FRI ✓ | SAT ✓ | ▲ — Indian

KARAHI DUBBA ☎020 8541 3666
51 Surbiton Road, Surbiton, KT1 2HG
Nearest Station: Surbiton
Perfect for a pre or post theatre meal, this is an ideal place to ensure stomach rumbling is kept at bay so you can focus on the entertainment. Supreme Punjabi cuisine served in modern surroundings.

25% OFF TOTAL | 8 | FRI ✓ | SAT ✓ — Indian/Punjabi

KHAN OF WALTON ☎01932 223 495
3 Simpson House, Walton-on-Thames, KT12 1QB
Nearest Station: Shepperton
Both novice and well-experienced diners will adore the opulent curries at this venue, which promise to be consistently bursting with flavour. From starters through to mains, you won't be disappointed.

2FOR1 2 COURSES | FRI | SAT — Indian

KHANAGE INDIAN KITCHEN ☎020 8648 7044
29 London Road, Morden, SM4 5HT
Nearest Station: Morden
Art lovers are in their element at this exquisitely decorated venue that oozes elegance. The modern surroundings complement the traditional food, such as the Lahori recipes which stand the test of time.

2FOR1 MAIN COURSE | FRI × | SAT × — Indian

KHAN'S RESTAURANT ☎020 7978 4455
159 Lavender Hill, Battersea, SW11 5QH
Nearest Station: Clapham Common
Sophisticated diners relish the elegant surroundings and refined service at this Indian eatery. Cooked to culinary impeccability, the cuisine is exceptional.

2FOR1 MAIN COURSE | FRI × | SAT × — Indian

KHAN'S RESTAURANT
☎01372 723 316
29 Upper High Street, Epsom, KT17 4QY
Nearest Station: Ewell East
Sophisticated diners relish the elegant surroundings and refined service at this Indian eatery. Cooked to culinary impeccability, the cuisine is exceptional.

2FOR1 MAIN COURSE | FRI × | SAT × — Indian

KHYBER PASS
☎01932 225 670
54 Terrace Road, Walton-on-Thames, KT12 2SA
Nearest Station: Walton-on-Thames
Feast on classic flavours and be filled with spiced aromas from a menu of favourite dishes and divine chef specialities. Everything you want from an Indian restaurant and takeaway.

2FOR1 3 COURSES | FRI ✱ | SAT ✱ | ✱ — Indian

THE KINGFISHER
01932 579 811
Chertsey Bridge Road, Chertsey, KT16 8LF
Nearest Station: Chertsey
This Vintage Inn oozes rural charm and rustic character. The picturesque surroundings provide the perfect backdrop for savouring the hearty, seasonal pub-food on the menu.

25% OFF TOTAL | FRI ✓ | SAT ✓ | SUN | ▲ — Modern British

KINGSTON LODGE HOTEL
☎020 8541 4481
94 Kingston Hill, Kingston-upon-Thames, KT2 7NP
Nearest Station: Norbiton
Experienced chefs give you the special treatment at this fine Brook group hotel-restaurant, showcasing a wide choice of expertly prepared dishes with an array of fine wines to complement the divine food.

25% OFF TOTAL | FRI ✓ | SAT ✓ — Brasserie

KISSE BAR
020 7924 3360
43 Lavender Hill, Clapham, SW11 5QW
Nearest Station: Clapham Common
A cocktail bar that combines gorgeous food and drink with great music to keep you dancing until late. Serves freshly prepared meals all day, from traditional breakfasts to a fine grill and salad menu.

2FOR1 MAIN COURSE | FRI ✓ | SAT ✓ | ✱ — European

KNIGHTS OF ST JOHN
☎020 7228 2202
137-139 St John's Hill, Wandsworth, SW11 1TD
Nearest Station: Wandsworth Town
Perfectly situated near Clapham Junction station, this chic bar and restaurant boasts tempting cocktails and a debonair European menu. Ideal venue for winding down after work or gearing up for the night.

50% OFF FOOD | 6 | FRI | SAT | ▲ — British

KOUCHIN
☎01784 420 120
8 Station Parade, Shepperton, TW15 2RX
Nearest Station: Ashford
Bringing traditional curries with a contemporary twist to the table, this venue promises to thrill diners with a selection of striking, zesty flavours.

2FOR1 MAIN COURSE | FRI ✓ | SAT ✓ — Indian

LA BELLE EPOQUE
☎020 8757 7777
Sofitel, Terminal 5, Heathrow Airport, TW6 2GD
Nearest Station: Heathrow Terminal 5
The awarding of 2 AA Rosettes in December 2012, shows the culinary delight of La Belle Epoque. The food is classic fine French Cuisine, with modern food trends incorporated, at it's very best.

25% OFF TOTAL | 4 | FRI ✓ | SAT ✓ — French

LA BUVETTE
☎020 8940 6264
6 Church Walk, Richmond, TW9 1SN
Nearest Station: Richmond
A passionate kitchen team that is dedicated to creating well-researched menus and regional French cooking. Enjoy classical dishes such as onglet steaks, scallops and escargots. Awarded 1 AA Rosette.

2FOR1 MAIN COURSE | FRI ✱ | SAT ✱ | SUN | ▲ — French

LA MANCHA PUTNEY
☎020 8780 1022
32 Putney High Street, Putney, SW15 1SQ
Nearest Station: Putney Bridge
Diners seeking a relaxing atmosphere with a sprinkling of fun need look no further than this Spanish eatery. Sip sangria and share over 50 plates of tapas with friends. A great place to start the weekend.

25% OFF TOTAL | 8 | FRI × | SAT × — Spanish

LA TASCA
☎020 8439 1002
52a High Street, Kingston-upon-Thames, KT1 1EU
Nearest Station: Kingston
Quintessentially Spanish, La Tasca's fresh and exciting menu offers something for everyone. Their tapas dishes are sincerely authentic, while their paellas always deliver on flavour.

25% OFF TOTAL | 8 | FRI ✓ | SAT × | ▲ — Spanish

LA VERANDA RISTORANTE
☎020 8647 4370
19a The Parade, Beynon Road, Carshalton, SM5 3RL
Nearest Station: Carshalton
A well-established Italian restaurant founded by two brothers who have worked hard to ensure high-quality food and excellent service always emerges at the top of the restaurant's agenda.

25% OFF TOTAL | 6 | FRI ✱ | SAT ✱ | SUN — Italian

LAMBOURNE BAR AND GRILL
☎020 8545 8661
263 The Broadway, Wimbledon, SW19 1SD
Nearest Station: South Wimbledon
A captivating vibrancy can be found in this popular bar and restaurant. Offers an impressive menu that strongly focuses on using local ingredients and seasonal produce.

25% OFF TOTAL | 10 | FRI × | SAT × | SUN | ▲ — British

LARDER RESTAURANT @ HILTON
☎020 8680 3000
Hilton Croydon, 101 Waddon Way, Croydon, CR9 4HH
Nearest Station: Waddon
This restaurant had a charming feel of a cosy country kitchen, albeit with a little more pizzazz. The menu is broadly British, with an emphasis on clear, strong flavours and fresh, seasonal produce.

50% OFF FOOD | 4 | FRI | SAT | ▲ — European

LE CHARDON
☎020 8673 9300
32 Abbeville Road, Clapham, SW4 9NG
Nearest Station: Clapham South
The majestically decorated interior goes hand in hand with magnificent food at this benign French restaurant. Try the classic moules mariniàres or the tender tuna steak for an unforgettable treat.

25% OFF TOTAL | 4 | FRI | SAT | ✱ — French

LE CHIEN QUI FUME
☎020 8979 7150
107 Walton Road, East Molesey, KT8 0DR
Nearest Station: Hampton Court
Influenced by the beauty of a similarly named Parisian restaurant, the owners of this wonderful establishment have a comparable attitude towards high quality food and amiable service.

25% OFF TOTAL | 4 | FRI × | SAT × | ▲ — French

LE PETIT NANTAIS
☎020 8979 2309
41 Bridge Road, Hampton Court, East Molesey, KT8 9ER
Nearest Station: Hampton Court
A well-established traditional bistro that will transport you to the heart of France itself. The beautiful cuisine will blow you away. The fillet steak, in particular, comes highly recommended.

25% OFF TOTAL | 4 | FRI ✱ | SAT ✱ | ▲ — French

LITTLE ITALY
☎020 8547 2133
2 Old London Road, Kingston-upon-Thames, KT2 6SN
Nearest Station: Kingston
Little Italy is situated at the end of the high street and is a reliably good Italian restaurant serving up all the classic pasta, pizza and risotto dishes diners love.

2FOR1 MAIN COURSE | FRI ✓ | SAT ✓ — Italian

LOCALE
☎020 8682 3553
225 Balham High Road, Balham, SW17 7BQ
Nearest Station: Tooting
Cool and collected Italian restaurant with all the classic dishes and flavours; hearty and flavourful pasta and risotto, and a line in beautifully seasoned meat and fish with smart accompaniments.

25% OFF TOTAL | 6 | FRI ✓ | SAT ✓ — Italian

LOCH FYNE
☎020 8255 6222
175 Hampton Road, Twickenham, TW2 5NG
Nearest Station: Fulwell
From the roadside oyster bar that once was, Loch Fyne restaurants now successfully inject energy and passion into great food and wonderful flavours, whilst ensuring their seafood is sustainably sourced.

25% OFF TOTAL | 4 | FRI ✱ | SAT ✱ | ▲ — Seafood

LOCH FYNE
☎01932 586 010

17 Portsmouth Street, Cobham, KT11 1JF
Nearest Station: Cobham

From the roadside oyster bar that once was, Loch Fyne restaurants now successfully inject energy and passion into great food and wonderful flavours, whilst ensuring their seafood is sustainably sourced.

25% OFF TOTAL | 4 | FRI ✱ | SAT ✱ — Seafood

THE LODGE HOTEL
☎020 8874 1598

Upper Richmond Road, Putney, SW15 2RN
Nearest Station: East Putney

Renowned for obvious reasons, this venue is ideally located near the Thames and offers a modish interior. Remove yourself from daily stresses in the plush lounges with friends.

2FOR1 MAIN COURSE | FRI ✓ | SAT × | SUN — International

THE LOFTY TURTLE
☎020 8878 1995

505-507 Upper Richmond Road West, East Sheen, SW14 7DE
Nearest Station: Mortlake

The Lofty Turtle's food selection is appropriately classic American, not only offering great burgers and steaks but super salads and classics taken from throughout the fifty states of the USA.

2FOR1 MAIN COURSE | FRI ✱ | SAT × | SUN — American

THE LONDON ROAD
☎020 8892 3328

68 London Road, Twickenham, TW1 3QS
Nearest Station: Twickenham

The London Road offers a wide variety of food, with lunch and dinner menus on offer. Light snack or hearty meal, there is something for all appetites.

2FOR1 3 COURSES | FRI ✓ | SAT × | SUN — British

LOVE FOOD
☎020 8940 1235

46 Hill Rise, Richmond, TW10 6UB
Nearest Station: Richmond

Love Food take their name seriously. Their passion for food is translated on the plate. Love Food never fails to deliver on service and quality. A hidden gem in Richmond.

2FOR1 3 COURSES | FRI ✓ | SAT ✓ — British

MACHAAN
☎020 8977 9111

5 High Street, Kingston-upon-Thames, KT1 4DA
Nearest Station: Hampton Wick

Taking Indian dining to another level, Machaan delivers rich cuisine brimming full of flavoursome spices and warm, creamy sauces. Taste and freshness runs through each and every dish.

25% OFF TOTAL | 2 | FRI × | SAT × — Authentic Indian

MAE PING THAI RESTAURANT
☎020 8545 0021

162 The Broadway, Wimbledon, SW19 1RX
Nearest Station: Wimbledon

Joy for those in the local area, Mae Ping Wimbledon serves traditional, wholesome Thai food as well as more modern interpretations of the cuisine. Popular dishes include the delicious pad thai goong.

2FOR1 MAIN COURSE | FRI × | SAT × — Thai

MA'JONG
01932 222 004

The Heart, Walton On Thames, KT12 1GH
Nearest Station: Walton-on-Thames

Ma'jong is the perfect place to catch-up with friends, a blend of stylish cocktail bar and fusion restaurant.The food at Ma'jong is of Asian and European descent, with a number of fusion dishes available.

2FOR1 MAIN COURSE | FRI ✓ | SAT ✓ | ✱ — Fusion

MANGO PALACE
☎020 8682 0009

114 Tooting High Street, Tooting, SW17 0RR
Nearest Station: Tooting Broadway

Specialists in South Indian and Sri Lankan cuisine; Mango Palace serve up an enticing variety of regional dishes amidst beautiful surroundings and a warm and welcoming atmosphere.

2FOR1 3 COURSES | FRI × | SAT × | ✱ — Indian

MANTOOS RESTAURANT
☎020 7738 1616

59 Battersea Bridge Road, Battersea, SW11 3AU
Nearest Station: Battersea Park

Specialising in Afghan and Persian cuisine, Mantoos provides something a little alternative for the discerning diner.The relaxed yet modern atmosphere makes for a sophisticated dining experience.

25% OFF TOTAL | FRI | SAT | SUN — Persian

MARKET HOUSE
020 7095 9443

443 Coldharbour Lane, Brixton, SW9 8LN
Nearest Station: Brixton

Market House is a bar, diner and music hall in central Brixton supporting local and independent suppliers of organic food, drinks, and sounds. Head on down to satisfy your appetite and quench that thirst.

2FOR1 2 COURSES | FRI × | SAT × | SUN — Modern British

MASALA KITCHEN
☎020 8870 2468

103 Easthill, Wandsworth, SW18 2QB
Nearest Station: Wandsworth Town

Traditional Indian and tandoori dishes are on offer at this popular restaurant in Wandsworth. A modern décor and interior design creates a welcoming ambience.

50% OFF FOOD | FRI ✓ | SAT ✓ — Indian

MASSALA
☎01932 865 005

19 Anyards Road, Cobham, KT11 2LW
Nearest Station: Cobham

Co-owned by its two main chefs, Massala is a fabulous Indian restaurant in Cobham whose primary focus is always on the quality of its dishes. The food here is fresh-flavoured and expertly spiced.

2FOR1 MAIN COURSE | FRI | SAT × — Indian

MAZAR RESTAURANT
☎020 7978 5374

11-12 Battersea Square, Battersea, SW11 3RA
Nearest Station: Clapham Junction

Mazar captures the taste of Lebanon in Battersea Square. Endorsing an Eastern vibe, this venue has a menu composed of Lebanese specialities and an extensive wine-list direct from its native vineyards.

2FOR1 2 COURSES | FRI × | SAT × — Lebanese

MEZZET
☎020 8979 4088

43 Bridge Road, Hampton Court East Molesey, KT8 9ER
Nearest Station: Hampton Court

Mezzet is a Lebanese restaurant and cocktail lounge in Bridge Road East Molesey - just a short walk from Hampton Court Palace. Family man Fadi sources produce locally and uses old Fenicien influences.

50% OFF FOOD | 4 | FRI × | SAT × — Middle Eastern

THE MINT IN BANSTEAD
01737 362 785

Park Road, Banstead, SM7 3DS
Nearest Station: Banstead

This Vintage Inn oozes rural charm and rustic character. The picturesque surroundings provide the perfect backdrop for savouring the hearty, seasonal pub-food on the menu.

25% OFF TOTAL | FRI ✓ | SAT ✓ | SUN — Modern British

THE MOGUL
☎01932 223 319

66 Terrace Road, Walton-on-Thames, KT12 2SA
Nearest Station: Walton-on-Thames

Popular with the locals, authentic Indian dishes are created with care and delivered efficiently. The relaxed, informal atmosphere makes this a wonderful place to enjoy your favourite Indian cuisine.

2FOR1 MAIN COURSE | FRI ✓ | SAT ✓ — Indian

MOIDULS OF STANLEY ROAD
☎020 8977 1933

200 Stanley Road, Teddington, TW11 8UE
Nearest Station: Fulwell

Moidul's of Stanley Road is one of the finest Indian and Bangladeshi restaurants in south west London.They have a passion for preparing quality food with the freshest of ingredients.

25% OFF TOTAL | 6 | FRI × | SAT × — Indian

MOIDULS OF TEDDINGTON
☎020 8977 4745

78 High Street, Teddington, TW11 8JD
Nearest Station: Teddington

Moidul's of Teddington is the latest string to leading local chef and restaurateur Moidul Hussain's bow. An innovative approach to Indian dining, Moidul's have brought fine Indian dining to Teddington.

25% OFF TOTAL | 6 | FRI × | SAT × — Indian

MOIDUL'S RAWALPINDI
☎020 8892 3010

62 King Street, Twickenham, TW1 3SH
Nearest Station: Twickenham

A local favourite with a wide range of Indian and Bangladeshi dishes, including various styles of curry, fresh fish dishes and regional specialities, crafted using locally sourced produce where possible.

2FOR1 3 COURSES | FRI × | SAT × — Indian

THE MONKEY PUZZLE 01372 744 060
Leatherhead Road, Chessington, KT9 2NE
Nearest Station: Chessington South
Beefeater Grill are one of the UK's best-loved restaurants welcoming guests for almost 40 years in over 130 locations nationwide. *Excludes Breakfast, Light Bites, Bar menu, set menus and all other offers.

2FOR1 MAIN COURSE | 6 | FRI ✓ | SAT ✗ | Modern British

MOOMBA KITCHEN AND BAR ☎020 8785 9151
5 Lacy Road, Putney, SW15 1NH
Nearest Station: East Putney
With its ranging menu and characterful vibe, Moomba's dishes are to savour, from a delicate but filling eggs benedict breakfast to a perfectly cooked loin of lamb with lentils and tzatziki for dinner.

25% OFF TOTAL | 4 | FRI ✗ | SAT ✗ | SUN | English and Continental

MOOMBA KITCHEN AND BAR ☎020 8332 6655
19 Hill Street, Richmond, TW9 1TN
Nearest Station: Richmond
With personal, friendly service and a distinctive ambience, Moomba serves up a tantalisingly wholesome food and drink menu, which has something for everyone.

25% OFF TOTAL | 4 | FRI ✗ | SAT ✗ | SUN | English and Continental

MUMBAI DELIGHT ☎020 7091 0043
51a South Lambeth Road, London, SW8 1RH
Nearest Station: Vauxhall
Deliciously fresh and spicy flavours are cooked up with impeccable service and a garnish of care to create an enjoyable and authentic Indian dining experience, bringing Mumbai's food revolution to London.

50% OFF FOOD | 4 | FRI | SAT ✱ | SUN | Indian

MYSTICA ☎01932 841 682
147-149 Station Road, Addlestone, KT15 2AT
Nearest Station: Weybridge
Moving forward with Indian cuisine is a key motive in the kitchen at Mystica. Stylish and chic, the ambience and décor match the sophistication of flavours and ingredients found in every dish.

2FOR1 MAIN COURSE | FRI ✓ | SAT ✓ | Indian

NAMADA ☎020 8870 5538
197-199 Replingham, Southfields, SW18 5LY
Nearest Station: Southfields
Proof is in the pudding, as it were, at this venture of acclaimed chef M. A. Bari. Fresh, subtle flavours speak cleanly. *Offer not available on take-away orders.

2FOR1 3 COURSES | FRI ✓ | SAT ✱ | Indian

NEW ANARKALI ☎020 8979 5072
158-160 Walton Road, East Molesey, KT8 0HP
Nearest Station: Hampton Court
Named after a courtesan dancer from Emperor Akbar's court, this venue offers a beautiful setting to enjoy the finest delicacies of India. Established 30 years ago, this prestigious venue is one of a kind.

2FOR1 3 COURSES | FRI ✓ | SAT ✓ | Indian

NEW SUNBURY TANDOORI ☎01932 781 818
98 Windmill Road, Sunbury-on-Thames, TW16 7HB
Nearest Station: Sunbury
Paying incredible attention to detail when it comes to the careful balancing of spices, chefs at this South Indian eatery offer diners different levels of spices to suit their palates.

2FOR1 2 COURSES | FRI ✓ | SAT ✓ | ✱ | Indian

NEW WORLD CHINESE RESTAURANT ☎020 8644 0078
1 Wrythe Lane, Carshalton, SM5 1AG
Nearest Station: St. Helier
Experience authentic flavour and indulge in finely crafted Chinese cuisine, feasting on an exemplary selection of delicious modern and traditional dishes, each influenced by the country's varying regions.

25% OFF TOTAL | FRI ✓ | SAT ✓ | SUN | Chinese

NOIYA ☎020 7228 7171
62 Lavender Hill, Clapham, SW11 5RQ
Nearest Station: Clapham Common
Intimate and romantic, the low-lighting at this eatery is undoubtedly soothing. Classic dishes with a contemporary twist excite and entice regulars, who rave avidly about the cuisine.

50% OFF FOOD | 6 | FRI ✓ | SAT ✓ | Indian

THE OLD FIRE STATION ☎020 8568 5999
55 High Street, Brentford, TW8 0AH
Nearest Station: Brentford
Start your night off with one of the famous flamed mojitos that will truly set your evening alight. Tender steaks and scrumptious sticky toffee puddings will have you coming back for more.

2FOR1 MAIN COURSE | FRI ✓ | SAT ✓ | British

ONAM ☎020 8767 7655
219 Tooting High Street, Tooting, SW17 0SZ
Nearest Station: Tooting Broadway
Great restaurant serving fine and tasty South Indian cuisine. Friendly, helpful staff will be happy to advise you should you be overwhelmed with choice having perused the well-selected menu.

50% OFF FOOD | 4 | FRI | SAT | Indian

ORIGIN ASIA ☎020 8948 0509
100 Kew Road, Richmond, TW9 2PQ
Nearest Station: Richmond
Austin-Powers-does-Asia is how we'd describe this stylish and kooky op-art inspired Indian restaurant, offering endless options of authentic cuisine, most popular for its classic take on delicious curries.

2FOR1 MAIN COURSE | FRI ✗ | SAT ✗ | Indian

THE OVAL TANDOORI ☎020 7582 1415
64-66 Brixton Road, Oval, SW9 6BP
Nearest Station: Oval
Good Food Guide-recommended restaurant serving contemporary Asian cuisine. Renowned for its tailor-made dishes to suit even the most temperamental of palates.

25% OFF TOTAL | 10 | FRI | SAT | ✱ | Indian

PALACE SPICE ☎020 7207 3925
139 Lavender Hill, Battersea, SW11 5QJ
Nearest Station: Clapham Junction
A popular Indian restaurant in Clapham, Palace Spice does all the classics very well, is attentively served and low-key in ambience. Altogether, it's a good, simple place to enjoy an evening and a tasty curry.

50% OFF FOOD | 10 | FRI ✱ | SAT ✱ | Indian

PALMYRA LEBANESE RESTAURANT ☎020 8948 7019
227 Sandycombe Road, Richmond, TW9 3LU
Nearest Station: Kew Gardens
A fabulous dining venue, serving up the finest Lebanese cuisine in the area. Delicious hot and cold mezze dishes are the highlights of the menu, alongside a choice of salads and traditional main courses.

2FOR1 MAIN COURSE | 6 | FRI ✓ | SAT ✓ | Lebanese

PANAHAR INDIAN ☎020 7228 8947
184 Lavender Hill, Wandsworth, SW11 5TQ
Nearest Station: Clapham Junction
Warm welcomes and delicious food at Panahar Indian Restaurant. Dishes are prepared to the highest standard, where only the freshest ingredients and quality spices are used.

2FOR1 MAIN COURSE | FRI ✗ | SAT ✗ | ✱ | Indian

PARK RESTAURANT @ THE PARK HOTEL ☎020 8614 9700
Park Road, Teddington, TW11 0AB
Nearest Station: Teddington
High-ceilinged hotel restaurant serving a classic à la carte menu. Favourites include the coq au vin with mash, the excellent boeuf bourguignon, and the straight-down-the-line steak and ale pie.

50% OFF FOOD | 6 | FRI ✓ | SAT ✓ | International

PEPPERS ☎020 8941 7138
175 High Street, Hampton Hill, TW12 1NL
Nearest Station: Fulwell
Celebrate the specialised "Dumpukht" style of cooking, originating from the Moghul Emperors. Focusing on clarity, the expert chefs at this venue focus only on cuisine that is fragrant and tantalising.

25% OFF TOTAL | 4 | FRI ✓ | SAT ✓ | Indian

PERSIAN HUT ☎020 8545 0900
325 Haydons Road, Wimbledon, SW19 8LA
Nearest Station: Haydons Road
Bringing the delicious fragrant flavours of the East to London, Persian Hut is an excellent choice for those seeking something different. The service is welcoming and efficient and the menu is a delight.

25% OFF TOTAL | 10 | FRI | SAT ✗ | Mediterranean

To understand what the restaurant icons mean, please see the inside back cover.

PREZZO

2FOR1 MAIN COURSE | FRI × | SAT ×

5 restaurants in South West London

28 High Street, Banstead, SM7 2LJ
Banstead — 01737 360 248

109-113 High Street, Shepperton, TW17 9BL
Shepperton — 01932 269 006

26 Station Way, Cheam, SM3 8SQ
Cheam — 020 8643 7490

The Rotunda, Clarence St, Kingston KT1 1QJ
Kingston — 020 8549 8687

44 Church Street, Weybridge, KT13 8DP
Weybridge — 01932 844 430

THE PIG AND WHISTLE
020 8874 1061
479-481 Merton Road, Earlsfield, SW18 5LD
Nearest Station: Southfields
Popular pub located in Earlsfield, where great food and a lively atmosphere guarantee it a fantastic reputation. Nachos, gourmet burgers and fish and chips feature as strong contenders on the menu.

50% OFF FOOD | 2 | FRI ✓ | SAT ✓ — British

PIZZA METRO PIZZA
020 7228 3812
64 Battersea Rise, Wandsworth, SW11 1EQ
Nearest Station: Clapham Junction
Italian chefs use their culture to inspire the dishes in the kitchen at Pizza Metro. Freshly prepared ingredients contribute to the tastiness of every dish, from the pizza to the tender meatballs.

50% OFF FOOD | 2 | FRI × | SAT × — Italian

PRINCESS OF INDIA
020 8646 8222
10 Morden Court Parade, London Rd, Merton, SM4 5HJ
Nearest Station: Morden
Come and enjoy an authentic restaurant where a selection of traditional Indian dishes are prepared for your pleasure, as well as delicious food for you to take away and dine in your own home.

2FOR1 MAIN COURSE | FRI ✓ | SAT ✓ | ✱ — Indian

PUKKA RESTAURANT
020 8671 8254
89 Streatham Hill, Streatham, SW2 4UD
Nearest Station: Streatham Hill
A warm welcome awaits you at the Pukka Brasserie. Guests will love the fantastically authentic Indian cuisine on offer, which can be fully enjoyed in pleasantly charming surroundings.

25% OFF TOTAL | 10 | FRI | SAT | ✱ — Indian

THE PURPLE CHILLI LOUNGE
020 7622 9400
72 Clapham Park Road, Lambeth, SW4 7BX
Nearest Station: Clapham Common
This venue is popular with the locals of Clapham and it is no surprise as to why. The Purple Chilli Lounge is constantly buzzing and the cuisine is mouth watering.

25% OFF TOTAL | 4 | FRI × | SAT × — Indian

Q VERDE
020 8332 2882
291 Sandycombe Road, Kew, TW9 3LU
Nearest Station: Kew Gardens
This beautiful family-owned restaurant is one of Kew's best kept secrets, with a rich flavourful menu to suit everyone's taste, complemented by an extensive and well-chosen wine list.

25% OFF TOTAL | 10 | FRI | SAT — Mediterranean

QUEEN OF INDIA
020 8785 6004
193 Lower Richmond Road, Putney, SW15 1HJ
Nearest Station: Putney Bridge
Queen of India is a restaurant dedicated to classic and contemporary south Indian cuisine. Everything is prepared traditionally and ground individually for each dish on the premises.

25% OFF TOTAL | 2 | FRI ✓ | SAT ✓ — Indian

RADHA KRISHNA BHAVAN
020 8682 0969
86 Tooting High Street, Tooting, SW17 0RN
Nearest Station: Tooting Broadway
Passionate and flavourful food. Specialising in dishes from the north and south of India this restaurant delivers the finest curries, firmly establishing itself as a flagship of Eastern sophistication.

2FOR1 2 COURSES | FRI | SAT — Indian

RAINTREE
020 8339 3737
162 Portsmouth Road, Thames Ditton, KT7 0XR
Nearest Station: Thames Ditton
When you are just in the mood for a bright, flavoursome curry, head to this vibrant Indian restaurant. The special chettinadu curry, made with twenty-three different spices, is sure to please.

2FOR1 3 COURSES | FRI ✱ | SAT ✱ — Indian

THE RAJ INDIAN CUISINE
020 8390 0251
163 Ewell Road, Surbiton, KT6 6AW
Nearest Station: Surbiton
Along with the wonderfully authentic Indian meals, the restaurant provides you with a special history behind your chosen dish, enriching your knowledge of Indian haute cuisine.

2FOR1 MAIN COURSE | FRI ✓ | SAT ✓ — Indian

THE RAVENSBURY ARMS
020 8648 9964
260 Croydon Road, Mitcham, CR4 4JA
Nearest Station: Mitcham
Well-kept ales and continental lagers, seasonal menus and an extensive wine list; these are just some of the great attributes of The Ravensbury Arms. Dine in the spacious lounge areas or large open garden.

2FOR1 3 COURSES | 4 | FRI | SAT | SUN — British

REGATTA RESTAURANT @ HOLIDAY INN
01932 899 988
Felix Lane, Shepperton, TW17 8NP
Nearest Station: Shepperton
The Regatta Restaurant offers diners an idyllic escape with the opportunity to sample a selection of traditional and international dishes including the speciality selection of steaks from the grill.

25% OFF TOTAL | 6 | FRI ✓ | SAT ✓ — International

RESHAM LOUNGE NORBURY
020 8764 4007
1538-1540 London Road, Norbury, SW16 4EU
Nearest Station: Norbury
Resham Lounge brings fine Indian cuisine to Norbury, serving this in beautiful, modern surroundings. A varied menu, coupled with a welcoming atmosphere, Resham Lounge is definitely an Indian to try.

2FOR1 3 COURSES | FRI × | SAT × | SUN — Indian

THE RESTAURANT
08433 575 514
The Bridge Hotel, Bridge Road, Chertsey, KT16 8JZ
Nearest Station: Chertsey
Carnivorous diners can sink their teeth into a notorious rack of sticky ribs, or devour sizzling fajitas with a kick. The view of the river is the perfect accompaniment to any dish, whatever you fancy.

2FOR1 MAIN COURSE | FRI ✓ | SAT × | SUN — International

RISTORANTE ICHNUSA
020 7350 0424
33 Lavender Hill, Battersea, SW11 5QW
Nearest Station: Clapham Common
At Ristorante Ichnusa,they offer their customers the authentic flavors of Sardinia, preparing the meals their grandmothers used to make them. Everyone can enjoy the real taste of Sardinia!

2FOR1 3 COURSES | FRI ✓ | SAT ✓ — Italian

REVOLUTION
☎020 8642 9264

1-3 High Street, Sutton, SM1 1DF

Nearest Station: Sutton

Let Great British bar food and every flavour of vodka under the sun tantalise your taste buds at this national bar chain. *Only valid on drinks purchased with food or while eating. Excludes champagne.

25% OFF TOTAL | ♟ 6 | FRI ✓ | SAT ✓ — British

RIVERSIDE VEGETARIA
☎020 8546 7992

64 High Street, Kingston-upon-Thames, KT1 1HN

Nearest Station: Kingston

Experience a culinary trip around the world with a cosmopolitan menu consisting of a wide variety of specialised vegetarian, gluten- and wheat-free dishes. One of Britain's best vegetarian restaurants.

2FOR1 3 COURSES | FRI 📱 | SAT 📱 | SUN | ▲ — Vegetarian

RIVIERA RESTAURANT
020 7978 5395

31-32 Battesrea Square, Battersea, SW11 3RA

Nearest Station: Clapham Junction

Captures the flavours and scent of the Mediterranean, offering a wide range of contemporary and traditional dishes which reflect the flavour of Italian cuisine.

2FOR1 MAIN COURSE | FRI ✓ | SAT ✓ — Italian

RODIZIO BRAZIL
☎020 7627 3747

62 Clapham High Street, Lambeth, SW4 7UL

Nearest Station: Clapham North

Try the unique Brazilian barbecue way of flaming and serving skewered meats, sausage and poultry. The juicy meats are specially marinated and grilled to perfection.

50% OFF FOOD | ♟ 4 | FRI ✓ | SAT ✓ — Brazilian

RODIZIO BRITTANIA
☎020 7720 9573

353 Wandsworth Road, South Lambeth, SW8 2JH

Nearest Station: Stockwell

An authentic Brazilian steakhouse, the proprietors of Rodizio Britannia bring the tastes of South America to London for an experience you'll find hard to forget.

2FOR1 MAIN COURSE | FRI ✓ | SAT ✓ | ▲ — Brazilian

THE ROYAL OAK
☎020 8891 1863

13 Richmond Road, Richmond, TW1 3AB

Nearest Station: Twickenham

A fantastic place to meet friends and family for great food and good times. An elegant interior creates a pleasing ambience, fully complementing the superb service and tasty food.

2FOR1 3 COURSES | FRI 📱 | SAT 📱 | SUN — British

RUPALI
☎020 8330 3046

376 Malden Road, Worcester Park, KT4 7NL

Nearest Station: Worcester Park

However you enjoy your curry, this authentic Indian restaurant offers something to suit every palate. Traditional favourite dishes appear alongside house specialities.

2FOR1 MAIN COURSE | FRI ✓ | SAT ✓ | SUN — Indian

SAI RESTAURANT
☎020 8947 2212

193 Worple Road, Merton, SW20 8RE

Nearest Station: Raynes Park

Inspired by the Pakistani region of Punjab, the recipes here are authentic and age-old. Appease a voracious stomach with a substantial dish from a dazzling menu.

2FOR1 3 COURSES | FRI 📱 | SAT 📱 — Indian/Punjabi

SAMRATT RESTAURANT
☎020 8788 9110

18-20 Lacy Road, Putney, SW15 1NL

Nearest Station: Putney

Enticing, traditional, classic yet cosmopolitan, this family-run restaurant provides authentic Indian cuisine using fresh ingredients and spices.

2FOR1 MAIN COURSE | FRI ✓ | SAT ✓ | * — Indian

SANTINI'S
☎020 8668 2159

64 Godstone Road, Kenley, CR8 5AA

Nearest Station: Kenley

A slice of Italy in the heart of Surrey. The returning customers indicate the high standards that can be found in both food and atmosphere at this delightful Italian restaurant.

25% OFF TOTAL | ♟ 8 | FRI ✓ | SAT ✓ | SUN — Italian

SANTOK MAA'S BHEL POORI HOUSE
☎020 8665 0626

848 London Road, Thornton Heath, CR7 7PA

Nearest Station: Thornton Heath

The team at Santok Maa's are committed to creating the purest vegetarian dishes possible. Enjoy a curry and handmade chapattis and taste Indian vegetarian at its finest.

25% OFF TOTAL | FRI ✓ | SAT ✓ — Indian

SARAGEMA
☎020 8288 0365

52-54 Banstead Road, Carshalton, SM5 3NW

Nearest Station: Carshalton Beeches

Priding themselves in authentic cooking methods and spices which are roasted in the kitchens of Saregama, the chefs at this idyllic venue cater for both the curry connoisseur or the novice.

2FOR1 MAIN COURSE | FRI × | SAT × — Indian

SERAFFINO
☎020 8647 0800

85-87 Manor Road, Wallington, SM6 0DE

Nearest Station: Wallington

Enjoy the live kitchen atmosphere at this cracking Italian restaurant in Wallington, where pizza tossing can be witnessed and the smells from the clay oven fill the room. A great place to dine.

25% OFF TOTAL | ♟ 6 | FRI 📱 | SAT 📱 — Italian

SERENDIP
020 8641 2199

69 Stonecot Hill, Sutton, SM3 9HJ

Nearest Station: St. Helier

Unique restaurant serving Indo-Sri Lankan cuisine in a cool, contemporary setting. Sri Lankan food is often overlooked, but what you'll find here is an excellent introduction to its distinctive flavours.

2FOR1 MAIN COURSE | FRI × | SAT × | SUN — Sri Lankan

SHANTI TANDOORI
☎01932 821 940

93 Queen Road, Weybridge, KT13 9UQ

Nearest Station: Weybridge

The fine selection of Indian and Bangladeshi dishes have provided this popular restaurant with an admirable local reputation. Balti specialities are not to be missed. *Offer excludes special event nights.

25% OFF TOTAL | ♟10 | FRI × | SAT × — Indian

THE SHY HORSE
01372 738 051

423 Leatherhead Road, Chessington, KT9 2NQ

Nearest Station: Chessington South

This Vintage Inn oozes rural charm and rustic character. The picturesque surroundings provide the perfect backdrop for savouring the hearty, seasonal pub-food on the menu.

25% OFF TOTAL | FRI ✓ | SAT ✓ | SUN | ▲ — Modern British

SQUARE OLIVE
☎020 8979 7676

2-6 Bridge Road, Hampton Court, KT8 9HA

Nearest Station: Hampton Court

Square Olive was born from a desire to unite friends and family over one of life's greatest pleasures; great food.For a unique and authentic Italian dining experience, look no further than Square Olive.

2FOR1 3 COURSES | FRI ✓ | SAT × — Italian

Gourmet Society discount applies to the à la carte menu only, unless stated otherwise.

SREE KRISHNA ☎020 8672 4250
192-194 Tooting High Street, Tooting, SW17 0SF
Nearest Station: Tooting Broadway
Experience the delights of South Indian cuisine, including vegetarian dishes and varieties such as the tantalising Karaikkudi regional specialities. Unique flavours and spices are infused into every dish.
2FOR1 MAIN COURSE | FRI ✱ | SAT ✱ | ▲ — Indian

THE STAG INDIAN RESTAURANT ☎020 7223 7516
96 Westbridge Rd, Battersea, SW11 3PH
Nearest Station: Battersea Park
A carefully selected menu draws on some of the most popular Indian dishes from the subcontinent. Marvel over the finest assortment of spices and high quality meats that are used in the kitchen.
25% OFF TOTAL | 8 | FRI ✓ | SAT ✓ | ✱ — Indian

THE STANWELL HOTEL ☎01784 252 292
171 Town Lane, Staines, TW19 7PW
Nearest Station: Heathrow Terminal 5
Award-winning Executive Chef Manuel Zamora delivers European cuisine at an impeccable standard in this elegantly decorated eatery. Guests can feast upon crab pancakes, home-made paté and tasty tapas.
2FOR1 MAIN COURSE | FRI ✓ | SAT ✓ — European

STEINS ☎020 8546 2411
56 High Street, Kingston-upon-Thames, KT1 1HN
Nearest Station: Kingston
Step into this cosy chalet, where the ultimate Bavarian experience is to be had. From escalopes to goulash, the menu captures the very essence of German and Austrian cuisine.
2FOR1 3 COURSES | FRI ✓ | SAT × | SUN — German

STEINS ☎020 8948 8189
55 Petersham Road, Richmond, TW10 6UX
Nearest Station: Richmond
Brilliant Bavarian outdoor restaurant by the banks of the Thames. Full bread baskets, rich eintopf soups, and a range of würste are on the cards; the place is a fine one to relax, exuding great character.
2FOR1 3 COURSES | FRI ✓ | SAT ✓ — German

SWAGAT ☎020 8940 7557
86 Hill Rise, Richmond, TW10 6UB
Nearest Station: Richmond
Fresh, contemporary and traditional Indian cuisine at its best. Experience extravagant flavours and original spices across the menu, while the extensive wine list incorporates a selection of champagnes.
2FOR1 MAIN COURSE | FRI ✱ | SAT ✱ | SUN | ✱ | ▲ — Indian

TACUBA ☎020 8673 5394
10 Bedford Hill, Balham, SW12 9RG
Nearest Station: Balham
Feast on delicious beef tacos in this fabulously stylish Mexican restaurant and bar. Sip on a fresh fruit cocktail and indulge in delicious dishes that originate from all over Mexico.
2FOR1 MAIN COURSE | FRI | SAT ✱ | ✱ — Mexican

TANDOORI MAHAL ☎020 8648 2926
35 Abbotsbury Road, Morden, SM4 5LJ
Nearest Station: Morden
Enjoy many rich and delectable dishes at this well-established and award-winning restaurant that provides patrons with great hospitality and freshly prepared, authentic and wholesome Indian food.
25% OFF TOTAL | 10 | FRI ✱ | SAT ✱ | ✱ — Indian

TASTE OF MOGUL ☎020 8892 3610
45-47 York Street, Twickenham, TW1 3LP
Nearest Station: Twickenham
This smart, contemporary restaurant boasts a menu that offers diners a gastronomic tour of India and Bangladesh's fabulous culinary regions. An exotic range and blend of cuisines available.
2FOR1 2 COURSES | FRI × | SAT × | ▲ — Indian

TASTE OF RAJ ☎020 8876 8271
130 Upper Richmond Road, Richmond, SW14 8DS
Nearest Station: Mortlake
Affable surroundings coupled with ample and flavoursome curries make for satisfied diners at Taste of Raj.
50% OFF FOOD | FRI ✓ | SAT ✓ — Indian

TATTENHAM CORNER 01737 351 454
Epsom Downs, Epsom, KT18 5NY
Nearest Station: Tattenham Corner
Beefeater Grill are one of the UK's best-loved restaurants welcoming guests for almost 40 years in over 130 locations nationwide. *Excludes Breakfast, Light Bites, Bar menu, set menus and all other offers.
2FOR1 MAIN COURSE | 6 | FRI ✓ | SAT × | ▲ — Modern British

THE TEA CUP ☎020 8914 8402
12 Brewers Lane, Richmond, TW9 1HH
Nearest Station: Richmond
Quintessentially British, this quaint tearoom-restaurant is the perfect place for a delicious cup of tea. Cakes and sweets a-plenty, this venue offers a charming afternoon dining experience.
50% OFF FOOD | 6 | FRI ✓ | SAT ✓ — International

STRADA

8 restaurants in South West London

25% OFF TOTAL

25% OFF TOTAL | 6 | FRI ✓ | SAT × | ▲

Address	Station	Phone
375 Lonsdale Road, Barnes, SW13 9PY	Barnes Bridge	☎ 020 8392 9216
11-13 Battersea Rise, SW11 1HG	Clapham Junction	☎ 020 7801 0794
102-104 Clapham High Street, SW4 7UL	Clapham North	☎ 020 7627 4847
13-15 Between Streets, Cobham, KT11 1AA	Cobham	☎ 01932 596 967
The Griffin Centre, Kingston-upon-Thames, KT1 1JT	Kingston	☎ 020 8974 8555
147 Upper Richmond Road, SW15 2TX	East Putney	☎ 020 8789 6996
26 Hill Street, Richmond, TW9 1TW	Richmond	☎ 020 8940 3141
91 High Street, Wimbledon, SW19 5EG	South Wimbledon	☎ 020 8946 4363

THAI GARDEN RESTAURANT
☎01932 846 824
47 High Street, Weybridge, KT13 8BB
Nearest Station: Weybridge
Thai Garden Restaurant has delicious food, great service and excellent atmosphere. All of these elements capture the spirit and essence of the great Thai cuisine.*Food must be consumed on premises.

2FOR1 3 COURSES | FRI × | SAT × | ✱ | ♣
Thai

THE THAI JASMINE
☎020 8642 2666
318 High Street, Sutton, SM1 1PR
Nearest Station: Sutton Common
With a highly experienced Thai chef manning the kitchen you will not be disappointed by the range of dishes and variety of tastes available. The North Eastern Thai dishes are spectacular.

25% OFF TOTAL | 4 | FRI ✱ | SAT ✱ | SUN | ✱
Thai

THAI SUNSET
☎020 3188 0004
39 High Street, Bushey, WD23 1BD
Nearest Station: Bushey
An exotic and exquisite taste of Thailand on your doorstep. Thai Sunset offers a whole host of the best regional delicacies of Thailand.

25% OFF TOTAL | 6 | FRI ✓ | SAT ×
Thai

THAI VENUE
☎020 8763 9626
200 Brighton Road, Coulsdon, CR5 2NF
Nearest Station: Smitham
A well-regarded, accommodating Thai restaurant that serves excellent food in satisfyingly comprehensive portions at a great price. Simple, sumptuously tasty, and thoroughly effective.

25% OFF TOTAL | 10 | FRI ✓ | SAT ✓ | ✱
Thai

THE THAMES COURT
01932 221 957
Towpath, Shepperton, TW17 9LJ
Nearest Station: Shepperton
This Vintage Inn oozes rural charm and rustic character. The picturesque surroundings provide the perfect backdrop for savouring the hearty, seasonal pub-food on the menu.

25% OFF TOTAL | FRI ✓ | SAT ✓ | SUN | ♣
Modern British

TOKO RESTAURANT
☎020 8687 6655
21 Abbotsbury Road, Morden, SM4 5LJ
Nearest Station: Morden
Expertly infusing the tastes of China, Japan, Thailand and Vietnam, guests can feast upon fresh sushi and generous portions of noodles. Health conscious guests can indulge, guilt-free, on the low-fat food.

25% OFF TOTAL | 2 | FRI ✱ | SAT ✱ | ♣
Japanese

TOPGOLF SURREY
☎01932 858 551
Moated Farm Drive, Addlestone, KT15 2DW
Nearest Station: Worcester Park
What better way to top off your game of golf than with a fantastic meal or a round of celebratory drinks. Head to the Bayview Café and Bar where you can find a variety of food available all day long.

50% OFF FOOD | 8 | FRI ✱ | SAT ✱ | ♣
American

THE TRAFALGAR ARMS
☎020 8127 4246
148-158 Tooting High Street, Tooting, SW17 0RT
Nearest Station: Tooting Broadway
This bustling South London restaurant is the perfect place to catch up with friends, offering the perfect blend of extraordinary food, exceptional drinks, comfortable atmosphere and first rate hospitality.

25% OFF TOTAL | 6 | FRI ✓ | SAT ✓
British

TUSCANY RISTORANTE
☎020 8990 1100
London Heathrow Marriott Hotel, Harlington, UB3 5AN
Nearest Station: Heathrow Terminals 1, 2, 3
Step into the theatre of a live open kitchen where this great food is accompanied by the very best Italian hospitality. Enjoy the intimacy of the restaurant and swim in the vast selection of fine wines.

25% OFF TOTAL | 6 | FRI 📱 | SAT 📱 | SUN | ✱ | ♣
Italian

VARANASI CHEFS
☎020 7228 3145
142 Battersea High Street, Battersea, SW11 3JR
Nearest Station: Clapham Junction
A stylish Battersea restaurant that endeavours to bring the cooking tradition of Baranasi to South London. An exotic, aromatic and flavourful menu offers subtle and sumptuous dishes.

50% OFF FOOD | 10 | FRI ✓ | SAT ✓ | ♣
Indian

VII HOTEL AND RESTAURANT
☎020 8754 0777
760-762 Bath Road, Cranford, TW5 9TY
Nearest Station: Hounslow West
VII Hotel and Restaurant are only a short journey by train or bus from many world famous London sights.Enjoy exquisite Indian dishes, freshly cooked with only the finest and freshest ingredients.

2FOR1 3 COURSES | FRI ✓ | SAT ✓ | ✱
Indian

VILLAGE TANDOORI
☎020 8673 5043
50 Abbeville Road, Clapham, SW4 9NF
Nearest Station: Clapham South
A highly popular restaurant in the heart of Clapham, with a large cohort of loyal diners. Serves up some truly tasty curry dishes, from a creamy korma to a spicy madras.

50% OFF FOOD | 4 | FRI × | SAT ×
Indian

VINES BAR & GRILL
☎020 8647 9207
13 Green Wrythe Lane, Sutton, SM5 2DS
Nearest Station: Carshalton
Tucked among the little row of shops on Green Wrythe Lane, Vines is a cosy little restaurant that serves good range of tasty, homely dishes from the classic bar & grill repertoire.

25% OFF TOTAL | 6 | FRI 📱 | SAT 📱 | ♣
Mediterranean

VITO'S RISTORANTE
☎020 7228 7673
175-177 Northcote Road, Battersea, SW11 6QF
Nearest Station: Clapham Junction
This lovely Italian restaurant is relaxed and always delivers service with a smile. The combination of appealing decor and traditional Italian cuisine make for a delightful dining experience.

2FOR1 3 COURSES | FRI × | SAT ×
Italian

VOJAN INDIAN CUISINE
☎01737 644 171
229 London Road North, Redhill, RH1 3BN
Nearest Station: Kingswood
Highly appraised for its healthy Indian dishes, Vojan is one of the most renowned restaurants in its area. Creating the most tantalising and decadent of flavours, this venue boasts expert chefs.

50% OFF FOOD | 4 | FRI ✓ | SAT ✓
Indian

THE WHEELWRIGHTS ARMS
☎020 8547 2990
60 Clarence Street, Kingston-upon-Thames, KT1 1NP
Nearest Station: Kingston
The Wheelwrights Arms is Kingston-upon-Thames' premium live sports venue and boasts four large screens, it serves traditional pub food and real ales, making it the perfect place to enjoy a sporting evening

2FOR1 3 COURSES | FRI × | SAT × | ♣
British

THE WILLIAM MORRIS
☎020 8540 0216
20 Watermill Way, Merton, SW19 2RD
Nearest Station: South Wimbledon
Watch the River Wandle meander by and kick back with a summer BBQ in the expansive beer garden. Celebrate a special occasion in style in the spacious function room.

50% OFF FOOD | 2 | FRI ✓ | SAT × | SUN
British

WINGS RESTAURANT @ HOLIDAY INN
☎020 8990 0000
Holiday Inn Heathrow, Bath Road, UB7 0DP
Nearest Station: Heathrow Terminals 1, 2, 3
Take care not to be distracted into missing your flight by the sophisticated, surprising contemporary dining on offer at the Heathrow Holiday Inn's Wings restaurant: it's a more-than-fleeting possibility.

50% OFF FOOD | 6 | FRI ✓ | SAT ✓
International

WOODLANDS PARK HOTEL
☎0845 072 7581
Oak Room, Woodlands Lane, Cobham, KT11 3QB
Nearest Station: Cobham
An elegant Hand Picked Hotels restaurant that offering a luxury dining experience. Ornate panelling and dark oak furnishings provide an intimate environment, perfect for a romantic meal. 1 AA Rosette.

25% OFF TOTAL | 4 | FRI ✱ | SAT ✱ | SUN | ✱
British

East Anglia

All restaurants listed within the M25 are listed within the Greater London region. Thus any Essex restaurants within the M25 are listed in the Greater London section

Cambridgeshire

BANGKOK CITY 01223 354 382
24 Green Street, Cambridge, CB2 3JX
Established in 1993, Bangkok City is Cambridge's longest running Thai restaurant, offering the finest seafood, fish, meat and vegetarian dishes to satisfy the most discerning diner.
50% OFF FOOD | FRI × | SAT × — Thai

THE BANYAN TREE 01733 570 111
9 Church Street, Werrington, Peterborough, PE4 6QA
With a menu that predominantly consists of Moghlai cuisine, this restaurant provides Indian food like you've never tasted before. An impressive selection of dishes are provided for the vegetarian diner.
25% OFF TOTAL | FRI ✱ | SAT ✱ | ▲ — Indian

BELLA ITALIA 01223 247 099
Cambridge Leisure Park, Cambridge, CB1 7DY
Accessible Italian cuisine on the British high street - indulge in authentic sharing platters, hand stretched pizzas and hearty pasta dishes, served with a healthy dose of gregarious Italian hospitality.
25% OFF TOTAL | ♟ 6 | FRI × | SAT × | SUN | ▲ — Italian

BELLA ITALIA 01223 367 507
The Watermill, Newnham Road, Cambridge, CB3 9EY
Accessible Italian cuisine on the British high street - indulge in authentic sharing platters, hand stretched pizzas and hearty pasta dishes, served with a healthy dose of gregarious Italian hospitality.
25% OFF TOTAL | ♟ 6 | FRI × | SAT × | SUN | ▲ — Italian

BLUE TIFFIN 01487 711 104
61 High Street, Huntingdon, PE26 1AB
Situated in the heart of Ramsey, Blue Tiffin provides their diners with a traditional Indian dining experience, serving a range of succulent dishes with a warm and friendly atmosphere.
2FOR1 3 COURSES | FRI ✓ | SAT ✓ — Indian

THE BRUNSWICK 01223 300 583
73 Newmarket Road, Cambridge, CB5 8EG
New restaurant and bar in the heart of Cambridge, where a warm welcome is always guaranteed. The Brunswick serves modern European food, local real ales and a fine selection of wines and spirits.
25% OFF TOTAL | ♟ 6 | FRI ▮ | SAT ▮ | SUN — European

CAFÉ ROUGE 01223 364 961
24-26 Bridge Street, Cambridge, CB2 1UJ
French sophistication on the British high street - enjoy seasonally changing French dishes and a continental wine selection, served in a relaxed environment with an undeniable flair of Parisian chic.
25% OFF TOTAL | ♟ 6 | FRI ✓ | SAT ✓ | ✱ | ▲ — French

CANTONESE KITCHEN 01354 657 777
22 Norwood Road, March, PE15 8QF
Decades of culinary experience are reflected in the Head Chef's delicious masterpiece dishes. Cantonese cuisine at its very best, with satay skewers and beef in black bean sauce coming in as favourites.
2FOR1 3 COURSES | FRI ✓ | SAT ✱ | ✱ — Cantonese

CASTLE LODGE HOTEL 01353 662 276
50 New Barns Road, Ely, CB7 4PW
Enter the snug, comfortable bar at this Ely guest house before settling in for one of their delicious home-made dinners.
25% OFF TOTAL | ♟ 2 | FRI ▮ | SAT ▮ | ✱ — British

THE CHERRY TREE 01353 741 111
8 Duck Lane, Haddenham, Ely, CB6 3UE
The Cherry Tree is a pub restaurant where you can enjoy a choice of freshly made dishes in a warm and relaxing atmosphere. There is a selection of real ales available to complement your meal.
2FOR1 MAIN COURSE | FRI ✓ | SAT × | SUN — European

THE CUCKOO 01733 239 638
20 Oundle Road, Alwalton, Peterborough, PE7 3UP
This Vintage Inn oozes rural charm and rustic character. The picturesque surroundings provide the perfect backdrop for savouring the hearty, seasonal pub-food on the menu.
25% OFF TOTAL | FRI ✓ | SAT ✓ | SUN | ▲ — Modern British

DOG IN A DOUBLET 01733 202 256
North Side, Thorney, Peterborough, PE6 0RW
A warmly loved place in Peterborough. Enjoy delicious food on the patio by the River Nene, or step inside where an open kitchen brings the natural patter of culinary creation to your ears.
25% OFF TOTAL | ♟ 6 | FRI ▮ | SAT ▮ | SUN — British

EMPEROR RESTAURANT 01733 310 190
195-197 Lincoln Road, Peterborough, PE1 2PL
With its popular reviews, Emperor Chinese Restaurant produces quality Chinese cuisine to loyal customers and first-time diners. Fine array of starters and mains can be accompanied by your favourite side.
2FOR1 MAIN COURSE | FRI ▮ | SAT ▮ | ▲ — Chinese

THE FALCON HOTEL 01733 351 001
London Street, Whittlesey, Peterborough, PE7 1BH
The Falcon Hotel is in Peterborough's historical district and oozes the characterful charm of the local area. At this 17th Century coaching inn, expect excellent menus and kind hospitality.
50% OFF FOOD | ♟ 4 | FRI ✓ | SAT ✓ | SUN — British

THE FITZWILLIAM ARMS 01733 267 913
Stamford Road, Marholm, Peterborough, PE6 7HX
This Vintage Inn oozes rural charm and rustic character. The picturesque surroundings provide the perfect backdrop for savouring the hearty, seasonal pub-food on the menu.
25% OFF TOTAL | FRI ✓ | SAT ✓ | SUN | ▲ — Modern British

THE GEORGE HOTEL 01487 815 264
65 High Street, Ramsey, PE26 1AA
With something for everyone, you can enjoy good food in relaxed surroundings. This is a family-run business and there is great emphasis on giving everyone a warm welcome and friendly service.
25% OFF TOTAL | ♟ 4 | FRI ✓ | SAT ✓ | SUN — British

GEORGES 01354 650 551
61 High Street, March, PE15 9JJ
For diners seeking hearty, wholesome cooking reminiscent of mother's own, this tavern offers traditional British meals that will undoubtedly appease voracious appetites.
2FOR1 3 COURSES | ♟ 4 | FRI ✓ | SAT ✓ — Traditional English

THE GRANARY 01733 235 794
Ham Lane, Orton Meadows, Peterborough, PE2 5UU
Beefeater Grill are one of the UK's best-loved restaurants welcoming guests for almost 40 years in over 130 locations nationwide. *Excludes Breakfast, Light Bites, Bar menu, set menus and all other offers.
2FOR1 MAIN COURSE | ♟ 6 | FRI ✓ | SAT × | ▲ — Modern British

THE GRILL ROOM 07789 527 925
2 Berkley Street, St Neots, PE19 2NA
The Grill Room at the Nag's Head Hotel hosts some of the finest dining experiences on offer. St Neots is proud to accommodate this terrific hotel, with delectable dishes making up a superb menu.
25% OFF TOTAL | ♟ 6 | FRI ✓ | SAT ✓ — Steakhouse

HOTEL DU VIN 01223 227 330
Trumpington Street, Cambridge, CB2 1QA
The finest, fresh local produce, simple European recipes, a stunning choice of wines; these are the elements of the trademark Hotel du Vin bistro. A quirky, stylish converted town building. 1 AA Rosette.
2FOR1 MAIN COURSE | FRI × | SAT × | SUN | ▲ — European

www.gourmetsociety.co.uk

IL GIRASOLE
☎ 01480 211 211

13 South Street, St Neots, PE19 2BW

Welcoming restaurant offering a wide range of delicious options to suit all tastes. Staff at this popular venue are friendly and attentive and the decor is cosy.

25% OFF TOTAL | 👤 4 | FRI × | SAT × | SUN | ▲ — Italian

THE JUNCTION RESTAURANT
☎ 08719 429 015

Holiday Inn, Bridge Road, Cambridge, CB4 9PH

The Holiday Inn Cambridge hosts a modern contemporary restaurant, where a British-themed menu offers delectable favourites and comforting treats. Imaginative international flavours also influence the food.

2FOR1 MAIN COURSE | FRI ✓ | SAT ✓ | SUN | ✱ | ▲ — English and Continental

KURRYZ
☎ 01733 245 666

2 Stewartby Avenue, Hampton Vale, Peterborough, PE7 8NJ

This venue delights in choosing genuine Indian dishes to suit the diners taste. Devoted to superb service, the staff will attend to every need whilst the clientele relax in the affable surroundings.

2FOR1 3 COURSES | FRI ✓ | SAT ✓ — Indian

LA RAZA
☎ 01223 464 550

Rose Crescent, Cambridge, CB2 3LL

Daytimes at La Raza see a selection of snacks and tapas dishes taking over the menu, while the evening brings in food for sharing. The seafood and meat paella options are superb.

25% OFF TOTAL | 👤 6 | FRI ✱ | SAT × | ▲ — Spanish

LA TASCA
☎ 01223 464 630

14-16 Bridge Street, Cambridge, CB2 1UF

Quintessentially Spanish, La Tasca's fresh and exciting menu offers something for everyone. Their tapas dishes are sincerely authentic, while their paellas always deliver on flavour.

25% OFF TOTAL | 👤 8 | FRI ✓ | SAT × | ▲ — Spanish

LAHORE TANDOORI
☎ 01733 555 399

539 Lincoln Road, Peterborough, PE1 2PB

A great Indian restaurant delivering fine cuisine, well-prepared and -presented, offering diners dishes filled with spice and rich, authentic aromas.

2FOR1 2 COURSES | FRI ✓ | SAT ✓ | ✱ — Indian

LAZY OTTER
☎ 01353 649 780

Cambridge Road, Stretham, Ely, CB6 3LU

Sip on your favourite wine and while away an afternoon watching the sleepy barge boats bobbing along the River Ouse. Enjoy home-made classics and Internationally inspired dishes.

50% OFF FOOD | 👤 2 | FRI ▯ | SAT ▯ | SUN — International

LINTON TANDOORI
☎ 01223 890 030

6-8 Bartlow Road, Linton, CB21 4LY

Warm welcomes and amiable smiles will greet you at the door in this local restaurant. The staff provide excellent service whatever the party size, while the delightful menu will tickle your taste buds.

2FOR1 MAIN COURSE | FRI ✓ | SAT ✓ | ✱ | ▲ — Indian

LOCH FYNE
☎ 01832 280 298

The Old Dairy, Elton, PE8 6SH

From the roadside oyster bar that once was, Loch Fyne restaurants now successfully inject energy and passion into great food and wonderful flavours, whilst ensuring their seafood is sustainably sourced.

25% OFF TOTAL | 👤 4 | FRI ✱ | SAT ✱ | ▲ — Seafood

LOCH FYNE
☎ 01223 362 433

The Little Rose, 37 Trumpington St, Cambridge, CB2 1QY

From the roadside oyster bar that once was, Loch Fyne restaurants now successfully inject energy and passion into great food and wonderful flavours, whilst ensuring their seafood is sustainably sourced.

25% OFF TOTAL | 👤 4 | FRI ✱ | SAT ✱ | ▲ — Seafood

MAI THAI
☎ 01223 367 480

Hobbs Pavilion, Park Terrace, Cambridge, CB1 1JH

A calm minimalist design creates a soothing ambience that will completely relax you. Warm weather encourages diners to eat outside, where you can enjoy views of Cambridge's most famous park.

25% OFF TOTAL | 👤 6 | FRI ✱ | SAT ✱ — Thai

MATTONI RESTAURANT
☎ 01733 241 246

114 Four Chimneys Crescent, Peterborough, PE7 8FH

Satisfy a ravenous appetite with an authentic crispy stone-baked pizza. Delivering a slice of Italy to Hampton, the chefs will even rustle up the dish of your desire should it be absent from the menu.

2FOR1 MAIN COURSE | FRI × | SAT × | SUN — Italian

THE MERRY MONK
☎ 01638 780 900

30 West Street, Isleham, Ely, CB7 5SB

Chefs here cook inspired, relaxed dishes with fresh flavours sourced from great local produce using meat and fish of exceptional quality. Tempting and familiar with a slight twist.

25% OFF TOTAL | 👤 4 | FRI × | SAT × | ✱ | ▲ — Classic British/French

METHI INDIAN TAKEAWAY
☎ 01480 471 157

Huntingdon Street, St Neots, PE19 1BG

Methi is a well-regarded Indian restaurant and takeaway in St Neots that's known for the high quality of its food, especially the rich, distinctly flavoured sauces.

2FOR1 MAIN COURSE | FRI × | SAT × | SUN — Indian

MOGHUL INDIAN CUISINE
01945 466 228

13a North Street, Peterborough, PE13 1NP

Moghul is a chirpy, unprepossessing Tandoori restaurant with a very accommodating selection of dishes, with the Kashmiri curries a particular favourite, alongside the fiery mirch massala.

2FOR1 MAIN COURSE | FRI × | SAT × | SUN — Indian

MONTAZ BAR AND RESTAURANT
☎ 01353 669 910

39-41 Market Street, Ely, CB7 4LZ

Delicious Indian and Bangladeshi cuisine garners a marvellous reputation for this popular restaurant. An ideal place to socialise or enjoy an intimate meal in stylish surroundings.

25% OFF TOTAL | 👤 4 | FRI ▯ | SAT ▯ | ▲ — Indian/Bangladeshi

NEEDHAMS RESTAURANT
☎ 01353 661 405

186 Main Street, Witchford, Ely, CB6 2HT

Nestled away in the village of Witchford, this beautifully converted farmhouse is home to a well-established restaurant with an impressive reputation. Dishes draw upon influences from around the world.

2FOR1 MAIN COURSE | FRI ✓ | SAT ✱ | SUN | ▲ — International

OLIVERS LODGE HOTEL
☎ 01480 463 252

50 Needingworth Road, St Ives, PE27 5JP

An extensive menu offers fresh fish and seasonal game amongst many other tasty dishes. Enjoy à la carte dining in an affable atmosphere, or opt for the bar menu for a lighter meal.

2FOR1 MAIN COURSE | FRI ✓ | SAT ✓ | ▲ — International

ORCHARDS RESTAURANT
☎ 01780 782 223

The Haycock Hotel, London Road, Wansford, PE8 6JA

Enjoy splendid views of the award-winning hotel gardens as you dine in this charming conservatory. A traditional British menu offers guests table d'hôte-style lunches and à la carte evening meals.

25% OFF TOTAL | 👤 10 | FRI ✓ | SAT ✓ — British

PAUL PRY
01733 571 234

1023 Lincoln Road, Walton, Peterborough, PE4 6AH

Quality pub classics with modern twists meets with a friendly and relaxed atmosphere to make this Table Table venue the perfect place for any occasion. * Excludes daytime & evening deals and festive menus

2FOR1 MAIN COURSE | FRI ✓ | SAT ✓ — Modern British

PREZZO
01353 659 832

12-14 High Street, Ely, CB7 4JZ

With a character all of its own, Prezzo oozes contemporary style and enduring charm. Signature pastas, stone-baked pizzas and classic Italian dishes promise a perfect dining choice for the whole family.

2FOR1 MAIN COURSE | FRI × | SAT × | ▲ — Italian

www.gourmetsociety.co.uk

Gourmet Society discount applies to the à la carte menu only, unless stated otherwise.

PREZZO
01733 348 081
2 Cowgate, Peterborough, PE1 1NA
With a character all of its own, Prezzo oozes contemporary style and enduring charm. Signature pastas, stone-baked pizzas and classic Italian dishes promise a perfect dining choice for the whole family.

2FOR1 MAIN COURSE | FRI × | SAT × | Italian

PREZZO
01223 314 954
32 Bridge Street, Cambridge, CB2 1UJ
With a character all of its own, Prezzo oozes contemporary style and enduring charm. Signature pastas, stone-baked pizzas and classic Italian dishes promise a perfect dining choice for the whole family.

2FOR1 MAIN COURSE | FRI × | SAT × | Italian

QUEENS HEAD INN
01780 784 006
54 Station Rd, Nassington, PE8 6QB
A lovely looking, beautifully located, even idyllic little hotel and pub. The Inn offers high-quality British cuisine in bright dining rooms.

25% OFF TOTAL | 8 | FRI × | SAT × | SUN | British

RED LION WHITTLESFORD BRIDGE HOTEL
01223 832 047
Station Road East, Cambridge, CB22 4NL
Red Lion Whittlesford Bridge Hotel offer locally sourced, contemporary, British food, cooked beautifully and simply, served in a traditional yet quirky setting.

25% OFF TOTAL | 10 | FRI ✓ | SAT | British

RESTAURANT @ HOLIDAY INN
01733 289 988
Peterborough West, Thorpe Wood, Peterborough, PE3 6SG
The restaurant at the 4-star Holiday Inn Peterborough West is renowned for its culinary delights. Visitors and locals alike can ease back after a long day with a delicious meal in this stylish restaurant.

25% OFF TOTAL | 6 | FRI ✓ | SAT ✓ | Contemporary

RIVERSIDE BRASSERIE
01223 259 988
DoubleTree by Hilton, Mill Lane, Cambridge, CB2 1RT
Overlooking the Cam and its punts, a hotel-based restaurant serving a broad based à la carte menu in fine, brasserie-style surroundings. *Offer also available on Afternoon Tea.

2FOR1 3 COURSES | FRI × | SAT × | SUN | International

RUBY CHINESE RESTAURANT
01487 710 057
64 High Street, Ramsay, PE26 1AA
In the pretty Fenland town of Ramsey, this restaurant specialises in the gamut of tastes true to Cantonese cuisine, focusing on fresh flavours and lush, juicy seafood.

25% OFF TOTAL | 4 | FRI ✱ | SAT ✱ | Chinese

SHAMPAN MASALA
01487 831 100
9 Greenways, Huntingdon, PE28 5UR
Shampan Marsala serves competitively priced food that is authentic and enjoyable. You can also enjoy a drink with your meal as Shampan Marsala is Sawtry's first licensed restaurant.

25% OFF TOTAL | FRI ✓ | SAT ✓ | ✱ | Indian

SHIRAZ RESTAURANT
01223 307 581
84 Regent Street, Cambridge, CB2 1DP
A delectable selection of Persian dishes occupies the menu at this wondrous restaurant. Watch as your food is vibrantly prepared over the charcoal grill before feasting by candlelight.

25% OFF TOTAL | 6 | FRI | SAT | SUN | ✱ | Persian

ST ANDREW'S BAR & RESTAURANT
01480 499 686
Hemingford Abbots Golf Complex, Huntingdon, PE28 9HQ
Situated perfectly in the Cambridge Golf and Conference Centre, St Andrew's Bar and Restaurant is perfect for bringing a day on the range to a close. A pint and a panini may be just the tonic.

25% OFF TOTAL | 10 | FRI ✓ | SAT | SUN | International

STRADA
01223 352 166
17 Trinity Street, Cambridge, CB2 1TB
Offering fresh, bold dishes inspired by flavours of Italian city life - Strada serves a selection of indulgent tastes, to those seeking a blissful escape to laidback Italian life. *excludes Pizzettas*

25% OFF TOTAL | 6 | FRI ✓ | SAT × | Italian

SULTAN TANDOORI RESTAURANT
01480 464 650
16 London Road, St Ives, PE27 5ES
Home-style Bangladeshi and Indian fine dining, that specialises in fish dishes. High quality and consistency is a key feature, producing mouth-watering flavours with unique herbs and spices every time.

2FOR1 3 COURSES | FRI ✱ | SAT ✱ | Indian

SWEET OLIVES
01733 562 572
5 Fletton Ave, Peterborough, PE2 8AX
Sophisticated eating with fine food at good value. A tantalising Mediterranean menu, crafted by creative chefs, offering huge choice. Fresh and delicious dishes that appeal to all.

2FOR1 MAIN COURSE | FRI ✓ | SAT ✓ | SUN | ✱ | Mediterranean

THE TAJ MAHAL
01733 348 840
37-39 Lincoln Road, Peterborough, PE1 2RH
Inspired by the architectural flawlessness of the Taj Mahal, this menu seeps perfection into all of its dishes. Passionate chefs prepare the cuisine lovingly, including a tempting selection of specials.

2FOR1 3 COURSES | FRI × | SAT × | Indian

TRAVELLERS REST
01223 276 182
Huntingdon Road, Girton, Cambridge, CB3 0DR
Beefeater Grill are one of the UK's best-loved restaurants welcoming guests for almost 40 years in over 130 locations nationwide. *Excludes Breakfast, Light Bites, Bar menu, set menus and all other offers.

2FOR1 MAIN COURSE | 6 | FRI ✓ | SAT × | Modern British

THE VAULTS
01223 506 090
14a Trinity Street, Cambridge, CB2 1TB
Renowned for cocktails, this effortlessly chic venue is perfect for occasions and nights with a touch of class. Serving tapas-sized portions, the menu hosts oriental fish cakes and crispy duck pancakes.

2FOR1 MAIN COURSE | FRI × | SAT × | Modern British

THE WHITE HORSE
01480 470 853
103 Great North Road, Eaton Socon, St Neots, PE19 8EL
Visit this wonderful Grade II listed building and enjoy traditional classics and new favourites, as well as a good selection of steaks from the grill. The ever-changing chef specials here are delicious.

25% OFF TOTAL | 4 | FRI × | SAT × | SUN | Modern Pub

Essex

AFFINITY 1777
01702 555 154
1777-1779 London Road, Leigh-on-Sea, SS9 2ST
Experience a delicious, seasonally changing menu coupled with efficient, courteous service. Ideal restaurant for reasonably priced, attractively presented food for all of the family.

50% OFF FOOD | 4 | FRI | SAT × | ✱ | British

ALBATTA
01206 618 121
18 Sir Isaacs Walk, Colchester, CO1 1JJ
Taste the Middle East in Colchester. The chefs at this restaurant prepare the most delectable of aromatic dishes with flair and finesse, making it a popular choice with the locals.

2FOR1 MAIN COURSE | FRI × | SAT × | Middle Eastern

THE ALBERT
01206 561 914
Cowdray Avenue, Colchester, CO1 1UT
Beefeater Grill are one of the UK's best-loved restaurants welcoming guests for almost 40 years in over 130 locations nationwide. *Excludes Breakfast, Light Bites, Bar menu, set menus and all other offers.

2FOR1 MAIN COURSE | 6 | FRI ✓ | SAT × | Modern British

AMY'S BAR
01279 680 800
Hilton Hotel, Round Coppice Road, Stansted, CM24 1SF
Whether waiting for a flight or resting after a long journey, Amy's Bar is ideal for a relaxing drink. Choose your tipple from a vast selection of international beers, choice wines and spirits.

2FOR1 3 COURSES | FRI ✓ | SAT ✓ | International

AMY'S RESTAURANT ☎01279 680 800
Hilton Hotel, Round Coppice Road, Stansted, CM24 1SF
Expect a blend of fine dining and relaxed surroundings at Amy's Restaurant, as guests choose from a varying menu of well-prepared International cuisine.

2FOR1 3 COURSES | FRI ✓ | SAT ✓ | ▲ — International

ASIA SPICE ☎01268 523 526
2 Cranes Farm Road, Basildon, SS14 3JF
Curry lovers will experience new taste sensations at Asia Spice. Traditional dishes are lavished with authentic spices to create food that is truly memorable and mouth-watering.

2FOR1 MAIN COURSE | FRI ✓ | SAT ✓ — Indian

BALKERNE GATE 01206 855 001
Ipswich Road, Colchester, Essex, CO4 9WP
Quality pub classics with modern twists meets with a friendly and relaxed atmosphere to make this Table Table venue the perfect place for any occasion. * Excludes daytime & evening deals and festive menus

2FOR1 MAIN COURSE | FRI ✓ | SAT ✓ — Modern British

BALTI KING ☎01245 264 038
190 Moulsham Street, Chelmsford, CM2 0LG
A wonderful Balti restaurant that serves good quality, honest dishes bursting full of flavour and delight.

50% OFF FOOD | FRI ✓ | SAT ✓ — Indian

BEAUVOIR ARMS ☎01268 711 115
Downham Road, Billericay, CM11 1QH
Beauvoir Arms serve the finest British and European cuisine. A passionate team of chefs, deliver quality food from the best locally sourced ingredients with everything prepared in house.

25% OFF TOTAL | FRI × | SAT × | ▲ — European

BELLA ITALIA 01708 890 776
Lakeside Shopping Centre, Thurrock, RM20 2ZN
Accessible Italian cuisine on the British high street - indulge in authentic sharing platters, hand stretched pizzas and hearty pasta dishes, served with a healthy dose of gregarious Italian hospitality.

25% OFF TOTAL | 6 | FRI × | SAT × | SUN | ▲ — Italian

BELLA ITALIA 01702 341 353
4-6 London Road, Southend-on-Sea, SS1 1TJ
Accessible Italian cuisine on the British high street - indulge in authentic sharing platters, hand stretched pizzas and hearty pasta dishes, served with a healthy dose of gregarious Italian hospitality.

25% OFF TOTAL | 6 | FRI × | SAT × | SUN | ▲ — Italian

BENGAL LANCERS 01279 793 131
2 High Street, Harlow, CM19 5HJ
Indian restaurant serving an eclectic range of regional Indian delicacies, providing diners with truly authentic dishes; well-prepared, rich in flavour, and crafted with the finest spices.

2FOR1 MAIN COURSE | FRI ✓ | SAT × | SUN | ✱ — Bangladeshi/Indian

BILASH ☎01245 352 690
7 Baddow Road, Town Centre, Chelmsford, CM2 0BX
A much-loved eatery in the heart of Chelmsford, Bilash is a hotspot for lovers of Indian cuisine. If you are looking for sensational Indian food, in a welcoming environment, look no further than Bilash.

2FOR1 2 COURSES | FRI × | SAT × — Indian

BIRD IN HAND ☎01787 222 557
Coggeshall Road, Earls Colne, Colchester, CO6 2JX
Dedicated to exceptional food and first-class service, the staff at this welcoming pub-restaurant ensure diners feel at home. *Not available in conjunction with other offers. À la carte menu only.

2FOR1 3 COURSES | FRI × | SAT ✱ | SUN — British

THE BLACK HORSE 01277 374 946
420 Ongar Road, Pilgrims Hatch, Brentwood, CM15 9JN
This Vintage Inn oozes rural charm and rustic character. The picturesque surroundings provide the perfect backdrop for savouring the hearty, seasonal pub-food on the menu.

25% OFF TOTAL | FRI ✓ | SAT ✓ | SUN | ▲ — Modern British

BOMBAY BUTLER INDIAN RESTAURANT ☎01279 816 492
7 Station Road, Stansted, CM24 8BE
Robust palates can contend with a fiery hot chili dish, whilst the more delicate of tastes savour a lightly spiced balti. This affably decorated and intimately lit restaurant is a fantastic night out.

2FOR1 MAIN COURSE | FRI × | SAT × — Indian

BOWLING GREEN 01255 831 430
Crown Green Roundabout, Colchester Rd, Weeley, CO16 9AD
Quality pub classics with modern twists meets with a friendly and relaxed atmosphere to make this Table Table venue the perfect place for any occasion. * Excludes daytime & evening deals and festive menus

2FOR1 MAIN COURSE | FRI ✓ | SAT ✓ — Modern British

THE BRASSERIE AT MARKS TEY ☎01206 210 001
Best Western, London Road, Colchester, CO6 1DU
Offering sophisticated brasserie-style food with a modern twist, guests can enjoy a relaxed three-course meal right down to informal light snacks. An ideal choice for business and leisure travellers.

2FOR1 MAIN COURSE | FRI ✓ | SAT 📱 | SUN | ▲ — Modern British

BUFFALO BOB'S STEAK AND RIB SHACK ☎01992 717 447
24a Sun Street, Waltham Abbey, EN9 1EE
It's all about beef at Buffalo Bob's Steak and Rib Shack. Succulent cuts of meat smothered in your chosen dressing or sauce are deliciously matched with tasty, appetising sides.

25% OFF TOTAL | 4 | FRI × | SAT × | ▲ — American

CAFÉ ELITE ☎01279 425 518
5 The Rows, Harlow, CM20 1BX
A cracking place for light to hearty breakfasts and home-made lunches and dinners. Stop and refuel after a morning of shopping, or chat amongst friends for that well needed catch up.

25% OFF TOTAL | 4 | FRI ✱ | SAT ✱ — British

CAFÉ MASALA ☎01702 589 494
187 Broadway, Thorpe Bay, SS1 3EX
When you visit Café Masala, you will immediately see that this is a restaurant that dares to be different. Quality food, professional service and a winning atmosphere mark it as a fine establishment in the area.

2FOR1 2 COURSES | FRI × | SAT × | ▲ — Indian

CHURCHILL'S ☎01702 468 646
7 Tylers Avenue, Southend-on-Sea, SS1 2BB
Buzzing venue that combines a bar and dancefloor with an excellent array of bar and grill-style fare. Try the excellent rack of ribs, florentine pasta, or their tasty tapas options.

50% OFF FOOD | 6 | FRI ✓ | SAT ✓ — International

COLNE VALLEY RESTAURANT ☎01787 223 380
110 High Street, Earls Colne, Colchester, CO6 2QX
Well-established local restaurant providing an excellent menu brimming full of staple Indian dishes alongside delectable vegetarian dishes and the more unusual options.

25% OFF TOTAL | 6 | FRI × | SAT × — Indian

THE CAMELIA HOTEL RESTAURANT ☎01702 587 917
178 Eastern Esplanade, Southend-on-Sea, SS1 3AA
A delicious boutique hotel with a light, spacious restaurant that features a selection of accomplished English and European dishes with an emphasis on local produce, including the daily caught Thames fish.

50% OFF FOOD | 4 | FRI ✓ | SAT ✓ — International

CAFÉ ROUGE

25% OFF TOTAL | ♟ 6 | FRI ✓ | SAT ✓ | ✱ | ▲

3 restaurants in Essex

219 Moulsham Street, Chelmsford, CM2 0LR
☎ 01245 250 588
59 High Street, Colchester, CO1 1DH
☎ 01206 541 839
Lakeside Shopping Ctr, Thurrock, RM20 2ZN
☎ 01708 890 857

THE CORIANDER ☎01245 353 060
10 Baddow Road, Chelmsford, CM2 0DG
The Coriander Restaurant pride themselves on their quality of food and delivery of service. They use a combination of Northern Indian and Bangladeshi flavours to create a taste sensation.

2FOR1 3 COURSES | FRI × | SAT × | ✱ | ▲ — Indian

THE CORNER LOUNGE ☎01245 505 880
1 Exchange Way, Chelmsford, CM1 1XB
Using ingredients sourced direct from Italy to create a menu of traditional and modern dishes, this family-run restaurant offers diners a truly authentic experience.

2FOR1 MAIN COURSE | FRI × | SAT × | ▲ — Italian

COUNTY KITCHEN ☎01245 455 700
County Hotel, Rainsford Road, Chelmsford, CM1 2PZ
Head Chef Wayne Browning is passionate about food, where it comes from and the quality is never compromised. Only the best ingredients from local farmers are used to create the dishes. 1 AA Rosette.

25% OFF TOTAL | ♟ 4 | FRI ✓ | SAT × | SUN | ▲ — European

THE CROWN 01206 231 946
Old Ipswich Road, Ardleigh, Colchester, CO7 7QR
This Vintage Inn oozes rural charm and rustic character. The picturesque surroundings provide the perfect backdrop for savouring the hearty, seasonal pub-food on the menu.

25% OFF TOTAL | FRI ✓ | SAT ✓ | SUN | ▲ — Modern British

DOSA PALACE RESTAURANT ☎01702 333 323
629 London Road, Westcliff-on-Sea, SS0 9PE
Sometimes, only Indian cuisine will do. The kitchen at Dosa Palace strive for perfection, capturing the essence of Indian street food mixed with authentic, home-style Asian recipes and ingredients.

25% OFF TOTAL | ♟ 6 | FRI × | SAT ✱ | ▲ — Indian

THE DUKE'S HEAD ☎01279 718 598
High Street, Hatfield Broad Oak, CM22 7HH
Quirky and quaint, this pub is traditionally friendly and welcoming. Feast upon classic British dishes prepared with gusto as you toast your feet by the log fire. *See online for further details.

2FOR1 MAIN COURSE | FRI ✱ | SAT × | SUN | ▲ — English/Gastro pub

DUNMOW'S CHINA GARDEN ☎01371 872 845
27 High Street, Great Dunmow, CM6 1AB
This elegant and family-run restaurant specialises in Peking, Szechuan and Cantonese cuisine. It's renowned for its delicious seafood dishes, excellent service and traditional style.

25% OFF TOTAL | ♟ 4 | FRI ✱ | SAT ✱ | SUN — Chinese

EL GUACA MEXICAN GRILL ☎01621 733 602
122 High Street, Maldon, CM9 5ET
El Guaca Mexican Grill does not disappoint. For an authentic Mexican fiesta, accompanied by thirst quenching beverages, enjoy the tasty delights of El Guaca with friends or family.

2FOR1 MAIN COURSE | FRI ✓ | SAT ✱ | ▲ — South American

FEAST OF BENGAL ☎01277 633 670
9 Meadow Rise, Billericay, CM11 2DN
The chef recommends that the more adventurous of palates try one of the duck curries for a memorable taste experience. For the traditional curry lovers, the menu is bursting with western favourites.

2FOR1 MAIN COURSE | FRI × | SAT × — Indian

THE FOWLER'S FARM 01376 551 560
Cressing Road, Braintree, CM77 8EZ
This Vintage Inn oozes rural charm and rustic character. The picturesque surroundings provide the perfect backdrop for savouring the hearty, seasonal pub-food on the menu.

25% OFF TOTAL | FRI ✓ | SAT ✓ | SUN | ▲ — Modern British

THE FOX AND RAVEN 01245 267 364
Barnes Mill Road, Chelmsford, CM2 6NL
This Vintage Inn oozes rural charm and rustic character. The picturesque surroundings provide the perfect backdrop for savouring the hearty, seasonal pub-food on the menu.

25% OFF TOTAL | FRI ✓ | SAT ✓ | SUN | ▲ — Modern British

GANDHI RESTAURANT ☎01277 630 600
3 Holly Court High Street, Billericay, CM12 9AP
Since 1983, this restaurant has been renowned for it's good food and service. The chef has been perfecting Indian dishes for 24 years and gained valuable experience whilst working in the restaurant trade.

2FOR1 3 COURSES | FRI × | SAT × | ✱ — Indian

THE GENERALS ARMS ☎01245 222 069
The Ridge, Little Baddow, Chelmsford, CM3 4SX
Nestled in breathtaking countryside, this pub is a hot spot for refuelling after an afternoon ramble. Whether it's a wholesome banquet or a light bite, there is an ample variety for every palate.

2FOR1 3 COURSES | FRI × | SAT × | SUN — British

THE GREYHOUND 01277 249 911
Magpie Lane, Little Warley, Brentwood, CM13 3DZ
This Vintage Inn oozes rural charm and rustic character. The picturesque surroundings provide the perfect backdrop for savouring the hearty, seasonal pub-food on the menu.

25% OFF TOTAL | FRI ✓ | SAT ✓ | SUN | ▲ — Modern British

THE GRILL ROOM @ DOWN HALL HOTEL ☎01279 731 441
Matching Road, Hatfield Heath, CM22 7AS
Informal dining throughout the day at this Hand Picked Hotels restaurant, with a stunning interior and abundance of natural light. Delivers a contemporary British menu that changes seasonally.

2FOR1 MAIN COURSE | FRI ▮ | SAT ▮ — European

GULSHAN RESTAURANT ☎01702 469 736
266 Sutton Road, Southend-on-Sea, SS2 5ET
Well-known local favourite that's known for its service, prices and consistent cooking. There's a wide-ranging menu that will keep you interested, while the restaurant's style is unashamedly old-school.

2FOR1 MAIN COURSE | FRI × | SAT × | SUN — Indian

HARLOW MILL 01279 442 545
Cambridge Road, Old Harlow, CM20 2EP
Beefeater Grill are one of the UK's best-loved restaurants welcoming guests for almost 40 years in over 130 locations nationwide. *Excludes Breakfast, Light Bites, Bar menu, set menus and all other offers.

2FOR1 MAIN COURSE | ♟ 6 | FRI ✓ | SAT × | ▲ — Modern British

HARRISONS RESTAURANT ☎01702 201 217
32 Main Road, Hockley, SS5 4QS
Harrisons Restaurant is located in Hockley, Essex where exquisite food, fine wine and local produce is served in sophisticated, comfortable surroundings.

2FOR1 3 COURSES | FRI ▮ | SAT × | SUN | ▲ — European

THE HAWK
01268 767 263
Hawk Hill, Battlesbridge, Wickford, SS11 7RJ
This Vintage Inn oozes rural charm and rustic character. The picturesque surroundings provide the perfect backdrop for savouring the hearty, seasonal pub-food on the menu.

25% OFF TOTAL | FRI ✓ | SAT ✓ | SUN | — Modern British

THE HAYWAIN
01268 554 500
High Road, Fobbing, Stanford Le Hope, SS17 9NR
Beefeater Grill are one of the UK's best-loved restaurants welcoming guests for almost 40 years in over 130 locations nationwide. *Excludes Breakfast, Light Bites, Bar menu, set menus and all other offers.

2FOR1 MAIN COURSE | 6 | FRI ✓ | SAT × | — Modern British

HORSE AND GROOM
01702 544 015
1 Southend Road, Rochford, SS4 1HA
The Horse and Groom is a 200 year old lovely pub serving real ales and excellent food which uses freah quality ingredients and locally sourced produce wherever possible.

50% OFF FOOD | 6 | FRI ✓ | SAT ✓ | — British

HUNTERS MEET
01279 730 549
Chelmsford Road, Hatfield Heath, CM22 7BQ
The restaurant was taken over by Lesley and Brendan in December 1990 after it had lain empty for some 14 months. It now has a reputation for its cuisine, its atmosphere and value for money.

25% OFF TOTAL | 4 | FRI × | SAT × | SUN | — British

INDIAN RUCHI
01277 630 933
9 High Street, Billericay, CM12 9BE
With an enviable central location, this Indian restaurant really does have everything going for it. Superbly fresh and tasty dishes can be enjoyed in a warm and friendly atmosphere.

2FOR1 MAIN COURSE | FRI ✓ | SAT ✓ | — Indian

JOHNNY'S CARIBBEAN HUT
01702 808 786
287 London Road, Westcliffe-on-Sea, SS0 7BX
Showcasing the very best of Caribbean cuisine, John's is always a hub of music and excitement.

25% OFF TOTAL | 2 | FRI ✓ | SAT × | SUN | ✱ | — Caribbean

THE KING'S HEAD
01277 637 135
Southend Road, Billericay, CM11 2PS
This Vintage Inn oozes rural charm and rustic character. The picturesque surroundings provide the perfect backdrop for savouring the hearty, seasonal pub-food on the menu.

25% OFF TOTAL | FRI ✓ | SAT ✓ | SUN | — Modern British

THE KING'S HEAD
01992 525 001
High Road, North Weald, Epping, CM16 6BU
This Vintage Inn oozes rural charm and rustic character. The picturesque surroundings provide the perfect backdrop for savouring the hearty, seasonal pub-food on the menu.

25% OFF TOTAL | FRI ✓ | SAT ✓ | SUN | — Modern British

LA TASCA
01708 890 855
Lakeside Shopping Centre, Thurrock, RM20 2ZP
Quintessentially Spanish, La Tasca's fresh and exciting menu offers something for everyone. Their tapas dishes are sincerely authentic, while their paellas always deliver on flavour.

25% OFF TOTAL | 8 | FRI ✓ | SAT × | — Spanish

LAKESIDE RESTAURANT
01279 506 475
Great Hallingbury Manor, Great Hallingbury, CM22 7TJ
Prepare to delight your taste buds with a unique country dining experience that's also excellent value for money. Attractive and exquisitely prepared food; the culmination of many years experience.

25% OFF TOTAL | 4 | FRI ✱ | SAT ✱ | SUN | — European

LAMPLIGHTS BRASSERIE
01702 345 247
Westcliff Parade, Westcliff-on-Sea, SS0 7QW
The Head Chef creates an abundance of dishes, regularly changed to guarantee fresh tastes. Spoil yourself with a weekend treat with a delicious meal out, ending it with the delicious Bramley apple pie.

50% OFF FOOD | 6 | FRI ✓ | SAT ✓ | — British

LATINO'S RESTAURANT
01702 555 010
205 London Road, Hadleigh, Benfleet, SS7 2RD
Great food and outstanding wines offered in a friendly and authentic athmosphere. An extensive menu offers diners everything from fresh tapas and paella to mouthwatering steaks.

25% OFF TOTAL | 4 | FRI | SAT ✱ | — Spanish

LE RAJ
01375 843 384
5-7 Broadway, Tilbury, Thurrock, RM18 7BP
Fine Indian dishes to savour and enjoy, whether you want an intimate meal or an easy takeaway. Exceptional standards and high-quality ingredients sets them apart from the competition.

2FOR1 MAIN COURSE | FRI | SAT | ✱ | — Indian

THE LEMON TREE
01206 767 337
48 St Johns Street, Colchester, CO2 7AD
Cooking the finest modern European cuisine, this restaurant focuses on warm welcomes and great food. The kitchen draws on the influences of guests' preferences to create amazingly satisfying dishes.

2FOR1 MAIN COURSE | FRI × | SAT × | — Modern British

LOCH FYNE
01245 293 620
109-111 Bond Street, Chelmsford, CM1 1GS
From the roadside oyster bar that once was, Loch Fyne restaurants now successfully inject energy and passion into great food and wonderful flavours, whilst ensuring their seafood is sustainably sourced.

25% OFF TOTAL | 4 | FRI ✱ | SAT ✱ | — Seafood

MAHARAJA
01268 794 541
358 London Road, Benfleet, Essex, SS7 1BG
Whilst serving all of the classic Indian staple dishes, Maharaja also offers a fine selection of seafood plucked from the Indian Ocean alongside ostrich, venison and other game dishes.

2FOR1 3 COURSES | FRI ✓ | SAT ✓ | — Indian

MALONE'S DINER
01621 840 007
8 High Street, Maldon, CM9 5PJ
Malones' diner is a fantastic American style family restaurant.They use high quality fresh produce to create meals that you won't forget in a hurry.

25% OFF TOTAL | FRI × | SAT × | ✱ | — American

MAMATAZ MAHAL TANDOORI
01702 341 046
440 London Road, Westcliff-on-Sea, SS0 9LA
Expect nothing less than exceptional hospitality at this beloved Indian venue. The culinary excellence is unmistakable and makes for a fantastic evening out with friends and loved ones.

2FOR1 2 COURSES | FRI ✓ | SAT ✓ | — Indian

MARCO'S BAR
01268 773 311
30 Eastwood Road, Rayleigh, Essex, SS6 7JQ
Marco's tapas has all the right zing and zest for a superb, ranging meal. It offers lunch and evening menus, along with a good array of bar snacks, in a warm, accommodating space.

25% OFF TOTAL | 4 | FRI | SAT | ✱ | — Spanish

MASONS RESTAURANT AND BAR
01277 261 331
155 Ingrave Road, Brentwood, CM13 2AA
An ideal place to eat with business clients over lunch, or wine and dine with family and friends in the evening. A wonderfully warm décor creates an intimate dining experience. *Not available on set menu.

2FOR1 MAIN COURSE | FRI | SAT ✱ | SUN | — Contemporary

MAYA'S WORLD BUFFET
01702 334 800
42-44 London Road, Southend on Sea, SS1 1NT
When you're finding it hard to pick and choose head to Maya's World Buffet where decisions won't be necessary. With such a wide variety, you can sample a little bite from every corner of the world.

25% OFF TOTAL | 4 | FRI | SAT | — International

THE MITRE
01621 891 379
2 The Street, Wickham Bishops, Whitham, CM8 3NN
An extremely popular traditional pub in the heart of Wickham Bishops. Enjoy hearty home-cooked dishes alongside quality ales, beers, spirits and wines in a warm environment.

25% OFF TOTAL | 10 | FRI ✓ | SAT ✓ | SUN | — British

To understand what the restaurant icons mean, please see the inside back cover.

MUGHAL DYNASTY
☎ 01702 470 443

1585 London Road, Leigh-on-Sea, SS9 2SG

A fragrant aroma of delicately spiced dishes, a taste that lingers on the tongue. A meal at Mughal Dynasty is Indian cuisine at its finest.

2FOR1 MAIN COURSE | FRI × | SAT × | ✱ — Indian

MUHINUR TANDOORI HOUSE
☎ 01992 766 333

1 Green Yard, Waltham Abbey, EN9 1RD

Deliciously tasty Indian cuisine will have you wanting to return here over and over again. Classic curries sit side by side with more unusual dishes, whilst the lower oil levels make much healthier dishes.

2FOR1 MAIN COURSE | FRI ✱ | SAT ✱ | ✱ — Indian

MUMBAI-SE
☎ 01702 330 575

12 Hamlet Court Road, Westcliff-on-Sea, SS0 7LX

Mirroring Mumbai's love affair with home-made food, simplicity produces the best results at this fabulous Indian restaurant. Minimal oil levels create great food that's good for you.

2FOR1 MAIN COURSE | FRI | SAT — Indian

NAKA THAI
☎ 01206 864 086

35 East Hill, Colchester, CO1 2QX

Authentic taste of Thailand in an unusual yet amiable setting. Step foot into the characteristically Tudor building, where you'll find a true sample of the East. Super staff provide warm welcomes to all.

25% OFF TOTAL | 6 | FRI ✓ | SAT ✓ | ✱ — Thai

THE OLIVE TREE
☎ 01255 473 931

66-68 Rosemary Road, Clacton-on-Sea, CO15 1TE

Indulge in divine Mediterranean cuisine at this popular and stylish restaurant. Prides itself on quality and value, also hosting superb entertainment nights with live music and traditional dancing.

25% OFF TOTAL | 10 | FRI ✓ | SAT × — Mediterranean

THE POLASH RESTAURANT
☎ 01621 782 233

169 Station Road, Burnham-on-Crouch, CM0 8HJ

A highly recommended restaurant that serves delightful food with a friendly smile. Curry lovers will enjoy the thought and effort that goes into every tasty dish.

2FOR1 MAIN COURSE | FRI | SAT | SUN | — Indian

THE POLASH RESTAURANT
☎ 01702 294 721

84-86 West Road, Southend-on-Sea, SS3 9DS

Great little Indian restaurant not far from the town's esplanades. Wide-ranging menu that's consistently tasty; all the old favourites done really well alongside some interesting specials.

2FOR1 MAIN COURSE | FRI | SAT — Indian

RADHUNI
☎ 01799 542 777

56 High Street, Newport, CB11 3QX

Combining the tastes of India and Bangladesh, this eatery promises to appease all of its diners. Both classic and unusual dishes align the carefully selected menu.

2FOR1 3 COURSES | FRI | SAT | SUN | — Indian

THE RARE COW
☎ 01245 420 399

11 Chequers Road, Writtle, Chelmsford, CM1 3NG

The Rare Cow is committed to providing great steak by sourcing produce from ethically sound farms, using 'season heaven'- a mixture of local and exotic salts and the char-grill to ensure steak perfection.

25% OFF TOTAL | 4 | FRI × | SAT × | — British

RBG @ PARK INN HARLOW
☎ 01279 829 988

Park Inn, Southern Way, Harlow, CM18 7BA

A grill bar that boasts tasty succulent steaks, fresh from the grill, and serves classic New York-style cocktails. Relax in the lavish surroundings and enjoy exceptional food and service.

50% OFF FOOD | 8 | FRI ✓ | SAT ✓ | — British

PREZZO

2FOR1 MAIN COURSE | FRI × | SAT × |

2-FOR-1 MAIN COURSE

12 restaurants in Essex

5 Market Hill, Halstead, CO9 2AR	☎ 01787 474 271
113-115 Bond Street, Chelmsford, CM1 1GD	☎ 01245 264 335
69 High Street, Maldon, CM9 5EP	☎ 01621 842 544
129-129A High Street, Brentwood, CM14 4RZ	☎ 01277 216 641
236 High Street, Epping, CM16 4AP	☎ 01992 570 056
Freeport Village, Charter Way, Braintree, CM77 8YH	☎ 01376 569 022
8 Baddow Road, Chelmsford, CM2 0DG	☎ 01245 358 533
39-41 High Street, Rayleigh, SS6 7EW	☎ 0126 877 5143
4 Marine Parade West, Clacton-on-Sea, CO15 1QZ	☎ 01255 223 894
1 Cross Street, Saffron Walden, CB10 1EX	☎ 01799 521 260
6 High Street, Billericay, CM12 9BQ	☎ 01277 658 273
1 Culver Street East, Colchester, CO1 1LD	☎ 01206 573 388

RBG @ PARK INN THURROCK
01708 719 988

Park Inn, High Road, Thurrock, RM16 5UE

Decked out in the Regency style, this hotel-based restaurant provides a calming and charming environment in which to enjoy their range of gourmet burgers, chargrilled dishes and homely classic desserts.

50% OFF FOOD | ♟ 6 | FRI ✓ | SAT ✓ — British

THE RED LION HOTEL
☎ 01206 577 986

High Street, Colchester, CO1 1DJ

In a restaurant set under the old timber beams of the Red Lion Hotel's former banqueting hall, diners can feast on suitably classic dishes with a modern twist.

25% OFF TOTAL | FRI ✓ | SAT ✓ — Traditional English

RESTAURANT @ BRANDY HOLE
☎ 01702 230 320

Pooles Lane, Hullbridge, Hockley, SS5 6QB

Fantastic setting overlooking the river Crouch; the wonderful views from The Brandy Hole provide an ambience as fresh as the menu.

2FOR1 MAIN COURSE | FRI ✓ | SAT ✓ | SUN — British

THE ROBIN HOOD
01255 476 785

211 London Road, Clacton-on-Sea, CO15 4ED

This Vintage Inn oozes rural charm and rustic character. The picturesque surroundings provide the perfect backdrop for savouring the hearty, seasonal pub-food on the menu.

25% OFF TOTAL | FRI ✓ | SAT ✓ | SUN | ▲ — Modern British

THE ROSE & CROWN
☎ 01206 271 251

Nayland Road, Great Horkesley, Colchester, CO6 4AH

Best Newcomer in East Anglia in the Great British Pub Awards, this place takes great pride in producing very simple yet delicious food including several cuts of steak served with hand cut chips.

2FOR1 3 COURSES | FRI ✓ | SAT ✱ | SUN — British

ROSE INN
☎ 01621 772 915

Burnham Road, Southminster, CM0 7BL

Forever in the hearts of its beloved locals, it is no surprise that this traditional roadside pub has stood the test of time. Dedicated to authentic British dishes, the Rose Inn promises flavour.

50% OFF FOOD | ♟ 4 | FRI ✓ | SAT ✓ — English/Gastro pub

THE ROYAL TIGER
☎ 01268 711 115

Old Southend Road, Rettendon Common, CM3 8EE

A fusion of Eastern cuisine and culture. Inspired by Royal Thailand and the Bengal tiger of India, the wonderful dishes they have on offer have been carefully selected and prepared for your enjoyment.

25% OFF TOTAL | FRI × | SAT ✓ | ▲ — Asian

THE RUNNING MARE
01245 253 031

Running Mare Lane, Chelmsford, CM2 8PN

This Vintage Inn oozes rural charm and rustic character. The picturesque surroundings provide the perfect backdrop for savouring the hearty, seasonal pub-food on the menu.

25% OFF TOTAL | FRI ✓ | SAT ✓ | SUN | ▲ — Modern British

RUSSELLS
☎ 01245 478 484

Bell Street, Great Baddow, Chelmsford, CM2 7JS

Undoubtedly dedicated, restaurant owner Barry is determined to give his diners a tantalising experience. Passionate about impeccable service, he and his staff provide an exquisite environment for dinner.

2FOR1 MAIN COURSE | FRI ✓ | SAT × | SUN | ▲ — British

SAND BAR & SEAFOOD COMPANY
☎ 01702 480 067

71 Broadway, Leigh-on-Sea, SS9 1PE

With a fast-growing reputation for fantastic food spreading far and wide, this restaurant offers a relaxed venue in which guests can enjoy a wonderful meal. A charming retreat from the bustling Broadway.

2FOR1 MAIN COURSE | FRI ✓ | SAT ✓ — Contemporary

SAPORI RESTAURANT
☎ 01245 268 179

Best Western Atlantic, New Street, Chelmsford, CM1 1PP

Italian for 'flavours', Sapori Restaurant takes heed of its name, infusing the cuisine with tasty, flavourful ingredients, using authentic Italian recipes. A slice of Italy brought straight to your table.

25% OFF TOTAL | ♟ 4 | FRI ✓ | SAT ✓ | ▲ — Italian

THE SECRET GARDEN
☎ 01621 850 396

1 Kings Head Centre, 38 High Street, Maldon, CM9 5PN

Whether guests are seeking a light bite for lunch or a hearty dinner, this English and Mediterranean inspired venue is sure to gratify. Fresh to order, the dishes use the most ambrosial of ingredients.

50% OFF FOOD | ♟ 2 | FRI × | SAT × — International

SHAAD
☎ 01245 256 003

34 Moulsham Street, Chelmsford, CM2 0HX

Known as a consistent provider of good, old-fashioned, thoroughly tasty curries in Chelmsford. Considered by some to be among the town's best, it'd be a shame to miss Shaad.

50% OFF FOOD | ♟ 6 | FRI ✱ | SAT ✱ — Indian

THE SHEPHERD & DOG
☎ 01206 272 711

Moor Road, Langham, Colchester, CO4 5NR

The Shepherd and Dog is widely renowned for its excellent food and outstanding quality. Serving an exquisite array of meat, fish and poultry dishes, the menu is well-balanced and offers something for all.

25% OFF TOTAL | FRI ✓ | SAT ✓ | ▲ — British

THE SHEPHERD & DOG
☎ 01702 258 279

Gore Road, Ballards Gore, Stambridge, Rochford, SS4 2DA

The Shepherd and Dog prides itself on food that is locally sourced and freshly prepared, the best quality ingredients and delicious seasonal menus. Make yourself at home in this traditional country pub.

50% OFF FOOD | ♟ 6 | FRI ✓ | SAT ✓ | SUN — British

THE SHIP INN
☎ 01277 840 201

Stock Road, West Hanningfield, Chelmsford, CM2 8LB

Sometimes the only thing that is guaranteed to satisfy is hearty, home-made pub classics. The Ship serves deliciously tasty food to a strong local following as well as visitors from afar.

2FOR1 3 COURSES | FRI ✱ | SAT ✱ | SUN | ▲ — English/Gastro pub

SOUTH RESTAURANT
☎ 01245 264 564

196 New London Road, Chelmsford, CM2 0AR

Modern and well-furnished restaurant serving an exciting, mouth-watering array of dishes by friendly staff. Provides quality dining in charming surroundings.

50% OFF FOOD | ♟ 4 | FRI ✓ | SAT ✓ | SUN | ▲ — British

SOUTHCHURCH TANDOORI
☎ 01702 615 666

565 Southchurch Road, Southend-on-Sea, SS1 2PN

Classic local Indian restaurant serving a brilliant array of the old favourite dishes, from baltis to tandoori recipes. Enjoy a meal that's brimming with sauce, sass and spice.

2FOR1 2 COURSES | FRI ✓ | SAT ✓ | ✱ — Indian

SPICE FUSION
☎ 01621 786 225

44 Station Road, Burnham-on-Crouch, CM0 8BQ

Contemporary Indian cuisine in a comfortable environment. Classic curry dishes are flavoursome and combine the freshest ingredients and spices to lock in exciting tastes.

50% OFF FOOD | FRI ✓ | SAT ✓ — Indian

STAR OF INDIA
☎ 01255 672 386

5 Connaught Avenue, Frinton-on-Sea, CO13 9PN

Set fair just up the way from the Esplanade, a popular little Indian restaurant, a family concern that does all the favourites with an emphasis on freshness of ingredient. Their experience is apparent.

2FOR1 MAIN COURSE | FRI × | SAT × — Indian

STRAWBERRY FIELD
01702 338 787

Thanet Grange, Southend-on-Sea, SS2 6GB

Quality pub classics with modern twists meets with a friendly and relaxed atmosphere to make this Table Table venue the perfect place for any occasion. * Excludes daytime & evening deals and festive menus.

2FOR1 MAIN COURSE | FRI ✓ | SAT ✓ — Modern British

www.gourmetsociety.co.uk

Gourmet Society discount applies to the à la carte menu only, unless stated otherwise.

STRADA

25% OFF TOTAL | 6 | FRI ✓ | SAT ×

4 restaurants in Essex

63 High Street, Billericay, CM12 9AX
01277 622 300
12 Baddow Road, Chelmsford, CM2 0DG
01245 491 991
19-20 North Hill, Colchester, CO1 1DZ
01206 542 854
Lakeside Shopping Ctr, Thurrock, RM20 2ZP
01708 890 038

TAJ MAHAL 2
01245 259 618
6 Baddow Road, Chelmsford, CM2 0DG
A wide ranging menu illustrating exactly what everyone loves about Indian cooking. The specialist chefs utilise traditional slow-cooking methods using a variety of techniques to create outstanding dishes.

2FOR1 3 COURSES | FRI | SAT — Indian

THE TANDOORI PARLOUR
01268 793 786
61-62 Hart Road, Thundersley, SS7 3PB
Light, colourful and charming tandoori restaurant. Excellent reputation not only for its atmosphere but for the fine food: a wide, appealing selection including the superb, spinach-based Bengali tar.

2FOR1 3 COURSES | FRI * | SAT * — Indian

TEMPLE FUSION AT CHELMSFORD
01245 248 201
Cross Keys, Boyton Cross, Chelmsford, CM1 4LP
Designed to give customers a comfortable and unique dining experience, the 'Indian Fusion' style cuisine contains dishes from the Indian sub-continent including Bangladesh, India and Nepal.

50% OFF FOOD | 4 | FRI | SAT — Indian

THAI HOUSE
01277 632 424
21B High Street, Billericay, CM12 9BA
Tucked away in Billericay this restaurant does a good line in the balanced flavours that you'll find in all the best Thai cuisine. Without frills, you'll enjoy simple rich flavours and a warm welcome.

2FOR1 MAIN COURSE | FRI ✓ | SAT ✓ | * — Thai

TRADER'S BAR AND RESTAURANT
01206 363 450
Holiday Inn, Eight Ash Green, Colchester, CO6 3QL
Trader's Restaurant at the Holiday Inn Colchester has a relaxed and informal feel to it, perfect for a relaxing evening out. The menu is made up of internationally inspired dishes.

25% OFF TOTAL | 8 | FRI ✓ | SAT ✓ — International

VOUJON
01375 892 555
Stanford Road, Orsett, RM16 3BL
A local treasure, Voujon serves divine curry to the area of Orsett. Spacious and open plan, this light and airy restaurant provides the perfect interior in which to enjoy a delectable Indian evening.

2FOR1 MAIN COURSE | FRI ✓ | SAT ✓ — Indian

THE WATERMILL
01268 522 227
Felmores, East Mayne, Basildon, SS13 1BW
Beefeater Grill are one of the UK's best-loved restaurants welcoming guests for almost 40 years in over 130 locations nationwide. *Excludes Breakfast, Light Bites, Bar menu, set menus and all other offers.

2FOR1 MAIN COURSE | 6 | FRI ✓ | SAT × — Modern British

WHEELERS TANDOORI
01268 757 868
458 London Road, Benfleet, SS7 1AW
Family owned Tandoori restaurant, where sumptuous flavours are a strong characteristic of the dishes on offer. Experienced chefs provide the very best takes on classic curries.

2FOR1 3 COURSES | FRI ✓ | SAT ✓ — Indian

THE WHITE HART
01787 237 250
Poole Street, Great Yeldham, CO9 4HJ
This pub's rural location is brilliantly reflected by its traditional style inside. The large timber-framed house is home to wood-beamed ceilings as well as tasty, classic pub food. Awarded 2 AA Rosettes.

2FOR1 MAIN COURSE | FRI ✓ | SAT | SUN — Fine Dining

WHITEHALL HOTEL
01279 850 603
Church End, Broxted, Dunmow, CM6 2BZ
A famous restaurant serving some of the finest dishes in the country, delivering a fantastic selection of fresh, mouth-watering cuisine in the magnificent surroundings of a luxurious hotel.

25% OFF TOTAL | FRI ✓ | SAT ✓ — Modern British

THE WINE CELLAR BAR AND BISTRO
01245 349 646
4 Dukes Street, Chelmsford, CM1 1HL
Situated in a quaint alleyway in front of Chelmsford Cathedral, The Wine Cellar is a unique and stylish place providing first-class food and wine. International beers take you on a whistle-stop world tour.

2FOR1 MAIN COURSE | FRI × | SAT × | SUN — British

THE WOODBINE INN
01992 713 050
Woodbine Inn Honey Lane, Waltham Abbey, EN9 3QT
The Woodbine Inn is a friendly old-fashioned English pub with a contemporary twist, listed in the Good Pub Guide and boosts real ales and fresh, home cooked food and locally sourced meat.

25% OFF TOTAL | 6 | FRI ✓ | SAT ✓ | SUN — British

YINGS ORIENTAL CUISINE
01268 771 688
156-158 High Street, Rayleigh, SS6 7BS
Chinese dishes and live entertainment are two of the highlights at Yings Oriental Cuisine. Efficient service and a lively atmosphere also ensure every dining experience is memorable.

25% OFF TOTAL | 6 | FRI × | SAT × | * — Chinese

Norfolk

AKAASH TANDOORI RESTAURANT
01362 692 614
22-23 Market Place, Dereham, NR19 2AX
Appealing Indian cuisine makes this restaurant a fantastic choice for the hungry diner. Serves a fine line in punchy curries and succulent tandoori meats, to be enjoyed alongside fresh sundries.

50% OFF FOOD | 6 | FRI × | SAT × — Indian

BAM BAM
01603 624 042
22 Tombland, Norwich, NR3 1RF
Asian food lovers are in their element at this well-decorated and modish eatery, dining on only the most authentic and scrumptious of dishes.

2FOR1 MAIN COURSE | FRI × | SAT × | SUN | * — British

BELUGA BAR & EATERIE
01603 624 042
2 Upper King Street, Norwich, NR3 1HA
Enjoy decadence and luxury without the guilt at this phenomenal bar and restaurant. Try the pork loin with a champagne and honey glaze as a sumptuous sample of this warm, eclectic menu.

2FOR1 MAIN COURSE | FRI ✓ | SAT ✓ | SUN — Fine Dining

BOMBAY NITE
01493 331 383
25a King Street, Great Yarmouth, NR30 2NZ
Popular for all the right reasons, this Indian eatery excellently prepares everything from mild, creamy delights to red hot dishes. Substantial and wholesome, the chefs guarantee satisfaction.

50% OFF FOOD | 4 | FRI × | SAT × — Indian

Bella Italia

Pizza ♥ Pasta ♥ Grill

25% OFF TOTAL | 6 | FRI × | SAT × | SUN | ✱ | ▲

8-10 Exchange Street, Norwich, NR2 1AT

☎ 01603 767 171

3 Red Lion Street, Norwich, NR1 3QF

☎ 01603 614 676

4AA Leisure, Riverside, Norwich, NR1 1EE

☎ 01603 615 584

THE BRASSERIE @ MECURE ☎ 08448 159 036

Boundary Road, Norwich, NR3 2BA

Consistent in providing quality accommodation, Mercure Hotels are well-recognised for providing welcoming stays. When in town, the Mercure Norwich Hotel is an ideal place to stay, dine, or a bit of both.

2FOR1 3 COURSES | FRI ✓ | SAT ✓ — International

BRASSERIE BAR & GRILL ☎ 01508 470 444

Dunston Hall Hotel, Ipswich Road, Norwich, NR14 8PQ

Located in a Victorian manor house surrounded by tranquil wooded parkland, the Brasserie offers the finest seasonal dishes with an excellent choice of wines, serving them an award of 1 AA Rosette.

25% OFF TOTAL | 10 | FRI ✱ | SAT ✱ | SUN | ▲ — Contemporary

BRUMMELLS ☎ 01603 625 555

7 Magdalen Street, Norwich, NR3 1LE

This double AA Rosette-rated restaurant serves exceptional seafood. It has been justly acclaimed for its attention to superlative produce and excellent cooking; the dining room is quirky and full of charm.

2FOR1 MAIN COURSE | FRI ▯ | SAT ▯ — Seafood

THE BUCK INN ☎ 01603 434 682

55 Yarmouth Road, Thorpe St Andrew, NR7 0EW

Charming pub in a serene part of Norfolk where you'll enjoy imaginative takes on pub favourites, cooked and presented with verve; stylishly done but losing none of the satisfying simplicity.

2FOR1 MAIN COURSE | FRI ✓ | SAT ✱ | SUN — British

CAFÉ ROUGE 01603 624 230

29 Exchange Street, Norwich, NR2 1DP

French sophistication on the British high street - enjoy seasonally changing French dishes and a continental wine selection, served in a relaxed environment with an undeniable flair of Parisian chic.

25% OFF TOTAL | 6 | FRI ✓ | SAT ✓ | ✱ | ▲ — French

CAFÉ ROUGE 01603 776 432

Intu Chapelfield, Merchant's Hall, Norwich, NR2 1SQ

French sophistication on the British high street - enjoy seasonally changing French dishes and a continental wine selection, served in a relaxed environment with an undeniable flair of Parisian chic.

25% OFF TOTAL | 6 | FRI ✓ | SAT ✓ | ✱ | ▲ — French

CAISTOR HALL HOTEL ☎ 01508 494 998

Caistor Lane, Caistor St Edmund, Norwich, NR14 8QN

Ivy-lined Georgian country house, elegant but unpretentious in style. The restaurant overlooks the gardens and serves sophisticated dishes from a range of European traditions; their John Dory stands out.

2FOR1 MAIN COURSE | FRI ✓ | SAT ✓ | ✱ | ▲ — International

CANTON ☎ 01953 717 110

Market Place, Market Street, Norwich, NR16 2AD

Indulge your senses and sample the sumptuous delights of renowned food and outstanding service. Set in a fantastic riverside location, this restaurant offers an excellent array of authentic Chinese fare.

2FOR1 MAIN COURSE | FRI ✱ | SAT ✱ | ▲ — Chinese

CHUTNEY AROMA OF INDIA ☎ 01603 305 300

23 Prince of Wales Road, Norwich, NR1 1BG

Chutney is a contemporary Indian restaurant and takeaway whose main concept is to create mouth-watering Indian, Bangladesh fusion cuisine with a healthy twist.

2FOR1 2 COURSES | FRI ▯ | SAT ▯ | ✱ — Indian

CONCORDE RESTAURANT ☎ 01603 410 544

Holiday Inn, Cromer Road, Norwich, NR6 6JA

Whether diners are looking for indulgent treats or healthy snacks, the Head Chef has carefully designed a well-rounded menu that appeals to both children and business lunches alike.

25% OFF TOTAL | 6 | FRI ✓ | SAT × | SUN — International

CONGHAM HALL HOTEL RESTAURANT ☎ 01485 600 250

Grimston, King's Lynn PE32 1AH

Stunning Norfolk manor in Georgian style. A kitchen garden produces 700 different herbs, salads and baby vegetables, picked daily for the chef, to create divine menus of imaginative dishes. 2 AA Rosettes.

25% OFF TOTAL | 4 | FRI ✓ | SAT × | ▲ — Fine Dining

DINE INDIA ☎ 01842 890 333

Thetford Road, Barnham, IP24 2PA

A perfect location for all the family, Dine India is an excellent establishment for those wishing to sample only the finest and most authentic in Indian cuisine.

25% OFF TOTAL | FRI ✓ | SAT × — Indian

FARMER BROWNS ☎ 01603 628 542

22 Tombland, Norwich, NR3 1RF

Expect the freshest of the fresh at Farmer Browns. A wonderful place to eat for lunch and dinner, where the produce is local and the menu imaginative. Serves everything from salmon to chicken livers.

2FOR1 MAIN COURSE | FRI ✱ | SAT ✱ — British

FRAZER'S RESTAURANT ☎ 01263 579 579

Sea Marge Hotel, 16 High St, Overstrand, NR27 0AB

Fresh, elegantly conceived seasonal menus in this AA Rosette-recognised beachfront restaurant, set in a stunning building in Overstrand on the Norfolk coast.

2FOR1 MAIN COURSE | FRI ✓ | SAT ✓ | SUN | ▲ — Fine Dining

IN 2 BLU ☎ 01263 838 383

The Links Country Park Hotel, Cromer, NR27 9QH

The Links Country Park Hotel has superb accommodation in beautiful surroundings and mouth watering food served in the contemporary restaurant.

2FOR1 MAIN COURSE | FRI ▯ | SAT ▯ | SUN | ▲ — Contemporary

KINGS ARMS CHINESE & THAI ☎ 01603 270 039

1 Panxworth Road, South Walsham, Norwich, NR13 6DY

Offers scrumptious Chinese and Thai dishes at reasonable prices. Carefully prepared and well-presented tasty food will have you coming back time and time again.

2FOR1 MAIN COURSE | FRI ✱ | SAT ✱ — Chinese/Thai

LA TASCA ☎ 01603 776 420

24 Tombland, Norwich, NR3 1RF

Quintessentially Spanish, La Tasca's fresh and exciting menu offers something for everyone. Their tapas dishes are sincerely authentic, while their paellas always deliver on flavour.

25% OFF TOTAL | 8 | FRI ✓ | SAT × | ▲ — Spanish

THE LAMB INN ☎ 01603 625 365

Orford Place, Norwich, NR1 3RU

The Lamb Inn is held dear by the locals and boasts hundreds of years of service. Complete with an abundance of international beer and cocktails, the menu vaunts delectable daily specials.

25% OFF TOTAL | 6 | FRI ✓ | SAT ✓ | ▲ — British

www.gourmetsociety.co.uk

Always mention your Gourmet Society card when booking a table.

THE LANGTRY
☎01603 469 347
79 Unthank Road, Norwich, NR2 2PE
Cool and calm pub in Norwich which serves superb quality Italian-style gourmet pizzas. With their perfectly done bases and vivid array of toppings, you're sure to savour these crisp, melting specialities.
2FOR1 MAIN COURSE | FRI ✓ | SAT ✓ | SUN — Brasserie

LOCH FYNE
☎01603 723 450
30-32 St Giles Street, Norwich, NR2 1LL
From the roadside oyster bar that once was, Loch Fyne restaurants now successfully inject energy and passion into great food and wonderful flavours, whilst ensuring their seafood is sustainably sourced.
25% OFF TOTAL | 4 | FRI ✱ | SAT ✱ | ▲ — Seafood

THE LODGE BAR & RESTAURANT
☎01362 638 466
Main Road, North Tuddenham, NR20 3DJ
An eclectic mix of old and new defines the nature and environment of The Lodge. The 19th-century building is now home to a delightful restaurant that serves first-class food and real ales.
2FOR1 MAIN COURSE | FRI × | SAT × | SUN | ▲ — British

MARKET BISTRO
☎01553 771 483
11 Saturday Market Place, King's Lynn, PE30 5DQ
This personal, close-knit bistro in King's Lynn serves food that is anything but impersonal: full, savoury flavours drawn out by chef Richard Golding who runs the restaurant with wife Lucy.
25% OFF TOTAL | 4 | FRI ✓ | SAT ✱ | SUN | ▲ — Modern British

THE MARSH HARRIER
01603 507 513
158 Ipswich Road, Norwich, NR4 6DX
This Vintage Inn oozes rural charm and rustic character. The picturesque surroundings provide the perfect backdrop for savouring the hearty, seasonal pub-food on the menu.
25% OFF TOTAL | FRI ✓ | SAT ✓ | SUN | ▲ — Modern British

NAMASTE INDIA
☎01603 662 016
2a Opie Street, Norwich, NR1 3DN
Combining informal service with a smile and Indian customs in a lively atmosphere, with melodious Indian music, Namaste India is a unique place to eat quality Vegetarian food, drink and meet friends.
2FOR1 3 COURSES | FRI × | SAT × | ▲ — Indian

THE NELSON
01603 214 438
Prince of Wales Road, Norwich, NR1 1DX
Quality pub classics with modern twists meets with a friendly and relaxed atmosphere to make this Table Table venue the perfect place for any occasion. * Excludes daytime & evening deals and festive menus
2FOR1 MAIN COURSE | FRI ✓ | SAT ✓ — Modern British

NIMMI
☎01842 761 260
17-19 Whitehart Street, Thetford, IP24 1AA
Sumptuous Indian dishes to be found on an extensive menu. Holding an astounding reputation for excellent food, meat lovers, vegetarians and sensitive palates are all successfully catered for.
25% OFF TOTAL | FRI ✱ | SAT ✱ — Indian

NUMBER 12
☎01603 611 135
12 Farmers Avenue, Norwich, NR1 3JX
A restaurant overflowing with charm and character. Well-maintained wooden floorboards and beamed ceilings are complemented by the neutral colour scheme. Enjoy a menu that offers flavoursome food.
25% OFF TOTAL | 2 | FRI × | SAT × | SUN — Modern British

THE OLD CROWN PUB AND RESTAURANT
☎01603 279 958
Crown Road, Buxton, NR10 5EN
A traditional, homely inn in Buxton that serves superbly cooked, full-flavoured meals using great fresh ingredients; it specialises in tender, striated and sumptuous steaks, simply and beautifully done.
2FOR1 3 COURSES | FRI ✓ | SAT ✓ — Traditional English

PREZZO
01603 660 404
2-6 Thorpe Road, Norwich, NR1 1RY
With a character all of its own, Prezzo oozes contemporary style and enduring charm. Signature pastas, stone-baked pizzas and classic Italian dishes promise a perfect dining choice for the whole family.
2FOR1 MAIN COURSE | FRI × | SAT × | ▲ — Italian

PREZZO
01553 777 616
22 Tuesday Market Place, King's Lynn, PE30 1JJ
With a character all of its own, Prezzo oozes contemporary style and enduring charm. Signature pastas, stone-baked pizzas and classic Italian dishes promise a perfect dining choice for the whole family.
2FOR1 MAIN COURSE | FRI × | SAT × | ▲ — Italian

PREZZO
01603 615 718
2-3 Tombland, Norwich, NR3 1HE
With a character all of its own, Prezzo oozes contemporary style and enduring charm. Signature pastas, stone-baked pizzas and classic Italian dishes promise a perfect dining choice for the whole family.
2FOR1 MAIN COURSE | FRI × | SAT × | ▲ — Italian

PRINCE OF INDIA
☎01603 616 937
19 Prince of Wales Road, Norwich, NR1 1BD
A highly recommended traditional-style restaurant. Simply good food with reasonable prices and attentive staff. Serves up some of the hottest curries in Norwich for all those who love their heat and spice.
2FOR1 MAIN COURSE | FRI ✓ | SAT ✓ — Indian

Q'S COFFEE SHOP AND BISTRO
☎01328 851 003
2 Quaker Lane, Fakenham, NR21 9BQ
Only a stone's throw away from the Norfolk coast, this quaint coffee shop and bistro is beautifully located in the town of Fakenham. Guests love the variety of snacks, lunches and dinners on offer.
2FOR1 MAIN COURSE | FRI ✓ | SAT ✓ | SUN | ▲ — British

RARE GRILL & STEAKHOUSE
☎01603 615 655
30-34 Unthank Road, Norwich, NR2 2RB
Unwind with a relaxed dining experience in this opulent but elegant restaurant, whose food is exceptionally tailored, unusually uncomplicated and extraordinarily delicious.
25% OFF TOTAL | 8 | FRI × | SAT × | ▲ — British

THE RED LION
☎01603 620 154
79 Bishopgate, Norwich, NR1 4AA
The Red Lion is traditional English pub in the heart of Norwich. The menu is fresh and seasonal, sourced from local producers where possible. Handmade pizzas are made to order there is a Sunday carvery.
2FOR1 3 COURSES | FRI ✓ | SAT ✓ | SUN — British

RED MOSSALA
☎01493 856 666
50 Marine Parade, Great Yarmouth, NR30 2EJ
Red Mossala is a superb place to dine when only curry will do. A terrific choice of Indian dishes feature alongside the usual sundries and breads, complete with Red Mossala's very own culinary style.
50% OFF FOOD | 4 | FRI × | SAT × — Indian

THE REFECTORY
☎01603 218 322
Norwich Cathedral, 12 The Close, Norwich, NR1 4DH
Support local suppliers and contribute to the upkeep of Norwich Cathedral by feasting on freshly prepared meals. Enjoy your lunch in the knowledge that all profits made here go towards a good cause.
2FOR1 MAIN COURSE | FRI ✓ | SAT ✓ | ▲ — English and Continental

RELISH
☎01508 470 548
Old Street, Newton Flotman, Norwich, NR15 1PD
Here at Relish, the kitchen uses only the freshest seasonal produce from personally vetted suppliers. All dishes are served with unmatchable bread baked in Woodbridge.
25% OFF TOTAL | 2 | FRI 🍷 | SAT 🍷 | ▲ — British

REVOLUCION DE CUBA
☎01603 857 565
7-9 Queen Street, Norwich, NR2 4TL
Revolucion De Cuba is causing a stir and for all the right reasons; mojitos meet burritos as day meets night. *Only valid on drinks purchased with food or while eating. Excludes champagne.
25% OFF TOTAL | 6 | FRI ✓ | SAT ✓ — Cuban

RIVAAJ
☎01953 883 884
11B High Street, Watton, IP25 6AB
The kind team at Rivaaj welcome you to a haven of subtle ambience and exquisite atmosphere along with superb food matched by the personal attention from staff makes it an enjoyable and unique experience.
2FOR1 3 COURSES | FRI ✓ | SAT ✓ | ✱ | ▲ — Indian

THE RIVERGARDEN
01603 703 900
36 Yarmouth Road, Thorpe St Andrew, Norwich, NR7 0EQ
Absorb the intimate and relaxing vibes of this small, candlelit restaurant where you will be delighted with the phenomenal cuisine on offer. The riverside location is perfect for a summer's day.

2FOR1 MAIN COURSE | FRI | SAT — British

ROYAL BENGAL
01603 406 633
Tills Road, Sprowston, Norwich, NR6 7QZ
An emphasis is placed on quality at the Royal Bengal. Carefully selected ingredients are equalled by well-rounded recipes and thoughtfully executed flavours.

25% OFF TOTAL | 10 | FRI × | SAT × — Indian

SAKURA
01603 663 838
5 White Lion Street, Norwich, NR2 1QA
Enjoy the innovative dining concept you'll find at this authentic Japanese restaurant. Grill your own meal on the built-in barbecue roaster while you sip a cold Japanese beer.

25% OFF TOTAL | 4 | FRI ✓ | SAT ✓ — Japanese

THE SHOWGROUND
01603 749 140
Dereham Road, New Costessey, Norwich, NR5 0TL
Quality pub classics with modern twists meets with a friendly and relaxed atmosphere to make this Table Table venue the perfect place for any occasion. * Excludes daytime & evening deals and festive menus.

2FOR1 MAIN COURSE | FRI ✓ | SAT ✓ — Modern British

SWALLOWTAILS RESTAURANT
01953 882 125
Broom Hall Country Hotel, Richmond Rd, Thetford, IP25 7EX
Small and neatly conceived restaurant in Saham Toney with its focus firmly on a range of tasty, fulsome home-cooked food prepared with local produce; a warm welcome and a delicious, leisurely meal await.

25% OFF TOTAL | 4 | FRI ✓ | SAT ✓ | SUN | * — British

THE SWAN INN
01692 630 316
10 Lower Street, Horning, Norfolk, NR12 8AA
This Vintage Inn oozes rural charm and rustic character. The picturesque surroundings provide the perfect backdrop for savouring the hearty, seasonal pub-food on the menu.

25% OFF TOTAL | FRI ✓ | SAT ✓ | SUN — Modern British

UPCHERS RESTAURANT
01263 824 555
The Dales Country Hotel, Upper Sheringham, NR26 8TJ
Enjoy refined flavours as clear as the sweeping stretch of Norfolk coastline from which this restaurant sits just a little inland. The quality and presentation are fit for its country house setting.

2FOR1 MAIN COURSE | FRI | SAT | SUN — British

VINES RESTAURANT
01603 879 567
Fakenham Road, Norwich, NR9 5QP
Ideally geared for a relaxing retreat, from the snug with its deep sofas to the pretty grounds, backing onto the River Wensum. The cuisine is smart and uncluttered, and the dining rooms full of light.

50% OFF FOOD | 2 | FRI * | SAT × | SUN — Fine Dining

WALNUT TREE SHADES
01603 622 910
Old Post Office Court, Norwich, NR2 1NG
Feast your eyes upon Tiffany lamps in this charming American-style diner whilst devouring steaks and ribs. Downstairs, music memorabilia line the walls and guests can enjoy the Wurlitzer-style jukebox.

2FOR1 3 COURSES | FRI * | SAT × — American

THE WARRENER
01842 826 120
Lynn-Wood, Brandon Road, Thetford, IP24 3PG
Quality pub classics with modern twists meets with a friendly and relaxed atmosphere to make this Table Table venue the perfect place for any occasion. * Excludes daytime & evening deals and festive menus.

2FOR1 MAIN COURSE | FRI ✓ | SAT ✓ — Modern British

THE WHITE HORSE INN
01953 888 857
Market Place, Kenninghall, NR16 2AH
The White Horse Inn is quintessentially English, providing classic food and real local ales to prove it. Shrouded in English charm and old country character.

2FOR1 3 COURSES | FRI ✓ | SAT ✓ | SUN | * — British

THE WINEPRESS @ WENSUM
01603 209 955
The Maids Head Hotel, 20 Tombland, Norwich, NR3 1LB
With a menu overseen by outstanding Executive Chef Daniel Galmiche, with his Michelin-starred experience, this hotel-based restaurant is unfussy in manner and precise in execution. 1 AA Rosette.

25% OFF TOTAL | 4 | FRI ✓ | SAT ✓ — European

THE WOOLIE
01603 219 544
2 Muspole Street, Norwich, NR3 1DJ
Kick start the weekend at this traditional venue, boasting 2 large TV screens showcasing sports and entertainment. Enjoy old favourites and an expansive selection of drinks, as The Woolie caters for all.

2FOR1 MAIN COURSE | FRI | SAT — British

Suffolk

A PASSAGE TO INDIA
01473 281 110
29 Fore Street, Ipswich, IP4 1JW
A Passage to India is an authentic Indian restaurant offering a wide selection of Indian, Bangladeshi and English Cuisine and a good selection of fine wines.

25% OFF TOTAL | FRI | SAT — Indian

ALATURKA TURKISH RESTAURANT
01473 233 448
9 Great Colman Street, Ipswich, IP4 2AA
Variety is simply one of Alaturka's pleasing qualities. Promising to tantalise and tempt with the delicious smells oozing from the kitchen, Alaktura's traditionally Turkish menu is fabulously fresh.

2FOR1 3 COURSES | FRI × | SAT × — Turkish

THE ARBORETUM
01473 222 177
43 High Street, Ipswich, IP1 3QL
Traditional pub which serves high-quality contemporary British food. Wide-ranging menu, sometimes surprising, and very appealing. Well-drilled staff are friendly and attentive; the atmosphere very relaxed.

2FOR1 MAIN COURSE | FRI ✓ | SAT ✓ | SUN — British

THE BEAGLE
01473 730 607
Hadleigh Road, Sproughton, Ipswich, IP8 3AR
This Vintage Inn oozes rural charm and rustic character. The picturesque surroundings provide the perfect backdrop for savouring the hearty, seasonal pub-food on the menu.

25% OFF TOTAL | FRI ✓ | SAT ✓ | SUN — Modern British

THE BEAR INN
01359 270 249
Tostock Road, Bury St Edmunds, IP30 9AG
Maintaining the right amount of traditional pub spirit and blending it with a contemporary charm, the Bear Inn is a great place to sup a fine ale or feast on modern British and European dishes.

25% OFF TOTAL | 4 | FRI * | SAT * — British

To understand what the restaurant icons mean, please see the inside back cover.

BEKASH TANDOORI
☎01473 741 121

10 Meredith Road, Ipswich, IP1 6EB

Fine little restaurant specialising in Bangladeshi and Indian food. Simple and effective menu, ranging from the classic vegetable curry to one of their speciality pathia dishes.

2FOR1 3 COURSES | FRI ✱ | SAT ✱ — Indian

THE BLACK SWAN
☎01986 788 204

Church Lane, Harleston, IP20 0ET

With over 15 years of experience, the Black Swan has put together a wonderful menu with produce from great local suppliers and growers, specialising in traditional and exotic steaks.

2FOR1 3 COURSES | FRI × | SAT × — British

BRASSERIE RESTAURANT AND BAR
01473 230 185

16 Falcon Street, Ipswich, IP1 1SL

Juicy, succulent steaks and fresh, melt-in-the-mouth fish make up an excellent, varied menu that offers something for all. An excellent wine and port selection accompanies a list of divine desserts.

2FOR1 3 COURSES | FRI ✱ | SAT × | ▲ — International

CAFÉ ROUGE
01284 764 477

59 Abbeygate St, Bury St Edmunds, IP33 1LB

French sophistication on the British high street - enjoy seasonally changing French dishes and a continental wine selection, served in a relaxed environment with an undeniable flair of Parisian chic.

25% OFF TOTAL | 👤 6 | FRI ✓ | SAT ✓ | ✱ | ▲ — French

CAMEO HOTEL COPDOCK
☎01473 209 988

Old London Road, Copdock, Ipswich, IP8 3JD

The Cameo Hotel offers a varied menu of dishes, that are all best washed down with a local cider, ale or a crisp glass of white wine. *Offer unavailable on Thursday and Sunday lunch.

50% OFF FOOD | 👤 2 | FRI 🍷 | SAT × | ▲ — British

THE CHEQUERS INN
☎01473 830 455

19 Stowmarket Road, Great Blakenham, Ipswich, IP6 0LP

Chequers Inn is a well-respected venue in Ipswich, providing excellent service and a fine selection of beers, wines and spirits. Head here for a well-deserved drink and a tasty bite to eat.

2FOR1 MAIN COURSE | FRI × | SAT × | SUN — British

CHURCH'S BISTRO
☎01473 219 138

The White House, Tower Church Yard, Ipswich, IP1 3BW

Quietly tucked away off the Ipswich main high street, Church's Bistro provides charming dining experiences. Contemporary British dishes from the chicken liver parfait to a superb steak for the meat lover.

25% OFF TOTAL | 👤 4 | FRI × | SAT × | ▲ — British

THE DUKE OF YORK
01394 386 347

Ipswich Road, Woodbridge, IP12 4BY

This Vintage Inn oozes rural charm and rustic character. The picturesque surroundings provide the perfect backdrop for savouring the hearty, seasonal pub-food on the menu.

25% OFF TOTAL | FRI ✓ | SAT ✓ | SUN | ▲ — Modern British

ELEMENTS RESTAURANT AND BAR
☎01473 232 400

Novotel Ipswich Centre, Grey Friars Rd, Ipswich, IP1 1UP

Health conscious diners will adore the vast selection of balanced dishes at this ideally located venue. Whether it's breakfast, a spot of lunch or a hearty dinner - this eatery tickles a lot of taste buds.

2FOR1 3 COURSES | 👤 8 | FRI 🍷 | SAT 🍷 — International

THE FOXBURROW
01502 572 441

249 Yarmouth Road, Lowestoft, NR32 4AA

Beefeater Grill are one of the UK's best-loved restaurants welcoming guests for almost 40 years in over 130 locations nationwide. *Excludes Breakfast, Light Bites, Bar menu, set menus and all other offers.

2FOR1 MAIN COURSE | 👤 6 | FRI ✓ | SAT × | ▲ — Modern British

THE GEORGE HINTLESHAM
☎01473 652 408

George Street, Hintlesham, Ipswich, IP8 3NH

At The George, they believe in wholesome home cooked food. The menu has been designed around family, all with individual tastes and fussiness, so hopefully you will find something for your entire family.

50% OFF FOOD | 👤 6 | FRI 🍷 | SAT 🍷 | SUN | ✱ | ▲ — International

GOLDEN SHIP INN
☎01473 230 030

Cliff Road, Ipswich, United Kingdom, IP3 0AX

The Golden Ship Inn is a restaurant serving authentic, fresh Chinese cuisine with a comfortable dining rooms and unique decor close to Ipswich's historic dock.

2FOR1 MAIN COURSE | FRI × | SAT × | SUN | ▲ — Chinese

INDIAN PALACE
☎01473 212 414

39 Upper Orwell Street, Ipswich, IP4 1HP

Inspired by the stunning southwesterly region of Kerala, the dishes are bursting with coconut, cardamom and cinnamon flavours. An expert balance of spices, seeds and chilies create the perfect dishes.

25% OFF TOTAL | 👤 4 | FRI × | SAT ✓ — Indian

JORNA INDIAN RESTAURANT
☎01473 680 635

29 Wherstead Road, Ipswich, IP3 9BN

Bringing both the firm favourite Indian dishes as well as some vivid new flavours to the floor, Jorna Restaurant has established an admirable reputation for quality, well-thought out cuisine.

2FOR1 MAIN COURSE | FRI × | SAT ✓ | ✱ — Indian

KINGS HEAD
☎01473 828 855

90 High Street, Hadleigh, IP7 5EF

Feast on classic favourites or indulge in the more modern dish in this wonderfully situated pub. A wood-burning stove and inglenook fire enhance the warm welcome that greets you at the door.

2FOR1 MAIN COURSE | FRI ✓ | SAT ✱ | SUN | ▲ — British

LEMON TREE BISTRO
☎01728 621 232

3 Church Street, Framlingham, IP13 9BE

A sensibly priced bistro that delivers a relaxing atmosphere for guests to enjoy amazing food, all day long. Perfectly placed just off the market square, this venue really has something for everyone.

25% OFF TOTAL | FRI ✱ | SAT 🍷 | ▲ — Modern European

LOCH FYNE
☎01473 269 810

Old Sub Station, 1 Duke St, Ipswich, IP3 0AE

From the roadside oyster bar that once was, Loch Fyne restaurants now successfully inject energy and passion into great food and wonderful flavours, whilst ensuring their seafood is sustainably sourced.

25% OFF TOTAL | 👤 4 | FRI ✱ | SAT ✱ | ▲ — Seafood

MAHARANI
☎01473 213 388

46 Norwich Road, Ipswich, IP1 2NJ

Classic Bangladeshi recipes underpin this acclaimed restaurant, supplemented by an ongoing openness to new tastes; it specialises in flavourful fish dishes and rich bhunas.

2FOR1 MAIN COURSE | FRI ✓ | SAT 🍷 — Indian

MANOR RESTAURANT
☎01473 684 241

Belstead Road, Ipswich, IP2 9HB

A smart, refined restaurant distinguished by some excellent food, from a menu whose basis is contemporary bistro cuisine, with a notable emphasis on modern British flavours.

50% OFF FOOD | 👤 4 | FRI ✱ | SAT ✱ | ▲ — British

MARCO PIERRE WHITE
☎01787 247 388

Market Place, Lavenham, CO10 9QZ

This elegant and historic Hotel is home to one of Marco Pierre White's prestigious eateries. Savour classic dishes prepared to culinary impeccability whilst sampling real ales from local breweries.

25% OFF TOTAL | 👤 6 | FRI × | SAT × | ✱ — Seafood/ International

MONTAZ
☎01638 665 007

30 Old Station Road, Newmarket, CB8 8DN

Curry lovers can feast upon both classic and unusual dishes at Montaz, one of the most exciting Indian restaurant chains around. Diners enjoy exceedingly good cuisine in a chic and beautiful setting.

25% OFF TOTAL | 👤 4 | FRI ✱ | SAT ✱ — Indian

THE OLD SCOTCH INDIAN RESTAURANT ☎01638 663 400
4 The Avenue, Newmarket, CB8 9AA
Fine Indian dining in Newmarket; classic flavours spruced up with contemporary flashes and served smartly and elegantly in these lovely old tea rooms.

25% OFF TOTAL | 10 | FRI | SAT | * — Indian

ORISSA ☎01284 719 116
108 Risbygate Street, Bury St Edmunds, IP33 3AA
A welcoming family-run establishment specialising in delivering the best of Indian flavours using fresh ingredients and passion. The popularity of Orissa speaks for itself, and is perfect for all diners.

2FOR1 MAIN COURSE | FRI × | SAT × — Indian

THE ORMONDE 01638 675 080
Fred Archer Way, Newmarket, Suffolk, CB8 7XN
Quality pub classics with modern twists meets with a friendly and relaxed atmosphere to make this Table Table venue the perfect place for any occasion. * Excludes daytime & evening deals and festive menus.

2FOR1 MAIN COURSE | FRI ✓ | SAT ✓ — Modern British

OYSTER REACH 01473 692 372
Bourne Hill, Wherstead, Ipswich, IP2 8ND
Beefeater Grill are one of the UK's best-loved restaurants welcoming guests for almost 40 years in over 130 locations nationwide. *Excludes Breakfast, Light Bites, Bar menu, set menus and all other offers.

2FOR1 MAIN COURSE | 6 | FRI ✓ | SAT × — Modern British

PIATTO ☎01502 711 711
23 Small Gate, Beccles, NR34 9AD
A brightly rustic Italian restaurant that prides itself on its well-decorated interior and fabulous cuisine. Deep-pan pizzas and divine pasta dishes will have you emerging satisfied.

25% OFF TOTAL | 10 | FRI | SAT | * — Italian

PLOUGH & FLEECE ☎01284 827 351
Great Green, Cockfield, IP30 0HJ
Run by Andy and Kerry pride themselves on their selection of ales and great food; this venue offers hearty home-made delights such as fish cakes and pies. The scenic beer garden is ideal for winding down.

50% OFF FOOD | FRI ✓ | SAT ✓ — British

THE RATTAN RESTAURANT ☎01394 285 621
The Marlborough Hotel, Sea Road, Felixstowe, IP11 2BJ
In-house restaurant of the Marlborough, a classic seafront hotel. Dishes range from a richly flavoured ham hock terrine or gravadlax starters, to classics like the Gressingham duck breast for your main.

25% OFF TOTAL | 6 | FRI ✓ | SAT ✓ — British

SPICE DEN ☎01502 514 499
89 High Street, Lowestoft, NR32 1XN
Spice Den is a traditional family run restaurant, situated in the market square. They offer a wide variety of traditional Asian dishes guaranteed to tantalise the taste buds.

25% OFF TOTAL | 4 | FRI × | SAT × — Indian

STRADA 01284 700 771
Cupola House, 7 The Traverse, Bury St Edmunds, IP33 1BJ
Offering fresh, bold dishes inspired by flavours of Italian city life - Strada serves a selection of indulgent tastes, to those seeking a blissful escape to laidback Italian life. *Excludes Pizzettas.

25% OFF TOTAL | 6 | FRI ✓ | SAT × — Italian

THE SUTTON PLOUGH ☎01394 411 785
Main Road, Sutton, IP12 3DU
Sutton is a charming village three miles from Woodbridge, playing home to the friendly and hospitable Sutton Plough. Having retained its original beams and log fires, the place has an inviting ambience.

25% OFF TOTAL | 4 | FRI ✓ | SAT ✓ — British

THE SWAN AT BURES ☎01787 228 121
1 Station Hill, Bures, CO8 5DD
Nestled in the picturesque village of Bures, the menu here includes light snacks and baguettes to pub classics such as the home-made burger and fish and chips.

25% OFF TOTAL | 10 | FRI | SAT — European

THE SWAN INN ☎01394 411 366
The Street, Alderton, IP12 3BL
A haven in which to unwind, the Swan Inn is characteristically British in appearance and captures the charming personality of its location. Serves impressive Indian cuisine.

2FOR1 MAIN COURSE | FRI × | SAT × | * — Indian

TAJ MAHAL ☎01473 257 712
40-42 Norwich Road, Ipswich, IP1 2NJ
Established in 1964, this is one of the oldest Indian restaurants in Suffolk. The place continues to use traditional ingredients when creating Indian dishes, along with their own flavoursome specialities.

2FOR1 3 COURSES | FRI | SAT — Indian

THAI PAVILION ☎01787 315 656
3 Friars Street, Sudbury, CO10 2AA
Accommodating Thai restaurant on the pretty Friars Street in Sudbury, where you can enjoy a warming meal of the fresh, eclectic and clean flavours that distinguish Thai cooking.

2FOR1 MAIN COURSE | FRI | SAT | SUN | * — Thai

PREZZO

2FOR1 MAIN COURSE | FRI × | SAT ×

2-FOR-1 MAIN COURSE

8 restaurants in Suffolk

54-55 Gainsborough Street, Sudbury, CO10 2ET	☎ 01787 880 852
1 Church Street, Woodbridge, IP12 1DS	☎ 01394 610 401
2 Exeter Road, Newmarket, CB8 8LT	☎ 01638 669 676
Ehringshausen Way, Haverhill, CB9 0BB	☎ 01440 767 878
146 High Street, Aldeburgh, IP15 5AQ	☎ 01728 454 452
9 Saltgate, Beccles, NR34 9AN	☎ 01502 715 036
35-36 Abbeygate Street, Bury St. Edmunds, IP33 1LW	☎ 01284 756 260
129-133 Hamilton Road, Felixstowe, IP11 7BN	☎ 01394 672 588

Wales

Clwyd

THE ASIA
01492 870 178
96 Gloddaeth Street, Llandudno, LL30 2DS
At The Asia, the team of experienced chefs showcase a real understanding and flair for proper Indian cuisine. Sample tasty dishes using a concoction of traditional and exotic ingredients.

25% OFF TOTAL | ♟ 6 | FRI × | SAT × | ✱ — Indian

BARRATT'S OF TYN RHYL
☎ 01745 344 138
167 Vale road, Rhyl, LL18 2PH
The oldest house in Rhyl, Barratts provides 4-star accommodation and hosts a well-renowned restaurant. Home cooked cuisine is lovingly and thoughtfully prepared for your enjoyment. 2 AA Rosettes.

25% OFF TOTAL | ♟ 4 | FRI ✓ | SAT ✓ | SUN | ✱ | ▲ — British

THE BEECHES
01978 853 214
Chester Road, Gresford, Nr Wrexham, LL12 8PW
Quality pub classics with a modern twist combine with a friendly and relaxed atmosphere to make this Table Table venue the perfect place for family gatherings or meeting friends.

2FOR1 MAIN COURSE | FRI ✓ | SAT ✓ — Modern British

BLACK PEPPERS
☎ 01978 261 143
18 Yorke Street, Wrexham, LL13 8LW
Mouth-watering Indian cuisine serves a local following as well as guests visiting Wrexham. Excellent signature flavours characterise dishes, which make them ever popular with regulars.

2FOR1 MAIN COURSE | FRI × | SAT × — Indian

COBDENS HOTEL & RESTAURANT
☎ 01690 720 243
Capel Curig, Snowdonia, LL24 0EE
Often considered 'The Mecca' for outdoor enthusiasts and sightseers in Northern Snowdonia. Head chef Andy Fowler has developed a menu prepared with excellent local produce and a touch of class.

2FOR1 MAIN COURSE | FRI × | SAT × | SUN — British

COUNTRY SPICE
☎ 01978 762 330
Asha House, Hawarden Road, Wrexham, LL12 9NW
Delectable Indian cuisine serves Country Spice with a well-deserved reputation in the area. Dine here for a satisfying fill of tasty curry dishes, from the more popular tastes to the less well-known.

2FOR1 MAIN COURSE | FRI ✱ | SAT ✱ | ✱ | ▲ — Indian

CROES HOWELL RESTAURANT BAR & GRILL
☎ 01244 570 570
Straight Mile, Rossett, Wrexham, LL12 0NY
Beautiful, modern restaurant with an open kitchen and fabulous countryside views. The menu is based on fresh seasonal ingredients, so visit them for an indulgent afternoon tea or a delicious evening meal.

25% OFF TOTAL | ♟ 2 | FRI ▯ | SAT ✱ | SUN | ▲ — Fine Dining

THE D RESTAURANT @ DAYS HOTEL
01244 830 332
Welsh Road, Sealand, Deeside, CH5 2HX
The D Restaurant at Days Hotel Chester North boasts a warm and welcoming atmosphere and a mouthwatering menu of locally-sourced foods for you to choose from whether it be for breakfast or dinner.

25% OFF TOTAL | ♟ 2 | FRI ✓ | SAT × | ▲ — British

THE GOLDEN LION
☎ 01244 571 020
Chester Road, Rossett, LL12 0HN
A traditionally adorned pub that has a phenomenal reputation for fantastic food. Feel completely at home in this cosy, warming establishment, where genial staff provide exceptional service.

2FOR1 MAIN COURSE | FRI × | SAT × | SUN | ▲ — European

GREEN PEA CAFÉ
☎ 01352 715 101
Basingwerk House, Holywell, CH8 7GH
Perfect for that something special at lunchtime or a much-needed coffee and cake afternoon treat, The Green Pea Café offers the perfect retreat from the great outdoors.

25% OFF TOTAL | ♟ 6 | FRI ✓ | SAT × | SUN — British

THE KINGS HEAD
☎ 01492 877 993
Old Road, Llandudno, LL30 2NB
Llandudno's oldest pub prides itself on serving great drinks, exceptional food and providing a lovely local atmosphere to locals and visitors alike. Enjoy hearty grub and excellent cask-conditioned ales.

2FOR1 MAIN COURSE | FRI × | SAT × | SUN — British

THE MOORS INN AND RESTAURANT
☎ 01978 755 365
Maes Maelor, Wrexham, LL11 5YL
This traditional inn celebrates the best of British cuisine, using only locally sourced ingredients. Catering for children and vegetarians, this pub welcomes a variety of diners with open arms and a smile.

2FOR1 MAIN COURSE | FRI ▯ | SAT ▯ | SUN — British

MORFA RHUDDLAN
01745 593 010
Castleview Retail Park, Marsh Road, Rhuddlan, LL18 5UA
Quality pub classics with a modern twist combine with a friendly and relaxed atmosphere to make this Table Table venue the perfect place for family gatherings or meeting friends.

2FOR1 MAIN COURSE | FRI ✓ | SAT ✓ — Modern British

THE RHYL BISTRO
☎ 01745 344 333
215 Wellington Road, Rhyl, LL18 1LR
The Rhyl Bistro is a well-established and locally renowned restaurant, dedicated to providing you with the very best dining experience. The quality of the cuisine is matched by the impeccable service.

25% OFF TOTAL | ♟ 4 | FRI × | SAT × | SUN | ✱ | ▲ — British

SERI INTAN
☎ 01745 856 000
145-151 High St, Prestatyn, LL19 9AS
Seri Intan is considered one of Prestatyn's best restaurants and has seen significant repeat business from locals.This Asian eatery delivers delicious Thai and Malaysian cuisine, bursting with flavours.

25% OFF TOTAL | ♟ 6 | FRI × | SAT × — Thai

SPICE OF INDIA
☎ 01745 827 355
Gwelfryn, Abergele Road, Bodelwyddan, LL18 5SR
Welcoming, simple and effective local Indian restaurant in Bodelwyddan. Spice of India has a broad-based menu of flavourful Indian dishes, classic curries and all the trimmings.

2FOR1 MAIN COURSE | FRI × | SAT × | SUN — Indian

TAMARIND THAI AT LYNDALE HOTEL
☎ 01492 515 429
410 Abergele Road, Colwyn Bay, LL29 9AB
Combining locally sourced produce with the spice and bite of classic Thai cuisine, this hotel-based restaurant sits close to the seafront in Colwyn Bay and promises excellent service in a serene setting.

25% OFF TOTAL | ♟ 4 | FRI ▯ | SAT ✱ | ✱ | ▲ — Thai

THE TANNERY
☎ 01492 641 655
Willow Street, Llanrwst, LL26 0ES
Characterised by fantastic service and culinary ambition, The Tannery is a great place to take a well-deserved rest and sample food cooked with passion and verve.

2FOR1 MAIN COURSE | FRI ▯ | SAT ▯ | ▲ — Welsh

TAVA
01829 270 491
Castle Street, Holt, LL13 9YL
Cool, laid-back Indian restaurant with something of the 1960's in its retro styling, yet with a very modern feel overall. Diverse and delicious cooking, with the sagwalla and razala curries standing out.

2FOR1 MAIN COURSE | FRI × | SAT × — Indian

THE VILLAGE MASSALA
☎ 01745 590 051
Station Road, Rhuddlan, LL18 5UA
A no-nonsense, welcoming place to enjoy a good curry in Rhuddlan. It's a simple and classic Indian restaurant that serves all the old favourites together with some fine contemporary dishes.

2FOR1 MAIN COURSE | FRI × | SAT × | SUN — Indian

VIRGILIOS PIZZERIA PORTUGUESE GRILL
☎ 01492 534 239
19 Penrhyn Road, Colwyn Bay, LL29 8LG
A deliciously authentic Mediterranean menu featuring dishes from Italy to Portugal made with expertise and skill and served in a remarkable setting.

2FOR1 3 COURSES | FRI × | SAT × — European

THE WYNNSTAY ARMS HOTEL ☎01978 822 187
High Street, Wrexham, LL14 6BL
The Wynnstay Arms Hotel has long held a reputation for its high standard of cuisine and the homely and cosy atmosphere in their Library and Restaurant.

50% OFF FOOD | 4 | FRI | SAT | SUN — British

ZARA RESTAURANT & BAR ☎01978 291 400
Ellice Way, Wrexham, LL13 7YH
Dine on imaginative dishes created to tempt your palate, including home-made desserts. This restaurant uses quality local Welsh produce to ensure guests have the very best dining experience.

25% OFF TOTAL | 6 | FRI ✓ | SAT ✓ — International

Dyfed

BARBUCCI ☎01554 777 791
10-12 Cwmfelin Road, Llanelli, SA14 9LR
There is only one reason why diners return time and time again to Barbucci Restaurant: for its fantastic Indian cuisine and excellently attentive service. Expert chefs create culinary delights.

2FOR1 3 COURSES | FRI ✓ | SAT × — Bangladeshi

BEST WESTERN DIPLOMAT HOTEL ☎01554 756 156
Felinfoel, Llanelli, SA15 3PJ
Imaginative presentation and complimenting flavours always excite guests and their palates. Enjoy seasonal menus including drinks on the terrace in the summer months.

25% OFF TOTAL | 2 | FRI ✓ | SAT ✓ | * — European

THE BOAR'S HEAD HOTEL ☎01267 222 789
120 Lammas Street, Carmarthen, SA31 3AE
The Boar's Head Hotel is situated in the centre of the thriving market town of Carmarthen. A variety of food is served throughout the day from the popular lunchtime carvery to the extensive evening menu.

25% OFF TOTAL | 6 | FRI | SAT — British

CON PASSIONATA ☎01267 243 240
16 Nott Square, Carmarthen, SA31 1PQ
A vibrant brasserie in the centre of Carmarthen, serving an eclectic mix of Welsh and European cuisine. Mixing good food and music, it's not one to miss.

50% OFF FOOD | 6 | FRI | SAT × | SUN — European

THE CONSERVATORY ☎01646 672 273
Lamphey Court, Lamphy, Tenby, SA71 5NT
With the restaurant having exceptional produce at their disposal, the quality here is something to enjoy and savour; the best of coast and country-crab, scallops, lobster and mussels from the local port.

2FOR1 MAIN COURSE | FRI ✓ | SAT × | SUN — International

THE FALCON INN ☎01974 241 633
Llanilar, Aberystwyth, SY23 4PA
The Falcon Inn is situated on the eastern edge of the pretty village of Llanilar. This locals' favourite serves up tasty, traditional pub food using fresh, local ingredients.

2FOR1 MAIN COURSE | FRI ✓ | SAT ✓ — British

THE FARMERS ARMS ☎01267 241 503
Llanybri, Carmarthen, SA33 5HJ
Food plays a very important role at The Farmers Arms and guests return again and again to savour the Thai and British cuisine. The chefs serve up simple yet superbly delicious dishes.

25% OFF TOTAL | 6 | FRI × | SAT × | SUN | * — Thai

THE GOGERDDAN ARMS ☎01239 810 784
Gogerddan, Cardigan, SA43 2HP
With some of Wales' sandiest beaches on their doorstep, The Gogerddan Arms is an ideal retreat in the countryside. From local steak and fish to burgers and salad - all food is sourced from local producers.

50% OFF FOOD | 6 | FRI × | SAT × | SUN — British

THE GEORGIAN RESTAURANT ☎01646 672 273
Lamphey Court, Lamphy, Tenby, SA71 5NT
Revelling in its impressive mansion home, the Georgian Restaurant at Lamphy Court is exceptional not only in location but also in its offerings of food and drink. Hearty food through and through.

2FOR1 MAIN COURSE | FRI ✓ | SAT × | SUN — International

LANGOSTINOS BRASSERIE ☎01554 773 711
1-6 Castle Buildings, Murray St, Llanelli, SA15 1AQ
A bright, relaxed and elegant brasserie-style steakhouse in Llanelli; contemporary cooking full of taste and complemented by the genial ambience and friendly service. Fresh and seasonal flavours.

2FOR1 3 COURSES | FRI | SAT | * — British

LLYS MEDDYG RESTAURANT ☎01239 820 008
East Street, Newport, SA42 0SY
2 AA Rosettes speak for the quality of this restaurant in Newport. Their cuisine has a beautiful sense of balance, complemented by fine produce sourced invariably from within a fifty-mile radius.

2FOR1 MAIN COURSE | FRI × | SAT × | SUN — British

THE MOORINGS RESTAURANT ☎01646 636 362
Dale Yacht Club, Haverfordwest, SA62 3RB
The Moorings Restaurant which is situated on the first floor of Dale Yacht Club, is a beautiful waterside eating and drinking establishment overlooking Dale Bay, newly reopened in April 2012.

2FOR1 3 COURSES | FRI × | SAT × | SUN — British

THE PEMBERTON 01554 740 092
Llandafen Road, Llanelli, SA14 9BD
Beefeater Grill are one of the UK's best-loved restaurants welcoming guests for almost 40 years in over 130 locations nationwide. *Excludes Breakfast, Light Bites, Bar menu, set menus and all other offers.

2FOR1 MAIN COURSE | 6 | FRI ✓ | SAT × — Modern British

QUBE RESTAURANT ☎01834 845 719
2 Tudor Square, Tenby, SA70 7AD
The Qube Restaurant is located in the heart of the beautiful walled resort town of Tenby. The dishes are all home made and freshly cooked to order, using locally sourced produce.

2FOR1 MAIN COURSE | FRI | SAT × — British

RESTAURANT 7TEEN & DELI ☎01267 229 599
17 Queen Street, Carmarthen, SA31 1JT
A fresh, innovative restaurant in Carmarthen with a focus on thorough, accomplished simplicity in its cooking, borne out by the clean, distinct and exceptionally full flavours that congregate in each dish.

25% OFF TOTAL | 2 | FRI ✓ | SAT * — British

THE STAG & PHEASANT INN ☎01269 844 000
Llandeilo Road, Llanelli, SA14 7SE
Fresh and locally sourced ingredients make up a delicious and varied menu at this long-established inn. Surrounded by miles of beautiful countryside, this rural retreat is definitely worth a visit.

25% OFF TOTAL | FRI ✓ | SAT ✓ — British

THREE HORSE SHOES ☎01550 721 201
6 High Street, Llandovery, SA20 0PT
Traditional fish & chips of the best quality and offers the highest quality of service available. Winning best chips in Llandovery 2006,7,8 and 9.

2FOR1 3 COURSES | FRI ✓ | SAT ✓ — British

TRUBSHAWS RESTAURANT ☎01554 756 156
Diplomat Hotel, Felinfoel, Llanelli, SA15 3PJ
Highly regarded locally, Trubshaws Restaurant in the Diplomat Hotel serves fresh and seasonal dishes in a bright and elegant dining room. No need to be diplomatic: enjoy and let your guard down.

25% OFF TOTAL | 6 | FRI ✓ | SAT ✓ — Modern European

VISTA LOUNGE ☎01554 773 711
Castle Buildings, Murray Street, Llanelli, SA15 1AQ
Bold, bright and ambitious with contemporary styling and a soft, buzz-filled atmosphere. The real emphasis though is on the home-cooked food, from classic British to European dishes.

25% OFF TOTAL | 4 | FRI | SAT | SUN — Modern European

Gourmet Society discount applies to the à la carte menu only, unless stated otherwise.

Glamorgan

ALMADA PORTUGUESE RESTAURANT ☎02920 226 242
146 Cowbridge Road East, Cardiff, CF11 9ND

Almada restaurant is bringing fresh Portuguese food to Canton. Perfect for a warm and friendly dining experience, Almada look forward to welcoming all customers, both old and new.

25% OFF TOTAL | Max 6 | FRI ☎ | SAT × | SUN | ✱ | ▲ — European

BAGLE BROOK 01639 813 017
Baglan Road, Baglan, Port Talbot, SA12 8ES

Beefeater Grill are one of the UK's best-loved restaurants welcoming guests for almost 40 years in over 130 locations nationwide. *Excludes Breakfast, Light Bites, Bar menu, set menus and all other offers.

2FOR1 MAIN COURSE | Max 6 | FRI ✓ | SAT × | ▲ — Modern British

BARAKAH TANDOORI INDIAN CUISINE 01792 879 995
42 Sterry Road, Swansea, SA4 3BR

Pleasant little tandoori restaurant that's more than sufficient if you're looking for a good, no-fussing neighbourhood curry. No great song and dance about this appealing restaurant, just a tasty meal.

2FOR1 MAIN COURSE | FRI × | SAT × | SUN — Indian

THE BARLEY MOW INN ☎01446 772 558
Craig Penllyn, Cowbridge, CF71 7RT

This country inn is steeped with character. Log burning fires providing winter warmth, and a relaxing patio to enjoy alfresco dining in the summer.

25% OFF TOTAL | Max 6 | FRI × | SAT ☎ | SUN — British

BELLA ITALIA 02920 472 009
Atlantic Wharf Leisure Park, Cardiff, CF10 4JY

Accessible Italian cuisine on the British high street - indulge in authentic sharing platters, hand stretched pizzas and hearty pasta dishes, served with a healthy dose of gregarious Italian hospitality.

25% OFF TOTAL | Max 6 | FRI × | SAT × | SUN | ▲ — Italian

BELLA ITALIA 02920 374 050
Old Brewery Quarter, St Mary's St, Cardiff, CF10 1AD

Accessible Italian cuisine on the British high street - indulge in authentic sharing platters, hand stretched pizzas and hearty pasta dishes, served with a healthy dose of gregarious Italian hospitality.

25% OFF TOTAL | Max 6 | FRI × | SAT × | SUN | ▲ — Italian

BELLA ITALIA 02920 399 466
6 High Street, Cardiff, CF10 1AW

Accessible Italian cuisine on the British high street - indulge in authentic sharing platters, hand stretched pizzas and hearty pasta dishes, served with a healthy dose of gregarious Italian hospitality.

25% OFF TOTAL | Max 6 | FRI × | SAT × | SUN | ▲ — Italian

BIG BLUE SPORTS BAR GRILL 02920 666 566
18-19 Trinity Street, Cardiff, CF10 1BH

The Big Blue Sports Bar & Grill in Cardiff is a great venue, suitable for any occasion. Offering everything from simple sandwiches and baguettes, to steaks, burgers and fish, fresh from the market.

2FOR1 MAIN COURSE | FRI ✓ | SAT ✓ | ✱ | ▲ — British

BLUE GARLIC ☎02920 623 465
35 Whitchurch Road, Cardiff, CF14 3JN

Piquant scents drift from the kitchen, enticing diners at Blue Garlic into matching the aromas with the dishes from the menu. Delectable Indian cuisine is sure to satisfy hungry curry lovers.

25% OFF TOTAL | Max 10 | FRI ✓ | SAT ✓ — Indian

THE BRASSERIE @ MERCURE ☎0844 815 9081
Mercure Swansea, Phoenix Way, Swansea, SA7 9EG

Tranquil lake views can be enjoyed at the Mercure Swansea Hotel, with the town centre being only a short distance away. Contemporary dining and international dishes dominate in the Hotel Brasserie.

2FOR1 3 COURSES | FRI ✓ | SAT ✓ — International

CAFÉ JAZZ ☎02929 387 026
21 St Mary Street, Cardiff, CF10 1PL

Get your weekly fix of jazz, blues and food at Café Jazz. Old, new, local and international sounds will soothe the soul as delicious food is devoured. Fine live performances to be expected.

25% OFF TOTAL | Max 4 | FRI ✓ | SAT ✓ | SUN | ▲ — European

CAFÉ ROUGE 02920 497 638
2 Mermaid Quay, Cardiff, CF10 5BZ

An attractive restaurant, a boulevard café or a Parisian-style wine bar; however you see Café Rouge, consistently excellent classic French dishes are always guaranteed.

25% OFF TOTAL | Max 6 | FRI ✓ | SAT ✓ | ✱ | ▲ — French

CAFÉ ROUGE 02920 236 574
13 Upper East Side, Cardiff, CF10 1EW

An attractive restaurant, a boulevard café or a Parisian-style wine bar; however you see Café Rouge, consistently excellent classic French dishes are always guaranteed.

25% OFF TOTAL | Max 6 | FRI ✓ | SAT ✓ | ✱ — French

THE CAPTAIN'S WIFE 02920 530 066
Beach Road, Swanbridge, Penarth, CF64 5UG

This Vintage Inn oozes rural charm and rustic character. The picturesque surroundings provide the perfect backdrop for savouring the hearty, seasonal pub-food on the menu.

25% OFF TOTAL | FRI ✓ | SAT ✓ | SUN | ▲ — Modern British

CARDAMOM INDIAN RESTAURANT 02920 233 506
442c Cowbridge Road, Victoria Park, Cardiff, CF5 1JN

Expect fine food and wonderfully friendly service in a hospitable environment. Warm welcomes and delicious Indian dishes make this a winning place to dine.

2FOR1 MAIN COURSE | FRI ✓ | SAT ✓ — Indian

CASA BIANCA ☎02920 492 817
175 City Road, Cardiff, CF24 3JB

Casa Bianca is a fusion of authentic Italian cuisine and fine dining. The ambience is intimate, with soft lighting, candles, music and crisp linen adorning every table.

25% OFF TOTAL | Max 4 | FRI ☎ | SAT ☎ — Italian

THE CASTELL MYNACH 01443 237 395
Llantrisant Road, Groesfaen, Pontyclun, CF72 8PN

Strada offers fresh, bold dishes inspired by flavours of Italian city life! Try the hand-stretched, stone baked pizzas, addictive pastas and risottos, great share plates and much more. *Excludes Pizzettas.

25% OFF TOTAL | FRI ✓ | SAT ✓ | SUN | ▲ — Modern British

COACH & HORSES 01633 680 070
Newport Road, Castleton, Nr Cardiff, CF3 2UQ

Beefeater Grill are one of the UK's best-loved restaurants welcoming guests for almost 40 years in over 130 locations nationwide. *Excludes Breakfast, Light Bites, Bar menu, set menus and all other offers.

2FOR1 MAIN COURSE | Max 6 | FRI ✓ | SAT × | ▲ — Modern British

DALCHINI ☎02920 471 224
10 Mackintosh Place, Cardiff, CF24 4RQ

Excellent-quality Indian food without the expensive price tag, Dalchini serves up seriously tasty curry to a large loyal following of diners. Supremely tasty dishes guaranteed.

2FOR1 MAIN COURSE | FRI × | SAT × | SUN | ▲ — Indian

THE DINING ROOM @ LLECHWEN HALL HOTEL ☎01443 742 050
Llechwen Hall Hotel, Nr Pontypridd, CF37 4HP

Awarded 1 AA Rosette, this is a fine place to enjoy a light lunch, substantial breakfast or a good dinner with excellent views across the valleys at this hotel tucked in a beautiful corner of South Wales.

50% OFF FOOD | Max 4 | FRI ✱ | SAT ✱ | ▲ — British

EL FARO TAPAS ☎01792 366 665
650 Mumbles Road, Swansea, SA3 4EA

Whether you are new to tapas or are already a fan of regional Spanish cuisine and are looking for new flavours to try, El Faro offers a unique, fun dining experience and truly delicious food.

2FOR1 3 COURSES | FRI ✓ | SAT × — Spanish

FFRESH BAR & RESTAURANT
☎02920 636 465

Wales Millennium Centre, Cardiff, CF10 5AL

Friendly staff deliver fresh and delicious lunches and dinners, along with an exceptional range of drinks. The home of great food at the heart of Cardiff Bay. *Offer not available for pre-theatre dining.

2FOR1 3 COURSES | FRI ✱ | SAT ✱ | SUN | ✱ | ▲ — Welsh

FILINI @ RADISSON BLU
☎02920 454 777

Radisson Blu Cardiff, Cardiff, CF10 2FL

Expect exquisite, modern Italian and Sardinian cuisine, as this popular restaurant merges local produce with Italian flavours to create mouth-watering dishes to delight the taste buds.

50% OFF FOOD | ♟6 | FRI ✓ | SAT ✓ — Italian

THE GLOBE INN
☎01656 773 344

2 Bridgend Road, Porthcawl, CF36 5RN

Explicitly known for its quality food and excellent service, the Globe Inn is a well-established place to drink and dine in Newton. Well worth travelling for, this is a great place for a family night out.

25% OFF TOTAL | ♟4 | FRI ✱ | SAT × | SUN — British

HAVELI
☎02920 482 882

157 City Road, Cardiff, CF24 3BQ

Using seductive spices, experienced chefs create innovative and contemporary pan-Asian cuisine. Fragrant, flavourful dishes are produced from fine ingredients and delivered in this stylish setting.

25% OFF TOTAL | ♟10 | FRI ✓ | SAT ✓ | ✱ — Pan-Asian

HAVELI
☎01443 449 779

Coedcae Lane, Pontyclun, CF72 9EW

By incorporating superb Indian cuisine, exceptional customer service and a luxurious setting, the team at Haveli hope to create a fine dining experience that is second to none.

25% OFF TOTAL | ♟8 | FRI ✓ | SAT ✓ — Indian

HENRY'S CAFÉ BAR
☎02920 224 672

Park Chambers, Park Place, Cardiff, CF10 3DN

An oasis for every type of person with a delicious, well-prepared menu ideal for lunch, dinner or a light snack. Henry's also boasts extensive wine and champagne lists and a choice of cocktails to die for.

25% OFF TOTAL | ♟10 | FRI ✓ | SAT ✓ | ▲ — European

HODGES BAR @ MERCURE
☎02920 435 000

Holland House, 24-26 Newport Rd, Cardiff, CF24 0DD

Enjoy a drink in an intimate setting while sampling a number of delicious refreshments and wholesome bar meals from this hotel-bar's extensive menu selection.

50% OFF FOOD | ♟4 | FRI ✓ | SAT × — International

HODGES RESTAURANT @ MERCURE
☎02920 435 000

Holland House, 24-26 Newport Rd, Cardiff, CF24 0DD

Guests can enjoy contemporary British cuisine including quality steaks and fresh seafood at this hotel-restaurant. Delicious food is served in an intimate and comfortable setting. Awarded 2 AA Rosettes.

50% OFF FOOD | ♟4 | FRI ✓ | SAT × — International

ICHIBAN
☎02920 668 833

201 Cowbridge Road East, Canton, Cardiff, CF11 9AJ

Get some welcome relief from stodgy takeaway fare and try some healthy, fresh Japanese cuisine at this eat-in restaurant. Ichiban is Japanese for 'number one', and sums up their top-notch food and service.

25% OFF TOTAL | ♟4 | FRI ✱ | SAT ✱ | SUN | ✱ — Japanese

INDUS
☎02920 226 687

147 East Cowbridge Road, Cardiff, CF11 9AH

Chef recommendations feature alongside traditional classic dishes in this superb Indian restaurant, from the authentic bhuna and korma dishes to the more unusual stuffed aubergines and koftas.

2FOR1 MAIN COURSE | FRI ✓ | SAT ✓ — Indian

K2 INDIAN RESTAURANT
☎01792 465 015

91-92 Mansel St, Swansea, SA1 5TZ

Providing treats for both the eyes and the palate, K2 Indian Restaurant successfully creates authentic dishes for every diner. Each entry on the menu will provide mouth-watering experiences.

2FOR1 MAIN COURSE | FRI ✓ | SAT ✓ — Indian

KAFELA
☎02920 611 633

65 Merthyr Road, Whitchurch, Cardiff, CF14 1DD

A warm and inviting Indian restaurant that combines its low-key, unassuming and cosy atmosphere with a good array of dishes that include excellent vegetarian options and signature specials.

2FOR1 MAIN COURSE | FRI ✱ | SAT ✱ — Indian

THE KINGS ARMS
☎02920 890 202

Church Road, Pentyrch, CF15 9QF

The Kings Arms is a traditional Welsh longhouse pub situated in the leafy village of Pentyrch. The delicious, fresh locally sourced food found on the menu is definitely worth a special trip.

25% OFF TOTAL | ♟6 | FRI ✓ | SAT ✓ | SUN | ▲ — British

KISMET INDIAN CUISINE
02920 481 665

24 City Road, Cardiff, CF24 3DL

A well-established Indian restaurant situated in Cardiff. Here the kitchen staff pride themselves on thorough, well-flavoured dishes that have been crafted from the most authentic of recipes.

50% OFF FOOD | FRI ✓ | SAT ✓ — Indian

LA BAGUETTE DU JOUR
☎01792 651 165

9 Caer Street, Castle Square, Swansea, SA1 3PP

Simple, high-quality lunches are the order of the day here at La Baguette du Jour, where an array of international flavours are created from fresh, with crisp, colourful ingredients.

2FOR1 3 COURSES | FRI ✓ | SAT ✓ | ▲ — International

LA LUPA
☎02920 223 697

155 Cowbridge Road East, Cardiff, CF11 9AH

La Lupa serves rustic Italian cuisine to a loyal following of locals in the area. The kitchen delicately put together individual flavours to create some of the tastiest food in Cardiff.

25% OFF TOTAL | ♟4 | FRI ▮ | SAT × | SUN | ▲ — Italian

LA TASCA
☎02920 230 087

The Old Brewery Quarter, Cardiff, CF10 1FG

Quintessentially Spanish, La Tasca's fresh and exciting menu offers something for everyone. Their tapas dishes are sincerely authentic, while their paellas always deliver on flavour.

25% OFF TOTAL | ♟8 | FRI ✓ | SAT × | ▲ — Spanish

LAS HAVANAS
☎02920 493 337

17-19 City Road, Roath, Cardiff, CF24 3BJ

An exciting, innovative and refreshing approach to Latin cooking, crafted with passion and flair. Traditional recipes, adapted into contemporary dishes that still retain their superbly authentic quality.

50% OFF FOOD | ♟4 | FRI ✓ | SAT ✓ | SUN | ✱ | ▲ — Tapas

LOCH FYNE
☎01446 776 070

Stalling Down, Cowbridge, CF71 7DT

From the roadside oyster bar that once was, Loch Fyne restaurants now successfully inject energy and passion into great food and wonderful flavours, whilst ensuring their seafood is sustainably sourced.

25% OFF TOTAL | ♟4 | FRI ✱ | SAT ✱ | ▲ — Seafood

THE LONGBOW
01443 233 952

Magden Park, Gwaun Elai, CF72 8XL

Beefeater Grill are one of the UK's best-loved restaurants welcoming guests for almost 40 years in over 130 locations nationwide. *Excludes Breakfast, Light Bites, Bar menu, set menus and all other offers.

2FOR1 MAIN COURSE | ♟6 | FRI ✓ | SAT × | ▲ — Modern British

THE LOUNGE BAR @ PARK INN
☎02920 589 988

Park Inn Cardiff North, Cardiff, CF23 9XF

This hotel lounge is the perfect place to enjoy a cocktail or draught beer with friends and colleagues, or for a nightcap and light snack before bed. Unwind in a casual and friendly atmosphere.

50% OFF FOOD | ♟10 | FRI ✓ | SAT ✓ — International

MAHARANI RESTAURANT
☎01792 648 509
81 St Helen's Road, Swansea, SA1 4BQ
Maharani Indian Restaurant serves up authentic Indian cuisine with a smile. They offer fresh and flavoursome curries. So when in Swansea and craving a curry, look no further than Maharani Indian Restaurant.

25% OFF TOTAL | 8 | FRI × | SAT × | SUN | * | Indian

MANGO HOUSE CARDIFF
☎02920 232 266
Grand Hotel, Westgate Street, Cardiff, CF10 1DD
Indian food lovers will be delighted with the freshly prepared recipes here, offering diners a wonderful array of dishes created from the flavours and spices of the subcontinent.

2FOR1 MAIN COURSE | FRI ✓ | SAT ✓ | * | Indian

MEZZA LUNA
☎02920 472 772
159 City Road, Cardiff, CF23 9JD
A friendly, open environment makes Mezza Luna a charming place to dine, without having to worry about pretence or formality. Live belly dancing performances make this a must.

2FOR1 MAIN COURSE | FRI × | SAT × | Moroccan/ Lebanese

MIA PORTO DUE
☎02920 227 147
Old Brewery Quarter, Cardiff, CF10 1FG
The Caramella family are known throughout Cardiff for their traditional Italian restaurants, and pride themselves in knowing about good food and wine, which Mia Porto Due most definitely has.

2FOR1 MAIN COURSE | FRI | SAT × | Mediterranean

MIMOSA KITCHEN & BAR
☎02920 491 900
Mermaid Quay, Cardiff Bay, Cardiff, CF10 5BZ
A contemporary menu that also features traditional Welsh favourites, delivered with first-class service and a drinks portfolio of choice wines, classic cocktails and a selection of beers and spirits.

25% OFF TOTAL | 10 | FRI ✓ | SAT × | SUN | Modern British

MONKEY CAFÉ AND BAR
☎01792 480 822
13-14 Castle Street, Swansea, SA1 1JF
A fun-filled atmosphere makes for the perfect environment to eat exciting hot and cold snacks and BBQ food. Food that tastes so good it'll have you swinging from the trees.

50% OFF FOOD | FRI ✓ | SAT ✓ | International

MR G'S SOUL KITCHEN
☎02921 328 969
106 Bute Street, Cardiff, CF10 5AD
Mr G's Soul Kitchen is one of Cardiff's greatest restaurants and hotspot, situated in the city's bay. Mr G's brings something different to the Capital; with its mix of tongue-tickling food for the soul.

50% OFF FOOD | 4 | FRI × | SAT × | Caribbean

MULBERRY STREET RESTAURANT
☎02920 564 646
48 Hight Street, Cardiff, CF5 2DZ
Worldwide flavours come into play on the Mulberry Street Restaurant menu. Enjoy sensational, inspired flavours and memorable textures. Food is cooked fresh to order, guaranteeing exceptional quality.

2FOR1 3 COURSES | FRI ✓ | SAT * | SUN | International

PANTRUTHYN FARM
01656 860 133
Pencoed, Bridgend, CF35 5HY
Quality pub classics with a modern twist combine with a friendly and relaxed atmosphere to make this Table Table venue the perfect place for family gatherings or meeting friends.

2FOR1 MAIN COURSE | FRI ✓ | SAT ✓ | Modern British

PARADISO CAFÉ BAR & RESTAURANT
☎02920 488 070
8-10 Crwys Road, Cardiff, CF24 4NJ
Stylish Café Bar Restaurant that combines a mix of affordable Mediterranean eating with innovative design. This bustling three-storey venue also has a sun terrace for alfresco dining, coffee and cocktails.

25% OFF TOTAL | FRI ✓ | SAT ✓ | Mediterranean

PARK HOUSE
☎02920 224 343
20 Park Place, Cardiff, CF10 3DQ
Fine restaurant serving modern British food that uses locally sourced ingredients that are as fresh as possible, including the finest meats and vegetables of the season.

25% OFF TOTAL | 4 | FRI ✓ | SAT ✓ | British

PEACHY KEENS
☎01792 463 222
Little Wind Street, Swansea, SA1 1ED
All-you-can-eat buffet that serves a sumptuous array of freshly prepared salads, delicious starters, authentic main courses, and mouth watering desserts from around the globe.

25% OFF TOTAL | 8 | FRI ✓ | SAT | International

PEARL OF THE ORIENT
☎02920 498 080
First Floor, Mermaid Quay, Cardiff Bay, CF10 5BZ
A formal fine dining experience is on offer at this delightful oriental restaurant. Live piano music enhances the characterful atmosphere, making this an ideal place to enjoy an array of dishes.

25% OFF TOTAL | 4 | FRI ✓ | SAT * | Oriental

PENTREBACH HOUSE
01443 693 616
Pentrebach, Merthyr Tydfil, CF48 4BD
Quality pub classics with a modern twist combine with a friendly and relaxed atmosphere to make this Table Table venue the perfect place for family gatherings or meeting friends.

2FOR1 MAIN COURSE | FRI ✓ | SAT ✓ | Modern British

PIPIS GREEK RESTAURANT
☎02920 229 016
31-32 Caroline Street, Cardiff, CF10 1FF
Pop into Pipis for a fresh coffee and croissant; perfect for a touch of the European charm in the morning. Offers freshly baked filo pastries stuffed full of tasty treats, such as spinach and feta cheese.

25% OFF TOTAL | 6 | FRI | SAT | SUN | * | Greek

THE PLYMOUTH ARMS
02920 569 173
St Fagans, Cardiff, CF5 6DU
This Vintage Inn oozes rural charm and rustic character. The picturesque surroundings provide the perfect backdrop for savouring the hearty, seasonal pub-food on the menu.

25% OFF TOTAL | FRI ✓ | SAT ✓ | SUN | Modern British

PORTO DUE SWANSEA
☎01792 475 767
8-14 College Street, Swansea, SA1 5AE
At Porto Due Swansea you can expect to enjoy a unique interactive dining experience where exquisite meals are served cooking at the table on super-heated natural volcanic stones.

2FOR1 MAIN COURSE | FRI | SAT | Mediterranean

PREZZO
02920 397 512
14 Bridge Street, St Davids, Cardiff, CF10 2EF
With a character all of its own, Prezzo oozes contemporary style and enduring charm. Signature pastas, stone-baked pizzas and classic Italian dishes promise a perfect dining choice for the whole family.

2FOR1 MAIN COURSE | FRI × | SAT × | Italian

PREZZO
02920 227 785
106 St Mary Street, Cardiff, CF10 9NQ
With a character all of its own, Prezzo oozes contemporary style and enduring charm. Signature pastas, stone-baked pizzas and classic Italian dishes promise a perfect dining choice for the whole family.

2FOR1 MAIN COURSE | FRI × | SAT × | Italian

PUCCINI
☎02920 493 031
120 Albany Road, Cardiff, CF24 3RU
Come dine at this calming oasis where an extensive tapas menu and a real assortment of Mediterranean dishes are on offer. A dining area reminiscent of Italy is the ideal setting for an intimate meal.

25% OFF TOTAL | 4 | FRI ✓ | SAT ✓ | SUN | * | Mediterranean

RAGLANS AT COPTHORNE HOTEL
☎02920 599 100
Copthorne Way, Culverhouse Cross, Cardiff, CF5 6DH
It's easy to see how this quietly stylish restaurant has won its 2 AA Rosettes. Great food and fine wine make an outstanding combination, whilst the lakeside setting is perfect for intimate dining.

25% OFF TOTAL | 6 | FRI ✓ | SAT ✓ | International

RAZZI RESTAURANT @ HILTON
☎ 02920 646 300

Hilton Hotel Cardiff, Kingsway, Cardiff, CF10 3HH

Experience a delicious and flavoursome menu featuring local specialities and the best of British and international cuisine, changed on a weekly basis to allow for the freshest ingredients.

25% OFF TOTAL | 6 | FRI | SAT | Welsh

RBG @ PARK INN
☎ 02920 589 988

Park Inn Cardiff North, Cardiff, CF23 9XF

Known for serving some of the best gourmet burgers in town, RBG at the Park Inn Hotel in Cardiff's city centre is a stylish and modern restaurant and grill. Delicious, convenient and affordable food.

50% OFF FOOD | 10 | FRI ✓ | SAT ✓ | ✱ | Contemporary

RESTAURANT AND BAR @ MERCURE
☎ 0844 815 9081

Mercure Swansea, Phoenix Way, Swansea, SA7 9EG

Unwind in The Restaurant and Bar at the Mercure Swansea over coffee or a bite to eat. The individually styled restaurant offers a wide selection of internationally inspired dishes.

2FOR1 MAIN COURSE | FRI ✓ | SAT × | SUN | International

REVOLUCION DE CUBA
☎ 0800 6300 860

The Friary, Cardiff, CF10 3FA

Grab your amigos and tuck into delicious Latin-influenced food, served seven days a week: from a sneaky lunchtime mojito and burrito to post-work street food and small plates.

25% OFF TOTAL | 6 | FRI × | SAT × | Cuban

SALTHOUSE ON THE SQUARE
☎ 01656 783 380

The Square, Porthcawl, CF36 3BW

Fresh, affordable food on offer at Salthouse on the Square. An eclectic blend of traditional and modern European dishes occupy a tastefully put-together menu. Relaxing lunches and memorable evenings.

25% OFF TOTAL | 4 | FRI ✱ | SAT ✱ | British

SPICE QUARTER
☎ 02920 220 075

The Old Brewery Quarter, Cardiff, CF10 1FG

A rare, authentic Indian dining experience. An exquisite selection of meals from traditional old favourites to exiting specials are created by original chefs recruited from Delhi and Bombay.

25% OFF TOTAL | 6 | FRI ✱ | SAT ✱ | Indian

STRADA
02920 482 112

24 Mermaid Quay, Cardiff, CF10 5BZ

Strada offers fresh, bold dishes inspired by flavours of Italian city life! Try the hand-stretched, stone baked pizzas, addictive pastas and risottos, great share plates and much more. *Excludes Pizzettas.

25% OFF TOTAL | 6 | FRI ✓ | SAT × | Italian

SURMA INDIAN RESTAURANT
☎ 01792 469 111

30 St Helens Road, Swansea, SA1 4AP

Effective recipes create deliciously popular and tasty Indian dishes at Surma Indian restaurant. Classic favourite curry dishes, such as the bhuna or the vindaloo, feature as strong contenders on the menu.

2FOR1 MAIN COURSE | FRI ✓ | SAT ✓ | ✱ | Indian

THE TRAVELLER'S REST
02920 859 021

Thornhill, Caerphilly, CF83 1LY

This Vintage Inn oozes rural charm and rustic character. The picturesque surroundings provide the perfect backdrop for savouring the hearty, seasonal pub-food on the menu.

25% OFF TOTAL | FRI ✓ | SAT ✓ | SUN | Modern British

TRIBE TRIBE
☎ 02920 666 111

169 Cowbridge Road, Cardiff, CF11 9AH

Enjoy an atmosphere that is contemporary yet relaxed, as excellent staff here strive to bridge the gastronomical divide between Africa and the rest of the world with an array of flavoursome dishes.

2FOR1 MAIN COURSE | FRI | SAT | SUN | ✱ | African

WALKABOUT
☎ 02920 727 930

65-74 St Mary's Street, Cardiff, CF10 1FA

Walkabout is famous for its characteristically Australian atmosphere and well-rounded menu. From live sport with a juicy burger to some Aussie kangaroo skewers, you'll find it hard to tear yourself away.

25% OFF TOTAL | 10 | FRI ✓ | SAT ✓ | International

WALKABOUT
☎ 01792 450 850

5-6 Castle Square, Swansea, SA1 1DW

Walkabout is famous for its characteristically Australian atmosphere and well-rounded menu. From live sport with a juicy burger to some Aussie kangaroo skewers, you'll find it hard to tear yourself away.

25% OFF TOTAL | FRI ✓ | SAT ✓ | International

WALSTON CASTLE
02920 593 896

Port Road, Nantisaf, Wenvoe, Cardiff, CF5 6DD

Beefeater Grill are one of the UK's best-loved restaurants welcoming guests for almost 40 years in over 130 locations nationwide. *Excludes Breakfast, Light Bites, Bar menu, set menus and all other offers.

2FOR1 MAIN COURSE | 6 | FRI ✓ | SAT × | Modern British

THE WATERFRONT
01792 452 514

The Waterfront Development, Langdon Rd, Swansea, SA1 8PL

Beefeater Grill are one of the UK's best-loved restaurants welcoming guests for almost 40 years in over 130 locations nationwide. *Excludes Breakfast, Light Bites, Bar menu, set menus and all other offers.

2FOR1 MAIN COURSE | 6 | FRI ✓ | SAT × | Modern British

Gwent & Monmouthshire

THE ASHBRIDGE
01633 876 678

Avondale Road, Pontrhydyrun, Cwmbran, NP44 1DE

Quality pub classics with a modern twist combine with a friendly and relaxed atmosphere to make this Table Table venue the perfect place for family gatherings or meeting friends.

2FOR1 MAIN COURSE | FRI ✓ | SAT ✓ | Modern British

BALTI NITE TANDOORI
☎ 01495 271 234

8 Gladstone Street, Cross Keys, NP11 7PA

Friendly, bright Indian restaurant not far from Crosskeys station. Does the simple things very well, with a good amount of kick where it's required and a classically broad range of dishes.

2FOR1 MAIN COURSE | FRI ✓ | SAT ✓ | Indian

THE BELL AT CAERLEON
☎ 01633 420 613

The Bell Inn, Newport, NP18 1QQ

Over 400 years old, The Bell takes pride in its ancient coaching inn setting in the beautiful Caerleon. The award-winning restaurant offers a seasonally rotating menu that makes use of local Welsh produce.

25% OFF TOTAL | 4 | FRI × | SAT × | ✱ | Welsh

THE BELL AT SKENFRITH
☎ 01600 750 235

The Bell, Skenfrith, Monmouth, NP7 8UH

With 2 AA Rosettes to its name, this restaurant is known for its ranging, fresh menu and superbly accomplished cooking, with a focus on sourcing local and seasonal classics.

2FOR1 3 COURSES | FRI ✱ | SAT ✱ | SUN | British

BISTRO PREGO
☎ 01600 712 600

7 Church Street, Monmouth, NP25 3BX

Swiftly gaining a reputation for excellence due to their outstanding range of fine food and wine, with a menu offering modern European dishes that are a real delight to the senses.

25% OFF TOTAL | 4 | FRI ✓ | SAT ✱ | Modern European

BLADES RESTAURANT
☎ 01291 622 497

Beaufort Hotel, Beaufort Square, Chepstow, NP16 5EP

A family-run restaurant where the staff pride themselves on their efficient and friendly service and great value for money. The modern à la carte menu has won the restaurant its award-winning status.

25% OFF TOTAL | 8 | FRI ✓ | SAT ✓ | SUN | ✱ | British

THE CLYTHA ARMS
☎ 01873 840 206

Clytha, Old Raglan Road, Abergavenny, NP7 9BW

Friendly and homely food-led pub between Raglan and Abergavenny; enjoy the finely cooked, eclectic dishes, from musky wild boar in rioja to a zippy Caribbean fruit curry with crayfish.

2FOR1 MAIN COURSE | FRI ✓ | SAT ✓ | SUN | International

To understand what the restaurant icons mean, please see the inside back cover.

THE COLDRA
01633 411 390
Chepstow Road, Langstone, Newport, NP18 2NX
Beefeater Grill are one of the UK's best-loved restaurants welcoming guests for almost 40 years in over 130 locations nationwide. *Excludes Breakfast, Light Bites, Bar menu, set menus and all other offers.

2FOR1 MAIN COURSE | 6 | FRI ✓ | SAT ✗ | ▲ — Modern British

THE DRAGONFLY
01633 810 611
Lakeside Drive, Coedkernew, Newport, NP10 8BB
This Vintage Inn oozes rural charm and rustic character. The picturesque surroundings provide the perfect backdrop for savouring the hearty, seasonal pub-food on the menu.

25% OFF TOTAL | FRI ✓ | SAT ✓ | SUN | ▲ — Modern British

THE FARMER'S DAUGHTER
☎ 01633 892 800
Croescarneinion Farm, Bassaleg, NP10 8RR
Fantastically personable and relaxed restaurant tucked away on the land of a working farm. With great care, attention to detail, and flexibility to diners' tastes, the restaurant is a distinctive treat.

25% OFF TOTAL | 4 | FRI ✓ | SAT ✱ | SUN | ✱ | ▲ — Welsh

THE GROES WEN INN
01633 400 978
Penhow, Caldicot, NP26 3AD
This Vintage Inn oozes rural charm and rustic character. The picturesque surroundings provide the perfect backdrop for savouring the hearty, seasonal pub-food on the menu.

25% OFF TOTAL | FRI ✓ | SAT ✓ | SUN | ▲ — Modern British

THE HALL INN
☎ 01291 672 381
Old Raglan Road, Gwehelog, NP15 1RB
Enjoy a friendly atmosphere, superb, flavoursome and savoury dishes of great pub fare, and a pleasingly diverse array of real ales, draughts, wines and spirits at the bar.

25% OFF TOTAL | 4 | FRI ✓ | SAT ✱ | SUN | ✱ | ▲ — British

HARPERS RESTAURANT & BAR
☎ 01633 412 777
The Holiday Inn, The Coldra, Newport, NP18 2YG
Enjoy a traditional Welsh breakfast, light lunch or a delicious evening meal at this great hotel-restaurant. Choose something sumptuous off the menu and unwind whilst perusing the ranging drinks menu.

25% OFF TOTAL | 6 | FRI ✓ | SAT ✓ — European

THE KOH I NOOR TANDOORI RESTAURANT
☎ 01633 258 028
164 Chepstow Road, Newport, NP19 8EG
The Koh-I-Noor specialise in traditional Indian, Bangladeshi, Balti and Tandoori dishes prepared from fresh ingredients and spices by expert staff.

25% OFF TOTAL | FRI ✗ | SAT ✗ | SUN | ✱ — Indian

LA CANTINA
☎ 01291 673 433
61 Bridge Street, Usk, NP15 1BQ
La Cantina are a local family run business who pride themselves on the quality of their food, service and value for money.Come and enjoy your meal in a friendly, relaxed continental atmosphere.

50% OFF FOOD | FRI ✓ | SAT ✓ — European

THE LODGE RESTAURANT @ CELTIC MANOR
☎ 01633 410 262
The Lodge Clubhouse, Coldra Woods, NP18 1HQ
In this restaurant at Celtic Manor, home of the 2010 Ryder Cup, you'll find luxury and comfort along with superb views. An accomplished, rustic British menu features succulent steaks and fresh seafood.

25% OFF TOTAL | 4 | FRI ✓ | SAT ✱ | SUN | ▲ — British

MANGO HOUSE MAGOR
☎ 01633 882 655
Glenroy House, Caldicot, NP26 3HY
Sample the flavour and spice of the Indian subcontinent through various well-prepared and sumptuous dishes. Traditional ingredients and recipes are used to create fine, high-quality cuisine.

2FOR1 MAIN COURSE | FRI ✓ | SAT ✓ | ✱ | ▲ — Indian

MINT LEAF
☎ 01633 892 377
68 Tregwilym Road, Newport, NP10 9EJ
Satisfying cuisine is on offer at the Mint Leaf, where house specials feature as strong contenders on a superbly put-together menu. Unusual, imaginative curries appear for the adventurous diner.

50% OFF FOOD | 4 | FRI ✗ | SAT ✗ — Indian

THE MISBAH
☎ 01600 714 940
9 Priory Street, Monmouth, NP25 3BR
The Misbah is a family-run restaurant offering authentic Bangladeshi cuisine and is located in a Grade II listed building in the heart of Monmouth, within the picturesque Wye valley.

2FOR1 MAIN COURSE | FRI ✗ | SAT ✗ | ▲ — Bangladeshi/Indian

MORGAN'S RESTAURANT
☎ 01291 635 265
St Pierre Park, Hayesgate, Chepstow, NP16 6YA
This restaurant's contemporary menu is inflected by the tender, hearty style of traditional Welsh cuisine. Enjoy the savoury, fresh flavours in the serene, rolling green of the South Wales countryside.

25% OFF TOTAL | 6 | FRI ▯ | SAT ▯ | ✱ | ▲ — International

THE MUGHAL SPICE
☎ 01291 623 222
13-14 Nelson Street, Chepstow, NP16 5HT
Impressive Indian restaurant serving a fine selection of Indian curry dishes, from tandoori to biryani and balti dishes. Range of rices, naans and sundries offer the perfect accompaniment to any choice.

25% OFF TOTAL | 4 | FRI ✗ | SAT ✗ | SUN | ✱ | ▲ — Indian

OLD FERRY INN
☎ 01291 622 474
Beachley, Chepstow, NP16 7HH
Valuing hospitality and service, this family-run business serves a variety of dishes: from hearty winter warmers to old pub favourites such as battered haddock and chips.

2FOR1 MAIN COURSE | FRI ✓ | SAT ✓ | SUN | ▲ — British

PEACHY KEENS
☎ 01633 262 222
62-65 Bridge St, Newport, NP20 1AZ
All-you-can-eat buffet that serves a sumptuous array of freshly prepared salads, delicious starters, authentic main courses, and mouth-watering desserts from around the globe.

25% OFF TOTAL | FRI ✓ | SAT ▯ — International

PHOENIX GARDEN
☎ 01633 431 166
9 High Street, Newport, NP18 1AG
Sizzling Chinese cuisine is on offer at the Phoenix Garden Restaurant in Newport, with a great selection of duck, chicken, beef and vegetable dishes all guaranteed to be fresh and flavoursome.

2FOR1 MAIN COURSE | FRI ✗ | SAT ✗ | SUN — Chinese

RAFTERS RESTAURANT @ CELTIC MANOR
☎ 01633 410 262
The Twenty Ten Clubhouse, Coldra Woods, NP18 1HQ
Occupied with modern elegance, this outstanding restaurant boasts a charming character that will be enjoyed by all guests. Be blown away by exquisite Welsh beef and fresh seafood. 1 AA Rosette.

25% OFF TOTAL | 4 | FRI ✓ | SAT ✱ | SUN | ▲ — British

THE RED LANTERN
☎ 01291 627 726
Bank Street, Chepstow, NP16 5EL
A fabulous restaurant that has introduced the great nuances of Chinese cuisine to the local area. Their Peking, Szechuan and Guangdong dishes are all delicious, whilst the fried Dover sole is incredible.

25% OFF TOTAL | 10 | FRI ✱ | SAT ✱ | ✱ | ▲ — Chinese

RESTAURANT 1862
☎ 0845 388 1861
Cross Ash, Nr Abergavveny NP7 8PB
The picturesque hamlet of Cross Ash is home to this truly gourmet cuisine experience brought guests by Owner and Head Chef Simon King; fine dining is very much his forte. Awarded 2 AA Rosettes.

2FOR1 MAIN COURSE | FRI ✓ | SAT ✱ — British

THE RIVERSIDE HOTEL
☎ 01600 715 577
Riverside Hotel, Cinderhill Street, Monmouth, NP25 5EY
A warm and lovely inn, where the restaurant is smart and accommodating and serves good, accomplished fare. You'll enjoy trying out the array of beers and ciders behind the bar to wash it all down.

25% OFF TOTAL | 4 | FRI ✓ | SAT ✓ | SUN | ▲ — British

THE THREE MUGHALS
☎ 01633 894 365
Western Valley Road, Rogerstone, Newport, NP10 9DS
India has its own distinctive cuisine that has drawn culinary influences from the country's multitude of historical intruders; this restaurant enhances each and every flavour and spice for your enjoyment.

25% OFF TOTAL | 4 | FRI ✗ | SAT ✗ | SUN — Indian

TONY'S PIZZERIA
01495 272 800
Risca Road, Crosskeys, Newport, NP11 7BT
Pizza is the hero at Tony's Pizzeria, but there also pastas and a selection of naughty sides to tempt your taste buds. If you haven't overindulged, be sure to try one of Tony's freshly blended milkshakes!

25% OFF TOTAL | FRI ✓ | SAT ✓ — Italian

ZEST RESTAURANT
01291 625 261
Marriott St Pierre Hotel, Chepstow, NP16 6YA
The second of two restaurants at the Marriott St Pierre offering contemporary dining in a relaxed environment. Start your day with a morning coffee and pastry, or join them for lunch and dinner.

25% OFF TOTAL | 6 | FRI ▮ | SAT ▮ | * | ▲ — English and Continental

Gwynedd

BAE ABERMAW
01341 280 550
Panorama Road, Barmouth, LL42 1DQ
The Bae Abermaw is one of the most elegant Victorian buildings in the area. Beautiful gardens and spectacular views accompany a delectable, home-cooked evening meal in the hotel's stylish dining area.

25% OFF TOTAL | 2 | FRI ✓ | SAT ✓ — British

BISHOPSGATE HOTEL AND RESTAURANT
01248 810 302
Castle Street, Beaumaris, LL58 8BB
This 18th Century town house makes for the perfect little hotel in Beaumaris, perfect for holidays or business trips. The AA Rosette restaurant is a fantastic place to feast on delicious Welsh produce.

2FOR1 3 COURSES | FRI ✓ | SAT × | * | ▲ — British

FRONOLEU COUNTRY HOTEL
01341 422 361
Tabor, Dolgellau, LL40 2PS
A converted stable, Fronoleu Country Hotel restaurant offers a wide selection of delicious dishes, both lunch time and evenings.Only the finest cuts of Welsh lamb, beef and game and local fish as in season

25% OFF TOTAL | 4 | FRI ✓ | SAT ✓ — British

LITTLE ITALY RISTORANTE ITALIANO
01407 831 905
Amlwch Business Parc, Amlwch, LL68 9BQ
A very warm welcome from Little Italy in Amlwch. As the only Italian restaurant on the Isle of Anglesey, they strive to provide the most authentic and simply the best Italian dining experience.

25% OFF TOTAL | 6 | FRI × | SAT × | * — Italian

PARC BRITANNIA
01248 679 070
Parc Menai Road, Parc Menai, Bangor, LL57 4FA
Quality pub classics with a modern twist combine with a friendly and relaxed atmosphere to make this Table Table venue the perfect place for family gatherings or meeting friends.

2FOR1 MAIN COURSE | FRI ✓ | SAT ✓ — Modern British

PLAS-YN-DRE
01678 521 256
23 High Street, Bala, LL23 7LU
You can't miss the grand exterior of one of Bala's favourite pub restaurants. Pop inside for proper pub-grub using only the freshest, locally sourced ingredients with stellar service from the staff.

25% OFF TOTAL | 8 | FRI ▮ | SAT ▮ — British

RISTORANTE PULCINELLA
01248 362 807
Pier Promenade, Bangor, LL57 2SW
This lovely, Italian eatery is tucked away by Bangor's historic Pier, but is instantly recognisable with its pretty blue and white exterior. Pop inside for one of the best pizzas in town.

25% OFF TOTAL | 4 | FRI ✓ | SAT × | SUN — Italian

THE ROYAL SPORTSMAN
01766 512 015
131 High Street, Porthmadog, LL49 9HB
With a kitchen committed to using fresh Welsh produce and with two AA Rosettes behind its name, The Royal Sportsman is worth a special visit. Sample Dan Owen's exceptional menu and expect flawless service.

2FOR1 MAIN COURSE | FRI × | SAT × | SUN | * — British

SEIONT MANOR HOTEL
0845 072 7550
The Llwyn y Brain Restaurant, Llanrug, LL55 2AQ
Mouth-watering, decadent, double-AA Rosette dining in this magnificent country house, part of the Hand Picked Hotels group. The dining hall is one of remarkable character and charm. 2 AA Rosettes.

25% OFF TOTAL | 6 | FRI ✓ | SAT * — British

TRECASTELL HOTEL
01407 830 651
Bull Bay, Amlwch, LL68 9SA
Refuel after a day of sailing at this elegant venue, boasting stunning views of the sea. Warmly hospitable, the staff present diners with a menu that celebrates the best of Anglesey's produce.

25% OFF TOTAL | 6 | FRI × | SAT × | SUN — International

TREMEIFION VEGETARIAN HOTEL
01766 770 491
Soar Road, Talsarnau, LL47 6UH
Barbara Heywood's passion for vegan and vegetarian food emanates through her wonderfully varied and tasty menu. Much of the fruit, herbs and vegetables used come from the surrounding garden and orchard.

25% OFF TOTAL | 10 | FRI ✓ | SAT ✓ | * — Vegetarian

TYWYN BALTI
01654 711 007
2 College Green, Tywyn, LL36 9BS
Tywyn Balti offers authentic Indian cuisine. Whatever the occasion, a formal dinner, birthday party, regular night out, Tywyn Balti has all the ingredients to make your celebration a success.

25% OFF TOTAL | 10 | FRI ✓ | SAT ✓ — Indian

YR HARBWR
01286 662 462
Doc Fictoria, Balaclava Road, Caernarfon, LL55 1SQ
Quality pub classics with a modern twist combine with a friendly and relaxed atmosphere to make this Table Table venue the perfect place for family gatherings or meeting friends.

2FOR1 MAIN COURSE | FRI ✓ | SAT ✓ — Modern British

Powys

BRADFORD ARMS HOTEL
01691 830 582
North Road, Llanmynech, SY22 6EJ
This restaurant is beautifully set in the stunning landscape touching on the Welsh-English border, and has a diverse menu that serves hearty, high-quality food.

2FOR1 MAIN COURSE | FRI ▮ | SAT ▮ — British

GULSHAN
01686 627 744
40b Broad Street, Newtown, SY16 2BQ
With attentive and knowledgeable staff, delectable Indian cuisine and an lovely ambience to match, book now to discover why Gulshan is Newtown's favourite restaurant.

25% OFF TOTAL | 10 | FRI × | SAT × — Indian

LLANGOED HALL
01874 754 525
Llyswen, Brecon, LD3 0YP
Welsh lamb and beef, home-grown garden herbs and vegetables and other local produce all contribute to the superb dishes on offer at Llangoed Hall. Fresh, light and wholly elegant place to dine.

25% OFF TOTAL | 6 | FRI ✓ | SAT ▮ | ▲ — European

THE RAILWAY INN FORDEN
01938 580 237
Forden, nr Welshpool, SY21 8NN
With a newly refurbished Mediterranean style restaurant, The Railway Inn offers a great choice of food to suit most tastes, fish, steak, vegetarian and specialising in Italian cuisine.

25% OFF TOTAL | 10 | FRI ✓ | SAT ✓ | * | ▲ — British

Gourmet Society discount applies to the à la carte menu only, unless stated otherwise.

West Midlands

Shropshire

BARON OF BUCKNELL ☎01547 530 549
Chapel Lawn Road, Bucknell, SY7 0AH
Idyllically located in the pretty village of Bucknell, the stunning views of the rolling hills add to the character and charm of this country inn. Expect welcomes as warm as the crackling log fire inside.

2FOR1 MAIN COURSE | FRI ✓ | SAT ✱ | SUN | ▲ — British

THE BOYNE ARMS ☎01746 787 214
Burwarton, Bridgnorth, WV16 6QH
Traditional family hospitality in a fresh environment, using local ingredients to create a range of versatile menus. Also boasts a relaxing bar area offering a wide selection of real ales and wines.

2FOR1 MAIN COURSE | FRI ✱ | SAT ✱ | SUN | ▲ — British

BRIDGEWATER ARMS 01939 290 377
Wem Road, Harmer Hill, Shrewsbury, SY4 3DS
Quality pub classics with modern twists meets with a friendly and relaxed atmosphere to make this Table Table venue the perfect place for any occasion. *Excludes daytime & evening deals and festive menus.

2FOR1 MAIN COURSE | FRI ✓ | SAT ✓ — Modern British

CAFÉ SAFFRON ☎01743 246 753
25 Hills Lane, Shrewsbury, SY1 1QU
Well-experienced in India and Bangladesh, the chef transfers his exceptional knowledge into a British kitchen. Feast upon classic dishes with a modern twist. *Booking is essential.

2FOR1 MAIN COURSE | FRI × | SAT × | ✱ | ▲ — Indian

THE CASTLE HOTEL ☎01588 638 403
The Castle Hotel, Market Square, Bishops Castle, SY9 5BN
Guests can soak up the Shropshire rays in stunning south facing gardens, admire the quaint fish ponds or relax by the open fire. The food is healthy, fresh and quintessentially British.

25% OFF TOTAL | 👤 2 | FRI × | SAT × | ▲ — British

THE CROWN COUNTRY INN ☎01584 841 205
Munslow, Craven Arms, SY7 9ET
Historical inn producing a variety of traditional and exotic fare, including an ever-changing selection of daily specials. Dishes make use of fine ingredients that satisfy all guests. 2 AA Rosettes.

25% OFF TOTAL | 👤 4 | FRI ✓ | SAT ✱ | SUN | ▲ — European

THE CROWN INN ☎01588 640 271
Newcastle-on-Clun, Ludlow, SY7 8QL
Being worn out from a day of cycling, fishing or walking in the Clun Valley, head to the Crown Inn where wholesome fare and real ales will take the edge off your exhaustion. Wholly relaxing place.

25% OFF TOTAL | 👤 8 | FRI ✓ | SAT ✓ | SUN | ✱ — English/Gastro pub

DILRAZ THE EASTERN EXPERIENCE ☎01746 765 888
63 Whitburn Street, Bridgnorth, WV16 4QP
Complete with a contemporary twist, the recipes endorsed at this venue stand the test of time. Combining a variety of flavours from across India, chefs are devoted to preparing food of exceptional quality.

2FOR1 MAIN COURSE | FRI ▯ | SAT ▯ | SUN — Indian

DORRINGTON OLD HALL ☎01743 719 100
Main Road, Dorrington, Shrewsbury, SY5 7JD
Steeped in historicism, this 13th Century building plays host to contemporary décor and an affable ambience. Persian-influenced, the menu is bursting with spicy soups and hearty stews.

2FOR1 MAIN COURSE | FRI × | SAT × | ✱ | ▲ — Persian

EUSTON WAY 01952 201 075
Euston Way, Telford, TF3 4LY
Beefeater Grill are one of the UK's best-loved restaurants welcoming guests for almost 40 years in over 130 locations nationwide. *Excludes Breakfast, Light Bites, Bar menu, set menus and all other offers.

2FOR1 MAIN COURSE | 👤 6 | FRI ✓ | SAT × | ▲ — Modern British

FEATHERS HOTEL ☎01584 875 261
Bull Ring, Ludlow, SY8 1AA
Creative and imaginative menus drawn up from quality local ingredients. This popular and well-regarded restaurant is in a beautiful setting and serves flavourful, textured food. Awarded 1 AA Rosette.

25% OFF TOTAL | 👤 6 | FRI ▯ | SAT ▯ | ✱ — Fine Dining

FORELLES AT FISHMORE HALL ☎01584 875 148
Fishmore Road, Ludlow, SY8 3DP
Chef David Jaram has composed a menu of locally sourced delights, such as the traditional Shropshire breakfast. This 3 AA Rosette venue boasts breathtaking views of orangeries and luscious landscapes.

50% OFF FOOD | 👤 6 | FRI ✓ | SAT ✓ — British

GARTELLS AT THE SUN INN ☎01938 561 211
Marton, Welshpool, SY21 8JP
Modern and stylish family-run restaurant that ranges eclectically through modern English and Mediterranean flavours, with a firm emphasis on fresh, local produce.

25% OFF TOTAL | 👤 2 | FRI ✱ | SAT ✱ | SUN — British

GOURMET PASTY CO. N/A
26 St Mary's Street, Newport, TF10 7AB
By combining freshly baked traditional Cornish pasties, quality home-made sandwiches, salads and soups, the Gourmet Pasty Co. is making its mark and standing out from the usual fast food market.

25% OFF TOTAL | 👤 2 | FRI ✓ | SAT ✓ | SUN — British

GRANARY GRILL BAR & RESTAURANT ☎01952 852 107
Weston Park, Weston-under-Lizard, Nr Shifnal, TF11 8LE
Set in the historical Granary building, chefs conjure up everything from succulent steaks to Mediterranean classics in an open kitchen. The wine list is bursting and the home-made lemonade is divine.

25% OFF TOTAL | 👤 4 | FRI × | SAT × | SUN | ▲ — Contemporary

HANNAH RESTAURANT AND CATERING ☎01948 666 699
5 Green End, Whitchurch, SY13 1AD
A superbly accomplished Indian restaurant whose experience tells in their range of classic and more esoteric dishes. Welcoming and devotedly family-friendly, this venue delivers a truly authentic curry.

2FOR1 MAIN COURSE | FRI ✓ | SAT ✓ | ✱ | ▲ — Indian

HAWKSTONE RESTAURANT ☎01948 841 700
Hawkstone Park, Shrewsbury, SY4 5UY
Hawkstone Park is deeply nestled in the heart of the country. This elegant hotel-restaurant offers an array of mouth-watering dishes, from fresh salmon and sole roulade to pan-fried calves liver.

50% OFF FOOD | FRI × | SAT × | SUN | ▲ — International

THE HAYWARD ☎01743 353 107
The Lion Hotel, Shrewsbury, SY1 1UY
Michelin-recognised, this award-winning venue specialises in British and European cuisine. The combination of passion with the finest quality ingredients ensure that diners are in for a memorable treat.

2FOR1 MAIN COURSE | FRI ✱ | SAT × | SUN | ▲ — British

LA ROSA ☎01952 254 666
19 Church St, Wellington, Telford, TF1 2DL
An enchanting restaurant suitably catering for every occasion, be it a romantic evening out or a business lunch. Guests will find a magical blend of Italian cuisine and amiable service.

25% OFF TOTAL | 👤 4 | FRI × | SAT × | ▲ — Italian

LOCH FYNE ☎01743 277 140
Talbot House, Market Street, Shrewsbury, SY1 1LG
From the roadside oyster bar that once was, Loch Fyne restaurants now successfully inject energy and passion into great food and wonderful flavours, whilst ensuring their seafood is sustainably sourced.

25% OFF TOTAL | 👤 4 | FRI ✱ | SAT ✱ | ▲ — Seafood

OSCARS DINER ☎01952 200 577
Odeon Cinema, Foregate, Telford, TF3 4NE
The ideal location to party, this 1950s movie-themed diner is an eating experience with a twist. The Titanic burger comes highly recommended for the brave and the hungry.

2FOR1 MAIN COURSE | FRI ✓ | SAT ✓ — American

OSWALD'S CROSS
01691 663 180
Rods Meadow, Maeys y Clawdd, Oswestry, SY10 8NN
Quality pub classics with modern twists meets with a friendly and relaxed atmosphere to make this Table Table venue the perfect place for any occasion. *Excludes daytime & evening deals and festive menus.

2FOR1 MAIN COURSE | FRI ✓ | SAT ✓ — Modern British

PEN-Y-DYFFRYN HALL
01691 653 700
Rhydycroesau, Oswestry, SY10 7JD
Healthy, locally sourced, and organic produce form the basis of this fine dining establishment, where game and other traditional delights appear on the menu. Awarded 2 AA Rosettes

25% OFF TOTAL | 10 | FRI ✓ | SAT ✓ — Fine Dining

PEPPERS
01948 666 338
A41-A49 Prees Heath, Whitchurch, SY13 3JT
Curry fans will be in their element at this Indian restaurant. A vast array of delicious delights occupy the menu, whilst the staff offer friendly smiles and efficient service.

25% OFF TOTAL | 10 | FRI * | SAT * | SUN — Indian

PIZZA TWO FOUR
01691 654 693
24 Leg Street, Oswestry, SY11 2NN
The place to go for for finely prepared and presented pizzas, delivered in a welcoming environment. A cosy family-friendly pizzeria and pasta restaurant proving to be a firm favourite with customers.

2FOR1 MAIN COURSE | FRI | SAT * | SUN | * — Italian

PREZZO
01691 650 932
30 Church Street, Oswestry, SY11 2SP
With a character all of its own, Prezzo oozes contemporary style and enduring charm. Signature pastas, stone-baked pizzas and classic Italian dishes promise a perfect dining choice for the whole family.

2FOR1 MAIN COURSE | FRI × | SAT × — Italian

THE RAJ MAHAL
01691 652 566
26 Leg Street, Oswestry, SY11 2NN
Modern Indian restaurant and takeaway with a classic feel, serving dishes from traditional favourites to distinctive specialities; full of verve, flavour and warm welcomes.

2FOR1 3 COURSES | FRI | SAT | * — Indian

RBG @ PARK INN TELFORD
01952 429 988
The Park Inn, Forgegate, Telford, TF3 4NA
An added bonus to the Park Inn hotel, this is great quality grill-bar that offers tasty steaks and classic New York style cocktails. Expect great food and fantastic service.

25% OFF TOTAL | 6 | FRI ✓ | SAT ✓ | * — English and Continental

RENAISSANCE RESTAURANT
01743 354 289
29a Princess Street, Shrewsbury, SY1 1LW
A combination of fine food and a subtly elegant ambience. The chefs expertly demonstrate traditional English culinary skills, producing outstanding dishes bursting with flavour and heavenly aromas.

25% OFF TOTAL | 4 | FRI ✓ | SAT ✓ | SUN — British

RENDEZVOUS AT THE PARK
01948 661 800
The Old Mill, Whitchurch, SY13 1SH
Indulge in an exquisite pan-fried sea bass or chicken liver parfait at this social venue. Catch-up with friends at the weekend whilst enjoying the beautiful surroundings.

2FOR1 3 COURSES | FRI * | SAT * | SUN — European

ROMOLO ITALIAN RESTAURANT
01743 233 244
Victoria Quay, Victoria Avenue, Shrewsbury, SY1 1HH
A vibrant, buzzing Italian restaurant perfect for those casual dinner dates or the more intimate of evenings. *3 courses must be ordered from the à la carte menu.

25% OFF TOTAL | 4 | FRI × | SAT × — Italian

SARACENS AT HADNALL
01939 210 877
Shrewsbury Road, Hadnall, Shrewsbury, SY4 4AG
A charming, listed 18th-century coaching inn now plays host to an outstanding restaurant offering the most beautifully prepared and presented British and International cuisine. Awarded 1 AA Rosette.

25% OFF TOTAL | 4 | FRI ✓ | SAT * | SUN — International

SAROS RESTAURANT
01746 762 848
12 Moat Street, Hightown, Bridgnorth, WV16 4EP
A menu to be thoroughly savoured. Indian and Bangladeshi cuisine is created with a twist that makes your favourite dishes even tastier. Combines excellent food with great prices.

2FOR1 MAIN COURSE | FRI * | SAT * | * — Indian

SHAPLA RESTAURANT
01584 875 153
58 Broad Street, Ludlow, SY8 1NH
A great Indian restaurant that presents an appealing menu. Tasty traditional dishes can be enjoyed in attractive surroundings.

2FOR1 MAIN COURSE | FRI ✓ | SAT ✓ | * — Indian

SIR STEPHENS BRASSERIE
01952 250 700
The Whitehouse Hotel, Wellington, Telford, TF1 2NJ
A superb hotel brasserie where the kitchen makes use of the very best English and international flavours and culinary styles. Regular diners rarely get bored with the ever-changing menu.

50% OFF FOOD | 6 | FRI ✓ | SAT ✓ | SUN — International

THE SUN AT NORBURY
01588 650 680
Norbury, Bishops Castle, SY9 5DX
A renowned 'restaurant with rooms', this inn is the perfect place to both eat and stay. Focusing on the quality of good food, dishes are tenderly prepared and carefully presented for your enjoyment.

25% OFF TOTAL | 4 | FRI ✓ | SAT | SUN | * — European

THE SWAN AT FORTON
01952 812 169
Eccleshall Road, Newport, TF10 8BY
The contemporary menu of this 18th Century inn hosts culinary delights such as Sicilian vegetable and goats cheese tartlet. For the more robust palate, the beer-battered haddock fillet is a must try.

2FOR1 3 COURSES | FRI | SAT — British

TASTE OF PARADISE
01952 825 505
2-4 High Street, Newport, TF10 7AN
Simple, unpretentious Indian takeaway in Newport with an industrious approach. Serves an array of dishes (try the balti methi or sylhet bahaar, for specialities) and a helpful, friendly service.

2FOR1 MAIN COURSE | FRI × | SAT × — Indian

THREE FISH
01952 822 981
Stafford Road, Newport, TF10 9BY
Beefeater Grill are one of the UK's best-loved restaurants welcoming guests for almost 40 years in over 130 locations nationwide. *Excludes Breakfast, Light Bites, Bar menu, set menus and all other offers.

2FOR1 MAIN COURSE | 6 | FRI ✓ | SAT × — Modern British

TRAITORS GATE BRASSERIE
01743 249 152
Castle Street, Shrewsbury, SY1 2BX
Hidden away from the hustle and bustle of the high street, quality is never amiss at this friendly brasserie. The ambience of the restaurant and the delicious food will inevitably help you unwind.

2FOR1 MAIN COURSE | FRI ✓ | SAT * | SUN | * — Mediterranean

THE WALLS
01691 670 970
Welsh Walls, Oswestry, SY11 1AW
With its vaulting, high-beamed dining space and crisp, colourful produce, the fundamentals of The Walls are very fine indeed. Superbly accomplished cooking and imaginative flavours top it off.

25% OFF TOTAL | 6 | FRI ✓ | SAT ✓ | SUN — British

THE WATERSIDE RESTAURANT
01746 780 437
The Mill Hotel, Bridgnorth, Aveley, WV15 6HL
The food here will ignite your taste-buds like never before. The flambé dishes come to life both in the kitchen and in the mouth, where fantastic flavours set fire to all of your senses.

2FOR1 MAIN COURSE | FRI | SAT | * — British

Gourmet Society discount applies to the à la carte menu only, unless stated otherwise.

Staffordshire

99 STATION STREET ☎01283 516 859
99 Station Street, Burton-upon-Trent, DE14 1BT
AA-Rosette winning Head Chef Daniel Pilkington crafts delicious, hearty food, and having been trained as a pastry chef delivers stunning desserts. All available with fine cheese and a compact wine list.
25% OFF TOTAL | ♟ 4 | FRI ▮ | SAT ✱ | SUN | ▲ — Modern British

ALBANI SPICE ☎01782 822 440
32 Market Place, Stoke-on-Trent, ST6 4AT
Experienced Head Chef delivers an array of Indian dishes, using everything from the hottest spices and creamiest sauces, to the tastiest lamb chops and the most succulent pieces of chicken.
2FOR1 MAIN COURSE | FRI ✓ | SAT ✓ — Indian

ARENA ☎01782 772 266
36 Market Street, Stoke-on-Trent, ST7 4AB
Popular Indian restaurant in Kidsgrove, known simply for its attentive and friendly service and a selection of tasty, filling dishes. Classic curries and some appealing specialities populate the menu.
2FOR1 MAIN COURSE | FRI × | SAT × | SUN — Indian

ARTHURS @ THE GRAIL COURT HOTEL ☎01283 741 155
Station Street, Burton-upon-Trent, DE14 1BN
Excellent food made with the freshest ingredients, whilst providing a high standard of service combined with comfortable surroundings. A sumptuous menu offering traditional English fare.
25% OFF TOTAL | ♟ 4 | FRI ✓ | SAT ✓ | SUN — Traditional English

BANK HOUSE HOTEL ☎01889 566 922
Church Street, Uttoxeter, ST14 8AG
Fantastically situated in the heart of the town centre, this restaurant has maintained all the characteristic features of the original bank that it once was. A wonderful À la carte menu is on offer.
2FOR1 MAIN COURSE | FRI ✓ | SAT ✓ | SUN | ▲ — European

THE BISTRO AT ASTON MARINA ☎01785 819 702
Lichfield Road [A51], Stone, ST15 8QU
Award-winning coffees and a dazzling selection of sophisticated liquors ensure this venue is a beverage haven. Savour British cuisine, sourced from traditional butcheries and local farm shops.
25% OFF TOTAL | ♟ 8 | FRI ▮ | SAT ▮ | SUN | ✱ — British

BISTRO LE COQ ☎01889 270 237
Station Road, Stowe by Chartley, Stafford, ST18 0LF
Thoroughly French bistro in the long-established Cock Inn. Bistro dishes are the stock-in-trade, with some brilliant regional specialities from the south of France. A great mix of rustic and lavish.
25% OFF TOTAL | ♟ 4 | FRI × | SAT × | ✱ — French

BLUE TIFFIN ☎01782 595 978
1003 Uttoxeter Road, Meir, Stoke-on-Trent, ST3 6HE
Blue Tiffin is proud to serve the local area with deliciously moreish Indian cuisine which has earned the restaurant a loyal following. The staff are dedicated to making every occasion special.
2FOR1 MAIN COURSE | FRI × | SAT × | SUN — Indian

BOLAKA SPICE ☎01538 373 734
41 Stockwell Street, Leek, ST13 6DH
Highly regarded Indian and Bangladeshi restaurant. Serves food that's full of colour, fresh and flavourful with distinctively accomplished cooking. Known for a good atmosphere and some eclectic specials.
2FOR1 3 COURSES | FRI ✱ | SAT ✱ — Indian/Bangladeshi

THE BULL'S HEAD 01543 480 214
Birmingham Road, Shenstone, Lichfield, WS14 0JR
This Vintage Inn oozes rural charm and rustic character. The picturesque surroundings provide the perfect backdrop for savouring the hearty, seasonal pub-food on the menu.
25% OFF TOTAL | FRI ✓ | SAT ✓ | SUN | ▲ — Modern British

CAFÉ INDIA ☎01785 841 144
Ivetsey Bank, Watling Street, Wheaton Aston, ST19 9QT
A comfortable setting in which romantic meals, special occasions and business dinners can be catered for. Offering a wide range of freshly cooked Indian and Bangladeshi dishes in pleasant surroundings.
2FOR1 MAIN COURSE | FRI ✱ | SAT ✱ | ▲ — Indian

THE CENTURION 01827 260 587
Watling Street, Wilnecote, Nr Tamworth, B77 5PN
Quality pub classics with modern twists meets with a friendly and relaxed atmosphere to make this Table Table venue the perfect place for any occasion. *Excludes daytime & evening deals and festive menus.
2FOR1 MAIN COURSE | FRI ✓ | SAT ✓ — Modern British

CHAMPAGNE INDIAN FUSION ☎01827 313 175
7a Aldergate, Nr Tamworth, B79 7DJ
Sharp design and vibrant colours set the tone for a good evening out, to which the food here matches up brilliantly. Dishes from India, Pakistan and Bangladesh; the hotter curries have a bit of pizzazz.
2FOR1 3 COURSES | FRI ✱ | SAT ✱ — Indian

CHANDLERS RESTAURANT ☎01543 416 688
Corn Exchange, Conduit Street, Lichfield, WS13 6JU
Featured in the Michelin Good Food Guide, this restaurant is renowned for using the finest fresh ingredients for a menu that boasts a great range of daily changing fish, among other treats.
2FOR1 MAIN COURSE | FRI ✓ | SAT ✓ | ▲ — English and Continental

COACHOUSE RESTAURANT ☎01543 428 614
Cross Keys, 42 Hill Street, Cannock, WS12 2DN
Specialising in authentic Caribbean cuisine, this restaurant is a real hidden gem, with a chef originating from the island of Jamaica demonstrating his wealth of cooking knowledge and experience.
50% OFF FOOD | ♟ 6 | FRI ✓ | SAT ✓ | ▲ — Caribbean

THE COLLIERS 01889 503 951
Power Station Road, Rugeley, WS15 1LX
Quality pub classics with modern twists meets with a friendly and relaxed atmosphere to make this Table Table venue the perfect place for any occasion. *Excludes daytime & evening deals and festive menus.
2FOR1 MAIN COURSE | FRI ✓ | SAT ✓ — Modern British

DARU CHINI ☎01785 851 978
1 Stafford Street, Eccleshall, Stafford, ST21 6BL
Modern Bangladeshi and Indian restaurant in a charming traditional building. Features an eclectic menu with fine standards of cooking and a sound eye for the quality of its ingredients. Try the fiery naga.
2FOR1 3 COURSES | FRI ✱ | SAT ✱ — Indian

DI MEZZO @ THE MIDDLE BELL ☎01283 716 979
33 Main Street, Barton-under-Needwood, DE13 8AA
Choose from a tasty menu which includes sharing boards, exquisite starters, and mouth-watering pizza and pasta dishes. Round off a wonderful meal with a selection of tempting home-made desserts.
50% OFF FOOD | ♟ 2 | FRI ▮ | SAT ▮ | SUN | ▲ — British

DILSHAD ☎01543 570 264
1 Ashworth House, Cannock Road, Chadsmoor, WS11 5DZ
Dig some fantastic curries at this Indian restaurant in Cannock; it's not just the warm welcome, but the superlative richness of the flavours in their dishes. Treat yourself to an unfussy, delicious meal.
2FOR1 MAIN COURSE | FRI ✓ | SAT ✓ | ✱ — Indian

DUNSLEY HALL HOTEL ☎01384 877 077
39 Dunsley Road, Kinver, DY7 6LU
Diners can experience locally sourced cuisine on a new level at this venue, where food is grown in the Victorian kitchen garden. Beautiful scenery and impeccable service make this eatery a reputable one.
2FOR1 MAIN COURSE | FRI ✓ | SAT × | SUN | ▲ — British

ENRICO'S ☎01283 533 230
New Street, Burton-upon-Trent, DE14 3QN
Sumptuous and authentic Italian food, ideal for a fine intimate meal or a family gathering. See what real Italian dishes should taste like at prices to suit all pockets.
25% OFF TOTAL | ♟ 8 | FRI ✱ | SAT ✱ | SUN | ✱ | ▲ — Italian

FOLLY RESTAURANT @ MERCURE
☎ 08448 159 018
Newton Park, Newton Solney, Burton-upon-Trent, DE15 0SS
Hearkening back to the period fictions of the late 18th and early 19th Century, this Staffordshire hotel is ideal for that traditionally British retreat. The Folly Restaurant pours forth timeless elegance.

2FOR1 3 COURSES | FRI ✓ | SAT ✓ — International

FOUR COUNTIES SPICE
01827 830 998
Ashby Road, No Mans Heath, Tamworth, B79 0PB
Whether you enjoy the more classic Indian staple dish, or are keen to try out a more modern take on the traditional cuisine, this fantastic restaurant offers it all. The Assamese dishes are delicious.

2FOR1 MAIN COURSE | FRI ✱ | SAT ✱ | ▲ — Indian

FOX AND HOUNDS
☎ 01543 480 257
44 Main Street, Shenstone, Lichfield, WS14 0NB
With many awards and a loyal following, this attractive restaurant has a real appeal about it. A varied menu offers delightful dishes that can be enjoyed in modern, comfortable surroundings.

2FOR1 MAIN COURSE | FRI ✗ | SAT ✗ | SUN — English and Continental

GILPINS BISTRO
☎ 01543 572 121
Watling Street, Cannock, WS11 1SH
Surrounded by stunning English countryside and offering a traditional dining and drinking experience, this bar and lounge is a great spot to end a day of sightseeing.

50% OFF FOOD | 2 | FRI ✓ | SAT ✓ — International

THE HANGING MANGOES
☎ 01782 825 635
114 Waterloo Road, Stoke-on-Trent, ST6 3HB
As the name suggests, The Hanging Mangoes serve the most mouth-watering of South Indian and Sri Lankan cuisine. Awaken the senses with bold colours and exotic textures, as the chefs cater specifically.

50% OFF FOOD | 4 | FRI ✗ | SAT ✗ | ▲ — South Indian/Sri Lankan

THE HATHERTON BAR @ MERCURE
☎ 01785 712 459
Hatherton House Hotel, Pinfold Lane, Stafford, ST19 5QP
A luxurious bar to match its location, The Hatherton Bar is situated in the Mercure Stafford Hotel and is a great place to relax and unwind over your favourite beverage while feasting on hot snacks.

50% OFF FOOD | 4 | FRI 📱 | SAT 📱 | ▲ — British

HEART OF INDIA
☎ 01782 662 673
5A Church St, Newcastle-under-Lyme, ST5 1QS
Efficient service and friendly welcomes are two characteristics of this fine Indian restaurant. Much like its sister venues, this Heart of India serves exotic dishes alongside classic curries.

50% OFF FOOD | FRI ✓ | SAT ✓ — Indian

THE HEDGEHOG
01543 415 789
Stafford Road, Lichfield, WS13 8JB
This Vintage Inn oozes rural charm and rustic character. The picturesque surroundings provide the perfect backdrop for savouring the hearty, seasonal pub-food on the menu.

25% OFF TOTAL | FRI ✓ | SAT ✓ | SUN | ▲ — Modern British

JOBA'S INN ARMINGTON
☎ 0182 759 500
134 Amington Road, Tamworth, B77 3PU
The chef has devised a menu to suit all palates by using a home-made special sauce on some dishes, as well as authentic herbs and spices to create a mouth watering meal.

2FOR1 MAIN COURSE | FRI 📱 | SAT ✗ | SUN | ✱ — Indian

KASHMIR GARDEN
☎ 01782 839 366
257 High Street, Tunstall, Stoke-on-Trent, ST6 5EG
Traditionally prepared and presented, this restaurant delivers quality Indian cuisine filled with rich flavours and delicate textures; a diverse menu of classic and speciality dishes.

25% OFF TOTAL | 10 | FRI ✱ | SAT ✱ — Indian

KETTUVALLAM
☎ 01283 529 250
1 Guild Street, Burton-upon-Trent, DE14 1NA
Filled with everything from enriching soups to beautiful slow-cooked curries, and well-spiced signature dishes, the menu here is far broader in scope than many Indian restaurants.

25% OFF TOTAL | 8 | FRI ✗ | SAT ✗ — Indian

KUDOS
☎ 01827 254 777
9 Coleshill Street, Fazeley, Tamworth, B78 3RB
This fine Indian restaurant delivers a menu of classic and fusion dishes alongside a wide range of drinks. Friendly staff endeavour to satisfy every diner, however discerning their palate.

25% OFF TOTAL | 8 | FRI ✓ | SAT ✱ | ✱ | ▲ — Indian

THE LADYBRIDGE
0182 754 414
Bonehill Road, Bitterscote, Nr Tamworth, B78 3HQ
Beefeater Grill are one of the UK's best-loved restaurants welcoming guests for almost 40 years in over 130 locations nationwide. *Excludes Breakfast, Light Bites, Bar menu, set menus and all other offers.

2FOR1 MAIN COURSE | 6 | FRI ✓ | SAT ✗ | ▲ — Modern British

LE JARDIN PUNJABI
☎ 01543 416 748
26 Bird Street, Lichfield, WS13 6PR
Punjabi dishes bursting with flavour. The restaurant's consistency in good food and wonderfully friendly service guarantees its popularity. The saag paneer comes highly recommended.

2FOR1 MAIN COURSE | FRI ✱ | SAT ✱ | SUN | ✱ — Indian

THE LODGE RESTAURANT
☎ 01384 221 000
Six Ashes Road, Halfpenny Green, Bobbington, DY7 5DP
Enjoy a substantial English dish whilst overlooking the south Staffordshire countryside. This converted barn offers nothing short of excellent quality food and service.

2FOR1 MAIN COURSE | FRI ✓ | SAT ✓ | SUN | ✱ | ▲ — Modern British

THE LONDON ROAD TAVERN
☎ 01782 622 878
73 London Road, Newcastle-under-Lyme, ST5 1NB
Family-run traditional pub well known for its hospitality, open atmosphere and an array of delicious home-cooked pub food. Their Sunday roasts are particularly well regarded, with the trimmings a treat.

2FOR1 MAIN COURSE | FRI ✓ | SAT ✓ | ▲ — British

LONGFORD HOUSE
01543 401 391
Watling Street, Cannock, WS11 1SJ
Beefeater Grill are one of the UK's best-loved restaurants welcoming guests for almost 40 years in over 130 locations nationwide. *Excludes Breakfast, Light Bites, Bar menu, set menus and all other offers.

2FOR1 MAIN COURSE | 6 | FRI ✓ | SAT ✗ | ▲ — Modern British

MASOONS MASSALA
☎ 01782 788 444
8 Congleton Road, Talke, ST7 1NE
Classic, simple, popular Indian restaurant that does a great range of flavourful, well-spiced and plentiful dishes. The menu is broad-based and appealing, and has won the restaurant a great many fans.

2FOR1 MAIN COURSE | FRI ✗ | SAT ✗ | SUN — Indian

MED BAR
☎ 01782 269 955
28 Cobridge Road, Hanley, Stoke-on-Trent, ST1 5JQ
Blending fresh, seasonal ingredients with authentic, regional Italian recipes, Med Bar produces some of the finest cuisine. Rich flavours and smooth textures characterise the food.

2FOR1 MAIN COURSE | 2 | FRI ✓ | SAT 📱 — Mediterranean

MERRY MONK
01283 749 921
Mercia Park, Burton-upon-Trent, DE14 2DQ
Beefeater Grill are one of the UK's best-loved restaurants welcoming guests for almost 40 years in over 130 locations nationwide. *Excludes Breakfast, Light Bites, Bar menu, set menus and all other offers.

2FOR1 MAIN COURSE | 6 | FRI ✓ | SAT ✗ | ▲ — Modern British

THE MESS
☎ 01902 851 694

3 Market Place, Stafford, ST19 9BS

Enjoy drinks and snacks in the daytime cafe, or wait until the evening transformation into a fine restaurant. *Not available on Saturday and Sunday Lunch.

25% OFF TOTAL | 👤4 | FRI ✓ | SAT ✓ | ▲ — British

MINSTERS BAR
☎ 01782 416 567

23-29 Glebe Street, Stoke-on-Trent, ST4 1HL

Minsters Bar and Bistro offers fresh, tasty and convenient food when you want it. From healthy baguettes to indulgent pizzas, the place offers a little ray of sunshine to any rainy day.

2FOR1 MAIN COURSE | FRI 📱 | SAT 📱 — British

MOAT HOUSE
☎ 08702 254 601

Best Western, Festival Way, Stoke-on-Trent, ST1 5BQ

Ideally located near Stoke, this hotel restaurant is modern and comfortable and offers a diverse range of breakfast, lunch and dinner options, inspired by modern international cuisines, for all the family.

25% OFF TOTAL | 👤6 | FRI ✓ | SAT ✓ — European

THE MOAT HOUSE
☎ 01785 712 217

Lower Penkridge Road, Acton Trussell, Stafford, ST17 0RJ

Luxury hotel and fine-dining venue presenting guests and visitors alike with an expert à la carte menu of modern British cuisine. Indulge in an unforgettable dining experience.

25% OFF TOTAL | 👤8 | FRI ✗ | SAT ✱ | SUN | ▲ — Modern British

MR MALIKS
☎ 01782 621 212

15 London Road, Newcastle-under-Lyme, ST5 1LQ

Welcome to Mr Maliks Authentic Indian Restaurant. Mr Maliks Restaurant is based in the heart of Newcastle Under Lyme town centre. Mr Malik specialises in genuine Indian Seafood and Tandoori recipes.

25% OFF TOTAL | 👤10 | FRI 📱 | SAT 📱 | ▲ — Indian

NETHERSTOWE HOUSE
☎ 01543 254 270

Netherstowe Lane, Lichfield, WS13 6AY

Netherstowe House was voted 'Restaurant of The Year' at the Taste of Staffordshire Good Food Awards 2012. The cuisine is classically based yet modern, with an emphasis on the finest seasonal produce.

50% OFF FOOD | 👤4 | FRI ✗ | SAT ✗ | ▲ — British

THE OLIVE TREE AT CHEADLE
☎ 01538 751 414

88 High Street, Cheadle, ST10 1AJ

Brilliant little tapas place and coffee bar in Cheadle. Tapas doesn't need to refer to Spanish food, but is a style of dining; here there's all sorts, including a fine line in trattoria-style Italian food.

25% OFF TOTAL | 👤8 | FRI 📱 | SAT 📱 | SUN | ✱ — Italian/ Mediterranean

OSTLER
☎ 01270 884 000

Best Western Manor House, Audley Road, Alsager, ST7 2QQ

Recognised with an AA Rosette, the Ostler combines hearty British fare with touches of Mediterranean influence; mouth-wateringly cooked meats and fish are combined with sharp, sassy accompanying flavours.

25% OFF TOTAL | 👤4 | FRI 📱 | SAT 📱 | SUN | ▲ — Fine Dining

PADMA LOUNGE BAR AND RESTAURANT
☎ 01543 502 101

8 High Green Court, Newhall St, Cannock, WS11 1GR

With quality spices direct from India, the food here clearly benefits as the chefs use them skilfully to delicately flavour the cuisine, giving diners an authentic culinary experience.

25% OFF TOTAL | 👤8 | FRI ✓ | SAT ✱ | ✱ — Indian

PASCAL AT THE OLD VICARAGE
☎ 01283 533 222

2 Main Street, Branston, Burton-upon-Trent, DE14 3EX

A monthly changing menu allows regular diners to consistently try new and exciting dishes. Drawing on French influences, the English cuisine demonstrates the owner's passion for delicious food.

25% OFF TOTAL | 👤4 | FRI ✓ | SAT ✱ | SUN | ▲ — Classic British/ French

PEAK WEAVERS
☎ 01538 383 729

King Street, Leek, ST13 5NW

Winner of the Taste of Staffordshire award and boasting an AA Rosette, this venue promises to source ingredients locally and entice diners with a romantic ambience. Treat yourself to an over-night stay.

2FOR1 MAIN COURSE | FRI 📱 | SAT 📱 | SUN | ✱ — British

PLAZA RESTAURANT
☎ 01543 506 016

4 Mill Street, Cannock, WS11 0DL

Everything you would expect from a fine Indian restaurant; exceptional food, pleasant surroundings and friendly service. Includes an extensive menu filled with Indian classics created in a proven style.

2FOR1 MAIN COURSE | FRI ✓ | SAT ✓ | ✱ — Indian

THE PLOUGH INN
☎ 01782 720 469

2 Ravens Lane, Stoke-on-Trent, ST7 8PS

A great little pub serving delicious food from a ranging menu, whilst a wide selection of drinks are also available. Friendly, efficient staff ensure all diners are catered for.

2FOR1 MAIN COURSE | FRI ✓ | SAT ✓ | SUN | ✱ — British

PORTOBELLO
☎ 0182 754 474

12 Silver Street, Tamworth, B79 7NH

Musky and refreshing wines are available from a menu laden with Old and New World bottles for you to try. An extensive À la carte menu offers exciting Italian dishes, from pizzas to steaks.

2FOR1 MAIN COURSE | FRI ✓ | SAT ✱ | ▲ — Italian

THE POST HOUSE
☎ 01785 231 450

35 Greenstreet, Mill Bank, Stafford, ST16 2HZ

A bustling cosmopolitan setting with an even more exciting menu, The Post House is perfect for both lazy lunches and more formal evenings out- be sure to check out the cocktail list!

2FOR1 MAIN COURSE | FRI ✱ | SAT ✗ | SUN | ✱ | ▲ — British

QARMA TANDOORI
☎ 01538 387 788

Cross Street Mill, Cross Street, Leek, ST13 6BL

Offering both classic Indian and Bangladeshi dishes and those not always found, such as the capsilla and the samber, this well-established restaurant is also popular for its wide range of thali dishes.

2FOR1 3 COURSES | FRI ✱ | SAT ✱ — Indian

THE RESTAURANT AT MODDERSHALL OAKS
☎ 01782 399 000

Moddershall, Stone, ST15 8TG

This venue boasts first-class service in aesthetically pleasing surrounds. Award-winning, the organic menu is contemporary and celebrates the distinct tastes of Staffordshire.

25% OFF TOTAL | 👤4 | FRI ✓ | SAT ✗ — Modern European

RESTAURANT GILMORE
☎ 01889 507 100

Strine's Farm, Beamhurst, Uttoxeter, ST14 5DZ

An exceptional farmhouse restaurant opened by a couple who have both spent over 25 years in the catering trade. The food dazzles, with an innovative approach to classical dishes. Awarded 2 AA Rosettes.

25% OFF TOTAL | 👤2 | FRI ✗ | SAT ✗ | SUN | ▲ — European

ROCESTER TANDOORI
☎ 01889 590 169

37 High Street, Rocester, Uttoxeter, ST14 5JU

Simple, classic tandoori restaurant in Rocester serving a selection of rich-flavoured, spicy, substantial and tongue-tingling subcontinental dishes.

2FOR1 MAIN COURSE | FRI ✓ | SAT ✓ | ✱ — Bangladeshi/Indian

ROYAL BENGAL RESTAURANT
☎ 0182 763 257

104a Lichfield Street, Nr Tamworth, B79 7QB

A refreshing combination of a simple elegant setting with a vast menu that offers many fantastic dishes. Try acharee curry or the sham special and you will soon be in a hurry to return to The Royal Bengal.

2FOR1 3 COURSES | FRI ✱ | SAT ✱ — Indian

RUCHI
☎ 01283 840 008

Bagot Street, Abbots Bromley, Rugeley, WS15 3DB

For a superbly authentic Indian meal in wonderful surroundings, The Ruchi delivers every time. The restaurant has an admirable reputation that draws in diners from the whole of Staffordshire.

25% OFF TOTAL | 👤10 | FRI 📱 | SAT ✓ | SUN | ▲ — Indian

SAKI SPICE TANDOORI RESTAURANT
☎ 01584 875 153

32 Waterloo Road, Burslem, Stoke-on-Trent, ST6 3ES

The Head Chef provides exciting new and traditional dishes that never disappoint. The divine king prawn moranjon is a traditional Bangladeshi dish and is exquisitely gratifying.

2FOR1 MAIN COURSE | FRI ✓ | SAT ✱ — Indian

SALEEM BAGH INDIAN CUISINE — 01543 505 089
Queen Square, Cannock, WS11 1EA

Saleem Bagh offers a distinctive dining experience, an exquisite taste of Bangladeshi, Indian, Pakistani cuisine and newly created fusion dishes taking inspiration from the far east.

2FOR1 MAIN COURSE | FRI × | SAT × | ✱ — Indian

SHAFFERS — ☎01782 212 212
60 Snowhill, Stoke-on-Trent, ST1 4LY

Warm, authentic Kashmiri food is matched by warm inviting welcomes provided by the staff at Shaffers. Expect to find delicious food and experience a fine evening of dining pleasure.

25% OFF TOTAL | ♟10 | FRI ✓ | SAT ✓ — Indian

THE SPREAD EAGLE — 01283 813 004
Church Rd, Rolleston-on-Dove, Burton-upon-Trent, DE13 9BE

This Vintage Inn oozes rural charm and rustic character. The picturesque surroundings provide the perfect backdrop for savouring the hearty, seasonal pub-food on the menu.

25% OFF TOTAL | FRI ✓ | SAT ✓ | SUN | ▲ — Modern British

THE STAFFORD BALTI — ☎01785 250 234
34 Mill Bank, Stafford, ST16 2QT

The Stafford Balti is a fine local restaurant, perfect for a well-rounded curry and evening out with friends. Indian spices and authentic flavours make this a popular spot for an Asian feast.

25% OFF TOTAL | ♟10 | FRI ▯ | SAT ▯ | ✱ | ▲ — Indian

THE STANHOPE — 01283 219 562
Ashby Road East, Nr Burton-upon-Trent, DE15 0PU

Quality pub classics with modern twists meets with a friendly and relaxed atmosphere to make this Table Table venue the perfect place for any occasion. *Excludes daytime & evening deals and festive menus.

2FOR1 MAIN COURSE | FRI ✓ | SAT ✓ — Modern British

THE STAR INN — ☎01785 850 279
Copmere End, Eccleshall, Stafford, ST21 6EW

The clientèle are forever thrilled by an ever-changing specials board and a hearty menu of old pub favourites appeases ravenous stomachs. Award-winning beers and real ales are in abundance.

25% OFF TOTAL | ♟4 | FRI ✳ | SAT ✳ | SUN | ▲ — British

THE SWAN — ☎01785 258 142
46 Greengate Street, Stafford, ST16 2JA

The Brasserie at The Swan Hotel serves some of the towns finest cuisine and you are guaranteed the pick of Staffordshire's local produce.

25% OFF TOTAL | ♟8 | FRI ✳ | SAT ✳ | ▲ — Brasserie

THE SWAN WITH TWO NECKS — ☎01543 490 251
40 Brook End, Longdon WS15 4PN

Exuding tradition, diners can feast upon a hearty ploughman's lunch or a wholesome home-made lasagne. Guests can enjoy pub favourites in the exquisite surroundings of the Staffordshire countryside.

2FOR1 3 COURSES | FRI × | SAT × — British

TAJ MAHAL — 01782 412 121
29 Liverpool Road, Stoke-on-Trent, ST4 1AN

A great quality, down-the-line Indian restaurant that serves a broad range of colourful, spicy and flavourful dishes with excellent service and a warm, accommodating ambience.

25% OFF TOTAL | ♟4 | FRI ▯ | SAT ▯ — Indian

THE TALBOT — 01782 512 608
73 Grange Road, Biddulph, Stoke-on-Trent, ST8 7RY

This Vintage Inn oozes rural charm and rustic character. The picturesque surroundings provide the perfect backdrop for savouring the hearty, seasonal pub-food on the menu.

25% OFF TOTAL | FRI ✓ | SAT ✓ | SUN | ▲ — Modern British

THE TAME OTTER — 0182 753 361
Lichfield Road, Hopwas, Nr Tamworth, B78 3AF

This Vintage Inn oozes rural charm and rustic character. The picturesque surroundings provide the perfect backdrop for savouring the hearty, seasonal pub-food on the menu.

25% OFF TOTAL | FRI ✓ | SAT ✓ | SUN | ▲ — Modern British

TASTE OF INDIA — ☎01782 316 060
70-74 Weston Road, Meir, Stoke-on-Trent, ST3 6AD

Whatever the occasion, the staff at this venue are devoted to exceedingly good service. Chefs blend the traditional with the unexpected to create an imaginative menu that is both fresh and tasty.

2FOR1 MAIN COURSE | FRI ✓ | SAT × — Indian

TEMPTATIONS — ☎01283 562 106
127 New Street, Burton-upon-Trent, DE14 3QW

Both locals and visitors from afar enjoy the exquisite flavours of Rajasthan and Bangladesh that find their way into each meal. The fish dishes and the Rongila Khama are deservedly popular.

2FOR1 MAIN COURSE | FRI ✳ | SAT ✳ | ✱ | ▲ — Indian

THE THREE CROWNS — 01785 819 516
Lichfield Road, Stone, ST15 8QU

This Vintage Inn oozes rural charm and rustic character. The picturesque surroundings provide the perfect backdrop for savouring the hearty, seasonal pub-food on the menu.

25% OFF TOTAL | FRI ✓ | SAT ✓ | SUN | ▲ — Modern British

THE THREE HORSESHOES — ☎01283 716 268
2 Station Road, Burton-upon-Trent, DE13 8DR

Delightful, home-made dishes make up a vast menu, which includes a delicious range of deserts. Ingredients are sourced locally wherever possible.

2FOR1 MAIN COURSE | FRI × | SAT × | SUN — British

WALKABOUT — ☎01782 281 543
38-42 Trinity Street, Hanley, Stoke-on-Trent, ST1 5LJ

Walkabout is famous for its characteristically Australian atmosphere and well-rounded menu. From live sport with a juicy burger to some Aussie kangaroo skewers, you'll find it hard to tear yourself away.

25% OFF TOTAL | ♟10 | FRI ✓ | SAT ✓ | ▲ — International

THE WATER BRIDGE — 01889 561 800
Derby Road, Uttoxeter, Staffordshire, ST14 5AA

Quality pub classics with modern twists meets with a friendly and relaxed atmosphere to make this Table Table venue the perfect place for any occasion. *Excludes daytime & evening deals and festive menus.

2FOR1 MAIN COURSE | FRI ✓ | SAT ✓ — Modern British

THE WOLSELEY ARMS — 01889 883 179
Wolseley Bridge, Stafford, ST17 0XS

This Vintage Inn oozes rural charm and rustic character. The picturesque surroundings provide the perfect backdrop for savouring the hearty, seasonal pub-food on the menu.

25% OFF TOTAL | FRI ✓ | SAT ✓ | SUN | ▲ — Modern British

To understand what the restaurant icons mean, please see the inside back cover.

Warwickshire

AGRA PALACE
☎02476 350 515
12 Abbey Green, Nuneaton, CV11 5DR
Dine in beautiful and comfortable private seating areas, taking advantage of perfectly crafted Indian dishes whilst sampling a selection of drinks, including globally selected wines.

2FOR1 MAIN COURSE | FRI ✓ | SAT ✱ | ▲ — Indian

AQUA FOOD & MOOD
☎01926 495 491
12-14 Jury St, Warwick, CV34 4EW
If you're unfamiliar with the warming, sumptuous and distinct flavours of Lebanese cooking, this is the place to draw you in. In an elegant setting, with superbly done dishes, you'll be hooked and crooked.

25% OFF TOTAL | ♟ 8 | FRI ✗ | SAT ✗ | ✱ — Lebanese

AVON SPICE
☎01789 267 067
7 Greenhill Street, Stratford-upon-Avon, CV37 6LF
The service is warm and welcoming, with perfect attention given to each individual group. Priding themselves on excellent quality and service is what makes Avon Spice Stratford-upon-Avon's favourite Indian

2FOR1 2 COURSES | FRI ✗ | SAT ✗ | ✱ — Indian

THE BELL AT SALFORD PRIORS
☎01789 772 112
Evesham Road, Salford Priors, WR11 8UU
Changing daily, the menu is varied, fresh and sure to tempt even the most discerning of guests. Offering a fine dining room, this venue is perfect for lunches or weekend treats.

2FOR1 3 COURSES | FRI ✗ | SAT ✗ | ▲ — British

BENGAL SPICE RESTAURANT
☎01788 540 222
318 Hillmorton Road, Hillmorton, Rugby, CV22 5BP
Good, unfussy restaurant specialising in North Indian food. Settle in to enjoy a simple, flavoursome meal at a good price. Through the rather retro frontage, you'll find a great welcome and a tasty dinner.

2FOR1 MAIN COURSE | FRI ✱ | SAT ✱ | ✱ — Indian

BEST WESTERN FALSTAFF HOTEL
☎01926 312 044
16 Warwick New Road, Leamington Spa, CV32 5JQ
Maintaining all of the original grace and character of the three Victorian mansions from which it was created, this hotel boasts a restaurant and bar where you can enjoy a relaxing vibe and a quality meal.

25% OFF TOTAL | ♟10 | FRI ✓ | SAT ✓ | ✱ | ▲ — European

BILASH
☎01926 858 423
86 Priory Road, Kenilworth, CV8 1LQ
Traditional Indian cooking using only the finest of ingredients to create incredible dishes. The ideal place for a memorable dining experience, where delicious food is served in a happy environment.

2FOR1 MAIN COURSE | FRI 📱 | SAT 📱 | ✱ — Indian

THE BLUE BOAR INN
☎01789 750 010
Temple Grafton, Stratford-upon-Avon, B49 6NR
Feast on traditional favourites as well as new tastes and experiences at this increasingly popular pub. Make sure you leave room for the deliciously divine home-made desserts which you won't want to miss.

2FOR1 MAIN COURSE | FRI ✱ | SAT ✱ | SUN | ▲ — English and Continental

BOMBAY TANDOORI
☎01926 420 521
38-40 Regent Street, Royal Leamington Spa, CV32 5EG
Having established an excellent reputation, The Bombay continues to provide quality food at reasonable prices. Karai and thali dishes are superb, although the chef will cater for all individual tastes.

2FOR1 3 COURSES | FRI ✱ | SAT ✱ | ✱ | ▲ — Indian

THE BRIDGE RESTAURANT
☎01676 522 442
Somers Road, Stonebridge, CV7 7PL
Calm, relaxing ambience to this smartly styled restaurant at Stonebridge Golf Club, where you can enjoy a delicious, sophisticated meal with views over the course and its gentle rolling green.

2FOR1 MAIN COURSE | FRI ✓ | SAT ✓ | SUN | ▲ — European

BROWNSOVER HALL HOTEL
☎01788 546 100
Old Brownsover, Brownsnover Lane, Rugby, CV21 1HU
Dramatically striking in appearance, the hotel takes full advantage of its situation within a Victorian mansion. Decadent dishes in the restaurant provide a suitable match for the magnificent surroundings.

25% OFF TOTAL | ♟ 2 | FRI 📱 | SAT ✱ | ▲ — British

THE BULL AT FURNACE END
☎01675 481 602
The Bull Coleshill Road, Furnace End, B46 2LG
The Bull is a family friendly pub and kitchen set in the tiny hamlet of Furnace End, housed in a historic building that has recently been given a new lease of life by a young and passionate team.

25% OFF TOTAL | ♟10 | FRI ✗ | SAT ✗ | SUN | ▲ — British

BUTLERS LEAP
01788 577 650
Clifton Road, Ridge Drive, Rugby, CV21 3TX
Quality pub classics with modern twists meets with a friendly and relaxed atmosphere to make this Table Table venue the perfect place for any occasion. *Excludes daytime & evening deals and festive menus.

2FOR1 MAIN COURSE | FRI ✓ | SAT ✓ — Modern British

CAFÉ ROUGE
01926 330 565
95-99 Regent Street, Leamington Spa, CV32 4NT
French sophistication on the British high street - enjoy seasonally changing French dishes and a continental wine selection, served in a relaxed environment with an undeniable flair of Parisian chic.

25% OFF TOTAL | ♟ 6 | FRI ✓ | SAT ✓ | ✱ | ▲ — French

CAFÉ ROUGE
01789 263 526
18 Sheep Street, Stratford-upon-Avon, CV37 6EF
French sophistication on the British high street - enjoy seasonally changing French dishes and a continental wine selection, served in a relaxed environment with an undeniable flair of Parisian chic.

25% OFF TOTAL | ♟ 6 | FRI ✓ | SAT ✓ | ✱ | ▲ — French

CHAPEL HOUSE HOTEL
☎01827 718 949
Friars Gate, Atherstone, CV9 1EY
Enjoy a range of tender and flavoursome dishes: melt-in-the-mouth meats and some fabulous sweetbreads. The restaurant also has an especial line in imaginative desserts. Awarded 1 AA Rosette.

2FOR1 MAIN COURSE | FRI ✓ | SAT ✓ | SUN | ✱ — Fine Dining

COCONUT LAGOON
☎01926 864 500
149 Warwick Road, Kenilworth, CV8 1HY
This acclaimed restaurant combines cuisine from several South Indian regions, presenting a gastronomic journey through the delicious legacy left by the diverse European influences on the region.

2FOR1 3 COURSES | FRI 📱 | SAT 📱 | SUN | ▲ — Indian

CROSSED KHUKRIS GURKHA
☎02476 344 488
115 Abbey Street, Nuneaton, CV11 5BX
The eclectic mix of flavours that comprise Nepalese cuisine is derived from the diverse make up of the country. Balancing flavour, texture and style in each dish, the chefs create culinary masterpieces.

2FOR1 MAIN COURSE | FRI 📱 | SAT ✱ — Nepalese

THE CURZON ARMS
☎01827 880 334
29 Main Road, Twycross, Atherstone, CV9 3PL
Owner John Newton is well-experienced in the restaurant profession and projects culinary excellence at every opportunity. Seasonally changing, this country pub menu is wholesome and traditionally British.

2FOR1 MAIN COURSE | FRI ✓ | SAT ✓ | SUN | ▲ — English/Gastro pub

DELHI PALACE
☎01926 420 944
51 High Street, Leamington Spa, CV31 1LN
Delicious, traditional and reasonably priced; the dishes at this terrific Indian restaurant are really something to write home about. Food fit for a king.

25% OFF TOTAL | ♟ 2 | FRI ✓ | SAT ✓ | SUN | ✱ — Indian

THE DUN COW
01788 810 305

The Green, Dunchurch, Rugby, CV22 6NJ

This Vintage Inn oozes rural charm and rustic character. The picturesque surroundings provide the perfect backdrop for savouring the hearty, seasonal pub-food on the menu.

25% OFF TOTAL | FRI ✓ | SAT ✓ | SUN | ▲ — Modern British

EPISODE
☎ 01926 883 777

64 Upper Holly Walk, Leamington Spa, CV32 4JL

Episode's philosophy on your plate, with the promise of serving only what they would want to eat themselves. Fresh, delicious produce sourced from the best possible places used to create fine dishes.

2FOR1 MAIN COURSE | FRI ✓ | SAT ✷ | SUN — British

ESSENCE OF INDIA
☎ 01926 632 766

15 Oxford Road, Marten, Rugby, CV23 9RH

As the name suggests, Essence of India focuses solely on using authentic Indian flavours and ingredients in their dishes to create genuine cuisine made with passion.

2FOR1 MAIN COURSE | FRI ✓ | SAT ✓ | ✱ — Indian

ETTINGTON CHASE
☎ 01789 740 000

Banbury Road, Stratford-upon-Avon, CV37 7NZ

Ettington Chase is characteristic of its setting. Charming, breathtaking and swarming in history, this hotel completely fits its location in Shakespeare's Country.

25% OFF TOTAL | 👤 6 | FRI ✓ | SAT ✓ | ▲ — British

EXOTICA BENGAL CUISINE
☎ 01788 551 584

68 Lower Street, Hillmorton, Rugby, CV21 4NU

Setting the standard high in this area, Exotica Bengal Cuisine offer a sensational menu combining classical and modern Bangladeshi dishes as well as European choices to cater for all tastes.

25% OFF TOTAL | 👤 4 | FRI ✓ | SAT ✷ | ✱ — Bangladeshi

FIVE RIVERS
☎ 01926 431 999

20-22 Victoria Terrace, Leamington Spa, CV31 3AB

Ambitious, imaginative Indian restaurant that combines the classic flavours with a flash of theatre; cool, bright dining and an inviting bar.

25% OFF TOTAL | FRI ✷ | SAT ✷ | ✱ — Indian

FUSION RESTAURANT
☎ 01788 535 686

The Grosvenor Hotel, Clifton Road, Rugby, CV21 3QQ

Indulge in a chic, stylish bar and brasserie restaurant of striking sophistication within this fine hotel. Boasts a delectable contemporary menu with extensive options of fine food and drink.

25% OFF TOTAL | FRI 📱 | SAT 📱 | ✱ | ▲ — Indian

THE GARDEN ROOM
☎ 01789 269 213

The Grosvenor, Warwick Rd, Stratford, CV37 6YT

An exquisite Georgian building steeped in its own history now plays home to this treasured hotel. Fantastically located, guests can take advantage of local attractions before dining and reclining.

2FOR1 MAIN COURSE | FRI ✓ | SAT 📱 | SUN — Modern British

THE GEORGE HOTEL
☎ 01608 661 453

High Street, Shipston-on-Stour, CV36 4AJ

This popular hotel-restaurant has created an exciting British menu, with temptations such as the real-ale battered fish and chips and chargrilled Hereford cross sirloin steak, all cooked to perfection.

25% OFF TOTAL | 👤 10 | FRI 📱 | SAT ✷ | SUN — British

THE GOLDEN CROSS
☎ 01789 772 420

Wixford Road, Ardens Grafton, Alcester, B50 4LG

With several areas to dine in and a home-cooked menu that offers something for all tastes, customers will be truly satisfied. Only the very best produce is used, with fresh fish coming in daily.

2FOR1 MAIN COURSE | FRI ✓ | SAT ✷ | SUN | ▲ — British

GRIFF HOUSE
02476 343 584

Coventry Road, Nuneaton, CV10 7PJ

Beefeater Grill are one of the UK's best-loved restaurants welcoming guests for almost 40 years in over 130 locations nationwide. *Excludes Breakfast, Light Bites, Bar menu, set menus and all other offers.

2FOR1 MAIN COURSE | 👤 6 | FRI ✓ | SAT ✗ | ▲ — Modern British

HARRINGTONS ON THE HILL
☎ 01926 852 074

42 Castle Hill, Kenilworth, CV8 1NB

There is nothing pretentious about this delightful venue, which offers a warm welcome and an uncomplicated, high-quality menu. Experience exceptional culinary skills in a small, almost rustic environment.

25% OFF TOTAL | 👤 2 | FRI 📱 | SAT ✷ | SUN | ✱ | ▲ — British

HELP OUT MILL RESTAURANT
☎ 01530 260 666

Heather Lane, Shackerstone, Nr Nuneaton, CV13 0BT

A hidden restaurant that is truly unique. Feel at home here, with the venue putting emphasis on ensuring their guests are completely relaxed. Enjoy their hugely popular carvery.

25% OFF TOTAL | 👤 4 | FRI ✓ | SAT ✓ — British

HONILEY COURT HOTEL
☎ 01926 484 234

Meer End Road, Honiley, Kenilworth, Warwick, CV8 1NP

This Brook hotel restaurant is popular with locals and guests alike, as the venue offers an extensive list of fine food, ideally complemented by a selection of wines from around the world.

25% OFF TOTAL | FRI ✓ | SAT ✓ — Modern British

KAVI
☎ 01926 858 331

Ramada Hotel, Chesford Bridge, Kenilworth, CV8 2LN

Luxury Indian dining in a well-placed location. Panoramic floor-to-ceiling windows provide outstanding views of the river Avon and the surrounding meadows.

25% OFF TOTAL | FRI 📱 | SAT 📱 | SUN | ▲ — Indian

THE KING'S HEAD
01789 840 206

Warwick Road, Wellesbourne, Warwick, CV35 9LX

This Vintage Inn oozes rural charm and rustic character. The picturesque surroundings provide the perfect backdrop for savouring the hearty, seasonal pub-food on the menu.

25% OFF TOTAL | FRI ✓ | SAT ✓ | SUN | ▲ — Modern British

THE LIME TREE RESTAURANT
☎ 01789 205 745

Campden Road, Stratford-upon-Avon, CV37 8LW

Whatever the time of day, The Lime Tree Restaurant's menu will tempt you with gastronomic delicacies and classic favourites, all complemented by a choice wine list.

2FOR1 3 COURSES | FRI ✗ | SAT ✗ | SUN — British

LOCH FYNE
☎ 01926 515 450

Clarendon House Hotel, High Street, Kenilworth CV8 1LZ

From the roadside oyster bar that once was, Loch Fyne restaurants now successfully inject energy and passion into great food and wonderful flavours, whilst ensuring their seafood is sustainably sourced.

25% OFF TOTAL | 👤 4 | FRI ✷ | SAT ✷ | ▲ — Seafood

THE MANOR GRILL
☎ 01789 205 478

Alveston Manor Hotel, Stratford-upon-Avon, CV37 7HP

Carnivorous diners can sink their teeth into prime Scottish beef, Norfolk pork or a well-deserved Sunday lunch. Boasting original Tudor features, guests can admire exposed beams and leaded windows.

50% OFF FOOD | 👤 4 | FRI ✓ | SAT ✓ | ✱ — British

MONCREIFFE RESTAURANT
☎ 01789 842 424

Walton Hall Hotel, Walton, Wellesbourne, CV35 9HU

Moncreiffe Restaurant has elegant surroundings and breathtaking views of the hotels gardens and surrounding countryside. Awarded two AA rosettes and featuring fresh local ingredients with seasonal menus.

25% OFF TOTAL | 👤 6 | FRI ✓ | SAT ✗ | ✱ — European

MR INDIA
☎ 01926 400 016

54 West Street, Warwick, CV34 6AN

Welcome to Mr India Warwick. Whatever the occasion, the staff at Mr. India invite you to come and enjoy a truly scrumptious Indian meal in the intimate atmosphere of their restaurant.

2FOR1 3 COURSES | FRI ✗ | SAT ✗ | ✱ — Indian

THE NEW BULLS HEAD
☎ 01789 268 832

9 Bull Street, Stratford-upon-Avon, CV37 6DT

The New Bulls Head is situated in the Old Town area of Stratford upon Avon. This family run establishment delivers an innovative menu that focuses on good quality food that aims to please all palates.

50% OFF FOOD | 👤 6 | FRI ✓ | SAT ✓ | SUN | ✱ — British

Gourmet Society discount applies to the à la carte menu only, unless stated otherwise.

NEWBOLD COMYN ARMS
☎ 01926 338 810
Newbold Terrace East, Leamington Spa, CV32 4EU
Roaring log fires for the winter and stunning countryside landscapes for the summer, this pub and restaurant is a fine place to eat and drink when exploring the Warwickshire area.

25% OFF TOTAL | ♟ 6 | FRI ✓ | SAT × | SUN — Bistro

NICOLINI'S RISTORANTE
☎ 01926 421 620
14 The Parade, Leamington Spa, CV32 4DW
Guests will be blown away by the subtle modern twists on traditional Italian dishes. Start the day with a delicious breakfast or take advantage of the extensive À la carte menus for dinner.

2FOR1 MAIN COURSE | FRI ✓ | SAT ✓ | ✱ | ▲ — Italian

THE OAK ROOM RESTAURANT
☎ 01789 450 123
Ettington Park Hotel, Stratford-upon-Avon, CV37 8BU
Under Head Chef Gary Lissemore's creative direction, this Hand Picked Hotels restaurant delivers full-flavoured fine dining in the luxurious surroundings of this country house setting. 2 AA Rosettes.

25% OFF TOTAL | ♟ 6 | FRI ✓ | SAT ✱ — Fine Dining

OTHELLO'S @ MERCURE
☎ 01789 294 997
Chapel Street, Stratford-upon-Avon, CV37 6ER
A well-loved aspect of the Shakespeare Hotel, which has maintained its original distinctive features while still appealing to the modern diner. A vibrant atmosphere and great food await you. 1 AA Rosette.

2FOR1 MAIN COURSE | FRI ▮ | SAT ✱ | ▲ — European

PANCHO TAPAS BAR
☎ 01926 400 809
5-6 The Knibbs, Smith Street, Warwick, CV34 4UW
Tucked away off Smith Street, Pancho takes "tapas" literally: a style of eating, not restricted to Spanish dishes. Includes sharing dishes from Thailand, Sweden and the USA. *Booking is essential.

25% OFF TOTAL | ♟ 6 | FRI ✓ | SAT ✓ — International

PREZZO
01926 431 833
25 Regent Grove, Leamington Spa, CV32 4NN
With a character all of its own, Prezzo oozes contemporary style and enduring charm. Signature pastas, stone-baked pizzas and classic Italian dishes promise a perfect dining choice for the whole family.

2FOR1 MAIN COURSE | FRI × | SAT × | ▲ — Italian

PREZZO
☎ 01789 290 933
22 Wood Street, Stratford-upon-Avon, CV37 6JF
With a character all of its own, Prezzo oozes contemporary style and enduring charm. Signature pastas, stone-baked pizzas and classic Italian dishes promise a perfect dining choice for the whole family.

2FOR1 MAIN COURSE | FRI × | SAT × | ▲ — Italian

PREZZO
☎ 01788 550 813
2 Regent Street, Rugby, CV21 2QF
With a character all of its own, Prezzo oozes contemporary style and enduring charm. Signature pastas, stone-baked pizzas and classic Italian dishes promise a perfect dining choice for the whole family.

2FOR1 MAIN COURSE | FRI × | SAT × | ▲ — Italian

QUEANS RESTAURANT
☎ 01926 315 522
15 Dormer Place, Leamington Spa, CV32 5AA
Refreshingly congenial service, a uniquely warm atmosphere and unsurpassed cuisine. A truly fine dining experience for any guest, with an astonishing sixteen home-made indulgent ice creams also on offer.

25% OFF TOTAL | ♟ 4 | FRI ✓ | SAT ✓ | SUN | ▲ — Fine Dining

QUILLS RESTAURANT
☎ 01789 271 000
Stratford Hotel, Arden St, Stratford-upon-Avon, CV37 6QQ
Quills keeps diners constantly brimming with anticipation over its ever changing menu. Trend-conscious, this contemporary restaurant reflects the seasons and its specialist suppliers.

25% OFF TOTAL | ♟ 6 | FRI ✓ | SAT ✓ — European

RAFFLES
☎ 01926 864 300
57 Warwick Road, Kenilworth, CV8 1HN
Britain's first colonial Malaysian restaurant brings a diverse range of exquisite cuisines together, all served in their own regal house style and ballroom setting. Delicious options available for all.

2FOR1 MAIN COURSE | FRI ▮ | SAT ▮ | SUN | ▲ — Malaysian

RAJDHANI
02476 352 254
1 Cambourne Dr, Horeston Grange, Nuneaton, CV11 6GU
Mouth-watering balti tandoori cuisine expertly prepared and cooked ensuring excellent flavours and spice. A family restaurant where a warm welcome and high standards are guaranteed.

25% OFF TOTAL | ♟ 4 | FRI ✓ | SAT ✱ — Indian

RED LION
01789 266 858
1 Warwick Rd, Bridgefoot, Stratford-upon-Avon, CV37 6YW
Quality pub classics with modern twists meets with a friendly and relaxed atmosphere to make this Table Table venue the perfect place for any occasion. *Excludes daytime & evening deals and festive menus.

2FOR1 MAIN COURSE | FRI ✓ | SAT ✓ — Modern British

THE REDGATE STEAK & ALEHOUSE
☎ 02476 383 384
Watling Street, Fenny Drayton, Nuneaton, CV10 0RY
Relax in style at this modern eatery, where emphasis is placed wholly on quality. Don't miss the 21 day-aged beef menu which provides you with a choice of 5 steaks in a variety of sizes.

25% OFF TOTAL | ♟ 4 | FRI ▮ | SAT ✱ — Steakhouse

REGENCY RESTAURANT
☎ 01676 522 735
The Manor Hotel Meriden, Main Road, Meriden, CV7 7NH
Offering a variety of dishes suitable for all palates and individual tastes, the owners proudly welcome you to enjoy their well-regarded, first-class food and service.

25% OFF TOTAL | ♟ 4 | FRI ✱ | SAT ✱ | SUN | ✱ — Fine Dining

ROBBIE'S OF WARWICK
☎ 01926 400 470
74 Smith Street, Warwick, CV34 4HU
Feast in this 15th-century timber-framed building, situated in the heart of the oldest part of town. Superlative international cuisine is created using the best of local produce by the talented Head Chef.

25% OFF TOTAL | ♟ 4 | FRI ▮ | SAT ▮ | ▲ — International

ROMNA
☎ 01788 544 882
39 Albert Street, Rugby, CV21 2SG
A well-designed Indian restaurant that serves classic favourites alongside distinctive local favourites all within a bright and welcoming environment. Try the Begum Bahar curries for a real delight.

2FOR1 3 COURSES | FRI ✱ | SAT ✱ — Indian

ROZANA TANDOORI
☎ 01926 428 620
28 Augusta Place, Leamington Spa, CV32 5EL
This busy, family-run Indian restaurant in Leamington Spa shows up well in its attention to detail. Generous portions, value for money and rich taste are the order of the day.

2FOR1 MAIN COURSE | FRI ✓ | SAT ✓ | ✱ — Indian

SAFFRON GOLD RESTAURANT
☎ 01926 402 061
Westage House, Market Street, Warwick CV34 4DE
A hugely popular Indian restaurant with an impressive, varied menu, offering traditional dishes whilst also providing the adventurous diner with many different choices.

25% OFF TOTAL | ♟ 4 | FRI ▮ | SAT ▮ | ✱ | ▲ — Indian

SEETAR TANDOORI
☎ 01926 851 585
55 Warwick Road, Kenilworth, CV8 1HN
Since opening its doors in 1989, Seetar Tandoori has become a cornerstone of Kenilworth's food map, with a dedication to authentic Indian cuisine and fantastic, friendly service. Join the loyal following.

2FOR1 MAIN COURSE | FRI ✓ | SAT ✓ | ✱ — Indian

SHAHPORAN BALTI
☎ 01788 568 892
149a Bilton Road, Rugby, CV22 7AS
A friendly, unpretentious balti place in Rugby where you can expect a full selection of classic Indian dishes. The flavours are rich and spicy, and the offerings generous.

2FOR1 MAIN COURSE | FRI × | SAT × | SUN — Indian

THE SHAKESPEARE
☎ 01926 421 212
56 Tavistock Street, Leamington Spa, CV32 5PW
Smart, lively pub-restaurant in Leamington Spa, where you can count on some great-quality, homely and fulsome dishes; the place buzzes, and is involved in local food festivals, so booking is a good idea.

25% OFF TOTAL | ♟ 2 | FRI ▮ | SAT ▮ | SUN — British

SOFTLEY'S ☎ 01455 290 464
2 Market Place, Market Bosworth, CV13 0LE
An intimate restaurant providing a comfortable atmosphere, where diners can enjoy quality dishes whilst overlooking the historical market place. Food is prepared using the best local ingredients.

25% OFF TOTAL | 👤4 | FRI ✓ | SAT ✱ | SUN | ▲ — European

SPA'S RESTAURANT ☎ 01926 425 522
Olympus Avenue, Tachbrook Park, Warwick, CV34 6RJ
Relaxed dining where guests can choose from a tasty menu offering a variety of European and international dishes. Ideal for visitors travelling to see the local historical sights.

25% OFF TOTAL | 👤4 | FRI ✓ | SAT ✓ | ▲ — European

SPICY AFFAIR ☎ 01926 338 883
4-6 Victoria Terrace, Leamington Spa, CV31 3AB
Setting out to bring a new twist to contemporary Asian cooking, Spicy Affair take you on a journey through the world of spices to experience culinary delights that you have never known before.

25% OFF TOTAL | 👤10 | FRI ✓ | SAT ✓ — Indian

STRADA 01926 420 094
90a Regents Court, Livery St, Leamington Spa, CV32 4AT
Offering fresh, bold dishes inspired by flavours of Italian city life - Strada serves a selection of indulgent tastes, to those seeking a blissful escape to laidback Italian life. *Excludes Pizzettas.

25% OFF TOTAL | 👤6 | FRI ✓ | SAT ✗ | ▲ — Italian

STRADA 01789 294 298
23 High Street, Stratford-upon-Avon, CV37 6AU
Offering fresh, bold dishes inspired by flavours of Italian city life - Strada serves a selection of indulgent tastes, to those seeking a blissful escape to laidback Italian life. *Excludes Pizzettas.

25% OFF TOTAL | 👤6 | FRI ✓ | SAT ✗ | ▲ — Italian

STUART RESTAURANT ☎ 01789 279 955
Barcelo Billesley Manor Hotel, Billesley, B49 6NF
Boasting 2 AA Rosettes, this manor oozes elegance and finesse. The fine-dining menu includes roast saddle of rabbit and soft Warwickshire duck eggs, served to perfection by chef Ales Maurer.

25% OFF TOTAL | FRI ✓ | SAT ✗ | SUN | ✱ — Fine Dining

STUDLEY SPICE ☎ 01527 850 077
75-77 Alcester Road, Studley, B80 7NJ
Guests will love the authentic Indian cuisine on offer in this relaxed restaurant. The mouth-watering dishes are guaranteed to satisfy every palate.

2FOR1 MAIN COURSE | FRI ✓ | SAT ✓ | ✱ — Indian

USHA ☎ 01789 297 348
28 Meer Street, Stratford-upon-Avon, CV37 6QB
Usha has an outstanding collection of accolades that can only be an encouragement to dine in this highly commended restaurant. Some of the finest aromatic Indian cuisine, produced in their clay oven.

2FOR1 MAIN COURSE | FRI ▮ | SAT ✱ | ✱ | ▲ — Indian

WARWICK SPICE ☎ 01926 491 736
24 Smith Street, Warwick, CV34 4HS
This restaurant revels in its reputation for high-quality, delicious food and unstinting consistency. The talents of the award-winning chef have casual diners soon becoming regulars.

2FOR1 MAIN COURSE | FRI ▮ | SAT ✱ — Indian/Bangladeshi

WILDWOOD KITCHEN ☎ 01789 262 910
10-11 Sheep Street, Stratford-upon-Avon, CV37 6EF
Wildwood Kitchen is a Italian pasta restaurant on Sheep Street in Stratford-upon-Avon and is a fun and laid-back dining venue divided into three separate dining areas.

2FOR1 MAIN COURSE | FRI ▮ | SAT ▮ | ▲ — Italian

WINDOWS ON THE WILD ☎ 0844 474 1777
Twycross Zoo, Burton Road, Atherston, CV9 3PX
To round off that perfect day at the zoo, head to Window on the Wild where the views of the bird aviary will provide some live entertainment while you dine. Delicious food and excellent service.

25% OFF TOTAL | 👤4 | FRI ✗ | SAT ✗ — Locally Sourced

West Midlands

24 CARAT BISTRO ☎ 0121 236 0519
27 Warstone Lane, Hockley, Birmingham, B18 6JQ
In the heart of Birmingham's Jewellery Quarter, this venue's aim is to provide good, home-cooked food at a modest price. A hidden gem serving everything from hearty breakfasts to traditional bread pudding.

25% OFF TOTAL | 👤4 | FRI ✓ | SAT ✱ | ▲ — British

ADDERLEY RESTAURANT ☎ 01675 470 468
Haunch Lane, Lea Marston, B76 0BY
Experience fine dining at its very best with the dinner or à la carte menu. Elegantly prepared dishes are served in the most stylish of settings. Excellence recognised with a double AA Rosette.

25% OFF TOTAL | 👤4 | FRI ✓ | SAT ▮ | ✱ | ▲ — Fine Dining

THE AGRABAD 0121 743 7883
884 Old Lode Lane, Solihull, B92 8LW
Renowned for its attentive and friendly staff, this Indian eatery prepares cuisine with a distinctive home-made taste. Dine at the pleasant restaurant or cosy up on the sofa at home with a tasty takeaway.

25% OFF TOTAL | 👤4 | FRI ✗ | SAT ✗ — Indian

AKBARS RESTAURANT 0121 452 1862
184 Hagley Road, Edgbaston, Birmingham, B16 9NY
A well-known Indian restaurant offering outstanding traditional cuisine. A busy buzz characterises the venue, meaning guests can enjoy high-quality food in an amiable atmosphere.

2FOR1 MAIN COURSE | FRI ✱ | SAT ✱ — Indian

AKRAM'S KASMIRI RESTAURANT ☎ 0121 433 4320
1526 Pershore Road, Stirchley, Birmingham, B30 2NW
Classic curries and favourite Indian dishes are on offer at this high-quality, good-value restaurant in Stirchley. The venue focuses on vibrant colours and distinctive flavours.

2FOR1 3 COURSES | FRI ✗ | SAT ✗ — Indian

AL FAISALS ☎ 0121 449 5695
136-140 Stoney Lane, Birmingham, B12 8AQ
Straight from the Heart of Kashmir, this regionally-inspired menu boasts expertly prepared balti curries. Mind-blowing flavours can be savoured in an unforgettable dining experience.

25% OFF TOTAL | FRI ✓ | SAT ✓ — Indian

ALBANY RESTAURANT & BAR ☎ 0121 634 6200
Smallbrook, Queensway, Birmingham, B5 4EW
Conveniently located city centre hotel that thrives upon its situation and plush facilities. The Albany Lounge Bar is the perfect place to unwind after a day exploring Birmingham, or to grab a bite.

50% OFF FOOD | 👤6 | FRI ✗ | SAT ✗ | SUN — European

AL-RABIE ☎ 0121 753 5599
392 Coventry Road, Birmingham, B10 0UF
The flavour of Lebanon, the savour of the Mediterranean; this is the secret that lies behind the recipes of Al-Rabie rich aromas and superb marinades, with every platter prepared freshly in front of you.

2FOR1 MAIN COURSE | FRI ✗ | SAT ✗ — Middle Eastern

AMERICANO ☎ 01902 424 433
The Connaught Hotel, Wolverhampton, WV1 4SW
The combination of gourmet cuisine with humble staff is the key to success at this steakhouse. Bursting with energy and enthusiasm, this venue is one of Wolverhampton's most exciting dining experiences.

25% OFF TOTAL | 👤10 | FRI ✓ | SAT ✓ | SUN | ✱ — American

ANNEXE ☎ 0121 236 1171
220 Corporation Street, Birmingham, B4 6QB
A venue edged with sophistication, this Birmingham brasserie looks great with its high, vaulting Victorian ceilings and elegant white linen. *Booking is essential. Always mention your Gourmet Society card.

25% OFF TOTAL | 👤2 | FRI ✗ | SAT ✗ | ✱ | ▲ — European

AQUA FOOD & MOOD
☎ 02476 229 551

14 Butts Street, Thomas Ct, Coventry, CV1 3GH

Infusing the cuisine of Italy and Lebanon, the dishes here are primarily healthy. Never compromising on the taste, the food is piquant and effortlessly chic.

25% OFF TOTAL | 8 | FRI × | SAT × | ✱ — Lebanese

ASHA'S RESTAURANT
☎ 0121 200 2767

12-22 Newhall Street, Birmingham, B3 3LX

Bollywood legend Asha Bhosle's first UK restaurant, delivering an impressive menu of Northwest Indian cuisine. The dishes on offer match the authentic venue, full of genuine colour, flavour and spice.

2FOR1 MAIN COURSE | FRI ✱ | SAT ✱ | ▲ — Indian

ASIAN FLAVOURS
☎ 02476 550 499

83 Far Gosford Street, Coventry, CV1 5DZ

Bright and brilliant Indian restaurant; one of the city's finest. Superb, understated modern style in its design, and a real freshness about the dishes, though with plenty of rich and spicy flavours.

50% OFF FOOD | FRI × | SAT × — Indian

ASIAN GRILL RESTAURANT
0121 354 7491

91 Park Road, Sutton Coldfield, B73 6BT

A delightful culinary experience where the passionate chefs have created an outstanding menu that fuses traditional and modern flavours and techniques. Thrill your palate with a taste of Southern Asia.

2FOR1 2 COURSES | FRI 📱 | SAT 📱 | ✱ — Indian

AWAY2DINE
☎ 0845 644 5244

252-260 Broad Street, Birmingham, B1 2HF

Moving serenely down the canal, in the process exposing long forgotten parts of the area to its guests, this mobile barge encourages guests to forget all about being in the city as they float Away2dine.

50% OFF FOOD | 4 | FRI ✓ | SAT ✓ — International

AZKA RESTAURANT
☎ 01384 423 806

53 High Street, Stourbridge, DY9 8LQ

Focussing on dishes from the Indian Subcontinent, Azka Balti has an extensive menu, comprising of favourite dishes from the whole region. Excellent food, impeccable service, you are bound to return.

2FOR1 MAIN COURSE | FRI ✓ | SAT ✓ | ✱ — Indian

BADGERS SETT
01562 883 120

Birmingham Road, Hagley, Nr Stourbridge, DY9 9JS

Beefeater Grill are one of the UK's best-loved restaurants welcoming guests for almost 40 years in over 130 locations nationwide. *Excludes Breakfast, Light Bites, Bar menu, set menus and all other offers.

2FOR1 MAIN COURSE | 6 | FRI ✓ | SAT × | ▲ — Modern British

BAILEY'S CARIBBEAN CUISINE
☎ 0121 359 2395

103 New Town Row, Birmingham, B6 4HG

At Baileys Caribbean Restaurant and Takeaway, you will always get a warm welcome. They offer a wide variety of traditional Caribbean breakfast, lunch and dinners for you to eat in or take away.

2FOR1 3 COURSES | FRI ✓ | SAT ✓ — Caribbean

BALTI BAZAAR
01384 353 800

1a Pedmore Road, Stourbridge, DY9 8DJ

A great balti restaurant in Lye. A popular place locally that has its stuff together, with a fine mix of attentive service, attention to detail and some rich, distinctive flavours among the curries.

2FOR1 MAIN COURSE | FRI 📱 | SAT × — Indian

BALTI COTTAGE
☎ 01675 464 122

107 High Street, Coleshill, Birmingham, B46 3BP

Bangladeshi cuisine has a world famous reputation for being rich and diverse. This warm, welcoming restaurant provides some of the very best dishes from across the South-East Asian subcontinent.

2FOR1 MAIN COURSE | FRI ✱ | SAT ✱ | ▲ — Bangladeshi/Indian

BALTI TOWERS
☎ 0121 559 5118

85 Long Lane, Halesowen, B62 9DJ

Bright and breezy Indian restaurant in Dudley with a loyal following off the back of their outstanding home-made sauces. Shows a great deal of know-how in the cooking, with a relaxed, low-key vibe.

50% OFF FOOD | 4 | FRI × | SAT × | ▲ — Indian

BANKS BISTRO
☎ 01902 238 433

40c Bath Road, Wolverhampton, WV1 4EP

Banks Bistro breathes elegance and sophistication. Offering convivial live music and a modern British menu that guarantees to get the taste buds tingling, this is a winning eatery all round.

25% OFF TOTAL | 4 | FRI ✓ | SAT × | SUN | ✱ | ▲ — French/European

BARAJEE
☎ 0121 643 6700

265 Broad Street, Birmingham, B1 2DS

A superb restaurant that offers creative menus in a modern, slightly retro venue. Indian and Bangladeshi cuisine is lovingly prepared to ensure it tastes its very best.

25% OFF TOTAL | 10 | FRI 📱 | SAT 📱 | ✱ — Indian

THE BARN
01564 782 144

Stratford Road, Hockley Heath, Solihull, B94 6NX

Beefeater Grill are one of the UK's best-loved restaurants welcoming guests for almost 40 years in over 130 locations nationwide. *Excludes Breakfast, Light Bites, Bar menu, set menus and all other offers.

2FOR1 MAIN COURSE | 6 | FRI ✓ | SAT × | ▲ — Modern British

BEACON VIEW BALTI RESTAURANT
☎ 07956 364 079

Beacon View Road, West Bromwich, B71 3NX

Beacon View Balti Restauant serves fine Indian cuisine. The chef's have over 25 years experience and pride themselves on their personal and professional service.

2FOR1 MAIN COURSE | FRI ✓ | SAT ✓ | ✱ — Indian

BEECHES BAR & GRILL
☎ 01675 442 277

Marsh Lane, Hampton in Arden, Solihull, B92 0AH

An impressive steak menu along with an array of grilled fish makes this a great place to dine. Try the unique 'wine flight' option, which allows guests to sample three distinct wines from around the world.

2FOR1 MAIN COURSE | FRI ✱ | SAT ✱ | SUN | ▲ — International

THE BELL INN
☎ 01675 463 380

12 Birmingham Road, Birmingham, B46 1AA

For tasty traditional meals and entertaining nights in a vibrant and friendly environment, try the Bell Inn. It makes for a highly enjoyable experience with friends.

2FOR1 3 COURSES | FRI ✓ | SAT ✓ — Traditional English

BENGAL BRASSERIE
☎ 01676 533 883

349-351 Kenilworth Road, Coventry, CV7 7DL

Locally renowned for its culinary excellence, the kitchen at Bengal Brasserie plays host to talented chefs who use exceptional ingredients and vibrant recipes. The tasty fish dishes are not to be missed.

25% OFF TOTAL | 10 | FRI ✓ | SAT ✓ — Indian

Bella Italia
Pizza ♥ Pasta ♥ Grill

25% OFF TOTAL | 6 | FRI × | SAT × | SUN | ✱ | ▲

4 restaurants in West Midlands

4 Belgrade Plz, Upr Well St, Coventry, CV1 4BF
☎ 02476 226 811

102 New Street, Birmingham, B2 4HS
☎ 0121 643 1548

10 Star City, Watson Rd, Birmingham, B7 5SB
☎ 0121 328 9696

The Touchwd Ctr, 25 Mill Ln, Solihull, B91 3GS
☎ 0121 711 8444

BENGAL DELIGHT
☎ 0121 454 7944

207 Hagley Road, Birmingham, B16 9RE

The Birmingham branch of Bengal Delights has gained the award-winning dishes and exceptional standards of service that were founded in its sister restaurants. Take away also available.

2FOR1 MAIN COURSE | FRI ▯ | SAT ▯ — Indian

BENGAL FUSION
☎ 01384 891 111

174 High Street, Lye, Stourbridge, DY9 8LN

Deliciously warming Bengali cuisine is served in a comfortable, contemporary setting. Tantalise your taste buds with an exceptional selection of starters, main dishes, and after-dinner delights.

25% OFF TOTAL | 10 | FRI ✱ | SAT ✱ — Indian

BENTLEY GREEN
01922 724 485

Bentley Road North, Walsall, WS2 0WB

Quality pub classics with modern twists meets with a friendly and relaxed atmosphere to make this Table Table venue the perfect place for any occasion. *Excludes daytime & evening deals and festive menus.

2FOR1 MAIN COURSE | FRI ✓ | SAT ✓ — Modern British

BENTLEY'S RESTAURANT
☎ 02476 633 733

The Brittania, Cathedral Square, Coventry, CV1 5RP

Adjoining the famous landmark of Coventry Cathedral, The Britannia is ideally located for rest, respite, dinner and drinks, while the restaurant has a well-deserved reputation for its irresistible food.

2FOR1 3 COURSES | FRI ✓ | SAT ✱ | SUN — British

THE BEWICK BAR @ MERCURE
☎ 02476 546 000

Main street, Brandon, Coventry, CV8 3FW

Elegant hotel and spa set in acres of beautiful grounds; the in-house Bewick Bar offers a range of wines, spirits and beers as well as a good selection of simple, tasty bar snacks and light meals.

50% OFF FOOD | 4 | FRI ✓ | SAT ✱ — International

BIG NANNY'S
☎ 0121 236 6831

27 Warstone Lane, Birmingham, B18 6JQ

Big Nanny's is a smart new Caribbean restaurant based in the heart of Birmingham?s historical Jewellery Quarter, serving authentic Caribbean cuisine with friendly service and a relaxed atmosphere.

25% OFF TOTAL | 4 | FRI ✓ | SAT ✓ | * | ▲ — Caribbean

BLUE BISTRO & RESTAURANT
☎ 02476 229 274

21 Spon Street, Coventry, CV1 3BA

Diners are transported back to the medieval period in this historic 1450 building. Guests enjoy the old wooden beams whilst indulging in a British menu which is ethically sourced and passionately prepared.

25% OFF TOTAL | 6 | FRI ✓ | SAT ✱ | SUN | ▲ — European

BLUE MANGO
☎ 02476 672 653

76 Albany Road, Earlsdon, Coventry, CV5 6JU

Expect familiar dishes cooked superbly and with a distinctive twist. Knowledgeable staff add to the welcoming vibrancy of the restaurant, whilst the stylish décor makes it an attractive place to dine.

2FOR1 MAIN COURSE | FRI ✓ | SAT ✓ — Indian

BLUE MANGO
☎ 0121 633 4422

5 Regency Wharf, Broad Street, Birmingham, B1 2DS

Blue Mango restaurant has vibrant city centre location in Birmingham with great reviews. They aim to offer diners excellent food alongside fantastic service.

25% OFF TOTAL | 4 | FRI ▯ | SAT ▯ | * | ▲ — Indian

BLUE ORCHID
☎ 02476 231 799

14 The Butts, Earlsdon, Coventry, CV1 3GR

The popularity of this restaurant testifies to the talent in the kitchen and the exquisite Thai and Indian food it serves. Among other favourite signature dishes, the meen mappas tetal is highly rated.

25% OFF TOTAL | FRI ✓ | SAT ✓ — Thai/Indian

THE BLUEBRICK
01902 875 300

Broad Gauge Way, Wolverhampton, WV1 1AA

Quality pub classics with modern twists meets with a friendly and relaxed atmosphere to make this Table Table venue the perfect place for any occasion. *Excludes daytime & evening deals and festive menus.

2FOR1 MAIN COURSE | FRI ✓ | SAT ✓ — Modern British

BOHEMIA
☎ 0121 471 2713

23 Oak Tree Lane, Selly Oak, Birmingham, B29 6JE

Bohemia's aim is purely and simply to provide modern and imaginative food, using fresh local produce, at a fair price. *Offer applies to set menu only. Members must purchase remaining courses.

2FOR1 MAIN COURSE | FRI ✓ | SAT ✓ | SUN | * | ▲ — Contemporary

BOMBAY PALACE
☎ 02476 677 851

64 Earlsdon Street, Coventry, CV5 6EJ

Fresh, bold flavours and innovative cooking techniques put Bombay Palace at the forefront of contemporary Indian gastronomy.

2FOR1 MAIN COURSE | FRI × | SAT × | * | ▲ — Indian

THE BRIDGE BAR & RESTAURANT
☎ 0870 400 7216

Holiday Inn, London Road, Coventry, CV8 3DY

A modern and friendly environment serving quality food from a menu that boasts a wide choice of international dishes for guests to choose from. Lounge bar also available for a full selection of beverages.

25% OFF TOTAL | 10 | FRI ✓ | SAT ✓ | * — International

THE BRIDGE RESTAURANT
☎ 0121 378 2442

Walmley Road, Sutton Coldfield, B76 1QX

An architecturally stunning building is home to an impressive Hand Picked Hotels group restaurant that produces exquisite cuisine. High standards have gained them 2 prestigious AA Rosettes.

25% OFF TOTAL | 6 | FRI ✱ | SAT ✱ | SUN — Fine Dining

BROOKES RESTAURANT
☎ 0121 623 9988

61 Homer Road, Solihull, B91 3QD

Brookes restaurant is tastefully decorated with a vibrant, contemporary feel yet with a welcoming and relaxed atmosphere for hotel guests, local diners and holidaymakers alike.

25% OFF TOTAL | 6 | FRI ✓ | SAT ✓ — International

25% OFF TOTAL

CAFÉ ROUGE

25% OFF TOTAL | 6 | FRI ✓ | SAT ✓ | * | ▲

7 restaurants in West Midlands

2 Belgrade Plaza, Coventry, CV1 4AJ
☎ 02476 222 550

The Waters Edge, Brindley Pl, Bham, B1 2HJ
☎ 0121 643 6556

The Bullring, Birmingham, B5 4BG
☎ 0121 616 1463

174-176 Wharfside St, Mailbox, Bham, B1 1RN
☎ 0121 665 6437

98 New Street, Birmingham, B2 4NS
☎ 0121 633 8125

42-44 High St, Harborne, Birmingham, B17 9NE
☎ 0121 426 4197

134 High Street, Solihull, B91 3SX
☎ 0121 711 8881

To understand what the restaurant icons mean, please see the inside back cover.

CAFÉ RICKSHAW
01902 425 353
20 Chapel Ash, Wolverhampton, WV3 0TN
Sumptuous Indian cuisine to be enjoyed in elegant and tasteful surroundings. While all of the dishes here are unique in taste and flavour, they're equal in quality and proportion.

25% OFF TOTAL | 10 | FRI ✓ | SAT ✓ | Indian

CARIB GRILL
0121 449 8818
2-4 St Mary's Row, Moseley, Birmingham, B13 8JG
Smart, up-market Caribbean restaurant that's known both for its warm atmosphere and for its excellent food. Begin with a rum punch and range through the jerk chicken, curry and other Caribbean delights.

2FOR1 MAIN COURSE | FRI ✱ | SAT × | SUN | Caribbean

CELEBRITY INDIAN RESTAURANT
0121 643 8969
44 Broad Street, Brindley Place, Birmingham, B8 1NZ
An appealing commingling of traditional and contemporary Indian cuisines, the food at Celebrity Indian Restaurant is the real star, even if the elegant, distinctive dining space vies for that crown.

2FOR1 MAIN COURSE | FRI ✓ | SAT × | ✱ | Indian

CHAOPHRAYA THAI RESTAURANT
0121 643 2424
Spiceal Street, Birmingham, B5 4BH
Inspired by the main waterway in Thailand, Chaophraya promises to breathe life into its diners through authentic, passionate cooking. An eclectic menu radiates colour and flavour from regional recipes.

2FOR1 MAIN COURSE | FRI | SAT × | Thai

CHILACAS BIRMINGHAM
0121 643 2707
Brindleyplace, The Waters Edge, Birmingham, B1 2HL
Chilaca's is all about capturing the energy, flavour, fire & passion of Mexican street food, served with flair and talent! They have got food for all tastes, from the mild to the extremely hot.

2FOR1 MAIN COURSE | 8 | FRI ✓ | SAT ✓ | Mexican

CHILLI 'N' CREME
01902 677 255
1 Holborn Centre, High Holborn, Sedgley, DY3 1SR
Popular Indian restaurant with a seductive combination of authentic Indian cuisine, great service and a warm atmosphere. Light, continental atmosphere; the cooking, in turn, is subtle and skilful.

2FOR1 MAIN COURSE | FRI ✓ | SAT ✓ | ✱ | Indian

CHINESE WOK
0121 544 0000
999 Wolverhampton Road, Oldbury, B69 4RJ
Newly established on the ground floor of Travellers Inn, Chinese Wok offers a Cantonese menu is prepared by experienced chefs who have adapted each dish to their own distinct taste and style

2FOR1 MAIN COURSE | FRI ✓ | SAT ✓ | Chinese

CITY CAFÉ
0121 633 6300
1 Brunswick Square, Brindley Place, Birmingham, B1 2H
Head Chef Neil Peers offers modern European dishes with seasonal menus, vegetarian choices and fine wines. The stylish restaurant and al fresco terraces both offer a pleasant atmosphere. 1 AA Rosette.

25% OFF TOTAL | 4 | FRI ✓ | SAT ✓ | European

CLUB BAR & LOUNGE
0121 351 3111
Ramada Jarvis, Penns Lane, Sutton Coldfield, B76 1LH
Enjoy a relaxing escape at the Ramada Birmingham and sample a quality international menu. From tasty smaller dishes to hearty main courses, this restaurant caters for every guest.

25% OFF TOTAL | 6 | FRI ✓ | SAT ✓ | International

CLUB ROOM
0844 815 9022
Ramada Jarvis, Penns Lane, Sutton Coldfield, B76 1LH
Offering contemporary bistro-style food whilst overlooking a picturesque lake, perfect for a relaxing break. The delicious menu offers temptations from starters through to desserts. Be sure to leave room.

25% OFF TOTAL | 6 | FRI ✓ | SAT ✓ | ✱ | Contemporary

THE CLUB ROOM RESTAURANT
0121 351 3111
Penns Lane, Sutton Coldfield, B76 1LH
Sample a tasty menu in this comfortable oak-beamed hotel-restaurant. Chefs use fresh seasonal produce, prepared in true brasserie style. A relaxed atmosphere makes for an enjoyable dining experience.

25% OFF TOTAL | 6 | FRI ✓ | SAT ✓ | International

THE COWSHED
01902 701 888
Clive Farm, Clive Road, Pattingham, WV6 7EN
Imaginative, contemporary British cuisine to be found in this characterful restaurant with oak beams and galleried balcony, all set on a working farm. Locally sourced and freshly cooked dishes.

25% OFF TOTAL | 10 | FRI | SAT ✱ | SUN | European

THE CROOKED HOUSE
01384 238 583
The Crooked House, Dudley, DY3 4DA
This intriguing venue is renowned for its level floors and leaning walls which create thrilling optical illusions such as marbles appearing to roll uphill. Try the local pheasant; delicious.

2FOR1 MAIN COURSE | FRI ✓ | SAT × | SUN | British

THE CROSS CAFÉ BAR
0121 449 6300
145-147 Alcester Road, Moseley, Birmingham, B13 8JP
One of Moseley's most popular venues; a perfect ambience yet completely unpretentious. Diligent and caring staff deliver clever but simple food. Also offers a variety of vegan and vegetarian dishes.

2FOR1 MAIN COURSE | FRI ✓ | SAT ✱ | SUN | International

CUCINA RUSTICA
0121 233 2277
24 Ludgate Hill, Birmingham, B3 1DX
Undoubtedly chic and modish, this Italian-inspired venue is centrally located for an ultimate cosmopolitan experience. Both classic and contemporary dishes are served by the most welcoming staff.

2FOR1 MAIN COURSE | FRI ✓ | SAT × | Italian

THE CURRY GARDEN RESTAURANT
0121 373 7173
16 York Road, Birmingham, B23 6TE
Established in 1976, this fine restaurant has 36 years of experience providing diners of the local area with outstanding Eastern Indian food. Expect a delicious menu and impeccable service.

2FOR1 MAIN COURSE | FRI ✓ | SAT ✓ | Indian

DEBULGE KITCHEN
0121 344 4714
353a Birchfield Road, Birmingham, B20 3BJ
Exciting and imaginative flavours characterise African cuisine; Debulge Kitchen provides an excellent sample of the Continent's very best dishes. From pounded yams to chicken and rice stew.

50% OFF FOOD | 2 | FRI ✓ | SAT ✓ | African

DEL VILLAGGIO
0121 643 1400
Unit 528, Bullring Shopping Centre, Birmingham, B5 4BE
Easygoing Italian restaurant in the Bullring. Serves a great range of Italian cuisine including the ever-popular pizzas, excellent steaks and tasty stuffed peppers. Convenient, spacious and lively.

2FOR1 MAIN COURSE | FRI ✓ | SAT × | SUN | Italian

DEOLALI BAR AND RESTAURANT
0121 442 2222
23A St Mary's Row, Moseley, Birmingham, B13 8HW
Offering dishes that perfectly represent the deliciousness of South Indian cuisine. Relax and unwind in a warm and comfortable environment as you enjoy a high-class dining experience.

25% OFF TOTAL | 4 | FRI ✓ | SAT ✓ | ✱ | Indian

DILKE ARMS
01922 746 456
Aldridge Road, Walsall, WS4 2JL
Quality pub classics with modern twists meets with a friendly and relaxed atmosphere to make this Table Table venue the perfect place for any occasion. *Excludes daytime & evening deals and festive menus.

2FOR1 MAIN COURSE | FRI ✓ | SAT ✓ | Modern British

'DINE' INDIAN & BANGLADESHI
01384 482 444
44 High Street, Brierley Hill, Dudley, DY5 3AE
A restaurant whose priorities simply lie in quality, flavour and service. With high-standard dishes created by an expert chef with 18 years experience, diners will not be disappointed.

25% OFF TOTAL | 8 | FRI ✓ | SAT ✓ | Indian

DIVINE RESTAURANT
0121 439 1140
325 Soho Road, Birmingham, B21 9SD
Divine is a family-run business who are proud of their authentic cooking style which originated in the heart of Africa. If you are not familiar with African cuisine, they can always suggest a dish for you to try!

2FOR1 MAIN COURSE | FRI ✓ | SAT ✓ | SUN | African

THE DOG INN
☎01675 481 318

Dog Lane, Nether Whitacre, Coleshill, B46 2DU

Superbly kept beers, fine food and a traditional atmosphere, all provided by a knowledgeable and welcoming landlady and her staff. Great value dishes, with guest ales added every week.

2FOR1 2 COURSES | FRI ✱ | SAT ✱ | SUN — British

DRAGON PHOENIX
☎02476 258 688

Hertford Place, Coventry, CV1 3JZ

Infusing the tastes of China, India and Italy, this buffet-style restaurant boasts mouth-watering oriental dishes and rustic pastas. Be sure to leave room for the luxurious and velvety chocolate fountain.

25% OFF TOTAL | 4 | FRI | SAT | ✱ — International

DRAGON VALE
☎01675 462 463

83 High Street, Coleshill, B46 3AG

This popular and lively Chinese restaurant serves classic dishes with traditional service in a beautiful surrounding. The extensive wine list and well-crafted menu offer something for everyone.

25% OFF TOTAL | 4 | FRI ✓ | SAT ✓ | ✱ — Chinese

THE DUCK
0121 452 5951

176 Hagley Road, Edgebaston, Birmingham, B16 9NY

Beefeater Grill are one of the UK's best-loved restaurants welcoming guests for almost 40 years in over 130 locations nationwide. *Excludes Breakfast, Light Bites, Bar menu, set menus and all other offers.

2FOR1 MAIN COURSE | 6 | FRI ✓ | SAT × | ▲ — Modern British

THE EDGBASTON PALACE HOTEL
☎0121 452 1577

198-200 Hagley Road, Edgbaston, Birmingham, B16 9PQ

What better place to dine than in this magnificent Victorian building situated in the leafy suburb of Edgbaston. Enjoy dining in the most beautiful surroundings.

2FOR1 3 COURSES | FRI | SAT | ✱ — European

EDMUNDS RESTAURANT
☎0121 633 4944

Six Brindleyplace, Birmingham, B1 2JB

Following a string of successful spells in the city, Chef Philipot has succeeded in injecting his passion for French cuisine to the menu at Edmunds; a long-standing favourite for any special occasion.

25% OFF TOTAL | 6 | FRI × | SAT × | SUN | ▲ | ✱ — Fine Dining

ELEMENTS BAR @ NOVOTEL
☎01902 871 100

Union Street, Wolverhampton, WV1 3JN

Elements Bar provides the perfect backdrop to a quiet, relaxed evening or an idyllic afternoon. Spend your time with friends or family as you eat from the snack menu and enjoy the extensive drink selection.

25% OFF TOTAL | 8 | FRI ✓ | SAT ✓ — British

ELEMENTS RESTAURANT @ NOVOTEL
☎01902 871 100

Union Street, Wolverhampton, WV1 3JN

Elements Restaurant offers a perfect accompaniment to the bar, perfect for those seeking something more substantial to eat. Old favourites have taken on a modern twist in the kitchen.

25% OFF TOTAL | 8 | FRI ✓ | SAT ✓ — British

THE ESTABLISHMENT BAR AND GRILL
☎02476 222 727

The Old County Hall, Coventry, CV1 5RN

The Establishment Bar and Grill have successfully retained a vintage yet contemporary feel, creating a homely environment in which guests can enjoy fine food. *This offer is available from 3pm onwards.

2FOR1 MAIN COURSE | FRI × | SAT × | ✱ — British

THE FAIRLAWNS RESTAURANT
☎01922 455 122

Fairlawns, Aston Road, Aldridge, WS9 0NU

Simple style accompanied by well-drilled, attentive service; an elegant, comfortable restaurant showing great precision in its cooking together with excellent sourcing. Fine English cuisine. 2 AA Rosettes.

25% OFF TOTAL | 10 | FRI ✓ | SAT × | SUN | ▲ — Modern European

FARADAYS RESTAURANT
☎01384 482 882

The Waterfront, Level St, Brierley, Dudley, DY5 1UR

Tremendous views of the waterfront marina enhance the overall appeal of this fine-dining hotel restaurant. Dine in elegance and style when visiting the Black Country.

50% OFF FOOD | 8 | FRI | SAT × — British

FILINI @ THE RADISSON BLU
☎0121 654 6000

12 Holloway Circus, Queensway, Birmingham, B1 1BT

Proclaiming a culinary philosophy of 'filini', this hotel-based restaurant produces uncluttered, clear flavours based on modern Italian cuisine.

25% OFF TOTAL | 2 | FRI ✓ | SAT ✓ — Italian

FLUTE RESTAURANT
☎0121 550 3415

179 Stourbridge Road, Birmingham, B63 3UD

Only fabulously fresh ingredients are carefully selected for the dishes at the Flute. Impeccable flavours, dynamic colours and creamy textures align the menu.

2FOR1 MAIN COURSE | FRI × | SAT × | SUN — Indian

THE FOX AND ANCHOR
01902 798 786

Brewood Road, Cross Green, Wolverhampton, WV10 7PW

This Vintage Inn oozes rural charm and rustic character. The picturesque surroundings provide the perfect backdrop for savouring the hearty, seasonal pub-food on the menu.

25% OFF TOTAL | FRI ✓ | SAT ✓ | SUN | ▲ — Modern British

FRENCH CONNECTION
☎01384 390 940

3 Coventry Street, Stourbridge, DY8 1EP

Highly regarded bistro that serves rounded, classic French dishes with a great emphasis on technique and precision; unstinting on French culinary tradition and keen to foreground its history and culture.

25% OFF TOTAL | 6 | FRI × | SAT ✱ | ▲ — French

GEORGE IN THE TREE
01676 533 118

Kenilworth Road, Balsall Common, Berkswell, CV7 7EX

Beefeater Grill are one of the UK's best-loved restaurants welcoming guests for almost 40 years in over 130 locations nationwide. *Excludes Breakfast, Light Bites, Bar menu, set menus and all other offers.

2FOR1 MAIN COURSE | 6 | FRI ✓ | SAT × | ▲ — Modern British

GINO RESTAURANT AND BAR
☎0121 212 1337

16 Frederick Street, Birmingham, B1 3HE

Gino is a unique venue in the heart of Birmingham, situated in the Jewellery Quarter. Relaxing at the bar or enjoying Mediterranean tapas and cocktails at the venue is a must.

50% OFF FOOD | 10 | FRI ✓ | SAT ✓ | ▲ — Mediterranean

THE GRILL ROOM
☎0800 400 9007

Holiday Inn B'ham Airport, Coventry Rd, B'ham, B26 3QW

The Grill Room doors open up to a world of devoted hospitality, fine cuisine and vibrant atmosphere. Meticulous preparation goes into every single order submitted to the kitchen.

25% OFF TOTAL | 6 | FRI ✓ | SAT ✓ — International

HABIBI
☎02476 220 669

142 Far Gosford Street, Coventry, CV1 5DY

An original Arabic restaurant that welcomes all to experience the sounds and tastes of the East. Offers an extensive halal menu that is freshly prepared. *Call on the day to check availability.

25% OFF TOTAL | 8 | FRI | SAT — Arabic

THE HERON'S NEST
01564 771 177

2110 Warwick Road, Knowle, Solihull, B93 0EE

This Vintage Inn oozes rural charm and rustic character. The picturesque surroundings provide the perfect backdrop for savouring the hearty, seasonal pub-food on the menu.

25% OFF TOTAL | FRI ✓ | SAT ✓ | SUN | ▲ — Modern British

HOGARTH'S HOTEL
☎01564 779 988

Four Ashes Road, Dorridge, B93 8QE

In a secluded venue set in acres of beautiful woodland, chefs passionately create exceptional food that appeals to all palates, delivering it in a hospitable and peaceful atmosphere.

25% OFF TOTAL | 4 | FRI | SAT | SUN — European

HOTEL DU VIN
☎0121 200 0600

Church Street, Birmingham, B3 2NR

The finest, fresh local produce, simple European recipes, a stunning choice of wines; these are the trademarks of a Hotel du Vin bistro. A distinctive venue with an ornate courtyard feature. 1 AA Rosette.

2FOR1 MAIN COURSE | FRI × | SAT × | SUN | ▲ — European

Gourmet Society discount applies to the à la carte menu only, unless stated otherwise.

handmade burger Cº

Waters Edge, Birmingham, B1 2JB
☎ 0121 665 6542

St. Martin's Square, Birmingham, B5 4BW
☎ 0121 633 3696

Upper Mill Lane Arcade, Solihull, B91 3GJ
☎ 0121 711 3004

2FOR1 MAIN COURSE | FRI ✓ | SAT ✗ | SUN

handmade burger Co.

handmade burger Co. are passionate about great, fresh, food and use only the finest ingredients for you to enjoy.

Famous for burgers handmade from traditionally reared, 100% prime Scotch beef, the chefs make over 40 varieties of hand pressed burgers everyday.

The sourdough burger buns come from a fourth generation family bakery and are made from a recipe developed in partnership.

The menu also boasts a wide selection of fabulous vegetarian options and a great range for children all made from the finest fresh ingredients.

HUB LOUNGE & BAR @ PARK INN ☎ 01922 639 100
Bescot Cresent, Walsall, WS1 4SE
Modern restaurant of clean lines, varnished wood and smart settings. Carved a niche for itself as a place to relax with friends, family or colleagues.

50% OFF FOOD | 6 | FRI ✱ | SAT ✱ — British

IL MICHELANGELO ☎ 0138 474 405
34 High Street, Brockmore, DY5 3XS
Divine Italian cuisine makes this a popular venue in which diners can enjoy the rustic, flavourful food on offer. Bright reds and vivid greens characterise the dishes in true Mediterranean style.

50% OFF FOOD | 4 | FRI × | SAT × — Italian

INDIA GATES ☎ 01902 401 500
6-8 Mount Pleasant, Wolverhampton, WV14 7LJ
Fine punjabi cuisine at India Gates, where butter chicken sits alongside a more fiery balti or chilli paneer. Traditional tandoori favourites are also exceptional, such as the delicious chicken tikka.

50% OFF FOOD | FRI ✓ | SAT ✓ — Indian

INDIANOS ☎ 0121 707 9055
2a Station Road, Acocks Green, Birmingham, B27 6DN
Superb Indian Restaurant serving authentic cuisine that will satisfy every diner. The food here is fresh and expertly spiced.

25% OFF TOTAL | 6 | FRI ✓ | SAT ✓ | ✱ — Indian

ISABELLAS RESTAURANT ☎ 0121 247 2010
856 Bristol Road, Selley Oak, Birmingham, B29 6HW
Nothing but fine, authentic Italian cuisine here, with an extensive menu offering guests a variety of dishes firmly rooted in Italy's rich culinary culture. Expect divine flavours and choice wines.

25% OFF TOTAL | 6 | FRI × | SAT × | SUN | ▲ — Italian

ITIHAAS ☎ 0121 212 3383
18 Fleet Street, Birmingham, B3 1JL
A smart and sophisticated venue delivering mouth-watering dishes following the traditions of Mogul and Maharaja India, where food was perceived as a pleasure rather than a necessity.

25% OFF TOTAL | 6 | FRI ✱ | SAT ✱ | ▲ — Indian

THE JEKYLL AND HYDE ☎ 0121 236 0345
28 Steelhouse Lane, Birmingham, B4 6BJ
Revamped city centre pub with a cutting edge drinks list, bespoke lunchtime sandwich selection and hearty gourmet pub meals. Also features a Victorian-inspired gin parlour.

2FOR1 MAIN COURSE | FRI × | SAT × | ✱ | ▲ — British

JENNY'S RESTAURANT ☎ 01922 630 983
Old Square, Walsall, WS1 1PY
When you fancy a quick bite to eat, a juicy burger or a fresh filling salad, head to Jenny's and let her cater to you. Delicious food and excellent service are guaranteed to be found here.

25% OFF TOTAL | FRI ✓ | SAT ✓ | ✱ — British

THE JEWEL RESTAURANT ☎ 01902 605 917
112 New Road, Willenhall, WV13 2AQ
The Jewel is a stylish, contemporary Balti restaurant located in Willenhall, which receives consistently excellent reviews from diners. The menu offers up fusion cuisine which will leave you delighted.

2FOR1 3 COURSES | FRI × | SAT × | SUN | ✱ | ▲ — Indian

JOJOLAPA RESTAURANT ☎ 0121 212 2511
55-59 Newhall Street, Birmingham, B3 3RB
Named after the Nepalese word meaning 'welcome', this venue is habitually inviting and hospitable. Enjoy an authentic dish of home-made kulfi whilst admiring the intricately carved panels of dark wood.

25% OFF TOTAL | 2 | FRI ✓ | SAT × | ▲ — Nepalese

KABABISH RESTAURANT ☎ 0121 355 5062
266 Jockey Road, Sutton Coldfield, B73 5XP
Relax and unwind in this tastefully decorated and elegantly lit restaurant. Exotic herbs and spices are distinctly blended using the traditional methods of the North West frontier of Pakistan.

25% OFF TOTAL | 8 | FRI ✱ | SAT ✱ | ▲ — Indian

KABABISH RESTAURANT ☎ 0121 449 5556
29 Woodbridge Road, Moseley, Birmingham, B13 8EH
Relax and unwind in this tastefully decorated and elegantly lit restaurant. Exotic herbs and spices are distinctly blended using the traditional methods of the North West frontier of Pakistan.

25% OFF TOTAL | 8 | FRI ✱ | SAT ✱ | ▲ — Indian

KABEN? ☎ 01384 484 827
The Blue Ball, Old High St, Stourbridge, DY5 1SE
Popular with the customers, this restaurant boasts a comprehensive menu of specialist dishes and traditional curries, alongside essential sundries and tasty desserts.

25% OFF TOTAL | 10 | FRI ✓ | SAT ✱ | ✱ | ▲ — Bangladeshi

KASTURI ☎ 0121 350 5100
498 College Road, Birmingham, B44 0HL
Kasturi has set new standards for serving authentic and high quality regional Indian food. The primary focus is healthy eating which is achieve by the careful selection of ingredients and cooking methods.

2FOR1 MAIN COURSE | FRI ✓ | SAT ✓ | ✱ — Indian

KINGSWINFORD BEEFEATER GRILL 01384 291 290
Dudley Road, Kingswinford, DY6 8WT
Beefeater Grill are one of the UK's best-loved restaurants welcoming guests for almost 40 years in over 130 locations nationwide. *Excludes Breakfast, Light Bites, Bar menu, set menus and all other offers.

2FOR1 MAIN COURSE | 6 | FRI ✓ | SAT × | ▲ — Modern British

KINNAREE THAI RESTAURANT ☎ 0121 665 6568
22 Waterfront Walk, Birmingham, B1 1SN
Enter an exotic, mystical atmosphere where the focus is placed on divine food in traditionally magical surroundings. The chicken and noodles in red curry soup is out of this world.

2FOR1 MAIN COURSE | FRI ✱ | SAT ✱ — Thai

KNOWLE INDIAN BRASSERIE ☎ 01564 776 453
1690 High Street, Knowle, Solihull, B93 0LY
A small intimate Indian restaurant that offers a large number of completely unique speciality dishes. Affable staff will cater to your every need.

25% OFF TOTAL | 4 | FRI ✱ | SAT ✱ | ▲ — Indian

LA CAVERNA HOTEL ☎ 0121 743 7917
2327 Coventry Road, Sheldon, B26 3PG
Renowned for its fabulous Italian cuisine served in a warm inviting environment. Fine seafood dishes such as the lobster soup and the scallops in bacon are especially popular.

25% OFF TOTAL | 2 | FRI ✓ | SAT ✓ — Italian

LA CC CAFE RESTAURANT & BAR ☎ 0121 786 2647
57 Stoney Lane, Birmingham, B25 8YG
Adventurous palates can sample generous boar steaks and octopus andalus at this genuine Spanish eatery. Family-run, this venue exudes intimacy and ambiance. Perfect for a romantic dinner for two.

25% OFF TOTAL | 4 | FRI ✓ | SAT ✓ — Spanish

LA FAVORITA ☎ 0121 771 4112
72 Alfred Street, Birmingham, B12 8JP
La Favorita is an Italian restaurant serving affordable, high quality Italian cuisine including 18 pizzas, a wide variety of pastas, fish and meat dishes and home made desserts.

25% OFF TOTAL | 4 | FRI × | SAT × | SUN | ▲ — Italian

LAHORE KARAHI CHINESE & BALTI ☎ 0121 773 7575
309 Highgate Road, Birmingham, B12 8DN
Britain's first dedicated halal Chinese restaurant, whose quality is attested by a series of endorsements - from Amir Khan to Prince Philip, to the Pakistan and England cricket teams.

2FOR1 2 COURSES | FRI ✓ | SAT ✓ — Chinese

LE RAJ ☎ 01384 251 222
31-35 Louise Street, Dudley, DY3 2UA
Passionate about Indian cuisine, Le Raj pride themselves on a menu abundant with choice. Boasting an assortment of curries and grills, this venue is also dedicated to impeccable service.

2FOR1 MAIN COURSE | FRI ✓ | SAT ✓ — Indian

THE LITTLE OWL
0121 781 0331

Bickenhill Parkway, Solihull, B40 1QA

This Vintage Inn oozes rural charm and rustic character. The picturesque surroundings provide the perfect backdrop for savouring the hearty, seasonal pub-food on the menu.

25% OFF TOTAL | FRI ✓ | SAT ✓ | SUN | ▲ — Modern British

THE LLOYDS INDIAN RESTAURANT
☎ 01564 775 777

7 Station Road, Knowle, Solihull, B93 OHL

Culinary pleasures need not be guilty ones when dining at this delightful Indian restaurant. The quality of the produce can be tasted in every divine dish, all exceptionally reasonable in price.

2FOR1 MAIN COURSE | FRI ✓ | SAT ✓ | ✱ | ▲ — Indian

LOCH FYNE
☎ 01564 732 750

The Bank House, High Street, Knowle, B93 0JU

From the roadside oyster bar that once was, Loch Fyne restaurants now successfully inject energy and passion into great food and wonderful flavours, whilst ensuring their seafood is sustainably sourced.

25% OFF TOTAL | 4 | FRI ✱ | SAT ✱ | ▲ — Seafood

LONGFELLOWS
☎ 0121 705 0547

255 Hampton Lane, Solihull, B91 2TJ

This versatile, welcoming restaurant specialises in imaginative and flavourful takes on English staples. Its line in succulent, seasonal game marks it out, along with its tender, tasty seafood dishes.

25% OFF TOTAL | 6 | FRI | SAT × | SUN | ▲ — British

MAA RESTAURANT
☎ 0121 355 0528

454 Chester Road North, Birmingham, B73 6RG

Hailed as one of the best Indian restaurants in Sutton Coldfield, Maa specialises in fine Indian Dining. Perfect for all occasions, all curry lovers are bound to agree that Maa is an excellent find.

2FOR1 3 COURSES | FRI × | SAT × | ✱ — Indian

THE MACDONALD ANSTY HALL HOTEL
☎ 02476 612 222

Main Road, Ansty, Coventry, CV7 9HZ

From the finest Scottish beef to corn-fed chicken and fresh wild fish, the produce is excellently sourced and creatively used, so that every dish is as outstanding as the next.

25% OFF TOTAL | 10 | FRI ✓ | SAT ✓ — European

MALABAR
☎ 0121 428 4466

103A High St, Harborne, Birmingham, B17 9NR

A wonderful Indian restaurant offering staple classics and more interesting, unusual dishes for the adventurous diner to sample. Staff are always happy to assist you in your choices.

2FOR1 MAIN COURSE | FRI × | SAT × — Indian

MALABAR
☎ 01902 332 080

315 Penn Road, Wolverhampton, WV4 5QF

A well-regarded Indian restaurant in Wolverhampton, Malabar specialises in fish dishes and some particularly accomplished entrées, complete with excellent service and décor to add a touch of charm.

2FOR1 MAIN COURSE | FRI ✓ | SAT ✓ | ✱ — Indian

MALMAISON
☎ 0121 246 5000

1 Wharfside Street, Mailbox, Birmingham, B1 1RD

This characterful Mal brasserie focuses on fresh local produce for its inviting and diverse menus; hearty, delicious game sourced from nearby on the Welsh border is stunning. Awarded 1 AA Rosette.

2FOR1 MAIN COURSE | FRI × | SAT × | SUN | ✱ | ▲ — European

MANGO SPICE
☎ 0121 308 0022

6a Hill Village Road, Sutton Coldfield, B75 5BA

This Indian restaurant testifies to the multiplicity of the continent's culinary and cultural traditions. You can count on a variety of vivid, fulsome and tasty dishes along with an accommodating ambience.

2FOR1 MAIN COURSE | FRI ✓ | SAT ✱ | ▲ — Indian

MARSTON FARM HOTEL
☎ 01827 872 133

Bodymoor Heath, Sutton Coldfield, B76 9JD

Set in the beautiful Warwickshire countryside, this Brook hotel's Courtyard Restaurant allows diners to sample a variety of mouth-watering meals coupled with warm, friendly service of the highest order.

25% OFF TOTAL | 10 | FRI ✓ | SAT ✓ — Traditional English

MASALA CLUB RESTAURANT
☎ 01676 533 210

235 Station Road, Balsall Common, Coventry, CV7 7EG

Try this lively, classy Indian restaurant and its superbly wide-ranging menu of aromatic starters and clear, distinctive main-course flavours.

25% OFF TOTAL | 10 | FRI ✱ | SAT ✱ | ✱ — Indian

MECHU GRILL
☎ 0121 710 4222

59 Summer Row, Birmingham, B3 1SS

Mechu's sleek, stylish setting combines with a real emphasis on clear, uncluttered flavours, with splashes of informality for a cool, comfortable evening out.

25% OFF TOTAL | 8 | FRI | SAT ✱ — Contemporary

THE MERMAID
01902 764 896

Bridgnorth Road, Wolverhampton, WV6 8BN

This Vintage Inn oozes rural charm and rustic character. The picturesque surroundings provide the perfect backdrop for savouring the hearty, seasonal pub-food on the menu.

25% OFF TOTAL | FRI ✓ | SAT ✓ | SUN | ▲ — Modern British

MILAN INDIAN CUISINE
☎ 0121 236 0671

93 Newhall Street, Birmingham, B3 1LH

This restaurant juxtaposes its basis in North Indian cooking with an openness to other flavours; it is known for its great array of vegetarian dishes and serves light, tasty food in a cosy ambience.

2FOR1 2 COURSES | FRI | SAT | ▲ — Indian

THE MINT
☎ 02476 226 111

13 Queens Road, The Butts, Earlsdon, Coventry, CV1 3GJ

A unique menu of modernised Indian Cuisine that still retains authentic flavour, yet combines with different accents from around the world, with a design and décor that embodies this creative style.

25% OFF TOTAL | 10 | FRI ✱ | SAT ✱ | ✱ | ▲ — Indian

MINT INDIAN AND BANGLADESHI CUISINE
☎ 0121 789 8908

Unit Three, Yew Tree Retail Park, Yardley, B25 8YP

Innovative, acclaimed Indian and Bangladeshi restaurant that supplements all the classics with distinctive house specialities; a real range from delicately spiced to bold and flavoursome dishes.

2FOR1 MAIN COURSE | FRI ✓ | SAT ✱ | ✱ | ▲ — Bangladeshi/Indian

MIYAKO TEPPANYAKI
☎ 0121 622 5183

Arcadian Centre, Ladywell Walk, Birmingham, B5 4ST

This restaurant showcases the full flavourful range of Japanese cuisine. Try the succulent fillet steak, cooked on the traditional Hibarchi; not to be outdone are its fresh, vibrant vegetarian dishes.

25% OFF TOTAL | 4 | FRI | SAT ✱ — Japanese

MOSELEY PARK
01902 397 755

Greenfield Lane, Wolverhampton, WV10 6TA

Quality pub classics with modern twists meets with a friendly and relaxed atmosphere to make this Table Table venue the perfect place for any occasion. *Excludes daytime & evening deals and festive menus.

2FOR1 MAIN COURSE | FRI ✓ | SAT ✓ — Modern British

NAGA NIGHTS
☎ 01902 424 511

31 School Street, Wolverhampton, WV1 4LR

A well-regarded establishment with a spice-filled and fragrant menu, rich in Indian classics, catering for all tastes and preferences. Delicious, authentic food delivered at a very high standard.

2FOR1 MAIN COURSE | FRI ✓ | SAT ✓ | ✱ — Indian

NATHANIELS
☎ 0121 449 9618

13 St Mary's Row, Moseley, Birmingham, B13 8HW

A seasonally changing à la carte menu and a deservedly popular lunch menu make this a perfect place to dine. Delicious steaks are to be devoured before moving on to the mind-blowing desserts.

2FOR1 2 COURSES | FRI | SAT | SUN | ▲ — British

NAZRAJ SIGNATURE BRASSERIE
☎ 02476 630 236

5 Station Square, Coventry, CV1 2GT

Passionate about giving customers an authentic taste of India, the chefs at this venue serve only the most flavoursome and fresh of dishes in a contemporary setting.

2FOR1 3 COURSES | FRI ✓ | SAT ✓ — Indian

NUTHURST GRANGE HOTEL
01564 783 972
Nuthurst Grange Lane, Hockley, B94 5NL
Enjoy the range of dining possibilities at this intimate and relaxed restaurant, from canapés with your pre-meal drinks, to petit fours with your coffee. Awarded 2 AA Rosettes.

2FOR1 MAIN COURSE | FRI | SAT | SUN — Fine Dining

THE OAK ROOM
02476 466 174
Nailcote Hall Hotel, Nailcote Lane, Berkswell, CV7 7DE
Renowned as one of Britain's most romantic hotels, the restaurant situated here acts as the perfect place for those special occasions. Make perfect memories in this 1 AA Rosette awarded restaurant.

2FOR1 2 COURSES | FRI | SAT | — Fine Dining

THE OAK ROOM RESTAURANT
0121 308 3751
Moor Hall Drive, Sutton Coldfield, B75 6LN
The Oak Room Restaurant was the original dining room of Sir Edward Ansell in the 1900s and it offers the perfect combination of delicious food and friendly attentive service.

2FOR1 MAIN COURSE | FRI × | SAT × | SUN | * | — European

THE OAKEN ARMS
01902 847 342
Holyhead Road, Oaken, Wolverhampton, WV8 2HX
This Vintage Inn oozes rural charm and rustic character. The picturesque surroundings provide the perfect backdrop for savouring the hearty, seasonal pub-food on the menu.

25% OFF TOTAL | FRI ✓ | SAT ✓ | SUN | — Modern British

THE OLIVE GROVE
02476 555 416
41 London Road, Coventry, CV1 2JP
Welcome to The Olive Grove.Whether it's tapas and a glass of wine you're after, or a fabulous setting to celebrate a special occasion, you'll feel completely treated at The Olive Grove.

25% OFF TOTAL | FRI × | SAT × | SUN | — Mediterranean

PAD THAI
0121 666 6669
86 Holloway Head, Birmingham, B1 1NB
Taking its name from the classic street-stall noodle dish, this wonderful Thai restaurant offers all the tastiness of the food and all the friendliness of Thai culture.

25% OFF TOTAL | 8 | FRI | SAT | * | — Thai

PAPRIKA GRILL HOUSE
0121 472 2137
9 Raddlebarn Road, Selly Oak, B29 6HJ
Succulent chunks of Chicken, seafood or vegetables are grilled on large skewers over an authentic charcoal barbecue. Hungry diners can feast on Mediterranean starters and wholesome side dishes.

2FOR1 MAIN COURSE | FRI × | SAT × | — Med/Meze

PAVAROTTI ITALIAN RESTAURANT
0121 743 3222
Blue ice plaza, Birmingham, B92 8JN
Step into the heart of Italy with a wholesome helping of creamy risotto or a crispy pizza. Vegetarians are generously catered for and local farm ingredients ensure genuine tastiness.

2FOR1 MAIN COURSE | FRI ✓ | SAT × — Italian

THE PAVILLION
0121 454 6621
The Quality Hotel, 166 Hagley Road, Edgbaston, WB16 9NZ
Browse the à la carte menu or head straight for the carvery at this wonderful hotel restaurant. Admire the garden views that are visible from the Pavilion and the Terrace Bar.

25% OFF TOTAL | FRI ✓ | SAT | * | — International

PLAYWRIGHTS
02476 231 441
4-6 Hay Lane, Cathedral Quarter, Coventry, CV1 5RF
Playwrights is a café, bistro and bar rolled into one. The menu offers an extensive selection of tasty bites which can be added to more substantial and delicious dishes.

25% OFF TOTAL | 4 | FRI | SAT | * | — International

THE PLOUGH
01217 442 942
Stratford Road, Shirley, Solihull, B90 4EP
Beefeater Grill are one of the UK's best-loved restaurants welcoming guests for almost 40 years in over 130 locations nationwide. *Excludes Breakfast, Light Bites, Bar menu, set menus and all other offers.

2FOR1 MAIN COURSE | 6 | FRI ✓ | SAT × | — Modern British

THE PLOUGH & HARROW HOTEL
0121 454 4111
135 Hagley Road, Edgbaston, Birmingham, B16 8LS
Just a stone's throw away from the city centre, this 18th-century building is now home to an ideally situated hotel and restaurant. Unwind over a fabulous cocktail or indulge in delicious food.

25% OFF TOTAL | 10 | FRI ✓ | SAT ✓ | — English and Continental

THE PLOUGH HARBORNE
0121 427 3678
21 High St, Harborne, Birmingham, B17 9NT
One fine gastro-pub on the outskirts of Birmingham. A hip local vibe and quirky, incisive dishes make this the sort of place that can easily become a favourite haunt.

2FOR1 MAIN COURSE | FRI ✓ | SAT ✓ — Modern Pub

POLASH
01675 462 868
85 High Street, Coleshill, Birmingham, B46 3AG
Quality Indian food cooked to perfection using fresh ingredients, ensuring every dish on their extensive menu is full of natural flavour and spice.

2FOR1 MAIN COURSE | FRI | SAT | * | — Indian

THE PORTLAND HOTEL
0121 455 0535
313 Hagley Road, Edgbaston, Birmingham, B16 9LQ
A restaurant that is equally as popular with non-residents as it is with hotel guests. Inexpensive meals are served in the most elegant of settings.

25% OFF TOTAL | 10 | FRI ✓ | SAT ✓ | * — English and Continental

PORTOBELLO RISTORANTE
01922 744 777
17-19 High Street, Aldridge, Walsall, WS9 8LX
Watch excellent chefs expertly prepare your food from the finest ingredients available in an open-plan kitchen. Ideal for lunch or a quiet evening meal, this Italian restaurant delivers fine, deluxe food.

25% OFF TOTAL | 4 | FRI | SAT | — Italian

PREZZO
0121 553 4482
14 New Square, West Bromwich, B70 7PP
With a character all of its own, Prezzo oozes contemporary style and enduring charm. Signature pastas, stone-baked pizzas and classic Italian dishes promise a perfect dining choice for the whole family.

2FOR1 MAIN COURSE | FRI × | SAT × | — Italian

PRIYA RESTAURANT
0121 448 8581
40-42 St Marys Row, Birmingham, B13 8JG
At Priya, they present Tandoori, Mughal and Bengali dishes as a sample of the variety of classic Asian food found across the Indian sub-continent. Enjoy the delicious food and attentive staff at Priya.

25% OFF TOTAL | 6 | FRI ✓ | SAT ✓ | * — Indian

THE PUNCHBOWL
01564 784 564
Mill Lane, Lapworth, Solihull, B94 6HR
Pop in for an impromptu lunch with friends, or relax over romantic candlelight with loved ones. The pub encompasses all the right traditional features, whilst delivering a modern style and atmosphere.

25% OFF TOTAL | 4 | FRI | SAT | SUN | — British

PUNJABI HAVELI
0121 745 3636
1558 Stratford Road, Hall Green, Birmingham, B28 9HA
A wonderful restaurant serving deliciously fresh Punjabi cuisine. Guests can taste authenticity and quality in every dish created by Head Chef Sukhdev Singh, who originates from the region of Punjab.

25% OFF TOTAL | 2 | FRI | SAT | * | — Indian

PURBANI TANDOORI RESTAURANT
01902 424 030
41-43 Birch Street, Wolverhampton, WV1 4JW
Good quality, simple and traditional Indian cuisine populates a menu showcasing all the classic Indian dishes. Made with quality ingredients, they provide rich and fragrant flavours.

25% OFF TOTAL | 4 | FRI ✓ | SAT ✓ — Indian

PURBOBAGH RESTAURANT
0121 785 1225
886 Washwood Heath Road, Birmingham, B8 2NB
The objective of the team at Purbobagh Restaurant is to create a dining establishment known for superb quality Indian food, first class ambiance and excellent service.

2FOR1 3 COURSES | FRI ✓ | SAT ✓ | * | — Indian

FIND MORE — ONLINE —

www.gourmetsociety.co.uk

THE PURPLE ROOMS
☎ 0121 702 2193

1076 Stratford Road, Hall Green, Birmingham, B28 8AD

The award-winning status of this restaurant reflects its culinary excellence, with a vast menu providing mouth-watering dishes in abundance. The superb fish curries are highly recommended.

2FOR1 MAIN COURSE | FRI ✓ | SAT ✓ | ▲ — Indian

QUICKEN TREE RESTAURANT
☎ 01676 543 300

Meriden Road, Fillongley, Coventry, CV7 8DX

The privacy, peace and sanctuary of the Quicken Tree affords a warm welcome to all guests, allowing you to dine in modern elegance. Select from a menu of traditional, home-cooked, hearty dishes.

2FOR1 MAIN COURSE | FRI ✓ | SAT ✓ — Fine Dining

RAJ INDIAN CUISINE
☎ 0121 357 8368

30 Birmingham Road, Great Barr, Birmingham, B43 6NR

Conveniently located, this classical Indian restaurant delivers sumptuous-tasting food from a greatly varied menu, with recommended dishes including the prawn Jhinga Mossalla.

25% OFF TOTAL | 4 | FRI ✷ | SAT ✷ | ✱ | ▲ — Indian

RANGA MATI
☎ 01902 305 635

75 Lichfield Road, Wolverhampton, WV11 1TW

Praised by locals, this Indian restaurant delivers an eclectic menu, with dishes originating from across the colourful sub-continent. Chef specialities come highly recommended.

2FOR1 MAIN COURSE | FRI × | SAT × | SUN — Indian

RASA RESTAURANT
☎ 0121 779 2773

3 Alcott Lane, Solihull, B37 7AT

Rasa's award-winning variety of dishes will delight your sense of taste, whilst pushing the boundaries of traditional Indian cuisine.

25% OFF TOTAL | 4 | FRI ▯ | SAT ▯ | ✱ | ▲ — Indian

RBG @ PARK INN BIRMINGHAM
☎ 0121 609 9988

Birmingham Road, West Bromwich, B70 6RS

A versatile hotel-based restaurant where you'll find everything from a well-accomplished full English breakfast, to a big, bold working lunch. Contemporary, stylish and sassy.

2FOR1 MAIN COURSE | FRI ✓ | SAT ✓ | SUN | ✱ | ▲ — English and Continental

RED FORT
☎ 01902 424 440

Fold Street, Wolverhampton, WV1 4LP

Vaunting a spacious interior, this venue boasts luxurious and elegant surrounds. Devour an authentic Punjabi dish bursting with tantalising flavours certain to appease grumbling stomachs.

2FOR1 MAIN COURSE | FRI ✓ | SAT ✓ | ✱ | ▲ — Indian/Punjabi

THE RED LION
0121 445 4162

Red Lion Street, Alvechurch, Birmingham, B48 7LG

This Vintage Inn oozes rural charm and rustic character. The picturesque surroundings provide the perfect backdrop for savouring the hearty, seasonal pub-food on the menu.

25% OFF TOTAL | FRI ✓ | SAT ✓ | SUN | ▲ — Modern British

THE RED LION
01564 702 946

Lady Lane, Earlswood, Solihull, B94 6AQ

This Vintage Inn oozes rural charm and rustic character. The picturesque surroundings provide the perfect backdrop for savouring the hearty, seasonal pub-food on the menu.

25% OFF TOTAL | FRI ✓ | SAT ✓ | SUN | ▲ — Modern British

RED OVEN
☎ 0121 429 2884

607A Bearwood Road, Birmingham, B66 4BJ

Red Oven is the first Indian Punjabi restaurant in Bearwood. They are unique in offering authentic Punjabi cuisine, all prepared using the freshest of ingredients combined with the Punjabi style of cooking.

2FOR1 3 COURSES | FRI × | SAT × | ✱ | ▲ — Indian

REGARDS
☎ 0121 455 6697

27 Chad Square, Edgbaston, Birmingham, B15 3TQ

Quality Indian cooking from a restaurant which prides itself on exceeding customers' expectations every time. Complete with a private dining area, this venue is an excellent choice whatever the occasion.

2FOR1 MAIN COURSE | FRI ✓ | SAT ✓ — Indian

THE REGENCY RESTAURANT
☎ 01902 311 311

53 Tettenhall Road, Wolverhampton, WV3 9NB

Set in a restored 18th-century school, this charming restaurant is regarded as one of Wolverhampton's best. The kitchen produces fine dishes such as the great rib-eye steak with a white wine pepper sauce.

25% OFF TOTAL | 2 | FRI × | SAT × | SUN | ✱ | ▲ — English and Continental

RESTAURANT @ GENTING CASINO
☎ 0121 454 3725

1 Norfolk Road, Birmingham, B15 3PS

The exclusive Genting Casino Edgbaston is well-reputed for its fine dining and warm welcomes. The stylish bar and restaurant will make any evening out highly memorable.

2FOR1 MAIN COURSE | FRI ▯ | SAT ▯ | SUN | ✱ | ▲ — British

THE RICKSHAW
☎ 01384 233 446

11 Porters Field, Dudley, DY2 7AT

Popular amongst loyal locals, the Rickshaw is a bustling venue with expert staff, fresh and relaxing decor and delicious meals cooked how you like it.

25% OFF TOTAL | FRI ✓ | SAT ✓ | ✱ — Indian

THE RIDGACRE
01215 534 910

New Gas Street, West Bromwich, B70 0NP

Quality pub classics with modern twists meets with a friendly and relaxed atmosphere to make this Table Table venue the perfect place for any occasion. *Excludes daytime & evening deals and festive menus.

2FOR1 MAIN COURSE | FRI ✓ | SAT ✓ — Modern British

ROSE OF KASHMIR
☎ 01384 235 673

179 Wolverhampton Street, Dudley, DY1 3AD

A restaurant where excellence is their start point and where every aspect of your dining experience becomes a feast for the eyes, the mouth and the soul.

2FOR1 3 COURSES | FRI ▯ | SAT ▯ | ✱ — Indian

ROYAL BENGAL
☎ 0121 643 8127

23 Smallbrook, Birmingham, B5 4HE

Offering flavourful and aromatic cuisine, the dishes here are prepared passionately and ooze authenticity. The attentive staff will help you select from the extensive wine list.

2FOR1 3 COURSES | FRI ✓ | SAT ✓ — Indian

THE ROYAL OAK
☎ 02476 501 077

Whitley Village, Coventry, CV3 4AL

A warm welcome awaits you at The Royal Oak, whether you wish to relax with friends for an evening drink or spend your lunchtime enjoying the best pub food that Coventry has to offer.

25% OFF TOTAL | 10 | FRI × | SAT × | SUN — Traditional English

ROYAL SPICE
☎ 0121 477 5223

953-955 Bristol Road S, Northfield, B31 2QT

Renowned for its fabulously flavoured balti dishes, this fine restaurant offers superbly authentic Indian and Bangladeshi dishes for all to enjoy. The popular five-course meal comes highly recommended.

25% OFF TOTAL | 10 | FRI ✷ | SAT ✷ — Bangladeshi/Indian

RUBY CANTONESE RESTAURANT
☎ 0121 429 8805

2A Barnsley Road, Edgbaston, Birmingham, B17 8ED

Delivering delicious Cantonese cuisine that successfully satisfies every time. Boasting a highly experienced chef, the kitchen produces favourite dishes from satay skewers to beef in black bean sauce.

2FOR1 MAIN COURSE | FRI ✓ | SAT ✓ — Cantonese

SAFARI BITES CUISINE
☎0121 333 4123

256 Great Lister Street, Birmingham, B7 4DA

A great place for those new to African cuisine to sample the best on offer, and a great chance for diners fond of it to try it once again. Regional favourites come strongly recommended.

25% OFF TOTAL | 4 | FRI ✱ | SAT✱ | SUN | ▲ — African

SAFFRON
☎0121 552 1752

909 Wolverhampton Road, Oldbury, B69 4RR

Vintage aromas and delicious flavours are exquisitely balanced in each and every dish. Valuing traditional methods of Indian cooking, the menu succeeds in serving extraordinarily appetising meals.

2FOR1 MAIN COURSE | FRI ✱ | SAT✱ | ▲ — Indian

SCOTTISH STEAK CLUB
☎0121 643 9191

Macdonald Burlington Hotel, Birmingham, B2 4JQ

Fine Scottish cuisine can be enjoyed as you take in the hustle and bustle of the outdoor Birmingham New Street. Succulent steaks and an excellent array of drinks maintain high standards of delivery.

2FOR1 MAIN COURSE | FRI ✓ | SAT✓ — British

THE SENATOR
☎01922 644 148

31 Bradford Street, Walsall, WS1 3QA

At the Senator, they offer a variety of African cuisine and a unique blend of tradition, with dishes from Nigeria, Kenya and Zimbabwe that include goat, grilled fish and authentic spices.

25% OFF TOTAL | FRI ✓ | SAT✓ | SUN — African

SHABAB'S
☎0121 440 2893

163 Ladypool Road, Birmingham, B12 8LQ

Nestled in the West Midlands Balti triangle, this venue does not disappoint its prestigious neighbours. Guaranteeing a fine-dining experience, Shabab's boasts a loyal following.

25% OFF TOTAL | 6 | FRI ✓ | SAT ✗ | ✱ — Indian

SHADES OF RAJ
☎0121 704 0353

52 Station Road, Solihull, B91 3RX

Presenting delicious dishes that focus on both taste and texture whilst maintaining an eye on healthy eating. The fine wine list will satisfy the desires of all budding wine connoisseurs.

25% OFF TOTAL | 10 | FRI ▯ | SAT ▯ | ✱ — Indian

SHAH'S BISTRO
☎0121 744 4123

135 Stratford Rd, Shirley, Solihull, B90 3AY

A great restaurant serving the finest cuisine from Bengal and India. Shah's chefs are passionate and creative, offering you flavours and dishes that culminate to a mouth-watering menu.

2FOR1 MAIN COURSE | FRI ✗ | SAT ✗ | ✱ — Indian

SHERWOODS INDIAN RESTAURANT
☎0121 733 7363

1492 Stratford Road, Hall Green, Birmingham, B28 9ET

Satisfy your senses and sample a true taste of India. The kitchen focuses its energy on producing high-quality food at great prices. The sizzling lamb balti is particularly popular.

2FOR1 3 COURSES | FRI ✱ | SAT✱ | ✱ | ▲ — Indian

SHIMLA PEPPERS BAR & RESTAURANT
☎01922 640 605

91 Ablewell Street, Walsall, WS1 2EU

Using cooking methods that date back to the Imperial food courts, the chefs devote themselves to taking diners on a culinary journey. No artificial colours or flavourings are used, only authentic spices.

50% OFF FOOD | 10 | FRI ✱ | SAT✱ | ▲ — Indian

SHIMLA PINKS
☎0121 633 0366

Fiveways Leisure Centre, Broad St, B'ham, B15 1AY

Incorporates new and exciting dishes amongst a menu of traditional Indian cuisine. The visually pleasing interior ensures you enjoy your meal in an outstanding setting. A beacon to curry lovers.

25% OFF TOTAL | FRI ✓ | SAT✓ — Indian

SHIMLA PINKS
☎0121 704 0344

44 Station Road, Solihull, B91 3RX

Incorporates new and exciting dishes amongst a menu of traditional Indian cuisine. The visually pleasing interior ensures you enjoy your meal in an outstanding setting. A beacon to curry lovers.

25% OFF TOTAL | FRI ✓ | SAT✓ — Indian

SIMLA
☎01543 360 600

29 High Street, Walsall, WS9 9LR

Established since 1998; Simla have managed to create a carefully crafted menu, that appeals to all palates. Using authentic Indian cooking methods, a truly traditional experience is masterfully achieved.

2FOR1 3 COURSES | FRI ✗ | SAT ✗ | ✱ | ▲ — Indian

SIMON'S CANTONESE & SEAFOOD
☎0121 580 9293

520 Chester Road, Little Aston, Walsall, WS9 0PU

Take it easy at the bar and enjoy a drink or two before taking your seat and enjoying fabulous Cantonese cuisine in a cosy and elegant environment. Also popular for its astoundingly good seafood dishes.

25% OFF TOTAL | 10 | FRI ✱ | SAT✱ | SUN | ✱ | ▲ — Chinese

SOFIAS ITALIAN RESTAURANT
☎01922 632 223

8 High Street, Walsall, WS1 1QW

Vibrant Italian restaurant situated in the town's Guildhall. Large open kitchen, beautiful architecture, and high-quality Italian food; plenty of pastas and pizzas, alongside lesser-known specialities.

2FOR1 MAIN COURSE | FRI ▯ | SAT ✗ | ▲ — Italian

SOUL FOOD PROJECT
☎0121 444 2081

106 High Street, Birmingham, B14 7JZ

A trailblazing Cajun Kitchen, specialising in food from America's Deep South. Expect jambalayas bursting with chorizo, chicken, crayfish and the rest, some fine vegetarian gumbos, and excellent po'boys.

2FOR1 MAIN COURSE | FRI ✓ | SAT ✗ | SUN — Southwestern American

SOUL FOOD PROJECT @ THE VICTORIA
☎0121 633 9439

48 John Bright Street, Birmingham, B1 1BN

A trailblazing Cajun Kitchen, specialising in food from America's Deep South. Expect jambalayas bursting with chorizo, chicken, crayfish and the rest, some fine vegetarian gumbos, and excellent po'boys.

2FOR1 2 COURSES | FRI ✓ | SAT ✗ | SUN — Southwestern American

SPICE BLUE INDIAN RESTAURANT
☎0121 373 4662

192 Sutton New Road, Birmingham, B23 6QU

Spice Blue Indian Restaurant is a popular haunt for locals that never fails to deliver. With traditional sumptuous curries and specialty Balti dishes, there is something on offer for even the fussiest of palates.

2FOR1 MAIN COURSE | FRI ▯ | SAT ▯ | ✱ — Indian

SPICE CLUB
☎0121 711 7070

697 Warwick Road, Solihull, B91 3DA

Scrumptious food, superb service and a personal touch are the reasons for Spice Club's popularity, making it one of the most well-cherished restaurants in Solihull.

2FOR1 MAIN COURSE | FRI ✗ | SAT ✗ — Indian

SPICE ROOM
0121 373 0044

358 Birmingham Road, Sutton Coldfield, B72 1YH

Spice Room is a vibrant restaurant that delights in serving a large array of bright and colourful Indian dishes. The fish specialities are especially worth a try, such as the chilli panga.

25% OFF TOTAL | 6 | FRI ▯ | SAT ✗ — Indian

SPICELAND
☎01902 425 444

58 Tettenhall Road, Wolverhampton, WV1 4SL

Knowledgeable staff ensure that no diner goes hungry at this Indian eatery. Whether it's an intimate meal for two or a special occasion, the loyal following indicates diners will return time after time.

2FOR1 MAIN COURSE | FRI ✓ | SAT✓ — Indian

SPICES OF INDIA
☎0121 643 3383

21 Smallbrook, Queensway, Birmingham, B5 4HE

Quality restaurant serving a fine array of Indian dishes, from classic curry staples to the more unusual choices. Fresh sundries and crispy starters will add great flavour to your evening.

2FOR1 MAIN COURSE | FRI ✓ | SAT✓ — Indian

SPICEWOODS
☎0121 742 6630

Solihull Ice Rink, Solihull, B92 8JN

With a menu consisting of much loved Indian favourites, freshly prepared using succulent cuts of meat and authentic spice blends, Spicewoods brings good, honest, authentic Indian cuisine to its clientèle.

25% OFF TOTAL | 10 | FRI ✗ | SAT ✗ — Indian

ST JOHN'S HOTEL
0121 711 3000

Warwick Road, Solihull, B91 1AT

Conveniently located close to Birmingham, the NEC, and local attractions such as Warwick Castle and Cadbury World, St Johns Hotel is a winning venue for your short break or business conference.

25% OFF TOTAL | 6 | FRI ✓ | SAT ✓ | ▲ — British

STAGESIDE BAR & RESTAURANT
0844 338 9000

Birmingham Hippodrome, Birmingham, B5 4TB

StageSide is a casual, brasserie-style experience with a lively bar and quick service. Pop in for a coffee or a tasty dish or two from their simple modern British menu. *Available evenings only, after 7pm.

25% OFF TOTAL | 10 | FRI ✓ | SAT ✓ | SUN | ✱ — European

STRADA
0121 212 2661

8 Quayside, Broad Street, Birmingham, B1 2EA

Offering fresh, bold dishes inspired by flavours of Italian city life - Strada serves a selection of indulgent tastes, to those seeking a blissful escape to laidback Italian life. *Excludes Pizzettas.

25% OFF TOTAL | 6 | FRI ✓ | SAT × | ▲ — Italian

STRADA
0121 643 7279

109 -111 Wharfside Street, Birmingham, B1 1XL

Offering fresh, bold dishes inspired by flavours of Italian city life - Strada serves a selection of indulgent tastes, to those seeking a blissful escape to laidback Italian life. *Excludes Pizzettas.

25% OFF TOTAL | 6 | FRI ✓ | SAT × | ▲ — Italian

STRESA
02476 238 110

The Butts, Earlsdon, Coventry, CV1 3GG

Relaxing, friendly atmosphere; the restaurant offers children the chance to make their own pizza. The food is warming and Mediterranean, focused on the quality of ingredients.

25% OFF TOTAL | 6 | FRI ✓ | SAT ✓ | ✱ | ▲ — Mediterranean

SURIYA
0121 373 2425

426 Kingstanding Road, Birmingham, B44 9SA

A local favourite for enthusiasts of pan-Asian cooking, Suriya can confidently assert their place as one of Birmingham's most popular Indian restaurants. A perfect combination of flawless gastronomy and un

2FOR1 MAIN COURSE | FRI × | SAT × | ✱ — Indian

THE SWALLOW'S NEST
01562 711 236

40 Bromsgrove Road, Romsley, Halesowen, B62 0LF

This Vintage Inn oozes rural charm and rustic character. The picturesque surroundings provide the perfect backdrop for savouring the hearty, seasonal pub-food on the menu.

25% OFF TOTAL | FRI ✓ | SAT ✓ | SUN | ▲ — Modern British

SWEET CHILLIES CUISINE
0121 443 2737

836 Yardleywood Road, Birmingham, B13 0JE

Excite your palate with delicious food from Bengal, the eastern region of India. Highly recommended for lovers of spice, yet chefs here also endeavour to cater for other guests and dietary requirements.

2FOR1 MAIN COURSE | FRI ✱ | SAT ✱ — Indian

THE SYLHET SPICE CUISINE
0121 444 6644

27-29 York Road, Kingsheath, Solihull, B14 7SA

Drawing on all the old favourites as well as a distinctive array of signature dishes, this Indian restaurant is firmly focused on authenticity and quality in its tastes from Bangladesh, India and Pakistan.

25% OFF TOTAL | 6 | FRI ✱ | SAT ✱ | SUN | ▲ — Indian

TAJ MAHAL
0121 643 8200

1 Hinckley Street, Birmingham, B5 4LJ

A traditional tandoori oven is used at the Taj Mahal restaurant, which works to produce the distinctive charcoal flavours of Indian dishes. Superb sauces and crisp sundries are also on offer.

2FOR1 MAIN COURSE | FRI ✓ | SAT ✓ | ✱ — Indian

TELION RESTAURANT
0121 236 3812

84 Bull Street, Birmingham, B4 6AB

Telion is a new Cafe - Deli, a Mediterranean experience which brings something different to your everyday lives. Delicious fresh food to make your day.

25% OFF TOTAL | FRI ✓ | SAT ✓ | SUN — Mediterranean

TERRACE RESTAURANT
0121 378 2442

Walmley Road, Sutton Coldfield, B76 1QX

A superb restaurant offering home-cooked treats inside a moated manor, and is a renowned member of the Hand Picked Hotels group, where each talented chef offers their own signature dish.

25% OFF TOTAL | 6 | FRI ✱ | SAT ✱ | SUN | ▲ — Brasserie

TIFFU'S
01902 324 340

2-3 High Street, Wolverhampton, WV5 9DN

Amiable staff and fine food make Tiffu's a great place to dine. Proudly presents genuine Bangladeshi cuisine of fine quality. Find characterful and distinctive dishes.

25% OFF TOTAL | 4 | FRI 📱 | SAT 📱 | ✱ — Bangladeshi

TIN TIN CHINESE RESTAURANT
0121 633 0888

9F Waters Edge, Brindley Place, Birmingham, BB1 2HL

Unique both in style and experience, Tin Tin maintains its status as the best for elegant Cantonese cuisine. The restaurant presents you with superb dishes cooked by a revolutionary team of chefs.

2FOR1 MAIN COURSE | FRI 📱 | SAT 📱 | ▲ — Chinese

TORINO PIZZA
02477 679 658

27 The Butts, Coventry, CV1 3GJ

Exciting toppings and freshly baked bases characterise the food on offer, while the staff are happy to cater to your own individual pizza cravings. Just the venue when only pizza will do.

50% OFF FOOD | FRI × | SAT × — Italian

TWICE THE SPICE
01384 232 425

97-98 High Street, Dudley, DY1 1QP

Good quality local Indian restaurant in Dudley. Enjoy a mouth-watering curry with fluffy naan and all the trimmings. Essential to phone at least 24 hours in advance.

2FOR1 3 COURSES | FRI ✱ | SAT ✱ | SUN | ✱ | ▲ — Indian

ULYSSES GREEK RESTAURANT
0121 622 3159

42a Bristol Street, Birmingham, B5 7AA

Established in 1986, this family-owned restaurant maintains its authentic and traditional Greek menu. In the heart of the city you can fully enjoy fine Greek and organic wines from Tripoli.

25% OFF TOTAL | 4 | FRI 📱 | SAT ✱ | ✱ — Greek

VALENTINO'S RESTAURANT
0121 427 2560

73 High Street, Harborne, Birmingham, B17 9NS

Deliciously simple yet delectably sophisticated, Valentino's offers a varied menu for all to enjoy, which is matched by the extensive wine list. The daily specials prove to be exceedingly popular.

25% OFF TOTAL | 6 | FRI 📱 | SAT 📱 — Italian

VENEZIA ITALIAN
0121 472 4423

523-525 Bristol Road, Birmingham, B29 6AU

Venezia has been serving great Italian cuisine since 2000 and are passionate about great food and wine, served in a vibrant, warm and friendly atmosphere, where the meu uses fresh ingredients and produce.

25% OFF TOTAL | 10 | FRI ✓ | SAT ✓ — Italian

VERVE BAR AND GRILL
0844 980 8042

Dolomite Avenue, Coventry Business Park, CV4 9GZ

The Verve Bar & Grill is a sleek and stylish restaurant located in the DeVere Village Hotel in Coventry, it is renown for its succulent steaks and great service.

50% OFF FOOD | 6 | FRI ✓ | SAT 📱 | SUN | ▲ — British

VERVE GRILL & OVEN
0844 980 0118

Stratford Road, Shirley, Solihull, B90 4GW

Seasonal classics cooked with imagination and served with style at this great little restaurant. Contemporary surroundings, attentive, knowledgeable and unrushed service goes with an emphasis on freshness.

2FOR1 MAIN COURSE | FRI ✓ | SAT ✓ | ✱ | ▲ — International

THE VICTORIAN RESTAURANT
0121 236 8312

16 Great Western Arcade, Birmingham, B2 5HU

The Victorian Restaurant serves freshly prepared classic British meals from winter-warming pies and grills, to light sandwiches and salads. You will be tempted by the delicious selection of cakes.

50% OFF FOOD | 6 | FRI 📱 | SAT 📱 — British

THE VILLAGE RESTAURANT 0121 327 7862
133 Alum Rock Road, Birmingham, B8 1NH
The most authentic and delectable cuisine is served at this Pakistani owned eatery. Guests can savour a delightful array of classic and specialty dishes, including an abundance of sumptuous sides.

2FOR1 MAIN COURSE | FRI ✓ | SAT × | ✱ — Pakistani

THE VINE 01902 894 829
High Street, Wombourne, Wolverhampton, WV5 9DT
This Vintage Inn oozes rural charm and rustic character. The picturesque surroundings provide the perfect backdrop for savouring the hearty, seasonal pub-food on the menu.

25% OFF TOTAL | FRI ✓ | SAT ✓ | SUN | ▲ — Modern British

THE VINE INN ☎01562 882 491
Vine Lane, Clent, Stourbridge, DY9 9PH
A new menu offers some traditional favourites such a steamed steak and kidney pudding and slow-cooked glazed pork belly as well as more unusual specialities such as wild boar, other game dishes and fish.

25% OFF TOTAL | FRI ✓ | SAT ✱ | SUN — British

WALKABOUT ☎0121 632 5712
Langley Building, Birmingham, B1 2DS
Walkabout is famous for its characteristically Australian atmosphere and well-rounded menu. From live sport with a juicy burger to some Aussie kangaroo skewers, you'll find it hard to tear yourself away.

25% OFF TOTAL | 👤2 | FRI ✓ | SAT ✓ | ▲ — Australian

WALKABOUT ☎01902 796 900
50 Queen Street, Wolverhampton, WV1 3BJ
Walkabout is famous for its characteristically Australian atmosphere and well-rounded menu. From live sport with a juicy burger to some Aussie kangaroo skewers, you'll find it hard to tear yourself away.

25% OFF TOTAL | 👤10 | FRI ✓ | SAT ✓ | ▲ — International

WALL HEATH TANDOORI ☎01384 287 402
4 High Street, Wall Heath, Kingswinford, DY6 0HA
Situated in Wall Heath's adjacent village Kingswinford, this restaurant offers pleasing Indian cuisine at affordable prices. Extremely popular with the local community, booking is recommended.

2FOR1 MAIN COURSE | FRI ✱ | SAT ✱ — Indian

WEST 12 RESTAURANT ☎0121 452 7007
12 Hagley Road, Edgbaston, Birmingham, B16 8SJ
Fine dining awaits you in the stylish West 12 restaurant and bar, which specialises in contemporary British cuisine such as Scottish beef and Welsh Lamb. A great place to relax and eat well.

25% OFF TOTAL | 👤6 | FRI ✓ | SAT ✓ | ▲ — European

THE WHITE HORSE 01675 470 227
Kingsbury Road, Curdworth, Sutton Coldfield, B76 9DS
This Vintage Inn oozes rural charm and rustic character. The picturesque surroundings provide the perfect backdrop for savouring the hearty, seasonal pub-food on the menu.

25% OFF TOTAL | FRI ✓ | SAT ✓ | SUN | ▲ — Modern British

THE WHITE LION 02476 332 841
Hawkes Mill Lane, Allesley, Coventry, CV5 9FQ
This Vintage Inn oozes rural charm and rustic character. The picturesque surroundings provide the perfect backdrop for savouring the hearty, seasonal pub-food on the menu.

25% OFF TOTAL | FRI ✓ | SAT ✓ | SUN | ▲ — Modern British

WING WAH CLUB ☎0121 327 7879
278 Thimble Mill Lane, Nechells, Birmingam, B7 5HD
Prestigious and boasting multiple awards, this fine-dining oriental eatery is aesthetically beautiful. Savour the delectable tastes of Cantonese, Szechuan and Peking cuisine at a surprisingly modest prices.

25% OFF TOTAL | 👤6 | FRI ✓ | SAT × | SUN | ▲ — Chinese

YE OLDE TOLL HOUSE RESTAURANT ☎01902 605 575
40 Walsall St, Willenhall, Wolverhampton, WV13 2ER
An unforgettable eating experience, here you will find imaginative dishes at affordable prices. The Old World interior encourages the maintenance of the restaurant's traditional splendour and atmosphere.

2FOR1 MAIN COURSE | FRI ✓ | SAT ✱ | ▲ — British

YUSRASS NICOBAR ☎0121 471 4696
608 Bristol Road, Birmingham, B29 6BQ
Spoil yourself with an evening of fine dining at this effortlessly chic Indian eatery. Whether you're treating the family or your colleagues, this venue caters to all parties and palettes.

25% OFF TOTAL | 👤10 | FRI ✓ | SAT ✓ — Multi-Cuisine

ZAGORA MOROCCAN RESTAURANT ☎0121 233 2484
4 Fletchers Walk, Birmingham, B3 3HJ
With its traditional Moroccan decor and deliciously spiced dishes, Zagora offers the perfect location for those seeking a taste of the exotic in the heart of Birmingham.

25% OFF TOTAL | 👤8 | FRI ▯ | SAT ▯ | ✱ — Med/Meze

Worcester/Herefordshire

ABDUL'S 01905 723 594
46 The Tything, Worcester, WR1 1JT
Friendly little balti restaurant in Worcester. Colourful and vibrant, they have all the basics down pat and offer a good selection of more esoteric dishes like the chicken kabolia with chickpeas and herbs.

2FOR1 MAIN COURSE | FRI × | SAT × | SUN — Indian

ARISHANA LOWERWICK ☎01905 339 338
51 Canada Way, Worcester, WR2 4XA
Located in the heart of Lower Wick, Worcester, Arishana is an unique dining experience. Modern décor and innovative artworks enhance the setting for you to enjoy your delicious Indian meal.

2FOR1 MAIN COURSE | FRI ▯ | SAT ▯ | ✱ — Indian

BEEFEATER GRILL REDDITCH 01527 590 916
Bordesley Lane, Redditch, B97 6AQ
Beefeater Grill are one of the UK's best-loved restaurants welcoming guests for almost 40 years in over 130 locations nationwide. *Excludes Breakfast, Light Bites, Bar menu, set menus and all other offers.

2FOR1 MAIN COURSE | 👤6 | FRI ✓ | SAT × | ▲ — Modern British

THE BLUE LAGOON ☎01386 429 383
8 Waterside, Evesham, R11 1BS
Melting and piquantly marinated slow-cooked meats populate the dishes of this Bangladeshi restaurant; the classics are there too, with the Boal Shatkora really standing out from the crowd.

2FOR1 MAIN COURSE | FRI ✱ | SAT ✱ | SUN | ✱ — Indian

BLUE STEAK ☎01527 510 710
Blue Inn Hotel, Redditch, B98 0SD
The menu at Blue Steak restaurant within the Blue Inn uses locally sourced produce and is prepared fresh on a daily basis. The specialty at the restaurant are steaks however there is also a large menu.

50% OFF FOOD | 👤10 | FRI ✓ | SAT ✓ — English/Gastro pub

THE BOMBAY PALACE ☎01905 613 969
38 The Tything, Worcester, WR1 1JL
Enjoy a tryst with this accommodating Indian restaurant in Worcester, where you'll find the gamut of classic curries, cooked well and drawing out all the fulsome and tasty aromas to savour.

2FOR1 MAIN COURSE | FRI ✓ | SAT ✓ | ✱ — Indian

THE BRAMBLINGS ☎01527 406 600
The Abbey Hotel, Hither Green Lane, Redditch, B98 9BE
Elegant dining with a focus on great service and innovative menus. A stylish atmosphere and a warm welcome is provided for all guests. The Sunday lunch carvery is very popular and pre-booking is a must.

25% OFF TOTAL | 👤4 | FRI ▯ | SAT ▯ | ✱ | ▲ — English and Continental

BRITISSERIE RESTAURANT ☎0121 447 7888
Hilton Bromsgrove, Birmingham Road, Bromsgrove, B61 0JB
French-inspired, this venue hosts both table d'hôte and à la carte menus. Rustic décor and fine cuisine make this brasserie popular with the Hilton hotel guests.

25% OFF TOTAL | 👤4 | FRI ▯ | SAT × | ✱ — Multi-Cuisine

CAFÉ MELA
☎ 0190 528 989
22 Foregate Street, Worcester, WR1 1DN
A haven for Indian food lovers, Café Mela serves up delicious dishes from the subcontinent. The chef specials, such as the South Indian garlic chilli chicken, come highly recommended.

2FOR1 MAIN COURSE | FRI ✓ | SAT ✓ — Indian

CAFÉ ROUGE
01905 613 055
5 Friar Street, Worcester, WR1 2LZ
French sophistication on the British high street - enjoy seasonally changing French dishes and a continental wine selection, served in a relaxed environment with an undeniable flair of Parisian chic.

25% OFF TOTAL | 6 | FRI ✓ | SAT ✓ | ✱ | ▲ — French

CLARIDGES RESTAURANT
☎ 01568 616 347
Best Western Talbot, 5 West Street, Leominster, HR6 8EP
Scrumptious food is served at the Claridges restaurant. The venue is an exceptional addition to the Best Western Talbot which offers guests a memorable stay.

50% OFF FOOD | 4 | FRI ✓ | SAT ✓ — British

THE COURT @ MERCURE
☎ 0844 815 9033
Habberley Road, Bewdley, Kidderminster, DY12 1LA
19th Century classic heritage is prominent at the Mercure Kidderminster Hotel. Beautifully lit, exquisitely decorated and classic features, the hotel is perfect for that well-deserved break from reality.

2FOR1 3 COURSES | FRI ✓ | SAT ✓ — Brasserie

THE DUCK INN AT OAKENSHAW
☎ 01527 540 106
Pheasant Lane, Redditch, B98 7YH
Talented chefs ooze passion for food and cook up a storm in the kitchen. They prepare a well-selected menu for guests to peruse, serving up beautifully presented dishes that will bring you back again.

2FOR1 MAIN COURSE | FRI × | SAT × | SUN — Fresh Fish/Pub Classics

FIELD'S RESTAURANT
☎ 01562 777 555
Stone Manor Hotel, Nr Stone, Kidderminster, DY10 4PJ
With an imaginative menu and fresh produce, the food created here is of the highest standard. Teamed with an extensive wine list, this venue serves up pleasurable dining experiences. 1 AA Rosette.

25% OFF TOTAL | 6 | FRI ✱ | SAT ✱ | SUN | ✱ | ▲ — European

FUSION BRASSERIE
☎ 01905 840 647
Hawbridge, Stoulton, Worcester, WR7 4RJ
A promise of good service, fresh food, fine wines, and friendly smiles in a relaxing atmosphere. This exciting restaurant is set in a unique 1960s 'retro pub', but the food is anything but old-fashioned.

25% OFF TOTAL | 6 | FRI ✓ | SAT ✱ | SUN | ▲ — Brasserie

FUSION TOO
☎ 01386 834 400
Cadbury House, Blackminster, WR11 7RE
Artisian rustic breads, juicy olives, sweet chilli fishcakes and brie and vegetable strudel can all be found and devoured in this Mediterranean style bistro. The second venue of Felice Tocchini.

25% OFF TOTAL | 6 | FRI ✱ | SAT × | SUN — Fusion

GAINSBOROUGH HOUSE HOTEL
☎ 01562 820 041
Bewdley Hill, Kidderminster, DY11 6BS
Well-regarded, luxurious restaurant in the Gainsborough House Hotel; its sweet, succulent carvery is a Sunday speciality.

25% OFF TOTAL | 10 | FRI ✓ | SAT ✓ | SUN | ▲ — Contemporary

GOLDEN CROSS INN
☎ 01432 880 274
Sutton St Nicholas, Hereford, HR1 3AZ
The Golden Cross is a family-run bar and restaurant, where a blend of the traditional with the contemporary has made this venue a success. Sample Herefordshire ciders and locally sourced produce.

50% OFF FOOD | 2 | FRI × | SAT × — British

THE GRANARY HOTEL
☎ 01562 777 535
Heath Lane, Shenstone, Kidderminster, DY10 4BS
Contemporary hotel and restaurant. The kitchen use only the finest, freshest ingredients, from their own kitchen garden, to produce exquisite dishes. Deserved 2 AA Rosette for cooking from the heart.

2FOR1 MAIN COURSE | FRI ✓ | SAT ✱ | SUN | ✱ | ▲ — International

THE GREAT HALL
☎ 01386 852 255
The Lygon Arms, High Street, Broadway, WR12 7DU
Classic French cooking gets a modern European twist at this two AA rosette establishment. An impressive setting with an even more impressive menu, the reputation of this restaurant speaks for itself.

25% OFF TOTAL | 4 | FRI × | SAT × | ▲ — Fine Dining

GREENS RESTAURANT
☎ 01299 405 222
Wharton Park Golf Club, Long Bank, Bewdley, DY12 2QW
A warm dining experience offered within the realms of a beautifully situated golf club. A weekly changing menu delivers fresh, high standard food coupled with a real emphasis on good hospitality.

25% OFF TOTAL | 4 | FRI ✓ | SAT ✓ | SUN | ▲ — British

JIMMY PICKLES
☎ 01386 555 900
76 High Street, Pershore, WR10 1DU
Set in the tranquil surroundings of the countryside, this exquisite Indian restaurant offers a heavenly selection of delicious dishes, rich in flavour and enhanced with selected spices.

25% OFF TOTAL | 4 | FRI × | SAT × — Indian

MONSOON INDIAN
☎ 01905 726 333
35 Foregate Street, Worcester, WR1 1EE
Speciality Indian dishes feature as strong contenders on a menu that is otherwise filled with classic, traditional favourites. Chefs are happy to add a spicy touch to mild dishes should you wish.

2FOR1 MAIN COURSE | FRI ✓ | SAT ✓ — Indian

NAMASTE INDIAN EATERY
☎ 01299 877 448
1 Lichfield Street, Stourport-on-Severn, DY13 9EU
Indian restaurant with a notable focus on hospitality. A wide range of traditional curries are on the menu, while specialities include their sizzling tawa dishes and the hot, tangy achari gust.

2FOR1 MAIN COURSE | FRI × | SAT × | SUN — Indian

THE NIGHTINGALE
01905 344 901
Evesham Road, Egdon, Worcester, WR7 4QS
This Vintage Inn oozes rural charm and rustic character. The picturesque surroundings provide the perfect backdrop for savouring the hearty, seasonal pub-food on the menu.

25% OFF TOTAL | FRI ✓ | SAT ✓ | SUN | ▲ — Modern British

OBILASH
☎ 01989 567 860
19a Gloucester road, Ross-on-Wye, HR9 5LQ
Obilash was established in 1980 and is a wonderful Indian family run restaurant located in Ross-on-Wye, where diners return time and again to enjoy the food and warm and attentive service.

2FOR1 3 COURSES | FRI ✓ | SAT × | ✱ — Indian

THE OLD RECTORY
☎ 01527 523 000
Ipsley Lane, Ipsley, Redditch, B98 0AP
A beautiful hotel and restaurant steeped in history. Having stood for over 500 years, The Old Rectory offers a beautiful blend of traditional features with modern décor.

2FOR1 MAIN COURSE | FRI ✱ | SAT × | SUN | ✱ — International

THE ORCHARD
01386 444 300
Twyford, Evesham, Worcestershire, WR11 4TP
Quality pub classics with modern twists meets with a friendly and relaxed atmosphere to make this Table Table venue the perfect place for any occasion. *Excludes daytime & evening deals and festive menus.

2FOR1 MAIN COURSE | FRI ✓ | SAT ✓ — Modern British

PASHA
☎ 01905 426 327
56 St John's, Worcester, WR2 5AJ
Outstanding Indian and Bengali dishes served in a modern interior boasting innovative artworks. Ensuring customer satisfaction at all times, the staff are amiable and will cater to your every need.

2FOR1 MAIN COURSE | FRI ✱ | SAT ✱ | ▲ — Indian

PENGETHLEY MANOR
☎ 01989 730 211
Pengethley Park, Ross-on-Wye, HR9 6LL
A luxurious venue where the warmth and grandeur of the restaurant is only exceeded by an astonishingly high standard of freshly sourced, elegant cuisine, for which they have won many accolades.

25% OFF TOTAL | 6 | FRI ✓ | SAT ✓ — Fine Dining

PIOS RESTAURANT
01386 554 038

White Horse Hotel, Churches Row, Pershore, WR10 1BH

In a combined pub-hotel, proprietor Pio creates and serves divinely authentic Italian dishes coupled with traditional background music. An elegant and incredibly tasty dining experience.

25% OFF TOTAL | 10 | FRI ✓ | SAT ✓ | ▲ — Italian

POACHERS RESTAURANT
01299 270 372

The Crown Inn, Hopton Wafers, Kidderminster, DY14 0NB

Nestled in Shropshire, this venue offers a snug place to dine whilst surrounded by exposed beams and roaring fireplaces. For an abundance of character and a warm welcome, be sure to make a reservation.

2FOR1 MAIN COURSE | FRI ✓ | SAT × | SUN | ▲ — British

PREZZO
01527 874 614

22-24 High Street, Bromsgrove, B61 8HQ

With a character all of its own, Prezzo oozes contemporary style and enduring charm. Signature pastas, stone-baked pizzas and classic Italian dishes promise a perfect dining choice for the whole family.

2FOR1 MAIN COURSE | FRI × | SAT × | ▲ — Italian

RAJKOT
0190 527 402

27 The Tything, Worcester, WR1 1JL

A luxurious dining experience delivering top-quality food, with a menu showcasing the finest Indian and Bangladeshi cuisine, in a dining room boasting exquisite décor and an intimate atmosphere.

2FOR1 MAIN COURSE | FRI ✓ | SAT ✓ — Indian

THE RAJPUT
01299 409 409

41 Load Street, Bewdley, DY12 2AS

A splendid place to enjoy fine dining in the midst of a pretty and peaceful Georgian town. Sophisticated use of Indian herbs and spices make every dish delectable and flavoursome.

25% OFF TOTAL | 6 | FRI ✱ | SAT ✱ | ▲ — Indian

RENT ROOM RESTAURANT
01299 270 372

The Crown Inn, Hopton Wafers, Kidderminster, DY14 0NB

Enjoy a light bite for lunch whilst overlooking the picturesque Shropshire landscape at this 16th Century coaching inn. For diners with a hearty appetite, the chefs kitchen specials come highly appraised.

2FOR1 MAIN COURSE | FRI ✓ | SAT × | SUN | ▲ — British

RILYS BROMSGROVE
01527 870 175

178 Kidderminster Road, Dodford, Bromsgrove, B61 9AJ

Distinctive flavours and fresh produce characterise the food at Rileys. Drawing on all aspects of Indian cuisine, Rileys guarantees high-quality service and luxurious dishes time and time again.

2FOR1 MAIN COURSE | FRI ✱ | SAT ✱ — Indian

RILYS EVESHAM
0138 645 289

2-3 Waterside, Evesham, WR11 1BS

The reopened Rilys offers guests a unique insight into real Indian cuisine, prepared and cooked by award winning chefs using only the freshest and highest quality ingredients.

2FOR1 MAIN COURSE | FRI ✱ | SAT ✱ — Indian

RILYS REDDITCH
0152 760 544

1B The Quadrant, Alcester Street, Redditch, B98 8AE

A new and fresh approach to distinctive food, fine wine and excellent customer service. Each dish combines rich and fragrant Indian flavours with a western approach, serving up a menu full of variety.

2FOR1 MAIN COURSE | FRI ✱ | SAT ✱ — Indian

THE ROBIN HOOD
01527 869 302

Rashwood, Droitwich, WR9 0BS

This Vintage Inn oozes rural charm and rustic character. The picturesque surroundings provide the perfect backdrop for savouring the hearty, seasonal pub-food on the menu.

25% OFF TOTAL | FRI ✓ | SAT ✓ | SUN | ▲ — Modern British

SEASONS RESTAURANT
01684 540 000

Colwall Park Hotel, Colwall, Malvern, WR13 6QG

Award-winning Head Chef James Garth produces modern British dishes with the finest local and seasonal ingredients. The restaurant has a contemporary feel for a wonderful evening meal. 2 AA Rosettes.

2FOR1 MAIN COURSE | FRI 📱 | SAT 📱 | ✱ — Fine Dining

SHROPSHIRE RESTAURANT
01299 270 372

The Crown Inn, Hopton Wafers, Kidderminster, DY14 0NB

One of three versatile dining options at the Crown Inn at Hopton, Shropshire Restaurant caters for the modern palate with contemporary, imaginative dishes making up an appealing menu.

2FOR1 MAIN COURSE | FRI ✓ | SAT × | SUN | ▲ — British

SPICE FUSION
01905 794 188

17 St Andrews Street, Droitwich, WR9 8DY

Take delight in great Indian food at Spice Fusion, whose name originates from the action in the kitchen. The chefs strive to produce well-rounded dishes that combine superb flavours and spices.

25% OFF TOTAL | 4 | FRI 📱 | SAT 📱 | ✱ — Indian

STANFORD RESTAURANT
01386 871 300

Best Western Salford Hall Hotel, Evesham, WR11 8UT

Located within the BEST WESTERN Salford Hall Hotel at Abbot's Salford, the elegant Stanford Restaurant offers modern English dishes with a European twist.

25% OFF TOTAL | 4 | FRI ✓ | SAT ✓ — British

STARTING GATE
01432 274 853

Holmer Road, Holmer, Hereford, HR4 9RS

Beefeater Grill are one of the UK's best-loved restaurants welcoming guests for almost 40 years in over 130 locations nationwide. *Excludes Breakfast, Light Bites, Bar menu, set menus and all other offers.

2FOR1 MAIN COURSE | 6 | FRI ✓ | SAT × | ▲ — Modern British

SWAN BLAKEDOWN
01562 700 229

9 Birmingham Road, Blakedown, Kidderminster, DY10 3JD

Priding themselves on excellent cuisine and prestigious wines, this traditional pub is constantly buzzing with life. Ideally located, this venue is a cracking night out.

25% OFF TOTAL | 2 | FRI × | SAT × — English/Gastro pub

THE SWAN INN
01562 823 008

Vicar Street, Kidderminster, DY10 1DE

A family run pub and winner of the Punch Taverns Quality Service Award 2012, each hearty meal is packed with flavour and texture at this cosy establishment. *Offer not available on the 'Not So Hungry' menu

2FOR1 MAIN COURSE | FRI × | SAT × | ▲ — British

TALBOT HOTEL
01531 632 963

New Street, Ledbury, HR8 2DX

Combining the very best hospitality and atmosphere, this lovely hotel and pub extends a warm welcome to every visitor, whilst delivering a menu filled with fine, home-made British cuisine.

25% OFF TOTAL | 4 | FRI × | SAT × | SUN — British

THREE PEARS
01905 451 240

Wainwright Way, Warndon, Worcester, WR4 9FA

Beefeater Grill are one of the UK's best-loved restaurants welcoming guests for almost 40 years in over 130 locations nationwide. *Excludes Breakfast, Light Bites, Bar menu, set menus and all other offers.

2FOR1 MAIN COURSE | 6 | FRI ✓ | SAT × | ▲ — Modern British

TRAVELLERS REST
01989 563 861

Ledbury Road, Nr Ross-on-Wye, HR9 7QJ

Beefeater Grill are one of the UK's best-loved restaurants welcoming guests for almost 40 years in over 130 locations nationwide. *Excludes Breakfast, Light Bites, Bar menu, set menus and all other offers.

2FOR1 MAIN COURSE | 6 | FRI ✓ | SAT × | ▲ — Modern British

TRUMPET INN
01531 670 277

Trumpet, Ledbury, HR8 2RA

A traditional country pub and restaurant offering locally produced, home-cooked food and superb cask ales including the famous Wadworth 6X. Enjoy wholesome food and drink with fine company.

25% OFF TOTAL | 4 | FRI × | SAT × | SUN — British

To understand what the restaurant icons mean, please see the inside back cover.

East Midlands

Derbyshire

ALISON HOUSE
01629 822 211
Intake Lane, Cromford, Matlock, DE4 3RH

A tranquil, renovated 18th-century country house with exquisite dining facilities. A high-quality and varied menu of home-cooked meals crafted with imagination and flair, including vegetarian dishes.

2FOR1 MAIN COURSE | FRI ✓ | SAT ✓ | SUN | ✱ — European

ASHOKA
01246 558 833
19 Hollywell Street, Chesterfield, S41 7SA

Lovely little Indian restaurant best described as a savvy place that knows how to serve a good curry. A welcoming restaurant with a menu that covers the classics and is especially strong with its lamb.

2FOR1 MAIN COURSE | FRI × | SAT × | ✱ | ▲ — Indian

BARCELO BUXTON PALACE
0129 822 001
Palace Road, Buxton, SK17 6AG

Dine in elegance and timeless style in the restaurant of the magnificent Palace Hotel; the focal point of Buxton's hospitality scene since 1868.

25% OFF TOTAL | 4 | FRI ▯ | SAT ✱ — International

BAY TREE
01332 863 358
4 Potter Street, Melbourne, DE73 8HW

Awarded 1 AA Rosette for its excellence and well-regarded in surrounding areas. Serving the best of New World cuisine and boasting an outstanding wine list, choose from snacks to à la carte.

25% OFF TOTAL | 4 | FRI ▯ | SAT ✱ | SUN — International

THE BLACK HORSE
01530 270 588
2 Top Street, Appleby Magna, Swadlincote, DE12 7AH

Boasting two elegant restaurants, this stunning 16th Century pub is steeped in historicism. Exposed beams, a variety of tempting ales and hearty European classics ensure a memorable dining experience.

25% OFF TOTAL | 4 | FRI ▯ | SAT ▯ | SUN — Modern European

THE BRASSERIE
0845 072 7502
The Priest House Hotel, Castle Donington, DE74 2RR

Positioned in the heart of the country, enjoy relaxed dining at this Hand Picked Hotels group venue, with The Brasserie especially popular for escaping life's hustle and bustle. 2 AA Rosettes.

25% OFF TOTAL | 4 | FRI ✓ | SAT ✓ | SUN — European

THE BREWERY TAP
01332 366 283
1 Derwent Street, Derby, DE1 2ED

A pub combining Victorian character with a touch of modern style; the roof terrace overlooking the river isn't bad either. Serves a range of excellent food and drink, from the classic pub food staples.

25% OFF TOTAL | 6 | FRI × | SAT × | SUN — British

BUCKINGHAM'S
01246 201 041
85 Newbold Road, Newbold, Chesterfield, S41 7PU

Restaurant overlooking the garden at this boutique hotel. A brilliantly distinctive experience, with food exceptional in both taste and presentation. *One card per party only on Saturday.

2FOR1 3 COURSES | FRI ✓ | SAT ✓ | SUN — British

BULL I' TH' THORN
0129 883 348
Ashbourne Road, Buxton, SK17 9QQ

Children, vegetarians and special diets are catered for at this well-rounded inn where everyone is welcome. Diners are spoilt for choice by the extensive menu, which can be washed down with a guest ale.

2FOR1 MAIN COURSE | FRI ✓ | SAT × | SUN — British

THE BULLS HEAD
01773 513 000
Denby Common, Denby, DE5 8PW

Boasts an extensive menu offering over 70 main course dishes including succulent, locally reared, farm-assured steaks and chicken specialities. *Check website for further details.

2FOR1 2 COURSES | FRI ✱ | SAT ✱ | SUN | ▲ — British

CARDAMOM CLUB
01332 867 840
The Pentagon Island, Derby, DE21 6DA

Cardamom Club provides an indulgent experience with leading service, tantalising food and fine champagnes- an Indian fine dining experience which exceeds all expectations.

50% OFF FOOD | FRI ✱ | SAT × | SUN | ▲ — Indian

THE CASTLE IN CASTLETON
01433 620 578
Castle Street, Castleton, Hope Valley, S33 8WG

The tasty pub food and fine selection of wines and ales that grace the bar at this picturesque Vintage Inn makes it an ideal location for all - just beware of the spooky local myths and legends!

25% OFF TOTAL | FRI ✓ | SAT ✓ | SUN | ▲ — Modern British

CRICKETTS INN
01283 760 359
Burton Road, Acresford, Swadlincote, DE12 8AP

Friendly, local, rooted inn. With a real attention to local sourcing and an investment in proper traditional home-cooking, this inn serves up some great pub fare and additional treats from local game.

25% OFF TOTAL | 4 | FRI × | SAT × | SUN | ✱ | ▲ — British

CURRY 2 NIGHT
01332 814 455
43-45 Borough Street, Castle Donington, DE74 2LB

Welcome to Curry Tonight, where you are bound to enjoy the refreshingly different Bangladeshi and Indian cuisine on offer. The atmosphere is relaxed and welcoming and the staff are more than happy to help.

25% OFF TOTAL | 4 | FRI × | SAT × | ✱ — Indian

DELHI 41
01246 268 638
530 Sheffield Road, Chesterfield, S41 8LP

Boasting an innovative menu, Delhi 41 is one of the most prestigious Indian and Bangladeshi restaurants in the area. Perfect for any occasion, the surroundings are cosmopolitan and modish.

2FOR1 2 COURSES | FRI ✓ | SAT ✓ — Indian

THE DERBYSHIRE
01773 812 000
Carter Lane East, South Normanton, Derby, DE55 2EH

In true Principal Hayley style, this fantastic hotel is one of its kind in the local area. Offering leading conference facilities as well as a fantastic atmosphere for those seeking a short break.

25% OFF TOTAL | 6 | FRI ✓ | SAT ✓ | ▲ — British

THE DOG AND PARTRIDGE COUNTRY INN
01325 343 183
Swinscoe, Ashbourne, DE6 2HS

Picturesque country inn set in the heart of the Derbyshire countryside. With an ideal location for ramblers and a dedication to good hospitality, this delightful pub has a coterie of loyal visitors.

2FOR1 MAIN COURSE | FRI ✓ | SAT ✓ — British

FAT CAT DERBY
01332 347 444
9 Friargate, Derby, DE1 1BU

Modern food meets a contemporary cocktail selection at Fat Cat, a sophisticated bar and restaurant serving wonderful food and drinks in plush, contemporary surroundings.

2FOR1 3 COURSES | FRI ▯ | SAT ▯ | ▲ — British

FINALE' THAI TAPAS AND DINING
01332 295 237
11 The Strand, Derby, DE1 1BE

Finale' offers customers a variety of fusion food including authentic Thai dishes and modern Thai tapas. The chef creates delicious freshly-made dishes using carefully selected ingredients.

25% OFF TOTAL | 4 | FRI × | SAT × — Thai

FISHERMAN'S REST
01773 828 771
Broadholme Lane, Belper, DE56 2JF

With one simple aim in mind, The Fisherman's Rest maintain and uphold their passion for simple, wholesome food and exceptional customer service. Hosts quiz nights, book clubs and live music events.

2FOR1 2 COURSES | FRI ▯ | SAT ▯ | SUN — European

GALLERY CAFÉ
01335 347 425
50 St John Street, Ashbourne, DE6 1GH

Award-winning café in Ashbourne that serves home-cooked food of the highest quality. Sumptuous patés go along with luxurious cakes in this characterful location, part of a contemporary art gallery.

25% OFF TOTAL | 2 | FRI ✓ | SAT ✓ — European

THE GEORGE HOTEL
☎ 01457 855 449
34 Norfolk Street, Glossop, SK13 7QU
Situated in the centre of Glossop, The George Hotel offers excellent pub grub combined with an extensive bar menu and specials board. All food is home made and from locally sourced produce.

2FOR1 MAIN COURSE | FRI ✓ | SAT ✱ | SUN | ✱ | ▲ — Modern Pub

GEORGE'S TRADITION BELPER
01773 828 662
18 Bridge Street, Belper, DE56 1AX
A generous helping of fish together with a wholesome portion of chunky British chips are on offer at this prestigious yet affordable venue. Look out for fishy delights such as plaice, haddock and sole.

25% OFF TOTAL | 8 | FRI × | SAT ✓ — British

GEORGE'S TRADITION CHELLASTON
01332 693 961
Unit 5 Royal Glen Park, Chellaston, DE73 5XE
A generous helping of fish together with a wholesome portion of chunky British chips are on offer at this prestigious yet affordable venue. Look out for Gourmet dishes such as zesty Lemon Sole.

25% OFF TOTAL | 8 | FRI × | SAT ✓ — British

GEORGE'S TRADITION ILKESTON
01159 301 515
184 Bath Street, Ilkeston, DE7 8FH
A generous helping of fish together with a wholesome portion of chunky British chips are on offer at this prestigious yet affordable venue. Guests receive exceptional service in agreeable surroundings.

25% OFF TOTAL | 8 | FRI × | SAT ✓ — British

THE GRAND BELPER
☎ 01773 823 885
8 Strutt Street, Belper, DE56 1UN
This spacious yet intimate restaurant serves traditional Indian cuisine cooked to your required taste. A warm welcome and fantastic service is always guaranteed and your visit will be one to remember.

2FOR1 MAIN COURSE | FRI ✓ | SAT × — Indian

THE GULSHAN
☎ 01332 523 553
165-171 Littlebank Road, Mickleover, DE3 0QF
Drawing on both traditional recipes and modern demands, The Gulshan serves Indian and Bangladeshi dishes for either dining in or taking away.

2FOR1 MAIN COURSE | FRI × | SAT × — Indian

HALLMARK HOTEL BRASSERIE
☎ 01332 345 894
Midland Road, Derby, DE1 2SQ
A lovely Victorian building, carefully brought up to date on the inside, is home to a welcoming and highly accomplished restaurant that features a delicious and ranging brasserie menu.

25% OFF TOTAL | 6 | FRI ✓ | SAT ✓ | ▲ — European

THE HANGING GATE
01773 550 467
34 Ashbourne Road, Shottle Gate, Belper, DE56 2LE
This Vintage Inn oozes rural charm and rustic character. The picturesque surroundings provide the perfect backdrop for savouring the hearty, seasonal pub-food on the menu.

25% OFF TOTAL | FRI ✓ | SAT ✓ | SUN | ▲ — Modern British

THE HEARTY OAK PUB AND KITCHEN
☎ 01142 891 322
22 Northern Common, Dronfield, S18 8XJ
As the name suggests, the Hearty Oak offers diners a variety of satisfying boozy dinners in a cosy environment. Head Chef Shaun White prides himself on good quality, local meats and seasonality.

2FOR1 MAIN COURSE | FRI ✱ | SAT ✓ | SUN | ▲ — British

THE HIGHWAYMAN
01246 566 330
Baslow Road, Eastmoor, Chesterfield, S42 7DA
Beefeater Grill are one of the UK's best-loved restaurants welcoming guests for almost 40 years in over 130 locations nationwide.*Excludes Breakfast, Light Bites, Bar menu, set menus and all other offers.

2FOR1 MAIN COURSE | 6 | FRI ✓ | SAT × | ▲ — Modern British

THE HOLLY BUSH
☎ 01530 270 943
Main Street, Oakthorpe, Swadlincote, DE12 7RB
Lovely village pub that is genial, warm, and proud of the freshness of their food. Besides being a great spot for a drink, you'll enjoy high-quality, unfussy and beautifully cooked dishes.

2FOR1 2 COURSES | FRI ✓ | SAT ✓ | SUN | ✱ | ▲ — European

THE KEGWORTH WHITEHOUSE HOTEL
☎ 01509 672 427
Packington Hill, Kegworth, DE74 2DF
The monthly changing menu here means that you're always able to try something new. Browse the extensive wine list which will undoubtedly provide you with an excellent drink to partner your meal.

25% OFF TOTAL | 6 | FRI ☎ | SAT ☎ | ✱ | ▲ — European

LAVINIA'S
☎ 0844 855 9111
Makeney Hall Hotel, Milford, Belper, DE56 0RS
A grand, beautiful Victorian country house in Belper with a light, open restaurant. Bay windows look out across the valleys and a range of modern English cuisine that looks to focus on seasonal produce.

2FOR1 3 COURSES | FRI ☎ | SAT ☎ — British

LE MISTRAL
☎ 01629 824 840
23 Market Place, Wirksworth, Matlock, DE4 4ET
Winner of 'Best International Restaurant in Derbyshire' 2009. A French-style café, bar and bistro serving top-quality, fresh food accompanied by a vast selection of wines, beers and espresso.

2FOR1 3 COURSES | FRI ☎ | SAT ✱ | ▲ — French

LE MISTRAL
☎ 01629 810 077
Bridge Street, Bakewell, DE45 1DS
A French-style café, bar and bistro serving top-quality, fresh food accompanied by a vast selection of wines, beers and espresso. For a slice of French charm, Le Mistral is the perfect place to dine.

2FOR1 3 COURSES | FRI ☎ | SAT ✱ | ▲ — French

THE LION PUB WITH ROOMS
☎ 01773 824 033
Bridge Street, Belper, DE56 1AX
This intimately furnished pub has everything you need for a comfortable, sophisticated dining experience, where the contemporary setting is matched by the menu of wholesome food and fine beverages.

25% OFF TOTAL | 6 | FRI ☎ | SAT × | ✱ | ▲ — Contemporary

THE MALLARD
01332 203 003
Southmead Way, Derby, DE22 3HN
Beefeater Grill are one of the UK's best-loved restaurants welcoming guests for almost 40 years in over 130 locations nationwide. *Excludes Breakfast, Light Bites, Bar menu, set menus and all other offers

2FOR1 MAIN COURSE | 6 | FRI ✓ | SAT × | ▲ — Modern British

MAURYAN
☎ 01332 365 691
11-13 Curzon Street, Derby, DE1 1LH
Mauryan Restaurant, in the heart of Derby city centre, has rapidly become a popular venue for diners seeking authentic Indian cuisine. High-quality ingredients make every dish fresh and tasty.

2FOR1 3 COURSES | FRI ✓ | SAT ✓ | ✱ | ▲ — Indian

MEXICO
☎ 01332 342 090
34-35 Sadler Gate, Derby, DE1 3NR
Although you can indulge in an exceptional burrito, steak quesadilla or chicken fajita at this Mexican joint, it pays to go off the beaten track for one of their truly fabulous 'especiales'.

25% OFF TOTAL | 6 | FRI ✓ | SAT ✓ | ✱ | ▲ — Mexican

MILEBURNE RESTAURANT
☎ 01332 864 170
2 Blanch Croft, Melbourne, DE73 8GG
A restaurant that does a superb job with its simple aim: good British food made with quality, locally sourced ingredients, all served in a laid-back and welcoming environment. A local treasure.

25% OFF TOTAL | 2 | FRI ✓ | SAT ☎ | SUN | ▲ — European

THE MOGUL RESTAURANT
☎ 01332 203 343
41-43 Green Lane, Derby, DE1 1RS
A traditional curry house with its own modest character. A menu full of moreish specialities and more popular subcontinental dishes; favourites include the paneer tikka and the achari lamb.

2FOR1 MAIN COURSE | FRI ☎ | SAT ☎ | ▲ — Indian/Bangladeshi

MUMBAI MASALA
☎ 01773 521 052
1A Cressy Rd, Alfreton, DE55 7BR
Mumbai Masala offers an intimate and relaxed dining experience. DET restaurant of year 2011 runner up. The restaurant is well reviewed, the staff are friendly and helpful and the food delicious.

2FOR1 MAIN COURSE | FRI × | SAT × | ✱ — Indian

Gourmet Society discount applies to the à la carte menu only, unless stated otherwise.

MUSHROOM HALL ☎01283 217 464
Main Street, Albert Village, Swadlincote, DE11 8EN
Steaks, lasagne's, local foods and a new guest ale every week. Relax in this lovely local village pub.

2FOR1 3 COURSES | FRI ▯ | SAT ▯ | SUN — Traditional English

NONSOLOVINO ☎01246 276 760
417 Chatsworth Rd, Brampton, Chesterfield, S40 3AD
Whilst sipping a glass of one of the many fine Italian wines that Nonsolovino has to offer, ponder over the delicious dishes that the extensive menu offers. A bright ambiance in an intimate setting.

25% OFF TOTAL | 6 | FRI × | SAT × | SUN | ▲ — Modern European

THE OASTHOUSE 01332 270 027
Foresters Park Centre, Sinfin Lane, Derby, DE23 8AG
Quality pub classics with a modern twist combine with a friendly and relaxed atmosphere to make this Table Table venue the perfect place for family gatherings or meeting friends.

2FOR1 MAIN COURSE | FRI ✓ | SAT ✓ — Modern British

OLD NAGS HEAD INN ☎01433 670 291
Grindsbrook Booth, Hope Valley, S33 7ZD
When exploring the villages and landscapes of the Peak District, what could be better than to take a well-earned break in a traditional pub. The Old Nag's Head is the perfect place to rest and feast.

2FOR1 3 COURSES | FRI ▯ | SAT ▯ — British

OPULENCE RESTAURANT ☎01332 546 080
Cathedral Quarter Hotel, St Marys Gate, Derby, DE1 3JR
Admirably located in a beautiful Victorian ballroom where stunning décor complements its traditional character. Wonderfully presented dishes make use of the freshest seasonal ingredients. 1 AA Rosette.

25% OFF TOTAL | 4 | FRI ✓ | SAT ✓ | ▲ — Contemporary

THE OTTER 01509 672 372
London Road, Kegworth, Derby, DE74 2EY
Situated on a site that has served a succession of pubs, this Vintage Inn combines a welcoming atmosphere with tasty food and fine drinks for the perfectly quintessential country pub experience.

25% OFF TOTAL | FRI ✓ | SAT ✓ | SUN | ▲ — Modern British

PEVERIL OF THE PEAK ☎01335 350 396
Thorpe, Ashbourne, DE6 2AW
A luxurious environment famed for award-winning food, creating an array of succulent dishes that have been prepared with the finest ingredients and cooked to perfection. A meal for every occasion.

25% OFF TOTAL | 4 | FRI ✓ | SAT ✓ | ✱ | ▲ — European

PITCHER & PIANO ☎01332 206 790
19-20 Friargate, Derby, DE1 1BX
Whether it's a sizzling summer BBQ in the glorious sunshine or a hearty Sunday Roast in the winter, this venue is the perfect destination. Increasingly popular, diners should book to ensure the best seats.

50% OFF FOOD | 4 | FRI ▯ | SAT ▯ — British

THE PLOUGH INN 01332 810 333
33 Hallgate, Diseworth, Derby, DE74 2QJ
By maintaining the herringbone masonry and the weathered beams, this delightful inn successfully radiates a warm and welcoming atmosphere. Tables and seating are spread across three main areas.

2FOR1 MAIN COURSE | FRI ✓ | SAT ✓ — British

PREZZO 01283 552 895
The Pipeworks, Coppice Side, Swadlincote, DE11 9FQ
With a character all of its own, Prezzo oozes contemporary style and enduring charm. Signature pastas, stone-baked pizzas and classic Italian dishes promise a perfect dining choice for the whole family.

2FOR1 MAIN COURSE | FRI × | SAT × | ▲ — Italian

THE RAJ RESTAURANT ☎01332 553 554
432 Kedleston Road, Allestree, Derby, DE22 2TF
Provides a warm welcome to all. The lavish bar area and the warm and cosy reception, complete with widescreen plasma TV, both ensure that the tone is set; subsequently, enjoy some classic Indian food.

2FOR1 MAIN COURSE | FRI × | SAT × | ✱ | ▲ — Indian

THE RESTAURANT ☎01332 810 649
The Priest House Hotel, Castle Donington, DE74 2RR
Travel through the magical woodlands and dine in this delightful Hand Picked Hotels restaurant. Discover the magnificence of its food and atmosphere. Awarded 2 AA Rosettes.

25% OFF TOTAL | 4 | FRI ✓ | SAT ✓ | SUN — British

REVOLUCION DE CUBA ☎01332 896 196
9 The Strand, Derby, DE1 1BJ
Grab your amigos and tuck into a vast Latin-influenced food menu served seven days a week; from a sneaky lunchtime Mojito and Burrito to after work street food and small plates.

25% OFF TOTAL | 6 | FRI ✓ | SAT ✓ — Mexican

THE RISLEY PARK ☎01159 392 313
Derby Road, Risley, DE72 3SS
With its magnificent décor and equally splendid menu, The Risley Park fully deserves its award-winning status and admirable reputation. The à la carte menu offers over 70 main courses to choose from.

2FOR1 2 COURSES | FRI ✷ | SAT ✷ | ▲ — British

THE ROSE AND CROWN 01332 782 921
Main Road, Morley, Ilkeston, DE7 6DG
Legend has it that the tower at the end of the garden used to be a look-out for hungry passersby - whilst things are now a little different, this pub keeps to its roots of home cooking and fine drinks.

25% OFF TOTAL | FRI ✓ | SAT ✓ | SUN | ▲ — Modern British

THE RUTLAND ARMS HOTEL ☎01629 812 812
The Square, Bakewell DE45 1BT
Beautifully located hotel whose dishes offer superb levels of taste right across the menu, with an AA Rosette truly attesting to its culinary excellence. After a walk in the Peaks, this is a great base.

2FOR1 MAIN COURSE | FRI ▯ | SAT ▯ — European

SAFFRON RESTAURANT ☎01332 344 786
7 Curzon Street, Derby, DE1 1LH
A well-established restaurant specialising in heavenly Indian and Bangladeshi cuisine. Tender meats and gratifying sauces will have you wishing you'd dined here before.

25% OFF TOTAL | 10 | FRI ✓ | SAT ▯ | ✱ — Indian

SAGE AT DONINGTON MANOR ☎01332 810 253
High Street, Castle Donington, DE74 2PP
An AA Rosette-winning restaurant maintaining many of its original period features. Head Chef Jeff Cadden has created a sophisticated menu of dishes complemented by an extensive wine list.

25% OFF TOTAL | 6 | FRI ▯ | SAT ▯ | ✱ — European

SAMUEL FOX COUNTRY INN ☎01433 621 562
Stretfield Road, Bradwell, Hope Valley, S33 9JT
A country inn serving traditional and modern British cuisine - the menu changes seasonally at the skilled hands of Chef James Duckett. The charming Hope Valley is an ideal backdrop to his delicious food.

25% OFF TOTAL | 4 | FRI ▯ | SAT × | SUN | ✱ — European

SA-TANG THAI RESTAURANT ☎01457 865 168
46-50 High Street West, Glossop, SK13 8BH
Recognised for its exceptional food and enchanting atmosphere, Sa-Tang Thai is a restaurant where modern takes on ancient recipes can be enjoyed just as much as the Asian art that surrounds you.

2FOR1 MAIN COURSE | FRI ✓ | SAT ✓ — Thai

SHALIMAR ☎01332 366 745
2-3 Midland Road, Derby, DE1 2SN
Excellent restaurant in Derby that serves first-class Indian cuisine to a great following of diners. The kitchen prides itself on great flavour, fine produce and authentic recipes.

2FOR1 MAIN COURSE | FRI ✓ | SAT ✓ — Indian

SHERWOOD RESTAURANT
☎01332 850 700

Beverley Road, Castle Donington, DE74 2SH

A superb hotel-restaurant offering a relaxing environment in which British and continental cuisine can be enjoyed. Medieval-style furnishings recall local legend Robin Hood.

25% OFF TOTAL | FRI ✓ | SAT ✓ | ▲ — European

SPICE COTTAGE
☎01629 815 489

4 portland square, Bakewell, DE45 1HA

Striking and fragrant aromas seep out of the doors of Spice Cottage. Experience a taste of the East with the expansive menu that leaves guests spoilt for choice but certain to return.

2FOR1 3 COURSES | FRI × | SAT × | ✱ — Indian

STONES RESTAURANT
☎0162 956 061

1c Dale Road, Matlock, DE4 3LT

Intimate dining in a relaxed setting; enjoy lunch, dinner, or a glass of wine from the extensive wine list. Fresh, appetising food made using local produce, with indulgent desserts. 2 AA Rosettes.

25% OFF TOTAL | 4 | FRI ✓ | SAT ✷ | ▲ — British

THYME RESTAURANT
☎01332 369 321

International Hotel, 288 Burton Rd, Derby, DE23 6AD

Clear-minded hotel-based restaurant that serves some superb, thoughtful and imaginative dishes; worth a visit for the sumptuous swordfish alone. Also caters for larger events.

25% OFF TOTAL | 10 | FRI × | SAT × | ✱ — European

WALKABOUT
☎01332 292 172

9-11 Market Square, Derby, DE1 3QE

Walkabout is famous for its characteristically Australian atmosphere and well-rounded menu. From live sport with a juicy burger to some Aussie kangaroo skewers, you'll find it hard to tear yourself away.

25% OFF TOTAL | 10 | FRI ✓ | SAT ✓ | ▲ — Australian

THE WONKY TABLE
☎01332 295 000

32-33 Sadler Gate, Derby, DE1 3NR

Family-run affair set on Sadler Gate, serving fresh-flavoured dishes with a local emphasis. *Runs only a set menu at lunch and not an a la carte, therefore the GS offer is restricted to evenings only.

25% OFF TOTAL | 4 | FRI ✓ | SAT × | ✱ | ▲ — English and Continental

YEW LODGE HOTEL
☎01509 672 518

33 Packington Hill, Kegworth, DE74 2DF

A double AA Rosette-winning hotel restaurant in beautiful countryside surroundings. Drawing on locally sourced ingredients, the food here is flavourful, accomplished and worthy of your time.

25% OFF TOTAL | 4 | FRI ✓ | SAT ▯ | ✱ | ▲ — British

ZEST
☎01332 381 101

16d George Street, Derby, DE1 1EH

Something of a cultural institution in the city, and recognised as one of its most stylish restaurants. Contemporary European and British cuisine of excellent quality, without fancy pretensions.

2FOR1 MAIN COURSE | FRI ✷ | SAT ✷ | ▲ — European

Leicestershire

1573 BAR AND GRILL
☎01162 516 879

Freeschool Lane, Leicester, LE1 4PB

A local independent restaurant serving a great array of beautifully cooked steaks, seafood, sandwiches and salads. In short, classic bar and grill cuisine of the very highest quality.

25% OFF TOTAL | 4 | FRI × | SAT × | SUN — British

AGRA FINE DINING
☎01162 542 657

63 London Road, Leicester, LE2 0PE

Found on London Road in Leicester, Agra Fine Dining offers exactly that; fine Indian cuisine. For a delicious Indian in traditional and relaxed surrounding, Agra Fine Dining is a winning find.

2FOR1 3 COURSES | FRI ▯ | SAT × | ✱ | ▲ — Indian

ASHOKA
☎01162 662 185

257 Melton Road, Leicester, LE4 7AN

At Ashoka a completely new experience in Indian cuisine awaits, providing traditionally popular dishes and new recipes, superbly crafted using the finest produce, herbs and spices.

2FOR1 3 COURSES | FRI ✓ | SAT ✓ | ✱ — Indian

ASPECTS AT THE PLOUGH
☎01162 863 307

7 Mill Hill, Enderby, LE19 4AL

Enjoy an English lunch with Indian specials, or celebrate the rich diversity of Indian cuisine in the evening with experienced and acclaimed chefs creating delicately spiced and authentic-tasting dishes.

25% OFF TOTAL | 2 | FRI × | SAT × | ✱ | ▲ — Indian

THE BADGER'S SETT
01162 367 999

Reservoir Road, Leicester, LE7 7GQ

The Badger's Sett Vintage Inn enjoys beautiful views over the local reservoir. These and the delicious food and extensive selection of wines and ales make for a quintessentially picturesque country pub.

25% OFF TOTAL | FRI ✓ | SAT ✓ | SUN | ▲ — Modern British

BANGLA LODGE
☎01162 848 894

77 Main Street, Cosby, Leicester, LE9 1UW

A welcoming, popular little restaurant in Cosby. Serves all the old favourites, does them well, and adds in a range of specialities that are worth a try. A solid, no-nonsense curry house.

2FOR1 3 COURSES | FRI ✷ | SAT ✷ | SUN — Indian

BANGLA LOUNGE
01455 615 111

91 Trinity Lane, Hinckley, LE10 0BJ

Modernised Indian cuisine that retains authentic flavours yet is crafted with a contemporary fusion approach. Executive chef Abdul Haque uses expert knowledge to create incredible Indian dishes.

2FOR1 MAIN COURSE | FRI ▯ | SAT ▯ | SUN — Bangladeshi

THE BANKER'S CLUB
☎01162 621 932

10 Friar Lane, Leicester, LE1 5RA

The Banker's Club is a new restaurant, lounge and bar, the historic bank building has been lovingly restored. The menu is seasonal with refined a la carte dishes together with lighter dining options.

50% OFF FOOD | 4 | FRI ▯ | SAT ▯ | SUN | ▲ — British

BARCELONETA
☎01162 708 408

54 Queens Road, Leicester, LE2 1TU

Authentic, lively restaurant serving fresh tapas and larger dishes complemented by a varied wine list. The proprietor sources many of the bottles directly from Spain.

25% OFF TOTAL | 4 | FRI × | SAT × — Mediterranean

BELLA ITALIA
01162 891 738

Meridien Leisure Park, Braunstone, LE19 1JZ

Accessible Italian cuisine on the British high street - indulge in authentic sharing platters, hand stretched pizzas and hearty pasta dishes, served with a healthy dose of gregarious Italian hospitality.

25% OFF TOTAL | 6 | FRI × | SAT × | SUN | ▲ — Italian

BELLA ITALIA
01162 548 936

15 Granby Street, Leicester, LE1 6EJ

Accessible Italian cuisine on the British high street - indulge in authentic sharing platters, hand stretched pizzas and hearty pasta dishes, served with a healthy dose of gregarious Italian hospitality.

25% OFF TOTAL | 6 | FRI × | SAT × | SUN | ▲ — Italian

BENGAL TANDOORI RESTAURANT
☎01509 621 000

35a Bridge Street, Loughborough, LE12 8PN

Succulent tandoori dishes, creamy sauces and spicy bases make up a popular menu at The Bengal Tandoori Restaurant. The kitchen offer a wide selection of curries ranging from the mild to the fiery.

2FOR1 MAIN COURSE | FRI × | SAT × — Indian

BISTRO LIVE
☎0845 331 1500

89-91 Charles Street, Leicester, LE1 1FA

Bright and buzzy place to enjoy live music, a fun evening out and a selection of remarkably tasty bistro-style food. *Essential to mention GS when booking. £10 entertainment fee is also required.

25% OFF TOTAL | FRI ✓ | SAT ✓ — International

BLACK BULL
☎ 01572 767 677

2 Teigh Road, Market Overton, LE15 7PW

Overlooking views of fields and the church in the picturesque village of Market Overton, this charming rural pub is the ideal spot for a pint of local beer and some delicious home-cooked food.

25% OFF TOTAL | 4 | FRI ✓ | SAT ✓ | SUN | ▲ — British

THE BOWSTRINGS
☎ 01162 758 215

1-3 Braunstone Gate, Leicester, LE3 5LH

Chic, upbeat & welcoming, The Bowstrings Bar is an unique bar which has created its home in one of the UK's most vibrant and cosmopolitan cities, Leicester. Quality pub food in a stylish environment.

25% OFF TOTAL | 10 | FRI × | SAT × | SUN | ✱ | ▲ — British

THE BRASSERIE @ MECURE
☎ 0844 815 9012

Granby Street, Leicester, LE1 6ES

Consistent in providing quality accommodation, Mercure Hotels are well-recognised for providing welcoming stays. The Leicester City Hotel exudes Victorian charm, serving international cuisine.

2FOR1 3 COURSES | FRI ✓ | SAT ✓ — International

BROWNS LANE RESTAURANT AND BAR
☎ 01509 217 227

2a Browns Lane, Loughborough, LE11 3HE

A two-storey restaurant and bar, where modern contemporary style plays a core role in the kitchen's ethos. English dishes that have been given a modern, creative twist are sure to impress every diner.

25% OFF TOTAL | 6 | FRI × | SAT × | SUN | ✱ | ▲ — British

THE BULL AND LION INN
☎ 01530 413 882

48 High St, Packington, Ashby De La Zouch, LE65 1WH

Great village pub where you'll enjoy a pint of the finest and some warming, filling food. A classic feel, rooted and down to earth, with a brilliant pie night. Booking, we should add, is essential.

2FOR1 MAIN COURSE | FRI 📱 | SAT 📱 | ✱ | ▲ — British

BUTT AND BARREL BAR
☎ 01536 771 370

Hunting Lodge Hotel, High Street, Cottingham, LE16 8XN

Spoil your friends with a relaxed dinner at the Butt and Barrel Bar, where the ambiance is soothing and the beverages are thirst-quenching.

2FOR1 MAIN COURSE | FRI ✓ | SAT × | SUN | ▲ — International

CAFÉ ROUGE
01162 518 067

Highcross Lane, Leicester, LE1 4SD

An attractive restaurant, a boulevard café or a Parisian-style wine bar; however you see Café Rouge, consistently excellent classic French dishes are always guaranteed.

25% OFF TOTAL | 6 | FRI ✓ | SAT ✓ | ✱ | ▲ — French

CHAMELEE INDIAN RESTAURANT
☎ 01162 771 179

Sycamore Street, Blaby, LE8 4FJ

Contemporary Indian restaurant serving food a cut above the standard fare. Light, spacious settings and colourful design; known for some excellent old favourites and one or two more eclectic gems.

2FOR1 3 COURSES | FRI 📱 | SAT 📱 — Indian

CHEIKHO'S ITALIAN
☎ 01162 711 933

9 Leicester Road, Oadby, Leicester, LE2 5BD

Chicken caccatura, ravioli di carne and vegetarian calzone are just a few of the delights featured on the menu. Family occasions or dinner dates; the extensive wine list ensures guests can truly unwind.

2FOR1 MAIN COURSE | FRI ✓ | SAT ✓ | SUN | ✱ — Italian

CHILACAS LEICESTER
01162 622 572

Highcross Shopping Centre, Leicester,LE1 4SD

Chilacas is all about capturing the energy, flavour, fire & passion of Mexican street food, served with flair and talent! They have got food for all tastes, from the mild to the extremely hot.

2FOR1 MAIN COURSE | 8 | FRI ✓ | SAT ✓ — Mexican

CHUTNEY IVY RESTAURANT AND BAR
☎ 01162 511 889

41 Halford Street, Leicester, LE1 1TR

Sleek white linen and smart modern furnishings at this fine Indian restaurant in the cultural quarter. Ranges from the Goan fish curry to the sweet chicken haryali; a touchstone for modern Indian food.

2FOR1 2 COURSES | FRI ✓ | SAT ✓ | SUN | ▲ — Indian

COLOURWORKS
☎ 01162 624 170

2 Westbridge Close, Leicester, LE3 5LW

This modern restaurant boasts a vibrant yet intimate atmosphere, gorgeous riverside views, and simply sublime food, offering diners a simple and unpretentious experience.

2FOR1 MAIN COURSE | FRI ✓ | SAT × | SUN | ✱ — European

THE CROWN AT ASFORDBY
☎ 01664 812 175

106 Main Street, Melton Mowbray, LE14 3SA

Excellent neighbourhood feel about this acclaimed pub in Asforby. Menu straight out of the top drawer of classic British pub food, with the fish pie and unbeatable mixed grill especially worthy of note.

2FOR1 3 COURSES | FRI 📱 | SAT 📱 | SUN | ▲ — British

DINE INDIA
☎ 01162 778 777

62 Main Street, Countesthorpe, LE8 5QX

Experience a warm welcome from the friendly staff of this highly popular restaurant, consistently voted among the best in the local area. The menu combines the traditional and the modern.

2FOR1 2 COURSES | FRI ✱ | SAT ✱ | SUN — Indian

DINING ROOM
☎ 01162 676 774

115 Wanlip Lane, Birstall, LE4 4GL

Tasty dishes all round are on offer at this sophisticated Indian restaurant, where experienced staff will be happy to advise you on the menu. Bring along your favourite tipple to accompany your meal.

25% OFF TOTAL | 4 | FRI × | SAT × — Indian

DIPALI RESTAURANT
☎ 01162 777 577

25 Lutterworth Road, Blaby, Leicester, LE8 4DW

Warm, low-lit Indian restaurant that has received some exceptional reviews in local media. Its menu features the classics whilst also going further afield with some distinctive, imaginative cooking.

2FOR1 3 COURSES | FRI ✓ | SAT ✓ — Indian

THE DRUID ARMS
☎ 01509 213 007

14 Pinfold Gate, Loughborough, LE11 1BE

Popular local pub on Pinfold Gate in Loughborough that is known for its friendly welcome and personal touch, as well as for a good range of classic English dishes.

2FOR1 MAIN COURSE | FRI ✓ | SAT ✓ — British

THE ELDERFLOWER RESTAURANT
☎ 01530 413 222

8 Mill Lane Mews, Ashby De La Zouch, LE65 1HP

Strong, British flavours meet classic French cooking in this well-received project by experienced chef Timothy Slack, delivering dishes cooked with flair and skill.

25% OFF TOTAL | 4 | FRI 📱 | SAT × | SUN | ✱ | ▲ — British

ENTROPY
☎ 01162 259 650

42 Hinckley Road, Leicester, LE3 0RB

Steeped in local history, this characterful restaurant is renowned as a landmark in the local area, serving great bistro-pub dishes and priding itself on quality food, drink and standards of care.

25% OFF TOTAL | 2 | FRI 📱 | SAT 📱 | SUN — European

EVEREST DINE
☎ 01162 510 555

61 Belgrave Gate, Leicester, LE1 3HR

Indulge in a variety of dishes from the extensive, mouth-watering menu of authentic Nepalese and Indian cuisine, whilst enjoying the warm and friendly ambiance, of pleasant service and modern interiors.

2FOR1 MAIN COURSE | FRI 📱 | SAT 📱 — Indian

FIELDS RESTAURANT
☎ 01162 886 161

299 Leicester Road, Wigston Fields, Leicester, LE18 1JW

A fine-dining restaurant with a superb à la carte menu, served to guests in a dining room that carries off a traditional vibe: classically dressed tables, calm lighting and tasteful decoration.

50% OFF FOOD | 10 | FRI ✓ | SAT ✓ | ▲ — European

FLINTLOCK RESTAURANT
☎01536 771 370
Hunting Lodge Hotel, High Street, Cottingham, LE16 8XN
Sooth a rapacious stomach with a substantial, wholesome dish. Guaranteeing quality cuisine every time, this restaurant vaunts an atmosphere in which to unwind.

2FOR1 MAIN COURSE | FRI ✓ | SAT × | SUN | ♟ — International

FOREST PARK
01162 394 677
Hinckley Road, Leicester Forest East, Leicester, LE3 3GD
Quality pub classics with a modern twist combine with a friendly and relaxed atmosphere to make this Table Table venue the perfect place for family gatherings or meeting friends.

2FOR1 MAIN COURSE | FRI ✓ | SAT ✓ — Modern British

THE FORGE INN
☎01162 871 702
Main Street, Glenfield, LE3 8DG
Smart and stylish dining pub where you can enjoy an eclectic range of well-cooked dishes at a sound price; try the classic old-fashioned bangers and mash, or a herby plate of delicious bass.

2FOR1 3 COURSES | FRI ✓ | SAT ✓ | SUN — Modern British

GHANDI
☎01142 349 966
348-352 South Road, Walkley, Sheepy Magna, S6 3FF
Committed little restaurant in Walkley that is gaining a solid reputation for its superb selection of dishes across the menu. Tasty, edgy marinades and sauces, with good quality cooking.

2FOR1 MAIN COURSE | FRI × | SAT × | SUN — Indian

THE GLOBE
☎01162 539 492
43 Silver Street, Leicester, LE1 5EU
Having recently undergone a major refurbishment, The Globe Leicester has a fresh new look. However, they remain synonymous with serving fresh, seasonal and locally sourced delicious food.

50% OFF FOOD | 6 | FRI ✓ | SAT × | SUN | ♟ — British

GOA
01455 850 099
55 Wood Stree, Earl Shilton, LE9 7NE
A Portuguese outpost for almost 500 years, the influence of colonial rule on the Indian state of Goa has created a wonderful cuisine of East-meets-West flavours, which this restaurant expertly recreates.

2FOR1 MAIN COURSE | FRI ✓ | SAT ✓ — Indian

GOLDEN AKASH TANDOORI
☎01162 559 030
159 London Road, Leicester, LE2 1EG
Close to Leicester's main concert hall and prominently placed, this Indian restaurant succeeds in its clear-minded aims: high-quality, flavourful Indian food in a congenial, welcoming environment.

25% OFF TOTAL | 10 | FRI | SAT — Indian

THE GOLDEN FLEECE
☎01664 840 275
77 Main Street, South Croxton, LE7 3RL
This idyllic country eatery serves local produce in a cosy setting complete with weekend entertainment. Pork belly risotto or baked gnocchi with spinach, the menu oozes undoubted taste and sophistication.

25% OFF TOTAL | 4 | FRI ✓ | SAT × | SUN | ♟ — British

THE GRANGE FARM
01162 715 088
Glen Road, Oadby, Leicester, LE2 4RH
This Vintage Inn oozes rural charm and rustic character. The picturesque surroundings provide the perfect backdrop for savouring the hearty, seasonal pub-food on the menu.

25% OFF TOTAL | FRI ✓ | SAT ✓ | SUN | ♟ — Modern British

HAMMER & PINCERS
☎01509 880 735
5 East Road, Loughborough, LE12 6ST
An outstanding restaurant in the picturesque village of Wymeswold, headed by Savoy-trained chefs Danny and his wife Sandra. In short, a family affair showing consummate imagination and skill.

2FOR1 MAIN COURSE | FRI ✱ | SAT ✱ | SUN — Modern European

HANDMADE BURGER CO.
01162 425 875
Unit R5 Highcross, Leicester, LE1 4SD
100% prime Scotch beef burgers, handmade in the restaurant daily, sourdough buns, delicious handmade relishes & a wide range of toppings giving you over 40 varieties to choose from. *Exclusions apply.

2FOR1 MAIN COURSE | FRI ✓ | SAT × | SUN — International

HERITAGE
☎01162 861 919
58 Leicester Road, Narborough, Leicester, LE19 2DG
Some of the best Indian food in the area, offering diners a wide variety of choice with a menu boasting options that go beyond ordinary venues. Relax and enjoy your food in a warm, authentic setting.

2FOR1 MAIN COURSE | FRI ✱ | SAT ✱ | SUN — Indian

HERMITAGE PARK HOTEL
☎01530 814 814
The Lamphouse, Whitwick Road, Coalville, LE67 3FA
Dine in the fully glazed atrium of this lovely hotel, with a menu of delectable dishes rooted in a range of European cuisines. Enjoy lunch or dinner with quality food and a selection of beverages.

25% OFF TOTAL | 10 | FRI ✓ | SAT ✓ | SUN — European

THE HORSESHOE INN
☎01572 722 564
83 Braunston Road, Oakham, LE15 6LE
Priding itself on home-made food, this venue caters for families and lovers of good pub favourites. Picturesque surroundings and a superb beer garden make this an all-round favourite.

2FOR1 MAIN COURSE | FRI ✓ | SAT ✓ — International

THE HUNTING LODGE
01509 412 337
38 South Street, Barrow Upon Soar, LE12 8LZ
Charismatic setting for this restaurant that delivers a huge range of popular British food. With several accompanying wines and beers to choose from, this is a contemporary venue for all to enjoy.

2FOR1 2 COURSES | FRI ✱ | SAT ✱ — British

THE INDIAN LOUNGE
☎01455 550 300
6 Weston Court, George Street, Lutterworth, LE17 4EG
With dishes standing out for their subtlety of flavour and quality of produce, it is no surprise that The Indian Lounge is highly reputable. Enjoy chef specialities such as the rajastani stew.

2FOR1 3 COURSES | FRI ✓ | SAT ✓ | ♟ — Indian

INDIAN OCEAN
01509 266 934
11 Swan Street, Loughborough, LE11 5BJ
Delight your senses with a taste of India as chefs create a menu filled with fragrant and flavoursome dishes. Food is prepared and presented with passion and care, making this venue truly worth a visit.

2FOR1 2 COURSES | FRI ✓ | SAT ✓ | ✱ — Indian

JAMES' CAFÉ BISTRO
☎01162 513 323
5 East Bond Street, Leicester, LE1 4SX
Innovative chefs prepare Mediterranean cuisine with lashings of French and Asian inspiration. The daily specials promise to tantalise the taste buds, whilst the less peckish can indulge in cake and coffee.

2FOR1 3 COURSES | FRI ✓ | SAT ✓ | ♟ — Mediterranean

THE JUNGLE CLUB
☎01162 661 054
21 Checketts Road, Leicester, LE4 5ER
A unique, versatile venue. Eclectic kind of place that caters to events large and small; with a menu ranging through an array of Indian dishes plus Indo-Chinese and English offerings.

2FOR1 MAIN COURSE | FRI × | SAT × | SUN | ✱ — Indian

KOH I NOOR
☎01509 231 059
29-35 Nottingham Road, Loughborough, LE11 1ER
An old favourite, crafting fine curries and an especially good line in dry dishes, marinated beautifully, and sizzling wildly on arrival. A cosy and welcoming place to eat a good, flavoursome curry.

2FOR1 MAIN COURSE | FRI ✱ | SAT ✱ — Indian

LA ZOUCH
☎01530 412 536
2 Kilwardby Street, Ashby De La Zouch, LE65 2FQ
A beautiful listed building offers the local area an outstanding place to dine. A loyal following indicates its excellence. *Offer also available on table d'hôte menu. Present your GS card on arrival.

2FOR1 3 COURSES | FRI ✓ | SAT ✱ | SUN | ♟ — British

LANGTON INN
01858 546 770
Melton Rd, West Langton, Market Harborough, LE16 7TG
Quality pub classics with a modern twist combine with a friendly and relaxed atmosphere to make this Table Table venue the perfect place for family gatherings or meeting friends.

2FOR1 MAIN COURSE | FRI ✓ | SAT ✓ — Modern British

To understand what the restaurant icons mean, please see the inside back cover.

LAUGHING BUDDHA
☎ 01509 236 868

3 Woodgate, Loughborough, LE11 2TY

A pleasing local restaurant serving traditional Cantonese and Peking-style cuisine in a lavishly spacious setting. Staff are passionate about serving first-rate food with outstanding hospitality.

25% OFF TOTAL | 4 | FRI × | SAT × | ✱ | ▲ — Chinese

LEEJA PALACE
☎ 01162 710 482

13 The Parade, Oadby, Leicester, LE2 5BB

Classically comfortable, modern and warm Indian restaurant that serves the gamut of Indian cuisine, juxtaposing traditional flavours with a modern twist.

25% OFF TOTAL | 4 | FRI ▯ | SAT × — Indian

THE LIME KILNS
☎ 01455 631 158

Watling Street, Burbage, LE10 3ED

Sip on a glass of wine and dine on delicious bar food whilst watching the waterway wildlife and colourful narrowboats. This old coaching house is a wonderful place to enjoy real ales and tasty treats.

25% OFF TOTAL | FRI ▯ | SAT ✱ | SUN — International

LITTLE INDIA
☎ 01162 478 251

St Peter's Road, Arnesby, LE8 5WJ

Regionally renowned Indian restaurant that goes beyond the staples with imaginative, eccentric and extremely tasty new recipes.

2FOR1 2 COURSES | FRI ✱ | SAT ✱ — Indian

LITTLE ITALY
☎ 01162 708 695

326 Welford Road, Knighton, Leicester, LE2 6EH

Family-run restaurant with full, rich tomato-based dishes along with a silky marinara as its speciality.

2FOR1 MAIN COURSE | FRI ▯ | SAT ▯ | SUN | ✱ | ▲ — Italian

THE MANOR HOUSE AT QUORN
☎ 01509 413 416

Woodhouse Road, Quorn, LE12 8AL

A wonderful, modern country pub where great beers and first-rate meals are served with a smile. The à la carte menu offers fine meats, poultry and game, guaranteeing its irresistibility.

25% OFF TOTAL | 4 | FRI ▯ | SAT ✱ | SUN — Contemporary

MARQUIS WELLINGTON
01162 540 542

139 London Road, Leicester, LE2 1EF

Set near Victoria Park in Leicester, the Marquis Wellington is a beautiful old building whose interior has been revamped in great style to produce a lovely atmosphere for a drink or a bite to eat.

2FOR1 MAIN COURSE | FRI ✓ | SAT ✓ — International

MR CHAN'S
☎ 01509 216 216

14 Bedford Square, Loughborough, LE11 2TP

An exceedingly popular restaurant serving outstanding Cantonese and Peking cuisine. Pay Mr Chan a visit if you like to be met by an impressive selection of dishes at affordable prices.

25% OFF TOTAL | 4 | FRI ✓ | SAT ✓ | ▲ — Chinese

NILA PALACE
☎ 01162 556 161

61 London Road, Leicester, LE2 2PZ

A regular dining spot for many locals, this Indian restaurant offers diners a staple menu of classic and modern dishes, as well as fresh sundries.

25% OFF TOTAL | 6 | FRI ✓ | SAT ▯ | ✱ — Indian

THE OBSERVATORY
01162 890 945

Meridian Business Park, Braunstone, Leicester, LE19 1LU

Beefeater Grill are one of the UK's best-loved restaurants welcoming guests for almost 40 years in over 130 locations nationwide. *Excludes Breakfast, Light Bites, Bar menu, set menus and all other offers.

2FOR1 MAIN COURSE | 6 | FRI ✓ | SAT × | ▲ — Modern British

THE PACKE ARMS
01509 889 106

Rempstone Road, Hoton, Loughborough, LE12 5SJ

Named for a local Victorian family, who restored the pub back in 1880, this Vintage Inn serves a fine selection of food and drinks. You can even see the original date stone above the front entrance!

25% OFF TOTAL | FRI ✓ | SAT ✓ | SUN | ▲ — Modern British

THE PAGET
☎ 01509 266 216

41 Oxford Street, Loughborough, LE11 5DP

Tucked away in a great location, this good old-fashioned pub does a fine line in ales. Don't overlook the great pub food: from excellent doorstop sandwiches to a massive Yorkshire with sausage and mash.

25% OFF TOTAL | 4 | FRI ✓ | SAT ✓ | ▲ — Traditional English

PAPRIKA WATERMEAD
☎ 01162 664 400

510 Melton Road, Leicester, LE4 7SP

Innovative menus here combine refined yet creative Indian cuisines, incorporating traditional favourites as well as new, original dishes with modern twists. A fresh approach to Indian dining.

2FOR1 3 COURSES | FRI × | SAT × — Oriental

PARADISE INDIAN RESTAURANT
☎ 01162 720 010

29 London Road, Oadby, Leicester, LE2 5DL

Real, authentic Indian cuisine is the order of the day at Paradise in Oadby, with its bright dining room and heady array of flavoursome dishes, from traditional favourites to more eclectic options.

2FOR1 3 COURSES | FRI ✱ | SAT ✱ | SUN — Indian

THE PLOUGH INN
☎ 01509 842 228

Main Street, Normanton on Soar, LE12 5HB

If you're looking for a cosy place to drink and eat hearty, classic pub food, this country inn is just what you need. Free moorings in the riverside garden make this a perfect stop for a boatman's lunch.

2FOR1 2 COURSES | FRI ✱ | SAT ✱ | SUN | ▲ — British

PREZZO
01162 513 343

22 Silver Street, Leicester, LE1 5ET

With a character all of its own, Prezzo oozes contemporary style and enduring charm. Signature pastas, stone-baked pizzas and classic Italian dishes promise a perfect dining choice for the whole family.

2FOR1 MAIN COURSE | FRI × | SAT × | ▲ — Italian

THE PRINTROOM
☎ 01509 634 100

60 Woodgate, Loughborough, LE11 2TZ

Drop in for an afternoon coffee, a rendezvous with friends or a business meeting. The Print Room offers the perfect backdrop for any occasion, with its stylish surroundings and vibrant atmosphere.

25% OFF TOTAL | 4 | FRI ▯ | SAT ▯ — British

QUORN EXCHANGE
☎ 01509 621 444

10-12 High Street, Quorn, LE12 8DT

Light and airy dining space in which to enjoy a panoply of contemporary and cosmopolitan cuisine. A focus on fine produce, rich flavours, and just the right wine to accompany.

2FOR1 MAIN COURSE | FRI ✱ | SAT ✱ | SUN — European

QUORN GRANGE
☎ 01509 412 167

88 Wood Lane, Quorn, LE12 8DB

The Buddon within the Quorn Grange hotel is a haven of tranquillity, offering exceptional food in an eclectic style designed to delight the most discerning palate. Fine dining in an informal environment.

25% OFF TOTAL | 8 | FRI ✓ | SAT ✓ | SUN | ▲ — Fine Dining

THE QUORNDON FOX
01509 413 134

46 High Street, Quorn, Loughborough, LE12 8DT

Legend has it the tower at the end of the garden used to be a look-out for hungry passersby - whilst things are now a little different, this Vintage Inn keeps to its roots of home cooking and fine drinks.

25% OFF TOTAL | FRI ✓ | SAT ✓ | SUN | ▲ — Modern British

THE RED COW
01162 387 878

Hinckley Road, Leicester, LE3 3PG

The Red Cow Vintage Inn started out as a small inn, situated in a row of cottages in a village near Leicester. Now, it welcomes its guests with an enticing selection of homely pub food and fine drinks.

25% OFF TOTAL | FRI ✓ | SAT ✓ | SUN | ▲ — Modern British

RED VEIL EXCLUSIVE INDIAN
☎ 01509 265 165

45 Nottingham Road, Loughborough, LE11 1ER

Tantalise your senses with a trip to this exclusive venue, filled with sensual music, lush surroundings, and most importantly extraordinary food exceeding all your culinary expectations.

25% OFF TOTAL | 2 | FRI ▯ | SAT ▯ | ✱ — Indian

REVOLUTION ☎01162 559 633
6b New Walk, Leicester, LE1 6TF
Let Great British bar food and every flavour of vodka under the sun tantalise your taste buds at this national bar chain. *Only valid on drinks purchased with food or while eating. Excludes champagne.

25% OFF TOTAL | 6 | FRI ✓ | SAT ✓ — British

REVOLUTION ☎01509 808 010
13-14 Baxter Gate, Loughborough, LE11 1TG
Let Great British bar food and every flavour of vodka under the sun tantalise your taste buds at this national bar chain. *Only valid on drinks purchased with food or while eating. Excludes champagne.

25% OFF TOTAL | 6 | FRI ✓ | SAT ✓ — British

THE ROBIN HOOD ☎01530 831 137
2 Spring Lane, Swannington, Coalville, LE67 8QQ
For superb home-cooked food, traditional ales and special food evenings, this is a wonderful choice.

2FOR1 MAIN COURSE | FRI ✓ | SAT ✱ | SUN | ✱ — International

THE ROYAL ARMS ☎01455 290 263
Main Street, Sutton Cheney, CV13 0AG
A warm and friendly welcome awaits guests at this beautifully situated village hotel and restaurant. Sample home-reared beef amongst other seasonal offerings from the à la carte or informal bar menu.

25% OFF TOTAL | 4 | FRI | SAT ✱ | SUN — British

RUCHITA INDIAN ☎01162 464 952
203 Uppingham Road, Leicester, LE5 4BQ
Ruchita contributes to Leicester's reputation for serving up the most memorable of curries. Find all of your favourite dishes packed full of locked in flavours and quality freshness.

2FOR1 MAIN COURSE | FRI ✓ | SAT ✓ | ✱ — Indian

RUTLAND & DERBY ☎01162 623 299
Millstone Lane, Leicester, LE15JN
'Tradition with ambition' is the ethos of this genteel pub. Wonderfully traditional food and award-winning ales can be enjoyed in light contemporary surroundings.

2FOR1 3 COURSES | FRI ✓ | SAT ✓ — European

SANTHI ☎01162 555 511
124 Granby Street, Leicester, LE1 1DL
A dedicated team of chefs have created an astounding fusion of Asian flavours to craft a confident, balanced menu, making a visit to Santhi a truly memorable dining experience.

25% OFF TOTAL | 4 | FRI | SAT — Indian

SAYONARA THALI RESTAURANT ☎01162 665 888
49 Belgrave Road, Leicester, LE4 6AR
Thalis is a vegetarian cuisine that combines dhal, curry, bread and pickles, served on a steel plate. Guests dine here because of its reliably good food, never lacking in fine, authentic taste.

25% OFF TOTAL | 10 | FRI ✓ | SAT ✓ — Vegetarian

SHAMIM ☎01162 628 188
54 Woodgate, Leicester, LE3 5GF
Locals do not have to go very far in order to delight in the vivacious array of Indian dishes that this restaurant has to offer. Shamim boast quality and authenticity at an affordable price.

2FOR1 MAIN COURSE | FRI × | SAT × | ✱ — Indian

SHEARSBY BATH ☎01162 478 202
Bruntingthorpe Road, Shearsby, Lutterworth, LE17 6PP
This elegantly decorated family-run establishment offering sublime dishes from the à la carte menu. Try the crab and mango millefeuille or deconstructed black forest gâteau: any choice is unforgettable.

2FOR1 3 COURSES | FRI | SAT | SUN — European

SHIMLA PINKS ☎01162 471 471
65-69 London Road, Leicester, LE2 0PE
Incorporates new and exciting dishes amongst a menu of traditional Indian cuisine. The visually pleasing interior ensures you enjoy your meal in an outstanding setting. A beacon to curry lovers.

25% OFF TOTAL | 10 | FRI ✓ | SAT ✓ — Indian

SHIRE RESTAURANT ☎01509 415 050
Quorn Country Hotel, 66 Leicester Rd, Quorn, LE12 8BB
The Shires Restaurant is a AA rosette restaurant offering elegant fine country dining in a 4 star 17th century country house hotel.

25% OFF TOTAL | 6 | FRI × | SAT × — Modern British

SLATE RESTAURANT ☎01162 374 406
61 Leicester Road, Loughborough, LE12 7AJ
Experience fine British comfort food and classic global dishes, all freshly prepared and well-presented. Simple, honest cooking that brings the flavours to the forefront of each dish. *1 card per party.

2FOR1 MAIN COURSE | FRI ✓ | SAT ✓ — British

THE SPICE KUBE ☎01162 460 079
310 Green Lane Road, Leicester, LE5 4PB
Modern and buzzy Indian restaurant with a warm welcome and plenty of atmosphere. Menu features all the old favourites. *Members must purchase individual dishes for discount to be applicable.

50% OFF FOOD | 8 | FRI ✓ | SAT ✱ — Indian

STANTON LAKES ☎01455 283 043
Broughton Road, Stoney Stanton, LE9 4JA
In idyllic surroundings guests can enjoy an array of excellently cooked dishes that reflect great quality and value for money. A unique venue suitable for individuals and all varieties of celebrations.

2FOR1 MAIN COURSE | FRI ✓ | SAT × | SUN | ✱ — British

STEAM TRUMPET ☎01530 231 258
286 Main Street, Thornton, Leicester, LE67 1AJ
Enjoy hearty home-cooked food while sampling one of the eight hand-pulled real ales, or the fine selection of continental lagers. A firm favourite with walkers and locals looking for something special.

25% OFF TOTAL | 4 | FRI ✓ | SAT ✓ — International

SYLHETI SPICE ☎01455 292 255
11 West End, Barlestone, CV13 0EJ
Classic Indian restaurant with simple, spacious design, serving a great range of beautifully prepared curries and other flavourful subcontinental dishes. A laid-back place for a good evening in company.

2FOR1 MAIN COURSE | FRI ✓ | SAT ✓ | ✱ — Indian

SYSONBY KNOLL HOTEL ☎01664 563 563
Sysonby Knoll Hotel, Melton Mowbray, LE13 0HP
Choose from a carefully selected array of specials, light lunch bites and leisurely dinners at this popular eatery. Vaunting views of the Wreake Valley, the ambiance is pleasant and the staff are warm.

2FOR1 3 COURSES | FRI ✓ | SAT × | SUN — European

TAJ MAHAL RESTAURANT ☎01162 540 328
12-14 Highfield Street, Leicester, LE2 1AB
Friendly and accommodating local Indian restaurant in Leicester with a line in flavoursome, deliciously spicy dishes. Generous portions, plenty of atmosphere and a comfortable dining space.

2FOR1 3 COURSES | FRI ✱ | SAT ✱ — Indian

TARBOUSH ☎01509 264 470
12a Market Street, Loughborough, LE11 3EP
Experience something different at this Middle-Eastern-inspired eatery. The menu offers Lebanese, Egyptian, Moroccan and Greek dishes so diners can be certain to go home with appeased stomachs.

25% OFF TOTAL | FRI | SAT — Middle Eastern

TASTE OF INDIA ☎01509 234 216
42 Church Gate, Loughborough, LE11 1UE
Classic Indian restaurant that does a good range of tasty curries with some more left-field options like the badhahi chicken or the tawa harin with venison.

2FOR1 3 COURSES | FRI ✱ | SAT ✱ — Indian

VALENTINOS RESTAURANT ☎01509 211 995
2-4 Nottingham Road, Loughborough, LE11 1EU
Beautiful little family-run restaurant that's begun to carve out a little niche for itself as a welcoming place for good Italian food. Modern, cosy atmosphere prevails, with a real warmth about the place.

25% OFF TOTAL | 4 | FRI ✓ | SAT ✓ | SUN | ✱ — Mediterranean

VERMONT RESTAURANT & BAR
☎ 01162 428 702
129 St Nicholas Circle, Leicester, LE1 5LX
Dine in the Vermont Restaurant, where delicious dishes from around the world make up a solid menu. New World wines provide the perfect accompaniment to any selection you make.

25% OFF TOTAL | 6 | FRI ✓ | SAT ✓ — European

THE VINE
01530 411 116
12 Bath Street, Ashby De La Zouch, LE65 2FH
Delicious food and drink served every day with seasonal menus using local ingredients. The Vine offers a warm welcoming atmosphere for a coffee, quick working lunch or a celebration a la carte meal.

25% OFF TOTAL | 4 | FRI × | SAT × | SUN | ✱ | ▲ — British

VINEE SPICE
☎ 01162 515 328
23 New Park Street, Leicester, LE3 5NH
Vaunting a 'Capital Curry Award', chef Vinnie cooks up a storm in the kitchen at this venue. Whether guests are seeking light lunch bites or substantial dinners, each dish is made lovingly.

2FOR1 MAIN COURSE | FRI ✓ | SAT ✓ | ▲ — Indian

VOJON RESTAURANT
☎ 01162 359 898
7 Stadon Road, Anstey, LE7 7AY
Habitual tranquility is what diners can expect at Vojon. Expert chefs blend sensational spices and the freshest of ingredients to create simmering curries and international cuisine.

2FOR1 MAIN COURSE | FRI ▯ | SAT ▯ | ▲ — Indian

VOUJON
☎ 01572 723 043
4 Burley Corner, High Street, Oakham, LE15 6DU
Flagship restaurant nestled in Oakham. Serves excellent Bangladeshi cuisine; the restaurant is stylish and colourful with high windows looking out over the town. Lovely place to dine on some fine curries.

2FOR1 MAIN COURSE | FRI ✓ | SAT ✓ | ✱ | ▲ — Bangladeshi/Indian

WALKABOUT
☎ 01162 515 816
30-32 Granby Street, Leicester, LE1 1DE
Walkabout is famous for its characteristically Australian atmosphere and well-rounded menu. From live sport with a juicy burger to some Aussie kangaroo skewers, you'll find it hard to tear yourself away.

25% OFF TOTAL | 10 | FRI ✓ | SAT ✓ | ▲ — International

THE WESTERN
☎ 01162 545 287
70 Western Road, Leicester, LE2 0QB
Classic real ale pub just off the Narborough Road. A good, old-school atmosphere together with a range of drinks and tasty pub-style food. Their signature is the range of cracking stone-baked pizzas.

2FOR1 MAIN COURSE | FRI × | SAT × | ▲ — International

THE WHIPPER-IN HOTEL
☎ 01572 756 971
The Market Place, Oakham, LE15 6DT
Savour a delicious meal at the renowned restaurant in the lovely and comfortable surroundings of this Brook hotel, boasting a cuisine that combines innovation with traditional use of methods and produce.

25% OFF TOTAL | FRI ✓ | SAT ✓ — Modern European

THE WHITE HORSE
☎ 01162 671 038
White Horse Lane, Birstall, Leicester, LE4 4EF
Local pub with a keen sense of its history on the Grand Union Canal. Serves warming, hearty and fulsome dishes; with awards for food and drink under its belt, The White Horse is worth taking for a hack.

25% OFF TOTAL | 4 | FRI × | SAT × | SUN | ▲ — British

THE WHITE LION
☎ 01858 880 260
Lutterworth Road, Lutterworth, LE17 6EP
Fine, classic village pub that serves up a warm welcome to locals and visitors alike. A great place to enjoy a quiet pint, and some fresh, wholesome traditional pub food to boot.

2FOR1 3 COURSES | FRI ✓ | SAT ✓ — English/Gastro pub

ZAMANIS
☎ 01530 560 719
11 Rushton Yard, Ashby De La Zouch, LE65 1AL
A favourite with the locals, Zamanis serves the finest quality Italian food and offers an excellent wine bar. *Advance booking mentioning Gourmet Society is essential. A la carte only.

25% OFF TOTAL | 4 | FRI ▯ | SAT ▯ | SUN | ✱ | ▲ — Italian

Lincolnshire

ABBEY PARKS FARM BISTRO
☎ 01205 821 610
Parks Farm, East Heckington, Boston, PE20 3QG
A cosy lunch beside the fire served by friendly staff will brighten a cold day; a cream tea on the patio or a private meal in the garden room for a special occasion: just a taste of what is on offer.

25% OFF TOTAL | 6 | FRI ✓ | SAT ✓ | SUN — British

THE ANCHOR
01724 870 030
Lakeside Parkway, Scunthorpe, DN16 3UA
Beefeater Grill are one of the UK's best-loved restaurants welcoming guests for almost 40 years in over 130 locations nationwide. *Excludes Breakfast, Light Bites, Bar menu, set menus and all other offers.

2FOR1 MAIN COURSE | 6 | FRI ✓ | SAT × | ▲ — Modern British

BINDI RESTAURANT
☎ 01476 570 777
22 London Road, Grantham, NG31 6EJ
Set in opulent surroundings, this exquisite Indian restaurant serves food to match with a mouthwatering section of regional and speciality dishes along with all the classics, prepared by expert chefs.

25% OFF TOTAL | 4 | FRI × | SAT × — Bangladeshi/Indian

BLUE BELL INN
☎ 01507 533 602
Main Road, Belchford, Horncastle, LN9 6LQ
Quality traditional fare mixed with some adventurous dishes for the more curious palates. The wine list is extensive and features guest wines each month; a treat for the sommelier in you.

2FOR1 MAIN COURSE | FRI ✓ | SAT ✸ | SUN — European

THE BRASSERIE AT THE HUMBER ROYAL
☎ 01472 240 024
Littlecoates Road, Grimsby, DN34 4LX
The very best produce that Lincolnshire has to offer is made use of at The Brasserie. Maintains the comfortability and contemporary vibes that can be found in the hotel itself.

2FOR1 MAIN COURSE | FRI ✓ | SAT × | SUN — International

CHANTRY'S RESTAURANT
☎ 0844 736 8612
The St. James Hotel, Grimsby, DN31 1EP
With plenty of experience under its wing, The St. James Hotel is held dear by locals and visitors alike. Friendly staff ensure a heart-warming experience at the bistro where the menu is expansive.

25% OFF TOTAL | 4 | FRI ✓ | SAT × — Traditional English

CHINA DELIGHT
☎ 01472 242 668
104 Cleethorpes Road, Grimsby, DN31 3HW
Charming restaurant that serves a range of Chinese, Thai and Japanese meals. Menu comprises a mix of dishes with familiar favourites sat comfortably alongside lesser-known delicacies.

50% OFF FOOD | 2 | FRI ▯ | SAT ▯ | ▲ — Chinese

CINNAMON BAY
☎ 01522 511 511
Odeon Multiplex, Brayford Wharf N., Lincoln, LN1 1YX
The patrons of this restaurant pride themselves on offering Indian cooking just as it would be in their own homes. With eyes firmly on authenticity of flavour, they serve up a mean array of great dishes.

25% OFF TOTAL | 6 | FRI ✸ | SAT ✸ — Indian

CROSS KEYS GRASBY
01652 628 247
Brigg Road, Grasby, DN38 6AQ
Beautiful rural pub offering a range of well-kept ales and excellent food made using locally sourced produce. A relaxed yet efficient approach to service and a warm and friendly atmosphere.

2FOR1 MAIN COURSE | FRI × | SAT × — British

ELIO'S ITALIAN RESTAURANT
☎ 01652 635 147
Market Place, Barton upon Humber, DN18 5DA
From Italy to Lincolnshire, the chef at this venue creates authentic dishes inspired by his Mediterranean heritage. Enjoy genuine recipes in a family-run, welcoming restaurant.

2FOR1 MAIN COURSE | FRI ✓ | SAT × | SUN | ▲ — Italian

THE GARDEN ROOM AT THE EDEN
☎ 01476 569 752

6 Market Place, Grantham, NG31 6LJ

Laid-back, ristorante-style conservatory along with a sleek contemporary interior, this Grantham restaurant serves highly accomplished, well-designed dishes without becoming over-fussy. A great find.

2FOR1 MAIN COURSE | FRI | SAT × | Classic British/French

THE GEORGE AND DRAGON
☎ 01507 588 255

High Street, Hagworthingham, PE23 4NA

Eclectic and classic cuisine, from a steak and ale pie to a tasty tiger prawn balti, in this idyll of a Lincolnshire country pub. If hunger be the dragon, it's laid to rest here.

25% OFF TOTAL | 10 | FRI | SAT * | SUN | Traditional English

GORKHA SQUARE RESTAURANT
☎ 01476 574 477

1 Wharf Road, Grantham, NG31 6BA

Whilst the authentic recipes are transported from thousands of miles, the ingredients most certainly are not. The kitchen prides itself on its use of fresh local produce and Nepalese influences.

2FOR1 3 COURSES | FRI × | SAT × | SUN | Indian

HANDMADE BURGER CO.
01522 524 420

The Glassmill, Brayford Wharf, Lincoln, LN1 1YX

100% prime Scotch beef burgers, handmade in the restaurant daily, sourdough buns, delicious handmade relishes & a wide range of toppings giving you over 40 varieties to choose from. *Exclusions apply.

2FOR1 MAIN COURSE | FRI ✓ | SAT × | SUN | International

HAVEN RESTAURANT SUPREME INNS
☎ 01205 822 804

Bicker Bar, Bicker, Boston, PE20 3AN

Superb home-cooked food, freshly prepared by experienced chefs using locally sourced produce. The spacious, beautifully refurbished dining space is a perfect venue, be it for business or pleasure.

25% OFF TOTAL | 4 | FRI | SAT | SUN | Classic British/French

JJ'S RESTAURANT
☎ 01754 762 928

1 Firbeck Avenue, Skegness, PE25 3JY

Superb cuisine and service in a relaxing environment, day or night. The mood gently changes during the evening as tables fill up with diners looking for a stylish venue to relax with friends and families.

2FOR1 2 COURSES | FRI ✓ | SAT ✓ | SUN | British

MACH RESTAURANT
☎ 01522 754 488

Wragby Road East, North Greetwell, Lincoln, LN2 4RA

Tranquilly situated on the edges of Lincoln, here you can enjoy a flavoursome array of classical and contemporary Indian recipes with knowledgeable and attentive staff to guide you.

2FOR1 2 COURSES | FRI | SAT | Indian

MACY'S BRASSERIE
☎ 01522 811 830

43 High Street, Navenby, Lincoln, LN5 0DZ

Macy's is light, bright, and geared perfectly for a cosy evening meal. With its homely feel, this restaurant sets a fine tone that is carried through to their crisp, delicious dishes.

25% OFF TOTAL | 2 | FRI ✓ | SAT × | * | European

MILL LODGE
01522 525 216

Lincoln Road, Lincoln, LN4 2RF

Quality pub classics with a modern twist combine with a friendly and relaxed atmosphere to make this Table Table venue the perfect place for family gatherings or meeting friends.

2FOR1 MAIN COURSE | FRI ✓ | SAT ✓ | Modern British

RAJDHANI
☎ 01472 290 881

31 Market Street, Cleethorpes, DN35 8LY

Classic Indian restaurant in Cleethorpes with a broad menu of classic dishes and more eclectic options - makhani, razella and Malayan curries alongside the Kashmirs, kormas and bhunas.

50% OFF FOOD | 2 | FRI * | SAT * | Indian

RED LION CAYTHORPE
☎ 01400 272 632

62 High Street, Caythorpe, Grantham, NG32 3DN

Open fireplaces, candlelight and cosy armchairs are all welcoming features at this classic pub. Their local reputation for fresh ingredients and quality food make this establishment an ideal eatery.

25% OFF TOTAL | FRI × | SAT × | SUN | British

STANTONS BRASSERIE
☎ 01476 514 334

Belton Woods Hotel, Belton, Grantham, NG32 2LN

Lively idyll in the Lincolnshire countryside, Belton Woods is home to this fine brasserie, focused on fresh and seasonal produce. This shines through in the dishes from their wide-ranging à la carte menu.

2FOR1 MAIN COURSE | FRI ✓ | SAT × | * | Modern British

THE SWAN HOLME
01522 509 859

Doddington Road, Lincoln, LN6 3RX

Situated close the rich Roman heritage of Lincoln, this Vintage Inn oozes rural charm, with its excellent selection of homely pub food and fine selection of world wines and cask-nurtured ales.

25% OFF TOTAL | FRI ✓ | SAT ✓ | SUN | Modern British

TATTERSHALL PARK
☎ 01526 268 597

53 Sleaford Road, Tattershall, LN4 4JG

Set in beautiful Lincolnshire countryside, Tattershall Park delivers quality, seasonal British cuisine in a modern, vibrant setting - with an outfit akin to that of a chic London bar.

2FOR1 2 COURSES | FRI * | SAT * | SUN | British

VOUJON
☎ 01780 757 030

26-27 Broad Street, Stamford, PE9 1PJ

Sister to the flagship Voujon in Oakham, this restaurant serves superb Bangladeshi cuisine from a very individual menu. Look out for Voujon Stanford's unique vegetarian dishes.

2FOR1 MAIN COURSE | FRI ✓ | SAT ✓ | * | Indian/Bangladeshi

WALKABOUT
☎01522 538 663
233-237 High Street, Lincoln, LN2 1AT
Walkabout is famous for its characteristically Australian atmosphere and well-rounded menu. From live sport with a juicy burger to some Aussie kangaroo skewers, you'll find it hard to tear yourself away.

25% OFF TOTAL | 10 | FRI ✓ | SAT ✓ | International

WANIA
☎01507 522 939
3-5 Bridge Street, Horncastle, LN9 5HZ
Classic Indian cuisine gets a contemporary twist at Wania, where quality ingredients and balanced flavours come together to create a balanced showcase of Indian cooking.

2FOR1 MAIN COURSE | FRI × | SAT × | Indian

WASHINGBOROUGH HALL
☎01522 790 340
Church Hill, Washingborough, Lincoln, LN4 1BE
Located in a magnificent Georgian manor house, the grand setting has been maintained. The food is traditionally British, cooked up with verve and accomplishment from quality, local produce. 1 AA Rosette.

2FOR1 MAIN COURSE | FRI ✓ | SAT × | SUN | * | European

WIG & MITRE
☎01522 538 902
32 Steep Hill, Lincoln, LN2 1LU
Priding itself on being a civilised and pleasant place, this venue adds a touch of class to the pub experience. Guaranteed to tempt even the most discerning of diners, the menu is bursting with choice.

25% OFF TOTAL | 6 | FRI ✓ | SAT ✓ | European

WINTERINGHAM FIELDS
☎01724 733 096
1 Silver Street, Winteringham, DN15 9ND
Situated in a 16th-century manor house, this is one of the most intimate and secretive places you could ever wish to stumble across. Its award-winning reputation is enough to challenge Europe's finest.

25% OFF TOTAL | 10 | FRI | SAT | SUN | British

WOODYS BAR & RESTAURANT
☎01507 450 079
Woodthorpe Hall Leisure Park, Woodthorpe, LN13 9HX
Woody's Bar & Restaurant is set within Woodthorpe Hall Leisure Park. The menu offers extensive choice to suit a wide range of tastes, all the food is home cooked.

2FOR1 MAIN COURSE | FRI * | SAT * | SUN | Traditional English

Northamptonshire

THE ABINGTON
☎01604 631 240
383 Wellingborough Road, Northampton, NN1 4EY
A fantastic meeting place for friends and family, The Abington is a great place to both start and end your evening out. Popular for lunch and dinner, the menu is well-balanced and appealing.

50% OFF FOOD | 8 | FRI ✓ | SAT ✓ | SUN | British

ALI'S
☎01536 403 732
9 Pytchley Court, Gretton Corby, NN17 2QD
Simplicity is key at this Tandoori restaurant in Corby. Ali's is well-established and well-reputed for maintaining high standards and producing tasty cuisine.

2FOR1 3 COURSES | FRI ✓ | SAT ✓ | Indian

THE ALTHORP COACHING INN
☎01604 770 651
Main Street, Great Brington, Northampton, NN7 4JA
A superb village setting, original oak beams and wooden floors throughout, give this wonderful establishment oodles of character. The menu is filled with inspirational home-cooked dishes.

25% OFF TOTAL | 10 | FRI × | SAT × | SUN | British

BALTI CHEF
☎01604 232 661
126 Wellingborough Road, Northampton, NN1 4DR
Reaching the culinary heights of traditional Indian cooking, Balti Chef hosts a kitchen brimming with talent and well equipped with authentic recipes and sound ingredients. Excellent curry selection.

25% OFF TOTAL | FRI × | SAT × | * | Indian

THE BARN RESTAURANT
☎01327 349 911
Old Dairy Farm Centre, Upper Stowe, NN7 4SH
A likeable place for a day out, beautifully set in the Northamptonshire countryside. The restaurant serves a range of hot and cold dishes in peaceful and picturesque surroundings.

50% OFF FOOD | 4 | FRI ✓ | SAT ✓ | SUN | Brasserie

BELLA ITALIA
01604 591 686
Sixfields Leisure, Weedon Road, Northampton, NN5 5QJ
Accessible Italian cuisine on the British high street - indulge in authentic sharing platters, hand stretched pizzas and hearty pasta dishes, served with a healthy dose of gregarious Italian hospitality.

25% OFF TOTAL | 6 | FRI × | SAT × | SUN | Italian

BLUE MOON
☎01604 627 861
1 Talbot Road, Northampton, NN1 4HZ
The excellent service is a perfect match for the superb food on offer at this Indian restaurant. The khaas roast comes highly recommended, as do the exceptional mouth-watering kebabs.

2FOR1 3 COURSES | FRI * | SAT * | Indian

BOLLYWOOD DREAMS
☎01536 443 779
67 Greenhill Rise, Corby, NN18 0LR
Fantastic Indian restaurant and takeaway in Corby, where the restaurant speciality dishes are a must for Indian cuisine fans. Offers plenty of exciting and unusual dishes for the adventurous.

2FOR1 3 COURSES | FRI ✓ | SAT ✓ | Indian

BOMBAY PALACE
☎01604 713 899
9-11 Welford Road, Kingsthorpe, Northampton, NN2 8AE
An amiable, friendly local restaurant that has a loyal following of diners from the surrounding area. Courteous staff provide you with fine, tasty and rich Indian food.

2FOR1 MAIN COURSE | FRI * | SAT * | Indian

BRABENEC'S RESTAURANT
☎01604 634 428
187 Wellingborough Road, Northampton, NN1 4EA
Look no further then Barbenec's for impeccable service in a mellow setting. Ran by a brother and sister duo, the cuisine is simple and honest. The belly of pork keeps diners returning time after time.

25% OFF TOTAL | 4 | FRI ✓ | SAT × | SUN | * | British

CAFÉ BANGLA
☎01933 411 994
86 High Street, Rushden, NN10 0PQ
A cosy restaurant on Rushden High Street serving an array of simple, unfussy Indian cuisine. Simple and comfortable in style, the service is quick and accommodating and the atmosphere excellent.

2FOR1 MAIN COURSE | FRI ✓ | SAT ✓ | SUN | Indian

CINNAMON
☎01604 580 680
2 Malvern Grove, Northampton, NN5 6AY
Colourful and contemporary Indian restaurant. The menu houses popular classics, but also does a special line in tandoori dishes together with a heady, long list of specialities.

2FOR1 3 COURSES | FRI | SAT * | Indian

THE COCK INN
☎01832 732 565
High Street, Denford, Kettering, NN14 4EQ
An inviting inn with quiet charm. All dishes are freshly prepared and cooked to order, with regularly updated menus and fresh fish delivered daily. A quality, informal, real country pub.

25% OFF TOTAL | 8 | FRI × | SAT * | SUN | * | British

THE DOG & DUCK
01933 278 606
London Road, Wellingborough, NN8 2DP
Beefeater Grill are one of the UK's best-loved restaurants welcoming guests for almost 40 years in over 130 locations nationwide. *Excludes Breakfast, Light Bites, Bar menu, set menus and all other offers.

2FOR1 MAIN COURSE | 6 | FRI ✓ | SAT × | Modern British

DOSA HUT
☎01604 636 480
18 Abington Square, Northampton, NN1 4AA
Originality and authenticity are at the heart of Dosa Hut and its ethos. Renowned for a fantastic dining experience, curry lovers are in their element with the extensive menu of Eastern delights.

25% OFF TOTAL | 10 | FRI ✓ | SAT | Indian

DUNKLEY'S
☎ 01604 810 546
Castle Ashby Station, Grendon Road, Whiston, NN7 1NP
Set in the scenic Northamptonshire countryside around the old goods sheds and carriages of Castle Ashby Station. This venue offers a delicious menu amongst the restored railway artefacts.

25% OFF TOTAL | 10 | FRI ✓ | SAT ✱ | SUN | ▲ — British

THE DYNASTY
☎ 01327 842 007
12 High Street, Long Buckby, NN6 7RD
Situated within a picturesque village, this venue provides a relaxing atmosphere where both food and staff are excellent. Offers an extensive Chinese menu, along with additional Thai and Malaysian dishes.

25% OFF TOTAL | 4 | FRI × | SAT ✱ | ✱ | ▲ — Chinese

EASTERN BALTI
☎ 01604 413 137
3 Fieldmill Square, Northampton, NN3 9AZ
Friendly, straightforward Indian takeaway in Northampton that's gotten itself a good reputation for swiftly producing some filling, substantial and spicy fare. Welcoming place for a good evening out.

2FOR1 MAIN COURSE | FRI ✓ | SAT ✓ | SUN — Indian

EASTERN SPICE
☎ 01933 650 044
56-60 High Street, Irthlingborough, NN9 5TN
A popular Indian restaurant with a convenient central location. Guests enjoy the week-night banquets that offer a fine selection of delicious meals. Mild to spicy dishes are on offer.

2FOR1 2 COURSES | FRI ▯ | SAT ▯ | ✱ — Indian

FEAST WORLD BUFFET
☎ 01536 480 032
34-36 Montagu Street, Kettering, NN16 8RU
Choose from the dishes on display and the chefs will also cook your meal in front of you at the famous Wok Station. Their enthusiasm, style and panache make each dining experience a truly memorable one.

25% OFF TOTAL | 10 | FRI ✓ | SAT ✓ — Asian

THE FOLLY INN
01327 354 031
London Road, Towcester, NN12 6LB
The Folly Inn is a pretty, quintessential thatched pub whose traditional charm is complimented by delightful food. Dishes are inspired by traditional British classics with a contemporary twist.

25% OFF TOTAL | 4 | FRI × | SAT × | SUN | ▲ — British

FUEL
☎ 01327 307 000
Barcelo Hotel, Sedgemoor Way, Daventry, NN11 0SG
With a keen investment in its extensive, well-conceived wine list, this hotel-based restaurant offers a tasty, diverse menu.

25% OFF TOTAL | 4 | FRI ✓ | SAT ✱ | ▲ — International

FUNKY SPICE
01933 222 522
31-33 Midland Road, Wellingborough, NN8 1HF
The dining room here is beautifully designed with elegant, crisp lines and warm tones making it a lovely place to settle in for the evening. The food, in turn, is well-prepared and distinctive in flavour.

2FOR1 MAIN COURSE | FRI × | SAT × | SUN — Indian

GIANBIAZ
☎ 01604 633 900
256 Wellingborough Road, Northampton, NN1 4EJ
A wide variety of the highest quality meats, fish and vegetarian dishes showcase the best of Italian cooking in a relaxing setting at this family-run establishment.

2FOR1 MAIN COURSE | FRI ✱ | SAT ✱ | SUN | ▲ — Italian

GRAND INDIAN
☎ 01933 413 141
105 High St South, Rushden, NN10 0RA
Simple, no-nonsense curry place in Rushden where you can get a great selection of dishes at a good price and in generous portions.

2FOR1 MAIN COURSE | FRI × | SAT × | SUN — Indian

THE GURKHAS RESTAURANT
☎ 01536 764 518
Harborough Road, Desborough, Kettering, NN14 2UG
Providing customers with fantastic Indian and Nepalese cuisine in authentic surroundings. Highly experienced owners deliver the ultimate in Indian restaurant dining, with full range of drinks available.

2FOR1 2 COURSES | FRI × | SAT × | SUN | ✱ | ▲ — Indian/Nepalese

IMPERIAL RAJ
☎ 01604 722 004
16a Kingsley Park Terrace, Northampton, NN2 7HG
Warm atmosphere suffused with scents of good cooking. Serves wide-ranging Indian cuisine with some esoteric specialities that include the superb laziz curry, served on a sizzler.

50% OFF FOOD | 4 | FRI ✱ | SAT ✱ — Indian

INDIAN BRASSERIE
☎ 01604 581 312
95 Weedon Road, St James, Northampton, NN5 5BG
Be tempted by an unrivalled range of authentic and imaginative fusion dishes, cooked to the highest standards, using only the finest and freshest ingredients.

2FOR1 2 COURSES | FRI ✱ | SAT ✱ | ▲ — Indian

KHUSHBOO
☎ 01280 701 555
73 High Street, Brackley, NN13 7BW
A comfortable and affable restaurant specialising in traditional Indian and Bangladeshi cuisine. Inviting staff warmly welcome you into this pleasant dining venue.

2FOR1 MAIN COURSE | FRI ✓ | SAT ✓ | ✱ — Indian

LA PAZIENZA
☎ 01604 949 017
268 Wellingborough Road, Northampton, NN1 4EJ
Enjoy dinner with friends or family, the welcoming friendly waiters at La Pazienza, provide a warm and cosy atmosphere, for you to enjoy authentic Italian wines and cuisine.

50% OFF FOOD | 4 | FRI ✓ | SAT ▯ | ▲ — Italian

LEOPOLD'S
☎ 08455 196 346
6 Abington Street, Northampton, NN1 2AJ
Leopold's is one of a kind in Northampton. Serving delicious coffee to go with exquisite hand-made Belgian chocolates, pastries and afternoon scones, the place has a rustic European feel to it.

50% OFF FOOD | 4 | FRI ✓ | SAT × | ▲ — British

MAHARAJA
☎ 01604 637 049
146-152 Wellingborough Road, Northampton, NN1 4DT
A fine Indian restaurant that uses only the finest produce, ingredients and fresh seasonal, native vegetables. Coupled with over 32 years experience this results in a meal prepared to the highest standard.

2FOR1 MAIN COURSE | FRI × | SAT × | ✱ — Indian

THE MOORINGS
☎ 01788 822 517
West Haddon Road, Crick, Northampton, NN6 7SQ
Accommodating restaurant by the canal in Crick with a line in characterful, rich flavours; from a smoky, mellow tripartite terrine for starters, to superb, fulsome pork belly with black pudding mash.

2FOR1 MAIN COURSE | FRI ▯ | SAT ▯ | SUN | ▲ — British

NEW DELHI COTTAGE
☎ 01604 766 144
25 St Leonard's Rd, Far Cotton, Northampton, NN4 8DL
A well-established restaurant serving fine Indian cuisine. The shatkora chicken, a dish made with Bangladeshi citrus fruits and blended spices, comes highly recommended.

25% OFF TOTAL | 4 | FRI × | SAT × | ✱ — Indian

NONNO PINO
☎ 01536 725 599
98 High Street, Burton Latimer, Kettering, NN15 5LA
The F-Word's Best Italian Restaurant in Northamptonshire, Nonno Pino has been serving up a little bit of Italy to Kettering for the last 7 years. This restaurant comes highly recommended.

25% OFF TOTAL | 4 | FRI ▯ | SAT ▯ | ▲ — Italian

OAKLEY HAY
01536 462 790
1 Little Colliers Field, Corby, NN18 9EZ
Beefeater Grill are one of the UK's best-loved restaurants welcoming guests for almost 40 years in over 130 locations nationwide.*Excludes Breakfast, Light Bites, Bar menu, set menus and all other offers.

2FOR1 MAIN COURSE | 6 | FRI ✓ | SAT × | ▲ — Modern British

ONE RESTAURANT AND BAR
☎ 01536 401 348
Best Rockingham Forest Hotel, Corby, NN17 1AE
Hotel-bar and restaurant set on the ground floor in stylish and contemporary surroundings. Guests have a great choice here, with delicious Modern British and brasserie options available.

2FOR1 MAIN COURSE | FRI ▯ | SAT ▯ | ▲ — Brasserie

To understand what the restaurant icons mean, please see the inside back cover.

PALASH BARI
☎01327 830 500
1 Watling Street, Fosters Booth, Towcester, NN12 8LB
In the sleepy village of Fosters Booth sits this delightful Indian restaurant, offering food that will truly wake up your senses. The 'Wine, Dine and Fly' package is certainly a special treat.
25% OFF TOTAL | FRI × | SAT ✱ | ✱ — Indian

PREZZO
☎01604 632 733
3 Wood Hill, Northampton, NN1 2DA
With a character all of its own, Prezzo oozes contemporary style and enduring charm. Signature pastas, stone-baked pizzas and classic Italian dishes promise a perfect dining choice for the whole family.
2FOR1 MAIN COURSE | FRI × | SAT × | ▲ — Italian

PREZZO
01536 485 415
Sheep Street, Kettering, NN16 0AQ
With a character all of its own, Prezzo oozes contemporary style and enduring charm. Signature pastas, stone-baked pizzas and classic Italian dishes promise a perfect dining choice for the whole family.
2FOR1 MAIN COURSE | FRI × | SAT × | ▲ — Italian

PURPLE MANGO
☎01536 206 229
56-58 Burghley Drive, Corby, NN18 8EB
Purple Mango in Corby is an established Indian restaurant, where curry classics and crisp, fresh starters make up a varied menu. The kitchen works hard to produce popular dishes superbly well.
50% OFF FOOD | 10 | FRI ✓ | SAT ✓ | ✱ — Indian

THE RAJ RESTAURANT
☎01536 513 606
46-50 Rockingham Road, Kettering, NN16 8JT
If you are looking for delicious Indian cuisine served in modern and stylish settings, then this is the place for you. Friendly service and smiles are brought to your table along with the flavoursome food.
2FOR1 2 COURSES | FRI × | SAT × | SUN | ✱ — Indian

RED HOT WORLD BUFFET
☎01604 586 527
Sixfields Leisure Park, Northampton, NN5 5QJ
The locals adore the international buffet that this popular venue has to offer. From Japanese to Mexican, the food is fresh and exquisite. With dishes from 6 cultures, make sure to leave room for dessert.
25% OFF TOTAL | 6 | FRI × | SAT × | ▲ — International

THE RESTAURANT & BAR
☎01536 416 666
Kettering Park Hotel & Spa, Kettering, NN15 6XT
The restaurant of this beautifully luxurious hotel certainly showcases the region's excellent produce by delivering creative daily menus. Boasts an enviable reputation along with an AA Rosette.
2FOR1 MAIN COURSE | FRI ✓ | SAT ✓ | ✱ | ▲ — British

RISTORANTE BERARDI
☎01536 211 985
42 Rockingham Road, Kettering, NN16 8JS
Perfect for families and friends, a relaxing atmosphere allows for a night of unwinding. Individual tastes are catered for such as gluten-free pasta, while chicken and fish specials to be savoured.
50% OFF FOOD | 4 | FRI ✓ | SAT × — Italian

ROADE HOUSE RESTAURANT AND HOTEL
☎01604 863 372
16 High Street, Roade, NN7 2NW
Award-winning, this Michelin featured eatery uses only seasonal ingredients to ensure optimum taste. Taking inspiration from an array of International cuisine, only honest food features on the menu.
2FOR1 MAIN COURSE | FRI ✓ | SAT × | SUN | ✱ — Modern British

THE ROYAL BENGAL
☎01536 510 747
64 Rockingham Road, Kettering, NN16 8JT
Known for its low-key buzz, a welcoming Indian restaurant that does tasty and satisfying curries. Does a fine job, first and foremost, of the old favourites; equally the specials here are worth a look.
2FOR1 2 COURSES | FRI ✓ | SAT ✓ — Indian

ROYAL TANDOORI
☎01536 265 391
88 Rockingham Road, Corby, NN17 1AE
Using passed-down recipes that stand the test of time, this traditional Indian restaurant guarantees a selection of favourites made by the well-experienced chefs for an authentic Indian experience.
2FOR1 MAIN COURSE | FRI 📱 | SAT 📱 — Indian

SAFFRON
☎01604 630 800
21 Castilian St, Northampton, NN1 1JS
A nouvelle-tandoori restaurant with a magnificent unique twist. Whilst you can still enjoy your favourite Indian and tandoori dishes, the menu also contains an exquisite range of venison and duck dishes.
2FOR1 MAIN COURSE | FRI ✓ | SAT ✓ | ✱ — Indian

SEDGEBROOK HALL
☎01604 821 666
Chapel Brampton, Northampton, NN6 8BD
A picturesque hotel to match its location, Sedgebrook Hall has maintained a perfect level of its Victorian heritage, whilst making room for the modern comforts that every guest deserves.
25% OFF TOTAL | 6 | FRI ✓ | SAT ✓ | ▲ — British

SONDES ARMS
☎01536 771 778
Main Street, Rockingham, Nr Corby, LE16 8TG
Step into the 1700s at the Sondes Arms, a historic coaching inn facing the picturesque castle of Rockingham. Oozing English charm, this venue was once the haunt of Charles Dickens. English cuisine served.
25% OFF TOTAL | 2 | FRI ✓ | SAT ✓ — British

TAJ MAHAL
☎01604 232 661
126 Wellingborough Road, Northampton, NN1 4DR
Well-liked Indian and Bangladeshi restaurant that goes about its business without undue bells and whistles. Known as a fine place to go for classic, homely Indian cuisine in generous portions.
25% OFF TOTAL | 2 | FRI ✓ | SAT × — Indian

TASTE OF SPICE
☎01604 754 999
38a Main Road, Duston, Northampton, NN5 6JF
Family-run business providing quality food and service. Spice up your evenings with a wide range of curries to suit all tastes, vegetarian and seafood varieties, and a selection of delicious desserts.
2FOR1 MAIN COURSE | FRI ✱ | SAT ✱ — Indian

THE TOLLEMACHE ARMS
☎01536 710 469
49 High Street, Harrington, NN6 9NU
The service is relaxed and friendly and a range of menus are offered to suit all tastes. The restaurant menu is carefully selected by Head Chef Mark Law using the finest local seasonal produce.
25% OFF TOTAL | 8 | FRI ✱ | SAT ✱ | SUN — British

THE TURNPIKE
01604 832 340
Harpole Turn, Weedon Road, Northampton, NN7 4DD
Beefeater Grill are one of the UK's best-loved restaurants welcoming guests for almost 40 years in over 130 locations nationwide. *Excludes Breakfast, Light Bites, Bar menu, set menus and all other offers.
2FOR1 MAIN COURSE | 6 | FRI ✓ | SAT × | ▲ — Modern British

VILLAGE GARDEN
☎01327 844 500
12 Market Place, Northampton, NN6 7RR
Make your way to the Village Garden with the knowledge that you'll be soon be feasting on delectable Indian dishes and moreishly fresh starters. Go for your favourite curry or try one of the chef specials.
25% OFF TOTAL | 6 | FRI 📱 | SAT 📱 | ✱ — Indian

THE VINEYARD
☎01604 633 978
7 Derngate, Northampton, NN1 1TU
The owners have created a unique and inviting dining experience bringing together simple modern decor and good old-fashioned service.
25% OFF TOTAL | 6 | FRI × | SAT × | SUN | ▲ — Continental

THE WINDHOVER
01604 847 859
Brampton Lane, Chapel Brampton, Northampton, NN6 8AA
Steeped in local heritage, this Vintage Inn provides a perfect back drop to enjoy quality pub food and a fine selection of wines and cask ales, either by the homely fire, or in the picturesque beer garden.
25% OFF TOTAL | FRI ✓ | SAT ✓ | SUN | ▲ — Modern British

WOODWARDS AT THE BOAT INN
☎01604 862 428
Stoke Bruerne, Towchester, NN12 7SB
An unexpectedly refined menu includes sublime duck breast, marvellous beef fillet, and gourmet steaks to provide a treat for any diner. Benefit from the experience and tradition at the core of this inn.

25% OFF TOTAL | 6 | FRI | SAT | SUN | British

Nottinghamshire

4550 MILES FROM DELHI
☎01159 475 111
Maid Marion Way, Nottingham, NG1 6HE
Experience Indian food as it is meant to be: fresh, invigorating and free from all artificial additives. Prepared by chefs from Delhi using the freshest herbs and spices; an ingenious fusion menu awaits.

25% OFF TOTAL | 8 | FRI ✓ | SAT × | * | Indian

ALLEY CAFÉ BAR
01159 551 013
1a Cannon Court, Long Row West, Nottingham, NG1 6JE
An eco-conscious café where inventive vegetarian cuisine showcases innovation, quality and choice. At night, world music DJs transform Alley into a hip, stylish bar.

25% OFF TOTAL | FRI ✓ | SAT × | Vegetarian

AMAZING THAI RESTAURANT
☎01159 243 011
32 Lower Parliament Street, Nottingham, NG1 3DA
Both city dwellers and guests from afar enjoy the centrality of this favourable Thai restaurant. Both meat lovers and vegetarians can enjoy an extensive menu that offers deliciously fresh, authentic food.

2FOR1 MAIN COURSE | FRI ✓ | SAT ✓ | * | Thai

THE APPROACH
☎01159 506 149
12-18 Friar Lane, Nottingham, NG1 6DQ
Vibrant venue in Nottingham that covers your day and night: stylish interior in which to settle for a drink at the end of the day; an atmospheric air in the evenings for live entertainment and tasty food.

2FOR1 MAIN COURSE | FRI ✓ | SAT * | Modern Pub

ASHIANA
☎01636 678 969
Bathly Lane, North Muskham, Newark, NG23 6HN
Traditional Indian cuisine in stylish and sophisticated surroundings. The wide ranging menu is inspired and prepared by the experienced chef to ensure the authentic taste of contemporary India.

25% OFF TOTAL | 6 | FRI | SAT | * | Indian

BALTI HOUSE
☎01159 472 871
35 Heathcote Street, Hockley, NG1 3AG
An accommodating Indian restaurant that has catered for the Bangladeshi cricket team and thrives on doing things differently. Serves up classic sauces alongside lighter, subcontinental summer dishes.

2FOR1 2 COURSES | FRI × | SAT × | Indian

BB'S RESTAURANT
☎01623 622 940
1 Bridge Street, Mansfield, NG18 1AL
A fantastic ristorante that delivers well-cooked dishes suitable for any Italian food lover. An extensive menu will have you completely spoilt for choice. A local treasure.

2FOR1 3 COURSES | FRI × | SAT × | SUN | Italian

BELLA ITALIA
01159 509 480
Cornerhouse, Forman Street, Nottingham, NG1 4DB
Accessible Italian cuisine on the British high street - indulge in authentic sharing platters, hand stretched pizzas and hearty pasta dishes, served with a healthy dose of gregarious Italian hospitality.

25% OFF TOTAL | 6 | FRI × | SAT × | SUN | Italian

BELLE & JEROME - BEESTON
☎01159 677 779
66 High Road, Beeston, Nottingham, NG9 2LF
Smooth roasted coffee by day, impressive wines by night: here at Belle and Jerome, the staff work hard to ensure that whatever time you visit, your experience is second to none. Charming and refined.

2FOR1 MAIN COURSE | FRI ✓ | SAT ✓ | SUN | * | European

BELLE & JEROME - WEST BRIDGFORD
☎01159 817 070
33 Central Avenue, West Bridgford, Nottingham, NG2 5GQ
Smooth roasted coffee by day, impressive wines by night: here at Belle and Jerome, the staff work hard to ensure that whatever time you visit, your experience is second to none. Charming and refined.

2FOR1 MAIN COURSE | FRI ✓ | SAT ✓ | SUN | * | Spanish

BIG POPPA'S
☎01157 524 173
64-66 Alfreton Road, Nottingham, NG7 3NN
Specialising in Jamaican cuisine, this Caribbean-inspired eatery is exploding with exotic flavour and authentic recipes. Start with a delicious red pea soup before devouring jerk pork and yam balls.

25% OFF TOTAL | 6 | FRI ✓ | SAT ✓ | Caribbean

BISTRO LIVE
☎01159 473 666
2 Barker Gate, The Lace Market, Nottingham, NG1 1JS
Bistro offers a complete night out of eating, drinking and dancing, culminating in live bands every evening. *Essential to mention GS when booking. £10 entertainment fee is also required.

25% OFF TOTAL | FRI ✓ | SAT ✓ | Bistro

THE BLUE BELL INN
☎01159 473 003
50 Upper Parliament Street, Nottingham, NG1 2AG
A great pub in the centre of Nottingham that offers a more laid-back experience of the city. Traditional in nature, The Blue Bell Inn serves fresh food and snacks alongside a well-stocked bar.

50% OFF FOOD | 10 | FRI ✓ | SAT ✓ | British

THE BLUE BELL INN
☎01777 249 410
Low Street, East Drayton, Retford, DN22 0LN
The Blue Bell Inn is located in East Drayton, Retford, Nottinghamshire. They have a wide selection of home cooked main meals and snacks with a mouthwatering selection of desserts to follow.

2FOR1 3 COURSES | FRI * | SAT * | British

THE BOATHOUSE
01159 473 419
Castle Bridge Road, Nottingham, NG7 1GX
Beefeater Grill are one of the UK's best-loved restaurants welcoming guests for almost 40 years in over 130 locations nationwide. *Excludes Breakfast, Light Bites, Bar menu, set menus and all other offers.

2FOR1 MAIN COURSE | 6 | FRI ✓ | SAT × | Modern British

BOBBIN'S RESTAURANT
☎01159 418 501
The Strathdon Hotel, Derby Road, Nottingham, NG1 5FT
Hotel restaurant serving an array of memorable and delicious dishes prepared by talented and inventive kitchen staff. * Also applies to the table d'hôte menu.

50% OFF FOOD | 6 | FRI ✓ | SAT ✓ | European

BOMBAY
☎01159 691 112
165 Hucknall Road, Nottingham, NG5 1FD
Well-known, longstanding Indian takeaway in Sherwood. They do an eclectic array of dishes, with nicely marinated tandoori sizzler dishes a speciality. The usual suspects are all present and correct.

2FOR1 MAIN COURSE | FRI × | SAT × | Indian

BOMBAY BRIDGFORD
☎01159 817 565
1a Radcliffe Rd, West Bridgford, Nottingham, NG2 5FF
Near to Trent Bridge cricket ground, enjoy an exceptional Indian meal, from regional specialities to traditional family recipes: delicate spices and aromas, the essence of culinary India.

25% OFF TOTAL | 6 | FRI * | SAT * | Indian

BOMBAY NIGHTS BRASSERIE
☎01159 162 121
352-356 Aspley Lane, Nottingham, NG8 5GB
This popular gem is renowned for tantalising, tasty curries. Diners return time and time again for its genuine Indian cuisine.

25% OFF TOTAL | 6 | FRI ✓ | SAT ✓ | SUN | * | Indian

BOTTLE & GLASS
☎01522 703 438
Harby-by-Lincoln, Newark, NG23 7EB
Celebrating the best of British, the menu is brimming with pub favourites. Attentive staff serve food by the roaring log fires and the candle-lit tables.

25% OFF TOTAL | 6 | FRI ✓ | SAT ✓ | European

Gourmet Society discount applies to the à la carte menu only, unless stated otherwise.

CAFÉ ILACHI
☎ 01623 551 111

19 King Street, Sutton-in-Ashfield, NG17 1AT

Devour generous kebabs at Café Ilachi. Whilst seafood lovers can banquet upon prawn papriki mirchi, non-fish eaters can enjoy a variety of house specials which are cooked to perfection.

2FOR1 MAIN COURSE | FRI ✓ | SAT × | SUN | ▲ — Indian

CAFÉ PIANO
☎ 01159 332 233

7a Main Road, Radcliffe-on-Trent, NG12 2FD

Buzzing café-restaurant in Radcliffe that's known especially for its atmosphere and as a spot to catch up with friends. Lively, sociable and featuring a good range of homely, hearty dishes.

2FOR1 MAIN COURSE | FRI × | SAT × | SUN — Italian

CAPOCCI
☎ 01159 473 622

57-58 Upper Parliament Street, Nottingham, NG1 2AG

Specialising in pre-theatre meals, business lunches and relaxed Saturday dining, all served in tasteful surroundings. Choose from a staggering array of Mediterranean and Italian country dishes and wines.

2FOR1 3 COURSES | FRI 📱 | SAT × | ✱ — International

THE CARNARVON
☎ 01623 559 676

Fackley Road, Teversal, Sutton In Ashfield, NG17 3JA

Superb British pub with contrasting décor producing an airy modern ambience. Guests can take advantage of the extensive menu and wide range of beverages on offer. *Check website for further details.

2FOR1 2 COURSES | FRI ✱ | SAT ✱ | ▲ — British

THE CARRINGTON RESTAURANT
☎ 01159 555 000

Best Western Westminster Hotel, Nottingham, NG5 2EF

Smartly turned-out hotel in Nottingham just a few minutes from the town centre. The in-house restaurant is low-key and traditional and features a range of dishes at a great price.

2FOR1 3 COURSES | FRI ✓ | SAT ✓ — British

CAST RESTAURANT
☎ 01158 523 898

Wellington Circus, Nottingham, NG1 5AF

Placing a British take on world cuisine; a contemporary twist adding unique flavours to carefully sourced produce. *Offer available Monday to Thursday from 8pm, Sunday 12.30pm till 5pm.

25% OFF TOTAL | 👤 4 | FRI × | SAT × | ✱ — European

THE CASTLE
01159 484 279

1 Castle Road, Nottingham, NG1 6AA

Classic-style pub with a modern edge. Picturesquely situated next to Nottingham Castle, serves a broad-based menu of bumper sandwiches, beef stews and decadent hickory chicken.

2FOR1 MAIN COURSE | FRI ✓ | SAT ✓ — International

CAUNTON BECK
☎ 01636 636 793

Caunton Village, Newark, NG23 6AB

Radiating culinary finesse, this sophisticated pub-restaurant hosts welcoming staff in stunning surroundings. Seasonal menus ensure diners are constantly catered for, and the food is fabulously fresh.

25% OFF TOTAL | 👤 6 | FRI ✓ | SAT ✓ — European

CHATTERLEY HOUSE HOTEL
☎ 01159 304 519

Coronation Road, Cossall, NG16 2RU

Wonderfully located on the edge of Cossall village, this is a restaurant that can be easily accessed from surrounding areas. Both the bar and the à la carte menu provide great food for lunch and dinner.

25% OFF TOTAL | 👤 6 | FRI 📱 | SAT 📱 | SUN | ▲ — Contemporary

CHINO LATINO
☎ 01159 477 444

41 Maid Marian Way, Nottingham, NG1 6GD

Multi award-winning restaurant offering delicious modern Pan-Asian cuisine and glamorous cocktails. Every appetite, big or small, will find something on the menu. *25% discount is not applied to cocktails.

25% OFF TOTAL | 👤 10 | FRI ✓ | SAT ✱ | SUN | ✱ — Pan-Asian

CHOW ORIENTAL
☎ 01623 633 822

2 St Peters Way, Clerkson Street, Mansfield, NG18 1BQ

Chow Oriental is a superb restaurant that draws upon the most characterful flavours from the Orient. Incredible Chinese dishes take precedent, with fresh meats and vegetables enhancing the flavours.

2FOR1 MAIN COURSE | FRI ✓ | SAT ✓ | ✱ | ▲ — Chinese

CHUTNEY
☎ 01159 241 743

41 Friar Lane, Nottingham, NG1 6DD

Chutney is a perfect blend of local Indian cuisine and a fine-dining restaurant. The menu offers traditional favourites and many chef's specialities. Locally acknowledged as a fantastic, buzzing venue.

25% OFF TOTAL | 👤 10 | FRI ✓ | SAT ✓ — Indian

COCK & HOOP
☎ 01158 583 232

The Lace Market, High Pavement, Nottingham, NG1 1HE

A quintessentially British pub in The Lace Market district that has great character and serves up wholesome British cooking. Cosy corners, comfy armchairs, and some excellent real ales.

25% OFF TOTAL | 👤 6 | FRI ✓ | SAT ✗ | SUN | ▲ — English/Gastro pub

COCKLIFFE HOUSE
☎ 01159 680 179

Burntstump Hill, Arnold, Nottingham, NG5 8PQ

Nestled within acres of rolling parkland, this breathtaking historic venue provides a private and intimate dining experience. The contemporary European menu is both sophisticated and locally sourced.

25% OFF TOTAL | FRI ✓ | SAT ✗ | SUN | ▲ — Fine Dining

COLWICK HALL
☎ 01159 500 566

Racecourse Rd, West Bridgford, Nottingham, NG2 4BH

The magnificent Colwick Hall is a Georgian country house nestled in acres of parkland, playing host to this colonial Malaysian restaurant. Exquisite cuisine is honoured with regal service.

25% OFF TOTAL | 👤 4 | FRI ✓ | SAT ✓ | ▲ — Malaysian

CROWNE PLAZA NOTTINGHAM
☎ 08719 429 161

Wollaton Street, Nottingham, NG1 5RH

You're sure to enjoy a finely cooked, deliciously flavoursome meal at this hotel-restaurant in Nottingham. *Offer available in the main restaurant only.

25% OFF TOTAL | 👤 6 | FRI ✓ | SAT ✓ — International

THE CUMIN
☎ 01159 419 941

62-64 Maid Marion Way, Nottingham, NG1 6BJ

Classy and atmospheric dining space near to Nottingham Castle, with a panoply of dishes focused on rich and silky North Indian cuisine, along with diasporic touches from East Africa. A distinctive treat.

2FOR1 MAIN COURSE | FRI ✓ | SAT ✓ | ✱ | ▲ — Indian

CURRY LOUNGE
☎ 01159 418 844

110 Upper Parliament Street, Nottingham, NG1 6LN

Situated in the heart of Nottingham city centre, this is one of the UK's most talked-about Indian restaurants. Experience the combination of truly authentic, home-cooked cuisine in a stylish setting.

2FOR1 MAIN COURSE | FRI ✓ | SAT ✗ | ✱ | ▲ — Indian

CUTLERS RESTAURANT
☎ 01636 703 399

The Grange Hotel, 73 London Road, Newark, NG24 1RZ

The Grange is a cosy hotel that houses the AA Rosette-rated restaurant 'Cutlers', providing an extensive à la carte menu combining traditional British cuisine with other exciting European flavours.

25% OFF TOTAL | 👤 4 | FRI ✓ | SAT ✓ | ✱ | ▲ — European

DAKOTA BAR & GRILL
☎ 01623 727 670

Holiday Inn, Lake View Drive, Nottingham, NG15 0EA

With their belief in fantastic food from local suppliers, cooked by exceptional emerging chefs, it's no surprise Dakota is a popular retreat. *Available from Thursday to Saturday, due to mid week set menu.

2FOR1 MAIN COURSE | FRI ✓ | SAT ✓ | SUN | ✱ | ▲ — British

DALYAN TURKISH RESTAURANT
☎ 01159 470 439

133-135 Mansfield Road, Nottingham, NG1 3FQ

Priding itself on being the only true Turkish restaurant in Nottingham. Dalyan introduces diners to the exciting and charismatic cuisine of Turkey; bringing you a range of dishes from across the country.

25% OFF TOTAL | 👤 6 | FRI ✱ | SAT ✱ | SUN | ▲ — Middle Eastern

DANUBE
☎ 01636 610 661

25 Castlegate, Newark, NG24 1AZ

Class and elegance pour forth from Danube, where European cuisine reigns free. Named after the river running through the centre of the Continent, Danube embraces the colours and flavours of European food.

2FOR1 2 COURSES | FRI ✓ | SAT ✗ | SUN — Eastern European

THE DRAWING ROOM
☎ 01777 860 077

22 The Square, Retford, DN22 6DQ

Freshly prepared, light and tasty meals at this lovely little café. Likened to something out of Agatha Christie, this is a great place to relax and enjoy a cup of tea in the afternoon.

2FOR1 3 COURSES | FRI ✱ | SAT ✗ — International

EASTWOOD HALL
☎ 01773 532 532

Eastwood, Nottingham, NG16 3SS

Much like its sister hotels, Eastwood Hall is everything Principal Hayley venues stand for. Oozing charm and capturing some of the local area's beauty, this hotel and conference venue offers it all.

25% OFF TOTAL | 👤 6 | FRI ✓ | SAT ✓ | ▲ — British

ELEMENTS BAR @ NOVOTEL
☎ 01159 465 111

Bostock Lane, Long Eaton, Nottingham, NG10 4EP

Take advantage of the ranging drinks list and comfortable furnishings at this Novotel Hotel venue, and simply relax. A friendly bar for all to enjoy, perfect for a nightcap.

50% OFF FOOD | 👤 10 | FRI ✓ | SAT ✓ | ▲ — British

ELEMENTS RESTAURANT @ NOVOTEL
☎ 01159 465 111

Bostock Lane, Long Eaton, Nottingham, NG10 4EP

Experience huge variety at this hotel-restaurant, with an exciting selection of dishes further enhanced by a range of sizes to cater to your desires, all served with a contemporary twist.

50% OFF FOOD | 👤 10 | FRI ✓ | SAT ✓ | ▲ — British

THE ELWES ARMS
01159 871 280

303 Oakdale Road, Carlton, Nottingham, NG4 1DH

A lively pub and restaurant with a great atmosphere. Coupling friendly, attentive staff with quality, wholesome food and value for money, this venue is sure to appeal to all.

25% OFF TOTAL | 👤 6 | FRI ✓ | SAT ✗ | SUN | ▲ — Fresh Fish/Pub Classics

EMILIOS GREEK RESTAURANT
☎ 01159 262 550

8 High Street, Arnold, Nottingham, NG5 7DZ

Emilios is a classic family restaurant cooking up fine Greek and Cypriot cuisine using the finest ingredients personally sourced by Emilios and his team.

25% OFF TOTAL | 👤 2 | FRI ✗ | SAT ✗ | SUN | ✱ | ▲ — Greek

FIVE RIVERS
☎ 01159 826 449

40 Gordon Road, West Bridgford, NG2 5LN

A refreshing concept in fusion Indian cuisine, bringing together the very best recipes from Eastern and Western cultures to provide an outstanding food experience.

2FOR1 MAIN COURSE | FRI ✗ | SAT ✗ | SUN | ✱ | ▲ — Indian

THE FOUNTAIN
☎ 01777 872 854

155 Lincoln Road, Tuxford, Newark, NG22 0JQ

Local game, farmed meat and vegetables from the kitchen garden feature highly on this classic menu. Quality assured, the dishes are subject to seasonal change to guarantee freshness.

2FOR1 MAIN COURSE | FRI ✗ | SAT ✗ | SUN — British

GEORGE'S TRADITION LONG EATON
01159 460 700

Boots Court, Long Eaton, NG10 3RJ

A generous helping of fish together with a wholesome portion of chunky British chips are on offer at this prestigious yet affordable venue. Guests receive exceptional service in agreeable surroundings.

25% OFF TOTAL | 👤 8 | FRI ✗ | SAT ✓ — British

HAVELI
☎ 01159 227 778

10 Attenborough Lane, Chilwell, Nottingham, NG9 5JW

The combination of expert chefs and hospitable staff guarantees that guests will have an experience to remember. Vaunting dishes worthy of an Asian domestic kitchen, the menu is dazzling.

2FOR1 MAIN COURSE | FRI ✗ | SAT ✗ — Indian

THE INDIAN CHEF
☎ 01777 839 234

A1 Northbound, Elkesley, Retford, DN22 8AT

Be tempted by the imaginative line in Indian and Bangladeshi curry dishes on offer at the Indian Chef. With a kitchen bursting full of talent, the chefs bring their homeland knowledge to Retford.

2FOR1 MAIN COURSE | FRI [icon] | SAT [icon] | ✱ | ▲ — Indian

INDIGO
☎ 01159 623 333

884 Woodborough Rd, Mapperley, Nottingham, NG3 5QR

Enjoy high-quality restaurant food in the comfort of your own home. Sensational traditional and contemporary Indian cuisine delivered to your door.

25% OFF TOTAL | 👤10 | FRI ✓ | SAT ✓ — Indian

LA TASCA
☎ 01159 599 456

9 Weekday Cross, The Lace Market, Nottingham, NG1 2GB

Quintessentially Spanish, La Tasca's fresh and exciting menu offers something for everyone. Their tapas dishes are sincerely authentic, while their paellas always deliver on flavour.

25% OFF TOTAL | 👤8 | FRI ✓ | SAT × | ▲ — Spanish

LAGUNA TANDOORI
☎ 01159 411 632

43 Mount Street, Nottingham, NG1 6HE

The restaurant's tandoori clay oven is its signature tool, religiously used to provide authentic, flavoursome dishes. Delicious Indian cuisine served by a charming, friendly team of staff.

25% OFF TOTAL | 👤6 | FRI ✓ | SAT ✱ | ▲ — Indian

THE LALON RESTAURANT
☎ 01159 816 030

A52 Radcliffe Road, Nottingham, NG12 2LF

Situated by a beautiful lake, the food at The Lalon provides a true sensory experience, allowing diners the opportunity to understand various tastes and smells from around the Indian Sub-Continent.

50% OFF FOOD | 👤4 | FRI ✓ | SAT ✓ | ✱ — Indian

LAZIZA
☎ 01159 383 888

4 Nottingham Road, Nuthall, NG16 1DP

Mellow Indian restaurant on the Nottingham Road with fine cooking and switched-on service. Serves an excellent array of dishes, among them the esoteric kaalan curry and a rich, creamy kashmiri balti.

50% OFF FOOD | 👤6 | FRI 📱 | SAT 📱 — Indian

LE MISTRAL
☎ 01159 410 401

2-3 Eldon Chambers, Nottingham, NG1 2GJ

A French-style café, bar and bistro serving top-quality, fresh food accompanied by a vast selection of wines, beers and espresso. For a slice of French charm, Le Mistral is the perfect place to dine.

2FOR1 3 COURSES | FRI 📱 | SAT × | ▲ — French

LE MISTRAL
☎ 01159 116 116

575 Mansfield Road, Sherwood, Nottingham, NG5 2JN

A French-style café, bar and bistro serving top-quality, fresh food accompanied by a vast selection of wines, beers and espresso. For a slice of French charm, Le Mistral is the perfect place to dine.

2FOR1 3 COURSES | FRI 📱 | SAT ✱ | ▲ — French

LOCH FYNE
☎ 01159 886 849

17 King Street, Nottingham, NG1 2AY

From the roadside oyster bar that once was, Loch Fyne restaurants now successfully inject energy and passion into great food and wonderful flavours, whilst ensuring their seafood is sustainably sourced.

25% OFF TOTAL | 👤4 | FRI ✱ | SAT ✱ | SUN | ▲ — Seafood

MARC & DAINA'S
☎ 01159 603 720

589a Mansfield Road, Sherwood, Nottingham, NG5 2FW

Relax and enjoy sensational French food, warm service and an unpretentious air. Marc and Daina use herbs and tomatoes from the restaurant's garden, where guests can also enjoy their meal.

25% OFF TOTAL | 👤4 | FRI ✓ | SAT ✓ — French

MEMSAAB
☎ 01159 570 009

Maid Marian Way, Nottingham, NG1 6HS

Highly acclaimed Indian restaurant in Nottingham; consistently regarded as among the best in the country by the likes of the Observer and Harden's, it deploys creative, skilful and subtle recipes.

25% OFF TOTAL | 👤2 | FRI × | SAT × | ▲ — Indian

MERCHANTS RESTAURANT
☎ 01158 523 232

The Lace Market Hotel, Nottingham, NG1 1HE

Double AA Rosette-rated restaurant that serves inventive and thrilling dishes using the best local and seasonal produce. The setting is lush and opulent, with a boudoir feel for a touch of satin and lace.

2FOR1 MAIN COURSE | FRI ✓ | SAT × | SUN | ✱ | ▲ — Fine Dining

MILLERS BARN
01159 519 971

Cinderhill Road, Notttingham, NG8 6AS

Beefeater Grill are one of the UK's best-loved restaurants welcoming guests for almost 40 years in over 130 locations nationwide. *Excludes Breakfast, Light Bites, Bar menu, set menus and all other offers.

2FOR1 MAIN COURSE | 👤6 | FRI ✓ | SAT × | ▲ — Modern British

THE MINT INDIAN
☎ 01623 659 911

Clerkson Street, Mansfield, NG18 1BQ

Diner's should be sure to sample one of the chef's signature dishes, made with the finest ingredients and prepared to culinary perfection. The classic palate will enjoy an array of traditional dishes.

2FOR1 MAIN COURSE | FRI ✓ | SAT ✓ — Indian

MINT LEAF PAN ASIAN CUISINE
☎ 01636 646 994

Lincoln Road, Newark, NG24 2NY

Smart, modern and inviting, this Indian restaurant is distinguished by an eclectic menu featuring some unusual specialities, and a genuine attention to detail. A tantalising experience to be remembered.

25% OFF TOTAL | 👤10 | FRI ✓ | SAT ✓ — Bangladeshi/Indian

MODHU MITHA
☎ 01623 651 203

11-15 Ratcliffe Gate, Mansfield, NG18 2JA

Contemporary Pakistani cuisine, such as the mango infused dacca lamb in kharai, makes Modhu Mitha such a popular eatery. Including classic Indian favourites, the menu is truly authentic.

2FOR1 2 COURSES | FRI × | SAT × — Indian

MOGAL-E-AZAM
☎ 01159 473 820

7-9 Goldsmith Street, Nottingham, NG1 5JS

This acclaimed Indian restaurant, one of the largest in the Midlands, specialises in the rich flavours of the tandoor, while also offering the range of classic Indian dishes, cooked to perfection.

2FOR1 MAIN COURSE | FRI 📱 | SAT × — Indian

MUMBAI FLAVOURS
☎ 01159 111 975

384 Radford Road, Nottingham, NG7 5GR

Deliciously authentic Indian cooking, bringing diners a blend of traditional and modern dishes. The tandoori options are a particular delight, while the fresh sundries complement any choice.

50% OFF FOOD | 👤4 | FRI ✓ | SAT ✓ — Indian

NOOR JAHAN
☎ 01159 476 449

41 Mansfield Road, Nottingham, NG1 3FB

A delightfully authentic Bangladesh restaurant in Nottingham, Noor Jahan caters well to the local people when only a curry will do. Serving firm favourites as well as the more unusual dishes.

25% OFF TOTAL | 👤8 | FRI 📱 | SAT 📱 | ✱ — Indian

THE ORCHID RESTAURANT
☎ 01159 140 038

Trent House, Trent Bridge, Nottingham, NG2 5GN

A fine selection of dishes from south east Asia appear alongside traditional Cantonese cuisine. Expect delicious flavours and quality produce in this family-run restaurant.

50% OFF FOOD | 👤4 | FRI × | SAT × — Chinese

PAPPAS RESTAURANT
☎ 01159 819 091

25 Radcliffe Road, West Bridgford, NG2 5FF

A well-established restaurant that is a result of a family's passion for good food, wine, music and dancing. A traditional Greek-Cypriot taverna that oozes character and spirit.

25% OFF TOTAL | 👤6 | FRI ✓ | SAT × | SUN | ✱ | ▲ — Greek

THE PARAMOUNT HOTEL
☎ 01159 621 621

328, Mansfield Road, Nottingham, NG5 2EF

A friendly, comfortable hotel offering fine Indian cuisine in its Balti restaurant. Find moreish curries alongside the English and seafood dishes, accommodating every appetite. Delicious food every time.

2FOR1 MAIN COURSE | FRI ✓ | SAT ✓ | ✱ — Indian

PITCHER & PIANO
☎ 01159 586 081

The Unitarian Church, Nottingham, High Pavement, NG1 1HN

Nosy through the exquisite collection of vintage bric-a-brac after a burger or a sandwich ready to burst. Complete with stained windows and gothic church candles, the ambiance is cosy and quaint.

25% OFF TOTAL | 👤4 | FRI ✓ | SAT 📱 | SUN | ▲ — British

PREZZO 01159 414 798
21-23 Forman Street, Nottingham, NG1 4AA
With a character all of its own, Prezzo oozes contemporary style and enduring charm. Signature pastas, stone-baked pizzas and classic Italian dishes promise a perfect dining choice for the whole family.

2FOR1 MAIN COURSE | FRI × | SAT × | ▲ — Italian

PREZZO ☎01159 585 780
8-10 Low Pavement, Nottingham, NG1 7DL
With a character all of its own, Prezzo oozes contemporary style and enduring charm. Signature pastas, stone-baked pizzas and classic Italian dishes promise a perfect dining choice for the whole family.

2FOR1 MAIN COURSE | FRI × | SAT × | ▲ — Italian

THE RED HEART 01159 215 896
Easthorpe Street, Ruddington, Nottingham, NG11 6LB
Located in the quaint village of Ruddington, the Red Heart focuses on what it does best - traditional heart pub grub. Perfect for a lunch date or post-work dinner.

2FOR1 MAIN COURSE | FRI ✱ | SAT × | SUN — British

THE ROCKET AT SALTWATER ☎01159 242 664
The Corner House, Burton St, Nottingham, NG1 4DB
An inventive and appealing menu is offered in this stunning restaurant; delight in panoramic views of the city and drinks from award-winning highly skilled bartenders in the rooftop cocktail lounge.

25% OFF TOTAL | ♟ 6 | FRI ▯ | SAT ✱ | SUN | ▲ — British

ROMAN WAY 01636 640 690
Lincoln Road, Newark, Nottinghamshire, NG24 2DB
Quality pub classics with a modern twist combine with a friendly and relaxed atmosphere to make this Table Table venue the perfect place for family gatherings or meeting friends.

2FOR1 MAIN COURSE | FRI ✓ | SAT ✓ — Modern British

SAVERA TANDOORI RESTAURANT ☎01159 781 904
365 Derby Road, Lenton Hillside, NG7 2EB
Exotic fragrant Indian spices are used to create traditional dishes originating from Northern India. Enjoy each dish's distinctive flavour and aroma.

25% OFF TOTAL | ♟ 2 | FRI × | SAT × | SUN | ✱ — Indian

SHALIMAR TANDOORI ☎01159 811 049
26 Tudor Square, West Bridgford, NG2 6BT
This cosy restaurant in West Bridgford is a favourite for local curry lovers. The menu spans a variety of dishes and the newly refurbished decor makes for a lovely experience.

2FOR1 3 COURSES | FRI × | SAT × | ✱ — Indian

SIMLA INDIAN RESTAURANT ☎01159 459 350
5 James Street, Kimberley, NG16 2LP
Simla enjoys a fantastic reputation, attracting visitors from far and wide who come for the top-quality Indian dishes. Old favourites to new flavour combinations, all offered at great value.

25% OFF TOTAL | FRI ✱ | SAT ✱ — Indian

SPAGHETTI AMORE @ THE OLD VOLUNTEER ☎01159 665 967
1 Caythorpe Road, Caythorpe, Nottingham, NG14 7EB
A lively, open-armed atmosphere and a thoroughly classic range of pub standards. This pub-restaurant has a great deal of charm, is extremely welcoming and forthcoming, and serves up a mean dinner.

25% OFF TOTAL | ♟10 | FRI ✱ | SAT ✱ — English and Continental

SPICE ☎01159 623 555
459 Westdale Lane, Mapperley, Nottingham, NG3 6DH
Quality Indian takeaway that serves a wide range of vibrant, flavourful, smooth and spicy dishes at good value.

25% OFF TOTAL | ♟10 | FRI ✓ | SAT ✓ — Indian

SPICES INDIAN RESTAURANT ☎01159 855 236
Wollaton Vale, Wollaton, Nottingham, NG8 2JA
Serving a wide array of delicious dishes in a beautifully relaxed atmosphere, Spices is the ideal venue for those seeking fantastic and unusual Indian food, and top quality service.

2FOR1 3 COURSES | FRI ▯ | SAT ✓ — Indian

THE SPRINGFIELD INN 01159 663 387
Old Epperstone Road, Lowdham, Nottingham, NG14 7BZ
Nestled in the heart of the Nottinghamshire countryside, in the village of Lowdham, this Vintage Inn welcomes its guests with its excellent and enticing selection of homely pub food and fine drinks.

25% OFF TOTAL | FRI ✓ | SAT ✓ | SUN | ▲ — Modern British

THEATRE ROYAL ☎01159 895 569
Theatre Square, Nottingham, NG1 5ND
Open for both matinée and evening performances, offering silver service and table d'hôte. Non-theatregoers are just as welcome to enjoy the delicious menu, highlighting some of the best European dishes.

25% OFF TOTAL | ♟ 2 | FRI ✱ | SAT ✱ — European

THE THORN TREE INN 01773 768 675
246 Nottingham Road, Woodlinkin, Nottingham, NG16 4HG
A generous helping of fish together with a wholesome portion of chunky British chips are on offer at this prestigious yet affordable venue. Guests receive exceptional service in agreeable surroundings.

25% OFF TOTAL | ♟ 8 | FRI × | SAT ✓ — British

THE TRENT LOCK 01159 725 159
Lock Lane, Sawley, Long Eaton, NG10 2FY
Taking its name from the Trent Lock, where three East Midlands counties meet, this Vintage Inn provides the perfect setting to enjoy quality pub grub and a fine selection of wines and cask ales.

25% OFF TOTAL | FRI ✓ | SAT ✓ | SUN | ▲ — Modern British

WALKABOUT ☎01159 410 990
11-15 Friar Lane, Nottingham, NG1 6DA
Walkabout is famous for its characteristically Australian atmosphere and well-rounded menu. From live sport with a juicy burger to some Aussie kangaroo skewers, you'll find it hard to tear yourself away.

25% OFF TOTAL | ♟10 | FRI ✓ | SAT ✓ | ▲ — International

WELBECK HOTEL ☎01158 411 000
Talbot Street, Nottingham, NG1 5GS
The relaxing Mediterranean feel is enhanced by the informal bar which overlooks the city, whilst night time sees the space intimately transformed as the tables are elegantly clothed and candlelit.

2FOR1 3 COURSES | FRI ✓ | SAT ✱ | ▲ — European

WOODBOROUGH HALL ☎01159 654 466
Bank Hill, Woodborough, NG14 6EF
Elegant and vibrant fine cuisine from a kitchen led by acclaimed chef Des Sweeney; the Hall is a sparkling setting, built around the time of the Restoration and maintaining an air of uncluttered splendour.

25% OFF TOTAL | ♟ 4 | FRI ▯ | SAT ▯ | SUN | ▲ — Fine Dining

YAADGAAR ☎01159 335 779
18a Shelford Road, Nottingham, NG12 2AG
With a blend of fragrant and exotic spices, this family-run establishment bring you some of India's most renowned and unique dishes from a chef with over 25 years of experience.

25% OFF TOTAL | ♟ 4 | FRI ▯ | SAT ▯ | ✱ — Indian

YIANNI'S ☎01159 856 648
67 Haydn Road, Nottingham, NG5 2LA
Enjoy a night of authentic Greek cuisine and hospitality at this restaurant. Dazzling platters for sharing, or some meltingly tasty meat and fish dishes, all earthy and fruity and full of flavour.

2FOR1 MAIN COURSE | FRI × | SAT × | SUN | ✱ | ▲ — Greek

To understand what the restaurant icons mean, please see the inside back cover.

North West

Cheshire

1852 RESTAURANT AT PECKFORTON CASTLE
☎01829 260 930
Peck'n Castle, Stonehouse Lane, Tarporley, CW6 9TN
An opulent location to enjoy finely cooked, imaginatively combined flavours making use of the strength of Cheshire's produce. Refined and elegant; awarded 3 AA Rosettes.
25% OFF TOTAL | 4 | FRI ✓ | SAT ✓ | SUN | ✱ | ▲ — British

A LA TURKA
☎01925 551 647
Victoria Buildings, Warrington, WA4 6LG
As the first Turkish restaurant in its area, A La Turka is extremely popular for its offerings. Serving only genuine Turkish cuisine, this contemporary venue does not fail to dazzle and delight its guests.
2FOR1 MAIN COURSE | FRI ✱ | SAT ✱ | ▲ — Turkish

THE AIDEN BYRNE BRITISH GRILL
☎0844 879 9038
Macdonald Craxton Wood Hotel, Ellesmere Port, CH66 9PB
Feast upon gourmet cuisine on the tranquil terrace at this classic country house. Devour British dishes and tempting desserts whilst savouring a cocktail. Expect food with a contemporary twist.
25% OFF TOTAL | FRI ✓ | SAT ✓ — International

ARTS RESTAURANT
☎01244 232 323
Mercure Chester East, Chester, CH3 5QL
Arts restaurant welcomes both walk-in diners and overnight guests. This contemporary hotel offers diners satisfying food whilst over-looking exquisite grounds.
2FOR1 MAIN COURSE | 4 | FRI ✓ | SAT × | SUN | ✱ | ▲ — International

ASIA FUSION
☎01244 322 597
104 Foregate Street, Chester, CH1 1HB
A contemporary restaurant that retains its Asian identity and cultural roots. Delicious fusion of cuisines offering guests variety in an array of flavours and spices, providing tremendous value for money.
25% OFF TOTAL | 10 | FRI ✓ | SAT ✓ — Asian

BAY LEAF
01925 823 707
Harpers Road, Warrington, WA2 0PB
An authentic Indian restaurant in Warrington. Has plenty of room for big parties, and carries a sound reputation for supplying consistent, high quality curries together with an excellent evening out.
2FOR1 3 COURSES | FRI ✱ | SAT ✱ — Indian

THE BEAR'S HEAD
01477 544 732
Newcastle Road South, Brereton, Sandbach, CW11 1RS
This Vintage Inn oozes rural charm and rustic character. The picturesque surroundings provide the perfect backdrop for savouring the hearty, seasonal pub-food on the menu.
25% OFF TOTAL | FRI ✓ | SAT ✓ | SUN | ▲ — Modern British

THE BEAR'S PAW
☎01270 526 317
School Lane, Warmingham, Sandbach, CW11 3QN
This characterful inn in picturesque Warmingham is a nexus for ales from local micro-breweries. Serves hearty, home-cooked meals, and boasts a warm, classic feel touched with a little contemporary style.
2FOR1 MAIN COURSE | FRI ✱ | SAT ✱ | SUN | ▲ — English/Gastro pub

BELLA ITALIA
01244 325 420
29 Eastgate Street, Chester, CH1 1LG
Accessible Italian cuisine on the British high street - indulge in authentic sharing platters, hand stretched pizzas and hearty pasta dishes, served with a healthy dose of gregarious Italian hospitality.
25% OFF TOTAL | 6 | FRI × | SAT × | SUN | ▲ — Italian

BELLA ITALIA
01513 573 251
5 Coliseum Way, Cheshire Oaks, Ellesmere Port, CH65 9HD
Accessible Italian cuisine on the British high street - indulge in authentic sharing platters, hand stretched pizzas and hearty pasta dishes, served with a healthy dose of gregarious Italian hospitality.
25% OFF TOTAL | 6 | FRI × | SAT × | SUN | ▲ — Italian

BELLA NAPOLI
☎01606 854 880
Warrington Road, Acton Bridge, CW8 4QT
Authentic Italian Restaurant in Northwich with an open kitchen which allows guests to watch the chefs as they work, bringing passion and theatre to the quirky olde-world dining room setting.
2FOR1 3 COURSES | FRI ✓ | SAT × | ▲ — Italian

BENGAL TIGER LILY
☎01625 890 379
Congleton Rd, Nether Alderley, SK10 4TD
A menu that combines old favourite curries with innovative dishes exclusive to the restaurant's kitchen. The staff aim to make every guest feel happy and satisfied with their meal.
2FOR1 3 COURSES | FRI ✱ | SAT ✱ — Indian

THE BOARS HEAD
☎01606 833 191
Kinderton Street, Middlewich, CW10 0JE
Country-walkers and over-night guests enjoy a traditionally charming experience at this historic hotel. Whether it's a classic evening meal or a hearty breakfast, diners will not be left unsatisfied.
2FOR1 3 COURSES | FRI ✓ | SAT ✓ — British

BOMBAY FRODSHAM
☎01928 734 099
13 High Street, Frodsham, WA6 7AH
Nestled in the centre of Frodsham, chefs at the Bombay devout themselves to quality and service through their expertise and talents. This Indian restaurant and takeaway is full of flavour and promise.
2FOR1 MAIN COURSE | FRI ✓ | SAT ✓ — Indian

THE BOUVERIE
☎01244 381 423
51 Garden Lane, Chester, CH1 4EW
This restaurant provides a great atmosphere for a couple of drinks or some of their bar-style food. It's a favourite with students, and the Sunday lunches, in particular, are a crowd-pleaser.
2FOR1 3 COURSES | FRI × | SAT × — European

THE BRASSERIE @ MERCURE
☎0844 815 9001
Whitchurch Road, Chester, CH3 5QL
Situated in the dearly treasured city of Chester, the Restaurant at the Chester Abbots Well Hotel is an elegant place to feast. Captures the city's unique blend of historical charm and a cosmopolitan buzz.
2FOR1 3 COURSES | FRI ✓ | SAT ✓ — British

BRIDGEFIELD CURRY LOUNGE
☎0161 304 8027
150 High Street, Stalybridge, SK15 1TN
The Bridgefield Curry Lounge is a modern yet authentic Indian Restaurant. Well known for their experienced chefs and top standard quality of food and service, customers are never dissatisfied!
2FOR1 MAIN COURSE | FRI ✓ | SAT ✓ | ▲ — Indian

BRITANNIA SPICE
☎0151 336 1774
18-19 The Parade, Parkgate, Neston, CH64 6SA
Boasting dishes from across the subcontinent, Britannia Spice is a classic Indian restaurant serving good quality, spice-laden and taste-drenched dishes.
2FOR1 MAIN COURSE | FRI ✱ | SAT ✱ | SUN — Indian

CAFÉ ROUGE
0151 357 1201
Cheshire Oaks Retail Park, Ellesmere Port, CH65 9JJ
An attractive restaurant, a boulevard café or a Parisian-style wine bar; however you see Café Rouge, consistently excellent classic French dishes are always guaranteed.
25% OFF TOTAL | 6 | FRI ✓ | SAT ✓ | ✱ — French

CAFÉ ROUGE
01244 315 626
29 Bridge Street, Chester, CH1 1NG
An attractive restaurant, a boulevard café or a Parisian-style wine bar; however you see Café Rouge, consistently excellent classic French dishes are always guaranteed.
25% OFF TOTAL | 6 | FRI ✓ | SAT ✓ | ✱ | ▲ — French

CAPRI RESTAURANT
☎01925 267 471
Knutsford Old Road, Warrington, WA4 2LD
This bijou restaurant really showcases the excellence of British produce and cuisine. It serves up classic dishes from quality ingredients with a great deal of skill and imaginative verve.
25% OFF TOTAL | 4 | FRI ✓ | SAT ✓ | ✱ | ▲ — British

THE CHESHIRE CAT
01244 332 200

Whitchurch Road, Christleton, Chester, CH3 6AE

This Vintage Inn oozes rural charm and rustic character. The picturesque surroundings provide the perfect backdrop for savouring the hearty, seasonal pub-food on the menu.

25% OFF TOTAL | FRI ✓ | SAT ✓ | SUN | ▲ — Modern British

CHETWODE ARMS
01925 730 203

Street Lane, Lower Whitley, WA4 4EN

A warm and cosy country pub with all the familiarities and comforts of home. Idyllically located in the heart of the countryside, local dishes like the Cheshire rabbit prove exceedingly popular.

25% OFF TOTAL | 6 | FRI ✓ | SAT ✱ | SUN — Traditional English

CHIANGMAI
01270 583 843

120-124 Nantwich Road, Crewe, CW2 6AT

Named after the largest and most culturally significant city in Northern Thailand, this restaurant is beautiful in authentic decoration, and offers a choice menu of classic and speciality Thai dishes.

2FOR1 MAIN COURSE | FRI × | SAT × | ▲ — Thai

CHILLIES INDIAN RESTAURANT & BAR
01925 411 104

4 St Austins Lane, Warrington, WA1 1HG

Sharafaet Ali, well-established in Pakistan, has expertly prepared the saporous menu. Boasting the concept of 'Spice it Yourself', curries are brought to the table with an assortment of spices to add.

2FOR1 2 COURSES | FRI ✓ | SAT × — Indian

THE CHIMNEYS
0151 327 5587

Hooton Green, Hooton, Ellesmere Port, CH66 5ND

This Vintage Inn oozes rural charm and rustic character. The picturesque surroundings provide the perfect backdrop for savouring the hearty, seasonal pub-food on the menu.

25% OFF TOTAL | FRI ✓ | SAT ✓ | SUN | ▲ — Modern British

THE CHURCH INN
01942 606 905

78 Newton Road, Lowton, Warrington, WA3 1DG

A traditional village pub serving great home cooked food which welcomes families and offers an outdoor children's play area and dining area.

25% OFF TOTAL | 6 | FRI ✓ | SAT ✓ — British

CIRO'S BRASSERIE
01244 570 560

Grosvenor Pulford, Wrexham Rd, Pulford, CH4 9DG

This Mediterranean-style restaurant offers modern European cuisine with an emphasis on using fresh local ingredients. The unique décor and al fresco coffee bar offer a delightful and elegant experience.

25% OFF TOTAL | 4 | FRI ✓ | SAT ✱ | SUN — Modern European

THE COTTON MILL BAR AND KITCHEN
01925 444 410

The Cottonmill, Warrington, WA1 2QZ

Effortlessly sophisticated, this venue boasts private booths for weekend drinks or a fine-dining restaurant in which to feast upon crispy pizzas and authentic pasta dishes.

50% OFF FOOD | 4 | FRI ▯ | SAT ▯ | SUN | ▲ — Modern British

CRABWALL MANOR HOTEL AND SPA
01244 851 666

Parkgate Road, Mollington, Chester, Cheshire CH1 6NE

Crabwall Manor is a Grade II listed building that oozes history and charm which dates back to before 1066. From cosy interiors to formal dining restaurants, there's a wide selection of seasonal dishes.

25% OFF TOTAL | 6 | FRI ✓ | SAT ▯ | ✱ — British

CRANAGE HALL
01477 536 666

Byley Lane, Cranage, Crewe, CW4 8EW

Principal Hayley hotels never fail to impress, and Cranage Hall is no exception. Revelling in its splendour and location, this hotel offers modern conference facilities and idyllic Cheshire landscapes.

25% OFF TOTAL | 6 | FRI ✓ | SAT ✓ | ▲ — British

CROWNE PLAZA
01244 899 988

Trinity Way, Chester, CH1 2BD

With a chef and team passionate for food, Silks Restaurant and Bar Lounge serves up a wide variety of dishes. Settle back in style here with a relaxed ambience and stunning views across the Welsh hills.

25% OFF TOTAL | 6 | FRI ✓ | SAT ✓ — International

CU RESTAURANT
0151 424 1616

Hillcrest Hotel, Cronton Lane, Widnes, WA8 9AR

Cu restaurant is set within the impressive Hillcrest Hotel, Cheshire. Head chef Andrew Ferguson and his team are proud to deliver seasonal menus that showcase innovative and modern cuisine.

50% OFF FOOD | 6 | FRI ✓ | SAT ✓ | ✱ — British

THE DINING ROOM AT THE FROG
01244 637 252

164 Liverpool Road, Chester, CH2 1BD

From breakfast and brunch through to lunch and dinner, the Dining Room at the Frog serves delicious, well-rounded cuisine. The menu features some sterling classics guaranteed to satisfy.

2FOR1 MAIN COURSE | FRI ▯ | SAT ▯ | SUN | ▲ — British

THE FARMHOUSE
01270 251 126

Coppenhall Lane, Woolstanwood, Crewe, CW2 8SD

Beefeater Grill are one of the UK's best-loved restaurants welcoming guests for almost 40 years in over 130 locations nationwide. *Excludes Breakfast, Light Bites, Bar menu, set menus and all other offers.

2FOR1 MAIN COURSE | 6 | FRI ✓ | SAT × | ▲ — Modern British

THE FARNDON
01829 270 570

High Street, Farndon, CH3 6PU

A delightful 16th-century building plays home to this wonderful village pub. Guests fall in love with the countryside location, while the Farndon burgers and home-made crumbles have all mouths watering.

25% OFF TOTAL | 6 | FRI ✱ | SAT ✱ | ▲ — British

FIESTA HAVANA
01244 347 878

39-41 Watergate Street, Chester, CH1 2LB

Smooth Latin style and infectious Caribbean rhythms pulse through Fiesta Havana. This popular bar and restaurant has built up a reputation for great tapas and fantastic cocktails.

50% OFF FOOD | 6 | FRI × | SAT × — Spanish

FRANCS BRASSERIE
01244 317 952

14 Cuppin Street, Chester, CH1 2BN

An original French bistro with a buzzing atmosphere, that keeps the very best of rustic ideas and throws in a few of their own. Although the French Franc is dead, Chester's Franc is most certainly alive.

25% OFF TOTAL | 2 | FRI ✓ | SAT ✱ | ✱ | ▲ — French

THE FROZEN MOP
01565 873 234

Faulkners Lane, Mobberley , Knutsford, WA16 7AL

This Vintage Inn oozes rural charm and rustic character. The picturesque surroundings provide the perfect backdrop for savouring the hearty, seasonal pub-food on the menu.

25% OFF TOTAL | FRI ✓ | SAT ✓ | SUN | ▲ — Modern British

THE GOSHAWK
01928 740 900

Station Road, Mouldsworth, CH3 8AJ

Back in the day, the Goshawk Inn was renowned for late-night dances and an easygoing manner. Now blends premium elements of food, drink, and hospitality; it's a little gem in the heart of the country.

2FOR1 MAIN COURSE | FRI × | SAT × | SUN | ▲ — British

THE GREEN DRAGON
01925 758 634

2 Mill Lane, Lymm, WA13 9SB

This Vintage Inn oozes rural charm and rustic character. The picturesque surroundings provide the perfect backdrop for savouring the hearty, seasonal pub-food on the menu.

25% OFF TOTAL | FRI ✓ | SAT ✓ | SUN | ▲ — Modern British

Gourmet Society discount applies to the à la carte menu only, unless stated otherwise.

THE GRILL @ THE DENE
☎01244 321 165
The Dene Hotel, Chester, CH2 3ND
Rare to well-done, the steaks here are made to order; if that isn't taking your fancy then there is an abundance of succulent alternatives. Pocket-friendly, this venue is a cracking eatery.

2FOR1 3 COURSES | FRI ✓ | SAT ✓ — Steakhouse

THE GUNNERY BRASSERIE
☎01829 749 333
The Gunnery Brasserie, Tarvin, CH3 8JA
Housed in a Grade II listed building, which has served the village since the early 19th century, the menu at The Gunnery is as homely and comforting as the atmosphere.

25% OFF TOTAL | 2 | FRI ✱ | SAT ✱ | SUN | ▲ — British

HILLTOPS RESTAURANT @ BEST WESTERN
☎01928 735 255
Forest Hills Hotel, Bellemonte Road, Frodsham, WA6 6HH
Indulge yourself in stunning panoramic views and delightful seasonal food with the fish menu locally recommended. Offers guests a range of experiences, from gourmet nights, tribute nights, and 80's nights.

2FOR1 3 COURSES | FRI ✓ | SAT ✓ | SUN | ▲ — International

THE HONEY BEE
01625 526 511
Wilmslow, Cheshire, SK9 4LT
This Vintage Inn oozes rural charm and rustic character. The picturesque surroundings provide the perfect backdrop for savouring the hearty, seasonal pub-food on the menu.

25% OFF TOTAL | FRI ✓ | SAT ✓ | SUN | ▲ — Modern British

INDIAN BRASSERIE
☎01244 381 657
151 Long Lane, Chester, CH2 1JF
Expert chefs lovingly prepare an enticing array of dishes, which have earned the venue a strong reputation. Diners must try the satkora ghosht - tender lamb infused with Bangladeshi citrus fruits.

25% OFF TOTAL | 6 | FRI × | SAT × | SUN | ▲ — Indian

INDIGO
☎01244 345 832
21 Frodsham Street, Chester, CH1 3JJ
Set in the historic city of Chester, Indigo offers great food and wine as well as a friendly and welcoming atmosphere.

25% OFF TOTAL | 4 | FRI | SAT — British

JUNCTION RESTAURANT
☎0871 942 9019
Wrexham Road, Chester, CH49DL
Admire the overwhelming Clwydian Welsh mountain range whilst savouring the delectable taste of contemporary International cuisine. Be sure to sample the Sunday roast with a crisp glass of wine.

25% OFF TOTAL | 8 | FRI ✓ | SAT | ✱ | ▲ — International

KOCONUT GROVE AT THE CHESHIRE CHEESE
☎01270 258 050
332 Crewe Road, Crewe, CW2 5AF
A place to enjoy authentic Indian food in Crewe. With courteous and attentive service, the staff will make your food experience at Koconut Grove a memorable one.

2FOR1 MAIN COURSE | FRI × | SAT × — Indian

KOCONUT GROVE CHESTER
☎01244 325 888
Ethos Court, Chester, CH1 3AE
A place to enjoy authentic Indian food in Crewe. With courteous and attentive service, the staff will make your food experience at Koconut Grove a memorable one.

2FOR1 MAIN COURSE | FRI × | SAT × — Indian

LA TASCA
☎01244 400 887
6–12 Cuppin Street, Chester, CH1 2BN
Quintessentially Spanish, La Tasca's fresh and exciting menu offers something for everyone. Their tapas dishes are sincerely authentic, while their paellas always deliver on flavour.

25% OFF TOTAL | 8 | FRI ✓ | SAT × | ▲ — Spanish

LOCH FYNE
☎01565 622 980
The Royal George, King Street, Knutsford, WA16 6GR
From the roadside oyster bar that once was, Loch Fyne restaurants now successfully inject energy and passion into great food and wonderful flavours, whilst ensuring their seafood is sustainably sourced.

25% OFF TOTAL | 4 | FRI ✱ | SAT ✱ | ▲ — Seafood

LOCH FYNE
☎01625 587 670
Brook Lane, Alderley Edge, SK9 7RU
From the roadside oyster bar that once was, Loch Fyne restaurants now successfully inject energy and passion into great food and wonderful flavours, whilst ensuring their seafood is sustainably sourced.

25% OFF TOTAL | 4 | FRI ✱ | SAT ✱ | ▲ — Seafood

THE LORD ELDON PUB
☎01565 652 261
27 Tatton Street, Knutsford, WA16 6AD
Quintessentially British, the Lord Eldon pub exudes charm and character. Perfect for a lite-bite after shopping in Cheshire or a hearty meal after a walk in the local country; this venue welcomes all.

2FOR1 MAIN COURSE | FRI ✓ | SAT ✓ — British

MAEGAEW
☎01565 631 621
48 King Street, Knutsford, WA16 6DT
Since opening in early 2007, Maegaew have been delighting diners with friendly service, great atmosphere and some of the best Thai cuisine for miles. Experience fresh, authentic dishes as truly intended.

2FOR1 MAIN COURSE | FRI × | SAT × — Thai

MD'S RESTAURANT
☎01244 400 322
38 Watergate Street, Chester, CH1 2LA
In this ambient 14th-century listed building, take in some fulsome food from a range of cultures: from duck leg with noodles for a starter, to a phlegmatic pan-fried halibut steak.

2FOR1 3 COURSES | FRI ✓ | SAT ✓ | SUN | ✱ — European

MITCHELLS WINE BAR & BRASSERIE
☎01829 771 477
Lynedale House, High Street, Tattenhall, CH3 9PX
At Mitchells you will enjoy hearty, homely Mediterranean food from a menu that is kept as fresh as the locally-sourced produce, changing each month to follow the seasons.

2FOR1 3 COURSES | FRI ✓ | SAT ✱ | ▲ — Mediterranean

MOJO BAR AND TAPAS
☎01925 576 576
15 Cairo Street, Warrington, WA1 1EE
Immerse yourself in authentic Spanish ambience, and sample the extensive menus and wine lists on offer at this fine tapas bar and restaurant. Exceptional food and service to match.

50% OFF FOOD | 4 | FRI | SAT | SUN | ▲ — Spanish

MOLLINGTON BANASTRE HOTEL
☎01244 851 471
Parkgate Road, Mollington, Chester, CH1 6NN
In a stately building and a beautiful locale, this Brook hotel restaurant offers accomplished, contemporary dining in formal but relaxed surroundings. Popular with locals and visitors alike.

25% OFF TOTAL | FRI ✓ | SAT ✓ — Traditional English

NAGS HEAD
☎01244 300 206
Chester Road, Chester, CH2 4JR
After a day exploring the beautiful Chester, guests can expect to experience fine dining in a cosy environment where the staff attend to every need.

2FOR1 MAIN COURSE | FRI × | SAT × | SUN | ▲ — British

THE OLIVE TREE
☎01928 732 290
22 Church Street, Frodsham, WA6 6QW
Offering an incredibly put together menu to its diners, the Olive Tree at Frodsham doesn't shy away from experimenting with flavours and putting an imaginative spin on otherwise traditional Italian dishes.

2FOR1 3 COURSES | FRI | SAT | SUN — Italian

OSWALDS @ HELTERSKELTER
☎01928 733 361
Helter Skelter, 31 Church Street, Frodsham, WA6 6PN
Ale lovers will wish they'd discovered this fantastic pub long ago. Serving over 20 different cask ales a week, guests will be spoilt for choice when it comes to choosing a drink to accompany their food.

2FOR1 2 COURSES | FRI | SAT ✱ | ▲ — British

THE PHEASANT INN
☎01829 770 434
Higher Burwardsley, Tattenhall, CH3 9PF
Spectacular views and great attention to detail in this popular and buzzing village pub where you can enjoy hearty and wholesome dishes. *See website for further details.

2FOR1 MAIN COURSE | FRI ✱ | SAT ✱ | SUN | ▲ — English/Gastro pub

PLUSH SPICE
☎01244 321 234

Newhall Road, Upton, Chester, CH2 1TB

An excellent new Indian restaurant already gaining a renowned reputation in Chester. Plush Spice delivers classic and contemporary dishes, all expertly prepared and presented to the highest standard.

2FOR1 MAIN COURSE | FRI × | SAT × | SUN — Indian

PRESTON BROOK
01928 716 829

Chester Road, Preston Brook, Runcorn, Cheshire, WA7 3BB

Quality pub classics with modern twists meets with a friendly and relaxed atmosphere to make this Table Table venue the perfect place for any occasion. *Excludes daytime & evening deals and festive menus.

2FOR1 MAIN COURSE | FRI ✓ | SAT ✓ — Modern British

PREZZO
0151 357 1394

Cheshire Oaks Village, Ellesmere Port, CH65 9HD

With a character all of its own, Prezzo oozes contemporary style and enduring charm. Signature pastas, stone-baked pizzas and classic Italian dishes promise a perfect dining choice for the whole family.

2FOR1 MAIN COURSE | FRI × | SAT × | ▲ — Italian

THE PURPLE PAKORA AT CONGLETON
☎01625 878 878

14 Lawton Street, Congleton, CW12 1RP

With a welcoming atmosphere and stunning choice of dishes; surrounded by the intoxicating scent of spices and mouth-watering tastes of India, enjoy the culinary journey that is The Purple Pakora.

2FOR1 2 COURSES | FRI × | SAT × | ✱ — Indian

THE DISLEY MASSALLA
☎01663 763 007

156 Buxton Road, Disley, SK12 2HG

With a welcoming atmosphere and stunning choice of dishes; surrounded by the intoxicating scent of spices and mouth-watering tastes of India, enjoy the culinary journey that is The Disley Massalla.

2FOR1 2 COURSES | FRI × | SAT × — Indian

THE PURPLE PAKORA AT MARPLE
☎0161 427 7748

10 Brabyns Brow, Marple Bridge, SK6 7DA

With a welcoming atmosphere and stunning choice of dishes; surrounded by the intoxicating scent of spices and mouth-watering tastes of India, enjoy the culinary journey that is The Purple Pakora.

2FOR1 2 COURSES | FRI × | SAT × | ✱ — Indian

THE PURPLE PAKORA AT POYNTON
☎01625 878 878

9 London Road South, Poynton, SK12 1JX

With a welcoming atmosphere and stunning choice of dishes; surrounded by the intoxicating scent of spices and mouth-watering tastes of India, enjoy the culinary journey that is The Purple Pakora.

2FOR1 2 COURSES | FRI × | SAT × | ✱ — Indian

RAJ TANDOORI
☎01514 242 850

210 Warrington Road, Widnes, WA8 0AX

Authentic and expertly prepared, the cuisine is both striking and fragrant. Explore a world of culinary excellence through vibrant colours and piquant flavours.

2FOR1 2 COURSES | FRI × | SAT × — Indian

RANULF RESTAURANT
☎0844 879 9082

Cobblers Cross Lane, Tarporley, CW6 0DJ

A fine Cheshire restaurant awarded 2 AA Rosettes for the quality of its food and service. Spacious, with a calm elegance about it, dishes focus on simple, accomplished cooking and exceptional produce.

2FOR1 MAIN COURSE | FRI ✓ | SAT × | SUN | ✱ — British

THE RED LION
01244 661 636

Church Road, Dodleston, Chester, CH4 9NG

This Vintage Inn oozes rural charm and rustic character. The picturesque surroundings provide the perfect backdrop for savouring the hearty, seasonal pub-food on the menu.

25% OFF TOTAL | FRI ✓ | SAT ✓ | SUN | ▲ — Modern British

THE RESTAURANT ON THE CRESCENT
☎01270 654 678

South Cheshire College, Crewe, CW2 8AB

If you're looking for a night to remember then the Restaurant on the Crescent can provide the perfect venue. Guarantees impeccable cuisine that offers a taste of the future.

25% OFF TOTAL | 6 | FRI × | SAT × | SUN — Bistro

RING O' BELLS
☎01244 335 422

Village Road, Christleton, CH3 7AS

At the heart of a pretty village, contemporary meets traditional in this high-quality pub. A classic gastro-pub menu delivered alongside new delectable signature dishes are sure to delight all guests.

2FOR1 3 COURSES | 2 | FRI ✱ | SAT ✱ | SUN | ▲ — English/Gastro pub

ROMAZZINO
☎01270 626 456

12a Love Lane, Nantwich, CW5 5BH

Their unique style of Italian food ensures that diners delight in the complete meal experience. Romazzino is a great place to have a light Lunch with colleagues, friends and family.

2FOR1 3 COURSES | FRI × | SAT × | ▲ — Italian

ROMAZZINO
☎01270 877 884

70-72 Crewe Road, Alsager, ST7 2HA

Their unique style of Italian food ensures that diners delight in the complete meal experience. Romazzino is a great place to have a light Lunch with colleagues, friends and family.

2FOR1 3 COURSES | FRI × | SAT × | ▲ — Italian

ROOKERY HALL HOTEL
☎08450 727 533

Rookery Hall Restaurant, Main Rd, Natwich, NCW5 6DQ

A beautifully located Hand Picked Hotels restaurant satisfying even the most discerning palates. The award-winning Head Chef creates masterpiece dishes in a charming Georgian mansion. 2 AA Rosettes.

25% OFF TOTAL | 6 | FRI ✱ | SAT ✱ | SUN | ✱ | ▲ — British

SAHIB INDIAN RESTAURANT
☎01925 757 576

4-6 The Cross, Lymm, WA13 0HP

Local favourite of an Indian restaurant tucked away through a pretty wrought iron side-gate. Friendly atmosphere and a great range of curries on the cards. Simple, unfussy and in plentiful portions.

2FOR1 MAIN COURSE | FRI ✱ | SAT ✱ — Indian

SHALIMAR RESTAURANT, BAR & LOUNGE
☎01625 444 845

13 Summerfields Village, Dean Row Road, Wilmslow

Shalimar's unparalleled blend of traditional Indian dishes and modern Indian cuisine will captivate your tastebuds and inspire your sense of the exotic.

2FOR1 2 COURSES | FRI × | SAT × — Indian

SHILLONG
☎01244 311 112

111 Boughton, Chester, CH3 5BH

Named after a hillside town in North East India, whose beauty and wonder is reflected in this amiable restaurant. The climate of Shillong is mirrored by a warm and welcoming atmosphere.

25% OFF TOTAL | 10 | FRI × | SAT × | SUN — Indian

SITAR RESTAURANT & WINE BAR
☎01625 521 355

26 Green Lane, Wilmslow, SK9 1LD

Perfect for any occasion, Sitar pride themselves on their 5-star rated kitchen in which expert chefs prepare delectable cuisine using prime ingredients.

25% OFF TOTAL | 10 | FRI ✓ | SAT ✓ — Indian

SPRINGWOOD PARK 01625 427 809
Springwood Way, Tytherington, Macclesfield, SK10 2XA
Quality pub classics with modern twists meets with a friendly and relaxed atmosphere to make this Table Table venue the perfect place for any occasion. *Excludes daytime & evening deals and festive menus.

2FOR1 MAIN COURSE | FRI ✓ | SAT ✓ — Modern British

THE STAMFORD BRIDGE INN ☎01829 740 229
Tarvin Road, Chester, Cheshire, CH3 7HN
Famous for its friendly hospitality and delicious home-cooked food, the lavish lounge area and the fabulous garden make this a wonderful place to drink and dine at any time of the year.

2FOR1 MAIN COURSE | FRI × | SAT × | SUN | ▲ — British

STEAK AND GRILL RESTAURANT ☎01925 752 233
The Lymm Hotel, Lymm, WA13 0JY
Perfect for informal dining, the Steak & Grill is a relaxed and comfortable contemporary restaurant in the heart of Cheshire, serving a diverse selection of freshly prepared dishes.

2FOR1 MAIN COURSE | FRI 📱 | SAT 📱 | * | ▲ — European

STOLEN LAMB GREEK RESTAURANT ☎01625 419 571
70a Grove Street, Wilmslow, SK9 1DS
The Stolen Lamb embraces old family recipes combining with new styles to offer the ultimate Greek dining experience. The traditional clay oven and coal fired BBQ give full flavour to their delectable food.

25% OFF TOTAL | FRI 📱 | SAT × | SUN | * — Greek

STONE CROSS 01942 273 422
Yew Tree Way, Golborne, Warrington, WA3 3JD
Quality pub classics with modern twists meets with a friendly and relaxed atmosphere to make this Table Table venue the perfect place for any occasion. *Excludes daytime & evening deals and festive menus.

2FOR1 MAIN COURSE | FRI ✓ | SAT ✓ — Modern British

STRADA 01625 418 698
22-24 Water Lane, Wilmslow, SK9 5AA
Offering fresh, bold dishes inspired by flavours of Italian city life– Strada serves a selection of indulgent tastes, to those seeking a blissful escape to laidback Italian life. *Excludes Pizzettas.

25% OFF TOTAL | 👤 6 | FRI ✓ | SAT × | ▲ — Italian

THE STRETTON FOX 01925 730 693
Spark Hall Close, Stretton, Warrington, WA4 4NU
This Vintage Inn oozes rural charm and rustic character. The picturesque surroundings provide the perfect backdrop for savouring the hearty, seasonal pub-food on the menu.

25% OFF TOTAL | FRI ✓ | SAT ✓ | SUN | ▲ — Modern British

SWADESH ☎01625 525 902
26-28 Green Lane, Wilmslow, SK9 1LD
Swadesh is well-known group of restaurants gradually growing in size across Greater Manchester. Popular for all the right reasons, its delicious Indian cuisine and amiable service bring in a devoted crowd.

2FOR1 MAIN COURSE | FRI × | SAT * — Indian

SYMPHONY RESTAURANT BAR & GRILL ☎01270 763 664
48 Congleton Road, Sandbach CW11 1HG
Sister restaurant to the Staffordshire Symphony Bar and Grill, this Sandbach venue is renowned across Cheshire for its fine wines and exquisite food. Charming, attentive staff cater to your every need.

25% OFF TOTAL | 👤 8 | FRI 📱 | SAT 📱 | ▲ — European

TERRACE BAR AND RESTAURANT ☎01625 889 988
Holiday Inn Manchester Airport, Wilmslow, SK9 4LR
The Terrace Bar and Restaurant is a superb addition to the Holiday Inn Manchester Airport, where guests can fill their boots before jetting off into the sun. Hearty dishes feature on the à la carte menu.

2FOR1 3 COURSES | FRI ✓ | SAT ✓ | * — Modern British

THE TERRACE RESTAURANT ☎01270 504 050
Macon Way, Crewe, CW1 6DR
With a range of intriguing Indian dishes, from dry gin-fried chicken to mutton rogan josh, along with a succulent grill menu, this hotel restaurant is smart, contemporary and accomplished in its touches.

2FOR1 MAIN COURSE | FRI * | SAT * | SUN | * — Indian

TONIC BAR 01625 501 273
27 Pickford Street, Macclesfield, SK11 6UJ
Chilled out venue with comfy sofas, friendly staff and a welcoming environment. Enjoy quality homemade food, draught beers, wine and cocktails.

25% OFF TOTAL | 👤 4 | FRI ✓ | SAT 📱 | SUN — International

TRADERS RESTAURANT @ HOLIDAY INN ☎0871 942 9070
Holiday Inn, Beechwood, Runcorn, WA7 3HA
In a relaxed and informal atmosphere diners can choose from a number of menus, whether it be à la carte dining or tasty bar snacks. Food can be adapted for dietary requirements, catering for all guests.

25% OFF TOTAL | 👤 6 | FRI ✓ | SAT ✓ | SUN | * — English and Continental

TRATTORIA BACI ☎01925 756 067
18 The Cross, Lymm, WA13 0HU
Trattoria Baci is a popular Italian restaurant with a lively atmosphere, located in the center of Lymm. Baci offers a wide range of high quality freshly prepared authentic Italian and Mediterranean food.

2FOR1 3 COURSES | FRI 📱 | SAT 📱 — Italian

THE VERDIN ARMS ☎01270 522 275
Nantwich Road, Wimboldsley, Middlewich, CW10 0LW
The Verdin Arms is a traditional pub in Wimboldsley offering classic British dishes and serves fresh local produce and locally sourced meat, has a good selection of cask ales and wines.

2FOR1 MAIN COURSE | FRI 📱 | SAT 📱 | SUN | * — British

VICEROY INDIAN ☎01625 573 006
22 Ingersley Road, Bollington, SK10 5RF
Cracking Indian restaurant with a smart modern dining room and a fine range of classic, delicious curries. Good reputation for consistently serving up very tasty dishes and an all-round satisfying evening.

2FOR1 MAIN COURSE | FRI × | SAT × | SUN | * — Indian

THE WHITE APRON ☎01925 444 894
27 Church Street, Warrington, WA1 2SS
The staff, sporting signature long white aprons, are devoted to providing fine dining experiences. Indulge in a Mediterranean-inspired dish with someone special at this romantically decorated eatery.

25% OFF TOTAL | 👤 4 | FRI ✓ | SAT ✓ | SUN | * | ▲ — Mediterranean

THE WILMSLOW TAVERN 01625 539 588
Dean Row Road, Wilmslow, SK9 2HA
Enjoy a great British roast at this wonderful Wilmslow tavern. Delicious home-cooked food will be sure to lure you back to this warmly welcoming restaurant and bar.

50% OFF FOOD | 👤 10 | FRI ✓ | SAT ✓ — Traditional English

YARA RESTAURANT ☎01625 584 040
29 London Road, Alderley Edge, SK9 7JT
Syrian and Lebanese cuisine has been brought to the affluent area of Alderley Edge by the founders of Yara Restaurant. Vine leaves and hummus to chicken kebabs and spinach filo pastries.

25% OFF TOTAL | 👤 4 | FRI × | SAT × — Lebanese

Cumbria

BERESFORD'S RESTAURANT ☎01539 488 488
Beresford Road, Windermere, LA23 2JG
Situated in some of England's finest scenery, this fabulous, forward-thinking restaurant serves a superbly crafted and great-tasting array of cuisine, the fresh fish being a particular highlight.

25% OFF TOTAL | 👤 6 | FRI ✓ | SAT * — Modern European

BORDER GATE 01228 532 073
Carleton, Carlisle, Cumbria, CA4 0AD
Quality pub classics with modern twists meets with a friendly and relaxed atmosphere to make this Table Table venue the perfect place for any occasion. *Excludes daytime & evening deals and festive menus.

2FOR1 MAIN COURSE | FRI ✓ | SAT ✓ — Modern British

BURN HOW GARDEN RESTAURANT
☎01539 446 226

Back Belsfield Road, Bowness-on-Windermere, LA23 3HH

Morecambe Bay potted shrimps, Lune Valley venison and Thornby Moor cheeses are just some of the locally sourced delights on the menu. Feast upon the freshest of British contemporary cuisine.

25% OFF TOTAL | 6 | FRI ✓ | SAT ✓ | * | British

DAMSON DENE
☎01539 568 676

Crosthwaite, Kendal, LA8 8JE

New culinary delights are brought to the menu on a daily basis by the restaurant's talented chefs. The kitchen has its own Victorian garden, which allows each dish to be made from the freshest produce.

50% OFF FOOD | 6 | FRI ✓ | SAT ✓ | * | Modern British

THE DROVE INN
☎01697 748 202

Roweltown, Carlisle, CA6 6LB

This pub has a varied menu filled with traditional British classics and dishes with a modern twist. Renowned for its speciality steaks, all cooked to suit your taste, this pub is very popular with diners.

50% OFF FOOD | 4 | FRI | SAT | * | British

THE ESTUARY RESTAURANT
☎01229 717 222

Pennington House, Main Street, Ravenglass, CA18 1SD

A fine hotel restaurant by the estuary in Ravenglassin. Fantastic menu with a range of recipes based on seasonal Cumbrian produce. Highly accomplished cooking in both presentation and distinct flavour.

2FOR1 3 COURSES | FRI | SAT | British

FOXES CAFÉ LOUNGE
07541 829 348

18 Abbey Street, Carlisle, CA3 8TX

A continental style café neatly nestled down the cobbles of Abbey Street, Foxes serves foamy cappuccinos, scrumptious smoothies and delicious cakes. Art shows and open mic nights give this place the edge.

50% OFF FOOD | FRI * | SAT * | SUN | Bistro

THE GILPIN BRIDGE
☎01539 552 206

Bridge End, Levens, Kendal, LA8 8EP

The Gilpin Inn is located close to Kendal, where the menu features fresh local ingredients cooked by a chef and run by a manager who have backgrounds in Michelin and Rosette restaurants.

2FOR1 MAIN COURSE | FRI ✓ | SAT ✓ | British

GOODY BLAKES RESTAURANT
☎01539 435 062

The Old Coach House Stock Lane, Cumbria, LA22 9SL

Goody Blake's is a contemporary and stylish restaurant in Grasmere, in the heart of the English Lake District, offering high quality food and warm and friendly service.

2FOR1 MAIN COURSE | FRI × | SAT × | SUN | * | International

GRAYTHWAITE MANOR HOTEL
☎01539 532 001

Fernhill Road, Grange over Sands, LA11 7JE

A beautiful country manor hotel with idyllic surroundings whose restaurant caters for every palate, whether it be for an informal meeting or an exquisite banquet. A comfortable fine dining experience.

25% OFF TOTAL | 10 | FRI ✓ | SAT ✓ | * | British

HALLMARK HOTEL BRASSERIE
☎01228 531 951

Court Square, Carlisle, CA1 1QY

Not just a sideline to the accommodation, this is an accomplished restaurant featuring a quality brasserie menu with dishes ranging from Thai stir fry to their rich and delicious venison stew.

25% OFF TOTAL | 6 | FRI ✓ | SAT ✓ | * | European

LAKE VIEW RESTAURANT
☎01768 777 285

Lodore Falls Hotel, Keswick, CA12 5UX

Charming restaurant overlooking Derwentwater, with cooking that lives up to the magnificent views. *2 for 1 on the 5 course seasonal menu. Maximum of 4 cards allowed per party.

2FOR1 3 COURSES | FRI ✓ | SAT * | * | British

To understand what the restaurant icons mean, please see the inside back cover.

LINTHWAITE HOUSE HOTEL & RESTAURANT ☎01539 488 600
Crook Road, Windermere, LA23 3JA
Talented young chef Richard Kearsley leads this triple AA Rosette kitchen, producing imaginative, technically superb dishes in this elegant and serene restaurant.

25% OFF TOTAL | 6 | FRI ✓ | SAT ✓ — Modern British

LUCYCOOKS DEMO AND DINE ☎01539 432 288
Church Street, Ambleside, LA22 0BU
Become a culinary master at this unusual venue where diners learn how to prepare delectable 4-course meals. Afterwards, guests attend a 'dinner party' to feast upon everything from Italian to Indian.

2FOR1 MAIN COURSE | FRI ✓ | SAT ✓ | SUN | ✱ — British

LUCY'S ON A PLATE ☎01539 430 427
Church Street, Ambleside, LA22 0BU
A quaint retreat for a delicious lunch or soothing evening meal, Lucy's on a Plate serves everything from hearty breakfasts to appetising afternoon treats. The evening menu changes on a daily basis.

2FOR1 MAIN COURSE | FRI × | SAT × | SUN — British

MANOR HOUSE PARK ☎01900 881 236
Edderside Road, Maryport, CA15 6RA
Manor House Park is a wonderfully located caravan park, perfect for those weekends away, whether it's peace and tranquility you're after, or a few days exploring the Lake District.

2FOR1 3 COURSES | FRI ✓ | SAT — British

NEWBY BRIDGE HOTEL ☎01539 531 222
Newby Bridge, Ulverston, LA12 8NA
Directly overlooking Lake Windermere in five acres of beautiful land, dining and resting at the Newby Bridge will be a real pleasure. A daily changing menu in the restaurant accommodates local produce.

25% OFF TOTAL | 6 | FRI ✓ | SAT ✓ | ✱ | ▲ — Modern British

NUMBER 23 CHURCH STREET RESTAURANT ☎0844 879 9144
23 Church Street, Bowness-on-Windermere, LA23 3DF
Contemporary style meets classic flavour at The Number 23 Church Street Restaurant, where elegance is central to the restaurant's key motive. British cuisine at its finest.

25% OFF TOTAL | 4 | FRI ✓ | SAT ✓ | ✱ | ▲ — Modern British

THE PENNY FARTHING ☎01228 521 970
Chapel Court, Carlisle, CA1 1NT
Coffee lovers can indulge in a delicious array of bursting baguettes, simmering curries and home-made quiches whilst enjoying an afternoon cup of their favourite beverage.

50% OFF FOOD | 4 | FRI ✓ | SAT × | SUN — International

THE PRIORY RESTAURANT AT SELLA PARK ☎01946 841 601
Sella Park, Seascale, CA20 1DW
Historically beautiful, this 16th Century hotel is set in acres of gardens in the Lake District. The freshest of locally sourced food is offered on the menu to deliver the perfect dining experience.

2FOR1 3 COURSES | FRI ✓ | SAT ✓ — International

RAFIKS ☎01228 599 889
141-145 Botchergate, Carlisle, CA1 1RZ
The art of sub continent cooking is presented to you with a blend of aromas and tastes. Rafiks will provide an experience that will involve all of your senses and transport you from Carlisle to Delhi.

2FOR1 3 COURSES | FRI × | SAT × — Indian

THE RESTAURANT AT LOVELADY SHIELD ☎01434 381 203
Lovelady Lane, Alston, CA9 3LX
Quaintly nestled in the foothills, this elegant country house hosts a menu that is brimming with an imaginative variety of sumptuous dishes that are British at heart with a continental edge. 2 AA Rosettes.

25% OFF TOTAL | 4 | FRI ✓ | SAT ✓ | ✱ — British

RIVERSIDE HOTEL ☎01539 734 861
Beezon Road, Kendal, LA9 6EQ
Enjoy river views in a luxury en-suite bedroom, or dine in the Riverside restaurant for ultimate pleasure. The kitchen makes use of its own produce from the garden to ensure every dish is fresh and tasty.

25% OFF TOTAL | 6 | FRI ✓ | SAT ✓ | ✱ | ▲ — Modern British

SPICE OF BENGAL ☎01539 431 250
3 Kelsick Road, Ambleside, LA22 0BZ
Both meat lovers and vegetarians can satisfy their curry cravings at this wonderful Indian restaurant. Affable waiting staff provide a friendly service and wide smiles.

25% OFF TOTAL | 10 | FRI | SAT | ✱ — Indian

THE TEMPLE THAI ☎01229 580 566
1 Cavendish Street, Ulverston, LA12 7AD
Traditionally cooked Thai cuisine that will enliven your senses. Maintaining their ethos of providing delicious, non-westernised dishes, this is a fabulous place to enjoy bona fide Thai food.

2FOR1 MAIN COURSE | FRI | SAT | ▲ — Thai

WAKEFIELD ARMS 01539 739 217
Maude Street, Kendal, Cumbria, LA9 4QD
Quality pub classics with modern twists meets with a friendly and relaxed atmosphere to make this Table Table venue the perfect place for any occasion. *Excludes daytime & evening deals and festive menus.

2FOR1 MAIN COURSE | FRI ✓ | SAT ✓ — Modern British

WINDER HALL ☎0190 085 107
Low Lorton, Cockermouth, CA13 9UP
Award-winning, Winder Hall offers sanctuary from the chaotic streets. Guests can take a relaxing stroll in the beautiful surroundings before indulging in naughty afternoon-tea treats on the terrace.

50% OFF FOOD | 4 | FRI ✓ | SAT ✓ | ✱ — Fine Dining

ZEST HARBOURSIDE ☎0194 666 981
West Strand, Whitehaven, CA28 7LR
Zest Harbourside delivers superb panoramic views of the harbour and marina to be enjoyed at any time of year, while the menu offers a vast and enjoyable list of dining options.

50% OFF FOOD | 4 | FRI × | SAT × — British

ZEST RESTAURANT ☎01946 692 848
Low Road, Whitehaven, CA28 9HS
Set in the picturesque town of Whitehaven, and more formal than its Harbourside sister, Zest places an emphasis on well-sourced produce that contributes to the tastiness of the British cuisine on offer.

2FOR1 3 COURSES | FRI ✓ | SAT × | ▲ — British

Greater Manchester

110 RESTAURANT AND BAR ☎0161 228 0077
Genting Club, 110 Portland St, Manchester, M1 4RL
Based in a casino, this venue delivers fine dining and gaming, for a throw of the dice beyond the typical. All dishes are a simple delight, created using fresh and fine ingredients.

25% OFF TOTAL | 10 | FRI ✓ | SAT ✱ | ▲ — European

24 BAR & GRILL ☎0161 238 4348
24 Princess Street, Manchester, M1 4LY
So named after its address, 24 Princess Street, Manchester is in the basement of the Arora Hotel, '24 Bar & Grill' is a new and well reviewed restaurant where the food is simple, seasonal and well prepared

25% OFF TOTAL | 8 | FRI ✓ | SAT | ▲ — British

48 KING STREET WEST RESTAURANT ☎0161 839 1929
47 King Street West, Manchester, M3 2PW
Renowned for its superb British cuisine, this restaurant offers a menu filled with sterling British dishes swirled with French accents. The glass-fronted dining room has an elegant, understated style.

50% OFF FOOD | 10 | FRI | SAT × | SUN | ✱ | ▲ — British

888 RESTAURANT ☎0161 277 6910
888 Oldham Road, Newton Heath, M40 2BS
Classic English cuisine with touches of flavour from other culinary cultures; a restaurant with a softly elegant ambience where you can enjoy the fulsome menu and an array of good wines and beers.

25% OFF TOTAL | 4 | FRI ✓ | SAT ✓ — English and Continental

AASTORIA ☎0161 819 5571
2 Empire Street, Cheetham Hill, M3 1JA
An authentic taste of Eastern Europe. Sample imaginative Ukrainian dishes, cooked by experienced chefs with passion and verve. Don't forget to sample the Eastern European selection of vodkas and beers.

50% OFF FOOD | 4 | FRI ✓ | SAT ✓ — European

ACHARI ☎01204 548 973
148 Crook Street, Bolton, BL3 6AS
Taking its name from Achar, the pickle which is traditionally the centrepiece to the Indian family dinner table, the emphasis is on an informal, relaxed dining experience.

2FOR1 MAIN COURSE | FRI | SAT × | SUN — Indian

AL BILAL ☎0161 257 0006
87 Wilmslow Road, Manchester, M14 5SU
A sophisticated and tranquil environment for diners to enjoy the culinary delights of well-prepared Indian cuisine, where the staff pride themselves in providing quality dishes and exemplary service.

25% OFF TOTAL | 10 | FRI ✓ | SAT ✓ — Indian

ANGON RESTAURANT ☎0161 485 4387
124 Turves Road, Cheadle, SK8 6AW
Brighten your day with a vibrant, exotic dish from this well-established venue. Perfect for any occasion, Angon has a loyal following of curry lovers.

2FOR1 MAIN COURSE | FRI | SAT — Indian

ANTELOPE INDIAN RESTAURANT ☎0161 790 7008
13 Manchester Road West, Walkden, M38 9EG
The Antelope employs 'East meets West' culinary expertise to create sophisticated and unique dishes. Offers a wide range of vegetarian and seafood options, each intertwined with a fusion of flavours.

2FOR1 MAIN COURSE | FRI ✓ | SAT ✓ | ✱ — Indian

APOTHECA ☎0161 834 9411
17 Thomas Street, Manchester, M4 1FS
Due to popular demand, Apotheca has recently extended the options of delectable delights it offers its diners, broadening their menu to offer taste-bud enlightenment to those who seek it.

25% OFF TOTAL | 4 | FRI ✱ | SAT × | SUN — International

ASIA LOUNGE ☎0161 764 7755
136 Rochdale Road, Bury, BL9 7BD
Asia Lounge have an experienced team of chefs who have devised an extensive menu featuring all your favourite Asian flavours. A warm welcome awaits from the friendly and efficient team at Asia Lounge.

2FOR1 MAIN COURSE | FRI ✓ | SAT ✓ — Asian

BAMFORD ARMS 0161 480 2968
Buxton Road, Stockport, SK2 6NB
Beefeater Grill are one of the UK's best-loved restaurants welcoming guests for almost 40 years in over 130 locations nationwide. *Excludes Breakfast, Light Bites, Bar menu, set menus and all other offers.

2FOR1 MAIN COURSE | 6 | FRI ✓ | SAT × — Modern British

BANGLA CITY ☎0161 368 6187
Grafton Street, Hyde, SK14 2AX
Modern and spacious Indian restaurant known as a great setting for an evening out. Lavish menu that serves up all the classics together with lots of good vegetarian dishes and some left-field options.

2FOR1 MAIN COURSE | FRI × | SAT × | SUN | ✱ — Indian

BANGLA VILLA RESTAURANT ☎0161 681 0073
476-478 Oldham Road, Failsworth, M35 0FH
Honest Indian cuisine is at the heart of this restaurant. Sensual and ample, the menu is certain to please. Guests are invited to unwind and treat their taste buds.

2FOR1 2 COURSES | FRI ✓ | SAT | ✱ — Indian

THE BANYAN TREE ☎0161 835 9906
Moho Building, Manchester, M15 4JY
Manchester's best kept secret is both chic and ambient. Combining the exotic with the modern, the venue serves delights such as pizzas on naan bread bases. Weekly quizzes make this a buzzing hotspot.

2FOR1 3 COURSES | FRI × | SAT ✓ — Asian

BAR EIGHT ☎0161 834 8488
Middle Warehouse, Manchester, M15 4NT
Bar Eight has been recently refurbished and has a varied menu with something for everyone. Enjoy a tipple in the sun alongside some delicious food and watch the world go by.

25% OFF TOTAL | 10 | FRI ✱ | SAT × | SUN — Spanish

THE BEACON AT DALTON ☎01695 622 771
Beacon Lane, Dalton, Wigan, WN8 7RR
Acclaimed Lancashire pub-restaurant whose dining room is light and breezy and whose food, ranging from pub grub to the contemporary à la carte menu, is smart, bright and fulsome in its flavours.

2FOR1 3 COURSES | FRI ✱ | SAT ✱ | SUN — English and Continental

BELLA CAFE BISTRO ☎01942 269 279
51 Railway Road, Leigh, WN7 4AA
Home-made soups and succulent British steaks guarantee this bistro a great reputation and a loyal holding of patrons. From sea bass with lime and garlic to creamy pastas, there's something for all.

2FOR1 3 COURSES | FRI | SAT — Italian

Bella Italia
Pizza ♥ Pasta ♥ Grill

25% OFF TOTAL | 6 | FRI × | SAT × | SUN

25% OFF TOTAL

4 restaurants in Greater Manchester

Middlebrook Retail Park, Bolton, BL6 6JA	☎ 01204 692 842
Arndale Shopping Centre, Manchester, M4 3AQ	☎ 01618 342 677
92-96 Deansgate, Manchester, M3 2QG	☎ 01618 324 332
11-13 Piccadilly, Manchester, M1 1LY	☎ 01612 362 342

Gourmet Society discount applies to the à la carte menu only, unless stated otherwise.

THE BIERKELLER
0845 533 3000
The Printworks, 29 Withy Grove, Manchester, M4 2BS
The Bierkeller Manchester is something a little different, a truly unique Bavarian experience. Be sure to give them a call to reserve a table for a night of wholesome Bavarian food, drink and music.

2FOR1 3 COURSES | FRI ✓ | SAT ✗ — European

BLUE TIFFIN
☎ 0161 628 2005
Laurel Trading Estate, Higginshaw Lane, Oldham, OL2
Traditional dishes have been given modern twists at this fine Indian restaurant. Eastern flavours, exotic spices and authentic recipes come together to make a whole menu full of delicious meals.

2FOR1 3 COURSES | FRI ✓ | SAT ✗ | ▲ — Indian

BOHEMIA BAR AND GRILL
☎ 0161 839 7099
Arch 8-9, Manchester, M3 4RU
Diners can customize their steaks to taste in this spacious cosmopolitan bar. Guests can choose sauces from classic peppercorn to exotic teriyaki glaze or treat friends to a hearty sharing platter.

2FOR1 MAIN COURSE | FRI ✗ | SAT ✗ | ▲ — Mediterranean

BOLLYWOOD MASALA
☎ 0161 832 1290
15-25 Liverpool Road, Manchester, M3 4NW
Infusing the extravagance of Bollywood with contemporary Indian cuisine, this venue stimulates the senses through bold colours, aromatic smells and dishes packed full of flavour.

50% OFF FOOD | 👤10 | FRI ✗ | SAT ✗ | SUN — Indian

BOMBAY CUISINE
☎ 0161 773 6311
401 Bury New Road, Prestwich, Manchester, M25 1AA
Tasty and unfussy above all, Bombay Cuisine serves a great range of classic curries, whether you go for a nice simple bhuna or something a little more eclectic from off the specials menu.

2FOR1 MAIN COURSE | FRI ✱ | SAT ✱ — Indian

THE BRASSERIE @ MERCURE
☎ 0844 815 9029
Manchester Road, Bolton, BL6 5RU
Step into the Mercure Bolton Georgian House Hotel and find a timeless elegance and a Brasserie that is modern, bright and vibrant. Stunningly presented dishes with appearances matching taste every time.

2FOR1 3 COURSES | FRI ✓ | SAT ✓ — British

THE BRASSERIE @ MERCURE
☎ 0844 815 9024
Portland Street, Manchester, M1 4PH
In the heart of the city, Mercure Manchester Piccadilly is perfect for exploration. The hotel Brasserie allows all-embracing views of the city centre and the bustling Piccadilly Gardens.

2FOR1 3 COURSES | FRI ✓ | SAT ✓ — British

BRAZA
☎ 01204 366 150
96 Great Moor Street, Bolton, BL3 6DS
Braza Persian Restaurant injects energy into traditional recipes, giving them a modern presence. Find colourful, exotic and fragrant dishes that employ exciting spices and ingredients.

2FOR1 3 COURSES | FRI ✓ | SAT ✓ — Persian

BUFFET METRO
☎ 0161 238 8686
61 Piccadilly, Manchester, M1 2AG
All-you-can-eat buffet, serving freshly prepared hot and cold Chinese dishes as well as a wide variety of dessert options to satisfy your sweet tooth.

50% OFF FOOD | FRI ✗ | SAT ✗ | ✱ | ▲ — Chinese

THE CEDAR TREE AT THE SHEAF
☎ 01706 842 626
1 Haugh Fold, Rochdale, OL16 3RF
Fantastic informal tapas bar, bustling and vibrant in a way that's meant to be. Mark your selections on your own personal menu before feasting on tasty tapas treats and sipping on your chosen wine.

25% OFF TOTAL | 👤6 | FRI ✓ | SAT ✗ — Mediterranean

CHANCELLORS HOTEL
☎ 0161 907 7414
Chancellors Way, Moseley Rd, Fallowfield, M14 6ZT
For a memorable dining experience and excellent food head to the Chancellors Hotel, situated in a fashionable suburb of Manchester. Contemporary British dishes with a European twist take precedent.

25% OFF TOTAL | 👤10 | FRI ✓ | SAT ✓ — Classic British/French

CHEADLE ROYAL
0161 491 5884
Royal Crescent, Cheadle, Cheshire, SK8 3FE
Quality pub classics with modern twists meets with a friendly and relaxed atmosphere to make this Table Table venue the perfect place for any occasion. *Excludes daytime & evening deals and festive menus.

2FOR1 MAIN COURSE | FRI ✓ | SAT ✓ — Modern British

CAFÉ ROUGE

25% OFF TOTAL | 👤6 | FRI ✓ | SAT ✓ | ✱ | ▲

25% OFF TOTAL

5 restaurants in Greater Manchester

651-653 Wilmslow Rd, Didsbury, Manchester, M20 6QZ — ☎ 0161 438 0444
82-84 Deansgate, Manchester, M3 2ER — ☎ 0161 839 0414
The Printworks, Manchester, M4 2BS — ☎ 0161 832 7749
137 The Orient, The Trafford Centre, Manchester, M17 8EQ — ☎ 0161 747 1927
The Lowry Outlet Mall, Salford Quays, M50 3AZ — ☎ 0161 877 3971

CHILLI GRILL
☎0161 249 3999
5a Wilbraham Road, Fallowfield, M14 6JS
Popular, prized local restaurant that serves supremely tasty chargrilled meats, sizzlingly seasoned and marinated with spicy, flavour-laden sauces. Great variety, value and ambience.

25% OFF TOTAL | 6 | FRI ✓ | SAT ✓ — Portuguese

THE CHINESE BUFFET
☎01942 820 277
63 Standishgate, Wigan, WN1 2UP
Extensive menu of authentic Chinese, Japanese and Thai cuisine that changes daily. Features high quality ingredients with a good attention to detail. *Offer is for the Grand Buffet (5pm to 10.30pm).

2FOR1 MAIN COURSE | FRI ✗ | SAT ✗ | SUN — Chinese

THE CHINESE BUFFET
☎01204 388 222
32 Bridge Street, Bolton, BL1 2EH
Extensive menu of authentic Chinese, Japanese and Thai cuisine that changes daily. Features high quality ingredients with a good attention to detail. *Offer is for the Grand Buffet (5pm to 10.30pm)

2FOR1 MAIN COURSE | FRI ✗ | SAT ✗ | SUN | ✱ — Chinese

CHOICE BAR & RESTAURANT
☎0161 833 3400
Castle Quay, Castlefield, Manchester, M15 4NT
Transferring the regional history of its location to its menu, Choice Bar and Restaurant brings you a traditional taste of Manchester working with the finest bespoke suppliers in the North West.

2FOR1 3 COURSES | FRI ✓ | SAT — Modern British

CHRISTIE FIELDS
0161 249 5000
Derwent Avenue, West Didsbury, Manchester, M21 7QS
Quality pub classics with modern twists meets with a friendly and relaxed atmosphere to make this Table Table venue the perfect place for any occasion. *Excludes daytime & evening deals and festive menus.

2FOR1 MAIN COURSE | FRI ✓ | SAT ✓ — Modern British

THE CHURCH INN
0161 624 6453
23 Chadderton Fold, Oldham, OL1 2RR
The Church Inn offers a variety of dishes including a tempting choice of desserts. The staff provide a smooth and efficient service ensuring everyone is greeted with a warm welcome.

2FOR1 MAIN COURSE | FRI | SAT | SUN — British

CIAO BELLA
☎0161 236 6631
42 Portland Street, Manchester, M1 4GS
Brilliant, distinctive Italian restaurant in Manchester. Chef Donato Loi serves up great dishes from family recipes; the pollo saltimbocca, for example, is wholesome, full-flavoured, rich and vibrant.

2FOR1 MAIN COURSE | FRI | SAT ✓ — Italian

CITY CAFÉ RESTAURANT, BAR & TERRACE
☎0161 242 1020
One Piccadilly Place, Manchester, M1 3DG
Award-winning chefs prepare a seasonal menu composed of locally sourced ingredients. Treat friends to a fruity cocktail on the expansive dining terrace and enjoy the breathtaking Manchester skyline.

25% OFF TOTAL | 6 | FRI ✓ | SAT ✓ | ✱ — European

COLISEUM RESTAURANT @ BEST WESTERN
☎0161 224 0461
Willow Bank Hotel, 340 Wilmslow Rd, Manchester, M14 6AF
A beautifully appointed restaurant, bar and lounge with the Roman themed Coliseum Restaurant, featuring delicious local and international cuisine.

50% OFF FOOD | 4 | FRI ✓ | SAT ✗ | ✱ — British

COURTYARD RESTAURANT
☎01204 591 131
The Last Drop Village, Bromley Cross, BL7 9PZ
A characterful venue with cobbled streets, craft shops, booksellers, antiquarians and stunning views of the moors. Cosy, traditional restaurant with a menu of local produce and deliciously unfussy food.

2FOR1 2 COURSES | FRI ✓ | SAT ✓ | ✱ — British

CRAZY WENDY'S THAI E SARN CLASSIC
☎0161 445 5200
210 Burton Road, West Didsbury, Manchester, M20 2LW
Something of a South Manchester institution, a long-established Thai restaurant with a bright, brash, utterly entertaining atmosphere, and a big range of exceptionally tasty Thai food.

2FOR1 MAIN COURSE | FRI ✗ | SAT ✗ — Thai

CURRY COTTAGE
☎0161 343 1271
1 Concord Way, Dukinfield, SK16 4DB
Expect staple Indian classics in an amiable atmosphere, where staff are happy to advise you on your choices. Their spicy chickpea vindaloo is definitely worth a try for the avid curry enthusiast.

50% OFF FOOD | 10 | FRI ✗ | SAT ✗ — Indian

DILLI
☎0161 929 7484
60 Stamford New Rd, Altrincham, WA14 1EE
Dilli's diners love their award-winning food that faithfully reconstitutes traditional Indian specialities. Adventurous culinary explorers will love the dishes from the regions of Chettinad and Mangalore.

25% OFF TOTAL | 8 | FRI ✓ | SAT ✓ — Indian

DIMITRI'S CAFE BAR
☎0161 434 5151
846 Wilmslow Road, Didsbury, M20 2RN
Short walk from the centre of Didsbury Village, Dimitri's provides traditional Mediterranean tasty dishes and delicious Mezes in a vibrant atmosphere - where any night can explode into a great time.

25% OFF TOTAL | 6 | FRI ✱ | SAT ✱ — Med/Meze

DIMITRI'S TAVERNA BAR
☎0161 839 3319
Campfield Arcade, Manchester, M3 4FN
From quick Dips to Meaty masterpieces, Seafood sensations, Vegetarian delights, traditional tapas and meze - Dimitri's Bar & Taverna is the place to be if you want to experience a great meal in a lively atmosphere.

25% OFF TOTAL | 6 | FRI ✱ | SAT ✱ — Med/Meze

DOUGH PIZZA KITCHEN
☎0161 834 9411
75-77 High Street, Manchester, M4 1FS
A stylish urban pizza parlour known for being exceptionally family-friendly but also for its exceptional array of toppings, characterful ambience and cool location. *Booking in advance is essential.

25% OFF TOTAL | 4 | FRI ✱ | SAT ✱ — Italian

THE DUKE WILLIAM INN
☎01204 778 657
Well Street, Bolton, BL2 5SQ
The Duke William Inn serves fresh, home-cooked food only, all sourced from local suppliers. Pub classics... in a proper pub!

50% OFF FOOD | 8 | FRI ✓ | SAT ✓ — British

EAST Z EAST
☎0161 834 3500
Blackfriars Street, Deansgate, Manchester M3 5BQ
Some of the city's finest Punjabi cuisine is to be had at this stylish, glamorous location by the river. A fabulous contemporary Indian dining experience; enjoy the vibe and outstanding food.

2FOR1 MAIN COURSE | FRI ✱ | SAT ✱ — Indian

EAST Z EAST
☎0161 244 5353
Pirincess Street, Manchester, M1 7DL
Some of the city's finest Punjabi cuisine is to be had at this vibrant but homely restaurant. A place that has long had a great name for its excellent ambience and top-notch authentic cooking.

2FOR1 MAIN COURSE | FRI ✱ | SAT ✱ — Indian

EDWARDOS @ THE CHURCH INN
☎0161 485 1897
90 Ravenoak Road, Stockport, SK8 7EG
Welcome to Edwardo's.More than just good food.Edwardo's at The Church Inn pride themselves on their extensive menu and locally sourced, fresh produce. Have a gander at their tantalising a la carte menu.

2FOR1 3 COURSES | FRI | SAT ✗ | SUN — British

FIND MORE
— ONLINE —
www.gourmetsociety.co.uk

EFES RESTAURANT
0161 236 1824
46 Princess Street, Manchester, M1 6HR
Relive your summer holidays with the home-cooked dishes that are as unique and authentic as it gets. Enjoy food, live music, and belly dancers at Manchester's original Turkish and Mediterranean taverna.

25% OFF TOTAL | 4 | FRI ✓ | SAT ✱ | ✱ | (tree) — Turkish

EVUNA
0161 819 2752
277-279 Deansgate, Manchester, M3 4EW
Central, stylishly conceived little restaurant that serves vivid, fulsome Spanish cuisine; it has a close, cosy vibe for an intimate dinner, while also catering for large events.

25% OFF TOTAL | 4 | FRI | SAT ✱ | (tree) — Spanish

EVUNA
0161 833 1130
79 Thomas Street, Manchester, M4 1LQ
Evuna is a fine Spanish wine house situated in the heart of Manchester. The restaurant aims to offer the finest in Spanish food and drink with food originating from the central regions in Spain.

25% OFF TOTAL | 4 | FRI × | SAT × | (tree) — Spanish

FAMILY LODGE INDIAN CUISINE
0161 442 4558
230 Wellington Road North, Stockport, SK4 2QN
Reputable for its mouth-watering dishes and pleasant atmosphere, the Bay Leaf is renowned as one of Stockport's best Indian restaurants. Offering delicious food in calming surrounds.

50% OFF FOOD | FRI ✓ | SAT ✓ — Indian

FIENO ITALIAN RESTAURANT
01942 245 327
15 Millgate, Wigan, WN1 1YB
Whether you are just popping in for a cup of coffee, a cocktail or to enjoy the extensive menu with friends or family, you can be assured of a warm welcome at the beautiful Fieno Italian restaurant.

2FOR1 2 COURSES | FRI ✓ | SAT ✓ | SUN — Italian

FREDERICK'S
01942 825 389
Mesnes Park, Wigan, WN1 1TU
Frederick's Ice Cream offers not only luxury ice cream but light snacks, paninis and made-to-order pizzas. Frederick's offers customers an excellent range of lunch or tea bites.

25% OFF TOTAL | FRI ✓ | SAT × | SUN — Italian

FREDERICK'S
0161 747 7778
Trafford Quays, Manchester, M41 7JA
Frederick's Ice Cream offers not only luxury ice cream but light snacks, paninis and made-to-order pizzas. Frederick's offers customers an excellent range of lunch or tea bites.

25% OFF TOTAL | 6 | FRI ✓ | SAT × | SUN — Italian

FUSION LOUNGE
01706 345 888
4-6 St Marys Gate, Rochdale, OL16 1DZ
A quality Chinese and Thai takeaway in Rochdale that does a great range of dishes, and has gained a healthy reputation locally for its food.

2FOR1 MAIN COURSE | FRI ✓ | SAT ✱ — Indian

GARAM MASSALA RESTAURANT
0161 488 4001
18 Station Road, Stockport, SK8 5AE
The Garam Massala is a well-cherished Indian restaurant in Cheadle Hulme. The staff ensure that the standards of service and food are never anything less than top quality.

2FOR1 3 COURSES | FRI ✓ | SAT ✓ — Indian

GARLIC INDIAN CUISINE
0161 368 4040
10 The Square, Hyde, SK14 2QR
Garlic Indian Cuisine comes highly recommended by locals. This popular haunt is hailed by many as the best Indian food in the area.With fresh poppadoms, delicious starters and quality curries, enjoy Garlic!

2FOR1 MAIN COURSE | FRI ✓ | SAT ✓ | ✱ | (tree) — Indian

GEORGE & DRAGON
0161 928 9933
Manchester Road, Altrincham, WA14 4PH
Quality pub classics with modern twists meets with a friendly and relaxed atmosphere to make this Table Table venue the perfect place for any occasion. *Excludes daytime & evening deals and festive menus.

2FOR1 MAIN COURSE | FRI ✓ | SAT ✓ — Modern British

GO PIZZA
0161 425 8225
Unit 17 The Arndale, Manchester, M4 3AQ
For those with a busy lifestyle, Go delivers fast fresh food from divine pizzas to delicious baguettes, all prepared to quality standards, providing excellent value for money.

2FOR1 MAIN COURSE | FRI ✱ | SAT ✱ | (tree) — Italian

GRANGE RESTAURANT @ MERCURE
0161 619 9004
Norton Grange Hotel, Manchester Rd, Castleton, OL11 2XZ
Opulently decorated, this venue is furnished with elegant oak tables and romantic lighting. Whether its a traditional cooked breakfast or a sumptuous dinner, the sophisticated diner is in their element.

25% OFF TOTAL | 4 | FRI ✓ | SAT ✓ — British

GREEN TEA RESTAURANT
0161 445 5395
222 Burton Road, Manchester, M20 2LW
A warm and friendly Chinese eatery with genuine décor and quality authentic cuisine. The tea menu is well populated as you would imagine, with options such as goji berry and the classic green tea.

50% OFF FOOD | 4 | FRI × | SAT × | ✱ | (tree) — Chinese

GRENACHE RESTAURANT
0161 799 8181
15 Bridgewater Road, Manchester, M28 3JE
Granche provides what can only be described as a decadent dining experience. This excellent restaurant has won a number of awards, including Best North West Restaurant in the 2013 Good Food Guide.

2FOR1 MAIN COURSE | 2 | FRI ✓ | SAT × | SUN | ✱ | (tree) — Fine Dining

GURKHA GRILL
0161 445 5444
194-198 Burton Road, West Didsbury, Manchester, M20 1LH
One of Manchester's best kept secrets, where divine Nepalese and Indian cuisine can be devoured in supreme surroundings. Home-made spices are added to traditional dishes, locking in unique flavours.

2FOR1 3 COURSES | FRI ✱ | SAT ✱ | SUN | ✱ — Nepalese

HABESHA RESTAURANT AND BAR
0161 228 7396
29-31 Sackville Street, Manchester, M1 3LZ
All freshly cooked, the dishes here are characterised by tenderly cooked meat or delicious, casseroled vegetables, with subtle and distinctive spices and a kick of heat where one is welcome.

50% OFF FOOD | 10 | FRI × | SAT × — African

THE HALE KITCHEN
0161 926 4670
149 Ashley Road, Altrincham, WA14 2UW
A charming, traditional menu of the best seasonal and local produce. With a relaxing atmosphere and a touch of glamour you can enjoy a meal or simply relax, sampling the eclectic range of drinks.

50% OFF FOOD | 8 | FRI ✓ | SAT ✓ — British

HARAPPA URBAN INDIAN CUISINE
0161 477 6757
106 Higher Hill Gate, Stockport, SK1 3QH
Specialist chefs combine tasty and exotic dishes from across the Asian subcontinent with healthy eating in mind. Maintaining original recipes, they create delicious and nutritious dishes full of flavour.

25% OFF TOTAL | 6 | FRI ✓ | SAT ✓ | ✱ | (tree) — Indian

HARDIES RESTAURANT @ HOLIDAY INN
01204 879 988
1 Higher Bridge Street, Bolton, BL1 2EW
This tastefully decorated gem gives diners a warm atmosphere. Delicious food is served all day in Hardies Restaurant from a wide-ranging menu, from succulent steak to those with an international twist.

25% OFF TOTAL | 6 | FRI ✓ | SAT ✓ — International

THE HARTSHEAD
01457 835 753
Mossley Road, Mossley, Ashton-under-Lyne, OL6 9AQ
This Vintage Inn oozes rural charm and rustic character. The picturesque surroundings provide the perfect backdrop for savouring the hearty, seasonal pub-food on the menu.

25% OFF TOTAL | FRI ✓ | SAT ✓ | SUN | (tree) — Modern British

HEALD GREEN BEEFEATER GRILL
0161 499 1944
Finney Lane, Heald Green, SK8 3QH
Beefeater Grill are one of the UK's best-loved restaurants welcoming guests for almost 40 years in over 130 locations nationwide. *Excludes Breakfast, Light Bites, Bar menu, set menus and all other offers.

2FOR1 MAIN COURSE | 6 | FRI ✓ | SAT × | (tree) — Modern British

HEATON PARK BEEFEATER GRILL 0161 720 6171
Middleton Road, Crumpsall, M8 6NP
Beefeater Grill are one of the UK's best-loved restaurants welcoming guests for almost 40 years in over 130 locations nationwide. *Excludes Breakfast, Light Bites, Bar menu, set menus and all other offers.

2FOR1 MAIN COURSE | ♟6 | FRI ✓ | SAT × | ▲ — Modern British

HENRY J BEANS ☎0161 827 7820
The Printworks, Dantzic Street, Manchester, M4 2AD
A unique brand that can best be described as a typical bar and grill. Simply classic American food complemented by a vast array of beverages, all served with flair in a vibrant and lively atmosphere.

25% OFF TOTAL | ♟6 | FRI 📱 | SAT ✱ | ▲ — North American

HUFFYS CAFEBAR & RESTAURANT ☎0161 419 9110
251 London Road, Hazel Grove, Stockport, SK7 4PL
A true all day joint, Huffys' homely tea and cake, light lunches, and evening menus of seasonal specials (from beer-battered fish to fajitas) are all served in its distinctively relaxed atmosphere.

2FOR1 MAIN COURSE | FRI ✱ | SAT × | ▲ — Traditional English

HUNGRY BUDDHA ☎0161 419 9831
16 London Road, Stockport, SK7 4AG
As the name suggests, the clientele at the Hungry Buddha banquet upon wholesome and authentic Chinese dishes. Treasured by locals, the food is piquant and sure to appease grumbling tummies.

25% OFF TOTAL | FRI ✓ | SAT ✓ | ▲ — Chinese

THE INDIAN CURRY COTTAGE ☎0161 973 8199
394 Washway Road, Sale, M33 4JH
Longstanding curry house in Sale that's managed to carve out a niche for itself with consistently high quality food over many years, together with a smart setting and smooth, efficient service.

2FOR1 3 COURSES | FRI ✱ | SAT ✱ — Indian

INDIAN OCEAN ☎0161 343 3343
Stamford Street East, Ashton-under-Lyne, OL6 6QH
This dining experience extends beyond a simple meal. Enjoy drinks in their spacious bar before or after your delicious food, that includes a blend of traditional recipes and British classics.

2FOR1 MAIN COURSE | FRI 📱 | SAT 📱 — Indian

INDIGO ☎0161 766 8040
703 Manchester Road, Bury, BL9 9SS
Regional North and South Indian dishes are tasty, delicious and bring diners back time and time again. Exceptional in quality and service, Indigo Bury is a must for curry lovers.

2FOR1 3 COURSES | FRI ✓ | SAT ✓ — Indian

ISLAMABAD GRILL ☎0161 257 3890
199-201 Wilmslow Road, Manchester, M14 5AQ
Feed a voracious stomach with the buffet at this Indian eatery. Aptly set on Manchester's curry mile, guests will adore this venue for quality cuisine and diversity. *Offer also includes the Buffet.

25% OFF TOTAL | ♟10 | FRI ✓ | SAT × — Indian

ITALIAN CORNER CAFE ☎0161 330 3440
1 Market Street, Ashton-under-Lyne, OL6 6BP
The menu here is typically Italian; many dishes are given a modern twist while others maintain their traditional roots meaning that every bite of your meal really is catered for. *Open lunchtimes only.

25% OFF TOTAL | ♟10 | FRI ✓ | SAT ✓ — Italian

JADE GARDEN ☎0161 445 6979
743 Wilsmlow Road, Didsbury, M20 6RN
Oriental food lovers can savour the sweet and sour tastes of China and Thailand in this Eastern inspired eatery. An abundance of dishes are cooked to impeccable standards by knowledgeable chefs.

2FOR1 MAIN COURSE | FRI ✓ | SAT ✓ — Chinese

JALFREZI ☎0161 439 9494
No.3 The Bramhall Centre, Bramhall, SK7 1AW
As the name suggests, this Indian eatery cooks up a cracking Jalfrezi. If that's not your preferred dish, the chefs guarantee guests will be spoilt for choice by the bursting menu.

2FOR1 MAIN COURSE | FRI ✱ | SAT ✱ | ✱ — Indian

JAMAL INDIAN RESTAURANT 01942 212 228
Anjou Boulevard Road, Wigan, WN3 0UL
Jamal is a cracking Indian restaurant not far from Wigan's DW stadium. It does all the classics right, and is a good place to enjoy a well-priced, satisfying curry.

2FOR1 MAIN COURSE | FRI × | SAT × — Indian

JAMUNA ☎0161 483 5379
405-407 Buxton Road, Stockport, SK2 7EY
Superb Indian restaurant that serves the local area with curry staples and tandoori classics. Friendly staff will help you choose from the extensive menu should you feel spoilt for choice.

2FOR1 3 COURSES | FRI × | SAT × | ✱ | ▲ — Indian

JANNAT ☎01942 829 335
51 Mesnes Street, Wigan, WN1 1QX
Choose from a wide variety of Indian dishes rich in spice and flavour, with choices to suit any taste. Relax in a warm and inviting atmosphere as you are attended to by polite and courteous staff.

2FOR1 MAIN COURSE | FRI ✓ | SAT ✓ — Indian

THE JASMINE HOUSE ☎0161 476 2005
269a Wellington Road South, Stockport, SK2 6NG
Superb Cantonese restaurant where you can sample tasty dishes from an extensive menu. With friendly staff and a warm inviting atmosphere, Jasmine House is well worth a visit.

25% OFF TOTAL | FRI 📱 | SAT 📱 | ✱ | ▲ — Chinese

JENNY'S RESTAURANT ☎0871 222 0018
Tib Street, Manchester, M4 1SH
Appease ravenous stomachs with a wholesome 3-course carvery at this renowned hotel. Jenny's is committed to preparing exquisite food and exceptional service at pocket-friendly prices.

50% OFF FOOD | ♟2 | FRI ✓ | SAT ✓ — International

JOHN MILNE 01706 299 999
Newhey Road, Milnrow, Rochdale, Lancashire, OL16 4JF
Quality pub classics with modern twists meets with a friendly and relaxed atmosphere to make this Table Table venue the perfect place for any occasion. *Excludes daytime & evening deals and festive menus.

2FOR1 MAIN COURSE | FRI ✓ | SAT ✓ — Modern British

KANTIPUR ☎0161 476 2688
238 Wellington Road South, Stockport, SK2 6NW
Nepalese cuisine is growing in popularity for its distinctive flavours; this restaurant is ahead of the curve with its authentic, beautifully realised dishes that ought to tempt you into something fresh.

2FOR1 3 COURSES | FRI ✱ | SAT ✱ — Nepalese

KHAN BABA INDIAN BAR & GRILL ☎0161 832 4883
73-83 Liverpool Road, Manchester, M3 4AQ
The moment you walk through these doors, you will enjoy the calming ambiance of the restaurant, take in the authentic aromas and savour the taste of freshly made-to-order dishes.

2FOR1 MAIN COURSE | FRI × | SAT × | SUN | ✱ — Indian

KHANDOKER BRAMHALL ☎0161 439 1050
10 Fir Road, Stockport, SK7 2NP
Serving delicious authentic cuisine from the subcontinent to the curry faithful with a potent combination of locally sourced produce and sumptuous Indian delicacies.

2FOR1 MAIN COURSE | FRI 📱 | SAT 📱 — Indian

KHANDOKER RESTAURANT ☎0161 434 3596
812 Kingsway, Manchester, M20 5WY
Enjoy a collection of authentic mouth-watering dishes from the Indian subcontinent, including divine, traditional delicacies. Quality food, service, and more than reasonable prices.

2FOR1 MAIN COURSE | FRI ✓ | SAT ✓ — Indian

To understand what the restaurant icons mean, please see the inside back cover.

KULSHI RESTAURANT
☎0161 747 1777

1 Stretford Road, Urmston, Manchester, M41 9JY

A mellow, cosy Bangladeshi restaurant in Urmston set in a grand old arched-roof beer hall. Choose from an eclectic menu that ranges from the delicately flavoured to the well spiced.

2FOR1 3 COURSES | FRI ✓ | SAT ✓ — Indian

KUSHOOM KOLY INDIAN RESTAURANT
☎0161 432 9841

6-8 Shaw Road, Stockport, SK4 4AE

Authentic Indian restaurant with an authentic setting. A local institution in Stockport, family-run since 1971 and well-known for its array of fine dishes, with traditional offerings and weekly specials.

2FOR1 3 COURSES | FRI 📱 | SAT ✱ — Indian

LA ROBERTO RESTAURANT
☎0161 478 3282

185 London Road, Stockport, SK7 4HJ

Experience something unique at this Romanian eatery where smoking charcoal-grilled steaks reign supreme. Expert chefs freshly prepare continental cuisine which can be enjoyed with a crisp glass of wine.

50% OFF FOOD | 8 | FRI × | SAT × | ▲ — Romanian

LA TASCA
☎0161 834 8234

76 Deansgate, Manchester, M3 2FW

Quintessentially Spanish, La Tasca's fresh and exciting menu offers something for everyone. Their tapas dishes are sincerely authentic, while their paellas always deliver on flavour.

25% OFF TOTAL | 8 | FRI ✓ | SAT × | ▲ — Spanish

LA TASCA
☎0161 749 9966

Unit R7A Trafford Centre, Manchester, M17 8EG

Quintessentially Spanish, La Tasca's fresh and exciting menu offers something for everyone. Their tapas dishes are sincerely authentic, while their paellas always deliver on flavour.

25% OFF TOTAL | 8 | FRI ✓ | SAT × | ▲ — Spanish

LAHORI SHAHENSHAH
☎0161 257 2534

131 Wilmslow Road, Manchester, M14 5AW

Nestled on Manchester's famous Curry Mile, this venue shines alongside its neighbours. Proud of their experienced chefs, Lahori Shahenshah offers hungry clientele curries to contend with.

2FOR1 MAIN COURSE | FRI × | SAT × | ✱ — Indian/Pakistani

LAST MONSOON INDIAN RESTAURANT
☎0161 476 4266

54 King Street West, Stockport, SK3 0DT

A unique fusion of Eastern cuisine from Bangladesh, India and Nepal along with some select European dishes for the less adventurous, prepared with new recipes and traditional cooking techniques.

25% OFF TOTAL | 6 | FRI ✓ | SAT ✓ | ✱ — Indian

LATINO LOUNGE
☎01204 591 122

122 Bradshaw Brow, Bolton, BL2 3DD

Blending tastes of Italy with the flavours of the Mediterranean, Latino Lounge serves superb fish, meat and vegetarian dishes, and is proud of its ability to cater for all appetites and palates.

2FOR1 3 COURSES | FRI ✓ | SAT × — Italian

LAVEEZA RESTAURANT
☎01204 771 914

212 Chorley New Road, Bolton, BL6 5NP

Laveeza is an Indian family run restaurant, serving only the finest in true Indian cuisine. All dishes are prepared with care & the same attention to detail as you would expect in a traditional Indian home

2FOR1 3 COURSES | FRI ✓ | SAT ✓ | ✱ | ▲ — Indian

LEE'S SPICE LOUNGE
☎0161 620 8922

73 High Street, Oldham, OL4 3BN

Providing an infusion of Bangladeshi, Punjabi, Nepalese and Sri Lankan tastes, the knowledgeable chefs consistently prepare dishes of an exceptional quality.

2FOR1 MAIN COURSE | FRI 📱 | SAT 📱 | ✱ | ▲ — Indian

LEGENDS RESTAURANT
☎01706 822476

Red Hall Hotel, Bury, BL9 5NA

Located on the northern outskirts of Manchester, Legends Restaurant really is a hidden gem.Their dedicated team of chefs produce British and European cuisine which is locally sourced where possible.

2FOR1 3 COURSES | FRI ✱ | SAT ✱ | SUN | ▲ — British

LOWRY'S BAR @ HILTON
☎0161 435 3000

Hilton Manchester Airport, Outwood Lane, M90 4WP

The perfect place to wind down with colleagues after a business meeting or conference, Lowry's Bar offers everything from coffees to fine wines and light meals.

50% OFF FOOD | 6 | FRI ✓ | SAT ✓ — International

LOWRY'S RESTAURANT @ HILTON
☎0161 435 3000

Hilton Manchester Airport, Outwood Lane, M90 4WP

Light and airy, contemporary and smooth, Lowry's Restaurant is a well-loved attribute of the Hilton at Manchester Airport. Feast on exquisite European dishes, washed down with one of the fine wines.

50% OFF FOOD | 6 | FRI ✓ | SAT ✓ — International

MANZIL RESTAURANT
☎0161 820 8555

29 Bury New Road, Manchester, M8 8EQ

Contemporary and stylish self-service restaurant that boasts an abudance of exotic and familiar dishes. The menu is laden with an exclusive selection of meat, fish, poutry and vegetarian options.

2FOR1 MAIN COURSE | FRI 📱 | SAT 📱 | SUN — Indian

THE MARCH HARE
0161 482 8638

Mill Lane, Cheadle Hulme, Cheadle, SK8 5PG

This Vintage Inn oozes rural charm and rustic character. The picturesque surroundings provide the perfect backdrop for savouring the hearty, seasonal pub-food on the menu.

25% OFF TOTAL | FRI ✓ | SAT ✓ | SUN | ▲ — Modern British

MARMARIS
☎0161 442 1891

29 Shaw Road, Stockport, SK4 4AG

As the name suggests, the cuisine at this venue is authentically Turkish. Refined palates will revel in the gourmet dishes that bring a taste of the Mediterranean to the table.

25% OFF TOTAL | 10 | FRI × | SAT × | ✱ — Turkish

MASTERCHEF TANDOORI
☎0161 431 0000

149 Heaton Moor Road, Stockport, SK4 4HY

As the name suggests, the chefs at this eatery are top-notch. Expert chefs recommend the biryani and karahi dishes which promise to take guests on an exotic culinary journey.

2FOR1 MAIN COURSE | FRI 📱 | SAT × — Indian/Pakistani

MCR RESTAURANT
☎0161 831 6000

Renaissance Hotel, Blackfriars St, Manchester, M3 2EQ

Striking hotel-restaurant with a smart, refined style about it. Features views across the city and fresh-faced, sophisticated modern hospitality, with a great range of excellent dishes.

50% OFF FOOD | 4 | FRI ✓ | SAT ✓ — International

MERSEY FARM
0161 9628 113

Carrington Lane, Ashton On Mersey, Sale, M33 5BL

Quality pub classics with modern twists meets with a friendly and relaxed atmosphere to make this Table Table venue the perfect place for any occasion. *Excludes daytime & evening deals and festive menus.

2FOR1 MAIN COURSE | FRI ✓ | SAT ✓ — Modern British

MILLON RESTAURANT
☎0161 620 6445

Westwood Business Centre, Oldham, OL9 6HN

The delicious food on offer at Millon Restaurant is not to be missed. Indian breads and sundries score highly, with the curry dishes proving to be a big hit with the regular diners.

2FOR1 2 COURSES | FRI × | SAT × | ✱ | ▲ — Indian

MOËT RESTAURANT & BAR
☎0161 838 0540

Selfridges, Exchange Square, Manchester, M3 1BD

Super stylish chic city centre champagne bar where you can enjoy that splash of sophistication on a day out at the shops, a bespoke visit for lunch, or simply to watch the world go by.

25% OFF TOTAL | 4 | FRI ✓ | SAT ✱ | ▲ — Modern European

MORTIMER'S
☎01942 824 180

34-45 King Street, Wigan, WN1 1BT

Mortimers is a cracking pub in the heart of Wigan which is great for a night out, to watch a match, and also to get some good old fashioned, satisfying pub food at a great price.

25% OFF TOTAL | 10 | FRI ✓ | SAT ✓ — Modern Pub

MURILLOS SPANISH RESTAURANT ☎0161 427 1200
48 Stockport Road, Stockport, SK6 6AB
Brimming with authentic Spanish delicacies, Murillo's Spanish Restaurant offers the finest regional cuisine and tantalising tapas in a vibrant setting. Superb Spanish food and warm, friendly service.
50% OFF FOOD | ♟ 6 | FRI ✗ | SAT ✗ — Spanish

THE NEW FAR PAVILION ☎0161 794 3801
249 Manchester Road, Swinton, M27 4TT
Popular, welcoming Indian restaurant to the north west of Salford that serves richly flavourful and generously proportioned Indian dishes. A place to be savoured and enjoyed.
2FOR1 MAIN COURSE | FRI ✗ | SAT ✗ | SUN | ✱ | ▲ — Indian

NEW SAGOR INDIAN RESTAURANT ☎0161 624 9268
274 Lees Road, Oldham, OL4 1PA
Chefs blend together aromatic and sensual spices to create only the tastiest of Indian dishes. Diners are promised a warm welcoming from staff in a vibrant atmosphere.
2FOR1 MAIN COURSE | FRI ✓ | SAT ✗ — Indian

NIDO DIDSBURY ☎0161 448 9503
786 Wilmslow Road, Manchester, M20 2DR
Set in the leafy suburb of Didsbury village, Nido is a great destination for tapas lovers. Whether you are looking for a romantic meal for two, or simply want to sit and watch the world go by - be sure to check out this gem.
2FOR1 3 COURSES | FRI ✗ | SAT ✗ | ▲ — Spanish

NING ☎0844 414 5484
92-94 Oldham St, Manchester, M4 1LJ
Sample Malaysian food that radiates honesty and simplicity. Unpretentious and genuine, the cuisine here is bursting with passion. Enjoy in modish, sleek surroundings that mirror chic Asian cities.
2FOR1 3 COURSES | FRI 📱 | SAT ✗ | ▲ — Malaysian

NISHAT LOUNGE ☎0161 652 4666
422-424 Middleton Road, Oldham, OL9 6PY
Not only does Nishat Lounge provide diners with genuine Indian cuisine at an exceedingly good standard, but they also promise to thrust diners into a culinary adventure alongside welcoming staff.
2FOR1 2 COURSES | FRI 📱 | SAT 📱 — Indian

THE NORTHERN QUARTER RESTAURANT ☎0161 832 7115
108 High Street, Manchester, M4 1HQ
Dine in the heart of Manchester's famous Northern Quarter. Characteristic of the area itself, this fabulous restaurant offers fulsome, fresh food and boasts an attractively vibrant atmosphere.
2FOR1 MAIN COURSE | FRI ✱ | SAT ✗ | SUN | ▲ — Modern British

THE ODDFELLOWS MELLOR ☎0161 449 7826
73 Moor End Road, Mellor, Stockport, SK6 5PT
Featured in the Michelin Guide 2013, The Oddfellows Mellor has been a favourite amongst diners for years. Freshly prepared, locally sourced British food with a modern twist.
2FOR1 2 COURSES | FRI ✱ | SAT ✱ — International

OKRA @ HOLIDAY INN ☎0161 743 0080
Liverpool Street, Salford, M5 4LT
Situated in the pleasant Holiday Inn, guests will enjoy the contemporary feel of the restaurant and the fine food on offer. European and pan-Asian cuisine is complemented by a fantastic selection of wines.
25% OFF TOTAL | ♟ 10 | FRI ✓ | SAT ✓ | ✱ — Pan-Asian

OKRA BAR @ HOLIDAY INN ☎0161 743 0080
Liverpool Street, Salford, M5 4LT
A quiet retreat in a vibrantly busy city, Okra Lounge Bar is a well-loved attribute of the Holiday Inn Manchester West. Find tasty hot and cold snacks as well as fruity or dry speciality cocktails.
25% OFF TOTAL | ♟ 6 | FRI ✓ | SAT ✓ — International

ORLANDO'S ☎01942 818 123
75-77 Market Street, Bolton, BL5 3AA
Carnivorous diners can sink their teeth into sticky ribs and healthy grills at this American-inspired eatery. Kick start the weekend with a cocktail or an ice cold beer.
2FOR1 MAIN COURSE | FRI 📱 | SAT 📱 | SUN — British

OVERSTUFFED PIZZERIA ☎0871 222 0018
Tib Street, Manchester, M4 1SH
Italian lovers can expect to find an array of classical dishes such as cannelloni and lasagne, to delightfully tasty bites such as ciabattas and salads. A fantastic addition to the Britannia Hotel.
50% OFF FOOD | FRI ✓ | SAT ✗ — Italian

PACIFICA-CANTONESE ☎0161 707 8828
5-7 Church Road, Eccles, M30 0DL
A well-regarded Cantonese restaurant serving eclectic, authentic dishes that range farther afield than usually seen in England; stylish, sassy and with flavours to savour.
25% OFF TOTAL | ♟ 6 | FRI ✗ | SAT ✗ | ▲ — Chinese

THE PALACE ☎0161 288 1111
Oxford Road, Manchester, M60 7HA
The Palace is situated in the heart of one of the UK's best-loved cities. While Manchester is a fantastic place to spend a break away, The Palace is an excellent starting point to kick off your stay.
25% OFF TOTAL | ♟ 6 | FRI ✓ | SAT ✓ | ▲ — British

PASSAGE TO INDIA ☎0161 787 7546
168 Monton Road, Monton, M30 9GA
Whether you want the comfort of your favourite Indian dish or you want to try something a little bit different, this superbly luxurious restaurant will cater for you.
2FOR1 2 COURSES | FRI 📱 | SAT 📱 | ▲ — Indian

PAVILION II ☎01706 526 666
231 Spotland Road, Rochdale, OL12 7AG
Having already gained an excellent reputation for Bangladeshi Cuisine. Pavilion II provides high quality cuisine, a vibrant atmosphere and first class service.
2FOR1 3 COURSES | FRI 📱 | SAT 📱 | ✱ — Indian

THE PEACOCK ROOM ☎01706 368 591
Crimble Lane, Bamford, Rochdale, OL11 4AD
An ever-evolving menu encapsulating modern English cuisine and peacocks freely roming outside make this stand out from the crowd. Enjoy 1 AA rosette quality food and a superb wine list.
25% OFF TOTAL | ♟ 4 | FRI ✓ | SAT ✗ | SUN | ▲ — Modern British

THE PEARL RESTAURANT & LOUNGE ☎0161 301 5680
119 Manchester Road, Audenshaw, M34 5PY
A restaurant for dining, a lounge for relaxing and a disco room for partying; The Pearl Restaurant has it all. Serves a great range of Asian dishes and more unusual delicacies.
2FOR1 2 COURSES | FRI ✓ | SAT ✗ | ✱ | ▲ — Indian

PERUGA AT WOODHEYS ☎01457 852 704
Glossop Road, Marple Bridge, Stockport, SK6 5RX
A unique venue set in an idyllic location, with breathtaking views over the Cheshire countryside and as far as the mountain ranges of North Wales. Peruga is certainly a hidden gem.
2FOR1 MAIN COURSE | FRI ✱ | SAT ✱ | SUN | ▲ — European

PICCOLO ITALIAN RESTAURANT & BAR ☎0161 428 5300
61a Church Road, Stockport, SK8 4NG
Piccolo Restaurant and Bar is in a converted Methodist chapel and serves authentic traditional and more modern Italian food.
25% OFF TOTAL | ♟ 6 | FRI ✗ | SAT ✗ | ✱ | ▲ — Italian

Gourmet Society discount applies to the à la carte menu only, unless stated otherwise.

THE PLACE HOTEL ☎ 0161 778 7744
Ducie Street, Manchester, M1 2TP
Place Hotel Manchester houses the Hotel's Restaurant and Bistro bar and offers a selection of relaxed dining and grander fine dining.

50% OFF FOOD | ♟ 4 | FRI × | SAT × — European

PODIUM RESTAURANT @ HILTON ☎ 0161 870 1600
Hilton Manchester, Deansgate, Manchester, M3 4LQ
Treat yourself to an aperitif and dine on locally reared Cheshire beef fillet with celeriac puree, roasted beetroot and a potted beef Scotch egg. All of which are firm favourites with the diners at Hilton.

25% OFF TOTAL | ♟ 8 | FRI ✓ | SAT × | ▲ — British

POTTERS ☎ 0161 746 8629
114 The Orient, Trafford Centre, Manchester, M17 8EH
Take a break and enjoy a dish from a menu of timeless British food. Something for the whole family, including a fantastic kids menu. Great food in relaxed and comfortable surroundings.

50% OFF FOOD | ♟ 4 | FRI ✓ | SAT ✱ | ▲ — British

PREZZO 0161 713 3742
Unit 1 Orange, Manchester, M50 2HF
With a character all of its own, oozes contemporary style and enduring charm. Signature pastas, stone-baked pizzas and classic Italian dishes promise a perfect dining choice for the whole family.

2FOR1 MAIN COURSE | FRI × | SAT × | ▲ — Italian

PREZZO 0161 835 9160
Unit 22-23 The Printworks, Manchester, M4 2BS
With a character all of its own, oozes contemporary style and enduring charm. Signature pastas, stone-baked pizzas and classic Italian dishes promise a perfect dining choice for the whole family.

2FOR1 MAIN COURSE | FRI × | SAT × | ▲ — Italian

PRIDE OF BENGAL ☎ 0161 406 6451
2 George Lane, Bredbury, Stockport, SK6 1AS
Loyal customers travel far and wide to taste the famous pepsilla, or the tasty chicken simla. Indian cuisine is served by a friendly team of staff, who are happy to help you choose from the menu.

2FOR1 MAIN COURSE | FRI ✓ | SAT ✓ | ▲ — Indian

QUAY HOUSE 0161 872 4026
The Quays, Salford Quays, Salford, Manchester, M50 3SQ
Beefeater Grill are one of the UK's best-loved restaurants welcoming guests for almost 40 years in over 130 locations nationwide. *Excludes Breakfast, Light Bites, Bar menu, set menus and all other offers.

2FOR1 MAIN COURSE | ♟ 6 | FRI ✓ | SAT × | ▲ — Modern British

RAYHOON PERSIAN RESTAURANT ☎ 0161 480 2114
30-34 St Petersgate, Stockport, SK1 1EB
Dedicated to creating memorable evenings out, the staff at Rayhoon are not only proud of the authentic food they serve but also of their ability to create the ultimate Persian experience.

25% OFF TOTAL | ♟ 6 | FRI 📱 | SAT 📱 | SUN | ✱ | ▲ — Persian

RBG @ PARK INN ☎ 01942 366 334
Park Inn, Sale Way, Leigh Sports Village, WN7 4JY
Step inside the comfortable and well-located Park Inn to find an outstanding bar and grill, where great food can be enjoyed. A delicious menu offers classic steaks and gourmet burgers.

25% OFF TOTAL | ♟ 10 | FRI ✓ | SAT ✓ | ▲ — Modern European

RBG @ PARK INN ☎ 0161 832 6565
4 Cheetham Hill Road, Manchester, M4 4EW
With a tempting selection of gourmet burgers, local dishes, light bites, and a variety of soups and salads, along with signature dishes from the grill this modern restaurant has something to offer everyone.

25% OFF TOTAL | ♟ 4 | FRI 📱 | SAT 📱 | ▲ — Steakhouse

RED CAFÉ ☎ 0161 868 8303
Manchester United Football Club, Manchester, M16 0RA
Football fans unite at The Red Café, Old Trafford. Pop in for a bite to eat before the big game, or simply sit back and take in the past and present football memorabilia that lines the restaurant.

50% OFF FOOD | ♟ 8 | FRI ✓ | SAT × — International

RED ROSE INDIAN RESTAURANT ☎ 0161 456 3638
173-175 London Road, Stockport, SK7 4HJ
Exuding energy, the menu is bursting with Indian and Continental delights. Experienced chefs create tantalising dishes to tempt and tease the taste buds. Enjoy the vibrant and vivacious atmosphere.

2FOR1 MAIN COURSE | FRI 📱 | SAT 📱 — Indian

RETREAT RESTAURANT ☎ 01204 849 313
319-321 Chorley New Road, Bolton, BL1 5BP
Delicate fish that will melt in your mouth and hearty chargrilled steaks make this a perfect place to dine. A calming atmosphere ensures every guest has a relaxing dining experience.

2FOR1 3 COURSES | FRI ✱ | SAT ✱ | ✱ | ▲ — British

REVOLUCION DE CUBA ☎ 0161 826 8266
South Central, Manchester, M2 5QR
Grab your amigos and tuck into a vast Latin-influenced food menu served seven days a week - from a sneaky lunchtime Mojito and Burrito to after work street food and small plates.

25% OFF TOTAL | ♟ 6 | FRI × | SAT × — Cuban

THE ROEBUCK INN ☎ 0161 624 7819
Brighton Road, Strinesdale, Oldham, OL4 3RB
In this charming Lancashire inn just near Strinesdale reservoir you'll enjoy a superb array of menus filled with classic pub-style fare, of an especial sophistication and quality.

2FOR1 3 COURSES | FRI ✓ | SAT ✱ | SUN — European

THE ROMPER ☎ 0161 427 1354
Ridge End, Marple, SK6 7ET
Edge-of-the-country pub with a keen sense of history, marked by a tastefully modern, relaxed atmosphere. Excellent food from among the classic British staples. *Friday & Saturday not available after 7pm.

2FOR1 3 COURSES | FRI ✓ | SAT ✓ | SUN — British

ROOM RESTAURANT ☎ 0161 836 2778
81 King Street, Manchester, M2 4AH
This unique, modern restaurant and cocktail bar is a stunning dining destination with 2 prestigious AA Rosettes. *Thursday bookings taken on the day. Unavailable on special event days.

25% OFF TOTAL | ♟ 6 | FRI × | SAT × | SUN | ▲ — British

ROYAL BALTI HOUSE ☎ 01204 573 515
78 Lower Market Street, Farnworth, Bolton, BL4 7NY
Firm local favourite with a classic balti house interior and a buzzy atmosphere. The food is excellent: massive range of dishes with a long-standing reputation for being full-flavoured and very satisfying.

2FOR1 3 COURSES | FRI ✱ | SAT ✱ — Indian

SADAGAR 0161 482 7171
45 Church Rd, Cheadle, SK8 4NG
Held dear by the locals, this long-established eatery serves up undoubtedly good curries. This green-fronted shop opens up an entire world of culinary flawlessness to all of its guests.

25% OFF TOTAL | ♟ 2 | FRI ✓ | SAT × — Indian

SAEED'S ☎ 0161 480 5164
84 Wellington Road South, Stockport, SK1 3SU
Guests can feast upon sizzling nirali and karahi dishes in this family-run Indian eatery. Using only the most traditional of recipes, this venue prepares an array of favourites.

25% OFF TOTAL | ♟ 4 | FRI × | SAT × | ✱ — Indian

SAME YET INN ☎ 0161 653 1430
145 Simister Lane, Prestwich, M25 2SF
A warm welcome and a comfortable relaxed atmosphere will add to your enjoyment of the quality food and drink served at Same Yet Inn. They are committed to providing customers excellent pub grub.

2FOR1 3 COURSES | FRI ✓ | SAT × | SUN — British

SAN LORENZO ☎ 01457 833 495
The Old Fire Station, Mossley, OL5 9BB
San Lorenzo brings Southern Italian cuisine with a strong Neapolitan influence to the heart of Mossley. Through the menu, the talented and passionate chefs showcase some of the best seasonal dishes around.

2FOR1 MAIN COURSE | FRI 📱 | SAT 📱 — Italian

SANGAM
☎ 0161 436 8809

202 Wilmslow Rd, Heald Green, Stockport, SK8 3BH

One of the two successful Sangam restaurants situated in Manchester. Popular for its delicious Indian cuisine and courteous service, guests will undoubtedly leave with an eye on their return.

2FOR1 MAIN COURSE | FRI ✓ | SAT ✱ — Indian

SANGAM
☎ 0161 446 1155

762 Wilmslow Rd, Didsbury, M20 2DR

Sangam Didsbury is every bit as attractive as its sister restaurant. Popular for its delicious Indian cuisine and courteous service, guests will undoubtedly leave desiring to return.

2FOR1 MAIN COURSE | FRI ✓ | SAT ✱ — Indian

SANGAM RESTAURANT
☎ 0161 225 5785

9-15 Wilmslow Road, Manchester, M14 5TB

One of the stars featuring on the famous Curry Mile, Sangam provides an excellent backdrop to a perfect night out. Consistently tasty Indian cuisine makes this a winning choice.

2FOR1 3 COURSES | FRI ✱ | SAT ✱ | SUN — Indian

SARAY
☎ 0161 881 8292

609 Wilbraham Road, Manchester, M21 9AN

Growing demands for Mediterranean and Middle Eastern cuisine in the Western world has encouraged restaurateurs to provide offerings of such tasty foreign flavours.

50% OFF FOOD | 6 | FRI ✱ | SAT ✱ | ▲ — Turkish

SAVOY SPICE
☎ 0161 406 9000

148 Stockport Rd, Stockport, SK6 3AN

Open, family-friendly modern Indian restaurant featuring a great range of dishes: classic curries alongside more eclectic, sophisticated subcontinental flavours. Try the balti silisa or shashi haleem.

2FOR1 MAIN COURSE | FRI ✱ | SAT ✱ — Indian

SIAM ORCHID
☎ 01612 361 388

54 Portland Street, Manchester, M1 4QU

One of Manchester's first Thai restaurants. Cosy and intimate, here you can enjoy scrumptious cuisine in calm and relaxed settings. Alternatively head to the bar which boasts full karaoke facilities.

2FOR1 2 COURSES | FRI ✱ | SAT ✱ | ▲ — Thai

SIMPLE BAR
☎ 0161 832 8764

44 Tib Street, Manchester, M4 1LA

In the bohemian Northern Quarter, Simple offers a laid back atmosphere for eating, drinking and socialising, mixing the style of a restaurant and ambiance of a bar to give you the best service possible.

25% OFF TOTAL | 4 | FRI × | SAT × | ▲ — British

SMOAK BAR & GRILL
☎ 0161 278 1000

Piccadilly, Manchester, M1 1LZ

A grill room and bar unlike anything sensed before. Incredible sunken bar demands to be tried whilst the best meats and fish are 'smoaked' over bespoke chippings creating a unique aroma and taste.

2FOR1 MAIN COURSE | FRI × | SAT × | SUN | ▲ — European

SOTTOVENTO RESTAURANT
☎ 01204 862 952

69 Worsley Road, Farnworth, BL4 9LU

Authentic Italian restaurant combining well-known favourites and rarer regional delicacies. With warm Mediterranean hospitality, it's a fantastic place to settle in, sit back and enjoy a fine meal.

2FOR1 3 COURSES | FRI ✓ | SAT × — Italian

THE SPICE LOUNGE
☎ 01942 494 909

Flax Mill, Brethertons Row, Wigan, WN1 1LL

Classic Indian restaurant in Wigan. Broad menu with a big range; much more in the way of eclectic specialities than your average curry house. The hot but sweet chilli madhu, or the imlee gosht, stand out.

2FOR1 3 COURSES | FRI ✱ | SAT ✱ — Indian

SPICE TOWER
☎ 0161 483 9988

198 Marple Road, Stockport, SK2 5EU

Always going the extra mile to provide outstanding service and fine food, Spice Tower uses excellent recipes, spices and ingredients to create superb Indian dishes.

2FOR1 MAIN COURSE | FRI × | SAT × | SUN — Indian

SPICY HUT RESTAURANT
0161 248 6200

35 Wilmslow Road, Manchester, M14 5BT

Combining the mouth-watering tastes of India and Pakistan, this venue is nestled in Manchester's renowned Curry Mile. *Offer excludes sizzlers. Cannot be used inconjunction with BYO offer.

2FOR1 MAIN COURSE | FRI × | SAT × | ✱ | ▲ — Indian/Pakistani

ST PETERSBURG
☎ 0161 236 6333

68 Sackville Street, Manchester, M1 3NJ

Fantastic Russian restaurant with an enviable reputation for the quality of its cuisine. Features a great range of authentic, traditional dishes: rich soups, stews and savoury pancakes. A pleasure to dine.

2FOR1 3 COURSES | FRI ✱ | SAT ✱ — Russian

STABLES RESTAURANT
☎ 0161 366 0300

276 Stockport Road, Hyde, SK14 5RF

Fine family-run restaurant that offers a relaxed and relaxing place to dine. Fresh and beautifully presented food from a wide-ranging Modern British menu has helped gain it a fine reputation locally.

25% OFF TOTAL | 8 | FRI × | SAT × | ✱ | ▲ — Modern British

STANDARD BALTI RESTAURANT
0161 748 2806

12 Higher Road, Urmston, M41 9BP

Standard Balti offers an array of excellent Indian dishes and has a great reputation for doing all the simple things well. The food is well spiced, uses quality ingredients, and comes in sizeble portions.

50% OFF FOOD | 10 | FRI ✱ | SAT ✱ — Indian

STAR OF BENGAL
☎ 01706 649 901

171 Yorkshire Street, Rochdale, OL12 0DR

A long-standing success of a restaurant, Star of Bengal offers tried and tested dishes to suit any taste buds. The Indian, balti and tandoori cuisine make this restaurant a Rochdale favourite.

2FOR1 3 COURSES | FRI ✱ | SAT ✓ — Indian

STEP IN INDIA
☎ 01706 345 888

4-6 St Mary's Gate, Rochdale, OL16 1DZ

Quality restaurant endeavouring to serve the finest Indian cuisine in a relaxing, contemporary atmosphere. Staff are attentive and offer diners their knowledge of the house specialities.

25% OFF TOTAL | FRI 📱 | SAT 📱 — Indian

STOCK
☎ 0161 839 6644

The Stock Exchange, 4 Norfolk St, Manchester, M2 1DW

Housed within Manchester's Edwardian former Stock Exchange, this inimitable Italian cuisine offers distinctive dishes, including the legendary steak Fiorentina, coupled with award-winning wines.

50% OFF FOOD | 2 | FRI 📱 | SAT ✱ | SUN | ▲ — Italian

STRESA
☎ 0161 876 5305

Ramada, Trafford Road, Salford Quays, M5 3AW

The ideal location for business lunches, match-day meals and pre-theatre dinners. Chefs create rustic Italian favourites and innovative dishes from a huge selection of meat, fish and vegetarian choices.

25% OFF TOTAL | 8 | FRI ✓ | SAT ✓ — Italian

SUHAG SPICE LOUNGE
☎ 01706 643 187

185 Yorkshire Street, Rochdale, OL12 0DR

Distinctive Indian restaurant in Rochdale that serves fresh and extremely flavourful dishes - deep, aromatic sauces; sweet, smoky or spice-laden marinades - with exceptional, attentive service.

2FOR1 2 COURSES | FRI 📱 | SAT 📱 | ✱ | ▲ — Indian

THE SUNAR GAW
☎ 01204 364 915

310 Manchester Road, Bolton, BL3 2QS

The Sunar Gaw is a popular Indian restaurant in Bolton that does a cracking range of curries and other delicacies, full in flavour and at an excellent price.

2FOR1 MAIN COURSE | FRI ✱ | SAT ✱ — Indian

SUNDORBON TANDOORI
☎0161 775 2812

40 Liverpool Road, Cadishead, M44 5AF

Good old-fashioned tandoori restaurant in Salford that serves an eclectic and very tasty array of dishes. Traditional curries, balti specials and some excellent Persian dishes, like the sweet-sour pathia.

2FOR1 3 COURSES | FRI ✱ | SAT ✱ — Indian

SWADESH
☎0161 941 5311

3 Richmond Rd, Bowdon, Altrincham, WA14 2TT

Sister restaurant to the Manchester Swadesh, this exclusive Indian restaurant offers vibrant cuisine in a stunningly furnished interior. Treasured ancient recipes provide deliciously authentic dishes.

2FOR1 MAIN COURSE | FRI ✗ | SAT ✱ — Indian

SWADESH
☎0161 236 1313

98 Portland St, Manchester, M1 4GY

Sister restaurant to Swadesh Bowden, this exclusive Indian restaurant offers vibrant cuisine in the very heart of the city. Treasured ancient recipes provide deliciously authentic dishes.

2FOR1 MAIN COURSE | FRI ✓ | SAT ✱ — Indian

SWINGING BRIDGE
0161 749 4184

Trafford Boulevard, Urmston, Manchester, M41 7JE

Quality pub classics with modern twists meets with a friendly and relaxed atmosphere to make this Table Table venue the perfect place for any occasion. *Excludes daytime & evening deals and festive menus.

2FOR1 MAIN COURSE | FRI ✓ | SAT ✓ — Modern British

TABLE TABLE MANCHESTER CITY CENTRE
01612 375 335

7-11 Lower Mosley Street, Manchester, M2 3DW

Quality pub classics with modern twists meets with a friendly and relaxed atmosphere to make this Table Table venue the perfect place for any occasion. *Excludes daytime & evening deals and festive menus.

2FOR1 MAIN COURSE | FRI ✓ | SAT ✓ — Modern British

TANDOORI NIGHTS MANCHESTER
☎0161 740 3100

252 Middleton Road, Manchester, M8 4WA

A popular local place on the edge of Heaton Park that does good, old-fashioned satisfying curries for hungry bellies and those looking for the makings of a good evening out.

2FOR1 3 COURSES | FRI ✓ | SAT ✓ — Indian

TASTE OF BENGAL
☎01257 473 119

11 High Street, Standish, Wigan, WN6 0HA

Good Indian restaurant in the centre of Standish. Cosy, welcoming place to dine with well-drilled service and warm hospitality. Plentiful, subtle food with a good kick where necessary.

2FOR1 3 COURSES | FRI ✱ | SAT ✱ — Indian

THAI BANANA
☎0161 248 7752

262 Wilmslow Road, Manchester, M14 6JR

Great Thai restaurant in a vibrant area of Manchester. Friendly, efficient service together with a fine range of authentic dishes. A cool noodle bar with excellent Thai-style noodle dishes and soups.

2FOR1 MAIN COURSE | FRI ✗ | SAT ✗ | ▲ — Thai

THE TOP TIER GRILL
☎01706 644 513

Soccer Village, Wild House Lane, Rochdale, OL16 3TW

Sports-themed restaurant venue that features tasty, unfussy food, cooked properly and served generously. Go for something off the grill menu like the lambs liver with red wine.

2FOR1 3 COURSES | FRI ✱ | SAT ✱ — British

TV21
0161 819 2221

10 Thomas Street, Manchester, M4 1DH

Good selection of home-made food at this trendy bar and restaurant in the Northern Quarter. TV, film and arts-themed venue. *Two courses must be ordered. Offer excludes 'Ladies Night' menus.

2FOR1 2 COURSES | FRI ✗ | SAT ✗ — Mexican

VASAMI
☎0161 480 7013

37 St Petersgate, Stockport, SK1 1DH

Revitalising a concept of the modern art of dining, Vasami demonstrates diverse style, slicing the core of Indian and Continental finesse with its vibrant atmosphere, efficient service and ambiance.

2FOR1 3 COURSES | FRI ✓ | SAT ✓ | ▲ — Indian

VERVE GRILL
0161 366 3700

Village Hotel Hyde, Captain Clark Road, Hyde, SK14 4QG

Authentically cosmopolitan, diners experience chic and modish décor at this contemporary venue. Boasting prime steaks and the 'Hot Rock Grill Experience', the menu is bursting with choice.

2FOR1 3 COURSES | FRI ✓ | SAT ✓ | SUN | ✱ — British

VIVA ESPANA
☎01204 438 235

12 Winter Hey Road, Horwich, BL6 7AA

A brilliantly welcoming little slice of Spain in Horwich. For a cosy, intimate setting, look no further than Viva Espana, where freshly prepared, Murcia-inspired tapas dishes are readily available.

25% OFF TOTAL | 6 | FRI ✓ | SAT ✗ | ▲ — Tapas

VOUJON
☎0161 682 4600

688-692 Manchester Road, Oldham, OL9 7ST

Experience a little piece of India in Lancashire, with a combination of classic Indian dishes and less well-known specialities guaranteed to enthral your taste buds. A must-visit restaurant.

25% OFF TOTAL | 10 | FRI ✱ | SAT ✱ | SUN | ▲ — Indian

WALKABOUT
☎0161 817 4800

13 Quay Street, Manchester, M3 3HN

Walkabout is famous for its characteristically Australian atmosphere and well-rounded menu. From live sport with a juicy burger to some Aussie kangaroo skewers, you'll find it hard to tear yourself away.

25% OFF TOTAL | 10 | FRI ✓ | SAT ✓ | ▲ — International

THE WATERSIDE RESTAURANT
☎01706 376 250

1 Inghams lane, Littleborough, Rochdale, OL15 0AY

The chef's passion for food can be fully tasted in the deliciousness of all the dishes on offer. Drawing produce from each Mediterranean country, the food here captures the intense flavour of the region.

2FOR1 2 COURSES | FRI | SAT ✱ — Mediterranean

WENDY'S THAI FUSION
☎0161 860 0002

359 Barlow Moor Road, Manchester, M21 8AZ

Thai Cuisine has never been at its finest since Wendy's Thai Fusion launched in Chorlton, Manchester. All dishes are freshly prepared and combine the best of local produce with wonderful Thai flavours.

2FOR1 MAIN COURSE | FRI ✗ | SAT ✗ | ▲ — Thai

WHITEGATE INN
0161 681 1373

Broadway, Chadderton, Oldham, OL9 8DW

Beefeater Grill are one of the UK's best-loved restaurants welcoming guests for almost 40 years in over 130 locations nationwide. *Excludes Breakfast, Light Bites, Bar menu, set menus and all other offers.

2FOR1 MAIN COURSE | 6 | FRI ✓ | SAT ✗ | ▲ — Modern British

THE WINEGLASS @ ETROP GRANGE HOTEL
☎0161 499 0500

Thorley Lane, Manchester Airport, M90 4EG

Outstanding food and first class service has always been at the heart of Etrop Grange and the WineGlass restaurant offers this and more by delivering exquisite food prepared with precision.

25% OFF TOTAL | 8 | FRI ✓ | SAT ✓ | ▲ — European

WINSTONS PIZZA
☎01695 627 692

190 Upholland Road, Billinge, WN5 7DJ

Something of a phoenix from the flames. Having garnered national acclaim for the original place, the owners retired only to succumb to the bug; this revamped pizza place is the happy result.

2FOR1 3 COURSES | FRI ✱ | SAT ✱ — British

THE WOODSIDE
0161 7027 246

501 Ellenbrook Road, Worsley, Manchester, M28 1ES

This Vintage Inn oozes rural charm and rustic character. The picturesque surroundings provide the perfect backdrop for savouring the hearty, seasonal pub-food on the menu.

25% OFF TOTAL | FRI ✓ | SAT ✓ | SUN | ▲ — Modern British

YABA AFRICAN RESTAURANT
☎0161 226 6998

110 Hulme High Street, Manchester, M15 5JP

You'll enjoy a wonderful culinary experience in this imaginative, thoughtful restaurant that serves brilliant authentic Caribbean and African cuisine; a truly welcoming, unique place to eat.

2FOR1 MAIN COURSE | FRI ✱ | SAT ✱ | SUN — African

THE YETIS' RETREAT ☎0161 637 0559
464 Didsbury Road, Stockport, SK4 3BS
At the Yeti's Retreat, they have created some excellent dishes for you to enjoy. Combining these products with the typical flair and colours of Nepalese cooking they bring you a Nepalese taste sensation.

25% OFF TOTAL | 4 | FRI × | SAT × | SUN | * — Nepalese

ZAIKA 0161 839 5111
2 Gt Northern Tower, Watson St, Manchester, M3 4EE
Sensational cuisine that will have your mouth watering as soon as you enter. A thoroughly extensive menu, offering food from the homes of regional gourmet families and Maharaja's areas.

2FOR1 MAIN COURSE | FRI ✓ | SAT ✓ — Indian

ZING AND ZEST INDIAN FOOD BAR ☎0161 343 2131
126 Oldham Road, Oldham, OL7 9AH
Sharp, aromatic and sumptuous, Zing & Zest offers a mix of traditional curries and contemporary dishes with a twist from a range of fresh and authentic ingredients from the exotic South East.

2FOR1 3 COURSES | FRI × | SAT × | * | ♣ — Indian

ZURRI INDIAN TAPAS ☎0161 338 3211
80-84 Market St, Staleybridge, SK15 2AB
A fabulous restaurant that draws on the vibrancy of Indian cuisine in its atmosphere, service and décor. Serves all the classic favourites alongside the more unusual offerings.

2FOR1 MAIN COURSE | FRI ☐ | SAT ☐ | * | ♣ — Authentic Indian

Lancashire

1725 ☎0152 466 898
28 Market Street, Lancaster, LA1 1HT
Deliciously fresh, home-made tapas to be enjoyed with cask ales, choice wines and continental lagers, all in one of Lancaster's oldest buildings. Open all week with a lunch, evening and tapas menu.

25% OFF TOTAL | 4 | FRI ✱ | SAT ✱ | ♣ — Spanish

AJ'S BISTRO ☎01253 626 111
65 Topping Street, Blackpool, FY1 3AF
A step aside from typical seaside fare, AJ's bistro serves filling dishes of full-throated flavour, from its fresh and refulgent seafood assiette to its lustrous, succulent steaks of various cuts.

2FOR1 MAIN COURSE | FRI ✓ | SAT ✓ | * | ♣ — British

AKASH TANDOORI RESTAURANT ☎01253 626 677
76 Topping Street, Blackpool, FY1 3AD
Refuel with a warming curry after exploring one of Britain's most favourable seaside resorts. The attentive staff ensure that diners enjoy an impeccable experience.

2FOR1 2 COURSES | FRI ☐ | SAT ☐ — Indian

AROMA ASIAN RESTAURANT ☎01282 434 403
56 Church Street, Burnley, BB11 2DL
An extensive menu is one of the key highlights at Aroma Asian Restaurant, where modern takes on Asian classics appeal to the masses. Tantalising seafood specialities are also extremely popular.

2FOR1 MAIN COURSE | FRI × | SAT × | * | ♣ — Indian

AYAAN CHILLIES ☎01253 620 233
42-44 Talbot Road, Blackpool, FY1 1LF
Just up from the Promenade in Blackpool, Ayaan Chillies is a fine little Indian restaurant with a good atmosphere. The food is simple, tasty and full of flavour, with a good spicy edge where it's needed.

2FOR1 3 COURSES | FRI ✱ | SAT ✱ — Indian

THE BALTI HOUSE RISHTON ☎01254 888 883
1-3 High Street, Blackburn, BB1 4JZ
This long-established restaurant has expanded after gaining an exceptional reputation. Classic or unique, the dishes will tickle everyone's taste buds. Guests are permitted to bring their own alcohol.

25% OFF TOTAL | 4 | FRI × | SAT × — Indian

BANGLA FUSION WINEBAR RESTAURANT ☎01772 610 800
Liverpool Old Road, Preston, PR4 5JQ
A plush dining space opens up invitingly at this fusion restaurant near Preston, whose array of dishes draw on an innovative and eclectic range of flavours from across the Eastern and Western canons.

25% OFF TOTAL | 4 | FRI ✓ | SAT ✓ | * — Bangladeshi/Indian

BAY LEAVES ☎01257 260 331
54 Park Road, Chorley, PR7 1QU
Cool, accommodating Indian restaurant in Chorley with a fine selection of traditional subcontinental cuisine. Fluffy rice and naan bread, tasty vegetable dishes and some good cuts of meat do the trick.

2FOR1 3 COURSES | FRI ✓ | SAT ✓ — Indian

BLACK LANE ENDS TAVERN ☎01282 863 070
Skipton Old Road, Colne, BB8 7EP
A true country pub with a strong following of locals and frequent visitors. Experience a warm welcome, home-cooked food, real ales and much more at this traditional and friendly venue.

25% OFF TOTAL | 10 | FRI ✱ | SAT ✱ | SUN — British

THE BLUE MALLARD 01704 893 954
Burscough Wharf, Burscough, L40 5RZ
Run by local lads Chris, Matthew and Leon, this venue overlooks the canal-side and offers guests a picturesque environment to savour regional dishes with a contemporary twist. *A la carte menu only.

2FOR1 MAIN COURSE | FRI ✱ | SAT × | SUN | ♣ — Modern British

BOONNAK THAI RESTAURANT ☎01253 290 647
60 Topping Street, Blackpool, FY1 3AQ
Good-quality, authentic Thai food. Recently taken over, the new management and kitchen offer guests the chance to sample expertly made dishes from a menu filled with classic and contemporary options.

50% OFF FOOD | 6 | FRI ☐ | SAT ☐ — Thai

THE BROUGHTON INN 01772 864 288
502 Garstang Road, Preston, PR3 5HE
This Vintage Inn oozes rural charm and rustic character. The picturesque surroundings provide the perfect backdrop for savouring the hearty, seasonal pub-food on the menu.

25% OFF TOTAL | FRI ✓ | SAT ✓ | SUN | ♣ — Modern British

BROUGHTON'S RESTAURANT ☎01772 864 087
Preston Marriott Hotel, Preston, PR3 5JB
This opulent 4-star hotel plays host to this fabulous eatery where an exciting blend of traditional and contemporary dishes align the menu. Locally sourced and seasonal, there is something for everyone.

2FOR1 MAIN COURSE | FRI ✓ | SAT ✓ | SUN — International

CALYPSO CARIBBEAN RESTAURANT ☎01254 261 020
The Wharf, Blackburn, BB1 5BY
Kick start the weekend with an exotic dish and some authentic music to get you in the mood. Cooking methods mirror those used in homes on the Caribbean Islands.

2FOR1 MAIN COURSE | FRI × | SAT × | * — Caribbean

THE CARTLAND RESTAURANT ☎01253 724 636
307-313 Clifton Drive, Lytham St Annes, FY8 1HN
This hotel restaurant is designed to serve the needs of The Bedford's guests; as a result, its superb, homely food is also exceptionally appealing for visiting diners. Absolutely worth a try.

25% OFF TOTAL | 10 | FRI ✓ | SAT ✓ | * — English and Continental

CASCADES ☎01253 624 947
80 Dickson Road, Blackpool, FY1 2BU
Cascades' meals are something quite special. Imaginatively conceived, skilfully prepared and beautifully presented, they raise a smile even before your first bite.

25% OFF TOTAL | 6 | FRI ✓ | SAT × — English and Continental

CINNAMON ☎01257 426 661
487 Preston Road, Standish, WN6 0QD
The fine, fresh ingredients on which Cinnamon prides itself can be discerned in the restaurant's range of distinctive, flavourful dishes.

2FOR1 MAIN COURSE | FRI ✱ | SAT ✱ | SUN | * | ♣ — Indian

To understand what the restaurant icons mean, please see the inside back cover.

DALTON ROOMS
☎ 01524 845 785

14 Dalton Square, Lancaster, LA1 1PL

Warm and friendly bar and grill in the heart of Lancaster specialising in great beers and wines, locally sourced traditional food and top quality live entertainment.

2FOR1 3 COURSES | FRI ✓ | SAT ✓ — International

EAST Z EAST
☎ 01772 200 084

29 Church Street, Preston, PR1 3BQ

Some of the city's finest Punjabi cuisine is to be had at this Preston venue. A fabulously contemporary Indian dining experience in its vibe and excellent range of curries, handis, grills and balti dishes.

2FOR1 MAIN COURSE | FRI ✱ | SAT ✱ — Indian

FARINGTON LODGE
☎ 01772 421 321

Stanifield Lane, Farington, Leyland, PR25 4QR

A hidden gem of a hotel, Farington Lodge is a beautifully decorated place to rest and dine. The restaurant is elegant and charismatic, with original fireplaces adding to its charm.

2FOR1 3 COURSES | FRI ✓ | SAT ✓ — British

THE FOX CUB
01772 617 841

Bridge House Farm, Liverpool Road, PR4 5JT

This Vintage Inn oozes rural charm and rustic character. The picturesque surroundings provide the perfect backdrop for savouring the hearty, seasonal pub-food on the menu.

25% OFF TOTAL | FRI ✓ | SAT ✓ | SUN | ▲ — Modern British

FREDERICK'S
01257 263 154

Bolton Road Dairies, Heath Charnock, PR7 4AL

Frederick's Ice Cream offers not only luxury ice cream but light snacks, paninis and made-to-order pizzas. Frederick's offers customers an excellent range of lunch or tea bites.

25% OFF TOTAL | FRI × | SAT × | SUN — Italian

FREDERICK'S
01257 232 070

3 Cunliffe Street, Chorley, PR7 2BA

Frederick's Ice Cream offers not only luxury ice cream but light snacks, paninis and made-to-order pizzas. Frederick's offers customers an excellent range of lunch or tea bites.

25% OFF TOTAL | FRI ✓ | SAT × | SUN — Italian

FRESCO FRESCO
☎ 01772 601 100

29-31 Town Road, Croston, PR26 9RA

Fresh by name, fresh by nature. By focusing on the quality of its produce, grown to order by a market gardener family friend, this Italian restaurant charms and delights with exuberantly tasty dishes.

2FOR1 MAIN COURSE | FRI 📱 | SAT × | ▲ — Italian

GREAT FORTUNE
☎ 01253 858 899

120 Victoria Road West, Thornton-Cleveleys, FY5 3LG

Chefs use only prime cuts of chicken, beef and pork to prepare simmering dishes of oriental cuisine. Friendly and efficient, the staff welcome diners with friendly smiles in an ambient atmosphere.

2FOR1 MAIN COURSE | FRI ✓ | SAT ✓ — Chinese

THE GRESSINGHAM RESTAURANT
☎ 01524 751 766

Thurnahm Hall, Lancaster, LA2 0DT

Step back in time at this 12th Century country house, perched proudly on 30 acres of estate. Whether guests are seeking casual dinner or a fine dining experience, the Jacobean great hall plays host to all.

25% OFF TOTAL | 4 | FRI ✱ | SAT ✱ — British

THE HASTINGS
☎ 01253 732 400

26 Hastings Place, Lytham, FY8 5LZ

A fresh, well-regarded restaurant in Lytham whose Head Chef Warrick Dodds leads a team of talented chefs preparing sophisticated, sumptuous and accomplished cuisine.

2FOR1 MAIN COURSE | FRI ✱ | SAT ✱ | SUN — European

THE HIDDEN GEM
☎ 01772 823 695

134 Church Street, Preston, PR1 3BT

The Hidden Gem serves some of the world's greatest dishes alongside a selection of the most delicious wines.They offer everything from fine Italian Cuisine to traditional English food.

50% OFF FOOD | FRI ✓ | SAT 📱 | ✱ — British

KASHTI RESTAURANT AND BAR
☎ 01772 824 444

1 Broadgate, Preston, PR1 8DX

Bringing the beautiful tastes of Bangladesh to Lancashire, guests dine on dishes cooked by energetic chefs. Passionate about food, Kashti guarantees quality with a side order of flair and panache.

2FOR1 3 COURSES | FRI × | SAT × | ✱ — Indian

KING KARAI
☎ 01772 736 838

28-30 Watery Lane, Preston, PR2 2NN

Experience an authentic North Indian meal in a venue with a great reputation, safe in the knowledge that the food will be flavoursome and made to perfection.

2FOR1 MAIN COURSE | FRI ✓ | SAT ✓ | ✱ | ▲ — Indian

KWIZEEN
☎ 01253 290 045

47-49 King Street, Blackpool, FY1 3EJ

Dine on a simple menu that delivers fresh, bold flavours created using local seasonal produce. Expect smart wooden flooring, cream-coloured walls, and smooth jazz playing in relaxed atmosphere.

2FOR1 MAIN COURSE | FRI 📱 | SAT 📱 — Italian

LA PIAZZA
☎ 01253 295 277

8 Cedar Square, Blackpool, FY1 1BP

With an enviable reputation for serving fine Italian cuisine, La Piazza is proud of its kitchen, where well-chosen ingredients and recipes take priority. Ideally located in Cedar Square.

2FOR1 3 COURSES | FRI ✓ | SAT × — Italian

MAI'DA BLACKBURN
☎ 01254 676 797

16 Eanam, Blackburn, BB1 5BY

Mai'da Blackburn is a fantastic restaurant that serves a fine line in Indian and Indo-Chinese cuisine. Popular with good reason, the food is superbly fresh and excels in taste and flavour.

2FOR1 3 COURSES | FRI ✓ | SAT ✓ — Indian

MAMMA MIA AT CROSSWAYS
☎ 01282 772 170

Whalley Road, Burnley, BB12 8JR

A top-quality restaurant serving fine Italian cuisine, complete with an on-site take away so guests can enjoy fresh culinary delights in their own home. Enjoy the beautiful terrace for al fresco dining.

2FOR1 MAIN COURSE | FRI ✓ | SAT ✷ | ✱ | ▲ — Italian

MANGIAMO
☎ 01254 760 770

108 Bolton Road, Darwen, BB3 1BZ

A cosy, charismatic ambience to this Italian ristorante provides a fit setting for its ranging menu of earthy, flavourful traditional recipes. Look out for the specials nights.

2FOR1 3 COURSES | FRI ✓ | SAT ✷ | ✱ — Italian

MARCO'S RESTAURANT
☎ 01524 844 445

26 North Road, Lancaster, LA1 1NS

Seafood lovers can feast on succulent treats, whilst the more classic of palettes can banquet on an award-winning oven-baked pizza. Bringing a little slice of Italy to Lancaster, this venue is a must.

2FOR1 MAIN COURSE | FRI 📱 | SAT 📱 — Italian

THE MED TAVERNA
☎ 01253 622 936

21a Church St, Blackpool, FY1 1HJ

Feta with a creamy texture yet distinctive taste, juicy olives, succulent meat kebabs and stuffed vine leaves make up extremely tasty dishes at this Greek and Mediterranean restaurant in Blackpool.

50% OFF FOOD | 6 | FRI ✓ | SAT ✓ — Mediterranean

THE MEETING HOUSE
☎ 01524 848 049

11-15 Meeting House Lane, Lancaster, LA1 1TJ

With an abundance of excellent produce available on their doorstep, this restaurant creates a delicious menu of local meats and vegetables with a variety of traditional favourites and seasonal options.

25% OFF TOTAL | 4 | FRI × | SAT × — British

MEHERIN
☎ 01253 855 840

7 Anchorsholme Lane East, Thornton-Cleveleys, FY5 3QH

With its impressive menu, it is no surprise that this eatery has gained a fantastic reputation for itself after opening in 2007. Chefs flamboyantly blend aromatic spices to create mouth-watering recipes.

2FOR1 MAIN COURSE | FRI 📱 | SAT 📱 — Indian

MORRIS DANCERS
01704 880 201

Southport Road, Scarisbrick, Ormskirk, L40 9RG

Beefeater Grill are one of the UK's best-loved restaurants welcoming guests for almost 40 years in over 130 locations nationwide. *Excludes Breakfast, Light Bites, Bar menu, set menus and all other offers.

2FOR1 MAIN COURSE | 6 | FRI ✓ | SAT × | ▲ — Modern British

THE NAAZ RESTAURANT
☎ 01772 626 695

Club Street, Bamber Bridge, Preston, PR5 6FN

Not only do the meals satisfy any curry craving, the Naaz is authentic, delicious cuisine in a cool and crisp environment that is perfect for sharing a sumptuous feast with family and friends.

2FOR1 2 COURSES | FRI × | SAT × | ✱ — Indian

THE NEW HOLLY
☎ 01524 793 500

Lancaster Road, Preston, PR3 0BL

Once a 17th Century coaching inn, the New Holly brings contemporary elegance to the Lancashire countryside. A modern pub menu features fine-dining options alongside succulent grill choices.

2FOR1 MAIN COURSE | FRI 📱 | SAT ✷ | SUN | ✱ — Modern Pub

NEW INN YEALAND
☎ 01524 732 938

40 Yealand Road, Carnforth, LA5 9SJ

Chefs are habitually hospitable at this classically British eatery. Grumbling stomachs are guaranteed to be gratified with a substantial dish.

2FOR1 3 COURSES | FRI ✷ | SAT × | SUN — British

THE NEW PRESIDENT HOTEL
☎ 01253 624 460

320-324 North Promenade, Blackpool, FY1 2JG

Prestigious and well-experienced, Head Chef Philip Whittle boasts cooking for the Queen in her private London club for 14 years. Over-looking the Irish Sea, this venue promises a fine dining experience.

2FOR1 MAIN COURSE | FRI ✓ | SAT ✓ | ✱ | ▲ — British

NEW SEASONS TAPAS BAR
☎ 01257 241 040

13 St Thomas's Road, Chorley, PR7 1HP

The award winning New Season Tapas Bar & Bistro offers fusion food from the Mediterranean , North Africa and Middle East, in tapas dishes and an evening a la carte menu, with an extensive cocktail menu.

25% OFF TOTAL | 8 | FRI × | SAT × | ▲ — Spanish

NORMAN JEPSON
01772 651 580

Bluebell Way, Fulwood, Preston, PR2 5PZ

Beefeater Grill are one of the UK's best-loved restaurants welcoming guests for almost 40 years in over 130 locations nationwide. *Excludes Breakfast, Light Bites, Bar menu, set menus and all other offers.

2FOR1 MAIN COURSE | 6 | FRI ✓ | SAT × | ▲ — Modern British

O'MARLEYS RED LION
☎ 01254 260 222

Whitebirk Road, Blackburn, BB1 3HY

O'Marleys Red Lion was a finalist in the Food Pub Of The Year Awards 2012. Serving hearty home-made dishes and a choice of ales, this pub is perfect for lunch or an evening meal.

2FOR1 MAIN COURSE | FRI × | SAT × | SUN — British

OTHELLO'S
☎ 01253 751 567

54 Talbot Street, Blackpool, FY1 1LR

A warm welcome awaits you as you enter the tasteful yet timeless surroundings of this Greek taverna in the heart of Blackpool.Othello's serves mouth watering Greek delights and provides attentive service.

50% OFF FOOD | 4 | FRI 📱 | SAT 📱 | ✱ — Mediterranean

OVER COFFEE
☎ 01254 391 191

70-72 Blackburn Road, Accrington, Blackburn, BB5 1LE

Over Coffee's café-bistro style design is part of its charm, and with a range of menus, from soup and nibbles to a full bistro menu in the evening, it has become a popular spot for locals to socialise.

2FOR1 3 COURSES | FRI ✓ | SAT ✓ — International

PARK HOTEL
☎ 01524 380 322

1 St Oswald Street, Lancaster, LA1 3AS

Architecturally astounding, this venue boasts over 100 years of historicism. The dishes are home-made and best enjoyed washed down with a real ale or a crisp wine.

2FOR1 MAIN COURSE | FRI ✓ | SAT ✓ — European

PENDLE INN
☎ 01282 614 808

Barley, Burnley, BB12 9JX

A good old-fashioned English pub where quality home-cooked dishes are the order of the day. Their fine selection ranges from black pudding with mustard sauce and apple compote to the excellent Pendle Pie.

2FOR1 3 COURSES | FRI ✷ | SAT ✷ — British

PIPERS RESTAURANT
☎ 01995 606 665

46-47 High Street, Garstang, Preston, PR3 1EA

A beautiful restaurant with a warm, cottage feel, serving devilishly tasty food. Boasts delicious dishes made from local produce with a variety of ingredients being of Fair Trade origin.

2FOR1 3 COURSES | FRI 📱 | SAT ✷ | ✱ | ▲ — British

THE PLOUGH
☎ 01524 751 337

Plough Inn, Main Road, Galgate, LA2 0LQ

From a steak and stout pie to a Chinese chicken salad, The Plough serves smart, eclectic dishes in a warm and accommodating ambience, aiming for the feel of a local for locals and non-locals alike.

25% OFF TOTAL | 4 | FRI 📱 | SAT ✷ | SUN | ✱ — Modern Pub

Gourmet Society discount applies to the à la carte menu only, unless stated otherwise.

PRESTON SWALLOW HOTEL ☎01772 877 351
Preston New Road, Preston, PR5 0UL
After enjoying the breathtaking scenery of the Lake District, unwind in this award-winning restaurant which offers a fine dining experience. An expansive array of exquisite wines and dishes align the menu.

2FOR1 3 COURSES | FRI ✓ | SAT ✓ — International

PROMENADE RESTAURANT @ HILTON ☎01253 623 434
North Promenade Sea Front, Blackpool, FY1 2JQ
Bright westward windows face out to sea in this open and elegant Blackpool hotel restaurant. Broad à la carte menu served in a fine dining room with soft-coloured colonnades and deep purple fabrics.

50% OFF FOOD | 6 | FRI ✱ | SAT ✱ | ▲ — International

THE PUNCHBOWL ☎01995 603 360
5-9 Church Street, Churchtown, Preston, PR3 0HT
From a Fylde sausage to a Thai-spiced monkfish fillet, The Punchbowl serves smart, eclectic dishes in a warm and accommodating ambience, aiming for the feel of a local for locals and non-locals alike.

25% OFF TOTAL | 4 | FRI 📱 | SAT ✱ | SUN | ✱ — Modern Pub

QUITE SIMPLY FRENCH ☎01524 843 199
27a St George's Quay, Lancaster, LA1 1RD
Committing itself to its name, this restaurant has an ever-changing menu bursting with magnificent French dishes for you to devour. *Offer excludes Lobster.

2FOR1 MAIN COURSE | FRI ✓ | SAT ✱ | SUN | ▲ — French

THE RAJ ☎01772 633 456
113 Lytham Road, Warton, PR4 1AD
A simple, effective restaurant that serves authentic Indian and Bangladeshi cuisine to Warton locals. It's gotten itself a sound reputation for some excellent curries, especially their thali dishes.

2FOR1 MAIN COURSE | FRI × | SAT × | SUN — Indian

RED LION 01253 354 942
Devonshire Road, Bispham, Blackpool, FY2 0AR
Beefeater Grill are one of the UK's best-loved restaurants welcoming guests for almost 40 years in over 130 locations nationwide. *Excludes Breakfast, Light Bites, Bar menu, set menus and all other offers.

2FOR1 MAIN COURSE | 6 | FRI ✓ | SAT × | ▲ — Modern British

THE RIVER WYRE 01253 893 428
Breck Road, Poulton-Le-Fylde, FY6 7JZ
This Vintage Inn oozes rural charm and rustic character. The picturesque surroundings provide the perfect backdrop for savouring the hearty, seasonal pub-food on the menu.

25% OFF TOTAL | FRI ✓ | SAT ✓ | SUN | ▲ — Modern British

THE SANDPIPER 01695 733 666
Holly Farm, Ormskirk Old Rd, Ormskirk, L39 0HD
This Vintage Inn oozes rural charm and rustic character. The picturesque surroundings provide the perfect backdrop for savouring the hearty, seasonal pub-food on the menu.

25% OFF TOTAL | FRI ✓ | SAT ✓ | SUN | ▲ — Modern British

SEAFARERS ☎01253 722 272
341-343 Clifton Drive South, Lytham St Annes, FY8 1LP
A great little restaurant on Clifton Road South, just up from the promenade in Lytham St Annes, Seafarers serves classic fish and chips in lovely surroundings.

2FOR1 3 COURSES | FRI ✓ | SAT ✓ — Seafood

SEAFOOD & STEAK RESTAURANT ☎01253 342 251
25 Bond Street, Blackpool, FY4 1BQ
Reaching for high levels of cooking and excellent standard of service, this restaurant does exactly what it says on the tin. The tastes of the sea meet the flavours of the land.

50% OFF FOOD | FRI 📱 | SAT 📱 — Steakhouse/ Seafood

THE SHOVELS INN ☎01253 700 209
Green Meadow Lane, Hambleton, FY6 9AL
This venue is the longest-standing pub in Hambleton, a fitting testament to their quality food, drinks, entertainment and exceptional customer service.

2FOR1 3 COURSES | FRI ✓ | SAT ✓ — British

SLICE OF SICILY 01772 750 040
7 Priory Lane, Preston, PR1 0AR
A deli, bistro and pizzeria in Preston. Friendly and open, the food is all about the quality of the ingredients: superb meats, cheeses and olives. *A minimum of 2 courses must be purchased.

2FOR1 3 COURSES | FRI 📱 | SAT 📱 — Italian

SPICE LOUNGE ☎01254 247 583
Wilpshire Road, Blackburn, BB1 4AD
The rich vibrancy of India is captured as chefs produce refined and creative Indian food. The menu incorporates classic favourites and new dishes that apply Eastern flavours with a Western touch.

2FOR1 3 COURSES | FRI ✱ | SAT ✱ | ✱ | ▲ — Indian

STEAK & GRILL @ TICKLED TROUT HOTEL ☎0844 879 9053
Preston New Road, Samlesbury, PR5 0UJ
Traditional favourites with a modern twist in the welcoming Tickled Trout restaurant. A range of fine British cuisine served in the excellent surroundings of this hotel, with its views across the Ribble.

50% OFF FOOD | 2 | FRI ✓ | SAT ✓ | ▲ — Bistro

STICKY CHOPS RESTAURANT ☎01772 933 865
Miller Arcade, Preston, PR1 2QY
A fun take on the American steakhouse, Sticky Chops is perfect for those who don't take dining too seriously.

50% OFF FOOD | 4 | FRI ✓ | SAT × — Chinese

STRAWBURY DUCK ☎01204 852 013
Overshores Road, Turton, BL7 0LU
Cosy up by the roaring log fires whilst nursing an award-winning ale at this Lancashire-based inn. Sample local favourites such as hearty black pudding, hash browns with poached egg, and crispy pancetta.

25% OFF TOTAL | 4 | FRI ✓ | SAT × | SUN | ✱ — British

SYKESIDE COUNTRY HOUSE HOTEL ☎01706 831 163
Rawtenstall Road End, Haslingden, BB4 6QE
Charming traditional hotel-based restaurant which serves a ranging menu of warming, delicious dishes; combined with the cosy and genial atmosphere, it's a place really to savour.

2FOR1 3 COURSES | FRI ✓ | SAT 📱 | SUN | ▲ — British

TERRY'S BALTI HOUSE ☎0871 811 5023
48 Clifton Street, Blackpool, FY1 1JP
Kick-start the evening with an exquisite Indian dish from Terry's Balti House before exploring one of Britain's best seaside resorts. Guaranteed to appease hungry diners with authentic cuisine.

2FOR1 2 COURSES | FRI ✓ | SAT ✓ — Indian

TOAST CAFE BAR & GRILL ☎01253 749 777
21-23 Wood St, Lytham St Annes, FY8 1QR
Toast Café Bar & Grill Restaurant is one of St Annes newest contemporary cafés and restaurants offering an extensive modern lunch café menu by day and an exclusive á la carte menu from 5pm every evening.

2FOR1 MAIN COURSE | FRI ✱ | SAT × | ✱ | ▲ — Mediterranean

TOAST CAFÉ BAR & GRILL ☎01253 749 777
28 Corporation Street, Blackpool, FY1 1EJ
Beautifully presented food, created fresh from high-quality ingredients. A perfect place for relaxing, dining and drinking in the heart of Blackpool.

2FOR1 MAIN COURSE | FRI ✱ | SAT ✱ | ✱ | ▲ — Mediterranean

TRADERS BRASSERIE ☎01254 602 022
The Globe Centre, Accrington, BB5 0RE
Support the talented chefs of the future at this elegant contemporary restaurant. Wonderful dishes are prepared by chefs-in-training, guaranteeing guests a first-class dining experience.

2FOR1 MAIN COURSE | FRI ✱ | SAT ✱ | SUN | ▲ — Brasserie

TRADERS RESTAURANT @ HOLIDAY INN ☎0871 942 9047
Holiday Inn, Lancaster, LA1 3RA
Modern takes on British classics make the menu at Traders Restaurant a fine attribute of the establishment. Clean, contemporary surrounds makes this an enjoyable place to dine.

50% OFF FOOD | 6 | FRI ✓ | SAT ✓ — British

VARDONS RESTAURANT
☎ 01257 269 221

Shaw Hill Hotel, Preston Road, PR6 7PP

Situated in a splendid Georgian mansion, Vardon's offers you award-winning dishes in the most delightful of settings. Look out over the golf course as your culinary delight is prepared.

25% OFF TOTAL | 4 | FRI ✓ | SAT ✓ | SUN — Fine Dining

THE VILLA COUNTRY HOUSE HOTEL
☎ 01772 804 040

Wrea Green, Preston, PR4 2PE

Whether it's a relaxed casual evening or a touch of formality that you're after, The Villa offers many options to diners who can enjoy a thoughtful, well-crafted menu prepared by chef Nigel Smith.

2FOR1 3 COURSES | FRI × | SAT × | SUN — Modern British

VUJON
☎ 01257 266 680

Eaves Green Road, Chorley, PR7 3QG

At Vujon, they take great pride in authentic quality cooking and exemplary standards of service. Varying from house specials and chef's recommendations, there is something on this menu for everyone.

2FOR1 2 COURSES | FRI × | SAT × | SUN | ✱ — Indian

WALKABOUT
☎ 01253 749 132

1-9 Queen Street, Blackpool, FY1 1NL

Walkabout is famous for its characteristically Australian atmosphere and well-rounded menu. From live sport with a juicy burger to some Aussie kangaroo skewers, you'll find it hard to tear yourself away.

25% OFF TOTAL | 10 | FRI ✓ | SAT ✓ — International

WALKABOUT
☎ 01282 455 714

10-14 Hammerton Street, Burnley, BB11 1NA

Walkabout is famous for its characteristically Australian atmosphere and well-rounded menu. From live sport with a juicy burger to some Aussie kangaroo skewers, you'll find it hard to tear yourself away.

25% OFF TOTAL | 10 | FRI ✓ | SAT ✓ — International

THE WALTON FOX
01772 323 364

Lostock Lane, Bamber Bridge, Preston, PR5 6BZ

This Vintage Inn oozes rural charm and rustic character. The picturesque surroundings provide the perfect backdrop for savouring the hearty, seasonal pub-food on the menu.

25% OFF TOTAL | FRI ✓ | SAT ✓ | SUN — Modern British

Merseyside

107 DINING ROOM
☎ 0151 342 3420

107 Telegraph Road, Wirall, CH60 0AF

Fusion dining at its best, the chefs prepare undoubtedly tasty dishes which are exquisitely presented. Al fresco dining is available all year, while the restaurant's interior has been designed for comfort.

2FOR1 3 COURSES | FRI × | SAT × — International

110 RESTAURANT AND BAR
0151 702 7610

Genting Club, Liverpool, L1 1RH

Set in the heart of the city centre, the 110 Restaurant offers a new culinary dining experience. Serving fresh soups, char-grilled steaks and creamy cheesecakes, this venue is perfect for every occasion.

2FOR1 3 COURSES | 10 | FRI ✱ | SAT ✱ | ✱ — European

1770 AT CIRCO
☎ 0151 709 0470

Britannia Pavilion, Albert Dock, Liverpool, L3 4AD

Roll up! Roll up! Ladies and gentlemen, the most amazing and spectacular Circo is the North West's most unique circus themed venue. Circo is the perfect place to relax for drinks and food.

2FOR1 3 COURSES | FRI ✱ | SAT × — British

ACADEMY RESTAURANT
☎ 0151 252 4512

Tradewind Square, Duke Street, Liverpool, L1 5BG

Support the talented chefs of the future at this terrific on-site restaurant. Wonderful dishes are prepared by chefs-in-training, guaranteeing guests a first-class dining experience.

2FOR1 MAIN COURSE | FRI ✱ | SAT × | SUN — Modern European

ALAM BALTI HOUSE
☎ 0151 643 8600

184 Bebington Road, Wirral, CH63 7NX

Alam Balti House is like a home from home in terms of comfort and relaxation; however when it comes to the food, you will be transported to a different continent entirely. Superb Indian cuisine.

2FOR1 2 COURSES | FRI ✱ | SAT ✱ | ✱ — Indian

ALMOND RESTAURANT AND BAR
☎ 0151 226 0021

16 Mill Lane, Liverpool, L12 7JB

An internationally inspired menu means that diners can follow the scent of their appetite after they've arrived. From Thai green curry to a braised lamb shank, there's something for everyone.

2FOR1 MAIN COURSE | FRI × | SAT × | ✱ — English and Continental

AUBERGE BRASSERIE
☎ 01704 530 671

1B Seabank Road, Southport, PR9 0EW

This lively and welcoming brasserie is decked out in traditional wood, vibrant red hues, sparkling mirrors and chandeliers. All the food is freshly prepared on the premises, from ice creams to breads.

2FOR1 3 COURSES | FRI × | SAT × | ✱ — Modern European

BEEF GRILL AND BAR
☎ 0151 342 196

154-158 Telegraph Road, Wirral, CH60 0AH

Highly reputable yet affordable, this is a venue that caters to a variety of taste buds. From succulent steaks to bursting burritos, fantastic service is always guaranteed.

2FOR1 MAIN COURSE | FRI ✓ | SAT ✓ — American

BEL PIATTO
☎ 0151 345 9694

1 Monument Place, Liverpool, L3 8JY

Divine Italian food served just how you like it: fresh, imaginative flavours created from traditional recipes. Creamy risottos, spicy pasta dishes and smooth wines make for a perfect dinner.

50% OFF FOOD | FRI ✓ | SAT ✓ | SUN — Italian

BELLA ITALIA
0151 707 2121

39 Ranelagh Street, Liverpool, L1 1JP

Accessible Italian cuisine on the British high street - indulge in authentic sharing platters, hand stretched pizzas and hearty pasta dishes, served with a healthy dose of gregarious Italian hospitality.

25% OFF TOTAL | 6 | FRI × | SAT × | SUN — Italian

BELLA ITALIA
01704 514 571

Ocean plaza, Marine parade, Southport, PR8 1SB

Accessible Italian cuisine on the British high street - indulge in authentic sharing platters, hand stretched pizzas and hearty pasta dishes, served with a healthy dose of gregarious Italian hospitality.

25% OFF TOTAL | 6 | FRI × | SAT × | SUN — Italian

THE BIERKELLER
08455 333 000

8 Thomas Steers Way, Liverpool Way, Liverpool, L1 8LW

The Bierkeller Liverpool is something a little different, a truly unique Bavarian experience. Be sure to give them a call to reserve a table for a night of wholesome Bavarian food, drink and music.

2FOR1 3 COURSES | FRI ✓ | SAT × — European

BLUE BAR & GRILL
☎ 0151 702 5831

Albert Dock, Liverpool, L3 4AE

Ideally situated on Liverpool's most prestigious dock, this venue is both sophisticated and chic. Not only is the menu fresh and diverse, the bar also provides fantastic late-night entertainment.

50% OFF FOOD | 6 | FRI × | SAT × | ✱ — International

BLUNDELL STREET
☎ 0151 709 5779

63-65 Blundell Street, Liverpool, L1 0AJ

Unique venue, a cabaret restaurant combining an eclectic range of dishes with equally eclectic live entertainment. A vibrant and fun place to enjoy the likes of Jamaican red snappers with fondant potato.

25% OFF TOTAL | 10 | FRI ✓ | SAT ✓ | SUN — European

BOLLYWOOD LOUNGE
☎ 0151 512 2521

33-37 Grange Road West, Birkenhead, CH41 4BY

Combining the vibrant colours of Bollywood dance with the tastes and aromas of India, Bollywood Lounge has created a unique take on Indian cuisine. Holds down a fantastic reputation in the area.

2FOR1 MAIN COURSE | FRI ▯ | SAT ▯ | ✱ — Indian

BROOKLYN'S AMERICAN RESTAURANT
☎ 0151 630 5779

Marine Point, King's Parade, New Brighton, CH45 2PB

Brooklyn's Restaurants aim to bring a fresh approach to dining; the very best from New York (huge menu choice, excellent service, fantastic quality and a great price) to the UK for the whole family.

2FOR1 3 COURSES | FRI × | SAT × | SUN | ▲ — American

CAFÉ ROUGE
0151 258 1879

Upper Floor Level, The Met Quarter, Liverpool L1 6AU

An attractive restaurant, a boulevard café or a Parisian-style wine bar; however you see Café Rouge, consistently excellent classic French dishes are always guaranteed.

25% OFF TOTAL | 6 | FRI ✓ | SAT ✓ | ✱ | ▲ — French

CAFÉ ROUGE
0151 709 8657

14 Paradise Street, Liverpool One, Liverpool L1 8JF

An attractive restaurant, a boulevard café or a Parisian-style wine bar; however you see Café Rouge, consistently excellent classic French dishes are always guaranteed.

25% OFF TOTAL | 6 | FRI ✓ | SAT ✓ | ✱ | ▲ — French

CAFÉ SEKANDER
☎ 0151 724 4300

156 Allerton Road, Liverpool, L18 6HG

If you're hungry for curry then head to Café Sekander for exciting culinary delights. Efficient and friendly staff are more than happy to cater to your every need.

2FOR1 MAIN COURSE | FRI × | SAT × | SUN — Indian

CAMBRIDGE HOUSE HOTEL
☎ 01704 538 372

4 Cambridge Road, Southport, PR9 9NG

A hotel that styles itself as a place of 'time honoured elegance', and this is nowhere more apparent than in their lovely dining rooms, where you can settle in to enjoy a fine range of traditional dishes.

2FOR1 3 COURSES | FRI ✓ | SAT ✓ | SUN | ✱ | ▲ — British

CASA MIA
☎ 0151 625 1503

1 Grange Road, West Kirby, CH48 4DY

A glowing restaurant specialising in lavish Italian cuisine. A brilliantly friendly atmosphere in which great food and wonderful wines can be enjoyed.

25% OFF TOTAL | 2 | FRI ✱ | SAT ✱ | SUN | ✱ — Italian

CHILLI POT
☎ 0151 236 7655

26 North John Street, Liverpool, L2 9RU

Undeniably good at what it does, Chilli Pot serves Thai cuisine perfect every time. From an aromatic noodle soup to crispy spring rolls, the dishes are spirited with truly fresh produce.

2FOR1 MAIN COURSE | FRI × | SAT × | SUN | ▲ — Thai

CHINA RESTAURANT
☎ 01704 548 972

85 Eastbank Street, Southport, PR8 1DG

Classic, accomplished local Chinese restaurant generating dishes with a depth of flavour, and an atmosphere that is calm, collected and accommodating.

25% OFF TOTAL | 10 | FRI ✓ | SAT ✓ — Chinese

CHINESE DELIGHT RESTAURANT
☎ 0151 920 8887

98 South Road, Waterloo, Liverpool, L22 0LY

Scrumptious traditional Chinese dishes can be enjoyed in stylish, relaxed surroundings. Reasonably priced meals make this an excellent place to dine with family and friends.

2FOR1 MAIN COURSE | FRI ▯ | SAT ▯ | ▲ — Chinese

CINNAMON RESTAURANT & BAR
☎ 0151 922 3370

211 Stanley Road, Bootle, L20 3DY

Cinnamon Restaurant offers an extensive menu filled with Indian and Turkish cuisine. All dishes are freshly made and the staff are well informed for those of you that like a suggestion from the menu.

2FOR1 2 COURSES | FRI ✓ | SAT ✓ — Indian

THE COUNTING HOUSE
☎ 01744 739 562

16 Hardshaw Street, St Helens, WA10 1RE

The Counting House in St Helens is a big, welcoming pub that shows a massive selection of live sport and combines that with some good old-fashioned pub/bar-style food.

50% OFF FOOD | 4 | FRI ▯ | SAT ▯ — British

CROMPTON'S
☎ 0151 709 7200

Ranelagh Place, Liverpool, L3 5UL

Cromptons is located in the internationally famous Adelphi Hotel which has been fully refurbished and is located in the heart of Liverpool City Centre and offers a French fine dining experience.

50% OFF FOOD | 10 | FRI ✓ | SAT ✓ | SUN | ✱ | ▲ — French

CROWNE PLAZA
☎ 0151 243 8000

St Nicholas Place, Princes Dock, Liverpool, L3 1QW

A fine attribute of the Crowne Plaza Liverpool, Plaza Brasserie serves up delicious dishes, created by chefs who draw upon modern international flavours and tastes. Contemporary, relaxing place to dine.

50% OFF FOOD | 4 | FRI ✓ | SAT ✓ — International

DERBY LODGE
0151 480 4440

Roby Road, Huyton, Liverpool, L36 4HD

Quality pub classics with modern twists meets with a friendly and relaxed atmosphere to make this Table Table venue the perfect place for any occasion. *Excludes daytime & evening deals and festive menus.

2FOR1 MAIN COURSE | FRI ✓ | SAT ✓ — Modern British

EAST Z EAST
☎ 0151 707 9377

Kings Dock, Liverpool, L3 4BX

As well as hosting mouth-watering curries, the menu also boasts grills and handis. The balti dishes have attracted a loyal following at this glamorous eatery which adds a touch of class to every dish.

2FOR1 MAIN COURSE | FRI ✱ | SAT ✱ | ▲ — Indian/Punjabi

ELEMENTS BAR @ NOVOTEL
☎ 0151 702 5100

40 Hanover Street, Liverpool, L1 4LN

Situated in the 4-star Hotel Novotel Liverpool, Elements Bar serves up some of the city's finest cuisine and provides a fantastic retreat for patrons who have spent the day exploring.

50% OFF FOOD | 4 | FRI ✓ | SAT ✓ — International

ELEMENTS RESTAURANT @ NOVOTEL
☎ 0151 702 5100

40 Hanover Street, Liverpool, L1 4LN

Situated in the 4-star Hotel Novotel Liverpool, Elements Restaurant is a fine accompaniment to the Elements Bar and Lounge. Serves up some really tasty dishes and a great array of drinks.

50% OFF FOOD | 4 | FRI ✓ | SAT ✓ — International

ELUDE
☎ 0151 227 3882

13-15 Porter Street, Docklands, Liverpool, L3 7BL

With rich roots in Liverpool's monumental legacy of popular music, this characterful restaurant serves contemporary European dishes prepared from a careful choice of quality produce.

2FOR1 3 COURSES | FRI ✓ | SAT ✓ | SUN | ✱ — European

EPHESUS
☎ 0151 709 3060

57 Blundell Street, Liverpool, L1 0AJ

Flaming Turkish kebabs, sizzling steaks and tender fillets of fish can be sniffed out before they are seen at this fabulous centrally located restaurant. Experienced chefs provide tasty dishes every time.

50% OFF FOOD | 4 | FRI ✓ | SAT ✓ — Turkish

GALA LEO CASINO
☎ 0151 709 8878

44 Chaloner Street, Liverpool, L3 4BF

Next to the world famous Albert Dock within the Gala Leo Casino, this restaurant offers a delectable and modern menu for diners to enjoy as well as the panoramic river views.

2FOR1 MAIN COURSE | FRI ✱ | SAT ✱ | ▲ — Modern British

GECKO MEDITERRANEAN KITCHEN & BAR
☎ 0151 707 7780

St Johns House, Queen Square, Liverpool, L1 1RH

Gecko, located in Queen Square and overlooking St Johns Gardens, is a Mediterranean restaurant. It is Liverpool's newest café bar, deli and restaurant offering a vast array of choice.

50% OFF FOOD | 4 | FRI × | SAT × | ▲ — Med/Meze

THE GLEGG ARMS
0151 342 1982

Chester Road, Heswell, Wirral, CH60 3SD

Beefeater Grill are one of the UK's best-loved restaurants welcoming guests for almost 40 years in over 130 locations nationwide. *Excludes Breakfast, Light Bites, Bar menu, set menus and all other offers.

2FOR1 MAIN COURSE | 6 | FRI ✓ | SAT ✗ | Modern British

GO PIZZA
0151 486 5744

John Lennon Liverpool Airport, Liverpool, M3 5NF

For those with a busy lifestyle, Go delivers fast fresh food from divine pizzas to delicious baguettes, all prepared to quality standards, providing excellent value for money.

2FOR1 MAIN COURSE | FRI ✱ | SAT ✱ | Italian

GOLDEN CASTLE
☎ 0151 944 2393

318 Stanley Road, Bootle, L20 3ET

A relaxed and convivial Chinese restaurant serving tasty, authentic and piquant dishes. Aromatic and classic, you'll enjoy your savoury Chinese meal.

2FOR1 MAIN COURSE | FRI ✓ | SAT ✱ | ✱ | Chinese

THE GRAND RESTAURANT
☎ 01704 873 389

126-128 Church Road, Formby, L37 7NH

The Grand Restaurant is an exclusive fine dining establishment that set to amaze guests with new taste sensations that entice aficionados of Indian cuisine.

2FOR1 3 COURSES | FRI ✓ | SAT ✓ | Indian

GULSHAN
☎ 0151 427 2273

544-548 Aigburth Road, Liverpool, L19 3QG

Situated in a quiet suburb of Merseyside, the proprietors of Gulshan have been bringing a taste of Indian to Liverpool since 1986. Elegant décor, amiable staff and original flavours are all highlights.

2FOR1 MAIN COURSE | FRI ✱ | SAT ✱ | ✱ | Indian

GUSTO TRATTORIA
☎ 01704 544255

58-62 Lord Street, Southport, PR8 1QB

Gusto Trattoria provides delicious, freshly cooked Italian cuisine. The restaurant's contemporary ambience and imaginative dishes have elevated them to becoming a firm favourite with diners in Merseyside.

2FOR1 MAIN COURSE | FRI ✗ | SAT ✗ | SUN | Italian

THE HESKETH ARMS
01704 509 548

Botanic Road, Southport, PR9 7NA

This Vintage Inn oozes rural charm and rustic character. The picturesque surroundings provide the perfect backdrop for savouring the hearty, seasonal pub-food on the menu.

25% OFF TOTAL | FRI ✓ | SAT ✓ | SUN | Modern British

INDIAN DELIGHT
☎ 0151 709 1722

83 Renshaw Street, Liverpool, L1 2SJ

Ravenous curry lovers can feast upon dishes infused with authenticity and imagination. Using only the freshest of ingredients, this venue oozes quality.

25% OFF TOTAL | FRI ✗ | SAT ✗ | Indian

INDIRA
☎ 0151 632 3978

36 Market Street, Hoylake, CH47 2AF

A superb Indian restaurant in Hoylake, Indira serves exquisite cuisine that wholly embraces the culinary culture of the subcontinent. Fill-up on spice-infused dishes and crisp, fresh sundries.

25% OFF TOTAL | 10 | FRI ✓ | SAT ✓ | ✱ | Indian

JADE GARDEN
☎ 0151 632 2421

75 Market Street, Hoylake, CH47 2BH

A firmly established family-run business offering deliciously tasty Chinese cuisine. Classic favourites are on offer in this amiable restaurant.

2FOR1 MAIN COURSE | FRI ✱ | SAT ✱ | Chinese

KERALA KITCHEN
☎ 0151 201 1121

27 Arrowepark Road, Wirral, CH49 0UB

Commitment to great flavour provides the true tastes and sumptuous experiences of South India, and providing these dining experiences is an accomplished ambition of Kerala Kitchen.

25% OFF TOTAL | 6 | FRI | SAT | ✱ | Indian

KNOTTY ASH BISTRO
☎ 0871 432 0500

216 East Prescot Rd, Liverpool, L14 5NG

The Knotty Ash Bistro caters to patrons who are well-deserving of superb food. Notes of French flavour come through in all of the dishes on offer, with the menu appealing to everyone's senses.

25% OFF TOTAL | 10 | FRI ✓ | SAT ✓ | ✱ | French

LA TASCA
☎ 0151 709 7999

4 Queens Square, Liverpool, L1 1RH

Quintessentially Spanish, La Tasca's fresh and exciting menu offers something for everyone. Their tapas dishes are sincerely authentic, while their paellas always deliver on flavour.

25% OFF TOTAL | 8 | FRI ✓ | SAT ✗ | Spanish

LADY JADE
☎ 0151 228 6888

19 St Oswalds Street, Old Swan, L13 5SA

An enchantingly exotic ambience awaits you at Lady Jade. Out-of-this-world Peking and Cantonese dishes are devoured by both regulars and guests from afar. The Hors d'oeuvres are incredible.

2FOR1 MAIN COURSE | FRI | SAT | ✱ | Cantonese

LIME LOUNGE @ HOLIDAY INN
☎ 0151 709 7090

Holiday Inn, Lime Street, Liverpool, L1 1NQ

After a long day exploring everything Liverpool has to offer, Lime Lounge offers a perfect retreat. Alternatively, begin your evening out on the town here: with great drinks and superb food on offer.

25% OFF TOTAL | 6 | FRI ✓ | SAT ✓ | British

THE LONDON CARRIAGE WORKS
☎ 0151 705 2222

Hope Street, Liverpool, L1 9DA

Exceptional chefs put their talents to full use at The London Carriage Works. Dedicated to sourcing the very best produce, culinary skills and fine ingredients marry together to make impressive dishes.

2FOR1 3 COURSES | FRI ✓ | SAT ✗ | International

THE LOUNGE @ CROWNE PLAZA
☎ 0151 243 8000

St Nicholas Place, Princes Dock, Liverpool, L3 1QW

Relax and unwind after a long day in the city in The Lounge at this Liverpool hotel lounge. A mouthwatering range of dishes, smooth coffees and a wide selection of beverages are all on offer.

50% OFF FOOD | 4 | FRI ✓ | SAT ✓ | International

MALMAISON
☎ 0151 229 5000

William Jessop Way, Princes Dock, Liverpool, L3 1QZ

Epitomising modern elegance, Malmaison Liverpool follows an inspired New York Gothic theme, ideally located by the riverside. A chic menu showcases local produce and delicious flavours. 1 AA Rosette.

2FOR1 MAIN COURSE | FRI ✗ | SAT ✗ | SUN | European

THE MANGO RESTAURANT AND WINE BAR
☎ 0151 254 2124

12 Dryden Road, Liverpool, L7 9PG

Mango Restaurant and Wine Bar draws on many popular dishes and brings them altogether on a well-executed menu. Specialises in producing international-inspired dishes, leaving no area of the map untouched.

2FOR1 3 COURSES | FRI ✗ | SAT ✗ | SUN | ✱ | British

MANZIL
☎ 0151 647 9911

67-75 Grange Road East, Birkenhead, CH41 5FD

Every visitor is sure to be impressed by the delectable Indian cuisine at Manzil Restaurant in Birkenhead. From a creamy masala to a spicy madras, diners are well-accommodated.

2FOR1 MAIN COURSE | FRI | SAT | ✱ | Indian

MAYUR
☎ 0151 709 9955

130 Duke Street, Liverpool, L1 5AG

A pleasant Indian dining experience can be expected at Mayur. The plush interior oozes opulence and sophistication, wilst every dish is bursting with intense rich flavour.

25% OFF TOTAL | 6 | FRI ✓ | SAT ✓ | Indian

To understand what the restaurant icons mean, please see the inside back cover.

MERCHANTS BAR & RESTAURANT
0151 702 7897
56-62 Castle Street, Liverpool, L2 7LQ
A sleek and modern restaurant, bar and cocktail lounge on Castle Street in Liverpool, Merchants makes best use of its stunning setting - high windows, marble columns - with a contemporary baroque style.

25% OFF TOTAL | 6 | FRI ✓ | SAT × | SUN | ✱ — British

MICHELANGELO'S ITALIAN RESTAURANT
0151 727 7380
The Blenheim Lakehouse Hotel, Liverpool, L17 4JE
Once home to the famous Beatles band member Stuart Sutcliffe, the beautiful Blenheim Lakeside Hotel now plays home to Michelangelo's Restaurant. Find melt-in-the-mouth Italian cuisine.

25% OFF TOTAL | 6 | FRI ✓ | SAT ✓ — Italian

MICKLE HEAD GREEN
01744 818 971
Lea Green, St Helens, WA9 4TT
Beefeater Grill are one of the UK's best-loved restaurants welcoming guests for almost 40 years in over 130 locations nationwide. *Excludes Breakfast, Light Bites, Bar menu, set menus and all other offers.

2FOR1 MAIN COURSE | 6 | FRI ✓ | SAT × — Modern British

MILLON
0151 729 0220
187 Allerton Road, Liverpool, L18 6HG
Specialising in flavourful tandoori dishes, this modern-styled restaurant serves tasty dishes with flavours from a range of Indian traditions. Try the chef's recommendations for their imaginative twists.

25% OFF TOTAL | 10 | FRI ✓ | SAT ✱ — Indian

NICOLA'S RISTORANTE
0151 928 2862
30 South Road, Liverpool, L22 5PQ
This eclectic restaurant brings a contemporary twist to traditional Italian fare, in an upbeat and friendly atmosphere.

25% OFF TOTAL | FRI | SAT — European

THE OLIVE GROVE GREEK TAVERNA
0151 342 9100
104-106 Telegraph Road, Wirral, CH60 0AQ
Ingredients are imported directly from Greece at this aptly named venue. Chefs promise to prepare dishes as authentic as those found in Greek villages, and guarantee to use age-old recipes.

2FOR1 3 COURSES | FRI × | SAT × | SUN — Greek

PACKET STEAMER
01515 311 497
Northern Perimeter Road, Merseyside, Bootle, L30 7PT
Beefeater Grill are one of the UK's best-loved restaurants welcoming guests for almost 40 years in over 130 locations nationwide. *Excludes Breakfast, Light Bites, Bar menu, set menus and all other offers.

2FOR1 MAIN COURSE | 6 | FRI ✓ | SAT × — Modern British

PAN AM BAR AND RESTAURANT
0151 702 5831
Albert Dock, Liverpool, L3 4AE
Overlooking Liverpool's prestigious Albert Dock and set in a Grade 1 listed building, Pan Am bar boasts the Taste of Merseyside Award. Diners can expect exquisite European food in a luxurious setting.

50% OFF FOOD | 6 | FRI × | SAT × | ✱ — International

THE PORTRAIT HOUSE
0151 632 4444
5-6 The Quadrant, Hoylake, Wirral, CH47 2EE
Named after the photographic studio it once was, this building is now home to talented chefs and happy customers. Enjoy the exquisite fusion of contemporary and classic cuisine.

2FOR1 MAIN COURSE | FRI | SAT × — International

PREZZO
01704 531 313
128 Lord Street, Southport, PR8 1AA
With a character all of its own, oozes contemporary style and enduring charm. Signature pastas, stone-baked pizzas and classic Italian dishes promise a perfect dining choice for the whole family.

2FOR1 MAIN COURSE | FRI × | SAT × — Italian

PREZZO
0151 691 0309
3 Marine Point, Wirral, CH45 2PB
With a character all of its own, oozes contemporary style and enduring charm. Signature pastas, stone-baked pizzas and classic Italian dishes promise a perfect dining choice for the whole family.

2FOR1 MAIN COURSE | FRI × | SAT × — Italian

THE PUNCHBOWL
0151 526 1018
Lunt Road, Liverpool, L29 7WA
This Vintage Inn oozes rural charm and rustic character. The picturesque surroundings provide the perfect backdrop for savouring the hearty, seasonal pub-food on the menu.

25% OFF TOTAL | FRI ✓ | SAT ✓ | SUN — Modern British

RADISSON BLU HOTEL LIVERPOOL
0151 966 1500
107 Old Hall Street, Liverpool, L3 9BD
Widely regarded as one of the top Liverpool restaurants, Filini offers modern Italian food. The restaurant merges the best local and Italian produce to create mouth-watering dishes.

25% OFF TOTAL | 10 | FRI ✓ | SAT × | SUN — Italian

RAGGAS
0151 222 4176
27 Lark Lane, Liverpool, L17 8US
The bold and vibrant tastes of the Caribbean are brought to Lark Lane, where genuine cuisine is served in a characteristically laid-back atmosphere.

2FOR1 MAIN COURSE | FRI | SAT — Caribbean

RICHARD FOX @ LEVERHULME HOTEL
0151 644 5555
Leverhulme Hotel, Port Sunlight, Wirral, CH62 5EZ
Award-winning Chef Richard Fox invites you to enjoy his seasonal menus in a modern, pristine, light and airy culinary setting that merges seamlessly with the elegant lines and contours of this lovely restored building.

25% OFF TOTAL | 8 | FRI ✓ | SAT ✓ — British

ROMIOS GREEK RESTAURANT
0151 727 7252
20 Lark Lane, Liverpool, L17 8US
Welcoming Greek taverna on Lark Lane. Traditional and unfussy in its hospitality, with a brilliant combination of classic Greek flavours on the menu: herbs, olive oil and slow-cooked tender meats.

25% OFF TOTAL | 6 | FRI × | SAT × — Greek

SANTORINI BAR & GRILL
0151 236 1881
Lombard Chambers, Liverpool, L3 9NG
Situated in Liverpool city centre, Santorini Bar and Grill is a beautiful restaurant dedicated to serving delicious, homemade Mediterranean and Mexican food using only the finest locally sourced produce.

50% OFF FOOD | 6 | FRI ✓ | SAT ✓ | SUN | ✱ — Mediterranean

SAVINA RESTAURANT
0151 708 9095
138 Duke Street, Liverpool, L1 5AG
Honest, modern cuisine is created from ingredients sourced from all over Mexico. Experience an abundance of varying tastes, flavours and spices as you enjoy a great evening out.

25% OFF TOTAL | 4 | FRI ✱ | SAT ✱ | ✱ — Mexican

SHAH JALAL TANDOORI
0151 606 1134
9 Arrowe Park Road, Wirral, CH49 0UB
A well-liked little Indian takeaway off Arrowe Park Road in Wirral, Shah Jalal is a welcoming place that does a fine selection of full-flavoured, tasty and spicy dishes.

2FOR1 MAIN COURSE | FRI | SAT | SUN — Indian

THE SIDE DOOR
0151 707 7888
29a Hope St, Liverpool, L1 9BQ
The Side Door is set over two floors of a handsome Georgian building. The team aim to bring their customers of traditional British and modern European dishes, using locally sourced produce whenever possible.

2FOR1 3 COURSES | FRI ✱ | SAT ✱ — European

SIGNALS RESTAURANT @ HOLIDAY INN
0151 709 7090
Holiday Inn Liverpool, Lime St, Liverpool, L1 1NQ
The Head Chef here has successfully built up a great reputation for creating superb classic and international dishes for guests. Seasonal table d'hôte menus are supported by an extensive wine list.

25% OFF TOTAL | 4 | FRI ✓ | SAT ✓ — International

SOMETHING SPECIAL
0151 678 1167
136 Ford Road, Birkenhead, CH49 0TQ
From Sunday lunches to vegetarian delights such as fillet au poivre, this eatery is bursting with energy and innovation. Diners must be sure to make room for the home-made meringue swan with blue curacao.

50% OFF FOOD | 6 | FRI ✓ | SAT ✓ — International

SPICE BRASSERIE
☎0151 427 1010

1-3 St Marys Road, Liverpool, L19 2NJ

Spice Brasserie pays homage to the spices and distinctive flavours of India, with popular curries appearing alongside dishes from across the subcontinent, often left unknown to the western world.

2FOR1 MAIN COURSE | FRI ✓ | SAT ✓ — Indian

SPICE CITY
☎0151 236 4443

18 Stanley Street, Liverpool, L1 6AF

Spice City is an Indian restaurant that goes above and beyond to understand the needs of their customers to ensure you return again and again. High quality Indian food and friendly and courteous service.

2FOR1 MAIN COURSE | FRI × | SAT × | * | ▲ — Indian

SPIGA
☎0170 453 9000

3-5 Bold St, Southport, PR9 0DD

A fresh Italian, Spiga offers the perfect balance between value and flavour. With generous portions and a modern look, the open kitchen allows you to witness your meal being prepared exactly as you like.

50% OFF FOOD | 10 | FRI ✓ | SAT ✓ — Italian

STAG AND RAINBOW
0151 228 4724

10 Queens Drive, West Derby, Liverpool, L13 0DL

Beefeater Grill are one of the UK's best-loved restaurants welcoming guests for almost 40 years in over 130 locations nationwide. *Excludes Breakfast, Light Bites, Bar menu, set menus and all other offers.

2FOR1 MAIN COURSE | 6 | FRI ✓ | SAT × | ▲ — Modern British

SURMA TANDOORI
☎0151 677 1331

271-273 Hoylake Road, Moreton, Wirral, CH46 0RL

A classic, popular Tandoori restaurant without unnecessary fripperies that serves a great range of fresh and flavourful Indian dishes with excellent service, in a comfortable, easygoing atmosphere.

2FOR1 MAIN COURSE | FRI ✓ | SAT * — Indian

TAJ MAHAL
☎01704 545 070

35-37 Bath Street, Southport, PR9 0DP

Specialising in balti and tandoori dishes, this restaurant delivers a fragrant and delicately spiced menu with wide-ranging choice. Expertly prepared food served in a contemporary, comfortable setting.

2FOR1 MAIN COURSE | FRI ✓ | SAT ✓ | * — Indian

TAPAS TAPAS
☎0151 949 1151

23 South Road, Waterloo, Liverpool

Warm lighting, low Latin music, hanging ham hocks and accessories; a restaurant with a rustic, homely atmosphere. The food too is simple and satisfying, with ranging flavours and textures: perfect tapas.

50% OFF FOOD | 2 | FRI × | SAT × | * | ▲ — Spanish

TAPAS TAPAS
☎0151 709 0999

14 Back Colquitt, Liverpool, L1 4DE

Authentic feel of an Andalucian tapas bar, with imported ham hocks hanging from the walls, wood beams and wall tiles from Seville. Popular venue that does a great selection of simple, tasty tapas dishes.

50% OFF FOOD | 2 | FRI × | SAT × | * | ▲ — Spanish

TJ'S RESTAURANT
☎0791 994 4488

The King Hary Hotel, 55 Blessington Rd, Liverpool, L4 0RY

Beautifully executed British cuisine with a wicked sense of humour, this is perfect for a decadent evening out. Block out the sounds of the town with rich, buttery dishes and the extravagant wine list.

2FOR1 MAIN COURSE | FRI ✓ | SAT ✓ | ▲ — British

TSO'S
☎0151 709 2811

4 Queens Square, Liverpool, L1 1HF

If you often find yourself spoilt for choice, TSO's is the place for you. Here you can sample an array of Chinese dishes all at excellent prices.*A la carte menu only.

25% OFF TOTAL | 6 | FRI ✓ | SAT ✓ | * — Chinese

VERVE GRILL
☎0844 980 8035

Fallows Way, Liverpool, L35 1RZ

This effortlessly chic venue is alluringly furnished with dark wooden furniture and plush leather seating. Devour a gorgonzola and mushroom pizza before giving in to a zesty lemon tart served with cream.

2FOR1 3 COURSES | FRI ✓ | SAT ✓ | SUN | * | ▲ — Bistro

THE VILLAGE INN
☎0151 520 3356

70 Haileybury Avenue, Liverpool, L10 6LP

Be it a leisurely drink with friends or a quiet evening meal with someone special, the Village Inn provides something for every circumstance. Delicious food on offer is complemented by fine beverages.

25% OFF TOTAL | 8 | FRI ✓ | SAT ✓ — British

VISTA RESTAURANT @ ATLANTIC TOWER
☎0871 376 9025

Chapel Street, Liverpool, L3 9RE

Complete with stunning views of the Liverpool Docks, this cosmopolitan venue serves everything from light lunches to intimate dinners. Offering British and European cuisine, the menu is sure to satisfy.

50% OFF FOOD | 6 | FRI ✓ | SAT × | ▲ — International

WALKABOUT
☎0151 708 0843

Concert Square, Liverpool, L1 4AN

Walkabout is famous for its characteristically Australian atmosphere and well-rounded menu. From live sport with a juicy burger to some Aussie kangaroo skewers, you'll find it hard to tear yourself away.

25% OFF TOTAL | 10 | FRI ✓ | SAT ✓ | ▲ — International

WAREHOUSE KITCHEN & BAR
☎01704 544662

30 West Street, Southport, PR8 1QN

An international menu with some eclectic flavour combinations, be it venison burger with red onion relish or grilled halibut. Awarded 1 AA Rosette. *Advance booking mentioning Gourmet Society is essential.

2FOR1 MAIN COURSE | FRI × | SAT × | SUN | ▲ — International

WHAT'S COOKING LIVERPOOL
☎0151 707 2023

24 Britannia Pavilion, Liverpool, L3 4AD

Located opposite the beautiful Albert Dock, this venue specialises in wholesome favourites such as plump and juicy burgers. Enjoy a classic dish whilst admiring the stunning Three Graces.

2FOR1 MAIN COURSE | FRI ☎ | SAT ☎ | ▲ — American

WIRRAL TANDOORI
☎0151 334 0024

18 Bromborough Village Road, Wirral, CH62 7ES

With 30 starters, diners are spoilt for choice from the word go. Expert chefs recommend the monkfish malabar, served to culinary perfection. Pocket-friendly, the menu boasts an array of chaats and puris.

2FOR1 MAIN COURSE | FRI ☎ | SAT ☎ — Indian

YASEMIN TURKISH RESTAURANT
☎0151 922 3370

211 Stanley Road, Liverpool, L20 3DY

Exquisitely furnished, this family venue provides clients with exceptional Turkish dishes inspired by the Ottoman heartland, alongside an international wine list.

50% OFF FOOD | 6 | FRI ✓ | SAT ✓ | SUN | * | ▲ — Turkish

YUKTI
☎0151 228 2225

393 Prescot Road, Liverpool, L13 3BS

At Yukti, they view cooking as an art form. The aim is to bring you modern Indian food that marries classic ingredients with more surprising twists to ensure you will have an original and enjoyable dining experience.

2FOR1 3 COURSES | FRI × | SAT × | ▲ — Indian

ZAGROS PERSIAN RESTAURANT
☎0151 708 6368

194 London Road, Liverpool, L3 8JN

Zagros Persian Restaurant has earned a reputation for providing attentive service and delicious food.This hidden gem is hailed by regulars as one of Liverpool's finest.

25% OFF TOTAL | FRI ✓ | SAT ✓ — Middle Eastern

ZEERA INDIAN RESTAURANT
☎0151 228 2716

164 Derby Lane, Liverpool, L13 6QQ

Zeera Indian Restaurant serves a whole host of curry dishes, sundries and sides to a happy and satisfied cohort of regular diners. The tasty plates on offer range from a mild korma to a spicy madras.

2FOR1 2 COURSES | FRI ✓ | SAT ✓ — Indian

North East

County Durham

THE ANCIENT UNICORN ☎01833 628 321
Main Street, Bowes, Barnard Castle, DL12 9HL
A welcoming retreat of a pub-restaurant whose array of crafted, palate-whetting regional specialities are worth the hike. Fine cuisine with dishes inspired by culinary nuances from around the world.

2FOR1 3 COURSES | FRI ✓ | SAT ✓ — British

BEACH TACO ☎0191 386 3889
87 North Road, Durham, DH1 4SR
Build your own Mexican feast at Beach Taco, where burritos, fajitas and tacos will grab your fancy. Cheesy quesadillas and creamy guacamole are also highlights, along with the addictive tortilla chips.

25% OFF TOTAL | 4 | FRI ✓ | SAT ✗ — Mexican

THE BEAMISH MARY INN ☎0191 370 0237
Beamish, Stanley, DH9 0QH
A well-cherished pub that serves the local village with a warm respite from the cold outdoors. The Beamish Mary Inn is shrouded in local history and is rich in tradition and British heartiness.

2FOR1 MAIN COURSE | FRI ✓ | SAT ✗ | SUN — British

BELLA ITALIA 0191 386 1060
20-21 Silver Street, Durham, DH1 3RB
Accessible Italian cuisine on the British high street - indulge in authentic sharing platters, hand stretched pizzas and hearty pasta dishes, served with a healthy dose of gregarious Italian hospitality.

25% OFF TOTAL | 6 | FRI ✗ | SAT ✗ | SUN | ▲ — Italian

THE BRIDGE ☎01833 627 341
Whorlton Village, Barnard Castle, DL12 8XD
The excitement of the city fused with quality local produce, by well-known North East chef Paul O'Hara. Extensive dish choice and a wine list assembled to complement the depth of flavour in the menu.

2FOR1 MAIN COURSE | FRI ✱ | SAT ✱ | SUN | ▲ — European

BROOMSIDE PARK 0191 370 6500
Broomside Lane, Belmont Industrial Est., Durham, DH1 1GG
Quality pub classics with a modern twist combine with a friendly and relaxed atmosphere to make this Table Table venue the perfect place for family gatherings or meeting friends.

2FOR1 MAIN COURSE | FRI ✓ | SAT ✓ — Modern British

CAFÉ INDIA ☎01429 275 252
21-23 Whitby Street, Hartlepool, TS24 7AB
Original Indian cuisine at its very best. Elegant surroundings transfer you to a stylish haven in which diners enjoy divine dishes that are served and devoured.

2FOR1 MAIN COURSE | FRI ✓ | SAT ✓ | ✱ — Indian

CAFÉ ROUGE 0191 384 3429
21 Silver Street, Durham, DH1 3RB
French sophistication on the British high street - enjoy seasonally changing French dishes and a continental wine selection, served in a relaxed environment with an undeniable flair of Parisian chic.

25% OFF TOTAL | 6 | FRI ✓ | SAT ✓ | ✱ | ▲ — French

CHANG THAI ☎01388 605 011
7 Market Place, Bishop Auckland, DL14 7NJ
Culinary delights will please all in this delightful Thai restaurant. Attentive staff proudly welcome you into this warm and inviting environment in which to savour the fine dishes.

2FOR1 3 COURSES | FRI ✱ | SAT ✱ | SUN | ✱ | ▲ — Thai

THE CHURCH MOUSE 0191 389 2628
Waldbridge, Chester Le Street, DH2 3SL
This Vintage Inn oozes rural charm and rustic character. The picturesque surroundings provide the perfect backdrop for savouring the hearty, seasonal pub-food on the menu.

25% OFF TOTAL | FRI ✓ | SAT ✓ | SUN | ▲ — Modern British

FILINI @ THE RADISSON BLU ☎0191 372 7200
Radisson Blu, Framwelgate Waterside, Durham, DH1 5TL
Uncluttered, clear flavours grounded in modern Italian cuisine based on the concept of simplicity and authenticity at this hotel-based restaurant.

25% OFF TOTAL | 2 | FRI ✓ | SAT ✓ — Italian

FOFFANO'S ☎01325 242 086
3-5 Bakhouse Hill, Darlington, DL1 5QA
A wonderfully authentic Mediterranean atmosphere showcasing a menu filled with classic Italian food and other sumptuous dishes. Everything is fresh and home made, in respect of the best Italian traditions.

2FOR1 3 COURSES | FRI ✓ | SAT ✱ | SUN — Italian/ Mediterranean

GARDEN OF INDIA ☎01325 467 975
43-44 Bondgate Roundabout, Darlington, DL3 7JJ
Hungry guests can expect substantial portion sizes at this eatery. Going back to the roots of Indian cooking, the Garden of India prepares genuine food in a British setting.

2FOR1 2 COURSES | FRI ✗ | SAT ✗ — Indian

HALL GARTH HOTEL ☎01325 300 400
Coatham Mundeville, Darlington, DL1 3LU
You needn't be staying at the Hall Garth to enjoy their fantastic restaurants. Food and drink have always been essential pleasures for guests at a country estate, and the dining here does not disappoint.

25% OFF TOTAL | 4 | FRI ✓ | SAT ✓ — European

HELME PARK ☎01388 730 970
Helme Park, Firtree, Bishop Auckland, DL13 4NW
Fine dining coupled with great prices, where guests can decide from a wide selection of well-prepared, flavourful dishes, with every item on the menu bearing a hallmark of quality.

25% OFF TOTAL | 4 | FRI 📱 | SAT ✱ | ✱ | ▲ — Italian

LA TASCA ☎0845 126 2958
58 Saddler Street, Durham, DH1 3NU
Quintessentially Spanish, La Tasca's fresh and exciting menu offers something for everyone. Their tapas dishes are sincerely authentic, while their paellas always deliver on flavour.

25% OFF TOTAL | 8 | FRI ✓ | SAT ✗ | ▲ — Spanish

MAXIMO'S ☎01429 839 299
The Old Brewery, Castle Eden, Hartlepool, TS27 4SU
A gorgeous restaurant complete with attentive and helpful staff, and a great choice of authentic and traditional dishes. Highly recommended in the area; simply first-class food.

25% OFF TOTAL | 4 | FRI ✱ | SAT ✱ | ▲ — Italian

MELANZANA ☎0191 384 0096
96 Elvet Bridge, Durham, DH1 3AG
This exquisite bistro boasts an enchanting view of Durham Cathedral and the River Wear. Coffee lovers can experience an authentic, creamy Italian masterpiece whilst tucking into a rustic dish.

2FOR1 MAIN COURSE | FRI 📱 | SAT 📱 — Italian

THE MINER'S ARMS 01207 560 428
41 Manor Road, Medomsley, Consett, DH8 6QN
Succulent rib-eye steaks can be devoured in this gastro-style pub which offers lunch and evening meals of tremendous quality. A weekly changing specials menu offers delicious alternatives.

25% OFF TOTAL | 2 | FRI ✓ | SAT ✱ | SUN | ▲ — English/Gastro pub

MONJU TANDOORI ☎01207 239 172
233 Park Road, Stanley, DH9 7QG
Long-established, classic Indian restaurant that has a good reputation for consistently producing the goods, with a menu that ranges through all the classics and specials like their Singapore curries.

2FOR1 MAIN COURSE | FRI ✗ | SAT ✗ | SUN — Indian

MORTON PARK 01325 373 340
Morton Park Way, Morton Park, Darlington, DL1 4PJ
Beefeater Grill are one of the UK's best-loved restaurants welcoming guests for almost 40 years in over 130 locations nationwide. *Excludes Breakfast, Light Bites, Bar menu, set menus and all other offers.

2FOR1 MAIN COURSE | 6 | FRI ✓ | SAT ✗ | ▲ — Modern British

OCHIS RESTAURANT ☎01325 282 675
30-32 Bondgate, Darlington, DL3 7JJ
Perfectly located in the heart of town, this is a popular place for both special occasions and spontaneous evenings out. Enjoy Caribbean and Mediterranean fine cuisine, with wines from around the world.

2FOR1 MAIN COURSE | FRI ✓ | SAT ✱ | ▲ — Caribbean

THE OLD FARMHOUSE 01325 332 191
Yarm Road, Darlington, DL2 1JZ
This Vintage Inn oozes rural charm and rustic character. The picturesque surroundings provide the perfect backdrop for savouring the hearty, seasonal pub-food on the menu.

25% OFF TOTAL | FRI ✓ | SAT ✓ | SUN | ▲ — Modern British

OLDFIELDS ☎0191 370 9595
18 Claypath, Durham, DH1 1RH
Superb food at great value for money, in a stylish and welcoming environment. Expect your every requirement to be dealt with efficiently and with exceptional hospitality. A wonderful place to relax.

25% OFF TOTAL | 6 | FRI ✱ | SAT ✱ | ▲ — International

POTENZA'S ☎01207 502 942
31-33 Medomsley Road, Consett, DH8 5HE
Potenza's have the best understanding of how to host an exceptional family meal. This, coupled with their hearty Italian food, makes for the perfect Italian dining experience for the whole family.

2FOR1 MAIN COURSE | FRI ✓ | SAT ✓ | ▲ — Italian

THE RED LION ☎01388 763 561
North Bitchburn Terrace, North Bitchburn, DL15 8AL
The owners specialise in serving up superb food in this warm and inviting pub. Serving four real ales, this is a popular place with locals who enjoy the good beer, great grub, and efficient service.

25% OFF TOTAL | 4 | FRI ✓ | SAT ✓ — British

RIVERSIDE RESTAURANT ☎01833 637 576
Bridge End, Barnard Castle, DL12 9BE
A warm and cosy place to come and enjoy a special dinner or a hearty lunch. Riverside has built a reputation for delivering wholesome food, properly prepared and filled with flavour.

2FOR1 MAIN COURSE | FRI ✓ | SAT ✱ | SUN — British

SEVEN STARS INN ☎0191 384 8454
High Street North, Shincliffe, Durham, DH1 2NU
A traditionally decorated restaurant; magical candlelight and divine tasting food make any evening spent here equal to perfection. The staff focus on ensuring your dining experience is completely relaxed.

25% OFF TOTAL | 4 | FRI ✱ | SAT ✱ | SUN | ✱ | ▲ — British

SPICE GARDEN DARLINGTON ☎01325 369 512
112-114 Parkgate, Darlington, DL1 1RX
An adventurous foray into contemporary Indian cuisine, Spice Garden caters for all palates and is committed to providing a top quality dining experience.

2FOR1 2 COURSES | FRI ✓ | SAT ✗ | ✱ — Indian

SPICE ISLAND ☎01388 777 775
100 Main Street, Shildon, DL4 1AQ
Visitors return time and time again to experience the pleasures of the food on offer here. Believing food to be one of life's exquisite pleasures, the Head Chef ensures every dish is made to perfection.

25% OFF TOTAL | 4 | FRI ✱ | SAT ✱ | SUN | ▲ — Indian

SPICE ISLAND ☎01833 630 575
9 Market Place, Barnard Castle, DL12 8NF
Passionately crafted fine Indian food filled with spice and flavour. Head Chef Babul Miah takes great care, pride and satisfaction in creating the finest cuisine available in a tranquil, stylish setting.

25% OFF TOTAL | 4 | FRI ✱ | SAT ✱ | SUN | ▲ — Indian

SPICE VENUE ☎01207 583 765
23 Newmarket Street, Consett, DH8 5LQ
A modern-style Indian restaurant held in high regard, offering a remarking array of flavoursome dishes to its guests. Fresh ingredients are used to create high-quality food every time.

25% OFF TOTAL | 10 | FRI ✱ | SAT ✱ | ✱ — Indian

SPICES ☎01429 865 888
16-18 Navigation Point, Hartlepool, TS24 0UG
Expect tasty curries and excellent service at this popular local restaurant. Whether you like your food deliciously spicy or mild yet flavoursome, Spices cater each dining option to suit your liking.

25% OFF TOTAL | 10 | FRI ✓ | SAT ✓ — Indian

TASTE OF INDIA ☎01388 451 452
20 Louisa Terrace, Bishop Auckland, DLI 9BP
Highly regarded Indian takeaway in Bishop Auckland featuring an array of distinctive, rich flavours on the menu. Simple balti curries and the more eclectic naga naga or amchoor are particular favourites.

2FOR1 MAIN COURSE | FRI ✗ | SAT ✗ | SUN — Indian

THE TAWNY OWL 01325 389 027
Neasham Road, Hurworth Moor, Darlington, DL2 1QE
This Vintage Inn oozes rural charm and rustic character. The picturesque surroundings provide the perfect backdrop for savouring the hearty, seasonal pub-food on the menu.

25% OFF TOTAL | FRI ✓ | SAT ✓ | SUN | ▲ — Modern British

TIA'S ☎0191 383 9001
84 Claypath, Durham, DH1 1RG
Saddle up for a Tex-Mex feast at this buzzy restaurant in Durham that serves all the classics with a bit of flair. The cocktail range is an extra treat. *Offer does not apply during happy hour (5pm-7pm).

25% OFF TOTAL | 6 | FRI ✓ | SAT ✱ | ▲ — Tex-Mex

THE VILLAGE INN ☎0191 527 1584
Sunderland Road, Durham, SR8 3AT
This country pub serves traditional British food in a relaxing and comfortable atmosphere. The staff are friendly and a warm welcome is guaranteed on every visit.

2FOR1 MAIN COURSE | FRI ✓ | SAT ✓ — British

WINGATE TANDOORI 01429 836 565
47 Front Street West, Wingate, TS28 5AA
Popular and low-key tandoori restaurant in Wingate. It caters to the neighbourhood without undue bells and whistles, and has a good reputation for simple, effective, spicy food.

2FOR1 MAIN COURSE | FRI ✗ | SAT ✗ | SUN — Indian

Northumberland

ARAMEE II ☎0166 183 3355
59 Front Street, Prudhoe, NE42 5AA
A totally unique Indian restaurant, not just in location but in quality of food and service. A simply delicious Indian experience from beginning to end.

2FOR1 MAIN COURSE | FRI | SAT ✱ | ▲ — Indian

BATTLESTEADS ☎01434 230 209
Wark, Hexham, NE48 3LS
Seasonal game, Cumbrian beef and Northumbrian lamb are just some examples of the fine produce used in the kitchen at Battlesteads. Cooked superbly, these local ingredients underpin some excellent dishes.

2FOR1 3 COURSES | FRI | SAT ✗ | SUN — British

BAWARCHI ☎0166 182 0869
3 Brewery Lane, Ponteland, NE20 9NZ
Creamy masala sauces and fiery madras dishes feature highly on the menu in this wonderful Indian restaurant, where fine dining meets a menu full of classic curry staples.

2FOR1 MAIN COURSE | FRI ✓ | SAT ✓ | ✱ — Indian

BISTRO EN GLAZE ☎0166 185 2185
Laburnum House, Wylam, NE41 8AJ
An impressive restaurant that attracts diners from near and far. Its regular clientèle from the surrounding areas testifies to the outstanding quality of the French-influenced food on offer.

25% OFF TOTAL | 2 | FRI | SAT ✱ — French

BLUE BELL RESTAURANT ☎0166 821 3543
1 Market Place, Belford, NE70 7NE
Award-winning dishes prepared by highly trained chefs. Dining in the garden restaurant or the hotel bar offer two very unique dining experiences, although scrumptious food can be found in both.

25% OFF TOTAL | 4 | FRI | SAT ✱ | ✱ | ▲ — British

THE BOYSON RESTAURANT ☎01670 795 000
Longhirst Hall, Morpeth, NE61 3LL
Set in beautiful woodland and gardens, The Boyson uses locally sourced or organically produced ingredients in creating their real honest food. Fresh and healthy, and without compromising on quality.

25% OFF TOTAL | 6 | FRI ✓ | SAT | ✱ — Fine Dining

THE CLARET JUG ☎01434 673 350
Slaley Hall Hotel, Hexham, NE47 0BX
Overlooking the Slaley Hall Hotel golf course, The Claret Jug offers more than spectacular views. Club house extraordinaire, this is the home of local must-try dishes, fresh ales and relaxing golfer's teas.

2FOR1 3 COURSES | FRI | SAT ✱ | ✱ | ▲ — British

THE CRASTER ARMS 0166 572 0272
The Wynding, Beadnell, NE67 5AX
Historic pub offers a range of local and continental beers along with a selection of fine wines, providing the perfect accompaniment to a delicious meal prepared by their talented kitchen brigade.

2FOR1 MAIN COURSE | FRI ✓ | SAT ✓ | SUN — British

DALCHINI ☎0166 560 6336
15 Narrowgate, Alnwick, NE66 1JH
Succumb to the temptations of Dalchini's mouth-watering cuisine and you won't regret it. Classic Indian dishes are on offer alongside more surprising treats, such as the tasty stuffed pepper starter.

2FOR1 MAIN COURSE | FRI ✓ | SAT ✓ — Indian

DOBSON RESTAURANT ☎01670 500 000
Macdonald Linden Hall Hotel, Morpeth, NE65 8XF
Inside a beautiful Georgian hotel surrounded by a golf course, this restaurant offers golfers and guests alike delectable and inspiring continental cuisine, teamed with impeccable service. 2 AA Rosettes.

25% OFF TOTAL | 4 | FRI ✓ | SAT ✱ | ✱ | ▲ — European

DUKE'S GRILL ☎01434 673 350
Slaley Hall Hotel, Hexham, NE47 0BX
In the Edwardian drawing room of Slaley Hall, chefs capture the essence of Northumberland's harvest from land, river and sea. Exquisite meals and the wide selection of wines will linger long in the memory.

2FOR1 3 COURSES | FRI | SAT ✱ | ✱ | ▲ — British

ESHOTT HALL ☎01670 787 454
Eshott, Morpeth, NE65 9EN
Eshott Hall is entirely unique; an elegant boutique property designed to give the discerning guest an unbeatable dining experience worthy of its AA rosette.

2FOR1 MAIN COURSE | FRI × | SAT × — British

GENERAL HAVELOCK INN ☎01434 684 376
9 Ratcliffe Road, Haydon Bridge, NE47 6ER
Full-blooded, hearty and fresh pub-style fare in a warm Northumberland inn. Backing onto the river, it's a lovely setting for a distinctive, delicious pub meal.

25% OFF TOTAL | 8 | FRI ✱ | SAT ✱ | SUN | ▲ — British

HADRIAN'S BRASSERIE ☎01434 673 350
Slaley Hall Hotel, Hexham, NE47 0BX
Stunning views and a menu to match. Perfect for an evening of exciting food and perfectly selected wine. An exquisitely designed restaurant, serving the freshest Northumberland produce.

2FOR1 3 COURSES | FRI | SAT ✱ | ✱ | ▲ — British

HARDY'S BISTRO ☎0166 560 2109
The White Swan Hotel, Alnwick, NE66 1TD
An informal atmosphere creates a relaxed ambience for diners to focus on enjoying the delicious food on offer. The bistro menu features steaks, curries and meat sharing platters.

2FOR1 MAIN COURSE | FRI ✓ | SAT ✓ | ✱ | ▲ — British

ITALIA PLUS ☎0166 962 2900
Coquetvale Hotel, Station Road, Rothbury, NE65 7QH
True Italian style is on offer at this wonderful hotel, providing guests with everything they need. Deliciously fresh dishes cooked to order by professional chefs. Great all-round dining.

25% OFF TOTAL | 6 | FRI ✓ | SAT ✱ — Italian

JOINERS ARMS ☎0166 557 6112
Newton-by-the-Sea, Alnwick, NE66 3EA
Genuine service combined with good quality food is what lies behind the success of the Joiners Arms. Cosy and warm, guests can unwind and relax upon entering the door.

2FOR1 MAIN COURSE | FRI ✓ | SAT × — British

MOOR FARM 0191 250 2770
Annitsford, Cramlington, NE23 7QA
Beefeater Grill are one of the UK's best-loved restaurants welcoming guests for almost 40 years in over 130 locations nationwide. *Excludes Breakfast, Light Bites, Bar menu, set menus and all other offers.

2FOR1 MAIN COURSE | 6 | FRI ✓ | SAT × | ▲ — Modern British

MULINOS ☎01670 353 311
79 Waterloo Road, Blyth, NE24 1BU
An enjoyable atmosphere in which excellent food can be relished. Pizzas, pastas and steaks are all available, as well as a wide range of wonderful tapas dishes that are incredibly popular.

2FOR1 MAIN COURSE | FRI ✓ | SAT ✓ | SUN — Italian/ Mediterranean

OAK ROOM RESTAURANT ☎01830 520 620
The Otterburn Tower, Otterburn, NE19 1NS
Admire the incredible stained glass windows, inglenook fireplaces and exposed oak panelling of this charming venue. Fresh beef, lamb and local game feature highly on the impeccable menu.

25% OFF TOTAL | 4 | FRI | SAT | ✱ — British

PREZZO 01670 733 508
Manor Walks Shopping Centre, Cramlington, NE23 6UL
With a character all of its own, Prezzo oozes contemporary style and enduring charm. Signature pastas, stone-baked pizzas and classic Italian dishes promise a perfect dining choice for the whole family.

2FOR1 MAIN COURSE | FRI × | SAT × | ▲ — Italian

THE SNOWY OWL 01670 736 111
Blagdon Lane, Cramlington, NE23 8AU
This Vintage Inn oozes rural charm and rustic character. The picturesque surroundings provide the perfect backdrop for savouring the hearty, seasonal pub-food on the menu.

25% OFF TOTAL | FRI ✓ | SAT ✓ | SUN | ▲ — Modern British

THE WANSBECK RESTAURANT ☎01670 841 210
Northumberland College, Ashington, NE63 9RG
Support the talented chefs of the future at this on-site restaurant. Wonderful dishes are prepared by chefs-in-training, guaranteeing guests a first-class dining experience. *Open College term times only.

25% OFF TOTAL | 4 | FRI ✱ | SAT ✱ | SUN | ▲ — British

Tyne and Wear

THE ALEXANDRA ☎0191 510 1100
Queen Alexandra Road, Sunderland, SR2 9PF
This fabulous eatery provides an extensive menu capturing the flavours and aromas of the Mediterranean by offering a range of contemporary and traditional dishes which reflect the variety of Italian food.

50% OFF FOOD | 4 | FRI ✓ | SAT ✓ | SUN — British

ALI'S KITCHEN ☎0191 265 5505
10 Heaton Road, Newcastle, NE6 1SD
Friendly staff and exotic Indian tastes wait for you at this wonderful Indian restaurant, in the heart of Heaton.

25% OFF TOTAL | 4 | FRI ✓ | SAT ✓ | ✱ — Indian

AMORE
☎0191 565 0077

11 Tavistock Place, Sunderland, SR1 1PB

An incredibly popular restaurant that serves Italian cuisine with a fiery modern edge. The smooth sounds of jazz on Tuesday evenings provide an evocative ambience.

25% OFF TOTAL | 4 | FRI ✱ | SAT ✱ | ▲ — Italian

THE ANGEL VIEW INN
0191 410 3219

Low Eighton, Gateshead, NE9 7UB

A real angel of the North, this great little pub is situated in the pretty countryside surrounding Low Eighton. Stone arches, high ceilings and a charming décor altogether make this a delightful choice.

25% OFF TOTAL | 6 | FRI ✓ | SAT × | SUN | ▲ — Multi-Cuisine

AROMA TANDOORI
☎0191 284 1117

215 High Street, Gosforth, Newcastle, NE3 1HQ

A great restaurant in Gosworth offering delightful Indian cuisine. While away an evening as you enjoy the many starters and curries that make up the menu.

2FOR1 MAIN COURSE | FRI ✓ | SAT ✓ | ▲ — Indian

AS YOU LIKE IT
☎0191 281 2277

Archbold Terrace, Jesmond, Newcastle, NE2 1DB

Whether you sample the renowned British comfort food or the more adventurous global offerings, the food on offer is simply exquisite, with four bars and live music to complete your night out in style.

2FOR1 2 COURSES | FRI ✓ | SAT ✱ | ▲ — European

THE BADGER
01661 871 037

Street Houses, Ponteland, Newcastle, NE20 9BT

This Vintage Inn oozes rural charm and rustic character. The picturesque surroundings provide the perfect backdrop for savouring the hearty, seasonal pub-food on the menu.

25% OFF TOTAL | FRI ✓ | SAT ✓ | SUN | ▲ — Modern British

BAR BLANC
☎0191 2815126

38-42 Osbourne Road, Jesmond, Newcastle, NE22 2AL

Bar Blanc is the in-house restaurant of Whites Hotel in Jesmond, Newcastle. It serves a great range of delicious Indian cuisine throughout the day, and a fine selection of English and Continental dishes.

25% OFF TOTAL | 4 | FRI ✓ | SAT ✓ — International

BIG MUSSEL
☎0191 232 1057

15 The Side, Quayside, Newcastle, NE1 3JE

Revel in seafood galore at this fabulous fish restaurant, from traditional fish and chips to the more elaborate sea bass with braised cabbage and bacon. *See the website for further info.

25% OFF TOTAL | 2 | FRI ✓ | SAT × — Seafood

BINDI
☎0191 274 5505

261 Whickham View, Newcastle, NE15 7HP

Simple, sprightly modern curry house in the west of Newcastle, Bindi does an eclectic range of Indian dishes, from the more familiar classics to some chef's specialities that are worth a try.

2FOR1 MAIN COURSE | FRI ▯ | SAT × | SUN — Indian

BLUE COBRA
☎08713 104 630

15-16 Green Terrace, Sunderland, SR1 3PZ

The menu at Blue Cobra blends trustworthy recipes with contemporary twists, creating a unique and exciting selection of dishes to choose from.

2FOR1 MAIN COURSE | FRI ▯ | SAT × | ✱ | ▲ — Indian

THE BOLDON LAD
☎0191 426 0302

Hedworth Lane, Jarrow, NE32 4LQ

Local pub serving a great line in hearty British cuisine. Home-made food is served daily alongside a huge variety of beers, wines and spirits.

25% OFF TOTAL | 6 | FRI ✓ | SAT × | ▲ — British

THE BRIDGE RESTAURANT
☎0191 233 1010

The Vermont Hotel, Newcastle, NE1 1RQ

Admire captivating views of the Castle Garth whilst savouring a delectable dish. Whether guests are kick-starting the day with breakfast or indulging in a well-deserved Sunday lunch, this venue has it all.

2FOR1 MAIN COURSE | FRI ✓ | SAT × | SUN | ▲ — European

CAFÉ BANGLA
☎0191 519 0929

2 St Bede's, Station Road, East Boldon, NE36 0LE

Popular and high-quality tandoori restaurant with a broad, bold range of curries and other subcontinental dishes.

25% OFF TOTAL | 10 | FRI ✱ | SAT ✱ | ▲ — Indian

CAFÉ ROUGE
0191 460 5502

Redmall, Intu Metrocentre, Gateshead, NE11 9XR

French sophistication on the British high street - enjoy seasonally changing French dishes and a continental wine selection, served in a relaxed environment with an undeniable flair of Parisian chic.

25% OFF TOTAL | FRI ✓ | SAT ✓ | ✱ — French

CAFÉ ROUGE
0191 230 2140

34-40 Grey Street, Newcastle, NE1 6AE

French sophistication on the British high street - enjoy seasonally changing French dishes and a continental wine selection, served in a relaxed environment with an undeniable flair of Parisian chic.

25% OFF TOTAL | 6 | FRI ✓ | SAT ✓ | ✱ — French

THE CHILLINGHAM
☎0191 265 3992

89-91 Chillingham, Newcastle, NE6 5XL

Constantly buzzing, this venue is authentically traditional and offers an assortment of both real and guest ales. With entertainment guaranteed, diners can enjoy good-quality food at an affordable price.

2FOR1 MAIN COURSE | FRI ✓ | SAT ✓ | SUN — British

CLASSICO RESTAURANT
☎0191 284 9900

235 High Street, Newcastle, NE3 1HQ

Classico serve exquisite authentic Italian food. They are passionate about great food and wine, served in a warm and friendly atmosphere, by people who care and deliver quality service.

2FOR1 3 COURSES | FRI ▯ | SAT × | SUN | ✱ | ▲ — Italian

CONVIVIUM RESTAURANT @ HOLIDAY INN
☎0871 423 4818

Great North Road, Newcastle, NE13 6BP

Relax and dine in the spacious and peaceful Holiday Inn Newcastle-upon-Tyne. A perfect haven for a sumptuous meal with choices on the menu to whet the appetite of the most discerning diner.

25% OFF TOTAL | 6 | FRI ✓ | SAT ✓ — International

CRAWCROOK TANDOORI
☎0191 413 3373

17-19 Main Street, Crawcrook, Ryton, NE40 4TX

A family restaurant with a cosmopolitan edge, serving modern yet authentic Indian food in a chic, contemporary setting. Expect a warm welcome and fine food.

25% OFF TOTAL | 10 | FRI ✓ | SAT ✓ — Indian

DA MIMMOS
☎0191 222 0659

6-10 Leazes Park Road, Newcastle, NE1 4PF

Modern Italian restaurant that rightly prides itself on its authenticity. Pasta and pizza dishes here are top notch; the range of other dishes are also excellent. *Offer unavailable on match days.

2FOR1 3 COURSES | FRI ✓ | SAT ✓ | ▲ — Italian

D'ACQUA
☎0191 565 1988

26-28 John Street, Basement, Sunderland, SR1 1JG

James Shadforth is a local chef with big ambitions and passion for the industry. He has worked his way up in kitchens from the age of 15 and now, only nine years later, presents the excellent D'ACQUA.

2FOR1 MAIN COURSE | FRI ✓ | SAT ✱ — Mediterranean

DARAZ
☎0191 281 8431

4 Holly Avenue West, Jesmond, Newcastle, NE2 2AR

Only the freshest herbs and spices are used in the preparation of the wide selection of dishes here, with Bangladeshi cuisine being the house speciality. A family-run restaurant with a great reputation.

2FOR1 MAIN COURSE | FRI ✓ | SAT ✓ — Bangladeshi

DAVID KENNEDY'S FOOD SOCIAL
☎0191 260 5411

The Biscuit Factory, Stoddart St, Newcastle, NE2 1AN

David Kennedy was North East Chef of the Year in 2007 and has brought his imaginative, accomplished cooking to this contemporary art gallery in Newcastle. Broad and informal, with cooking of rare quality.

25% OFF TOTAL | 4 | FRI ✓ | SAT × | SUN | ▲ — Brasserie

DAYS OF THE RAJ
☎ 0191 284 9555

49 Great North Road, Gosforth, Newcastle, NE3 2HH

Combining the best of Eastern and Western cultures, this Indian cuisine is a subtle mixture of exotic flavours achieved by the blending of authentic spices. Flavoursome dishes to suit all tastes.

2FOR1 MAIN COURSE | FRI 📱 | SAT 📱 | SUN — Indian

DIVAN KHANAH
☎ 0191 417 7700

Spout Lane, Washington, NE38 7HP

Long-running Indian restaurant in Washington that's won itself a loyal base of fans over the years for its excellent array of dishes, consistently high standards in terms of flavour and generous portions.

2FOR1 MAIN COURSE | FRI × | SAT × | SUN — Indian

ESSY'S
☎ 0191 455 4477

Pier Block Yard, South Pier, South Shields, NE33 2JX

Essy's is located on the Pier in a beautiful small building with a wonderful view. Enjoy delectable Italian food served alongside chef's specials such as the 'black pudding tower'.

25% OFF TOTAL | 👤 4 | FRI ✓ | SAT ✓ | SUN — Italian

THE FALCON'S NEST
0191 236 7078

Rotary Way, North Brunton, Newcastle, NE3 5EH

This Vintage Inn oozes rural charm and rustic character. The picturesque surroundings provide the perfect backdrop for savouring the hearty, seasonal pub-food on the menu.

25% OFF TOTAL | FRI ✓ | SAT ✓ | SUN | ▲ — Modern British

FRANCO'S
☎ 0191 281 3434

1 Brentwood Mews, Jesmond, Newcastle, NE2 3DH

This restaurant has it all: style, atmosphere, quality food and excellent service. Owned by an Italian couple who combine their passion for food and hospitality to provide a venue fit for any occasion.

2FOR1 MAIN COURSE | FRI 📱 | SAT ✱ | ▲ — Italian

FREGATE RESTAURANT
☎ 0191 427 0999

Best Western Sea Hotel, Sea Rd, South Shields, NE33 2LD

Light, bright dining area with stunning sea views for a calm, relaxed meal; classic, clean and sophisticated flavours throughout the well-conceived menu. *Offer also available on the 'Super 8' menu.

25% OFF TOTAL | 👤 6 | FRI ✓ | SAT ✓ | ✱ | ▲ — British

FREYA'S RESTAURANT AT ASPERS
☎ 0191 255 0400

The Gate, Newgate Street, Newcastle, NE1 5TG

A casual eating environment throughout the day. Late breakfast, lunch and dinner are all covered with delicious menus offering dishes ranging from tempting steaks to delectable grilled fish.

2FOR1 3 COURSES | FRI ✓ | SAT ✱ | SUN — International

THE GODFATHER
☎ 0191 232 6171

3 Market Street, Newcastle, NE1 6JE

This venue caters for couples as well as larger parties, providing an authentic atmosphere. The menu contains many traditional and contemporary dishes, along with the chef's delicious specialities.

2FOR1 3 COURSES | FRI 📱 | SAT 📱 — Italian

THE GREENHOUSE BRASSERIE
☎ 0191 490 2414

Quarryfield Road, Gateshead, NE8 3BE

Ideal place to enjoy top-quality, modern British food. Dishes are reasonably priced and made from the very best seasonal ingredients, served in a relaxed environment. A local favourite.

2FOR1 MAIN COURSE | FRI ✓ | SAT ✓ | SUN — British

GREEN'S BRASSERIE
☎ 0191 213 0070

Gosforth, Parkway, Newcastle, NE12 8ET

A brasserie situated within a health club boasting a full menu of excellently balanced light and main meals. First-rate food complete with a wide range of alcoholic and soft drinks.

25% OFF TOTAL | FRI ✓ | SAT ✓ — European

HANDMADE BURGER CO.
0191 261 4589

The Gate, Newgate Street, Newcastle, NE1 5TG

100% prime Scotch beef burgers, handmade in the restaurant daily, sourdough buns, delicious handmade relishes and a wide range of toppings giving you over 40 varieties to choose from. *Exclusions apply.

2FOR1 MAIN COURSE | FRI ✓ | SAT × | SUN — International

HANDMADE BURGER CO.
0191 460 5086

48a Garden Walk, Metro Centre, Gateshead, NE11 9XZ

100% prime Scotch beef burgers, handmade in the restaurant daily, sourdough buns, delicious handmade relishes and a wide range of toppings giving you over 40 varieties to choose from. *Exclusions apply.

2FOR1 MAIN COURSE | FRI ✓ | SAT × | SUN — International

HIMALAYA
☎ 0191 251 3629

33 Esplanade, Whitley Bay, NE26 2AL

A locally popular venue offering quality Indian cuisine, good value and ocean views. Time and time again this restaurant delivers quality food, with classic dishes from tikka to tandoori.

2FOR1 MAIN COURSE | FRI ✓ | SAT ✓ | SUN — Indian

HORTON GRANGE
☎ 01661 860 686

Berwick Hill, Newcastle, NE13 6BU

Appreciate the beautiful scenery and enjoy excellent dishes created with quality produce. Imaginative menus provide something for all, and includes seasonal specialities, such as the grilled halibut.

25% OFF TOTAL | 👤 4 | FRI ✓ | SAT ✱ | SUN — International

HOTEL DU VIN
☎ 0191 229 2215

Allan House, City Road, Newcastle, NE1 2BE

The finest, freshest local produce, simple European recipes and a stunning choice of wines; these are the elements of the trademark Hotel du Vin bistro. Recognised with a double AA Rosette.

2FOR1 MAIN COURSE | FRI ✓ | SAT ✱ | SUN — Bistro

IMPERIAL DRAGON
☎ 0191 262 8788

86 High Street East, Wallsend, NE28 7RH

The vastness and diversity of China's geography is reflected in the eclectic cuisine showcased here, with a cooking style that produces delicious results.

2FOR1 MAIN COURSE | FRI ✓ | SAT ✱ | ✱ — Chinese

INDIGO
☎ 0191 454 8882

104-106 Ocean Road, South Shields, NE33 2JF

Honesty and simplicity are key to this venue's ethos. Focusing on quality service and excellent flavours, it is no wonder Indigo has an abundance of regular clientèle along with newcomers every night.

25% OFF TOTAL | 👤 6 | FRI ✓ | SAT ✓ | ✱ — Indian

IT'S ALL GREEK 2 ME
☎ 0191 251 0622

Watt's Road, Whitley Bay, NE26 1BQ

Sit down and relax, enjoy original cuisine, and listen to Greek music. With a picturesque location on the entrance to Whitley Bay beach, this restaurant offers you unbeatable atmosphere and delicious food.

2FOR1 MAIN COURSE | FRI × | SAT × — Mediterranean

JACK SPRATS CAFÉ
☎ 0191 265 7708

413 Chillingham Road, Heaton, Newcastle, NE6 5QU

A vegetarian restaurant serving tasty snacks, seasonal dishes and home-made cakes, to be accompanied with a smooth coffee or juicy smoothie. Breads, cheeses and wines line the menu.

50% OFF FOOD | 👤 2 | FRI 📱 | SAT 📱 — Vegetarian

JASHN
☎ 0191 488 8505

Whickham Bank, Newcastle, NE16 3BP

A blend of classic and contemporary cuisine lines the menu here, with every dish delicately spiced and flavoured.

25% OFF TOTAL | FRI ✓ | SAT 📱 | ✱ — Indian

KAMAL BALTI HOUSE
☎ 0191 226 1726

277-279 Stanhope Street, Fenham, Newcastle NE4 5JU

The Kamal Balti House specializes in authentic Indian cuisine, there is a wide selection of dishes and the service friendly, staff accommodating and atmosphere warm.

2FOR1 2 COURSES | FRI × | SAT × | ✱ — Indian

KESAR
☎ 0191 259 5976

76-78 Church Way, North Shields, NE29 0AA

Brings elegant Indian cuisine to the city. Well-recognised for its award-winning status and delicious dishes.

2FOR1 2 COURSES | FRI ✱ | SAT ✱ | ✱ — Indian

KOH-I-NOOR
☎0191 232 5379

26 Cloth Market, Newcastle, NE1 1EE

A late night, family-run restaurant with an owner boasting 18 years experience. Heavenly rich and fragrant dishes that cater for all tastes: the ideal spot for celebrations before a night on the town.

2FOR1 2 COURSES | FRI ✓ | SAT ✓ | ✱ — Indian

LA TASCA
☎0191 230 4006

106 The Quayside, Newcastle, NE1 3DX

Quintessentially Spanish, La Tasca's fresh and exciting menu offers something for everyone. Their tapas dishes are sincerely authentic, while their paellas always deliver on flavour.

25% OFF TOTAL | 8 | FRI ✓ | SAT ✗ | ▲ — Spanish

LA VITA
☎0191 265 0044

210 Heaton Road, Heaton, Newcastle, NE6 5HP

An impressive restaurant offering a menu bursting with tremendously good, classic Italian dishes. A specials board offers delightful variations, such as a corking lamb shank in red wine sauce.

2FOR1 MAIN COURSE | FRI ✓ | SAT ✓ — Italian

LB RESTAURANT
☎0191 230 3780

1a Clayton Street West, Newcastle, NE1 5EE

Great thought and a large amount of culinary influence goes into every dish at LB Restaurant. Offers guests a menu that is bursting to the brim of Indian specials and classic favourites.

25% OFF TOTAL | 10 | FRI ✓ | SAT ✓ — Indian

LIBERTY BROWN
☎0191 516 9009

10 Hylton Retail Park, Sunderland, SR5 3XG

Exotic and healthy cuisine is served in a cosy yet stylishly chic environment. From North African vegetable tangine to home-made game sausages, this venue provides a little something for everyone.

2FOR1 MAIN COURSE | FRI ✗ | SAT ✗ — Italian

LIBRARY AND PRINT ROOM
☎01661 886 500

Matfen Hall, Matfen, Newcastle, NE20 0RH

This restaurant has 2 AA Rosettes attesting to the quality of its food. Overlooking the 18th green of Matfen Hall's golf course, the Library and Print Room serves fabulous food in an idyllic setting.

2FOR1 2 COURSES | FRI ▮ | SAT ▮ — British

LIGHT OF ASIA
☎01642 470 135

15 Queen Street, Redcar, TS10 1AB

Whether diners are seeking a little something to get them through the day or a weekend treat, Light of Asia cooks up vivacious and vibrant curries to satisfy hungry tummies.

2FOR1 MAIN COURSE | FRI ✓ | SAT ✓ — Indian

LIGHT OF INDIA
☎0191 234 5556

120-122 High Street East, Wallsend, NE28 7RH

Highly recommended by locals, Light of India uses fresh ingredients and traditional recipes to create a diverse range of Indian culinary delights for down-to-earth prices.

2FOR1 3 COURSES | FRI ✓ | SAT ✓ | ✱ — Indian

LITTLE SAIGON
☎0191 233 0766

6 Bigg Market, Newcastle, NE1 1UW

Vietnam's long history and vibrant culture has left a legacy of truly inspirational cuisine, showcased here among the eclectic array of beautiful, healthy dishes concocted out of exotic ingredients.

25% OFF TOTAL | 4 | FRI ✱ | SAT ✱ — Vietnamese

LOCH FYNE
☎01912 559 320

West Avenue, Gosforth, Newcastle, NE3 4ES

From the roadside oyster bar that once was, Loch Fyne restaurants now successfully inject energy and passion into great food and wonderful flavours, whilst ensuring their seafood is sustainably sourced.

25% OFF TOTAL | 4 | FRI ✱ | SAT ✱ | ▲ — Seafood

THE LOUNGE BISTRO AND BAR
☎0191 511 6270

Sunderland College, Sunderland, SR5 5DB

Situated at the Hylton Campus of Sunderland College, The Lounge Bistro and Bar is one of the UK's top chef training colleges in the UK. Head here to sample the very best that new talent has to offer.

25% OFF TOTAL | 4 | FRI ✱ | SAT ✱ | ▲ — Modern British

THE MAGPIE ROOM
☎0844 372 1892

St James' Park, Newcastle, NE1 4ST

This restaurant serves food in the function room at St James Park, home of the renowned institution, Newcastle United FC. Enjoy a thoroughgoing four-course Sunday lunch before your tour of the stadium.

25% OFF TOTAL | 2 | FRI ✓ | SAT ✓ — British

MALMAISON
☎0191 245 5000

Quayside, Newcastle, NE1 3DX

Striking and charismatic décor in a brasserie whose focus is on fresh, locally sourced produce and a contemporary, stylish ambience. Enjoy this sassy Newcastle Mal and its distinctive style. 1 AA Rosette.

2FOR1 MAIN COURSE | FRI ✗ | SAT ✗ | SUN | ▲ — European

MANDARIN
☎0191 261 7960

14 Stowell Street, Newcastle, NE1 4XQ

Set in Newcastle's Chinatown, the Mandarin draws on piquant flavours from the many traditions and techniques of Chinese cuisine; it provides the classics, while adding innovative original tastes.

25% OFF TOTAL | 4 | FRI ✓ | SAT ✱ | ▲ — Chinese

THE MED
☎0191 597 4109

4 Grangerville South, Newcastle, NE4 6UH

Combining Turkish, Kurdish and Greek cooking methods, the chefs exert innovation and imagination. Vegetarians can give into vegetable moussaka and guvec, then finish off with a sumptuous Turkish delight.

25% OFF TOTAL | FRI ▮ | SAT ▮ — Mediterranean

MING DYNASTY
☎0191 514 2578

7 High Street West, Sunderland, SR1 3EX

A lively, central Chinese restaurant that draws especially on the clear, fresh flavours of Cantonese cuisine, along with a full range of bright, classic Chinese dishes.

25% OFF TOTAL | 6 | FRI ✓ | SAT ✓ — Chinese

MODERN TANDOORI
☎0191 234 2749

174 High Street West, Wallsend, NE28 8HZ

This place is a must for lovers of Bangladeshi and Indian cuisine, with the rich, vibrant, and flavoursome cuisine always being perfectly cooked and beautifully presented.

25% OFF TOTAL | 10 | FRI ✓ | SAT ✓ | ✱ — Indian

THE MOGUL RAJ
☎01661 821 550

15-17 Merton Way, Ponteland, NE20 9PY

The fantastic Indian dishes served here are worth travelling that extra mile for. Once you discover its satisfying tastiness, you will be reluctant to share your chosen dish.

2FOR1 MAIN COURSE | FRI ▮ | SAT ▮ | SUN — Indian

MR LYNCH
☎0191 281 3010

Archbold Terrace, Newcastle, NE2 1BF

Music lovers are in their element with the fantastic entertainment this venue has to offer. Seven nights a week, guests can indulge in a dance accompanied by a wholesome, home-made dish.

2FOR1 MAIN COURSE | FRI ✓ | SAT ✗ — British

MRS ALI
☎0191 281 9988

11-17 Archbold Terrace, Jesmond, NE2 1DB

This contemporary pan-Asian restaurant revels in its attention to detail with an observance of classic Indian tradition and an onus on hospitality to go with their use of natural, fresh herbs and spices.

2FOR1 MAIN COURSE | FRI ✓ | SAT ✓ — Indian

NANCY'S BORDELLO
☎0191 260 2929

13 Argyle Street, Newcastle, NE1 6PF

With an exquisite décor mirroring that of a boutique, stripped floorboards, plush vintage armchairs and antique lamps create a retro ambiance in which to indulge in home-made cuisine after a game of pool.

2FOR1 MAIN COURSE | FRI ✓ | SAT ✗ — Mediterranean

NEW BENGAL
☎0191 284 1295

232 High Street, Gosforth, Newcastle, NE3 1HH

Cosy, accommodating Indian restaurant in Gosforth where you'll find the air rich with the scent of fresh spices and the menu filled with everything from old favourites to house specialities.

2FOR1 MAIN COURSE | 8 | FRI ✱ | SAT ✱ — Indian

To understand what the restaurant icons mean, please see the inside back cover.

NOOSH RESTAURANT
0191 232 4663
St Nicholas Street, Newcastle, NE1 1PE
Contemporary European meets classic Middle Eastern cuisine at this savvy restaurant. There are some scintillating dishes to be found here, all based on strong local knowledge and supplier relationships.
2FOR1 MAIN COURSE | FRI | SAT | International

OLIVIANA'S
0191 232 5537
5-7 The Side, Quayside, Newcastle, TNE1 3JE
Reasonably priced Italian cuisine can be expected at Oliviana's. While away the evening over your favourite dish and a bottle of fine wine.
25% OFF TOTAL | 4 | FRI | SAT | Italian

PARADISO
0191 221 1240
1 Market Lane, Newcastle, NE1 6QQ
Discreetly hidden down a quaint cobbled street, this restaurant epitomises Italian stylishness. Lamb shank with mustard and leek mash and Moroccan monkfish are just two of the tasty treats you can try.
2FOR1 2 COURSES | FRI | SAT | Mediterranean

PIAZZA LATINA
0191 487 5810
592-596 Durham Road, Newcastle, NE9 6HX
Piazza Latina is a fusion of Italian, Continental and Mexican cuisine. The menu offers a vast and varied choice of freshly prepared dishes, using only the best ingredients which are delivered fresh each day.
2FOR1 MAIN COURSE | FRI ✓ | SAT ✓ | SUN | Italian

PITCHER & PIANO
0191 232 4110
108 Quayside, Newcastle, NE1 3DX
Passion for the best service, premium drinks and great food, and a commitment to creating a contemporary, cool ambience define the character of life at this modern bar.
25% OFF TOTAL | 2 | FRI ✓ | SAT | SUN | British

PIZZERIA 395
01912 610 481
33a Groat Market, Newcastle, NE1 1UQ
Situated in the heart of the bustling Groat market, Newcastle, you are invited to join the amiable staff at 395 pizzeria. Great cuisine of exceptional quality produced in a family-run kitchen.
2FOR1 MAIN COURSE | FRI ✓ | SAT ✓ | SUN | Pizza

THE PLATE RESTAURANT
0191 236 4111
Marriott Hotel Gosforth Park, Newcastle, NE3 5HN
Boasting 12 acres of parkland and an enviable location, the Marriott at Gosworth Park offers guests everything they need for a perfect stay. Fine dining can be found in the 1 AA Rosette winning restaurant.
25% OFF TOTAL | 8 | FRI | SAT ✓ | SUN | International

PLAZA TANDOORI
0191 257 4344
4 Palace Building, Grand Parade, Tynemouth, NE30 4JS
Besides an adherence to its name - that is, a specialisation in tandoori - this Bangladeshi restaurant walks a mile in the eclectic's shoes: trout and duck dishes supplement the staple chicken and lamb.
2FOR1 MAIN COURSE | FRI | SAT | Indian

PRIMA
0191 233 1011
40-46 Side, Newcastle, NE1 3JA
Undoubtedly authentic, the Italian cuisine is genuinely rustic. Gorge on creamy pastas, home-made pizzas and quality cuts of meat smothered in flavourful sauces.
25% OFF TOTAL | 8 | FRI | SAT × | Pizza

RASA NEWCASTLE
0191 232 7799
27 Queen street, Newcastle, NE1 3UG
Inspired by the authentic home cooking of beautiful, spice-rich Kerala, this restaurant's passion is food prepared with devotion, love, and the finest ingredients.
2FOR1 MAIN COURSE | FRI ✓ | SAT ✓ | Indian

RENDEZ VOUS BAR
0871 376 9029
County Hotel, Neville Street, Newcastle, NE1 5DF
Set in The County Hotel Newcastle, the Rendez Vous bar is tall and bright, and a great place to settle in for a glass of wine or a cocktail, together with some light bites and bar snacks.
50% OFF FOOD | 6 | FRI ✓ | SAT ✓ | British

RENDEZ VOUS RESTAURANT
0871 376 9029
County Hotel, Neville Street, Newcastle, NE1 5DF
Bustling city centre restaurant in the County Hotel. Friendly, open welcome both for hotel guests and those looking for a good bite to eat. Menu of British and European dishes cooked in an open kitchen.
50% OFF FOOD | 6 | FRI ✓ | SAT ✓ | British

RESTAURANT KRAKOW
0191 261 0197
2-6 Shakespeare Street, Newcastle, NE1 6AQ
Day-by-day Polish cuisine is becoming more popular in the UK, and this restaurant brings a taste of Eastern Europe to Newcastle with pork loins, chicken schnitzel and meatballs all featured on the menu.
25% OFF TOTAL | 10 | FRI | SAT | Polish

RETREAT RESTAURANT
0191 229 5237
Tyne Metropolitan College, Wallsend, NE28 9NJ
Treat yourself to an opulent 5-course fine dining experience at a pocket-friendly price. Prepared by the most innovative and talented trainee chefs, the cuisine is so popular that booking is essential.
2FOR1 2 COURSES | FRI | SAT × | SUN | British

ROMNA TANDOORI
0191 251 3583
43 Esplanade, Whitley Bay, NE26 2AE
Offering first-rate authentic Indian cuisine, this restaurant is one of the best for value in Whitley bay. A varied menu delivers classic dishes that are cooked to perfection time and time again.
2FOR1 3 COURSES | FRI ✓ | SAT ✓ | Indian

RUPALI RESTAURANT
0191 232 8629
6 Bigg Market, Newcastle, NE1 1UW
Providing a range of mild to extremely spicy Indian dishes. For the brave only, the infamous 'curry hell' is free for those who succeed in eating every mouthful of the world's hottest curry.
2FOR1 2 COURSES | FRI ✓ | SAT ✓ | Indian

SALSA TAPAS BAR
0191 221 1022
89 Westgate Road, Newcastle, NE1 4AE
Sample enticing tapas dishes such as minted lamb meatballs, tempura battered brie and tiger prawns in garlic. Meet with friends over a jug of Sangria and enjoy informal social grazing in a chilled out style.
25% OFF TOTAL | 2 | FRI ✓ | SAT × | Spanish

SHAHE
0191 285 1801
30 Wansbeck Road, Gosforth, NE3 3HQ
'Shahe' means 'royal': the wide variety of dishes and delicate flavours of India ensure this restaurant lives up to its name. Richly decadent food is served in lavish, palace-style surroundings.
2FOR1 MAIN COURSE | FRI | SAT | Indian

SHAHIRA RESTAURANT
0191 273 5688
498 Westgate Road, Newcastle, NE4 9HD
House specials from the makhani to the chilli masala dish make this a must-visit Indian and Tandoori restaurant. Find the ideal drink from an extensive list to match your chosen dish.
2FOR1 3 COURSES | FRI ✓ | SAT × | SUN | Bangladeshi

SHIRAZ RESTAURANT
0191 222 1363
39b Groat Market, Newcastle, NE1 1UG
A very warm welcome to SHIRAZ, the home of great tasting, authentic Indian cuisine, set in beautiful, contemporary surroundings in the heart of Newcastle city centre.
2FOR1 2 COURSES | FRI ✓ | SAT × | Indian

SILK ROOM RESTAURANT
0191 260 3506
Trinity Gardens, Newcastle, E1 2HF
This popular bar and restaurant is a breath of fresh air to the dining scene on Newcastle Quayside. Mouth-watering cuisine is served in intimate boutique surroundings.
2FOR1 MAIN COURSE | FRI | SAT | Contemporary

SIMPLY GREEK TAVERN
0191 222 0035
2-4 Bigg Market, Newcastle, NE1 1UW
Step inside this classic taverna and you're transported as if to Greece. From the whitewash walls to the delectable, herby delicacies on the menu, the owners ensure you have a truly Greek experience.
2FOR1 2 COURSES | FRI | SAT | Greek

SINGH'S INDIAN RESTAURANT
☎0191 272 2992

20 Stanhope Street, Newcastle, NE4 6BH

Beautifully presented, the cuisine at Singh's oozes genuine Indian character. The knowledgeable staff serve exceptional food by candlelight and will take delight in helping guests choose the perfect dish.

25% OFF TOTAL | 10 | FRI ✓ | SAT ✓ — Indian

SIX AT THE BALTIC
☎0191 440 4948

BALTIC Centre, Gateshead Quays, Gateshead, NE8 3BA

Offers a striking menu of simply cooked dishes; you'll enjoy the visual and olfactory qualities of their contemporary British cuisine. *Advance booking mentioning Gourmet Society is essential.

2FOR1 2 COURSES | FRI ✓ | SAT ✱ | ▲ — British

SONNY'S ITALIA
☎0191 296 0755

Front Street, North Shields, NE30 4DX

Widely travelled and experienced chef Ken leads the kitchen of this Riviera-style restaurant, serving classical, homely Mediterranean food and drink in a vibrant and welcoming atmosphere.

2FOR1 MAIN COURSE | FRI ✓ | SAT ✱ — Italian

SPICE BOLLYWOOD
0191 460 9449

Unit 16-17, The Studio, Gateshead, NE11 9YG

Offers patrons all the classic Indian dishes, like onion bhajis and lamb curry. Immersed in a Bollywood setting diners can enjoy sumptuous food in an authentic atmosphere.

2FOR1 3 COURSES | FRI ✓ | SAT ✱ — Indian

THE STAR OF SIAM
☎0191 512 0905

101 Durham Road, Houghton-le-Spring, DH5 9QT

Diners are promised service with a smile at this long-established Thai venue. Whether guests are novices or well-experienced curry lovers, the cuisine is sure to tantalise the palate.

25% OFF TOTAL | 8 | FRI ✓ | SAT × — Thai

THE STONEBROOK
0191 270 2704

Edmund Road, Holystone, Newcastle, NE27 0UN

Quality pub classics with a modern twist combine with a friendly and relaxed atmosphere to make this Table Table venue the perfect place for family gatherings or meeting friends.

2FOR1 MAIN COURSE | FRI ✓ | SAT ✓ — Modern British

STRADA
0191 261 6070

Old Eldon Square, Newcastle, NE1 7JG

Strada offers fresh, bold dishes inspired by flavours of Italian city life! Try the hand-stretched, stone baked pizzas, addictive pastas and risottos, great share plates and much more. *Excludes Pizzettas.

25% OFF TOTAL | 6 | FRI ✓ | SAT × | ▲ — Italian

TANDOORI INTERNATIONAL
☎0191 456 2000

97 Ocean Road, South Shields, NE33 2JL

Family-run for two generations hailing from the Sylhet region of Bangladesh; the chefs here are particular masters of Sylheti cuisine and masala dishes.

2FOR1 MAIN COURSE | FRI ✓ | SAT ✱ | ✱ — Indian

TAVISTOCK ITALIA
☎0191 567 1786

Roker Hotel, Roker Terrace, Sunderland, SR6 9ND

Stunning in architecture and style, this Victorian building is now home to an impressive hotel and restaurant. Head to heaven with the chicken and cranberry parfait or the wild mushroom and truffle soup.

2FOR1 3 COURSES | FRI ✱ | SAT ✱ — European

TAVISTOCK ITALIA
☎0191 456 5670

Stanhope Road, Newcastle, NE33 4SS

Complete with retro décor, the ambiance is ideal for unwinding after a long week. Guests can devour bursting potato skins, authentic pizzas and naughty-but-nice tiramisu loaded with chocolate.

50% OFF FOOD | 6 | FRI × | SAT × | ▲ — Italian

THAI SIAM
☎0191 232 0261

16 Stowell Street, Newcastle, NE1 4XQ

For those who already have a firm favourite, the à la carte menu offers a large variety of Thai dishes for your satisfaction; alternatively, the set banquets are a great way to sample a bit of everything.

25% OFF TOTAL | 4 | FRI ✓ | SAT ✱ | ▲ — Thai

THROWING STONES
☎0191 565 3939

Glass Centre, Liberty Way, Sunderland, SR6 0GL

Characterful café and restaurant at the National Glass Centre; acclaimed in its own right as a leading restaurant in the North East, it serves a diversity of dishes with verve and passion.

25% OFF TOTAL | 2 | FRI ✓ | SAT × | SUN — British

TRACKSIDE RESTAURANT
☎0191 210 5300

Greyhound Stadium, Foss Way, Byker, Newcastle, NE6 2XJ

Trackside restaurant at the Newcastle Greyhound Stadium. Just the place to enjoy the best seats in the house for a great evening at the dogs, with some simple, tasty food while you're at it.

50% OFF FOOD | FRI × | SAT × | SUN | ▲ — British

TRACKSIDE RESTAURANT
☎0191 568 6205

Greyhound Stadium, Newcastle Road, Sunderland, SR5 1RP

Sunderland Dogs is a great night out, needless to say, which is improved even more by the Trackside Restaurant, serving a range of tasty, freshly cooked dishes to accompany your evening at the races.

50% OFF FOOD | 2 | FRI ✱ | SAT ✱ — British

VENETO
☎0191 413 6444

Parsons Drive, Ryton, Gateshead, NE40 3RA

A fresh venue that boasts a classic pizzeria menu and many other classic options to choose from. Wonderful, friendly staff serve quality food in a relaxed and casual atmosphere, catering for all tastes.

2FOR1 MAIN COURSE | FRI ✱ | SAT ✱ — Italian/ Mediterranean

VINCENZO'S
☎0191 240 0300

16 Addycombe Terrace, Heaton, Newcastle, NE6 5DP

A traditional Italian restaurant offering an authentic taste to its diners, with well-prepared and -presented dishes and a high-class specials board. A local favourite for both couples and families alike.

2FOR1 2 COURSES | FRI ✓ | SAT ✱ — Italian

WHITES HOTEL
☎0191 281 5126

38-42 Osbourne Road, Newcastle, NE2 2AL

A warm, inviting hotel that thrives on its friendly service and decadent interior. Dine in the hotel's best attribute, Bar Blanc, where wine bar chic blends with a fabulous Indian restaurant.

25% OFF TOTAL | FRI ✓ | SAT ✓ — Indian

WHITLEYBAY TANDOORI RESTAURANT
☎0191 252 9483

40 Esplanade, Whitley Bay, NE26 2AE

Whitley Bay Tandoori does just as it says on the tin, with a bright and hospitable ambience playing host to the full gamut of classic Indian dishes, and an especial line in tandoori recipes.

2FOR1 MAIN COURSE | FRI ✓ | SAT ✓ | ✱ — Indian

East Yorkshire

ALISHAAN
☎01482 847 255

205 Hallgate, Cottingham, HU16 4BB

Homely place to eat that stands out for its simple quality and range of choice. A restaurant that has regularly received accolades in the local media, with the focus consistently on the quality of cooking.

50% OFF FOOD | 4 | FRI ✱ | SAT ✱ | ▲ — Indian

BARINDA BAR & GRILL
☎01482 500 800

61 Boothferry Road, Hull, HU3 6UA

Smart and well-organised neighbourhood Bangladeshi restaurant that's won itself a good local reputation for the range of its menu and the quality of its cooking.

50% OFF FOOD | 4 | FRI ✱ | SAT ✱ — Bangladeshi

BEVERLEY ARMS HOTEL
☎01482 869 241

North Bar, Beverley East, HU17 8DD

Dine in the classically decorated restaurant of this hotel, a former coach house dating back to 1794. Guests and in-the-know locals are invited to feast on a wide range of traditional dishes.

25% OFF TOTAL | FRI ✓ | SAT ✓ — Traditional English

THE BLACK PRINCE
☎01482 845 872

18 The Parkway, Cottingham, HU16 5DG

The Black Prince is a pristine establishment with friendly welcoming staff and hearty pub grub. They are hard working team, dedicated to providing tasty food and high quality service.

2FOR1 3 COURSES | FRI ✱ | SAT✱ — British

THE BRASSERIE @ MECURE
☎0844 815 9037

Grange Park Hotel, Grange Park Lane, Hull, HU10 6EA

When hunger strikes, the Hull Grange Park Brasserie Restaurant will serve you and cater to your needs. Here you'll find a vibrant and open place to feed your appetite with a well-accomplished menu.

2FOR1 3 COURSES | FRI ✓ | SAT✓ — British

BURLINGTONS RESTAURANT
☎01262 400 383

91 High Street, Bridlington, YO16 4PN

A restaurant run by husband and wife offering food that incorporates influences from all over the world. Co-owner and chef David injects Thai twists and Italian freshness into some very English dishes.

25% OFF TOTAL | 4 | FRI ✓ | SAT✱ | SUN | ▲ — Contemporary

CINNAMON INDIAN RESTAURANT
☎01482 323 113

17 Anlaby Road, Hull, HU1 2PJ

Opulent surroundings set the scene for some truly exquisite Indian dishes. Cinnamon's chefs use only seasonal ingredients to ensure authenticity and freshness. Guests can expect a warm welcome.

50% OFF FOOD | 4 | FRI ✓ | SAT✓ — Indian

THE DERWENT ARMS
☎0190 441 3498

39 The Village, Osbaldwick, YO10 3NP

Situated in the village of Osbaldwick in York, The Derwent Arms is well known in the local area as a great meeting point and public house. *Offer is not valid on a Tuesday evening.

2FOR1 MAIN COURSE | FRI × | SAT× | SUN — English/Gastro pub

DINE ON THE ROWE
☎01482 502 269

12-14 Butcher Row, Beverley, HU17 0AB

A restaurant in Beverley that serves beautiful brasserie-style food from fresh, local produce. Look in particular for the succulent Givendale steaks, hung for four weeks and cooked to perfection.

25% OFF TOTAL | 6 | FRI × | SAT× | ▲ — British

DOMINIC'S RESTAURANT
☎01482 507 070

254 Hull Road, Hull, HU4 7RR

Renowned for obvious reasons, flair and panache seep from the doors of Dominic's. Hospitality being key to their work ethos, staff welcome a variety of guests. Meat dishes and pastas feature highly menu.

25% OFF TOTAL | 10 | FRI × | SAT× | ✱ | ▲ — Italian

FUDGE RESTAURANT
☎01482 441 019

93 Princes Avenue, Hull, HU5 3QP

From the delicious mains to the decadent desserts, the menu here sings with an appreciation of homely, hearty goodness. A vibrant, friendly place to enjoy a light bite or something more substantial.

2FOR1 3 COURSES | FRI ✓ | SAT× — Brasserie

THE GARDENERS
☎01964 562 625

Hull Road, Coniston, Hull, HU11 5AE

A charming country inn set amidst beautifully peaceful farmland, The Gardeners is the ideal place to take advantage of country classic dishes and mouth-watering cuisine.

50% OFF FOOD | 2 | FRI ✓ | SAT✓ | SUN | ▲ — British

HANDMADE BURGER CO.
01482 212 711

110 Ferensway, Hull, HU2 8LN

100% prime Scotch beef burgers, handmade in the restaurant daily, sourdough buns, delicious handmade relishes and a wide range of toppings giving you over 40 varieties to choose from. *Exclusions apply.

2FOR1 MAIN COURSE | FRI ✓ | SAT× | SUN — International

JUNCTION RESTAURANT @ HOLIDAY INN
☎01482 386 299

Holiday Inn Hull, Castle Street, Hull, HU1 2BX

Guests will be impressed by the different dining options available to them at Holiday Inn Hull. The bar offers light, informal meals while the restaurant serves up some wholesome British fare and seafood.

25% OFF TOTAL | FRI ✓ | SAT✓ — International

THE KETCH
01482 651 255

Great Gutter Lane West, Willerby, Hull, HU10 6DP

Beefeater Grill are one of the UK's best-loved restaurants welcoming guests for almost 40 years in over 130 locations nationwide. *Excludes Breakfast, Light Bites, Bar menu, set menus and all other offers.

2FOR1 MAIN COURSE | 6 | FRI ✓ | SAT× | ▲ — Modern British

THE KINGSWOOD
01482 820225

Kingswood Retail Park, Kingston Upon Hull, HU73 3DD

Quality pub classics with a modern twist combine with a friendly and relaxed atmosphere to make this Table Table venue the perfect place for family gatherings or meeting friends.

2FOR1 MAIN COURSE | FRI ✓ | SAT✓ — Modern British

LOUNGE BAR @ HOLIDAY INN
☎01482 386 300

Holiday Inn Hull, Castle Street, Hull, HU1 2BX

Holiday Inn Hull makes full use of its prime location. This relaxing, spacious lounge overlooks the Marina, providing the perfect backdrop to a balmy afternoon. Light meals and dinner drinks on offer.

25% OFF TOTAL | FRI ✓ | SAT✓ — International

LUCCA BAR AND KITCHEN
☎01482 470 088

84 Princes Avenue, Hull, HU5 3QJ

At Lucca Bar & Kitchen, they are passionate about fine dining and hospitality. They are committed to providing outstanding food and service, in a friendly inviting atmosphere.

25% OFF TOTAL | 4 | FRI ✱ | SAT✱ | SUN | ▲ — Italian

MAHARAJAH RESTAURANT
☎01482 224 647

245 Holderness Road, Hull, HU8 8TB

Specialising in fulfilling those curry cravings, Maharajah prepare velvety korma and spicy chicken balti. An abundance of tempting starters and hot naans ensure diners go home gratified.

25% OFF TOTAL | 8 | FRI ✓ | SAT✓ | ✱ — Indian

MIAH'S RESTAURANT
☎01405 761 751

1 Government Street, Goole, DN14 5AN

Skilled chefs prepare traditional curries with a zesty, contemporary twist. Guaranteeing to please every palate, Miah's boast a loyal following of regulars.

2FOR1 MAIN COURSE | FRI × | SAT× — Indian

MIRCHI RESTAURANT
☎01482 871 537

6 Ladygate, Beverley, HU17 8BH

Specialising in Indian cuisine, the korahi and balti dishes come highly appraised. For the more adventurous, bold flavours and colours are captured by the house specials and fish dishes.

2FOR1 2 COURSES | FRI ✓ | SAT✓ | ✱ — Indian

PREZZO
☎01482 223 277

St Stephens Ferensway, Hull, HU2 8LN

With a character all of its own, Prezzo oozes contemporary style and enduring charm. Signature pastas, stone-baked pizzas and classic Italian dishes promise a perfect dining choice for the whole family.

2FOR1 MAIN COURSE | FRI × | SAT× | ▲ — Italian

PREZZO
01482 866 334

65-66 Saturday Market, Beverley, HU17 8AJ

With a character all of its own, Prezzo oozes contemporary style and enduring charm. Signature pastas, stone-baked pizzas and classic Italian dishes promise a perfect dining choice for the whole family.

2FOR1 MAIN COURSE | FRI × | SAT× | ▲ — Italian

PRINCE OF INDIA
☎01482 845 777

119 Hall Gate, Cottingham, HU16 4DA

Providing memorable dining experiences, the kitchen and waiting staff at the Prince of India work together to achieve first-class service and outstanding Indian food.

25% OFF TOTAL | 10 | FRI | SAT | ✱ — Indian

RAJ PAVILION
☎01482 581 939

56a-58 Beverley Road, Kingston-upon-Hull, HU3 1YE

Vivid and stylish modern Indian restaurant, serving a cracking range of dishes. Known for its marinades, korahi dishes and excellent specialities such as the Bangladeshi favourite, dil pasand gaggot.

2FOR1 3 COURSES | FRI ✱ | SAT✱ — Indian

ROTTANA ☎01482 471 390

175-177 Newland Avenue, Hull, HU5 2EP

The menu here is full of Turkish delights ranging from mezes and salads to flavoursome plates of grilled chicken, lamb & vegetarian dishes, using only the finest ingredients.

2FOR1 3 COURSES | FRI ✓ | SAT ✓ — Middle Eastern

SIMPLY INDIAN RESTAURANT ☎01405 869 618

Main Street , Pollington, Goole, DN14 0DN

Simple by name, simple by nature, yet guaranteed to exceed your expectations. Creating classic flavours from fresh produce, their philosophy may be straightforward, but their dishes are masterpieces.

2FOR1 2 COURSES | FRI × | SAT × — Indian

TAMAN RIA TROPICANA ☎01482 345 640

45-47 Princes Avenue, Hull, HU5 3RX

Popular Malaysian and Indonesian restaurant in Hull. Serves a fabulous range of dishes, from fresh and light mee laksa curried soup to the hot sambal or superb Java curry. Eclectic, colourful flavours.

2FOR1 3 COURSES | FRI ✱ | SAT ✱ | ▲ — Malaysian

VERVE GRILL ☎01482 642 422

Village Hotel, Priory Way, Hull, HU4 7DY

In-house restaurant of the Village Hotel; combines a smart, sleek dining space with some classic grill fare, from simple flatbreads to a majestic chateaubriand and all that comes in between.

25% OFF TOTAL | 6 | FRI ✓ | SAT ✓ | SUN | ✱ | ▲ — Steakhouse

VOUJON ☎01482 505 924

248 Hull Road, Anlaby, Hull, HU4 7RS

Distinctive flavours and a unique blend of spices make every dish sumptuous and unique at this Indian restaurant. Although the atmosphere is informal, the staff never fail to offer first-class service.

2FOR1 3 COURSES | FRI × | SAT × — Indian

North Yorkshire

701 RESTAURANT @ HOLIDAY INN ☎0871 942 9261

Holiday Inn Harrogate, Kings Road, Harrogate, HG1 1XX

Set in the heart of town, the Holiday Inn Harrogate boasts its own hidden retreat - Restaurant 701. The restaurant provides a modern yet warm atmosphere as well as elevated views of the famous spa town.

25% OFF TOTAL | 6 | FRI ✓ | SAT ✓ — International

ABBEY RESTAURANT @ HOLIDAY INN ☎0871 942 9261

Holiday Inn Harrogate, Kings Road, Harrogate, HG1 1XX

Light and airy hotel restaurant that serves a good range of well-cooked dishes for a relaxed evening meal. Slow-braised lamb shank is their order of the day.

2FOR1 3 COURSES | FRI ✱ | SAT ✱ | ▲ — International

AKASH TANDOORI RESTAURANT 0190 463 3550

10 North Street, York, YO1 6JD

Right in the heart of York, Akash is a well-supported, popular tandoori restaurant that combines a good eye for quality and detail with a welcoming, congenial atmosphere.

2FOR1 MAIN COURSE | FRI × | SAT × | SUN — Indian

THE ALICE HAWTHORN ☎01423 330 303

The Green, Nun Monkton, YO26 8EW

Rustic and warm, the ambience is second to none. With a frequently changing seasonal menu - you'll always be in for a treat at The Alice Hawthorne.

2FOR1 3 COURSES | FRI × | SAT × | SUN | ▲ — European

AMBIENCE CAFE BISTRO ☎07946 224 960

40 Gillygate, York, YO31 8JE

Ambience is an adorable Bistro in the heart of York where attention to detail is key. Chef and proprietor, Guy, uses only the freshest ingredients from local suppliers to prepare the delicious dishes served here.

50% OFF FOOD | 2 | FRI ▯ | SAT × | SUN | ✱ — International

THE APPLETREE COUNTRY INN ☎01751 433 189

Marton, York, YO62 6RD

A beautiful country pub with dining areas of great character, each hosting an open fire place and the menu is updated regularly and changes as and when seasonal produce becomes available.

25% OFF TOTAL | 6 | FRI ✓ | SAT × — British

BED RESTAURANT ☎01423 568 600

20 Kings Road, Harrogate, HG1 5JW

Stay in Bed and dine in style. Whatever the attire or occasion, receive a warm welcome and leave fully satisfied. The only problem is deciding who to take with you.

2FOR1 MAIN COURSE | FRI ✓ | SAT ✱ | SUN | ✱ | ▲ — British

BEECHWOOD CLOSE HOTEL ☎0190 465 8378

19 Shipton Road, York, YO30 5RE

The Beechwood Close Hotel is an impressive 20th century house set in its own magnificent grounds in York. The restaurant & bar serves classic British dishes with an evening a la carte menu.

25% OFF TOTAL | FRI ▯ | SAT ▯ | SUN — British

BELLA ITALIA 0190 461 1221

89 Low Petergate, York, YO1 7HY

Accessible Italian cuisine on the British high street - indulge in authentic sharing platters, hand stretched pizzas and hearty pasta dishes, served with a healthy dose of gregarious Italian hospitality.

25% OFF TOTAL | 6 | FRI × | SAT × | SUN | ▲ — Italian

BENEDICTS ☎01677 422 122

The Lodge, 88 Bedale Road, Bedale, DL8 1DT

Overlooking the blissful and serene orchard, Benedicts provides a relaxed setting in which to dine. Using the finest local produce, the menu is bursting with traditional regional dishes.

2FOR1 MAIN COURSE | FRI ✓ | SAT ✓ — Traditional English

BENGAL SPICE ☎01423 502 610

21 Cheltenham Cresent, Harrogate, HG1 1DH

Offering Indian and Bangladeshi cuisine that will exceed all of your expectations. Whether you enjoy delicate flavours or fiery spices, the authenticity of each dish will really set your night on fire.

2FOR1 MAIN COURSE | FRI ▯ | SAT ▯ — Indian

THE BILTMORE BAR & GRILL ☎0190 461 0075

29 Swinegate, York, Y01 8AZ

Opulent dining in sumptuous surroundings in which guests can devour the delicious English and French dishes. *Advance booking mentioning Gourmet Society is essential.

2FOR1 MAIN COURSE | FRI × | SAT × | SUN | ✱ | ▲ — European

BLACKWELL OX INN ☎01347 810 328

Huby Road, Sutton-on-the-Forest, YO6 1DT

Chef Steven Holding delivers simple, classic food in this gorgeous North Yorkshire inn; local produce is a key focus, and you can wash the lot down with a robust pint of the finest. Awarded 1 AA Rosette.

25% OFF TOTAL | 4 | FRI ✓ | SAT ✓ | SUN — Modern British

THE BLUE BELL INN ☎01944 738 204

Weaverthorpe, Malton, YO17 8EX

A popular restaurant, well known for its excellent food and cosy ambience. Modern English cuisine guarantees a delicious dining experience.

2FOR1 MAIN COURSE | FRI ✓ | SAT ✱ | ▲ — Modern British

BLUE CRUSH 01723 362 450

Kepwick House, Peasholm Gap, Scarborough, YO12 7TN

Diners feast their eyes upon the stunning views of the shimmering sands at North Bay Beach, whilst filling up on excellent food at an affordable price. Fish lovers should try the freshly catch of the day.

2FOR1 MAIN COURSE | FRI × | SAT × | SUN — British

THE BOAR'S HEAD ☎01729 840 217

9 Main Street, Long Preston, Nr. Skipton, BD23 4ND

The Boars Head is a beautifully located traditional pub and hotel that revels in its village location without compromising on its proximity to landmark towns. Firm favourites appear on the menu.

2FOR1 MAIN COURSE | FRI ✱ | SAT ✱ | SUN — International

BOMBAY SPICE ☎0190 461 3300
58 Goodram Gate, York, YO1 7LF
A warm, charming Indian restaurant in York whose menu delivers all the traditional favourites along with some esoteric delights; the knowledgeable staff will have you up to speed on these in no time.

2FOR1 2 COURSES | FRI ✓ | SAT ✓ — Indian/Bangladeshi

BOMBAY SPICE ☎01723 354 324
9-10 Queen Street, Scarborough, YO11 1HA
Popular Indian restaurant close to the seafront. Specialises in North Indian dishes and does a good range from mildly flavourful offerings to the hotter end of the spectrum.

2FOR1 MAIN COURSE | FRI ✱ | SAT ✱ — Indian

THE BULL INN ☎0167 747 0678
Church Street, Ripon, HG4 5JQ
Village pub with a classic look tucked away in the pretty village of Ripon. Inside, it reveals itself to be a food-led delight, serving an excellent selection of freshly cooked and plentiful dishes.

2FOR1 3 COURSES | FRI ✱ | SAT ✱ — British

CAFÉ INDIGO ☎01642 677 144
24 Castlegate Mill, Stockton-on-Tees, TS18 1BZ
Stunning surroundings, sensational views and sumptuous food make this an ideal place for lunch and dinner. Relying on the subtlety of fragrant herbs and spices, each dish has an abundance of flavour.

2FOR1 MAIN COURSE | FRI ✓ | SAT ✓ — Indian

CEDAR COURT ☎01423 858 585
Park Parade, Harrogate, HG1 5AH
Harrogate hotel in the grand style. Elegant but unpretentious venue with an excellent restaurant. It serves a brasserie-style menu that draws on British recipes and has a good eye for produce.

2FOR1 3 COURSES | FRI ✓ | SAT ✓ — European

THE CHASE GRILL @ THE YORK MARRIOT ☎0190 477 0603
Tadcaster Road, York, YO24 1QQ
Bright red button-back banquettes and colourful design, with long tables ideal for a company gathering, or low-key, intimate ones for a quiet one-to-one. Serves grill-style cuisine, tasty and neatly done.

50% OFF FOOD | 4 | FRI ✱ | SAT ✱ — International

THE CHEQUERS INN ☎01423 359 637
Bilton-in-Ainsty, York, YO26 7NN
An idyllic country pub serving freshly prepared and locally sourced homemade food accompanied by great beers, wines and spirits.

2FOR1 MAIN COURSE | FRI ✕ | SAT ✕ | SUN | ✱ | ▲ — British

CAFÉ ROUGE

25% OFF TOTAL | 6 | FRI ✓ | SAT ✓ | ✱ | ▲

3 restaurants in North Yorkshire

21-29 Beulah Street, Harrogate, HG1 1QH
☎ 01423 500 043

3 Coney Street, York, YO1 9QL
☎ 0190 465 3264

Adams Hse, 52 Low Petergate, York, YO1 7HZ
☎ 0190 467 3293

CILANTRO ☎01751 472 233
21 Market Place, Pickering, YO18 7AE
Passion and sophistication are at the forefront of this restaurants ethos. Stylishly chic, Cilantro prepares only the most delectable and rich of Indian cuisine.

2FOR1 MAIN COURSE | FRI ✓ | SAT ✓ | ✱ | ▲ — Indian

CLASSICS BAR @ HOLIDAY INN ☎0871 942 9261
Kings Road, Harrogate, HG1 1XX
A comfortable, cosy bar that serves a good range of light bites to eat in the welcoming surroundings of Harrogate's Holiday Inn.

2FOR1 3 COURSES | FRI ✱ | SAT ✱ | ▲ — Bistro

THE CLIFTON HOTEL ☎01723 375 691
Queen's Parade, North Bay, Scarborough, YO12 7HX
Hotel-restaurant with an excellent local reputation for fine food and good service. Residents and guests alike can take breakfast, lunch and dinner in this charming, traditionally furnished restaurant.

2FOR1 3 COURSES | FRI ✓ | SAT ✱ | SUN — British

CLOCKTOWER ☎01423 871 350
Rudding Park, Follifoot, Harrogate, HG3 1JH
If food is your passion look no further than Clocktower. Yorkshire produce cooked to perfection and a monthly Food Heroes menu uses principal ingredients that arelocally sourced. Awarded 2 AA Rosettes.

2FOR1 3 COURSES | FRI | SAT ✱ | SUN | ▲ — British

CLOISTERS RESTAURANT @ MONKBAR HOTEL ☎0190 463 8086
St Maurices Road, Monkbar, YO31 7JA
Treat yourself to a seasonal dish after a day of exploring the beautifully historic city of York. Welcoming a variety of guests, the staff will happily accommodate dietary requirements.

2FOR1 MAIN COURSE | FRI ✓ | SAT ✓ — British

THE COPPER HORSE RESTAURANT ☎01723 862 029
15 Main Street, Seamer, Scarborough, YO12 4PS
Cosy and welcoming pub-style restaurant with a unique theatrical theme. Decked out with memorabilia dating back to the 1950s, it's a characterful place to enjoy their wide-ranging traditional menu.

2FOR1 MAIN COURSE | FRI ✱ | SAT ✱ | ▲ — British

DA-CLAUDIO ☎01723 354 648
4 Harcourt Place, Scarborough, YO11 2EP
A blend of innovative and traditional Italian cuisine is served with a wine choice to complement every dish. The friendly service, pleasant atmosphere and novel menu complete the dining experience.

2FOR1 2 COURSES | FRI ✓ | SAT ✓ — Italian

THE DAWNAY ARMS ☎01944 728 365
West Heslerton, Malton, YO17 8RQ
Exuding tradition, this inn prides itself in offering genuine cosy ambiance by the roaring log fire. Unwind in a comfy chair and indulge in a classic British dish that really hits the spot.

2FOR1 MAIN COURSE | FRI ✓ | SAT ✓ | ✱ — British

THE DEVONSHIRE FELL HOTEL ☎01756 729 000
Burnsall Village, Skipton, BD23 6BT
With crisp, clear flavours a hallmark of the menu here, together with delightful presentation, the look, texture and taste of the dishes at this award-winning restaurant are outstanding. 2 AA Rosettes.

2FOR1 3 COURSES | FRI ✱ | SAT ✱ — International

THE DORMOUSE 0190 464 0682
Clifton Park Avenue, York, YO30 5PA
This Vintage Inn oozes rural charm and rustic character. The picturesque surroundings provide the perfect backdrop for savouring the hearty, seasonal pub-food on the menu.

25% OFF TOTAL | FRI ✓ | SAT ✓ | SUN | ▲ — Modern British

DROVERS REST @ THE FLEECE ☎01944 758 464
9-11 Westgate, Rillington, Malton, YO17 8LN
Boasting high-class, seasonally varied dining, this conveniently located pub is an ideal place to bring the family. Places exciting English cuisine at the heart of the menu.

2FOR1 3 COURSES | FRI ✓ | SAT ✓ | SUN — British

EASTERN PARADISE
☎01287 622 698
8 Amber Street, Saltburn-by-the-Sea, TS12 1DT
An excellent independently owned restaurant that has become an established part of the town's 21st-century landscape. A wide selection of classic dishes served with a list of drinks and a personal touch.

25% OFF TOTAL | 4 | FRI ✓ | SAT ✱ | ✱ — Chinese

ELIANO'S BRASSERIE
☎01642 868 566
20 Fairbridge Street, Middlesbrough, TS1 5DJ
Bringing a wealth of experience from restaurants across Europe, owner Rosa leads this exciting Italian restaurant serving homely, flavoursome food in a classic setting.

2FOR1 MAIN COURSE | FRI | SAT | SUN | — Italian

FILMORE AND UNION HARROGATE
☎01423 560 988
3 Station Square, Harrogate, HG1 1TB
Home of the Health Kitchen, the salads, juice remedies, artisan breads, seafood, tagines, pastas and pastries are all presented beautifully and the fresh ingredients make for a delicious dining experience.

25% OFF TOTAL | 4 | FRI × | SAT × | SUN — British

FILMORE AND UNION YORK
☎0190 465 4123
62a Low Petergate, York, YO1 7HZ
Lovers of vegetarian, gluten-free and dairy-free foods, Filmore & Union set out to prove their meals can be healthy and yet gloriously delicious in a chic restaurant with a view of The Minster.

25% OFF TOTAL | 4 | FRI × | SAT × | SUN — British

FILMORE AND UNION YORK STATION
☎0190 465 4123
Platf 8, York Station, Station Road, York, YO24 1AB
Pick up a healthy salad, bagel, soup or juice at platform 8 of the railway station for that boost you need on a busy day.

25% OFF TOTAL | 4 | FRI × | SAT × | SUN — British

THE FOX AND ROMAN
0190 470 8720
58 Tadcaster Road, Dringhouses, York, YO24 1LR
This Vintage Inn oozes rural charm and rustic character. The picturesque surroundings provide the perfect backdrop for savouring the hearty, seasonal pub-food on the menu.

25% OFF TOTAL | FRI ✓ | SAT ✓ | SUN | — Modern British

THE GEORGE & DRAGON INN
☎01969 663 358
Aysgarth, Leyburn, DL8 3AD
Idyllically situated in the stunning Yorkshire Dales National Park, The George and Dragon Inn embraces the nearby spectacle of the Aysgarth falls. Real local ales and exquisite, fine-dining dishes.

25% OFF TOTAL | 4 | FRI ✱ | SAT ✱ | SUN — British

GEORGE AND DRAGON
☎01977 661 319
Doncaster Road, Whitley, DN14 0HY
Traditional, hearty pub food for when any other meal just won't do, delivered by a committed team who relish the opportunity of extending a warm welcome and offering quality service to every guest.

25% OFF TOTAL | 10 | FRI ✓ | SAT ✓ — Modern Pub

THE GEORGE AT WATH
☎01765 641 324
Main Street, Ripon, YO7 4LX
The menu hosts an abundance of seasonal and local produce, providing guests with an authentic taste of Yorkshire. Devour roasted duck in sweetcorn cream whilst unwinding by the roaring log fire.

2FOR1 MAIN COURSE | FRI ✓ | SAT ✓ | SUN — British

GREEN'S OF WHITBY
☎01947 600 284
13 Bridge Street, Whitby, YO22 4BG
Green's multi award winning Restaurant & Bistro has one of those enviable, picturesque settings, nestled close to the busy fishing harbour of this charming, bustling coastal town in Whitby.

25% OFF TOTAL | 2 | FRI ✱ | SAT ✱ | — Seafood

THE GRILL ROOM AT THE GRAND
☎0190 438 0038
The Grand Hotel and Spa, Station Rise, York, Y01 6HT
A pristine, well-decorated interior provides a dining haven in which you can enjoy wholesome British dishes. Classic favourites appear alongside more adventurous gastronomic delights.

25% OFF TOTAL | 4 | FRI × | SAT × | SUN | ✱ — Modern British

HACKNESS GRANGE COUNTRY HOUSE HOTEL
☎01723 882 345
Hackness, Scarborough, YO13 0JW
Enjoying an excellent reputation for the food, wines and service alike, this restaurant offers menus of exceptional modern British cuisine, constructed from the freshest of local ingredients.

2FOR1 3 COURSES | FRI ✓ | SAT ✱ | SUN — British

HOTEL DU VIN
☎01423 856 800
Prospect Place, Harrogate, HG1 1LB
The finest, freshest local produce, simple European recipes, a stunning choice of wines; these are the elements of the trademark Hotel du Vin bistro. Enjoy amazing views with glass in hand. 2 AA Rosettes.

2FOR1 MAIN COURSE | FRI × | SAT × | SUN | — European

HOTEL DU VIN
☎0190 455 7350
89 The Mount, York, YO24 1AX
The finest, freshest local produce, simple European recipes and a stunning choice of wines; these are the elements of the trademark Hotel du Vin bistro. A beautiful grade II listed venue. 1 AA Rosette.

2FOR1 MAIN COURSE | FRI × | SAT × | SUN | — European

IVY RESTAURANT
☎0190 464 4744
The Grange Hotel, 1 Clifton, York, YO30 6AA
An unpretentious approach to top-quality dining, with a stylish, modern dining room pairing a relaxed ambience. Enjoy divine food, skilfully cooked from the freshest seasonal ingredients. 2 AA Rosettes.

25% OFF TOTAL | 6 | FRI ✓ | SAT × | SUN | ✱ | — Brasserie

JAIPUR SPICE
☎01423 502 610
Cheltenham Parade, Harrogate, HG1 1DH
The menu is extensive and the food is cooked using the freshest ingredients and herbs and spices. The waiters are charming and friendly ensuring all customers receive service of the highest standard.

2FOR1 MAIN COURSE | FRI | SAT | ✱ — Indian

J'S @ 636 - PARKMORE HOTEL
01642 786 815
636 Yarm Road, Eaglescliffe, Middlesborough, TS16 0DH
The restaurant of this tastefully converted Victorian house serves classic dishes made with the finest local produce from the nearby village of Yarm and the surrounding areas.

2FOR1 3 COURSES | FRI ✓ | SAT ✓ | SUN | — European

KENNEDY'S
0190 462 0222
1 Little Stonegate, York, YO1 8AX
A lively cosmopolitan area is home to this unique bar and restaurant. The stylish contemporary atmosphere attracts an eclectic clientèle.

2FOR1 3 COURSES | FRI | SAT — Contemporary

THE KESTREL
01423 797 979
Wetherby Road, Plompton, Knaresborough, HG5 8LY
This Vintage Inn oozes rural charm and rustic character. The picturesque surroundings provide the perfect backdrop for savouring the hearty, seasonal pub-food on the menu.

25% OFF TOTAL | FRI ✓ | SAT ✓ | SUN | — Modern British

KILBY'S AT MERCURE YORK
☎0844 815 9038
Shipton Road, Skelton, York, YO30 1XW
Kilby's Restaurant is a fantastic attribute of this Hotel, where dashing views of the northern countryside are taken advantage of. Own-grown herbs and fresh produce make exceptional flavours.

2FOR1 3 COURSES | FRI ✓ | SAT ✓ — British

LA TASCA
☎01423 566 333
1 John Street, Harrogate, HG1 1JZ
Quintessentially Spanish, La Tasca's fresh and exciting menu offers something for everyone. Their tapas dishes are sincerely authentic, while their paellas always deliver on flavour.

25% OFF TOTAL | 8 | FRI ✓ | SAT × | — Spanish

LA TASCA
☎0190 452 1100
21 Back Swinegate, York, YO1 8AD
Quintessentially Spanish, La Tasca's fresh and exciting menu offers something for everyone. Their tapas dishes are sincerely authentic, while their paellas always deliver on flavour.

25% OFF TOTAL | 8 | FRI ✓ | SAT × | — Spanish

LASTINGHAM GRANGE
01751 417 345

Lastingham Grange Hotel, High St, Lastingham, YO62 6TH

There is a restful and friendly atmosphere at the Grange, which has a reputation for good food and personal, courteous service. It has a spacious lounge with an open fire and a beautiful dining room.

25% OFF TOTAL | 4 | FRI ✓ | SAT × | SUN | British

LE JARDIN
01423 507 323

7 Montpellier Parade, Harrogate, HG1 2TJ

Family-run restaurant, whose dining area overlooks Montpellier Gardens in Harrogate. Its homely ambience ideally sets off the restaurant's traditional, locally sourced food.

2FOR1 3 COURSES | FRI ✓ | SAT ✓ | French/European

LEVEN RESTAURANT
0845 072 7440

Crathorne Hall Hotel, Crathorne, TS15 0AR

Enjoy double AA Rosette dining in the elegant surroundings of this Hand Picked Hotels' grand country house. The beautiful dining room creates a special ambience, ideal to mark any special occasion.

25% OFF TOTAL | 10 | FRI ✓ | SAT ✓ | Fine Dining

THE LIME HOUSE RESTAURANT
0190 463 2734

55 Goodramgate, York, YO1 7LS

It is easy to see how this award-winning restaurant gained its popular reputation. The owners identify culinary variety as being vital for a successfully satisfying menu.

25% OFF TOTAL | 4 | FRI ✓ | SAT ✱ | SUN | ✱ | International

LOCH FYNE
0190 465 0910

Foss Bridge Street, Walmsgate, York, YO1 9TJ

From the roadside oyster bar that once was, Loch Fyne restaurants now successfully inject energy and passion into great food and wonderful flavours, whilst ensuring their seafood is sustainably sourced.

25% OFF TOTAL | 4 | FRI ✱ | SAT ✱ | Seafood

THE LONGBOAT
0190 454 4491

28-40 Blossom Street, York, YO24 1AJ

Quality pub classics with a modern twist combine with a friendly and relaxed atmosphere to make this Table Table venue the perfect place for family gatherings or meeting friends.

2FOR1 MAIN COURSE | FRI ✓ | SAT ✓ | Modern British

LUNA PIENA
01947 600 200

31-33 Skinner Street, Whitby, YO21 3AH

Congenial kind of a restaurant in Whitby. Simple style and superb presentation strike you immediately, while the tastes keep up with appearances, featuring rich, clear flavours across a broad-based menu.

2FOR1 3 COURSES | FRI ✓ | SAT ✱ | Italian

MALTON SPICE
0165 369 1222

24-26 Castlegate, Malton, YO17 7DT

Malton Spice serves up a wide array of delicious dishes, all featuring fresh ingredients. For an authentic Indian meal in a warm and welcoming environment, Malton Spice is an excellent choice.

50% OFF FOOD | FRI ✓ | SAT ✓ | Indian

MASSALA
01642 250 145

118 Borough Road, Middlesbrough, TS1 2ES

Massala offers a diverse, mouth-watering range of curries in a classy, cosy dining room, with quick, friendly and attentive service.

2FOR1 2 COURSES | FRI ✱ | SAT ✱ | Indian

THE MILLFIELD
0190 478 7630

White Rose Close, Nether Poppleton, York, YO26 6RL

Beefeater Grill are one of the UK's best-loved restaurants welcoming guests for almost 40 years in over 130 locations nationwide. *Excludes Breakfast, Light Bites, Bar menu, set menus and all other offers.

2FOR1 MAIN COURSE | 6 | FRI ✓ | SAT × | Modern British

MIRCHI RESTAURANT
01759 305 027

13 Railway Street, York, YO42 2QR

The expansive menu provides curry lovers with a gamut of dishes. Whether diners are seeking traditional favourites or something unusual, Mirchi is sure to appease large appetites.

2FOR1 3 COURSES | FRI ✓ | SAT ✓ | Indian

MOHUJOS
01642 881 478

113 Station Road, Billingham, TS23 2RL

Mohujos distinguishes itself with its range of lively Mexican dishes. Particularly prized are their chilli con carne, home-made piri piri sauce, and rich, Mexican-inflected take on chicken parmesan.

2FOR1 2 COURSES | FRI | SAT ✱ | Mexican

MUCKLES
01423 858 153

11 West Park, Harrogate, HG1 1BL

Take time out for some classically hearty, well-cooked English pub food at this characterful inn in Harrogate. Welcoming, accommodating and well-located, it promises a treat of an evening.

25% OFF TOTAL | FRI ✓ | SAT ✓ | English/Gastro pub

NASEEB RESTAURANT
01642 714 466

59-61 High Street, Middlesbrough, TS9 5AB

Traditional restaurant bringing you the truly outstanding and varied cuisines of Kerala, Goa, Karnataka and Andhra Pradesh, all under one roof. Welcome to a south Indian gastronomic oasis.

2FOR1 3 COURSES | FRI ✓ | SAT ✓ | Indian

THE NELSON INN
01423 500 340

Skipton Road, Hampsthwaite, Harrogate, HG3 2BU

This Vintage Inn oozes rural charm and rustic character. The picturesque surroundings provide the perfect backdrop for savouring the hearty, seasonal pub-food on the menu.

25% OFF TOTAL | FRI ✓ | SAT ✓ | SUN | Modern British

NOSH & NAWAAB
0175 670 0060

25 New Market Street, Skipton, BD23 2JE

Situated in the beautifully adorned Boutique 25, both hotel guests and external visitors can take delight in the food on offer at Nosh & Nawaab. Fine Indian and Pakistani dining is a sure thing.

2FOR1 MAIN COURSE | FRI | SAT | Fine Dining

THE OLD DEANERY
01765 600 003

Minster Road, Ripon, HG4 1QS

The bright sparkle of this treasured Yorkshire jewel is not to be missed. Its award-winning status is just one reason to dine in this unforgettable restaurant. Priceless cuisine in heavenly surroundings.

2FOR1 MAIN COURSE | FRI ✓ | SAT | Fine Dining

OODLES NOODLES BAR AND CAFÉ
01642 243 809

136 Linthorpe Road, Middlesbrough, TS1 3RA

A wide range of deliciously tempting hot dishes are on offer in this New York-style noodle bar. Super sandwiches are also on offer, with the 'Hot Provencette' proving to be an exceedingly popular choice.

25% OFF TOTAL | 6 | FRI | SAT | ✱ | Pan-Asian

THE PARK
01423 878580

Hornbeam Park Avenue, Harrogate, HG2 8RA

Quality pub classics with a modern twist combine with a friendly and relaxed atmosphere to make this Table Table venue the perfect place for family gatherings or meeting friends.

2FOR1 MAIN COURSE | FRI ✓ | SAT ✓ | Modern British

THE PIANO RESTAURANT
0190 464 4456

The Churchill Hotel, 65 Bootham, York, YO30 7DQ

High, arched windows look out onto the gardens from this spectacular dining room. A hotel restaurant whose menu is broad and imaginative, and whose quality almost goes without saying. 2 AA Rosettes.

2FOR1 3 COURSES | FRI ✓ | SAT | ✱ | European

PREZZO
0190 462 4474

1-3 Clifford Street, York, YO1 9RG

With a character all of its own, Prezzo oozes contemporary style and enduring charm. Signature pastas, stone-baked pizzas and classic Italian dishes promise a perfect dining choice for the whole family.

2FOR1 MAIN COURSE | FRI × | SAT × | Italian

PREZZO
01423 520 447

2-4 Albert Street, Harrogate, HG1 1JG

With a character all of its own, Prezzo oozes contemporary style and enduring charm. Signature pastas, stone-baked pizzas and classic Italian dishes promise a perfect dining choice for the whole family.

2FOR1 MAIN COURSE | FRI × | SAT × | Italian

THE RAJ YORK
☎ 0787 316 4874

21 Bootham Street, York, YO30 7BW

An authentic Indian restaurant that never fails to deliver, offering a wide variety of Indian food ranging from traditional dishes to house specialities. Expect fine cuisine and reasonable prices.

25% OFF TOTAL | 6 | FRI × | SAT × — Indian

RESTAURANT 55
☎ 01723 365 921

49-55 Eastborough, Scarborough, YO11 1NH

Hugely popular seafood establishment offering diners amazingly fresh food and spectacular views of the south bay. There are numerous delectable fish, salad, and shellfish dishes on the menu.

2FOR1 3 COURSES | FRI | SAT — British

RICHARDSON'S RESTAURANT
☎ 0134 782 5400

Burn Hall Hotel, Tollerton Rd, Huby, York, YO61 1JB

Situated in the divine Burn Hall Hotel, Richardson's Restaurant serves mouth-watering meals complemented by a finely selected wine list. Locally sourced produce is a key ingredient in the kitchen.

50% OFF FOOD | 4 | FRI | SAT — International

ROYAL TANDOORI
☎ 01723 354 324

9-10 Queen Street, Scarborough, YO11 1HA

Taste authentic cuisine with every bite as this restaurant brings diners a menu packed with fresh and flavoursome dishes, from quality staple curries to delicious chef specialities.

2FOR1 MAIN COURSE | FRI | SAT — Indian

THE ROYAL YORK
☎ 0190 465 3681

Station Parade, York, YO24 1AA

Built on an old Viking road, this pub fully encompasses the history of the local area. Just minutes from York Minster Cathedral, this is a quaint little pub perfect for lunch or dinner after a day in York.

25% OFF TOTAL | 6 | FRI ✓ | SAT ✓ | ▲ — British

SANGTHAI
☎ 0190 472 8462

Church Cottage, Escrick, York, YO19 6EX

Ingredients fresh from Thailand, Sangthai provide diners with authentic oriental cuisine. The menu is vast and bursting with exotic, aromatic flavours.

2FOR1 MAIN COURSE | FRI ✓ | SAT ✓ — Thai

SHABAB
☎ 01423 560 674

7 Cheltenham Parade, Harrogate, HG1 1DD

Boasting cooking methods that closely mirror Asian domestic kitchens, this venue oozes authenticity in exotic surroundings. Guests will never find artificial colourings or ready made pastes in the dishes.

2FOR1 MAIN COURSE | FRI ✓ | SAT ✓ — Indian

SIDINGS RESTAURANT
☎ 0190 447 0221

Station Lane, York, YO30 1BT

Brilliant concept of a restaurant, built around five Pullman railway carriages and featuring sleeper-car accommodation, sophisticated diner-car dining, and a further trattoria-style restaurant to boot.

2FOR1 3 COURSES | FRI ✱ | SAT ✱ — European

SKIPTON BALTI
☎ 01756 793 960

1b Court Lane, Off New Market St, Skipton, BD23 1DD

Relaxed Indian restaurant serving a diverse menu. Spacious and welcoming interior, carefully lit, and setting a great tone for the evening. Accomplished cooking, lots of flavour and generous portions.

2FOR1 MAIN COURSE | FRI × | SAT × | SUN — Indian

SO! BAR AND EATS
☎ 01765 601 369

6 Old Market Square, Ripon, HG4 1EQ

So! Bar & Eats in Ripon is an award winning, independently run bar & restaurant, offering a range of high quality freshly prepared food to meet every occasion, in a contemporary bar environment.

2FOR1 3 COURSES | FRI ✱ | SAT ✱ — British

SO! BAR AND EATS
☎ 01423 863 202

1 Silver Street, Knaresborough, HG5 8AJ

An award-winning, independently-run bar and restaurant offering an innovative and contemporary menu, perfect for everything from fine-dining to sharing feasts. A modern, relaxed spot for any occasion.

2FOR1 3 COURSES | FRI ✱ | SAT ✱ — British

SPICE 4U
☎ 01751 473 334

41 Hungate, Pickering, YO18 7DG

A family-owned restaurant bringing authentic Indian cuisine to both the people of Wetherby and visitors from afar. Regular guests enjoy the genuine taste of the East in their classic and speciality dishes.

2FOR1 2 COURSES | FRI ✓ | SAT ✓ — Indian

STRADA
0190 467 2999

75 Low Petergate, York, Y01 7HY

Strada offers fresh, bold dishes inspired by flavours of Italian city life! Try the hand-stretched, stone baked pizzas, addictive pastas and risottos, great share plates and much more. *Excludes Pizzettas.

25% OFF TOTAL | 6 | FRI ✓ | SAT × | ▲ — Italian

THE TALPORE
01642 671 573

White Water Way, Thornaby, Stockton-on-Tees, TS17 6QB

Beefeater Grill are one of the UK's best-loved restaurants welcoming guests for almost 40 years in over 130 locations nationwide. *Excludes Breakfast, Light Bites, Bar menu, set menus and all other offers.

2FOR1 MAIN COURSE | 6 | FRI ✓ | SAT × | ▲ — Modern British

TANDOORI NIGHT
☎ 01748 826 677

3 Castle Hill, Richmond, DL10 4QP

Classic Indian cuisine served in a picturesque village. Renowned for its helpful staff and atmospheric surroundings, this venue offers quality, authentic dishes created to delight your taste buds.

2FOR1 3 COURSES | FRI | SAT — Indian

TANDOORI NIGHTS
☎ 0190 461 2017

21-22 Boothan, York, YO3 07BW

Curry lovers can feast on classic Indian dishes or tantalise their taste buds with something completely unique. Whatever the occasion, Tandoori Nights promises an exceptional night out.

2FOR1 2 COURSES | FRI | SAT | ✱ — Indian

THE TANGLEWOOD
☎ 0190 446 8611

Malton Road, York, YO32 9TW

A gastro-pub in York with a theatrical twist. Features an appealing menu with traditional British food at centre stage. Versatile restaurant with nostalgic stage and screen memorabilia lining the walls.

2FOR1 MAIN COURSE | FRI ✱ | SAT ✱ | ▲ — British

THAI ELEPHANT
☎ 01423 530 099

13-15 Cheltenham Parade, Harrogate, HG1 1DD

Charming, forthcoming Thai restaurant whose range of dishes is as popular as its warm welcome to diners. Thai cuisine's vivid, vibrant colours are brought out to the full.

25% OFF TOTAL | 6 | FRI | SAT — Thai

THE THREE CUPS
01759 377 381

York Road, Stamford Bridge, York, YO41 1AX

This Vintage Inn oozes rural charm and rustic character. The picturesque surroundings provide the perfect backdrop for savouring the hearty, seasonal pub-food on the menu.

25% OFF TOTAL | FRI ✓ | SAT ✓ | SUN | ▲ — Modern British

THE THREE HORSESHOES
☎ 01423 506 302

Ripon Road, Harrogate, HG3 2DH

The aromatic smells of home-cooked food ooze out of the kitchen at this snug country pub. Always fully stocked, the bar boasts a varied selection of real ales which ensure locals return on a regular basis.

2FOR1 MAIN COURSE | 4 | FRI ✓ | SAT ✓ | SUN — Traditional English

TOWER RESTAURANT @ HILTON
☎ 0190 446 4727

The Hilton York, 1 Tower Street, York, YO1 9WD

The Tower Restaurant is within the Hilton Hotel, a smart but relaxed dining venue; it serves local and European dishes; Breakfast, lunch, and table d'hôte or à la carte dinners are available.

25% OFF TOTAL | 4 | FRI | SAT — British

VENNELLS RESTAURANT
☎ 01765 689000

7 Silver Street, Masham, HG4 4DX

Laura and the front of house team welcome you into the elegant surroundings of award winning Vennell's. The menu is fine dining at its best. Jon's food is simple but cooked well and is all locally sourced.

25% OFF TOTAL | 10 | FRI | SAT | ✱ — British

To understand what the restaurant icons mean, please see the inside back cover.

WALKABOUT
☎01642 248 682
28-32 Corporation Road, Middlesbrough, TS1 2RX
Walkabout is famous for its characteristically Australian atmosphere and well-rounded menu. From live sport with a juicy burger to some Aussie kangaroo skewers, you'll find it hard to tear yourself away.

25% OFF TOTAL | 10 | FRI ✓ | SAT ✓ | International

THE WHITE LODGE HOTEL
☎01723 514 771
The White Lodge Hotel, Filey, YO14 9JX
Savour succulent crab, salmon and sea trout fresh from Filey Bay. Boasting a contemporary international menu, this venue guarantees to appease grumbling stomachs.

2FOR1 3 COURSES | FRI ✓ | SAT ✓ | ✱ | English and Continental

WILLIAM AND VICTORIA RESTAURANT
☎01423 521 510
6 Cold Bath Road, Harrogate, HG2 0NA
Family-run restaurant with a distinctive blend of traditional splendour and splashes of modern style. Serves a menu of well-known favourites and often-overlooked classics; a fine place to dine.

25% OFF TOTAL | 6 | FRI ✓ | SAT ✗ | SUN | ✱ | British

THE WORSLEY ARMS HOTEL
☎01653 628 234
High Street, Hovingham, YO62 4LA
Maintaining its historical purpose of providing comfort for travellers, this is a pleasing place to rest and dine. Old World charm exudes from all aspects of this hotel.

2FOR1 MAIN COURSE | FRI ✗ | SAT ✱ | British

South Yorkshire

23 BAR AND RESTAURANT
☎0114 272 2323
3 West One Plaza, Fitzwilliam St, Sheffield, S1 4JB
An unprecedented dining and drinking environment that delivers a committed service and fine British cuisine. An award-winning venue that takes pride in every aspect of guests' dining experience.

2FOR1 3 COURSES | FRI ✓ | SAT ✓ | British

7 SPICES BALTI
☎0114 275 7695
120 Mayfair Court, Sheffield, S3 8PP
7 Spices Balti is a lavish, spacious Indian restaurant in Sheffield. Beautifully lit and well-adorned for comfort and relaxation, the staff at the restaurant ensure every guest is well catered for.

2FOR1 MAIN COURSE | FRI | SAT | ✱ | Indian

THE ADMIRAL RODNEY
0114 233 6121
592 Loxley Road, Loxley, Sheffield, S6 6RU
This Vintage Inn oozes rural charm and rustic character. The picturesque surroundings provide the perfect backdrop for savouring the hearty, seasonal pub-food on the menu.

25% OFF TOTAL | FRI ✓ | SAT ✓ | SUN | Modern British

AKDENIZ GREEK RESTAURANT
☎01302 830 212
45a Doncaster Road, Doncaster, DN3 2BU
From meze to tapas, this Mediterranean venue is the perfect place to sample new flavours. Liven up your weekend with some cracking entertainment, from belly dancing to live music.

25% OFF TOTAL | 4 | FRI | SAT ✗ | SUN | ✱ | Greek

AL SHAMI LEBANESE
☎0114 327 3135
45 The Wicker, Sheffield, S3 8HT
Well known in the local area for their delicious food; all of the dishes served at Lebanese Al Shami are created on the premises from the finest ingedients.

25% OFF TOTAL | 6 | FRI ✓ | SAT ✓ | Middle Eastern

ANTIBO SHEFFIELD
☎0114 272 7222
The Plaza, Fitzwilliam St, Sheffield, S1 4JB
Antibo Sheffield is typically characteristic of its sister venues. Focusing wholly on providing high quality Italian cuisine, Antibo never fails to impress with its great menu and seriously tasty food.

2FOR1 3 COURSES | FRI | SAT ✗ | Italian

ARENA SQUARE
0114 243 2320
3 Arena Court, Attercliffe, Sheffield, S9 2LF
Quality pub classics with a modern twist combine with a friendly and relaxed atmosphere to make this Table Table venue the perfect place for family gatherings or meeting friends.

2FOR1 MAIN COURSE | FRI ✓ | SAT ✓ | Modern British

AYESHA'S INDIAN CUISINE
☎0114 266 6002
407 Ecclesall Road, Sheffield, S11 8PG
Brilliant little Indian restaurant. Stresses that it's a forward-thinking, even avant-garde place, and while the classics are all there, there's some fantastic more unfamiliar dishes across the board.

2FOR1 MAIN COURSE | FRI ✗ | SAT ✗ | ✱ | Indian

BABYLON RESTAURANT
☎0114 272 9031
408 Pitsmoor Road, Sheffield, S3 9AY
The very best of Middle Eastern cuisine in a relaxed setting. Friendly staff serve you your chosen dishes, from a mixed grill to a creamy curry. Crispy, fresh naan breads are also brought to the table.

25% OFF TOTAL | FRI ✓ | SAT ✓ | Indian

BALTI KING
☎0114 266 6655
216 Fulwood Road, Sheffield, S10 3BB
Just as it says on the label, Balti King specialises in traditional balti. Staggeringly, the restaurant offers a choice of over 700 dishes, all easily navigable, and altogether promising a great curry.

2FOR1 MAIN COURSE | FRI ✓ | SAT ✓ | ✱ | Indian

BANGLA COTTAGE
☎0114 285 3439
481 Langsett Road, Sheffield, S6 2LN
Indian restaurant known especially for its welcome and for the consistently high standards of their cooking. There's all the range you need, with a good eye for flavour that helps it stand out.

2FOR1 3 COURSES | FRI ✱ | SAT ✱ | Indian

BARLEY TWIST
01302 304 050
High Fishergate, Doncaster, DN1 1QZ
Quality pub classics with a modern twist combine with a friendly and relaxed atmosphere to make this Table Table venue the perfect place for family gatherings or meeting friends.

2FOR1 MAIN COURSE | FRI ✓ | SAT ✓ | Modern British

BAYLEAVES RESTAURANT
☎0114 240 1919
129 High Street, Ecclesfield, S35 9UA
Touch of elegance about this Indian restaurant in Sheffield. Serves a range of accomplished, aromatic and neatly seasoned dishes. Their butter chicken is a real delight, as is the tandoori mixed grill.

2FOR1 3 COURSES | FRI | SAT | Indian

BELLA ITALIA
0114 243 1923
Valley Centertainment, Sheffield, S9 2EP
Accessible Italian cuisine on the British high street - indulge in authentic sharing platters, hand stretched pizzas and hearty pasta dishes, served with a healthy dose of gregarious Italian hospitality.

25% OFF TOTAL | 6 | FRI ✗ | SAT ✗ | SUN | Italian

BENGAL KITCHEN
☎011 4255 5008
96-98 The Dale, Woodseats, Sheffield, S8 0PS
Situated in Woodseats, Bengal Kitchen invites you to come and enjoy a drink in their luxurious bar, whilst enjoying all the delights that Bangladeshi and Indian cuisine has to offer.

25% OFF TOTAL | 4 | FRI ✓ | SAT ✓ | Indian

BLESS'ED JAMAICAN SPICE
☎0114 3270202
127-129 Abbeydale Road, Sheffield, S7 1FE
Perfectly blended spices are cooked up in rich sauces, with succulent meats in a homely accommodating environment, to create a dining experience that is truly reflective of the Caribbean way of life.

2FOR1 MAIN COURSE | FRI ✓ | SAT ✓ | South American

BLOO 88
☎0114 270 6264
182 West street, Sheffield, S1 4ET
Situated in a 19th Century building, Bloo 88 is ever-popular not only for its location but for its contemporary take on delicious pizzas, from the all-day breakfast topping to the Shanghai surprise.

2FOR1 MAIN COURSE | FRI ✓ | SAT ✓ | Pizza

THE BOAT INN — 01302 858 500
Nursery Lane, Sprotborough, Doncaster, DB5 7NB

This Vintage Inn oozes rural charm and rustic character. The picturesque surroundings provide the perfect backdrop for savouring the hearty, seasonal pub-food on the menu.

25% OFF TOTAL | FRI ✓ | SAT ✓ | SUN — Modern British

BOLLYWOOD RESTAURANT — ☎01709 739 520
192 Bawtry Road, Rotherham, S66 1AA

Adding an innovative spin to the classic curry, Bollywood Restaurant transfers the glitz and glamour of India's biggest film industry into their zesty dishes. The affable staff are sure to appease.

25% OFF TOTAL | 10 | FRI × | SAT × | ✱ — Indian

THE BRECKS — 01709 543 216
Wickersley Road, Rotherham, S65 3JB

Beefeater Grill are one of the UK's best-loved restaurants welcoming guests for almost 40 years in over 130 locations nationwide. *Excludes Breakfast, Light Bites, Bar menu, set menus and all other offers.

2FOR1 MAIN COURSE | 6 | FRI ✓ | SAT × — Modern British

CARBROOK HALL — 0114 244 0117
537 Carbrook, Sheffield, S9 2FJ

With a historical tale to tell, Carbrook Hall dates back to 1176 and was rebuilt in 1462. Having maintained its original character, the staff here work hard to maintain traditional public house standards.

2FOR1 MAIN COURSE | FRI ✓ | SAT ✓ | SUN — British

THE CHILLI LODGE — ☎01226 792 300
Knabbs Lane, Silkstone Common, Barnsley, S75 4RD

Chic and contemporary, this Indian restaurant in Silkstone Common takes great care with the taste of its classic favourites while also taking seriously its aim to produce innovative and tasty new dishes.

2FOR1 MAIN COURSE | FRI ✱ | SAT ✱ | ✱ — Indian

CLAY OVEN — ☎0114 230 8312
139-141 Oakbrook Road, Sheffield, S11 7EB

Superb Indian restaurant serving all the staple dishes that you would expect to find on the menu. Specialising in vegetarian dishes, Clay Oven is proud of its local reputation.

2FOR1 3 COURSES | FRI ✱ | SAT ✱ — Indian

THE COCK INN — ☎0114 286 2373
5 Bridge Hill, Sheffield, S35 0FL

The team at the Cock Inn overjoyed to serve you up their delicious home cooked quality British cuisine. Be sure to check out their delightful new tea room for a scone and cup of tea.

2FOR1 3 COURSES | FRI × | SAT × — British

CUNNINGHAMS RESTAURANT & THE LOUNGE — ☎0114 276 8822
Holiday Inn Royal Victoria Hotel, Sheffield, S4 7YE

Chefs at this hotel-restaurant pride themselves on attention to detail, and use only the very best seasonal ingredients to create dishes of excellent quality. Timeless elegance in a luxurious setting.

25% OFF TOTAL | 6 | FRI ✓ | SAT ✓ — European

THE CUTLER'S HOTEL — 0114 273 9939
George Street, Heart of the City, Sheffield, S1 2PF

Relaxing place to encamp whether you're visiting the city or stretching out into the Yorkshire countryside. Mezzanine restaurant with a retro ambience, serving a broad selection of international dishes.

2FOR1 3 COURSES | FRI ✓ | SAT ✓ — International

DARCY'S BRASSERIE @ MOSBOROUGH HALL — ☎0114 248 4353
Mosborough Hall Hotel, High St, Mosborough, S20 5EA

A calm oasis of a restaurant which offers contemporary dining in opulent surroundings. The excellence of the food and atmosphere at Darcy's ensures a regular crowd of fans.

2FOR1 3 COURSES | FRI × | SAT × | ✱ — British

THE DOVECOTE MOOR INN — 0114 262 1031
Hathersage Road, Dore, Sheffield, S17 3AB

This Vintage Inn oozes rural charm and rustic character. The picturesque surroundings provide the perfect backdrop for savouring the hearty, seasonal pub-food on the menu.

25% OFF TOTAL | FRI ✓ | SAT ✓ | SUN — Modern British

EL PASO — ☎0114 273 9523
8 Cumberland Street, Sheffield, S1 4PT

A dazzling array of Latin American and Mexican dishes ensures that El Paso is a splendid eatery for every palate. Diners enjoy authentic décor in a contemporary and modish environment.

2FOR1 3 COURSES | FRI | SAT | ✱ — Mexican

ELEMENTS BAR @ NOVOTEL — ☎0871 310 4954
50 Arundel Gate, Sheffield, S1 2PR

Elements Bar provides the perfect backdrop to a quiet, relaxed evening or an idyllic afternoon. Spend your time with friends or family as you eat from the snack menu and enjoy the extensive drink selection.

2FOR1 3 COURSES | FRI ✓ | SAT ✓ — International

ELEMENTS RESTAURANT @ NOVOTEL — ☎0871 310 4954
51 Arundel Gate, Sheffield, S1 2PR

Elements Restaurant offers a perfect accompaniment to the bar, perfect for those seeking something more substantial to eat. Old favourites have taken on a modern twist in the kitchen.

2FOR1 3 COURSES | FRI ✓ | SAT ✓ — International

EVEREST RESTAURANT — ☎0114 258 2975
59-61 Chesterfield Road, Sheffield, S8 0RL

This award-winning eatery has a solid reputation for tantalising flavours in traditional recipes. With over 30 years experience, this venue guarantees a fantastic night out.

25% OFF TOTAL | 4 | FRI ✱ | SAT ✱ | ✱ — Indian

THE FOX HOUSE — 01433 630 374
Longshaw, Sheffield, S11 7TY

This Vintage Inn oozes rural charm and rustic character. The picturesque surroundings provide the perfect backdrop for savouring the hearty, seasonal pub-food on the menu.

25% OFF TOTAL | FRI ✓ | SAT ✓ | SUN — Modern British

GLASS HOUSE — 01226 209170
Shambles Street, Gateway Plaza, Barnsley, S70 2SB

Quality pub classics with a modern twist combine with a friendly and relaxed atmosphere to make this Table Table venue the perfect place for family gatherings or meeting friends.

2FOR1 MAIN COURSE | FRI ✓ | SAT ✓ — Modern British

GO FRESH FOOD — 0151 486 5744
The Oasis Food Court, Meadowhall, Sheffield, S9 1EP

As the name suggests, this eatery is dedicated to providing fresh food fast. Created with the busy diner in mind, GO prepare bursting sandwiches and overloaded pizzas to suit.

2FOR1 MAIN COURSE | FRI ✱ | SAT ✱ — Italian

THE GOLDEN BALL INN
01709 726 911

Turner Lane, Whiston, Rotherham, S60 4HY

This Vintage Inn oozes rural charm and rustic character. The picturesque surroundings provide the perfect backdrop for savouring the hearty, seasonal pub-food on the menu.

25% OFF TOTAL | FRI ✓ | SAT ✓ | SUN | ▲ — Modern British

GULSHAN BALTI HOUSE
☎ 0114 275 8589

50 The Wicker, Sheffield, S3 8JB

Punjabi-style cuisine is at the heart of this restaurant's menu. Chefs promise to seduce and tantalise taste buds with an array of fresh and fragrant flavours cooked in authentic cast iron woks.

2FOR1 MAIN COURSE | FRI 📱 | SAT 📱 | ✱ — Indian

HALF MOON
☎ 0114 244 4753

71 Mather Road, Sheffield, S9 4GP

The Half Moon offers a warm welcome to regulars as well as visitors. The staff work hard to provide an excellent service alongside great, quality food served in a relaxed and cosy atmosphere.

2FOR1 3 COURSES | FRI ✓ | SAT × | SUN — British

HANDMADE BURGER CO.
0114 256 8945

The Oasis, Meadowhall, Sheffield, S9 1EP

100% prime Scotch beef burgers, handmade in the restaurant daily, sourdough buns, delicious handmade relishes and a wide range of toppings giving you over 40 varieties to choose from. *Exclusions apply.

2FOR1 MAIN COURSE | FRI ✓ | SAT × | SUN — International

HANDMADE BURGER CO.
0114 242 4023

Valley Centertainment, Sheffield, S9 2EP

100% prime Scotch beef burgers, handmade in the restaurant daily, sourdough buns, delicious handmade relishes and a wide range of toppings giving you over 40 varieties to choose from. *Exclusions apply.

2FOR1 MAIN COURSE | FRI ✓ | SAT × | SUN — International

THE HARE AND TORTOISE
01302 867 329

329 Bawtry Road, Doncaster, DN4 7PB

This Vintage Inn oozes rural charm and rustic character. The picturesque surroundings provide the perfect backdrop for savouring the hearty, seasonal pub-food on the menu.

25% OFF TOTAL | FRI ✓ | SAT ✓ | SUN | ▲ — Modern British

HESTIA RESTAURANT
☎ 0114 268 3131

190-192 Northfield Road, Sheffield, S10 1QU

Hestia saves guests the trouble of travelling abroad by bringing a taste of the Mediterranean to Sheffield. Be transported to Europe with culinary classics such as paella and beef stifado.

2FOR1 MAIN COURSE | FRI ✓ | SAT ✓ | ✱ | ▲ — Mediterranean

INDUS
☎ 0114 243 1690

688-690 Attercliffe Road, Sheffield, S9 3RP

With over 40 years of experience, Indus is an established part of Sheffield dining culture, having matured over the years into a fine modern restaurant with traditional values and an outstanding menu.

25% OFF TOTAL | 👤 4 | FRI ✓ | SAT 📱 | ✱ — Indian

THE INN AT TROWAY
☎ 01246 417 666

Snowdon Lane, Troway, Sheffield, S21 5RU

Hearty pub classics prepared by chefs who are passionate about local produce. Rustic originality is maintained at the core of this fantastic award-winning pub.

2FOR1 MAIN COURSE | FRI ✓ | SAT × | SUN — Modern Pub

ITALIAN KITCHEN
☎ 01142 664 168

349 Ecclesall Road, Sheffield, S7 2QD

Families are welcomed with open arms at this venue, where scrumptious Italian treats are served up on the heart of Eccallsall road. Independently owned, the chefs are long-established and authentic.

25% OFF TOTAL | 👤 6 | FRI ✓ | SAT × | ▲ — Italian/ Mediterranean

KASHMIRI AROMA WOODSEATS
☎ 01142 587 780

798 Chesterfield Road, Woodseats, Sheffield, S8 0SF

Authentic and exquisite cuisine showcasing the diverse culture of Indian and its culinary delights. The menu is extensive, offering vegetarian and non-vegetarian food that is all halal.

2FOR1 MAIN COURSE | FRI ✱ | SAT ✱ | ▲ — Indian

KENWOOD HALL
☎ 0114 258 3811

Kenwood Road, Sheffield, S7 1NQ

A stunning conference venue and hotel just one mile outside of the city of Sheffield. Drawing on both its countryside setting and city location, Kenwood Hall is fantastic in setting and appearance.

25% OFF TOTAL | 👤 6 | FRI ✓ | SAT ✓ | ▲ — British

LA TASCA
☎ 0114 256 9986

3a The Oasis, Meadowhall, Sheffield, S9 1EP

Quintessentially Spanish, La Tasca's fresh and exciting menu offers something for everyone. Their tapas dishes are sincerely authentic, while their paellas always deliver on flavour.

25% OFF TOTAL | 👤 8 | FRI ✓ | SAT × | ▲ — Spanish

LA TASCA
☎ 0114 266 6242

519 Ecclesall Road, Sheffield, S11 8PR

Quintessentially Spanish, La Tasca's fresh and exciting menu offers something for everyone. Their tapas dishes are sincerely authentic, while their paellas always deliver on flavour.

25% OFF TOTAL | 👤 8 | FRI ✓ | SAT × | ▲ — Spanish

LA TAVERNA
☎ 01302 364 557

30 Hall Gate, Doncaster, DN1 3NL

Highly reputable for its Mediterranean cuisine, La Taverna serves up a delectable menu of vibrant Italian dishes. Expect an excellent level of service and welcoming staff.

2FOR1 MAIN COURSE | FRI 📱 | SAT 📱 | ✱ | ▲ — Italian

THE LAKESIDE
01302 361 134

South Entry Drive, White Rose Way, Doncaster, DN4 5PJ

Beefeater Grill are one of the UK's best-loved restaurants welcoming guests for almost 40 years in over 130 locations nationwide. *Excludes Breakfast, Light Bites, Bar menu, set menus and all other offers.

2FOR1 MAIN COURSE | 👤 6 | FRI ✓ | SAT × | ▲ — Modern British

LAKESIDE RESTAURANT
☎ 01302 844 113

Tyram Hall, Doncaster, DN7 6DR

Priding themselves on habitual hospitality, the staff at this restaurant promise guests an unforgettable dining experience. The surroundings are vivacious and the menu guarantees authenticity.

2FOR1 MAIN COURSE | FRI 📱 | SAT 📱 | ✱ — Indian

LANCERS INDIAN TAKE AWAY
☎ 0114 265 5553

36c Birley Moor Road, Sheffield, S12 4WD

Good old-fashioned curry house set back from the main road. Does an eclectic, delicious selection of dishes at great prices, and in sizeable portions. Simple, effective, and very popular as a result.

2FOR1 MAIN COURSE | FRI × | SAT × | SUN — Indian

LE BAR @ THE CAMPANILE HOTEL
☎ 01302 370 770

Doncaster Leisure Park, Bawtry Road, Doncaster, DN4 7PD

A neat bar in the Campanile Hotel Doncaster provides the perfect space in which to relax and unwind after a day exploring the area. Enjoy your favourite beverage alongside tasty bar snacks.

50% OFF FOOD | 👤 8 | FRI × | SAT × — French

LOCH FYNE
☎ 0114 270 3940

Glossop Road, Sheffield, S10 2HQ

From the roadside oyster bar that once was, Loch Fyne restaurants now successfully inject energy and passion into great food and wonderful flavours, whilst ensuring their seafood is sustainably sourced.

25% OFF TOTAL | 👤 4 | FRI ✱ | SAT ✱ | ▲ — Seafood

THE LORD NELSON
☎ 01226 762 324

Barnsley Road, Sheffield, S36 7JA

Treat yourself to a 3-course meal from a menu that boasts an array of starters, mains and scrumptious desserts. Locally sourced and home-made, the food is guaranteed to really hit the spot.

25% OFF TOTAL | 👤 6 | FRI 📱 | SAT 📱 | SUN — British

MAHARAJ RESTAURANT
☎ 0114 266 4193

22-24 Commonside, Sheffield, S10 1GB

This Sheffield-based restaurant is a firm city favourite, well known for its Indian offerings and fine flavours. Imaginative spices and ingredients characterise the cuisine on offer.

2FOR1 MAIN COURSE | FRI × | SAT × | SUN | ✱ | ▲ — Indian

MARIOS TRATTORIA 01709 550 503
52 Kimberworth Road, Rotherham, S61 1AE
Mario's Trattoria is a delightful Italian restaurant serving a fine line in excellent, authentic dishes. Delectable pastas, succulent meats and fine breads make up a terrific menu.
2FOR1 MAIN COURSE | FRI | SAT | SUN ✱ — Italian

MARKET BRASSERIE @ HOLIDAY INN 0871 942 9061
High Road, Warmsworth, DN4 9UX
Preludes offers a sumptuous choice of mouth-watering dishes for the most discerning diner. Sit back, relax and enjoy the modern surroundings that make this restaurant a favourite for locals and guests alike.
25% OFF TOTAL | 6 | FRI | SAT — International

THE MOSSBROOK 01246 432 771
Sheffield Road, Eckington, Sheffield, S21 4FP
This Vintage Inn oozes rural charm and rustic character. The picturesque surroundings provide the perfect backdrop for savouring the hearty, seasonal pub-food on the menu.
25% OFF TOTAL | FRI ✓ | SAT ✓ | SUN — Modern British

NEW INDIA GARDEN TANDOORI RESTAURANT 0114 250 0059
659-661 London Road, Heeley, Sheffield, S2 4HT
Only prime cuts of lean lamb and succulent chicken breast go into the dishes at this exquisite Indian eatery. The menu vaunts genuinely tasty dishes that will surely tantalise curry lovers.
2FOR1 MAIN COURSE | FRI ✓ | SAT ✓ | ✱ — Indian

NIRMAL RESTAURANT 0114 272 4054
189-193 Glossop Road, Sheffield, S10 2GW
Quality Indian food is on offer at Nirmal Restaurant, where friendly staff make the overall experience a positive one. Fine line in familiar curries and chef specials.
2FOR1 MAIN COURSE | FRI ✓ | SAT ✓ | ✱ — Indian

THE OLD PUMP 0114 289 0296
Hackney Lane, Sheffield, S18 7TD
Serving the local community, this traditional pub also provides for visitors and is an ideal meeting place for families and friends to eat, relax and take in the stunning views across the open countryside.
2FOR1 2 COURSES | FRI ✓ | SAT ✓ | SUN — British

THE OLD RED LION 0114 246 8307
210 Main Street, Sheffield, S35 8PR
Spoil yourself with contemporary cuisine in a traditionally British environment. Choose creamy leek an gorgonzola risotto or a bean cassoulet from the à la carte menu by the Michelin-trained chef.
2FOR1 MAIN COURSE | FRI ✓ | SAT ✓ | SUN — British

THE ORIGINAL DILRAJ 01226 202 606
8-12 High Street, Dodworth, Barnsley, S75 3RF
Great Indian restaurant offering consistently excellent hospitality and proper, tasty Indian cuisine. Avoids the trap of being stodgy; oils, creams and heavy spices are used sparingly to keep things fresh.
2FOR1 MAIN COURSE | FRI ✓ | SAT ✓ — Bangladeshi/Indian

THE ORIGINAL INDIAN GARDEN 0114 250 0059
659-661 London Road, Sheffield, S2 4HT
Chingri maache St Martin, a king prawn and white fish fusion in an aromatic sauce, is just one of the tempting chef specials. Complete with platters, tandoori starters and warm naans, the menu is bursting.
2FOR1 MAIN COURSE | FRI | SAT | ✱ — Indian

PANAHAR 0114 263 0106
478 Fulwood Road, Sheffield, S10 3QD
Spoilt for choice, diners have the excruciating task of selecting a dish out of the 100 on offer at this authentic eatery. Using a spectacular array of spices, the cuisine here is exceedingly flavoursome.
25% OFF TOTAL | 2 | FRI × | SAT × | SUN — Indian

PARK VIEW RESTAURANT AND BAR 01709 580 004
Park Road, Rotherham, S64 8JH
Park View offers traditional British dining with our vast menu featuring a delicious choice of starters, pasta dishes, pizza, steak, homemade pie, chicken and fish dishes- there is always something to tempt you
50% OFF FOOD | FRI ✓ | SAT ✓ — British

PARKGATE INDIAN RESTAURANT 01709 525 502
21 Broad Street, Rotherham, S62 6AW
A modern and contemporary restaurant which serves a delicious combination of North Indian and Bangladeshi cuisine. The menu at Parkgate incorporates many classic dishes, as well as many more authentic dishes.
2FOR1 MAIN COURSE | FRI ✓ | SAT ✓ — Indian

PARTHENONAS 0114 258 5050
290-292 London Road, Sheffield, S2 4NJ
Authentic cuisine and a lively atmosphere to be enjoyed any day of the week. Cold and hot starters, such as the dips and pitta bread or the calamari, make excellent entrées before the moussaka.
50% OFF FOOD | 10 | FRI × | SAT ✓ — Greek

PORTOFINO ITALIAN 0114 255 5655
617 London Road, Sheffield, S2 4HT
The succulent lemon chicken or the juicy fillet steak are more than enough to get any meat-eater's taste buds tingling here. For the classic option, Italian dishes are also served with a variety of wines.
25% OFF TOTAL | 4 | FRI ✱ | SAT ✱ | SUN | ✱ — Italian

PREZZO 0114 244 7477
Valley Centertainment, Sheffield, SS9 2EP
With a character all of its own, Prezzo oozes contemporary style and enduring charm. Signature pastas, stone-baked pizzas and classic Italian dishes promise a perfect dining choice for the whole family.
2FOR1 MAIN COURSE | FRI × | SAT × — Italian

PREZZO 0114 267 0565
631-633 Eccleshall Road, Sheffield, S11 8PT
With a character all of its own, Prezzo oozes contemporary style and enduring charm. Signature pastas, stone-baked pizzas and classic Italian dishes promise a perfect dining choice for the whole family.
2FOR1 MAIN COURSE | FRI × | SAT × — Italian

THE QUAYS BAR @ HILTON 0114 252 5500
Hilton Sheffield, Victoria Quays, Sheffield, S4 7YA
The Quays Bar at the Hilton Sheffield is the perfect place to have a drink before heading to the restaurant, or to wind down at the end of the day. Serves lighter snacks and meals for a daytime treat.
50% OFF FOOD | 10 | FRI ✓ | SAT ✓ — British

THE QUAYS RESTAURANT @ HILTON 0114 252 5500
Hilton Sheffield, Victoria Quays, Sheffield, S4 7YA
The Quays Restaurant at the Hilton Sheffield provides a great place to rest, drink and dine with loved ones or business colleagues. Contemporary British cuisine on offer in a warm and spacious dining area.
50% OFF FOOD | 10 | FRI ✓ | SAT ✓ — British

RBG @ PARK INN 01302 760 710
The Park Inn, White Rose Way, Doncaster, DN4 5PD
Park Inn Doncaster is proud to play home to this stylish RBG restaurant, where quality food is always on the table. The gourmet burgers and the blackened salmon salad feature highly on the favourites list.
25% OFF TOTAL | 4 | FRI × | SAT × | ✱ — British

RBG @ PARK INN 01709 760 666
The Park Inn, Manvers Park, Wath-upon-Dearne, S63 7EQ
A tempting menu hosts a fantastic selection of gourmet burgers, signature grill dishes, soups and salads at this spacious hotel restaurant. Enjoy everything the bar has to offer before or after your meal.
2FOR1 3 COURSES | FRI ✓ | SAT ✓ — American

REVOLUCION DE CUBA 0114 279 9250
1 Mappin Street, Sheffield, S1 4DT
Welcome to the world of rum, where 1930's Havana meets Miami Beach. Revolucion De Cuba is causing a stir and for all the right reasons; mojitos meet burritos as day meets night.
25% OFF TOTAL | 6 | FRI × | SAT × — Cuban

THE ROBIN HOOD 0114 287 1010
Main Street, Sheffield, S26 3XJ
The Robin Hood Inn is a perfect example of an English pub found in Aughton, with plenty of draught ales and beers available. The traditional menu is packed full of mouth-watering pub classic.
25% OFF TOTAL | FRI | SAT | SUN — British

SAKUSHI JAPANESE RESTAURANT
☎01142 737 399

27 Campo Lane, Sheffield, S1 2EG

Sakushi is Sheffield's first city centre sushi and noodle bar. Whether you are after a quick bite to eat or a relaxed meal. The traditional food is delicately prepared by hand in the open kitchen.

50% OFF FOOD | 4 | FRI * | SAT * — Japanese

SHIMUL TANDOORI
☎0114 235 9911

329 Meadowhead, Sheffield, S8 7UP

Cracking little Indian restaurant with a menu that covers all the usual suspects and does them very well. The choice is excellent, and the atmosphere accommodating and relaxed.

2FOR1 MAIN COURSE | FRI × | SAT × | * — Indian

STRADA
0114 279 5948

Leopold Square, Sheffield, S1 2JG

Strada offers fresh, bold dishes inspired by flavours of Italian city life! Try the hand-stretched, stone baked pizzas, addictive pastas and risottos, great share plates and much more. *Excludes Pizzettas.

25% OFF TOTAL | 6 | FRI ✓ | SAT × — Italian

TULIP LOUNGE
01142 765 870

21-23 North Church St, Sheffield, S1 2DH

A highlight of the Cathedral Quarter in Sheffield, the Tulip Lounge is one of the most popular venues in the city. With a variety of menus to choose from, you'll never be short of choice.

2FOR1 3 COURSES | FRI | SAT — British

RADHUNI
☎0114 258 2581

186 London Road, Sheffield, S2 4LT

Contemporary Indian cuisine that will completely stimulate your palate. Kind, welcoming staff are happy to ensure you have a pleasing dining experience.

2FOR1 MAIN COURSE | FRI ✓ | SAT ✓ | * — Indian

VIRAAJ
☎0114 250 9066

743 Chesterfield Road, Woodseats, Sheffield, S8 0SL

Welcoming and comfortable restaurant providing diners with a varied menu of deliciously authentic Indian dishes, each crafted with the finest herbs and spices by accomplished chefs.

2FOR1 MAIN COURSE | FRI × | SAT × — Indian

VITO'S ITALIAN RESTAURANT
☎0114 233 3574

284 South Road, Sheffield, S6 3TE

Vito's offers a delightful tour of some of Italy's treasures. Vito, the proprietor, offers dishes representing the best from his native southern Italy.

25% OFF TOTAL | FRI × | SAT × | * — Italian

WALKABOUT

25% OFF TOTAL | 10 | FRI ✓ | SAT ✓

3 restaurants in South Yorkshire

1-3 Church Street, Barnsley, S70 2AB
☎ 01226 733 864

5 Priory Walk, Doncaster, DN1 1TS
☎ 01302 328 188

Carver Street, Sheffield, S1 4FS
☎ 0114 241 3400

THE WICK AT BOTH ENDS
0114 272 3039

149-151 West Street, Sheffield, S1 4EU

As the name suggests, this is a venue in which to completely indulge yourself. Diners watch as their favourite dishes are made before their eyes, including home-made chicken burgers with garlic and thyme.

2FOR1 MAIN COURSE | FRI ✓ | SAT ✓ | SUN — Modern British

YE OLDE MUSTARD POT
☎01226 761 155

Mortimer Road, Midhopestones, Sheffield, S36 4GW

Ye Olde Mustard Pot is the perfect place for either a relaxing pub lunch or a more intimate evening out, there is the simplicity of a traditional menu but with a number of new and exciting twists.

2FOR1 MAIN COURSE | FRI | SAT * | SUN — Traditional English

West Yorkshire

THE 1875 RESTUARANT
☎01943 871 811

Station Road, Menston, Leeds, LS29 6JH

Gastronomic pleasures to be enjoyed as you journey to India without even leaving your seat. The food at The 1875 will launch you into a culinary whirlwind of Indian treats and sensational flavours.

2FOR1 MAIN COURSE | FRI ✓ | SAT ✓ — Fine Dining

A TASTE OF TRINIDAD
☎0113 219 5668

152 Chapeltown Road, Leeds, LS7 4EE

The menu includes dishes such as chicken dhalpouril rotti and goat paratha roti. This is just a small selection of the delicious and healthy dishes available which are all cooked Trinidad style.

2FOR1 3 COURSES | FRI ✓ | SAT ✓ — Caribbean

AIOLIS RESTAURANT @ HOLIDAY INN
☎0113 385 3792

Wakefield Road, Garforth, Leeds, LS25 1LH

Thoughtful, creative cuisine, vegetarian dishes and healthy food options help this stylish restaurant stand out. An industrious place that caters for family dining, business and simple, friendly company.

50% OFF FOOD | FRI ✓ | SAT ✓ — International

APADANA PERSIAN
☎01484 511 118

9 Viaduct Street, Huddersfield, HD1 5DL

Apadana is the one and only Persian restaurant in Huddersfield. Apadana has a menu bursting with Iranian flavours, an atmosphere exuding the beauty and warmth of Iran with its friendly helpful staff.

2FOR1 MAIN COURSE | FRI × | SAT × — Middle Eastern

ARABIAN HOUSE RESTAURANT
☎0113 240 0349

159 Roundhay Road, Leeds, LS8 5AJ

Offering an exciting and innovative range of tasty, well thought out Arabic, Middle Eastern and Moroccan cuisine. Exquisite spices and flavours are locked in every dish.

25% OFF TOTAL | 4 | FRI ✓ | SAT ✓ — Middle Eastern

AROMA
☎0192 443 7733

58-60 Bradford Road, Dewsbury, WF13 2DU

Stylish surroundings and excellent food make Aroma superb choice for an authentic Indian dining experience in Dewsbury. The menu is famed throughout the area with the tastiest selection of dishes.

2FOR1 MAIN COURSE | FRI ✓ | SAT ✓ | * — Indian

AROOJE
☎0192 422 0075

Market Street, Normanton, WF6 2AR

Synonymous with quality Indian food, Arooje pleases curry lovers from all around by crafting authentic dishes using the best local produce, fresh herbs and carefully selected whole spices.

2FOR1 3 COURSES | FRI | SAT — Indian

ASHIANA BRADFORD
☎01274 652 141

48 Tong Street, Bradford, BD4 9LU

Ashiana is a haven for fans of traditional Pakistani fare. Drawing on years of experience, the owner has devised a menu compiled solely of Kashmir and Punjab dishes.

2FOR1 3 COURSES | FRI × | SAT × | * — Indian

THE ASPLEY
01484 544250

St Andrews Road, Huddersfield, HD1 6SB

Quality pub classics with a modern twist combine with a friendly and relaxed atmosphere to make this Table Table venue the perfect place for family gatherings or meeting friends.

2FOR1 MAIN COURSE | FRI ✓ | SAT ✓ — Modern British

AWADH RESTAURANT
☎ 01274 725 565

1060 Manchester Road, Bradford, BD5 8NN

Awadh covers gourmet delicacies from all four major regions of India. The highly experienced chefs bring you a true taste of the subcontinent, creating an eclectic menu that guarantees satisfaction.

2FOR1 MAIN COURSE | FRI × | SAT × — Indian

BABY JUPITER
☎ 0113 242 1202

The Basement, 11 York Place, Leeds, LS1 2DS

Retro bar in Leeds that mixes a nice buzz, some brilliant music and an array of drinks with a good range of pub- and bar-style food that you can enjoy for a lunch or make part of your evening out.

2FOR1 MAIN COURSE | FRI × | SAT × | SUN — Locally Sourced

BALOOSHAI
☎ 01484 664 455

Eastgate, Holmfirth, HD9 6PA

An authentic menu overflows with fantastic regional recipes, as well as some old favourites collected from all over India, lovingly prepared in full view of the restaurant in the open plan kitchen.

25% OFF TOTAL | 10 | FRI ✓ | SAT ✓ | ✱ — Indian

BALOOSHAI CENTRAL
☎ 01484 559 055

Viaduct Street, Huddersfield, HD1 5DL

Ever-popular Indian restaurant tucked away under some old railway arches. Take them on trust and be guided through pickles, poppadoms, pakoras, parathas and puris, among others.

2FOR1 3 COURSES | FRI × | SAT × | ✱ | ▲ — Indian

BAR RISA
☎ 0113 247 1759

The Cube, Albion Street, Leeds, LS2 8ER

Vibrant and contemporary spot in the centre of Leeds combining a relaxed ambience with some classic bar food. Cumberland sausages with creamy mash, rich lasagne and great nachos all hit the spot.

2FOR1 MAIN COURSE | FRI ✱ | SAT ✱ — British

THE BAY HORSE
01756 797 711

Snaygill, Bradley, Keighley, BD20 9HB

This Vintage Inn oozes rural charm and rustic character. The picturesque surroundings provide the perfect backdrop for savouring the hearty, seasonal pub-food on the menu.

25% OFF TOTAL | FRI ✓ | SAT ✓ | SUN | ▲ — Modern British

Bella Italia
Pizza ♥ Pasta ♥ Grill

25% OFF TOTAL | 6 | FRI × | SAT × | SUN | ✱ | ▲

4 restaurants in West Yorkshire

Xscape, Colorado Way, Castleford, WF10 4TA
☎ 01977 514 200

145 Briggate, Leeds, LS1 6BR
☎ 0113 245 4630

Kirkstall Road, Leeds, LS4 2DG
☎ 0113 220 5818

Centre 27 Retail Pk, Birstall, Leeds, WF17 9TB
☎ 01924 422 374

THE BEEHIVE
☎ 0113 201 7171

Main Street, Thorner, Leeds, LS14 3DE

Operating on the principle of 'real value for money' this cosy village restaurant offers a casual and relaxed dining experience. Without fuss, but absolutely with quality food and wine.

2FOR1 MAIN COURSE | FRI ✱ | SAT ✱ | SUN | ▲ — British

BIANCO
☎ 0113 246 5225

40 Great George Street, Leeds, LS1 3DL

Restaurant filled with vibrant colours and bright lights to match the colourful Italian cuisine on offer. Bianco hosts a real taste of Italy, serving well-designed pizzas and creamy pasta dishes.

2FOR1 3 COURSES | FRI ✓ | SAT × — Italian

THE BIERKELLER
08455 333 000

Sovereign House, 123 The Headrow, Leeds, LS1 5RD

The Bierkeller Leeds is a truly unique experience with finest selection of draught German beers served in steins by waiting staff in traditional Bavarian clothing and hearty authentic regional food.

2FOR1 3 COURSES | FRI ✓ | SAT × — European

BLACK BULL
☎ 01924 885 022

21 Barr Lane, Wakefield, WF4 4JJ

Priding themselves on simple, honest food, the Black Bull dedicates its menu to wholesome British classics. Expect the most hearty of dishes, all of which are sourced locally for freshness.

2FOR1 MAIN COURSE | FRI ✓ | SAT ✓ | SUN — Carvery

THE BRASSERIE @ MERCURE
☎ 0844 815 9004

Bradford Bankfield Hotel, Bradford Rd, Bingley, BD16 1TU

Mercure Bradford North Hotel oozes gothic grandeur; with its magnificent appearance the hotel has the ability to cause a breathtaking experience. For a touch of the modern, head to the Brasserie.

2FOR1 3 COURSES | FRI ✓ | SAT ✓ — British

THE BRASSERIE @ MERCURE
☎ 0844 815 9020

Leeds Parkway Hotel, Otley Road, Leeds, LS16 8AG

Located in the Gold Acre Nature Park Reserve and only three miles from the Yorkshire Dales, the Mercure Leeds is great for city fun and country escape. Vibrant lunches and intimate dinners on offer.

2FOR1 3 COURSES | FRI ✓ | SAT ✓ — British

BRASSERIE 1 AT THE CRAIGLANDS HOTEL
☎ 01943 430 001

Craiglands Hotel, Cow Pasture Road, Ilkley, LS29 8RQ

Set in a Victorian house out on the eastern flank of Ilkley, a restaurant with an open ambience about it, lending itself to a comfortable lunch or low-key evening meal. Serves broad, tasty brasserie fare.

2FOR1 3 COURSES | FRI ✓ | SAT ✓ — Brasserie

THE BRASSERIE AT BEWLEYS HOTEL LEEDS
☎ 0113 245 2030

7 City Walk Sweet Street, Leeds, LS11 9AT

Situated in the contemporary Bewleys Hotel in Leeds, The Brasserie offers a specially selected menu which draws on the unique flavours of the season. Ingredients are sourced locally.

2FOR1 3 COURSES | FRI ✓ | SAT ✓ | SUN | ✱ — European

BRASSERIE AT MERCURE WETHERBY HOTEL
☎ 0844 815 9067

Leeds Road, Wetherby, LS22 5HE

The Brasserie at the Mercure Wetherby relishes its ability to aid relaxation and dining enjoyment. Lovers of great food and wine will not be disappointed with the friendly service complementing your meal.

2FOR1 3 COURSES | FRI ✓ | SAT ✓ — British

BRASSERIE AT WEST PARK
☎ 0113 275 6333

269 Otley Road, Leeds, LS16 5LN

Stylish restaurant that offers a seductive, modern brasserie menu with an emphasis on locally sourced meats and seasonal produce. A balanced place both in terms of atmosphere and as far as flavour goes.

2FOR1 MAIN COURSE | FRI ✓ | SAT ✓ | SUN | ▲ — French

BRETTS FISH RESTAURANT
☎ 0113 232 3344

12-14 North Lane, Headingley, Leeds, LS6 3HE

Step inside this beautiful ivy-covered Victorian house and expect to be blown away by the fish and chips. Icelandic haddock and chips made from Lincolnshire potatoes make up the signature dish.

25% OFF TOTAL | FRI ▮ | SAT ▮ — Seafood

To understand what the restaurant icons mean, please see the inside back cover.

THE BRIDGE
☎01937 580 115

Walshford, Wetherby, Leeds, LS22 5HS

Steeped in history, offering a truly unique experience. Diners are given a choice of various appealing dishes, freshly prepared, and served in a dining room complete with fascinating historical features.

2FOR1 3 COURSES | FRI ✓ | SAT ✓ | SUN | ▲ — British

THE BROWN CALF KITCHEN @ THE BROWN COW
☎01274 564 345

The Island Bridge, Bingley, BD16 2QX

This historic 17th Century venue provides a cracking night of entertainment with a Tuesday quiz, Saturday night entertainment and live bands. Renowned for exceptional food, the Brown Cow is a hot spot.

2FOR1 3 COURSES | FRI 📱 | SAT 📱 | SUN | ▲ — British

THE BULL'S HEAD
☎01484 847 225

Blackmoorfoot, Huddersfield, HD7 5TR

A special dining experience offering great food, fine wine and superb service with value and flair. The Bull's Head is a cosy country pub with 3 cask ales on rotation.

2FOR1 MAIN COURSE | FRI × | SAT × | SUN | * | ▲ — British

CAFÉ ROUGE
0113 246 1620

2 The Light, The Headrow, Leeds, LS1 8EH

French sophistication on the British high street - enjoy seasonally changing French dishes and a continental wine selection, served in a relaxed environment with an undeniable flair of Parisian chic.

25% OFF TOTAL | 6 | FRI ✓ | SAT ✓ | * | ▲ — French

THE CALVERLEY ARMS
0113 255 7771

Calverley Lane, Calverley, Pudsey, LS28 5QQ

This Vintage Inn oozes rural charm and rustic character. The picturesque surroundings provide the perfect backdrop for savouring the hearty, seasonal pub-food on the menu.

25% OFF TOTAL | FRI ✓ | SAT ✓ | SUN | ▲ — Modern British

CALVERLEY GOLF AND COUNTRY CLUB
☎0113 256 9244

Woodhall Lane, Leeds, LS28 5QY

A warm welcome always awaits at the Calverley Golf & Country Club and they are proud of their reputation for being the friendly golf club. All are welcome to sample the hospitality and welcoming ambience.

25% OFF TOTAL | 4 | FRI ✓ | SAT ✓ | SUN | * | ▲ — International

THE CALVERLEY GRILL AT OULTON HALL
☎0113 282 1000

Rothwell Lane, Leeds, LS26 8HN

Excellent melding of tradition and contemporaneity at this fine-dining restaurant. Set in a magnificent country house hotel, the cuisine is fresh, acute, and thoughtfully accompanied. 2 AA Rosettes.

2FOR1 MAIN COURSE | FRI × | SAT × | * | ▲ — Fine Dining

CASINO RED
☎0845 838 1833

3 Northumberland Street, Huddersfield, HD1 1DT

After working up an appetite in the casino, head to the restaurant for a hunger-filling meal and a well-deserved glass of wine. The best place to spend the first of your winnings.

50% OFF FOOD | 4 | FRI ✓ | SAT ✓ — Indian

CHARCO'S BRADFORD
☎01274 743 742

375-377 Leeds Road, Bradford, BD3 9LY

Enjoy a delicious menu packed with peri-peri chicken, seasoned with their own unique marinade of herbs and Chile spices then flame-grilled to perfection for a tastier, healthier dining option.

25% OFF TOTAL | FRI ✓ | SAT ✓ — Portuguese

CHARCO'S LEEDS
☎0113 217 0809

162 Woodhouse Lane, Leeds, LS2 9HB

Enjoy a delicious menu packed with peri-peri chicken, seasoned with their own unique marinade of herbs and Chile spices then flame-grilled to perfection for a tastier, healthier dining option.

25% OFF TOTAL | FRI ✓ | SAT ✓ — Portuguese

CHARCO'S ROUNDHAY ROAD
☎0113 240 4060

228-230 Roundhay Road, Leeds, LS8 5AA

Enjoy a delicious menu packed with peri-peri chicken, seasoned with their own unique marinade of herbs and Chile spices, then flame grilled to perfection for a tastier, healthier dining option.

25% OFF TOTAL | FRI ✓ | SAT ✓ — Portuguese

CHINI INDIAN RESTAURANT
☎0113 245 2025

20 Merrion Street, Leeds, LS1 6PQ

In this traditional restaurant in the centre of Leeds, established in 1970 and family run ever since, only the highest quality of Indian dining is provided.

25% OFF TOTAL | 10 | FRI 📱 | SAT 📱 | * | ▲ — Indian

CHINO LATINO
☎0113 380 4080

Boar Lane, Leeds, LS1 5NS

Trailblazing pan-Asian restaurant. Stylishly designed, all gun-metal greys, crimsons and creams, the restaurant serves eclectic dishes to an urbane crowd. *25% discount is not applied to cocktails.

25% OFF TOTAL | 10 | FRI × | SAT × | * — Pan-Asian

CILANTRO
☎0113 269 2000

378 Harrogate Road, Leeds, LS17 6PY

Passion and sophistication are at the forefront of this restaurants ethos. Stylishly chic, Cilantro prepares only the most delectable and rich of Indian cuisine.

25% OFF TOTAL | 10 | FRI ✓ | SAT ✓ | ▲ — Indian

CITY 3 BAR @ HILTON
☎01274 734 734

Hilton Bradford, Hall Ings, Bradford, BD1 5SH

International dining in the restaurant of a luxury Bradford hotel. The bar serves a range of simple, very tasty light options alongside its eclectic range of beers, wines and spirits.

50% OFF FOOD | 6 | FRI ✓ | SAT ✓ — International

CITY 3 RESTAURANT @ HILTON
☎01274 734 734

Hilton Bradford, Hall Ings, Bradford, BD1 5SH

International dining in the restaurant of a luxury Bradford hotel. The restaurant offers a range of flavour from a standing table d'hôte menu, as well as some excellent 'Taste of Yorkshire' dishes.

50% OFF FOOD | 6 | FRI ✓ | SAT ✓ — International

THE COURTYARD RESTAURANT
☎0113 285 4646

The Pastures, Bradford, BD4 0RP

Ivy-clad former vicarage set in the quaint village of Tong offers a comfortable country welcome to both locals and visitors. The hotel's restaurant has a varied, globally inspired menu.

25% OFF TOTAL | 6 | FRI 📱 | SAT 📱 | * | ▲ — Modern European

THE COW AND CALF
01943 607 335

Hangingstone Road, Ilkley, LS29 8BT

This Vintage Inn oozes rural charm and rustic character. The picturesque surroundings provide the perfect backdrop for savouring the hearty, seasonal pub-food on the menu.

25% OFF TOTAL | FRI ✓ | SAT ✓ | SUN | ▲ — Modern British

THE CROWN
☎01422 349 270

31 Crown Street, Halifax, HX1 1TT

Diners must be sure to start their dining experience with the chef's special bandhor bhaji. All dishes are prepared using the finest of aromatic and effluvious spices to ensure authenticity.

2FOR1 MAIN COURSE | FRI × | SAT × | * | ▲ — Indian

CYRUS
☎01274 728 728

Morley Street, Bradford, BD7 1AF

Persian and Greek is infused to create a unique dining experience. The moussaka comes highly appraised, as does the pastitsio. Quality guaranteed, the staff believe good food brings people together!

2FOR1 MAIN COURSE | FRI 📱 | SAT 📱 | * — Mediterranean

DESI BUFFET
☎01484 549 775

80 Blacker Road, Huddersfield, HD1 5HN

Desi Buffet is a great Indian option in Huddersfield. They have a tasty selection of morsels available to tempt your taste buds. A perfect place for a family meal.

25% OFF TOTAL | 4 | FRI × | SAT × | SUN | * | ▲ — Indian

DICK HUDSONS
01274 552 121

Otley Road, Bingley, BD16 3BA

This Vintage Inn oozes rural charm and rustic character. The picturesque surroundings provide the perfect backdrop for savouring the hearty, seasonal pub-food on the menu.

25% OFF TOTAL | FRI ✓ | SAT ✓ | SUN | ▲ — Modern British

DIGBY'S @ THE NEW ELLINGTON
☎ 0844 815 9838
23-25 York Place, Leeds, LS1 2EY
Digby's is a restaurant with impeccable taste. Enter a world of passionate and sumptuous dining with award-winning culinary expertise from Anton Scoones.

25% OFF TOTAL | FRI ✓ | SAT ✗ | ▲ — International

DISTRIKT
☎ 0113 243 3674
7 Duncan Street, Leeds, LS1 6DQ
Distrikt, renowned for its tapas, combines a love for underground electronic music with an eclectic mix of Middle Eastern, Mediterranean and British influences in its fresh, locally sourced food.

2FOR1 MAIN COURSE | FRI ✓ | SAT ✱ | SUN — Mediterranean

THE DOG AND GUN INN
☎ 01535 643 159
Denholme Road, Oxenhope, BD22 9SN
17th-century coaching inn whose dining room has spectacular views across Bronte country in West Yorkshire. Good home-cooked food and superb, award-winning beers are the order of the day.

2FOR1 MAIN COURSE | FRI ✱ | SAT ✱ | SUN | ▲ — Modern Pub

DOUGH BISTRO
☎ 0113 278 7255
293-295 Spen Lane, West Park, Leeds, LS16 5BD
Restaurant in what was once a bakery, with exposed brick walls, wooden floors and bohemian charm. Fine ingredients are a hallmark, as is the seasonal, thoughtful character of the menu.

25% OFF TOTAL | 👤 2 | FRI ✓ | SAT ✓ — British

THE DUKE OF YORK
☎ 01422 203 615
West Street, Halifax, HX3 7LN
Situated along a well-recommended walkers trail through Stone Chair, the Duke of York is not only ideally located but is also brimming with historical beauty worthy of its Grade II listing

2FOR1 3 COURSES | FRI 📱 | SAT ✱ | SUN | ▲ — British

EAST BAR & GRILL
☎ 0113 257 9991
Richardshaw Lane, Pudsey, Leeds, LS28 6BN
Spectacular modern Indian restaurant in Pudsey. Warm tones, smart use of space and splashes of offbeat pattern make up the setting; in turn, the food is outstanding, with an acclaimed, eclectic menu.

2FOR1 3 COURSES | FRI ✱ | SAT ✱ — Indian

EAST INDIA RESTAURANT
☎ 0113 260 2530
Crossgates Shopping Centre, Leeds, LS15 8ET
A great little Indian restaurant set just off the main drag in the Crossgates centre. Bright place with a low-key buzz about it; serves tasty traditional curries and some left-field regional dishes.

2FOR1 MAIN COURSE | FRI ✱ | SAT ✱ — Indian

FILMORE AND UNION WETHERBY
☎ 01937 580 135
61 Market Place, Wetherby, LS22 6LN
Home of the Health Kitchen, the salads, juice remedies, artisan breads, seafood, tagines, pastas and pastries are all presented beautifully and the fresh ingredients make for a delicious dining experience.

25% OFF TOTAL | 👤 4 | FRI ✗ | SAT ✗ | SUN — British

THE FISHERMAN AT BINGLEY
☎ 0127 451 1886
Wagon Lane, Bingley, BD16 1TS
This traditional Yorkshire alehouse offers a British but modern menu which features exceptional meat, poultry, game and fish dishes and is updated with the seasons.

50% OFF FOOD | 👤 10 | FRI ✓ | SAT ✓ — British

THE FOX & HOUNDS
☎ 01937 842 192
Hall Park Road, Walton, Wetherby, LS23 7DQ
Food-led pub with all their dishes cooked to order, grounded in a real attention to the quality of the produce. Friendly and efficient service combines with classic, fresh-flavoured fare.

2FOR1 3 COURSES | FRI ✗ | SAT ✗ | SUN — British

THE FOXGLOVE
01484 602 101
36a Penistone Road, Kirkburton, Huddersfield, HD8 0P
This Vintage Inn oozes rural charm and rustic character. The picturesque surroundings provide the perfect backdrop for savouring the hearty, seasonal pub-food on the menu.

25% OFF TOTAL | FRI ✓ | SAT ✓ | SUN | ▲ — Modern British

FRANGANOS
☎ 01422 365 566
10-12 Crown Street, Halifax, West Yorkshire, HX1 1TT
Tasty flame-grilled peri peri chicken is the house speciality at Franganos. Zingy chicken dishes cooked and served in a variety of different ways appear on a quirky, vibrant menu.

25% OFF TOTAL | 👤 2 | FRI ✓ | SAT ✓ — Portuguese

GALLERY FORTYONE
☎ 0113 274 0041
41-43 Commercial Road, Leeds, LS5 3AW
Exciting, vibrant Mediterranean cuisine on Commercial Road in Leeds. Find a vast wine selection and a menu that reflects the flavours, ingredients and recipes from sun-drenched countries.

25% OFF TOTAL | 👤 4 | FRI 📱 | SAT ✗ | ✱ | ▲ — Mediterranean

THE GASCOIGNE ARMS
0113 281 2265
2 Main Street, Barwick in Elmet, Leeds, LS15 4JQ
A great place for a piled-high plate of some classic, unpretentious but completely satisfying pub grub. Settle in for a Sunday lunch or make an evening of it with a pint to wash down your dinner.

25% OFF TOTAL | 👤 4 | FRI ✓ | SAT ✓ — English/Gastro pub

THE GEORGIAN RESTAURANT
☎ 0845 072 7564
Wood Hall Hotel, Trip Lane, LS22 4JA
Offering classic dishes with a touch of flair, this Hand Picked Hotels venue will have you spoilt for choice. The wine list includes Old World classics and intriguing New World arrivals. 2 AA Rosettes.

25% OFF TOTAL | 👤 6 | FRI ✱ | SAT ✱ | ✱ — British

GIORGIO'S RISTORANTE ITALIANO
☎ 0113 278 2030
70-72 Otley Road, Leeds, LS6 4BA
Juicy olives, handmade pizzas, garlic king prawns and lemon lamb cutlets are just a few of the incredibly tasty dishes available on the menu at Giorgio's Italian restaurant.

2FOR1 3 COURSES | FRI ✓ | SAT ✓ — Italian

THE GOLDEN COCK
☎ 01484 664 863
2 The Village, Huddersfield, HD4 6UD
Guests can dine informally in the Bistro, which offers traditional pub favourites and Continental specialities to share, or enjoy a more extensive menu in the Brasserie.

2FOR1 MAIN COURSE | FRI ✗ | SAT ✗ | SUN | ✱ | ▲ — European

GRANGEMOOR RESTAURANT
☎ 0844 736 8609
The Old Golf House, New Hey Rd, Huddersfield, HD3 3YP
Restaurant with breathtaking views, perfect for an enjoyable family dinner or intimate meal. Excellent modern cuisine complemented by a well-stocked bar, and al fresco dining.

25% OFF TOTAL | 👤 6 | FRI ✓ | SAT ✓ | ✱ | ▲ — Modern European

GUIDE POST HOTEL RESTAURANT & BAR
☎ 0845 409 1350
Common Road, Low Moor, Bradford, BD12 0ST
A warm and welcoming restaurant offering a varied selection of fine British fare and hearty alternatives. The Head Chef Steve Hartshorne has cultivated a varied selection of menus to suit every taste.

2FOR1 3 COURSES | FRI ✗ | SAT ✗ — British

HALIFAX BEEFEATER GRILL
01422 386 530
Broad Street Plaza, Halifax, HX1 1YA
Beefeater Grill are one of the UK's best-loved restaurants welcoming guests for almost 40 years in over 130 locations nationwide. *Excludes Breakfast, Light Bites, Bar menu, set menus and all other offers.

2FOR1 MAIN COURSE | 👤 6 | FRI ✓ | SAT ✗ | ▲ — Modern British

HANDMADE BURGER CO.
01924 366 522
Trinity Walk, Wakefield, WF1 1QU
100% prime Scotch beef burgers, handmade in the restaurant daily, sourdough buns, delicious handmade relishes and a wide range of toppings giving you over 40 varieties to choose from. *Exclusions apply.

2FOR1 MAIN COURSE | FRI ✓ | SAT ✗ | SUN — International

HANDMADE BURGER CO.
0113 246 1742
Trinity Leeds, Trinity East, Leeds, LS1 5ER
100% prime Scotch beef burgers, handmade in the restaurant daily, sourdough buns, delicious handmade relishes and a wide range of toppings giving you over 40 varieties to choose from. *Exclusions apply.

2FOR1 MAIN COURSE | FRI ✓ | SAT ✗ | SUN — International

THE HARE AND HOUNDS
01924 493 814
Liley Lane, Mirfield, WF14 8EE
This Vintage Inn oozes rural charm and rustic character. The picturesque surroundings provide the perfect backdrop for savouring the hearty, seasonal pub-food on the menu.

25% OFF TOTAL | FRI ✓ | SAT ✓ | SUN | ▲ — Modern British

HASAN'S RESTAURANT
☎ 0113 278 8990
352-354 Kirkstall Road, Leeds, LS4 2HQ
Boasting an impressive menu, the kitchen at Hasan's thrives upon its ability to cook up delicious Indian dishes made from the finest ingredients and tastiest spices. Meat, fish and vegetarian dishes.

2FOR1 3 COURSES | FRI × | SAT × | ▲ — Indian

HENRY'S CAFÉ BAR
☎ 0113 245 9424
10 Greek Street, Leeds, LS1 5RU
An oasis for every guest with a delicious, well-prepared menu ideal for lunch, dinner or a light snack. Henry's also boasts an extensive wine and champagne list and a choice of cocktails to die for.

25% OFF TOTAL | 👤10 | FRI ✓ | SAT ✓ — European

THE HUNSWORTH
01274 862828
Whitehall Road, Cleckheaton, Bradford, BD19 6HG
Quality pub classics with a modern twist combine with a friendly and relaxed atmosphere to make this Table Table venue the perfect place for family gatherings or meeting friends.

2FOR1 MAIN COURSE | FRI ✓ | SAT ✓ — Modern British

ISTANBUL MANGAL
☎ 0113 266 2682
41 Street Lane, Leeds, LS8 1AP
Traditionally Turkish, the portions are generous and certain to appease grumbling stomachs. Attentive and knowledgeable staff will advise guests on the expansive menu bursting with Mediterranean treats.

25% OFF TOTAL | 👤6 | FRI × | SAT × | SUN | ▲ — Turkish

JANNAT RESTAURANT
☎ 01484 548 001
Gamma House, Huddersfield, HD1 4AA
A genuine Punjabi restaurant where you won't find the normal fare. Instead, each unique meal is traditionally cooked with secret recipes from the Punjab to cultivate the perfect dish.

2FOR1 3 COURSES | FRI ✓ | SAT ✓ — Indian

JEWEL OF INDIA
☎ 01943 467 138
1 Bridge Street, Otley, LS21 1BQ
There is an extensive menu to choose from with a wide choice of dishes all cooked and prepared exactly to your taste. The staff do their utmost to make your visit a pleasurable experience.

25% OFF TOTAL | 👤6 | FRI × | SAT × | ✱ — Indian

JURYS INN LEEDS
☎ 0113 283 8800
Kendell Street, Brewery Wharf, Leeds, LS10 1NE
Jurys Inn Leeds is ideally located in the city centre, so when you are feeling a little peckish after your busy day of work or sightseeing, be sure to head on down to the in-house contemporary restaurant.

2FOR1 MAIN COURSE | FRI ✓ | SAT ✓ | ✱ — British

KALABASH
☎ 0113 249 2324
258 Harehills Lane, Leeds, LS8 5DH
A vibrant taste of the Caribbean is brought to Yorkshire. Impeccable service and an exceptional standard of cuisine ensure that this exotic eatery enchants its diners.

50% OFF FOOD | 👤10 | FRI ▯ | SAT ▯ — Caribbean

KAMRAN BALTI HOUSE
☎ 01422 345 678
27 Union Street, Halifax, HX1 1PR
Classic Indian cuisine is on offer at this highly reputable local restaurant, with a fine line in traditional dishes that blend the best spices with the finest produce.

2FOR1 3 COURSES | FRI × | SAT × — Indian

KASHMIRI AROMA ILKLEY
☎ 01943 865 554
Coutances Way, Burley-in-Wharfedale, Ilkley, LS29 7HQ
An aromatic, fragrant and spice-filled menu that reflects the cultural diversities of India. Choose to dine à la carte or sample the tantalising buffet selections. Fine Indian dining and hospitality.

2FOR1 MAIN COURSE | FRI ✱ | SAT ✱ | ▲ — Indian

KEBABEESH
☎ 01274 617 188
165 Newline, Bradford, BD10 0BN
Bringing a taste of Lahore to the table, the long-established chefs prepare authentic Pakistani cuisine which promises to have diners returning time after time.

2FOR1 MAIN COURSE | FRI ✱ | SAT ✱ — Indian

KERALA CAFÉ
☎ 01274 595 367
139-141 Bradford Road, Bradford, BD18 3TB
Outstanding reviews and a highly loyal cohort of diners pays homage to this exceptional south Indian restaurant in Bradford. Exquisite flavours are created from fine blends of unusual spices.

2FOR1 MAIN COURSE | FRI ▯ | SAT ▯ | ✱ — South Indian/Sri Lankan

THE KEYS
☎ 01484 516 677
The Crypt of St Peters, Huddersfield, HD1 1BU
A distinctive place to eat, set in the crypt of St Peter's parish church. And the British, bistro-style cuisine is superb. *The Keys only opens lunchtimes.

2FOR1 3 COURSES | FRI ✓ | SAT ✓ — British

LA BRASSERIE @ CEDAR COURT HOTEL
☎ 01924 276 310
Denby Dale Road, Calder Grove, Wakefield, WF4 3QZ
In-house restaurant for the Cedar Court Hotel. Serves a sumptuous array of dishes with primarily British and French influences. Duo of salmon and sea bass or scallop and crab tian stand out from the crowd.

2FOR1 3 COURSES | FRI ✓ | SAT ✓ — British

LA CANTINA 44
☎ 0113 368 0066
1a Austhorpe Road, Cross Gates, Leeds, LS15 8QR
La Cantina 44's vast selection of dishes ensures a comprehensively satisfied palate. The restaurant offers superb Mediterranean cuisine made from the freshest ingredients.

2FOR1 2 COURSES | FRI ▯ | SAT ▯ | ✱ | ▲ — Mediterranean

LA TASCA
☎ 0113 244 2205
4 Russell Street, Leeds, LS1 5PT
Quintessentially Spanish, La Tasca's fresh and exciting menu offers something for everyone. Their tapas dishes are sincerely authentic, while their paellas always deliver on flavour.

25% OFF TOTAL | 👤8 | FRI ✓ | SAT × | ▲ — Spanish

LAKESIDE RESTAURANT
☎ 01943 467 818
Chevin Country Park Hotel, Yorkgate, Otley, LS21 3NU
Overlooking a beautiful lake, whether you peer out from the cosy restaurant or pop onto the patio outside, it's a truly idyllic setting to enjoy a menu filled with refined and delicious food.

2FOR1 3 COURSES | FRI × | SAT × | ▲ — European

LAZY LOUNGE
☎ 0113 244 6055
29 Wellington Street, Leeds, LS1 4JY
An exclusive wine bar in the heart of the city's financial district. Sample a wonderful, unknown wine, or choose a comforting glass of your favourite. An exemplary menu offers great food.

25% OFF TOTAL | 👤4 | FRI ▯ | SAT ▯ | SUN — English and Continental

LE BAR @ THE CAMPANILE HOTEL
☎ 01924 201 054
Monckton Road, Wakefield, WF2 7AL
Cosmopolitan yet comfortable, the menu at this stylish eatery is delicious and best enjoyed with a beverage from the extensive bar menu. Treat friends to a crisp glass of wine after exploring the city.

50% OFF FOOD | 👤8 | FRI ✓ | SAT ✓ — International

LE RESTAURANT @ THE CAMPANILE HOTEL
☎ 01274 683 683
6 Roydsdale Way, Bradford, BD4 6SA
Simple, contemporary and classic-clean, Le Restaurant at the Campanile Bradford is characteristic of its setting. Drawing on French flavours and recipes, diners can enjoy delicious, good quality food.

50% OFF FOOD | 👤4 | FRI ✓ | SAT ✓ — International

LE RESTAURANT @ THE CAMPANILE HOTEL
☎ 01924 201 054
Monckton Road, Wakefield, WF2 7AL
French inspired, this venue offers a mouth-watering buffet of entrées and desserts. 3 Michelin-starred Chef Pierre Gagnaire shines in this contemporary and healthy restaurant in the Campanile Hotel.

50% OFF FOOD | 👤8 | FRI ✓ | SAT ✓ — International

LEEDS CITY MUSEUM
0113 224 3732
Millenium Square, Leeds, LS2 8BH
During your visit to Leeds City Museum, you will inevitably want to find time to eat before you progress with your day. Make your way to the restaurant where you will find lots of tasty treats.

2FOR1 MAIN COURSE | FRI ✓ | SAT ✗ — British

LEENA'S
☎ 01484 646 466
17-19 Lidget Street, Lindley, Huddersfield, HD1 4HT
A gem of an Indian restaurant in Huddersfield, with a menu that covers the gamut of old classic curries, as well as a good range of distinctive specialities.

2FOR1 MAIN COURSE | FRI ✗ | SAT ✗ | SUN | ♣ — Pakistani

LOCH FYNE
☎ 0113 391 7550
The Old Post Office, 2 City Square, Leeds, LS1 3ES
From the roadside oyster bar that once was, Loch Fyne restaurants now successfully inject energy and passion into great food and wonderful flavours, whilst ensuring their seafood is sustainably sourced.

25% OFF TOTAL | 4 | FRI ✱ | SAT ✱ | ♣ — Seafood

THE LOCKWOOD
01484 428 804
1 Woodhead Road, Lockwood, Huddersfield, HD4 6ER
Generous Sunday lunches with huge, fluffy boulders of Yorkshire pudding sidling up to succulent slices of roast beef; the rest of the traditional menu is well worth a visit, any day of the week.

2FOR1 MAIN COURSE | FRI ✓ | SAT ✓ | ✱ | ♣ — Traditional English

MALMAISON
☎ 0113 398 1000
1 Swinegate, Leeds, LS1 4AG
Striking and charismatic décor in this brasserie whose focus is on fresh, locally sourced produce and a contemporary, stylish ambience. Enjoy this stylish Leeds Mal and its distinctive style. 1 AA Rosette.

2FOR1 MAIN COURSE | FRI ✗ | SAT ✗ | SUN | ♣ — European

MAMSY'S
☎ 0113 230 2575
225 Hyde Park Road, Leeds, LS6 1AH
Vibrant new café serving authentic Thai cuisine in a family atmosphere. Feel at home as you enjoy a quick lunch or relaxing evening meal, not forgetting to take in the picturesque views of Hyde Park.

2FOR1 MAIN COURSE | FRI ✓ | SAT ✓ | ✱ — Thai

THE MANSION
☎ 0113 269 1000
Mansion Lane, Roundhay, Leeds, LS8 2HH
Enjoy delightful views of the 700 acres in which this classical building is situated in. Guests will be overwhelmed by the interior magnificence and grandeur of this listed venue.

25% OFF TOTAL | 2 | FRI | SAT ✱ | SUN — British

MASSALA LOUNGE
☎ 01484 680 742
57 Huddersfield Road, Holmfirth, HD9 3JH
Friendly and welcoming restaurant serving an excellent Indian and Bangladeshi menu that features classic curries and freshly made sundries. Spice lovers should definitely sample the house specialities.

2FOR1 3 COURSES | FRI ✗ | SAT ✗ — Indian

THE MET
☎ 0113 245 0841
King Street, Leeds, LS1 2HQ
Situated in a magnificent listed building, this Principal Hayley hotel oozes retro charm with its terracotta architecture and central location within the vibrant and dynamic city of Leeds.

25% OFF TOTAL | 6 | FRI ✓ | SAT ✓ | ♣ — British

THE MUSEUM CAFÉ
0113 263 7915
Leeds City Museum, Leeds, LS2 8BH
Priding themselves on local sourcing, Leeds City Museum Café uses only fresh ingredients. Classic dishes consumed on the roof terrace means this venue is the perfect end to a day of sightseeing.

2FOR1 MAIN COURSE | FRI ✱ | SAT ✱ — Modern British

NASH'S FISH RESTAURANT
☎ 0113 285 5960
Nash's Fish Restaurant, Leeds, LS2 8JE
Awarded an AA Rosette in 2011 for its quality of produce and superb menu, Nash's brings the characteristically British fish and chips to the area and takes it to a whole new level.

2FOR1 3 COURSES | FRI ✓ | SAT ✱ — British

THE NEEDLESS INN
☎ 01924 472 986
Scotchman Lane, Morley, LS27 0NZ
Situated between two busy town centres, this ideally located inn is a great place for a rest away from the hustle and bustle of everyday life. Enjoy views of country fields as you feast on daily specials.

2FOR1 MAIN COURSE | FRI ✱ | SAT ✗ | SUN | ♣ — English and Continental

THE NEW INN IN SCARCROFT
0113 289 2748
Wetherby Road, Scarcroft, Leeds, LS14 3AT
This Vintage Inn oozes rural charm and rustic character. The picturesque surroundings provide the perfect backdrop for savouring the hearty, seasonal pub-food on the menu.

25% OFF TOTAL | FRI ✓ | SAT ✓ | SUN | ♣ — Modern British

THE NORTHERN MONKEY
0113 242 6630
115 The Headrow, Leeds, LS1 5JW
Quirky, open bar combining a cool modern style with a range of contemporary pub-grub classics. Try the stonking home-made burger, satisfyingly hot peri peri chicken, or an excellent sharing platter.

50% OFF FOOD | 2 | FRI ✗ | SAT ✗ | SUN — English/Gastro pub

THE OLD BRIDGE HOTEL
☎ 01484 681 212
Market Walk, Holmfirth, HD9 7DA
From juicy burgers to char-grilled steaks, filling salads to hot sandwiches, the Old Bridge Hotel serves a wide range of delicious dishes however big or small your appetite.

2FOR1 MAIN COURSE | FRI ✗ | SAT ✗ | SUN — European

THE OLD STEPS BAR & BISTRO
☎ 0113 245 0482
26 York Place, Leeds, LS1 2EY
Lunchtime is the speciality of The Old Steps with a daily changing menu of top quality regional French dishes and British favourites at modest prices. All dishes are prepared by French chef, Raphael Ganet.

25% OFF TOTAL | 4 | FRI ✗ | SAT ✗ | SUN | ♣ — European

THE OLD TRAMSHED
☎ 01274 582 111
199 Bingley Road, Saltaire, BD18 4DH
A pub-restaurant that prides itself on using fresh, local produce and offering up superb cask ales, this is a great place to sit back, relax, drink and eat whether you're from nearby or visiting Saltaire.

2FOR1 3 COURSES | FRI ✱ | SAT ✱ | SUN | ♣ — English/Gastro pub

THE OLIVE TREE
☎ 0113 274 8282
74-76 Otley Road, Leeds, LS6 4BA
The third branch of the Olive Tree, Headingley has a modern setting arranged over two floors. Head Chef Orhan has been creating Greek dishes at the Olive Tree for the last 5 years.

2FOR1 MAIN COURSE | FRI ✓ | SAT ✓ — Greek

THE OLIVE TREE GREEK RESTAURANT
☎ 0113 256 9283
55 Rodley Lane, Rodley, LS13 1NG
Weekend Bouzouki performances bring this place to life. Put on your dancing shoes if you are a willing participant, or sit back and be jovially entertained as you feast on traditional Greek dishes.

2FOR1 MAIN COURSE | FRI ✓ | SAT ✓ — Greek

THE OLIVE TREE RESTAURANT
☎ 0113 269 8488
188-190 Harrogate Road, Leeds, LS7 4NZ
Emphasising the importance of food and wine that were celebrated during the Ancient Greek Bacchanalia, The Olive Tree Restaurant serves delicious mezes, traditional dips and crispy filo pastries.

2FOR1 MAIN COURSE | FRI ✓ | SAT ✓ — Greek

OMARS BALTI HOUSE
☎ 01274 414 188
46 Great Horton Road, Bradford, BD7 1AL
Restaurant specialising in dishes from the Northern Punjab and frontier. The cracking chicken ladosh (with peas and cashews), and the fine jaipuri punjabi are well worth a look from among the specials.

2FOR1 MAIN COURSE | FRI ✱ | SAT ✱ — Indian

THE OTHELLO
☎ 01924 371 355
86 Kirkgate, Wakefield, WF1 1TB
Othello's offers a relaxing & friendly environment in which to enjoy a meal, or a drink and a chat. Their friendly staff are always eager to please customers.

50% OFF FOOD | 8 | FRI ✓ | SAT ✓ — British

THE PARK ROW BAR AND BRASSIERE
0113 243 2300
23 The Headrow, Leeds, LS1 5RD
Indulge in a menu of pub classics and enjoy quality food at this stylish venue. With a relaxing ambience, this is a perfect chance for a well-deserved break from hectic city living.

2FOR1 MAIN COURSE | FRI ✓ | SAT × | ✱ — European

PREZZO
0113 246 1910
16-18 The Light, Leeds, LS1 8TL
With a character all of its own, Prezzo oozes contemporary style and enduring charm. Signature pastas, stone-baked pizzas and classic Italian dishes promise a perfect dining choice for the whole family.

2FOR1 MAIN COURSE | FRI × | SAT × | ▲ — Italian

QUEEN
0113 231 9394
134 Oldfields Lane, Leeds, LS12 4EU
After receiving a hearty welcome, customers can relax and soak up the vibrant atmosphere. Queen is the perfect place to unwind and dine on a delicious array of classic British dishes.

2FOR1 3 COURSES | FRI ▯ | SAT ▯ | SUN — British

RED CHILLI II
☎ 01924 384 433
148-150 Kirkgate, Wakefield, WF1 1TU
Well-regarded Indian restaurant with an eclectic menu featuring not only chicken, lamb and prawn but also duck, venison, fish and the like. Popular and friendly place, fresh flavours and good portions.

2FOR1 3 COURSES | FRI ✓ | SAT ✓ — Indian

THE RED KITE
01924 251 542
Denby Dale Road, Wakefield, WF4 3BB
This Vintage Inn oozes rural charm and rustic character. The picturesque surroundings provide the perfect backdrop for savouring the hearty, seasonal pub-food on the menu.

25% OFF TOTAL | FRI ✓ | SAT ✓ | SUN | ▲ — Modern British

RED PEPPER INDIAN RESTAURANT
☎ 0113 230 1101
4-6 The Avenue, Alwoodley, Leeds, LS17 7BE
This restaurant has a modern, contemporary look but has kept the characteristics of the Otley branch. The menu is filled with Indian classics and special dishes unique to Red Pepper.

25% OFF TOTAL | 👤10 | FRI ▯ | SAT ▯ | SUN | ✱ — Indian

RING O BELLS
☎ 01274 832 296
212 Hilltop Road, Thornton, BD13 3QL
A traditional pie and a thirst-quenching pint is sometimes all you need. This Yorkshire pub offers a relaxed, family friendly atmosphere in which top quality food is always guaranteed.

2FOR1 2 COURSES | FRI ✓ | SAT ✓ | SUN | ▲ — English/Gastro pub

THE RISING SUN & PALM COURT BAR
☎ 01977 554 766
Whitwood Common Lane, Castleford, WF10 5PT
This family friendly pub and restaurant serves delicious, home made, Spanish and Italian dishes.

25% OFF TOTAL | 👤4 | FRI ▯ | SAT ▯ | SUN | ▲ — Spanish

ROCK CAFÉ HUDDERSFIELD
01484 300 004
11-13 Ramsden Street, Huddersfield, HD1 2SX
Share nachos and barbecue ribs with friends, whilst sipping a fruity cocktail. Hungry appetites are gratified with bursting pies and overloaded lasagnes at this American-themed bar. *Food served until 7pm.

25% OFF TOTAL | 👤8 | FRI ✓ | SAT ✓ | SUN — British

ROOTS AND FRUITS
☎ 0113 242 8313
10-11 Grand Arcade, Leeds, LS1 6PG
Only happy faces can be seen coming from Roots and Fruits. Providing healthy vegetarian dishes, GM free cakes and a great range of teas, this eatery has a lot going for it.

2FOR1 MAIN COURSE | FRI ✓ | SAT ✓ — Vegetarian

THE ROUNDHAY FOX
0113 269 3352
Princes Avenue, Roundhay, Leeds, LS8 2EP
This Vintage Inn oozes rural charm and rustic character. The picturesque surroundings provide the perfect backdrop for savouring the hearty, seasonal pub-food on the menu.

25% OFF TOTAL | FRI ✓ | SAT ✓ | SUN | ▲ — Modern British

ROYAL GREEN CURRY
01924 671 123
61b Westgate End, Wakefield, WF2 9RL
Royal Green Curry, in the heart of Wakefield, offers the very finest in Thai and Chinese cuisine. With an extensive menu, the dishes are beautifully presented and perfect for an authentic dining experience.

25% OFF TOTAL | 👤10 | FRI ✓ | SAT ✓ — Thai

ROYAL SAFFRON
☎ 01943 461 277
42 Bond Gate, Otley, LS21 1AD
Dine on quality Indian cuisine and choose from a varying menu that delivers a fusion of traditional and modern flavours. This restaurant provides outstanding service as well as excellent value for money.

50% OFF FOOD | FRI ✓ | SAT × — Indian

THE RUSSIAN RESTAURANT
☎ 01274 733 121
15 Manor Row, Bradford, BD1 4PB
Drawing on an eclectic wealth of flavours, this restaurant offers a sweeping span of Russian cuisine, where each of the four corners has its own take on Russian culinary expression.

2FOR1 3 COURSES | FRI × | SAT × — Russian

SALUTE AT THE WHITE SWAN
☎ 0113 282 0508
Church Street, Rothwell, LS26 0QL
Rustic, well-loved Italian dishes feature proudly on the Salute menu. Enjoy your favourite company as you become immersed in the friendly, neighbourhood atmosphere that the venue emits.

25% OFF TOTAL | 👤4 | FRI ▯ | SAT × | ▲ — Italian

SEVEN BAR AND GRILL
☎ 0113 2172 352
7 Blenheim Terrace, Leeds, LS2 9HZ
Inspired by tapas, guests can share platters of tortillas and stuffed peppers at this cosmopolitan eatery. Sip fresh and fruity cocktails whilst treating yourself to a night of music and dancing.

25% OFF TOTAL | 👤4 | FRI ✓ | SAT ✓ | SUN — British

SHABAB
☎ 0113 242 7012
1 Bishopgate Street, Leeds, LS1 5DY
Boasting cooking methods that closely mirror Asian domestic kitchens, this venue oozes authenticity in exotic surroundings. Guests will never find artificial colourings or ready-made pastes in the dishes.

2FOR1 MAIN COURSE | FRI ✓ | SAT ✓ | ✱ — Indian

SHALIMAR RESTAURANT
☎ 0113 269 2000
378 Harrogate Road, Leeds, LS17 6PY
Shalimar Restaurant's speciality lies in providing a traditional Indian dining experience. If you are looking for a mouth-watering curry in Leeds, Shalimar Restaurant is the place to go!

25% OFF TOTAL | 👤6 | FRI ✓ | SAT ✓ — Indian

SHAMA RESTAURANT
☎ 0127 458 2312
2a Commerical Street, Shipley, Bradford, BD18 3SR
Big, friendly Indian restaurant in Shipley that's known for the flavour of its curries, the range of options on the menu, the great atmosphere and value for money. A popular place for a good curry.

2FOR1 MAIN COURSE | FRI × | SAT × | SUN — Indian

SHOOTERS SPORTS BAR
☎ 0113 243 2300
123 The Headrow, Leeds, LS1 5RD
A sociable venue delivering food and entertainment on a grand scale with bars, big screens, pool tables and a dining area. Enjoy a selection of appetising meals whilst soaking up the lively atmosphere.

2FOR1 MAIN COURSE | FRI ✓ | SAT × | SUN | ✱ | ▲ — International

THE SOVEREIGN
01484 609 725
172-174 Penistone Road, Shepley, Huddersfield, HD8 8BE
This Vintage Inn oozes rural charm and rustic character. The picturesque surroundings provide the perfect backdrop for savouring the hearty, seasonal pub-food on the menu.

25% OFF TOTAL | FRI ✓ | SAT ✓ | SUN | ▲ — Modern British

SPICE HOUSE
☎ 0113 260 5098
249 Selby Road, Cross Gates, Leeds, LS15 7JR
A simple, unfussy neighbourhood Indian place on the Selby Road out towards Halton. Serves a good selection of curries and other subcontinental dishes.

2FOR1 3 COURSES | FRI ✓ | SAT ✓ — Indian

THE SPICE QUARTER
☎ 0113 246 9241

Electric Press Building, Leeds, LS2 3AD

Spice Quarter Buffet Restaurant brings 4 cuisines to 1 destination. Famous dishes from India, Italy, Thailand and China combine to offer something special for every food-lover.

2FOR1 MAIN COURSE | FRI × | SAT × | ✱ | ▲ — Indian

THE STROOM RESTAURANT
☎ 0113 257 0140

9 Chapeltown, Pudsey, Leeds, LS28 7RZ

Enjoy locally produced ingredients with a modern twist in a stylish and contemporary location. The Stroom Restaurant is perfect for romantic meals for two or for high-spirited family gatherings.

25% OFF TOTAL | 👤 6 | FRI ✓ | SAT × | SUN | ▲ — European

THE SUN INN
☎ 01924 848 603

62 Barnsley Road, Flockton, Wakefield, WF4 4DW

Great spot for traditional food and drink with a menu of classic pub grub, Sunday roasts and hearty ales. Has a twist in the tail, with a delicious tapas menu to add to the mix. Weekly guest ales on tap.

25% OFF TOTAL | 👤 6 | FRI 📱 | SAT 📱 — Mediterranean

SWEET SPICE CARIBBEAN CUISINE
☎ 01484 536 315

111 Bradford Road, Huddersfield, HD1 6DZ

Curried goat, jerk chicken and steamed fish have proven to be popular entries on the menu. An adventurous diners dream, there is plenty on offer in terms of imaginative Caribbean cuisine.

2FOR1 MAIN COURSE | FRI × | SAT × — Caribbean

THAI EDGE
☎ 0113 243 6333

7 Calverley Street, Leeds, LS1 3DY

Thai Edge encapsulates contemporary Oriental design and exotic Thai cuisine. All palates are catered for, whether you prefer subtle sophisticated flavours or hot and spicy tastes.

2FOR1 MAIN COURSE | FRI ✓ | SAT ✱ | SUN | ✱ | ▲ — Thai

THAI ERAWAN
☎ 0113 240 1010

629 Roundhay Road, Leeds, LS8 4AR

Lovely, light restaurant in Leeds with lots of charm, splashes of colour and subtle lighting. Serves a great selection of Thai dishes, great for the novice but also for the more seasoned veteran.

2FOR1 3 COURSES | FRI 📱 | SAT 📱 — Thai

TRADERS RESTAURANT @ HOLIDAY INN
☎ 01924 230 600

M1 Jct. 40, Queens Drive, Ossett, Wakefield, WF5 9BE

Comfortable restaurant at the Holiday Inn at Wakefield. You'll enjoy a range of traditional and contemporary dishes cooked confidently for a breadth of occasions, whether formal or relaxed.

25% OFF TOTAL | 👤 10 | FRI ✓ | SAT ✓ — British

UNICORN INN
☎ 0113 282 2366

Main Street, Carlton, Wakefield, WF3 3RW

Welcoming place that does a fine selection of tender steaks, a great mixed grill and other traditional classics. A traditional pub with a focus on its steaks, but with fine seafood and vegetables to boot.

50% OFF FOOD | 👤 10 | FRI ✓ | SAT ✓ — British

THE VEDAS
0170 681 4009

26-32 Rochdale Rd, Todmorden, OL14 7LD

High-class Indian restaurant, where simple, low-key colours make it an accommodating place to eat. A wide-ranging menu features some fresh-tasting, very appealing specialities alongside the usual suspects.

2FOR1 MAIN COURSE | FRI 📱 | SAT × — Indian

VERVE
☎ 01484 549 333

3 Byram Street, Huddersfield, HD1 1BX

Relaxing can be hard to do in the midst of a busy week, however head to Verve and you'll need no excuse to unwind. Try the halloumi burger or meat sharing platter for something extra special.

50% OFF FOOD | 👤 6 | FRI ✓ | SAT ✓ | ▲ — British

VERVE GRILL @ VILLAGE HOTEL
☎ 0844 980 8031

Village Leisure Hotel, 186 Otley Rd, Leeds, LS16 5PR

Classic dishes adopt stylish and imaginative twists in this wonderful hotel restaurant, where the menu changes to reflect the seasons. The hotel is ideally located to explore all that Leeds has to offer.

2FOR1 3 COURSES | FRI ✓ | SAT ✓ — Contemporary

WALKABOUT
☎ 0113 205 6500

67-81 Cookridge Street, Leeds, LS2 3AW

Walkabout is famous for its characteristically Australian atmosphere and well-rounded menu. From live sport with a juicy burger to some Aussie kangaroo skewers, you'll find it hard to tear yourself away.

25% OFF TOTAL | 👤 10 | FRI ✓ | SAT ✓ | ▲ — International

WALLIS SIMPSON RESTAURANT
☎ 01422 342 342

42-46 Horton Street, Halifax, HX1 1QE

Relaxing, bright place for drinks and snacks. Complementing the café is a wood-panelled restaurant which offers a variety of menu choices including English and European dishes.

2FOR1 MAIN COURSE | FRI ✓ | SAT ✓ | ✱ | ▲ — British

WEETWOOD HALL'S BRASSERIE
☎ 0113 230 6000

Otley Road, Leeds, LS16 5PS

Enjoy a refreshing glass of wine, a frothy cappuccino or a delicious light meal in an environment that is perfect during the day for one-to-one meetings. Free wi-fi is available for a working lunch.

25% OFF TOTAL | 👤 4 | FRI ✱ | SAT ✱ | ▲ — Brasserie

THE WRENS HOTEL
☎ 0113 245 8888

61a New Briggate, Leeds, LS2 8JD

At The Wrens, they serve you food they would be happy to eat themselves, all their food is freshly made in house. Serving the best in British cuisine.

2FOR1 3 COURSES | FRI ✓ | SAT × | SUN — British

THE WYKE LION
01274 674 756

Whitehall Road, Wyke, Bradford, BD12 8LL

This Vintage Inn oozes rural charm and rustic character. The picturesque surroundings provide the perfect backdrop for savouring the hearty, seasonal pub-food on the menu.

25% OFF TOTAL | FRI ✓ | SAT ✓ | SUN | ▲ — Modern British

THE YARD
☎ 01943 609 606

30a Brook Street, Ilkley, LS29 8DE

Casque Marque-accredited bar with excellent reputation maintained by fabulous food. Try the 'Yorkshire tapas' or home-made fish fingers. *Advance booking mentioning Gourmet Society is essential.

2FOR1 MAIN COURSE | FRI ✓ | SAT ✓ — English/Gastro pub

YEADON STOOPS
0113 250 4284

Victoria Avenue, Bayton Lane, Yeadon, Leeds , LS19 7AW

Beefeater Grill are one of the UK's best-loved restaurants welcoming guests for almost 40 years in over 130 locations nationwide. *Excludes Breakfast, Light Bites, Bar menu, set menus and all other offers.

2FOR1 MAIN COURSE | 👤 6 | FRI ✓ | SAT × | ▲ — Modern British

YOYO BAR & RESTAURANT
☎ 01274 599 880

Rosse Street, Off Saltaire Road, Shipley, BD18 3SW

Offering Japanese, Chinese and Thai cuisine, as well as catering for children and alternate dietary needs, this restaurant ensures everyone is satisfied. Cocktails and light bites available.

2FOR1 MAIN COURSE | FRI ✓ | SAT 📱 | ✱ | ▲ — Asian

YOYO CAFE BAR
☎ 01274 727 287

29 Chapel Street, Little Germany, Bradford, BD1 5DT

From macro (a global agglomeration of flavours) to micro (focusing on locally sourced ingredients) this fusion café bar in Bradford does everything with panache; bright, convivial and vibrant.

2FOR1 MAIN COURSE | FRI 📱 | SAT 📱 | SUN — European

ZEST BAR AT THE MARRIOTT
☎ 01274 530 053

Marriott Hollins Hill, Baildon, Shipley, BD17 7QW

Casual yet stylishly chic, this French-inspired bar at the Marriott Hollins Hall offers an informal atmosphere in which to dine, drink and relax. Perfect for both in-house guests and non-residents.

2FOR1 3 COURSES | FRI ✓ | SAT ✓ — International

ZEST RESTAURANT AT THE MARRIOTT
☎ 01274 530 053

Marriott Hollins Hill, Baildon, Shipley, BD17 7QW

A stylish lounge bar and restaurant based in the Marriott Hollins Hall Hotel serving brasserie-style food with an informal atmosphere.

2FOR1 3 COURSES | FRI ✓ | SAT ✓ — International

To understand what the restaurant icons mean, please see the inside back cover.

Scotland

Aberdeenshire

210 BISTRO 01224 211 857
210 South Market Street, Aberdeen, AB11 5PQ
A unique venue that meets the exacting standards of the business community and casual diners. The perfect place to enjoy both traditional and contemporary recipes, or simply relax with friends.

2FOR1 MAIN COURSE | FRI ✓ | SAT ✓ | SUN | * | — Bistro

THE ATHENAEUM 01224 595 585
5-9 Union Street, Aberdeen, AB11 5BU
The grandeur of the building's interior is transferred to the design within this beautifully adorned restaurant. Admire the local artwork that decorates the venue whilst sampling tasty, creative dishes.

25% OFF TOTAL | 4 | FRI ✓ | SAT ✓ — Contemporary

THE ATRIUM INDIAN RESTAURANT 01224 581 117
401-405 Union Street, Aberdeen, AB11 6BX
At the Atrium, the belief is that Indian cuisine should be constantly evolving and adopting new ideas. For those seeking top-quality Indian food with a modern twist, look no further than The Atrium.

25% OFF TOTAL | 8 | FRI ✓ | SAT ✓ — Indian

BELLA ITALIA 01224 592 253
Queens Link Leisure Park, Aberdeen, AB24 5EN
Accessible Italian cuisine on the British high street - indulge in authentic sharing platters, hand stretched pizzas and hearty pasta dishes, served with a healthy dose of gregarious Italian hospitality.

25% OFF TOTAL | 6 | FRI ✗ | SAT ✗ | SUN | — Italian

BOLLYWOOD TANDOORI 01224 587 700
367 Union Street, Aberdeen, AB11 6BT
Bollywood Tandoori, a fine Indian Restaurant in Aberdeen, a dream name after India's huge film industry where the chef has more than 20 years experience, there is wide selection of delicious dishes.

25% OFF TOTAL | FRI ✓ | SAT ✗ | * — Indian

CAFÉ ROUGE 01224 647 335
Bon Accord Centre, George Street, Aberdeen, AB25 1HZ
French sophistication on the British high street - enjoy seasonally changing French dishes and a continental wine selection, served in a relaxed environment with an undeniable flair of Parisian chic.

25% OFF TOTAL | 6 | FRI ✓ | SAT ✓ | * | — French

CARMELITE BAR AND GRILL 01224 589 101
Stirling Street, Merchant Quarter, Aberdeen, AB116JU
Making use of the best Scottish suppliers of local produce, the Head Chef passionately creates fantastic dishes for your enjoyment. The succulent Aberdeen beef and tasty Shetland lamb are both heavenly.

2FOR1 MAIN COURSE | FRI ✓ | SAT ✓ — Scottish

THE COCK AND BULL RESTAURANT 01358 743 249
Ellon Road, Balmedien, Aberdeen, AB23 8XY
An intimate inn where food is made from fresh ingredients. The menu also benefits from seasonal changes and is complemented by the chef's daily specials. Awarded 1 AA Rosette for its excellence.

2FOR1 3 COURSES | FRI | SAT * | SUN | — International

FRANCO'S RESTAURANT 01330 826 093
40 High Street, Banchory, AB31 5SR
A different kind of experience for lunch and dinner with a menu that focuses on local food in conjunction with some of the most traditional Italian dishes. A taste of Italy delivered to perfection.

2FOR1 2 COURSES | FRI * | SAT * | * | — Italian

GADIE'S RESTAURANT 01464 851 573
Ryehill, Oyne, Insch, AB52 6QS
A light, airy interior creates a refreshing atmosphere at Gadie's, where traditional Scottish cuisine is never absent from the menu. Outstanding deli platters and hearty burgers are strong contenders.

25% OFF TOTAL | FRI ✓ | SAT ✓ | * | — Scottish

THE GREEN INN 01339 755 701
9 Victoria Road, Ballater, Aberdeen, AB35 5QQ
Come and sample The Green Inn's wonderful fusion of French, Indian and Thai Cuisine, amidst the delightfully quaint Aberdeenshire countryside.

2FOR1 MAIN COURSE | FRI ✓ | SAT ✓ | * — International

HANDMADE BURGER CO. 01224 580 400
Union Square Shopping Centre, Aberdeen, AB11 5RG
100% prime Scotch beef burgers, handmade in the restaurant daily, sourdough buns, delicious handmade relishes and a wide range of toppings giving you over 40 varieties to choose from. *Exclusions apply.

2FOR1 MAIN COURSE | FRI ✓ | SAT ✗ | SUN — International

LA TASCA 01224 212 001
367 Union Street, Aberdeen, AB11 6BT
Quintessentially Spanish, La Tasca's fresh and exciting menu offers something for everyone. Their tapas dishes are sincerely authentic, while their paellas always deliver on flavour.

25% OFF TOTAL | 8 | FRI ✓ | SAT ✗ | — Spanish

LOCKER ROOM BAR AND RESTAURANT 01224 592 900
Gamola Golf Ltd, Trinity Quay House, Aberdeen, AB11 5PZ
Whether you are popping in for lunch or want to be wined and dined, guests can do it all at The Locker Room, whilst also getting in a round of golf!

25% OFF TOTAL | 2 | FRI ✓ | SAT ✓ | — British

MANZIL ABERDEEN 01224 645 015
22-24 King Street, Aberdeen, AB24 5AX
At Manzil, each meal is prepared with care and served with pride. The menu consists of classic and modern dishes from a cuisine guaranteed to tantalise your taste buds. Delicious food and superb service.

2FOR1 MAIN COURSE | FRI | SAT ✗ | * | — Indian

MILL OF MUNDURNO 01224 821 217
Ellon Road, Murcar, Bridge of Don, Aberdeen, AB23 8BP
Quality pub classics with a modern twist combine with a friendly and relaxed atmosphere to make this Table Table venue the perfect place for family gatherings or meeting friends.

2FOR1 MAIN COURSE | FRI ✓ | SAT ✓ — Modern British

MONTMARTRE RESTAURANT FRANCAIS 01224 584 599
58-60 Justice Mill Lane, Aberdeen, AB11 6EP
Enjoy fine French cuisine which uses locally sourced produce and prepared by a team of experienced chefs. Sample traditional and contemporary French gastronomy complemented by a selection of fine wines.

2FOR1 3 COURSES | FRI ✗ | SAT ✗ | SUN | — European

OGILVIES RESTAURANT 01779 471 121
Fraserburgh Road, Peterhead, AB42 3BN
Set within its own extensive gardens, this purpose-built hotel is the owner of 105 beautiful bedrooms, a luxurious spa and award-winning kitchen. The restaurant offers fine meals you'll want to savour.

25% OFF TOTAL | 4 | FRI ✓ | SAT ✓ | — British

PREZZO 01224 593 009
Union Square Shopping Centre, Aberdeen, AB11 5RG
With a character all of its own, Prezzo oozes contemporary style and enduring charm. Signature pastas, stone-baked pizzas and classic Italian dishes promise a perfect dining choice for the whole family.

2FOR1 MAIN COURSE | FRI ✗ | SAT ✗ | — Italian

RBG @ PARK INN 01224 592 999
Park Inn, 1 Justice Mill Lane, Aberdeen, AB11 6EQ
An extensive menu that takes in a number of different international flavours. The gourmet burgers are a particular treat, though don't overlook the likes of their blackened salmon salad

2FOR1 MAIN COURSE | FRI ✓ | SAT ✓ | SUN | — British

SPRINGFIELD'S RESTAURANT 01224 498 337
161 Springfield Road, Aberdeen, AB15 7AQ
Showcasing entertainment and sports events on the HDTV screens, this venue is a cracking night out with a touch of class. Perfect for a sumptuous dinner, the food promises freshness.

50% OFF FOOD | 4 | FRI ✗ | SAT ✗ | * | — Scottish

SUNSET BAR AND DINER
01224 595 910

Sunset Boulevard, Codona's Park, Aberdeen, AB24 5ED

Retro American family diner offering huge party platters, old favourites, world famous chicken wings and fantastic desserts. Something for everyone, with great options for adults and kids alike.

2FOR1 MAIN COURSE | FRI ✓ | SAT ✱ | ▲ — American

CHILLIES INDIAN CUSINE
01569 739 120

Bridge Croft, Newtonhill, AB39 3NN

Friendly local Indian restaurant in Newtonhill that's known for its charming neighbourhood atmosphere and a good range of flavourful Indian dishes. Simple, unfussy and tasty cuisine.

2FOR1 MAIN COURSE | FRI × | SAT × | SUN — Indian

Angus

WESTPORT BAR & FUNCTION SUITE
01382 221 634

64-66 North Lindsay Street, Dundee, DD1 1PS

Westport Bar and Junction Suite invite you to join them for a meal. With a great selection of drinks and friendly, efficient staff, celebrate festivities in style at Westport Bar.

2FOR1 MAIN COURSE | FRI ✱ | SAT ✱ | ▲ — British

APEX CITY QUAY HOTEL AND SPA
01382 202 404

1 West Victoria Dock Road, Dundee, DD1 3JP

Close to the sights and sounds of Dundee and boasting Quayside views, The Apex City Quay Hotel also hosts the Metro Brasserie. An internationally inspired menu infused with a touch of Scottish flavour.

25% OFF TOTAL | ♟10 | FRI ▮ | SAT ✱ | ▲ — Modern British

THE BLUE MARLIN
01382 534 001

Camperdown Street, City Quay, Dundee, DD1 3JA

A kitchen that plays home to a chef who appreciates good quality food made from excellent ingredients. The menu makes full use of the prime catch of the local coastal waters and the finest Scottish beef.

2FOR1 MAIN COURSE | FRI ▮ | SAT ✱ | SUN — Seafood

BOMBAY JOE'S
01382 776 448

44 Gray Street, Broughty Ferry, Dundee, DD5 2BJ

Well-regarded Indian restaurant, previously a finalist in the Sunday Post's Restaurant of the Year Award (2009). Lots of flavour, generous portions, and plenty of spice and kick where it's needed.

2FOR1 3 COURSES | FRI ✱ | SAT ✱ — Indian

CAFFÈ CINO @ HILTON
01382 229 271

Hilton Dundee, Earl Grey Place, Dundee, DD1 4DE

Low-key, laid-back place to enjoy a good coffee and a fresh pastry, or otherwise a fine light lunch. Warm and modern in style, a hotel-based restaurant with baby grand and a touch of flair about it.

50% OFF FOOD | ♟10 | FRI ✓ | SAT ✓ | ▲ — International

THE CAMBUSTAY IN DUNDEE
01382 480 286

8 Dalhousie Road, Broughty Ferry, Dundee, DD5 2SQ

This Vintage Inn oozes rural charm and rustic character. The picturesque surroundings provide the perfect backdrop for savouring the hearty, seasonal pub-food on the menu.

25% OFF TOTAL | FRI ✓ | SAT ✓ | SUN | ▲ — Modern British

THE CRAIGTON COACH INN
01382 370 223

Craigton of Monikie, Dundee, DD5 3QN

A rural restaurant of some repute with an emphasis on local, fresh produce and attentive, polite staff. The steak pie is a notable delight among their range of dishes renowned for their excellent taste.

2FOR1 2 COURSES | FRI ✓ | SAT ✱ — British

DISCOVERY QUAY
01382 203 240

Riverside Drive, Dundee, DD1 4XA

Quality pub classics with a modern twist combine with a friendly and relaxed atmosphere to make this Table Table venue the perfect place for family gatherings or meeting friends.

2FOR1 MAIN COURSE | FRI ✓ | SAT ✓ — Modern British

DROVERS INN
01307 860 322

Memus, By Fofar, DD8 3TY

Snuggled into the little village of Memus, the quaint location of the Drovers Inn encourages regular visits. Hearty meals and characterful ales set this place apart as a fine choice for an evening out.

25% OFF TOTAL | ♟6 | FRI ✓ | SAT ▮ | ▲ — Scottish

THE GARDEN ROOM AT THE LANDMARK
01382 641 122

The Landmark Hotel, Kingsway West, Dundee, DD2 5JT

Recently refurbished site where there is a distinct emphasis on flavour and freshness, with ingredients sourced from local markets and regions. Both the service and wine list complement the food on offer.

2FOR1 MAIN COURSE | FRI ✓ | SAT ▮ | SUN — Scottish

GOURDIE CROFT
01382 561 115

Kingsway West, Dundee, DD2 5JU

Beefeater Grill are one of the UK's best-loved restaurants welcoming guests for almost 40 years in over 130 locations nationwide. *Excludes Breakfast, Light Bites, Bar menu, set menus and all other offers.

2FOR1 MAIN COURSE | ♟6 | FRI ✓ | SAT × | ▲ — Modern British

JAHANGIR RESTAURANT
01382 202 022

1 Session Street, Dundee, DD1 5DN

The staff here are dedicated to providing diners with excellent food and service ensuring your experience is not only one to remember but one to ensure you visit time and again.

2FOR1 2 COURSES | FRI ✓ | SAT × | ✱ — Indian

METRO BRASSERIE
0845 365 0002

Apex City Quay Hotel, Dundee, DD1 3JP

Metro bar and brasserie is located in the Apex City Quay Hotel and overlooks Dundee City Quay. The menu has an international flavour, with influences of Italy, South America, the Pacific Rim & Scotland.

25% OFF TOTAL | ♟6 | FRI ✓ | SAT ✓ — Scottish

RIVERFRONT RESTAURANT @ HILTON
01382 229 271

Hilton Dundee, Earl Grey Place, Dundee, DD1 4DE

Long, high windows give out across the River Tay at this hotel restaurant. Serves a broad selection of dishes throughout the day in a fine ambience, with a beautiful summer terrace when the sun shines.

50% OFF FOOD | ♟10 | FRI ✓ | SAT ✓ | ▲ — International

SAFFRON INDIAN CUISINE
01241 437 737

28-30 Millgate, Arbroath, DD11 1NW

Well-respected Indian restaurant that serves a wide variety of delicious dishes. Saffron brings an authentic taste of Indian cuisine in friendly, comfortable surroundings.

2FOR1 MAIN COURSE | FRI ✱ | SAT ✱ | ✱ | ▲ — Indian

SHEHZAD INDIAN RESTAURANT
01382 200 265

24 Castle Street, Dundee, DD1 3AF

Great restaurant serving fantastic Indian and tandoori dishes, such as the special house thali dish or the tandoori chicken. A warm, inviting and spacious place to dine.

2FOR1 3 COURSES | FRI ✓ | SAT ✓ — Indian

Argyll

ASKNISH BAY RESTAURANT
01852 200 233

Loch Melfort Hotel, Arduaine, PA34 4XG

Choose from fresh langoustines, lobster, crab, and select cuts of meat and game at this highly applauded fine-dining venue. Escape the city and enjoy the finest views on the West Coast. 2 AA Rosettes.

2FOR1 MAIN COURSE | FRI ✓ | SAT × | ✱ — Fine Dining

BULAS BAR & BISTRO
01855 811 606

The Ballachulish Hotel, Ballachulish, PH49 4JY

Fantastic restaurant near to Glencoe. The traditional Gaelic bulas is their speciality: a rich, warming one-pot stew with various permutations. Fine alternatives like their lamb steaks also make a mark.

2FOR1 3 COURSES | FRI ✱ | SAT ✱ — Scottish

Gourmet Society discount applies to the à la carte menu only, unless stated otherwise.

CHARTROOM II BISTRO
☎ 01852 200 233
Loch Melfort Hotel, Arduaine, PA34 4XG

Overlooking the spectacular Asknish Bay, head to the Chartroom II and indulge in magical sunsets and memorable food. Well known for its langoustines, scallops and Highland beef burgers.

2FOR1 MAIN COURSE | FRI ✓ | SAT × | * — Bistro

THE GLENCOE HOTEL
☎ 01855 811 245
Glencoe Village, Ballachulish, PH49 4HW

Superb hotel restaurant with stunning views out over Loch Leven. Combines a relaxed atmosphere for debriefing over a drink and something to eat, with some excellent dishes across the wide-reaching menu.

50% OFF FOOD | 👤 6 | FRI 📱 | SAT 📱 — Scottish

Ayrshire

AYR INDIA @ ALLOWAY PLACE
☎ 01292 261 026
1a Alloway Place, Ayr, KA7 2AA

While the original restaurant focuses on traditional food, the emphasis here is firmly placed on contemporary dishes, while still providing quality and authentic flavours.

2FOR1 MAIN COURSE | FRI × | SAT × — Indian

AYR INDIA TANDOORI RESTAURANT
☎ 01292 263 731
10 Seafield Road, Seafront, Ayr, KA7 4AD

A menu showcasing everything delicious about traditional Indian cuisine, complete with attentive staff and the right beverages. For a true taste of the subcontinent in Scotland, this is the place to go.

2FOR1 MAIN COURSE | FRI × | SAT × | * — Indian

AYR SPICE
☎ 01292 441 413
22 Ayr Road, Minishant, KA19 8EX

Set in a beautiful old church building in Minishant, Ayr Spice is a welcoming, homely kind of Indian restaurant. The menu features a range of traditional dishes, with the handi bhuna curry their signature.

2FOR1 MAIN COURSE | FRI 📱 | SAT × | SUN — Indian

THE BRASSERIE @ MERCURE
☎ 0844 815 9005
Mercure Ayr Hotel, Dalblair Road, Ayr, KA7 1UG

In the heart of the Scottish Burns country, views of the Isle of Arran are a first-class feature of the Mercure Ayr Hotel. The Brasserie is modern without shying away from classic restaurant features.

2FOR1 3 COURSES | FRI ✓ | SAT ✓ — British

GARFIELD'S TAPAS & WINE BAR
☎ 01294 463 155
59 Princes Street, Ardrossan, KA22 8DE

An exciting take on classic Spanish tapas, this restaurant utilises local Scottish produce to create the ultimate in fusion cooking.

25% OFF TOTAL | 👤 4 | FRI 📱 | SAT 📱 — Spanish

THE RUPEE ROOM
☎ 01292 283 002
26A Wellington Square, Ayr, KA7 1HH

Opening in 1999, this friendly curry house has since established itself as one of the finest contemporary Indian restaurants in the West of Scotland, serving a wide range of cuisine from Northern India.

2FOR1 3 COURSES | FRI ✓ | SAT ✓ — Indian

SHIMLA PALACE
☎ 01563 559 444
43 Titchfield Street, Kilmarnock, KA1 1QS

Quality-assured Indian cuisine is always served at Shimla Palace. Like home from home, the restaurant is softly decorated to create a calm, relaxed and informal dining atmosphere.

2FOR1 3 COURSES | FRI ✓ | SAT ✓ | * — Indian

Clackmannanshire

AZAD TANDOORI
☎ 01259 725 600
2b Shillinghill, Alloa, FK10 1JT

A great Indian and Pakistani restaurant and takeaway in Alloa, offering the finest quality produce and exquisite traditional recipes. Staple classic dishes feature on a menu alongside tandoori options.

2FOR1 3 COURSES | FRI × | SAT × — Indian

Dumfriesshire

THE ANVIL RESTAURANT & BAR
☎ 01461 338 257
Gretna Hall Hotel, Gretna, DG16 5DY

Based in a charming hotel, The Anvil Restaurant & Bar is ideal for both relaxation and for an appetising evening meal, which can be accompanied by fine wines from their extensive range.

50% OFF FOOD | 👤 2 | FRI × | SAT × — International

BLACKADDIE COUNTRY HOUSE HOTEL
☎ 0165 950 270
Blackaddie Road, Sanquhar, DG4 6JJ

Beautiful hotel on the banks of the Nith and a fine restaurant that boasts 2 AA Rosettes. The Head Chef comes with Michelin-star experience; as you would expect, the balance and quality are exceptional.

2FOR1 3 COURSES | FRI 📱 | SAT 📱 — Fine Dining

BOMBAY CUISINE
☎ 01683 220 900
Lower Craignelder, High Street, Moffat, DG10 9ED

Drawing on family recipes, this popular local Indian restaurant in Moffat specialises in Punjabi regional cuisine. The tawa sizzler and their range of tandoori dishes lead the way.

2FOR1 MAIN COURSE | FRI × | SAT × | SUN — Indian

KNOCKINAAM LODGE
☎ 01776 810 471
Portpatrick, Dumfries, DG9 9AD

Informal, Michelin-starred dining at its best. Long-serving chef Tony Pierce feeds guests with a superb menu featuring locally-sourced Scottish ingredients brought together with classic, French finesse.

25% OFF TOTAL | FRI ✓ | SAT ✓ — Scottish

SOLWAY GATE
01387 249 785
Annan Road, Dumfries, DG1 3JX

Quality pub classics with a modern twist combine with a friendly and relaxed atmosphere to make this Table Table venue the perfect place for family gatherings or meeting friends.

2FOR1 MAIN COURSE | FRI ✓ | SAT ✓ — Modern British

Dunbartonshire

THE BALLOCH HOUSE
01389 752 579
Balloch Road, Balloch, Alexandria, G83 8LQ

This Vintage Inn oozes rural charm and rustic character. The picturesque surroundings provide the perfect backdrop for savouring the hearty, seasonal pub-food on the menu.

25% OFF TOTAL | FRI ✓ | SAT ✓ | SUN | ▲ — Modern British

THE BOAT HOUSE
☎ 01389 755 565
De Vere Cameron House Hotel, Loch Lomond, G83 8QZ

The décor here is a nod to New England style, with an open kitchen and wood-burning oven, offering a friendly dining experience. Choose from local seafood, great meat dishes, and tasty stone-baked pizzas.

25% OFF TOTAL | 👤 8 | FRI × | SAT × | SUN | * | ▲ — Mediterranean

THE CAMERON GRILL ☎01389 755 565
De Vere Cameron House Hotel, Loch Lomond, G83 8QZ
Stylish and informal, with an emphasis on Scotland's larder of fresh produce, this is the main restaurant at the luxurious Cameron House. Sample some of Scotland's tastiest steaks. Awarded 1 AA Rosette.

25% OFF TOTAL | 8 | FRI × | SAT × | SUN | * | — Scottish

THE CLARET JUG ☎01389 755 565
De Vere Cameron House Hotel, Loch Lomond, G83 8QZ
Apart from providing golfers with the ideal place to gather in style after a round of golf, The Claret Jug also serves a choice of delights - from light bites to classic favourite dishes.

25% OFF TOTAL | 8 | FRI × | SAT × | SUN | * | — Bistro

CUCINA ☎01389 755 455
The Galleries, Balloch Road, Balloch, G83 8SS
This friendly and contemporary Italian restaurant offers attentive service, fantastic imported ingredients and a great atmosphere. Their varied menu offers delicious steaks, pizzas, fish and pasta dishes.

25% OFF TOTAL | 4 | FRI | SAT | * — Italian

GOLDEN STAR TANDOORI ☎01389 721 077
100 Balloch Road, Balloch, G83 8SR
Acclaimed Indian restaurant just by the shore of Loch Lomond which specialises in the clarified, spicy flavours of Punjabi cooking, while also drawing in influences from other Indian regional cuisines.

2FOR1 MAIN COURSE | FRI * | SAT * | — Indian

East Lothian

THE DOLPHIN INN ☎01316 653 354
10 Whitecraigs Road, Musselburgh, EH21 8PG
A family-owned establishment, The Dolphin Inn is a classic village pub featuring an appealing conservatory restaurant. Freshly cooked food and friendly staff are also appealing factors.

25% OFF TOTAL | 6 | FRI × | SAT × | SUN — British

JOHN PAUL AT THE MARINE ☎01620 897 313
Macdonald Hotel and Spa, Cromwell Road, EH39 4LZ
Sitting comfortably on the east coast of Scotland, this hotel restaurant is renowned for not only its coastal location but also its appealing menu and excellent dishes. Perfection found in every offering.

2FOR1 MAIN COURSE | FRI | SAT | * | — Modern British

KASHMIR VALLEY ☎01875 614 888
95 High Street, Tranent, EH33 1LW
Classic Indian restaurant serving diners an array of tasty and extremely popular curry dishes, as well as house specials and mouth-watering seafood options, all to be enjoyed with delicious sundries.

2FOR1 3 COURSES | FRI ✓ | SAT ✓ — Indian

MADISONS ☎01316 536 699
Olive Bank Retail Park, Musselburgh, EH21 6RE
With a menu that changes fortnightly and daily specials, all using locally sourced ingredients of the highest quality, the best flavours are guaranteed to be packed into Madisons' food.

50% OFF FOOD | 6 | FRI | SAT | — British

Fife

BELLA ITALIA 01383 729 133
Fife leisure Park, Whimbrel Place, Dunfermline, KY11 8EX
Accessible Italian cuisine on the British high street - indulge in authentic sharing platters, hand stretched pizzas and hearty pasta dishes, served with a healthy dose of gregarious Italian hospitality.

25% OFF TOTAL | 6 | FRI × | SAT × | SUN | — Italian

BELLA ITALIA 01334 476 268
39 Bell Street, St Andrews, KY16 9UR
Accessible Italian cuisine on the British high street - indulge in authentic sharing platters, hand stretched pizzas and hearty pasta dishes, served with a healthy dose of gregarious Italian hospitality.

25% OFF TOTAL | 6 | FRI × | SAT × | SUN | — Italian

BUFFET KING ☎01383 624 222
41 Carnegie Drive, Dunfermline, KY12 7AN
Take your pick from a wide selection of Chinese and oriental dishes alongside tasty sides and starters. Here you'll find food so good, you'll be glad of the opportunity to fill your boots.

25% OFF TOTAL | 8 | FRI ✓ | SAT ✓ | * — Chinese

CHOPSTICKS ☎01383 411 993
157 Queensferry Road, Rosyth, KY11 2PP
Locally renowned Chinese restaurant that delivers high-quality, classic dishes including options that cater for various dietary requirements. Each choice here represents excellent value for money.

25% OFF TOTAL | 4 | FRI | SAT × | * — Chinese

EVEREST INN ☎01383 840 400
78 Hospital Hill, Dunfermline, KY11 3AT
Renowned for its traditional Nepalese and Indian cuisine, this venue boasts an expansive menu overloaded with choice. Vaunting a 'Best Indian Food in Fife' award, the dishes ooze authenticity.

2FOR1 MAIN COURSE | 6 | FRI ✓ | SAT ✓ | SUN | * — Indian

THE FETTYKIL FOX 01592 749 613
Leslie Roundabout, Glenrothes, KY6 3EP
This Vintage Inn oozes rural charm and rustic character. The picturesque surroundings provide the perfect backdrop for savouring the hearty, seasonal pub-food on the menu.

25% OFF TOTAL | FRI ✓ | SAT ✓ | SUN | — Modern British

GALLAGHERS ☎01592 206 090
Hendry Road, Kirkcaldy, KY2 5DE
Find light snacks, bar lunches and fulfilling evening meals at Gallaghers in Kirkcaldy. Pool tables, Sky TV and live entertainment make for an informal, relaxed evening.

2FOR1 MAIN COURSE | FRI * | SAT × | SUN | — Scottish

HOTEL DU VIN ☎01334 472 611
40 The Scores, St Andrews, KY16 9AS
The finest, freshest local produce, simple European recipes, a stunning choice of wines; these are the elements of the trademark Hotel du Vin bistro. Recently Refurbished, be wined and dined in style.

2FOR1 MAIN COURSE | FRI × | SAT × | SUN | — European

MAISHA ☎01334 476 666
5 College Street, St Andrews, KY16 9AA
A choice selection of Indian and seafood dishes appears on a well thought out menu at Maisha. Situated in the famous St Andrews, this is a fantastic place to eat delectable food after a day exploring.

25% OFF TOTAL | 10 | FRI ✓ | SAT ✓ — Indian

MEHEK ☎01383 515 008
250 High Street, Cowdenbeath, KY4 9NP
For quality Indian cuisine, head down to Mehek in Cowdenbeath. Creamy sauces and fiery flavours line the menu, while classic dishes are exquisitely produced to the highest of standards.

2FOR1 MAIN COURSE | FRI | SAT — Indian

THE PRINCE INDIAN RESTAURANT ☎01592 268 881
231 High Street, Kirkcaldy, KY1 1JF
Welcoming and friendly staff enhance your experience at The Prince Indian. Exotic flavours and spices will guarantee to bring you back time and time again.

2FOR1 2 COURSES | FRI × | SAT × — Indian

SPRINGFIELD TAVERN ☎01334 653 305
The Cross, Springfield, Cupar, KY15 5SJ
A wonderful pub offering both locals and guests from afar great food and a vast selection of beverages.

2FOR1 MAIN COURSE | FRI | SAT | SUN | — British

TASTE OF INDIA ☎01383 411 667
130 Admiralty Road, Dunfermline, KY11 2QJ
A Taste of India is a delightful local restaurant that caters to both regular and first time diners. Classic curry choices sit alongside imaginative, well-rounded dishes that draw on the flavours of India.

25% OFF TOTAL | FRI | SAT | Indian

TASTE OF INDIA ☎01333 422 530
1-3 Branch Street, Leven, KY8 4NL
The Taste of India in Leven offers traditional tandoori Indian cuisine to an extremely high standard. All of the dishes are freshly prepared by their chef with the finest of ingredients.

25% OFF TOTAL | 4 | FRI ✓ | SAT ✓ | Indian

THE VICEROY ☎07715 381 935
1 Queen Anne Street, Dunfermline, KY12 7BA
This outstanding restaurant deserves its enviable reputation as a superb Indian eatery. Talented chefs with outstanding culinary abilities make up one of the finest kitchen teams in the area.

2FOR1 MAIN COURSE | FRI ✓ | SAT × | Indian British

WOOD MILL RESTAURANT ☎01383 841 698
Linburn Road, Dunfermline, KY11 4UH
A creative, seasonally inspired menu guarantees The Wood Mill its impressive status as a fine place to eat. Fantastic fish, succulent steaks and superb pasta dishes feature highly.

2FOR1 MAIN COURSE | FRI × | SAT ✓ | British

Highlands

BOAT BISTRO ☎01479 831 258
Boat Hotel, Boat Of Garten, PH24 4BH
With a superb location, talented chefs and a well-stocked wine cabinet all in its favour, there are few things that the owners of Boat Bistro could more desire for their establishment. 2 AA Rosettes.

25% OFF TOTAL | 8 | FRI ✓ | SAT ✓ | Locally Sourced

THE SNOW GOOSE 01463 701 921
Stoneyfield, Inverness, IV2 7PA
This Vintage Inn oozes rural charm and rustic character. The picturesque surroundings provide the perfect backdrop for savouring the hearty, seasonal pub-food on the menu.

25% OFF TOTAL | FRI ✓ | SAT ✓ | SUN | Modern British

ADAM'S DINING ROOM ☎01463 790 461
The Culloden House Hotel, Inverness, IV2 7BZ
Highly rated and regarded restaurant at the stately Culloden House that serves outstanding, double AA rosette-winning cuisine including fine, musky game and superbly flavourful local produce.

25% OFF TOTAL | 4 | FRI ✓ | SAT ✓ | Fine Dining

ASH ☎01463 231 926
18 Academy Street, Inverness, IV1 1LG
A venue providing diners ample opportunity to sample glorious Scottish highland and internationally renowned cuisine. Courteous service perfectly complements the superb range of delicious food on offer.

2FOR1 MAIN COURSE | FRI | SAT * | * | Scottish

BELLA ITALIA 01463 230 138
1 Bridge Street, Inverness, IV1 1HG
Accessible Italian cuisine on the British high street - indulge in authentic sharing platters, hand stretched pizzas and hearty pasta dishes, served with a healthy dose of gregarious Italian hospitality.

25% OFF TOTAL | 6 | FRI × | SAT × | SUN | Italian

THE BRASSERIE @ MERCURE ☎0844 815 9006
Mercure Hotel, Church Street, Inverness, IV1 1DX
The Mercure Inverness Hotel is a superb place to while away a few days of rest and retreat. The Brasserie serves traditional and contemporary dishes with British flavours and international imagination.

2FOR1 3 COURSES | FRI ✓ | SAT ✓ | British

CRAIGDARROCH HOUSE HOTEL ☎01456 486 400
Foyers, Loch Ness, Inverness, IV2 6XU
Log fires and stunning views over Loch Ness are just two fine attributes of this exquisite Highland hotel. The restaurant is small and intimate and serves up some truly delectable dishes.

50% OFF FOOD | 4 | FRI ✓ | SAT ✓ | European

INDIAN OCEAN INVERNESS ☎01463 237 755
64 Academy Street, Inverness, IV1 1LP
At Indian Ocean, you will be tempted by an unrivalled range of authentic and imaginative Indian cuisine. The menu is cooked to the highest standards, using only the freshest ingredients.

2FOR1 MAIN COURSE | FRI | SAT | Indian

KOOL RUNNINGS ☎01463 230 856
14 Church Street, Inverness, IV1 1EA
Unwind to the soothing sounds of reggae whilst tucking in to authentic jerk chicken or sumptuous goat curry. Using soulful recipes, this heart-warming venue welcomes guests with open arms and a smile.

2FOR1 3 COURSES | FRI | SAT | Caribbean

LA TORTILLA ASESINA ☎01463 709 809
99 Castle Street, Inverness, IV2 3EA
With a menu boasting over 40 tapas dishes it is no wonder that this authentic Spanish restaurant has a wonderful reputation. Affable, knowledgeable staff are happy to help if you are spoilt for choice.

25% OFF TOTAL | 4 | FRI | SAT | SUN | Spanish

LOCH NESS HOUSE 01463 701 111
Glenurquhart Road, Inverness, IV3 5TD
Beefeater Grill are one of the UK's best-loved restaurants welcoming guests for almost 40 years in over 130 locations nationwide. *Excludes Breakfast, Light Bites, Bar menu, set menus and all other offers.

2FOR1 MAIN COURSE | 6 | FRI ✓ | SAT × | Modern British

LOCH NESS LODGE ☎01456 459 469
Brachla, Loch Ness, Inverness, IV3 8LA
This fine-dining establishment utilises its wonderful seasonal range of produce to create creative, contemporary dishes, happily tailoring the menu to please each guest. Awarded 2 AA Rosettes.

25% OFF TOTAL | 4 | FRI ✓ | SAT ✓ | Fine Dining

MUCKRACH LODGE HOTEL & RESTAURANT ☎01479 851 257
Dulnain Bridge, Nr Grantown-on-Spey, PH26 3LY
The restaurant at Muckrach Lodge is one of the hotel's finest attributes. Oozing contemporary elegance, this is a perfect place to drink and dine in an oasis of calm.

50% OFF FOOD | 4 | FRI ✓ | SAT ✓ | Modern European

ROYAL TANDOORI ☎01479 811 199
43 Grampian Road, Aviemore, PH22 1RH
Holding an excellent reputation with both locals and tourists, this Indian restaurant offers outstanding cuisine for all to enjoy. Spicy curry fans will love the challenge of the 'roof-lifter' dish.

25% OFF TOTAL | 10 | FRI ✓ | SAT ✓ | * | Indian

SPICE TANDOORI ☎01463 241 919
2 Castle Road, Inverness, IV2 3AA
Incredibly tasty tandoori, creamy curries and superb sundries make the Spice Tandoori a great choice of restaurant. Diners will not be disappointed by the fine line of delicious dishes available here.

2FOR1 MAIN COURSE | FRI ✓ | SAT × | SUN | Indian

CARRON RESTAURANT ☎01520 722 488
Cam-allt, Strathcarron, IV54 8YX
Indulge in picturesque views over the Loch as your meal is prepared in front of you on a chargrill. Steak and local seafood are heavenly choices, whilst the dessert trolley must not be missed.

2FOR1 MAIN COURSE | FRI ✓ | SAT ✓ | SUN | Scottish

TIGH AN EILEAN HOTEL RESTAURANT ☎01520 755 251
Main Street, Shieldaig on Loch Torridon, IV54 8XN
Drawing on the flavours and produce of Scotland, the chef at Tigh an Eilean Hotel adds a modern twist to the well-famed dishes. Certain international tastes are exposed on the menu. 2 AA Rosettes.

25% OFF TOTAL | 10 | FRI ✓ | SAT ✓ | * | Seafood/ International

Lanarkshire

ANNLANN RESTAURANT @ THISTLE ☎0871 376 9043
Thistle Glasgow Hotel, Cambridge Street, Glasgow, G2 3HN

Expansive and contemporary space in the Thistle Hotel Glasgow. Warm colours set against bright white linen contribute to an elegant ambience. Serves some simple, delicious British and European dishes.

50% OFF FOOD | ♟10 | FRI ✓ | SAT ✓ | European

ASHOKA ASHTON LANE ☎0141 337 1115
19 Ashton Lane, Glasgow, G12 8SJ

Take a saunter down the cobbled stones of Ashton Lane and be enticed by the intoxicating aromas and spice-filled dishes of the amazing Ashoka restaurant. Authentic and most certainly irresistible.

2FOR1 MAIN COURSE | FRI ✱ | SAT ✱ | ✱ | ▲ | Indian

ASHOKA AT THE MILL ☎0141 876 0458
500 Corselet Road, Darnley, Glasgow, G53 7RN

A stunning Ashoka restaurant that combines a historic medieval farmhouse setting with a classy contemporary twist in its vast interior; the heavenly food bursts with flavour and freshness.

2FOR1 MAIN COURSE | FRI ✓ | SAT ✱ | ✱ | ▲ | Indian

ASHOKA AT THE QUAY ☎0141 429 4492
The Quay Leisure Park, Glasgow, G5 8NP

Another addition to the superb Ashoka restaurants, taking diners on a culinary adventure with a delicious range of authentic Indian dishes to choose from on their mouth-watering menu.

50% OFF FOOD | ♟4 | FRI ✓ | SAT ✓ | ▲ | Indian

ASHOKA BEARSDEN ☎0141 570 0075
9 Kirk Road, Bearsden, Glasgow, G61 3RG

Simplistic yet stylish interior coupled with the finest Indian food, this Ashoka restaurant demonstrates continued quality and exceptional service, sending ripples of delight throughout the community.

2FOR1 MAIN COURSE | FRI ✱ | SAT ✱ | ▲ | Indian

ASHOKA SHAK COATBRIDGE ☎01236 437 181
Showcase Leisure park, Coatbridge, Glasgow, SG69 7TS

With a legendary reputation for quality and service, Ashoka Shak truly delivers authentic Indian delights and invites diners to set out on an exciting journey of culinary discovery.

2FOR1 2 COURSES | FRI ✓ | SAT ✱ | ✱ | ▲ | Indian

ASHOKA SOUTH SIDE ☎0141 637 0711
268 Clarkston Road, Glasgow, G44 3EA

Another Ashoka restaurant bursting with Eastern promise, perfect for curry lovers and even the uninitiated. A range of authentically crafted dishes with tastes and spices to suit every preference.

2FOR1 MAIN COURSE | FRI ✱ | SAT ✱ | ✱ | ▲ | Indian

ASHOKA WEST END ☎0141 339 3371
1284 Argyle Street, Glasgow, G3 8AB

Immortalised as a famous culinary landmark, the Ashoka West End restaurant acts like a magnet to Glasgow's colossal curry eating fraternity, showcasing a vast array of freshly made, authentic dishes.

2FOR1 MAIN COURSE | FRI ✱ | SAT ✱ | ✱ | ▲ | Indian

ATRIUM BAR @ RADISSON ☎0141 204 3333
Radisson Blu Hotel, 301 Argyle Street, Glasgow, G2 8DL

Cool blues, long windows and deep brown sofas create a warm, inviting ambience for guests to drink and dine in. Smooth coffees, fruity cocktails and chunky sandwiches line the menu.

25% OFF TOTAL | ♟4 | FRI ✓ | SAT ✓ | International

THE AUCHINAIRN TAVERN ☎0141 772 1399
137 Auchinairn Road, Glasgow, G64 1NF

Good simple food is served up by new chef Alex. The friendly team help create the perfect environment to relax and chill-out. So put your feet up and let the staff at the 'Tavern' do the hard work for you.

2FOR1 3 COURSES | FRI ✓ | SAT ✗ | SUN | ▲ | British

THE BABY GRAND ☎0141 248 4942
3 Elmbank Gardens, Glasgow, G2 4NQ

The Baby Grand has been a Glasgow institution for over 25 years and is a favourite for eating out. From succulent chicken to deliciously tasty steak-frites, every diner will find something for them.

25% OFF TOTAL | ♟2 | FRI ▯ | SAT ▯ | ✱ | Bistro

THE BAGIO CAFÉ BAR @ MERCURE ☎0844 815 9103
Mercure Glasgow City Hotel, Ingram St, Glasgow, G1 1DQ

The bright lights of Scotland's most vibrant city can be taken full advantage of by the visitors of Mercure Glasgow City Hotel. After a day of exploration, head to the hotel's Bagio Café Bar.

2FOR1 3 COURSES | FRI ✓ | SAT ✓ | British

BANANA LEAF ☎0141 334 4445
76 Old Dumbarton Road, Glasgow, G3 8RE

Catering to the Glaswegian demands for south Indian cuisine, Banana Leaf serves a delicious fusion of various Indian flavours for diners who wish to avoid the more westernised curry scene.

25% OFF TOTAL | ♟4 | FRI ✗ | SAT ✗ | Indian

BANANA LEAF ☎0141 423 9692
105 Albert Drive, Glasgow, G41 2SU

Catering to the Glaswegian demands for South Indian cuisine, the second Banana Leaf serves a delicious fusion of various Indian flavours for diners who wish to avoid the more westernised curry scene.

25% OFF TOTAL | ♟4 | FRI ✗ | SAT ✗ | Indian

BELLA ITALIA 0141 221 5321
96 Hope Street, Glasgow, G2 6PH

Accessible Italian cuisine on the British high street - indulge in authentic sharing platters, hand stretched pizzas and hearty pasta dishes, served with a healthy dose of gregarious Italian hospitality.

25% OFF TOTAL | ♟6 | FRI ✗ | SAT ✗ | SUN | ▲ | Italian

BELLA ITALIA 0141 886 7645
Xscape, Braehead, Glasgow, G51 4FB

Accessible Italian cuisine on the British high street - indulge in authentic sharing platters, hand stretched pizzas and hearty pasta dishes, served with a healthy dose of gregarious Italian hospitality.

25% OFF TOTAL | ♟6 | FRI ✗ | SAT ✗ | SUN | ▲ | Italian

BELLINI ☎0141 649 6096
67-69 Kilmarnock Road, Shawlands, Glasgow, G41 3YR

A casual yet sophisticated atmosphere with a menu delivering a contemporary take on classic Italian tastes. An ideal destination all day whether it be for fresh coffee, a light lunch, or exquisite dinner.

2FOR1 MAIN COURSE | FRI ✓ | SAT ✓ | Italian

BLACK BEAR 0141 773 1133
601 Hamilton Road, Uddington, Glasgow, G71 7SA

Beefeater Grill are one of the UK's best-loved restaurants welcoming guests for almost 40 years in over 130 locations nationwide. *Excludes Breakfast, Light Bites, Bar menu, set menus and all other offers.

2FOR1 MAIN COURSE | ♟6 | FRI ✓ | SAT ✗ | ▲ | Modern British

THE BLIND PIG ☎0141 357 5482
116-122 Byres Road, Glasgow, G12 8TB

Expect only the best in local produce as The Blind Pig takes inspiration from around the world, matching it with the best classic dishes, all made with a commitment to the freshest and best ingredients.

2FOR1 MAIN COURSE | FRI ✗ | SAT ✗ | International

BLUE RUPEE ☎0141 634 0019
163 Eastkilbride Road, Burnside, Glasgow, G73 5EA

Guests will love the rich Indian dishes that make up the vastly diverse menu at this great restaurant. Attentive and accommodating service is guaranteed.

2FOR1 3 COURSES | ✱ | Indian

THE BOATHOUSE ☎01236 829 201
Auchinstarry Marina, Kilsyth, G65 9SG

An admirably located pub and restaurant that overlooks the beautiful marina and the Campsie Fells. Rest and relax in one of the luxurious bedrooms or simply come and dine on divine lunches and dinners.

2FOR1 MAIN COURSE | FRI ✓ | SAT ✱ | SUN | ▲ | European

To understand what the restaurant icons mean, please see the inside back cover.

THE BRASSERIE
☎0141 222 2929

27 Washington Street, Glasgow, G3 8AZ

Convivial, lively in-house restaurant at this hotel in Glasgow. Standing menu features a good range of brasserie-style dishes cooked with great accomplishment and emphasis on clarity of flavour.

2FOR1 3 COURSES | FRI ☎ | SAT ☎ — Scottish

BUKHARAH RESTAURANT
☎0141 330 1550

923 Sauchiehall Street, Glasgow, G3 7TQ

With a menu that is subject to daily change, fresh cuisine is guaranteed every time. Start the evening with a renowned 'Bilberry' cocktail before indulging in a vegetable sabzi prepared by the expert chef.

25% OFF TOTAL | 👤10 | FRI × | SAT × | ▲ — Indian

CABIN BAR @ THISTLE
☎0872 376 9043

Thistle Glasgow Hotel, Cambridge St, Glasgow, G2 3HN

Informal place to have light bites, sandwiches and other bar food options in a friendly and personal setting. A centrally located hotel that's modern, light and sharp in design.

50% OFF FOOD | 👤4 | FRI ✓ | SAT ✱ — European

CAFÉ DARNA
☎0141 353 6528

175 St Georges Road, Glasgow, G3 6JA

Tasty Indian and Moroccan cuisine makes Café Darna a popular place to dine in Glasgow. Tandoori specials add a fantastic touch to the menu, with firm favourite curry dishes featuring highly as well.

2FOR1 MAIN COURSE | FRI ☎ | SAT ☎ — Moroccan

CAFE INDIA
☎0141 552 5115

9 Albion Street, Merchant City, Glasgow, G1 1LH

Café India offers a unique dining experience with constantly evolving menus and a carefully matched wine list and organic Scottish beer selection, designed to reflect an ethos of innovation and creativity.

25% OFF TOTAL | FRI ✓ | SAT × | ▲ — Indian

CAFÉ ROUGE
0141 243 2055

20 Royal Exchange Square, Glasgow, G1 2AB

French sophistication on the British high street - enjoy seasonally changing French dishes and a continental wine selection, served in a relaxed environment with an undeniable flair of Parisian chic.

25% OFF TOTAL | 👤6 | FRI ✓ | SAT ✓ | ✱ — French

CAFE SHABAB
☎01698 383 429

138 Manse Road, Wishaw, ML2 9BD

Cafe Shabab offers a wide array of beautiful Indian dishes. The restaurant is known for its curries, offering a full 'heat spectrum', all created with homemade spice blends.

2FOR1 3 COURSES | FRI ✓ | SAT × — Indian

CAFÉ SPICE
☎01236 755 123

76 Stirling Street, Airdrie, ML6 0AS

Classic mouth-watering Indian recipes are used to create both new and traditional dishes at this fantastically authentic restaurant. The outstanding food and service will ensure you leave with a smile.

2FOR1 MAIN COURSE | FRI ✓ | SAT ✱ | ▲ — Indian

CAFE TASTE
☎0141 435 4813

1515 Dumbarton Road, Glasgow, G14 9XQ

The team at Cafe Taste have hand picked the best products and ingredients from many places, from the best quality meats to tasty fair trade coffee. A passion for quality and service.

50% OFF FOOD | FRI ✓ | SAT ✓ — International

THE CASTLE
0141 955 7901

Greenlaw Crookfur Road, Newton Mearns, G77 6NP

Beefeater Grill are one of the UK's best-loved restaurants welcoming guests for almost 40 years in over 130 locations nationwide. *Excludes Breakfast, Light Bites, Bar menu, set menus and all other offers.

2FOR1 MAIN COURSE | 👤6 | FRI ✓ | SAT × | ▲ — Modern British

CINNAMON CAMBUSLANG
☎0141 641 9595

252 Main Street, Cambuslang, Glasgow, G72 7EG

Cinnamon's creators have been at the forefront of Indian cooking in Scotland since the 1960s. This family run establishment has proved to be extremely popular with locals and out-of-town diners alike.

25% OFF TOTAL | FRI × | SAT × | SUN | ✱ | ▲ — Indian

COLLAGE RESTAURANT
☎0141 225 2046

Radisson Blu Hotel, 301 Argyle Street, Glasgow, G2 8DL

Sir Peter Blake and Roy Ackerman join together to deliver a combination of art and food. A blend of Mediterranean and Scottish cuisine with a modern twist will delight the most experienced diner.

25% OFF TOTAL | 👤4 | FRI ✓ | SAT ✓ | ▲ — European

COTTIERS
☎0141 357 5825

93 Hyndland Street, Glasgow, G11 5QE

Situated in a converted church building, Cottiers is a wonderful restaurant accommodating a vibrant Scottish menu. A well-designed interior makes this a beautiful place to dine.

25% OFF TOTAL | 👤10 | FRI ✓ | SAT ✓ | ✱ | ▲ — Scottish

CROOKED LUM
01355 222 809

Brunel Way, The Murray, East Kilbride, G75 0JY

Beefeater Grill are one of the UK's best-loved restaurants welcoming guests for almost 40 years in over 130 locations nationwide. *Excludes Breakfast, Light Bites, Bar menu, set menus and all other offers.

2FOR1 MAIN COURSE | 👤6 | FRI ✓ | SAT × | ▲ — Modern British

Di Maggio's

7 restaurants in Lanarkshire

25% OFF TOTAL

25% OFF TOTAL | 👤6 | FRI ✱ | SAT ✱ | ▲

21 Royal Exchange Square, Glasgow, G1 3AJ	☎ 0141 248 2111
1038 Pollokshaws Road, Glasgow, G41 3EB	☎ 0141 632 7924
163 West Nile Street, Glasgow, G1 3RL	☎ 0141 333 4999
61 Ruthven Lane, Glasgow, G12 9BG	☎ 0141 357 0874
42 Gateside Street, Hamilton, ML3 7JQ	☎ 01698 891 828
1 Rochsolloch Road, Airdrie, ML6 9BG	☎ 01236 766 561
Stroud Road, East Kilbride, G75 0YA	☎ 01355 242 222

CROWNE PLAZA GLASGOW
☎0871 942 9091
Congress Road, Glasgow, G3 8QT
Guests at this hotel have a choice of two dining options, with cuisine from around the world. Views over the Clyde can be enjoyed in One Restaurant; snacks and drinks are served in the Quarterdeck Bar.

25% OFF TOTAL | 6 | FRI ✓ | SAT ✓ — International

CURRYOKE CLUB
☎0141 258 7720
100 Stobcross Road, Glasgow, G3 8QQ
Situated on the banks of the River Clyde, Curryoke Club is the only place to spend that much anticipated evening out. Provides a winning blend of delicious Indian food with a party atmosphere.

2FOR1 MAIN COURSE | FRI ✓ | SAT × | SUN | ▲ — Indian

DIVA RESTAURANT
☎0141 952 0354
Steward Street, Clydebank, G81 4AD
One of the most reputable in the area, this restaurant has a loyal clientele who return time after time for the tantalising cuisine which is sure to appease the appetites of hungry diners.

25% OFF TOTAL | 4 | FRI ✱ | SAT ✱ | ✱ | ▲ — Indian

THE DOVECOTE
01236 725 339
4 South Muirhead Road, Cumbernauld, Glasgow, G67 1AX
Beefeater Grill are one of the UK's best-loved restaurants welcoming guests for almost 40 years in over 130 locations nationwide. *Excludes Breakfast, Light Bites, Bar menu, set menus and all other offers.

2FOR1 MAIN COURSE | 6 | FRI ✓ | SAT × | ▲ — Modern British

FALAFEL PETRA
☎0141 334 1414
27 Gibson Street, Glasgow, G12 8NX
Offering a mouth-watering range of authentic Middle Eastern cuisine with a strong Jordanian influence, FalaFel Petra is a delicious piece of Lebanon in the heart of Glasgow.

25% OFF TOTAL | FRI ✓ | SAT ✓ | ✱ — Middle Eastern

FIREBIRD RESTAURANT
☎0141 334 0594
1321 Argyle Street, Glasgow, G3 8TL
Delightful neighbourhood bar and bistro for smooth experiences. Having enjoyed the sights and sounds of the city, head to Firebird for a microbrewery pint or crispy-base pizza as you watch the world go by.

2FOR1 MAIN COURSE | FRI ✱ | SAT × | SUN | ▲ — Mediterranean

FOUR SEASONS
☎0141 332 2666
87 Cambridge Street, Glasgow, G3 6RU
The finest fresh ingredients are used with authentic oriental spices, to create traditional Chinese meals with a modern twist. Perfect for business lunches, pre-theatre appetisers or romantic dinners.

25% OFF TOTAL | 6 | FRI | SAT | ▲ — Chinese

GRAND CENTRAL
☎0141 240 3700
99 Gordon Street, Glasgow, G1 3SF
An iconic addition to the city, Grand Central stands as Glasgow's much-loved hotel. A four-star venue that offers the perfect backdrop to a weekend stay or important business conference.

25% OFF TOTAL | 6 | FRI ✓ | SAT ✓ | ▲ — British

THE GREEN CHILLI CAFÉ
☎0141 337 6378
1293 Argyle Street, Glasgow, G3 8TL
The Green Chilli Café is an Indian Tapas Restaurant in the heart of Glasgow's West End, where old traditional recipes from India are served in small simple dishes.

25% OFF TOTAL | 10 | FRI ✓ | SAT × — Indian

THE GRILL BAR @ JURYS INN
☎0141 314 4800
Jurys Inns, 80 Jamaica Street, Glasgow, G43 2PJ
When you are feeling a little peckish after your busy day of work or sightseeing, be sure to head on down to the recently refurbished bar and restaurant, The Grill Bar, serving up tasty Scottish cuisine.

2FOR1 MAIN COURSE | FRI ✓ | SAT ✓ | ✱ | ▲ — British

GUY'S RESTAURANT & BAR
☎0141 552 1114
24 Candleriggs, Merchant City, Glasgow, G1 1LD
Held in high regard, this venue offers a great ambience and friendly staff that really enhance the dining experience, not forgetting the simply delicious food that is superb value for money.

2FOR1 3 COURSES | FRI ✱ | SAT ✱ | ▲ — Modern British

HANDMADE BURGER CO.
0141 886 5896
Braehead Shopping Centre, Glasgow, G51 4BP
100% prime Scotch beef burgers, handmade in the restaurant daily, sourdough buns, delicious handmade relishes and a wide range of toppings giving you over 40 varieties to choose from. *Exclusions apply.

2FOR1 MAIN COURSE | FRI ✓ | SAT × | SUN — International

HANDMADE BURGER CO.
0141 881 8780
Silverburn, Barrhead Road, Glasgow, G53 6AF
100% prime Scotch beef burgers, handmade in the restaurant daily, sourdough buns, delicious handmade relishes and a wide range of toppings giving you over 40 varieties to choose from. *Exclusions apply.

2FOR1 MAIN COURSE | FRI ✓ | SAT × | SUN — International

HEERA INDIAN RESTAURANT
☎0141 248 8333
15-17 Kent Road, Glasgow, G3 7EH
Heera Indian Restaurant, the home of award winning Indian Chef PJ. Enjoy the magic of an award winning curry in the heart of Glasgow. Fresh, healthy and delicious dishes for you to try!

2FOR1 3 COURSES | FRI ✓ | SAT ✓ — Indian

INDIA GATE
☎0141 423 9988
679 Pollokshaws Road, Glasgow, G41 2AB
Classic Indian dishes on offer at this quality restaurant, where the chefs proudly produce firm favourite dishes to a cohort of diners. The staff will enhance your overall enjoyment of the evening.

2FOR1 3 COURSES | FRI ✓ | SAT ✓ — Indian

INDIAN GALLERY
☎0141 332 3355
450 Sauchiehall Street, Glasgow, G2 3JD
Indian dining at its finest. Lunch, evening and à la carte menus include traditional and modern Indian and Asian dishes for you to enjoy.

2FOR1 MAIN COURSE | FRI ✓ | SAT ✓ — Indian

KABANA
☎0141 420 3233
64 Seward Street, Glasgow, G41 1HJ
Nested near Kinning Park is Kabana, a fine Indian dining restaurant that combines the traditional Indian charm along with wholesome, satisfying and elevating experience.

2FOR1 2 COURSES | FRI × | SAT × | SUN — Indian

KAMA SUTRA
☎0141 332 0055
331 Sauchiehall Street, Glasgow, G2 3HW
A fantastic eatery extremely popular with local curry lovers, serving up a superb selection of quality Indian dishes that are rich in flavour and authentic aroma. All available to eat in or takeaway.

2FOR1 2 COURSES | FRI ✓ | SAT ✓ | ▲ — Indian

LA BONNE AUBERGE & BAR
☎0141 352 8300
Holiday Inn Glasgow Theatreland, Glasgow, G1 2RL
The eclectic atmosphere and casual, relaxed surrounds of this excellent restaurant, combined with its AA Rosette-awarded cuisine, offers a truly memorable Glasgow dining experience.

25% OFF TOTAL | 6 | FRI × | SAT × — International

LA TASCA
☎0141 204 5188
39-43 Renfield Street, Glasgow, G2 1JS
Quintessentially Spanish, La Tasca's fresh and exciting menu offers something for everyone. Their tapas dishes are sincerely authentic, while their paellas always deliver on flavour.

25% OFF TOTAL | 8 | FRI ✓ | SAT × | ▲ — Spanish

LA TASCA
☎0845 126 2964
Silverburn Shopping Centre, Glasgow, G53 6QR
Quintessentially Spanish, La Tasca's fresh and exciting menu offers something for everyone. Their tapas dishes are sincerely authentic, while their paellas always deliver on flavour.

25% OFF TOTAL | 8 | FRI ✓ | SAT × | ▲ — Spanish

LAS RAMBLAS TAPAS
☎0141 942 1380
5 Kirk Lane, Bearsden, Glasgow, G61 3RU
With food being of such importance to the people of Spain, it is easy to see how tapas has become a way of life. Las Ramblas Tapas recognises the appeal of tapas-style dining and brings it to Bearsden.

2FOR1 MAIN COURSE | FRI × | SAT × — Spanish

LE BAR @ THE CAMPANILE HOTEL ☎ 0141 287 7700
10 Tunnel Street, Glasgow, G3 8HL
A neat bar in the Campanile Hotel Glasgow provides the perfect space in which to relax and unwind after a day exploring the city. Enjoy your favourite beverage alongside tasty bar snacks.

50% OFF FOOD | 8 | FRI ✓ | SAT ✓ — French

LE BAR @ THE CAMPANILE HOTEL ☎ 0141 886 1347
2 Row Avenue, Glasgow, G51 4SY
A neat bar in the Campanile Hotel Glasgow Airport provides the perfect space in which to relax and unwind before or after you fly. Enjoy your favourite beverage alongside tasty bar snacks.

50% OFF FOOD | 8 | FRI ✓ | SAT ✓ — International

LE RESTAURANT @ THE CAMPANILE HOTEL ☎ 0141 287 7700
10 Tunnel Street, Glasgow, G3 8HL
A simply elegant restaurant at the Hotel Campanile, situated in a vibrant part of a fantastic city. Quality produce contributes to a seasonal menu that provides guests with delicious savoury flavours.

50% OFF FOOD | 8 | FRI ✓ | SAT ✓ — French

LE RESTAURANT @ THE CAMPANILE HOTEL ☎ 0141 886 1347
2 Row Avenue, Glasgow, G51 4SY
Savour modern and contemporary dishes that take influence from France and the Mediterranean, with chefs here presenting seasonal dishes and local favourites. Great British food with a French accent.

50% OFF FOOD | 8 | FRI ✓ | SAT ✓ — International

THE LEEBURN 01355 586451
5 Lee Burns Court, Nerston, East Kilbride, G74 3XB
Quality pub classics with a modern twist combine with a friendly and relaxed atmosphere to make this Table Table venue the perfect place for family gatherings or meeting friends.

2FOR1 MAIN COURSE | FRI ✓ | SAT ✓ — Modern British

MAJESTIC INDIA ☎ 01236 613 333
68 Main Street, Cumbernauld, G67 2RX
Diners who are seeking to gratify their rumbling tummies with pocket-friendly cuisine will adore the menu. With quality at the forefront of their ethos, the chefs prepare authentic and tasty dishes.

2FOR1 3 COURSES | FRI 📱 | SAT 📱 | ✱ | ▲ — Indian

MALMAISON ☎ 0141 572 1000
278 West George Street, Glasgow, G2 4LL
This former Church has become one of Glasgow's most heavenly dining and resting venues. With great food and service, it's easy to see how Malmaison has gained such a faithful congregation. 1 AA Rosette.

2FOR1 MAIN COURSE | FRI × | SAT × | SUN | ▲ — European

MAMA'S RASOI ☎ 0141 222 2632
82 Howard Street, Glasgow, G1 4EE
Mama's Rasoi, which means mother's kitchen, offers a authentic Indian cuisine from various parts of India. *Must order a minimum of 3 courses per person.

2FOR1 3 COURSES | FRI 📱 | SAT 📱 | SUN | ▲ — Indian

MARQUIS BAR ☎ 0141 7640 123
1082 Shettleston Road, Glasgow, G32 7PW
The Marquis Bar do not claim to be a fancy gastro pub but they do endeavour to serve honest, value for money and above all tasty and fresh food.

2FOR1 3 COURSES | FRI ✓ | SAT ✓ | SUN | ▲ — British

MASALA TWIST ☎ 0141 339 3777
192-194 Byres Road, Glasgow, G12 8SN
Expect first-class service at this colourful restaurant, as you indulge in a menu bursting with rich flavours and delicate spices. Enjoy authentic Indian dishes in a relaxed, casual atmosphere.

2FOR1 MAIN COURSE | FRI ✓ | SAT × — Indian

MIRAGE RESTAURANT ☎ 0141 889 4477
59 Broomlands Street, Paisley, Glasgow, PA1 2NH
Creativity is key in the kitchen at Mirage, where a fine selection of curries, tandoori dishes and meaty kebabs occupy a well-thought out menu. A tastefully decorated interior encourages return visits.

2FOR1 MAIN COURSE | FRI ✓ | SAT ✓ — Indian

MISTER SINGH'S INDIA ☎ 0141 204 0186
149 Elderlie Street, Glasgow, G3 7JR
A popular restaurant that often caters for business and executive lunches. An eclectic blend of clientèle fills the restaurant each evening, where scrumptious curries and crispy naan breads are devoured.

2FOR1 MAIN COURSE | FRI ✓ | SAT ✱ | ▲ — Indian

ML ONE ☎ 01698 232 323
1 Enterprise Way, Motherwell, ML1 2TX
Support the talented chefs of the future at this terrific on-site restaurant. Wonderful dishes are prepared by chefs-in-training, guaranteeing guests a first-class dining experience.

2FOR1 MAIN COURSE | FRI 📱 | SAT ✱ | SUN — Modern European

NEW PEARL OF INDIA ☎ 0141 632 7700
100 Cathcart Road, Mount Florida, Glasgow, G42 9XJ
The New Pearl of India is a fantastic place to dine, with authentic mouth-watering Indian cuisine served on a daily basis. The staff are proud of the quality of food and level of service on offer.

50% OFF FOOD | FRI ✓ | SAT ✓ | ▲ — Indian

NEWHOUSE HOTEL 01698 860 277
Edinburgh Road, Newhouse, Motherwell, ML1 5SY
Quality pub classics with a modern twist combine with a friendly and relaxed atmosphere to make this Table Table venue the perfect place for family gatherings or meeting friends.

2FOR1 MAIN COURSE | FRI ✓ | SAT ✓ — Modern British

ONE TEN BAR & GRILL ☎ 0141 353 0800
Marks Hotel, Glasgow, 110-114 Bath Street, G2 2EN
Chic fine-dining and modern cocktail offerings make One Ten Bar & Grill a firm favourite in Glasgow. Chef specials are created with imagination and can be enjoyed with great ease.

2FOR1 3 COURSES | FRI × | SAT × — International

ORION WAY 0141 764 2655
30-40 Westhorn Drive, Cambuslang, Glasgow, G32 8EY
Quality pub classics with a modern twist combine with a friendly and relaxed atmosphere to make this Table Table venue the perfect place for family gatherings or meeting friends.

2FOR1 MAIN COURSE | FRI ✓ | SAT ✓ — Modern British

PAPA TONY'S ☎ 0141 332 3800
283 Sauchiehall Street, Glasgow, G2 3HQ
Papa Tony's restaurants are a unique combination of extraordinary Italian cuisine, beautiful décor and affordable prices - the perfect family restaurant providing quality Italian food, firmly rooted in tradition.

25% OFF TOTAL | FRI ✓ | SAT × | ▲ — Italian

PAPA TONY'S THE QUAY ☎ 0141 237 4818
Springfield Quay, Glasgow, G5 8NP
Papa Tony's restaurants are a unique combination of extraordinary Italian cuisine, beautiful décor and affordable prices - the perfect family restaurant providing quality Italian food, firmly rooted in tradition.

25% OFF TOTAL | FRI ✓ | SAT × | ▲ — Italian

PINK TURBAN 01698 375 835
157 Wishaw Road, Waterloo, Wishaw, ML2 8EN
Alongside the old favourites, the restaurant has some excellent specialities, not least the majestic 'Turban special', with chicken and lamb tikka, mince and prawns in a fantastically rich bhuna sauce.

2FOR1 MAIN COURSE | FRI × | SAT × | ▲ — Indian

PJ'S INDIA ☎ 0141 248 8333
15 Kent Road, Charring Cross, Glasgow, G3 7EH
Culinary genius is provided here as an experienced team deliver rich, fragrant Indian cuisine. Diners are offered an à la carte menu or gastronomic buffet, both excellently crafted with passion and spice.

25% OFF TOTAL | 10 | FRI 📱 | SAT 📱 | ✱ | ▲ — Indian

THE POUR HOUSE
0141 221 4449
1038-1042 Argyle Street, Glasgow, G3 8LX
Fantastic gourmet pub grub is the serving of the day at the Pour House. From a hearty Scottish steak and ale pie to a gourmet three bean and goats cheese burger, the menu is filled with tasty treats.

2FOR1 3 COURSES | FRI ✓ | SAT ✓ — British

PREZZO
0141 881 1467
Silverburn Shopping Centre, Barrhead Road, Glasgow, G53 6AG
With a character all of its own, Prezzo oozes contemporary style and enduring charm. Signature pastas, stone-baked pizzas and classic Italian dishes promise a perfect dining choice for the whole family.

2FOR1 MAIN COURSE | FRI × | SAT × — Italian

PREZZO
0141 248 9815
35 St Vincent Place, Glasgow, G1 2ER
With a character all of its own, Prezzo oozes contemporary style and enduring charm. Signature pastas, stone-baked pizzas and classic Italian dishes promise a perfect dining choice for the whole family.

2FOR1 MAIN COURSE | FRI × | SAT × — Italian

PREZZO
0141 886 2437
Braehead Shopping Centre, Kings Inch Rd, Glasgow, G51 4BP
With a character all of its own, Prezzo oozes contemporary style and enduring charm. Signature pastas, stone-baked pizzas and classic Italian dishes promise a perfect dining choice for the whole family.

2FOR1 MAIN COURSE | FRI × | SAT × — Italian

PREZZO
0141 773 3378
Glasgow Fort Shopping Park, Glasgow, G34 9DL
With a character all of its own, Prezzo oozes contemporary style and enduring charm. Signature pastas, stone-baked pizzas and classic Italian dishes promise a perfect dining choice for the whole family.

2FOR1 MAIN COURSE | FRI × | SAT × — Italian

PUNJABI CHARING CROSS
0141 221 3926
157-159 North Street, Glasgow, G3 7DA
The Punjabi has been established since the early 1970's serving the Southside of Glasgow for over 30 years. The chefs, who are real Punjabis endeavour to produce quality Indian food to authentic recipes.

25% OFF TOTAL | FRI ✓ | SAT ✓ | ✱ — Indian

PUNJABI TADKA
01355 260 681
3 The Boardwalk, East Kilbride, G75 0YW
A great place to dine where you will find traditional authentic Indian dishes in an affable environment. Staff are happy to cater to your tastes and every need.

2FOR1 MAIN COURSE | FRI ✓ | SAT ✓ — Indian

RASOI INDIAN KITCHEN
0141 339 2068
120 Dumbarton Road, Glasgow, G11 6NY
Specialising in classic Indian cuisine, Rasoi Indian Kitchen caters to both regular diners alongside visitors from afar. Highly experienced chefs create the most delectable curry dishes.

2FOR1 3 COURSES | FRI × | SAT × — Indian

RAWALPINDI TANDOORI
0141 332 4180
321 Sauchiehall Street, Glasgow, G2 3HW
This traditional family-run restaurant offers divinely tasty Indian cuisine in an authentic interior, delivering a dining experience attractive to families, couples, and late-night socialites.

2FOR1 MAIN COURSE | FRI ✓ | SAT ✓ | ✱ — Indian

REDCHILLIES INDIAN TAPAS
0141 222 2128
57 Union Street, Glasgow, G1 3RB
Indian tapas, allowing guests to choose from a range of sumptuous scaled-down classic dishes to share with friends and family. Experience Indian cuisine in delicious bite-sized dishes.

2FOR1 MAIN COURSE | FRI | SAT — Indian

S.J @ SNOOKS STEAKHOUSE
0141 876 0229
Westboune Centre, Barrhead, Glasgow, G78 1LR
Relax in warm, friendly surroundings whilst enjoying a tasty steak; the mains here are always nothing short of perfection. The Rossini - fillet on a crouton base topped with Madeira sauce - is a must.

2FOR1 3 COURSES | FRI ✓ | SAT ✓ — Scottish

SAFFRON
0141 881 3870
232a Main Street, Glasgow, G78 1SN
Saffron offers the tastiest Indian dishes to a loyal following of regular diners. From a creamy korma to a hot and fiery balti, all appetites and palates are well catered for.

2FOR1 MAIN COURSE | FRI | SAT | ✱ — Indian

SAPPORO TEPPANYAKI
0141 553 4060
2-6 Ingram Street, Merchant City, Glasgow, G1 1HA
Unique dining experience as a range of fresh, flavourful Japanese dishes are prepared with flair and theatricality before your eyes. One of the most entertaining and tastiest meals out in the city.

2FOR1 2 COURSES | FRI ✱ | SAT ✱ — Japanese

SHEZAN TANDOORI
0141 649 4776
1096 Cathcart Road, Glasgow, G42 9XW
Dine in contemporary surroundings at the Shezan Tandoori. Guests enjoy the excellent quality of the Indian cuisine, while the affable waiting staff provide smiles and efficient service.

25% OFF TOTAL | 10 | FRI ✓ | SAT | ✱ — Indian

SHIMLA PINKS
0141 423 4488
777 Pollokshaws Road, Glasgow, G41 2AX
Drawing on the vibrant energy its name radiates, the Shimla Pinks team have built a shrine for diners by bringing supremely tasty Indian dishes and serving them in modern surroundings.

2FOR1 3 COURSES | FRI ✓ | SAT ✓ — Indian

SINGH'S LITTLE INDIA
0141 636 1000
71 Kilmarnock Rd, Shawlands, Glasgow, G41 3YR
Fine Indian staples line the menu at this well-loved restaurant in Shawlands. Concerning themselves with the comfort and happiness of their patrons, the staff serve classic curries with a smile.

2FOR1 3 COURSES | FRI ✓ | SAT ✓ — Indian

SPICE GARDEN
0141 429 4422
11-17 Clyde Place, Glasgow, G5 8AA
Spice Garden pride themselves on using the freshest ingredients to create a range of contemporary recipes. They offer unique surroundings, an exquisite Indian menu with exceptional taste and service.

25% OFF TOTAL | FRI ✓ | SAT ✓ | ✱ — Indian

SUTHERLANDS
0141 357 4711
973 Sauchiehall Street, Glasgow, G3 7TQ
Great value for money and a wonderful experience whatever the occasion. Taking advantage of Scotland's extensive larder, dishes are made fresh using carefully sourced ingredients by an experienced team.

25% OFF TOTAL | 4 | FRI ✓ | SAT ✓ | SUN | ✱ — Scottish

TAAL
01357 522 555
2 Bridge Street, Strathaven, ML10 6AN
Taal offers a magnificent dining experience. Using only the best and freshest ingredients, the dishes are created from traditional Indian recipes that have been passed through the generations.

25% OFF TOTAL | 4 | FRI × | SAT × | SUN | ✱ — Indian

TASTE INDIAN CUISINE
0141 772 4154
27 St Mungo Street, Bishopbriggs, G64 1QT
A fantastic family-run restaurant in Bishopbriggs, where special family recipes have been transported to the Taste kitchen. Dishes such as jalfrezi, padeena and rogan josh are all cooked from scratch.

2FOR1 3 COURSES | FRI × | SAT × — Indian

TORRES
0141 332 6789
327 Sauchiehall Street, Glasgow, G2 3HW
Light, colourful booths and stripped-back Catalan style. A convivial atmosphere geared towards company, sharing and shooting the breeze. The eclectic Spanish tapas menu is wide-ranging and delicious.

50% OFF FOOD | 6 | FRI × | SAT × — Tapas

THE UPLAWMOOR HOTEL
0150 585 0565
Neilston Road, Uplawmoor, Glasgow, G78 4AF
A hotel that has been lovingly maintained by its owners and staff. With its AA Rosette restaurant, the place is highly reputable and guests can be assured that their stay will be thoroughly enjoyable.

2FOR1 MAIN COURSE | FRI ✓ | SAT × — International

URBAN BAR AND BRASSERIE
☎0141 248 5636
23-25 St Vincent Place, Glasgow, G1 2DT
Presenting classic dishes in the chef's own inimitable contemporary style, the fine menu is matched by this award-winning restaurant's stunning setting and elegant ambience. 1 AA Rosette.

2FOR1 MAIN COURSE | FRI 📱 | SAT ✱ | ▲ — European

VESPBAR
0141 204 0060
14 Drury Street, Glasgow, G2 5AA
Sporting a retro style Italian café interior, Vespbar serves pizza by the metre! A trend which has taken off in London. Thanks to Vespbar, Glaswegians can now get a slice of the action.

50% OFF FOOD | 👤 6 | FRI ✓ | SAT ✓ | ▲ — Italian

THE VICEROY
☎0141 429 2222
480 Paisley Road, Glasgow, G5 8RE
Retreat for a good quality curry at this Indian restaurant in Glasgow. Warm and welcoming service provides dishes with classic flavours; at root it's a good, honest local curry house.

25% OFF TOTAL | 👤 4 | FRI ✓ | SAT ✱ — Indian

WALKABOUT
☎0141 332 8209
128 Renfield Street, Glasgow, G2 3AL
Walkabout is famous for its characteristically Australian atmosphere and well-rounded menu. From live sport with a juicy burger to some Aussie kangaroo skewers, you'll find it hard to tear yourself away.

25% OFF TOTAL | 👤 10 | FRI ✓ | SAT ✓ | ▲ — International

WAXY O`CONNORS
☎0141 354 5154
44 West George Street, Glasgow, G2 1DH
A name making itself felt around the UK for its choice group of charismatic, buzzy pubs. This Glasgow venue has a brilliant atmosphere and serves simple, substantial and very tasty food.

2FOR1 3 COURSES | FRI 📱 | SAT ✱ — International

WEST HIGHLAND GATE
0141 956 7835
103 Main Street, Milngavie, Glasgow, G63 6JQ
Beefeater Grill are one of the UK's best-loved restaurants welcoming guests for almost 40 years in over 130 locations nationwide. *Excludes Breakfast, Light Bites, Bar menu, set menus and all other offers.

2FOR1 MAIN COURSE | 👤 6 | FRI ✓ | SAT × | ▲ — Modern British

WINDOWS RESTAURANT
☎0141 354 5070
44-46 West George Street, Glasgow, G2 1DH
A rooftop restaurant in Glasgow serving some very good dishes from only the fines local produce. Seasonal menus accompany the stunning view across Glasgow's rooftops.

25% OFF TOTAL | 👤 4 | FRI 📱 | SAT 📱 | ✱ | ▲ — British

TRADERS RESTAURANT @ HOLIDAY INN
0141 847 8240
Holiday Inn, Abbotsinch Paisley, Glasgow, PA3 2TE
Traders Restaurant is located in the Holiday Inn at Glasgow Airport and provides a Continental buffet from 5am, cooked breakfast from 6am and in the evening there is an a la carte menu.

50% OFF FOOD | 👤 4 | FRI ✓ | SAT ✓ | ✱ — Modern British

THE OSPREY
0141 639 7453
Stewarton Road, Newton Mearns, Glasgow, G77 6NP
This Vintage Inn oozes rural charm and rustic character. The picturesque surroundings provide the perfect backdrop for savouring the hearty, seasonal pub-food on the menu.

25% OFF TOTAL | FRI ✓ | SAT ✓ | SUN | ▲ — Modern British

THE RED DEER
01236 795 861
Auchinkilns Roundabout, Auchinkilns, Glasgow, G68 9A
This Vintage Inn oozes rural charm and rustic character. The picturesque surroundings provide the perfect backdrop for savouring the hearty, seasonal pub-food on the menu.

25% OFF TOTAL | FRI ✓ | SAT ✓ | SUN | ▲ — Modern British

THE STABLES
0141 777 6088
Glasgow Bridge, Kirkintilloch, Glasgow, G66 1RH
This Vintage Inn oozes rural charm and rustic character. The picturesque surroundings provide the perfect backdrop for savouring the hearty, seasonal pub-food on the menu.

25% OFF TOTAL | FRI ✓ | SAT ✓ | SUN | ▲ — Modern British

THE TICKLED TROUT
01360 621 968
878 Boclair Road, Milngavie, Glasgow, G62 6EP
This Vintage Inn oozes rural charm and rustic character. The picturesque surroundings provide the perfect backdrop for savouring the hearty, seasonal pub-food on the menu.

25% OFF TOTAL | FRI ✓ | SAT ✓ | SUN | ▲ — Modern British

Midlothian

GEORGE STREET BAR AND GRILL
☎0131 527 4637
George Street, Edinburgh, EH2 4HQ
Inspired by grand European cafés and brasseries, with a stunning interior to reflect the stylish local architecture, experience some of the best dining in the city at George Street Bar and Grill.

25% OFF TOTAL | 👤 6 | FRI ✱ | SAT × | ▲ — European

110 RESTAURANT AND BAR
☎0131 228 4446
124 Dundee Street, Edinburgh, EH11 1AF
Those with both a passion for fine dining and a love of casino gaming should take heed of this fantastic establishment. Theatricality and decadence go hand in hand perfectly at 110 Restaurant.

2FOR1 MAIN COURSE | FRI × | SAT × | ✱ | ▲ — European

AGUA RESTAURANT
☎0845 365 0002
Apex City Hotel, 61 Grassmarket, Edinburgh, EH1 2HJ
Agua bar and restaurant in Edinburgh city centre is situated in the Apex City Hotel, in the heart of Edinburgh Grassmarket. This city centre restaurant has an AA rosette award and offers quality food.

50% OFF FOOD | 👤 6 | FRI ✓ | SAT ✓ | ▲ — Scottish

AL DENTE RESTAURANT
☎0131 652 1932
139 Easter Road, Edinburgh, EH7 5QA
Pure Italian food, unadulterated by cream or pre-cooked pasta, always fresh and delicious. Both the food and surroundings are authentic, everything one would expect in a traditional Italian restaurant.

2FOR1 MAIN COURSE | FRI 📱 | SAT 📱 | SUN | ✱ — Italian

ANN PURNA
☎0131 662 1807
44-45 St Patricks Square, Edinburgh, EH8 9ET
A popular feature on the Edinburgh scene since the early 1990s, this restaurant serves delicious Gujarati-influenced vegetarian cooking in an unfussy dining space that is both homely and comfortable.

25% OFF TOTAL | 👤 4 | FRI ✱ | SAT ✱ | ✱ — Indian

THE ATHOLL AT THE HOWARD
☎0131 557 3500
34 Great King Street, Edinburgh, EH3 6QH
An expertly composed Scottish menu serves the ambrosial beauty of this Georgian setting extremely well. The Atholl has gradually evolved into a much sought-after Edinburgh restaurant. 1 AA Rosette.

25% OFF TOTAL | 👤 6 | FRI ✓ | SAT ✓ | ▲ — Scottish

BABYLON
☎0131 555 6927
1 Albert place, Edinburgh, EH7 5HN
Located in the heart of Edinburgh, the newly-opened Babylon is a unique Kurdish restaurant serving a fusion of mouth-watering Mediterranean and Middle Eastern dishes.

25% OFF TOTAL | FRI × | SAT × | ▲ — Middle Eastern

BAR ROMA
☎0131 226 2977
39a Queensferry Road, Edinburgh, EH6 6EP
A well-established family restaurant, neatly nestled in the busy West End of Edinburgh city. Drawing on Roman influences, the Italian food on offer is guaranteed to be explosive in colour and variety.

25% OFF TOTAL | 👤 8 | FRI ✱ | SAT ✱ | ▲ — Italian

www.gourmetsociety.co.uk

BAY OF BENGAL RESTAURANT
☎0131 225 2361

164 High Street, Edinburgh, EH1 1QS

Ideally located restaurant for those exploring Edinburgh's famous Royal Mile, Bay of Bengal serves delicious Indian, Bangladeshi, vegetarian and Halal dishes to a cohort of regular and visiting diners.

2FOR1 MAIN COURSE | FRI ✓ | SAT ✓ — Indian

BELLA ITALIA
0131 225 4808

9-11 Hanover Street, Edinburgh, EH2 2DL

Accessible Italian cuisine on the British high street - indulge in authentic sharing platters, hand stretched pizzas and hearty pasta dishes, served with a healthy dose of gregarious Italian hospitality.

25% OFF TOTAL | 6 | FRI ✗ | SAT ✗ | SUN | — Italian

BELLA ITALIA
0131 225 2044

54-56 Northbridge, Edinburgh, EH1 1SB

Accessible Italian cuisine on the British high street - indulge in authentic sharing platters, hand stretched pizzas and hearty pasta dishes, served with a healthy dose of gregarious Italian hospitality.

25% OFF TOTAL | 6 | FRI ✗ | SAT ✗ | SUN | — Italian

BELLA ITALIA
0131 555 6700

Ocean Terminal, Ocean Drive, Leith, Edinburgh, EH6 7DZ

Accessible Italian cuisine on the British high street - indulge in authentic sharing platters, hand stretched pizzas and hearty pasta dishes, served with a healthy dose of gregarious Italian hospitality.

25% OFF TOTAL | 6 | FRI ✗ | SAT ✗ | SUN | — Italian

B'EST
☎0131 556 6040

16 Drummond Street, Edinburgh, EH8 9TX

French in style and evocatively so, B'est breathes comfortability so much it's hard to believe it that hasn't always existed. Classic flavours and effortlessly delicious dishes will have you returning.

25% OFF TOTAL | 10 | FRI ✓ | SAT ✓ — European

BIJOU BISTRO
☎0131 538 0664

2 Restalrig Road, Edinburgh, EH6 8BN

A bustling café offering a carefully thought out, and specially selected menu that provides delicious dishes to come as starters or mains. *BYO policy not valid where GS card is used.

25% OFF TOTAL | 4 | FRI ✗ | SAT ✗ — Bistro

BLUE PARROT CANTINA
☎0131 225 2941

49 St Stephen Street, Edinburgh, EH3 5AH

With traditional dishes such as nachos, fajitas and chimichanga's, the chefs at Blue Parrot Cantina are passionate about creating delicious, Mexican comfort food using fresh quality ingredients.

2FOR1 3 COURSES | FRI ✗ | SAT ✗ — Mexican

BOMBAY SPICE
☎0131 555 3007

138-140 Duke Street, Edinburgh, EH6 8HR

Bombay Spice serves terrific Indian cuisine at great quality prices. Choose your favourite dish to satisfy those curry cravings, or branch out and try something new from the extensive menu.

2FOR1 MAIN COURSE | FRI ✓ | SAT ✓ | * — Indian

BOND NO 9
☎0131 555 5578

84 Commercial Street, Leith, Edinburgh, EH6 6LX

Its situation in one of the oldest parts of the city provides this delightful restaurant and bar with a charismatic character and personality. A charming environment that offers luscious comfort.

2FOR1 3 COURSES | FRI ✗ | SAT ✗ — European

THE BRASSERIE
☎0131 333 1275

The Brasserie, Ingliston, Edinburgh, EH28 8LX

Enjoy classically traditional British cuisine in a beautiful Hand Picked Hotel. Passion and care goes into every dish, accompanying the outstanding ingredients.

25% OFF TOTAL | 4 | FRI * | SAT * | SUN — British

THE BRASSERIE @ MERCURE
☎0844 815 9017

Princes Street, Edinburgh, EH2 2DG

The Brasserie, with its grand leather chairs and warm décor, serves delicious cuisine in amiable surroundings. International flavours feature heavily on the menu alongside juicy meats and creamy pastas.

2FOR1 3 COURSES | FRI ✓ | SAT ✓ — British

BRIDGE RESTAURANT
☎0131 472 3000

The Carlton Hotel, North Bridge, Edinburgh, EH1 1SD

Grand hotel-based restaurant overlooking the Royal Mile. The restaurant serves a brasserie-style menu in relaxing surroundings, with an array of refined contemporary European cuisine.

50% OFF FOOD | 4 | FRI * | SAT * — British

BRITANNIA SPICE
☎0131 555 2255

150 Commercial Street, Edinburgh, EH6 6LB

Causing a positive stir in the area, Britannia Spice draws on the various distinctive flavours of Asia and uses them to create exciting dishes. Indian, Nepalese, Bangladeshi and Thai meals on offer.

2FOR1 MAIN COURSE | FRI ✓ | SAT ✗ | — Indian

CACIOPEPE
☎0131 220 6733

87 Hanover Street, Edinburgh, EH2 1EE

Caciopepe offers you the mood and atmosphere of a classic Italian brassiere. Here you will experience classic Italian dishes prepared using only the finest ingredients. *Not available on Rugby match days.

50% OFF FOOD | 4 | FRI ✓ | SAT ✓ | — Italian

CAFÉ EXPRESS @ HOLIDAY INN
☎0871 942 9026

134 Corstorphine Road, Edinburgh, EH12 6UA

An ideally located hotel, perfect for making the most of the beautiful Edinburgh. For an informal dining option, the Holiday Inn's Café Express provides light meal and drink options.

25% OFF TOTAL | 6 | FRI ✓ | SAT ✓ — European

CAFÉ ROUGE
0131 225 4515

43 Frederick Street, Edinburgh, EH2 1EP

French sophistication on the British high street - enjoy seasonally changing French dishes and a continental wine selection, served in a relaxed environment with an undeniable flair of Parisian chic.

25% OFF TOTAL | 6 | FRI ✓ | SAT ✓ | * | — French

CAFÉ ST HONORE
☎0131 226 2211

34 North West Thistle Street Lane, Edinburgh, EH2 1EA

Neatly snuggled down a cobbled lane in the heart of the city's New Town, this restaurant is a dream for food lovers. Lavish French décor reflects the longstanding friendship between Scotland and France.

25% OFF TOTAL | 6 | FRI | SAT * — French

CAFFE CENTRO
☎0131 225 3419

38 George Street, Edinburgh, EH2 2LE

Whether you are after a simple appetizer, light lunch or full meal, Caffe Centro is sure to cater for your every need. Splendid location and attentive service. *Not available during August.

50% OFF FOOD | FRI ✓ | SAT ✓ — Italian

THE CALEY SAMPLE ROOM
☎0131 337 7204

42-58 Angle Park Terrace, Edinburgh, EH11 2JR

A welcoming venue, the Caley Sample Room is a place where fresh food and superb beers and wines can be enjoyed. Relish the opportunity to spend time with loved ones in a warm and inviting atmosphere.

25% OFF TOTAL | 4 | FRI ✗ | SAT ✗ | SUN | — British

THE CAMBRIDGE BAR & GRILL
☎0131 226 2120

20 Young Street, Edinburgh, EH2 4JB

Strongly established and well frequented, the Cambridge Bar & Grill is renowned for its tasty gourmet burgers and stylish food offerings. Craft bottled beers and Brooklyn draught lager are also highlights.

2FOR1 MAIN COURSE | FRI ✓ | SAT ✓ | — American

CARGO
☎0131 659 7880

129 Fountainbridge, Edinburgh, EH3 9QG

Split-level venue on Fountainbridge; versatile location where you might just as easily enjoy a gala dinner as a simple cocktail or big night out. Good range of bistro-style selections and grill-style fare.

2FOR1 3 COURSES | FRI ✗ | SAT ✗ | SUN | — Bistro

CHANNINGS RESTAURANT
☎0131 315 2226

12-16 South Learmonth Gardens, Edinburgh EH4 1EZ

A first-class neighbourhood bistro offering superb taste combinations in its many dishes. 1 AA Rosette. *Offer applies to a la carte, dinner and all-day menu.

25% OFF TOTAL | 6 | FRI ✓ | SAT ✓ | — European

To understand what the restaurant icons mean, please see the inside back cover.

CHINA TOWN RESTAURANT
0131 228 3333
3 Atholl Place, Edinburgh, EH3 8HP
An outstanding Cantonese restaurant which comes second to none with its chic décor and contemporary cuisine. Speciality seafood dishes such as the sea bass and halibut will blow you away.

25% OFF TOTAL | 6 | FRI ✱ | SAT ✱ | ✱ | ▲ — Cantonese

CLASSIC'S RESTAURANT
0131 629 9987
10 Windsor Street, Edinburgh, EH7 5JR
Traditional Indian spices and herbs are intrinsic to the flavours of the specialities served here. The menu journeys from succulent kebabs to rich curries and flavourful rice-based dishes.

25% OFF TOTAL | 8 | FRI ✓ | SAT ✓ — Indian

CRAIG'S RESTAURANT @ THE KING JAMES
0871 376 9016
107 Leith Street, Edinburgh, EH1 3SW
Boasting an expansive Scottish and European menu, Craig's restaurant offers contemporary cuisine in modern surroundings. Graze over a light dish or a hearty meal before resuming the Edinburgh sightseeing.

50% OFF FOOD | FRI ✓ | SAT ✓ | ▲ — British

CRANSTON'S RESTAURANT
0131 556 4648
Old Waverley Hotel, 43 Princes Street, Edinburgh, EH2 2BY
Whilst revelling in its splendid view of Edinburgh Castle, Cranston's Restaurant maintains a sense of modesty and unpretentiousness. Hosts a fantastic menu that accommodates traditional Scottish fare.

25% OFF TOTAL | 6 | FRI ✓ | SAT ✓ | ▲ — International

CURRY CAFE
0131 556 8435
30 Elm Row, Edinburgh, EH7 4AH
The cuisine at the Curry Cafe combines subtle tastes with an emphasis on fresh ingredients and exotic spices, delicately blended to create special and mouth-watering dishes.

25% OFF TOTAL | 2 | FRI ✱ | SAT ✱ — Indian

DARIO'S PIZZA & SPAGHETTI HOUSE
0131 229 9625
85-87 Lothian Road, Edinburgh, EH3 9AW
Situated in the heart of Edinburgh's theatre district, Dario's is a long established Italian restaurant that serves a wide variety of classic dishes. *Not available during August.

50% OFF FOOD | FRI ✓ | SAT ✓ — Italian

DHABA DINER
0131 667 7308
32b West Nicolson Street, Edinburgh, EH8 9DD
Leisurely dinners or speedy lunches, this Indian eatery specialises in humble, honest cuisine. Consistently buzzing, diners are in for a cracking night out at this authentic eatery.

25% OFF TOTAL | 8 | FRI ▯ | SAT ▯ — Indian

DIVINO ENOTECA
0131 225 1770
5 Merchant Street, Edinburgh, EH1 2QD
Divino is a round-trip ticket to Italy at a fraction of the price. Cosy and intimate, its location is steeped in tradition and rich history. Delicious regional Italian cuisine with an extensive wine list.

25% OFF TOTAL | 6 | FRI × | SAT ✱ | SUN — Italian

EL QUIJOTE TAPAS RESTAURANT
0131 478 2856
13a Brougham Street, Edinburgh, EH1 1DR
A number of years ago, a group of Spanish friends set up camp in Edinburgh, determined to bring an honest taste of Spain to the area. Serves less well known but equally delicious tapas dishes.

25% OFF TOTAL | 4 | FRI × | SAT × | SUN | ▲ — Tapas

ELBOW BAR & KITCHEN
0131 556 5662
133-135 East Claremont Street, Edinburgh, EH7 4JA
Elbow aim simply to deliver good value, top quality food in a comfortable atmosphere. Boasting an imaginative menu, this is the place to enjoy a casual eating experience throughout the day.

2FOR1 2 COURSES | FRI ▯ | SAT ▯ | ▲ — European

ELEMENTS BAR AND RESTAURANT
0131 656 3500
Novotel, 80 Lauriston Place, Edinburgh, EH3 9DE
Modern flavours and classic favourites are all on offer at the Elements Restaurant. A great place to rest and dine in Edinburgh, here you'll find comfort and luxury are a firm focus.

50% OFF FOOD | 6 | FRI ✓ | SAT ✓ | ▲ — British

ELLIOT'S
0845 365 0002
Apex Waterloo Place Hotel, Edinburgh, EH1 3BH
Elliot's bar and restaurant is located in Edinburgh's Apex Waterloo Place Hotel where dishes are made with locally sourced seasonal ingredients. The restaurant has an extensive wine list.

50% OFF FOOD | 4 | FRI ▯ | SAT ▯ | ▲ — Scottish

ESK VALLEY
0131 561 9000
Melville Dykes Road, Dalkeith, Midlothian, Scotland, EH18 1AN
Quality pub classics with a modern twist combine with a friendly and relaxed atmosphere to make this Table Table venue the perfect place for family gatherings or meeting friends.

2FOR1 MAIN COURSE | FRI ✓ | SAT ✓ — Modern British

THE EVEREST
0131 229 1348
52 Home Street, Edinburgh, EH3 9NA
The knowledgeable staff will ensure that no diner goes hungry. Seafood lovers will delight in the speciality menu which includes green herb trout and kantipur king prawns, all locally sourced.

2FOR1 3 COURSES | FRI ✓ | SAT ✓ — Indian

FATMA'S
0131 554 4000
92 Commercial Street, Edinburgh, EH6 6LX
Sample from the most extensive Lebanese wine selection in Scotland whilst enjoying delicious Lebanese food prepared using traditional techniques in this stylish and welcoming restaurant.

25% OFF TOTAL | FRI ▯ | SAT ▯ | SUN — Middle Eastern

GLASS AND THOMPSON
0131 557 0909
2 Dundas Street, Edinburgh, EH3 6HZ
Glass & Thompson is an elegant delicatessens cafe located close to Edinburgh city centre, though you wouldn't know it from the relaxed atmosphere . *Open at lunchtime only. Mention GS on arrival.

2FOR1 3 COURSES | FRI ✓ | SAT × | SUN — British

GOOD SEED BISTRO
0131 337 3803
101-102 Dalry Road, Edinburgh, EH11 2DW
Good Seed Bistro serves up top-notch modern British food with continental influences. The friendly, welcoming atmosphere, unpretentious decor and delicious food is bound to see you return.

25% OFF TOTAL | 8 | FRI ✓ | SAT ✓ | SUN — British

HANDMADE BURGER CO.
0131 561 8253
LE3A Second Floor Ocean Terminal, Edinburgh, EH6 6JJ
100% prime Scotch beef burgers, handmade in the restaurant daily, sourdough buns, delicious handmade relishes and a wide range of toppings giving you over 40 varieties to choose from. *Exclusions apply.

2FOR1 MAIN COURSE | FRI ✓ | SAT × | SUN — International

THE HAWES INN
0131 331 1990
7 Newhalls Road, South Queensferry, EH30 9TA
This Vintage Inn oozes rural charm and rustic character. The picturesque surroundings provide the perfect backdrop for savouring the hearty, seasonal pub-food on the menu.

25% OFF TOTAL | FRI ✓ | SAT ✓ | SUN | ▲ — Modern British

HEIGHTS RESTAURANT
0845 365 0002
Apex International Hotel, Edinburgh, EH1 2HS
Heights Restaurant is located in Apex International Hotel offering great Scottish cuisine and wonderful views of Edinburgh Castle.

50% OFF FOOD | 6 | FRI ✓ | SAT × — Scottish

HEWAT'S RESTAURANT
0131 466 6660
19-21b Causewayside, Edinburgh, EH9 1QF
A fantastically run restaurant where the owners wholly focus on bringing the very best to the table. Combines classic French flavours with the very best aspects of Scottish cuisine.

25% OFF TOTAL | 4 | FRI ✓ | SAT × | SUN | ▲ — Modern British

HOTEL DU VIN
0131 247 4900
11 Bistro Place, Edinburgh, EH1 1EZ
The finest, freshest local produce, simple European recipes, a stunning choice of wines; these are the elements of the trademark Hotel du Vin bistro. Awarded 2 AA Rosettes.

2FOR1 MAIN COURSE | FRI × | SAT × | SUN — European

THE HOWGATE RESTAURANT ☎ 01968 670 000
Howgate, Penicuik, EH26 8PY
Home-made fish cakes, delicate parcels of goats cheese and crusty ciabattas are some of the highlights at the Howgate. Traditional meets contemporary. *One card per party only.

2FOR1 MAIN COURSE | FRI ✓ | SAT ✓ — International

HYDE OUT ☎ 0131 221 0632
2 Fountainbridge Square, Edinburgh, EH6 6PW
Hyde Out is a sophisticated venue that features three areas, a Bang & Olufsen sound system and unique decor including a glass chandelier, with excellent reviews for food and service.

2FOR1 MAIN COURSE | FRI × | SAT × — Scottish

IGGS RESTAURANT ☎ 0131 557 8184
15-19 Jeffrey Street, Edinburgh, EH1 1DR
Twenty years on and the team at Igg's continue to evolve their modern Spanish cuisine using the finest ingredients imported directly from Spain alongside the best of local, seasonal Scottish produce.

25% OFF TOTAL | 8 | FRI ✓ | SAT ✓ | SUN — Spanish

IGNITE BENGALI & INDIAN RESTAURANT ☎ 0131 228 5666
272-274 Morrison Street, Edinburgh, EH8 9EZ
Situated in the heart of Edinburgh's West End, Ignite offers one of the most talked about fine-dining experiences in the Scottish capital. *Offer unavailable on rugby match nights.

25% OFF TOTAL | 10 | FRI ▮ | SAT ▮ — Indian

IMAN'S ☎ 0131 221 1115
Gilmore Place, 4-8 Lochrin Buildings, Edinburgh, EH3 9NB
Great little Punjabi restaurant on Nicholson Square. Has itself a good following based on a friendly, family-run atmosphere, as well as its range of dishes. Their 'Mum's home-cooked specials' win the day.

2FOR1 3 COURSES | FRI ✱ | SAT ✱ | SUN — Indian

INDIAN CAVALRY CLUB ☎ 0131 220 0138
22 Coates Crescent, Edinburgh, EH3 7AF
Having been serving food for many years previous, the Indian Cavalry Club is certainly experienced enough to bring its new Indian additions to the menu. Excellent approach to Asian cooking.

2FOR1 MAIN COURSE | FRI ✓ | SAT × | SUN | ▲ — Indian

IRIS ☎ 0131 220 2111
47a Thistle Street, Edinburgh, EH2 1DY
Nestled discreetly on Thistle Street, Iris is a low-key yet stylish boutique restaurant boasting a myriad of exquisite attributes. A modern European menu has a distinctive Mediterranean flavour.

2FOR1 MAIN COURSE | FRI × | SAT × | ▲ — European

KAMA SUTRA 0131 229 7747
105-109 Lothian Road, Edinburgh, EH3 9AN
Feed the senses at this seductive venue, where the soothing music and sultry surroundings will help you unwind. The menu is vast and will tempt the palates of even the most discerning of diners.

2FOR1 MAIN COURSE | FRI ✓ | SAT ✓ — Indian

THE KHUKURI ☎ 0131 228 2085
8 West Maitland Street, Edinburgh, EH12 5DS
At The Khukuri, locally sourced ingredients, combined with Himalayan herbs ensure delicious and authentic Nepalese cuisine. The team invite you to enjoy Nepali food and warmest hospitality.

2FOR1 MAIN COURSE | FRI ▮ | SAT ▮ — Nepalese

KUBLAI KHAN MONGOLIAN BBQ ☎ 0131 555 0005
43 Assembly Street, Edinburgh, EH6 7BQ
Drawing inspiration from the Mongolian warriors of the 13th century, Khublai Khans Mongolian Restaurant offers a genuinely unique, fun and relaxed dining experience with a lively, interactive atmosphere.

25% OFF TOTAL | 4 | FRI × | SAT × | SUN | ✱ | ▲ — Asian

LA STAZIONE ☎ 0131 337 7582
Ryries Bar, 1 Haymarket Terrace, Edinburgh, EH12 5EY
A little piece of Italy has been preserved for the upper floor of the traditional Haymarket pub, Ryries. The Head Chef cooks up many Italian delights from penne arrabiata to tagliatelle salmone.

2FOR1 MAIN COURSE | FRI ✓ | SAT ✱ | SUN | ✱ | ▲ — Italian

LA TASCA ☎ 0131 220 0011
9 South Charlotte Street, Edinburgh, EH2 4AS
Quintessentially Spanish, La Tasca's fresh and exciting menu offers something for everyone. Their tapas dishes are sincerely authentic, while their paellas always deliver on flavour.

25% OFF TOTAL | 8 | FRI ✓ | SAT × | ▲ — Spanish

LA TASCA ☎ 0131 558 8894
Unit 2 Omni, Greenside Place, Edinburgh, EH1 3AA
Quintessentially Spanish, La Tasca's fresh and exciting menu offers something for everyone. Their tapas dishes are sincerely authentic, while their paellas always deliver on flavour.

25% OFF TOTAL | 8 | FRI ✓ | SAT × | ▲ — Spanish

LADY NAIRNE 0131 661 3396
228 Willowbrae Road, Edinburgh, EH8 7NG
Beefeater Grill are one of the UK's best-loved restaurants welcoming guests for almost 40 years in over 130 locations nationwide. *Excludes Breakfast, Light Bites, Bar menu, set menus and all other offers.

2FOR1 MAIN COURSE | 6 | FRI ✓ | SAT × | ▲ — Modern British

THE LITTLE PANDA ☎ 0131 555 4435
Unit 84, Ocean Terminal, Edinburgh, EH6 6JJ
Perfect for a shopping-break in Ocean Terminal, or especially for those looking for a fresh and alternative approach to Chinese cuisine - The Little Panda's innovative approaches are a must-taste!

2FOR1 3 COURSES | FRI × | SAT × — Chinese

LOCH FYNE ☎ 0131 559 3900
25 Pier Place, Leith, Edinburgh, EH6 4LP
From the roadside oyster bar that once was, Loch Fyne restaurants now successfully inject energy and passion into great food and wonderful flavours, whilst ensuring their seafood is sustainably sourced.

25% OFF TOTAL | 4 | FRI ✱ | SAT ✱ | ▲ — Seafood

THE LONGSTONE INN ☎ 0131 455 7807
30 Longstone Road, Edinburgh, EH14 2BH
The Longstone Inn is a true traditional Scottish pub. It is truly at the heart of the community and it is this community vibe that makes The Longstone Inn such a delightful pub.

2FOR1 3 COURSES | FRI ✓ | SAT × | SUN — British

LOTUS INDIAN RESTAURANT AND BAR ☎ 0131 662 9212
79 Buccleuch Street, Edinburgh, EH8 9LS
Lotus Indian Restaurant provides you with a warm beautiful place to dine with your friends and family.

2FOR1 3 COURSES | FRI ▮ | SAT ▮ — Indian

MADOGS STEAKHOUSE ☎ 0131 235 3408
38 George Street, Edinburgh, EH2 2LE
With a focus on quality steak and burgers, Madogs offers an extensive menu in a energetic atmosphere, live music and an impressive cocktail menu. *Offer not available during August.

50% OFF FOOD | FRI ✓ | SAT ✓ — American

MALMAISON ☎ 0131 468 5000
1 Tower Place, Leith, Edinburgh, EH6 7DB
Edinburgh Mal is a gorgeous riverside property, inviting you to feast from a well-constructed menu. Favouring local produce with dazzling choice wines, meals here are to be lingered over. 2 AA Rosettes.

2FOR1 MAIN COURSE | FRI × | SAT × | SUN | ▲ — European

MALONE'S IRISH BAR ☎ 0131 226 5954
14 Forrest Road, Edinburgh, EH1 2QN
A traditional Irish bar that pays homage to the traditional Irish forms of celebration. Live music and brilliant vibes, Malone's serves delicious authentic fare, from a Guinness stew to bacon with cabbage.

2FOR1 MAIN COURSE | FRI ✓ | SAT × | SUN — North American/ Irish

MAMMA'S AMERICAN PIZZA CO. ☎ 0131 225 6464
30 Grassmarket, Edinburgh, EH1 2JU
Indulge in a vast menu packed with an exceptional range of starters, main courses and desserts; however, a visit to Mamma's wouldn't be complete without one of their fresh stone-baked pizzas.

2FOR1 3 COURSES | FRI ▮ | SAT ▮ — Pizza

THE MELVILLE INN
0131 660 4925
Melville Nursery, Lasswade, Edinburgh, EH18 1AR
This Vintage Inn oozes rural charm and rustic character. The picturesque surroundings provide the perfect backdrop for savouring the hearty, seasonal pub-food on the menu.

25% OFF TOTAL | FRI ✓ | SAT ✓ | SUN | ♣ — Modern British

METRO WEST END RESTAURANT
☎ 0845 365 0002
Apex European Hotel, Edinburgh, EH12 5LQ
Do lunch or dinner at Metro West End restaurant, situated in Edinburgh city centre, and enjoy great food and great service at great prices. More than anything, Metro West End has an unmistakable air of fun

50% OFF FOOD | 6 | FRI ✓ | SAT ✓ — Scottish

MUMBAI MANSION
☎ 0131 229 7173
250 Morrison Street, Edinburgh, EH3 8DT
Mumbai Mansion was established in 2009 by executive chef Salim Haider. The aim is to bring you the ultimate fine dining experience with the highest quality of traditional Indian cuisine.

2FOR1 MAIN COURSE | FRI ✓ | SAT ✓ — Indian

NAMASTE KATHMANDU
☎ 0131 220 2273
17-19 Forrest Road, Edinburgh, EH1 2QH
Using carefully selected Nepalese herbs and spices, and the best local Scottish produce, particularly meats, Namaste Kathmandu aim to create a truly excellent dining experience.

50% OFF FOOD | 6 | FRI × | SAT × — Indian

NEWTOWN BAR
☎ 0131 538 7775
26b Dublin Street, Edinburgh, EH3 6NN
A cracking joint in central Edinburgh, the Newtown Bar is the place to head to when pub-food cravings kick in. Live music and traditional roast dinners are a Sunday highlight.

2FOR1 3 COURSES | FRI × | SAT × — Modern Pub

NORTH BRIDGE BRASSERIE
☎ 0131 622 2900
20 North Bridge, Edinburgh, EH1 1TR
Paul Hart serves a seasonal, Scottish cuisine with a strong focus on locally-sourced ingredients. Whatever the occasion North Bridge will leave a lasting impression thatÕll make you return again and again.

2FOR1 MAIN COURSE | FRI ✓ | SAT × — Scottish

PASSAGE TO INDIA
☎ 0131 556 4547
20 Union Place, Edinburgh, EH1 3NQ
A cracking Indian restaurant across from the Edinburgh Playhouse Theatre. Serves finely flavoured, subtly spiced dishes, specialising in particular in Punjabi cuisine.*Offer not available during festivals.

2FOR1 3 COURSES | FRI | SAT | * — Indian

PEPE NERO
☎ 0131 228 3228
169 Gilmore Place, Edinburgh, EH3 9PW
Pepe Nero is a restaurant with a difference. The menu consists of a range of recipes, from traditional Italian to original dishes created using the special flair of the talented chefs.

2FOR1 MAIN COURSE | FRI ✓ | SAT ✓ — Italian

PREZZO
0131 552 4356
25 Pier Place, Leith, Edinburgh, EH6 4LP
With a character all of its own, Prezzo oozes contemporary style and enduring charm. Signature pastas, stone-baked pizzas and classic Italian dishes promise a perfect dining choice for the whole family.

2FOR1 MAIN COURSE | FRI × | SAT × | ♣ — Italian

PREZZO
☎ 0131 557 5346
7-9 North Bridge, Edinburgh, EH1 1SB
With a character all of its own, Prezzo oozes contemporary style and enduring charm. Signature pastas, stone-baked pizzas and classic Italian dishes promise a perfect dining choice for the whole family.

2FOR1 MAIN COURSE | FRI × | SAT × | ♣ — Italian

PRINCE BALTI HOUSE
☎ 0131 657 1155
11 Seafield Road East, Edinburgh, EH15 1EB
A highly skilled team of chefs put their talents to use in The Prince Balti House kitchen. A mouth-watering range of delicacies from Bangladesh, Nepal and India are all on offer.

2FOR1 3 COURSES | FRI ✓ | SAT ✓ | ♣ — Indian

THE PRINCE OF INDIA
☎ 0131 337 2213
88 Haymarket Terrace, Edinburgh, EH12 5LQ
Attentive chefs take pride in both the presentation and taste of each and every dish they produce in the kitchen. Well thought out Indian cuisine that is sumptuous, delicious, and incredibly tasty.

2FOR1 3 COURSES | FRI ✓ | SAT ✓ — Indian

QUATTRO ZERO
☎ 0131 220 5622
40-41 Queensferry Street, Edinburgh, EH2 4RA
Quattro Zero is a restaurant, bar, pizzeria and takeaway located in Edinburgh serving fresh, delicious food with friendly service. *Offer not available on rugby match days.

50% OFF FOOD | 4 | FRI ✓ | SAT ✓ | ♣ — Italian

RAJ RESTAURANT ON THE SHORE
☎ 0131 553 3980
91 Henderson Street, Edinburgh, EH6 6ED
Fusing the exotic tastes of India and Bangladesh together, this restaurant boasts an 'International Indian Chef of the Year Competition' award. Enjoy a fruity shisha in the relaxing hookah lounge.

25% OFF TOTAL | 6 | FRI × | SAT × — Indian/Bangladeshi

REAL RAJPUT INDIAN CUISINE
☎ 0131 220 2335
209-213 High Street, Edinburgh, EH1 1PE
With a focus on your dining experience, the menu features eclectic specialties alongside the traditional Indian cuisines. *Not available during Edinburgh festival.

25% OFF TOTAL | 6 | FRI ✓ | SAT ✓ | ♣ — Indian

RESTAURANT AT THE BONHAM
☎ 0131 274 7444
35 Drumsheugh Gardens, Edinburgh, EH3 7RN
A sophisticated venue rooted in French tradition coupled with expertly sourced, seasonal Scottish produce. Minimalist décor ensures the 2 AA rosette-rated food is the definite focus.

25% OFF TOTAL | 6 | FRI | SAT | SUN | ♣ — European

THE ROSEHIP
☎ 0131 225 8028
43 Rose Street, Edinburgh, EH2 2NH
Here at The Rosehip we offer traditional pub food and over 200 single malt whiskies, all served with a smile. Find us on Rose Street in the heart of New Town. *Not available during Edinburgh festival.

2FOR1 3 COURSES | FRI ✓ | SAT ✓ | ♣ — British

RYAN'S CELLAR BAR
☎ 0131 226 7005
2 Hope Street, Edinburgh, EH2 4DB
A modern Scottish à la carte menu is on offer at this characterful bar. The venison with port and juniper berry jus is phenomenal, while the regular jazz nights provide popular entertainment.

2FOR1 MAIN COURSE | FRI | SAT | * | ♣ — Scottish

SAMBUCA ITALIAN RESTAURANT
☎ 0131 667 3307
101-103 Causeway Side, Edinburgh, EH9 1QG
A family-run affair, Sambuca combines delicious food with gregarious Italian hospitality to create an unforgettable dining experience. *Not available during Edinburgh festival.

2FOR1 MAIN COURSE | FRI × | SAT × | ♣ — Italian

SAMPANS RESTAURANT @ HOLIDAY INN
☎ 0871 942 9026
133 Corstorphine Road, Edinburgh, EH12 6UA
The beautiful Edinburgh has so much to offer, and the Holiday Inn can really help you make the most of it. Dine in Sampans Restaurant, where dim sum and decadent Asian curries line the menu.

25% OFF TOTAL | 6 | FRI ✓ | SAT ✓ — European

SHEZAN TANDOORI
☎ 0131 557 5098
25 Union Street, Edinburgh, EH1 3NQ
To kill those curry cravings, head to Shezan Tandoori, where you are sure to find all of your staple favourites alongside a decent menu of sundries, vegetable dishes and crisp, fresh starters.

50% OFF FOOD | 2 | FRI × | SAT × — Indian

STRADA
0131 225 2213
15 Castle Street, Edinburgh, EH2 3AH
Strada offers fresh, bold dishes inspired by flavours of Italian city life! Try the hand-stretched, stone baked pizzas, addictive pastas and risottos, great share plates and much more. *Excludes Pizzettas.

25% OFF TOTAL | 6 | FRI ✓ | SAT × | ♣ — Italian

THE STREET
☎0131 556 4272

2 Picardy Place, Edinburgh, EH1 3JT

Offbeat style at this bar-restaurant. Cool, quirky place to eat and drink, with a broad-based menu ranging from nachos to olives and fries, together with some simple hearty pasta dishes and sandwiches.

2FOR1 3 COURSES | FRI ✱ | SAT ✱ — European

SURUCHI
☎0131 556 6583

14a Nicolson Street, Edinburgh, EH8 9DH

Suruchi offers a truly celebratory Indian atmosphere for diners to enjoy fabulous flavours from the length and breadth of the subcontinent.

2FOR1 MAIN COURSE | FRI | SAT | ✱ — Indian

SURUCHI TOO
☎0131 554 3268

121 Constitution Street, Leith, Edinburgh, EH6 7AE

Wholesome dishes from every corner of India with spices, herbs, and flavours to lure any diner into a true Indian atmosphere. A comprehensive wine list is also offered to enhance your dining experience.

2FOR1 MAIN COURSE | FRI | SAT — Indian

TRADERS RESTAURANT @ HOLIDAY INN
☎0871 942 9026

132 Corstorphine Road, Edinburgh, EH12 6UA

When staying somewhere as beautiful as Edinburgh, you want to make the most of it. Traders Restaurant at Holiday Inn offers spectacular views of the Pentland Hills and tasty international dishes.

25% OFF TOTAL | 6 | FRI ✓ | SAT ✓ — Chinese

THE TURQUOISE THISTLE RESTAURANT
☎0131 556 5577

Hotel Indigo, 51-59 York Place, Edinburgh, EH1 3JD

With a passionate Head Chef and a kitchen jam-packed full of fresh local produce, the Turquoise Thistle offers delicious food and a fantastic wine list. Imaginative dishes make up a well-prepared menu.

25% OFF TOTAL | FRI ✓ | SAT ✓ — Scottish

THE VERANDAH
☎0131 337 5828

17 Dalry Road, Edinburgh, EH11 2BQ

Pushing past some of the Indian restaurant clichés, this award-winning place has well earned its reputation as 'Best Indian Restaurant' according to the Scottish Good Food Guide.

2FOR1 MAIN COURSE | FRI ✓ | SAT ✓ — Indian/Bangladeshi

THE VILLAGE
☎0131 558 8488

103-105 Brunswick Street, Edinburgh, EH7 5HR

The Village is the place for desi(traditional) curry and shisha. At The Village, they combine a blend of the traditional Asian and modern Indian cooking, a cuisine which offers customers a diverse variety.

25% OFF TOTAL | 4 | FRI | SAT — Indian

VIVA MEXICO
☎0131 226 5145

41 Cockburn Street, Edinburgh, EH1 1BS

A real family affair, Viva Mexico opened over 26 years ago and continues to bring an impressively authentic taste of Mexico to the bustling city of Edinburgh. Trusty family recipes are relied upon.

2FOR1 MAIN COURSE | FRI ✓ | SAT ✓ — Mexican

THE VOODOO ROOMS
☎0131 556 7060

19a West Register Street, Edinburgh, EH2 2AA

Get your fill of the fantastic food on offer at The Voodoo Rooms before making the most of the exhilarating beats and intoxicating rhythms that give this place its popular reputation.

50% OFF FOOD | 2 | FRI × | SAT × — Modern Pub

ZEST
☎0131 556 5028

15 North St , Andrew Street, Edinburgh, EH2 1HJ

A fine restaurant adding to the wealth of eateries in Edinburgh city centre. Serving tasty Indian cuisine, Zest is suitably located to round off a day out exploring, or to start a night out in town.

2FOR1 3 COURSES | FRI ✓ | SAT ✓ — Indian

ZUCCA
☎0131 221 9323

15-17 Grindlay Street, Edinburgh, EH3 9AX

A restaurant that sets its stall out to serve homely, high quality Italian cuisine cooked with the freshness, simplicity and earthiness that characterise the best food from out of Italy.

25% OFF TOTAL | 10 | FRI ✓ | SAT ✓ | SUN | ✱ | ▲ — Italian

GUCHHI INDIAN SEAFOOD AND BAR
☎0131 555 5604

9-10 Commercial Street, Edinburgh, EH6 6JA

Guchhi is a contemporary Indian seafood restaurant in the heart of Leith, Edinburgh The restaurant presents a varied menu from shellfish platters with an Indian twist and tandoori crab to classic Indian.

2FOR1 MAIN COURSE | 4 | FRI | SAT — Indian

THE FAR PAVILIONS
☎0131 332 3362

10-12 Craigleith Road, Edinburgh, EH4 2DP

Offering the real cooking of India and Pakistan, The Far Pavilions aim to offer our customers a relaxed and convivial environment in which to enjoy good food in the pleasure of good company.

2FOR1 MAIN COURSE | FRI × | SAT × | ▲ — Indian

Morayshire

XORIATIKI ELGIN
☎01343 546 868

87-91 High street, Elgin, IV30 1EA

You won't be disappointed with the mouth-watering menu at Xoriatiki. Based in the centre of Elgin, customers visit from surrounding areas and beyond for an authentic unforgettable Greek experience.

50% OFF FOOD | 4 | FRI ✓ | SAT ✓ — Greek

DARROCH RESTAURANT
☎01343 543 077

Eight Acres Hotel, Morriston Road, Elgin, IV30 6UL

Just out to the north west of Elgin, a noted retreat from the bustle that serves hearty, down-to-earth food. Local produce is a priority, although their menu features dishes from around the world.

50% OFF FOOD | 4 | FRI ✓ | SAT ✓ — Scottish

Perthshire

63 TAY STREET RESTAURANT
☎01738 441 451

63 Tay Street, Perth, PH2 8NN

In the heart of historic Perth, culinary delights await with a menu strongly emphasising seasonality, complemented by New World wines and a fair amount of older classics. Awarded 2 AA Rosettes.

25% OFF TOTAL | 6 | FRI ✓ | SAT ✱ | SUN | ▲ — Modern European

THE BRASSERIE @ MERCURE
☎0844 815 9105

Mercure Perth Hotel, West Mill Street, Perth, PH1 5QP

With the fractured outline of the Highlands in the background and the city of Perth closeting the hotel, the mood-lit Brasserie Restaurant is warmly inviting, especially on chilly Scottish evenings.

2FOR1 3 COURSES | FRI ✓ | SAT ✓ — British

GAVIN'S BISTRO
☎01738 623 355

The New County Hotel, 22-30 County Place, Perth, PH2 8EE

Creamy cappuccinos and smooth lattes are to be enjoyed alongside the delicious home-made scones and muffins on offer at Gavin's Bistro. Bright and soothing, the place is relaxed and laid-back.

2FOR1 MAIN COURSE | FRI | SAT — Bistro

THE GLOVER ARMS
01738 624 888

Crieff Road, Huntingtower Park, Perth, PH1 3JJ

This Vintage Inn oozes rural charm and rustic character. The picturesque surroundings provide the perfect backdrop for savouring the hearty, seasonal pub-food on the menu.

25% OFF TOTAL | FRI ✓ | SAT ✓ | SUN | ▲ — Modern British

THE GURKHA
☎01738 622 563

36 South Methven Street, Perth, PH1 2UQ

Nepalese cuisine holds a character all of its own, with influences from the neighbouring China and India making an impact on flavours. Gurkha Restaurant focuses on the tastiest dishes.

2FOR1 MAIN COURSE | FRI ✓ | SAT ✓ | ✱ — Indian/Nepalese

MAZA INDIAN BUFFET RESTAURANT ☎01738 447 980
222-224 High Street, Perth, PH1 5PA
A popular, classic Indian restaurant in Perth whose specialities include a nentara full of spice and flavour; all the gamut of dishes you would expect are also here in this accommodating restaurant.

25% OFF TOTAL | 10 | FRI ✓ | SAT ✓ — Indian

NURJAHAN INDIAN RESTAURANT ☎01738 635 030
70 Tay Street, Perth, PH2 8NN
Yours will be yet another heart won by Nurjahan restaurant. Indulge in original authentic Indian cuisine in beautiful surroundings. Diners can expect to be warmly welcomed and well looked after.

25% OFF TOTAL | 4 | FRI ✓ | SAT ✓ — Indian

OLD MASTERS ☎01738 551 171
Murrayshall House Hotel, New Scone, Perth, PH2 7PH
Delivering a refined dining experience in a relaxed traditional atmosphere, the award winning Old Masters restaurant has held two AA rosettes for its cuisine constantly for the past fifteen years.

25% OFF TOTAL | FRI ✓ | SAT ✓ | ▲ — Scottish

OPUS ONE RESTAURANT ☎01738 623 355
New County Hotel, 22-30 County Place, Perth, PH2 8EE
Passionate about sourcing local produce from Perthshire's larder, this restaurant regularly use it in their seasonal dishes, creatively prepared and executed with meticulous precision and flair.

25% OFF TOTAL | 10 | FRI ✓ | SAT ▮ | SUN — Modern European

RIVER VIEW RESTAURANT ☎01350 727 219
Atholl Arms Hotel, Bridgehead, Dunkeld, PH8 0AQ
Expect nothing less than spectacular food and service at the River View Restaurant, situated in the equally spell-bounding Atholl Arms Hotel. Proudly reinforces its Scottish heritage through the cuisine.

25% OFF TOTAL | 4 | FRI ✓ | SAT ✓ — Scottish

SHERAY PUNJAB RESTAURANT ☎01764 664 277
97 High Street, Auchterarder, PH3 1BJ
Sheray Indian restaurant is located in Auchterarder, which is easily accessible, only 10 minutes from Perth and Stirling and offers authentic Punjab cooking with a home-style flavour.

25% OFF TOTAL | 8 | FRI × | SAT × | ✱ | ▲ — Indian

TABLA INDIAN RESTAURANT ☎01738 444 630
173 South Street, Perth, PH2 8NY
Perth's only authentic Indian restaurant, Tabla use fresh, farm-grown spices from India for truly traditional flavour. Well-presented restaurant that provides a warm and welcoming dining experience.

2FOR1 MAIN COURSE | FRI ▮ | SAT ▮ | ▲ — Indian

Renfrewshire

AJUBA ☎0150 532 2718
133 Main Road, Paisley, PA5 9ES
Perfect for families and couples alike, Ajuba serves up a wide selection of the finest Indian dishes. You certainly won't struggle for choice at this tastefully decorated restaurant.

2FOR1 MAIN COURSE | FRI × | SAT × | SUN | ✱ | ▲ — Indian

BOWFIELD HOTEL & COUNTRY CLUB ☎0150 570 5225
Bowfield Hotel, Howwood, PA9 1DZ
Characteristic of its country location, Bowfield Hotel and Country Club delights in its setting as well as its close proximity to the city of Glasgow. A well-recommended restaurant resides on site.

25% OFF TOTAL | 4 | FRI ✓ | SAT ✱ — European

EXOTIC INDIA ☎0141 886 3377
65 Ferry Road, Renfrew, PA4 8SH
Aromatic Indian spices, authentic recipes and traditional cooking methods all go towards creating the finest dishes at Exotic Indian Restaurant. Enjoy your favourite curry in full comfort.

2FOR1 MAIN COURSE | FRI ✓ | SAT ✓ — Indian

HEERA ☎0141 886 3222
14-16 Porterfield Road, Renfrew, PA4 8HJ
Long-established Indian restaurant going from strength to strength. Uncluttered, colourful design makes for a comfortable ambience; their tandoori dishes and specialities like the pardesi curry stand out.

2FOR1 MAIN COURSE | FRI × | SAT × | SUN — Indian

Scottish Borders

THE BLACK BULL LAUDER ☎01578 722 208
Market Place, Lauder, TD2 6SR
The Black Bull Hotel in Lauder is an independent, family-owned hotel with dining rooms and bar, offering seasonal food and a warm welcome in a stylish 18th century coaching inn.

2FOR1 MAIN COURSE | FRI ▮ | SAT ▮ — Scottish

SIAMESE KITCHEN ☎01361 883 470
12 Murray Street, Duns, TD11 3DE
An exciting marriage of eastern and western gastronomic influences, creating a cuisine that is uniquely alternative. Eye-wateringly hot to mild and refined dishes also available.

2FOR1 3 COURSES | FRI ✱ | SAT ✱ | ▲ — Thai

SUTHERLAND RESTAURANT ☎01721 725 750
Cringletie House Hotel, Edinburgh Road, Pebbles, EH45 8PL
One of Scotland's finest, awarded 3 prestigious AA Rosettes, The Sutherland Restaurant at Cringletie House, welcomes diners to enjoy innovative and imaginative French cuisine in a spectacular setting.

25% OFF TOTAL | 4 | FRI ✓ | SAT ✓ | ✱ — European

THE MELGUND ☎01450 374 148
11 Melgund Place, Hawick, TD9 9HY
An impressively furnished bar and restaurant providing tempting meals and a pleasing drinks selection. Expect genial service and a lovely warm welcome on arrival.

2FOR1 3 COURSES | FRI ✓ | SAT ✓ | ▲ — International

THE SUNRISE ☎01835 863 503
51 High Street, Jedburgh, TD8 6DQ
An accommodating Indian restaurant in Jedburgh where you're sure to enjoy the great range of classic, flavourful curries and leftfield specialities.

25% OFF TOTAL | 6 | FRI ▮ | SAT ▮ | ✱ | ▲ — Indian

THE TWEED RESTAURANT ☎01835 822 261
Dryburgh Abbey Hotel, Melrose, TD6 0RQ
The Tweed Restaurant has many appealing features; the magnificent view of its River namesake is certainly one of them. The menu draw upon the flavours belonging to Scotland and presents them in every dish.

2FOR1 3 COURSES | FRI ✓ | SAT ✓ | ✱ — Scottish

THE PLACE RESTAURANT ☎01750 778 174
73 High Street, Selkirk, TD7 4BZ
A new and exciting eatery in Selkirk, The Place is a relaxed and friendly restaurant offering traditional but exciting and innovative cooking. Quite simply, The Place is 'The Place to Be'.

2FOR1 MAIN COURSE | FRI ▮ | SAT ▮ | SUN | ✱ | ▲ — British

TASTE OF SPICE ☎0175 020 210
3 Market Place, Selkirk, TD7 4BT
Taste a variety of exotic flavours and spices at this fantastic Indian restaurant, where staff are happy to cater for large and small parties and any occasion. Supreme dishes made from fine ingredients.

2FOR1 MAIN COURSE | FRI ✓ | SAT × | SUN — Indian

Stirlingshire

CAFÉ CIRCA ☎01786 841 683
The Scottish Antiques Centre, Doune, FK16 6HG
Hot bustling bistro where you can find a cool calm moment with an array of gorgeously cooked, well-prepared and -presented dishes derived from high quality local Scottish produce.
25% OFF TOTAL | 4 | FRI | SAT — Scottish

CAFE CONTINENTAL ☎01786 824 234
Riverview, High Street, Dunblane, FK15 0EE
Café Continental are proud of their seasonal changing menu, an amazing combination of their best a la carte and brasserie dishes using great, local ingredients in partnership with the finest suppliers.
25% OFF TOTAL | 4 | FRI | SAT — European

EAST INDIA COMPANY ☎01786 447 770
7 Viewfield Place, Stirling, FK8 1NQ
A name that calls up a whole history. The restaurant is known for its mouth-watering, beautifully flavoured dishes. It has won a regular following in the town and continues to thrive.
2FOR1 3 COURSES | FRI ✓ | SAT ✓ — Indian

KAMA SUTRA STIRLING 01786 470 999
50 Uppercraig, Stirling, FK8 2DS
Feed the senses at this seductive venue, where the soothing music and sultry surroundings will help you unwind. The menu is vast and will tempt the palates of even the most discerning of diners.
2FOR1 MAIN COURSE | FRI ✓ | SAT ✓ — Indian

PAPARAZZI BISTRO ☎01786 834 969
84 Henderson Street, Bridge of Allan, Stirling, FK9 4HA
Paparazzi operates a dual dining experience. By day, the restaurant offers exceptional snacks and meals and by night, the evening menu is sure to impress, heavily Italian themed and hand made delights.
25% OFF TOTAL | 6 | FRI ✓ | SAT ✓ — Italian

PIERRES RESTAURANT ☎01324 635 843
140 Grahams Road, Falkirk, FK2 7BZ
Traditional Scottish food created with the best of Scottish produce and the principles of French cuisine. Offering a widely varying menu specialising in seafood, this restaurant produces gratifying dishes.
25% OFF TOTAL | 4 | FRI | SAT ✱ | SUN | ▲ — Scottish

RANA'S INDIAN RESTAURANT 0845 833 4243
37 Friars St, Stirling, FK8 1HA
Rana serves delectable cuisine to a room full of happy diners. From chicken chat to a mixed tandoori grill, the starters taste as good as they sound. The mains range from dopiaza to chilli masala.
2FOR1 MAIN COURSE | FRI | SAT | ✱ | ▲ — Indian

THE ROSEBANK 01324 611 842
Main Street, Camelon, Falkirk, FK1 4DS
Beefeater Grill are one of the UK's best-loved restaurants welcoming guests for almost 40 years in over 130 locations nationwide. *Excludes Breakfast, Light Bites, Bar menu, set menus and all other offers.
2FOR1 MAIN COURSE | 6 | FRI ✓ | SAT × | ▲ — Modern British

SPICE GARDEN ☎0845 833 4239
23 Allan Park, Stirling, FK8 2LY
Spice Garden is a stylish and modern Indian restaurant located in the centre of Stirling. It is an ideal place to relax and unwind whilst enjoying authentic Indian food.
25% OFF TOTAL | 2 | FRI × | SAT × | ▲ — Indian

TAIYUAN ☎01324 629 223
4 Weir Street, Falkirk, FK1 1RA
Offers first-class service and high-quality food. The staff at Taiyuan are happy to help you decide on a dish should the extensive Chinese menu leave you feeling spoilt for choice.
25% OFF TOTAL | 4 | FRI | SAT | ▲ — Chinese

THE WHEELHOUSE ☎01324 673 490
Millennium Wheel Drive, Falkirk, FK1 4AD
The panoramic windows allow you to take in the world outside whilst being warmly and comfortably seated in the restaurant's pleasant interior. The kitchen makes use of some of the finest fresh food.
2FOR1 MAIN COURSE | FRI ✓ | SAT ✱ | SUN | ▲ — European

West Lothian

ASHOKA SHAK ☎01506 416 622
26 Mcarthur Glen Outlet, Livingston, EH54 6QX
Spicing up the lives of curry lovers in Livingston and visitors alike, the Ashoka Shak - complete with a grand design - delivers authentic Indian dishes cooked to perfection.
2FOR1 3 COURSES | FRI ✓ | SAT ✓ — Indian

THE BRASSERIE @ MERCURE ☎0844 815 9102
Mercure Livingston Hotel, Almondview, Livingston, EH54 6QB
Enjoy an excellent dining experience and fantastic international dishes at this fine hotel-restaurant. A comprehensive wine list provides a bottle to complement every culinary option.
2FOR1 3 COURSES | FRI ✓ | SAT ✓ — British

CATHAY CUISINE ☎01506 409 988
25 Main Street, Livingston, EH54 8BE
Cathay Cuisine is the perfect venue for diners wishing to indulge in Chinese treats and Orient specials. Head here with friends for that long awaited catch-up.
25% OFF TOTAL | FRI ✓ | SAT ✓ — Chinese

CLASSIC INDIA ☎01506 410 786
3c Howden West Road, Livingston, EH54 6AA
Classic India is situated in the heart of Livingston and serves a cracking array of traditional and more eclectic Indian dishes, with the emphasis on simple quality and lots of flavour.
2FOR1 MAIN COURSE | FRI | SAT — Indian

DEER PARK 01506 439 202
Deer Park Avenue, Knightsbridge, Livingston, EH54 8AD
Beefeater Grill are one of the UK's best-loved restaurants welcoming guests for almost 40 years in over 130 locations nationwide. *Excludes Breakfast, Light Bites, Bar menu, set menus and all other offers.
2FOR1 MAIN COURSE | 6 | FRI ✓ | SAT × | ▲ — Modern British

JEREMY WARES @ HOUSTOUN HOUSE ☎0844 879 9043
Macdonald Houstoun House, Uphall, EH52 6JS
In our 16th Century tower, you'll enjoy award-winning cuisine at Jeremy Wares at Houstoun House. It's the perfect setting to enjoy a menu featuring traditional Scottish food with a modern twist.
2FOR1 MAIN COURSE | FRI × | SAT × | ✱ | ▲ — Scottish

K2 INDIAN RESTAURANT ☎01506 676 750
28a Glasgow Road, Bathgate, EH48 2AG
Punjabi-style cuisine is on offer at this wonderful contemporary restaurant in Bathgate. Classic curry dishes can be enjoyed in this comfortable, relaxed environment.
2FOR1 3 COURSES | FRI ✓ | SAT ✓ — Indian

LIVINGSTON'S RESTAURANT ☎01506 846 565
52 High Street, Linlithgow, EH49 7AE
A prestigious restaurant with an enviable reputation. Testimony to its success, Livingston's has thrived for nineteen years and has won a number of accolades for its cuisine, including 2 AA Rosettes.
2FOR1 MAIN COURSE | FRI × | SAT × | SUN | ▲ — European

THE OATRIDGE HOTEL AND GRILL ☎01506 856 465
2-4 East Main Street, Broxburn, EH52 5DA
Whether you are looking for somewhere to stay or simply for something to eat, The Oatridge Hotel and Grill offers it all. The classic British menu is infused with the finest flavours of Scotland.
25% OFF TOTAL | 6 | FRI ✓ | SAT ✓ | ▲ — British

To understand what the restaurant icons mean, please see the inside back cover.

Ireland

The Gourmet Society has continued to bring you great savings at hundreds of quality restaurants throughout Northern Ireland and Eire.

Enjoy hundreds of local, independent establishments - from restaurants and bars, to cafés and pubs. Whether you are in a traditional pub or contemporary urban kitchen, here in Ireland you will find some of the freshest, finest food in the world. Excellent seafood, beef, lamb and pork are crafted into exquisite dishes thanks to the combination of skilful local suppliers, inspired chefs and a rich culinary heritage.

Discover all participating Gourmet Society restaurants in Ireland by visiting www.gourmetsociety.co.uk.

The Offers & How it Works

As a Gourmet Society member you'll get up to 50% off meals by showing your card.

When you check the restaurant listings you will see a variety of icons. Although most restaurants welcome Gourmet Society members throughout the week and the weekend, some restrictions may apply. Each listing has the following symbols for your confirmation. Let's take a look at what they mean..

It's simple

Choose & Check - Find a restaurant and check the offer. Visit www.gourmetsociety.co.uk or use the mobile app. Make sure the offer is available on the day you wish to use it.

Call & Book - Call the restaurant to book your table and let them know that you will be using your Gourmet Society card.

Dine & Save - Enjoy your meal, show your membership and get the discount. It's that simple!

Don't forget!

Always check the individual restaurant's offer and availability prior to booking. Restaurants may exclude bank holidays and other special days.
Full details are available for every restaurant online at
www.gourmetsociety.co.uk